W.E.B. GRIFFIN

THREE COMPLETE NOVELS

ALSO BY W.E.B. GRIFFIN

Blood and Honor

Honor Bound

BROTHERHOOD OF WAR
Book I: The Lieutenants
Book II: The Captains
Book III: The Majors
Book IV: The Colonels
Book V: The Berets
Book VI: The Generals
Book VII: The New Breed
Book VIII: The Aviators

THE CORPS
Book I: Semper Fi
Book II: Call to Arms
Book III: Counterattack
Book IV: The Battleground
Book V: Line of Fire
Book VI: Close Combat
Book VII: Behind the Lines

BADGE OF HONOR
Book I: Men in Blue
Book II: Special Operations
Book III: The Victim

W.E.B. GRIFFIN

THREE COMPLETE NOVELS

The Witness
The Assassin
The Murderers

G. P. PUTNAM'S SONS

New York

G. P. Putnam's Sons
Publishers Since 1838
200 Madison Avenue
New York, NY 10016

Library of Congress Cataloging-in-Publication Data
Griffin, W.E.B.
Three complete novels / W.E.B. Griffin.
p.   cm.
Contents: The witness—The assassin—The murderers.
ISBN 0-399-14238-X
1. Detective and mystery stories, American.   2. Police—Pennsylvania—
Philadelphia—Fiction.   3. Philadelphia (Pa.)—Fiction.   I. Title.
PS3557.R489137A6   1997
813'.54—dc21   96-46327 CIP

Printed in the United States of America
1   3   5   7   9   10   8   6   4   2

Book design by Jennifer Ann Daddio

CONTENTS

For Sergeant Zebulon V. Casey,
    Internal Affairs Division,
Police Department, Retired, the City of Philadelphia.
    He knows why.

THE
WITNESS

1.

The Day After New Year's Day Reception given by Taddeus Czernich, who was the police commissioner of the City of Philadelphia, was considered by Staff Inspector Peter F. Wohl as a lousy idea whose time had unfortunately come.

New Year's Eve is not a popular festive occasion so far as the police of Philadelphia are concerned. For one thing, almost no police are free to make merry themselves, because they are on duty. On New Year's Eve all the amateur drunks are out in force, with a lamentable tendency to settle midnight differences of opinion with one form of violence or another, and/or to run their automobiles through red lights and into one another, which of course requires the professional services of the Police Department to put things in order.

New Year's Day is worse. Philadelphia greets the New Year with the Mummer's Parade down Broad Street. There are massive crowds of people, many of whom have ingested one form of antifreeze or another, to control. Pickpockets and other thieves, who have been anxiously awaiting the chance to ply their trades, come out of the woodwork.

For a very long time, the Day After New Year's Day was a day on which every police officer who did not absolutely have to be on duty stayed home, slept late, and tried to forget how he had spent New Year's Eve and New Year's Day.

But then, during the reign of Police Commissioner Jerry Carlucci, that all changed. Jerry Carlucci had decided that it behooved him to make some gesture to the senior commanders of the Department in token of his appreciation for their faithful service during the past year.

He would, he decided, have a Commissioner's Reception at his home, and invite every captain and above in the Department. It would have been nice to invite all the white shirts, but there were just too many lieutenants; they would have to wait until they got themselves promoted. Since New Year's Day was out of the question, because everybody was working, the Day After New Year's Day was selected.

By the time Commissioner Czernich had assumed office, following the election of Jerry Carlucci as mayor of the City of Brotherly Love, the Commissioner's Reception on the Day After New Year's Day had become a tradition.

The wives, of course, loved it. Because their husbands had been working, they hadn't had the chance to do anything special on New Year's Eve. Now, through the gracious invitation of the commissioner, they had the opportunity to get all dressed up and meet with the other ladies in a pleasant atmosphere.

If the senior officers of the Philadelphia Police Department, who had really looked forward to doing nothing more physically exerting than walking from the bedroom to their chair in front of the TV in the living room, didn't like it, too bad.

Marriage was a two-way street. It was not too much to ask of a husband that he put on either his best uniform (uniforms were "suggested") or his good suit and spend three hours in the company of his spiffed-up spouse, who had spent New Year's watching the TV.

What wives thought of the affair was not really germane for Staff Inspector Wohl, who did not have one, had never had one, and had absolutely no desire to change that situation anytime soon.

There was a Mrs. Wohl at the reception, however, in the role of wife. She was Mrs. Olga Wohl, whose husband was Chief Inspector Augustus Wohl, Retired.

Mrs. Wohl had actually said to Staff Inspector Wohl, "Peter, if you were married, your wife would be here with you. She would love it."

Peter Wohl had learned at twelve that debating his mother was a no-win arrangement, so he simply smiled at her.

"And you should have worn your uniform," Mrs. Wohl went on. "You look so nice in it. Why didn't you?"

Wohl was wearing a nearly new single-breasted glen plaid suit, a light blue, button-down collar shirt, and a striped necktie his administrative assistant had told him was also worn by members of Her Britannic Majesty's Household Cavalry. He was a pleasant-looking thirty-five-year-old who did not much resemble what comes to mind when the term "cop" or "staff inspector" comes up.

"It didn't come back from the cleaners."

That was not the truth, the whole truth, and nothing but the truth. Staff Inspector Wohl's uniform was hanging in one of his closets. He had bought it when he had been promoted to lieutenant, and the epaulets were adorned with a golden bar. Now the epaulets carried the golden oak leaf (like an army major's) of a staff inspector, but the uniform still looked almost brand-new. He had seldom worn it as a lieutenant, or as a captain, and he rarely wore it now. He had last worn it six months before at the inspector's funeral Captain Richard F. "Dutch" Moffitt had earned for himself by getting killed in the line of duty. It would not have bothered Staff Inspector Wohl if his uniform remained in his closet, unworn, until the moths ate it down to the last button hole.

"Well, you certainly have no one to blame but yourself for that."

"You're right, Mother," he said, reaching for another shrimp.

The food at the Commissioner's Day After New Year's Day Reception was superb. This was less a manifestation of either Commissioner Czernich's taste or his generosity toward his guests but rather of the high esteem in which Commissioner Czernich and the police generally were held by various citizens of the City of Brotherly Love.

This, too, was a legacy from the reign of Jerry Carlucci as police commissioner. At the very first Commissioner's Reception to which then Sergeant Wohl had gone (under the mantle of then active Chief Inspector Wohl), the food had been heavily Italian in flavor. When the mayor's many friends in the Italian community had heard that Jerry was having a party for the other cops on the Day After New Year's Day, it seemed only right that they sort of help him out.

You can say a lot of things, many of them unpleasant, about Jerry Carlucci, but nobody ever heard of him taking a dime. And on what he's making as commissioner, he can't afford to feed all them cops. Angelo, call Salvatore, and maybe Joe Fierellio, too, and tell them I'm gonna make up some pasta and a ham, and maybe some pastry, and send it out to Jerry Carlucci's house, for the Day After New Year's Day cop party he's giving, and ask them maybe they want to get in on it.

By the time Commissioner Carlucci's Second Annual Day After New Year's Day Reception was held, the Commissioner's many friends in the other ethnic communities of the City of Brotherly Love had learned what the Italians had done. The repast of the Second Reception had been multinational in scope. By the time of Commissioner Carlucci's last Day After New Year's Day Reception (three years before; two days after which he had to resign to run for mayor), being *permitted* to make a little contribution to the Commissioner's Day After New Year's Day Reception carried a certain cachet among the city's restauranteurs, fish mongers, pastry bakers, florists, and wholesale butchers.

"When did you start drinking that?"

"Right after the waiter filled the glass."

"I mean, start drinking champagne?"

"As soon as I heard it was free, Mother."

"Don't be a smarty-pants, Peter. It gives me a headache, is what I mean."

"Then if I were you, I wouldn't drink it."

A tall, muscular, intelligent-faced young man, who looked to be in his late twenties, walked up to them.

"Good afternoon, Inspector," he said, and nodded at Olga Wohl. "Ma'am."

"Hello, Charley," Wohl said. "Do you know my mother?"

"No, I don't. I know Chief Wohl, ma'am."

"Mother, this is Sergeant Draper. He's Commissioner Cohan's driver."

"Nice to meet you," she said. "Are you having a nice time?"

"Yes, ma'am. Inspector, when you have a minute, the commissioner would like to have a word with you."

"Which commissioner, Charley?" Wohl asked. "Your commissioner, or that one?"

He raised his glass in the direction of half a dozen men gathered in a knot. One of them was the Hon. Jerry Carlucci. The others were Chief Inspector Augustus Wohl, Retired, Chief Inspector Matt Lowenstein, Chief Inspector Dennis V. Coughlin, Captain Jack McGovern, and Police Commissioner Taddeus Czernich.

"Mine, sir," Sergeant Draper said, a little chagrined. "Commissioner Cohan is over thataway." He pointed with an inclination of his head.

"Tell him I'll be right with him."

"Yes, sir."

"Where, by the way," Olga Wohl asked as soon as Draper was out of earshot, "is your driver?"

"I don't have a driver, Mother. I am a lowly staff inspector."

"You know what I mean. The Payne boy. Your father likes him."

"Oh, you mean, my *administrative assistant?*"

"You know very well what I meant. Shouldn't he be here?"

"I believe Officer Payne is having dinner with his parents."

"He should be here. He could meet people."

"He already knows people."

"I mean the *right* people."

"He already knows the right people. He told me that he and his father were going to play golf with H. Richard Detweiler and Chadwick T. Nesbitt this morning."

"Really?"

Chadwick T. Nesbitt III and H. Richard Detweiler were chairman of the board and president, respectively, of Nesfoods, International, which had begun more than a century before as Nesbitt Potted Meats and was now Philadelphia's largest single employer.

"Now if *I* were interested in social climbing, I probably could have talked myself into an invitation."

"You don't play golf."

"I could learn."

"He's a policeman now, Peter. It doesn't matter who his family is."

"Mother, I have no intention of telling them, but I'll bet you a dollar to a doughnut that if Jerry Carlucci or the commissioner knew where Matt is, they would be delighted."

Mrs. Wohl sniffed; Peter wasn't sure what it meant.

"I'd better go see what Cohan wants," Wohl said. "Can I trust you to go easy on the booze?"

"You ought to be ashamed of yourself, Peter Wohl!"

"I'll be right back," Wohl said. "I hope."

Deputy Commissioner-Administration Francis J. Cohan was a fair-skinned, finely featured, trim man of fifty or so. He was dressed in a suit almost identical to Peter Wohl's, but instead of the blue button-down collar shirt and striped necktie, he wore a stiffly starched white shirt and a tie bearing miniature representations of the insignia of the International Association of Chiefs of Police.

"Happy New Year, Commissioner," Wohl said. "You wanted to see me, sir?"

"Happy New Year, Peter," Cohan said, smiling and offering his hand. "Yes, I did. Why don't we get ourselves a fresh drink and find a quiet corner someplace? What is that, champagne?"

"Yes, sir."

"When did you start drinking that?"

"As soon as I saw the bottles with 'Moet et Chandon' on them. This is first-class stuff."

"It gives me a headache."

"May I say I admire your taste in suits, Commissioner?"

Cohan chuckled. "I noticed," he said. "Makes us look like the Bobbsey Twins, doesn't it?"

"Did you ever notice, sir, that when a man goes someplace and sees someone else with a suit like his, he thinks, 'Well, he certainly has good taste,' but if a woman sees somebody with a dress like hers, she wants to go home?"

"Don't get me started on the subject of women," Cohan said, and put his hand on Wohl's arm and led him to the bar. "Sometimes I think the Chinese had the right idea. Just keep enough for breeding purposes and drown the rest at birth."

Commissioner Cohan ordered a fresh Scotch and water. "And bubbly for my son here. You'd better give him two. Those look like small glasses, and this may take some time."

The bartender served the drinks.

"Tad Czernich said he has a little office off the hall; that we could use that," Cohan said. "Now let's see if we can find it."

I sense, Peter Wohl thought, *that while this little chat is obviously important—Czernich knows about it—it doesn't concern anything I've either done wrong or have not done.*

Commissioner Czernich's home office was closet-sized. There was barely room for a desk, an upholstered "executive" chair, and a second, straight-backed, metal chair. Wohl thought, idly, that it was probably used by Czernich only to make or take telephone calls privately. There were three telephones on the battered wooden desk.

Cohan sat in the upholstered chair.

"Have you got room enough to turn around and close the door?" he asked.

"If I suck in my breath."

Wohl closed the door behind him and sat down, feeling something like a schoolboy, in the straight-backed chair.

"Peter, the sequence in which this happened was that I was going to talk to you first, then, if you were amenable, to Tad, and if *he* was amenable, *then* to the mayor. It didn't go that way. I got here as the mayor did. He wanted to talk to me. I had to take the opportunity; he was in a good mood. So the sequence has been reversed."

Which means that I am about to be presented with a fait accompli; Carlucci has apparently gone along with whatever Cohan wants to do, and whether I am amenable or not no longer matters.

"You're aware, I'm sure, Peter, that the great majority of FBI agents are either Irish or Mormons?"

"I know one named Franklin D. Roosevelt Stevens that I'll bet isn't either Irish or Mormon," Peter said.

Cohan laughed, but Peter saw that it was with an effort.

"Okay," Cohan said. "Strike 'great majority' and insert 'a great many.' "

"Yes, sir. I've noticed, come to think of it."

"You ever hear the story, Peter, about why is it better to get arrested by an Irish FBI agent than a Mormon FBI agent?"

What the hell is this, a Polish joke?

"No, sir. I can't say that I have."

"Let's say the crime is spitting on the sidewalk, and the punishment is death by firing squad. You know they really do that, the Mormons in Utah, execute by firing squad?"

"Yes, sir. I'd heard that."

"Okay. So here's this guy, spitting on the sidewalk. If the Mormon FBI guy sees him, that's it. Cuff him. Read him his Miranda and stand him up against the wall. The law's the law. Spitters get shot. Period."

"I'm a little lost, Commissioner."

"Now, the Irish FBI agent: He sees the guy spitting. He knows it's against the law, but he knows that he's spit once or twice himself in his time. And maybe he thinks that getting shot for spitting is maybe a little harsh. So he either gets something in his eye so he can't identify the culprit, or he forgets to read him his rights."

"And therefore, be nice to Irish FBI agents?"

"What follows gets no further than Czernich's closet, okay?"

"Yes, sir."

"You know Jack Malone, don't you?"

"Sure."

Before Chief Inspector Cohan had been named a deputy commissioner, Sergeant John J. Malone had been his driver. Wohl now remembered that Malone had been on the last lieutenant's list. He couldn't remember where he had been assigned. If, indeed, he had ever known.

"And?"

"What do I think of him? Good cop. Smart. Straight arrow."

"Not always smart," Cohan said.

"Oh?"

"Assault is a felony," Cohan said carefully. "A police officer who is found guilty of committing any crime, not just a felony, is dismissed. A Mormon FBI guy would say, 'That's the law. Fire him. Put the felon in jail.' "

But you're Irish, right?

"You may have noticed, Peter, that I'm Irish," Cohan said.

"Who did he hit?"

"It's not important, but you'd probably hear anyway. A lawyer named Howard B. Candless."

Wohl shrugged, signaling he had never heard of him.

"Jack did quite a job on him," Cohan said. "Knocked a couple of teeth out. Caused what the medical report said were 'multiple bruises and contusions.' They kept Candless in the hospital two days, worrying about a possible concussion."

"Why?" Wohl asked. "That doesn't sound like Malone."

"And when he was finished with the lawyer, Jack had a couple too many drinks and went home and slapped his wife around."

"On general principles?"

"Jack is a very simple guy. He believes that when a woman marries one man, she should not get into another man's bed."

"Jesus Christ!"

"They kept her in the hospital overnight; long enough to make Polaroid pictures of her bruises and contusions. That's important."

"But he's not going to be charged? Or did I get the wrong impression?"

"It took some doing. He wasn't charged."

Malone wasn't charged because Deputy Commissioner Cohan is his rabbi. Every up-and-coming police officer has a rabbi. My father was Jerry Carlucci's rabbi. Jerry Carlucci was Denny Coughlin's rabbi. Denny Coughlin, it is said, is my rabbi. Even Officer Matthew M. Payne has a rabbi, I have lately come to realize—me.

The function of a rabbi is to select a young officer and guide him through the mine-fields of police department politics, try to see that he is given assignments that will broaden his areas of expertise and enhance his chances of promotion. And, of course, when he gets in trouble, to try not only to fix it, so he doesn't get kicked off the cops, but to try to ensure that he won't do what he did again.

"He was lucky to have you as a friend," Wohl said.

"He's a good man," Cohan said. "And a good cop."

"Yes, sir, I think so."

"I had him assigned to Major Crimes Division, to the Auto Squad," Cohan said. "And I arranged for him to stay there after he made lieutenant. All this took place, you understand, right around the time they were making up the lieutenant's list. If there had been an Internal Affairs report—"

"I understand," Wohl said. "What's his status with his wife?"

"They were divorced. I was a little slow on that one, Peter. A little naive. I thought the lawyer had gone along with withdrawing the assault charges because he was either ashamed of what he had done, didn't want the story repeated around the courtrooms, and/or didn't want to have any scandal floating around Mrs. Malone, who he intended to marry."

"But?"

"It would not have solved his purpose to have Jack locked up or even fired. That might have tended to make the judge feel a little sympathetic toward Jack when he got him in court and showed the judge the color photos of Mrs. Malone's swollen, black-and-blue face. And, Jesus, tell it all, the bruises on her chest and ass. Jack literally kicked her ass all over the house."

"Oh, Christ! Who was the judge?"

"Seymour F. Marshutz," Cohan said. "Marshutz cannot conceive of a situation—don't misunderstand me, I'm not defending what Jack did, not for a minute—where slapping a wife around is not right up there with child molesting. I tried to talk to him, I've known Sy Marshutz for years, and got absolutely nowhere."

"And?"

"She got everything, of course: the house, everything in it, and almost every other damn asset they had. All he took was his clothes and an old junk car. She got custody, of course, because the way Sy Marshutz sees it, while playing the whore is bad, it's not as bad as violence, and Jack has limited visitation privileges."

I wonder what I'm supposed to do with Lieutenant Jack Malone. That's obviously what this is about; this is not marital notes from all over.

"I had a long talk—lots of long talks—with Jack. I chewed his ass. I held his hand. For all I know, if Marilyn had done to me what his wife did to Jack, maybe I'd have taken a swing at her too. Anyway, I told him his life wasn't over, and that if I were him, I'd give everything I have to the job for a while, that thinking about what happened was only—you know what I mean, Peter."

"Yes, sir."

"So he took me literally. He's working all the time. He's got a room in a hotel, the St. Charles, on Arch at 19th?"

"Faded grandeur," Wohl said without thinking.

"Yeah," Cohan said. "Okay. Anyway. All he does is work and watch TV in the hotel room."

"No booze?"

"A little of that. We had a talk about that too. I think he's had more to drink in the last year than he's had up to now. That isn't a problem."

"But there is one."

"Yeah. Now he sees a car thief behind every bush."

"I don't follow you, sir."

"All work and no play hasn't made Jack a dull boy, Peter," Cohan said solemnly, "it's put his imagination in high gear, out of control."

"Is this any of my business, sir?"

"He thinks Bob Holland is a car thief."

Bob Holland was Holland Cadillac Motor Cars. And Bob Holland Chevrolet. And Holland Pontiac-GMC. And there was a strong rumor going around that Broad Street Ford and Jenkintown Chrysler-Plymouth were really owned by Robert L. Holland.

"Is he?"

"Come on, Peter," Cohan said. "You're not talking about some sleazeball used car dealer here."

"I gather Jack has nothing but a hunch to go on?"

"He went to Charley Gaft and asked for permission to surveil all of Holland's show-rooms," Cohan said. "And when Gaft turned him down, he came to me. Ten minutes after Bob called me and told me he was worried about him."

Captain Charles B. Gaft commanded the Major Crimes Division.

"I'm afraid to ask what all this has to do with me, Commissioner. What do you want me to do, have Highway Patrol keep an eye on Bob Holland's showrooms? Or sit on Jack Malone?"

"Peter," Cohan said, almost sadly, "your mouth has a tendency to run away with itself. It's only because I've known you, literally, since you wore short pants and because I know what a good police officer you are that I don't take offense. But there are those—people of growing importance to you, now that you're moving up—who would think that was just a flippant remark and unbecoming to a division commander."

Oh, shit!

"Commissioner, it was flippant, and I apologize. I have no excuse to offer except the champagne."

"Now, I already said, I understand your sense of humor, Peter. But maybe you'd better watch that champagne. It sneaks up on you."

"Yes, sir. But I do apologize."

"It never happened. Getting back to Jack. He's under a strain. He's working too hard. But he's a fine police officer and worth saving, and that's why I'm asking you for your help."

I'll be a sonofabitch. He rehearsed that little speech. That's what he planned to say to me to see if I would stand still for whatever he wants. It was supposed to be delivered before he went to see Czernich and Carlucci.

"Whatever I can do, Commissioner."

I say nobly, aware that I have absolutely no option to do or say anything else.

"I knew I could count on you, Peter. What I'm going to do is send Jack over to you—"

Shit! But what else did I expect?

"—and have Tony Lucci transferred to Jack's job on the Auto Squad in Major Crimes."

Lieutenant Anthony J. Lucci, who had been Mayor Carlucci's driver as a sergeant, had been sent to Special Operations on his promotion to lieutenant. It was a reward for a job well done, which by possibly innocent coincidence gave His Honor the Mayor a window on the inner workings of Special Operations, reports delivered daily.

Every black cloud has a silver lining. I get rid of Lucci. What's that going to cost me? Is he telling the truth about Malone not having a bottle problem, or am I going to have to nurse a drunk?

"Now, I have no intention of trying to tell you how to run your division, Peter, or what to do with Jack Malone when you get him—"

But?

"—but if you could find something constructive for him to do that would keep him from thinking he's been assigned to the rubber-gun squad, I would be personally grateful."

"So far as I'm concerned, Commissioner, even after what you've told me, Jack Malone is a good cop, and I'll find something worthwhile for him to do."

"What was Lucci doing?"

"He's my administrative officer. He also makes sure the mayor knows what's going on."

Cohan looked sharply at Wohl, pursed his lips thoughtfully for a moment, and then said, "So I've heard. Jack won't feel any obligation to do that, Peter."

"Thank you, sir."

"Your father is in good spirits, isn't he?" Cohan said. "I had a pleasant chat with him a couple of minutes ago."

Our little chat is apparently over.

"I think he'd go back on the job tomorrow, if someone asked him."

"The grass is not as green as it looked?"

"I think he's bored, sir."

"He was active all his life," Cohan said. "That's understandable."

Cohan pushed himself out of the seat and extended his hand.

"Thank you, Peter," he said. "I knew I could count on you."

"Anytime, Commissioner."

GENERAL: 0565 01/02/74 FROM COMMISSIONER PAGE 1 OF 1
***********CITY OF PHILADELPHIA***********
************POLICE DEPARTMENT***********
TRANSFERS:
EFFECTIVE 1201 AM JANUARY 3, 1974
LIEUTENANT ANTHONY S. LUCCI: REASSIGNED FROM SPECIAL OPERATIONS DIVISION TO MAJOR CRIMES DIVISION AS COMMANDING OFFICER AUTO SQUAD.
LIEUTENANT JOHN J. MALONE: REASSIGNED FROM AUTO SQUAD, MAJOR CRIMES DIVISION TO SPECIAL OPERATIONS DIVISION.
TADDEUS CZERNICH
POLICE COMMISSIONER

2.

The day began for Police Officer Charles McFadden at five minutes before six A.M. when Mrs. Agnes McFadden, his mother, went into his bedroom, on the second floor of a row house on Fitzgerald Street, near Methodist Hospital in South Philadelphia, snapped on the lights, walked to his bed, and rather loudly announced, "Almost six. Rise and shine, Charley."

Officer McFadden, who the previous Tuesday had celebrated his twenty-third birthday, was large-boned and broad-shouldered and weighed 214 pounds.

He rolled over on his back, shielded his eyes from the light, and replied, "Jesus, already?"

"Watch your mouth, mister," his mother said sharply, and then added, "If you didn't keep that poor girl out until all hours, you just might not have such trouble getting up in the morning."

With a visible effort Charley McFadden hauled himself into a sitting position and swung his feet out of bed and onto the floor.

"Mom, Margaret didn't get *off work* until half past ten."

"Then you should have brought her straight home, instead of keeping her up all night," Mrs. McFadden said, and then marched out of the room.

Margaret McCarthy, R.N., a slight, blue-eyed, redheaded young woman, was the niece of Bob and Patricia McCarthy, who lived across Fitzgerald Street and had been in the neighborhood, and good friends, just about as long as the McFaddens, and that meant even before Charley had been born.

Margaret and Charley had known each other as kids, before her parents had moved to Baltimore, and Agnes remembered seeing her after that, on holidays and whenever else her family had visited, but she and Charley had met again only a couple of months ago.

Margaret had gone through the Nurse Training Program and gotten her R.N. at Johns Hopkins Hospital in Baltimore, and now she was enrolled at Temple University to get a college degree.

As smart as Margaret was, Agnes McFadden wouldn't have been at all surprised if she wound up as a doctor.

Anyway, Charley and Margaret had bumped into each other and started going out, and there was no question in Agnes's mind that it was only a matter of time until Charley popped the question. She wouldn't have been surprised if they were waiting for one of two things, Margaret finishing her first year at Temple, or Charley taking the examination for detective. Or maybe both.

Agnes and Rudy McFadden approved of the match. She wasn't sure that the McCarthys were all that enthusiastic. Bob McCarthy was the sort of man who held a grudge, and Agnes thought he was still sore at Charley for taking out the windshield of his brand-new Ford with a golf ball, playing stickball in the street, when Charley was still a kid.

And Agnes knew full well all the nasty things Bob McCarthy had had to say about Charley when Charley had first gone on the cops and they'd made him work with the drug people.

The truth was, Agnes realized, that Charley did look and act like a bum when that was going on. He wore a beard and filthy, dirty clothes, and he was out all night, every night, and he'd hardly ever gone to church.

Anybody but Bob McCarthy, Agnes often thought, would have put that all behind him, and maybe even apologized, after Charley had caught the drug addict who had shot Captain Moffitt, and gotten a citation from Police Commissioner Czernich himself, and they'd let him wear a uniform like a regular cop. But people like Bob McCarthy, Agnes understood, found it very hard to admit they were wrong.

Charley McFadden took a quick shower and shave and splashed himself liberally with Bahama Lime aftershave, a bottle of which had been Margaret's birthday gift to him.

He put on fresh underwear, went to the head of the stairs, and called down, "Don't make no breakfast, Mom. We're going out."

"I already made it," she said. "Why don't you bring her over here? There's more than enough."

"We're meeting some people," Charley replied.

That was not true. But he wanted to have breakfast with Margaret alone, not with his mother hanging over her shoulder.

There was a snort of derision from the kitchen.

Charley went into his room and put on his uniform. There was a blue shirt and a black necktie (a pretied tie that clipped on; regular ties that went around the neck could be grabbed), breeches, motorcycle boots, a leather jacket, a Sam Browne belt from which were suspended a holster for the service revolver, a handcuff case, and an attachment that held a nightstick. Finally, bending his knees to get a good look at himself in the mirror over his chest of drawers, Charley put squarely in place on his head a leather-brimmed cap. There was no crown stiffener.

This was the uniform of the Highway Patrol, which differed considerably from the uniform of ordinary police officers. They wore trousers and shoes, for example, not breeches and boots, and the crowns of their brimmed caps were stiffly erect.

Highway Patrol was considered, especially by members of the Highway Patrol, as the elite unit of the Philadelphia Police Department.

In the ordinary course of events, a rookie cop such as Officer McFadden (who had been a policeman not yet two years) would be either walking a footbeat or working a van in a district, hauling sick fat ladies down stairwells for transport to a hospital, or prisoners between where they were arrested and the district holding cell and between there and the Central Cell Room in the Roundhouse. He would not ordinarily be trusted to ride around in a district radio patrol car. He would be working under close supervision, learning the policeman's profession. The one thing a rookie cop would almost certainly not be doing would be putting on a Highway Patrolman's distinctive uniform.

But two extraordinary things had happened to Officer Charles McFadden in his short police career. The first had been his assignment, right from the Academy, to the Narcotics Bureau.

Narcotics had learned that one of the more effective—perhaps the most effective—

means to deal with people who trafficked in proscribed drugs was to infiltrate, so to speak, the drug culture.

This could not be accomplished, Narcotics had learned, by simply putting Narcotics Division police officers in plainclothes and sending them out onto the streets. The faces of Narcotics Division officers were known to the drug people. And bringing in officers from districts far from the major areas of drug activity and putting them in plainclothes didn't work either. Even if the vendors of controlled substances did not recognize the face of an individual police officer, they seemed to be able to "make him" by observing the subtle mannerisms of dress, behavior, or speech that, apparently, almost all policemen with a couple of years on the job seem to manifest.

There was only one solution, and somewhat reluctantly Narcotics turned to it. One or two young, brand-new police officers were selected from each class at the Police Academy and asked to volunteer for a plainclothes and/or undercover assignment with Narcotics.

A cop with a week on the job (or, less often, just-graduated-from-the-Academy rookie) was not going to be recognized on the street because he had not been on the street. Nor had he been a cop long enough to acquire a cop's mannerisms.

Few rookies, whose notions of police work were mostly acquired from television and the movies, refused such an opportunity to battle crime. When asked, Officer Charley McFadden had accepted immediately.

Some, perhaps even most, such volunteers don't work out when they actually go on the streets. The tension is too much for some. Others simply cannot physically stomach what they see in the course of their duties, and some just prove inept. They are then, if they hadn't graduated from the Academy, sent back to finish their training, or, if they have graduated, sent to a district.

Charley McFadden proved to be the exception. He was a good undercover Narc virtually from almost the first day, and got even better at it with experience, and after he had grown a beard, and come to look, in his mother's description, "like a filthy bum."

After three months on the job, he was paired with Officer Jesus Martinez, a slight, intense Latino who had been on the job for six months longer than Charley, and had learned the mannerisms of a successful middle-level drug dealer to near perfection.

They were an odd couple, the extra large Irishman and the barely over the height and weight minimums Latino. Behind their backs, they were known by their brother Narcotics Bureau officers as Mutt & Jeff, after the cartoon characters.

But they were good at what they did, and not only their peers understood this. Their lieutenant at the time, Dave Pekach, led them to believe that if they kept up the good work, he would do his very best to keep them in Narcotics even when their identities had become known on the street.

That was important. They didn't tell the rookies at the time they were recruited, but what usually happened when undercover Narcs became, inevitably, known on the street was that they were reassigned to a district. There, they picked up their police career where it had been interrupted. That is to say they now got to work a wagon and haul sick fat ladies down narrow stairways and prisoners down to Central Cell Room.

The way to become a detective in the Philadelphia Police Department was not the way it was in the movies, where a smiling police commissioner handed a detective's badge to the undercover rookie who had just made a really good arrest. In Philadelphia, it doesn't matter if you catch Jack the Ripper with the knife in his hand, you wait until you have two years on the job, and then you take the examination for detective, and if you pass, when your number comes up, then, and only then, you get to be a detective.

What Lieutenant Dave Pekach had offered them, instead of being sent to some damned district to work school crossings and turn off fire hydrants, was a chance to stay in Narcotics as plainclothes officers until they had their time in to take the detective exam.

Charley and Jesus would have killed to convince Lieutenant Pekach what good under-cover Narcs they were, what good plainclothes cops they could be, if that would keep them from going out to some damned district in uniform.

And it almost came to that.

Captain Richard F. Moffitt, off duty and in civilian clothing, had walked in on a rob-bery in progress in a diner on Roosevelt Boulevard.

The doer, to Captain Moffitt's experienced eye, was a strung-out junkie, a poor, skinny, dirty Irish kid who had somehow got hooked on the shit and was, with a thirty-dollar Sat-urday Night Special .22 revolver, trying to score enough money for a hit, or something to eat, or probably both.

"I'm a police officer," Captain Moffitt said gently. "Put the gun down, son, before somebody gets hurt."

The doer, subsequently identified as a poor, skinny Irish kid who had somehow gotten hooked on a pharmacist's encyclopedia of controlled substances, and whose name was Gerald Vincent Gallagher, fired every .22 Long Rifle cartridge his pistol held at Captain Moffitt, and managed to hit him once.

That was enough. The bullet ruptured an artery, and Captain Richard F. Moffitt died a minute or so later, slumped against the wall of the diner.

The killing of any cop triggers a deep emotional response in every other police-man. And "Dutch" Moffitt was not an ordinary cop. He was a captain. He was the son of a cop. His brother had been a cop, and it was immediately recalled that the brother, a sergeant, had been shot to death while answering a silent alarm.

And Captain Dutch Moffitt had been the commanding officer of Highway Patrol. High-way Patrol had been organized years before to do what its name implied. The first Highway Patrolmen had patrolled the highways throughout the city on motorcycles. The breeches, boots, and leather jackets of Highway Patrol motorcyclists were still worn, although radio patrol cars now outnumbered motorcycles.

Highway Patrol had become, beginning with the reign of Captain Jerry Carlucci (and later with the blessing of Inspector Carlucci, and Chief Inspector Carlucci, and Deputy Commissioner Carlucci, and Commissioner Carlucci, and now Mayor Carlucci), a spe-cial force.

Although the Philadelphia *Ledger,* which did not approve of much that Mayor Carlucci did, was prone to refer to the Highway Patrol as "Carlucci's Commandos" and even as his "Jackbooted Gestapo," just about everyone else in Philadelphia recognized Highway Patrol and its officers, who rode two men to an RPC, and who did most of their patrolling in high-crime areas of the city, as something special.

Getting into Highway was difficult. As a general rule of thumb, an officer had to have four or five years, good years, on the job. It helped to be about six feet and at least 175 pounds, and it helped if you had come to the attention of someone who was (or had been) a Highway supervisor—that is, a sergeant or better—and he had decided that you were a better cop than most. An assignment to Highway was seen by many as a good step to take if you wanted to rise above sergeant elsewhere in the Police Department.

Every police officer in Philadelphia reacted emotionally to the murder of Captain Dutch Moffitt—*If the bad guys can get away with shooting a cop, what's next?*—but it was taken as a personal affront by every man in Highway.

The result was that eight thousand police officers, most especially including every member of the Highway Patrol, were searching for Gerald Vincent Gallagher.

He was found by two rookie cops, working undercover in Narcotics, whose names were Charley McFadden and Jesus Martinez. And it wasn't a question of just stumbling onto the dirty little scumbag, either. On their own time, not even getting overtime, they had staked out Pratt Street Terminal, where Charley McFadden had an idea the miserable pissant would eventually show up.

And he had, and Charley and Jesus had chased the scumbag down the elevated tracks until Charles Vincent Gallagher had slipped, fallen onto the third rail, fried himself, and then been cut into many pieces under the wheels of a train.

Once they'd gotten their pictures in the newspaper, of course, Jesus's and Charley's effectiveness as undercover Narcs came to an end. And at a very awkward time for them, as Lieutenant David Pekach, having been promoted to captain, had been transferred out of Narcotics, and his replacement, a real shit heel, in their judgment, immediately made it clear that he felt no obligation to honor Lieutenant Pekach's implied promise to keep them in Narcotics in plainclothes if they did a good job on the job.

They had, however, also come to the attention of Chief Inspector Dennis V. Coughlin, who was arguably the most influential of the seven chief inspectors in the Department. Denny Coughlin saw in Charley McFadden something of himself. In other words, a good, hardworking Irish Catholic lad from South Philadelphia who was obviously destined to be a better than average cop. And Coughlin knew that once a rookie had worked the streets undercover, he regarded being put back in uniform as a demotion.

So he arranged for Officer McFadden to be assigned, temporarily, to the 12th District, in plainclothes, to work on an auto burglary detail. Chief Coughlin felt no such kinship for Officer Martinez—for one thing, the little Mexican didn't look big enough to be a real cop, and for another, Coughlin was made vaguely uneasy by someone who had the same name as the Son of God himself—but fair was fair, and he arranged for Jesus Martinez to be similarly assigned.

Then when Mayor Carlucci had set up Special Operations and given it to Peter Wohl, the problem of what to do with McFadden and Martinez was, as far as Denny Coughlin was concerned, solved. He sent them over to Special Operations. Peter Wohl was a smart cop; he'd figure out something useful for them to do.

The subordination of Highway Patrol to the new Special Operations Division had been regarded by many, most, Highway guys as bullshit. It was wondered, aloud, why the mayor, who *was* a real Highway guy, had let the commissioner get away with it.

Giving command of Special Operations (and thus, Highway) to Staff Inspector Peter Wohl made it even worse. Everybody knew what staff inspectors did. Not that locking up judges and city commissioners and other big shots like that on the take wasn't important, but it wasn't the same thing as being out on the street, one-on-one, with the worst scumbags in Philadelphia.

Wohl seemed to prove what a Roundhouse asshole he was when he was reliably quoted as saying that anyone who willingly got on a motorcycle wasn't playing with a full deck. Every Highway Patrolman had to go through extensive motorcycle training ("Wheel School") and prove he could really ride a motorcycle, and they didn't like some Roundhouse politically savvy supercop making fun of that.

That was all bad enough, but what really pissed people off, the straw that broke the fucking camel's back, so to speak, was Wohl's probationary Highway Patrolman idea. Wohl said that he would approve the transfer into Highway of outstanding young cops who didn't have four or five years on the job. He would put them to work under a Highway supervisor for six months. At any time during the six months, the supervisor could recommend, in writing, that the rookie be transferred out of Highway. But he had to give his reasons. In other words, if the rookie didn't screw up, he was in. He would get himself sent to Wheel School and if he got through that, he could go buy himself a pair of boots, breeches, and a crushed-crown brimmed cap.

The first two probationary Highway Patrolmen were Officers Jesus Martinez and Charles McFadden.

Officer Charley McFadden pulled open the top left-hand drawer of his dresser and took his Smith & Wesson Military & Police .38 Special caliber service revolver from under a pile of Jockey shorts and slipped it into his holster.

Then he went down the stairs two at a time.

"See you later, Mom!" he called at the bottom.

"Ask Margaret if she'd like to come to supper," Agnes McFadden said. "If you can spare the time for your mother."

"I'll ask," Charley said, and went out the door.

He ran across Fitzgerald Street, down two houses, and up the steps to the porch. The door opened as he got there.

Margaret was wearing her nurse suit. Sometimes she did, and sometimes she didn't. Charley wasn't sure exactly how that worked, but he did know that she was a real knockout in her starched white uniform. Not that she wasn't in regular clothes too, of course. But there was something about that white uniform that turned Charley on.

"Hi!" she said.

"Hi!"

She stood on her toes and kissed him. Chastely, but on the lips.

She had an armful of books.

"How come the books?"

"Classes in the morning," she said. "Then I agreed to fill in at the emergency room from one to seven."

"I get off at four," he said, disappointed.

"I need the money," she said, and then corrected herself. "*We* need the money. And I'm getting double-time."

They went down the stairs. Charley unlocked the door of his Volkswagen.

"Good morning, Margaret!" Agnes McFadden called from the white marble steps in front of her door.

"Morning, Mrs. McFadden."

"Why don't you come to supper?"

"I'd love to, but I can't. I'm working. Can I have a raincheck?"

"Yeah, sure."

Charley closed the door after her, and then went around the front and got behind the wheel.

"So what are you going to do today?"

"I got court," Charley replied. "Which means I get off at four."

"I told you, they're paying me double-time."

"How come?"

"Because it's less than twenty-four hours since my last overtime tour. I got overtime yesterday too."

"You're not getting enough sleep," Charley said.

"So tonight, after I meet you in the FOP at seven-fifteen, and we have dinner, I go to bed early."

The Fraternal Order of Police, on Spring Garden Street, was just a couple of minutes' walk from Hahnemann Hospital on North Broad Street in downtown Philadelphia.

"Yeah," he said. "This isn't a hell of a lot of fun, is it?"

"Most people are broke when they get married, and have to go in debt. We won't be."

"To hell with it. Let's get married and go in debt."

She laughed and leaned over and kissed him again.

They had breakfast in the medical staff cafeteria at Temple Hospital. The food was good and reasonable and there was a place to park the Volkswagen. As long as she was wearing a nurse's uniform and her R.N. pin, she could eat there. When she was in regular clothes, for some reason, they wouldn't let her do that.

Charley sometimes felt a little uncomfortable when he was in his Highway uniform and they ate there. He had the feeling that some of the medical personnel had started believing the bullshit the Philadelphia *Ledger* had been printing about the cops generally, and Highway specifically. The *Ledger* had really been on Highway's ass, with that "Carlucci's Commandos" and "Gestapo" bullshit, so it wasn't really surprising. People believe what they read.

He thought that if he was really a Highway guy, maybe he wouldn't be so sensitive about it. Nobody in the world knew it but Margaret, but the truth was, he didn't like Highway. What he really wanted to be was a detective.

If I was in here in plainclothes, nobody would give me a second look; they would think I was a doctor, or a pill salesman, or something.

When they finished breakfast, Charley got in the Volkswagen and drove to Highway headquarters at Bustleton and Bowler Streets in Northeast Philadelphia.

There, he met his partner, Police Officer Gerald "Gerry" D. Quinn, who was thirty-three, had been on the job eleven years and in Highway for five years.

The very first day he and Quinn had gone on patrol together, they had stopped a '72 Buick for speeding. It had turned out to be stolen. The case was finally coming up for trial today.

They stood roll call, and then drew a car, Highway 22, a year-old Chevrolet with 97,000-odd miles on its odometer. If by some miracle the trial went off as scheduled, they could then go on patrol. They drove downtown to City Hall at the intersection of Broad and Market Streets and parked just outside the southeast corner entrance.

Just off the southeast stairwell is Court Attendance, an administrative unit of the Police Department, which tries to keep track of which police officer is to testify at what time in which courtroom. They checked in there, learned where they were supposed to go to testify, and then went to the stairwell itself, where a blind concessionaire brewed what most police agreed was the worst coffee in the Delaware River Basin. They shot the bull with other cops for a while, and then went upstairs to their courtroom to wait for their case to be called.

The day began for Staff Inspector Peter Frederick Wohl at about the same time, a few minutes before six, as it had for Officer Charles McFadden.

Wohl was wakened by the ringing of one of the two telephones on the bedside table in his bedroom in his apartment. His over-a-six-car-garage apartment had once been the chauffeur's quarters of a turn-of-the-century mansion on the 800 block of Norwood Street in Chestnut Hill. The mansion itself had been divided into luxury apartments.

"Inspector Wohl," he said, somewhat formally. The phone that had been ringing was the official phone, paid for by the Police Department.

"Six o'clock, sir. Good morning."

It was the voice of the tour lieutenant at Bustleton and Bowler. The voice was familiar, and so was the face he could put to it—that of a lieutenant newly assigned to Special Operations—but he could not come up with a name.

"Good morning," Wohl said, as cheerfully as he could manage. "How goes the never-ending war against crime?"

The lieutenant chuckled.

"I don't know about that, sir. But I can report your car is back from the garage. Shall I have someone run it over to you?"

For the first time, Wohl remembered what had happened to his car, an unmarked nearly brand-new Ford LTD four-door sedan. The sonofabitch had just died on him. He had been stopped by the red light at Mount Airy and Germantown Avenue on the way home from Commissioner Czernich's soiree, and when the light changed, the Ford had moved fifteen feet forward and lurched to a stop.

When he tried to start it, the only thing that happened was the lights dimmed. The radio still worked, happily. He had called for a police tow truck, and then asked Police Radio to have the nearest Highway or Special Operations car meet him.

By the time the tow truck reached him, a Highway RPC, a Highway sergeant, and the

Special Operations/Highway lieutenant were already there. The lieutenant had driven him home.

Wohl sat up and swung his feet out of bed, hoping to clear his brain.

"Let me think," he said.

If they sent somebody over with his car, it would be someone who should be out on the street, or someone who was going off-duty, and thus should not be doing a white shirt a favor.

On the other hand, he was reluctant to drive his personal car over to Bustleton and Bowler for a number of reasons, not the least of which was that it might get "accidentally" bumped by a Highway Patrolman who believed Peter Wohl to be the devil reincarnate.

Peter Wohl's personal automobile was a twenty-three-year-old Jaguar XK-120 drop-head roadster. He had spent four years and more money than he liked to think about rebuilding it from the frame up.

And even if I did drive it over there, he finally decided, *when the day is over I will be back on square one, since I obviously cannot drive both the Jag and the Department's Ford back here at the same time.*

"Let me call you if I need a ride, Lieutenant," Wohl said. "If you don't hear from me, just forget it."

"Yes, sir. I'll be here."

Wohl hung up the official telephone and picked up the one he paid for and dialed a number from memory.

"Hello."

"Peter Wohl, Matt. Did I wake you?"

"No, sir. I had to get out of bed to take a shower."

"You sound pretty chipper this morning, Officer Payne."

"We celibates always sleep, sir, with a clear conscience and wake up chipper."

Wohl chuckled, and then asked, "Have you had breakfast?"

"No, sir."

"I'll swap you a breakfast of your choice for a ride to work. The Ford broke last night. They fixed it and took it to Bustleton and Bowler."

"Thirty minutes?"

"Thank you, Matt. I hate to put you out."

"You *did* say, sir, *you* were buying breakfast?"

"Yes, I did."

"Thirty minutes, sir."

3.

Officer Matthew M. Payne had just about finished dressing when Wohl called. Like Wohl, he was a bachelor. He lived in a very nice, if rather small, apartment on the top floor of a turn-of-the-century mansion on Rittenhouse Square. The lower floors of the building, owned by his father, now housed the Delaware Valley Cancer Society.

A tall, lithely muscled twenty-two-year-old, Payne had graduated the previous June from the University of Pennsylvania and had almost immediately joined the Police Department. He was assigned as "administrative assistant" to Inspector Wohl, who commanded the Special Operations Division of the Philadelphia Police Department. It was a plainclothes assignment.

He put the telephone back into its cradle and then walked to the fireplace, where he tied his necktie in the mirror over the mantel. He put his jacket on and then went back to the fireplace and took his Smith & Wesson "Undercover" .38 Special five-shot revolver and its ankle holster from the mantelpiece and strapped it to his ankle.

Then he left the apartment, went down the narrow stairs to the fourth floor, and got on the elevator to the parking garage in the basement.

There he got into a new silver Porsche 911, his graduation present from his father, and drove out of the garage, waving at the Holmes Security Service rent-a-cop as he passed his glassed-in cubicle. For a long time the rent-a-cop, a retired Traffic Division corporal, was the only person in the building who knew that Payne was a policeman.

There had been a lot of guessing by the two dozen young women who worked for the Cancer Society about just who the good-looking young guy who lived in the attic apartment was. He had been reliably reported to be a stockbroker, a lawyer, in the advertising business, and several other things. No one had suggested that he might be a cop; cops are not expected to dress like an advertisement for Brooks Brothers or to drive new silver Porsche 911s.

But then Officer Payne had shot to death one Warren K. Fletcher, thirty-one, of a Germantown address, whom the newspapers had taken to calling "the Northwest serial rapist" and his photograph, with Mayor Jerry Carlucci's arm around him, had been on the front pages of all the newspapers, and his secret was out.

He was not an overly egotistical young man, but it seemed to him that after the shooting, the looks of invitation in the eyes of the Cancer Society's maidens had seemed to intensify.

There were two or three of them he thought he would like to get to know, in the biblical sense, but he had painful proof when he was at the University of Pennsylvania that *"hell hath no fury like a woman scorned"* was more than a cleverly turned phrase. A woman scorned who worked where he lived, he had concluded, was too much of a risk to take.

Matt Payne drove to Peter Wohl's apartment via the Schuylkill Expressway, not recklessly, but well over the speed limit. He was aware that he was in little danger of being stopped (much less cited) for speeding. The Schuylkill Expressway was patrolled by officers of the Highway Patrol, all of whom were aware that Inspector Wohl's administrative assistant drove a silver Porsche 911.

Wohl was waiting for him when Payne arrived, leaning against one of the garage doors.

"Funny, you don't look celibate," Wohl said as he got in the car.

"Good morning, sir."

"Let's go somewhere nice, Matt. I know I'm buying, but the condemned man is entitled to a hearty meal."

"I don't think I like the sound of that," Matt replied.

"Not you, me. Condemned, I mean. They want me in the commissioner's office at ten. I'm sure what he wants to know is how the Magnella job is going."

Officer Joseph Magnella, twenty-four, had been found lying in the gutter beside his 22nd District RPC (radio patrol car) with seven .22 bullets in his body. Mayor Carlucci had given the job to Special Operations. A massive effort, led by two of the best detectives in the department, to find the doers had so far come up with nothing.

"Nothing came up overnight?" Matt asked softly.

"Not a goddamned clue, to coin a phrase," Wohl said bitterly. "I told them to call me if anything at all came up. Nobody called."

Payne braked before turning onto Norwood Street.

"How about The Country Club?" he asked.

The Country Club was a diner with a reputation for good food on Cottman Avenue in the Northeast, along their route to Bustleton and Bowler.

"Fine," Wohl said.

Wohl bought a copy of the *Ledger* from a vending machine as they walked into the restaurant, glanced at the headlines, and then flipped through it until he found what he was looking for.

"Somewhat self-righteously," he said, handing the paper to Matt, "the *Ledger* comments editorially on the incompetence of the Police Department, vis-à-vis the murder of Officer Magnella."

The waitress appeared and handed them menus.

"Breakfast steak, pink in the middle, two fried eggs, sunny side up, home fries, an English muffin, orange juice, milk, and coffee," Payne ordered without looking at the menu.

"If you're what you say you are, where do you get the appetite?" Wohl said, and added, "Toast and coffee, please."

"I have high hopes," Payne replied. "You have to eat, Inspector."

"Who do you think you are, my mother?"

"Think of the starving children in India," Payne said. "How *they* would love a breakfast steak."

"Oh, Jesus," Wohl groaned, but after a moment added, "Okay. Do that twice, please, miss."

Payne read the editorial and handed the newspaper back.

"You didn't expect anything else, did you?" Payne asked.

"I can ignore those bastards when they're wrong. But it smarts when they're right."

"Harris and Washington will come up with something."

"He said, not really believing it."

"I believe it."

"As a matter of fact, the longer they don't come up with something, the greater the odds are that they won't," Wohl said.

The waitress delivered the coffee, milk, and orange juice, sparing Payne having to respond. He was grateful; he hated to sound like a cheerleader.

Wohl ate everything put before him, but absently. He volunteered no further conversation, and Payne decided he should keep his mouth shut.

They were halfway between The Country Club and Special Operations headquarters when Wohl decided to tell Payne about Lieutenant Jack Malone.

"We're getting a new lieutenant this morning," he said. "And Lucci's being transferred out."

"That sounds like bad news-good news."

"Lieutenant Malone used to be Commissioner Cohan's driver. Cohan is behind the transfer."

"Then it's good news-good news?"

"Not necessarily," Wohl said. "Cohan sprung this on me at Commissioner Czernich's reception. Malone's had some personal problems, and in a manner of speaking has been working too hard. Cohan wants to take some of the pressure off him. He's had the Auto Squad in Major Crimes; that's where Lucci's going. It's a good job. Cohan's afraid that Malone will think he's been shanghaied to us. Which means that I have—"

"Has he?" Payne interrupted. "Been shanghaied to us?"

"I used the wrong word. *Punished* would be better. He's been shanghaied in the sense that he didn't ask for the transfer, and probably doesn't like the idea, but I'm not really sure if he just needs some of the pressure taken off, or whether Cohan is sending him a message. Cohan made it plain that he expects me to put him to work doing something worthy of his talent."

"What did he do?" Payne asked.

Why the hell did I tell him any of this in the first place?

"He caught his wife in bed with a lawyer and beat them up."

"Both of them?"

"Yeah, both of them. But that's not why he's being sent to us, I don't think. The pressure began to affect his work."

"I don't think I understand."

And aside from that, the problems, personal or professional, of a lieutenant are really none of the business of a police officer. But I started this, didn't I? And Payne is really more than a run-of-the mill young cop, isn't he?

"He's got a wild idea that Bob Holland is involved in auto theft," Wohl said.

"Holland Cadillac?" Matt asked, a hint of incredulity in his voice.

"Yeah."

"Is he?"

"I don't know. It strikes me as damned unlikely. If I had to bet, I'd say no. Why should he be? He's got a dealership on every other corner in Philadelphia. Presumably, they're making money. He sold the city the mayor's limousine. Hell, my father bought his Buick from him; he gives a police discount, whatever the hell that is. And Commissioner Cohan obviously doesn't think so; he thinks that the pressure got to Malone and his imagination ran away with him."

"He was at the club yesterday. I saw him in the bar with that congressman I think is light on his feet."

"Holland?" Wohl asked, and when Payne nodded, he went on, "Which club was that?"

"We played at Whitemarsh Valley."

"So Holland has friends in high places, right? Is that what you're driving at?"

"It would explain why the commissioner wants him out of the Auto Squad."

"Yeah," Wohl agreed a moment later. "Well, if Holland is doing hot cars, that's now Lucci's concern, not Malone's."

And I will make sure that Lieutenant Jack Malone clearly understands that.

"What are you going to do with him?" Payne asked.

"We now have a plans and training officer," Wohl said. "His name is Lieutenant John J. Malone."

"What's he going to do?"

"I haven't figured that out yet," Wohl said.

When Payne pulled into the parking lot, it was half past seven. The cars of Captain Mike Sabara, Wohl's deputy, and Captain Dave Pekach, the commanding officer of Highway Patrol, were already there. Payne wondered if Wohl had sent for them—the normal duty day began at eight—or whether they had come in early on their own.

Once inside the building, Wohl, Sabara, and Pekach went into Wohl's office and closed the door. Payne understood that his presence was not desired.

He told the sergeant on the desk that if the inspector was looking for him, he had gone to park his car and to get the inspector's car.

When he came back and sat down at his desk, Wohl's phone began to ring.

"Inspector Wohl's office, Officer Payne."

"My name is Special Agent Davis of the FBI," the caller said. "Inspector Wohl, please."

"I'm sorry, sir, the inspector is tied up. May I have him call you back?"

"I wonder if you would please tell him that Special Agent in Charge Davis wants just a moment of time, and see if he'll speak to me?"

There was a tone of authority in Davis's voice that got through to Matt.

"Hold on, please, sir," he said, and walked to the closed door. He knocked and then, without waiting, opened it.

"Sir, there's a Special Agent Davis—'Special Agent in Charge' is actually what he said—on twenty-nine. He said he wants 'just a moment of your time.' You want to talk to him?"

"For your general information, Officer Payne, Special Agent in Charge Davis is the high priest of the FBI in Philadelphia," Wohl said. "Yes, of course, I'll talk to him." He picked up the telephone, pushed one of the buttons on it, and said, "Hello, Walter. How are you?"

Payne closed the door and went back to his desk.

When he got out of bed, at quarter past seven, John J. "Jack" Malone almost immediately learned that among a large number of other things that had gone wrong recently in his life he could now count the plumbing system of the St. Charles Hotel, where he resided. Specifically, both the hot and cold taps in his bathroom ran ice-cold.

While he fully understood that the St. Charles was not in the league of the Bellevue-Stratford or the Warwick, neither was it a fleabag, and considering what they were charging him for his "suite" (a bedroom, a tiny sitting room, and an alcove containing a small refrigerator, a two-burner electric stove, and a small table), it seemed to him that the least the bastards could do was make sure the hot water worked.

There was no question that it was not working. That, until he just now had been desperately hoping, it was not just the time required to get hot water up from the basement heater to the tenth floor. The damned water had been running full blast for five minutes and it was just as ice-cold now as it had been when he first turned it on.

A shower, under the circumstances, was clearly out of the question. Shaving was going to be bad enough (he had a beard that, even with a hot-towel preshave soak, wore out a blade every time he sawed it off); he was not going to stand under a torrent of ice water.

At least, he consoled himself, he had nobly kept John Jameson in his bottle last night. He had not so much as sniffed a cork for forty-eight hours, so he would not reek of old booze when he presented himself to Staff Inspector Peter Wohl and announced he was reporting for duty. All he would smell of was twenty-four hours' worth of flaking skin plus more than a little nervous sweat. It was possible that a liberal sprinkling of cologne would mask that.

Possible or not, that was his only choice.

He had slept in his underwear, so he took that off, rubbed his underarms briskly with a stiff towel, and then patted himself there and elsewhere with cologne. The cologne, he was painfully aware, had been Little Jack's birthday gift to Daddy. Little Jack was nine, Daddy, thirty-four.

Three weeks before, the Honorable Seymour F. Marshutz of the Family Court had awarded Daddy very limited rights of visitation (one weekend a month, plus no more than three lunch or supper visits per month, with the understanding that Jack would give Mrs. Malone at least three hours' notice, preferably longer, of his intention to exercise the lunch/supper privilege) in which to be Daddy.

He tore brown paper from around three bundles from the laundry before he found the one with underwear in it, and then put on a T-shirt and boxer shorts. Then he went to the closet for a uniform.

The uniform was new. The last time he'd worn a uniform, he had been a cop in the 13th District. He'd worn plainclothes as a detective in South Detectives, and then when he'd made sergeant, he'd been assigned as driver to Chief Inspector Francis J. Cohan, another plainclothes assignment. When Chief Cohan had been made deputy commissioner-Operations, as sort of a reward for a job well done, Cohan had arranged for Jack Malone to be assigned to the Major Crimes Division, still in plainclothes. When he'd made lieutenant, four months before, he had gone out and bought a new uniform, knowing that sooner or later, he would need one. As commanding officer of the Auto Squad, it was up to him whether or not to wear a uniform; he had elected not to.

Sooner had come much quicker than he expected. Captain Charley Gaft, who commanded Major Crimes, had called him up yesterday and told him he was being transferred, immediately, to Special Operations, and suggested he use the holiday to clean out his desk in Major Crimes.

"Can I ask why?"

"Career enhancement," Captain Gaft replied, after a just barely perceptible hesitation.

That was so much bullshit.

"I see."

There had been a tone in his voice that Captain Gaft had picked up on.

"It could be a number of things," Gaft offered.

"Sir?"

"You know Tony Lucci?" Gaft asked.

"Yes, sir."

Tony Lucci, as a sergeant, had been Mayor Jerry Carlucci's driver. When he had made lieutenant (four places under Jack Malone on the list), he had been assigned to Special Operations. The word was that he was the mayor's spy in Special Operations.

"He's taking over for you here, and you're replacing him at Bustleton and Bowler. I was told about both transfers, not asked, but it seems possible to me that the mayor may have been interested in seeing that Tony got an assignment that would enhance his career."

"Oh, it was *his* career enhancement you were talking about?"

"Maybe Lucci knows when it's best to back off, Jack."

"Are we talking about Holland here?"

"I'm not. I don't know about you."

Malone did not reply.

"You're being *transferred,* Jack," Captain Gaft went on. "You want a little advice, leave it at that. Maybe it was time. Sometimes people, especially people with personal problems, get too tied up with the job. That sometimes gets people in trouble. That didn't happen to you. Maybe if you weren't being transferred, it would have. Am I getting through to you?"

"Yes, sir."

He's really a good guy. What I really did was go over his head. If you go over a captain's head, even if you're right, you'd better expect trouble. I went over his head, and nobody thinks I'm right, and it could be a lot worse. There are a lot of assignments for a lieutenant a lot worse than Lucci's old job in Special Operations—whatever Lucci's job was.

Gaft didn't stick it in me, although everybody would have understood it if he had. Or Cohan took care of me again. Or both. More than likely, both. But there is sort of a "this is your last chance, Malone, to straighten up and fly right" element in this transfer.

"You're expected at Bustleton and Bowler at eight-thirty. In uniform. Maybe it would be a good idea to clear out your desk here today. Any loose ends we can worry about later."

"Yes, sir," Malone had said. "Captain, I enjoyed working for you."

"Most of the time, Jack, I enjoyed having you work for me. When you get settled out there with the hotshots, call me, and we'll have lunch or something."

"I'll do that, sir. Thank you."

"Good luck, Jack."

Malone had bought only one new uniform when he'd made lieutenant. There had not been, thanks to his lawyer's money-up-front business practice, enough money for more than one. Now he would need at least one—and preferably two—more. But that was his problem, not the Police Department's. He would just have to take the one he had to a two-hour dry cleaners, until, by temporarily giving up unimportant things, like eating, he could come up with the money to buy more. EZ-Credit was something else that had gone with Mrs. John J. Malone.

Malone examined himself in the none-too-clear mirror on the chest of drawers. He did not especially like what he saw. Gone was the trim young cop, replaced by a lieutenant who looked like a lieutenant.

Chubby, Malone thought. *Hairline retreating. A little pouchy under the eyes. Is that the beginning of a jowl?*

He left his suite and walked down the narrow, dimly lit corridor to the elevator, which, after he pushed the button, announced its arrival with an alarming combination of screeches and groans.

He stopped by the desk, which was manned by a cadaverous white male in a soiled maroon sports coat.

"There's no hot water."

"I know, they're working on it," the desk clerk said, without raising his eyes from the Philadelphia *Daily News.*

"If it's not fixed by the time I get home from work, I'll blow up the building," Malone said.

The desk clerk raised his eyes from the *Daily News.*

"I didn't know you were a cop," he said.

"Now you do. Get the hot water fixed."

Malone found his car, on the roof of which someone had left two beer cans and the remains of a slice of pizza. It was a seven-year-old Ford Mustang. There had once been two cars registered in his name, the other a 1972 Ford station wagon. Ellen now had that.

I should have the station wagon. And I should have the house. She was the one fucking around. She should be living in that goddamned hotel and driving this piece of shit.

Look on the bright side. No alimony. And, what the hell, she needed something to carry Little Jack around in.

He knocked the beer cans and pizza off the roof and got in. He went east to North Broad Street, and then out North Broad to Roosevelt Boulevard. Eight blocks down Roosevelt Boulevard he made a lane change that did not meet the standards of a brother police officer.

There was the growl of a siren, and when he looked in the mirror, he saw a cop waving him over.

A Highway Patrol car. Only Highway RPCs had two cops in them.

He nodded his head to show that he understood the order, and as soon as he could safely do so pulled to the side.

The Highway Patrolman swaggered over to the Mustang, only at the last moment noticing that there was a gold bar on the epaulets of Malone's blue jacket.

"Good morning, sir," the Highway Patrolman said.

"Good morning."

"Lieutenant, your turn signal's inoperative. I thought you'd like to know."

"Yes. Thank you very much. I'll have it checked."

The Highway Patrolman saluted and walked back to his car.

Malone moved the turn signal lever.

The goddamn thing really is broken. Did I use the sonofabitch, and it didn't work, or was I just weaving through traffic in this rusty piece of shit, and he stopped me for that?

Moot point, Lieutenant. Either today, or tomorrow, or the day after that, one of those two guys is going to see me at Bustleton and Bowler, and I will become universally known as the New Lieutenant Who Drives Not Only Recklessly But in a Real Piece of Shit of an Ancient Mustang.

Malone hadn't been to Highway Patrol Headquarters, at Bustleton and Bowler Streets, not far from the North Philadelphia Airport, in a long time. It had been busy then, he remembered, because it shared the building with the headquarters of the 7th District, but it had been nothing like it was now.

There were the cars and vans of the 7th District; the cars and motorcycles of Highway Patrol; a flock of cars, marked and unmarked, that obviously belonged to Special Operations; and even a stakeout van. His hope of finding a parking space reserved for LIEU-TENANTS or even OFFICIAL VISITORS had been wishful thinking. He had trouble just driving through the parking lot. The only empty space he saw was marked RESERVED FOR COMMISSIONER.

He drove around the block and tried again. This time a turnkey (an officer assigned to make himself useful in the parking lot) waved him down and pointed out a parking spot reserved for a sergeant.

It was crowded inside too, but finally he managed to give his name to a sergeant at a desk just inside a door marked HEADQUARTERS, SPECIAL OPERATIONS.

"Welcome to the circus, Lieutenant," the sergeant said. "I saw the teletype. The inspector's office is through that door."

On the other side of the door was a small room, barely large enough for the two desks it held back-to-back. One of them was not occupied. There was a sign on it, CAPTAIN MICHAEL J. SABARA.

There was a young plainclothes cop at the other one. When he saw Malone he stood up.

"Lieutenant Malone?"

"Right."

"The inspector's expecting you, sir. I'll see if he's free."

"Thank you."

The plainclothes cop stuck his head in an interior door, and Malone heard his name spoken.

Then the door opened and Staff Inspector Peter Wohl came out. Malone had seen him around before, but now he was surprised to see how young he was.

He's no older than I am. And not only a staff inspector, but a division commander. Is he really that good? Or is it pull?

"I'm Inspector Wohl, Lieutenant," Wohl said. "Now that I see you, I know we've met, but I can't remember where."

"Yes, sir."

"I hate to make you cool your heels, but I've got something that really won't wait. Officer Payne will get you a cup of coffee. Be careful he doesn't pour it in your lap."

"Yes, sir."

Payne? Oh, hell, yes! This is the kid who blew the brains out of the Northwest serial rapist.

Wohl disappeared behind his door again.

"How do you take your coffee, Lieutenant?"

"In a cup, please, if that's convenient," Malone said.

"Yes, sir," Payne said, chuckling.

"I don't know why I said that," Malone said. "I wasn't trying to be a smart-ass."

"I think you'll be right at home around here, Lieutenant," Payne said.

Payne went to a coffee machine sitting on top of a file cabinet and a moment later handed Malone a steaming china cup.

"There's sugar and what is euphemistically known as nondairy creamer," he said.

"Black's fine," Malone said. "Thank you."

He remembered a story that had gone around the Department about the time Captain Dutch Moffitt had been shot, and Special Operations had been formed and given to Peter Wohl.

Dutch Moffitt's deputy had been a well-liked lieutenant named Mike Sabara. It was presumed that, after the scumbag killed Dutch, Mike Sabara would take over as Highway commander. Instead, the job went to newly promoted Captain Dave Pekach. Sabara was named Wohl's deputy commander of Special Operations. It quickly went around Highway that Wohl had told Sabara he could either wear plainclothes or a regular uniform, but he didn't want to see him in Highway breeches and boots. And then Wohl had announced a new recruiting policy for Highway, outstanding young cops who didn't have four, five years on the job. The first two "probationary" Highway Patrolmen were the two Narcs who got the critter who killed Captain Moffitt.

The idea that just anybody could get into Highway had enraged most Highway Patrolmen.

Well, maybe the two guys who caught the scumbag who shot down Captain Dutch Moffitt were entitled to a little special treatment, but letting just about anybody in Highway—

A delegation, someone had told Malone, three Highway sergeants and two longtime Highway Patrolmen, went to see Captain Sabara: Couldn't Sabara have a word with Wohl and tell him how what he was doing was really going to fuck Highway up? Nothing against the inspector personally; it's just that he just doesn't *know* about *Highway*.

Captain Sabara, a phlegmatic man, announced he would think about it.

Two days later one of the sergeants who had gone to Captain Sabara to ask him if he could have a word with Staff Inspector Wohl had to go see Captain Sabara again. His emotional state was mingled fury and gross embarrassment.

"I wouldn't bother you with this, Captain, but nobody knows where Captain Pekach is."

"What's the problem?"

"You know about the parade? Escort the governor to Constitution Hall?"

Sabara nodded. "Twelve wheels. At the airport no later than eleven-thirty. Something wrong?"

"Captain, we brought the bikes here. We went inside for a cup of coffee, before the inspection. When we went back out, there was only ten wheels."

"You're not telling me somebody stole two Highway bikes?"

"Stole, no. Some wiseass is fucking around. When I find out who, I'll have his ass. But what do we do now?"

"Everybody else is outside, where they're supposed to be?"

"Yes, sir."

Captain Sabara, with the sergeant following, strode purposefully out of his office and then out the side door of the building, where he found ten Highway motorcycles lined up neatly, their riders standing beside them.

"Whose wheels are missing?" he demanded.

Two Highway Patrolmen, holding their plastic helmets in their hands and looking more than a little sheepish, stepped forward.

"What did you do, leave the keys in them?"

One patrolman nodded, embarrassed. The second began to explain, "Captain, who the hell's going to steal a Highway—"

He was stilled in midsentence by one of Captain Mike Sabara's nearly legendary frosty glances.

Sabara kept up his icy look for about thirty seconds, and then there came the sound of two motorcycles, approaching at high speed.

"Who the fuck—?" the sergeant asked, only to find that Captain Sabara's cold eyes were now on him.

Two Highway wheels, ridden by guys in complete Highway regalia, including plastic helmets with the face masks down, appeared just outside the parking lot on Bustleton Street, and slid to a stop on squealing tires. Now their sergeant's stripes were visible.

They sat there a moment, revving the engines, and then, one at a time, entered the parking lot, where, simultaneously, they executed a maneuver known to the motorcycling fraternity as a "wheelie." This maneuver involves lifting the front wheel off the ground and steering by precisely adjusting the balance of what is now a powered unicycle by shifting the weight of the body.

It is a maneuver that only can be successfully accomplished by a rider of extraordinary skill. In the interest of rider safety and vehicle economy, the maneuver is forbidden by the Police Department except for instructional purposes by Wheel School instructors.

After passing one way through the parking lot, the two cyclists dropped the front wheel gently back onto the ground, simultaneously negotiated a turn, and then simultaneously executed another wheelie, in the other direction. A final gentle lowering on the front wheel, a final gentle, precise turn, and then the two rode to the center of the parked motorcycles and stopped. They revved the engines a final time, kicked the kickstands in place in a synchronized movement, and then swung off the machines.

The first rider raised his face mask and then removed his helmet.

Jesus H. Christ, it's Pekach! I knew he had been in Highway, but I didn't know he could ride a wheel that good!

"For obvious reasons," Captain Pekach announced solemnly, "I think I should remind all of you that Departmental regulations require that the keys to motorcycles be removed when they are left unattended."

The second rider now raised his mask and removed his helmet.

"Anyone who willingly gets on one of those things," Staff Inspector Peter Wohl announced, "is obviously not playing with a full deck."

Then he and Captain Pekach walked into the building.

Captain Sabara had turned to the sergeant who had reported the missing wheels to him.

"Did I ever tell you, Sergeant, that when I first came to Highway the sergeant I replaced was Inspector Wohl?"

Then he turned and walked into the building.

Malone thought it was a great story. But it was more than that. Wohl knew how to deal with people. After the wheelie demonstration, and after the word had spread that Wohl had been the youngest sergeant ever in Highway, there had been no more bitching that he didn't understand how things were in Highway.

And, Malone thought, it had been a nice touch for Wohl to come out of his office himself to apologize for being tied up. Most division commanders wouldn't have done that; they would have told their driver to have the newcomer wait.

And what Payne had said, "you'll be right at home around here," was interesting too. Maybe this Special Operations assignment will turn out all right after all.

4.

At five minutes past one that afternoon, Abu Ben Mohammed pushed open one of the double doors giving access to the business premises of Goldblatt & Sons Credit Furniture & Appliances, Inc., which occupied all of a three-story building on the north side of South Street, between South 8th and South 9th Streets in South Philadelphia.

Abu Ben Mohammed, according to police records, had been born, as Charles David Stevens, at the Temple University Hospital, in North Philadelphia, twenty-four years, six months, and eleven days earlier. On the occasion of his most recent arrest, he had been described as a Negro Male, five feet nine inches tall, weighing approximately 165 pounds, and with no particular deformities or scars.

Goldblatt & Sons had a doorman, Albert J. Monahan, who was fifty-six, Red Monahan had been with Goldblatt & Sons for thirty-eight years. He went way back to when it had been Samuel Goldblatt Fine Furniture, when Mr. Joshua Goldblatt (now treasurer) and Mr. Harold Goldblatt (now secretary) had been in short pants, and Mr. Samuel Goldblatt, Jr. (now president), then known as "Little Sammy," had been just another muscular eighteen-year-old working one of the trucks delivering merchandise alongside Red.

Before he'd had his heart attack, three years before, Red Monahan had worked his way up to warehouse supervisor. In addition to the portions of the third floor and of the basement of the building on South Street used to warehouse, there was a five-story warehouse building on Washington Avenue two blocks away.

Red had been responsible for checking merchandise as it came in, filling orders from the store to be loaded on trucks, and in moving merchandise back and forth between the store and the warehouse.

Old Mr. Goldblatt had still been alive when Red had his heart attack, although he was getting pretty fragile. But he insisted on being taken to the hospital to see Red, and Young Mr. Sam had, nervously, loaded him into his Buick and taken him.

Old Mr. Goldblatt had told Red that he was too mean an Irishman to die, or even to stay sick for very long, and anyway not to worry. The store had good hospital insurance and what that didn't pay, the store would. And he could consider himself retired, at full pay, from that moment. Anyone with thirty-five years with the store was entitled to take it easy when the time came.

Red told Old Mr. Goldblatt that he didn't want to retire; everybody he knew who retired was dead in a year or eighteen months. And what the hell would he do, anyway, sit around the house all day?

Old Mr. Goldblatt told Red that there would be a job for him at the store as long as he wanted one, and then when he was back in the Buick he told Young Mr. Sam that he was to figure out something for Red to do that wouldn't be a strain on him, but that would also keep him busy.

"No make work. Red's got pride."

"Jesus Christ, Pop!"

"Just do it, Sammy. Let me know what you come up with."

What Young Mr. Sam came up with was what he called "floor walker." When he was a kid, there had been floor walkers in Strawbridge & Clothier, John Wanamaker's, and other top-class department stores. What they did was literally walk the floor, keeping an eye on customers, stock, and employees.

Goldblatt & Sons had never had such people, but once he thought of it, it struck Young Mr. Sam as a pretty good idea. For one thing, Red was a genial Irishman, charming, silver-haired. People liked him. For another, nobody knew more about the stock than Red did. If when people came through the door, Red could be there to greet them with a smile and find out whether they were interested in a bedroom suite, or a refrigerator, or a rug, or whatever, then he could point them in the right direction. "Appliances are on the second floor, right up the stairs." "Carpets are on the third floor, you'll find the elevator right over there."

The first problem was to think of a new term to describe what he would be doing. Young Mr. Sam didn't think Red would like to be a floor walker. He finally came up with "merchandise counselor." Red's face stiffened when he heard that, but he heard Young Mr. Sam out, listening to Sam explain what would be expected of him.

"You mean like a doorman, Sam, right? To make sure the customers don't get away?"

"Yeah."

"That sounds like a pretty good idea," Red had said.

Having Red Monahan working as the doorman turned out to be a very good idea, better than Young Mr. Sam would have believed when he first thought of it.

Red started out by telling people, "Bedroom suites are in the front of the third floor. Take the elevator and when you get up there ask for Mrs. Lipshutz." Or "Wall-to-wall carpeting is in the back of the store. Ask for Mr. Callahan."

The next step was to have the salespeople waiting downstairs near the door. Red would march the customer over to Mrs. Lipshutz or whoever and introduce her with a naughty little wink: "Mrs. Lipshutz is our bedroom expert."

And when somebody came in sore because the Credit Department hadn't credited their account, or because the leg had come off a kitchen chair, or something, Red would be the soul of sympathy and calm them down.

And he kept the undesirables out. There were a lot of drunks around South Street, particularly on Friday nights, when the store was open until nine P.M. and he discouraged them from coming in the store. And he kept the religious loonies from bothering the customers too. The ones who just wanted to pass out their literature were bad enough, but the ones who just about demanded money to plant trees in Israel, or save souls for Jesus in the Congo, or to buy tickets for the Annual Picnic of the 3rd Abyssinian Baptist Church, things like that, had been, pre-Red the Doorman, a real pain in the ass.

Now Red either discouraged them before they got through the doors, or got rid of the really determined ones with a couple of bucks from a roll of singles he got, as needed, from petty cash.

Abu Ben Mohammed, when Red Monahan greeted him at the door, told him he wanted to see about some wall-to-wall carpet.

"You saw the ad in the paper, I guess?" Red asked.

"Huh?"

"We're having a special sale," Red explained. "Twenty-five percent off everything we have in stock, plus free pad and installation."

"No kidding?"

"Absolutely," Red said. "You picked the right day to get yourself some carpet."

He guided Abu Ben Mohammed over to where Phil Katz, who was Old Mr. Sam's nephew, was sitting with the other salespeople on the tufted blue velvet couch and matching armchairs that a sign advertised as "Today's Special! Three-Piece Suite! $99 Down! No Payment Until March!"

"Mr. Katz," Red began, which caused Phil Katz to break off his conversation with Mr. Callahan in midsentence and get to his feet with a smile in place.

"Mr. Katz," Red went on, "this is Mr.—I didn't catch your name?"

"I didn't tell you," Abu Ben Mohammed replied.

"This gentleman," Red Monahan went on, "is interested in some wall-to-wall carpeting."

"Well, this is your day," Mr. Katz said, "we're running a special sale. Why don't we ride up to the carpet department and let me show you what we have?"

Mr. Katz thought he might have a live one. He had, of course, noticed that Abu Ben Mohammed was wearing what he thought of as African clothes. Over a purple turtleneck sweater and baggy black trousers, Abu Ben Mohammed was wearing a brightly colored dashiki. Perched on the back of his head was sort of a black yarmulke, neatly and rather brightly embroidered in a yellow and green pattern. He was also wearing a trench coat over his shoulders. Maybe they didn't have overcoats in North Africa, Mr. Katz thought, or maybe this guy just didn't have an African coat to handle the chill of January in Philadelphia.

What was important was that he was into the African thing, and the Africans were deep into carpets. They put them two and three deep on the floors, and sometimes they even upholstered their walls with them.

What was just about as important was that he had come into the store today. The furniture business just about died after Christmas; it was Phil Katz's personal opinion that the store was just pissing money down the toilet with their advertisements in the Philadelphia *Daily News* for the "After Christmas" and "New Year's" sales. People had spent their money (or used up their credit, which was the same thing) buying Christmas presents. They had no money to do anything but start paying the bills they had run up for Christmas.

But there were exceptions to every rule, and this guy in the dashiki just might be one of them. Mr. Katz had heard that the blacks who had become Muslims had to stop drinking and smoking and gambling, which meant this guy might just have the money to cover the floors of his apartment with carpet.

He led Abu Ben Mohammed to the elevator, slid the door shut, and took him up to the third floor.

Five minutes after Abu Ben Mohammed entered the store, a man subsequently identified as Hector Carlos Estivez, twenty-four, five feet nine inches tall, and weighing 140 pounds, and again with no distinguishing marks or features, came in.

He told Red Monahan that he wanted to look at a washer-drier combination, and was turned over by Red to Mrs. Emily Watkins, who was forty-eight, and had worked for fifteen years in the Credit Department of Goldblatt & Sons before deciding, three years before, that she could make more money on the floor, on a small salary plus commission, than she could at her desk. She had asked Young Mr. Sam for a chance to try, and to his surprise, she had done very well, probably, he had finally decided, because women did most of the buying of washers and driers and other appliances, and probably trusted another woman more than they would a man.

Mrs. Watkins led Mr. Estivez up the stairs to the second floor, and then to the rear of the building, where the washer-driers were on display. She was not nearly as enthusiastic about her chances to make a sale to her potential customer as Mr. Katz had been about his. She had been in the credit business a long time, and had a feel for who would have credit and who wouldn't. Mr. Estivez did not strike her as the kind of man who held a steady job. But on the other hand, he might have hit his number or something and might have the cash.

In a similar manner, over the next twenty minutes, seven more potential customers pushed open the door from South Street into Goldblatt & Sons Credit Furniture & Appliances, Inc., were greeted by Red Monahan and turned over to a member of the sales force.

One of them, the third to come in the store, was a woman. She was later identified as Doris M. (Mrs. Harold) Martin, fifty-two, of East Hagert Street in Kensington. She had come in to look at carpet for her upstairs corridor and bedrooms after having seen the Goldblatt & Sons advertisement in that day's *Daily News*. Red Monahan introduced Mrs. Martin to Mrs. Irene Dougherty, who took her by elevator to the third floor.

The other six people to come in were all men. Two of them wore clothing suggesting they were either Muslims or at least had some connection with an African culture. All of them were, according to the race codification then in use by the Philadelphia Police Department, Negroid. Two of them, however, had such pale skin pigmentation that there was some question whether they were "really colored" or "maybe Puerto Rican or Mexican, or something like that."

The last of the six men to enter the store, at approximately 1:32 P.M., described as a "black male, approximately six feet tall, thirty years of age, and weighing approximately one hundred seventy-five pounds," was wearing a "dark blue, waist-length woolen jacket similar in appearance to the U.S. Navy pea coat."

Immediately upon entering Goldblatt & Sons, this suspect, subsequently identified as Kenneth H. Dorne, aka "King," aka Hussein El Baruca, turned and began to bolt the door shut.

"Hey, friend," Red Monahan asked as he walked up to him, "what are you doing?"

"Shut your face, motherfucker!" Hussein El Baruca replied, simultaneously drawing a large, blue in color, large-caliber semiautomatic pistol (probably a Colt Model 1911 or 1911A1 .45-caliber service pistol) and pointing it at Red Monahan.

"Hey, you don't really want to do this—" Red Monahan said, whereupon Hussein El Baruca struck him, with a slashing backward motion of his right arm, in the face with the pistol, with sufficient force to knock him down and, it was subsequently learned, to cause a crack in Mr. Monahan's full upper denture.

Then he raised the pistol to a nearly vertical position and fired it three times. One of the bullets struck a fluorescent lighting fixture on the ceiling, smashing a bulb, which caused broken glass and then a cloud of powder, from the interior coating of the bulb, to float down from the ceiling. Then, the fixture itself tore loose at one end, causing a short-circuit in the wiring. There was a flash of light, and then that entire line of lighting fixtures, one of two running from the front of the store to the rear, went off, reducing the light on the ground floor by half.

"On your fucking bellies or I'll blow your fucking heads off!" Hussein El Baruca ordered.

The three salespeople, two men and a woman, waiting for customers in the living-room suite, and Red Monahan complied with the order. The woman crossed herself, and her lips moved in prayer as she got onto her knees and then lay on the floor.

Hussein El Baruca then turned back to the double doors and closed the venetian blinds on them. There was a large display window on either side of the entrance. A complete bedroom set was on display in one window, and a compete bedroom set in the other. The "walls" behind the furniture in each window blocked the view of the interior of the store to passersby, and with the blinds on the doors now closed, there was no way anyone on South Street could look into Goldblatt & Sons Credit Furniture & Appliances, Inc.

The sound of the three pistol shots fired by Hussein El Baruca was muffled somewhat by the upholstered furniture on the ground floor, and because the store was open from the front to the rear, where the Credit Department was located. But it was loud enough to be heard on the second floor, where it was correctly interpreted by Hector Carlos Estivez as the signal he had been expecting.

He took what was probably a Smith & Wesson Military & Police .38 Special caliber revolver from where he had concealed it in the small of his back, held it in both hands at arm's length, and fired two shots at the glass viewing port of a Hotpoint drier that was sitting on the floor approximately six feet from him, and two feet to the left of Mrs. Emily Watkins.

Mrs. Watkins yelped and covered her mouth with both hands.

Hector Carlos Estivez, when he saw that he missed the glass viewing port with one of his shots, and that the second had cracked but not smashed or penetrated the glass, said, "Shit!" and fired a third time. This time the thick, tempered glass of the viewing port broke.

"On the floor, bitch!" Hector Carlos Estivez said, and Mrs. Watkins, now whimpering, dropped to her knees and then spread herself on the floor.

The shots from Estivez's revolver were audible to Abu Ben Mohammed on the third floor, where Phil Katz was explaining to him that trying to get by with bottom-of-the-line cheap carpet was really not economy at all.

"It's just like tires," Mr. Katz was saying, "what you're really buying is wear. You— What the hell was that?"

"You're being robbed, motherfucker, that's what it is," Abu Ben Mohammed said, taking a large-caliber, single-action, Western-style revolver with plastic "pearl" grips from beneath his dashiki. He pushed the hammer back, cocking the pistol, and then fired at a three-foot-tall, stainless-steel cigarette receptacle that had been placed beside the elevator door.

A hole appeared near the top of the receptacle, which then slowly tilted to one side, as if in a slow-motion picture, and then fell, dislodging a sand-filled glass tray, which shattered upon striking the metal elevator threshold.

"Jesus H. Christ!" Phil Katz said.

"Lay down on the floor," Abu Ben Mohammed ordered.

"What?"

"On the fucking floor, you heard me."

"Yes, sir."

The executive offices of Goldblatt & Sons Credit Furniture & Appliances, Inc., those of Mr. Samuel Goldblatt, Jr., and Mr. Harold Goldblatt, the secretary, and their secretary, Mrs. Blanche Steiner, forty-four, were at the right rear of the building. Mr. Joshua Goldblatt, the treasurer, maintained his office in the Credit Department on the ground floor.

The sound of Abu Ben Mohammed's pistol shot attracted the attention of Mr. Samuel Goldblatt, Jr., who looked up from the work on his desk, and then stood up. When the executive offices had been built, one-way glass panels providing a view of the third-floor showroom had been installed. But they had never really worked, and eventually had been almost entirely covered up by a row of filing cabinets. The only way to see what was going on on the floor was to open the door and look.

Mr. Goldblatt did so, and found himself looking into the barrel of Abu Ben Mohammed's revolver.

"Hands up, honky!"

"Yes, sir," Mr. Goldblatt said.

"Oh, my *God!*" Mrs. Steiner said, thereby attracting Abu Ben Mohammed's attention.

"Out here, bitch!"

"Do what he says, Blanche," Mr. Goldblatt said.

Abu Ben Mohammed then took careful aim at Mrs. Steiner's IBM typewriter and fired. The machine seemed to lift slightly off the desk and then settled back. There was a faint screeching noise, and then, a short-circuit within the typewriter having caused a fuse to blow, the overhead lights in the executive office went out. Desk lamps on Mr. Goldblatt's and Mrs. Steiner's desks continued to burn and produced sufficient light to see.

"Oh, my *God!*" Mrs. Steiner wailed.

"Please don't hurt anyone," Mr. Goldblatt pleaded. "We'll do whatever you want us to do."

Abu Ben Mohammed then struck Mr. Goldblatt on the head, with a downward slashing motion of his pistol, causing him to fall to his knees and also causing a small cut on the (bald) top of his head.

"Get the money and some rope," Abu Ben Mohammed ordered.

"What?" Mrs. Steiner asked.

"There's no money up here," Mr. Goldblatt said. "Honest to God there isn't!"

"Bullshit!" Abu Ben Mohammed said. "Get the fucking money!"

Mr. Goldblatt reached into the hip pocket of his trousers and came out with his wallet, which he handed to Abu Ben Mohammed.

"Take this," he said.

Abu Ben Mohammed took the wallet, and from it not less than one hundred twenty dollars and not more than two hundred dollars and put the bills in a pocket of his dashiki. Then he threw the wallet at Mr. Goldblatt.

"Give him your purse, Blanche," Mr. Goldblatt said.

"Go get it," Abu Ben Mohammed said to Mrs. Steiner, and then added to Mr. Goldblatt, "If you're lying to me, if we find any money in that office, I'm going to blow your fucking honky head off."

"I swear to God, believe me, we don't keep any money up here."

"Then what's that fucking safe for?"

"Business papers. Look for yourself."

"Don't you tell me what to do, you honky motherfucker!" Abu Ben Mohammed said, and swung his pistol at Mr. Goldblatt's head again. Mr. Goldblatt was able to ward off most of the force of this blow with his hands, suffering only a minor bruise to his left hand.

Mrs. Steiner took her purse from a desk drawer and offered it to Abu Ben Mohammed. A coin purse contained approximately sixteen dollars in bills, and there was approximately sixty dollars in her wallet. Abu Ben Mohammed removed these monies and placed them in a pocket of his dashiki.

On the second floor, meanwhile, Hector Carlos Estivez had startled Mrs. Emily Watkins by ordering her to remove her shoes and stockings. When she had done so, he used one of the stockings to bind her hands behind her back. He then told her to lie down again, on her stomach, and when she failed to so quickly enough to satisfy him, he pushed her so that she fell.

A minute or so later Mrs. Watkins was ordered to get up, and when she was not able to get to her feet quickly enough to satisfy Hector Carlos Estivez, he kicked her in the side, and then jerked her to an upright position.

She saw then for the first time Mr. Ted Sadowsky, a Goldblatt employee specializing in televisions and stereo equipment, who had been in the front part of the building. He was being held at gunpoint, probably a Colt Police Positive .38 Special caliber snub-nosed revolver (or the Smith & Wesson equivalent) by a suspect subsequently identified as Randolph George Dawes, aka Muhammed el Sikkim, Negro Male, twenty-four, five feet nine inches, 160 pounds.

"Tie the cocksucker up," Hector Carlos Estivez said to Muhammed el Sikkim, and handed him Mrs. Watkins's other stocking.

Muhammed el Sikkim tied Mr. Sadowsky's hands behind his back with Mrs. Watkins's stocking, and then led the two of them to the stairway between the passenger and freight elevators and took them to the third floor, where he ordered them to get on the floor on their stomachs.

"No fucking rope and no fucking money," Abu Ben Mohammed said to Muhammed el Sikkim.

"Use stockings. Tell that kike bitch to take hers off."

Mrs. Steiner was then forced to remove her panty hose, which were torn apart at the crotch and one part of them then used to tie her arms behind her back. Mr. Samuel Goldblatt was then tied in a similar manner, with the other leg of Mrs. Steiner's panty hose, and he and Mrs. Steiner were then forced to lie on their stomachs beside Mr. Sadowsky and Mrs. Watkins.

Within the next five minutes, all Goldblatt employees, plus the one customer in the store, Mrs. Doris Martin, were brought to the third floor by the perpetrators. These included the three employees on duty in the first-floor Credit Department, the remaining salespeople, and Mr. Monahan.

From this point, inasmuch as all Goldblatt employees (including Mr. Samuel Goldblatt, Jr.) and Mrs. Martin were lying on their stomachs on the floor of the third floor of the Goldblatt Building with their arms bound behind them, the only witnesses to the perpetrators' actions on the first and second floors of the Goldblatt Building were the perpetrators themselves.

What is known is that three (or four) of the perpetrators (almost certainly including Abu Ben Mohammed, and probably including Hector Carlos Estivez and Muhammed el Sikkim) went to the Credit Department on the first floor and

(a) Removed approximately four hundred eighty dollars in bills and coins-in-rolls from the cashier's cash drawer.

(b) Broke into the interior compartments (three) of the safe. The safe itself was open at the time the robbery began. There was no cash in the safe.

(c) Emptied the contents of a wastebasket (mostly waste paper) into the safe and set it afire.

Sometime during this period, Mr. John Francis Cohn, forty-nine, of Queen Lane in East Falls, supervisor of the Maintenance Department of Goldblatt & Sons Credit Furniture & Appliances, Inc., apparently entered the building via a door on Rodman Street, the narrow alley at the rear of the building. This self-closing door was closed to the public and was normally locked. Mr. Cohn had a key.

Apparently, Mr. Cohn then descended to the basement of the store by the stairwell between the freight and passenger elevators. He then uncrated (or completed uncrating) a special, demonstration model Hotpoint washing machine, constructed of a plastic material so that the interior of the apparatus was visible, and, using a hand truck, put the machine onto the freight elevator.

He then apparently ascended to the second floor, where he had received instructions to install the machine in the Washer and Drier Department.

He moved the machine to the rear of the second floor, and then apparently became aware that there were no salespeople on duty. (Or possibly wished to ascertain precisely where he was to set up the machine.) He then got back onto the freight elevator and descended to the first floor, and opened the door and the elevator gate.

At this point, apparently, he saw the perpetrators and attempted to flee by moving the elevator. At this point, the perpetrators saw him, and at least two of them then fired their weapons at him.

Mr. Cohn was struck by four bullets, two of .38 Special caliber and two of .45 Colt Automatic Pistol caliber. Three additional .38 Special caliber and one additional .45 ACP bullets were later found in the woodwork of the elevator.

Mr. Cohn fell inward into the elevator.

The perpetrators then entered the stairwell and went to the third floor. They reported to the others that they "had blown away a honky motherfucker on the elevator," and that the cash register had contained "only a lousy five hundred fucking dollars."

A conversation, within hearing, but out of sight of the victims, was then held, during which one of the perpetrators announced he had found an inflammable fluid and soaked some carpet with it, and that he was going to "burn the fucking place down, and the honkies with it."

Another perpetrator was heard to say, "It's time to get the fuck out of here."

The perpetrators then, without further discussion, apparently ignited the inflammable fluid that had been poured upon a stack of carpet, descending to the first floor by means of the stairwell between the freight and passenger elevators, exited the building via a fire door in the rear of the building opening onto the alley (Rodman Street).

Opening of the fire door set off an alarm, which both caused bells mounted on the front and rear of the building and in the finance and executive offices to begin to ring, and was connected with the Holmes Security Service. A Holmes employee then

(a) Telephoned the Police Radio Room,
(b) Attempted to telephone the Goldblatt Building to verify that the alarm had not been accidentally triggered, and on failing to have anyone answer the telephone,
(c) Contacted a Holmes patrol unit in the area, informing him of the triggering of the alarm in the Goldblatt Building.

The Radio Room of the Philadelphia Police Department is on the second floor of the Police Administration Building at Eighth and Race Streets in downtown Philadelphia.

"Police Emergency," the operator, a thirty-seven-year-old woman named Janet Grosse, said into her headset.

"This is Holmes," the caller said. "I have a signal of a fire door audible alarm at Goldblatt Furniture, northwest corner, 8th and South."

The call from Holmes Security Service was treated exactly as any other call for help would be treated, except of course that Mrs. Grosse, who had worked in Police Radio for eleven years, seemed to recognize the voice of the Holmes man and made a subconscious decision from the phrasing of the report that it was genuine, and not coming from someone who got his kicks sending the cops on wild-goose chases.

"Got you covered," she said, which was not exactly the precise response called for by regulations.

Eighth and South streets, Mrs. Grosse knew, was in the 6th Police District, which has its headquarters at 11th and Winter Streets. She looked up at her board and saw that Radio Patrol Car 611 was available for service.

She opened her microphone.

"Six Eleven, northwest corner, 8th and South, Goldblatt's Furniture, an audible alarm."

RPC 611 was a somewhat battered 1972 Plymouth with more than 100,000 miles on its odometer. When the call came, Officer James J. Molyneux, Badge Number 6771, who had been on the job eighteen years, had just turned left off South Broad Street onto South Street.

He picked up his microphone.

"Six Eleven, okay."

Officer Molyneux turned on his flashing lights, but not the siren, and held his hand down on the horn button to clear the traffic in front of him.

At just about this time, the ringing of the alarm bell had attracted the attention of Police

Officer Johnson V. Collins, Badge Number 2662, who was then on foot patrol (Beat Two) on South Street between 10th and 11th Streets.

Officer Collins was equipped with a portable radio, and heard Mrs. Grosse's call to RPC 611. He took his radio from its holster and spoke into it.

"Six Beat Two," he said. "That's on me. I've got it."

Mrs. Grosse immediately replied, "Okay, Six Beat Two. Six Eleven, resume patrol."

Officer Molyneux, without responding, turned off his flashing lights, but, having nothing better to do, continued driving down South Street toward Goldblatt & Sons Credit Furniture & Appliances, Inc.

Officer Collins walked purposefully (but did not run or even trot; audible alarms went off all the time) down South Street to the Goldblatt Building. It was only when he found the doors closed and the venetian blinds closed that he suspected that anything might be out of the ordinary. Business was slow, but Goldblatt's shouldn't be closed.

He glanced up the street and saw RPC 611 coming in his direction. Now trotting, he went to the corner of South and South Ninth Streets, stepped into the street, and raised his arm to attract the attention of the driver of 611. He recognized Officer Molyneux.

He made a signal for Molyneux to cover the front of the building, and when he was sure that Molyneux understood what was being asked of him, Collins trotted down South Ninth Street to Rodman Street, which was more of an alley than a street, and then to the rear of the Goldblatt Building.

The fire door had an automatic closing device, but it had not completely closed the door. Collins was able to get his fingers behind the inch-wide strip of steel welded to the end of the door to shield the crack between door and jamb and pull the door open.

He took several steps inside the building, and then saw the body lying in the freight elevator and the blood on the elevator's wall.

"Jesus, Mary, and Joseph!" he breathed, and reached for his radio.

"Six Beat Two, Six Beat Two, give me some backup here, I think I've got a robbery in progress! Give me a wagon too. I've got a shooting victim!"

Then, suddenly remembering that portable radios often fail to work inside a building, he went back into the alley and repeated his call.

"What's your location, Six Beat Two?" Police Radio replied.

"800 South Street. Goldblatt Furniture."

The first response was from Officer Molyneux.

"Six Eleven, I'm on the scene. In front."

He was drowned out by the Police Radio transmission. First there were three beeps, and then Mrs. Grosse announced, "800 South Street. Assist officer. Holdup in progress. Report of shooting and hospital case."

Then there came a brief pause, and the entire message, including the three beeps, was repeated.

The response was immediate:

"Six A, in." Six A was one of the two 9th District sergeants on duty. He was responsible for covering the lower end of the district, from Vine Street to South Street. The other sergeant (Six B) covered the upper end of the district from Vine to Poplar Streets.

"Six Oh One, in." Six Oh One was one of the 9th District's two-man vans.

"Highway Twenty-Two, in on that."

"Six Ten, in," came from another 6th District RPC.

"Six Command, in," came from the car of the 6th District lieutenant on duty, who was responsible for covering the entire district.

Officer Collins replaced his radio in its holster, drew his service revolver, and, with his mouth dry and his heart beating almost audibly, went, very carefully, back into the building.

5.

Officers Gerald Quinn and Charles McFadden had spent all of the morning hanging around the sixth-floor hallway outside Courtroom 636 in City Hall waiting to be called to testify. The assistant DA sent word, however, that they probably would be, and asked them not to leave the building until he gave them permission or until the court broke for lunch.

That meant that in addition to the lousy coffee served by the concessionaire in the stairwell, they would have to eat lunch in some crowded greasy spoon restaurant nearby.

They went back to Courtroom 636 a few minutes before two. The assistant district attorney told them they would not be needed. By the time they had gone back downstairs and checked out through Court Attendance, it was a few minutes after two.

They went out and found their car. Quinn got behind the wheel and cranked the battered Chevrolet. The radio warmed almost immediately, and came to life:

"BEEP BEEP BEEP. 800 South Street. Assist officer. Holdup in progress. Report of shooting and hospital case.

"BEEP BEEP BEEP. 800 South Street. Assist officer. Holdup in progress. Report of shooting and hospital case."

Quinn had the siren howling and the lights flashing even before McFadden could pick up the microphone.

When he had it in his hand, he said, "Highway Twenty-Two in on that."

Mrs. Janet Grosse's—Police Radio's—second call about the robbery of Goldblatt & Sons Credit Furniture & Appliances, Inc.—

"Beep Beep Beep. 800 South Street. Assist officer. Holdup in progress. Report of shooting and hospital case.

—was also picked up by one of the several police frequency radios in an antennae-festooned Buick, a new one, registered to Michael J. O'Hara of the 2100 block of South Shields Street in West Philadelphia.

Mr. O'Hara had just a moment before entered the Buick after having taken luncheon (a cheese-steak sandwich, a large side order of french fries, and three bottles of Ortlieb's beer) at Beato's on Parrish Street, in the company of Sergeant Max Feldman, of the 9th District.

When the call came, Mr. O'Hara was filling out a small pointed document that he would, on Friday, turn in to the administrative office of the Philadelphia *Bulletin,* the newspaper by which he was employed. It would state that in the course of business he had entertained Sergeant Feldman at luncheon at a cost of $23.50, plus a $3.75 tip, for a total of $27.25. In due course, a check would be issued to reimburse Mr. O'Hara for this business expense.

Actually, Mr. O'Hara had not paid for the lunch, and indeed had no idea what it had cost. Sergeant Feldman's money was no good at Beato's, and the management had picked up Mr. O'Hara's tab as a further courtesy to Sergeant Feldman.

But several months before, Casimir J. Bolinski, LLD, had renegotiated Mr. O'Hara's contract for the provision of his professional services to the *Bulletin.* Among other stipulations, the new contract required the *Bulletin* to reimburse Mr. O'Hara for whatever expenses he incurred in carrying out his professional duties, specifically including the entertainment of individuals who, in Mr. O'Hara's sole judgment, might prove useful to him professionally.

Since Casimir had gone to all that trouble for him, it seemed to Mr. O'Hara that it would be ungrateful of him not to turn in luncheon expense vouchers whether or not cash had actually changed hands. Anyway, Mr. O'Hara reasoned, if Beato's hadn't grabbed the tab, he *would* have paid it.

Mr. O'Hara's profession was journalism. Specifically, he was the *Bulletin*'s top crime reporter. Arguably, he was the best crime reporter in Philadelphia or, for that matter, between Boston and Washington.

Dr. Bolinski had enjoyed a certain fame—some said "notoriety"—as a linebacker for the Green Bay Packers professional football team before hanging up the suit and joining the bar and entering the legal specialization field of representing professional athletes.

Bull Bolinski had surprised a lot of people, including Mickey O'Hara, who had known him since they were in the third grade at Saint Stephen's Parochial School at 10th and Butler, with his near-instant success at big-dollar contract negotiations.

"What it is, Michael," The Bull had once explained to him over a beer, "is that the fuckers think I'm just a dumb fucking jock. That gives me a leg up on the bastards."

The Bull was the only person in the world except Mickey's mother who called Mr. O'Hara "Michael." Mickey, similarly, was the only person in the world save Mrs. Bolinski who called The Bull "Casimir." The Bull's mother didn't even call him Casimir; usually it was Sonny, but often she called him "Bull" too.

That went back to Saint Stephen's, too, where Sister Mary Magdalene, the principal, had a thing about Christian names. You either used the name you got when you were baptized, or you took a crack across the hand, bottom, or a stab into the ribs from Sister Mary Magdalene's eighteen-inch steel-reinforced ruler.

Casimir had been in town eight months before and had been deeply shocked to learn how little Michael was being compensated for his services by the *Bulletin.*

"Jesus, Michael, you got a fucking Pulitzer Prize, and that's all those cheap bastards are paying you? That's fucking outrageous!"

"Casimir, you may have been a hot shit ball player, and you may be a hot shit lawyer now, but you don't know your ass from left field about newspapers."

"Trust me, Michael," The Bull had said confidently. "I can handle those bastards."

Somewhat uneasily, Mr. O'Hara had placed the financial aspects of his career into Dr. Bolinski's hands. To his genuine surprise, the *Bulletin* was now paying him more money than he had ever expected to make, and there were fringe benefits like the Buick (previously he had driven his own car and been reimbursed at a dime a mile) and the expense account.

While it would not be fair to say that Mickey O'Hara was happy to hear that someone had been illegally deprived of their property at gunpoint, or that somebody had gotten themselves shot, neither would it be honest to say that he was beside himself with vicarious sorrow.

It had been a damned dull week, so far, and so far the line of type reading, *"By Michael J. O'Hara, Bulletin Staff Writer"* had not appeared on the front page of the *Bulletin.* A good shooting would probably fix that.

Mickey finished filling out the expense account chit, shoved the pads of forms back into the glove compartment, and got the Buick moving.

Mickey knew the streets of the City of Philadelphia as well as any London taxi driver knows those of the city on the Thames. He turned left onto 26th Street and headed south toward the Art Museum and moved swiftly down the Benjamin Franklin Parkway toward City Hall. The pedestrian traffic around City Hall was frustrating, but his pace picked up as he headed south on Broad Street toward South Street. As he turned east on South Street, he could see flashing lights a few blocks ahead.

He drove expertly. That is to say, he was not reckless. But he paid absolutely no attention to the posted speed limits, and paused for red lights only long enough to make sure he could get across the intersection without getting hit.

He was not worried about being cited for violation of the Motor Vehicle Code. His chances of being charged with speeding or running a red light or reckless lane changing were about as great as those of Mayor Jerry Carlucci's.

Mickey O'Hara was regarded by the Police Department as one of their own. To be sure, there was always some stiff-necked prick who would point out that all Mickey O'Hara was, was a goddamn civilian and entitled to no special privileges. But for every one of these, there were two or three cops, driving RPCs or walking beats, or captains and inspectors, who had known Mickey for twenty years and had come to believe that he was on the side of the cops, and told the prick where to head in.

When the Emerald Society had a function, and there was a head table, Mickey O'Hara was routinely seated at it. The Fraternal Order of Police club, downtown, off North Broad Street, had an ironclad rule that the only way a civilian could get past the door was in the company of a member. Except for Mickey O'Hara, who could be expected to drop in once a night for a beer, sitting at a stool near the cash register that might as well have had his name on it, because it was tacitly reserved for him.

The thing about Mickey, it was said, was that he never betrayed a confidence. If you told him something was out of school, you would never see it in the newspaper.

There was a white-capped (Traffic Division) cop diverting traffic away from South Street onto South 9th Street when Mickey O'Hara's Buick appeared.

He waved Mickey through, winked at him as he passed, and then furiously blew his whistle at the car behind him, who thought he wanted to follow Mickey.

Mickey pulled up behind a car he recognized as belonging to Central Detectives. Some of the chrome letters that had once spelled out CHEVROLET had fallen off; now it read CHE RO   T. He had seen it the night before downtown; a lawyer from Pittsburgh had been mugged and stabbed coming out of a bar. The detective had told Mickey what had happened, and when Mickey had asked him, "What do you think?" the detective had said, "It's a start, but the bastards breed like rabbits."

Mickey took a 35-mm camera from the passenger-side floor and got out. He saw that South Street was jammed with police vehicles of all descriptions. There were three 6th District RPCs, cars assigned to one of the 6th District sergeants and the 6th District lieutenant captain, a Highway RPC, a 6th District van and two stakeout vans, the Mobile Crime Lab vehicle, and a number of unmarked cars. One of the unmarked cars was a brand-new Chevrolet Impala, telling Mickey that a captain (or better) with nothing more important to do had come to the crime scene, and was more than likely getting in the way. The other unmarked cars were battered; that meant they were from Central Detectives.

Obviously (people were standing around) whatever had happened here was over. The stakeout vans, which are manned by specially trained policemen who are equipped with special weapons (rifles, shotguns, machine guns, et cetera) and equipment, and called into use in situations where ordinary armament (handguns) is likely to be inadequate, were not going to be needed.

Then Mickey saw a familiar face, that of Homicide Detective Joe D'Amata, and knew that something serious had happened. The "hospital case" in the Police Radio call hadn't needed a hospital.

Mickey stepped over the Crime Scene barrier and walked toward another familiar face. He now knew who was driving the new Impala.

"I didn't know they let old men like you go in on real jobs," Mickey said.

Chief Inspector Matt Lowenstein, a short, stocky man with large, dark eyes, who commanded the Detective Division, took a black, six-inch cigar from between his lips and looked coldly at Mickey.

"If there's one thing I can't stand, it's a laugh-a-minute Irishman," he said. "I knew if I didn't get out of here, something unpleasant, like you showing up, would happen."

"Things a little slow at the Roundhouse, are they? Or are you trying to recapture your youth by patrolling the streets?"

"I was driving by, all right? Up yours, O'Hara."

Despite the exchange, they were friends. Matt Lowenstein met Mickey O'Hara's criteria for a very good cop. Not all senior supervisors did. O'Hara admired Lowenstein for being an absolute straight arrow, who protected his men like a mother hen.

On Lowenstein's part, he not only respected O'Hara professionally, but when his son had been bar mitzvahed, not only had Mickey shown up (his gift had been *The Oxford Complete Dictionary of the English Language*) but the event had been reported on the front page of the Sunday Social Section, complete with a three-column picture of Lowenstein and his son via Mickey's influence at the *Bulletin*.

"So before you go back to the rocking chair, you going to tell me what happened? Why are you here?"

"I told you, I was nearby and heard the call," Lowenstein said. "It's a strange one, Mickey. Six, eight guys, A-rabs—"

"Real Arabs?" Mickey interrupted.

"They kept saying 'motherfucker.' That's Arabian, isn't it?"

Mickey chuckled. "I think so," he said solemnly.

"They came in the place one at a time, spread out through the building, and then pulled guns. They shot up the place, God only knows why, and then tried to set some rugs on fire. The maintenance man walked in while it was going on, and they killed him."

"He try to do something or what?"

Lowenstein shrugged.

"Don't know yet. You want to have a look?"

"I'd like to, Matt," Mickey said.

Lowenstein pursed his lips. A surprisingly loud whistle came from between them. A dozen people turned to look, including the uniformed cop guarding access to the Goldblatt crime scene.

"He's okay," Lowenstein said, pointing to Mickey O'Hara.

"Thanks," Mickey said.

"Sylvia said if you can watch your filthy mouth, you can come to dinner."

"When?"

"How about tonight?"

"Fine. What time and what can I bring?"

"Half past six. You don't have to bring anything, but take a shave and a shower."

"Didn't The Dago tell you you were supposed to cultivate the press?"

"No. But I'll tell you what I did hear: You finally found some girl willing to be seen in public with you. Bring her, if you want."

"Okay. I was going to anyway," Mickey said, and touched Lowenstein's arm and walked past the cop into Goldblatt & Sons Credit Furniture & Appliances, Inc.

As Michael J. O'Hara walked into Goldblatt & Sons Credit Furniture & Appliances, Inc., on South Street, four blocks away, on 11th Street, near Carpenter, three law enforcement officers in civilian clothing were having their lunch in Shank & Evelyn's Restaurant.

They were Staff Inspector Peter Wohl and Officer Matthew Payne of the Philadelphia Police Department, and Walter Davis, a tall, well-built, well-dressed (in a gray pin-striped, three-piece suit) man in his middle forties, who was the special agent in charge (the "SAC") of the Philadelphia Office of the Federal Bureau of Investigation.

Shank & Evelyn's Restaurant was not the sort of place Walter Davis had had in mind when he had telephoned Wohl early that morning to ask if he was free for lunch. Davis had had in mind the Ristorante Alfredo, in downtown Philadelphia, in part because the food was superb and the banquettes would provide what he considered to be the necessary privacy he sought, and also because he thought it would provide an opportunity to needle the management a little.

There was no question in Davis's mind (or for that matter in the minds of any peace officer with the brains to find his rear end with both hands) that Ristorante Alfredo was owned by persons connected with organized crime, otherwise known as "the Mob" and sometimes as "the Mafia."

Davis was sure that there would be someone in the restaurant who would recognize him and Wohl, whom Davis believed to be as bright and competent a Philadelphia cop as they came, and note and report to his superiors that they had been taking lunch together.

If that had caused Ricco Baltazari, who held the restaurant license for Ristorante Alfredo, or Vincenzo Savarese, "the businessman" who actually owned it, some uncomfortable moments wondering what the head of the FBI and the head of Special Operations were up to, together, that would have added a little something to the luncheon.

But that had not come to pass. Wohl had accepted the invitation, and said that since he would be at the Roundhouse at about lunchtime, he would just stop by the FBI office when he was finished with his business and pick Davis up.

The Administration Building of the Philadelphia Police Department, at 8th and Race Streets, was universally called "the Roundhouse" because its architect had been fascinated with curves, and everything in the building was curved, right down to the elevators.

Wohl's own office was at Bustleton and Bowler Streets in Northeast Philadelphia, from which he commanded the Special Operations Division, which consisted of the Highway Patrol and a newly formed, somewhat experimental unit of above-average uniformed and plainclothes cops.

The original idea was that Special Operations, which like the Highway Patrol had city-wide responsibility, would move into high-crime areas of the city, and overwhelm the problem with manpower, special equipment and techniques, and an arrangement with the district attorney to hustle the arrested through the criminal justice procedure.

That was being done, but politics had inevitably entered the picture almost immediately. First, there had been the murder of Jerome Nelson, whose father, Arthur J. Nelson, was chairman of the board of the Daye-Nelson Corporation, which owned (among other newspapers and television stations) the Philadelphia *Ledger* and WGHA-TV.

When a Homicide Division lieutenant, Edward M. DelRaye, had been truthfully tactless enough to inform the press that the police were looking for a Negro Male, Pierre St. Maury, a known homosexual known to be living with young Nelson in his luxury Society Hill apartment, in connection with the killing, the *Ledger* and its publisher had declared war on both the Police Department and the Hon. Jerry Carlucci, mayor of the City of Philadelphia.

Mayor Carlucci had "suggested" to Police Commissioner Taddeus Czernich that the investigation of the Nelson murder be turned over to Peter Wohl's Special Operations Division.

The case had more or less solved itself when two other Negro Homosexual Males had been arrested in Atlantic City in possession of Jerome Nelson's Visa and American Express cards, and had been charged by New Jersey authorities with the murder of Pierre St. Maury, whose body had been found near Jerome Nelson's abandoned Jaguar in the wilds of New Jersey.

SAC Davis knew that, for reasons that could only be described as political, Mayor Carlucci had "suggested" to Commissioner Czernich that Peter Wohl's Special Operations Division be given responsibility for three other situations that had attracted a good deal of media attention, much of it (all of it, in the case of the *Ledger)* unfavorable.

The first of these, a serial murderer-rapist in Northwest Philadelphia, had been resolved, to favorable publicity, when a police officer assigned to Special Operations had not only shot the murderer-rapist to death, but done so when the villain actually had his next intended victim tied up, naked, in the back of his van.

The other two highly publicized cases had not gone at all well. One was the apparently senseless murder of a young police officer who had been on patrol near Temple University. A massive effort, still ongoing, hadn't turned up a thing, which gave Arthur Nelson's *Ledger* an at least once-a-week opportunity to run an editorial criticizing the Police Department generally, Special Operations specifically, and Mayor Carlucci in particular.

Davis was sure that the pressure on Wohl to find the cop killer must be enormous.

The third case had been that of a contract hit of a third-rate mobster, Anthony J. DeZego, also known as "Tony the Zee," on the roof of a downtown parking garage. Ordinarily, the untimely demise of a minor thug would have been forgotten in twenty-four hours, but this particular thug had been in the company of a young woman named Penelope Detweiler when someone had opened up on him with a shotgun. The Detweiler girl's father was president of Nesfoods International and one of the rocks upon which the cathedral of Philadelphia society had been built. Not only had this young woman been wounded during the attack on Mr. DeZego, but it had come out that she was not only carrying on with Tony the Zee, but also addicted to heroin.

Obviously, since it wasn't their fault that their precious child had not only been shacking up with a married thug, but had been injecting and inhaling narcotics, it had to be somebody's fault. Since the police were supposed to stop that sort of thing it was obviously the fault of the police. For a few days, the influence of Nesfoods International had allied itself with Mr. Nelson and his newspaper in roundly condemning the Police Department and the mayor.

But then that had stopped, with Mr. Detweiler making a 180-degree turn. Davis had no idea how Mayor Carlucci (or possibly Peter Wohl) had pulled that off, but what had happened was that Detweiler had made a speech not only praising the police, but also starting, with a large contribution of his own, a rewarding fund to catch whoever had murdered the young cop in his patrol car.

Special Agent Davis knew that Mr. Detweiler's change of heart had nothing to do with the cops having caught whoever had killed DeZego and seriously wounded his daughter. That was never going to happen. The DeZego murder and the Detweiler aggravated assault cases would almost certainly never be officially closed.

There had been a report from the FBI's Chicago office that a known contract hit man meeting the description of the DeZego killer had been found in the trunk of his car with three .45-caliber bullets having passed through his cranial cavity. There was little question in anyone's mind that the DeZego/Detweiler hit man had himself been hit, probably to shut his mouth, but knowing something and being able to prove it were two entirely different things.

Special Agent in Charge Davis had been meaning to have lunch with Peter Wohl, to chat, out of school, about these cases, even before he had learned, within the past fortyeight hours, that the Nelson case was not, in something of an understatement, over. It was in fact the reason he had asked Staff Inspector Wohl to break bread with him, preferably in some quiet restaurant, like Ristorante Alfredo, where they could talk in confidence.

Davis had been summoned to Washington two days before and informed that after a review of the facts, the United States Attorney for the Eastern District of Pennsylvania had brought the case of the two Negro Males who had kidnapped Pierre St. Maury, taken him against his will across a state border, and then shot him to death before a federal Grand Jury and secured an indictment against them under the Lindbergh Act.

Davis had been informed that it behooved him to do whatever he could to assist the deputy attorney general in securing a conviction. He had been told that the case had attracted the interest of certain people high in the Justice Department. Davis did not need to be reminded that the deputy attorney general of the United States, before his appointment, had been a senior partner of the law firm that represented the Daye-Nelson Corporation.

Davis had been on the telephone when Wohl had appeared at his office, and Wohl consequently had had to cool his heels for fifteen minutes before Davis could come out of his office to greet him, and apologize for getting hung up.

This would have annoyed Peter Wohl in any case, when all things were going fine in his world. Today that wasn't the case. He had just come from the Roundhouse, where he had had a painful session with Mayor Carlucci and Commissioner Czernich, witnessed by Chief Inspectors Matt Lowenstein (Detective Division) and Dennis V. Coughlin concerning the inability of the Special Operations Division to come up with even *one* fucking thing that might lead them to find whoever had put four .22 Long Rifle bullets into the chest, and one into the leg, of Police Officer Joseph Magnella.

He had not been in the mood to be kept waiting by anybody, and Special Agent Davis had seen this on his face.

It was unfortunate, Davis had thought, that Wohl first of all looked too young to be a staff inspector of police (he was, in fact, Davis had recalled, the youngest staff inspector in the Department), and second, he seemed to have a thing about not introducing himself by giving his rank or even identifying himself as a police officer unless it was absolutely necessary.

If he had told the receptionist that he was "Staff Inspector Wohl," Davis thought, she would certainly have taken him into the staff coffee room as a professional courtesy. But apparently, he had not done so; the receptionist had said, "There's a man named Wohl to see you." And so she had pointed out a chair in the outer office to him and let him wait.

And then, no sooner had Davis put on his topcoat and hat, as they were literally walking out of the reception room to the elevators, than there had been another "must-take" telephone call.

"Peter, I'm sorry."

"Why don't we try this another time? You're obviously really too busy."

"Wait downstairs, I'll only be a minute."

It had been at least ten minutes. When he walked out onto the street, Wohl had been leaning against the fender of his official Plymouth, wearing a visibly insincere smile.

"Well, Walter, here you are!"

"You know how these things go," Davis replied.

"Certainly," Wohl said. "I mean, my God, FBI agents aren't expected to have to eat, are they?"

"How does Italian sound, Peter?"

"Italian sounds fine," Wohl replied and opened the back door of the car for him. Only then did Davis see the young man behind the wheel of the Ford.

A plainclothesman, he decided. *He's too young to be a detective.*

He realized that the presence of Wohl's driver was going to be a problem. He didn't want to talk about the murder-kidnapping case, especially the political implications of it, in front of a junior police officer.

Wohl slammed the door after Davis and got in the front seat.

"Shank & Evelyn's, Matt," he ordered. "Eleventh and Carpenter."

"Yes, sir," the young cop said.

"Officer Payne, this is Special Agent—Special Agent *in Charge,* excuse *me*—Davis."

"How do you do?" Payne said.

"Nice to meet you," Davis said absently, forcing a smile. He had begun to suspect that the luncheon was not going to go well. "Peter, I was thinking about Alfredo's—"

"That's a Mob-owned joint," Wohl said, as if shocked at the suggestion. "I don't know about the FBI, but we local cops have to worry about where we're seen, isn't that so, Officer Payne?"

"Yes, sir, we certainly do," the young cop said, playing straight man to Wohl.

"Besides, the veal is better at Shank & Evelyn's than at Ristorante Alfredo, wouldn't you say, Officer Payne?"

"Yes, sir, I would agree with that."

"Officer Payne is quite a gourmet, Walter. He really knows his veal."

"Okay, Peter, I give up," Davis said. "I'm sorry about making you wait. I really am. It won't happen again."

"I have no idea what you're talking about, Walter. Anyway, Officer Payne and I don't have anything else to do but wait around to buy the FBI lunch, do we, Officer Payne?"

"Not a thing, sir."

"I'm buying the lunch," Davis said.

"In that case, you want us to go back and stand around on the curb for a while?"

"So, how are things, Peter?" Davis said, smiling. "Not to change the subject, of course?"

"Can't complain," Wohl said.

Davis had seen that they had turned left onto South Broad and were heading toward the airport.

"Where is this restaurant?" Davis asked.

"In South Philly. If you want good Italian food, go to South Philly, I always say. Isn't that so, Officer Payne?"

"Yes, sir," Officer Payne replied. "You're always saying that, sir."

"So tell me, Officer Payne, how do you like being Inspector Wohl's straight man?"

Officer Payne turned and smiled at Davis. "I like it fine, sir," he said.

Nice-looking kid, Davis thought.

A few minutes later Payne turned off South Broad Street, and then onto Christian, and then south onto 11th Street. A 3rd District sergeant's car was parked in a Tow Away Zone at a corner.

"Pull up beside him, Matt," Wohl ordered, and, when Payne did so, rolled down the window.

What Davis thought of as a real, old-time beat cop, a heavyset, florid-faced sergeant in his fifties, first scowled out of the window and then smiled broadly. With surprising agility, he got out of the car, put out his hand, and said, "Goddamn, look who's out slumming. How the hell are you, Peter—Inspector?"

He saw me, Davis thought, *and decided he should not call Wohl by his first name in front of a stranger, who is probably a senior police official.*

"Pat, say hello to the headman of the FBI, Walter Davis," Wohl said. "Walter, Sergeant Pat McGovern. He was my tour sergeant in this district when I got out of the Academy."

"Hello, sir, an honor I'm sure," McGovern said to Davis.

"How are you, Sergeant?"

McGovern looked at Payne, decided he wasn't important, and nodded at him.

"Anything I can do for you?" McGovern asked.

"Where can we find a place to park?" Wohl asked.

"Going in Shank & Evelyn's?"

"Yeah."

"You got a parking place," Sergeant McGovern said. He raised his eyes to Matt Payne. "Back it up, son, and I'll get out of your way."

"Good to see you, Pat."

"Yeah, you too," McGovern said as he started to get back in his car. "Say hello to your old man. He all right?"

Davis remembered that Wohl's father was a retired chief inspector.

"If anything, meaner."

"Impossible," McGovern said, and then got his car moving.

Payne moved into the space vacated, and Davis and Wohl got out of the car.

"Peter," Davis said quietly, touching Wohl's arm. "Could we send your driver someplace else to eat?"

"Is this personal, Walter?"

Davis hesitated a moment before replying.

"No. Not really."

"He's good with details," Wohl said, nodding toward Payne.

Which translates, Davis thought, a little annoyed, *that Wohl's straight man doesn't go somewhere else to eat.*

Shank & Evelyn's Restaurant was worse for Davis's purposes than he could have imagined possible. The whole place was smaller than his office, and consisted of a grill, a counter with ten or twelve stools, and half a dozen tables, at the largest of which, provided they kept their elbows at their sides, four people could eat.

What I should have done, Davis thought, annoyed, *was simply get in my car and drive out to Wohl's office at Bustleton and Bowler. This is a disaster.*

They found seats at a tiny table littered with the debris of the previous customers' meals. A massively bosomed waitress with a beehive hairdo first cleaned the table and then took their orders. Wohl ordered the veal, and somewhat reluctantly, Davis ordered the same.

"Sausage, *hot* sausage, and peppers, please, extra peppers," Matt Payne said.

"Frankie around?" Wohl asked her.

"In the back," the waitress said.

Wohl nodded.

A minute or so later, a very large, sweating man in a chef's hat, T-shirt, and white trousers came up to the table, offering his hand.

"How the hell are you, Peter?"

"Frankie, say hello to Walter Davis and Matt Payne," Wohl said. "This is Frankie Perri."

Frankie gave them a callused ham of a hand.

"Matt works for me," Wohl went on. "Walter runs the FBI. He said he'd never met a Mob guy, so I said I could fix that and brought him here."

"He's kidding, I hope you know," Frankie said.

"Yes, of course," Davis said uncomfortably.

"With a name like Frankie Perri, the FBI figures you have to be in the Mafia," Wohl said.

"Kiss my ass, Peter," Frankie Perri said, punching Wohl affectionately on the arm. "I'm going to burn your goddamn veal."

He put out his hand to Davis, and nodded at Matt.

"Nice to meet you, Mr. Davis. Come back. Both of you."

"Thank you," Davis said, and then when he was gone, he said, "What do you call that, Peter, community relations?"

"What's on your mind, Walter?"

"The government is going to try Clifford Wallis and Delmore Travis for murder/kidnapping under the Lindbergh Act."

"Who?" Matt Payne asked.

Wohl glanced at him, a flicker of annoyance in his eyes.

"New Jersey's got them," Wohl said, "with a lot of evidence, on a murder one. They might plea-bargain that down to manslaughter one, but no further. That's good for twenty-to-life, anyway. Why?"

"They violated federal law, Peter."

"Come on."

"Let us say there is considerable interest in this case rather high up in the Justice Department."

"You mean that Arthur Nelson wants them prosecuted," Wohl said.

Davis, who had been sitting back in his chair with his left hand against his cheek, moved the hand momentarily away from his face, a tacit agreement with Wohl's statement.

"Why?" Wohl asked, visibly thinking aloud.

"People get paroled on a state twenty-to-life conviction after what, seven years?" Davis said.

"And he wants to make sure they do more than seven years for the murder of his son. You got enough to try them?"

"We have enough for a Grand Jury indictment."

"That's not what I asked."

"I grant, it's pretty circumstantial," Davis said. "That's why I'm turning to you for help, Peter."

"Would you think me cynical to suspect that someone's leaning on you about this, Walter?"

"Yes," Davis said, smiling. "But they called me to Washington yesterday, and both of the telephone calls that delayed this little luncheon of ours concerned this case."

The waitress with the beehive hairdo delivered three large plates with sliced tomatoes and onions just about covering them.

When she had gone, Wohl took a forkful, chewed it slowly, and then asked, "So how can I help, Walter? More than the established, official routine for cooperation with the FBI would be helpful?"

"I need what you have as soon as I can get it, and I want everything you have, not just what a normal request for information would produce."

The waitress delivered three round water glasses, now scarred nearly gray by a thousand trips through the dishwasher. She half filled them, from a battered stainless-steel water pitcher, with a red liquid.

"Frankie said his grandfather made it over in Jersey," the waitress said.

Wohl picked up his glass, then stood up, called "Frankie," and, when he had his attention, called "Salud!" and then sat down again.

Walter Davis, thinking, *Oh, God, homemade Dago Red!* took a swallow. It was surprisingly good.

"You're almost certainly drinking an alcoholic beverage on which the applicable federal tax has not been paid," Wohl said. "Does that bother you?"

"Not a damned bit, to tell you the truth," Davis said. He stood up, called "Frankie" and then "Salud!" and then sat down, looking at Wohl, obviously pleased with himself.

Wohl chuckled, then looked at Matt Payne.

"Matt, when we get back to the office, round up everything in my files on the Nelson murder case. Make a copy of everything. Then go to Homicide and do the same thing. Then find Detective Harris and photocopy everything he has. Have it ready for me in the morning."

"Yes, sir," Matt Payne said.

"I'll take a look at it, see if anything is missing, and then you can take it to the FBI. Soon enough for you, Walter?"

"Thank you, Peter. 'Harris,' you said, was the detective on the job? Any chance that I could talk to him?"

"You, or one of your people?"

"Actually, I was thinking of one of my people."

"Tony Harris is the exception to the rule that most detectives really would rather be FBI agents, Walter. I don't think that would be very productive."

"I thought everybody loved us," Davis said.

"We all do. Isn't that so, Officer Payne?"

"Yes, sir. We all love the FBI."

The waitress with the beehive hairdo delivered their meal.

The veal was, Walter Davis was willing to admit, better than the veal in Ristorante Alfredo. And the homemade Chianti was nicer than some of the dry red wine he'd had at twenty-five dollars a bottle in Ristorante Alfredo.

But he knew that neither the quality of the food nor its considerably cheaper than Ristorante Alfredo prices were the reasons Peter Wohl had brought him here for lunch.

6.

Under the special agent in charge (the "SAC") of the Philadelphia Office of the Federal Bureau of Investigation were three divisions, Criminal Affairs, Counterintelligence, and Administration. Each division was under an assistant agent in charge, called an "A-SAC."

It was SAC Davis's custom to hold two daily Senior Staff Conferences, called "SSC"s, each business day, one first thing in the morning, and the other at four P.M. Participation at the SSCs was limited to the SAC and the three A-SACs. The conferences were informal. No stenographic record was made of them, except when the SAC could not be present, and one of the A-SACs was standing in for him. The SAC naturally wanted to know what he had missed, so a steno was called in to make a written record.

If one of the A-SACs could not make a SSC, one of his assistants, customarily, but not always, the most senior special agent in that division, would be appointed to stand in for him.

This was very common. The A-SACs were busy men, and it was often inconvenient for them to make both daily SSCs, although they generally tried to make at least one of them, and took especial pains not to miss two days' SSCs in a row.

But it was a rare thing for SAC Davis to find, as he did when he returned to his office from lunch with Staff Inspector Wohl and Officer Payne, all three A-SACs waiting outside his office for the afternoon SSC.

He was pleased. In addition to whatever else would be discussed, he intended to discuss the upcoming trials of Clifford Wallis and Delmore Travis. The political aspects were mind-boggling. Washington was going to be breathing down his neck on this one, and not only the senior hierarchy of the FBI, joining which was one of SAC Davis's most fond dreams, but the higher—*highest*—echelons of the Department of Justice.

If he handled this well, it would reflect well upon him. If he dropped the ball (or someone he was responsible for dropped it), there would be no chance whatever that he would be transferred to Washington and named a deputy inspector. And from what he had seen of the situation, there was a saber-toothed tiger behind every filing cabinet, just waiting to leap and bite off somebody's ass.

This sort of a case was the sort of thing one should discuss with the A-SACs personally, not with one of their subordinates. With all three of the A-SACs present at this SSC, it would not be necessary to call a special SSC.

Davis waited until he had heard all the reports of what was going on in the Criminal, Administrative, and Counterintelligence Divisions, and made the few decisions necessary before getting into what he was now thinking of as the "Wallis/Travis Sticky Ball of Wax."

Then he gave a report, the essentials and the flavor, of both the personal conference he had had in Washington the day before and the two telephone calls he had had that morning before going off to lunch with Staff Inspector Wohl and his straight man.

"I had lunch today with Staff Inspector Wohl of the Philadelphia Police Department," he announced. "Everybody know who Wohl is?"

The three A-SACs nodded.

"I didn't go through you, Glenn," he explained to Glenn Williamson, A-SAC (Administration). "I know Peter Wohl, and this was unofficial. But I think you should open a line of communication with Captain— What's his name?"

"Duffy. Jack Duffy, Chief," Williamson furnished. Williamson was a well-dressed man of forty-two who took especial pains with his full head of silver-gray hair.

"—Duffy of—what's his title, Glenn?"

"Assistant to the commissioner, Chief."

"—whatever—as soon as possible. Either this afternoon, or first thing in the morning," Davis finished.

For reasons SAC Davis really did not understand, cooperation between the Philadelphia Police Department and the Federal Bureau of Investigation was not what he believed it should be. Getting anything out of them was like pulling teeth. When he had found the opportunity, he had discussed the problem with Commissioner Czernich. Czernich had told him that whenever he wanted anything from the Department, he should contact Captain Duffy, who would take care of whatever was requested. It had been Davis's experience that bringing Duffy into the loop had served primarily to promptly inform Czernich that the FBI was asking for something; it had not measurably speeded up getting anything. The reverse, he thought, might actually be the case.

But now that Duffy was in the loop, Duffy would have to be consulted.

"Yes, sir."

"You might mention I had an unofficial word with Wohl. Whatever you think best."

"Yes, sir. How did it go with Wohl, sir?"

"Very interesting man. He had his straight man with him. I was thinking of a lunch at Alfredo's, and we wound up in a greasy spoon in South Philadelphia."

"His straight man, sir?" A-SAC (Criminal Affairs) Frank F. Young asked. Young was a redhead, pale-faced, and on the edge between muscular and plump.

"His driver. A young plainclothes cop named Payne. They have a little comedy routine they use on people Wohl's annoyed with. I had to keep Wohl waiting twice, you see—"

"Oh, you met Payne, Chief?" A-SAC (Counterintelligence) Isaac J. Towne asked. He was a thirty-nine-year-old, balding Mormon, who took his religion seriously, a tall, hawk-featured man who had once told Davis, perfectly serious, that he regarded the Communists as the Antichrist.

"You know him?" Davis asked, surprised.

"I know about him," Towne replied. "Actually, I know a good deal about him. Among other things, he's the fellow who blew the brains of the serial rapist all over his van."

"Oh, really?" A-SAC Young asked, genuine interest evident in his voice. Davis knew that Young had a fascination for what he had once called "real street cop stuff"; Davis suspected he was less interested in some of the white-collar crime that occupied a good deal of the FBI's time and effort.

"How is it you know 'a good deal about him,' Isaac?" Davis asked.

"Well, when I saw the story in the papers, the name rang a bell, and I checked my files. We had just finished a CBI on him." (Complete Background Investigation.)

"He'd applied for the FBI?"

"The Marine Corps. He was about to be commissioned."

"Apparently he wasn't?"

"He flunked the physical," Towne said. "His father, his *adoptive* father, is Brewster Cortland Payne."

"As in Mawson, Payne, Stockton, McAdoo and whatever else?"

"And Lester. Right, Chief."

SAC Davis found that fascinating. He was himself an attorney, and although he had never actively practiced law, he was active in the Philadelphia Bar Association. He knew enough about the Bar in Philadelphia to know that Mawson, Payne, Stockton, McAdoo & Lester was one of the more prestigious firms.

"His 'adoptive' father, you said?"

"Yes, sir. His father was a Philadelphia cop. A sergeant. Killed in the line of duty. His mother remarried Payne, and Payne adopted the boy."

That would stick in your mind, Davis thought, *a street cop killed in the line of duty.*

"I wonder why he became a cop?" Davis wondered aloud, and then, without waiting for a reply, asked, "You say he was the man who shot the serial rapist?"

"Right, Chief. In the head, with his service revolver. Blew his brains all over the inside of his van."

And that, too, would stick in your mind, wouldn't it, Isaac?

"I seem to remember seeing something about that in the papers," Davis said. "But as I was saying, Wohl, once he'd made his annoyance with me quite clear, was very cooperative. He's going to photocopy everything in his files and have this Payne fellow bring it over here tomorrow."

The three A-SACs nodded their understanding.

"I just had a thought," Davis went on. "Do you happen to recall precisely why Payne failed the Marine Corps physical?"

Isaac Young searched his memory, then shook his head. "No."

"Can you find out?" Davis ordered. "The FBI is always looking for outstanding young men."

"Right, Chief," Isaac Young said.

"And when Officer Payne delivers the material from Inspector Wohl, I think one of us should receive it. Tell the receptionist. Make sure she understands. Show him around the office."

"Right, Chief," Young said.

I mean, after all, Davis thought, *why would a bright young man of good family want to be a cop when he could be an FBI agent?*

And if that doesn't turn out, it can't hurt to have a friend—especially a kid like that, who must hear all sorts of interesting things in the Department.

Matt Payne, feeding documents into the Xerox machine, jumped when Peter Wohl spoke in his ear.

"I have bled enough for the city for one day," Wohl announced. "I am going home and get into a cold martini or a hot blonde, whichever comes first."

"Yes, sir." Matt chuckled. "I'll see you in the morning."

"One of the wounds from which I'm bleeding has to do with what you're doing—"

"Sir?" Matt asked, confused.

"I just got off the phone with Commissioner Czernich," Wohl went on. "I don't know what Davis's agenda really is, and I wondered why he came to me with the request for all that stuff. One possibility was that he didn't want the commissioner to know he was asking for it. With that in mind, I called the commissioner and told him where and with whom we had lunch—" He saw the confused look still on Payne's face and stopped.

"I'm—I don't follow you, Inspector," Matt said.

"For reasons I'm sure I don't have to explain, we are very careful what we pass to the FBI," Wohl said.

I haven't the faintest idea what he's talking about.

"Yes, sir."

"Nothing goes over to them unless the commissioner approves it. Denny Coughlin or Matt Lowenstein might slip them something quietly, but since career suicide is not one of my aims, I won't, and Davis must know that."

"So why did he ask you?"

"Right. So I called the commissioner. The commissioner told me I had done the right thing in calling him, and that I should use my good judgment in giving him whatever I felt like giving him."

"Okay," Matt said thoughtfully.

"Two minutes after I hung up, Czernich called back. 'Peter,' he said, 'I've been thinking it over, and I think I know why Davis went directly to you.' So I said, 'Yes, sir?'

and he said, 'It's because you and the Payne kid look more like FBI agents than cops. Hahaha!' And then he hung up."

"Jesus!" Matt said.

"It may well be Polish humor," Wohl said. "But I'm paranoid. The moral to this little story is that I want you to clearly understand you are to pass nothing to the FBI, or the feds generally, unless I tell you to. Clear?"

"Yes, sir."

"Okay. Then I will say good night."

"I'll see you in the morning, sir."

"God willing, and if the creek don't rise," Wohl said solemnly, and walked out of the room.

Matt Payne finished making copies of the documents he had taken from the file, stuffed the copies into a large manila envelope, and then returned the originals to their filing cabinet.

It was quarter to four. He would still have to see Detective Tony Harris, and then go downtown to Homicide and see if their files contained something he hadn't found, or would get from Harris. He would not be able to quit at five.

Tony Harris was not in the closet-sized office he shared with Detective Jason Washington. Washington, he knew, had taken the day off; he had a place at The Shore that always seemed to need some kind of emergency repair.

He really should, he thought, talk to Washington about the file Wohl wanted to pass to the FBI. Washington had worked with Harris on the Nelson job. He remembered over-hearing Washington telling Wohl he would be back sometime in the afternoon.

The tour lieutenant, Harry Jensen, a Highway guy, said that Harris was out on the street somewhere. Both he and Washington were running down increasingly less promising leads to find whoever had shot down Joe Magnella, the young 22nd District cop. Wohl, Matt thought, had not really been kidding when he had said he had bled enough for the city for one day; the pressure on him to find the Magnella doers was enormous.

Payne went to Special Operations communications and tried to raise Harris on the radio. There was no reply, which meant that Harris was either working and away from his car, or that he had hung it up for the day.

That left Homicide, and opened the question of how to get there. He could go to the sergeant and get keys to one of the Special Operations cars. Or he could see if he could catch a ride downtown in either a Special Operations car or a Highway car. In either case, when he was finished at the Roundhouse, that would leave him downtown and his personal car here.

There was no reason for him to come back here, except to get his car, because it would be long past quitting before he finished at Homicide and finally ran Harris down, if he managed to do that.

He went back to Lieutenant Jensen and told him that if Inspector Wohl called for him, to tell him that he had gone to Homicide in his own car, and was going to quit for the day when he finished there.

"The inspector know where to reach you?"

"I'll either be home or I'll call in," Matt said.

"But you *are* going to Homicide?"

"Yes, sir."

Lieutenant Jensen, Matt suspected, was one of a large number of people, in and out of Highway, who nursed a resentment toward him. That a rookie should have a plainclothes assignment as administrative assistant to a division commander was part of it; and part of it, Matt knew, was that he had about as powerful a rabbi, in the person of Chief Inspector Dennis V. Coughlin, as they came.

He had once discussed this with Detective Jason Washington, who had said it was clear to him that the only option Matt had in the circumstances was to adopt a "fuck you" philosophy.

"You didn't ask for the assignment, Matt, the mayor set that up. And it's not your fault that Denny Coughlin looks on you as the son he never had. If people can't figure that out for themselves, fuck 'em."

In time, Matt hoped, the resentment would pass.

He drove downtown via North Broad Street, and was surprised, until he considered the hour, to find a spot in the parking area behind the Roundhouse.

If I were a cynical man, he thought, *I might be prone to suspect that not all of the captains, inspectors, and chief inspectors who toil here in The Palace scrupulously avoid leaving their place of duty before five P.M.*

He entered the Roundhouse by the rear door, waved his ID at the corporal behind the thick plastic window, and the corporal pushed the button that triggered the solenoid in the door to the lobby.

He got in one of the curved elevators and rode it up one floor, and then walked down the curved corridor to the Homicide Bureau.

He had been here often before, and twice under more or less involuntary conditions. The first time, which ranked among the top two or three most unpleasant experiences of his life, had been an eight-hour visit following his shooting of Warren K. Fletcher, aka the Northwest serial rapist.

He had been "interviewed" by two very unpleasant Homicide detectives, under the cold eye of a Homicide captain named Henry Quaire, all three of whom seemed to feel that the shooting was not a good shooting. It had not helped at all that both Peter Wohl and Denny Coughlin had established themselves in Quaire's office during the "interview." By the time the "interview" was over, Matt was beginning to wonder whose side the Homicide guys were on.

The second time was when an asshole Narcotics sergeant had actually suspected (with nothing more, really, to go on than the Porsche) that Matt was (a) involved with drugs, and therefore (b) connected with the shotgun slaying of a Mafia guy named Tony DeZego.

That was all the bastard had. And all Matt had done to arouse his suspicion was to have driven into the crime scene a minute or two after the shooting had taken place. You didn't have to be Sherlock Holmes to figure out that if Matt had been involved, he wouldn't have been the one who had sent his date to call the *shooting, hospital case* in.

This afternoon, however, all was sweetness and light. He had no sooner got to the railing barring access to the interior of the Homicide Bureau than he heard his name being called, and then saw Captain Quaire smiling and waving him inside.

Quaire offered his hand.

"How are you, Payne? Inspector Wohl called. We've been expecting you."

"How are you, sir?"

"I had them pull the files," Quaire said, tapping a stack of folders on his desk.

"I appreciate that," Matt said.

"I would have had them Xeroxed," Captain Quaire said, "but I didn't know what you already had."

"I got a bunch," Matt said, holding up the well-stuffed manila envelope.

Quaire picked up the folders on his desk and carried them to an unoccupied desk in the outer office and sat there as Matt went through the Homicide files on the Nelson murder.

There were only three things—none of which looked important—in the Homicide files that Matt hadn't already found at Bustleton and Bowler, but it took half an hour to find them.

"I didn't think there'd be much," Captain Quaire said as Matt was making copies. "Anything else we can do for Special Operations?"

"I need to use the phone, sir," Matt said. "I'm supposed to see if Mr. Harris has anything."

"Oh, yes, *Mr.* Harris," Quaire said, dryly sarcastic. *"Mr.* Harris used to work here, you know."

"He's told me," Matt said, smiling.

Quaire laughed.

"Help yourself," Quaire said, pointing to a telephone.

Matt called Harris's number at Special Operations. There was no answer. Then he called Police Radio and asked the operator if she could contact W-William Four and ask him to call Homicide.

A minute later she reported there was no response from W-William Four.

"Thank you," Matt said, and hung up.

"For your general information, Officer Payne," Captain Quaire said, "in my long experience with *Mr.* Harris, when he worked here, you understand, it is often difficult to establish contact with him at the cocktail hour."

"Thank you, sir. I'll remember that."

"Why don't you try him at his apartment in an hour or so?"

"I will," Matt said.

Two detectives walked into the room. One of them, a slightly built, natty, olive-skinned man, Matt recognized. He was a Homicide detective, Joe D'Amata. The other one, a large, heavy, round-faced man, he didn't know.

"What have you got, Joe?" Captain Quaire said.

"High noon at the OK Corral, Captain," D'Amata said. "Whaddaya say, Payne? How are you?"

"Hello, Joe."

"He calls Tony Harris 'Mr.', " Captain Quaire said. "That tell you anything?"

"Tony Harris is much older than I am," D'Amata said, grinning. He turned to the other detective. "You know Payne, don't you?"

The other detective shook his head no.

"Jerry Pelosi, Central Detectives, Matt Payne, Special Operations, also known as 'Dead Eye.' "

"I know *who* he is, I just never met him. How are you, Payne?" Pelosi said, offering Matt a large, muscular hand and a smile.

"Hi," Matt said, and then, to keep D'Amata from making further witty reference to the shooting, he asked, "What's this 'OK Corral' business?"

" 'High Noon at the OK Corral,' " D'Amata corrected him. "The current count of bullets fired and found at Goldblatt's, not counting what the medical examiner will find in Mr. Cohn—three, maybe four—is twenty-six."

"Jesus," Captain Quaire said.

"And they're still looking."

"What's Goldblatt's?" Matt asked.

"Furniture store on South Street," Pelosi explained. "Robbery and murder. Early this afternoon."

"And a gun battle," Matt offered.

"No," D'Amata said, as much to Captain Quaire as to correct Payne. "Not a gun battle. Nobody took a shot at them. Nobody even had a gun. The doers just shot the place up, for no reason that I can figure."

Quaire looked between the two detectives. When his eyes met Pelosi's, Pelosi said, "What *I* can't figure, Captain, is why they hit this place in the first place. They never have much cash around, couple of hundred bucks, maybe a thousand tops. They could have hit any one of the bars around there, and got more. And why did they hit it now? I mean, right after the holidays, there's no business?"

"You have any idea who the doers are?" Quaire asked.

"No, but we're working on that," D'Amata said. "The victims are still a little shaky. I want them calm when I show them some pictures."

Quaire nodded.

"I'd better get out of here," Matt Payne said, suspecting he might be in the way. "Thank you for your help, Captain. And it was nice to meet you."

"Same here," Pelosi replied.

"Anytime you want to sell that piece of shit you drive around in, Payne, cheap, of course, call me," D'Amata said, punching Matt's shoulder.

Matt got as far as the outer door when Captain Quaire called his name. Matt turned.

"Yes, sir?"

"If you manage to find him," Quaire said. "Give our regards to *Mr.* Harris. Tell him we miss his smiling face around here."

"Yes, sir," Matt said. "I'll do that."

On the way to the lobby in the elevator, Matt thought first, *If they didn't like me, they would not tease me.* Teasing, he had learned, was not the police way of expressing displeasure or contempt.

And then he thought, *Shit, I'll be out all night looking for Harris.*

And then a solution to his problem popped into his mind. He crossed the lobby to the desk and asked the corporal if he could use the telephone.

"Business?"

"No, I'm going to call my bookie," Matt said.

The corporal, not smiling, pushed the telephone to him. Matt dialed, from memory, the home telephone of Detective Jason Washington.

7.

Detective Jason Washington was sitting slumped almost sinfully comfortably in his molded plywood and leather chair, his feet up on a matching footstool, when the telephone rang. The chair had been, ten days before, his forty-third birthday gift from his daughter and son-in-law. He had expected either a necktie, or a box of cigars, or maybe a bottle of Johnnie Walker Black. The chair had surprised him to begin with, and even more after he'd seen one in the window of John Wanamaker's Department Store with a sign announcing that the Charles Eames Chair and Matching Footstool was now available in Better Furniture for $980.

A glass dark with twelve-year-old Scotch rested on his stomach. Whenever anything disturbing happened, it was Jason Washington's custom to make himself a drink of good whiskey. He would then sit down and think the problem over. During the thought process, he never touched the whiskey. The net result of this, he sometimes thought, was that he wasted a lot of good whiskey.

"Hello," he said to the telephone. He had a very deep, melodious voice. When she was little, his daughter used to say he should be on the radio.

"Mr. Washington, this is Matt."

Officer Matthew M. Payne had the discomfiting habit of calling Detective Washington "Mr." At first, Washington had suspected that Payne was being obsequious, or perhaps even, less kindly, mocking him in some perverse manner known only to upper-class white boys. He had come to understand, however, that Matt Payne called him "Mr.," even after being told not to, as a manifestation of his respect. Washington found this discomfiting too.

"Hello, Matt."

"I hate to bother you at home, but I have a little problem. Is this a bad time for me to call?"

I am sitting here alone with a bottle of Johnnie Walker Black Label, just hoping for something to brighten my day.

"What is it, Matt?"

"The feds are going to try the two guys who carved up Jerome Nelson."

What the hell is he talking about?

"Run that past me again?"

"The inspector and I had lunch with the FBI SAC, Mr. Davis. He told the inspector the feds are going to try the doers of the Nelson job for kidnapping. He asked the inspector for what we have on the job. The inspector told me to Xerox everything we have in the files, what Homicide has, and to check with Mr. Harris. I just left Homicide. I can't find Harris. The inspector wants it all on his desk first thing in the morning."

The first thought Jason Washington had was, *Has Wohl lost his mind? If Czernich finds out he has been slipping material to the FBI, he'll be on the phone to Jerry Carlucci two seconds later, and ten seconds after that, Wohl will be teaching "Police Administration" at the Academy.*

This was immediately followed by the obvious rebuttal: *Either Czernich is in on this, or Wohl has his own agenda; the one thing Peter Wohl is not is a fool.*

And then: *Interesting, the way he calls the FBI guy "Mr."; Wohl "the inspector"; and, the first time, Harris "Mr." But that title of respect dropped off the second time he got to Tony. Since he knows that Tony is a first-rate detective, it has to be something else. A little vestigial Main Line snobbery, because Tony dresses like a bum? Or has the kid figured out that Tony has a bottle problem? One possibility is that he called Tony at home—if a furnished room can be called a home—and Tony was incoherent, and he'd rather not deal with that.*

"Why don't you bring what you have here, Matt? I'll have a look at it; see if it's all there."

"Yes, sir," Matt Payne said. "Thank you. I'm on my way."

Washington broke the connection with his finger and dialed Tony's number. There was no answer.

Meaning he's not there. Or that he's there, passed out.

He took a well-worn leather-bound notebook from his pocket, found the number of the Red Rooster, Tony Harris's favorite bar, and dialed it. Tony wasn't there. Washington left word for him to call him at home. It was possible, even likely, that Wohl would want to see him in the morning. Wohl, being Wohl, probably knew all about Tony's bottle problem, but it would not do Tony any good if Wohl saw him with the shakes.

He hung up, looked at the drink he had left sitting on the table beside his chair, and took the first swallow from it.

Jason and Martha Washington lived in an apartment on the tenth floor of a luxury building on the parkway. A wall of ceiling-to-floor windows in the living room gave them a view of the Art Museum, the Schuylkill River, and West Philadelphia.

Martha Washington was a commercial artist who made just about as much money as he did. Now that their daughter, Barbara, was gone, married to a twenty-five-year-old electronics engineer at RCA, across the Delaware in Jersey, who made as much money as his in-laws did together, the Washingtons were, as Jason thought of it, "comfortable."

Not only did they have the condo at The Shore, but Martha had a Lincoln; the furniture in the apartment was all they wanted; and Martha was starting to buy (and sell at often amazing profit) art. It had been a long time, he thought, since there had been an angry or hurt look in Martha's eyes when he walked in wearing a Tripler or Hart, Shaffner & Marx new suit.

They no longer had to think about the costs of getting Barbara a good education. That need had been removed from the financial equation when the graduate student of engineering had snatched her from her cradle the week before he graduated and RCA started throwing money at him.

Ten minutes later the doorman announced that a Mr. Payne was calling.

"If he's wearing shoes, send him up, please."

Washington timed his walk to the door precisely; he opened it as Matt got off the elevator.

"Sorry to bother you with this at home," Matt said.

"Come on in, Matt. I am drinking from the good stuff; make yourself one."

"What's the occasion?"

"Let me see what you have," Washington said, putting out his hand for the manila envelope. "You know where the booze is."

Matt headed for the liquor cabinet.

He is, with the possible exception of Peter Wohl, the only one of my brothers in blue who is not awed and/or made uncomfortable by this apartment.

Washington sat down on a leather upholstered couch and took the photocopies from the envelope and went through them. Payne sat in an armchair watching him.

"I think everything's there, Matt," Washington said, finally.

"Thank God," Matt said. "Thank you."

"You couldn't find Tony, you said?"

"He didn't answer the radio—twice, and he didn't answer the phone at his apartment."

"You ever been to his apartment?"

Matt shook his head no.

Then he hasn't found Tony mumbling incoherently into his booze. Moot point, he will learn eventually.

"Anything interesting going on at Homicide?"

"They had a murder of a guy during a robbery at a furniture store on South Street."

"I heard the call," Washington said.

The *officer needs assistance shooting hospital case* call had been on the air when he switched on the police radio in his unmarked police car as he came off the Benjamin Franklin Bridge into Philadelphia from New Jersey. By the time he reached the parkway, he had heard Matt Lowenstein calling in that he was at the scene. That too was very interesting. The chief of the Detective Division would ordinarily not go in on a robbery, or even a murder. Neither was uncommon in Philadelphia. He finally decided that Lowenstein had coincidentally been somewhere near without anything else important to do.

The car issued to Jason Washington by the Philadelphia Police Department was a new, two-tone (blue over gray) Ford LTD four-door sedan. It had whitewall tires, elaborate chrome wheel covers, and powder blue velour upholstery. There were only eight thousand odd miles on the odometer, and the car still even smelled new.

Detectives (like corporals, only one step above the lowest rank in the Police Department hierarchy) are not normally given brand-new cars to drive, much less to take home after work, but Jason Washington was not an ordinary detective.

Until recently, he had been able to take more than a little pride in his reputation of being the best detective in the Homicide Bureau, which was tantamount to saying that he was arguably the best detective in the entire Philadelphia Police Department, as it is generally conceded that the best detectives are assigned to Homicide.

Washington had not willingly given up his assignment to Homicide. He had been transferred (he thought of it as "shanghaied") to the just-then-formed Special Operations Division over his somewhat bluntly stated desire not to be transferred.

There had been a number of advantages in being assigned to Homicide. There was of course the personal satisfaction of simply knowing that you *were* a Homicide detective. That satisfaction was of course buttressed if you could believe that you were probably the best Homicide detective in the Bureau.

Jason Washington was not plagued with extraordinary humility. While he was perfectly willing to admit there were a number of very good detectives in Homicide, he could not honestly state that he knew of any who were quite as professionally competent as he was.

And the money was good, because of overtime. As a Homicide detective, he had taken home as much money as a chief inspector. Chief inspectors, he knew, often put in as many hours as he did, but under Civil Service regulations, they didn't get paid for it; they were given "compensatory time off" that they never seemed able to find time to take.

And chief inspectors (and other Police Department supervisors) spent a good portion of their time handling administrative matters that had little to do with catching critters, marching them through the judicial process, and seeing them sentenced and packed off to the pokey.

In Homicide, all Jason Washington had had to do was catch critters, either on jobs that had come to him via the Wheel, or on jobs that the Wheel had given to others, but on which he had been asked to "assist."

(The Wheel wasn't really a wheel, but rather a piece of lined paper, on which, at the beginning of each tour, each Homicide detective's name was written. As each homicide came to the attention of the Homicide Bureau, the job was given to the detective whose name was at the head of the list. He would not be given another job until every other detective listed on the Wheel had, in turn, been given one.)

While Jason Washington was at least as good as any other Homicide detective while working the crime scene, and certainly at least as knowledgeable as any other Homicide detective in the use of the high-tech techniques now available to match fibers, determine that a particular bullet had been fired from a particular weapon, and so on, his real strengths, he believed, were psychological and intellectual.

He believed, with more than a little reason, that he had no peers in interrogation. He could play, with great skill, any number of roles when interviewing a suspect. If the situation demanded it, Washington, who stood well over six feet and weighed 220 pounds, could strike terror into the heart of most human beings who had previously believed they were not afraid of the Devil himself. Or, with equal ease, he could assume the role of sympathetic uncle who understood how, through no fault of his own, the suspect had found himself in a situation where striking the deceased in the forehead with a fire axe had seemed a perfectly reasonable thing to do under the circumstances, and that the decent thing to do now was put the whole unfortunate incident behind him (or her) by making a clean breast of it.

Intellectually, Washington believed that both by natural inclination (perhaps genetic) and by long experience, he had no equal in discovering anomalies. An anomaly, by definition, is a deviation, modification, mutation, permutation, shift, or variation from the norm. If there was one tiny little piece of the jigsaw puzzle that didn't fit, Jason Washington could find it.

He had, in other words, been perfectly happy as the acknowledged best detective in Homicide when Jerome Nelson had been found in his apartment on Society Hill dead of multiple wounds probably inflicted by one of his own matched set of teak-handled Solingen kitchen knives.

The Wheel had assigned the case to Detective Anthony C. "Tony" Harris, who was not only a good friend of Washington's, but, in Washington's judgment, the second-best detective in Homicide. As soon as the case had come in, and as soon as Jerome Nelson's position in society had become known, Jason Washington had felt sure that he would soon be involved with it himself. Tony certainly would want some help, and would naturally turn to Jason Washington, or Captain Henry C. Quaire, who commanded the Homicide Bureau, would order him to work with Tony.

It hadn't happened quite that way. The Honorable Jerry Carlucci, mayor of the City of Brotherly Love, had taken the job away from the Homicide Bureau and given it to the newly formed Special Operations Division. Jason Washington's initial reaction to that had mirrored that of Captain Quaire and Chief Inspector Matt Lowenstein, who commanded the Detective Division that included the Homicide Bureau: righteous indignation that once more The Dago had put his goddamn nose in where it had no business.

Mayor Carlucci's notorious penchant for issuing orders directly to various divisions (for that matter, to individual officers) of the Police Department, instead of letting the commissioner run it, was, in a sense, understandable. Before winning, in his first bid for elective office, the mayoralty, The Dago had been police commissioner. He had, in fact, held every rank in the Philadelphia Police Department except policewoman. He therefore believed that he knew at least as much about running the Police Department as anyone else. And he had read the statutory functions of the mayor, which quite clearly stated that he was responsible for supervising "the various departments of the city."

On a secondary level, his parochial indignation as a Homicide detective aside, Jason Washington had thought that he understood The Dago's game plan, and that it would work. The Dago had turned out to be a better politician than anyone ever thought he would be.

Jason Washington and Jerry Carlucci went way back together. Carlucci had done a year in Homicide as a lieutenant, before he passed the captain's examination and moved to Highway Patrol. It was only fair to acknowledge that Carlucci had been a good lieutenant—he had been an all-around good cop, no one ever denied that—one proof of which being that even back then he had been smart enough to exercise only the barest minimum of supervision over Detective Jason Washington.

When, rarely, they bumped into each other, Washington could count on a bear hug and being greeted either by his Christian name or as "Ol' Buddy," or both. Jason Washington, who did not like to be hugged by anyone except his wife and daughter, and disliked being called "Ol' Buddy" by anyone, always smiled and referred to The Dago as "Mr. Mayor."

The way Washington had seen the assignment of the Nelson job to Special Operations seemed to make sense. Carlucci had just set up Special Operations. It was his. What had become a big-deal murder in the newspapers, because of the victim, was actually just a routine homicide. The odds were that the job would be closed in a week or two by Homicide. But that would not earn The Dago any favorable space in the newspapers. That's what Homicide was supposed to do, solve homicides.

But if Jerry Carlucci's Special Operations solved the Nelson job, His Honor the Mayor could, and would, claim the credit.

And Washington had seen that The Dago had carefully hedged his bet: Special Operations was commanded by Peter Wohl, who not only had been a sergeant in Homicide, but was, in Washington's judgment (and that of a lot of other knowledgeable people), one of the smartest cops in the Department. Before The Dago had formed Special Operations and given it to Peter Wohl, Wohl had been the youngest (ever) staff inspector in the department.

Staff inspectors ranked immediately above captains. With the exception, now, of Wohl, they operated within the Internal Affairs Division, and were charged with, primarily, investigations of corruption within and outside the Police Department. Wohl, just before being given Special Operations, had sent two judges and a city councilman to the state penitentiary for some rather imaginative income augmentation.

Washington had reasoned that Carlucci had decided that Wohl would have no trouble finding who had punctured Jerome Nelson so thoroughly, and that Special Operations—thus the mayor—would get the credit.

Washington had underestimated both Carlucci and Wohl. To make sure that Wohl did indeed catch the critters who had punctured Nelson with his own imported butcher knives, he gave him blanket authority to transfer to Special Operations anybody he thought he needed. Wohl had immediately decided that he needed Detectives Washington and Harris, and over howls of protest from the chief inspector of the Detective Division, the commanding officer of the Homicide Bureau, and Detectives Harris and Washington, they had been transferred to Special Operations.

Wohl was not only a good cop, but a good guy, and he had assured both Washington and Harris that he would see they could make as much overtime money as they had in Homicide, and done other things to soothe their ruffled feathers. They would work directly for him (and his deputy, Captain Mike Sabara) rather than under some sergeant, and had even arranged for the both of them to draw brand-new cars (normally reserved for at least captains) from the Police Garage.

He would not, however, promise (as Washington asked) to return them to Homicide once they caught whoever had murdered Jerome Nelson.

That job had just about solved itself when two critters had been caught by the cops in Atlantic City using Nelson's credit cards, but by then a looney tune in Northwest Philadelphia had started abducting and then carving up women, and the process had been repeated: Jerry Carlucci had called a press conference to announce he had given the job of apprehending the Northwest serial rapist to Special Operations, and Wohl had given it to Washington and Harris.

Washington and Harris had just about identified the psychopath who was carrying women off in the back of his van when, in one of those lucky breaks that sometimes happen, his van had been spotted by the rookie cop Wohl had had dumped in his lap by Chief Inspector Dennis V. Coughlin and was using as his driver.

Denny Coughlin, in what some people would call blatant nepotism but which Jason Washington felt perfectly sensible, had sent Officer Matthew M. Payne right out of the Police Academy to Special Operations, his intention clearly being to keep the kid from getting hurt before he came to his senses and quit the cops.

The kid had been born Matthew Mark Moffitt, three months after his father, Sergeant John Xavier Moffitt, had gotten himself shot to death answering a silent alarm. Sergeant Moffitt and Denny Coughlin had gone through the Academy together, and Coughlin had wept shamelessly at his funeral and when he had become the baby's godfather three months later.

Washington had always had the private opinion that Denny Coughlin had been more than a little sweet on the widow. If he had been (or, for that matter, if he still was; he had never married), he hadn't been able to do anything about it, for six months after Sergeant Moffitt had been killed, his widow got a job working as a trainee-secretary for Lowerie, Tant, Foster, Pedigill and Payne, a large and prestigious law firm. She hadn't worked more than a month or so when, pushing the kid in a stroller by the Franklin Institute on a Sunday afternoon, she met Brewster Cortland Payne II, walking his kids.

Payne recognized her vaguely from work; she was one of the girls in the typing pool. He spoke to her, and Patty Moffitt replied, because she had seen him at work too. He was the only son of one of the two founding partners of the law firm.

Within half an hour, Brewster Cortland Payne II learned that Mrs. Moffitt was a widow, and Patty Moffitt learned that his kids were motherless: Mrs. Payne had been killed in an auto accident returning from the Payne lodge in the Poconos some months before.

A month later Patricia Moffitt, enraging her family, her late husband's family, and the Payne family establishment, became Mrs. Brewster C. Payne II. Nice Irish Catholic Widows do not marry Main Line WASPs in an Episcopal Church, nor let their fatherless children be adopted by WASPs, nor become Episcopalians.

Similarly, Main Line WASPs, scions of distinguished families, and heirs apparent to prestigious law firms, do not consort with—much less marry—little Irish typists from Kensington. Brewster C. Payne II resigned from the family law firm and set up his own practice in a two-room office with his bride functioning as his secretary.

That was twenty-odd years ago. Mrs. Brewster C. Payne II (who had borne Mr. Payne two additional children) was now a Main Line Matron of impeccable reputation, and Brewster C. Payne, Attorney At Law, was now the presiding partner of Mawson, Payne, Stockton, McAdoo & Lester, Lawyers, whose offices and eighty-four junior partners and associates occupied two entire floors of the Philadelphia Savings Fund Society Building, and were arguably the most successful and unquestionably one of the two or three most prestigious law firms in the city.

Mrs. Payne had done what she could (in Jason Washington's opinion, taken the extra step, and then a couple more) to see that her son did not lose contact with either her late husband's family or with her late husband's best friend, Dennis V. Coughlin.

Her late husband's family were cops. John X. Moffitt's father and grandfather had been cops, and his brother (Richard C., known as "Dutch") was a cop. Her ex-mother-in-law, known as Mother Moffitt, a formidable German/Irish lady in her late sixties, had a father and two brothers who had retired from the Department.

Seven months before, when Captain "Dutch" Moffitt had been given a police funeral presided over by the cardinal archbishop of Philadelphia at Saint Monica's Church, Mother Moffitt had let the world know that she had not forgiven her ex-daughter-in-law for leaving Holy Mother Church and taking her son with her. Patricia Moffitt Payne's name had been conspicuously absent not only from the list of family members entitled to sit in a reserved pew but from the list of Friends of the Family as well.

When Denny Coughlin had told the inspector working the door that the entire Payne family was to be seated inside and up front in Saint Monica's if that meant evicting members of the City Council, Mother Moffitt had pretended Patty Payne and her husband and their kids were invisible.

Three days later Matthew M. Payne had walked into the City Administration Building across from City Hall, taken the exam, and joined the cops.

There was nothing that either Brewster C. Payne or Chief Inspector Dennis V. Coughlin could do about it. The two, who over the years had become friends, had a long talk over lunch at the Union League Club. They agreed that Matt's motives were fairly obvious: The fact that his uncle Dutch had been killed obviously had a lot to do with it, and so did the results of a physical examination that found something wrong with his eyes and would keep him from becoming a second lieutenant in the Marine Corps when he graduated from the University of Pennsylvania.

He could prove his challenged masculinity by becoming a cop, in the footsteps of his real father, uncle, and grandfather.

Adoptive father and godfather agreed that what Matt really should do was go on to law school, but they also agreed that he was just as hardheaded as his mother when he wanted to do something, and could not be talked out of joining the cops.

It was to be hoped that when the emotions caused by Dutch's death and the Marine Corps rejection had time to simmer down, he would come to his senses. They were both agreed that Matt was a more levelheaded kid than most. With a little bit of luck that would happen before he was close to graduating from the Police Academy.

It didn't happen. He did well in the Academy.

Dennis V. Coughlin, as a sergeant, had gone to Patricia Moffitt's apartment to tell her that her husband had just been shot to death. He had no intention of going to Patricia Moffitt Payne to tell her her son had just been killed as a cop. The most influential of the seven chief inspectors had a word with the chief of Personnel, and Officer Payne was assigned to Special Operations.

There, after Denny Coughlin had a quiet word with Peter Wohl, Officer Payne was assigned duties as a sort of clerk/driver, the hope now being that when he saw what police work was really like, he would finally come to his senses, quit the cops, and go to law school.

What Jason Washington hadn't already known of Matt Payne's background had been filled in by Peter Wohl when he gave him Payne as a gofer. The investigation of the Northwest Philadelphia serial rapist/murderer had become very intense. Washington needed someone to run errands, make telephone calls, and otherwise save his time.

Payne had gone with Washington to Bucks County, where the body of the latest victim had been found. Washington had gotten a description of the man, his van, the license plate number, and had made plaster casts of the van's tire tracks. Within hours, they would know who they were looking for.

Washington had sent Payne back to Philadelphia with the tire casts and orders to tell Peter Wohl of the latest developments before he quit for the day. Payne had dropped off the tire casts at the laboratory in the Roundhouse, and then turned in the unmarked police car he had been driving at Special Operations headquarters at Bustleton and Bowler Streets.

In his own car, on the way to Wohl's apartment in Chestnut Hill, Payne had spotted the van. There was no way he could call for backup. In the very first time he had ever attempted to exercise his authority as a police officer, Payne had walked up to the van.

The driver had then tried to run him over. Payne had jumped out of the way, but the van had wiped out the rear end of Payne's Porsche 911 and then raced away.

Payne had fired five shots, all the cylinder of his snub-nosed Smith & Wesson Undercover held. One bullet, in what Jason Washington believed (and, more important, Payne realized) was blind luck, had struck the van driver in the back of the head.

The van had crashed into a tree. When Payne jerked the door open, he found the looney-tune's next intended victim, already stripped naked and trussed up like a Christmas turkey, under a tarpaulin on the back.

When Police Radio had put out the *beep beep beep, assist officer, shots fired, hospital case* the second response had been "M-Mary One in on the shots fired."

M-Mary One was the radio call assigned to Jerry Carlucci's official Cadillac. The mayor had been on the way to his Chestnut Hill home after speaking at a dinner in South Philadelphia.

The lifelong cop in Jerry Carlucci could no more resist responding to an *assist officer shots fired* than he could pass up a chance to speak to a group of potential voters. Then, too, he sensed that there were a lot of voters out there who liked to see pictures in the newspapers, or on television, of their mayor at a crime scene, personally leading the war against crime.

Mickey O'Hara had also been working the streets that night. The next morning's *Bulletin* had a three-column picture of Mayor Carlucci, standing so that the snub-nosed revolver on his belt was visible under his jacket, with his arm around Officer Payne's shoulder. In the accompanying story by Michael J. O'Hara, *Bulletin* Staff Writer, Officer Payne was described by the mayor as both "administrative assistant" to Peter Wohl and as "the type of well-educated, dedicated, courageous young police officer" now, under his direction, being recruited for the Police Department.

The mayor's description of Matt Payne as Wohl's administrative assistant had erased any notions Wohl might have had to transfer Officer Payne someplace else.

He had joked about it to Washington: "Thank God for our mayor. I didn't even know what an administrative assistant was, and now I have one." But Washington sensed that Wohl was really not at all displeased.

For one thing, a "driver," analogous to an aide-de-camp for a general officer in the military services, was a perquisite of inspectors, chief inspectors, and deputy commissioners. Wohl was only a staff inspector, but he was also the only division commanding officer who was not at least an inspector. Before the mayor's off-the-cuff designation of Matt Payne as his "administrative assistant," Wohl had not had a driver, and there would have been cracks about delusions of glory from the corps of inspectors and chief inspectors, more than a few of whom thought they should have been given command of Special Operations, if he had asked for one.

But most important, Washington thought, was that Wohl needed not only a driver, but one like Matt Payne. It may have sounded like bullshit when The Dago said it for the papers, but Washington could find nothing wrong with the notion of young police officers who were in fact well educated, dedicated, and courageous.

"Detective D'Amata said it was 'high noon at the OK Corral' at the furniture store," Matt Payne said.

There he goes again. "Detective D'Amata," said with respect, instead of just D'Amata, or for that matter "Joe." Joe D'Amata would not be at all annoyed to be called by his first

*name by Matt. So far as D'Amata's concerned, Matt stopped being a rookie when he shot
the serial rapist.*

"Meaning what?"

"He said the doers really shot the place up. He said they found twenty-six bullets."

"There was a gun battle?"

"No. That's what he said was interesting. They just shot off their guns. Not even the
victim had a gun."

"There was just the one victim?"

"He was the maintenance man; he walked in on it."

"They have a lead on the doers?"

"I think Detective D'Amata has a good idea. He said that the witnesses were still pretty
shaky; he wanted them to calm down a little before he showed them pictures."

"That may work, and it may not," Washington said. "A lot of people, with good reason,
are nervous about having to go to court and point their fingers. Particularly at scumbags
like these, a gang of them."

"Yes, sir," Matt said.

Washington met his eyes.

"I am not going to tell you anymore not to call me 'sir,' " he said.

"Sorry," Matt said, throwing up his hands. "It just slips out."

"Let me show you what the postman brought today," Washington said. He went to the
table by the door and returned with a postcard and handed it to Matt.

It was a printed form, Number 73–41 (Revised 3/72), issued by the Personnel Department of the City of Philadelphia, headed FINAL RESULTS OF EXAMINATIONS. It informed
Jason Washington that his Final Average on the Examination for Police Sergeant was
96.52 and that his Rank on List was 3.

"Jesus!" Payne exclaimed happily.

"You asked what the occasion was," Washington said.

"Well, congratulations!" Matt said enthusiastically. "I didn't even know you had taken
the examination."

"I'd almost forgotten I had," Washington said.

Matt looked at him with curiosity in his eyes, but did not ask.

"Two days after Wohl shanghaied me to Special Operations," Washington explained,
"I put my name in. I almost didn't take it. I never cracked a book."

"But you came in third," Matt said.

"As I said, Officer Payne, you may now call me 'sir.' "

"Well, I think this is splendid!"

Spoken like a true Main Line WASP. "Splendid."

"Splendid?" Washington asked dryly.

"I think so."

"Thank you, Matt," Washington said.

"So what happens to you now? Will they transfer you?"

"I devoutly hope so," Washington said. "Back to Homicide."

"I'd hate to see you go."

*Now that I think about it, I'm not so sure I want to go back to Homicide. Not as a
sergeant.*

"I don't think Peter Wohl will let me go anywhere until we catch the cop killer," Washington said.

"Is that the way that works? It's up to the inspector?"

"No. The way it works is that assignments of newly promoted people are made by Personnel. They evaluate the individual in terms of vacancies, his future career, and the good
of the Department. After a good deal of thought and paper-pushing, they reach a decision,
and the promotee—is that right, 'promotee'?"

"Why not?" Matt chuckled.

"—the *promotee* gets his new assignment. Providing, of course, that certain members of the hierarchy, Denny Coughlin, for example, and Matt Lowenstein, people like that, and, of course, our own beloved commander, P. Wohl, agree. If they don't like the promotee's assignment, they somehow manage to get it changed to one they do like. The operative words are 'for the good of the Department.' "

"I think I understand," Matt said.

There was the sound of a key in the door. Jason Washington started toward it, but it opened before he could reach it.

It was a very tall, sharply featured woman, her hair drawn tight against an angular skull.

She looks, Matt thought, *like one of the Egyptian bas-reliefs in the museum.*

Martha (Mrs. Jason) Washington, wearing a flowing pale green dress, stepped into the apartment. Behind her was the doorman, carrying a very large framed picture, wrapped in kraft paper.

"Take that from him, please," she ordered.

Washington put his hand in his pocket, gave the doorman a couple of dollar bills, and relieved him of the picture.

"Hello, Matt," Martha Washington said.

"Good evening," Matt said.

"What's this?" Jason asked.

"I thought you could tell from the shape," she said. "It's a bathtub."

Jason Washington tore the kraft paper away. It was a turn-of-the-century oil painting of a voluptuous nude, reclining on her side.

"Finally, some art I can understand and appreciate," Washington said.

"Inspector Wohl's got one almost just like that," Matt said.

"That figures," Martha said. "That's to sell, Jason, not for you to ogle; don't get attached to it. I found it in one of those terribly chic places off South Street. I think he needed the money to pay the rent. I bought it right, and I think I know just where to get rid of it."

"Well, *I* like it," Matt said. "How much do you want for it?"

"You're too young," she said. "And besides, it would enrage your liberated female girlfriends."

"Yeah," Matt said, considering that. The prospect seemed to please him.

She seemed to see his whiskey glass for the first time.

"Are we celebrating something?" she asked.

"Yes, indeed," Matt said.

"Good evening, Matthew," Jason Washington said. "Nice of you to drop by."

"Just what's going on here?"

"Good night, Mrs. Washington," Matt said.

"Jason?" Mrs. Washington asked. There was a hint of threat in her voice.

"I took the sergeant's exam," Jason said.

"Well, it's about damned time," she said. "And you think you passed? Is that what you're celebrating?"

"Not exactly," Matt heard Jason Washington say as he pulled the door closed after him.

8.

Chief Inspector Matt Lowenstein lived in a row house on Tyson Avenue, just off Roosevelt Boulevard in Northeast Philadelphia, with his wife, Sarah, and their only child, Samuel Lowenstein, who was fifteen.

It was the only home they had ever had. The down payment had been a wedding gift from Sarah's parents. The Lowensteins had been married three weeks after Matt, with three years on the job, had been promoted to detective. His first assignment as a detective had been to Northeast Detectives, not far away at Harbison and Levick Streets.

Sarah, at the time of her marriage, had been employed as a librarian at the Fox Chase Branch of the Philadelphia Public Library. Shortly afterward, she had become librarian at Northeast High School, at Cottman and Algon, and had held that job, with the exception of the three years she had taken off to have their son, ever since.

Sarah was active in women's affairs of Temple Sholom, a reformed congregation at Large Street and Roosevelt Boulevard, but had long since given up hope of getting Matt to take a more active role in the affairs of the synagogue.

While what Matt said—that he did not have an eight-to-five, five-day-a-week job, but was on call twenty-four hours a day seven days a week, and thus could really not get involved like somebody who had a regular job—was true, Sarah suspected that if he did have a regular job, he would have found another excuse not to get involved.

There was absolutely no pressure from Rabbi Stephen Kuntz, who had replaced the retiring Rabbi Schneider just before Samuel was born, for Matt to take a greater role in the affairs of the congregation, which, in the beginning, had surprised Sarah, for Matt and the new young rabbi had quickly become close. And then she came to understand that *was* the reason.

The rabbi had a surfeit of homes offering him sumptuous meals on tables set with silver and the good china, with everyone on their good behavior, listening with polite attention as he discoursed on the moral issues of the day. Her home, she was sure, was the only home in the rabbi's congregation where he was greeted by the man of the house calling out, "Lock up the booze, the rabbi's here."

She didn't think the rabbi sat with his tie pulled down and his shoes off in anyone else's basement, sucking beer from the bottleneck watching the fights on TV, or arguing politics loudly, or laughing deep in his belly at Lowenstein's recounting of the most recent ribald story of the *schwartzes* or the Irishers or the wops in the Roundhouse.

The rabbi needed a respite from the piety of the congregation, and Matt gave it to him. That was a contribution to the congregation, too, more important, Sarah had come to understand, than having Matt serve on the Building Committee or whatever.

And it worked the other way too. When Matt had been a lieutenant in the 16th District, and had to shoot a poor, crazy hillbilly woman who had already used a shotgun to kill her husband and was about to kill a cop with it, and was as distraught as Sarah had ever seen him, Rabbi Steve had gone off with him and Denny Coughlin to the Jersey shore for four days.

All three of them had bad breath and bloodshot eyes when they came back, but the terrible look was gone from Matt's eyes and that was all, Sarah thought, that really mattered.

Rabbi Kuntz had "dropped by" ten minutes before Lowenstein came home, fifteen minutes late, to announce that he had run into Mickey O'Hara and invited him and his girlfriend for supper.

"You could have called," Sarah said. "They have telephones all over. What time's he coming?"

"*They*. He's bringing his girlfriend. I told him half past six."

"If I had a little warning, I could have made a roast or something. Now I don't know what I'm going to do."

"Go to the deli," Lowenstein said, grinning at Kuntz. "Mickey's a smarter Irisher. He likes Jew food."

"You're terrible," Sarah said. "You think that would be all right?"

"Of course it would," Lowenstein said. "Get cold cuts and hot potato salad."

"Well, all right, I suppose."

"You really like that coffee, or would you rather have a beer? Or a drink?"

"I think I'll finish the coffee and go," the rabbi said.

"Don't be silly. Mickey's always good for a laugh. You look like you could use one."

"I'd be in the way."

"Beer or booze?"

"Beer, please."

"Don't be polite. I'm going to have a stiff drink. It's been a bad day."

"Beer anyway."

"Samuel's not home yet, so don't go in the basement," Sarah said as she took her coat off a hook by the rear door. "You wouldn't hear the doorbell."

"Where is he?"

"He called and said he would be studying with the Rosen girl, Natalie."

"That's what they call that now, 'studying'?"

"He must have had a bad day, Rabbi, excuse him, please," Sarah said, and went out the door.

"A bad bad day?" Kuntz asked. "Or an ordinary, run-of-the-mill bad day?"

Lowenstein took a bottle of beer from the refrigerator and handed it to Kuntz, and then made himself a stiff Scotch, with very little ice or water, before replying.

"Maybe in the middle of that," Lowenstein said, raising his drink and adding *"Mazel tov."*

"Mazel tov," the rabbi replied.

"I spent a painful hour and a half—closer to two, really—before lunch with the commissioner and the mayor," Lowenstein said. "Most of it strained silence, which is actually worse than an exhibition of his famous Neapolitan temper."

"What about?"

"That young Italian cop who got himself shot down by Temple University. You know what I'm talking about?"

Kuntz nodded. "It's been in the papers."

"Has it really?" Lowenstein said bitterly. "There was another editorial in today's *Ledger,* you see that one?"

Kuntz nodded.

"We have no idea who shot him or why," Lowenstein said. "Not even a hunch. And the mayor, who is angry at several levels, first, giving him the benefit of the doubt, as a cop, and then as an Italian, and then, obviously, as a politician, getting the flak from the newspapers, and not only the *Ledger,* is really angry. Frustrated, maybe, is the better word."

"Which makes him angry."

"Yeah."

"And he's holding you responsible?"

"He took the job away from me—technically away from Homicide, but it's the same thing—and gave it to Special Operations. I think he now regrets that."

"Special Operations isn't up to the job?"

"You know Peter Wohl? Runs Special Operations?"

Kuntz shook his head no.

"Very sharp cop. His father is a retired chief, an old pal of mine. Peter was a sergeant in Homicide. He was the youngest captain in the Department, and is now the youngest staff inspector. Just before Carlucci gave him Special Operations, he put Judge Findermann away."

"I remember that," Kuntz said. "So why can't he find the people who did this?"

"For the same reason I couldn't; there's simply nothing out there to find."

"But wouldn't you have more resources in the Detective Division? More experienced people?"

"Wohl took the two best homicide detectives away from Homicide, with the mayor's blessing," Lowenstein said. "And I passed the word that anything else he wants from the Detective Division, he can have. The way it works is that if you don't get anything at the scene of the crime, then you start ringing doorbells and asking questions. Wohl's people have run out of doorbells to ring and people to question. Hell, there's a twenty-five-thousand-dollar reward out—Nesfoods International put it up—and we haven't gotten a damned thing out of that, either."

"And the mayor knows all of this?"

"Sure. And I think one of the reasons he's so upset is that he knows he couldn't do any better himself. But that doesn't get the newspapers off his back. I had a very unkind thought in there this morning: The only reason Carlucci isn't throwing Peter Wohl to the wolves—"

"This man Wohl was there?"

"Yeah. Wohl and Denny Coughlin too. As I was saying, the only reason he hasn't already thrown Wohl to the wolves is because he knows that whoever he would send in to replace him wouldn't be able to do a damned thing Wohl hasn't already done. And he—Carlucci—would look even worse if his pinch hitter struck out."

"Yes, I see."

"Shooting a cop is like shooting the pope," Lowenstein said. "You just can't tolerate it. So you throw all the resources you can lay your hands on at the job. We've done that, and that hasn't been good enough. But there's other crimes in the city, and you can't keep it up. Not even if it means that for the first time in the history of the City of Philadelphia, a cop killer will get away with it."

"Really? This has never happened before?"

"Never," Lowenstein said. "Not once. And, at the risk of repeating myself, you can't let anyone get away with shooting a cop."

"So what will happen?"

Lowenstein shrugged his shoulders and threw up his hands in a gesture of helplessness.

"And two other little items to brighten my day came to my attention," he said. "One connected to the Magnella—that's the name of the young cop—job. Interesting problem of ethics. You know Captain Frieberg, Manny Frieberg?"

"Sure."

"He's got the 9th District. One of my boys. Good cop. There are those that say I'm his rabbi."

"I've heard the term," Rabbi Kuntz said with a chuckle.

"He came to see me just before I went to see the mayor. At half past three this morning, one of his cars answered a call about a body in a saloon parking lot. It wasn't a body. It was a passed-out drunk. Specifically, it was one of the hotshot homicide detectives I mentioned a moment ago, who were transferred from Homicide to Peter Wohl. He passed out, fortunately, between the barroom door and his car, so he didn't have a chance to run into the cardinal archbishop or a station wagon full of nuns."

Kuntz chuckled, and then asked, "Does he have a drinking problem?"

Lowenstein ignored the question.

"When they tried to wake him up," he went on, "he got belligerent, so they took his gun away from him and locked him up in a district holding cell. When Manny came in, he turned him loose and then came to see me."

"You said 'ethical problem'?"

"If he worked for me, I'd know how to deal with him. I'd tell him if I heard he had so much as sniffed a cork for six months, he would be on the recovered stolen car detail forever."

"I don't know what that means."

"Two kinds of stolen cars are recovered. The ones some kids took for a joyride and ditched, or ones that somebody has stripped and abandoned. In either case, it has to be investigated. Lots of forms that no one will ever see again have to be filled out. It's the worst job a detective can get. For a Homicide detective, it would be the worst thing that could possibly happen to him."

"But?"

"He doesn't work for me. So what do I do, go tell Peter Wohl? Since he doesn't work for me, it's none of my business, right? And I don't know how Peter would handle it. He's under a hell of a lot of pressure, and he would not be pleased to hear that one of the two men he's forced to rely on has a bad bottle problem."

"Is that what it is? The man is an alcoholic?"

"Maybe not yet, but almost. What happened is that his wife caught him in the wrong bed. The judge awarded the wife everything but his spare pair of socks. He's living in a cheap room out by the University, eating baked beans out of the can. And the ex-wife is using his money to support a boyfriend."

"How sad," Kuntz said.

The doorbell played "Be It Ever So Humble."

"That's O'Hara," Lowenstein said, looking at his watch. "He has only one virtue, punctuality. The subject we were on is now closed, okay?"

Kuntz nodded.

Lowenstein left the kitchen and returned in a moment leading Mickey O'Hara, who had a bottle in a brown bag in his hand, and a young woman.

"If I knew the rabbi was going to be here, I'd have brought two of these," Mickey said, handing the bag to Lowenstein. He pulled a bottle of Johnnie Walker Black Label Scotch from it.

"Hello, Mickey, how are you?" Kuntz said.

"I won't say you shouldn't have done this, because you should have," Lowenstein said.

"Don't let it go to your head, the *Bulletin*'s paying for it."

The young woman with Mickey O'Hara, Kuntz thought (almost simultaneously realizing that it was not a kind thought), was not what he would have expected. She was—he searched for the word and came up with—wholesome. More than that. She was tastefully, conservatively dressed, with just the right amount of makeup. She had a full head of well-coiffured dark brown hair.

And she was, Kuntz saw, more than a little surprised, even shocked, at the exchange between Lowenstein and O'Hara.

"I'm Stephen Kuntz," he said.

"Eleanor Neal," she said. "How do you do?"

"If you understand that these two are old friends," Kuntz said, "it explains a good deal."

She smiled. "And is there a reason Mickey called you a rabbi?"

"I happen to be a rabbi," Kuntz said.

"Oh?" she said.

"I'm Matt Lowenstein. Don't mind Mick and me. Welcome to Chez Lowenstein."

"Thank you for having me," Eleanor said.

"I just got to ask this," Lowenstein said.

"No, you don't," Mickey said.

"Mick!" Eleanor protested.

"What he's going to ask is 'what is a nice girl like you doing going out with me?' "

"Well, I don't think he would have asked that, but if he did, I would have said that finally you're introducing me to your friends."

"What I was going to ask," Lowenstein said, more than a little lamely, "was how is it he's never brought you here before?"

"Why haven't you, Mick?" Eleanor asked.

"Well, you're here now, and that's all that counts," Kuntz said.

"And if you'll make us a drink, I'll give you something else," O'Hara said.

"Excuse me," Lowenstein said, sounding genuinely contrite. "What can I fix you, Miss Neal?"

"Eleanor, please," she said. "Would you happen to have any white wine?"

"Absolutely," Lowenstein said, and took a bottle from the refrigerator.

"No, I don't mind helping myself to the Scotch, thank you very much," O'Hara said.

"There's an open bottle," Lowenstein said.

"Yeah, but you've refilled it with cheap hootch so often the neck is chipped," O'Hara said, and pulled the cork from the bottle he had brought.

Kuntz laughed.

"Hey, you're supposed to be on my side," Lowenstein protested.

"I am a simple man of God trying my very best to bring peace between the warring factions," Kuntz said piously.

"I think you have your work cut out for you," Eleanor said.

Lowenstein handed her a glass of wine, and then turned to O'Hara.

"Okay. What else have you got me that somebody else paid for?"

O'Hara took an envelope from his inside jacket pocket and handed it to him. Lowenstein, suspiciously, took it from the envelope and unfolded it. Then his expression changed.

"What the hell is this?"

"It was delivered to the *Bulletin*, left with the girl downstairs in an enveloped marked 'urgent.' "

"Where's the envelope?" Lowenstein snapped.

"With the original. You *did* notice that was a copy?"

"Where's the original?"

"I had a messenger take it, and the envelope, to Homicide." Lowenstein handed the sheet of paper to Kuntz.

ISLAMIC LIBERATION ARMY

There Is No God But God,
And Allah Is His Name

PRESS RELEASE:
Be advised that the events at Goldblatt's Furniture Store today were conducted by troops of the Islamic Liberation Army.
It was the first battle of many to follow against the infidel sons of Zion, who for too long have victimized the African Brothers (Islamic and other) and other minorities of Philadelphia.
Death to the Zionist oppressors of our people!
  Freedom Now!
  Muhammed el Sikkim
  Chief of Staff
  Islamic Liberation Army

"What in the world is this?" Kuntz asked when he had read it.

"There was a robbery, and a murder, at Goldblatt's furniture store on South Street this afternoon," Lowenstein said.

"But what's *this?*"

"The Islamic Liberation Army just confessed to the job," O'Hara said dryly.

"What's the Islamic Liberation Army?" Kuntz asked.

"Offhand," Lowenstein said, "I would guess it's half a dozen *schwartzer* stickup artists who saw Malcolm X on TV, smoked some funny cigarettes, and then went to Sears, Roebuck and bought themselves bathrobes."

Kuntz saw the look of confusion on Eleanor's face.

"May I show her this?" he asked.

"Sure," O'Hara said. "It's not like it's a secret or anything."

"Did the other papers get this, Mickey, do you think, or just Philly's ace crime writer?" Lowenstein asked.

"I didn't ask, but I'll bet they did."

"What's a—what did you say before, 'Schwartz'?" Eleanor asked.

"*Schwartzes,*" Lowenstein explained. "It's Yiddish. Means 'blacks.' "

"I don't understand," Kuntz confessed.

"Offhand, Rabbi," O'Hara said, "it's obviously one of two things: a group of master criminals cleverly trying to get Sherlock Holmes here and his gumshoes off their trail, or the opening salvo of the Great Race War."

"What the hell *is* it, if you're so smart, wiseass?" Lowenstein asked.

"Or it could be a couple of guys named O'Shaughnessy and Goldberg, college kids, maybe, trying to pull the chain of the newspapers," O'Hara said.

"You really think so?" Lowenstein asked, his tone of voice making it clear that possibility had not occurred to him.

"I really don't know what to think, Matt," Mickey replied.

"What did you *write?*"

"About the Islamic Liberation Army, you mean?"

"Yes."

"Nothing."

"*Nothing?*"

"Just because somebody sends me a piece of paper that says they're the Islamic Liberation Army and that they've declared war on the Jews doesn't make it so. *You* tell me you think the Islamic Liberation Army shot up Goldblatt's and murdered that maintenance man, and I'll write it. But not until."

"You got that after the robbery, right?"

"Of course," O'Hara said. "And Joe D'Amata told me that the Central Detective is on the job, Pelosi?"

"Jerry Pelosi," Lowenstein furnished.

"He's got a damned good idea who the doers are. And he doesn't think they're a bunch of looney-tune amateur Arabs."

Lieutenant Jack Malone was not equipped with the necessary household skills for happy bachelorhood. He was the fourth of five children, the others all female. Jack and his father (a Fire Department captain) had met what the Malone family perceived to be the responsibility of the male gender: They moved furniture, washed the car, cut the grass, painted, and even moved the garbage cans from beside the kitchen door to the curb, and then moved them back.

But the other domestic tasks in the house were clearly feminine responsibilities, and Mrs. Jeannette Malone and her daughters shopped, cooked, laundered, ironed, made beds, set and cleaned the table, and washed the dishes.

This arrangement lasted until, a week after he graduated from North Catholic High School, Jack enlisted in the Army. For four years thereafter, except for the making of his bunk in the prescribed manner and shining of boots and brass, the Army took over for his mother and sisters. He ate in mess halls. Once a week he carried a bag full of dirty clothing to the supply room and picked up last week's laundry, now washed, starched, and pressed by an Army laundry for a three-dollar-a-month charge.

When he got out of the Army, he immediately took both the Fire Department and Police Department tests. The Police Department came up first, and he became a cop. He really had not wanted to be a fireman, although, rather than hurt his father's feelings, he would have joined the firemen if that test had come back first.

He lived at home until, fifteen months after he got out of the Army, he had married Ellen Fogarty. Ellen had been reared under a comparable perception of the roles and responsibilities of the sexes in marriage. The man went to work, and the woman kept house. The only real difference, aside from the joys of the marriage bed, in living with

Ellen as opposed to living with his mother and sisters was that Ellen put some really strange food on the table. Mexican, Chinese, even *Indian*-Indian, things like that.

He had pretended to like it, and after a while he had even grown used to it.

When he had reentered the single state, he was for the first time in his life forced to fend for himself. Obviously, he could not move back into his parents' house. For one thing, his sister Deborah had married a real loser who couldn't hold a job for more than three months at a time, and Charley and Deborah and their two kids were "until things worked out for Charley" living in the house.

But that wasn't the only reason he couldn't live there. His father had made it clear that he believed he wasn't getting the whole story about what had gone wrong with Jack and Ellen. Good Catholic girls like Ellen from decent families don't suddenly just decide to start fucking some lawyer; there are two sides to every story, and since he wasn't getting Ellen's that was because Ellen was too decent to tell anybody what Jack had done that made her do it.

The only time in ten years and four months of marriage that Jack had laid a hand on Ellen was that one time, after he'd knocked Howard Candless around, and then gone home to tell her, and ask her why, and she had screamed, so mad that she was spitting in his face, that because whenever he touched her, she wanted to puke.

He couldn't be any sorrier about that than he was, sorry and ashamed, but it had happened, and there was no taking it back. And it had happened only once.

His mother had cried when she heard about it, which was even worse than having her yell at him, and his sisters, every damned one of them, had made it plain they believed the reason Ellen had done what she had done was that he had been regularly knocking Ellen around all the time, and she'd finally had enough.

That had really surprised him and made him wonder about his brothers-in-law. Was the reason his sisters were so quick to jump on the idea that he was regularly knocking Ellen around because they were regularly getting it from their husbands? It wasn't such a far-out idea when he thought about it. If his sisters were getting slapped around, they would have kept it to themselves, knowing full well that their father and their brother would have kicked the living shit out of their husbands.

And if that was the case, Jack Malone reasoned, that would explain why they were almost happy to find out that Jack Malone was no better than their husbands.

And Ellen had jumped on that, and made it sing like a violin. When she had taken Little Jack to see Grandma, she had told Grandma she didn't think it would do anyone any good, least of all Little Jack, to dwell on what had happened between them. All she thought was that Little Jack's father needed help, and she really hoped he could get it.

In the eyes of Grandma and his sisters, that made Ellen just about as noble as the Virgin Mary.

So not only could he not move back into his parents' house, he really hated to go over there at all.

So into the St. Charles Hotel. In some ways, it was like when he made sergeant in the Army and he had gotten his own room. The big differences were that he couldn't get his laundry done for three bucks a month, and there was no mess hall passing out free "take all you want, but eat what you take" meals.

The one uniform Jack had bought when he made lieutenant came with two pairs of pants, so he still had a freshly pressed pair to wear on the job tomorrow. Tomorrow night, depending on whether he spilled something on the jacket or not, he would have to have it at least pressed, but that wasn't a problem for tonight.

What he would have liked to do tonight was go out and have a couple of beers, beers hell, drinks, and then a steak with a glass of red wine or two with that, and then maybe a nightcap or something afterward.

What he did was what he could afford to do. He went to Colonel Sanders's and bought the special (a half breast, a leg, a couple of livers, a roll, and a little tub of coleslaw) for $1.69 and took it back to the St. Charles. There he took off his clothes and ate it in his underwear, watching the TV, washing it down with a glass of water from the tap.

He fell asleep watching a rerun of *I Love Lucy* and woke up to the trumpets and drum-roll announcing *Nine's News at Nine.*

He could taste all of the Colonel's Seventeen Secret Herbs and Spices in his mouth, and his left leg had gone to sleep. He hobbled around the room flexing and shaking his left leg.

He put the remnants of the $1.69 Special in the wastebasket under the sink in the toilet, and then tested the water. It ran rusty red for a couple of seconds, burped, and then turned hot.

He took a hot shower, thinking that simply because there was hot water now there was no guarantee that there would be hot water in the morning.

He was now wide awake. He knew that even if he could force himself to go to sleep, he would almost certainly wake up at say half past four and, if that happened, never get back to sleep.

He put on a pair of blue jeans and a sweatshirt and a pair of sneakers and left the room.

There was a tavern on the corner of 18th and Arch. He certainly could afford a beer.

He pushed open the door and looked inside and changed his mind. A bunch of losers sitting around staring into the stale, getting warm beer in their glasses. Nobody was having a good time.

He acted like he was looking for somebody who wasn't there, and went back out onto 18th Street.

He knew where he wanted to go, and what he wanted to do, and walked to where he had parked his car and got in it.

Am I doing this because I didn't want to belly up to the bar with the other losers, or is this what I really wanted to do in the first place?

He drove up North Broad Street until he came to the Holland Pontiac-GMC showroom. The lights were on, but there was no one in the showroom. They closed at half past nine.

He turned left and made the next left, which put him behind the Pontiac-GMC show-room building and between it and a large concrete block building on which was lettered, HOLLAND MOTOR COMPANY BODY SHOP.

It was a factory-type building. The windows were of what he thought of as a chicken wire reinforced glass. They passed light, but you couldn't see through them.

The Holland Motor Company Body Shop was going full blast.

It was a twenty-four-hour-a-day, seven-day-a-week operation. Part of this was because they fixed the entire GM line of cars in this body shop, not just Pontiacs and GMCs. And part of it was because, to help the working man who needed his car to drive to work, you could bring your crumpled fender to the Holland Motor Car Body Shop in installments, leaving it there overnight and getting it back in the morning. They would straighten the fender one night, prime it the second, and paint it the third night, or over the weekends.

And the other reason they were open twenty-four hours a day, seven days a week, Lieutenant Jack Malone was convinced, was because the Working Man's Friend had a hot car scam of some kind going.

Malone had no facts. Just a gut feeling. But he *knew.*

I don't care if he and Commissioner Czernich play with the same rubber duck, the sonofabitch is a thief. And I'm going to catch him.

He circled the block, and then found a place to park the rusty old Mustang in the shadow of a building where he would not attract attention, and from which he could keep his eyes on the door to the Holland Motor Company Body Shop.

Something, maybe not tonight, maybe not this week, maybe not this fucking year, but something, sometime, sooner or later, is going to happen, and then I'll know how he's doing it.

He lit a cigarette, saw that it was his next to last—

Fuck it, I smoke too much anyway—

—and settled himself against the worn-out and lumpy cushion and started to look.

9.

When Officer Charles McFadden finished his tour at four, he went looking for Officer Matthew Payne. When he went through the door marked HEADQUARTERS, SPECIAL OPERATIONS, Payne was not at his desk. And there was no one sitting at the sergeant's desk either.

Charley sat on the edge of Payne's desk, confident that one or both of them would turn up in a minute; *somebody* would be around to answer the inspector's phone.

A minute or so later, the door to the inspector's office opened and a slight, fair-skinned, rather sharp-featured police officer came out. He was in Highway regalia identical to Officer McFadden's, except that there were silver captain's bars on the epaulets of his leather jacket. He was Captain David Pekach, commanding officer of Highway Patrol.

McFadden pushed himself quickly off Payne's desk.

"Hey, whaddaya say, McFadden?" Captain Pekach said, smiling, and offering his hand.

"Captain," McFadden replied.

"Where's the sergeant?" Pekach asked.

"I don't know," Charley said. "I came in here looking for Payne."

"The inspector's got him running down some paperwork. I don't think he'll be back today. Something I can do for you?"

"No, sir, it was— I wanted to see if he wanted to have a beer or something."

"You might try him at home in a couple of hours," Pekach said. "I really don't think he'll be coming back. Do me a favor, Charley?"

"Yes, sir."

"Stick around for a couple of minutes and answer the phone until the sergeant comes back. He's probably in the can. But somebody should be on that phone."

"Yes, sir."

"The inspector's gone for the day. Captain Sabara and I are minding the store."

"Yes, sir," McFadden said, smiling. He liked Captain Pekach. Pekach had been his lieutenant when he had worked undercover in Narcotics.

The door opened and a sergeant whom McFadden didn't know came in.

"You looking for me, sir?"

"Not anymore," Pekach said, tempering the sarcasm with a little smile.

"I had to go to the can, Captain."

"See if you can find Detective Harris," Pekach said. "Keep looking. Tell him to call either me or Captain Sabara, no matter what the hour."

"Yes, sir."

Pekach turned and went back into the office he shared with Captain Mike Sabara. Then he turned again, remembering two things: first, that he had not said "So long" or something to McFadden; and second that McFadden and his partner had answered the call on the shooting at Goldblatt's furniture.

He reentered the outer office just in time to hear the sergeant snarl, "What do you want?" at McFadden.

"Officer McFadden, Sergeant," Pekach said, "for the good of the Department, you understand, was kind enough to be standing by to answer the telephone. Since, you see, there was no one else out here."

The sergeant flushed.

"Come on in a minute, Charley," Pekach said. "You got a minute?"

"Yes, sir."

Pekach held the door open for Charley and then followed him into the office.

Captain Michael J. Sabara, a short, muscular, swarthy-skinned man whose acne-scarred face, dark eyes, and mustache made him appear far more menacing than was the case, looked up curiously at McFadden.

"You know Charley, don't you, Mike?" Pekach asked.

"Yeah, sure," Sabara said, offering his hand. "How are you, McFadden?"

At least this one, he thought, *looks like a Highway Patrolman.*

The other one, in Captain Sabara's mind, was Officer Jesus Martinez; the *other* of the first two probationary Highway Patrolmen. Jesus Martinez was just barely over Departmental height and weight minimums. It wasn't his fault, but he just didn't look like a Highway Patrolman. He looked, in Captain Sabara's opinion, like a small-sized spic dressed up in a cut-down Highway Patrol uniform.

"Charley, you went in on that shots fired, hospital case at Goldblatt's, didn't you?" Pekach asked.

"Yes, sir. Quinn and I were at City Hall when we heard it."

"What did you find?"

"Nothing. They were long gone—they had stashed a van out in back—when we got there."

"You hear anything on the scene about the doers?"

"Spades in bathrobes," McFadden said, "Is what we heard. Dumb spades. They—Goldblatt's—don't keep any real money in the store."

"What do you think about this?" Captain Sabara said, and handed him a photocopy of the press release that had been sent to Mickey O'Hara at the *Bulletin.*

"What the hell is it?" McFadden asked.

"What do you think it is, Charley?" Pekach asked.

"I think it's bullshit. *If* this thing is real, and they're going to have a war with the Jews, how come the guy they shot was an Irishman?"

"Good question," Pekach said. "If you had to guess, Charley, what would you say?"

"Jesus, Captain, I don't know. I don't think this Liberation Army is for real—is it?"

"That seems to be the question of the day, Charley," Pekach said, and then changed the subject. "I don't seem to see you much anymore. How do you like Highway?"

"It's all right, I guess," Charley replied. "But sometimes, Captain, I sort of miss Narcotics."

"Narcotics or undercover?" Pekach pursued.

"Both, I guess."

"If you don't catch up with Payne tonight, I'll tell him you were looking for him," Pekach said.

McFadden understood he was being dismissed.

"Yes, sir. Good night, Captain." He faced Sabara and repeated, "Captain."

Sabara nodded and smiled.

When McFadden had closed the door behind him, Sabara said, "There are three hundred young cops out there with five, six years on the job who would give their left nut to be in Highway, and that one says, 'It's all right, I guess.' "

"But *your* three hundred young cops never had the opportunity to work for *me* in *Narcotics,*" Pekach said.

"Oh, go to hell," Sabara chuckled. "You're no better than he is."

"He wasn't much help, was he?"

"No, he wasn't. Did you think he would be?"

"Wohl said he thought we should find out what we could about Goldblatt's. I was trying."

"You really think Special Operations is going to wind up with that job?"

"I wouldn't be surprised. Carlucci probably sees a story in the newspapers, 'Mayor Carlucci announced this afternoon that the Special Operations Division arrested the Islamic Liberation Army—' "

"All eight of them," Sabara interrupted. "That's if there *is* an Islamic Liberation Army. And anyway, Highway could handle it without the bullshit."

"That's my line, Mike. Write this on your forehead: '*Pekach* is Highway, *I'm* Special Operations.' "

Sabara chuckled again. "What the hell is Wohl up to?"

"I guess he's just trying to cover his ass," Pekach replied. "In case he does—in other words, we do—get that job."

Charley McFadden drove home, took a bottle of Schlitz from the refrigerator, carried it into the living room, sat on the couch, and dialed Matt Payne's apartment. It rang twice.

"Matthew Payne profoundly regrets, knowing what devastating disappointment it will cause you, that he is not available for conversation at this time. If you would be so kind as to leave your number at the beep, he will know that you have called."

"Shit!" Charley said, laughing, and hung up.

"Watch your mouth, Charley!" his mother called from the kitchen.

Charley hoisted himself out of the couch and went up the stairs, two at a time, to his bedroom. He took his pistol from its holster, put it in the sock drawer of his dresser, and took his snub-nosed Colt .38 Special and its holster out of the drawer. Then he took off his uniform. He rubbed the Sam Browne belt and its accoutrements with a polishing cloth, took a brush to his boots, and then arranged everything neatly in his closet, where, with the addition of a clean shirt, it would be ready for tomorrow.

Then he dressed in blue jeans and a sweatshirt that had WILDWOOD BY THE SEA and a representation of a fish jumping out of the water painted on it. He slipped his feet into loafers and completed dressing by unpinning his badge from his leather jacket and pinning it to a leather badge and ID case and putting that in his left hip pocket, and by slipping the spring clip of the Colt holster inside his trousers just in front of his right hip.

He went down the stairs three at a time, grabbed a quilted nylon zipper jacket from a hook by the front door, and, quickly, so there would be no opportunity for challenge, called out, "I'm going down to Flo & Danny's for a beer, Ma. And then out for supper."

Flo & Danny's Bar & Grill was on the corner. He slid onto a bar stool and Danny, without a word, drew a beer and set it before him.

"How they hanging, kid?"

"One lower than the other."

Charley looked at his watch. It was quarter to six. He had to meet Margaret at the FOP at seven. It would take fifteen minutes to drive there. There was plenty of time.

Maybe too much. She doesn't like it when I smell like a beer tap.

"Danny, give me an egg and a sausage," he said.

Harry fished a purple pickled egg and a piece of pickled sausage from two glass jars beside the cash register and delivered them on a paper napkin. Charley took a bite of the egg, and walked to the telephone and put the rest of his egg in his mouth as he dropped a dime in the slot and dialed a number.

"Hello."

"You and your goddamn wiseass answer machine messages. Where have you been?"

"Running errands."

"You want to have a beer or something?"

"Just one. I got a date."

"Me too. At seven."

"You want to come here? Where are you?"

"Home. FOP?"

"Fifteen minutes?"

"Good."

Matt Payne hung up.

Charley paid for the beer, the egg, and the sausage, and got in his car and drove to the FOP. Matt Payne's Porsche was already in the parking lot, and he found him at the bar.

There was just time to order a beer and have it served when he heard Margaret's soft voice in his ear.

"Hi!"

"Well, as I live and breathe, Florence Nightingale," Matt said, smiling.

"Hello, Matt."

"You're early," Charley said.

"You make it sound like an accusation," Matt said.

"Get off early?" Charley asked.

"Not exactly."

"What's that mean?"

"I mean, I went in, and they said they really needed me from midnight till six."

"They told you to come in," Charley said indignantly.

"And I get an hour, at time-and-a-half, just for coming in," Margaret said. "Plus double-time for midnight to six."

"You're not really going to go in at midnight?" Charley asked incredulously.

"Yes, of course I am," Margaret said. "I told you, it's double-time."

"If I were you, I'd tell them where to stick their double-time."

"Charley!"

"May I make a suggestion?" Matt asked.

"Huh?" Charley asked.

"What, Matt?" Margaret asked, a touch of impatience in her voice.

"If you're going to fight like married people, why don't you go get married?"

"I'm with him," Charley said.

"We just can't, Matt," Margaret said. "Not right now."

"It is better to marry than to burn," Matt quoted sonorously. "Saint Peter."

"No, it's not," Margaret said. "Saint Peter, I mean."

"It was one of those guys," Matt said. "Saint Timothy?"

"So what do we do now?" Charley asked.

"I don't know about you, but I'm going home to get some sleep. You can stay with Matt."

"I'll take you home," Charley said flatly. "He's got a date."

"You don't have to take me home."

"I'll take you home, *and* to work."

"You don't have to do that."

"You're not going walking around North Broad Street alone at midnight."

"Don't be silly."

"Listen to him, Margaret," Matt said.

"Oh, God!" she said in resignation.

Charley got off the bar stool.

"Let's go," he said.

"We'll have to get together real soon, Margaret, and do this again," Matt said.

"You can go to hell too," Margaret said, but she touched his arm before she left.

Matt watched as the two of them walked across the room, and then signaled for another drink.

He did not have a date. But when Charley had called, he had realized that he did not want to sit in a bar somewhere and watch television with Charley.

What he wanted to do was get laid. He had been doing very poorly in that department lately. If he was with Charley, getting laid was, now that Charley had found Margaret, out of the question. Charley was a very moral person.

The trouble, he thought, as he watched the bartender take a bill and make change, *is that men want to get* laid *and women want a* relationship. *Since I don't want a relationship, consequently, I'm not getting laid very much.*

As he took his first sip of the fresh drink, he considered the possibility of hanging around the FOP and seeing what developed. There were sometimes unattached women around the bar. Some of them had a connection with either the police or the court establishment, clerks, secretaries, girls like that. And some were police groupies, who liked to hang around with cops.

Rumor had it that the latter group screwed like minks. The trouble there was the groupies, so to speak, had their groupies, cops who liked to hang around with girls who screwed like minks.

The demand for their services, Matt decided, *overwhelmed the supply. If I try to move in on what looks to be someone else's sure thing for the night, I'm liable to get knocked on my ass.*

And the others, the secretaries and the clerks, the nice *girls, some of whom seemed to have been looking at me with what could be interest, were, like the vast majority of their sisters, not looking to get laid, but rather for a relationship.*

Back to square one.

And if I have another of these, I am very likely to forget this calm, logical, most importantly sober analysis of the situation and wind up either in a relationship, or engaged in an altercation with a brother officer in the parking lot, or, more likely, right here on the dance floor, which altercation, no matter who the victor, would be difficult to explain when, inevitably, Staff Inspector P. Wohl heard about it.

He finished his drink, picked up his change, and walked across the room to the stairs leading up to the street.

Was that really invitation in that well-stacked redhead's eyes or has my imagination been inflamed by this near-terminal case of lakanookie?

He got in the Porsche and drove home. There were, he noticed when he drove in the underground beneath the building that housed both the Delaware Valley Cancer Society and Chez Payne, far more cars in it than there normally were at this hour of the night. Ordinarily, it was just about deserted.

Parking spaces twenty-nine and thirty, which happened to be closest to the elevator, had been reserved by the management for the occupant of the top-floor apartment. The management had been instructed to do so by the owner, less as a courtesy to his son, who occupied the top-floor apartment, than, the son had come to understand, because a second parking spot was convenient when the owner's wife or other members of the family had some need to park around Rittenhouse Square.

Tonight, a Cadillac Fleetwood sedan was parked in parking space twenty-nine, its right side overflowing into what looked like half of parking space thirty. The Payne family owned a Cadillac Fleetwood, but this wasn't it.

Matt managed to squeeze the Porsche 911 into what was left of parking space thirty. But when he had done so, there was not room enough between him and the Cadillac to open the Porsche's driver's side door. It was necessary for him to exit by the passenger side door, which, in a Porsche 911, is a squirming feat worthy of Houdini.

He got on the elevator and rode it to the third floor and got off. The narrow corridor between the elevator and the stairs to his apartment was crowded with people.

A woman he could never remember having seen before in his life rushed over to him, stuck something to his lapel, cried, "Oh, I'm so glad you could come!" and handed him a glass of champagne.

"Thank you," Matt said. The champagne glass, he noticed, was plastic.

"We're circulating *downward* tonight," the woman said.

"Are we?"

"Yes, isn't that clever?"

"Mind-boggling," Matt replied.

The woman walked away.

Nice ass for an old woman; I wonder if there's anybody here under, say, thirty?

"Hello, Mr. Payne."

It was one of the Holmes Security rent-a-cops. Matt knew he was a retired police sergeant, and it made him a little uncomfortable to be called "Mr." by a sergeant.

"I bet you know what's going on here," Matt said, smiling at him.

The retired cop chuckled. "I saw the look on your face. This is a party for the people who worked on the Cancer Society Ball."

"I have no idea what that means, but thanks anyway."

"You know, the ones who sold tickets, did all the work. And, of course, gave money."

"Oh," Matt said.

He saw a very pretty face, surrounded by blond hair in a pageboy. She was looking at him with unabashed curiosity. All he could see was the head and shoulders. The lady was on her way down the narrow stairway to the second floor.

Oh, that's what she meant by "circulating downward."

"I just came from the FOP," Matt said. "I wondered where everybody had come from."

"This is better than the FOP," the Holmes man said. "Here the booze is free. There's a bar in the lobby."

"But I don't belong."

"They don't know that. That lady gave you a badge, and you got by me. *I* keep the riffraff out."

The pretty face in the blond pageboy was no longer in sight.

"Well, maybe I *should* do my part for the noble cause," Matt said.

You're wasting your time. But on the other hand, nothing ventured, nothing gained.

The blonde was not on the second floor. He went down to the lobby and saw the bar.

What I will do is get a drink, and then go upstairs.

There was a small wait in line, and then he found himself facing the bartender.

"Scotch, please. Water."

"Any preference?"

Matt looked and saw that whatever else it did, the Opera Ball Club or whatever the hell it was really served fine booze.

"Famous Grouse, please. Easy on the water."

He became aware, in less time than it takes to tell, first of an exotic perfume, then of an expanse of white flesh that swelled with exquisite grace before disappearing beneath a delicate brassiere, and then of warm breath on his ear.

"I hope you won't be offended by me saying so, but your gun is showing," the voice behind the warm breath on his ear said in almost a whisper.

It was the blonde in the pageboy.

For the first time he noticed that she was wearing a hat.

If half an ounce of black silk and silk netting can be called a hat, he thought.

What the hell did she say about a gun? God, I bet she has nice teats!

"I beg your pardon?"

She smiled, and laughed softly, and tugged on his arm, pulling his head down.

"Your gun, " she said. "It's showing."

This time when he smelled her breath, he picked up the smell of alcohol. Gin, he thought. He looked down at his leg and saw that his trouser leg was hiked up, caught by the butt of the pistol in his ankle holster.

Shit!

When I had to climb out of the goddamn car because of that asshole in the Cadillac in both my parking places, that's when it happened.

He squatted and rearranged his trouser leg.

"Thank you."

"I don't think anybody else noticed," she said. "It was only because I was going downstairs that I saw it. You know what I mean?"

"Thank you for telling me."

"Could I ask you a question? Out of pure idle—there being not much else to think about around here—curiosity?"

"Sure?"

"How many of you are there here tonight?"

What the hell is that supposed to mean?

"How many do you see?"

"That's why I'm asking," she said, laughing. "I'm curious."

Matt held up three fingers.

"Let's start with the easy things. How many fingers?"

"Three, wise guy," she said. "And I only see one of you. That's why I'm asking how many others there are of you. Just out of idle curiosity."

"As far as I know, I am the only one like me here tonight."

"The only one in regular clothes, you mean."

"What?"

"I mean not counting him," she said, pointing to a Holmes Security man taking invitations by the door, "and the one I saw you talking to upstairs."

"Oh. I'm not a rent-a-cop. I had no idea what you were talking about."

"Then what are you doing walking around with a gun strapped to your leg? Your *ankle?*"

"I'm a cop."

"Are you really?"

He nodded.

"A detective, you mean? There are police here, too, in addition to—what did you say, the rent-a-cops?"

"No. Not a detective. A cop. Off duty."

"You're pulling my leg. Aren't you?"

"Boy Scout's honor," Matt said, holding up three fingers.

"And you're active in, a sponsor, of the Cancer Society Ball?"

"Regretfully, no."

"Then what are you doing here?"

"You mean, *here?*" Matt said, and nodded his head to take in the lobby.

"Yes."

"I got off the elevator and a lady told me she was so glad I could come, pinned this thing on me, and handed me a glass of champagne."

She laughed and took his arm, which caused contact between his elbow and her bosom.

"All right, wise guy," she said. "What were you doing getting off the elevator?"

"I live here," Matt said.

"You live here?"

He nodded. "In what Charles Dickens would call the 'garret.' "

She let go of his arm and stepped in front of him and looked at him intently.

"And your name is Matt—*Matthew*—Payne, right?"

"Guilty," Matt said. "You have the advantage, mademoiselle, on me."

"Don't go away," she said, and then asked, "What is that?"

"Famous Grouse."

He watched as she went to the bar and returned with another drink for him, and what, to judge by the gin on her breath, was a martini on the rocks.

She handed him the Scotch and took a swallow of her martini.

"I needed that," she said. "The way they were talking about you—'Poor Patricia's *Boy*'—I thought you'd have acne and wear short pants."

"Who was talking about me?"

"It was the only interesting conversation I heard here tonight. You'll never guess who lives upstairs: Poor Patricia Payne's Boy, they sent him to UP and he paid them back by joining the cops right after he graduated. He's the one who shot the serial rapist in the head."

"Oh."

"And it's madam, not mademoiselle, by the way. I'm sort of married."

"What does 'sort of married' mean?"

"Among other things, that he's not here tonight," she said. "Can we let it go at that?"

"Sure."

"Did you really?"

"Did I really what?"

"Shoot that man in the head?"

"Jesus!"

"I'll take that as a yes," she said, and took another sip of her martini. "Is that the gun you did it with?"

"Does it matter?"

"Answer the question."

"Yes, as a matter of fact, it is. Can we change the subject to something more pleasant, like cancer, for example?"

"So you live upstairs, do you? In what Charles Dickens would call the 'garret'?"

"That's right."

"Are you going to ask me if I want to go to your apartment and look at your etchings, Matthew Payne?"

"I don't have any etchings," he said.

"I'll settle for a look at your gun," she said.

"I beg your pardon?"

"You heard me," she said. "You show me what I want to see, and I will show you what you—judging by the way you've been looking down my front—want to see."

"Jesus!"

"Actually, it's Helene," she said, and took his hand. "Deal?"

"If you're serious," he said. "The elevator is over there."

"With a little bit of luck, there will be no one on it but you and me," Helene said. "Do you have some gin, or should I bring this with me?"

"I have gin," he said.

She put her glass down, put her hand under his arm, and steered him to the elevator.

When it stopped at the lobby floor, the tiny elevator already held four people, but they squeezed on anyway. Matt was aware of the pressure of her breasts on his back, and was quite sure that it was intentional.

On the third floor, he unlocked the door to his stairwell and motioned for her to precede him. At the top, when he had turned on the lights, she turned to him and smiled.

"Dickens would have said 'tiny garret.' "

"And he would have been right."

"Make me a drink—martini?"

"Sure."

"But first, show me the gun."

He squatted, took the revolver from its holster, opened the cylinder, and ejected the cartridges.

"Those are the bullets, the same kind?"

"Cartridges," he corrected automatically.

"Let me see one."

He dropped one in her hand. She inhaled audibly as she touched it, and then rolled it around in the upturned palm of her hand.

"Show me how it goes in," she said.

He took the cartridge back and dropped it in the cylinder.

"It takes five," he said.

He unloaded it again, dropped the cartridge in his pocket, and handed her the revolver.

As he poured gin over ice in his tiny kitchen, he could see her looking at the gun from all angles. Finally, she sniffed it, and then sat down, disappearing from sight behind the bookcase that separated the "living area" from the "dining area," at least on the architect's plans.

When he went into the living area, she was sitting on the edge of his couch. The pistol was on the coffee table. She was running her fingers over it. To do so, she had to lean forward, which served to give him a good look down her dress.

"I found that very interesting," she said, reaching up for her drink. " 'Exciting' would be a better word."

"We try to please," he said. He picked up the pistol and carried it to the mantel over the fireplace. He was now more than a little uncomfortable. He didn't like her reaction to the pistol, and suspected that she was somehow excited by the knowledge that he had killed someone with it.

There's a word for that, and it's spelled P E R V E R S E.

When he turned around, she was on her feet, walking toward him.

"How old are you, Poor Patricia Payne's Boy Matthew?"

"Twenty-two."

"I'm pushing thirty," she said. "Which does pose something of a problem for you, doesn't it?"

"I don't know what you mean."

She laughed, just a little nastily.

"As does the fact that I am behaving very oddly indeed about your gun, not to mention the fact that I am married. Right?"

He could think of nothing whatever to say.

"So we will leave the decision up to you, Matthew Payne. Do I say good night and thank you for showing me your etchings, or do I take off my dress?"

"Do what you want to do," Matt said.

She met his eyes, and pushed her dress off one shoulder and then the other, and then worked it down off her hips.

Then she walked to him, put her hands to his face, and kissed him. And then he felt her hand on his zipper.

When Margaret McCarthy got in Charley McFadden's Volkswagen he could almost immediately smell soap. He glanced at her and saw that her hair was still damp.

Charley immediately had—and was as immediately shamed by—a mental image of Margaret naked in her shower.

"You didn't have to do this, you know," Margaret said.

"What? You got some guy waiting for you at the hospital?"

"Absolutely, and in my uniform we're going to a bar somewhere."

"I'll break his neck," Charley said.

"What I meant, honey," Margaret said, "was that you didn't have to stay up just to drive me to work."

I really like it when she calls me "honey."

"I don't want you wandering around North Broad Street alone at midnight," Charley said. "Are we going to argue about this again?"

"No, Charley."

"Call me 'honey' again," Charley said. "I like that."

"Just 'honey.' Not 'sugar'? How do you feel about 'saccharine'?"

"Now you're making fun of me."

"No, honey, I'm not," Margaret said, and leaned over and kissed him on the cheek.

"I like that too," he said.

"Well, I'd do it more often if I didn't wear lipstick. When I go on duty, no lipstick, and you get a little smooch."

"Now you know why I had to drive you to work," Charley said.

She laughed.

"What are you going to do now? Go home? Or go back to the FOP and have a couple of beers with Matt?"

"If I went to the FOP and Payne was still there, I would have to carry him home. Anyway, he had a date."

"A date? He doesn't have a girl, does he?"

"He has lots of them. Jesus, with that car, what did you expect?"

"A lot of girls, including this one, don't really care what kind of a car a fellow drives."

"There's not a lot of girls like you."

"Is that the voice of experience talking?"

"Maybe, maybe not. Matt was really bananas about one girl. A rich girl, like him. He met her when Whatsername, the girl whose father owns Nesfoods, got married."

"What happened?"

"She was a rich girl. She thought he was nuts for wanting to be a cop. Instead of like, a lawyer, something like that."

"So why does he want to be a cop?"

"I thought a lot about that. What it is, I think, is that he likes it. It's got nothing to do with him not getting in the Marines, or that his father, his real father, was killed on the job. I think he just likes it. And he's working for Inspector Wohl. He gets to see a lot of stuff. I don't think he'd stick around if they had him in one of the districts, turning off fire hydrants."

"You really like him, don't you?"

"Yeah. We get along good."

"You going to ask him to be your best man when we get married?"

Charley had not thought about a best man.

"Yeah," he said. "I guess I will, if I live that long."

"Are we going to start on that subject again?"

"I'm not starting anything. That's just the truth."

"We want to have some money in the bank when we get married."

"I'd just as soon go in hock like everybody else," Charley said. "Jesus, baby, I go nuts sometimes thinking about you."

"Like when, for example?"

"Like now, for example. Since you asked. I smell your soap, and then I—"

"Then you what?"

"I think of you taking a shower."

"Those are carnal thoughts."

"You bet your ass they are," Charley said. "About as carnal as they get."

There was a long silence.

"I guess I shouldn't have said that. Sorry."

"You think you could live six weeks the way things are?"

"What happens in six weeks?"

"The semester's over. I could skip a semester. I wouldn't want to be a just-married, and work a full shift, and try to go to school. But I could skip a semester."

"Jesus, baby, you mean it?"

"I'll call my mother in the morning and tell her we don't want to wait anymore."

"Jesus! Great!"

"I get those thoughts too, honey," Margaret said. She reached over and caught his hand.

At the hospital, when she kissed him, she kissed him on the mouth and gave him a little tongue, something she didn't hardly ever do.

Where the fuck am I?

I was thinking about that, and what she said about her having those kind of thoughts, carnal thoughts too, and drove right across Broad Street without thinking where I'm supposed to be going.

"Shit!" he said, and slowed abruptly, and made the next left.

There's Holland's body shop. That means I'm behind Holland Pontiac-GMC, just a block off North Broad. That's not so bad. I could have wound up in Paoli or somewhere not thinking like that.

And then something wrong caught his eye. There was a guy sitting in a beat-up old Mustang in an alley.

If I hadn't been looking to see where the fuck I was, I would never have seen him.

What's wrong about it? Well, maybe nothing. Or maybe he's drunk. Or dead. Or maybe not. Now that I think of it, he was smoking a cigarette. People don't sit in alleys smoking cigarettes at midnight. Not around here.

He made the next right, and the next, and pulled to the curb.

Fuck it, McFadden. It ain't any of your business, and you ain't Sherlock Holmes.

Fuck fuck it!

Charley turned off the headlights and got out of the car. He took his wallet ID folder from his pocket and folded it back on itself, so the badge was visible, and then he took the snub nose from its holster, and held it at arm's length down along his leg so that it would be kind of hard to see.

Then he went in the alley, and sort of keeping in the shadows walked down close to the Mustang.

Piece of shit, that car.

Moving very quickly now, he walked up to the driver's window. He tapped on the window with his badge.

He scared shit out of the guy inside, who jumped.

The window rolled down.

"Excuse me, sir. I'm a police officer. Is everything all right?"

"I'm a Three-Six-Nine," the man said. "Everything's okay. On the job."

Oh, shit. He's probably a Central Detective on stakeout. Why didn't you mind your own fucking business?

Fuck fuck fuck it. Maybe he ain't.

"Let me see your folder, please," Charley said, and pulled the door open so the light would come on. It didn't.

Lieutenant Jack Malone thinking, *This big fucker, whoever he is, smells something wrong, and he's got his gun out,* very slowly and nonthreateningly found his badge and photo ID and handed it to Officer Charles McFadden.

"Lieutenant, I'm sorry as hell about this."

"Don't be silly. You were just doing your job. I suppose I did look a little suspicious."

"I didn't know what the fuck to think, so I thought I'd better check. Sorry to bother you, sir."

"No problem, I told you that," Malone said. "But I don't want this on the record. You call it in?"

"No, sir. I'm in my own car. No radio."

"Just keep this between ourselves. What did you say your name was?"

"McFadden, sir."

"You work this district?"

"No, sir. I'm Highway."

"Well, I'll certainly tell Captain Pekach how alert you were. But I don't want anyone else to know you saw me here. Okay?"

"Yes, sir. I understand. Good night, sir."

Charley stuffed his pistol back in its holster and walked back up the alley.

Nice guy. I really could have got my ass in a crack doing that. But he understood why I did it. Malone was his name. I wonder where he works. He said he knows Captain Pekach.

And then he got back in the Volkswagen, and there was still a faint smell of Margaret's soap, and he started to think about her, and her in the shower, and what she had said about her having those kinds of thoughts too, and Lieutenant Malone and the rusty piece of shit he was driving were relegated to a far corner of his mind.

10.

The time projected on the ceiling by the clever little machine that had been Amelia Payne, M.D.'s birthday present to her little brother showed that it was quarter past eleven.

It should be later than that, Matt thought, *considering all that's happened.*

He bent one of the pillows on the bed in half and propped it under his head. Then he reached down and pulled up the blanket. The sheet that covered him wasn't enough; he felt chilled.

He could hear the shower running in the bath, and in his mind's eyes saw Helene at her ablutions, and for a moment considered leaping out of bed and getting in the shower with her.

He sensed that it would be a bad idea, and discarded the notion.

Three times is a sufficiency. At the moment, almost certainly, the lady is not burning with lust.

Well, two and a half, considering the first time was more on the order of premature ejaculation than a proper screw.

With an effort, she had been very kind about that. He was not to worry. It happened sometimes. But she had been visibly pleased at his resurgent desire, or more precisely when El Wango had risen phoenixlike from the ashes of too-quickly burned passion.

And clearly done his duty: There is absolutely no way that she could have faked that orgasm.

Orgasms?

Passion followed by sleep, followed by slowly becoming delightedly aware that what one is fondling in one's sleep is not the goddamn pillow again, but a magnificent real live boob, attached to a real live woman.

One who whispered huskily in the dark "Don't stop!" when, ever the gentleman, I decided that copping a feel was perhaps not the thing to do under the circumstances.

And El Wango, God bless him, had risen to the occasion, giving his all for God, Mother, and Country, as if determined to prove that what good had happened previously was the norm, and that "oh, shit" spasm earlier on a once-in-a-century aberration.

She had said, "I'll be sore for a week," which I understand could be a complaint, but which, I believe, I will accept as a compliment.

The drumming of the shower died, and he could hear the large gurgle as the water went down the drain, and he could hear other faint sounds, including what he thought was the sound of his hairbrush clattering into the washbasin.

And then she came out. In her underwear, but still modestly covering herself with a towel.

"You're not leaving?" Matt said. "The evening is young."

"The question is what about the Opera Ball people?"

She sat on the edge of the bed, keeping the towel in place.

I was right. Thrice, or even twice and a half, is a more than a sufficiency, it is a surfeit.

"I haven't heard the elevator in a while. I guess they're all gone. Would you like me to take you home?"

"I have a car."

"Where?"

"In the garage in the basement."

"Parked right next to the elevator?"

"How did you know that?"

"You're the Cadillac in my parking spot. Spots. The gods—the Greco-Roman ones, who understand this sort of thing—obviously wanted us to get together."

"I don't know about that, but I do know what got us together. It's spelled G I N. As in, I should know better than to drink martinis."

"Are you sorry?"

"Yes, of course I'm sorry," Helene said. "I expect you hear this from all your married ladies, but in my case it's true. I normally don't do things like this."

"Well, I'm glad you made an exception for me," Matt said. "And just for the record, you're my first married lady. I would like to thank you for being gentle with me, it being my first time."

She laughed, and then grew serious.

"I would like to say the same thing," she said. "But you're the third. And I decided just ninety seconds ago, the last."

"I didn't measure up?"

"That's the trouble. You—left nothing to be desired. Except more of you, and that's obviously out of the question."

"Why is it obviously out of the question?"

She got up suddenly from the bed, dropped the towel, and walked out of the bedroom, snapping, "I'm married," angrily over her shoulder.

She'll be back, Matt thought confidently. *She will at least say good-bye.*

But she did not come back, so he picked up the towel she had dropped and put it around his waist and went looking for her.

She was gone.

I don't even know what her last name is.

During his military service Staff Inspector Peter F. Wohl had learned that rubber gloves were what smart people wore when applying cordovan shoe polish to footwear, otherwise you walked around for a couple of days with brown fingernails. When the last pair had worn out, the only rubber gloves he could find in the Acme Supermarket had been the ones he now wore, which were flaming pink in color and decorated in a floral pattern. At the time, their function, not their appearance, had seemed to be the criterion.

Now he was not so sure. Mrs. Samantha Stoddard, the 230-pound, fifty-two-year-old Afro-American grandmother who cleaned the apartment two times a week had found them under the sink and offered the unsolicited opinion that he better hope nobody but her ever saw them. "I *know* you like girls, Peter. Other people might wonder."

Mrs. Stoddard felt at ease calling Staff Inspector Wohl by his Christian name because she had been doing so since he was four years old. She still spent the balance of the week working for his mother.

When the telephone rang, at ten past seven in the morning, Wohl was standing at his kitchen sink, wearing his pink rubber gloves, his underwear, an unbuttoned shirt, and his socks, examining with satisfaction the shine he had just caused to appear on a pair of loafers. At five past seven, as he prepared to slip his feet into them, he had discovered that they were in desperate need of a shine.

From the sound of the bell, he could tell that it was his official telephone ringing. He headed for the bedroom, hurriedly removing the flaming pink rubber gloves as he did so. The left came off with no difficulty; the right stuck. Before he got it off, he had cordovan shoe polish all over his left hand.

"Shit!" he said aloud, adding aloud, "Why do I think this is going to be one of those days?"

Then he picked up the telephone.

"Inspector Wohl."

"Matt Lowenstein, Peter. Is there some reason you can't meet me at Tommy Callis's office at eight?"

"No, sir."

"Keep it under your hat," Lowenstein said, and hung up.

Wohl replaced the handset in its cradle, but, deep in thought, kept his hand on it for a moment. Thomas J. Callis was the district attorney. He could think of no business he— that is to say Special Operations, including Highway Patrol—had with the district attorney. If something serious had happened, he would have been informed of it.

A wild hair appeared—Tony Harris was on a spectacular bender; he could have run into a school bus or something—and was immediately discarded. He would have heard of that too, as quickly as he had learned that they had held Tony overnight in the 9th District holding cell.

He shrugged, and dialed the Special Operations number. He told the lieutenant who answered that he would be in late. He did not say how late or where he would be. Lowenstein had told him to keep the meeting at the DA's office under his hat.

He looked at his watch, then shook his head. There was no time to go somewhere for breakfast.

He returned to the kitchen, put a pot of water on the stove to boil, and got eggs and bread from the refrigerator. He decided he would not make coffee, because that would mean having to clean the pot, technically a brewer his mother had given him for Christmas. It made marvelous coffee, but unless it was cleaned almost immediately, it turned the coffee grounds in its works to concrete and required a major overhaul.

When the water boiled, he added vinegar, then, with a wooden spoon, swirled the water around until it formed a whirlpool. Then, expertly, he cracked two eggs with one hand and dropped them into the water. By the time they were done, the toaster had popped up. He took the eggs from the water with a slotted spoon, put them onto the toast, and moved to his small kitchen table. Time elapsed, beginning to end: ten minutes.

"If I only had a cup of coffee," he announced aloud, "all would be right in my world."

Then it occurred to him that if he was to meet with the district attorney, a suit would be in order, not the blazer and slacks he had intended to wear. And if he wore a suit, shoes, not loafers, would be in order.

The whole goddamn shoe-shining business, including the polish-stained left hand, had been a waste of time and effort.

He returned to the sink, and washed his hands with a bar of miracle abrasive soap that was guaranteed to remove all kinds of stain. The manufacturers had apparently never dealt with cordovan shoe polish.

Or, he thought cynically, *they knew damned well that very few people would wrap up a fifty-cent bar of soap and mail it off to Dubuque, Iowa, or wherever, for a refund. Particularly since they wouldn't have the address in Iowa, having thrown the wrapping away when they took the soap out.*

He took his pale blue shirt off, replaced it with a white one, and put on a dark gray, pinstriped suit.

"Oh, you are a handsome devil, Peter Wohl," he said as he checked himself in the mirror. "I wonder why you don't get laid more than you do?"

He arrived downtown at the district attorney's office with five minutes to spare, having exceeded the speed limit over almost all of the route.

As he looked at his watch, he thought the hour was odd. He didn't think the district attorney was usually about the people's business at eight A.M. Had Callis summoned Lowenstein at this time? Probably not. If Callis had wanted to see them, somebody would have called him too. The odds were that Lowenstein had called Callis and told him he had to see him as soon as possible, and then when Callis had agreed, Lowenstein had called him.

Why?

Chief Inspector Matt Lowenstein, Detective Joe D'Amata of Homicide, and another man, obviously a detective, were in Callis's outer office when Peter walked in.

"I was getting worried about you," Lowenstein greeted him.

"Good morning, Chief, I'm not late, am I?"

"Just barely," Lowenstein said. "You know Jerry Pelosi, don't you?"

"Sure. How are you, Pelosi?"

They shook hands.

The mystery is over. Pelosi's the Central Detectives guy working the Goldblatt job. This is about that.

There was no chance to ask Chief Lowenstein. A large, silver-haired, ruddy-faced man, the Hon. Thomas J. Callis, district attorney of Philadelphia, swept into his outer office, the door held open for him by Philadelphia County Detective W. H. Mahoney. The district attorney had in effect his own detective bureau. Most of them, like Mahoney, were ex–Philadelphia Police Department officers. A detective bodyguard-driver was one of the perks of being the district attorney.

"Hello, Matt," Callis said. "How the hell are you?"

A real pol, Wohl thought. Wohl did not ordinarily like politicians, but he was of mixed emotions about Callis. He had worked closely with him during his investigation—

In those happy, happy, days when I was just one more staff inspector—

—of Judge Findermann and his fellow scumbags, and had concluded that Callis was deeply offended by the very notion of a judge on the take, and interested in the prosecution for that reason alone, not simply because it might look good for him in the newspapers.

"And Peter," Callis went on, "looking the fashion plate even at this ungodly hour."

"Good morning, Mr. Callis."

"Tommy! Tommy! How many times do I have to tell you that?"

"Tommy," Wohl said obediently.

"Detective D'Amata I know, of course, but I don't think I've had the pleasure—"

"Detective Jerry Pelosi," Lowenstein offered, "of Central Detectives."

"Well, I'm delighted to meet you, Jerry," Callis said, sounding as if he meant it, and pumping his hand.

Callis turned and faced the others, beaming as if just seeing them gave him great pleasure.

"Well, let's get on with this, whatever it is," he said. "Are we all going in, Matt?"

"Why not?" Lowenstein said, after a just perceptible pause. "Mahoney knows when to keep his mouth shut, don't you, Mahoney?"

"Yes, of course he does," Callis said. "Well then, come on in. Anybody want some coffee?"

"I would kill for a cup of coffee," Wohl said.

"Figuratively speaking, of course, Peter?"

"Don't get between me and the pot," Wohl replied.

"Black, Inspector?" Mahoney asked.

"Please," Wohl said.

"My time is your time, Matt, providing this doesn't last more than thirty minutes," Callis said.

"You heard about the Goldblatt job?" Lowenstein asked.

"You mean the—what was it?—'Islamic Liberation Army'? It was all over the tube. The *Ledger* even ran a photo of their press release on the front page of the second section. Who the hell are these nuts, Matt?"

"Between Pelosi and D'Amata we have a pretty good idea who they are," Lowenstein said.

"Good idea or names?"

"Names. On almost all of them, anyway."

"Witnesses?"

"There were twenty-odd people in Goldblatt's," Lowenstein replied.

"That's not what I asked."

"We have one *good* witness," Lowenstein said carefully. "A Goldblatt employee. Worked like sort of a doorman. Albert J. Monahan. Pelosi showed him pictures and he positively identified all of them."

"A moment ago you said there were twenty-odd people in Goldblatt's."

"They don't want to get involved. In other words, they're scared. That press release and the way the press swallowed it, hook, line, and sinker, made things worse."

"So if you catch these guys, you have *one* witness?"

"There's no question of 'if' we catch them, Tommy," Lowenstein said. "The question is how, and what we do with them."

"Let's cut to the chase," the district attorney said.

"Okay. Two things bug me about this job," Lowenstein said. "First, something that's been building up the last couple of years. Witnesses not wanting to get involved. A lot of scumbags are walking around out there because witnesses suddenly have developed trouble with their memories."

Callis nodded. "They're afraid. I don't know what to do about it."

"In a minute, I'll tell you. The second thing is I don't like the idea of a bunch of *schwartzer* thugs dressing up like Arabs—"

"Americans of African descent, you mean, of course, Chief?" Callis interrupted softly.

"—and announcing they're not really stick-up artists—in this case, murderers—but soldiers in some liberation army."

"And blaming the Jews for all their troubles?"

"Yeah. Blaming *us* Jews for all their troubles," Lowenstein said. "That bothers me personally, but I'm here as the chief inspector of Detectives of the City of Philadelphia. Okay?"

"No offense, Matt."

"I called Jason Washington last night—" Lowenstein said, and then interrupted himself. "I tried to call you, Peter, but all I got was your answering machine. Then I called your driver, and all I got there was a smart-ass message on his answering machine. So I gave up and called Washington without checking with you. I hope you're not sore. I thought it was necessary."

"Don't be silly," Wohl said. "But if you are referring to Officer Payne, he is my administrative assistant, not my driver. Only full inspectors and better get drivers."

"I don't think it will be too long, Chief," Callis said, "before Peter is a full inspector, do you?"

"What about Washington, Chief?" Wohl asked.

"He has a relationship with Arthur X," Lowenstein went on. "I asked him to call him."

Arthur X, a Negro male, thirty-six years of age, 175 pounds, who shaved his head, and wore flowing robes, had been born Arthur John Thomlinson. He had replaced Thomlinson with X on the basis that Thomlinson was a slave name. Arthur X was head of the Philadelphia Islamic Temple, which was established in a former movie palace on North Broad Street.

He had converted an estimated three thousand people to his version of Islam. The men wore suits and ties, and the women white robes, including headgear that covered most of their faces.

"And?" Tommy Callis asked.

"He told Jason he never heard of the Islamic Liberation Army."

"Did Jason believe him? Do you?"

"Yeah."

"Why?"

"He and Jason have an understanding. He doesn't lie to Jason, and Jason doesn't lie to him. Jason said he had the feeling that Arthur didn't like their using the term 'Islamic.' That's his word."

"He didn't volunteer who he thought these people might be, by any chance?"

"Jason didn't ask. He said if he asked, and Arthur told him—Jason said he didn't think Arthur knew, but he certainly could find out—then we would owe him one. I told you, Tommy, we already know who they are."

"So why did you have Washington call Arthur X?"

"To make sure that when we go to pick these scumbags up, we wouldn't be running into the Fruit of Islam screaming religious and/or racial persecution."

The Fruit of Islam was a group, estimated to be as many as one hundred, of Arthur X's followers, all at least six feet tall, who served as Arthur X's bodyguard.

"So when are you going to pick these people up?" Tommy Callis asked.

"That's what I wanted to talk to you about," Lowenstein said. "I want to do it like Gangbusters."

"I don't know what that means, Matt," Callis said carefully.

"I want warrants issued for all the people that Mr. Monahan has identified from photographs. I want them—this is where Peter and the Highway Patrol come in—picked up all at one time, say tomorrow morning at six. I then want Mr. Monahan to pick them out of a lineup, one at a time, as soon as possible, after the arraignment, before the preliminary hearing. I want them charged with first-degree murder and armed robbery. Then I want to run them past a municipal court in the Roundhouse who is not going to release them on their own recognizance or on two-bit bail. I want you to run them past the Grand Jury just as soon as that can be arranged, and then I want them on the docket just as soon as that can be arranged. Unless there is some reason not to, I want them all tried together, and I want one of the best assistant DAs in the Homicide Unit, preferably the head man, to prosecute. I would not be unhappy if you could find the time to prosecute yourself, Tommy."

Tommy Callis thought that over a minute.

"You have *one* witness."

"He's a good one. Credible."

"One," Callis repeated.

"You're suggesting those thugs would get to him?"

"What have they got to lose? It's already murder one. And he could get sick, or drop dead or something."

"That's where Peter comes in again. Right now, I've got a couple of Northwest Detectives on Mr. Monahan. That's just to be sure. Just as soon as this thing starts, I want Peter to *conspicuously* protect Mr. Monahan."

"Meaning what?"

"A Highway car parked around the clock in front of his house. If he insists on going to work, Highway will take him back and forth, and park in front of Goldblatt's while he's working."

"He could still have a heart attack, or something."

"And he could get struck by lightning," Lowenstein said. "Anything's possible. I think it's more possible that we could come up with a couple, maybe six, eight, ten more witnesses."

"Explain that to me, Matt."

"Peter will also put Highway people on the other witnesses."

"What for?" Callis asked, without thinking.

"To protect them, of course. We are dealing with dangerous people here. While the witnesses, if they are to be believed, can't identify the doers, the doers don't know that."

"Christ, Matt, I don't know," Callis protested.

"Once they come to understand that they are in some danger whether or not they testify, they may decide that the only way they can *really* protect their asses is by making sure these scumbags are put away. An assistant DA, with good persuasive skills, might be able to jolt their memories a little. I also thought I would ask Peter to have Washington have a word with the witnesses."

"The Afro-American witnesses, you mean?"

"All of them. Jason is a formidable sonofabitch, in addition to being very persuasive."

"You're suggesting, 'Here is this big black *good* guy, who will protect me from the *bad* black guys'?" Callis asked.

"Why not?" Lowenstein said. "And I'm going to suggest to Peter that when we make the arrests, it might be a good idea to use black Highway guys. A couple of them, anyway, at each site."

"Yeah," Wohl said thoughtfully. "Good idea."

Callis thought about that a moment.

"I presume Commissioner Czernich thinks this is a good idea?" he asked, finally.

"I haven't had the opportunity to discuss this with the commissioner," Lowenstein said.

"What?" Callis asked disbelievingly.

"Commissioner Czernich is a very busy man," Lowenstein said. "And besides, he won't fart unless The Dago tells him to. Or authorize anything that's not in the book. If I went to Tad Czernich, he would check with The Dago before he said anything. And I know, and so do you, Tommy, that the mayor would rather not know about this until it was over."

Callis looked at his watch.

"My God, and it's only quarter after eight!"

"The early bird gets the worm," Lowerstein said.

"You haven't said much about this, Peter."

"I haven't had anything to say."

"Well, what *do* you think about this?"

"If Special Operations is called upon by Chief Lowenstein to assist the Detective Division, we would of course do so."

Callis picked up his coffee cup and found that it was empty. He held it up impatiently and Sergeant Mahoney quickly went to take it from him.

He tapped his fingertips together impatiently for a moment, said "Christ!" and then picked up one of the two telephones on his desk.

"Ask Mr. Stillwell to come in here, please," he said. "Tell him it's—just ask him to come in right away, please."

Wohl glanced at Lowenstein, whose eyebrows rose in surprise. When he saw Wohl looking at him, he gave a barely perceptible shrug.

Farnsworth Stillwell was an assistant district attorney. Generally speaking, there were three kinds of assistant district attorneys, young ones fresh from law school, who took the job to pay the rent and gain experience, and left after a few years; the mediocre ones who had just stayed on because the hoped-for good offer had not come; and the ones who stayed on because they liked the job and were willing to work for less than they could make in private practice.

Farnsworth Stillwell did not fall into any of the three categories. He came from a wealthy, socially prominent family. He had gone from Princeton into the Navy, become a pilot, and earned the Distinguished Flying Cross and some other medals for valor flying off an aircraft carrier off Vietnam. He had been seriously injured when he tried to land his damaged aircraft on returning to his carrier after a mission.

There had been six months in a hospital to consider what he wanted to do with his future now that a permanently stiff knee had eliminated the Navy and flying. He had decided on public service. He'd gone to law school, found and married a suitable wife, and then decided the quickest way to put himself in the public eye was by becoming an assistant district attorney.

He was, in Peter Wohl's judgment, smart—perhaps even brilliant—in addition to being competent. He was tall, thin, getting gray flecks in his hair, superbly tailored, and charming.

Wohl had come to know him rather well in the latter stages of the Judge Findermann investigation, and during the prosecution. There had been overtures of friendship from Stillwell. Without coming out and saying so, Stillwell had made it clear that he thought that he and Wohl, as they rose in the system, could be useful to each other.

Obviously, Stillwell was going places, and Wohl was fully aware of the political side of being a cop, particularly in the upper ranks. But he had, as tactfully as he could manage, rejected the offer.

There was something about the sonofabitch that he just didn't like. He couldn't put his finger on it, and vacillated between thinking that he just didn't like politicians, or archetypical WASPs (and that consequently he was making a mistake), and a gut feeling that there was a mean, or perhaps corrupt, streak in Stillwell somewhere. Whatever it was, he knew that he did not want to get any closer to Farnsworth Stillwell, professionally or personally, than he had to.

He wondered now, as they waited for Stillwell to show up in Callis's office, what Matt Lowenstein thought of him.

"You wanted to see me, boss?" Stillwell called cheerfully as he strode, with an uneven gait, because of his knee, into Callis's office.

Then he saw Lowenstein first, and then Wohl, D'Amata, and Pelosi.

"Chief Lowenstein," he said. "How nice to see you. And Peter!"

He went to each and pumped their hands, and then turned to D'Amata and Pelosi.

"I'm Still Stillwell," he said, putting out his hand.

"Joe D'Amata, of Homicide," Lowenstein offered, "and Jerry Pelosi of Central Detectives."

"Sit down," Callis ordered, tempering it with a smile. "Matt's got a wild idea. I want your reaction to it."

"Chief Lowenstein is not the kind of man who has wild ideas," Stillwell said. "*Unusual,* perhaps. But not wild."

Nice try, Wohl thought, somewhat unkindly, *but a waste of effort. Matt Lowenstein wouldn't vote Republican if Moses were heading the ticket.*

"Tell the man about your *unusual* idea, Matt," Callis said.

Lowenstein laid out, quickly but completely, what he had in mind.

"What do you think of the chief's idea, Peter?" Stillwell asked.

Covering your ass, Still?

"We know what we think about it," Callis said. "What we want to know is what *you* think about it."

Thank you, Mr. District Attorney.

"All right. Gut reaction. Off the top of my head. I love it."

"Why?" Callis asked.

" 'District Attorney Thomas J. Callis announced this afternoon that he will bring the six, eight, whatever it is, members of the gang calling themselves the Islamic Liberation Army before the Grand Jury immediately, and that he is confident the Grand Jury will return murder and armed robbery indictments against all of them.' "

"You *were* listening when Lowenstein said they have just the one witness?"

"Yes. And I was also listening when he said he thought other witnesses might experience a miraculous return of memory."

"You want to put your money where your mouth is?" Callis asked.

"Am I going to be allowed to take part in this?"

"It's yours, if you want it," Callis said.

"I've got a pretty heavy schedule—"

"Meaning you really don't want to get involved, now that you've had ten seconds to think it over?"

"Meaning, I'll have to have some help with my present calendar."

"No problem," Callis said. "That can be arranged."

Callis, Wohl thought unkindly, but with a certain degree of admiration, *has just pulled a Carlucci. If this works, he will take, if not all, at least a substantial portion of the credit. And if it goes wrong, that will be Farnsworth Stillwell's fault.*

Or Matt Lowenstein's fault. Or mine.

Probably the latter. When you get to the bottom line, Farnsworth Stillwell is smarter than either Lowenstein or me. Or at least less principled. Or both.

"Keep me up-to-date on what's going on," Callis said. "And later today, Still, I'll want to talk to you about the municipal court judge."

"Right, Chief," Stillwell said. "Gentlemen, why don't we go into the conference room and work out some of the details?"

"Thank you, Tommy," Lowenstein said.

Callis grunted. When he gave his hand to Peter Wohl, he said, "You'd better hope your people can protect Mr. Monahan, Peter. For that matter you'd better hope he doesn't have a heart attack."

When Officer Matthew Payne walked into the Special Operations Office, the sergeant had given him the message that Inspector Wohl had called in at 7:12 to say that he would not be in until later, time unspecified.

Office Payne sat down at his desk and opened the *Bulletin*. He had just started to read Mickey O'Hara's story about the robbery and murder at Goldblatt & Sons Credit Furniture & Appliances, Inc., when, startling him, the newspaper was snatched out of his hands.

Officer Charles McFadden was standing there, looking very pleased with himself.

"Jesus Christ, Charley!"

"Gotcha, huh?"

"Why aren't you out fighting crime?"

"Need a favor."

"Okay. Within reason."

"Be my best man," Charley said.

"I have this strange feeling you're serious."

"Margaret's going to call her mother this morning; we're going to get married in six weeks."

"Yeah, sure, Charley. I'd be honored."

"Thank you," Charley said very seriously, shook Matt's hand enthusiastically, and walked out of the office.

When he was gone, Matt picked up and read the *Bulletin* and then the *Ledger*. Both carried stories about the robbery of Goldblatt's. The *Ledger* story was accompanied by a photograph of a press release from the Islamic Liberation Army, claiming responsibility. Mickey O'Hara's story in the *Bulletin* hadn't mentioned the Islamic Liberation Army.

Matt found that interesting. He allowed himself to hope that the press release was a hoax, on which the *Ledger* had bit, and which would show them up for the assholes they were.

The society pages of both newspapers (called "LIVING" in the *Ledger*) carried stories of the festivities of the Delaware Valley Cancer Society on Rittenhouse Square, complete with photographs of some of the guests, standing around holding plastic champagne glasses. Matt hoped that he would find Helene's picture, and then, in the caption, her last name. He examined each of them carefully but was unable to find a picture of Helene.

Of course not. While this momentous occasion was being photographed for posterity, Helene and I were thrashing around in our birthday suits on my bed. It's a shame I don't have a picture of that for my memory book.

The telephone rang.

"Good morning. Inspector Wohl's office, Officer Payne."

"You're remarkably cheerful," Wohl's voice said.

"Yes, sir. Every day, in every way, things are getting better and better."

"I gather you were not alone in your monastic cell last night?"

"Yes, sir. That's true."

"I'm in the DA's office, Matt. Get word to Pekach and Sabara that I want to see them in my office at half past eleven. Tell them to keep lunch free too."

"Yes, sir."

"In the upper right drawer of my desk, you'll find a ring of keys. They're to the elementary school building at Frankford and Castor."

"Yes, sir?"

"Get a car and take Lieutenant Malone over there. Tell him I want his assessment of the building as a headquarters—listen carefully: for Special Operations headquarters and Special Operations; for Special Operations headquarters and Highway; and for Special Operations headquarters, Special Operations, *and* Highway. All three possibilities. Got it?"

"Yes, sir. I understand."

"Don't help him," Wohl said.

"Sir?" Matt asked, confused.

"I want to know what you think too, separately," Wohl said. "Get him back in time for the eleven-thirty meeting."

"Yes, sir. What would you like me to do with the stuff for the FBI?"

"You have it all?"

"Yes, sir. I couldn't run Mr. Harris down, but I asked Mr. Washington to have a look at it, and he said I found everything they'd want."

"Leave it on my desk. Maybe I'll have time—I'll have to make time—to look at it before eleven-thirty. You have to be damned careful what you hand the FBI. Call them, and tell them they'll have it this afternoon."

"Yes, sir."

"And see if you can get word to Washington to be there at half past eleven."

"Just Mr. Washington?"

"Just Mr. Washington" Wohl repeated, and hung up.

Matt called Captain Sabara, Captain Pekach, Detective Washington—*now Sergeant Washington*—and finally the FBI office. He got through to everybody but SAC Davis, who was not available to come to the telephone. Matt left word that the material Inspector Wohl was sending would be there that afternoon.

Then he went to the Special Operations dispatcher and asked for a car. When he had the keys, he went and looked for Lieutenant Malone.

11.

The building at Frankford and Castor Avenues, according to what was chiseled in stone over the front door and on a piece of granite to the left of the door, had been built in 1892 as the Frankford Grammar School.

Plywood had been nailed over the glass portion of the doors and many of the ground-floor windows, the ones from which, Matt Payne decided, the local vandals had been successful in ripping off the wire mesh window guards.

The front doors were locked with two massive padlocks and closing chains looped around the center posts of the door. When Matt finally managed to get one padlock to function, he turned to Lieutenant Jack Malone.

"Why don't we just stop here and go back and tell the inspector that a detailed survey of these premises has forced us to conclude they are unfit for human habitation?"

"They obviously are, but we are talking about *police* habitation," Malone said. "The standards for which are considerably looser."

Matt jerked the door open. It sagged and dragged on the ground; the top hinge had pulled loose from the rotten frame.

He bowed and waved Malone past him.

Malone chuckled. From what he had seen of Payne, he liked him. He was not only a pleasant kid, but he'd already proven he was a cop. And Malone had heard the gossip. He knew that Payne's father had been a sergeant, killed on the job, and that he had a very important rabbi in Chief Inspector Dennis V. Coughlin.

Not that he needed one, Malone thought, as close as Payne was to Inspector Wohl. Wohl was a powerful man in the Department. In his present uncomfortable circumstances, that could mean he could get his career back on track, or begin thinking of leaving the Department as soon as he had his twenty in, or maybe even before.

And since Payne was close to Wohl, the same thing applied to him. He could help, or he could hurt. Malone had waked up wondering what kind of trouble he was already in, thanks to that zealous Highway cop who had spotted him keeping an eye on Holland's body shop.

Wohl hadn't said anything to him about keeping his nose out of Auto Squad's business now that he was assigned to Special Operations. Malone knew that he was supposed to be smart enough to figure that out himself. There was little chance that Wohl hadn't heard about it, however.

They didn't send me to Special Operations without talking to Wohl about Poor Jack Malone, who has personal problems, and who incidentally had somehow acquired the nutty idea that Robert L. Holland, respectable businessman and pal of everybody important from Mayor Jerry Carlucci down, was a car thief.

The smart thing for me to have done was just forget the whole damned thing and make myself useful around Special Operations. A good year on this job, and the word would get around that I had gotten through my personal problems and could now, again, be trusted not to make an ass of myself and the Department. That word, coming from Wohl, would straighten everything out.

The worst possible scenario would be for the Highway cop, McFadden, he said his name was, to tell his lieutenant that he had checked out a suspicious car parked near Holland's body shop and found the new lieutenant, Malone, in it. If that happened, there was a good chance that the lieutenant would "mention" that to either Sabara or Pekach. Or maybe to Inspector Wohl himself. In any event, Wohl would hear about it.

At that point, Wohl would have to call me in and tell me to straighten up and fly right or find myself another home. Wohl was not about to put himself in a position where the brass would jump on his ass for letting Poor Jack Malone run around making wild accusations about a friend of the mayor's.

I think I could probably talk myself out of the first time. Yes, sir. I'm sorry, sir. I realize I was wrong, sir. It won't happen again, sir.

And I couldn't let it happen again, which would mean that sonofabitch would continue to get away with it.

That's the worst possible scenario. That doesn't mean it will go down that way. For one thing, the odds are, because McFadden probably walked away thinking he had made a fool of himself, that he had walked into, and almost fucked up, a stakeout where he had no business, that McFadden won't mention what happened to anybody, least of all his lieutenant.

That, I suppose, is the best possible scenario. What will really happen is probably somewhere in between. Whatever it is, since I can't do a fucking thing about it, there's no point in worrying about it.

That puts me back to what I do next. The smart thing to do obviously, since I nearly got caught doing something that really threatens my career, is don't do that no more.

But I'm a cop, and Holland is a thief, and what cops are supposed to do is lock up thieves.

Maybe Wohl, if I went to him, would understand. He understands that some thieves are fucking pillars of the community. Christ, he locked up Judge Findermann, didn't he?

You're dreaming, Poor Jack Malone. You don't have anything to go on except a gut feeling, and if you said that to Wohl, you'd soon be commanding officer of the rubber-gun squad.

Inside the outer doors was a small flight of stairs. Malone went up that, and then through a second set of doors. He heard scurrying noises that experience told him was the sound of rats.

I wonder what the hell they eat in here? It doesn't look like anybody has been in here in years.

He waited for a moment, to let his eyes adjust to the dim light, and then went left down a corridor. The ancient hardwood floor squealed and creaked under his weight. There was a sign with PRINCIPAL still lettered on a door. He pushed that open and looked inside.

There was a counter inside, and several open doors, through which he could see rooms that could be used as Wohl's and Sabara's office.

"We could put the boss in there, I suppose," he said.

"Jesus!"

"And you, Officer Payne," Malone said. "I can see your desk right there by the hole in the wall."

"Do they really think we can use this place?" Payne asked.

"I think the inspector is desperate," Malone said. "We're sitting in each other's laps at Bustleton and Bowler."

"Well, there's a big enough parking lot. Already fenced in. We could start with that, I suppose, and build on it."

"Where?" Malone asked, and then went to a window and looked out where Payne pointed.

"I was reading the grant, and there's—"

"What?"

"The Justice Department Grant," Payne said. "That's where we got the money for Special Operations. A. C. T. It stands for Augmented Crime Teams."

Interesting. He's probably the only guy in Special Operations besides Wohl and Sabara who ever heard of the grant, much less read it.

"You were saying?"

"There's money in there, available on application, for capital improvement. About a hundred grand, if I remember correctly. The question is, would fixing this dump up be considered a 'capital improvement'?"

"I don't know," Malone said. "It's a thought."

"I'll mention it to the inspector," Payne said.

Malone went back in the corridor and down it and into another room. It was a boys' room.

"Well, there's something else we could start with and build on," Malone said. "I saw a Highway guy this morning who's small enough to use one of those urinals."

"Hay-zus," Payne chuckled.

"What?"

"Hay-zus—Jesus—Martinez. He's a quarter of an inch and maybe two pounds over Department minimums."

"How did he get in Highway? Most of those guys are six feet something."

"He was one of the two of the inspector's first probationary Highway Patrolmen. He was a Narc. He and his partner were the ones who caught the guy who killed Dutch Moffitt. The inspector gave him a chance to see if he could make Highway, and he did."

"Oh, yeah. I remember that. The doer got himself run over by an elevated train, right?"

"Right."

"I remember Dutch Moffitt too. He was a real pisser. Big, good-looking guy. He screwed everything in skirts. What did they say?—'that he'd screw a snake if he could get it to hold still.' Did you know him?"

So that's why I have not been wallowing in Episcopalian remorse for having taken someone else's wife into my bed! My Moffitt genes have overwhelmed all my moral training.

"Dutch was my uncle," Payne said.

"Oh, Christ!" Malone said. "Payne, I'm sorry. I meant no offense."

"None taken," Payne said. "Dutch was—Dutch."

"If I'd have known he was your uncle, I wouldn't have—"

"Lieutenant, it's all right," Matt said. "But I would like to make a suggestion."

"Shoot."

"I think we have seen enough of this ruin to know that without spending a hell of a lot of money on it, it's useless. Why don't we go back and tell the inspector that? Maybe there is money in the grant we could get."

"Agreed. I'm freezing."

"Presuming we can get the door to shut, let's go find a cup of coffee."

Inspector Wohl was walking to the door of the building at Bustleton and Bowler as Matt Payne and Jack Malone drove up. He saw them and waited for them to get out of their car.

"Well, if it isn't the real estate squad," Wohl greeted them. "How did that go?"

"Well, we cut it sort of short, sir," Payne said. "The building is falling down. Unless we can get the money to fix it from ACT Capital Improvement, I think we should tell the City 'thank you, but no thank you.' "

He did not get the smile he expected.

"How many rooms?" Wohl asked. "Did you find someplace that could be used as a holding cell? Will the roof take antennae?"

"We didn't get that far, sir," Payne said.

"Go that far this afternoon when you come back from the FBI," Wohl said. "I didn't send you over there for a casual look. The building is ours, and there is money in the ACT Grant."

"I'm sorry, sir," Matt said.

"It's my fault, Inspector," Malone said.

"No, it's not," Wohl said flatly. "Matt, for Christ's sake, do me the courtesy of listening carefully to what I'm saying in the future."

"Yes, sir," Matt said.

"We'll take care of it, sir," Malone said.

"No, 'we' won't," Wohl said. "*He* will. *He* will come in in the morning with a sketch of the building, including dimensions. Indicate on it where people might fit. See what shape the furnace is in. *If* there is a furnace. You get the idea, and I don't care if you're there all night, Matt."

"Yes, sir."

"I don't see Jason Washington's car. Did you get in touch with him?"

"Yes, sir. He said he would be here."

"I want you in on this, Malone," Wohl said, and walked ahead of them into the building.

Well, the kid fucked up, sorry about that was the first thing Malone thought. This was immediately followed by, *Now he has to do it all himself,* and finally with a sudden insight: *If Wohl knows the kid can examine that building by himself, then there was no reason for him to send me over there in the first place. Except maybe to compare what the both of us had to say; in other words, to see if I am as smart as the kid. I'll be a sonofabitch.*

Jason Washington was standing by the door to Wohl's office.

"Got a minute, Inspector?" he asked.

"Yeah, sure," Wohl said. He looked over his shoulder. "You two go on in."

Captain Mike Sabara and Captain Dave Pekach were in Wohl's office, sitting on the couch in front of a small coffee table.

"Slide over, Dave, and make room for Malone," Sabara said, "otherwise we'll have Washington on here with us. Malone isn't nearly as broad in the beam."

"Your pal McFadden was looking for you, Payne," Pekach said as he made room for Malone. "Did he find you?"

"When was he looking?"

"Last night."

"Yeah. And he came looking for me again this morning. I am to be the best man at his wedding."

Christ, Malone thought, *maybe I'll get the worst possible scenario. If McFadden and Payne are pals, that's just as dangerous as McFadden telling his lieutenant he saw me staking out Holland's body shop. Damn!*

"Are you going to ask me to be your best man, David?" Sabara asked innocently.

"What?"

"Well, a nice Polish boy like you can't just go on living in sin indefinitely, can you?"

"Fuck you, Mike!" Pekach flared.

What the hell is that all about?

"If you feel that way, you can just get somebody else to be your best man," Sabara said.

"Goddammit, knock it off!"

"Play nice, children," Wohl said, coming into the room.

"He's always on my ass about Martha," Pekach said.

"Get off Captain Pekach's ass about Martha, Captain Sabara," Wohl said.

"Yes, sir," Sabara said, seemingly chastised. "What time is it, David?"

Without thinking, Pekach held up his wrist and opened his mouth.

"Nice watch, Dave," Sabara said innocently. "Where did you say you got it?"

"You sonofabitch!" Pekach flared.

It was too much for Wohl; he started to laugh, and when he did, Payne joined in.

Pekach looked like he was about to erupt, but finally started to laugh too, shaking his head.

"You bastards!"

"Show Malone your watch, Dave," Wohl said.

Pekach looked uncomfortable, but finally held up his wrist. Around it was a heavy gold strap attached to a gold Omega chronograph.

Jesus, Malone thought, *that's worth three, four thousand dollars!*

"My—lady friend—gave it to me," he explained. There was a touch of pride in his voice. "These guys are just jealous."

"I certainly am," Jason Washington said. "That's worth thirty-nine ninety-five if it's worth a dime."

There was more laughter, and then Wohl ended it. "Recess is over, children," he said, "class has begun."

They all looked at him.

"I might as well start with that, and get it out of the way. We now have the school building at Frankford and Castor. We have it because the Board of Education no longer wants it, and the reason they no longer want it—confirmed by Malone and Payne, who were over there this morning—is because it's falling down. The upside of that is that as part of the ACT Grant there is money for capital improvements. So as soon as possible, say day after tomorrow, we're going to start making it habitable—"

Malone had noticed that Captain Sabara had raised his hand—like a kid wanting the teacher's attention.

"Yes, Mike?" Wohl asked, interrupting himself.

"Figuratively speaking, you mean, Inspector?"

"No."

"Inspector, we're going to have to let the City put out specifications, get bids, open bids, all that stuff."

"No. Matt read the small print and showed me where it says we don't have to go through that for 'emergency repairs.' 'Emergency repairs' was not more precisely defined. I have decided that it means anything but beautification and additions. Fixing broken windows, plumbing, getting a new furnace—that's emergency repairs because we can't use the building with no heat, or no plumbing, or broken windows. Okay?"

"Department of Public Buildings isn't going to like it. They have their list of friendly folks who do work like that."

"I can't help that. We have to get out of here. And Commissioner Czernich—not Public Buildings—has the authority to spend the ACT Grant money."

"And he knows what you're going to do?"

"He will when he gets the bills."

"Inspector, you're asking for trouble," Sabara said.

"The bottom line is that we have to get out of here, Mike. If it goes before the mayor, and I suppose it eventually will, I'm betting he'll decide that I did the right thing and will tell Public Buildings to shut up."

"And if he doesn't decide that?"

"Then the new commanding officer of Special Operations will have a heated and air-conditioned office in a building he would not have had if his predecessor hadn't screwed up."

"It's liable to cost you your promotion, Peter," Sabara said.

"I appreciate your concern, Mike. But (a) I'm not sure if I'm in line for promotion and (b) I've made this decision. Okay?"

"Yes, sir."

"Item two," Wohl said. "Last night, Chief Inspector Lowenstein called one of our people—all right, Jason Washington—and asked him to do something he thought had to be done. Jason agreed to do it, then tried to find me to tell me, ask me, and couldn't—my fault, he should have been able to find me—and then went ahead and did it."

"What did Lowenstein want?" Pekach asked.

Wohl ignored the question and went on: "Okay. This is now official policy. As soon as Matt has the chance, he'll write it up, and I want it circulated to all supervisors. But I want this word passed immediately. Only three people, besides me, are authorized to take action when the assistance of Special Operations or Highway is asked for by anyone else. They are Captain Sabara for Special Operations, Captain Pekach for Highway, and Sergeant Washington for Special Investigations."

"Special Investigations?" Pekach asked, and then, *"Sergeant* Washington? When did that happen?"

"Washington made sergeant yesterday," Wohl said. "Special Investigations is a little younger. I thought it up about five minutes ago."

"Well, my God, Jason," Pekach said. "Congratulations. I didn't know you even took the examination."

He stood up and gave Washington his hand. The others followed suit.

"The word to be passed is that our supervisors don't—no matter who makes the request—do anything for anybody else unless, in your areas of responsibility, you know about it and approve. That means we have to be available twenty-four hours a day, seven days a week, to make the decision. And if you're not going to be available, you have to make sure I am. Okay?"

"Don't misunderstand me, Inspector," Captain Pekach said. "But there's a reason for this, right?"

"Yes, of course there is," Wohl said impatiently. "I don't want Matt Lowenstein, or anyone else, thinking they can just call up here and give our people things to do."

"It's hard to tell Matt Lowenstein no, Inspector," Jason Washington said.

"Especially if you hope to go back and work for him, right?" Wohl responded.

Washington's face tightened.

"I thought it was important, Inspector," Washington said.

"Just don't forget where you work, Jason. For whom you work."

"I suppose that means I won't be going back to Homicide?"

"The question came up as soon as the commissioner got the exam results. He called me and said he thought Lowenstein and Quaire would like to have you back in Homicide and how did I feel about that? I told him over my dead body. He said, joking of course, that

Chief Lowenstein could probably arrange that, and I replied, joking of course, that if he did, the funeral procession would make a detour through the mayor's office, where the corpse would make a final protest."

Sabara chuckled.

"I'm glad you're amused, Mike," Wohl said.

"What I was thinking was, you really don't want to get promoted, do you?"

"I would like to be commissioner, all right? And I think the way to get myself promoted is to do a good job here."

"Hey, take it easy. I'm on your side. I'm one of the good guys."

"If you say so," Wohl said, and then he went on, "Item three: the Islamic Liberation Army."

"Don't tell me they gave us that too?" Pekach asked.

"No. Right now, it's a Homicide job. And properly so. What Lowenstein wanted Jason to do, and what, for the record, Jason quite properly agreed to do, was get in touch with Arthur X to ask him, so to speak, if when the Islamic Liberation Army is picked up, the arresting officers will face the Fruit of Islam, screaming religious and/or racial persecution."

"So they know who they are?" Pekach said.

"Yes, they do. What Chief Lowenstein told the district attorney was going to happen was that Highway would pick all these people up first thing tomorrow morning. They will be run through a lineup, lineups, so that they can be positively identified by the one good witness Homicide has. By then, the DA will have made sure that the municipal court judge doesn't turn these thugs loose on their own recognizance. He will then arrange to get them before the Grand Jury for indictment, and then on the docket. The district attorney has assigned Assistant District Attorney Farnsworth Stillwell to the case."

"What did Arthur X say?" Sabara asked.

"I don't think he considers the gentlemen in question to be bona fide coreligionists," Washington said. "The phrase he used was 'punk niggers.' "

There was a moment's silence.

"Inspector," Pekach said thoughtfully, "I get the feeling that there's something about this that bothers you. I guess I'm just dense—"

"As I was saying to Officer Payne just a few minutes ago, Captain Pekach, listening carefully to what I say may be the thing to do."

Jesus, Wohl can be a sarcastic prick! Jack Malone thought. Then, *Why am I surprised? He's no older than I am, and a staff inspector, a division commander. You don't get to be either as Mr. Nice Guy.*

This was followed by: *If he finds out that I'm still after Bob Holland, which now seems even more likely, with Payne and McFadden being pals, Christ only knows what he'll do.*

"Chief Lowenstein also told the district attorney," Wohl went on, "that Highway will conspicuously protect his one witness, with the idea being that the other witnesses, perhaps counseled by Sergeant Washington, may suddenly have their memories unfogged by coming to realize that the only way they can really cover their asses is to help put the Islamic Liberation Army away, by testifying."

"But Chief Lowenstein did not, I gather, confer with you before he decided what Highway was going to do, right?" Jason Washington asked.

"Sergeant Washington has just won the Careful Listener of the Week Award," Wohl said.

"But he's like that, you know that," Sabara said.

"He may be like that with other people, but he's not going to be like that with me," Wohl said.

"That puts me in the same boat with Dave. I'm lost."

"Special Operations is going to make the arrests," Wohl said. "And Special Operations is going to protect Homicide's one witness. Not Highway."

"And if Special Operations blows it?" Sabara asked.

"We have here an armed robbery, during which a murder occurred. We know who the doers are. The suspects are under surveillance at this moment by Homicide detectives. At five o'clock tomorrow morning, they will tell Sergeant Washington where these people are. At that point, police officers, with warrants, will be sent to assist the Homicide detectives in arresting them. If the police officers in question cannot accomplish this without difficulty, then perhaps they shouldn't be cops, and their supervisors, by whom I mean you and me, Mike, shouldn't be supervisors."

Sabara didn't reply.

"Two things," Wohl said. "I don't want anybody in Highway, or anywhere else, hearing about this before it happens. And I don't want a big deal made of it. I'm not putting Highway down or Special Operations up. I'm treating the robbery and shooting at Goldblatt's like any other robbery where things got out of hand and somebody got killed. The Homicide Bureau found out who did it, and uniformed officers are going to help them make the arrests. I don't want to dignify a bunch of thugs by calling them an army."

"What about the press?"

"We owe Mickey O'Hara one. Actually, we owe Mickey O'Hara a couple of dozen. When you decide where this thing will start, Mike, call Mickey and suggest he might find it interesting to be there."

"Just Mickey?"

"Just Mickey."

"Do we know where these guys are? I mean are they all in one area, or all over the city?" Sabara asked.

"Mostly in Frankford, the Whitehall area," Jason Washington said. "One of them is in West Philadelphia."

"Where'd you get that?" Wohl asked.

Washington met his eyes and then said, "I talked to Joe D'Amata."

"One of Sergeant Washington's responsibilities as head of the Special Investigations Section will be to keep in touch with the Detective Division, and especially Homicide," Wohl said. "Matt, make sure you put that in when you write the job description."

"Yes, sir. Sir, can I say something?"

"At your peril, Officer Payne."

"There's a parking lot, actually a playground, behind the school building. You could use that as a place to meet."

"We're going to need—" Sabara said, pausing to do the mental arithmetic, "—space to park fifteen, sixteen cars, plus what, four wagons and a couple of stakeout trucks. That big?"

"Yes, sir."

"I don't want stakeout acting like the 2nd Armored Division invading Germany," Wohl said. "They should be available, but—"

"I understand," Sabara said.

"Matt, on your way to the FBI," Wohl said, "swing past the school building and make sure the parking lot will be big enough. And then call Captain Sabara and tell him."

"Yes, sir."

"Jesus," Wohl said angrily. "I haven't looked at this stuff yet."

He flipped through the photocopied documents for the FBI quickly and then looked up at Payne.

"You'd better leave now," Wohl said. "I wouldn't want the FBI to think I had forgotten them. And we won't need you in on this. Get the building dimensions, and whatever other information about that place you think we can use, and be here at eight in the morning." He paused and looked at the others. "By that time, we should have eight thugs, more or less, on their way, without fuss, to the Roundhouse. Then we can turn to important things, like making our new home habitable."

"Yes, sir," Matt said, and got up and started to leave.

"Matt!" Wohl called after him.

"Yes, sir?"

"Don't you think it would be a good idea to take this stuff with you?" Wohl asked innocently, pointing at the stack of copies of the Jerome Nelson job.

"Yes, sir," Matt said. His face flushed. He took the documents from Wohl's desk and walked out.

As he closed the door, he heard Wohl say, "If I didn't know better, I might suspect Young Matt's in love."

"How about 'in rut'?" Sabara said.

Matt closed the door on their laughter.

"May I help you, sir?" Miss Lenore Gray, who was twenty-six, tall, slim, auburn-haired, and the receptionist at the FBI office, asked, smiling a bit more brightly than was her custom at what she judged to be a very well-dressed, nice-looking young man.

"My name is Payne," Matt said. "I'm a police officer. I have some documents for Mr. Davis."

Lenore had been told to be on the lookout for a Philadelphia cop named Payne, and to call SAC Davis (or, if he was out of the office, A-SAC [Criminal Affairs] Frank F. Young, or if he was out too, one of the other A-SACs) when he showed up.

She had expected a cop in uniform, not a good-looking young man like this in a very nice blue blazer.

"I'm sorry, but Mr. Davis is not in the office," she said. "Just a moment, please."

She pushed buttons on her new, state-of-the-art telephone system that caused one of the telephones on the desk of A-SAC (Criminal Affairs) Frank F. Young to ring. She did not want to go through the hassle of telling A-SAC Young's secretary why she wanted to talk to him.

"Frank Young."

"This is Miss Gray at reception, Mr. Young. Officer Payne of the police is here."

"Tell him I'll be right out," Young said.

"Mr. Young will be out in a moment," Lenore said with a smile. "Mr. Young is our A-SAC, Criminal Affairs."

"As opposed to romantic?" Matt asked.

He was obviously making a joke, but it took Lenore a moment to search for and find the point.

"Oh, aren't you terrible!" she said.

"You *do* have an A-SAC, Romantic Affairs?"

"No," Lenore said. "But it sounds like a marvelous idea."

"I'm Frank Young," Young announced, coming into the reception area with his hand out. "The chief had to leave, I'm afraid, and you're stuck with me. Come on in."

Matt was surprised. He had considered himself an errand boy, delivering a package, and errand boys are not normally greeted with a smile and a handshake.

"Thank you," Matt said.

Young led him into the brightly lit, spacious interior, and then into his own well-furnished office, through the windows of which he could see Billy Penn atop City Hall. He could not help but make the comparison between this and Inspector Wohl's crowded office, and then between it and the new home of Special Operations at Frankford and Castor.

In the icy cold, dark recesses of which, I will now spend the next three or four hours, with my little tape measure.

"I'm sure this is just what we asked for," Young said, "but I think it would be a good idea if I took a quick look at it. Can I have my girl get you a cup of coffee?"

"Thank you," Matt said. "Black, please."

The coffee was served in cups and saucers, with a cream pitcher and a bowl of sugar cubes on the side, which was certainly more elegant, Matt thought, than the collection of chipped china mugs, can of condensed milk, and coffee can full of little sugar packets reading *McDonald's* and *Roy Rogers* and *Peking Palace* in Peter Wohl's office coffee service.

There were more surprises. Assistant Special Agent in Charge Young was more than complimentary about the completeness of the Nelson files Matt had brought him. They would be very helpful, he said, and the FBI was grateful.

Then, with great tact, he asked Matt all sorts of questions about himself, why he had joined the cops, how he liked it, whether he liked law enforcement in general—*"I don't really know why I asked that. You seem to have proven that you take to law enforcement like a duck to water. I think everybody with a badge in Philadelphia was delighted when you terminated Mr. Warren K. Fletcher's criminal career."*—and what his long-term career plans were.

"I intend to work myself up through the ranks," Matt said solemnly, "to police commissioner. And then I will seek an appropriate political office."

Young laughed heartily. "Jerry Carlucci's going to be a tough act to follow. But why not? You've got the potential."

If I didn't know better, Matt thought, *I'd think he was about to offer me a job.*

Then came the question: *I am being charmed. Why should they bother to charm me? All I am is an errand-boy-by-another-name to Wohl.*

Young then offered to give him a tour of the office, which Matt, after a moment's indecision, accepted. For one thing, he was curious to see what the inside of an FBI office looked like. And maybe they would actually ask him for something. In any event, the school building could wait.

He was introduced to another A-SAC, whose name he promptly forgot, and to a dozen FBI agents, some singly and some in groups. Every time, A-SAC Young used the same words, "This is the Philadelphia plainclothesman who terminated Mr. Warren K. Fletcher's criminal career."

And everyone seemed pleased to have the opportunity to shake the hand that held the gun that terminated the criminal career of Mr. Warren K. Fletcher.

I really don't know what the hell is going on here, but there is some reason I'm being given the grand tour. It may be that Young is being nice to Wohl through his errand boy; or that he is genuinely impressed with the guy who shot Fletcher—if he knew the circumstances, of course, he would be far less impressed—or, really, that they are going to offer me a job. But it's damned sure they don't give the grand tour to every cop from the Department who shows up here with a pile of records.

The subject of employment with the FBI did not come up. A-SAC Young walked him to the elevator, shook his hand, and said that he was sure he would see Matt again and looked forward to it.

When he was on the street again, Matt saw that the skies were dark. It was probably going to snow.

Not only is it going to be bitter cold in that goddamn building, it's going to be dark. Shit!

He drove back to Bustleton and Bowler, and turned in the Department car. He couldn't keep it overnight without permission, and he didn't want to ask Wohl for permission, so it was either turn it in now or when he was finished with the measuring job, and now seemed to be better than later.

On the way to the Frankford and Castor building, he remembered thinking that it was going to be dark, as well as cold, inside the building. He would need more than a flashlight. He could go back and draw a battery-powered floodlight from supply, but he didn't want to go back.

He drove down Frankford Avenue until he found a hardware store, and went in and bought the largest battery-powered floodlight they had, plus a spare battery. Then he bought a fifty-foot tape measure.

It then occurred to him that he would need something that provided more space than his pocket notebook. He found a stationery store and bought a clipboard, two mechanical pencils, and a pad of graph paper.

He was carrying all this back to his car when a Highway car suddenly pulled to the curb, in the process spraying his trousers and overcoat with a mixture of snow, soot, grime, and slush.

The driver's door opened and the head and shoulders of Officer Charles McFadden appeared.

"I thought those were your wheels," McFadden said, nodding up the street toward where Matt had parked his Porsche. "What the hell are you doing?"

"I'm on a scavenger hunt. The next thing on my list is the severed head of an Irishman."

McFadden laughed.

"No shit, Matt, what are you doing?"

"Would you believe I am going to measure the school building at Frankford and Castor?"

"I heard we were getting that," McFadden said. "And Inspector Wohl's making you measure it?"

"Right."

"All by yourself?"

"Right."

"Have fun," McFadden said, and got behind the wheel again.

Matt could see in the car. Officer McFadden was explaining to Officer Quinn why Officer Payne was wading through the slush with a floodlight, a tape measure, and a clipboard. To judge by the look on Officer Quinn's face, he found this rather amusing.

Officer McFadden put the Highway RPC in gear and stepped on the accelerator. The rear wheels spun in the dirty slush, spraying same on Officer Payne.

12.

There was a telephone in Lieutenant Jack Malone's suite in the St. Charles Hotel, through which, by the miracle of modern telecommunications, he could converse with anyone in the whole wide world, with perhaps a few minor exceptions like Ulan Bator or Leningrad.

He had learned, however, to his horror, when he paid his first bill for two weeks' residency, that local calls, which had been free on his home phone, and which cost a dime at any pay station, were billed by the hotel at fifty cents each.

Thereafter, whenever possible, Lieutenant Malone made his outgoing calls from a pay station in the lobby.

When he dropped the dime in the slot this time, he knew the number from memory. It was the fourth time he'd called since returning to the hotel shortly before six.

"Hello?"

"Officer McFadden, please?"

"You're the one who's been calling, right?"

"Yes, ma'am."

"Well, he hasn't come home," Mrs. Agnes McFadden said. "I don't really have any idea where he is. You want to give me a number, I'll have him call back the minute he walks in the door."

"I'll be moving around, I'm afraid," Malone said. "I'll try again. Thank you very much."

"What did you say your name was?"

Malone broke the connection with his finger.

"My name is Asshole, madam," he said softly, bitterly. "Lieutenant J. Asshole Malone."

He put the handset back and pushed open the door.

He was not going to get to talk to Officer McFadden tonight, and he would not try again. He had carefully avoided giving McFadden's mother his name—she had volunteered her identity on the first call.

When Officer McFadden finally returns home, his mother will tell him that some guy who had not given his name had called four times for him, but had not said what he wanted or where he could be reached.

McFadden will be naturally curious, but there will be no way for him to connect the calls with me.

On the other hand, if I did call back, and finally got through to him, he would know not only who I am, but whatever I had in mind was important enough that I would try five times to get through to him.

Under those circumstances, there would be no way I could casually, nonchalantly, let it be known that I would be grateful if he didn't tell his pal Payne that I was staking out Holland's body shop. I already know he has an active curiosity, and if I said please don't tell Payne, that's exactly what he will do. And Payne would lose no time in telling Wohl.

That triggered thoughts of Payne in a different area: *The poor bastard's probably still over there in that falling-down building, stumbling around in the dark, measuring it.*

That was chickenshit of Wohl, making him do that. He sent me over there to look it over. I should not have let myself be talked out of doing what I was sent to do by a rookie cop, even if the rookie works for Wohl. I'm a lieutenant, although there seems to be some questions at all levels about just how good a lieutenant. But he's taking the heat for what I did, and that's not right.

If I were a good guy, I'd get in the car and go over there and help him. But Wohl might not like that. He sent the kid over there to rap his knuckles and Wohl might not like it if I held his hand.

Fuck Wohl! A man is responsible for his actions, and other people should not take the heat for them.

He walked out of the lobby of the St. Charles Hotel and found his car and started out for the school building at Frankford and Castor.

Halfway there, he had another thought, which almost made him change his mind: *Am I really being a nice guy about this? A supervisor doing the right thing? Or am I trying to show Payne what a nice guy I am, so that if I get the chance to ask him not to tell Wohl that I am watching Holland, he will go along?*

You can be a conniving prick, Jack Malone, always working the angles, he finally decided, *but this is not one of those times. You are going there because Payne wouldn't be there if you hadn't been a jackass.*

When he reached the building, he at first thought that he was too late, that Payne had done what he had to do and left, because the building was dark. But then he saw, on the second floor, lights. Moving around.

A flashlight. No. A floodlight. Too much light for a flashlight. That's Payne.

Stupid, you know the lights aren't turned on!

He had another *stupid* thought a moment later, when he turned off Frankford Avenue onto Castor Avenue. There was a Porsche 911, what looked like a new one, parked against the curb, lightly dusted by the snow that had begun to fall as he had driven out here.

If there is a more stupid place to park a car like that, I don't know where the hell it would be. When the jackass who owns that car comes back for it, he'll be lucky to find the door handles.

He pulled his Mustang to the curb behind a battered Volkswagen, and added to his previous judgment: *Because of the generosity of the Porsche owner, the Bug is probably safe. Why bother to strip a Bug when you can strip a Porsche?*

It occurred to him, finally, as he got out of the car that possibly the Porsche was stolen. Not stolen-stolen, never to show up again, but stolen for a joyride by some kids who had found it with the keys in the ignition.

Maybe I should find a phone and call it in.

Fuck it, it's none of my business. A district RPC will roll by here eventually and he'll see it.

Fuck it, it is my business. I'm a cop, and what cops do is protect the citizenry, even from their own stupidity. As soon as I have a word with Payne, I will call it in.

There was now a layer of snow covering the thawed and then refrozen snow on the steps to the building, and he slipped and almost went down, catching himself at the last moment.

When he straightened up, he could see Payne's light, now on the first floor. He stopped just outside the outer door. The light grew brighter, and then Payne appeared. Except it wasn't Payne. It was a Highway cop.

McFadden!

Payne appeared a moment later.

I should have guessed he might be over here helping out his buddy.

All of a sudden, he was blinded by the light from one of the lamps.

"Who are you?" McFadden demanded firmly, but before Malone could speak, McFadden recognized him, and the light went back on the ground. "Hello, Lieutenant. Sorry."

"How's it going?" Malone asked, far more cheerfully than he felt.

"Aside from terminal frostbite, you mean?" Payne said. "Did Wo—Inspector Wohl send you to check on me?"

"No. I just thought you might be able to use some help. You're finished, I guess?"

"Yes, sir. McFadden's been helping me. Do you know McFadden, Lieutenant?"

"Yeah, sure. Whaddaya say, McFadden?"

"Lieutenant."

"Well, at least let me buy you fellas a hamburger, or a cheese-steak, something, and a cup of coffee," Malone said, adding mentally, *said the last of the big spenders.*

"Well, that's very kind, Lieutenant," Payne said. "But not necessary. We're going over to my place and, presuming our fingers thaw, make a nice drawing, drawings, for Inspector Wohl. I thought we'd pick up some ribs on the way."

"It'd be my pleasure," Malone said. "Where do you live?"

"Downtown. Rittenhouse Square."

"I live at 19th and Arch," Malone said. "We're all headed in the same direction. And I haven't had my dinner. Why don't you let me buy the ribs?"

He looked at Payne and saw suspicion in his eyes.

"Why don't we all go to my place for ribs?" Payne said, finally.

"Where's your car?" Malone asked.

"We're parked over there," McFadden said, and pointed to where Malone had parked behind the Volkswagen.

"I want to find a phone," Malone said. "And call that Porsche in."

"Why?" Payne asked, obviously surprised.

"I have a gut feeling it's wrong," Malone said. "A Porsche like that shouldn't be parked in this neighborhood."

"That's Payne's car, Lieutenant," McFadden said. "Nice, huh?"

Malone thought he saw amusement in McFadden's eyes.

"Very nice," Malone said.

"Lieutenant," Payne said. "You're sure welcome to come with us. I appreciate your coming out here."

"I haven't had my dinner."

"You'd better follow me, otherwise there will be a hassle getting you into the garage," Payne said.

"I'm sorry?" Malone asked.

"The parking lot in my building," Payne said. "There's a rent-a-cop—it would be easier if we stuck together."

"Okay. Sure," Malone said.

The little convoy stopped twice on the way to Payne's apartment, first in a gas station on Frankford Avenue, where Payne made a telephone call from a pay booth, and then on Chestnut Street in downtown Philadelphia. There Payne walked quickly around the nose of his Porsche and into Ribs Unlimited, an eatery Jack Malone remembered from happier days as a place to which husbands took wives on their birthdays for arguably the best ribs in Philadelphia, and which were priced accordingly.

In a moment Payne came back out, trailed by the manager and two costumed rib-cookers in red chef's hats and white jackets and aprons, bearing large foil-wrapped packages and what looked like a half case of beer.

Payne opened the nose of his Porsche, and everything was loaded inside. Payne reached in his pocket and handed bills to the manager and the two guys in cook's suits. They beamed at him.

Payne closed the nose of his Porsche, got behind the wheel, and the three-car convoy rolled off again.

I didn't know Ribs Unlimited offered takeouts, Malone thought, and then, *Jesus Christ, me and my big mouth: When I offer to pay for the ribs, as I have to, I will have to give him a check, because I have maybe nineteen dollars in my pocket. A check that will be drawn against insufficient funds and will bounce, unless I can get to the bank and beg that four-eyed asshole of an assistant manager to hold it until payday.*

Five minutes later they were unloading the nose of the Porsche in a basement garage.

Payne's apartment, which they reached after riding an elevator and then walking up a narrow flight of stairs, was something of a disappointment.

It was nicely furnished, but it was very small. Somehow, after the Porsche, and because it was on Rittenhouse Square, he had expected something far more luxurious.

McFadden carried the case of beer into the kitchen, and Malone heard bottles being opened.

"Here you are, Lieutenant," he said. "You ever had any of this? Tuborg. Comes from Holland."

"Denmark," Payne corrected him, tolerantly.

Malone took out his wallet.

"This is my treat, you will recall," he said. "What's the tab?"

"This is my apartment," Payne said with a smile. 'You owe us a cheese-steak."

"I insist."

"So do I," Payne said, and put the neck of the Tuborg bottle to his lips.

"Well, okay," Malone said, putting his wallet back in his pocket.

Did he do that because he is a nice guy? Or because he is the last of the big spenders? Or was I just lucky? Or has Wohl had a confidential chat with him about The New Lieutenant, and his problems, financial and otherwise?

"You two eat in the living room," McFadden ordered, "so I can have the table in here."

"Among Officer McFadden's many, many other talents," Payne said cheerfully, "he assures me that he is the product of four years of mechanical drawing in high school. He is going to prepare drawings of that goddamn old building that will absolutely dazzle Inspector Wohl."

McFadden smiled. "My father works for UGI," he said. "My mother wanted me to go to work there as a draftsman." (United Gas Industries, the Philadelphia gas company.)

"My father's a fireman," Malone said. "I was supposed to be a fireman."

"Let's eat, before they get cold," Payne said. "Or do you think I should stick them into the oven on general principles?"

McFadden laid a hand on the aluminum. "They're still hot. Or warm, anyway."

He opened one of the packages. Payne took plates, knives and forks, and a large package of dinner-sized paper napkins from a closet.

"You going to need any help?" he asked McFadden.

"No," McFadden said flatly. "Just leave me something to eat and leave me alone."

"You'd better put an apron on, or you'll get rib goo all over your uniform," Payne said.

"They call that barbecue sauce," McFadden said. " 'Rib goo'! Jesus H. Christ!"

Payne handed him an apron with MASTER CHEF painted on it. Then he began to pass out the ribs, coleslaw, baked beans, salad, rolls, and other contents of the aluminum-wrapped packages.

A piece of paper fluttered to the floor. Malone picked it up. It was the cash register tape from Ribs Unlimited. Three complete Rib Feasts at $11.95 came to $35.85. They had charged Payne retail price for the BEER, IMPORT, which, at $2.25 a bottle, came to $27.00. With the tax, the bill was nearly seventy dollars.

And Payne had tipped the manager and both cooks. Christ, that's my food budget for two weeks.

"Fuck it," McFadden said. "Eat first, work later. McFadden's Law."

He sat down and picked up a rib and started to gnaw on it.

"That makes sense," Payne said. "Sit down, Lieutenant. They do make a good rib."

"I know. I used to take my wife there," Malone said without thinking.

McFadden silently ate one piece of rib, and then another. He picked up his beer bottle, drank deeply, burped, and then delicately wiped his mouth with a paper napkin.

"Are you going to tell me, Lieutenant, what's going on at half past four tomorrow morning at that school building?" McFadden suddenly asked. *"He* won't tell me."

"What makes you think something's going on?"

"The word is out that something is," McFadden said.

"Can I tell you without it getting all over Highway before half past four tomorrow morning?" Malone replied, after a moment's hesitation.

"Then you'd better not tell me, Lieutenant," McFadden said. "Not that I would say anything to anybody—just between you, me, and the lamppost, Lieutenant, the only thing Highway has going for me is that it keeps me from doing school crossing duty in a district—but Highway is going to find out, and I wouldn't want you to think I was the one who told them."

"He's right, Lieutenant," Payne said. "If Charley knows something's going to happen, so does everybody in Highway, and they will snoop around until they find out what."

"As Lieutenant Malone, I can't tell you," Malone said. "But we're off duty, right? And you're Charley, and I'm Jack, and this won't go any further?"

He saw Payne's eyes appraising him.

Is he going to go to Wohl first thing in the morning? "Inspector, I think I should tell you that that new lieutenant can't keep his mouth shut."

Fuck it, I sense an opening here to get to McFadden. If I can get McFadden to agree not to tell Wohl about finding me at Holland's, Payne will probably, or at least possibly, fall in line. And if he doesn't, if I blow this, things can't get any worse than they are now.

"Okay, Jack," McFadden said. "Out of school, what's going on in the morning?"

Malone saw Payne's eyes flash between him and McFadden and back again.

Shit! He's suspicious as hell.

"If I did, Payne, would you feel you had to tell Inspector Wohl I told him?"

Payne met his eyes. Then he picked up his bottle of beer and took a pull at it.

"Lieutenant," Payne said. "I don't really know what the hell is going on here."

"I beg your pardon?"

"We're out of school, right?"

"Absolutely."

"No, then. I would *not* tell the Inspector you told Charley about what's going on at half past four in the morning. I was going to tell him anyway. I was just pulling his chain, not telling him before. That's not what's bothering me."

"What is, then?"

"You showed up at the school tonight, for one thing. 'Call me Jack,' and 'Let me buy you fellas a cheese-steak,' for some more."

Christ, I'm losing control. Am I just bad at this? Or are these two a lot smarter than I gave them credit for being?

"I went out to the school because I thought you were taking heat for something that was my responsibility."

"What do you want from us, Lieutenant?" Payne asked, both his tone of voice and the look in his eyes making it clear he hadn't bought that at all. "Has it got something to do with Charley finding you snooping around Holland's body shop?"

Christ, he already knows! What did I expect? Well, fuck it, I blew it.

"Are you going to tell Inspector Wohl about that?" Malone asked.

"Unless you can come up with a good reason I shouldn't," Payne said.

Malone glanced at McFadden. He recognized the look in McFadden's eyes. He had seen it a hundred times. A cop who knew that the suspect had been lying all along had just told him he knew he had been lying all along, and was waiting to see what reaction that would cause.

And I am the guy they caught lying.

When all else fails, tell the truth.

"Holland is dirty," Malone said.

"How do you know?" McFadden asked, picking up another rib.

"You've been on the street," Malone said, meeting McFadden's eyes. "You *know* when you know someone's dirty."

"Yeah," McFadden said. "But sometimes when you know, you're wrong."

Charley McFadden's response surprised Matt Payne.

What the hell are they talking about? Some kind of mystical intuition?

"I *know*, McFadden," Malone said.

McFadden seemed to be willing to give Malone the benefit of the doubt.

Because he's a lieutenant? Or because Charley was on the street? Is there something to this intuition business that these two, real cops as opposed to me, understand and I don't?

And then Officer Matthew M. Payne had a literally chilling additional thought.

I knew. Jesus H. Christ, I knew. When I saw Fletcher's van, I knew it was wrong. I told myself, consciously, that all it was, was a van, but I knew it was dirty. If I hadn't subconsciously known it was dirty, hadn't really been careful, Warren K. Fletcher would have run over me. The only reason I'm alive and he's dead is because, intuitively, *I knew the van was dirty.*

"You want to tell us about it?" McFadden asked.

"You know Tom Lenihan?" Malone asked.

McFadden shook his head no.

"He's Chief Coughlin's driver," Matt offered, and corrected himself. *"Was.* He made lieutenant."

"Right," Malone said. "Now he's in Organized Crime."

"What about him?"

"We go back a ways together. When he made lieutenant, he bought a new car. For him new. Actually a year-old one with low mileage. I went out to Holland Pontiac-GMC to help him get it."

"And?"

"He got a Pontiac Bonneville. They gave him a real deal, he said."

"That doesn't make Holland a thief," Matt Payne said.

"Holland himself came out. Very charming. A lot of bullshit."

"What's wrong with that?" Charley asked.

"Holland has six, seven dealerships. Why should he kiss the ass of a new police lieu-tenant who just bought a lousy used Bonneville?"

"Maybe because he knew he worked for Denny Coughlin," Matt thought out loud.

"Same thought. Why should a big-shot car dealer kiss the ass of even Denny Coughlin?"

"That's all you have?" McFadden asked.

"Two reasons," Matt said. "One he likes cops, which I doubt, or because he's getting his rocks off knowing he's making a fool of the cops."

"What the fuck are *you* talking about?" Charley challenged.

"That's the gut feeling I had," Malone said.

"I don't know what the fuck either one of you is talking about," McFadden said.

"Tell me some more," Matt said. "What do you think? How's he doing it? Why?"

"I don't know *exactly* how he's doing it," Malone said. "But I have an idea why, how it started. A lot of car dealers are dirty. I mean, Christ, you know, they make their living cheating people. The only reason they don't cheat more, which is stealing, is because they don't want to get arrested."

"Okay," McFadden said. "So what?"

"So they all know how to steal something, cheating on a finance contract, swapping radios and tires around, buying hot parts for repair work," Malone said. "Now let's say Holland, maybe early on, maybe that's the reason he's so successful, figured out a way to steal cars. He's so successful, the thievery is like business, so the thrill is gone."

"Jesus, Lieutenant," McFadden said, his tone suggesting that Malone had just asked him to believe the cardinal archbishop was a secret compulsive gambler.

"Let him talk, Charley," Matt said, on the edge of sharpness.

"I also read somewhere that some thieves really want to get caught," Malone said. "And I read someplace else that some thieves really do it for the thrill, not the money."

"So you see Bob Holland as a successful thief who gets his thrills, his sense of superi-ority, by being a friend of the cops?"

"No wonder they think you're crazy," McFadden said, and then, realizing that he had spoken his thought, looked horrified.

"I don't think—" Matt said. "I'm not willing to join them."

"Who's them?" McFadden asked.

"Those who suggest Lieutenant Malone is crazy to think Bob Holland could be a thief," Payne said.

McFadden looked at Payne, first in disbelief, and then, when he saw that Payne was serious, with curiosity.

"Based on what, you think he's stealing and selling whole cars?" McFadden asked.

"I know how," Malone said. "I just haven't figured out how to get Holland yet."

"Great!" McFadden said. "Then you *don't* know, Lieutenant."

"I do know," Malone said. "Tom Lenihan is driving a stolen car."

"How do you know that?" McFadden asked, on the edge of scornfully.

"Because the VIN tag and the secret mark on his Bonneville are different," Malone said. "I looked."

The VIN tag is a small metal plate stamped with the Vehicle Identification Number and other data, which is riveted, usually where it can be seen through the windshield, to the vehicle frame.

"No shit?" McFadden asked.

"What's the secret mark?" Matt asked, curiosity having overwhelmed his reluctance to admit his ignorance.

"The manufacturer's stamp," Malone said, "in some place where it can't be seen, unless you know where to look, either all the numbers, or some of the numbers, on the VIN tag. So that if the thief swaps VIN tags, you can tell."

If he knows that, Matt wondered, *why doesn't he just go arrest Holland?*

"Does Lieutenant Lenihan know?" Charley asked.

"No," Malone said.

"Why?"

"Because I didn't tell him. If I told him, he would go to the Auto Squad, and they would get a warrant and go out there. I don't want some body shop mechanic, or even the guy that runs the body shop, taking the rap for this, I want Holland."

"Holland probably hasn't been in the body shop for years, and can prove it," McFadden said. "You're sure they're doing this in the body shop?"

"Where else?"

"Well, let's figure out how he's stealing cars, and then we can figure out how to catch him," Charley said.

"Stealing and selling," Matt corrected him.

"Hypo-something," McFadden said. "What is that you're always saying, Matt?"

"Hypothetically speaking," Matt furnished.

"Right," McFadden said. "Okay. From the thief's angle. You steal a car, and you can do what with it?"

"Strip it or chop it," Malone said.

"What's the difference?" Matt asked.

"A quick strip job means you take the tires and wheels, the radio, the air-conditioner compressor, the battery, anything you can unbolt in a hurry. A chop job is when you take maybe the front clip—you know what that is?"

"The fenders and grill," Matt answered.

"Sometimes the whole front end, less the engine," Malone said. "Engines have serial numbers. Or the rear end, or the rear quarter panels. Then you just dump what's left. Clip job or strip job."

"Or you get the whole car on a boat and send it to South America or Africa, or someplace," McFadden said. "You don't think that's what Holland is doing, do you, Lieutenant?"

"Holland is selling whole cars."

"With legitimate VIN tags," McFadden said. "Where's he get those?"

"From wrecks," Malone said. "There's no other place. He goes—*he* doesn't go, he sends one of his people—to an insurance company auction—"

"A what?" Matt interrupted.

"You run your car into a tree," Malone explained. "The insurance company decides it would cost too much to fix. They give you a check and take your car. Once a week, once every other week, they—not just one insurance company, a bunch of them—have an auction. The wrecks are bought by salvage yards, body shops, people like that."

"And Holland just takes the VIN off the wreck and puts it on the stolen car, right, and says it's been repaired, and puts it on one of his lots?" Matt asked.

"That's how I see it," Malone said.

"Well, if we know that," Matt asked, "what's the problem? All we have to do is—"

"Let me tell you, Payne, all we have to do," Malone said, more than a little contempt in his tone. "Let me give you a for example. For example, we take Tom Lenihan's car. We go back to Holland with it and say it's stolen, and where did you get it? They say, *'Gee, whiz, we didn't know it was stolen. We carefully checked the VIN tag when we bought it at the insurance auction. See, here's the bill of sale.'* So then we go to the insurance auction, and they say, *'That's right, we auctioned that car off for ABC Insurance, and sure, we checked the VIN tag. No, we didn't check for the secret stamping, there's no law says we have to, all the law says we have to do is check the VIN tag and fill out the forms for the*

Motor Vehicle Bureau. We did that. Besides, we are respectable businessmen, and we resent you hinting we're a bunch of thieves.' "

"Oh," Matt said, chagrined.

"If we went out there tomorrow morning, with Tom Lenihan's Pontiac, which we *know* is stolen, you know what would happen? First of all, nobody would get arrested. Lenihan would have to give the car up, because it's stolen. The original owner would get it back, but would have trouble with Motor Vehicles because the VIN tag doesn't match the stamped ID on the frame somewhere. Holland would piss his pants, he was so sorry that this happened to an honest man like himself and an honest man like Lenihan. He would give Lenihan another car, maybe even a better one, to show what a good guy he is. Holland would then have his lawyer sue the auction for selling him a hot car. It would take years to get on the docket. There would be delays after delays after delays. Finally it either would die a natural death or the auction would settle out of court, and as part of the deal, both parties would agree never to divulge the amount of the settlement. You getting the picture, Payne?"

"Yes, sir."

"And then he wouldn't steal any more cars until he figured we didn't have the time to watch him anymore," Malone said.

"Then how do you plan to catch Holland, Lieutenant?" McFadden asked.

"I've got a couple of ideas."

"That's what I'm asking," McFadden said.

"If Inspector Wohl finds out I haven't listened to all the good advice I've been given to forget Holland, in other words, if you tell him you saw me at the body shop, or Payne tells him about tonight, what's the difference?"

"The only people I told about you being outside the body shop is Matt and Hay-zus."

Jesus, he has told somebody!

"Who's—what did you say?"

"Hay-zus, Jesus in English, Martinez. He was my partner when we was undercover in Narcotics."

"And how many people do you think he's told, since you told him?"

"Nobody. I told him to keep it under his hat until I had a chance to ask Payne."

"So what about you, Payne?" Malone asked. "Are you going to get on the phone to Wohl the minute I leave here, or wait until tomorrow morning, or what?"

"It's an interesting ethical question," Matt said. "On one hand, for reasons I don't quite understand, I would *really* like to see Holland caught. On the other, so far as Wohl is concerned, my primary loyalty is to him—"

"Your primary loyalty should be to the Police Department," Malone interrupted. "You're a cop. It's your duty to catch crooks."

Matt met Malone's eyes, but didn't respond.

"That's the reason you would really like to see Holland caught. You're a cop," Malone went on.

"And on the other hand, Inspector Wohl trusts me," Matt said. "I like that. I admire him. I don't want to betray whatever confidence he has in me."

"So you are going to tell him?"

"I don't do very well deciding ethical questions when I've had four bottles of beer," Matt said. "I think I'd better sleep on this."

"I see."

"I won't, if I decide I have to tell him, tell him about tonight. If I tell him anything, it will be just that Charley saw you staking out Holland's body shop. Maybe that can slip my mind too. I don't want to decide that, either way, tonight. But if I do decide to tell him, I'll tell you before I do."

"Fair enough," Malone said.

He stood up and offered Matt in his hand.

"Thank you."

"For the ribs, you mean," Matt said.

"Yeah, for the ribs," Malone said. Then he leaned over and shook McFadden's hand. Charley nodded at him, but said nothing.

Malone found his coat and walked out of the apartment.

"I wonder if he really has some ideas about catching Holland, or whether that was just bullshit," McFadden said.

"Why couldn't he tell—who did he work for in Auto Squad?"

"That's part of Major Crimes. Major Crimes is commanded by a captain. I forget his name."

"Why couldn't he tell him what he told us?"

"You really don't understand, do you?" McFadden said. "Sometimes, you're smart, Matt, and sometimes you're dumber than dog shit."

"I prefer to think of it as 'inexperienced,' " Matt said. "Answer the question."

"Okay. Don't Make Waves."

"Meaning what?"

"Meaning the Auto Squad and Major Crimes has enough, more than enough, already to do without getting involved in something that might turn against them. It's not as if people are going to die because Holland is stealing cars. Who the hell is really hurt except the insurance company?"

"I could debate that: *You* are. Your premiums are so high because cars are stolen and have to be paid for."

"And sometimes," Charley said, smiling at him, "you sound like the monks in school. Absolute logic. You're absolutely right. But it don't mean a fucking thing in the real world. Whoever runs Major Crimes decided he didn't want to go after Bob Holland because there are other car thieves out there he *knows* he can catch, car thieves who *will* go to jail, and who don't call the mayor by his first name. You understand?"

"Yeah, I guess so."

"Don't get me wrong, Matt. For the record, I hope, when you settle your *ethical problem,* that you decide you don't have to tell Wohl. I'd like to go after Holland."

"Help Malone, you mean?"

"Yeah. Don't you?"

"Yeah. I would. But I think it would be stupid. And probably dangerous."

"To your job, you mean? I don't think you'd be likely to get shot or anything trying to catch Holland."

"Yeah, to my job. I like my job."

"Right. You get your rocks off stumbling around fall-down buildings in the dark with a tape measure, right?"

"You'd better finish those drawings while you can still draw a reasonably straight line."

"Yeah. Jesus, it's getting late, isn't it?"

He sat down at the table. Matt went around picking up the remnants of the meal and the empty beer bottles. When he opened the cabinet under the sink, to put rib bones in the garbage can, he saw the martini glass. It had Helene's lipstick on it. It had somehow gotten broken when they had been thrashing around on the couch.

As the memories of that filled his mind's eye, he felt a sudden surge of desire.

My God, I'd like to be with her again!

"You going to tell me what's happening at half past four tomorrow morning?" Charley asked.

"They know who the doers are on that Goldblatt furniture job—"

"The Islamic Liberation Army?"

"—and they're going to pick them up all at once."

"Highway, you mean?"

"No. Special Operations. ACT."

"Jesus, that's interesting. How come not Highway?"

"A couple of reasons. I think Wohl wants Special Operations—the ACT guys—to do something on their own. And I think he's concerned that this Islamic Liberation Army thing could get out of hand."

"What do you mean, 'out of hand'?"

"He doesn't want a gang of armed robbers to get away with it, or get special treatment, because they're calling themselves a liberation army."

"That liberation army business is bullshit, huh?"

"Yeah. And finally, Chief Lowenstein told Wohl he wanted Highway to pick up these guys. I think Wohl wants to make the point that he will take requests, or suggestions, from Lowenstein, but not orders. In other words, if Lowenstein had said he wanted ACT to make the arrests, Wohl would have sent Highway."

"If the ACT guys blow it, Wohl'll have egg on his face."

"Yeah," Matt said, "and if you should happen to be around Castor and Frankford at that time of the morning, Wohl would figure out where you heard what was happening and I would have egg, or worse, on mine."

"Yeah, I suppose. Shit! Okay. I won't be there."

Matt finished cleaning up and then stood and looked over Charley's shoulder as he worked. It became quickly apparent that Charley was a quite competent draftsman.

I didn't learn a damned thing in high school, for that matter in college, that has any practical value.

"I wish I could do that," Matt said.

"So do I," McFadden said. "Then I could get the fuck out of here."

13.

At 3:45 the next morning Officer Matthew M. Payne, in his bathrobe, was watching the timer on his combination washer-drier. It had twenty-five minutes to run.

At approximately 3:25 Officer Matthew M. Payne had experienced what the Rev. H. Wadsworth Coyle of Episcopal Academy had, in a euphemistically titled course (Personal Hygiene I), euphemistically termed a "nocturnal emission." The Reverend Coyle had assured the boys that it was a natural biological phenomenon, and nothing to be shamed about.

It had provoked in Officer Payne a mixed reaction. On one hand, it had been a really first-class experience, with splendid mental imagery of Helene, right down to the slightly salty taste of her mouth on his, and on the other, a real first-class pain in the ass, having to get out of goddamn bed in the middle of the goddamn night to take a goddamn shower and then wash the goddamn sheets so the maid would not find the goddamn tell-tale spots on the goddamn sheets.

"Fuck it!" Officer Payne said, aloud and somewhat angrily. He draped his bathrobe carefully on the stove, went into his bedroom, and dressed. The last item of his wardrobe was his revolver and his ankle holster, which he had deposited for the night on the mantelpiece over the fireplace.

Picking up the revolver triggered another mental image of the superbly bosomed Helene, but a nonerotic, indeed somewhat disturbing, one: the way she had handled the gun, and even the cartridges. That had been weird.

He went down the stairs, and then rode the elevator to the basement. When he drove out of the garage onto Manning Street, he saw that not only was it snowing, but that it had apparently been snowing for some time. Small flakes, which were not melting, and which suggested it was going to continue to snow for at least some time.

He made his way to North Broad Street, and drove out North Broad to Spring Garden, and then right on Spring Garden to Delaware Avenue, and then north on Delaware to Frankford Avenue and then out on Frankford toward Castor.

Except for a few all-night gas stations and fast-food emporia, the City of Philadelphia seemed to be asleep. The snow had not yet had time to become soot-soiled. It was, Matt thought, rather pretty.

On the other hand, there was ice beneath the nice white snow, and twice he felt the wheels of the Porsche slipping out of control.

And there is a very good chance that when I get out there, Inspector Wohl will remind me that he said he would see me at eight o'clock in the office, not here at four-fifteen, remind me that he has suggested it would well behoove me to listen carefully to what he says, and send me home.

There was a white glow, of headlights and parking lights reflecting off the fallen and falling snow in the school building parking lot. And just as he saw an ACT cop open the door of an RPC standing at the curb to wave a flashlight to stop him, Matt saw Inspector Wohl, Captain Sabara, and Lieutenant Malone standing in the light coming through the windshield of a stakeout van.

Malone and Sabara were in uniform. Wohl was wearing a fur-collared overcoat and a tweed cap. He looked, Matt thought, like a stockbroker waiting for the 8:05 commuter train at Wallingford, not like the sort of man who would be in charge of all this police activity.

Matt pushed the button and the window of the Porsche whooshed down.

"I'm a Three Six Nine," he said to the ACT cop. "I work for Inspector Wohl."

The cop waved him through, and Matt turned into the parking lot and found a place to park the car.

As he walked across the snow, which crunched under his shoes, toward them, he was aware that they were looking at him. He decided that there was a good chance that Wohl would be sore he had come here.

"Good morning," Matt said.

Wohl looked at him a good thirty seconds before speaking, then said, "There's a thermos of coffee in the stakeout van, if you'd like some."

"Thank you," Matt said.

When he came back out of the van, Mickey O'Hara was standing with the others.

"You know Officer Payne of the Building Measuring Detail, don't you, Mickey?" Wohl asked, straight-faced.

"Whaddaya say, Payne?" Mickey said. "Relax, I'm not going to play straight man to your boss."

A lieutenant whose name Matt could not recall walked up and with surprising formality saluted.

"Everything's in place, Inspector," he said.

Matt was pleased to see that Wohl was somewhat discomfited by the lieutenant's salute, visibly torn between returning it, like an officer returning a soldier's salute, or not.

"You check with West Philly?" Wohl asked after a moment, making a vague gesture toward his tweed cap that could have been a salute, but did not have to be.

"Yes, sir. Two cars, a sergeant, a stakeout truck, and a van."

"Can you make it over there in thirty"—looking at his watch—"seven minutes?"

"Yes, sir."

"Well, you—" Wohl interrupted himself. Captain Pekach, in full Highway uniform, walked up. The lieutenant saluted again. Pekach, although he looked a little surprised, returned it.

"Good morning," Pekach said.

Wohl ignored him.

"Lieutenant, when did you get out of the Army?" he asked.

"I've been back about four months, sir."

"What were you?"

"I had a platoon in the First Cavalry, sir."

"That worries me," Wohl said. "Let me tell you why. We are policemen, not soldiers. We are going to arrest some small-time robbers, not assault a Vietcong village. I'm a little worried that you don't understand that. I don't want any shooting, unless lives are in danger. I would rather that one or two of these scumbags get away—we can get them later—than to have anybody start shooting the place up. Did Captain Sabara make sure you understood that?"

"Yes, sir. I understand."

"I am about to promulgate a new edict," Wohl said. "Henceforth, no one will salute the commanding officer of Special Operations unless he happens to be in a uniform."

"Yes, sir," the lieutenant said. "I'm sorry, Inspector. I didn't know the ground rules."

"Go and sin no more," Wohl said with a smile, touching his arm. "Take over in West Philly. Get going at five o'clock, presuming you think they're ready."

"Yes, sir," the lieutenant said.

He walked away.

"Good morning, David," Wohl said to Pekach. "Captain Sabara and myself are touched that you would get out of your warm bed to be with us here."

"I figured maybe I could help," Pekach said.

"You and Officer Payne," Wohl said dryly. He looked at his watch. "H-hour in thirty-five minutes, men," he added in a credible mimicry of John Wayne.

"What happens at H-hour, General?" Mickey O'Hara asked.

"We know the whereabouts, as of fifteen minutes ago, of all eight of the people who stuck up Goldblatt's and murdered the maintenance man—"

"Ah, the Islamic Liberation Army," Mickey interrupted, "I thought that's what this probably was."

"The eight suspects in the felonies committed at Goldblatt's is what I said, Mr. O'Hara," Wohl said. "I didn't say anything about any army, liberation or otherwise."

"Pardon me all to death, Inspector, sir, I should have picked up on that."

"As I was saying," Wohl went on. "Shortly after five, the officers you see gathered here will assist detectives of the Homicide Bureau in serving warrants and taking the suspects into custody. Simultaneously. Or as nearly simultaneously as we can manage."

"I would have expected Highway," Mickey said.

"You are getting the ACT officers of Special Operations," Wohl said.

"How exactly are you going to do the arrests?" Mickey asked. "It looks like an army around here."

"Seven of the eight suspects are known to be in this area, in other words, around Frank-ford Avenue. One of them is in West Philly. Two ACT cars, each carrying two officers, will go to the various addresses. There will be a sergeant at each address, plus, of course, the Homicide detective who has been keeping the suspects under surveillance. We antici-pate no difficulty in making the arrests. But, just to be sure, there are, under the control of a lieutenant, stakeout vans available. One per two sergeants, plus one more in West Philly. Plus four wagons, three here and one in West Philly."

"Okay," Mickey said.

"At Captain Sabara's suggestion," Wohl went on, "when the arrests have been made, the suspect will be taken out the back of his residence, rather than out the front door. There he will be loaded into a van and taken to Homicide."

"Instead of out the front door, where there might be angry citizens enraged that these devout Muslims are being dragged out of their beds by honky infidels?"

"You got it, Mickey," Wohl said. "What do you think?"

"I think Lowenstein thinks you were going to use Highway," Mickey said.

"Chief Lowenstein does not run Special Operations," Wohl replied.

"May I quote you?"

"I wish you wouldn't," Wohl said. "If you need a quote, how about quoting me as saying these suspects have no connection with the fine, law-abiding Islamic community of Philadelphia."

Mickey O'Hara snorted.

"Where do you think I might find something interesting?" O'Hara asked.

"One of the suspects is a fellow named Charles D. Stevens," Wohl said. "Word has reached me that he sometimes uses the alias Abu Ben Mohammed. Rumor has it that he fancies himself to be the Robin Hood of this merry band of bandits. Perhaps you might find that a photograph of Mr. Stevens, in handcuffs and under arrest, would be of interest to your readers."

"Okay, Peter," Mickey chuckled. "Thank you. Who do I go with?"

"Officer Payne," Wohl said, "please take Mr. O'Hara to Lieutenant Suffern. Tell him that I have given permission for you and Mr. O'Hara to accompany his team during the arrest of Mr. Stevens."

"Yes, sir," Matt said.

"You will ensure that Mr. O'Hara in no way endangers his own life. In other words, he is not, repeat not, to enter the building in which we believe Mr. Stevens to be until Mr. Stevens is under arrest."

"Ah, for Christ's sake, Peter!" O'Hara protested.

"You listened carefully, didn't you, Officer Payne, to what I just said?"

"Yes, sir."

"If necessary, you will sit on Mr. O'Hara. Clear?"

"Yes, sir."

Lieutenant Ed Suffern, a very large, just short of fat, ruddy-faced man, pushed himself off the fender of his car when he saw Mickey O'Hara and Matt Payne walking up.

"How are you, Mickey?" he said, smiling, offering his hand, obviously pleased to see him. "I'm a little surprised to see you."

"Officially, I just happened to be in the neighborhood."

"Yeah," Suffern said, chuckling. "Sure."

"Got a small problem, Ed," O'Hara said. "How am I going to get to see you catching— whatsisname?—*Abu Ben Mohammed* with Matt Payne sitting on my shoulders?"

"What?"

"Wohl says I can't go in the building until you have this guy in cuffs, and he sent Payne along with orders to sit on me if necessary."

"I wondered what he was doing here," Suffern said. "No problem. Here, let me show you."

He opened the door of his RPC and took a clipboard from the seat.

"Somebody give me a light here," he ordered, and one of the ACT cops took his flashlight from its holster and shined it on the clipboard. It held a map.

"This is Hawthorne Street," he said, pointing. "Mr. Abu Whatsisname—his real name is Charles D. Stevens, Wohl tell you that?"

O'Hara nodded.

"—lives here, just about in the middle of the block." He pointed. "There's a Homicide detective, he has the warrant, sitting here, right now. This is the way we're going to do this: One ACT car, with two cops and the Homicide guy, will go to the front door. Another ACT car, with two ACT guys and the sergeant, will go around to the back, via the alley here." He pointed again. "When they're in place, the sergeant will give the word. The Homicide guy will knock or ring the bell or whatever. We'll give him thirty seconds to open the door. Then they'll take both doors. When they have him in cuffs, they'll take him out the back. There's a wagon, here." He pointed again, this time to a point a block away. "The van will start for the alley the moment he hears they're going in. They'll put Abu Whatsisname in the van, with one cop from each of the ACT cars, and get out of the neighborhood. The same thing, the same sort of thing, will be going on here in the 5000 block of Saul Street. Two ACT cars, a sergeant, and a Homicide detective will pick up Kenneth H. Dorne, also known as 'King' Dorne, also known as Hussein Something. When they have *him,* the sergeant will call for the wagon. When both of these guys are in the van, they'll be taken to Homicide. Got it?"

"Yeah," Mickey said thoughtfully.

"So there's no problem, Mickey," Lieutenant Suffern finished. "I'll put you and Payne in my car. We'll go into the alley behind Stevens's house, from the other direction. I'll let you two out, and I'll go in with the sergeant when he takes the back door. When you see us coming out, you can make your pictures. Okay?"

"Can you give me a list of the names?" O'Hara asked. "I really hate to spell people's names wrong. And point them out to me, so I know who's who?"

"Absolutely," Suffern said.

Lieutenant Suffern, Officer Payne thought, *is entertaining hopes that the next issue of the* Bulletin *will carry a photograph of Lieutenant Ed Suffern with the just arrested felon in his firm personal grip.*

"Payne," Lieutenant Suffern said, "if answering this puts you on a spot, don't answer it. Are we really going to move in here?" He waved in the general direction of the school building.

"I think so," Matt said. "I think the Board of Education wants to get rid of it."

"My mother went to school in there," Suffern said. "I thought they were going to tear it down."

"Okay," Inspector Peter Wohl's voice suddenly came over, with remarkable clarity, all the loudspeakers in all the vehicles in the playground. "Let's go do it."

There was the sound of starters grinding, and then an angry voice.

"I'm going to need a jump start here!"

Headlights came on, their beams reflecting off the still-falling snow.

Suffern opened the rear door of his car and waved Mickey O'Hara and Matt in. The hem of Matt's topcoat got caught in the door, and the door had to be reopened and then closed again.

The cars and vans began to roll out of the playground, onto Frankford Avenue. Most turned left, but some turned right. Matt looked at his watch. It was twenty minutes to five.

At ten minutes to five, they drove down Hawthorne Street. There were a number of cars, their roofs and windshields now coated with snow, parked on the street.

If this snow keeps up, Matt thought, *these cars are going to be buried.*

The headlights of a rusty and battered Chrysler flicked on and off quickly.

"That's the Homicide guy," Lieutenant Suffern said, and then added, "That wasn't too smart."

"Maybe he's just glad to see you," Mickey O'Hara said. "How long has he been there?"

"Probably since midnight," Suffern said. "When he tries to get out of the car, he'll probably be frozen stiff."

Suffern made the next right, turned his headlights off, and then turned right again into the alley and stopped.

Matt started to open the door.

"We got a couple of minutes," Suffern said, stopping him. "Better to stay in the car."

"Right," Matt said.

Said Officer Payne, the rookie, who don't know no better.

"I want to get out," O'Hara said. "If I just jump out of the car, my lens is likely to fog over."

"Okay, Mick," Suffern said obligingly. "But stick close to the walls, huh?"

O'Hara got out and Matt followed him, carefully closing the car's door. Suffern put the car in gear and inched away from them, stopping fifty yards farther down the alley.

It took Matt's eyes a minute to adjust to the darkness, but gradually the alley took shape. They were standing between two brick walls, but thirty feet away, the alley was lined with wooden fences. There was what looked like a derelict car parked against one wall, between them and Suffern's car. Matt wondered how Suffern had managed to get past it in the dark.

And then, as he looked at Mickey O'Hara, who was wiping the lens of his 35-mm camera with a handkerchief, the hair on the back of Matt's neck began to curl.

What the hell is the matter with me? Abu Ben Whatsisname is sound asleep in his bed. He won't know what hit him when those guys come crashing into his house. And I am a good hundred yards from where the action is going to be anyway.

But he pulled off his right glove, stuffed it into the pocket of his topcoat, and then quickly knelt and took his revolver from the ankle holster on the inside of his left leg. Hoping that Mickey O'Hara hadn't seen him, he quickly put it, and the hand that held it, into his topcoat pocket.

And then there was first a creaking, tearing noise, like a board being split, somewhere down the alley, and then the sound of crunching snow.

A moment later he saw something moving.

It has to be a cat, or a dog, or something—

Then he realized that what was coming down the alley toward them was too large to be a dog.

Everything shifted into slow motion.

"Stop!" Matt heard himself say. He had trouble finding his voice. "Police officer—"

"Out of my way, motherfucker!" an intensely angry voice called.

There followed a series of orange flashes, accompanied by sharp cracks.

"Jesus, Mary, and Joseph!" Mickey O'Hara said softly.

Matt was slapped in the face and then, a half second later, with terrifying force, in his right calf. He felt himself falling hard against the brick wall to his side.

As a voice from the recesses of his brain told him, *Hold it in both hands,* he pulled his revolver from his topcoat pocket. He got it free and up as he slid to the ground.

There was no way to hold the pistol with both hands. He fired instinctively. And then again. And a third time.

There was a grunt from the vague figure coming down the alley, and then the figure stood erect. Matt fired again. The figure took two more steps, and then fell forward.

Matt tried to get on his feet by pushing himself up the wall, but his hands slipped and his leg seemed unstable. He got on all fours, and somehow, that way, managed to get on his feet.

Now holding the pistol in both hands, Matt moved unsteadily toward the fallen figure.

You only have one cartridge left! Don't fuck this up!

The man on the ground was writhing in pain. Matt saw his pistol—*a semiautomatic, probably a Colt .45*—on the ground, half buried in snow. The man made no move for it. Matt hobbled to it and put his foot on it and nearly fell down.

There was a white flash, and he turned quickly toward it, pistol extended.

It was Mickey O'Hara's goddamn camera!

"Easy, kid!" Mickey said, fear in his voice.

Matt aimed the pistol at the man on the ground.

A moment later the camera flash went off again.

"Fuck you, O'Hara!" Matt heard himself shout furiously.

Now there were lights, all kinds of lights, headlights, flashing red and blue lights, portable floodlights.

He looked down the alley and saw an RPC squeeze past Lieutenant Suffern's car, and then, in his headlights, Suffern, his pistol drawn, running down the alley.

Suffern hoisted the skirt of his coat and holstered his pistol and came out with handcuffs. He put his knee in the back of the man on the ground and grabbed his arm to handcuff him.

The man screamed in pain.

The Special Operations car slid to a stop and two cops jumped out.

Suffern came to Matt, said, "Jesus!" and touched his face.

"You can put your pistol away, Payne," Suffern said, and then raised his hand and gently forced Matt's arm down.

Matt looked at him. He saw something sticky on Suffern's fingers, and then touched his face. His fingers, too, came away bloody.

He squatted to feel his calf, and fell down.

Suffern ran to the RPC, slid behind the wheel, and found the microphone.

"This is Suffern, get the van here, now!" he called, then: "This is Team A Supervisor. We have had a shooting. We have an officer down. We have a suspect down."

Matt, at the moment he was aware he was lying facedown in the snow, felt hands on his shoulders. He felt himself being first rolled over, and then being held up in a slumping position.

He put his hands to his eyes, and wiped away the bloody slush over them. He could see one of the Special Operations cops looking down at him with concern in his eyes.

"You all right?"

"Shit!"

He heard the wail of a siren in the distance, and then other sirens.

"Suffern, where are you?" Wohl's voice came over the radio.

"In the alley behind the scene."

"Who's down?"

"Payne and the suspect."

"On my way."

Matt saw Suffern's face now, close to his.

"Just take it easy, the van's on the way. We'll have you in a hospital in two minutes."

Mickey O'Hara's flashgun went off again.

"Get that fucking camera out of here, Mickey!" Suffern said angrily.

"You all right, Matt?" O'Hara asked.

"I'm shot, for Christ's sake!"

There was the sound of squealing brakes, of clashing gears, and tires slipping on the ice and snow.

Matt looked over his shoulder and saw a van backing into the alley.

"Here's the van," Suffern said, quite unnecessarily.

Matt felt something scrubbing at his face. When his vision cleared, he saw the cop who had rolled him over throwing a bloody handkerchief away and being handed another. He put the fresh handkerchief to Matt's forehead.

"Can you hold that?" he asked.

Matt put his hand to it.

Two more cops appeared, carrying a stretcher.

"Get me to my feet," Matt said. "I don't need that."

They ignored him. He felt himself being unceremoniously picked up and then dumped onto the stretcher. Then he was lifted up and carried to the van. The feet of the stretcher screeched as it was pushed inside.

"Where do you think you're going, Mickey?" someone asked.

"Where does it look like?" O'Hara replied, and then he was sitting on the floor of the van beside Matt.

And then something else was thrown in the van. Matt looked and saw that it was the man he had shot. He was unconscious.

Two uniformed cops, neither of whom Matt recognized, scrambled inside. The van's rear doors slammed closed, and then a moment later, there was the sound of the front doors slamming. The engine raced and the siren began to wail again.

"Is he dead?" Matt asked.

"I don't know," Mickey replied, and then matter-of-factly turned and put his fingers to the unconscious man's jugular. "Not yet, anyway," he added.

"Look at my leg," Matt said.

"What's wrong with your leg?"

"You tell me."

He propped himself up, awkwardly, and watched as Mickey pulled his trouser leg up.

"Looks like you got it there too," Mickey said. "Not much blood. It hurt?"

"No, not much," Matt said. "It feels like I got hit with a rock or something."

"There's only one hole," Mickey said. "The bullet's probably still in there. I don't think anything is broken."

When Matt let himself fall back on the stretcher, he saw that the man he had shot was bleeding from the nose and mouth. There was a froth of bloody bubbles on his lips. Matt looked away, wondering if he was going to be sick to his stomach.

Matt suddenly started to shiver. Mickey looked around the interior of the van.

"Hand me one of those blankets," he ordered.

A gray, dirt-spotted blanket appeared, and O'Hara draped it over him.

"Throw one on him too," Matt Payne ordered.

Two minutes or so later the van leaned on its springs as it made a turn, then bounced over a curb. It stopped and the doors were jerked open.

Three men in hospital whites and a nurse with a purple, sequin-decorated sweater thrown over the shoulders of her whites peered into the van. One of the men grabbed the handles of the stretcher and Matt felt himself sliding down the van's floor.

Once the stretcher was out of the van, he felt himself being moved, and then he realized he had been transferred to a gurney; he could feel the cold plastic beneath the thin sheet on his stomach.

"Get the handcuffs off him!" he heard his nurse order angrily. "He's unconscious, for Christ's sake!"

Matt's gurney began to move into the hospital. There were two sets of doors. The gurney slammed into the outer set, and then the inner set.

"Out of the way!" the nurse's voice called, and Matt's gurney was moved to the wall, where it stopped. He saw a second gurney being pushed, at a trot, by two of the attendants, down the corridor.

And then Staff Inspector Peter Wohl's face appeared next to his.

"How are you doing?"

"I'm all right," Matt said.

Why the hell did I say that?

"They'll take care of you in a minute."

"Why not now?"

"Because the guy you shot is in a lot worse shape than you are," Wohl said matter-of-factly.

"Is he going to live?"

"I don't think they know yet."

"Shit, my car!"

"What about your car?"

"It's in the playground. With the keys in it."

"I'll take care of it," Wohl said. "Don't worry about it."

"I think I'm going to be sick to my stomach."

All of a sudden, Matt found himself looking at Peter Wohl's stomach.

He must have had to squat to get down to me.

"Get me a towel or a bucket or something," Wohl ordered.

Matt rolled on his side, and then completely over, onto his back.

That's better. Now I won't have to throw up.

He propped himself up on his elbows, and then the nausea came so quickly he barely had time to get his head over the edge of the gurney.

He now felt faint, and his leg began to throb.

The gurney began to move. He looked up and back and saw that he was being towed by a very tall, six feet six or better, very thin black man in hospital greens.

He was pulled into a cubicle walled by white plastic curtains.

A new face appeared in his. Another black one.

"I'm Dr. Hampton. How you doing?"

"Just fine, thank you."

Dr. Hampton removed the handkerchief, jerking it quickly off, and painfully prodded Matt's forehead.

"Nothing serious," he said. "It will have to be sutured, but that can wait."

"What about my leg?"

"I'll have a look," Dr. Hampton said, and then ordered: "Get an IV in him."

Somebody got him into a sitting position and he felt his topcoat and jacket being removed, and then his shirt.

"I'm cold."

He was ignored.

He felt a blood pressure apparatus being strapped around his left arm, and then his right arm was held firmly immobile as a nurse searched for and found a vein.

"Nothing broken. There's no exit wound. There's a bullet in there somewhere. Prep him and send him up to Sixteen."

"Yes, Doctor," the nurse said.

Peter Wohl watched as the gurney with Matt on it was wheeled out of the Emergency treatment cubicle, and then ran after the doctor he had seen go into the cubicle.

"Tell me about the man you just had in there," he said.

"Who are you?" Dr. Hampton asked.

"I'm Inspector Wohl."

"You don't look much like a cop, Inspector."

"What do you want to do, see my badge?"

"No. Take it easy. I suppose I said that because I was just thinking he doesn't either. Look like a cop, I mean."

"Actually," Wohl said, "he's a pretty good cop. How badly is he injured?"

"A good deal less seriously than most people I see who have been shot with a large-caliber weapon," Dr. Hampton said, and then went on to explain his diagnosis and prognosis.

Wohl thanked him, and then went to one of the pay phones mounted on the wall between the outer and inner doors of the Emergency entrance and took first a dime from his pocket and then his wallet. Inside the wallet was a typewritten list of telephone numbers, on both sides of a sheet of paper cut to the size of a credit card, and then coated with Scotch tape to preserve it.

He dropped a dime in the slot and then dialed one of the numbers. There was an answer, surprisingly wide awake, on the third ring: "Coughlin."

"Chief, this is Peter Wohl."

"What's up, Peter?"

"Matt Payne has been shot."

There was a just perceptible pause.

"Bad?"

"He's got a .45 bullet in his calf. It apparently was a ricochet off a brick wall. And his face was hit, the forehead, probably by a piece of bullet jacket. It slit the skin. Not serious, take a couple of stitches."

"But the bullet in the leg *is* serious?"

"There's not much damage. I don't know for sure what I'm talking about, but what I think happened was that the bullet hit the wall, a brick wall, and lost most of its momentum, and then hit him. It's still in him. They just took him into the operating room."

"Where is he?"

"Frankford Hospital."

"What the hell happened, Peter?"

I have just become the guy who is responsible for getting Denny Coughlin's godson, the son he never had, shot.

"At five o'clock this morning, we picked up the doers of the Goldblatt job."

" 'We' presumably meaning Highway," Coughlin said coldly. "I didn't know that Matt was in Highway. When did that happen?"

"ACT Teams from Special Operations, working with Homicide, made the arrests. Simultaneously—"

"Not Highway?"

"No, sir. Not Highway."

"Go on, Peter."

"Mickey O'Hara was there. I invited him. I sent Matt with him to make sure Mickey didn't get in the way, get himself hurt. One of the doers, a scumbag named Charles D. Stevens, apparently saw either the cars, or more likely the Homicide guy sitting on him, and then the cars. As the ACT cars were getting in place, he—this is conjecture, Chief, but I think this is it—made his way to either the next house, or the house next to that, and tried to get away through the alley. O'Hara and Matt were at the head of the alley. He—Stevens—started shooting. And got Matt."

"Did you get Stevens?"

"Matt got Stevens. He shot at him four times and hit him twice. Once in the arm, and once in the liver. Stevens was brought here. I have the feeling he's not going to live."

"But Matt is in no danger?"

"No, sir. I don't even think there is going to be much muscle damage. As I said, I think the bullet lost much of its momentum—"

"That's nice," Coughlin said.

"He's more worried about his car than anything else, Chief."

"What about his car?"

"We formed up in the playground of the school at Castor and Frankford. Matt went to the scene with Lieutenant Suffern. And left his car, with the keys in it, in the playground."

"You're taking care of it, I suppose?"

"Yes, sir."

"Have you called the commissioner?"

"No, sir. Chief Lowenstein is doing that."

"Lowenstein was there?"

"No, sir. But he heard about it, and told me he would take care of calling the commissioner."

"Is the Department going to look bad in this, Peter?"

"No, sir. I don't see how. The other seven arrests went very smoothly. They're all down at 8th and Race already. As soon as I get off the phone, I'm going down there."

"Have you notified Matt's family?"

"No, sir. I thought I should call you before I did that."

"Well, at least your brain wasn't entirely disengaged," Coughlin said. And then, immediately, "Sorry, Peter. I shouldn't have said that."

"Forget it, Chief. I don't think I have to tell you how bad I feel about this. And I know how you feel about Matt."

"I've been on the job twenty-seven years and I've never been hurt," Coughlin said. "Matt's father gets killed. His uncle Dutch gets killed, and now he damned near does."

"I thought about that too, Chief."

"I'll take care of notifying his family," Coughlin said. "You make sure nobody else gets carried away with procedure and tries to."

"I've already done that, Chief."

"You're sure he's going to be all right?"

"Yes, sir."

"Keep yourself available, Peter. You say you're going to be at Homicide?"

"Yes, sir. Mr. Stillwell asked me to be there."

"Farnsworth Stillwell?"

"Yes, sir."

"When you can break loose, it might be a good idea to go back to the hospital; to have a word with Matt's family."

"Yes, sir, I'd planned to do that."

"Well, don't blame yourself for this, Peter. These things happen."

"Yes, sir."

Coughlin, without another word, hung up. He swung his feet out of bed, pulled open the drawer of a bedside table, and took out a telephone book. He dialed a number.

"Police Department."

"Let me speak to the senior officer on duty."

"Maybe I can help you."

"This is Chief Inspector Dennis V. Coughlin. Get the senior police officer present on the telephone!"

"This is Lieutenant Swann. Can I help you?"

"This is Chief Inspector Dennis V. Coughlin—"

"Oh, sure. How are you, Chief?"

"I need a favor."

"Name it."

"You know where the Payne house is on Providence Road in Wallingford?"

"Sure."

"Their son is a police officer. He has just been shot in the line of duty. He is in Frankford Hospital. I am about to notify them. I would consider it a personal favor if you would provide an escort for them from their home to the Philadelphia city line. I'll have a car meet you there."

"Chief, when the Paynes come out of their driveway, a car will be sitting there."

"Thank you."

"He hurt bad?"

"We don't think so."

"Thank God."

"Thank God," Denny Coughlin repeated, and, unable to trust his voice any further, hung up.

He walked into the kitchen, poured an inch and a half of John Jameson's Irish whiskey in a plastic cup, drank it down, and then reached for the telephone on the wall. He dialed a number from memory. It took a long time to answer.

Please, God, don't let Patty answer.

"Hello?"

"Brewster, this is Denny Coughlin."

"Is something wrong, Denny?" Brewster Cortland Payne, suddenly wide awake, asked.

"What is it?" a familiar female voice came faintly over the telephone.

"Matt's got himself shot," Denny Coughlin said very quickly. "Not seriously. He's in Frankford Hospital. By the time you get dressed, there will be a police car waiting in your driveway to escort you to the hospital. I'll meet you there."

"All right."

"My God, I'm sorry, Brewster."

"Yes, I know. We'll see you there, Denny."

The phone went dead.

Coughlin broke the connection with his finger and then dialed another number from memory.

"Highway."

"This is Chief Coughlin."

"Yes, sir."

"I have cleared this with Inspector Wohl. A Media police car is about to escort a car to the city line. I want a Highway car to meet it and take it the rest of the way to Frankford Hospital. Got that?"

"Yes, sir."

"Thank you," Coughlin said, and hung up. Then he went into his bedroom and started to get dressed. As he was tying his shoes, he suddenly looked up, at the crucifix hanging over his bed.

"It could be worse. Thank you," he said.

14.

Shortly after Mr. Michael J. O'Hara appeared in the city room of the Philadelphia *Bulletin* at a little after six A.M., the *Bulletin*'s city and managing editors decided that since they had an exclusive (the term "scoop" is considered déclassé by modern journalists) in Mr. O'Hara's coverage of the shooting during the arrest of the Islamic Liberation Army, together with some really great pictures, it clearly behooved them to run with it.

The front pages of Sections A and B were redone. On Page 1A, a photograph of the President of the United States shaking hands with some foreign dignitary in flowing robes was replaced with a photograph of the cop bleeding all over himself as he held his gun on the guy who had shot him. Under it was the caption:

> Special Operations Officer Matthew M. Payne, blood streaming from his wounds, holds his pistol on Charles D. Stevens, whom he had just bested in an early morning gun battle in Frankford. Stevens was one of eight men, alleged to be participants in the murder-robbery on Goldblatt's furniture store, whom police rounded up at dawn. Payne collapsed moments after this photo was taken. Full details on Page 1B. [Bulletin Photograph by Michael J. O'Hara.]

Most of Page 1B was redone. When finished it had three photographs lining the top, and a headline reading, EXCLUSIVE BULLETIN COVERAGE OF EARLY MORNING SHOOTOUT.

Below the photographs—which showed Matt Payne being held up by the ACT cop; Charles D. Stevens being rolled into Frankford Hospital on a gurney; and Matt Payne, his face caked with blood, on his gurney in the corridor at Frankford Hospital—was the story:

> By Michael J. O'Hara
> Bulletin Staff Writer
>
> Blood stained the freshly fallen snow in an alley in Frankford early this morning after Charles D. Stevens chose to shoot it out with the cops rather than submit to arrest and picked the wrong cop for his deadly duel.
>
> Stevens, who sometimes calls himself Abu Ben Mohammed, is one of eight suspects in the murder-robbery of Goldblatt's Furniture earlier this week. It was the intention of Staff Inspector Peter Wohl, commanding the Special Operations Division, to arrest all eight suspects at once, and in the wee hours, to minimize risks to both the public and his officers.

Seven of the eight carefully orchestrated arrests went smoothly. But, as this reporter and Officer Matthew M. Payne, administrative assistant to Inspector Wohl, waited in a dark alley behind Stevens's house in the 4700 block of Hawthorne Street for the meticulously planned arrest procedure to begin, Stevens suddenly appeared in the alley, a blazing .45 automatic in his hand.

As this reporter dove for cover, two of Stevens's bullets struck Payne, who had been assigned to escort this reporter during Stevens's arrest. Payne went down, but he was not out. Somehow, Payne managed to get his own pistol into action. When the shooting was over, Stevens was critically, possibly fatally, wounded, and the young cop he had tried to gun down without warning was standing over him, blood dripping from his own wounds.

This was not the first battle for his life fought by Payne, who is twenty-two and a bachelor. Three months ago, while attempting to arrest Warren K. Fletcher, the Northwest Philadelphia serial rapist, Fletcher, who had his latest victim in his van, tried to run over the young policeman. Moments later he was dead of a bullet in the brain fired by the then six-months-on-the-police-force rookie.

Payne, who collapsed moments after making sure Stevens posed no further threat, was taken to Frankford Hospital, where he underwent surgery for the removal of the bullet in his leg. His condition is described as "good."

Stevens, who was also rushed to Frankford Hospital by police, is in intensive care, his condition described as "critical" by hospital authorities.

Chief Inspector Matt Lowenstein, who commands the Detective Division, under whose overall command the mass arrest took place, said that Stevens, if he lives, will have assault with a deadly weapon and resisting arrest added to the other charges, which include first-degree murder, already lodged against him.

"I regret that force was necessary," Chief Lowenstein said. "Inspector Wohl and his men took every step they could think of to avoid it. But I cannot conceal my admiration for this young officer (Payne) who bravely stood up to this vicious criminal."

By 6:45 A.M., the appropriate plates had been replaced on the presses, and with a deep growl, they began to roll again.

It was the opinion of the managing editor that they could probably sell an additional thirty-five or forty thousand copies of the paper. Blood and shooting always sold.

How that goddamn O'Hara manages to always be in on things like this is a mystery, but giving the sonofabitch his due, he always is, and he probably is worth all the money we have to pay him.

Hector Carlos Estivez was in the first of the vans carrying the prisoners to arrive at the Police Administration Building at 8th and Race Streets in downtown Philadelphia. The others arrived over the next fifteen minutes.

The van carrying Mr. Estivez entered the parking lot at the rear of the Roundhouse, and immediately backed up down the ramp leading to the Central Cell Room.

The driver and his partner got out and went to the rear of the van. They found Homicide detective Joe D'Amata, who had driven in his own car from Frankford, waiting for them. The driver opened the rear door of the van and Mr. Estivez, who had been handcuffed, was helped out of the van.

Detective D'Amata took one of Mr. Estivez's arms, and one of the officers who had been in the back of the van with him took the other.

Mr. Estivez was then led through the Cell Room to an elevator, and taken in it to the Homicide Bureau on the third floor.

There were several people standing just outside the office of Captain Henry C. Quaire, commanding officer of the Homicide Bureau. Mr. Estivez recognized only one of them, Sergeant Jason Washington. The others were Farnsworth Stillwell, an assistant district attorney of Philadelphia County; Staff Inspector Peter Wohl; and Captain Quaire himself.

Mr. Estivez was taken to a small room furnished with an Early American–style chair and a small table. There was a window with one-way glass in one wall of the room. The chair was made of steel and was bolted to the floor. One end of a pair of handcuffs was looped through a hole in the chair seat.

Mr. Estivez's handcuffs were removed. Detective D'Amata told him to sit down and, when he had done so, put Mr. Estivez's left wrist in the handcuff cuffed to the chair.

Mr. Estivez was then left alone.

He looked with a mixture of contempt and uneasiness at the one-way glass window. There was no way of telling if someone was on the other side, looking in at him.

A minute or so later the door to the room opened, and Detective D'Amata returned. On his heels came Sergeant Jason Washington, Staff Inspector Wohl, and Assistant District Attorney Stillwell.

"Which one is this one?" Sergeant Washington inquired.

"This is Mr. Hector Carlos Estivez," Detective D'Amata replied.

Sergeant Washington, a carefully calculated (and in fact, once practiced before a mirror) look of contempt, scorn, and dislike on his face, then took two steps toward Mr. Estivez. Mr. Estivez, who was sitting, had to look up at him. There was no way that Mr. Estivez could not be aware of Washington's considerable bulk.

Sergeant Washington then squatted down, so that his face was on a level with Mr. Estivez, and examined him carefully for twenty seconds or so.

He then grunted, stood erect, said, "Okay, Hector Carlos *Estivez*. Fine," and scribbled something in his notebook.

This was a little psychological warfare, Jason Washington having long ago come to believe that the greatest fear is the fear of the unknown.

Washington knew he enjoyed a certain fame (perhaps notoriety) in the criminal community. There was a perhaps fifty-fifty chance that Estivez knew who he was. And even if he didn't, Washington was sure that the sight of a very large, very well-dressed black man in an obvious position of police authority would be unnerving.

Jason Washington then covered his mouth with his hand and said softly, so that Mr. Estivez could not understand him, "Obviously a pillar of his community, wouldn't you say?"

The remark caused Wohl to smile, which was Washington's intention. He had long ago also come to believe that knowing that one is the source of amusement, but not knowing specifically how, is also psychologically disturbing, particularly if the person amused holds great—if undefined—power over you.

At that point, Inspector Wohl, Assistant District Attorney Stillwell, and Sergeant Washington left the interview room, closing the door behind them and leaving Detective D'Amata alone with Mr. Estivez.

"Mr. Estivez," Detective D'Amata said, "you have been arrested on warrants charging you with murder and armed robbery. Before I say anything else, I want to make sure that you are aware of your rights under the Constitution."

He then took a small card from his jacket pocket and read Mr. Estivez his rights under the Miranda Decision. Mr. Estivez had seen them enough on television to know them by heart, but he listened attentively anyway.

"Do you understand the rights I have pointed out to you?" Detective D'Amata said.

"Yeah," Mr. Estivez said. "I'm not going to say one fucking word without my lawyer."

"That is your right, sir," Detective D'Amata said.

He then left Mr. Estivez alone in the interview room again.

"Mr. Estivez," Detective D'Amata said dryly to Mssrs. Washington, Wohl, and Stillwell, "has elected to exercise his rights under the Miranda Decision."

"Really?" Wohl replied with a smile.

"So what happens now?" Farnsworth Stillwell asked. "We're not going to run into trouble with the Six-Hour Rule, are we?"

The Pennsylvania Supreme Court had issued another ruling designed to protect the innocent from the police. It had decreed that unless an accused was brought before an arraignment judge within six hours of his arrest, any statement he had made could not be used against him.

"Correct me if I'm wrong, Counselor," Jason Washington said with more than a hint of sarcasm in his voice, "but as I understand the Six-Hour Rule, it does not prohibit the use of a statement inadmissible against the individual who made it being used against other participants in the offense."

"Yes, of course, you're right," Stillwell said. It was obvious he did not like being lectured on the law.

"We'll take him back downstairs, process him, and send him over to the House of Detention," D'Amata replied.

"What I'm going to do, Inspector, unless you have something else in mind," Jason Washington announced, "is give them all day to thoughtfully consider their situation, and maybe get a little sound advice from the legal profession. Then, after they have had their supper, and are convinced that nothing further is going to happen to them today, starting at six-fifteen, I'm going to run them all through the lineup, for a positive identification by Mr. Monahan. Then I will give them the rest of the night to consider their situation, now that they know we have a witness, and then starting at eight tomorrow morning, I will interview them."

"Have at it, Jason," Wohl said.

"By then, I think we can count on somebody going to Mr. Stillwell to make a deal," Washington said. "There's seven of them. I think the odds are pretty good that at least one of them will try to save his skin."

Farnsworth Stillwell, whose wordless role in the little playlet had been orchestrated by Sergeant Washington, had played along for several reasons. For one thing, he had never seen how something like this was actually carried out, and he was curious. For another, when he had worked with Wohl during the investigation and prosecution of Judge Findermann, he had come to understand that Wohl was anything but a fool, and it logically followed from that that if Wohl was willing to play along with Washington, there was probably a good reason for it.

Secondly, the one bit of specific advice he had been given by District Attorney Thomas J. Callis had concerned Jason Washington.

"Not only does he know how to deal with, in order words, read, this kind of scum, but he has forgotten more about criminal law than you know. So don't make the mistake of trying to tell him how to do his job. I can't imagine Washington doing anything dumb, but if he does, Wohl will catch him at it, and he will take 'suggestions' from Wohl. Understand?"

The idea of getting one or more of the seven to testify against the others to save himself had a positive appeal. The State had only Monahan as a witness, which was rather frightening to consider. If this case went down the toilet, he would have egg all over his face. People with egg on their faces only rarely ever get to become the governor.

Kenneth H. Dorne, aka "King," aka Hussein El Baruca, in handcuffs, a uniformed police officer on each arm, was led into Homicide and taken into a second, identical interview room and cuffed to the steel chair.

"Here we go again," D'Amata said. "Anyone want to bet that this one will announce that he has been thinking of his aged mother and wants to make a clean breast of the whole thing?"

D'Amata, Wohl, and Washington waited until Mr. Estivez had been uncuffed from his steel chair, cuffed behind his back, and led out of Homicide before going into the second interview room. Stillwell followed them.

The only thing that bothered him was how long this process was taking. He had sched-

uled a press conference to announce the arrest of these people, and the determination
of Assistant District Attorney Farnsworth Stillwell to prosecute them to the full extent of
the law, for nine o'clock, and two things bothered him about that: Should he take Wohl
and Washington with him, or, more accurately, *ask* them, one of them, or both, to come
along?

*Having Washington in the picture—literally the picture, there were sure to be photog-
raphers—might be valuable, vis-à-vis the Afro-American voters, somewhere down the
pike. Wohl, however, was a little too attractive, well dressed, well spoken, and with a
reputation. The goddamn press was likely to be as interested, even more interested, in
what he had to say than they would be in Farnsworth Stillwell.*

*And finally, is there going to be time to get from here to my office in time to meet the
press?*

The little playlet was run again, and a few minutes later, Wohl, Washington, and Stillwell were standing outside Captain Quaire's office again.

"I don't want to bubble over with enthusiasm," Washington said. "But I have a feeling
that Mr. Dorne may decide that being a religious martyr is not really his bag."

Detective D'Amata came out of the interview room, and announced, surprising no one,
that Kenneth H. Dorne, aka "King," aka Hussein El Baruca, had also elected to avail
himself of his right to legal counsel before deciding whether or not he would answer any
questions.

"What about him, Joe?" Washington said.

"You picked up on that too, huh, Jason?" D'Amata replied. "Yeah. Maybe. Maybe
after the lineup. I wouldn't bet on it."

"I'm tempted to," Stillwell said. "Sergeant Washington's insight into things like that is
legendary."

The flattery, he decided, after looking at Washington's face, *had not gone wide of
the mark.*

"If you and Inspector Wohl could find the time," he went on, having made that decision, "I'd like you to come help me deal with the press. I asked the ladies and gentlemen
of the press to be at the office at nine."

"I'll beg off, thank you just the same," Washington said. "I want a good look at the
others."

"Peter?"

"No, thank you. I live by the rule never to talk to the press unless I have to. And
anyway, I want to go back to Frankford Hospital. The officer who was shot works for me."

"I'm going up there too," Washington said. "When I'm finished here."

"Tragic, tragic," Stillwell said. "Thank God, he's alive."

"Yes," Washington said.

"Would you call my office, Sergeant, when you're finished? I'd really like to hear your
assessment of these people."

"Certainly."

Farnsworth Stillwell offered Wohl and Washington his hand.

"Thank you very much for letting me share this with you," he said. "It's been a—an
education. I've never been in here before."

"This is where it happens, Mr. Stillwell," Washington said.

Stillwell rode the elevator down to the main lobby and started for the parking lot, but as
he reached the door, he had a second thought, one he immediately recognized to be a first-
rate idea.

He turned and went to the desk, asked permission of the sergeant to use the telephone,
and dialed his office number.

"When the press arrives," he ordered. "Give them my apologies, and tell them I have
gone to Frankford Hospital to visit the police officer who was shot this morning. I feel I

have that duty. Tell them that too. And tell them if they come to the hospital, I'll meet with them there."

When he hung up, he had another idea, even better, and pulled the telephone to him again and dialed his home.

"Darling," he said when his wife answered, "I'm glad I caught you. Something has come up. I'm going to Frankford Hospital, to visit with the cop who got himself shot this morning—"

"What are you talking about?"

"—I'll tell you all about it in the car. I want you there with me. The press will be there."

There was twenty seconds of silence.

"Darling, this is important to me," he said firmly. "I'll be waiting outside for you in fifteen minutes."

He hung up thinking, somewhat petulantly, *If she really wants to be the governor's wife, she damned well had better learn that there is no free lunch, that certain things are going to be required of her.*

"Mother," Officer Matt Payne said, "why don't you get out of here? I'm all right, and there's nothing you can do for me here."

Patricia and Brewster C. Payne had been in the Recovery Room when Matt was taken there from the surgical suite. It was strictly against hospital policy, but the chairman of the board of trustees of Frankford Hospital entrusted his legal affairs to Mawson, Payne, Stockton, McAdoo & Lester. A telephone call to him had resulted not only in a telephone call to the senior staff physician, but the physical presence of that gentleman himself, three minutes later, to make sure that whatever Brewster Payne thought the hospital should do for his son was being done.

Aside from access to the Recovery Room, the only request Brewster Payne had made was that Matt be given a private room, something the senior staff physician had already decided to provide to spare some other patient from the horde of people who had come to the hospital to see Matt Payne.

The mayor, the police commissioner, two chief inspectors, and their respective entourages, plus a number of less senior police officers, plus representatives of the print and electronic media had begun to descend on the hospital at about the same time screaming sirens on two Highway Patrol cars had announced the arrival of the Payne family.

While the press could be required to wait in the main lobby, the others immediately made it plain they would wait right where they were, overflowing the small waiting room on the surgical floor, until Officer Payne was out of surgery and his condition known.

And when that had come to pass—the removal of a bullet from the calf musculature was a fairly simple procedure, routinely handled by surgical residents half a dozen times on any given weekend—and Young Payne was taken to the Recovery Room, the Hospital Security Staff was unable to deter the mayor's driver from carrying out his assigned mission—"Go down and bring the press up here. They'll want a picture of me with Payne when he wakes up."

The senior staff physician was able to delay the picture taking until the staff had put Young Payne in a private room, and after the mayor had taken the necessary steps to keep the public aware that their mayor, in his never-ceasing efforts to rid the streets of Philadelphia of crime, was never far from the action, he left, and so did perhaps half of the people who had arrived at about the time he had.

"You'll need pajamas," Patricia Payne said to her son. "And your toilet things—"

"I won't be in here long," Matt said.

"You don't know that," Patricia Payne said, and looked at her daughter, Amelia.

"I don't know how long they're going to keep him, Mother," she replied. "But I'll find out. I'll call you at home and let you know. And I'll go by his apartment and get him what he needs. I have to come back out here anyway. You and Dad go on home."

"I suppose he should rest," Patricia Payne gave in. She leaned over her son and kissed him. "Do what they tell you to do, for once."

"Yes, ma'am," Matt said.

"If you need anything, Matt," Brewster Payne said, "I'm as close as that phone."

"Thank you, Dad. I don't think I'll need anything."

"I'll call as soon as I have a chance to go home, change, and get to the office."

"Go on, you two, get out of here," Amelia Payne said.

They left.

"Thank you," Matt said when the door had closed.

"Don't look so pleased with yourself, you sonofabitch," Amy Payne snapped. "I did that for them, not you."

"Wow!"

"You *bastard!* Are you trying to drive Mother crazy, or what?" She dipped into an extra-large purse, came out with a copy of the *Bulletin,* and threw it at him. "I hope she doesn't see that!"

The front page showed Matt, bloody-faced, holding his gun on Charles D. Stevens.

"Hey, I didn't do this on purpose. That bastard was shooting at me."

"That bastard died thirty minutes ago. You can carve another notch on your gun, Jesse James."

"He died?" Matt asked, wanting confirmation.

"I didn't think Mother needed to know that."

She looked at him. Their eyes met.

"How do you feel about that?" she asked.

"I'm not about to wallow in remorse, if that's what you're hoping. He was trying to kill me."

"And almost did. Do you have any idea how lucky you are? Have you ever seen what a .45-caliber bullet does to tissue?"

"I just found out."

"No, you didn't. The bullet that hit you had lost most of its energy bouncing off a wall."

"Amy, I wasn't trying to be a hero. This just happened. I can't understand why you're sore at me."

"Because, you *ass,* of what you're doing to Mother. When are you going to come to your senses, for her sake, if nothing else?"

Matt was not given time to form a reply. The door opened, and a nurse put her head in.

"Are you a family member?"

"I'm Dr. Payne," Amy replied, not at all pleasantly. "What do you want?"

"Mr. Payne's grandmother and aunt are here, Doctor. They'd like to see him."

"Let them come in, I'm leaving."

The nurse pushed the door open. A stout, somewhat florid-faced woman in her sixties, her gray hair done up in a bun, followed by a blond woman in her late thirties, came into the room.

"Hello, Mother Moffitt," Amy Payne said. "Jeannie."

"Hello, Amy," the younger woman replied.

The older woman flashed Amy a cold look, nodded, and said, "Miss Payne."

"It's *Dr.* Payne, Mrs. Moffitt," Amy said, and walked out of the room.

"Hello, Grandma," Matt said.

"Your grandfather, your father, and your uncle Richard would be proud of you, darling," Gertrude Moffitt said emotionally, walking to the bed and grasping his hand.

"Hello, Aunt Jeannie," Matt said.

"I'm just sorry you didn't kill the man who did this to you," Mother Moffitt said.

"I apparently did," Matt said. "They told me he died half an hour ago."

"Then I hope he burns in hell."

"Mother Moffitt!" Jeannie Moffitt protested. "For God's sake."

"I have lost two sons to the scum of this city. I have no compassion in my heart for them, and neither should you."

"I'm just grateful Matt's not more seriously injured," Jeannie said.

"Chief Coughlin called and told me," Mother Moffitt said. "Your mother apparently couldn't be bothered."

"She was upset, for God's sake!" Jeannie Moffitt protested. "You, of all people, should understand that."

"No matter what trials and pain God has sent me, I take pride in always having done my duty."

Jeannie Moffitt shook her head, and she and Matt exchanged a smile.

"So, how are you, Matty?" she asked.

"Aside from that, Mrs. Lincoln, how was the play?"

Jeannie Moffitt laughed.

"What was that? I don't understand that," Mother Moffitt said.

"A little joke, Grandma," Matt said.

The nurse stuck her head through the door again.

"I'm afraid you'll have to leave now," she said.

"I just got here," Mother Moffitt said indignantly.

"Doctor's orders," the nurse said, and walked to the side of Matt's bed. "Mr. Payne needs rest."

"*Officer Payne,* thank you," Mother Moffitt said.

"Do you need anything, Matty?" Jeannie asked.

"Not a thing, thank you."

"I'll come back, of course, if Jeannie can find the time to bring me," Mother Moffitt said.

"Of course I will. You know that."

"It's a terrible thing when the only time I get to see him is in a hospital bed with a bullet in him," Mother Moffitt said.

She bent and kissed his cheek and marched out of the room. The nurse went to the door and turned and smiled.

"Dr. Payne said to tell you, you owe her one," she said.

"Thank both of you," Matt said.

"There's some other people out here to see you. You feel up to it?"

"Who?"

"A Highway Patrolman, some kind of a big-shot cop named Coughlin, and a man from the district's attorney's office. And his wife."

"The district attorney?"

"I think he said *assistant.* And his wife. I can run them off."

"No. I'm all right. Isn't this thing supposed to hurt?"

"It will. When it starts to hurt, ring for a nurse."

"I'm also hungry. Can I get something to eat?"

"I can probably arrange for something," she said. "So you want to see them?"

"Please."

Chief Inspector Dennis V. Coughlin, Officer Charles McFadden, and Assistant District Attorney and Mrs. Farnsworth Stillwell filed into the room.

"Hey, Charley," Matt said. "Uncle Denny."

"I'm Farnsworth Stillwell, Officer Payne," the assistant district attorney said, walking up to the bed with his hand extended, "and this is Mrs. Stillwell."

"How do you do?" Matt said politely. He had previously had the pleasure of making Mrs. Stillwell's acquaintance. He not only knew her Christian name, but a number of other intimate details about her.

Her name was Helene, and the last time he had seen her, she was putting her clothing back on in his apartment, to which they had gone from the Delaware Valley Cancer Society's cocktail party.

"Hello," Helene said. "I'm a little vague about the protocol here. Is it permitted to say I'm so sorry you've been shot?"

"This is my first time too," Matt said. "I'm a little fuzzy about the protocol myself."

She walked to the bed and offered him her hand.

"I'm sorry you've been shot."

"Thank you. So am I," Matt said.

"Are you all right?"

"Just fine."

"We're all sorry you've—this has happened," Farnsworth Stillwell said. "And I must tell you, I feel to some degree responsible."

"Nonsense," Denny Coughlin said. "No one is responsible except the man who pulled the trigger."

"I'm sorry we didn't bring you anything," Helene Stillwell said. "But I didn't know who you were, what you would be like, and at this time of the morning—"

"It was good of you to come," Matt said.

Helene finally took her hand back.

"We wanted you to know that we were concerned," Stillwell said, "concerned and grateful."

"I think we should let Officer Payne get some rest, darling," Helene said.

"There are some members of the press outside who would like to have our picture together," Farnsworth Stillwell said. "Would you feel up to that?"

Matt looked at Denny Coughlin, who shrugged and then nodded his head.

"Sure," Matt said.

A photographer came into the room. He asked if the bed could be cranked up, and when it had, he suggested that Mr. Stillwell get on one side of him, and Mrs. Stillwell on the other. When they had done so, he suggested that they get closer to Matt. "It feels a little awkward, but the picture comes out better."

When they had moved into the desired positions, they had to swap sides, so that Assistant District Attorney Stillwell and Officer Payne could shake hands. Mrs. Stillwell, in order to get closer, put her arm behind Officer Payne's shoulders, a position that pressed her breast against his arm, and for a moment allowed her fingers to caress the back of his neck.

And then the flashbulb went off, Farnsworth Stillwell told Officer Payne that if he needed anything, anything at all, all he had to do was let him know, and they were gone.

"I don't like that sonofabitch," Denny Coughlin said, "but I wouldn't be surprised if he really does get to be governor."

"Really?" Matt asked.

"So how are you, Matty?" Denny Coughlin asked.

"Worried about my car," Matt said, looking at Charley.

"I got it downstairs," Charley said. "Aside from no radio, doors, or seats, it's okay."

"You'd better be kidding."

"I got it downstairs, all in one piece. Inspector Wohl asked me to ask you where you want it."

"In the garage under the apartment, please."

"You got it. You need anything else?"

"Can't think of anything."

"I'll come see you when I get off. But I'd better get going now. Quinn's sitting in the car about to shit a brick."

"Thanks, Charley," Matt said.

Dennis V. Coughlin closed the door after McFadden, and then exhaled audibly. He walked to the bed and sat down on it.

"Jesus, Matty, you gave us a scare. What the hell happened?"

This is more than a godfather, more than my blood father's buddy, doing his duty, Matt suddenly realized. *This man loves me.*

He remembered that his father, the other father, the only one he had ever known, Brewster C. Payne, had told him that he believed Dennis V. Coughlin had always been in love with his mother.

"Lieutenant Suffern let us out of his car in the alley behind Stevens's house—"

"You and O'Hara?"

"Yeah. We were waiting for the ACT team and the sergeant to bring Stevens down so Mickey could get a picture. Then I heard a noise, a creaking noise, like wood breaking. I think now it was Stevens coming over a fence. Anyway, all of a sudden, there he was shooting at us."

"He shot first?"

"He shot first."

"That makes it justifiable homicide. You're absolutely sure he shot first?"

"Hey, I thought you were here to comfort me on my bed of pain, not interview me?"

"Are you in pain?" Coughlin asked, concern and possibly even a hint of pity—or maybe shame—in his voice.

"No, Uncle Denny, I'm not," Matt said, and touched the older man's shoulder. After a moment, Coughlin's hand came up and covered his.

"It'll probably start to hurt later, Matty," he said. "But they'll give you something for it. I'm sure."

Their eyes met.

Coughlin stood up.

"I got to go. You need anything, you know how to reach me."

15.

A motherly, very large black woman wearing a badge identifying her as a licensed practical nurse delivered a fried egg on limp toast sandwich, a container of milk, and a Styrofoam cup of coffee.

"Lunch is at eleven-thirty," she announced. "Unless you like beans and franks you won't be thrilled."

"Thank you."

"You know how to work the TV clicker?"

She showed him, walked to the door to leave, and then turned.

"I heard what happened," she said. "Good for you. Animals like that bum you shot are taking over the city."

Matt found the controls for the bed, adjusted the back to his satisfaction, and turned on the television. Not surprising him at all, there was nothing on that he would watch if he were not in a hospital bed feeling lousy and with his leg wrapped up like that of an Egyptian mummy.

If it were Saturday morning, he thought, *at least I could watch the teenagers flopping their boobs around on that dance show on WCAU-TV.*

He settled for a quiz show, quickly deciding that the participants had been chosen not for their potential ability to call forth trivia but rather on their ability to jump up and down, shrieking with joy, when they were awarded a lifetime supply of acne medication.

His calf began to feel prickly, as if it had fallen asleep, and it seemed to him he could feel blood pumping through it.

The door opened and a handsome young man with long blond hair entered, bearing a floral display.

"Where do you want this, buddy?"

"On that dresser, I suppose."

The handsome young man jerked the card free from the display and tossed it onto the bed and left.

The card read, "Best Wishes for a Speedy Recovery. Fraternal Order of Police."

Officer Payne was surprised at how much the gesture touched him.

There was no question about it now, he *could* feel the beating of his heart in his calf.

The moron on television, even though he had eagerly pushed the I-know-the-answer button, erroneously located Casablanca in Tunisia, the you-goofed foghorn sounded, and the moron's face registered as much sorrow as if his mother had just been run over by a truck.

The door opened again, to another florist's deliveryman, this one bearing two floral displays. One of the cards read, "Mother, Dad, & House Apes." The second, "Charley & Margaret."

He was aware that he had audibly let his breath out, and then that it was more than that; he had moaned. Every time his heart made his leg throb, it hurt.

Well, why am I surprised? They told me it would start to hurt.

With some effort (the device, at the end of an electrical cord, had fallen off the back of the bed when he had raised it), he found the button to summon the nurse.

A minute or so later, the door opened, but it was not an angel of mercy with the wherewithal to deaden his pain, but another delivery person, this one female, fat, and bearing an expensively wrapped package.

"You're the one who got shot, aren't you?" she greeted him. "I seen it in the newspaper."

Whoopee! Ring the you-got-it-right! siren. You have just won a year's supply of Acne Free!

"I guess I am."

The package contained a pound of Barricini assorted chocolates and a copy of Art Buchwald's latest book. The card read, "Ask the nurse to explain the big words to you. Amy."

Jesus Christ, I hurt! Where the hell is that goddamn nurse?

The nurse's head appeared in the partially opened door. A new one. This one was blond, and had intelligent hazel eyes in a very attractive face.

"Is there a problem?" she asked.

Nice voice. Deep. Soft. I wonder what the rest of her looks like?

"Actually, there are two."

"Oh?"

"I hurt."

"And?"

"Nature calls."

"Bowels or bladder?"

"Bladder," he said, and then reconsidered. "Probably both."

God, what a perfectly wonderful way to begin a romantic conversation.

The head withdrew from the door, and the door closed.

"I give you my personal guarantee," Mr. Robert Holland announced sincerely from the television screen, "that you'll never get a better deal anywhere in the Delaware Valley than you'll get from me. Step into any one of our locations today, and one of our sales counselors of integrity will prove it to you."

"You hypocritical fucking thief!" Officer Payne responded indignantly.

The nurse returned, more quickly than Matt had expected, carrying a tray with a tiny paper cup on it, and two stainless-steel devices, one under her arm, which reminded Matt of the phrase "form follows function."

The rest of her was as attractive as her face. She was tall, and lithe, and moved with grace.

Scandinavian, he thought. *Or maybe one of those Baltic countries, Latvia, Estonia. Maybe Polish? Jesus, she's attractive!*

She put the functional utensils on the bed beside him, and then half filled a plastic glass with water from a carafe. Then she handed him the tiny paper cup. There was one very small pill, half the size of an aspirin, in it.

"What's this?"

"Demerol."

"Will it work?"

"The doctor apparently thinks so."

Matt shrugged, then reached into the cup for the pill. He lost it between the cup and his lip.

The nurse shook her head, and then when Matt was unable to find it in the folds of his sheets found it for him.

"Watch," she said. She picked up the cup, stuck out her tongue, and then mimed upending the pill cup onto her tongue.

"Think you can manage that?"

"I'll give it a good shot."

She dropped the pill into the paper cup and handed it to him.

"How do I know you don't have some loathsome disease?" Matt asked.

"She said you'd probably be trouble," the nurse said.

"Who's she?"

"Margaret McCarthy," the nurse said. "Trust me. Take your pill."

He succeeded in getting the pill into his mouth and then swallowing it.

"How do you know Margaret?"

"We're going for our BSs at Temple together," the nurse said.

"Are you going to tell me what to call you, or am I going to have to ask Margaret?"

"You can call me Nurse," she said.

"Here I am, in pain, and you won't even tell me your name?"

"Lari," she said. "Lari Matsi."

"What is that, Estonian?"

"*Estonian?* No. Finnish."

"I never met a Finn before."

"Now you have."

"How come Margaret mentioned me?"

"She knew I worked here, and she called me and said you and Prince Charming were buddies."

"How long is that little pill going to take to work?"

"A couple of minutes. You do know how to work those?" She nodded at the bedpans. "You won't need a demonstration?"

"No."

"Ring when you're through," she said. "They'll come take them away for you."

"They'll?"

"I'm a surgical nurse," Lari said. "I've graduated from bedpan handling."

"I see. Then we're just ships passing in the night?"

"I'll be back when the doctor, doctors, come to see you."

She walked out of the room. The rear view was as attractive as the front.

Matt picked up one of the bedpans.

I don't really want to use that goddamn thing, and I really don't want to use the other flat one.

He looked around the room. There were two doors. One of them had to be a bathroom.

He tried moving his wounded leg. It hurt like hell, but he could raise it.

I can stagger over there, hopping on one leg. I don't have to stand on it.

It proved possible, but considerably more painful than he thought it would be. By the time he had arranged himself on the commode, he was covered with a clammy sweat.

The telephone began to ring.

Goddammit! That's probably Dad. He said he would call when he finally got to the office. Well, I'll just have to call him back.

After a long time, it stopped ringing.

Three minutes later, he pushed open the bathroom door, which took considerably more effort than he thought it would.

Lari was standing there.

"I thought you would probably try something stupid like that," she said. "Put your arm around my shoulders."

Using Lari as a crutch, he made his way back to the bed. She watched him get in and then rearranged the thin sheet over him.

"Does this mean I don't get a gold star to take home to Mommy?"

"I'd have gotten you a crutch if you had asked for one," she said. "If that was uncomfortable, it's your own fault."

"Uncomfortable, certainly, but far more dignified."

Finally, he got her to smile. He liked her smile.

"You should start feeling a little drowsy about now," she said. "That should help the pain."

"I don't suppose I could interest you in waltzing around the room with me again?"

"Not right now, thank you," she said, and smiled again, and left, taking the bedpans with her.

He lowered the head of the bed, and then shut the television off. He was feeling drowsy, but the leg still hurt.

The telephone rang again. He picked it up.

"Dad?"

"No, not Dad," Helene's voice said.

"Oh. Hi!"

"That went far more smoothly than one would have thought, didn't it?"

"I guess."

"It's a good thing I didn't know who he was taking me to see. I just ten minutes ago saw the *Bulletin.*"

"I've seen it," he said. "It's not a very good likeness."

"Oh, I think it is. I thought it rather exciting, as a matter of fact. Not as exciting as being in the room with you like that, but exciting."

"Jesus!"

"If I thought there was any way in the world to get away with it, I'd come back. Would you like that?"

"Under the circumstances, it might not be the smartest thing to do."

" 'Faint heart ne'er won fair maiden,' " she quoted.

Matt was trying to find a reply to that when he realized that she had hung up.

"Jesus H. Christ!" he said, and put the phone back in its cradle.

He recalled the pressure of her breast against his arm, and her fingers at the back of his neck. And other things about Helene.

He looked down at his middle.

"Well," he said aloud. "At least that's not broken."

Martha Washington was sitting on the narrow end of the grand piano in the living room looking out the window when she heard the key in the door and knew her husband had come home.

She looked at her watch, saw that it was a few minutes after three, and then turned to look toward the door. She didn't get off the piano.

"Hi!" she called.

Jason came into the living room pulling off his overcoat. He threw it onto the couch. When it was wet, as it was now, that tended to stain the cream-colored leather, but Martha decided this was not the time to mention that for the five hundredth time.

"How come I get hell when I set a glass on there, and you can sit on it?" he greeted her en route to the whiskey cabinet.

"Because *I* don't drip on the wood and make stains," she said.

He turned from the whiskey cabinet and smiled. That pleased her.

"How's Matt?" she asked.

"Apparently he was lucky; he's not seriously hurt. I haven't seen him."

"Why not?"

"Because when I went to the hospital this morning it looked like Suburban station at half past five. Even Farnsworth Stillwell—*and* his wife—were there. I thought I'd have a chance to go back, but I haven't."

"Are you going to tell me what happened? That picture of Matt in the paper was horrifying!"

"From what I have been able to piece together, he wasn't even supposed to be there, but he showed up when they were getting ready to go, and Wohl sent him with Mickey O'Hara. They were in an alley behind the bastard's house, waiting for the detectives and the cops to go in, when the sonofabitch showed up in the alley, shooting. He was a lousy shot, fortunately—"

"He got Matt!"

"With a ricochet, it hit a brick wall first. If it had hit Matt first, he'd be—a lot worse off."

"He was covered with blood in the newspaper."

"Minor wound, scratch, really, in the forehead. The head tends to bleed a lot."

"The radio said the man died," Martha said. "Poor Matt."

" 'Poor Matt'?"

"It will bother him, having taken someone's life."

"The last one he shot didn't bother him that I could see."

"That you could see."

Jason's face wrinkled as he considered that.

"Touché," he said, finally.

"I got him a box of candy. I didn't know what else to get him."

"You could have given him the picture of the naked lady. I know he'd like that."

She looked at him a minute, smiled, and said, "Okay. I will."

"Really?"

"Why not?" she asked.

"You're not thinking of taking it to the hospital?"

"Are we going to the hospital?"

"Yeah. Well, I thought maybe if you took off early and were here when I came home, you might want to go up there with me."

"I was about to go without you," she said. "You didn't call all day."

"I was busy," he said, and then added, "I found Tony."

"Oh?"

"In a bar in Roxborough. Specifically, in the back of a bar in Roxborough."

"Oh, honey!"

"I was right on the edge of taking him to a hospital. God, he looked awful. But I managed to get him to go home. I put him to bed. I just hope he stays there."

"Does Inspector Wohl know?"

He shook his head no.

"Well, maybe with all this—"

"He won't find out? You underestimate Peter Wohl."

"What's going to happen?"

"Drunks don't really reform until they hit bottom. Tony's pretty close to the bottom. Maybe I should have left him there and let him face Wohl. Maybe that would straighten him out."

"You know you couldn't do that."

"No," he agreed.

"The picture's in the spare bedroom."

"You really want to take it to the hospital?"

"If it will make him feel better, why not?"

When Jason and Martha Washington got off the elevator carrying the oil painting of the naked voluptuous lady, Jason found that Officer Matthew M. Payne had, in addition to the two uniformed cops guarding his door, other visitors, none of whom he was, in the circumstances, pleased to see.

Chief Inspector Matt Lowenstein and Staff Inspector Peter Wohl were standing in the corridor outside Matt's room, in conversation with a tall, angular man wearing a tweed jacket, a trench coat, gray flannel slacks, loafers, and the reserved collar affected by members of the clergy.

Lowenstein had seen them; there was no option of getting back on the elevator.

"Chief," Jason said.

"I'm glad you're here. I was about to suggest to Inspector Wohl that we try to find you," Lowenstein said, then changed his tone of voice from business to social: "Hello, Martha. It's been a long time."

"How are you, Chief Lowenstein?" Martha asked, giving him her hand.

"Reverend Coyle, may I introduce some other friends of Matt Payne's? Detective and Mrs. Jason Washington."

"That's *Sergeant* Washington, Chief," Wohl corrected him. "How are you, Martha?"

"Christ," Lowenstein said. "That's right, I forgot. Well, let me then be among the last to congratulate you, Jason."

"I'm very pleased to meet you," the Reverend H. Wadsworth Coyle said, enthusiastically pumping their hands in turn.

"Reverend Coyle," Lowenstein said, "has been telling us that he was Matt's spiritual adviser at Episcopal Academy—"

"Yes, indeed," Coyle interrupted him. "And just as soon as I heard of this terrible, terrible accident, I—"

"—so perhaps you had better explain what that picture is you're carrying," Lowenstein concluded.

Wohl looked amused.

"Inspector Wohl has one very much like this, Reverend," Martha Washington replied, "which Matt admires. He asked me to see if I could find him one as much like it as possible, and I have. I thought it might cheer him up."

Wohl no longer looked amused, but Lowenstein did.

"Very nice," the Reverend Coyle said, not very convincingly.

"They gave him something, for the pain, I suppose," Wohl said. "He's sleeping. We're waiting for him to wake up. But I think you could stick your head in, maybe he's just dozing."

"Martha," Lowenstein said, "your husband is not the silent gumshoe of legend. Why don't you stick your head in? That way, if Matt's asleep, he'll stay that way."

"Perhaps the both of us?" the Reverend Coyle said.

"Go on, Reverend," Lowenstein said. There was something in his eyes that kept Jason from challenging the "suggestion" not to go in.

As Mrs. Washington, trailed by Reverend Coyle, disappeared into Matt's room, Lowenstein took a paper from his pocket and handed it to Washington.

ISLAMIC LIBERATION ARMY

There Is No God But God,
And Allah Is His Name

PRESS RELEASE:

Allah has taken our Beloved Brother Abu Ben Mohammed into his arms in
Heaven. Blessed be the Name of Allah!
But the cold-blooded murder of our Beloved Brother Abu Ben Mohammed
by the infidel lackeys of the infidel sons of Zion, who call themselves police,
shall not go unpunished!
Death to the murderers of our Brother!
Death to those who bear false witness against the Brothers of the Islamic
Liberation Army in their Holy War against the infidel sons of Zion, who for
too long have victimized the African Brothers (Islamic and other) and other
minorities of Philadelphia.
Death to the Zionist oppressors of our people and the murderers who call
themselves police!

Freedom Now!

Abdullah el Sikkim
Chief of Staff
Islamic Liberation Army

Washington read it, then looked at Lowenstein.

"Sent by messenger to Mickey O'Hara at the *Bulletin,*" Lowenstein said. "And to the other papers, and the TV and radio stations."

"The question, obviously, is, who sent this?" Washington said. "And the immediate next question is, is it for real, or are we dealing with kooks?"

"I think we have to work on the presumption that there's something to it," Wohl said.

"What's something?"

"The first question that occurred to me was who did we miss, maybe how many, when we picked up those people this morning?" Wohl went on.

"There were eight people in the store; eight people Mr. Monahan identified from photographs; the eight people we had warrants for."

"There was probably, almost certainly," Lowenstein said, "a ninth man. Who drove the van."

"*Muhammed* el Sikkim is a guy named Randolph George Dawes," Washington said. "Little guy." He held up his hand at shoulder level. "Who is this *Abdullah* el Sikkim? His brother?"

"Dawes has two brothers," Lowenstein said. "One of them is nine years old. The other one's in Lewisburg."

"He could be the one guy we missed, the one driving the van," Wohl said. "Or he could be any one of any number of people we don't know about."

"Well, whoever he is, he's guilty of plagiarism," Washington said. "A lot of this," he dropped his eyes to the sheet of paper and read, " 'infidel sons of Zion, who for too long have victimized the African Brothers (Islamic and other) and other minorities of Philadelphia,' and some more of it too, I think, is right out of the first press release."

"He also used the phrase 'death to' more than once," Lowenstein said.

"He says 'murderers,' not 'murderer,' " Wohl injected. "Does that mean he doesn't know Matt shot Dawes?"

"It was all over the papers, and TV too," Washington said. "I can't see how he can't know. Are we taking this as a bona fide threat to Matt?"

"It seems to me the first thing we have to do is find this *Abdullah* el Sikkim," Lowenstein said. "Did you get anything out of the ones we arrested about more people being involved?"

"I'm letting them stew until after supper," Washington replied. "I'm going to start running them through lineups at half past six."

"Why haven't you done that already?" Lowenstein demanded.

"Because I think I will get more out of them after they have been locked up, all alone, all day," Washington explained. "The adrenaline will have worn off. They may even be a little worried about their futures by half past six. That's the way I called it, but I could go down there right now, Chief, if you or Inspector Wohl think I should."

"You're a sergeant now, Jason, a supervisor, but since you don't have anybody but Tony Harris to supervise, I guess it's your job," Wohl said. "I won't tell you how to do it."

Washington met his eyes.

"Are you going to tell Matt about this?" he asked.

"The question we wanted to ask you," Wohl said, "for quotation, I think I should tell you, at a five o'clock meeting with the commissioner, was, do we take this thing seriously? Are they really going to try to kill Matt, and/or the witnesses, which right now is Monahan, period?"

"So you asked *us* if we thought it should be taken seriously," Lowenstein said. "Why the hell are we letting these scumbags get to us, the three of us, this way?"

"And the next question was going to be," Wohl went on, "did Monahan go ahead and make a positive ID of these people after the threat was made? Obviously, since you're not going to run the lineup until half past six, that can't be answered."

"The reason the three of us are upset by this," Washington said thoughtfully, "is that as much as we don't want to believe it, as incredible as this whole Islamic Liberation Army thing sounds, we have a gut feeling that these people are perfectly serious. They *are* just crazy enough, or dumb enough, to try to kill Matt and Monahan."

Lowenstein took a fresh cigar, as thick as his thumb and six inches long, from his pocket. He bit off the end, and then took a long time lighting it properly.

"Harry will be back in a minute," he said finally. "I sent him to have a talk with Hospital Security. He's a retired Internal Affairs sergeant. I want whatever he can give us to keep this under control."

Detective Harry McElroy was Chief Inspector Lowenstein's driver.

"I want to get plainclothes people to guard Matt," Wohl said. "A lot of uniforms are going to signal these idiots—and the public—that we're taking them seriously."

"You mean you don't want us to look scared," Lowenstein said. "OK. Good point. But protecting Monahan is something else. You did intend, Peter, to put Highway on him and his wife twenty-four hours a day?"

"Special Operations will continue to provide two police officers to guard Mr. Monahan and his wife around the clock," Wohl said, and then when he saw the look on Lowenstein's face went on: "To take the ACT people off that job—they *are* police officers, Chief—as a result of this 'press release' would both signal the Liberation Army that we're afraid of them, and send the message to the ACT cops that I don't have any faith in them."

"I hope your touching faith is justified, Peter," Lowenstein said. "If they get to Monahan, either kill him, or scare him so that he won't testify, this whole thing goes down the tube, the scumbags go free, and the whole police department, not just you, will have egg all over its face."

"I intend to protect Mr. Monahan," Wohl said, a little sharply. "I'm even thinking about shotguns."

"You have enough ex–Stakeout people who are shotgun qualified?" Lowenstein asked.

Unlike most major city police departments, which routinely equip police officers with shotguns, Philadelphia does not. Only the specially armed Stakeout unit is issued shotguns.

"I've got people finding out," Wohl said.

"I'll call the range at the Police Academy, Peter," Lowenstein said. "Have ten of your people there in an hour. The Range Training Officers will be set up to train and certify them in no more than two hours."

"Thank you," Wohl said, simply.

"I hope Harry gets something from hospital security," Washington said. "How long is Matt going to be in here, anyway?"

"Not long," Wohl said. "They'll probably let him go tomorrow."

"That soon?" Washington asked, surprised.

"The new theory is that the more he moves around, the quicker he'll heal," Lowenstein said.

The door to Matt's room opened.

"Matt's awake," Martha Washington announced.

"Jason," Lowenstein said quickly, softly, "when somebody asks, as somebody surely will, how you're coming with the ones we have locked up, could I say that I don't know, the last I heard you were off to see Arthur X?"

"You're reading my mind again, Chief," Washington said.

"And there's one more thing you could do that would help, Jason," Wohl said.

"What's that?"

"Find Tony Harris and sober him up. I'd like him in on this."

Washington's face registered momentary surprise, then he met Wohl's eyes.

"I've found him. I'm working on sobering him up."

"Are you going to come in here or not?" Martha asked.

The three men filed into Matt's room. He was sitting up in bed.

"I'll be running along now," the Reverend Coyle said. "The hospital doesn't like to have a patient have too many visitors at once."

"Thank you for coming to see me," Matt said politely.

"Don't be silly," the Reverend Coyle said. "You feel free to call me, Matt, whenever you want to talk this over."

"I will, thank you very much," Matt said.

Jason Washington caught Martha's eye and made a barely perceptible gesture.

"I'll be outside," she said.

Matt looked from one to the other.

Lowenstein finally broke the silence.

"How much dope are you on?"

"One tiny little pill of Demerol whenever they feel I should have one."

"Could you do without it?"

"Why?"

"Your judgment is impaired when you're on Demerol."

"Am I going to need my judgment in here?"

Lowenstein handed him the press release.

Matt read it, and looked at Lowenstein.

"Jesus, are they serious?" he asked.

Lowenstein shrugged.

"I think we should err on the side of caution," Wohl said. "In this case meaning having a pistol in your bedside table might be a good idea."

Matt felt a cramp in his stomach.

Jesus, is that fear?

"The sergeant from the Mobile Crime Lab took my pistol," Matt said, desperately hoping his voice did not betray him, that he sounded like a matter-of-fact cop explaining something.

Simultaneously, Chief Inspector Lowenstein and Staff Inspector Wohl reached into the pockets of their topcoats and came out with identical Smith & Wesson Chief's Special snub-nosed .38 Special caliber revolvers.

Matt took the one Wohl had extended to him, butt first. He laid it on the sheet and covered it with his hand.

"One should be enough, don't you think?" he said. "You just happened to have spares with you, right?"

He's frightened, Wohl thought. *He's cracking wise, but he's frightened.* Then he grew angry. *Those dirty sonsofbitches!*

"Harry McElroy is arranging with hospital security to make sure nobody even knows where you are in here, much less gets close to you," Lowenstein said. "I think that threat is pure bullshit. But better safe than sorry."

"Yes, of course," Matt said.

"Just make sure no one knows you have a weapon," Wohl said. "The hospital would throw a fit."

"You'll be out of here tomorrow, or the day after," Washington said. "Even if this is not fantasy on the part of these people, they won't look for you in Wallingford. You are going to Wallingford, right?"

"I was, but not now," Matt said. "Christ, I don't want my family to hear about this!"

"It'll be in the papers," Wohl said. "They'll hear about it."

"I'll go to my apartment," Matt said, "not Wallingford."

"You in the phone book?" Lowenstein asked.

"No, sir."

"What I think this is intended to do, Payne," Lowenstein went on, "is frighten Mr. Monahan. I think they're trying to get him to think that if they can threaten a cop— You take my meaning?"

"Yes, sir."

"I can't believe they'd come after you. If they were serious about revenge, they wouldn't have given a warning."

"Yes, sir."

On the other hand, Matt thought, *if they did kill me, that would really send Mr. Monahan a message.*

The pain in his stomach had gone as quickly as it had come.

Jesus, that Demerol must be working. I'm not even afraid anymore. This is more like watching a cops-and-robbers show on TV. You know it's not real.

And then he had a sudden, very clear image of the orange muzzle blasts in the alley, and heard again the crack of Abu Ben Mohammed's pistol, and felt again getting slammed in the calf and forehead, and the fear, and the cramp in his stomach, came back.

"I'll have a talk with your father, Matt," Wohl said. "And put this in perspective. If you'd like me to."

"Please," Matt said.

"I'm sure McElroy has arranged with the switchboard to put through only calls from your family and friends," Lowenstein said. "But some calls may get through—"

"Calls from whom?" Matt interrupted.

"I was thinking of the press, those bastards are not above saying they're somebody's brother, but now that I think of it, these people may try to call you too."

"In either case, hang up," Wohl said. "No matter what you would say, it would be the wrong thing."

"Yes, sir."

"And above all," Wohl said, "as the hangman said as he led the condemned man up the scaffold steps, try not to worry about this."

"Oh, God!" Washington groaned, and then they all laughed.

A little too heartily, Matt thought. *That wasn't that funny.*

16.

The Honorable Jerry Carlucci, mayor of the City of Philadelphia, sat in the commissioner's chair at the head of the commissioner's conference table in the commissioner's conference room on the third floor of the Roundhouse rolling one of Chief Inspector Matt Lowenstein's big black cigars in his fingers. His Honor was visibly not in a good mood.

One indication of this was the manner in which he had come by the cigar.

"Matt, I don't suppose you have a spare cigar you could let me have, do you?" the mayor had politely asked.

Lowenstein knew from long experience that when The Dago was carefully watching his manners, it was a sure sign that he was no more than a millimeter or two away from throwing a fit.

"Thank you very much, Matt," the mayor said very politely.

Police Commissioner Taddeus Czernich, a large, florid-faced man sitting to the mayor's immediate left, next to Chief Inspector Dennis V. Coughlin, produced a gas-flame cigarette lighter, turned it on, and offered it to the mayor.

"No, thank you, Commissioner," the mayor said, very politely, "I'm sure Matt will offer me a match."

He turned to Lowenstein, sitting beside Peter Wohl on the other side of the table. Lowenstein handed him a large kitchen match and the mayor then took a good thirty seconds to get the cigar going. Finally, exhaling cigar smoke as he approvingly examined the coal on the cigar, he said, very politely, "Well, since we are all here, do you think we should get going? Why don't you just rough me in on this, Commissioner, and then I can ask specific questions of the others, if there's something I don't quite understand."

"Yes, sir," Commissioner Czernich said. "Should I start, sir, with the Goldblatt robbery and murder?"

"No, start with what happened at five o'clock this morning. I know what happened at Goldblatt's."

"Chief Lowenstein asked the assistance of Inspector Wohl, that is, Special Operations, in arresting eight men identified by a witness as the doers of the Goldblatt job. They obtained warrants through the district attorney. The idea was to make the arrests simultaneously, and at a time when there would be the least risk to the public and the officers involved, that is at five o'clock in the morning."

"And the operation presumably had your blessing, Commissioner?"

"I didn't know about it until it was over, Mr. Mayor."

"You and Lowenstein had a falling-out?" Carlucci demanded, looking from one to the other. "You're not talking to each other? What?"

"It was a routine arrest, arrests, Jerry," Lowenstein said. "There was no reason to bring the commissioner in on it."

"Just for the record, Matt, correct me if I'm wrong, this is the first time we've arrested the Islamic Liberation Army, right? Or any other kind of army, right? So how is that routine?"

"Just because eight *schwartzers* call themselves an army doesn't make them an army," Lowenstein said. "So far as I'm concerned, these guys are thieves and murderers, period."

"Yeah, well, tell that to the newspapers," Carlucci said. "The newspapers think they're an army."

"Then the newspapers are wrong," Lowenstein said.

"And it never entered your mind, Peter," Carlucci asked, turning to Wohl, "to run this past the commissioner and get his approval?"

"Mr. Mayor, I thought of it like Chief Lowenstein did. It was a routine arrest."

"If it was a routine arrest—don't hand me any of your bullshit, Peter, I was commanding Highway when you were in high school—Homicide detectives backed up by district cops would have picked these people up, one at a time. Did you see what the *Daily News* said?"

"No, sir."

The mayor jammed his cigar in his mouth, opened his briefcase, took out a sheet of Xerox paper, and read, "They said, 'A small army of heavily armed police had their first battle with the Islamic Liberation Army early this morning. When it was over, Abu Ben Mohammed was fatally wounded and Police Officer Matthew M. Payne, who two months ago shot to death the Northwest Philadelphia serial rapist, was in Frankford Hospital suffering from multiple gunshot wounds. The police took seven members of the ILA prisoner.' "

He looked at Wohl.

"I didn't see that," Wohl said.

"Maybe you should start reading the newspapers, Peter."

"Yes, sir."

"Just don't give me any more bullshit about a routine arrest. If this thing had been handled like a routine arrest none of this would have happened."

"You're right," Lowenstein said angrily. "Absolutely right. If I had tried to pick up these scumbags one at a time, using district cops, we'd have three, four, a half dozen cops in Frankford Hospital, or maybe the morgue. And probably that many civilians."

"Yeah?"

"Yeah. We took a goddamn arsenal full of guns away from these people. The only reason they didn't get to use them was because we hit them all at once. If we had taken them one at a time, by the time we got to the second or third one, they would either have been long gone, in Kansas City or someplace, if we were lucky. Or, if we were unlucky, they would have done what this scumbag Stevens did, come out shooting."

There were very few people in the Police Department, for that matter in city government, who would have dared to tell the mayor in scornful sarcasm that he was right, absolutely right, and then explain in detail to him why he was wrong. Matt Lowenstein was one of them. But there was doubt in the minds of everyone else in the conference room that he was going to get away with it this time.

He and the mayor glared at each other for a full fifteen seconds.

"Is that his name? Stevens? The dead one?" the mayor finally asked, almost conversationally.

"Charles David Stevens," Lowenstein furnished.

The mayor turned his attention to Staff Inspector Wohl again: "Presumably you were aware of this 'arsenal of weapons'? That being the case, how come you didn't use Highway?"

"I didn't want the *Ledger* complaining about excessive force by 'Carlucci's Jackbooted Gestapo,' " Wohl replied evenly. "Highway was alerted, in case they would be needed, and there were also stakeout units available. Neither was needed, which was fine with me; I didn't want an early morning gun battle."

Carlucci thought that over for a long moment before replying: "I'm not sure I would have taken that kind of chance, Peter."

"We also have to submit quarterly reports to the Justice Department on how we're spending the ACT Grant funds. I thought that reporting that ACT-funded cops had assisted Homicide in the arrest of eight individuals charged with murder and armed robbery would look good."

"I still think I would have used Highway," the mayor said. "You *did* have a gun battle."

"I haven't had a chance to figure that out yet," Wohl said. "I don't think Stevens spotted the Homicide detective. Possibilities are that he got up to take a leak, and looked out his window, just as the units were moving into place."

"You said possibilities."

"Or somebody saw all the activity at the school playground, or as they were moving from the playground, and called Stevens."

"Somebody who?"

"Maybe the same somebody who issued the second press release."

"So you don't have all of them?"

"No. What Jason Washington is doing, right now, is trying to find out how many there are. He hopes Arthur X will tell him."

"What does Intelligence have to say about these people? Or Organized Crime?" Carlucci asked.

"Intelligence has nothing on the Islamic Liberation Army, period," Lowenstein answered. "And until they pulled this job, none of these people did anything that would make them of interest to Organized Crime. They had their names, or some of them, but with no ties to anyone serious. They're—or they were—small-time thieves."

"Czernich," the mayor said, "maybe you'd better have a talk with Intelligence. I find it hard to believe that one day last week, out of the clear blue sky, these bastards said, 'Okay, we're now the Islamic Liberation Army.' Intelligence should have something on them."

"Yes, sir," Commissioner Czernich said.

"But you are," the mayor said, looking at Lowenstein, "taking this second so-called press release seriously?"

"I don't think we should ignore it," Lowenstein replied.

"The newspapers aren't going to ignore it, you can bet your ass on that," Carlucci said.

"There's almost certainly at least one more of them," Wohl said. "Somebody was driving the van. Washington maybe can get a lead on him after he runs the seven of them through lineups."

"He hasn't done that yet?" Carlucci asked incredulously.

"He wanted them to have all day to consider their predicament. He'll start the lineups at half past six."

"There was an implied threat against Matt Payne in that second press release," Chief Inspector Dennis V. Coughlin said. It was the first time he had spoken. "How are you going to handle that?"

"Not specifically," the mayor said. "What it said was—" he went into his briefcase again for another photocopy and then read, " 'Death to the murderers of our Brother.' Murderers, plural, not Payne by name."

"Maybe that was before he knew Matt shot him," Coughlin said.

"Denny, I know how you feel about that boy—" Carlucci said gently.

"Chief, he's a cop," Wohl interrupted, "and I don't want to give these people the satisfaction of thinking that they have scared us to the point where we are protecting a cop—"

"He's in a goddamn hospital bed!" Coughlin flared. "I don't give a good goddamn what these scumbags think."

"We had a talk with hospital security," Lowenstein said. "We changed his room. They're screening his phone calls. And Peter loaned him a gun."

"—And," Wohl went on, "and, purely as a routine administrative matter, while he is recovering, I'm going to ask Captain Pekach of Highway to rearrange the duty schedules of Officers McFadden and Martinez so that they can spend some time, off duty, in civilian clothes, with Matt."

Coughlin looked at him, with gratitude in his eyes.

"And I wouldn't be surprised if other friends of his looked in on him from time to time," Wohl said.

"You, for example?" Carlucci asked, chuckling, "And maybe Denny?"

"Yes, sir. And maybe Sergeant Washington."

"Satisfied, Denny?" the mayor asked.

"I never thought I'd see the day in Philadelphia, Jerry," Coughlin said, "when scumbags would not only threaten a cop's life, but send out a press release announcing it."

"I think the press release is bullshit," Lowenstein said. "I think it's intended to scare Monahan."

"He the witness? Will it?" Carlucci asked.

"He's the only one with any balls," Lowenstein said. "And no. I don't think he'll scare."

"But we can forget the others, right? So we'd better hope this one doesn't scare. Or get himself killed."

"I haven't given up on the other witnesses," Lowenstein said. "Washington hasn't talked to them yet. I mean *really* talked to them."

"Don't hold your breath," Carlucci said.

"It seems to me," Commissioner Czernich said, "that our first priority is the protection of Mr. Monahan."

The mayor looked at him and shook his head.

"You figured that out all by yourself, did you?" he asked.

Then he closed his briefcase and stood up.

There is a price, Wohl thought, *for being appointed police commissioner.*

Commissioner Czernich waited until the mayor had left the conference room. Then, his face still showing signs of the flush that had come to it when Carlucci had humiliated him, he pointed at Lowenstein and Wohl.

"That's the last time either one of you will pull something like that harebrained scheme you pulled this morning without coming to me and getting my permission. The last time. Am I making myself clear?"

"Yes, sir," Wohl said.

"Whatever you say, Commissioner," Lowenstein said.

"And I want Highway in on the protection of Mr. Monahan, Wohl. We can't take any chances with him."

"Yes, sir."

Commissioner Czernich looked sternly at each man, and then marched out of his conference room.

"Remember that, Peter," Coughlin said. "No more harebrained schemes are to be pulled without the commissioner's permission."

"Jesus," Wohl said, and then laughed, "I thought that's what he said."

"Well, it made him happy," Lowenstein said. "It gave him a chance to give an order all by himself."

"*Two* orders," Coughlin replied. "You heard what he told Peter. He wants Highway in on protecting Monahan."

"That's the exception proving the rule. That makes sense."

"I'm not so sure," Wohl said.

"Now you're not making sense," Lowenstein said.

"The first priority, agreeing with the commissioner, is to protect the Monahans. The second priority is to make the Monahans feel protected. I decided the best way I could do that, during the day, when Mr. Monahan's at work, is with two plainclothes officers in an unmarked car. A blue-and-white sitting in front of Goldblatt's all day would give people the impression we're afraid of the ILA—" He interrupted himself. "That's dangerous. Did you hear what I said?"

"I heard," Lowenstein said.

"I called these scumbags the ILA. I don't want to get in the habit of doing that."

"No, we don't," Coughlin agreed.

"There is another car, a blue-and-white, with uniformed officers, at his house," Wohl went on. "There will be one there, twenty-four hours a day, from now on. That will reassure Mrs. Monahan, and if an associate of *these felons* should happen to ride by the Monahan house, they will see the blue-and-white."

"Okay," Lowenstein said. "I see your reasoning. So what are you going to do?"

"Obey the order he gave me," Wohl said. "Have a Highway car meet Washington and the unmarked car at Goldblatt's and go with them when they bring Mr. Monahan here to the Roundhouse. Unless I heard the commissioner incorrectly, he only said he wanted 'Highway *in* on protecting Mr. Monahan.' "

"You're devious, Peter. Maybe you *will* get to be commissioner one day."

"I'm doing the job the best way I can see to do it," Wohl said.

"I think you're doing it right," Coughlin said.

"We won that encounter in there, Peter," Lowenstein said. "I think Czernich expected both of us to be drawn and quartered. I think Czernich is disappointed. So watch out for him."

"Yeah," Wohl said.

"I'd appreciate being kept up-to-date on what's happening," Coughlin said.

"I'll have Washington call you after the line-up. Lineups."

"Lineups. Lineups, for Christ's sake," Lowenstein said, chuckling. He touched Wohl's arm, nodded at Coughlin, and walked out of the room.

"I appreciate your concern for Matt, Peter," Coughlin said.

"Don't be silly."

"Well, I do," Coughlin said, and then he left.

Wohl started to follow him, but as he passed through the commissioner's office, the commissioner's secretary asked him how Matt was doing, and he stopped to give her a report.

In the elevator on the way to the lobby, he remembered that he had promised Matt to have a word with his father. He stopped at the counter, asked for a phone book, and called Mawson, Payne, Stockton, McAdoo & Lester.

Brewster C. Payne gave him the impression he had expected him to call. He asked where Wohl was, and then suggested they have a drink in the Union League Club.

"Thank you, I can use one," Peter said.

"I think we can both use several," Payne said. "I'll see you there in a few minutes."

Wohl started to push the telephone back to the corporal on duty, and then changed his mind and dialed Dave Pekach's number and explained why a Highway car was going to have to be at Goldblatt's.

Lari Matsi came into Matt Payne's, carrying a small tray with a tiny paper cup on it.

"How's it going?" she asked.

"I'm watching *The Dating Game* on the boob tube. That tell you anything?"

"Maybe you have more culture than I've been giving you credit for," she said. "Anyway, take this and in five minutes you won't care what's on TV."

"I don't need that, thank you."

"It's not a suggestion. It's on orders."

"I still don't want it," he said.

She was standing by the side of the bed. She looked down at it, and grew serious.

"I don't think you're supposed to have that in here."

He followed her eyes, and saw that she was looking at the revolver Wohl had given him, its butt peeking out from a fold in the thin cotton blanket.

He took the revolver and put it inside the box of Kleenex on the bedside table.

"Okay?" he asked.

"No. Not okay. You want to tell me what's going on here?"

"Like what? I'm a cop. Cops have guns."

"They moved you in here, and your name is not Matthews, which is the name on the door."

"I don't suppose you'd believe that I'm really a rock-and-roll star trying to avoid my fans?"

"Do you really think somebody's going to try to—do something to you?"

"No. But better safe than sorry."

"I suppose this is supposed to be exciting," she said. "But what I really feel is that I don't like it at all."

"I'm sorry you saw the gun," he said. "Can we drop it there?"

"You don't want the Demerol because it will make you drowsy, right?"

He met her eyes, but didn't reply.

"This was going to be your last one, anyway," Lari said. "I could get you some aspirin, if you want."

"Please."

"Are you in pain?"

"No."

"If anybody asks, you took it, okay?" she asked. "It would be easier that way."

She went to the bathroom, and in a moment, with a mighty roar, the toilet flushed.

"Thank you," he said when she came out.

"I'll get the aspirin," she said, and went out.

She came back in a minute with a small tin of Bayer aspirin.

"These are mine," she said. "You didn't get them from me. Okay?"

"Thank you."

"There's a security guard at the nurses' station, I guess you know. He's giving everybody who gets off the elevator the once-over."

"No, I didn't."

"In the morning, they're going to send you a physical therapist, to show you how to use crutches," she said. "When she tells you the more you use your leg, the more quickly it will feel better, trust her."

"Okay."

"I'll see you around, maybe, sometime."

"Not in the morning?"

"No. I won't be coming back here. I'm only filling in."

"I'd really like to see you around, no maybe, sometime. Could I call you?"

"There's a rule against that."

"You don't know what I have in mind, so how can there be a rule against that?"

"I mean, giving your phone number to a patient."

"I'm not just any old patient. I'm Margaret's Prince Charming's buddy. And, anyway, don't you ever do something you're not supposed to?"

"Not very often," she said, "and something tells me this is one of the times I should follow the rules."

She walked out of the room.

Matt watched the door close slowly after her.

"Damn!" he said aloud.

The door swung open again.

"My father is the only Henry Matsi in the phone book," Lari announced, "but I should tell you I'm hardly ever home."

Then she was gone again.

"Henry Matsi, Henry Matsi, Henry Matsi, Henry Matsi," Matt said aloud, to engrave it in his memory.

A minute or so later the door opened again, but it was not Lari. A chubby, determinedly cheerful woman bearing a tray announced, "Here's our supper."

"What are we having?"

"A *nice* piece of chicken," she said. "Primarily."

She took the gray cover off a plate with a flourish.

"And steamed veggies."

"Wow!" Matt said enthusiastically. "And what do you suppose that gray stuff in the cup is?"

"Custard."

"I was afraid of that."

Five minutes later, as he was trying to scrape the custard off his teeth and the roof of his mouth with his tongue, the door opened again.

A familiar face, to which Matt could not instantly attach a name, appeared.

"Feel up to a couple of visitors?"

"Sure, come on in."

Walter Davis, special agent in charge, Philadelphia Office, FBI, came into the room, trailed by A-SAC (Criminal Affairs) Frank Young.

"We won't stay long, but we wanted to come by and see if there was anything we could do for you," Davis said as Matt finally realized who they were.

You could tell me you just arrested the guy who wants to get me for shooting Charles D. Stevens. That would be nice.

What the hell are they doing here? What do they want?

Mr. Albert J. Monahan was talking with Mr. Phil Katz when Sergeant Jason Washington came through the door of Goldblatt & Sons Credit Furniture & Appliances, Inc., on South Street. Mr. Monahan smiled and seemed pleased to see Sergeant Washington. Mr. Katz did not.

"Good evening," Washington said.

"How are you, Detective Washington?" Mr. Monahan replied, pumping his hand.

Mr. Katz nodded.

"I guess you heard—" Washington began.

"We heard," Katz said.

"—we have the people who were here locked up," Washington continued. "And I hope Detective Pelosi called to tell you I was coming by?"

"Yes, he did," Monahan said.

"What I thought you meant," Katz said, "was, had we heard about what the Islamic Liberation Army had to say about people 'bearing false witness.' "

"We really don't think they're an army, Mr. Katz."

Katz snorted.

"Do what you think you have to, Albert," Mr. Katz said, and walked away.

"He's a married man, with kids," Al Monahan said, "I understand how he feels."

"Are you about ready, Mr. Monahan?" Washington asked.

"I've just got to get my coat and hat," Monahan replied. "And then I'll be with you."

Washington watched him walk across the floor toward the rear of the store, and then went to the door and looked out.

Things were exactly as he had set them up. He questioned whether it was really necessary, but Peter Wohl had told him to "err on the side of caution" and Washington was willing to go along with his concern, not only because, obviously, Wohl was his commanding officer, but also because of all the police brass Washington knew well, Peter Wohl was among the least excitable. He did not, in other words, as Washington thought of it, run around in circles chasing his tail, in the manner of other supervisors of his acquaintance when they were faced with an out-of-the-ordinary situation.

There were three cars parked in front of Goldblatt's. First was the Highway car, then Washington's unmarked car, and finally the unmarked car that carried the two plainclothes officers.

Both Highway cops, one of the plainclothesmen, and the 6th District beat cop were standing by the fender of Washington's car.

"Okay," Mr. Monahan said in Washington's ear, startling him a little.

Washington smiled at him, and led him to the door.

When they stepped outside, one of the Highway cops and the plainclothesmen stepped beside Mr. Monahan. As Washington got behind the wheel of his car, they walked Monahan between the Highway car and Washington's, and installed him in the front seat.

The beat cop, as the Highway cop and the plainclothesmen got in their cars, stepped into the middle of the street and held up his hand, blocking traffic coming east on South Street, so that the three cars could pull away from the curb together.

The Highway car in front of Washington had almost reached South 8th Street and had already turned on his turn signal when Washington saw something dropping out of the sky.

He had just time to recognize it as a bottle, whiskey or ginger ale, that big, then as a bottle on fire, at the neck, when it hit the roof of the Highway car and then bounced off, unbroken, onto South Street, where it shattered.

The Highway car slammed on his brakes, and Washington almost ran into him. As he slammed his hand on the horn, the unmarked car behind him slammed into his bumper.

Washington signaled furiously for the Highway car to get moving. It began to move again the instant there was a sound like a blown-up paper bag being ruptured, and then a puff of orange flame.

Those dirty rotten sonsofbitches!

"Jesus, Mary, and Joseph!" Mr. Monahan said.

Washington's hand found his microphone.

"Keep moving!" he ordered. "The beat cop'll call it in. Go to the Roundhouse."

Washington looked in his mirror. The unmarked car behind him was still moving, already through the puddle of burning gasoline.

"What the hell was it, a fucking Molotov cocktail?" an incredulous voice, probably, Washington thought, one of the Highway guys, came over the radio.

"Can you see, Mr. Monahan, if the car behind us is all right?" he asked.

"It looks okay."

Washington picked up the microphone again.

"Okay. Everything's under control," he said.

In a porcine rectum, he thought, *everything's under control. What the* hell *is going on here? This is* Philadelphia, *not Saigon!*

17.

The tall, trim, simply dressed woman who looked a good deal younger than her years stood for a moment in the door to the lounge of the Union League Club, running her eyes over the people in the room, now crowded with the after-work-before-catching-the-train crowd.

Finally, with a small, triumphant smile, she pointed her finger at a table across the room against the wall.

"There," she announced to her companion.

"I see them," he replied.

She walked to the table, with her companion trailing behind her, and announced her presence by reaching down and picking a squat whiskey glass up from the table.

"I really hope this is not one of those times when you're drinking something chic," she said, taking a healthy swallow.

Mr. Brewster Cortland Payne, who had just set the drink (his third) down after taking a first sip, looked up at his wife and, smiling, got to his feet.

Patricia Payne sat down in one of the heavy wooden chairs.

"I needed that," she said. "Denny has been trying to convince me, with not much success, that we don't have anything to worry about. Has Inspector Wohl been more successful than he has?"

"I hope so," Peter Wohl said. "Good evening, Mrs. Payne. Chief."

"Peter," Chief Inspector Dennis V. Coughlin said. "Brewster."

Brewster C. Payne raised his hand, index finger extended, above his shoulders. The gesture was unnecessary, for a white-jacketed waiter, who provided service based on his own assessment of who really mattered around the place, now that they were letting every Tom, Dick, and Harry in, was already headed for the table.

"Mrs. Payne, what can I get for you?"

"You can get Mr. Payne whatever he was drinking, thank you, Homer," she said. "I just stole his."

"Yes, ma'am," the waiter said with a broad smile. "And you, sir?"

"The same please," Coughlin said.

"To answer your question, Pat," Brewster C. Payne said, "Yes. Peter has been very reassuring."

"Did he reassure you before or after you heard about the Molotov cocktail?" Patricia Payne asked.

"I beg your pardon?"

"I was in the bar of the Bellevue-Stratford, being reassured by Denny," she said, "when Tom Lenihan came running in and said, if I quote him accurately, 'Jesus Christ, Chief, you're not going to believe this. They just threw a Molotov cocktail at the cars guarding Monahan.' "

"My God!" Payne said.

"At that point, I thought I had better get myself reassured by *you,* darling, so I called the office and they said you had come here. So Denny brought me. So how was *your* day?"

Both Wohl and Payne looked at Chief Coughlin, and both shared the same thought, that they had never seen Coughlin looking quite so unhappy.

"Oh, Denny, I'm sorry," Patricia Payne said, laying her hand on his. "That sounded as if I don't trust you, or am blaming you. I didn't mean that!"

"From what I know," Coughlin said, "what happened was that when Washington picked up Monahan at Goldblatt's to take him to the Roundhouse, somebody tossed a bottle full of gasoline down from a roof, or out of a window. It bounced off the Highway car, broke when it hit the street, and then caught fire."

"Anyone hurt?" Wohl asked.

"No. The burning gas flowed under a car on South Street and set it on fire."

"Monahan?"

"I got Washington on the radio. He said Monahan was riding with him. They were behind the Highway car, and one of your unmarked cars was behind them. Monahan is all right. He's at the Roundhouse right now. The lineups at the Detention Center will go on as scheduled, as soon as they finish at the Roundhouse."

"What are they doing over there?" Wohl asked.

"I suppose Washington thought that was the best place to go; Central Detectives will want to get some statements, put it all together. And the lab probably wants a look at the Highway car they hit with the bottle. Maybe pick up another car or two to escort them to the Detention Center."

If you were thinking clearly, Peter Wohl, you would not have had to ask that dumb question.

"I think I'd better get over there," Wohl said.

Coughlin nodded.

"Peter, I called Mike Sabara and told him I thought it would be a good idea if he sent a Highway car over to Frankford Hospital. I hope that's all right with you."

"Thank you. That saves me making a phone call," Wohl said. He got to his feet. "Mrs. Payne," he began, and then couldn't think of what to say next.

She looked up at him and smiled.

"Peter—you don't mind if I call you Peter?"

"No, ma'am."

"Peter, as I walked over here with Denny, I thought that I couldn't ask for anyone better than you and Denny to look out for Matt."

"Absolutely," Brewster C. Payne agreed.

"Patty, we'll take care of Matt, don't you worry about that," Denny Coughlin said emotionally.

"Sit down, Peter," Brewster C. Payne said, "and finish your drink. I'm sure that everything that should be done has been done."

"He's right. Sit down, Peter," Chief Coughlin chimed in. "Right now, both of us would be in the way at the Roundhouse."

Wohl looked at both of the men, and then at Patricia Payne, and then sat down.

The Police Department records concerning Captain David R. Pekach stated that he was a bachelor, who lived in a Park Drive Manor apartment. Captain Pekach had last spent the night in his apartment approximately five months before, that is to say four days after he had made the acquaintance of Miss Martha Peebles, who resided in a turn-of-the-century mansion set on five acres at 606 Glengarry Lane in Chestnut Hill.

Miss Peebles, who had a certain influence in Philadelphia (according to *Business Week* magazine, her father had owned outright 11.7 percent of the anthracite coal reserves of the United States, among other holdings, all of which he had left to his sole and beloved daughter), had been burglarized several times.

When the police had not only been unable to apprehend the burglar, but also to prevent additional burglaries, she had complained to her legal adviser (and lifelong friend of her father) Brewster Cortland Payne, of Mawson, Payne, Stockton, McAdoo & Lester.

Mr. Payne had had a word with the other founding partner of Mawson, Payne, Stockton, McAdoo & Lester, Colonel J. Dunlop Mawson, who handled the criminal side of their practice. Colonel Mawson had had a word with Police Commissioner Taddeus Czernich about Miss Peebles's problem, and Commissioner Czernich, fully aware that unless Mawson got satisfaction from him, the next call the sonofabitch would make would be to Mayor Carlucci, told him to put the problem from his mind, he personally would take care of it.

Commissioner Czernich had then called Staff Inspector Peter Wohl, commanding officer of the Special Operations Division, and told him he didn't care how he did it, he didn't want to hear of one more incident of any kind at the residence of Miss Martha Peebles, 606 Glengarry Lane, Chestnut Hill.

Staff Inspector Wohl, in turn, turned the problem over to Captain Pekach, using essentially the same phraseology Commissioner Czernich had used when he had called.

Working with Inspector Wohl's deputy, Captain Mike Sabara, Captain Pekach had arranged for Miss Peebles's residence to be placed under surveillance. An unmarked Special Operations car would be parked on Glengarry Lane until the burglar was nabbed, and Highway RPCs would drive past no less than once an hour.

Captain Pekach had then presented himself personally at the Peebles residence, to assure the lady that the Philadelphia Police Department generally and Captain David Pekach personally were doing all that was humanly possible to shield her home from future violations of any kind.

In the course of their conversation, Miss Peebles had said that it wasn't the loss of what already had been stolen, essentially bric-a-brac, that concerned her, but rather the potential theft of her late father's collection of Early American firearms.

Captain Pekach, whose hobby happened to be Early American firearms, asked if he might see the collection. Miss Peebles obliged him.

As she passed him a rather interesting piece, a mint condition U.S. Rifle, model of 1819 with a J.H. Hall action, stamped with the initials of the proving inspector, Zachary Ellsworth Hampden, Captain, Ordnance Corps, later Deputy Chief of Ordnance, their hands touched.

Shortly afterward, Miss Peebles, who was thirty-six, willingly offered her heretofore zealously guarded pearl of great price to Captain Pekach, who was also thirty-six, who took it with what Miss Peebles regarded as exquisite tenderness, and convincing her that she had at last found what had so far eluded her, a true gentleman to share life's joys and sorrows.

And so it was that when Captain David Pekach, after first having personally checked to see that there was a Highway RPC parked outside Goldblatt & Sons Credit Furniture & Appliances, Inc., on South Street, under orders to obey whatever orders Sergeant Jason Washington might issue, left his office at Bustleton and Bowler for the day, he did not head for his official home of record, but rather for 606 Glengarry Lane in Chestnut Hill.

When he approached the house, he reached up to the sun visor and pushed the button that caused the left of the double steel gates to the estate to swing open. Three hundred yards up the cobblestone drive, he stopped his official, unmarked car under the two-car-wide portico to the left of the house and got out. There was a year-old Mercedes roadster, now wearing its steel winter top, in the other lane, pointing down the driveway.

Evans, the elderly, white-haired black butler (who, with his wife, had been in the house when Miss Martha had been born, and when both of her parents had died), came out of the house.

"Good evening, Captain," he said. "I believe Miss Martha's upstairs."

"Thank you," Pekach said.

As Pekach went into the house, Evans got behind the wheel of the unmarked car and drove it to the four-car garage, once a stable, a hundred yards from the house.

There was a downstairs sitting room in the house, and an upstairs sitting room. Martha had gotten into the habit of greeting him upstairs with a drink, and some hors d'oeuvres in the upstairs sitting room.

He would have a drink, or sometimes two, and then he would take a shower. Sometimes he would dress after his shower, and they would have another drink and watch the news on television, and then go for dinner, either out or here in the house. And sometimes he would have his shower and he would not get dressed, because Martha had somehow let him know that she would really rather fool around than watch the news on television.

Tonight, obviously, there would be no fooling around. At least not now, if probably later. Martha, when she greeted him with a glass dark with Old Bushmills and a kiss that was at once decorous and exciting, was dressed to go out. She had on a simple black dress, a double string of pearls, each the size of a pencil eraser, and a diamond and ruby pin in the shape of a pheasant.

"Precious," she said, "I asked Evans to lay out your blazer and gray slacks. I thought you would want to look more or less official, but we're going out for dinner, and I know you don't like to do that in uniform, and the blazer-with-the-police-buttons seemed to be a nice compromise. All right?"

He had called Martha early in the morning, to tell her that Matt Payne, thank God, was not seriously injured. He knew that she would have heard of the shooting, and would be concerned on two levels, first that it was a cop with whom he worked, and second, perhaps more important, that Matt was the son of her lawyer. He told her that he would be a little late getting home; he wanted to put in an appearance at Frankford Hospital.

"I'd like to go too, if that would be all right," she said.

He had hesitated. He could think of no good reason why she should not go to see Payne. After all, Payne's father was her lawyer, and they probably more or less knew each other, but he suspected that Martha was at least as interested in appearing as David Pekach's very good lady friend as she was in offering her sympathy to Matt Payne.

He had tried from the beginning, and so far unsuccessfully, to keep Martha away from his brother officers. Every sonofabitch and his brother in the Police Department seemed to think his relationship with the rich old maid from Chestnut Hill was as funny as a rubber crutch.

Martha, he knew, had sensed that he was keeping their personal life very much separate from his professional life. One of the astonishing things about their relationship was that he knew what she was thinking. The flip side of that was that she knew what he was thinking too.

He had hesitated, and lost.

"Precious, if that would in any way be embarrassing to you, just forget it."

"Don't be silly. How could it be embarrassing? I'll come by the house right from work and pick you up."

"All right, if you think it would be all right," Martha had said, her pleased tone of voice telling him he had really had no choice. "And then we'll go out for dinner afterward? Seafood?"

"Seafood sounds fine," he had said.

He had spent a good deal of time during the day considering his relationship with Martha, finally concluding that while the way things were was fine, things could not go along much longer unchanged.

Sometimes, he felt like a gigolo, the way she was always giving him things. It wasn't, he managed to convince himself, that he had fallen for her because she was rich, but that didn't make her just another woman. There was no getting away from the fact that she was a rich woman.

How could he feel like a man when she probably spent more money on fuel oil and having the grass cut at her house than he made?

But when he was with her, like now, he could not imagine life without her.

Jesus, just being around her makes me feel good!

"Was that all right, precious, having Evans lay out your blazer?"

"Fine," Captain David Pekach said, putting his arm around Miss Martha Peebles and kissing her again.

"Precious, behave," she said, when he dropped his hand to her buttock. "We don't have time."

The blazer to which she referred was originally the property of her father.

When Evans and his wife (after an initial three- or four-week period during which their behavior had been more like that of concerned parents rather than servants) had finally decided that Dave Pekach was going to be good for Miss Martha, they had turned to being what they genuinely believed to be helpful and constructive.

Dave Pekach now had an extensive wardrobe, formerly the property of the late Alexander Peebles. No one had asked him if he wanted it, or would even be willing to wear what he had at first thought of as a dead man's clothes. It had been presented as a fait accompli. Evans had taken four suits, half a dozen sports coats, a dozen pairs of trousers, and the measurements Martha had made of the new uniform Dave had given himself as a present for making captain to an Italian custom tailor on Chestnut Street.

Only minor adjustments had been necessary, Evans had happily told him. Mr. Alex had been, fortunately, just slightly larger than Captain Pekach, rather than the other way.

The buttons on the blazer, which bore the label of a London tailor, and which to Dave Pekach's eyes looked unworn, had been replaced with Philadelphia Police Department buttons.

"You have no idea what trouble Evans had to go to for those buttons!" Martha had exclaimed. "But it was, wasn't it, Evans, worth it. Doesn't the captain look nice?"

"The captain looks just fine, Miss Martha," Evans had agreed, beaming with pleasure.

It had not been the time to bring up the subjects of being able to buy his own damned clothing, thank you just the same, or being unable to comfortably wear a dead man's hand-me-downs.

And the trouble, Dave Pekach thought, as he walked into the bedroom carrying his drink in one hand and a bacon-wrapped oyster in the other, and saw the blazer hanging on the mahogany clothes horse, *is that I now think of all these clothes as mine.*

He unbuckled his Sam Browne belt and hung it over the clothes horse, and then stripped out of his uniform, tossing it onto a green leather chaise lounge, secure in the knowledge that in the morning, freshly pressed, it (or another, fresh from the cleaners) would be on the clothes horse.

And that I'm getting pretty used to living like this.

When he came out of the glass-walled shower, Martha was in the bathroom. He was a little confused. Sometimes, when she felt like fooling around, she joined him, but not all dressed up as she was now.

"Captain Sabara called," Martha announced. "He wants you to call. I wrote down the number."

She extended a small piece of paper, but snatched it back when he reached for it.

"Put your robe on, precious," she said. "You'll catch your death!"

He took a heavy terry-cloth robe (also ex–Alexander Peebles, Esq.) from the chrome towel warmer, shrugged into it, took the phone number from Martha, and went into the bedroom, where he sat on the bed and picked up the telephone on the bedside table.

Martha sat on the bed next to him.

"Dave Pekach, Mike," he said. "What's up?"

Martha could hear only Dave's side of the conversation.

"They did *what?* . . .

"Monahan okay? . . .

"Anyone else hurt? . . .

"Where's Wohl? . . .

"Okay. If you get in touch with him, tell him I'm on my way to the Roundhouse. It should take me twenty minutes, depending on the traffic. Thanks for calling me, Mike."

He put the telephone back in its cradle and stood up.

He saw Martha's eyes, curiosity in them, on him.

She never pries, he thought. *She's pleased when I tell her things, but she never asks.*

"When they started to take Monahan, the witness to the Goldblatt job, from Goldblatt's to the Roundhouse, they were firebombed."

"Firebombed?"

"Somebody threw a whatdoyoucallit? A Molotov cocktail, a bottle full of gas."

"Was anyone hurt?"

He looked at the green leather chaise lounge where he'd tossed his uniform. It had already been removed.

Damn!

He started to put on the clothing Evans had laid out for him, and remembered she had asked a question.

"No. Not as far as Sabara knew. I sent a Highway RPC down there. I can't imagine anybody trying to firebomb a Highway car." He looked at her, and added, "I'll have to go down there, to the Roundhouse."

"Of course," she said, and then, a moment later, "I suppose that means I should make arrangements for my dinner? And about seeing the Payne boy?"

"I don't know how long I'll be," he said. "You'd probably have to wait around—"

"I don't mind," Martha said very evenly.

Pekach suddenly realized that a very great deal depended on his response to that.

"On the other hand, if you came along, it would save me coming all the way back out here to get you. You sure you wouldn't mind waiting?"

"I don't have anything else to do," she said. "Why should I?"

Dave Pekach understood that he had come up with the proper response. He could see it in her eyes, and then confirmation came when she impulsively kissed him.

When they went out under the portico, the Mercedes was there. He looked at the garage. Not only had the Department's car been put away, but a snowplow sat in front of the garage door where it had been put.

He went to the Mercedes and put his hand on the door, and then remembered his manners and went around and held the passenger-side door open for Martha.

I have been manipulated, he thought. *Why am I not pissed off?*

As Peter Wohl looked for a place to park at Frankford Hospital, he saw two Highway cars, the first parked by the main entrance, and the second near the Emergency entrance.

Jesus Christ, has something happened?

His concern, which he recognized to contain more than a small element of fear for Matt Payne's well-being, immediately chagrined him.

You're getting paranoid. They have this clever thing called "police radio." You have one. If something had happened, you'd have heard about it.

He had trouble finding a place to park and finally decided he had as much right to park by the main entrance as the Highway RPC did. He wasn't here to visit an ailing aunt.

He walked past the "Visitors Register Here" desk by holding out his leather badge-and-photo-ID case to the rent-a-cop on duty. But when he walked across the lobby toward the bank of elevators he saw that the hospital rent-a-cops had set up another barrier, a guy sitting behind a table you had to get past before you could get on an elevator.

This time, holding out the leather folder and murmuring the magic words "police officer" didn't work.

"Excuse me, sir," the rent-a-cop said, getting to his feet after Wohl had waved the leather folder in front of him. "I don't see your visitor's badge."

Another rent-a-cop he hadn't noticed before stepped between Wohl and the elevator.

"I don't have one," Wohl said. "I'm a police officer." He gave the rent-a-cop a better look at his identification.

"Who are you going to see?"

"Matthew M. Payne," Wohl said. "He's on the surgical floor."

"I'm sorry, sir, there's no patient here by that name," the rent-a-cop said.

He had not, Wohl noticed, checked any kind of a list before making that announcement.

He chuckled. "I'm *Inspector* Wohl," he said. "The police officers keeping an eye on Officer Payne work for me."

"Just a moment, sir," the rent-a-cop said, and sat down at his table and dialed a number. A moment later he said, "You can go up, sir."

"You guys are really doing your job," Wohl said. "Thank you."

The compliment, which was genuine, didn't seem to make much of an impression on either of the rent-a-cops.

When Wohl stepped off the elevator, there was a Highway Patrolman Wohl could not remember having seen before, and a Highway Sergeant he had seen around and whose name came to him almost instantly.

"Hello, Sergeant Carter," Wohl said, smiling, extending his hand. "For a while there, I didn't think they were going to let me come up here."

"Good evening, sir," Sergeant Carter said. "You know Hughes, don't you?"

"I've seen him around," Wohl said, offering his hand. "How are you, Hughes?"

"Inspector."

Then Wohl saw something he didn't like. Behind Hughes, leaning against the wall, was a short-barreled pump shotgun.

I don't think that's a Remington 870, Wohl thought automatically. *Probably an Ithica.*

"Do you really think we're going to need the shotgun?" Wohl asked.

"My experience is, Inspector," Carter said, "that if you have a shotgun, you seldom need one."

Wohl smiled.

Now, how am I going to tactfully tell him to get it out of sight without hurting his feelings?

The first time he had seen Carter, shortly after assuming command of Highway, Wohl had taken the trouble of reading his name on the name tag and committing it to memory. First impressions *did* matter, and he had been favorably impressed with his first look at Carter. He was a good-looking guy, tall and lean, about as black as Jason Washington, who wore his uniform not only with evident pride, but according to the regulations. Highway guys were prone—Sergeant Peter Wohl had himself been prone—to add little sartorial touches to the prescribed uniform that sometimes crossed the line into ludicrous.

Most commonly this was a crushed brim cap four sizes too small, shined cartridges (and/or extra cartridges), patent leather boots, and Sam Browne belt, that sort of thing. Carter looked like he could pose for a picture with the caption "The Prescribed Uniform for a Highway Patrol Sergeant."

"I understand that the Secret Service guys guarding the President carry their shotguns in golf bags," Wohl said. "To keep from frightening the voters. Is there some way you can think of to get that out of sight, but handy?"

"Not offhand, but I'll come up with something. You said 'handy,' Inspector. Does that mean you take this threat seriously?"

"They threw a Molotov cocktail at Sergeant Washington. You would have to be serious, or crazy, to do something like that. Yeah, I take them seriously. These people want two things, I think. To get themselves in the newspapers and to frighten off the witnesses to the Goldblatt job. They're already facing murder one. From their perspective, they have more to gain than to lose from killing a cop."

"Did it scare off the witness?"

"It made him mad," Wohl laughed. "I just talked to Jason Washington. He said Mr. Monahan couldn't wait to get over to the Detention Center and identify these creeps."

"I looked in on Payne," Carter said. "I wondered if he was—if he had a gun. I didn't think I should ask him. I didn't know how much he knows about what the ILA has threatened."

"Do me a favor, Sergeant," Wohl said. "Don't use the term 'ILA.' Don't call these scumbags an army. That's just what they want. They're thieves and murderers, that's all."

"Sorry," Carter said. "I see what you mean."

"And pass that word too," Wohl said. "To answer your question: Yes, he's got one. The Mobile Crime Lab guys took his to the laboratory, so I loaned him one."

"How long is he going to be in here?"

"I'm not sure that I know what I'm talking about, but I think he'll be out of here tomorrow. Apparently, the doctors think the sooner you're moving around, the better it is."

"And then what?"

"It's sort of a delicate question. We don't want these lunatics to think they have frightened us silly. Payne is, after all, a cop. Captain Pekach is working out some kind of an arrangement where Payne's friends can keep an eye on him in plainclothes, maybe on overtime."

"I'd be happy to take a little of that, if you need somebody."

Wohl chuckled. "You'd look a little out of place, Sergeant, but thank you anyway."

"Because I'm black, you mean?"

"No. Because you're what—thirty-five? And because you look like a cop. The three guys who are going to sit on Payne are his age."

"And white?"

I can't let that pass.

"Tiny Lewis is as black as you are," Wohl said coldly. "He's also as old as Payne. He's one of the three. And since we're on this sensitive minority kick, Hay-zus Martinez is the second one. That means only one of the three will be what these scumbags would call a honky."

"No offense, Inspector. I didn't mean that the way it sounded."

"Okay. I hope not. But just for the record, the only color I see in a cop is blue."

"Yes, sir."

Wohl saw that Carter looked genuinely unhappy.

Did I have to jump on his ass that way? Was it because this whole thing has got me more upset than I should let it?

The elevator door whooshed open again. The Highway cop with the shotgun, who had been leaning against the wall, straightened, and then relaxed when he recognized Captain David Pekach.

"Inspector," Pekach said, somewhat stiffly. "Sergeant Carter." He nodded at the Highway cop standing against the wall.

Martha Peebles, smiling a little uneasily, stood behind him.

Nice-looking woman, Wohl thought.

"Hello, Dave."

"Inspector, I don't think you know Miss Peebles," Pekach said, slowly and carefully, as if reciting something polite he had memorized, and then he blurted, "my fiancée."

"No, I don't," Wohl said, and, catching the look on Martha Peebles's face, decided, *I'll bet that's the first time he ever used that word.* Confirmation came when he looked at Pekach, whose face was now red.

"How do you do?" Martha Peebles said, offering Wohl her hand.

Classy, Wohl decided. *Just what Dave needs.*

"I'm very pleased to meet you," Wohl said.

"Honey," Pekach went on, "this is Sergeant Carter and Officer Hughes."

They nodded at one another.

"I hope I'm not intruding, Inspector," Martha Peebles said. "Matt Payne's father is an old family friend."

"We were at the Roundhouse, and they told me I'd just missed you; that you were coming here," Pekach said. "We were already on our way here when Sabara called and told me what happened."

"I'm sure Matt will be delighted to see you," Wohl said. "Why don't you go on in? I'd like a quick word with Dave."

He pointed toward Matt's door. Martha walked to it, opened it a crack, peered in, and then pushed the door fully open and went in.

Pekach waited until the automatic closing device had closed the door and then looked at Wohl.

"Well, what do you think?"

"About the security arrangements for Matt or Miss Peebles?"

Pekach flushed again, and then smiled.

"Both," he said.

"Frankly, I can't see what a beautiful woman like that sees in an ugly Polack like you, but they say there's no accounting for taste."

"Thanks a lot."

"And so far as the security arrangements are concerned, it looks to me as if Sergeant Carter has things well in hand," Wohl said.

Why am I uneasy saying that?

"What about when Payne leaves the hospital?"

"We're working on that. Question one, to be answered, is when he will be leaving. We can talk about that in the morning."

Why didn't I just say we're going to have Lewis, McFadden, and Martinez sit on him?

Wohl put his hand on Pekach's arm and led him to Matt Payne's door.

18.

"I'm sorry, we have no patient by that name," the hospital operator said.

"But I know he's there," Helene Stillwell said snappishly. "I *visited* him this morning."

"One moment, please," the operator said.

"Damn!" Helene said.

A male voice came on the line: "May I help you, ma'am?"

Helene hung up.

They're monitoring his calls. Obviously. After that threat to—what did it say?

She dropped her eyes to the *Ledger,* which she had laid on the marble top of the bar in the sun room, and found what she was looking for. It was in a front-page story with the headline ISLAMIC LIBERATION ARMY THREATENS REVENGE FOR POLICE SHOOTING.

"Death to the Zionist oppressors of our people and the murderers who call themselves police!" she read aloud. "My God!"

Under the headline was a photograph of Matt and Mayor Jerry Carlucci, with the caption "Officer M. M. Payne, of Special Operations, apparently the target of the ILA threat, shown with Mayor Jerome Carlucci three months ago, shortly after Payne shot to death Germantown resident Warren K. Fletcher, allegedly the 'North Philadelphia serial rapist.' "

Looking at Matt's face, she had a sudden very clear mental image of his gun, and the slick, menacing cartridges for it, which was then replaced by the memory of his naked body next to hers, and of him and the eruption, the explosion, in her, which had followed.

"Christ!" she said softly, and reached for the cognac snifter on the marble.

There was the clunking noise the garage door always made the moment the mechanism was triggered. When she looked out the glass wall at the end of the sun room, she saw Farny's Lincoln coupe waiting for the garage door to open fully.

I didn't see him come up the drive, she thought, and then: *I wonder what he's doing home so early.*

Helene went behind the bar, intending to give the cognac snifter a quick rinse and to put the bottle away. But then she changed her mind, splashed more Rémy Martin in the glass and drank it all down at a gulp. Then she rinsed the glass and put the Rémy Martin bottle back on the shelf beneath the bar.

Before Farny came into the house, there was time for her to fish in her purse for a spray bottle of breath sweetener, to use it, replace it, and then move purse and newspaper to the glass-topped coffee table. She had seated herself on the couch and found and lit a cigarette by the time she heard the kitchen door open and then slam.

He always slams that goddamn door!

"I'm in here," she called.

He didn't respond. She heard the sound of his opening the cloak closet under the stairs, the rattling of hangers, and then the clunk of the door closing.

He appeared in the entrance to the sun room.

"Hello," he said.

"Hi," Helene said. "I didn't expect you until later."

"I've got to go way the hell across town to the Detention Center," he said. "I thought it made more sense to get dressed now. I may have to call you and ask you to meet me at the Thompsons'. All right?"

She nodded. "I've been thinking about having a drink. Specifically, a straight cognac. Does that sound appealing?"

"Very tempting, but I'd better not. I don't want someone sniffing my breath over there."

"You don't mind if I do? I think I'm fighting a cold."

"Don't fight too hard. You heard what I said about you maybe having to drive yourself to the Thompsons'?"

"Why don't I just skip the Thompsons'?"

"We've been over this before. Thompson is important in the party."

"You make him, you make the both of you sound like apparatchiks in the Supreme Soviet," Helene said.

"That's the second, maybe the third, time you made that little joke. I don't find it funny this time, either."

"You're certainly in a lousy mood. Has it to do with—what did you say? 'The Detention Center'? What is that, anyway?"

She got up and walked to the bar, retrieved her glass and the bottle of Rémy Martin, and poured a half inch into the snifter.

"The Detention Center is where they lock people up before they're indicted, or if they can't make bail. Essentially, it's a prison in everything but name."

"What are you going to be doing there?"

"The one witness we have to the robbery and murder at Goldblatt's is going to try to pick the guilty parties out in line-ups. Washington—that great big Negro detective?—has scheduled it for half past six. Christ only knows how long it will take."

"I think you're supposed to say 'black,' not 'Negro,' " Helene said.

"Whatever."

"Have you seen the paper?"

"I wasn't in it, my secretary said."

"I meant about the Islamic Liberation Army threatening reprisal, revenge, whatever."

"I heard about it," he said, and then followed her pointing finger and went and picked up the *Ledger.*

She waited until he had read the newspaper story, and then asked, "Do they mean it?"

"Who the hell knows?" he said, and then had a thought. "Going over to see that kid was a good idea. I don't know if I knew it or not, but I didn't make the connection. You do know who his father is?"

"Tell me."

"Brewster Cortland Payne, of Mawson, Payne, Stockton, McAdoo & Lester."

"He's important in the party too, I suppose?"

"Helene, you're being a bitch, and I'm really not in the mood for it."

"Sorry."

"But to answer your question, yes. He is important in the party. And if this political thing doesn't work out, Mawson, Payne, Stockton, McAdoo & Lester is the sort of firm with which I would like to be associated."

"Then maybe we should have gotten him a box of candy or something."

He looked at her and took a moment to consider whether she was being sarcastic again.

"It's not too late, I suppose," Helene said.

He considered that a moment.

"I think that's a lost opportunity," he said.

Damn, it would have given me an excuse to go see him.

"Well, maybe we could have him for drinks or dinner or something," Helene said. "If it's important."

"We'll see," Farnsworth Stillwell said. "I'm going to get dressed."

He had just started up the stairs when the telephone rang. Helene answered it.

"Mr. Farnsworth Stillwell, please," a female voice said. "Mr. Armando Giacomo is calling."

"Just a moment, please," Helene said, and covered the mouthpiece with her hand.

"Are you home for a Mr. Giacomo?" she called.

"Armando Giacomo?" Stillwell asked, already coming back into the room.

She nodded. "His secretary, I think."

Stillwell took the phone from her.

"This is Farnsworth Stillwell," he said, and then, a moment later, "How are you, Armando? What can I do for you?"

The charm is on, Helene thought, *Armando Whatsisname must be somebody else important in the party.*

"Well, I must say I'm surprised," Stillwell said to the telephone. "If I may say so, Armando, hiring you is tantamount to saying 'I'm guilty as sin and need a genius to get me off.' "

There was a reply that Helene could not hear.

He's wearing one of his patently insincere smiles. Whatever this was about, he doesn't like it.

"Well, I'll see you there, then, Armando," Stillwell said. "I'm going to change my clothes and go over there. Helene and I are having dinner with Jack Thompson, and I have no idea how long the business at the Detention Center will take. I appreciate your courtesy in calling me."

He absentmindedly handed her the handset.

"What was that all about?" Helene asked.

"That was Armando C. Giacomo," he said.

"So the girl said. Who *is* Armando C. Giawhatever?"

A look of annoyance crossed his face, but he almost visibly made the decision to answer her.

"The top two criminal lawyers in Philadelphia, in my judgment, and practically everyone else's, are Colonel J. Dunlop Mawson of the aforementioned Mawson, Payne, Stockton, McAdoo & Lester and Armando C. Giacomo. Giacomo telephoned to tell me he has been retained to represent the people the police arrested this morning."

"That's bad news, I gather."

"Frankly, I would rather face some public defender six months out of law school, or one of the less expensive members of the criminal bar," Stillwell said. "I don't want to walk out of the courtroom with egg all over my face. I'll have to give this development some thought."

He turned and left the room and went to their bedroom on the second floor.

Farnsworth Stillwell had several disturbing thoughts. Armando C. Giacomo was very good, and consequently very expensive. Like Colonel J. Dunlop Mawson, he had a well-earned reputation for defending, most often successfully and invariably with great skill, people charged with violation of the whole gamut of criminal offenses.

But, like Mawson, Giacomo seldom represented ordinary criminals, for, in Stillwell's mind, the very good reason that ordinary criminals seldom had any money. They both drew their clientele from the well heeled, excluding only members of the Mob.

If he was representing the Islamic Liberation Army, he certainly wasn't doing it *pro bono publico;* he was being paid, well paid. By whom? Certainly not by the accused themselves. If there was money around to hire Armando C. Giacomo, it challenged Matt Lowenstein's (and Peter Wohl's) theory that the Islamic Liberation Army was nothing more than a group of thugs with a bizarre imagination.

Farnsworth Stillwell had a good deal of respect for Armando C. Giacomo, not all of it based on his professional reputation. On a personal basis, he regarded Giacomo as a brother in the fraternity of naval aviators. They hadn't flown together—Giacomo had flown in the Korean War, Stillwell in Vietnam—but they shared the common experience of Pensacola training, landing high-performance aircraft on the decks of aircraft carriers, flying in Harm's Way, and the proud self-assurance that comes with golden wings pinned to a blue Navy uniform.

Stillwell did not really understand why a man who had been a naval aviator would choose to become a criminal lawyer, except for the obvious reason that, at the upper echelons of the specialty, it paid very well indeed.

He was forced now to consider the unpleasant possibilities, starting with the least pleasant to consider, that Armando C. Giacomo was a better, more experienced lawyer than he was.

I will have absolutely no room for error in the courtroom.

Or, for that matter, in all the administrative garbage that has to be plowed through before we get into court.

Christ, why didn't I keep my mouth shut when Tony Callis brought this up? When am I going to learn that whenever something looks as if the gods are smiling on me, the exact opposite is true?

Farnsworth Stillwell had been told by Sergeant Jason Washington that the lineups were going to start at the Detention Center at half past six.

Stillwell often joked that his only virtue was punctuality. The truth was that he believed punctuality to be not only good manners, but good business practice. He made a genuine effort to be where he was supposed to be when he was supposed to be there. He expected reciprocity on the part of people with whom he was professionally associated, and demanded it from both his subordinates and those who ranked lower in the government hierarchy than he did.

He had never been to the Detention Center before, so in order to be on time, he had taken the trouble to locate it precisely on a map, and to leave his house in sufficient time to arrive on time.

When he pulled into one of the Official Visitor parking spots at the Detention Center, it was 6:28.

He entered the building, and went to the uniformed corrections officer sitting behind a plate-glass window.

"Assistant District Attorney Stillwell," he announced. "To meet Sergeant Washington."

"He's not here yet," the corrections officer, a small black woman, said. "You can take a seat and wait, if you like."

He smiled at her and said, "Thank you."

He sat down on a battered bench against the wall, more than a little annoyed.

He and Helene were due at Jack Thompson's at eight, and he intensively disliked the idea of arriving there late. He had told Helene that if he wasn't back, or hadn't called, by half past seven, she was to drive to the Thompsons'.

He now regretted that decision. The way she was throwing the cognac down, the possibility existed that the headlines in tomorrow's *Bulletin* and *Ledger* and *Daily News* would not concern the ILA, but rather something they knew their readers would really like to read, "Assistant District Attorney Stillwell's Wife Charged in Drunken Driving Episode."

If the lineups were to begin at half past six, Stillwell fumed, *obviously some preparatory steps had to be taken, and therefore Washington should have arrived, with the witness in tow, at whatever time before half past six was necessary in order for him to do what he had to do so that they could begin on schedule.*

Stillwell was aware that one of his faults was a tendency to become angry over circumstances over which he had no control. This seemed to be one of them. He told himself that Washington was not late on purpose, that things, for example delays in traffic because of the snow, sometimes happened.

Washington will be along any moment, with an explanation, and probably an apology, for being tardy, Stillwell thought, taking just a little satisfaction in knowing that he was being reasonable.

At quarter to seven, however, when Sergeant Washington had still not shown up, or even had the simple courtesy to send word that he would be delayed, Farnsworth Stillwell decided that he had been patient enough.

While he thought it was highly unlikely that Staff Inspector Peter Wohl would know where Sergeant Washington was and/or why he wasn't at the Detention Center when he was supposed to be, calling Wohl would at least serve to tell him (a) that his super detective was unreliable, time-wise, and (b) that Farnsworth Stillwell did not like to be kept waiting.

He asked the female corrections officer behind the plate-glass window if he could use the telephone.

"It's for official business only, sir."

Farnsworth Stillwell had a fresh, unpleasant thought. There was no one else here.

Armando C. Giacomo was supposed to be here, and certainly there would be others besides Washington and the witness.

Had the whole damned thing been called off for some reason, and he had not been told?

"Are you sure Sergeant Washington isn't here? Could he be here and you not be aware of it?"

"Everybody has to come past me," she said. "If he were here, I'd know it."

"May I have the telephone, please?"

"It's for official business only, like I told you before."

"I'm Assistant District Attorney Stillwell. This is official business."

She gave him a look that suggested she doubted him, but gave in.

"I'll have the operator get the number for you, sir."

"I don't know the number. I want to talk to Inspector Wohl of Special Operations."

The corrections officer obligingly searched for the number on her list of official telephones. It was not listed, and she so informed Farnsworth Stillwell.

"Check with information."

Information had the number.

"Special Operations, may I help you?"

"This is Assistant District Attorney Stillwell. Inspector Wohl, please."

"I'm sorry, sir. Inspector Wohl has gone for the day."

"Do you have a number where he can be reached?"

"Just one moment, sir."

"This is Lieutenant Kelsey. May I help you, sir?"

"This is Assistant District Attorney Stillwell. It's important that I get in touch with Inspector Wohl."

"I'm sorry, the inspector's gone for the day. Is there something I can do for you, Mr. Stillwell?"

"Do you have a number where he can be reached?"

"No, sir."

"You mean you have no idea where he is?"

"The inspector is on his way to Frankford Hospital, sir. But until he calls in, I won't have a number there for him."

"What about Sergeant Washington?"

"Are you referring to Detective Washington, sir?"

"I understood he was promoted."

"Well, what do you know? I hadn't heard that."

"Do you know where he is?"

"He's at the Detention Center, sir. I can give you that number."

"I'm at the Detention Center. He's not here. That's what I'm calling about."

"Hold one, sir," Lieutenant Kelsey said.

The pause was twenty seconds, but seemed much longer, before Kelsey came back on the line.

"They're at Cottman and State Road, Mr. Stillwell. They should be there any second now."

"Thank you."

"Should I ask Inspector Wohl to get in touch with you when he calls in, sir?"

"That won't be necessary, thank you very much," Farnsworth Stillwell said.

He put the telephone back in its cradle, and slid it back through the opening in the plate-glass window. He walked to the door as the first of the cars in what had become a five-car convoy rolled up.

Heading the procession was a Highway Patrol Sergeant's car. A second Highway Patrol RPC with two Highway cops followed him. The third car was Jason Washington's nearly new Ford. Stillwell saw a man in the front seat beside him, and decided that he must be

Monahan The Witness. There was another unmarked car, with two men in civilian clothing in it behind Washington's Ford, and bringing up the rear was another Highway RPC.

The sergeant leading the procession stopped his car in a position that placed Washington's car closest to the entrance of the Detention Center. Everyone except Monahan The Witness got quickly out of their cars. The Highway Patrolmen stood on the sidewalk as the plainclothes went to the passenger side of Washington's car and took him from the car. Washington and the Highway Sergeant moved to the entrance door of the building and held it open.

Sergeant Jason Washington saw Farnsworth Stillwell and nodded.

"Good evening, Mr. Stillwell," he said.

"You told me this was going to take place at half past six. It's now"—he checked his watch—"four past seven."

"We were delayed," Washington said.

"Were you, indeed?"

"We were Molotov-cocktailed, is what happened," the man Stillwell was sure was Monahan The Witness said.

"I beg your pardon?"

"Mr. Stillwell," Washington said, "this is Mr. Albert J. Monahan."

Stillwell smiled at Monahan and offered his hand.

"I'm Farnsworth Stillwell, Mr. Monahan. I'm very pleased to meet you."

"Can you believe that?" Monahan said. "A Molotov cocktail? Right on South Street? What the hell is the world coming to?"

What is this man babbling about? A Molotov cocktail is what the Russians used against German tanks, a bottle of gasoline with a flaming wick.

"I'm afraid I don't quite understand," Stillwell said.

"As we drove away from Goldblatt's," Washington explained, "party or parties unknown threw a bottle filled with gasoline down—more than likely from the roof—onto a Highway car that was escorting us here."

"I will be *damned!*" Farnsworth Stillwell said.

My God, wait until the newspapers get hold of that!

"The bottle bounced off the Highway car, broke when it hit the street, and then caught fire," Washington went on.

"Was anyone hurt?"

"I understand a car parked on South Street caught fire," Washington said. "But no one was hurt. We went to the Roundhouse. I knew Central Detectives and the laboratory people would want a look at the Highway car."

"You could have called," Stillwell said, and immediately regretted it.

Washington looked at him coldly, but did not directly respond.

"I'm going to explain to Mr. Monahan how we run the lineup, lineups," Washington said. "And show him the layout. Perhaps you'd like to come along?"

"Yes, thank you, Sergeant, I'd appreciate that," Stillwell said. He smiled at Washington. Washington did not return it.

"The way this works, Mr. Monahan," he said, "is that the defense counsel will try to question your identification. One of the ways they'll try to do that is to attempt to prove that we rigged the lineup, set it up so that you would have an idea who we think the individual is. Lead you, so to speak. You follow me?"

"Yeah, sure."

"So we will lean over backward to make sure that the lineups are absolutely fair."

"Where do you get the other people?" Monahan said. "The innocent ones?"

"They're all volunteers."

"Off the street? People in jail?"

"Neither. People being held here. This is the Detention Center. Nobody being held here has been found guilty of anything. They're awaiting trial. The other people in the lineup will be chosen from them, from those that have volunteered."

"Why do they volunteer?"

"Well, I suppose I could stick my tongue in my cheek and say they're all public-spirited citizens, anxious to make whatever small contribution they can to the criminal justice system, but the truth is I don't know. If they had me in here for something, I don't think I'd be running around looking for some way I could help, particularly if all I got out of it was an extra ice cream chit or movie pass. And, of course, most of the people being held here don't volunteer. As for the ones that do, I can only guess they do it because they're bored, or figure they can screw the system up."

"How do you mean?"

"Let's say there's a guy here who has a perfect alibi for the Goldblatt job; he was in here. So he figures if he can get in the lineup, and somehow look nervous or guilty and have you point him out, the guy who did the Goldblatt job walks away, and so does he; he has a perfect alibi."

"I'll be goddamned," Monahan said.

"So it's very important to the good guys, Mr. Monahan," Washington said, "that before you pick somebody out you be absolutely sure it's the guy. It would be much better for you not to be able to recognize somebody in the lineup than for you to make a mistake. If you did that, it would come out in court and put in serious question every other identification you made. You understand, of course."

"Yeah," Monahan said thoughtfully, then added: "I'll be damned."

Washington pushed open a door and held it open as Monahan and Stillwell walked through it.

Stillwell found himself in a windowless, harshly lit room forty feet long and twenty-five wide. Against one of the long walls was a narrow platform, two feet off the floor and about six feet wide. Behind it the wall had been painted. The numbers 1 through 8 were painted near the ceiling, marking where the men in the lineup were to stand. Horizontal lines marked off in feet and inches ran under the numbers. Mounted on the ceiling were half a dozen floodlights aimed at the platform. There was a step down from the platform to the floor at the right.

Facing the platform were a row of folding metal chairs and two tables. A microphone was on one table and a telephone on the other.

There were a dozen people in the room, four of them in corrections officer's uniforms. A lieutenant from Major Crimes Division had a 35-mm camera with a flash attachment hanging around his neck. There were two women, both holding stenographer's notebooks.

I wonder how it is that I was left sitting outside on that bench when everyone else with a connection with this was in here?

Stillwell recognized Detectives D'Amata and Pelosi and then a familiar face. "The proceedings can now begin," Armando C. Giacomo announced sonorously, "the Right Honorable Assistant District Attorney having finally made an appearance."

Giacomo, a slight, lithe, dapper man who wore what was left of his hair plastered to the sides of his tanned skull, walked quickly to Stillwell and offered his hand.

"Armando, how are you?" Stillwell said.

"Armando C. Giacomo is, as always, ready to defend the rights of the unjustly accused against all the abusive powers of the state."

"Presuming they can write a nonrubber check, of course," Jason Washington said. "How are you, Manny?"

"Ah, my favorite gumshoe. How are you, Jason?"

Giacomo enthusiastically pumped Washington's hand.

They were friends, Stillwell saw, the proof being not only their smiles, but that Washington had called him "Manny." He remembered hearing that Giacomo was well thought of by the cops because he devoted the *pro bono publico* side of his practice to defending cops charged with violating the civil rights of individuals.

"Aside from almost getting myself fried on the way over here, I'm fine. How about you?"

"Whatever are you talking about, Detective Washington?" Giacomo asked.

"Detective Washington is now Sergeant Washington," Stillwell said.

"And you stopped to celebrate? Shame on you!"

"We was Molotov-cocktailed, is what happened," Albert J. Monahan explained.

"You must be Mr. Monahan," Giacomo said. "I'm Armando C. Giacomo. I'm very happy to meet you."

"Likewise," Monahan said.

"What was that you were saying about a Molotov cocktail?"

"They threw one at us. Off a roof by Goldblatt's."

Giacomo looked at Washington for confirmation. Washington nodded.

"Well, I'm very glad to see that you came through that all right," Giacomo said.

"I came through it pissed, is the way I came through it. That's fucking outrageous."

"I absolutely agree with you. Terrible. Outrageous. Did the police manage to apprehend the culprits?"

"Not yet," Washington said.

"Mr. Giacomo, Mr. Monahan," Washington said, "is here to represent the people we think were at Goldblatt's."

"And you're friends with him?"

"Yes, we're friends," Giacomo said solemnly. "We have the same basic interest. Justice."

Jason Washington laughed deep in his stomach.

"Manny, you're really something," he said.

"It is not nice to mock small Italian gentlemen," Giacomo said. "You ought to be ashamed of yourself."

Washington laughed louder, then turned to Joe D'Amata: "Are we about ready to do this?"

"Yeah. We have seven different groups of people." He pointed toward the door at the end of the platform.

Washington turned to Monahan: "If you'll just have a chair, Mr. Monahan—"

Detective Pelosi smiled at Monahan and put his hands on the back of one of the folding chairs. Monahan walked to it and sat down.

Washington waved Giacomo ahead of him and headed for the door. Stillwell followed them.

There were two corrections officers and eight other people in a small room. The eight people were all Hispanic, all of about the same age and height and weight. One of them was Hector Carlos Estivez.

"Okay with you, Manny?" Washington asked.

Armando C. Giacomo looked at the eight men very carefully before he finally nodded his head.

"That should be all right, Jason," he said, and turned and walked out of the room. Washington and Stillwell followed him.

Giacomo sat down in a folding chair next to Monahan. Washington sat on the other side of him, and Stillwell sat next to Washington.

"Okay, Joe," Washington said.

"Lights," D'Amata ordered.

One of the corrections officers flicked switches that killed all the lights in the room except the floodlights shining on the platform. The people in the room would be only barely visible to the men on the platform.

"Okay," D'Amata ordered. "Bring them in."

The door to the room at the end of the platform opened, and eight men came into the room and took the two steps up to the platform.

"Stand directly under the number, look forward," D'Amata ordered. The men complied.

The Major Crimes lieutenant with the 35-mm camera walked in front of the men sitting in the chairs. He took three flash photographs, one from the left, one from the center, and one from the right.

"You didn't have to do that, Jason," Giacomo said.

"Oh, yes, I did, Manny," Washington said. "I only get burned once."

I wonder what the hell that's all about, Stillwell thought, and then the answer came to him: *I will get copies of those photographs. If Giacomo suggests during the trial that Monahan was able to pick out Estivez because the other people in the lineup were conspicuously different in age, or size, or complexion, or whatever, I can introduce the pictures he's taking.*

He remembered what Tony Callis had said about Washington having forgotten more about criminal law than he knew.

"Number one, step forward," D'Amata ordered when the photographer had stepped out of the way.

"Number three," Albert J. Monahan said positively.

"Just a moment, please, Mr. Monahan," Washington said.

"Number three is one of them. I recognize the bastard when I see him."

"Mr. Monahan," Washington said, "I ask you now if you recognize any of the men on the platform."

"Number three," Monahan said impatiently. "I told you already."

"Can you tell us where you have seen the man standing under the number three on the platform?" Washington asked.

"He's one of the bastards who came into the store and robbed it and shot it up."

"You are referring to January third of this year, and the robbery and murder that occurred at Goldblatt's furniture store on South Street?"

"Yes, I am."

"There is no question in your mind that the man standing under number three is one of the participants in that robbery and murder?"

"None whatever. That's one of them. That's him. Number three."

"Mr. Giacomo?" Washington asked.

Armando C. Giacomo shook his head, signifying that he had nothing to say.

"Jason?" Joe D'Amata asked.

"We're through with this bunch," Washington said.

"Take them out," D'Amata ordered.

A corrections officer opened the door at the end of the platform and gestured for the men on the platform to get off it.

That man didn't show any sign of anything at all when Monahan picked him out, Stillwell thought. *What kind of people are we dealing with here?*

"Mr. Monahan," Giacomo said. "I see that you're wearing glasses."

"That's right."

"Before this is all over, I'd be grateful if you would give me the name of your eye doctor."

"You're not going to try to tell me I couldn't see that bastard? Recognize him?"

"I'm just trying to do the best job I can, Mr. Monahan," Giacomo said. "I'm sure you understand."

"No, I don't," Monahan said. "I don't understand at all."

19.

Lieutenant Jack Malone had just carefully rewrapped the aluminum foil around the remnants of his dinner—two egg rolls and beef-and-pepper—and was about to shoot it, basketball-like, into the wastebasket under the writing desk in his room in the St. Charles Hotel when his telephone rang.

He glanced at his watch as he reached for the telephone. Quarter past seven. Sometimes Little Jack would telephone him around this hour. His first reaction was pleasure, which was almost immediately replaced with something close to pain:

If it is Little Jack, he's liable to ask again why I'm not coming home.

"Peter Wohl, Jack," his caller said. "Am I interrupting anything?"

"No, sir."

"Sorry to bother you at home, but I want to talk to you about something."

"Yes, sir?"

"Have you had dinner?"

"Yes, sir."

"Would you mind watching me eat? I've got to get something in my stomach."

"Not at all."

"You know Ribs Unlimited on Chestnut Street?"

"Yes, sir."

"Can you meet me there in—thirty, thirty-five minutes?"

"Yes, sir, I'll be there."

"At the bar, Jack. Thank you," Wohl said, and hung up.

What the fuck does Wohl want? Is this going to be one of those heart-to-heart talks better held in an informal atmosphere? Has word finally got to him that I was watching Holland's body shop?

"Malone, you disappoint me. A word to the wise should have been sufficient. Get Bob Holland out of your mind. In other words, get off his case."

Malone pushed himself out of bed and started to dress. He really hated to wear anything but blue jeans and a sweater and a nylon jacket, *because sure as Christ made little apples, if I put on a suit and shirt, I will get something—slush or barbecue sauce, something—on them and have to take them to the cleaners.*

"But on the other hand," he said aloud as he took a tweed sports coat and a pair of cavalry twill trousers from the closet, "one must look one's best when one is about to socialize with one's superior officer. Clothes indeed do make the man."

When he got outside the hotel, he saw that the temperature had dropped, and frozen the slush. He decided to walk. It wasn't really that close, but if he drove, he might not be able to find a place to park when he came back, and he had plenty of time. Wohl had said thirty, thirty-five minutes.

Now I won't soil my clothes, I'll slip on the goddamn ice and break my fucking leg.

Ribs Unlimited, despite the lousy weather, was crowded. There was a line of people waiting for the nod of the headwaiter in the narrow entrance foyer.

Malone stood in the line for a minute or two, and then remembered Wohl had said "in the bar."

The headwaiter tried to stop him.

"I'm meeting someone," Malone said, and kept walking.

He found an empty stool next to a woman who was desperately trying to appear younger than the calendar made her, and whose perfume filled his nostrils with a scent that reminded him of something else he hadn't been getting much—any—of lately.

When the bartender appeared, he almost automatically said "Ortleib's" but at the last moment changed his mind.

"John Jameson, easy on the ice," he said.

Fuck it, I've been a good boy lately. One little shooter will be good for me. And one I can afford.

Wohl appeared as the bartender served the drink.

"Been waiting long?"

"No, sir, I just got here."

"What is that?"

"Irish."

"I feel Irish," Wohl said to the bartender. "Same way, please. Not too much ice."

A heavyset man appeared, beaming.

"How are you, Inspector?"

"How are you, Charley?" Wohl replied. "Charley, this is Lieutenant Jack Malone. Jack, Charley Meader, our host."

"You work with the Inspector, Lieutenant?" Meader said, pumping Malone's hand.

"Yes, sir," Malone said.

"I've got you a table in the back anytime you're ready, Inspector," Meader said.

"I guess we could carry our drinks, right?" Wohl said. "When I get mine, that is."

"Whatever you'd prefer," Meader said, and waited until the bartender served Wohl.

"House account that, Jerry," he said.

"Very kind, thank you," Wohl said.

"My pleasure, Inspector. And anytime, you know that."

He patted Wohl on the shoulder and shook hands with both of them.

"Whenever you're ready, Inspector, your table's available," Meader said. "Good to see you. And to meet you, Lieutenant."

Wohl waited until he had gone, then said, "There was once a Department of Health inspector who led Charley Meader to believe that he would have far less trouble passing his inspections if he handed him an envelope once a week when he came in for a free meal."

"Oh," Malone said.

"Charley belongs to the Jaguar Club," Wohl went on. "You know I have a Jaguar?"

"I've seen it."

"1950 SK-120 Drophead Coupe," Wohl said. "So he came to me after a meeting one night and said he had heard I was a cop, and that he didn't want to put me on the spot, but did I know an honest sergeant, or maybe even an honest lieutenant. He would go to him, without mentioning my name, and tell him his problem."

"A long time ago?"

"Just before they gave me Special Operations," Wohl said.

"He didn't know you were a staff inspector?"

"No. Not until I testified in court."

"So what happened?"

"The next time the Health Department sleazeball came in, I was tending bar and I had a photographer up there." He gestured toward a balcony overlooking the bar and smiled. "I put a microphone in the pretzel bowl. Hanging Harriet gave the Health Department guy three to five," Wohl said.

Hanging Harriet was the Hon. Harriet M. McCandless, a formidable black jurist who passionately believed that civilized society was based upon a civil service whose honesty was above question.

"No wonder he buys you drinks."

"The sad part of the story, Jack, is that Charley really was afraid to go to the cops until he found one he thought *might* be honest."

Wohl took a swallow of his drink, and then said, "Let's carry these to the table. I've got to get something to eat."

The headwaiter left his padded rope and showed them to a table at the rear of the room. A waiter immediately appeared.

"The El Rancho Special," Wohl ordered. "Hold the beans. French fries."

"What's that?"

"Barbecued beef. Great sauce. You really ought to try it."

"I think I will," Malone said.

"Yes, sir. And can I get you gentlemen a drink?"

"Please. The same thing. Jameson's, isn't it?"

"Jameson's," Malone offered.

"And I don't care what Mr. Meader says, I want the check for this," Wohl said.

The waiter looked uncomfortable.

"You're going to have to talk to Mr. Meader about that, sir."

"All right," Wohl said. He waited until the waiter left, and then said, "Well, you can't say I didn't try to pay for this, can you?"

Malone chuckled.

Wohl reached in the breast pocket of his jacket and came out with several sheets of blue-lined paper and handed them to Malone.

"I'd like to know what you think about that, Jack. I don't have much—practically no—experience in this sort of thing."

"What is it?"

"How to protect Monahan, the witness in the Goldblatt job, and Matt Payne. Monahan positively identified everybody we arrested, by the way. Washington called me just after I called you."

The protection plan was detailed and precise, even including drawings of Monahan's house, Matt's apartment, and the areas around them. That didn't surprise Malone, for he expected as much from Wohl. His brief association with him had convinced him that he really was as smart as his reputation held him to be.

But he was surprised at the handwriting. He had read somewhere, years before, and come to accept, that a very good clue to a man's character was his handwriting. From what he had seen of Wohl, what he knew about him, there was a certain flamboyance to his character, which, according to the handwriting theory, should have manifested itself in flamboyant, perhaps even careless, writing. But the writing on the sheets of lined paper was quite the opposite. Wohl's characters were small, carefully formed, with dots over the *i*'s, and neatly crossed *t*'s. Even his abbreviations were followed by periods.

Maybe that's what he's really like, Malone thought. *Beneath the fashionable clothing and the anti-establishment public attitude, there really beats the heart of a very careful man, one who doesn't really like to take the chance of being wrong.*

"You have three officers at Monahan's house when he's there," Malone said, but it was meant as a question, and Wohl answered it.

"Two two-man Special Operations RPCs," Wohl said. "Four cops. One car and three cops at Monahan's. The fourth officer will be the guy wearing the rent-a-cop uniform in the garage on Rittenhouse Square."

"He'll have the second car with him at Payne's place?" Malone asked.

Wohl nodded, and went on. "I think Monahan's at the greatest risk. There is a real chance that they will try to kill him. And I don't want everybody there just sitting in a car. I want one man, all the time, walking around. It's cold as hell now, so they can split it up any way they want."

"I understand."

"Payne's apartment is really easy to protect. After five-thirty, the main door is locked. There's a pretty good burglar alarm not only on the door, but on the first-, second-, and third-floor windows. There's a key for the elevator from the basement. They haven't been using it, but starting tomorrow, they'll have to."

"Payne gets out of the hospital tomorrow?"

"Right. Before lunch. He'll go to the Roundhouse for the Homicide interviews—Chief Coughlin got Chief Lowenstein to hold off on that, kept them out of Frankford Hospital, but it has to be done—and then he'll go to his apartment. We'll give the officer in the rent-a-cop uniform a shotgun; he can stay inside that little cubicle with it. And, of course, we'll have one of the three guys with Payne around the clock. I don't think that's going to be a problem. Monahan might be."

"And district and Highway cars will make passes by both places all night, right?"

"District, Highway, and Special Operations," Wohl said. "There should be at least one of them going by both places at least once an hour, maybe more often. And if Monahan keeps insisting on going to work, by Goldblatt's during the day."

"I don't want to sound like I'm polishing the apple, Inspector, but I can't think of a thing I'd do differently."

"Good," Wohl said. "Because, until further notice, you're in charge. I told Captain Sabara and Captain Pekach that they are to give you whatever you think you need."

"Yes, sir," Malone said. "I met McFadden, and I've seen Martinez, but I don't know this man Lewis."

"Great big black kid," Wohl said. "He just came on the job, sort of."

"Sort of?"

"He worked Police Radio for four, five years before he came on the job, while he was in college. His father is a cop. He made lieutenant on the list before yours. He used to be a sergeant in the 18th District."

"Great big guy? Mean as hell, and goes strictly by the book?"

"That's him."

"And the young one's in Highway?"

"No. He's been working as a gofer for Detective Harris. Frankly—don't misunderstand this, he's a nice kid and he'll probably make a very good cop—he's in Special Operations because the mayor made a speech at some black church saying Czernich had assigned him to Special Operations. The same sort of thing that Carlucci did with Payne. Carlucci told the newspapers Payne was my administrative assistant, so I named Payne my administrative assistant. Carlucci told the people at the church that Czernich had assigned this well-educated, highly motivated young black officer to Special Operations, so Czernich assigned him to us—"

The waiter delivered two plates heaped high with food. The smell made Malone's mouth water.

"I'll get your drinks, gentlemen," the waiter said.

"—so not knowing what to do with him," Wohl went on, "I gave him to Harris. He needed a gofer. We still don't have a fucking clue about who shot that young Italian cop, Magnella. That's what Harris is working."

Malone, who had heard the gossip about Detective Tony Harris being on a monumental bender, wondered if Wohl knew.

Wohl started eating.

"The idea, if I didn't make this clear," he said a moment later, "is that with three young cops, in plainclothes, one of whom is actually Payne's buddy, it will look, I hope, that they're just hanging around with him."

"I got that. Instead of a protection detail, you mean?"

"Right. I don't want these scumbags to get the idea that they're worrying us as much as they are."

"How long is this going to go on?"

"So far as Monahan is concerned, I don't know. At least until the end of the trail, and probably a little longer. Stillwell is going to go before the Grand Jury as soon as he can, probably in the next couple of days, and then they're going to put it on the docket as soon as that can be arranged. Giacomo will do his damnedest to get continuances, of course, but with a little bit of luck, we'll have a judge who won't indulge him. As far as Payne is concerned: He's a cop. As soon as he's back for duty, we'll call off official protection. Encourage him to do his drinking and wenching in the FOP."

Malone nodded and chuckled.

"There is also a chance that we'll be able to get our hands on the people who are issuing the press releases. I want the people on Monahan's house to take license numbers, that sort of thing."

"That wasn't in here," Malone said, tapping the lined paper Wohl had given him, "but I thought about it."

"There is also a chance, a very slim one, that we can get some of the other witnesses to agree to testify. Washington's going to talk to them. And I'm sure that Stillwell will probably try too. If we can get more people to come forward—"

"Which is exactly what these scumbags are worried about, what they're trying to prevent," Malone said, and then, really surprising Wohl, said bitterly, "Shit!"

Then, having heard what he said, and seeing the look on Wohl's face, he explained.

"Second table from the headwaiter's table. My wife. Ex-wife."

Wohl looked, saw a not-especially-attractive woman, facing in their direction, across a table from a man with long, silver-gray hair, and then turned to Malone.

"That the lawyer?"

"That's him."

"What I think you should do, Jack," Wohl said, "is smile and act as if you're having a great time. I'm only sorry that I'm not a long-legged blonde with spectacular breastworks."

Malone looked at him for a moment, and then picked up his glass.

"Whoopee!" he said, waving it around. "Ain't we having fun!"

"What do you say, kiddo?" Mickey O'Hara asked as he stuck his head into Matt Payne's room. "Feel up to a couple of visitors?"

"Come on in, Mickey," Matt said. He had been watching an especially dull program on public television hoping that it would put him to sleep; it hadn't. He now knew more of the water problems of Los Angeles than he really wanted to know.

Mickey O'Hara and Eleanor Neal came into the room. O'Hara had a brown bag in his hand, and Eleanor carried a potted plant.

"I hope we're not intruding," Eleanor said, "but Mickey said it would be all right if I came, and I wanted to thank you for saving his life."

"Matt, say hello to Eleanor Neal," Mickey said.

"How do you do?" Matt said, a reflex response, and then: "I didn't save his life."

"Yeah, you did," Mickey said. "But for a moment, in the alley, I thought you had changed your mind."

Matt had a sudden, very clear mental picture of the fear on Mickey's face and in his eyes, right after it had happened, when he had, startled by the flash from Mickey's camera, turned from the man he had shot and pointed his revolver at Mickey O'Hara.

"What does that mean?"

"Not important," Mickey said. He pulled a bottle of John Jameson Irish whiskey from the brown paper bag. "Down payment on what I owe you, Matt."

"Hey, I didn't save your life, okay? You don't owe me a damned thing."

Mickey ignored him. He bent over and took two plastic cups from the bedside table, opened the bottle, poured whiskey in each cup, and then looked at Matt.

"You want it straight, or should I pour some water in it?"

"I'm not sure you should be giving him that," Eleanor said.

"He's an Irishman," Mickey said. "It'll do him more good than whatever else they've been giving him in here."

"Put a little water in it, please, Mickey," Matt said.

Mickey poured water from the insulated water carafe into the paper cup and handed it to Matt.

"Here's to you, Matt," he said, raising his glass.

"Cheers," Matt said, and took a swallow.

Maybe the booze will make me sleepy, or at least take the edge off the pain in the god-damn leg.

And then: *Does he really think I saved his life, or is that bullshit? Blarney.*

"How do you feel, Matt?" Mickey asked.

"I'm all right," Matt said. "I get out of here tomorrow."

"So soon?" Eleanor asked, surprised.

"Current medical wisdom is that the sooner they get you moving around, the better," Matt said.

"You going home?" Mickey said.

"If by 'home' you mean my apartment, yes, of course."

"I was thinking of—where do your parents live, Wallingford?"

"My apartment."

"You know getting in to see you is like getting to see the gold at Fort Knox?" Mickey asked. Matt nodded. "So you know what these people have been up to?"

Matt nodded again.

"The Molotov cocktail, the press release, the second one? All of it?"

Matt nodded again.

"What do you think, Mickey?" he asked.

"I know a lot of black guys, and a lot of Muslims," Mickey said. "Ordinarily, I can get what I want to know out of at least a couple of them. So far, all I get is shrugs when I ask about the Islamic Liberation Army. That could mean they really don't know, or it could mean that they think I'm just one more goddamn honky. I'd watch myself, if I were you."

"I was thinking—with what they have on television, there's been a lot of time for that—about what the hell they're after."

"And?"

"In the thirties, during the Depression, when Dillinger and Bonnie and Clyde were running around robbing banks, killing people, there was supposed to be some support for them; people thought they were Robin Hood."

"From what I've heard about Bonnie, she was no Maid Marion," Mickey said.

"What does that mean?" Eleanor asked.

"Not important," Mickey said. "For that matter, Clyde wasn't exactly Errol Flynn, either. What is it you're saying, Matty, that they're after public support?"

Matt nodded.

"A political agenda?"

"Why else the press releases?"

"That's pretty sophisticated thinking for a bunch of stickup guys who have to have somebody read the Exit sign to them."

"Somebody wrote those press releases," Matt argued. "For their purpose—getting themselves in the newspapers and on TV—they were, by definition, effective. At least one of them can write. And plan things, like the gasoline bomb."

"What do you mean, 'plan the gasoline bomb'? Anybody knows how to make one of those. *That* I would expect from these people."

"When and where to throw it," Matt said. "They had to be watching Goldblatt's. One man, just standing around, would have been suspicious. So they had a half a dozen of them, plus of course the guy on the roof who threw it."

O'Hara grunted.

"Unless, of course, Matty, they have somebody inside the cops, inside Special Operations, who just called them and told them when Washington was going to pick up Monahan. *That* suggests an operation run by people who know what they're doing."

"You really think that's possible?" Matt asked, genuinely shocked. "That they have somebody inside?"

O'Hara never got the chance to reply. The door opened again and Mr. and Mrs. Brewster C. Payne walked in.

"Hi!" Matt said.

"How are you, honey?" Patricia Payne asked.

"Just fine," Matt said. "Mother, you didn't have to come back. I'm getting out of here tomorrow."

She held up her arm, around which was folded a hang-up bag.

"In your underwear?"

"It's the cocktail hour, I see," Brewster C. Payne said.

"Dad, do you know Mickey O'Hara?"

"Only by reputation. How are you, Mr. O'Hara?"

"Are you allowed to have that?" Patricia Payne asked.

"Probably not, but I can't see where it will do any harm," Brewster Payne said. He smiled at Eleanor. "I'm Brewster Payne, and this is my wife."

"I'm Eleanor Neal."

"How do you do?" Patricia Payne said.

"Can I offer you a little taste, Mr. Payne?" Mickey asked.

"Is there a glass?"

"How do you know they aren't giving you some medicine that will react with that?" Patricia Payne asked.

"All I'm taking is aspirin," Matt replied.

Mickey made drinks for the Paynes.

Patricia Payne nodded her thanks, sipped hers, and said, "I have this terrible premonition that some two-hundred-pound nurse is going to storm in here, find the party in progress, yell for the guards, and I will win the Terrible Mother of the Year award."

"I thought bringing Matt a little taste was the least I could do for what he did, saving my life, for me."

Thank you, Mickey O'Hara.

"It was very kind of you, Mr. O'Hara," Brewster Payne said.

And thank you, Dad, for cutting off the colorful story of my courage in the face of death.

"Call me Mickey, please."

"Mickey."

"Mickey, we should be going," Eleanor said. "We've been here long enough."

"You're right," Mickey said. He tossed his drink down, shook hands all around, and opened the door for Eleanor.

"Interesting man," Brewster Payne said as the door closed after them.

"He's supposed to be the best police reporter on the Eastern Seaboard."

"He has a Pulitzer, I believe," Brewster Payne said, and then changed the subject. "Denny Coughlin tells me you insist on going to your apartment when they turn you loose?"

"Yes, sir."

"How much do you know of what else has happened?"

"I know about the threats, and the firebomb. Is there something else?"

"No. I just didn't know how much you knew. Just before we came here, Dick Detweiler phoned. They wanted to come see you—he called earlier, as soon as he heard what had happened—but I told him you were getting out in the morning."

"Thank you."

"He also volunteered to send out to Wallingford as many of Nesfoods plant security people as would be necessary for as long as would be necessary. The point of this is that if the reason you don't want to come home is because of your concern for your mother and me, that won't be a problem. Dick would really like to help."

"I'm a cop," Matt said. "I'm not about to let these scumbags run me out of town."

"I told you that's what he would say," Patricia Payne said.

"And I'll have people with me," Matt said.

"That was explained to us in great detail by Denny Coughlin. Having said that, I think Denny would be more comfortable if you were in Wallingford."

"I'm going to the apartment, Dad," Matt said.

"The police are taking these threats seriously, honey," Patricia Payne said. "Getting in to see you is like trying to walk into the White House."

"I suspect Uncle Denny had a lot to do with whatever security there is here," Matt said. "In his godfather, as opposed to chief inspector of police, role."

"I think that probably has a lot to do with it," Brewster Payne agreed, smiling. "Okay. You change your mind—I suspect you'll get claustrophobia in your apartment—and we'll get you out to the house."

The door opened again, and a nurse came in. She was well under one hundred pounds, but she was every bit as formidable and outraged as the two-hundred-pounder Patricia Payne had imagined.

"Liquor is absolutely forbidden," she announced. "I should think you would have known that."

"I tried to tell my wife that," Brewster C. Payne said, straight-faced, "but she wouldn't listen to me."

Matt laughed heartily, and even more heartily when he saw the look on his mother's face. Each time his stomach contracted in laughter his leg hurt.

Jason Washington was waiting for Peter Wohl when he walked into the building at Bustleton and Bowler at five minutes to eight the next morning.

"Morning, Jason."

"Can I have a minute, Inspector?"

"Sure. Come on in the office. With a little bit of luck, there will be hot coffee."

"How about here? This will only take a yes or a no."

"Okay. What's on your mind?"

"Captain Sabara told me he wants Tiny Lewis—you know who I mean?"

"Sure."

"—on the security detail for Matt Payne. I'd rather he got somebody else."

"You have something for Lewis to do?"

Washington nodded.

"You got him. You discuss this with Sabara?"

"No."

"I'm sure he would have let you have Lewis."

"He would have asked why."

"You're losing me."

"I didn't know if he knew Tony Harris has been at the bottle."

"What's that got to do with Lewis?"

"Harris is sober. If we can keep him that way for the next seventy-two hours, I think we can keep him that way more or less indefinitely. Lewis will be with Harris all day, with orders to call me if Tony even looks at a liquor store."

"And at night?"

"Martha likes him. We have a room at the apartment. He can stay with us for a while."

"Martha is a saint," Wohl said.

"No," Washington said, "it's just—"

"Yeah," Wohl interrupted coldly. "Only a saint or a fool can stand a dedicated drunk, and Martha's not a fool."

"He's a good cop, Inspector."

"That's what I've been thinking, with one part of my mind, for the last three or four days. The *other* part of my mind keeps repeating, 'He's a drunk, he's a drunk, he's a drunk.' "

"I think it's under control," Washington said.

"It better be, Jason."

"Thanks, Inspector," Washington said.

"You got something going now? I'd like you to sit in on what Malone has set up for Matt and Monahan. They're supposed to be waiting for me in my office."

"I can make time for that," Washington said.

Wohl led the way to his office. Sabara was standing by his desk, a telephone to his ear.

"He just walked in, Commissioner," Sabara said. He covered the mouthpiece with his hand. "This is the third time he called."

Wohl nodded and took the telephone from him.

"Good morning, Commissioner. Sorry you had to call back."

The others in the room could hear only Wohl's end of the conversation:

"I'm sure Mr. Stillwell has his reasons. . . .

"I checked with the hospital fifteen minutes ago. We're planning on taking him out of there at about half past ten. . . .

"Yes, sir. . . .

"I can stop by your office as soon as the interview is over, Commissioner. . . .

"I'm sure everyone else— No. I don't know about O'Hara, come to think of it. But everyone involved but O'Hara has given a statement, sir. I'll check on O'Hara right away and let you know, sir. . . .

"Yes, sir. I'll see you in your office as soon as they've finished with Payne. Good-bye, sir."

He put the telephone in its cradle, but, deep in thought, did not take his hand off it.

He finally shrugged and looked at the others.

"Stillwell wants to run Matt Payne, the shooting, past the Grand Jury. It probably makes sense, if you think about it—"

He paused, thinking, *I wonder why that sonofabitch didn't tell me—*

"—they will decline to indict, and then Giacomo can't start making noise about a police cover-up."

"It was a good shooting," Sabara said. "Stevens—what does he call himself?"

"Abu Ben Mohammed," Wohl furnished.

"—came out shooting. It wasn't even justifiable force, it was self-defense."

"I guess that's what Stillwell figures," Wohl said, and then changed the subject. "Jack has polished my rough plan to protect Matt and Monahan. I'd like to hear what you think of it. Jack?"

Malone took the protection plan, which he had just had typed up and duplicated, from his jacket pocket.

Is he trying to give me credit for this to be a nice guy, Malone wondered, *or trying to lay the responsibility on me in case something goes wrong?*

20.

Matt had been told "The Doctor" would be in to see him before he would be discharged, and therefore not to get dressed.

"The Doctor" turned out to be three doctors, accompanied, to Matt's pleasant surprise, by Lari Matsi, R.N.

No one acted as if there was a live human being in the bed. He was nothing more than a specimen.

"Remove the dressing on the leg, please," a plump doctor with a pencil-line mustache Matt could not remember ever having seen before ordered, "let's have a look at it."

Lari folded the sheet and blanket back, put her fingers to the adhesive tape, and gave a quick jerk.

"Shit!" Matt yelped, and then, a moment later, added, "Sorry."

Lari didn't seem to notice either the expletive or the apology.

The three doctors solemnly bent over and peered at the leg. Matt looked. His entire calf was a massive bruise, the purple-black of the bruise color coordinated with the circus orange antiseptic with which the area had apparently been painted. There was a three-inch slash, closed with eight or ten black sutures. A bloody goo seemed to be leaking out.

"Healing nicely," one doctor opined.

"Not much suppuration," the second observed.

Pencil-line mustache asked, "What do I have him on?"

Lari checked an aluminum clipboard, announced something ending in "—mycin, one hundred thousand, every four hours," and handed Pencil-line mustache the clipboard. He took a gold pen from his white jacket and wrote something on it.

"Have that filled before he leaves the hospital," he ordered.

"Yes, Doctor," Lari said.

Pencil-line mustache pointed at Matt.

Lari reached over and snatched the bandage on Matt's forehead off.

He didn't utter an expletive this time, but it took a good deal of effort.

Pencil-line mustache grunted.

"Nice job," Doctor Two opined. "Who did it?"

"Who else?" Doctor One answered, just a trifle smugly.

Pencil-line mustache looked from one to the other. Both shook their heads no.

Pencil-line mustache finally acknowledged that a human being was in the bed.

"You will be given a medication before leaving—"

" 'Medication'?" Matt interrupted. "Is that something like medicine?"

"—which should take care of the possibility of infection," Pencil-line went on. "The dressing should be changed daily. Your personal physician can handle that. Your only problem that I can see is your personal hygiene, in other words, bathing. Until that suppuration, in other words that oozing, stops, I don't think you should immerse that leg, in other words, get it wet."

"I see," Matt said solemnly.

"The best way to handle the problem, in my experience, is with Saran Wrap. In other words, you wrap the leg with Saran Wrap, holding it in place with Scotch tape, and when you get in the bathtub, you keep the leg out of the water."

"Do I take the bandage off, or do I wrap the Saran Wrap over the bandage?"

"Leave the dressing—that's a *dressing,* not a bandage—on."

"Yes, sir."

"In a week or so, in his good judgment, whatever he thinks is appropriate, your personal physician will remove the sutures, in other words those stitches."

"In other words, whatever he decides, right?"

"Right," Pencil-line said. A suspicion that he was being mocked had just been born.

"Got it," Matt said.

"Nurse, you may replace the dressing," Pencil-line said.

"Yes, Doctor," Lari said.

Pencil-line nodded at Matt. His lips bent in what could have been a smile, and he marched out of the room. Doctors One and Two followed him.

"You're a wise guy, aren't you?" Lari said when they were alone.

"No. I'm a cop. A wise guy is a gangster. Who was *that* guy, in other words, Pencilline, anyway?"

"Chief of Surgery. He's a very good surgeon."

"In other words, he cuts good, right?"

She looked at him and smiled.

"You told me you weren't coming back," Matt said.

"I go where the money is. They were shorthanded, probably because of the lousy weather, so they called me."

"I'm delighted," Matt said. "But we're going to have to stop meeting this way. People will start talking."

"How's the pain?" she asked, pushing a rolling cart with bandaging material on it up to the bed.

"It's all right now. It hurt like hell last night."

"It's bruised," she said. "But I think you were very lucky."

"Yeah, look at the nurse I got."

"Have you ever used a crutch before?"

"No. Do I really need one?"

"For a couple of days. Then you can either use a cane, or take your chances without one. When I finish bandaging this, I'll get one and show you how to use it."

"That's not a bandage, that's a dressing."

"I'm bandaging it with a dressing," Lari said, and smiled at him again.

It was, he decided when she had finished, a professional dressing. And she hadn't hurt him.

"What happens now?"

"I get your prescription to the pharmacy, get your crutch, show you how to use it, and presuming you don't break your leg, then—I don't know. I'll see if I can find out."

Charley McFadden, in civilian clothes, blue jeans and a quilted nylon jacket, came into the room as Matt was practicing with the crutch.

"Hi ya, Lari," he said, obviously pleased to see her.

"Hello, Charley," she said. "What are you doing here?"

"I'm going to carry Gimpy here to the Roundhouse. Can he operate on that crutch?"

"Why don't you ask me?" Matt asked.

"You wouldn't know," Charley said.

"He'll be all right," Lari said.

"Are you here officially?" Matt asked.

"Oh, yeah. Unmarked car—Hay-zus is downstairs in it—whatever overtime we turn in, the works. Even a shotgun. And on the way here, I heard them send a Highway RPC here to meet the lieutenant. You get a goddamn—sorry, Lari—convoy."

"When?"

"Whenever you're ready."

"When is that going to be, Lari?" Matt asked.

"As soon as you get dressed," she said. "I'll go get a wheelchair."

Matt was amused and touched by the gentleness with which Charley McFadden helped him pull his trouser leg over his injured calf, tied his shoes, and even offered to tie his necktie, if he didn't feel like standing in front of the mirror.

Lari returned with the wheelchair, saw him installed in it, put his crutch between his legs, and then insisted on pushing it herself.

"Hospital rules," she said when McFadden stepped behind it.

"I like it," Matt said. "In China, they make the females walk three paces behind their men. This is even better."

"You're not my man," Lari said.

"We could talk about that."

What the hell am I doing? Making a pass at her when two minutes ago I was won-dering how I could get Helene back in the sack?

Both Highway cops on duty at the nurses' station by the elevator greeted Matt by name, and then got on the elevator with them.

Lieutenant Malone was waiting in the main lobby when the door opened.

"There's a couple of press guys," he said to the Highway cops, nodding toward the door. "Don't let them get in the way."

Matt saw two men, one of them wearing earmuffs and both holding cameras, just out-side the hospital door.

Lari rolled him up the side of the circular door.

"End of the line," she said.

Chief Inspector Dennis V. Coughlin came through the revolving door, trailed by a very large, neatly dressed young man whom Matt correctly guessed was Coughlin's new driver.

"Morning, Matt," he said.

"Good morning."

"You two make a hand seat," Coughlin ordered. "Put him in back of my car. There's more room."

Coughlin's official car was an Oldsmobile Ninety-Eight.

"I can walk."

"It's icy out there, and you're no crutch expert," Coughlin said.

"Thanks for everything," Matt said to Lari. "I'll see you around."

She crossed her arms under her breasts and nodded.

Charley and Coughlin's driver made a seat with their crossed hands. Matt lowered him-self into it, Coughlin pushed open a glass door, and they carried him out of the lobby.

"How do you feel, Payne?" one of the reporters called to him, in the act of taking his picture.

"I'm feeling fine."

"Any regrets about shooting Charles Stevens?"

"What kind of a question is that? What the hell is the matter with you people?" Denny Coughlin flared.

The interruption served to give Matt time to reconsider the answer—"Not a one"—that had come to his lips.

"I'm sorry it was necessary," he said.

Matt saw that he was indeed being transported in a convoy. There was a Highway Patrol RPC, an unmarked car *(probably Malone's,* he thought), Coughlin's Oldsmobile, and behind that another unmarked car with Jesus Martinez behind the wheel.

They set him on his feet beside the Oldsmobile. Coughlin's driver opened the door, and Matt got in.

"Let him sit sideward with his leg on the seat," Coughlin ordered. "McFadden, you ride in your car."

"There's plenty of room back here," Matt protested. "Get in, Charley."

Charley looked at Coughlin for a decision.

"Okay, get in," Coughlin said.

By the time Coughlin had gotten into the front seat, his driver had gotten behind the wheel and started the engine.

Coughlin turned in his seat and put his arm on the back of it.

"You haven't met Sergeant Holloran, have you, Matt?"

"What do you say, Payne?" the driver said.

"Thanks for the ride," Matt said.

"You're McFadden, right?" Holloran asked, turning his head to look at McFadden. "The guy who ran down the guy who shot Dutch Moffitt?"

"Yeah. How are you, Sergeant?"

"While we're doing this, Matty," Coughlin said, "and before I forget it, Tom Lenihan called and asked if it would be all right if he went to the hospital, and I told him you had enough visitors, but he said to tell you hello."

"Thank you."

"There's been another development, one I just heard about, which is the reason I came to the hospital myself," Coughlin said.

Bullshit, Uncle Denny. You wanted to be here.

"What?"

"Stillwater is going to run you past the Grand Jury."

"I don't know what that means."

"Once they take a case before the Grand Jury, and the Grand Jury declines to issue a true bill, that's it."

"I don't know what that means, either."

"It means the facts of the case will be presented to a Grand Jury, who will decide that there is no grounds to take you to trial."

"That doesn't always happen?"

"Normally, in a case like this, the district attorney will just make the decision, and that would be the end of it. But with Armando C. Giacomo the defense counsel—"

"Who's—what was that name?"

"Armando C. Giacomo. Very good criminal lawyer. Half a dozen one way, six the other if he or Colonel Mawson is the best there is in Philadelphia."

"You never heard of him?" Charley McFadden asked, genuinely surprised, which earned him a no from Matt and a dirty, keep-out-of-this look from Coughlin.

"The assistant DA, Stillwell, or maybe Tom Callis, the DA himself, is probably worried that Giacomo will start hollering 'police whitewash' or 'cover-up.' Giacomo couldn't do that if you had been before the Grand Jury and they hadn't returned a true bill. You understand all this?"

"I think so."

"It gets a little more complicated," Coughlin said. "I called your father as soon as I heard about this, and he said Colonel Mawson would be in the Roundhouse for your interview."

"Good."

Whatever the hell this Grand Jury business is all about—it never came up when I shot Fletcher—I am very unlikely to get screwed with J. Dunlop Mawson hovering protectively over me.

"Maybe good and maybe not," Coughlin said. "If you had done something wrong, then having Mawson there to protect your rights would be fine. So let me ask you again, Matty, you already told me, but let me ask you again: You didn't shoot at Stevens until he had shot at you, right?"

"Right."

"Did you shoot at him before or after you got hit?"

"After."

"You're absolutely sure about that?"

"Absolutely."

"And that's what Mickey O'Hara will say?"

"He was there. He saw what happened."

"That being the case, you have done absolutely nothing wrong," Coughlin said.

"I already had that figured out," Matt said, which earned him a painful look.

"Let me tell you how this works, Matty," Coughlin said. "You have civil rights, even if you are a cop—"

Well, that's nice to know.

"—in other words, when you are interviewed by Homicide, you don't have to say anything at all, and you have the right to have an attorney present. Miranda. You understand?"

Matt nodded.

"Some cops, if they're worried, will want a lawyer. The FOP will provide one. If you figure you need one, you could have an FOP lawyer. Or Colonel Mawson—"

What the hell is he leading up to?

"—but on the other hand, you don't have to have a lawyer. Just answer the questions in the interview as honestly as you can."

"Are you telling me I shouldn't ask for a lawyer?"

"I'm telling you that Armando C. Giacomo, if you have a lawyer, especially if you have Colonel Mawson, is probably going to try to twist that around so it looks as if you were reluctant to tell the Homicide people what really happened, to make it look as if the only reason you didn't get indicted by the Grand Jury is because Mawson was there when you were interviewed."

"You *are* telling me I should tell Colonel Mawson 'thanks, but no thanks'?"

"I'm telling you that you have to make up your mind what's best for you and the Police Department."

Jesus H. Christ!

STATEMENT OF: P/O Matthew Mark Payne, Badge 7701

DATE AND TIME: 1105 A.M. Jan. 5, 1973

PLACE: Homicide Bureau, Police Admin. Bldg.

CONCERNING: Death by Shooting of Charles David Stevens, aka Abu Ben Mohammed

IN PRESENCE OF: Captain Henry C. Quaire; Detective Kenneth J. Summers, Badge 4505

INTERROGATED BY: Det. Alonzo Kramer, Badge 1967

RECORDED BY: Mrs. Jo-Ellen Garcia-Romez

I am Detective Kramer of the Homicide Bureau

We are questioning you concerning your involvement in the fatal shooting of Charles David Stevens, also known as Abu Ben Mohammed. We have a duty to explain to you and to warn you that you have the following legal rights:

A. You have the right to remain silent and do not have to say anything at all.

B. Anything you say can and will be used against you in court.

C. You have a right to talk to a lawyer of your own choice before we ask you any questions, and also to have a lawyer here with you while we ask questions.

D. If you cannot afford to hire a lawyer, and you want one, we will see that you have a lawyer provided to you, free of charge, before we ask you any questions.

E. If you are willing to give us a statement, you have a right to stop anytime you wish.

1. Q. Do you understand that you have a right to keep quiet and do not have to say anything at all?
    A. Yes, I do.

2. Q. Do you understand that anything you say can and will be used against you?
    A. Yes, I do.

3. Q. Do you want to remain silent?
    A. I'll tell you anything you want to know.

4. Q. Do you understand you have a right to talk to a lawyer before we ask you any questions?
    A. Yes, I do.

5. Q. Do you understand that if you cannot afford to hire a lawyer, and you want one, we will not ask you any questions until a lawyer is appointed for you free of charge?
    A. Yes, I do.

6. Q. Do you want to talk to a lawyer at this time, or to have a lawyer with you while we ask you questions?
    A. I don't want a lawyer, thank you.

7. Q. Are you willing to answer questions of your own free will, without force or fear, and without any threats and promises having been made to you?
    A. Yes, I am.

8. Q. State your name, city of residence, and employment?
    A. Matthew M. Payne, I live in Philadelphia, and I am a police officer.

9. Q. State your badge number and duty assignment?
    A. Badge Number 7701. Special Operations Division.

10. Q. What is your specific assignment?
    A. I am administrative assistant to Inspector Wohl.

11. Q. That is Staff Inspector Peter Wohl, commanding officer of the Special Operations Division?
    A. That's right.

12. Q. Were you on duty at approximately five A.M. January 4 of this year?
    A. Yes, I was.

13. Q. What was the nature of your duty at that time and place?
    A. Inspector Wohl ordered me to accompany Mr. Mickey O'Hara of the Bulletin during an arrest that was taking place.

14. Q. That is Mr. Michael J. O'Hara, a police reporter employed by the Philadelphia Bulletin?
    A. That's correct.

15. Q. Were you in uniform and armed at this time?
    A. I was in civilian clothing. I was armed.

16. Q. Why were you in civilian clothing?
    A. I am in a plainclothes assignment.

17. Q. You do not then normally wear a uniform on duty?
    A. No, sir.

18. Q. With what type weapon were you armed?
    A. A Smith & Wesson Undercover revolver.

19. Q. That is a five-shot .38 Special caliber short-nosed revolver?
    A. Correct.

20. Q. Was that weapon issued to you by the Police Department for use in your official duties?
    A. No.

21. Q. Where did you get that revolver?
    A. Colosimo's Gun Store.

22. Q. That revolver is your personal property?
    A. Yes.

23. Q. Have you been issued a revolver or other weapon by the Police Department for use in your duties?
    A. Yes.

24. Q. Since you were on duty, why were you not carrying that weapon?
    A. I have permission to carry the Undercover.

25. Q. From whom?
    A. From Inspector Wohl.

26. Q. For what purpose?
    A. It's easier to conceal, more concealable, than the Police Special.

27. Q. The Police Special being the .38 Special Caliber Smith & Wesson Military and Police revolver with four-inch barrel issued to you by the Police Department?
    A. Yes.

28. Q. Have you undergone any official instruction, testing, and/or qualification involving the Smith & Wesson Undercover revolver with which you were armed on January 3 of this year?
    A. I went through the prescribed course at the Police Firearms Range before I was authorized to carry the Undercover revolver.

29. Q. With what type of cartridge was your Undercover revolver loaded at the time and date we're talking about?
    A. Standard Remington .38 Special cartridges, with a 158-grain round nose lead bullet.

30. Q. Where did you get that ammunition?
    A. It was issued to me.

31. Q. It is the standard ammunition prescribed by regulation for the Undercover revolver?
    A. So far as I know, for both of them. The Military and Police and the Undercover.

32. Q. What were your specific orders in regard to Mr. O'Hara?
    A. Inspector Wohl told me to take Mr. O'Hara to Lieutenant Suffern.

33. Q. That is Lieutenant Edward J. Suffern, who is assigned to Special Operations?
    A. Yes, sir.

34. Q. Go on.
    A. Inspector Wohl told me to take Mr. O'Hara to Lieutenant Suffern, and to tell him that he had authorized Mr. O'Hara to accompany Lieutenant Suffern during the arrest, but that Mr. O'Hara was not to enter the building where Stevens was until he had been arrested.

35. Q. Who is Stevens?
    A. Charles David Stevens. Also known as Abu Ben Mohammed. A warrant had been issued for his arrest in connection with an armed robbery and murder at Goldblatt's furniture store.

36. Q. Were you charged with serving this warrant?
    A. No. It was to be served by a Homicide detective, backed up by men under Lieutenant Suffern.

37. Q. You took Mr. O'Hara to Lieutenant Suffern?
    A. Yes, I did.

38. Q. And then what happened?
    A. Lieutenant Suffern said that Mr. O'Hara and myself should accompany him. When the time came, we got in his car and went with him.

39. Q. Where did you go with Lieutenant Suffern in his car?
    A. To the alley behind Stevens's house.

40. Q. I now show you a map of the Frankford area of Philadelphia. Would you please mark on the map where you were taken by Lieutenant Suffern?
    A. All right.
(See Map marked as Attachment 1.)

41. Q. And then what happened?
    A. Mr. O'Hara got out of the car.

42. Q. Why, if you know, did Mr. O'Hara get out of the car?
    A. He said he didn't want his camera lens to become fogged as he was afraid it might if he jumped out of the car when the arrest was made.

43. Q. Go on.
    A. I got out of the car too.

44. Q. Did you have Lieutenant Suffern's permission to do so?
    A. My orders were to accompany Mr. O'Hara. So I got out of the car too.

45. Q. What comment, if any, did Lieutenant Suffern have about either of you getting out of the car?
    A. I seem to recall he told Mickey, Mr. O'Hara, to stick close to the wall.

46. Q. What, if anything, did you or Mr. O'Hara do at this time?
    A. Mr. O'Hara wiped the lens of his camera with his handkerchief.

47. Q. And what, if anything, happened next?
   A. I heard noise, what sounded like wood breaking, in the alley in the direction of Stevens's house. After a moment, I detected movement in the alley.

48. Q. Had you, at that time, drawn your weapon?
   A. Not drawn it. I had taken it from my ankle holster and put it in my overcoat pocket.

49. Q. Your weapon, was it in sight or not?
   A. No. It was not.

50. Q. Why did you take your weapon from its holster and put it in your pocket?
   A. Because I thought I could get at it easier that way if I needed it.

51. Q. Then you anticipated having need of your weapon?
   A. No. I was just being careful.

(Chief Inspectors Lowenstein and Coughlin became additional witnesses to the interrogation at this point.)

52. Q. Did Mr. O'Hara see you take your weapon from your ankle holster?
   A. I don't know if he did or not.

53. Q. How about Lieutenant Suffern?
   A. I don't know. I don't believe so.

54. Q. Go on.
   A. Where were we?

55. Q. You and Mr. O'Hara were in the alley, you said. You said you detected movement.
   A. Okay. I realized that what I was seeing was a man coming in my direction. So I called to him to stop.

56. Q. Did you identify yourself as a police officer?
   A. I said, Stop. Police Officer.

57. Q. At this time, did you recognize the person in the alley as Mr. Charles D. Stevens?
   A. No.

58. Q. Had you, previous to this occasion, ever seen Mr. Charles D. Stevens?
   A. No.

59. Q. Had you ever seen a photograph of Mr. Stevens and/or were you familiar with his description?
   A. No.

60. Q. Then you did not recognize the individual coming toward you as Mr. Stevens?
   A. No. But it didn't matter. It was too dark. All I saw was somebody coming down the alley.

61. Q. But you shot at him. Why did you shoot at him?
   A. Because he shot at me, because he had shot me. Jesus Christ!

62. Q. (Captain Quaire) Take it easy, Payne.
   A. Yes, sir. Sorry.

63. Q. (Detective Kramer) Did you see any weapon in Mr. Stevens's hand?
   A. Not until he was down.

64. Q. How did you know he, Stevens, was shooting at you?
   A. He was the only one in the alley. I didn't know who it was until later. I saw flashes. I was hit.

65. Q. What was the response of the individual you now know to be Charles David Stevens to your order, Stop. Police officer?
   A. He screamed, Get out of my way, motherfucker.

66. Q. Those precise words?
   A. That's a direct quote. For some reason, I remember it very clearly.

67. Q. (Captain Quaire) Payne, spare us the sarcasm.
   A. Yes, sir.

68. Q. (Detective Kramer) You said, screamed. That suggests pain.
   A. Strike, screamed. Insert, shouted angrily.

69. Q. He angrily shouted, Get out of my way, motherfucker, or words to that effect. Is that what you mean to say?
   A. He angrily shouted, Get out of my way, motherfucker. Those exact words.

70. Q. And then what happened?
   A. Then he started shooting.

71. Q. You're sure it was Charles D. Stevens who started shooting?
   A. I am sure the man in the alley started shooting. He was subsequently identified as Charles D. Stevens.

72. Q. And?
   A. He hit me. I got my gun out and started shooting back at him.

73. Q. Until he shot at you, your pistol was out of sight, in your overcoat pocket. Is that what you're telling me?
   A. Right.

74. Q. How many times did you fire your weapon?
   A. Four times.

75. Q. You're sure?
   A. I'm sure.

76. Q. Was there any indication that any of your bullets struck Mr. Stevens?
   A. Yes. He went down. Somebody, I don't remember who, subsequently told me I had hit him twice.

77. Q. By, went down, do you mean he fell down in the alley?
   A. Yes.

78. Q. What, if anything, did you then do?
   A. I went to him to make sure he was down.

79. Q. You have stated you were wounded. Where were you wounded?
    A. In the forehead and left calf.

80. Q. Since you were wounded, how did you manage, as you said you did, to go to Mr. Stevens?
    A. I don't know. Hobbled over, I suppose.

81. Q. Hobbled? What do you mean by, hobbled?
    A. When I was shot, I fell down, fell against a wall, and then fell down. I had trouble getting to my feet. I was, sort of, on all fours.

82. Q. Sort of on all fours?
    A. Yes, sort of on all fours. I finally got to my feet and went to the man I had shot.

83. Q. What did you do when you reached Mr. Stevens?
    A. I stepped on his gun.

84. Q. What type of weapon was this? Could you identify it?
    A. It looked to me like an Army Colt .45 automatic, the Army service pistol.

85. Q. But you're not sure?
    A. I didn't closely examine it.

86. Q. Why not?
    A. I was otherwise occupied, for Christ's sake.

87. Q. (Captain Quaire) Watch it, Payne.

88. Q. (Detective Kramer) Was Stevens holding the weapon when you stepped on it?
    A. No. He had dropped it, and it was half buried in the snow. I stepped on it to make sure he couldn't pick it up.

89. Q. Did you see him drop it?
    A. No.

90. Q. Then how do you know the pistol you stepped on was dropped by Mr. Stevens?
    A. Didn't you say I could stop answering questions whenever I wanted? Okay. I want to stop answering questions.

91. Q. (Captain Quaire) Is something bothering you, Payne?
    A. Yes, sir. This guy's stupid questions are bothering me. How do I know it was dropped by Mr. Stevens? Who else could have dropped it, the good fairy?

92. Q. (Detective Kramer) We're just trying to clear this up as best we can, Payne.
    A. I'm sorry I lost my temper.

93. Q. (Chief Inspector Coughlin) How long have you been discharged from the hospital, Officer Payne? I think that should be made note of in this interview.
    A. I came here directly from the hospital. I don't know how long. Maybe an hour.

94. Q. (Detective Kramer) The first time you saw the .45 automatic pistol you stepped on was when you found it in the snow. Is that correct?
   A. Yes.

95. Q. You saw a pistol in the hand of the man subsequently identified to you as Charles D. Stevens, is that correct?
   A. Correct.

96. Q. But you cannot positively identify the pistol you stepped on near Mr. Stevens after you shot him as the same pistol you saw earlier in his hand, is that correct?
   A. Yes, that's correct.

97. Q. Did you see Mr. Stevens fire the pistol you saw him holding in his hand?
   A. Yes. He shot me with the pistol he held in his hand.

98. Q. Did Mr. Stevens say anything to you when you went to him in the alley after you shot him?
   A. No.

99. Q. What happened after you stepped on the pistol?
   A. Mickey O'Hara was there. He took a couple of pictures, and then Lieutenant Suffern showed up and handcuffed Mr. Stevens.

100. Q. Was Mr. Stevens conscious?
   A. Yes.

101. Q. Could you tell anything of the nature of his wounds?
   A. No.

102. Q. Did you attempt to render first aid to Mr. Stevens?
   A. No.

103. Q. What happened to you then?
   A. I was put onto a stretcher, loaded in a van, and taken to Frankford Hospital.

104. Q. Do you know what happened to Mr. Stevens at that time?
   A. He was in the same van as I was. He was taken to Frankford Hospital with me.

105. Q. (Chief Inspector Coughlin) Considering your weakened physical condition, Officer Payne, do you feel up to answering any more questions at this time?
   A. I would rather not answer any more questions at this time.

106. Q. (Detective Kramer) You understand, Officer Payne, that we will be asking you more questions when your physical condition permits?
   A. Yeah.

107. Q. Thank you, Payne.

21.

There was a Mercury station wagon with a Rose Tree Hunt Club decal in the rear window parked beside Matt Payne's silver Porsche in the underground parking lot of the building on Rittenhouse Square when the convoy rolled in.

"My mother's here," Matt said.

"I thought she might be," Chief Inspector Dennis V. Coughlin said matter-of-factly, and then added, to Sergeant Holloran, "Francis, we can get him upstairs. You take the car around and park it in front."

"Yes, sir. You want me to come up, Chief?"

Coughlin hesitated just perceptibly.

"Yeah. You might as well see the layout."

The Highway Patrol RPC had dropped out, but otherwise, the convoy was the same as the one that had carried Matt to the Roundhouse. Malone's car had led the way from the Roundhouse, followed by Coughlin's Oldsmobile, and Jesus Martinez in a second unmarked Special Operations Ford.

Holloran stopped the car as near as he could get to the elevator. Charley McFadden got out and then turned to help Matt get out and onto his feet.

Coughlin got out of the front seat.

"You and me lock wrists, McFadden," Coughlin ordered. "I don't think Martinez could handle Matt."

"Hey. I'm not a cripple. I can manage," Matt said, standing on his good leg and waving the crutch. "I've got to learn to use this thing anyway."

Coughlin looked doubtful, but finally walked to Martinez.

"Park that wherever you can find a place," he ordered.

Matt, with Charley McFadden hovering around him, made his way to the elevator door, where Malone was waiting. He pushed the button to open the door, waited for Matt and McFadden to get in, and then joined them. When the door started to close, Matt leaned against the elevator wall, and then stuck his crutch into the opening, holding the door open.

Coughlin walked quickly to the door and then stopped.

"You got room for one more?" he asked.

"The more the merrier," Matt said.

Coughlin got in. The door closed.

Sergeant Carter was on the third-floor landing when the door opened.

He saluted Coughlin.

"Good morning, Chief," he said, and then nodded at Malone. "Lieutenant."

"Carter, isn't it?" Coughlin said, offering his hand.

"Yes, sir. I was here, checking the arrangements, and Mrs. Payne—she and your father are in your apartment, Payne—said you would be coming. So I thought I had better wait."

"Everything seems to be all right. The rent-a-cop in the garage is one of ours, isn't he?"

"Yes, sir. And we have a man in the lobby, downstairs, in a Holmes uniform."

"I see a problem," Matt said. "Getting up those stairs."

They all turned to look at the flight of stairs leading up to the attic apartment. They were steep and narrow.

"We could put a rope around your neck and haul you up," McFadden said cheerfully. "Or you could get on my back and I could carry you up piggyback."

"Or," Matt said, handing McFadden the crutch, "I can do this."

He sat down on the stairs, and then, using his arms and one good leg, started pushing himself up the stairs.

Thirty seconds later, he turned to see how far he had to go and found himself looking at the hem of a woman's slip and skirt. He craned his neck and identified the woman.

"I didn't know shrinks made house calls," he said.

"Only when the patient is an unquestioned danger to himself," Amelia Payne, M.D., said without missing a beat. "To judge by the way you did that, you've had some practice scuttling along like a crab." She turned and called, "Sound the trumpet. Our hero is home."

"Amy!" Patricia Payne said.

Matt got to his feet, and leaned against the wall at the head of the stairs.

"Where's your crutch?" Patricia Payne asked.

"Here," McFadden said, coming up the stairs and handing it to him. He stuck it under his arm and made it to the couch. His mother leaned over and kissed him.

"You all right?"

"I'm fine," he said. "Hi, Dad."

"How are you doing?" Brewster C. Payne said.

"If Amy didn't guzzle it down, there was a bottle of Scotch here."

"And I brought one," Brewster Payne said. "And a drink seems like a fine idea."

"That would depend on what they're giving him," Amy said.

"The Mayo Clinic has been heard from," Matt said.

"Let me see it, Matt," Amy said firmly.

He fished in his pocket and handed her the bottle of capsules from the hospital pharmacy.

Denny Coughlin and Jack Malone were now standing at the head of the stairs. Patricia Payne went and kissed Coughlin on the cheek, and then Coughlin introduced Malone.

"What is that stuff they gave him, Amy?" Coughlin asked.

"Just an antibiotic, Uncle Denny," Amy said. "I'm very sorry to report that alcohol is not contraindicated."

Brewster Payne laughed. "You and Lieutenant Malone will have a little taste, Denny?"

"Not for me, thank you," Malone said.

"I will, thank you."

"I still have the bottle of Jameson's you gave me, Uncle Denny," Matt said.

"I'll have a little of that, then, please," Coughlin said.

"So will I," Patricia Payne said. "In fact, I'll even make them."

Sergeant Carter and Jesus Martinez appeared at the head of the stairs. Martinez was wearing an electric blue suit, a shirt with very long collar points, and a yellow necktie. But what caught everyone's attention was that he held a pump shotgun in each hand.

"Hay-zus," Matt said. "Why don't you put those in that closet?" He pointed. "I guess everybody's met Sergeant Carter. Does everybody know Hay-zus Martinez?"

Patricia Payne made a valiant, but failed, effort to conceal her surprise at Officer Martinez.

"Matt's spoken of you often, Mr. Martinez," she said when he turned from putting the shotguns in a tiny closet at the head of the stairs. "I'm glad you'll be looking out for him."

"Yes, ma'am," Martinez said.

"We're about to have a drink. Can we offer you something?"

"No, ma'am, thank you."

"Officer Martinez, Amy," Coughlin said, "was with Charley McFadden when they caught the man who was responsible for what happened to Dutch Moffitt."

"I know who he is," Amy said, not very pleasantly. "Are those shotguns really necessary?"

"Probably not, Miss Payne," Malone said. "It's one of those cases where it's better to take the extra precaution."

"It's *Doctor* Payne," Amy said.

"Sorry."

"Ease off, Amy," Matt said sharply.

Patricia Payne came out of the kitchen with two glasses. She handed one to Denny Coughlin and the other to Matt.

"Thank you," Matt said, and took a sip, and then turned and set the glass on the chair at the end of the couch.

The red light on his telephone answering machine was blinking. He shifted on the couch and stretched to push the button that would play his messages.

"Matt—" Brewster Payne said, stopping him.

"Dad?"

"There's some pretty unpleasant stuff on there," Brewster C. Payne said. "The only reason I didn't erase them was because I thought they would be of interest to Denny. Maybe you'd better wait until your mother and Amy have gone."

"Don't be silly, Brewster," Patricia Payne called from the kitchen. "I'm not a child, and I've already heard them."

"What are you talking about, Dad?" Amy asked.

Holloran appeared at the head of the stairs.

"Sorry, Chief, I had trouble finding a place to park."

"Push the button, Matt," Patricia Payne ordered. "Get it over with."

There were, it was later calculated when the tape was transcribed, forty-one messages on the tape, all that the thirty-minute tape would hold. Four of the messages were from people known to Matt Payne. One was a recorded offer to install vinyl siding at a special price good this week only. One was a cryptic message, a female voice saying, "You know who this is, call me after nine in the morning." Matt recognized the voice to be Helene Stillwell's, but had the presence of mind in the circumstances to shrug and shake his head and smile, indicating he had no idea who it might be.

The other thirty-five messages recorded on his machine were from persons unknown to him.

The voices were different (later voice analysis by police experts indicated that four individuals, three males and one female, had telephoned several times each), but the gist of the messages was that Matt Payne, variously described as a motherfucker, a honky, a pig, and a cocksucker (each noun coming with various adjectival prefixes, most commonly "fucking," "goddamn," and "motherfucking"), was going to be killed for having murdered Abu Ben Mohammed.

Patricia Payne, except to pass drinks around, stayed in the kitchen while the tape played. Amy, after the first thirty seconds or so, came and sat beside Matt on the couch, took a notebook from her purse, and made notes.

The policemen in the apartment looked either at the floor or the ceiling, and seemed quite uncomfortable. Sergeant Holloran's and Officer McFadden's faces quickly turned red with embarrassment and stayed that way, even after the tape suddenly cut off in midsentence and began to rewind.

"Nice friends you have, Matthew," Amy Payne broke the silence. "You ever hear what happens to people who roll around with the pigs in the mud?"

"I wonder how they got the number?" Matt asked. "I'm not in the book."

"There are ways to get unlisted numbers," Denny Coughlin said absently. "I'll want to take the tape with me, Matt, and see what the lab boys can make of it."

"Well, the thing to do is have Matt's number changed," Brewster C. Payne said.

"Some of that was spontaneous," Amy said thoughtfully. "But some, maybe most, seemed to me to be rehearsed, perhaps even read."

"What did you say, Amy?" Coughlin asked.

"If you know what to listen for, Uncle Denny," Amy said, "you sometimes can hear things in people's voices. I said, I think that some of those people called and said whatever came into their minds, but others, I think, seemed to be reading what they said, or at least had a good idea of what they were going to say before they said it. Oddly enough, those are the ones who sounded awkward or hesitant."

"Interesting," Coughlin said, not very convincingly. "I'd rather not have that number changed, Brewster. Maybe we can get Matt another line—that will take a day or two, probably—"

"No, it won't," Payne said.

"What won't?"

"Getting Matt another line. I think I know who to call."

"What I was saying, Brewster, is that I would like to leave that line as it is, and record what calls come in."

"Oh, I see what you mean."

"Have you got a spare tape for the machine, Matty?"

Matt considered that a minute, then replied, "No. I don't think so."

"Let's take it apart and see what we need," Coughlin said.

Matt opened the telephone recorder and removed the tape cassette and handed it to Coughlin.

Brewster C. Payne reached for the telephone and dialed a number.

"Mr. Arnold, please," he said. "Brewster Payne calling." There was a brief pause, and then he went on: "Jack, for reasons I would rather not get into, I need another telephone line installed in my son's apartment, in the Delaware Valley Cancer Society Building on Rittenhouse Square, right away." There was another pause. "No, I don't mean first thing tomorrow. In the next hour or so is what I had in mind."

Matt saw Denny Coughlin smiling.

"No, I am not kidding," Brewster Payne went on. "You told me, Jack, to call you if I ever needed something. This is that call." There was one last pause. "Two hours would be fine, Jack. His name is Matthew M. Payne and it's the apartment in the attic. Thank you very much."

He turned somewhat triumphantly from the telephone.

"Two hours, Denny."

"You are an amazing man," Coughlin said.

"How kind of you to recognize that," Payne said smugly.

Patricia Payne groaned.

"I wonder where we can get one of these?" Coughlin said, examining the tape cassette.

"I bought that in the electronics store on Walnut and 15th," Matt said.

"Okay. We'll take Officer Martinez with us when we go, and he can bring it back. Until we get another tape in there, just don't answer the phone. Better yet, take it off the hook."

He picked up his drink and drained it.

"Patty, Brewster," he said."Matt's in good hands. You have nothing to worry about."

"Good try, Denny," Patricia Payne said. "But not a very successful one."

"Let's go," Coughlin said. He looked at Matt Payne. "I'll check in with you later, Matty."

"Thank you, Uncle Denny."

"Have you got any special orders for me, Chief?" Sergeant Carter said.

"No. You know what to do. Do it."

"Carter, why don't you and I take a run past Mr. Monahan's house?" Malone said.

"He's at Goldblatt's, sir. I checked."

"I want to check the arrangements at his house," Malone said tartly. "I know where he is."

"Yes, sir."

"It was nice to meet you, Mrs. Payne," Malone said. "Mr. Payne."

"It was nice to meet you, Lieutenant," Patricia Payne said, "and you too, Sergeant Carter. Thank you."

"Yes, ma'am," Carter said.

In a few moments everyone but the Paynes and Charley McFadden had gone down the steep stairway.

"Are you hungry, Matt?"

"I think there's some ribs in the refrigerator," Matt said.

"There's more ribs in the refrigerator than you know," she said. "I stopped off at Ribs Unlimited—I know how you like their ribs—on my way here and got you some."

"Then take yours home with you or give them to Amy."

"Why don't I heat them all up, and we can have lunch? I haven't had anything to eat, either."

"I've got to get back to the office," Brewster Payne said.

"Can you drop me at Hahnemann, Dad?" Amy asked.

He nodded.

At the head of the stairs, Amy turned and pointed her finger at Matt.

"For once in your life, Matt, do what people tell you."

"Yes, ma'am."

"Well, then, the three of us can eat the ribs," Patricia Payne said with forced cheerfulness.

"Four," Charley McFadden said. "Hay-zus will be back in a couple of minutes."

"The four of us, then," she agreed.

The telephone rang. Matt reached to pick it up, then stopped.

They all watched it wordlessly until, after seven rings, it stopped.

I have the strangest feeling that was Helene, Matt thought.

Charley McFadden suddenly got up from his chair and started down the stairs.

"Where are you going?"

"From now on," Charley called, "I think we should keep that door locked."

Matt glanced at his mother. She looked very sad. When she sensed his eyes on her, she smiled.

"He really is large, isn't he?"

Jesus Martinez came back to the apartment almost an hour later, as Matt's mother was cleaning up the kitchen.

"They don't make that model anymore," he said. "I have been in every electronics store in Center City trying to find these."

He held up three tape cassettes.

The telephone had rung twice more while they had been eating. They hadn't answered it.

It rang again almost immediately after Matt had installed a new tape.

"What are we supposed to do?" McFadden asked. "Answer it? Or let the machine answer it?"

"Let the machine do it," Martinez said. "I think the chief wants the recording."

With the machine reconnected, it was possible to hear the caller's message.

It was a variation of the previous calls, no more scatologically obscene than the others, but enough, because of Patricia Payne—whom McFadden thought of as Matt's Mother—to cause McFadden to blush with embarrassment and his face to tighten in anger.

"I can rig that thing so we don't have to listen to that crap—sorry, Mrs. Payne," he said.

"That might be a good idea," she said. "But I'm leaving anyway, if that's what's bothering you."

"I'd like to get my hands on that guy," McFadden said.

"So would I," she said. "But don't you see, Charley, that's what they're trying to do, make us angry?"

"They're succeeding," Charley said.

She put her hat and coat on, and then went and stood before Matt, who was sprawled in an overstuffed leather armchair, his bad leg resting on a pillow sitting on the matching ottoman.

"After I leave, maybe you can get Charley to hang your artwork," she said.

"What?" Matt asked, and then understood. "Oh, that. How did it get here?"

"Your dad and I brought it from the hospital," she said.

"Thank you."

"Now, there's plenty of food there for breakfast and sandwiches, and I'll bring more when I come tomorrow. But for dinner, your father called the Rittenhouse Club, and they'll bring you anything you want to eat."

"I don't like Rittenhouse Club food in the Rittenhouse Club," Matt said. "Why should I have them haul it over here?" He saw the hurt look in her eyes and added, "I'm in a lousy mood, sorry, Mother."

"Are you in pain?"

He shook his head no.

"They do a very nice mixed grill, and you like their London broil, I know you do, and besides, beggars can't be choosers." She leaned over and kissed him.

"Ignore him," Patricia Payne said to Charley and Jesus. "Make him feed you."

"Yes, ma'am," Charley said. "I will."

When he came back up the stairs after locking the door after her, McFadden asked, "What artwork is she talking about?"

"There's a great big picture of a naked woman in his bedroom," Jesus said.

"No shit?"

"It was a gift from Mrs. Washington," Matt said. "Mrs. Washington and I think of it as a splendid example of Victorian art."

"I gotta see this," Charley said, and went into the bedroom.

He returned carrying the oil painting.

"Over the fireplace, right?"

"Why not?" Charley said.

McFadden went to the fireplace, leaned the picture against it, and then took something from the mantelpiece. He walked to Matt with a snub-nosed revolver in the palm of each hand.

"Maybe you'd better keep these—one of them, anyway—with you. What are you doing with two?"

"One of them belongs to Wohl. He loaned it to me in the hospital. The shooting team took mine away from me. I just got it back."

McFadden sniffed the barrel of one of the revolvers and then the other.

"This must be yours," he said. "I'll clean it for you, if you have the stuff. Otherwise, you'll fuck up the barrel."

"There's cleaning stuff in one of the drawers in the kitchen," Matt said.

"You got any bullets? There's none in this."

"*Cartridges,* Charley. *Bullets* are the little lead things that come out the end. There's a box with the cleaning stuff."

"Fuck you, clean your own pistol," Charley said, laid both pistols beside the answering machine, and returned to the oil painting. He picked it up and held it in place over the fireplace, turning his head for approval.

"Great," Matt said.

"What are you going to do when your mother comes back?"

"Mother will modestly avert her eyes," Matt said.

"You got a brick nail?"

"What's a brick nail?"

"A nail you can drive in bricks. You can't do that with regular nails, asshole, they bend."

"No."

There was a knock at the door at the foot of the stairs.

Jesus erupted from his chair and went to the closet and took the shotgun from it.

"It's probably Wohl or Washington," Matt said.

"Who's there?" Jesus called.

"Telephone company."

Jesus went down the stairs. In a moment, he returned, followed by two telephone company technicians, one of whom was visibly curious and made more than a little uncomfortable by Jesus's shotgun.

"Where do you want your phone?" one of them asked.

"One here and one in the bedroom, please," Matt said.

"Is something going on around here?" the other one asked, curiosity having overwhelmed him.

"Like what?" Charley asked.

"Hey, you're the cop who shot the Liberation Army guy, aren't you?" the first one asked.

"Just put the goddamn phone in," Jesus snapped.

"What the hell is wrong with you? I just asked, is all."

It took forty-five minutes to install the two telephones. The installers refused a drink, but accepted Matt's offer of coffee.

"It's cold as a bitch out there," one said.

When they were gone, Martinez said, "That's not going to work."

"What's not going to work?"

"Having people knock on the door, and we ask who is it, and then go down and open the door."

"Why not?" Charley asked.

"What we need is an intercom," Jesus said. "They ring the bell, we ask the intercom who's there. I saw one in the store where I bought the tapes."

"Who would put it in?" Charley asked.

"I would."

"Do you really think it's necessary?" Matt said. "More to the point, do you think that anybody's really going to try to come up here?"

"They threw the firebomb at Monahan," Charley said.

"Jesus," Matt said.

"Save your money, if you want to," Jesus said. "They cost twenty-four ninety-five."

"You can install it?" Matt asked.

"You got a screwdriver, a drill, and a staple machine, I can install it."

"I think I've got a screwdriver, but I don't have a drill or a staple machine."

"You don't have a drill?" McFadden asked, surprised.

"No."

"How about a hammer? You're going to need a hammer for the brick nails."

"No hammer, either."

"Hay-zus can get a hammer and the brick nails and the drill and the staple machine when he gets the intercom," Charley said.

"Don't forget the screwdriver," Matt said, and shifted on the couch and took out his wallet.

"What the fuck, Payne, if they don't kill you, it'll come in handy later," Jesus said as he took three twenties. "If you've got some broad up here, and some other broad comes to see you, you could tell her you're busy on the intercom."

"I could also just not answer her knock," Matt said.

"You want the intercom or not? You're not doing me any favors."

"I want the intercom, Hay-zus, thank you."

Martinez returned in a little over half an hour, his arms full of kraft paper bags.

"Goddamn sidewalks are all ice," he said. "I almost busted my ass, twice."

"How would you like to be walking a foot beat in this weather?" McFadden asked.

"How about standing at Broad and Vine in a white cap, directing traffic?" Martinez said as he put the packages on the coffee table.

In one of the bags was a Philadelphia *Daily News*. He tossed it on Matt's lap.

"In case you don't know where you are," he said. "This is an 'undisclosed location.' "

"What?"

"You're on the front page," Jesus said.

Matt unfolded the newspaper. There was a photograph of him being carried to Coughlin's car at Frankford Hospital. Beneath it was the caption:

> COP UNDER DEATH THREAT—As heavily armed police stand by, Officer Matthew M. Payne, whose life has been threatened by the Islamic Liberation Army, is carried from Frankford Hospital to a police car that took him to an undisclosed location. Payne was wounded in the gun battle in which he shot to death ILA member Abu Ben Mohammed. (See ILA, Page 5)

Charley leaned over Matt's shoulder and read the caption.

"Well, the bastards got what they wanted, didn't they?" he asked. "The front page of the *News,* and we sure look like we're scared of them."

"I don't know about *you* being scared, white boy," Matt heard himself say, "but *we* are."

McFadden looked at him curiously, and after a moment said seriously, "You'll be all right, buddy. You can take that to the bank."

There was a moment's awkward silence, which Jesus finally broke.

"The first thing you have to decide is where you want this end of the intercom."

"How about on the kitchen wall?"

"Why not?"

Matt was impressed with the skill with which Jesus installed the intercom. He seemed to know exactly what he was doing. It reminded him of Charley's mechanical drawing skill, and that made him consider his own practical ineptitude.

Matthew Mark Payne, B.A., Cum Laude, University of Pennsylvania, you don't have one salable skill, something you could find a paying job doing, except being a cop, and, truth to tell, you ain't too good at that.

By half past five, the intercom was installed and tested.

"Anybody else getting hungry?" Matt asked as Jesus—workmanlike, Matt thought— neatly coiled the leftover wire and put the tools back in their boxes.

"I could eat something," Jesus said.

"I'm going to finish hanging your naked lady picture," Charley said, "and then leave. I'm going to have supper with Margaret. I'll be back at midnight and relieve Hay-zus."

"Bring her back here, and her friend Lari too, and we'll send out for food."

"No," Charley said. "For one thing, I wouldn't bring a nice girl like her anyplace where there's a naked lady hanging on the wall."

"You're kidding!"

"Her uncle and aunt are feeding us," Charley said. "We have to go there."

"Don't break your ass on the way to the subway," Jesus said.

"You don't have your car, do you?" Matt asked, and, when Charley shook his head, asked, "where is it, Bustleton and Bowler?"

"Yeah."

"Why don't you leave it there and take the Porsche?"

"I don't know, Matt. I'd hate to tear it up."

"You can't leave a Porsche sit," Matt said. "And I damned sure can't drive it. Where'd you put the keys?"

"Jesus, I forgot!" Charley said, and pulled them from his trouser pocket.

"Take the car. Just try to keep it under a hundred and ten."

"Well, okay," Charley said, trying and failing to give the impression he would drive the Porsche only as a favor to Matt.

Five minutes after Charley left, the intercom was first put to use.

"Let me in, Hay-zus," Charley's voice announced mechanically from the speaker in the kitchen. "It's me."

Jesus went down and unlocked the door and Charley followed him back up the stairs.

"Wouldn't start?" Matt asked.

"The front tires are slashed," McFadden announced. "And they got the hood and doors with a knife or something."

"Jesus H. Christ!" Matt exploded.

"Did you look at the car when we came here?" Charley asked.

"No. Except to see that it was there. My mother's car was there. You couldn't see it clearly."

"Shit!"

The bell rang.

Martinez went into the kitchen.

"Who's there?"

"Peter Wohl."

"Just a minute, Inspector."

Wohl appeared at the head of the stairs carrying a large paper bag.

"I thought the patient might like a beer," he said, and then, when he saw the look on Matt's face, asked, "What's going on?"

"Those fuckers slashed my tires and did a scratch job on my hood and doors," Matt said. "Charley just found it that way."

Wohl walked into the kitchen and started putting the beer into the refrigerator.

"You just found this out, McFadden?"

"Yes, sir. I went down to get the car, and I saw it was down in front."

"And you didn't see any damage to it when they brought Matt here?"

"No, sir."

"We didn't look," Matt said.

"I just walked past it myself," Wohl said, "and didn't see anything out of the ordinary."

Wohl came into the living room and picked up the telephone beside Matt. He dialed a number from memory.

"This is Inspector Wohl," he announced. "Let me speak to the senior supervisor present."

I wonder who he's calling? Matt thought.

"Inspector Wohl, Lieutenant. We have a case of vehicular vandalism. The vehicle in question belongs to Officer Payne. I rather doubt we'll be able to find the vandals, but I want a complete investigation, especially photographs. Even dust the damned car for fingerprints. We may get lucky. It's in the parking lot under the Delaware Valley Cancer Society Building on Rittenhouse Square. Payne lives in the top-floor apartment. I'll be here with him."

He put the telephone down.

"Inspector, I'm supposed to meet my girl," Charley said uncomfortably.

"Well, I guess that will have to wait, won't it?" Wohl snapped. "Central Detectives are on their way. Obviously, they'll want to talk to you."

"Yes, sir."

"No. Wait a minute," Wohl said, exhaling audibly. "What exactly did you see, Charley, when you went down to the garage?"

"When I started to unlock the door, I saw the nose was down. So I looked at the tires. And then I saw what they did to the hood and doors with a knife or something."

"You're coming on at midnight, right?"

"Yes, sir."

"I'll tell the detectives what you told me," Wohl said. "Go ahead, Charley. I didn't mean to snap at you like that."

"That's okay, sir."

He hurried down the stairwell as if he was afraid Wohl would change his mind.

Wohl lost his temper, Matt thought. *He was nearly as mad as I am about the car. No. That's impossible. Nobody can be nearly as fucking outraged as I am.*

"Inspector, I was about to send out for supper for Hay-zus and me," Matt said. "Will you have something with us?"

"No pizza."

"Actually, I was thinking of either a London broil or a mixed grill. My father fixed it with the Rittenhouse Club."

"In that case, Officer Payne, I gratefully accept your kind invitation."

22.

Lieutenant Foster H. Lewis, Sr., was of two minds concerning Officer Foster H. Lewis, Jr. On one hand, it was impossible to feel like anything but a proud father to see one's son and namesake drive up to the house in an unmarked car, wearing a very nice looking blazer, gray flannel slacks, a starched white shirt, and a regimentally striped necktie and know that Tiny had a more responsible job after having been on the job less than a year than he had had in his first five years on the job.

But there were two problems with that. The first being that he had hoped—and for a long time believed—that Tiny would spend his life as Foster H. Lewis, M.D. But that hadn't come to pass. Tiny had been placed on Academic Probation by the Temple University Medical School and reacted to that by joining the cops.

And then the Honorable Jerry Carlucci had put his two cents in, in what Foster H. Lewis, Sr., believed to be an understandable, but no less contemptible, ploy to pick up a few more Afro-American voters. The mayor had told a large gathering at the Second Abyssinian Baptist Church that, as one more proof that he was determined to see that the Police Department afforded Afro-Americans equal opportunities within the Department, that he had recommended to Commissioner Czernich that Officer Foster H. Lewis, Jr., son of that outstanding Afro-American police Lieutenant, Foster H. Lewis, Sr., be assigned to Special Operations.

It was said that if The Mayor looked as if he might be about to fart, Commissioner Czernich instantly began to look for a dog to blame, and, in case he couldn't find one, pursed his lips to apologize for breaking wind.

Lieutenant Lewis thought that Special Operations was a good idea, and he would have been proud and delighted to see Tiny assigned there *after* he'd done a couple of years in a district, working a van, walking a foot beat, riding around in an RPC, learning what being a cop was all about. Sending Tiny over there before he'd found all the little inspection stickers on his new uniform was really—unless, of course, you were interested in Afro-American votes—a lousy idea.

And then Staff Inspector Peter Wohl, for whom Lieutenant Lewis had previously had a great deal of respect, had compounded the idiocy. Instead of sending Tiny out to work with experienced Special Operations uniformed officers, from whom he could have learned at least some of what he would have to know, he had put him in plain clothes and given him to Detective Tony Harris for use as a gofer.

At the time, Harris had been working on two important jobs, the Northwest Philadelphia Serial Rapist, and the murder of Officer Magnella near Temple University. It could be argued that Harris needed someone to run errands, and to relieve him of time-consuming chores, thus freeing his time for investigation. And certainly, working under a really first-class homicide detective would give Tiny experience he could get nowhere else.

But only as a temporary thing. It now looked as if it was becoming permanent. The serial rapist had been shot to death by another young, college-educated, Special Operations plainclothesman. Harris was now devoting his full time to the Officer Magnella job.

   And in Lieutenant Lewis's judgement, that was becoming a dead end. In his opinion, if those responsible for Magnella's murder were ever apprehended, it would not be because of brilliant police work, or even dull and plodding police work, but either because of the reward offered, or simple dumb luck: Someone would come forward and point a finger.

   Tiny Lewis rang the door buzzer, as he had been doing to his father's undiminished annoyance since he was fourteen, to the rhythm of *Shave-And-A-Haircut-Two Bits,* and Lieutenant Lewis walked from the window to the door to let him in.

   "Hi ya, Pop."

   "Come in."

   "Hi ya, Mom?" Tony said, considerably louder.

   The men shook hands.

   "I'm in the kitchen, honey."

   "Nice blazer," Lieutenant Lewis said. "New?"

   "Yeah. It is nice, isn't it?"

   Tiny walked past his father into the kitchen, put his arms around his mother, who weighed almost exactly one-half as much as he did, and lifted her off the floor.

   "Put me down!" she said, and turned to face him. "Don't you look nice!"

   "Thank you, ma'am," he said. "It's new."

   She fingered the material. *"Very* nice."

   "What are we eating?"

   "Roast pork."

   "Pork goes nicely, he said, apropos of nothing whatever, with beer."

   "Help yourself," she laughed. "You know where it is."

   "You're driving a department car," Lieutenant Lewis said.

   "Yes, I am."

   "You know what it would do to your record if you had an accident and had been drinking," Lieutenant Lewis said, and immediately regretted it.

   "Well, then, I guess I better not have an accident. You want a beer, Dad?"

   "Yes, please."

   "I saw your boss earlier this evening," Lieutenant Lewis said.

   "Sergeant Washington?"

   "I meant Inspector Wohl," Lieutenant Lewis said. "Do you consider Jason Washington your boss?"

   "They formed a Special Investigations Section. He's in charge. I'm in it."

   "Doing what?"

   "Baby-sitting honkies," Tiny said, with a smile.

   "And what does that mean?" Lieutenant Lewis snapped.

   "You know a Highway sergeant named Carter?"

   Lieutenant Lewis nodded.

   "That's what he said, that I was 'baby-sitting honkies.' "

   "Foster, I have no idea what you're talking about."

   "You heard about these screwballs calling themselves the Islamic Liberation Army threatening to get Matt Payne for blowing away one of them?"

   Lewis nodded.

   "Well, Wohl's got some people sitting on him—"

   "You might well form the habit, Foster, of referring to Inspector Wohl as Inspector Wohl," Lewis said.

   He received a look of tolerance from his son, who went on, "—and I was supposed to be one of them. But then *Sergeant* Washington went to *Inspector* Wohl and said he'd rather I stick with *Detective* Harris, and *Inspector* Wohl said okay, he'd get somebody else, and *Sergeant* Carter—"

   "Your sarcasm is becoming offensive."

"—heard about it, apparently. Anyway, he struck up a conversation with me, said he'd heard I was going to be one of the guys—the other two are McFadden and Martinez, the ex-Narcs who ran down the junkie who shot Captain Moffitt?"

He waited to see understanding on his father's face, and then went on:

"—sitting on Payne, and then that I wasn't, and how come? And I said, mine not to reason why, mine but to do what the Great Black Buddha orders—"

"Is that what you call Jason Washington?" Mrs. Lewis interrupted. "That's terrible! You ought to be ashamed of yourself!"

"Think about it, Mom," Tiny said, unrepentant.

She did, and laughed, but repeated, "That's terrible."

"And?" Lieutenant Lewis prompted.

"And Carter said, 'I don't suppose it matters, in either case, what you're doing is baby-sitting a honky.' "

"Which means what?"

"How the hell do I know, Pop?"

"Watch your tone of voice, please."

"Sorry, Dad."

"I don't ordinarily listen to gossip—"

"Watch your father's nose grow, honey."

"—but the word is that Harris is having a problem with liquor. Is that what Carter means about baby-sitting?"

"I guess so. He's been on a bender. Washington's taking care of him."

"How, taking care of him?"

"I keep him out of bars during the day, and at night he's staying with the Washingtons."

"Martha must love that," Mrs. Lewis said.

"Jason and Tony Harris have been close for years," Lieutenant Foster said, thoughtfully. "Is that how you feel about it, Foster? That you're baby-sitting a honky?"

"Hey, Pop. Tony Harris has been good to me. And Matt Payne is sort of a friend of mine."

" 'Sort of a friend'?" Mrs. Lewis asked.

"Well, I haven't been invited to the Rose Tree Hunt Club yet, but yeah. We're friends. We get along well. If Harris wasn't sick, I would have liked to be one of the guys sitting on him."

"I don't like the idea of one police officer using the word 'honky' to describe another," Lieutenant Lewis said.

"Pop, I didn't use it. Carter did."

"You repeated it."

"My mistake," Tiny said, a hint of anger in his voice. "Where did you see Wohl—*Inspector* Wohl?"

"You know that your friend Payne is being protected in his apartment?"

Tiny nodded.

"I was supposed to have the midnight-to-eight tour before—*my boss*—got me out of it."

"I was driving by and saw some activity in the garage. A lab van, specifically. So I stopped. Someone, presumably the lowlifes who are calling themselves a Liberation Army, did a job on his car."

"What kind of a job?"

"Slashed the tires. Scraped the paint."

"That's going too far!" Tiny said. "That's absolutely sacrilegious! That's not an automobile, it's a work of art!"

"Now it's a work of art with flat tires and a scratched paint job," Lieutenant Lewis said.

"And Wohl was there?"

"*Inspector* Wohl was there. And nearly as offended by the desecration of the work of art as you are."

"What kind of a car are you talking about?" Mrs. Lewis asked.

"A Porsche 911."

"Very expensive," Lieutenant Lewis said. "Only rich people can afford them—lawyers, *doctors,* people like that—"

"Stop, Foster!" Mrs. Lewis said. "Not one more word!"

"What's the matter with you?"

"You know damned well what's the matter. You are not going to needle him the rest of his life about not being a doctor! He wants to be a cop. What's wrong with that? I'm married to a cop. You should be proud that he wants to do what you do!"

Lieutenant Lewis looked at Officer Lewis.

"The lady used profane language, Officer Lewis. Did you pick up on that?"

"Yes, sir. I heard her."

"I guess that means she's serious, huh?"

"Yes, sir, I guess it does."

"Then maybe you and I better get another beer and go in the living room until she calms down, what do you think?"

"I think that's a fine idea, sir."

"Don't try to make a joke of it, Foster. I meant every word I said!"

"I somehow had the feeling you did," Lieutenant Foster said.

When Chief Inspectors Dennis V. Coughlin and Matthew Lowenstein and Staff Inspector Peter Wohl filed into the Commissioner's Conference room at eight-ten the next morning, The Honorable Jerry Carlucci, Mayor of the City of Brotherly Love, was already there, his back to them, looking out the window, supporting himself on both hands.

Commissioner Taddeus Czernich, holding a cup of coffee in his hands, stood by the open door to his office. Coughlin, Lowenstein, and Wohl stood behind chairs at the table, waiting for the Mayor to turn around.

He took his time in doing so, prompting each of them, privately, to conclude that the first psychological warfare salvo had been fired.

Finally, he turned around.

"Good morning," he said. "I'm aware that all of you have busy schedules, and that in theory, I should be able to get from Commissioner Czernich all the details of whatever I would like to know. But since there seems to be some breakdown in communications, I thought it best to ask you to spare me a few minutes of your valuable time."

"Good morning, Mr. Mayor," Lowenstein said. "I'm sure I speak for all of us when I say I'm sorry you fell out of the wrong side of the bed this morning."

Carlucci glared at him for a moment.

"Oh, for Christ's sake, sit down, all of you," he said. "I know you're doing your best." He looked at Czernich. "Can we get some coffee in here, Tad?"

"Yes, sir. There's a fresh pot."

"I was reading the overnights," the mayor said. "Did you notice that some wiseass painted *'Free The Goldblatt's Six'* on a wall at the University?"

"Those villains we have," Coughlin said.

"No kidding?"

"The railroad cops caught three of them doing it again on the Pennsy Main Line right-of-way. You know those great big granite blocks where the tracks go behind the stadium? They had lowered themselves on ropes. Two they caught hanging there. They squealed on the third one."

"Who were they?"

"College kids. Wiseasses."

"The judge ought to make them clean it off with a toothbrush," Carlucci said. "But that's wishful thinking."

"Mike Sabara told me when I called him just before I came here that there's 'ILA' painted all over North Philadelphia," Wohl said. "I don't think that's college kids, and I would like to know who did that."

"What do you mean?"

"How much of it is spontaneous, and how much was painted by the people who issued those press releases."

"Let's talk about the ILA," Carlucci said. "Now that it just happened to come up. What do we know today about them that we didn't know yesterday?"

"Not a goddamn thing," Coughlin said. "I was over at Intelligence yesterday. They don't have a damned thing, and it's not for want of trying."

"They're harassing Monahan. And for that matter, Payne, too. Telephone calls to Goldblatt's from the time they open the doors until they close."

"What about at his house?" Carlucci asked.

"Telephone calls. The same kind they're making to Matt Payne's apartment."

"Driving by Monahan's house? Anything like that?"

"Nothing that we've been able to get a handle on. Nobody hanging around, driving by more than once."

"What have you got on Monahan, at his house?"

"Three uniformed officers in an unmarked car. One of the three is always walking around."

"Supervised by who?"

"A lieutenant named Jack Malone. He came to Special Operations from Major Crimes."

"Where he got the nutty idea that Bob Holland is a car thief," the mayor said. "I know all about Malone. Is he the man for the job, Peter? This whole thing would go down the toilet if we lose Monahan as a witness, or lose him, period. Christ, what that bastard Nelson and his *Ledger* would do to me if that happened."

"Malone strikes me, Mr. Mayor, as a pretty good cop who unfortunately has had some personal problems."

The mayor looked at Wohl for a moment and then said. "Okay. If you say so. You say they're harassing Payne? How? What's going on with him?"

"He has an apartment on the top floor of the Delaware Valley Cancer Society Building on Rittenhouse Square. There's an underground garage with a Holmes rent-a-cop at the entrance, and, during the day, there's a Holmes rent-a-cop in the lobby. There's a pretty good burglar alarm system. We have an officer wearing a Holmes uniform, replacing the Holmes guy, in the garage at night."

"That's all?"

"And we have somebody with Payne all the time."

"Two of them are those kids from Narcotics who ran down the punk who shot Dutch Moffitt," Chief Inspector Coughlin said. "McFadden and Martinez. They're friends, and in regular clothes. We don't want to give the impression that we're—"

"Baby-sitting a cop, huh?" the mayor interrupted. "I get the point."

"They call him, these sleazebags," Wohl said, "every fifteen minutes or so. Say something dirty, and hang up. No time to trace the call."

He took a tape cassette from his pocket and held it up.

"What's that?"

"A recording of the calls," Wohl said. "I'm going to take it to the lab."

"That sounds as if we're chasing our tails," the mayor said. "What do they hope to find?"

"We're trying everything we can think of, Mr. Mayor," Wohl said.

"Sometime yesterday afternoon, they got to his car," Coughlin said. "Slashed the tires, and did a job with a knife or a key, or something on the paint job."

"And nobody saw anything?" the mayor said, unpleasantly.

"All we can do is guess," Wohl said.

"So guess."

"Somebody came in the front door during business hours, rode the elevator down to the garage, slashed the tires, et cetera—the car is parked right by the elevator, it wouldn't have taken more than thirty seconds, a minute, tops—got back on the elevator, rode back to the lobby floor, and walked out."

"The rent-a-cop in the garage didn't see anything?"

"He can't see where the car is parked."

"I don't suppose anybody bothered to check the car for prints, call the lab people?"

"I did, Mr. Mayor," Wohl said. "They took some pictures, too. Should I have them send you a set?"

"No, Peter, thank you. They would just make me sick to my stomach. I don't like these people thumbing their noses at the cops."

They all knew Jerry Carlucci well enough to recognize the signals for an impending eruption, and they all waited for it to come. It was less violent, however, than any of them expected.

"Okay. Now I'll tell you what's going to happen," he said, and pointed his finger at Dennis V. Coughlin. "You, Denny—and this should in no way be construed as a suggestion that Wohl isn't doing the job right, but he's a Staff Inspector and you're a Chief—are going to go to Intelligence and Organized Crime and light a fire under them. I said before and I'm saying now that these clowns didn't wake up one morning and say, 'Okay, today we're the Islamic Liberation Army, we're going to go out and make fools of the police and incidentally stick up a furniture store.' They came from somewhere, and I want to know where, and I want to know who the other ones of them are, the ones issuing these goddamned press releases."

"Yes, sir," Coughlin said.

The mayor turned to Matt Lowenstein. "You're the Chief Inspector of Detectives. Get out there and detect. Whatever you're doing now isn't working."

Lowenstein's face flushed, but he didn't reply.

"And you, Peter: I won't start telling you how to run Special Operations. If you're comfortable having a guy who beats up on his wife and has paranoid ideas about Bob Holland in charge of protecting the only goddamned witness we have, okay. I'm sure you're smart enough to understand that it's your ass if this goes wrong."

"Yes, sir, I understand."

"And you will, all three of you, keep Commissioner Czernich up to date on what's going on. I'm sick and tired of calling him up and having him tell me, 'I don't know, Jerry. I haven't talked to Wohl or Lowenstein or Coughlin today.' "

"Yes, sir," the three of them replied almost in unison.

The mayor ground out his cigar in the ashtray in front of him, stood up, and walked out of the room without another word.

"When the police department looks bad," Commissioner Czernich said, "it makes all of us, but especially the mayor, look bad. I think we should all keep that in mind."

"You're right, Tad," Matt Lowenstein said. "You're absolutely right."

He turned his face so Czernich couldn't see him and winked at Coughlin and Wohl.

At just about the same time, Officer Charles McFadden looked over Officer Matthew Payne's shoulder at what was being stirred in a small stainless-steel pot and offered:

"I always wondered how they made that shit."

"I gather that creamed beef is not a regular part of your diet?"

"I eat in restaurants all the time, but I never had it in a house before."

"But then, until you met me, you never knew that people had indoor toilets, did you?"

"Fuck you."

"What's his name?" Matt asked, softly, nodding toward the living room, where a large, muscular young man with a crew cut sat facing the television.

"Hartzog," Charley furnished quietly.

"You sure you don't want some of this, Hartzog?" Matt called, raising his voice. "There's more than enough."

"It's okay. I ate just before I came over," Hartzog replied.

Matt began to swirl the boiling water in another stainless-steel pot.

"What the hell are you doing now?"

"I am about to poach eggs. Eggs are these unborn chickens in the obloid white containers you see in my hand."

"In there?" Charley asked, genuinely surprised as Matt skillfully cracked eggs with one hand into the swirling water.

"As you see," Matt said.

"My mother uses a little pan. It's got little cups you put the eggs in."

"Is that so?"

"I'll be damned," Charley said, peering into the pan. "That works, don't it?"

"Just about every time," Matt said. "Now, if you will be so good as to take the English muffins from the toaster—"

Matt split the English muffins, laid a half on each of two plates, ladled creamed beef on top of them, and then added, using a pierced spoon, two poached eggs on top.

"Maybe you are good for something," Charley said, taking the plates and carrying them into the living room.

Matt, using a cane, hobbled after him. He lowered himself into the armchair and Charley handed him his plate.

"Oh, good!" Matt said. "We're in time for today's episode of Mary Trueheart, Girl Nymphomaniac."

Officer Hartzog looked at him without comprehension.

"I got the Today Show on there. Is that all right?"

"Fine," Matt said.

"Is there really such a thing?" Charley asked.

"As what?"

"As a nymphomaniac."

"Yeah, sure."

"How come I never met one?"

"They only go after men whose dicks are longer than two inches," Matt said.

"Then I guess you never met one, either, huh?"

In point of fact, I have. Or at least it could be argued that Helene's peculiar sexual appetites might, using the term loosely, qualify her as a nymphomaniac. But somehow, Charley, I don't think you would approve if I told you about her.

"One works downstairs," Matt said. "Brunette. Name of Jasmine."

"No shit?" Charley asked, fascinated, and then saw the look on Matt's face. "Bullshit."

"There was one when I was in junior high school," Officer Hartzog said. "They caught her fucking the janitor. They arrested him and sent her off to a girl's home someplace."

The door buzzer sounded.

"Who the hell can that be?" Charley wondered aloud.

Hartzog got up and went to get his shotgun, which he had leaned against the wall at the head of the stairs. Charley went to the intercom in the kitchen.

"Who's there?"

"My name is Young."

"What can we do for you?"

"I'd like to see Matt Payne."

"What for?"

"Am I speaking with a police officer?"

"What kind of question is that?"

"This is Special Agent Frank F. Young of the FBI. Would you let us in, please?"

"I know him, Charley," Matt called. "Let him in."

Hartzog went down the stairs, two at a time, carrying his shotgun.

There was the sound of multiple footsteps on the stairs, and then Young appeared, followed by another neatly dressed, hat-wearing, clean-cut man who didn't look any older than Matt or Charley.

"Hello, Matt," Young said with a smile. "I see you're in good hands."

"How are you, Mr. Young?"

What the fuck do you want?

"I apologize for the hour, but we had to be in this neck of the woods, and I thought we'd take the opportunity to drop by."

"Can we offer you coffee?"

"Love a cup. It's bitter cold out there. This is Special Agent Matthews."

Matthews walked up to Matt, offered his hand, and said, "Jack Matthews. I've wanted to meet you."

"How are you?" Matt said. "The large one is Officer Charley McFadden. The other's Officer Hartzog."

They shook hands. Hartzog put the shotgun back and sat down where he had been sitting watching television.

"Charley, will you get the FBI some coffee?"

"Yeah, sure."

"You've wanted to meet him, too, Jack," Young said. "Officer McFadden is the man who located, and ran to earth, the individual who shot Captain Moffitt."

"Yes, I have," Matthews said. "I'm one of your fans, McFadden. That was good work."

Charley looked uncomfortable.

"You want something in your coffee, or black?" he responded.

"Black for me, please."

"A little sugar for me, if you have it, please," Young said.

"You want some more, Matt? Hartzog?"

"Please," Matt said.

"Not now, thanks," Hartzog said.

"How do you feel, Matt?" Young asked.

"I feel all right."

"No pain in the leg?"

"Only when I forget and step on it."

"It'll take a while," Young said. "It could have been a lot worse. .45, wasn't it?"

"Apparently a ricochet," Matt said.

Charley passed out the coffee.

"They must be taking this ILA threat pretty seriously," Young said. "Judging by the fact that you have two men on you."

"I'm off duty," McFadden said. "Hartzog came on at eight. Just one."

"Matt, is there somewhere we could have a word?" Young asked.

What the hell is this all about?

"We can go in my bedroom."

"Please," Young said, smiling. "You need any help?"

"No. I just move a little slowly."

He pushed himself out of the chair and, using a cane, made his way to his bedroom.

Young followed and closed the door after them.

"Nice apartment."

"It gets a little crowded with more than me in it."

Young smiled dutifully, then said, seriously, "Matt, I won't ask you if I can trust your discretion, but you didn't get this from me, all right?"

"All right."

"I heard yesterday that a charge has been brought that you have violated the civil rights of Charles David Stevens, and that Justice will ask us to conduct an investigation."

"What?" Matt asked, incredulously.

"It's becoming a fairly standard tactic. All it does as far as we're concerned—in cases like yours—is waste manpower. From their standpoint, the only thing I can imagine is that they hope the very charge will sow a seed of doubt in some potential juror's mind. If the FBI is investigating, the police, the police officer, must have done something wrong."

"Who brought the charges?" Matt asked, angrily.

"One of the civil rights groups, I don't remember which one. But it's more than safe to say that Armando C. Giacomo is behind it."

"What, exactly, am I being charged with?"

"Violating the civil rights of Stevens by taking his life unlawfully, or excessive force, something like that."

"That sonofabitch was trying to kill me when I shot him!"

"Don't get all excited. The investigation will bring all that out. There's also a story that they're going to take you before the Grand Jury. Is that right?"

Why don't I want to tell him?

"I've heard they are."

"Well, that may—more than likely *will*—take the wind out of their sails. I can't imagine a Grand Jury returning a true bill under the circumstances. As I say, what I really think they're after is sowing that seed of doubt. Where there's smoke, there must be fire, so to speak."

"I will be goddamned!"

"As well as I can, there's an ethical question here, of course, I will keep you advised. More specifically, when I hear something I think you ought to know, I'll have Matthews pass the word to you. He's one of the good guys."

"Jesus!" Matt said. "That's absolute bullshit! He tries to kill me. I defend myself, and *I'm* accused of violating *his* civil rights."

"It's a crazy world. But don't worry too much about it. Remember, you didn't do anything wrong."

"Yeah."

"Do you play chess?"

What the hell has that got to do with anything?

"Yes, I play chess."

"So does Matthews. That would give him an excuse to come here."

Why is he doing this?

"I very much appreciate your telling me this, Mr. Young."

"Frank, please. What the hell, we have different badges, but we're both cops, right?"

I really would like to believe that. I wonder why I don't?

Young looked at his watch.

"Gotta get moving," he said, and offered Matt his hand.

When Matt followed him back into the living room, Matthews was holding the Queen of a set of green jade chess pieces Matt had been given for his fifteenth birthday.

"Interesting set," Matthews said. "Do you play much?"

"Some."

"We'll have to have a game sometime."

"Anytime. I'll be here."

"I might surprise you, and just come knocking some night."

"I wish you would."

23.

"How are you, Inspector?" Lieutenant Warren Lomax greeted Peter Wohl cheerfully, offering his hand. "What can we do for you?"

Lomax was a tall, quite skinny man in his early forties. He had been seriously injured years before in a high-speed-chase accident as a Highway Patrol sergeant, and pensioned off.

After two years of retirement, he had (it was generally acknowledged with the help of then Commissioner Carlucci) managed to get back on the job on limited duty. He'd gone to work in the Forensics Laboratory as sort of the chief clerk. There, he had become fascinated with what he saw and what the lab did, actually gone back to school at night to study chemistry and electronics and whatever else he thought would be useful, and gradually become an expert in what was called "scientific crime detection."

Three years before he had managed to get himself off limited duty, taken and passed the lieutenant's exam, and now the Forensics Lab was his.

Wohl thought, as he always did, that Lomax looked like a sick man (he remembered him as a robust Highway sergeant), felt sorry for him, and then wondered why: Lomax obviously didn't feel sorry for himself, and was obviously as happy as a pig in mud doing what he was doing.

"How are you, Warren?" Wohl said, and handed him the cassette tape from Matt Payne's answering machine with his free hand.

"What's this?" Lomax asked.

"The tape from Officer Matt Payne's answering machine. Payne told me that Chief Coughlin wanted to run them through here. And as I had to come here to face an irate mayor anyhow, I brought it along."

"Christ, Carlucci even called me, wanting to know if I had heard anything about the— what is it—the Islamic Liberation Army."

"Had you?"

"The first I ever heard of them was in the newspapers. Who the hell are they, anyway?"

"I wish I knew," Wohl said. "You come up with anything on Payne's car?"

Lomax turned and walked stiffly, reminding Wohl that the accident had crushed his hip, to a desk and came back with a manila folder.

"My vast experience in forensics leads me to believe a. that the same instrument was used to slice his tires and fuck up his paint job, and b. that said instrument was a pretty high-quality collapsible knife, probably with a six-inch blade."

"How did you reach these conclusions, Dr. Lomax? And what is a collapsible knife?"

"A *switchblade,*" Lomax said, "is like a regular penknife, the blade folds into the handle, except that it's spring loaded, so that when you push the button, it springs open. A *collapsible* knife is one where the blade slides in and out of the handle. Some are spring loaded, and some you have to push. You follow me?"

Wohl nodded.

"Okay. Switchblades aren't much good for stabbing tires, particularly high-quality tires like the Pirellis on Payne's car. They're slashing instruments. The blades are thin. You try to stab something, like the walls of tires, the blade tends to snap. Payne's tires were stabbed, more than slashed. The contour of the penetration, the holes, shows that the blade was pretty thick on the dull side. A lot of switchblades are just thin pieces of steel sharpened on *both* sides. Hence, a collapsible knife of pretty good quality. Six inches long or so because there's generally a proportion between blade width and length. The same instrument because we found particles of tire rubber in the scratches in the paint. And, for the hell of it, the size and depth of the scratches indicates a blade shape, the point shape, confirming what I said before."

"I am dazzled," Wohl said.

"Now all you street cops have to do is find the knife, and there's your doer. There can't be more than eight or ten thousand knives like that in Philadelphia. Forensics is happy to have been able to be of service."

Wohl slid photographs out of the folder and looked at them.

"I hate to think what it's going to cost to have that car repainted," he said.

"Well, I have a nice heel print of who I suspect is the doer," Lomax said. "Heel and three clear fingers, right hand. Maybe you can get him to pay to have it painted."

Wohl looked at him curiously.

"It's in a position suggesting that he laid his hand on the hood, left side, when he bent over to stick the knife in the ninety-dollar tire," Lomax said, and then pointed to one of the photographs. "There."

"Well, when we have a suspect in custody," Wohl said, "I'm sure that will be very valuable."

Lomax laughed. Both knew that while the positive identification of an individual by his fingerprints has long been established as nearly infallible—fingerprints are truly unique—it is *not* true that all you have to do to find an individual is have his fingerprint or fingerprints. Trying to match a fingerprint without a name to go with it, with fingerprints on file in either a police department or in the FBI's miles of cabinets in Washington, and thus come up with a name, is for all practical purposes impossible.

"What's on here?" Lomax asked, picking up the cassette tape.

"I don't know. I didn't hear it. I don't think anybody has. They're calling there every fifteen minutes or so, so McFadden—one of the guys sitting on Payne—fixed it so that the machine worked silently."

"You want to hear it?"

"Not particularly," Wohl said, and then reconsidered. He looked at his watch. "Maybe I'd better," he said. "Let me have the phone, will you, please, Warren?"

Lomax pushed a telephone to him, and Wohl dialed a number.

"This is Inspector Wohl. Have Detective Harris call me at 555-3445."

When he had put the phone down, Lomax asked, "He getting anywhere with the Magnella job?"

"Not so far."

"How's he doing?"

"If you mean, Warren, 'is he still on a bender?' he better not be. Christ, is that all over the Department?"

"People talk, Peter."

"The word is gossip, and cops do it more than women," Wohl said.

"I was having my own troubles with good ol' Jack Daniel's for a while," Lomax said. "I'm sympathetic."

"I sometimes wonder if people weren't so sympathetic if the people they feel sorry for would straighten themselves out."

"He's a good cop, Peter."

"So I keep telling myself," Wohl said. "But then I keep hearing stories about him waving his gun around and getting thrown in a holding cell to sober up."

"You heard that, huh?"

"Let's play the tape."

Lieutenant Lomax had methodically made notes on seventeen recorded messages when his telephone rang. He answered it, then handed it to Wohl. "Tony Harris."

"Where are you working, Harris?" Wohl asked. There was a pause while Harris told him. Wohl thought a moment, then said, "Okay. Meet me at the Waikiki Diner on Roosevelt Boulevard at noon. If you get there before I do, get us a booth."

He hung up without waiting for a reply.

"Would you think me a racist if I told you I suspect all of these calls were from those of the Afro-American persuasion?" he asked.

"What did you expect?" Lomax replied. "Two kinds, though, I think. Some of these sleazeballs have gone past the sixth grade."

"Yeah, I sort of noticed that. A little affectation in the diction."

"And not all of them are black, I don't think."

"No?"

"At least not on the first tape. There was a very sexy lady on tape one. 'You know who this is,' she said, in a very sultry voice indeed, 'call me in the morning,' or 'after nine in the morning.' Something like that."

"Now you're a racist. How do you know the sexy lady isn't black?"

"I doubt it. This was a pure Bala Cynwyd, Rose Tree Hunt Club accent. She talked with her teeth clenched."

Wohl chuckled. "I think one might reasonably presume that if one is young, good-looking, rich, and drives a Porsche, one might reasonably expect to get one's wick dipped."

"Even a Porsche with slashed tires?" Lomax quipped, and then started the tape again.

The fifth message next played was, "Darling, he's gone out again, thank *God,* and I'm sitting here with a *martini*—and you *know* what *they* do to me—thinking of all the things I'd like to do to you. So if you get this before eight-thirty, call me, and we can at least *talk.* Otherwise, call me after nineish in the morning."

Wohl could see the lady, teeth clenched, talking. He even had a good idea of what she looked like. Blond hair, long, parted in the middle and hanging to her shoulders. She was wearing a sweater and a pleated skirt. From Strawbridge & Clothier in Jenkintown.

"I wonder what she has in *mind* to *do* to Officer Payne?" Lomax asked, teeth clenched. "Something frightfully *naughty,* wouldn't you say?"

"We gonna stick a .45 down your throat, motherfucker, and blow your fucking brains out your ass!"

"On the whole, I think I prefer the lady's offer," Wohl said.

"Yeah," Lomax said.

"Her voice," Wohl thought aloud, "sounds vaguely familiar."

"If he who has gone out again, thank *God,"* Lomax said, in a credible mimicry, "finds out, Payne is going to have a bullet in both legs."

"We gonna cut your cock off and shove it down your throat, motherfucker!"

"I think that's more or less what the lady has in mind," Wohl said. "Except that she wants to bite it off and shove it down her own throat."

"Peter, you're a dirty old man."

"Shut if off, I've heard enough," Wohl said. "I'm on my way to 'counsel' Detective Harris. I shouldn't have a mind full of lewd images."

"I don't think you missed anything. I'll play the whole thing to be sure. But that's about what the first one had on it."

"Why do you think they're doing this, Warren?"

"I don't know," Lomax said thoughtfully. "Just to be a pain in the ass, maybe. Or they get their jollies talking nasty to a cop."

"Wouldn't that get dull after a while? How many times can you say 'fuck you'?"

"I had the feeling, too, that it's organized. Some of them sound like they're reading it."

"That brings us back to why?"

"It could be, playing a psychiatrist, that they're getting a little worried, and calling Payne and Goldblatt's makes them think they're doing something useful for the revolution."

"You think they're really revolutionaries?"

"They don't sound like bomb throwers. Christ, I've listened to enough of them. *They* sound either really bananas, or very calm, as if they're going about God's work. These clowns don't even sound particularly angry."

"Yeah," Wohl said. "Well, thanks, Warren. It was good to see you."

"I got some really dirty tapes back there, Peter," Lomax said, gesturing toward a row of file tapes, "and some blue movies, now that we know you react to them. Come back anytime."

Martha Peebles woke thinking that she was—to her joyous surprise; four months before she would have given eight to five that she would end her life as a virginal spinster—not only a woman in love, but a *betrothed* woman.

David—sweet, shy David—had never actually proposed, of course, getting down on his knees and asking her to be his bride, giving her an engagement ring. But that didn't matter. He knew in his heart as she knew in hers that they were meant for each other, that it was ordained, perhaps by God, that they share life's joys and pains together, that they be man and wife.

Getting down on his knees wasn't David's style. She could not, now that she had time to think about it, imagine her father getting down on his knees either. And she already had an engagement ring. It had been her mother's. *And it looked so good on her finger!*

She got out of bed and put on a robe and went into the bath and watched David shave and then get dressed, and, hanging on his arm, her head against his shoulder, walked with him downstairs for breakfast.

Evans gave her, she thought, a knowing look.

Well, have I got a surprise for you! It's not what you think at all.

Evans disappeared into the kitchen, and then returned a moment later with the coffee service.

"Good morning, Miss Martha, Captain," he said. "It's cold out, but nice and clear. I hope you slept well?"

"Splendidly, thank you," Martha said. "Evans, Captain Pekach and I have a little announcement."

David looked uncomfortable.

"I saw the ring when you came in, Miss Martha," Evans said. "Your mother and dad would be happy for you."

He held out his hand to David.

"May I offer my congratulations, Captain?"

"Thank you," David said, getting to his feet, visibly torn between embarrassment and pleasure.

Harriet Evans came through the swinging door to the kitchen and wrapped her arms around Martha.

"Oh, honey baby, I'm so happy for you," she said, tears running down her cheeks. "I knew the first time I saw you with the captain that he'd be the one."

"I knew the first time I saw him that he was the one," Martha said.

Harriet touched Martha's face and then went to Pekach and hugged him.

David's embarrassment passed. He was now smiling broadly.

I will never be as happy ever again as I am at this moment, Martha thought.

She waited until Evans and Harriet had gone to fetch the rest of breakfast, and then asked, "Precious, would you do something for me?"

"Name it," he said, after a just perceptible hesitation.

"I know how you feel about people and parties, precious. But I do want to share this with *someone.*"

"Who?" David asked suspiciously.

"I was thinking we could have a very few people, Peter Wohl, for example, in for cocktails and dinner. Nothing elaborate—"

"*Wohl?*"

"Well, he is your boss, and he was the first one who knew."

"Yeah, I guess he was."

"And he's not married, and I suspect that he's under terrible pressure—"

"You can say that again."

"Well?"

"Well, what?"

"Would you ask him?"

"For when?"

"For tonight."

"I'll ask him."

"And maybe Captain and Mrs. Sabara?"

"I can ask."

And I will think of one more couple. Somebody who can do David some good. I would like to ask Brewster and Patricia Payne, but with their boy in the condition he is, that probably isn't a good idea. I'll think of someone. Since my husband-to-be wants to be a policeman, it is clearly the duty of his wife-to-be to do everything in her power to see that he becomes commissioner.

"You ask the minute you get to work, and call me and tell me what they said."

"That sounds like a wifely order."

"Yes, I guess it does. Do you want to change your mind about anything?"

Smiling broadly, he shook his head no.

She got up and went to his end of the table and stood behind his chair and put her arms around him.

And so it was that when Assistant District Attorney Farnsworth Stillwell finally managed to get Staff Inspector Peter Wohl on the telephone at half past one that afternoon, Wohl was able to make the absolutely truthful statement, "Well, that's very kind of you, Farnsworth, but I have previous plans."

He was to take cocktails and dinner with Miss Martha Peebles and her fiancé at Miss Peebles's residence, primarily because when Dave Pekach asked him, Pekach took him by surprise, and he could think of no excuse not to accept that would not hurt Pekach's feelings.

Until Stillwell had called, he had taken some consolation by thinking that the food would probably be good, and even if that didn't happen, he would be able to satisfy his curiosity about what the inside of the mansion behind the walls at 606 Glengarry Lane looked like.

Now he was extremely grateful to have been the recipient of Miss Peebles's kind invitation.

I may even carry her flowers.

"Can't you get out of it?" Stillwell insisted. "Peter, this is important. Possibly to both of us."

You for sure, and me possibly. Fuck you, Stillwell.

"I just can't. One of my men is having a little party to celebrate his engagement. I have to be there. You understand."

"Which one of your men?"

You are a persistent bastard, aren't you?

"Captain David Pekach, as a matter of fact."

Farnsworth Stillwell laughed, which surprised Wohl.

"I wondered what the hell that was all about. I'll see you there, Peter," he said, and hung up.

What the hell does he mean by that?

Farnsworth Stillwell broke the connection with his finger and dialed his home. "Helene, call the Peebles woman back, tell her that I was able to rearrange my schedule and that we'll be able to come after all."

Margaret McCarthy, trailed by Lari Matsi, came up the narrow staircase into Matt Payne's apartment. Both of them were wearing heavy quilted three-quarter-length jackets and earmuffs.

"I could have come and picked you up," Charley McFadden said.

"Next time, take him up on it," Lari said. "It's *cold* out there."

Jesus Martinez came up the stairs.

"Hay-zus, you don't know Lari, do you?" Margaret said. "Hay-zus Martinez, Lari Matsi."

"How are you?" Martinez said.

"I didn't catch the name?" Lari replied.

"It's 'Jesus' in Spanish," Charley offered.

"Oh," Lari said, and smiled.

"I don't think we've met," Margaret said, smiling, to the third young man in the room. "And Charley's not too good about introducing people."

He was wearing a mixed sweat suit, gray trousers and a yellow sweatshirt, on which was painted, STOLEN FROM THE SING SING PRISON ATHLETIC DEPARTMENT. There was little doubt in her mind that he was a cop; a shoulder holster with a large revolver in it was hanging from the chair that he was straddling backward. He stood up and put out his hand.

"Jack Matthews," he said.

"Where's Matt?"

"In his bedroom with a woman," Charley said.

"He thought you'd never ask," Jack Matthews said.

"What are you talking about?" Margaret said, not quite sure her leg was being pulled.

"You asked where Matt was, and I told you. He's in his bedroom with a woman."

"I don't believe you."

"Probably with his pants off," Charley added, exchanging a pleased smile with Jack Matthews. Jesus Martinez shook his head in disgust.

Amy Payne came out of Matt's bedroom, saw the women in the living room, and smiled.

"Hi! I'm Amy," she said. "Matt'll be out in a minute, presuming he can get his pants on by himself."

Officer McFadden and Special Agent Matthews for reasons that baffled all three women found this announcement convulsively hilarious. Even Jesus smiled.

"Just what's going on around here, Charley?" Margaret demanded.

"Let me take it from the beginning," Amy said. "I'm Amy Payne. Matt's sister. I happen to be a doctor. And knowing my idiot brother as I do, I felt reasonably sure that he would not change his dressings, and that's what I've been doing."

"Not very funny at all, Charley," Margaret said, but she could not keep herself from smiling.

Lari dipped into an enormous purse and held up a plastic bag full of bandages and antiseptic.

"I don't know him as well as you do, Doctor," she said. "But that's why I'm here too. He is that category of patient best described as a pain-in-the-you-know-what. I was filling in on the surgical floor at Frankford when they brought him in."

"Well, that was certainly nice of you," Amy said. "Apparently, you don't know my brother very well. If you did, you would encourage gangrene."

"No," Lari said. "That would put him back in the hospital. Anything to prevent that."

They smiled at each other.

Matt came into the room, supporting himself on a cane.

"Oh, good!" he said. "Everybody's here. Choir practice can begin."

"I promised Mother I would see that you were eating," Amy said. "What are your plans for that?"

"We're going out for the worst food in Philadelphia," Matt said. "You're welcome to join us, Amy."

"I know I shouldn't ask, but curiosity overwhelms me. Where are you going to get the worst food in Philadelphia?"

"At the FOP," Matt replied. "As a special dispensation, because I have been a very good boy, I have permission to go there, providing I don't drink too much and I come directly home afterward."

"Actually, I'm looking forward to it," Jack Matthews said. "I've never been there."

"I think I'll pass, thank you just the same," Amy said.

"You're a cop, and you've never been to the FOP?" Lari Matsi asked.

"Oh, come on, Amy," Matt said. "I'll even buy you a chili dog."

"I haven't had supper," Amy said. "For some perverse reason, a chili dog has a certain appeal to me."

"How is it," Lari pursued, "that you've never been to the FOP?"

"He's not a *real* cop," Charley said. "More like a Junior G-man."

"In deference to the ladies, Officer McFadden," Jack Matthews said, "I will not suggest that you attempt a physiologically impossible act of self-impregnation."

Matt laughed. After a moment, Amy did too, and then Lari.

"Then what's the gun for?" Lari asked.

"I work for the Justice Department," Jack replied.

"He's an FBI agent, Lari," Matt said.

"Oh, really?"

Matt saw the way Lari was looking at Jack Matthews, and knew that whatever chance there might have been for him to know Lari Matsi in the biblical sense had just gone up in smoke.

"Are you here *officially?*" Amy asked. "I mean, are you part of Matt's bodyguard, or whatever it's called?"

"Actually, I came to play chess," Jack said. "But these evil people pressed intoxicants on me. Have I shattered your faith in the FBI?"

"Yeah," Amy said, smiling.

Yeah, you are here officially, Matt thought, *or at least quasi-officially. You came here, under cover of playing chess, to tell me that yes, indeed, the rumors are true. I am to be investigated by the FBI regarding formal charges made that I violated the civil rights of Charles David Stevens, Esq., by shooting the murderous sonofabitch.*

"Has any thought been given to how we're going to get Matt—I guess I mean all of us—from here to the FOP?" Amy asked. "I don't have my car."

"No problem," Charley said. "We—Hay-zus and me—have an unmarked car downstairs. We'll take Matt in that. The rest of you can ride with Jack in his G-man wagon."

"That should work," Lari Matsi said.

And I will bet twenty dollars to a doughnut that when the convoy gets under way, Lari will be in the front seat of same with J. Edgar Hoover, Junior, both of them wondering how they can get rid of Amy and Margaret.

Oh, what the hell. There's always Helene.

Staff Inspector Peter F. Wohl left his office at Bustleton and Bowler Streets a few minutes after half past five.

On the way to his apartment in the 800 block of Norwood Street in Chestnut Hill, Wohl decided that tonight was a good opportunity to give the Jag a little exercise. He hadn't had it out of the garage since the lousy weather had started.

Among its many not-so-charming idiosyncrasies, the Jag frequently expressed its annoyance at being ignored for more than forty-eight hours at a time by absolutely refusing to start when the person privileged to have the responsibility for its care and feeding finally came to take it out.

Driving it back and forth to Martha Peebles's house—plus maybe a run past Monahan's house on the way home, just to check—would be just long enough a trip to give it a good warm-up, get the oil circulating, and get the flat spots out of the tires.

He thought again that if there was only room to *safely* park a car like the Jag at Bustleton and Bowler, he could drive it to work every other day or so. He made a mental note to tell Payne, when he came back on duty, and could devote some attention to the "new" school building at Frankford and Castor, to make sure that, as a prerogative of his exalted rank and position, the commanding officer of Special Operations have reserved for him a parking place that was at once convenient and would provide a certain protection against getting its fenders dinged.

When he reached the garages behind the mansion he put his city-owned car in the garage, and then took a shovel and started to clear the ice and snow away from the doors of the Jag's garage. He finally got the door open, but it was even more difficult than he thought it would be. The snow had melted and frozen into ice and thawed and refrozen. He had, he thought, actually *chiseled* his way through the ice into the garage, rather than *shoveled* his way through the snow.

He got behind the wheel and put the key in the ignition. To his delighted surprise, the engine caught immediately. It ran a little roughly, but it ran. It would not, as he had worst-scenario predicted, refuse to start until he had run the battery down and then recharged it.

"Good girl," he said.

He sat there, running the engine just above idle until the engine temperature gauge needle finally moved off the peg. He shut the engine off, opened the hood and checked the oil and brake fluid, looked at the tires, and then closed the doors, locked them, and went up the stairs at the end of the building to his apartment.

He showered and shaved, put on a glen plaid suit, and wondered—he had little experience in this sort of thing—if he was expected to bring a gift to the affair, and if so, what?

To hell with it.

He put on his overcoat, which had a collar of some unidentified fur, and a green felt snap-brim hat.

There were no messages on his answering machine, which surprised him. He called Special Operations and told the lieutenant on duty that he would be at the residence of Miss Martha Peebles in Chestnut Hill from fifteen minutes from now until he advised differently.

Then he went down and got back in the Jaguar. It started immediately. All was right with the world, he told himself, until he glanced at his watch and saw that he was not due at Glengarry Lane for almost an hour.

What the hell, I'll check on the people sitting on Monahan now, instead of later.

When he reached the neighborhood, he drove slowly east on Bridge Street, looking up Sylvester Street at the intersection. There was an unmarked car parked at the curb. He could see the heads of two men in the car, one of them wearing a regular uniform cap, the other what he thought of as a Renfrew of the Royal Canadian Mounted Police cap.

He turned left into the alley behind the row of houses of which, he now remembered. Mr. and Mrs. Albert J. Monahan occupied the sixth from this corner.

He had gone perhaps fifty yards into the alley when a uniformed officer stepped into it and, somewhat warily, Wohl thought approvingly, motioned for him to stop.

Wohl braked and rolled down the window.

"Good evening, sir," the cop began, and then recognized him. "Oh, it's you, Inspector."

"This way to the North Pole, right?" Wohl said, and offered his hand through the window. The cop laughed dutifully.

"Aside from frostbite, how's things going?" Wohl asked with a smile.

"Quiet as a tomb, Inspector."

An unfortunate choice of words, but I take your point.

"I guess everybody but cops are smart enough to stay inside, huh?"

"Sure looks that way. Anything I can do for you, Inspector?"

"No. I just thought I'd better check on what was going on. Mr. Monahan is very important."

"Well, we're sitting on him good. There's either a Highway or a district RPC by here every fifteen to twenty minutes. Or a supervisor, or both. Sergeant Carter drove through the alley just a couple of minutes ago."

"But nothing out of the ordinary?"

"Not a thing."

"Well, then, I guess I can go. Good to see you. I'm sorry you have to march around in the snow and ice, but I think it's necessary."

"I've been telling myself the guys in Traffic do this for twenty years," the cop said. "Good evening, sir."

Wohl smiled, rolled up the window, and drove the rest of the way down the alley, looking at the rear of the Monahan house as he went past.

He turned left from the alley onto Sanger Street, and then left again onto Sylvester Street. He would stop and say hello to the two cops in the car.

Now there were two unmarked cars on Rosehill Street.

That's probably Sergeant Carter.

The cop with the Renfrew of the Royal Canadian Mounted Police cap got— surprisingly quickly, Wohl thought—from behind the wheel and stepped into the street, signaling him to stop.

Christ, I hope they're not stopping every car that comes down the street!

This time there was no recognition in the cop's eyes when Wohl rolled the window down and looked up at him.

"Sir," the cop said, "you're going the wrong way down a one-way street. May I see your driver's license, please?"

Wohl took his leather ID folder from his pocket and passed it out the window.

"Maybe you could give me another chance, Officer," he said. "I'm usually not this stupid."

"Oh, Jesus, Inspector!"

"I honest to God didn't see the one-way sign," Wohl said. "Who's that in the back of the RPC? Sergeant Carter?"

"Lieutenant Malone, sir."

"Let me pull this over—turn it around, I guess—I'd like a word with him."

"Yes, sir."

Wohl turned the car around and parked it, and then went and got in the back of the unmarked car.

"We all feel a little foolish, Inspector," Malone said when Wohl got in the backseat of the RPC. "We should have recognized you."

Wohl saw that Malone was in civilian clothing.

"You don't feel half as foolish as I do," Wohl said. "If I had been doing ninety in a thirty-mile zone, that I would understand. But going the wrong way down a one-way street—"

"I'll let you go with a warning this time, Inspector," the cop who had stopped him said, "but the next time, right into Lewisburg!"

Everyone laughed.

"Something on your mind, Inspector?" Malone asked.

"Just wanted to check on Monahan, that's all."

"He's been home about an hour and a half," the cop who had stopped Wohl said. "I don't think he'll be going out again tonight in this weather."

"How are you working this?" Wohl asked, and touched Malone's knee to silence him when it looked like Malone was going to answer.

"Simple rotation," the second cop answered. "One of us walks for thirty minutes— when the wind's really blowing, only fifteen minutes—and then one of us takes his place. We do a four-hour tour, and then go on our regular patrols."

"Your reliefs showing up all right?"

"Yes, sir."

"Does the man walking the beat have a radio?"

"We all have radios."

"Can you think of any way to improve what we're trying to do? Even a wild hair?"

"How about a heated snowmobile?"

"I'll ask Commissioner Czernich in the morning about a snowmobile. Don't hold your breath. But I meant it, anybody got any ideas about something we should, or should not, be doing?"

Both cops shook their heads.

"Well, I can see that I'm not needed here," Wohl said. "I guess everybody understands how important Monahan is as a witness?"

"Yes, sir," they said, nearly in unison.

"Can I have a word with you, Lieutenant?"

"Yes, sir, certainly."

Wohl shook hands with both cops and got out of the car. Malone followed him to the Jaguar.

"Yes, sir."

"You have anything else to do here?"

"No, sir."

"Any hot plans for tonight? For dinner, to start with?"

"No, sir."

"Okay, Jack. Get in your car and follow me."

"Where are we going?"

"Somewhere where it's warm, and where, I suspect, there will be a more than adequate supply of free antifreeze."

24.

Miss Martha Peebles had decided that it would be better to receive her and Captain Pekach's guests in the family (as opposed to the formal) dining room of her home. For one thing, it had been her father's favorite room. She had good memories of her father and his friends getting up from the dinner table and moving to the overstuffed chairs and couches at the far end of the room for cognac and cigars and coffee.

Tonight, she would more or less reverse that. She had had Evans and his nephew Nathaniel set up a little bar near the overstuffed furniture. Nathaniel would serve drinks first, before they moved to the dining table for the meal. Then, after they had eaten, they could move back.

Besides, she reasoned, the formal dining room was just too large for the few people who would be coming. When she was a little girl, for her eleventh birthday party, it had been converted into a roller-skating rink.

But her father had preferred the family dining room, and it seemed appropriate for tonight. And she thought that her father would appreciate the arrangements she had made.

She was convinced that her father would have liked David, and vice versa. They were men. And if he liked David, her father would also like David's friends, Inspector Wohl and Captain Sabara.

Daddy probably wouldn't like Farnsworth Stillwell any more than I do, she thought, but she could clearly hear his voice telling her, *"Like it or not, kitten, you are who you are, and from time to time, you have to go through the motions and put up with people of your own background."*

And, besides, now that Stillwell had entered politics, he might turn out to be useful to David.

Captain and Mrs. Michael J. Sabara were the first to arrive. As Evans led them into the family dining room, Martha had the thought—which she instantly recognized as unkind and regretted—that Mrs. Sabara was a trifle overdressed. Captain Sabara was dressed almost exactly as David was, that is to say in a blazer and gray slacks, and that pleased her.

"I'm Martha Peebles," she said, offering her hand to Mrs. Sabara. "I'm so glad you could come on such short notice."

"Your home is beautiful!" Mrs. Sabara said.

"David calls it the fortress," Martha said. "But I grew up here, and I guess I'm used to it."

Sabara and Pekach shook hands, although they had seen each other only two hours before.

"Why don't you have Nathaniel make Captain and Mrs. Sabara something to chase the chill, David?"

As they approached the bar, Captain Sabara said, "I told you I didn't need a tie. Dave's not wearing one."

"When you come to a house like this," Mrs. Sabara said firmly, "you wear a necktie." Then she turned to Pekach. "She's beautiful, David."

"Yeah," Pekach said. "Look, Lois, don't say anything about us being engaged. I think she wants to make an announcement."

Lois Sabara put her index finger before her lips.

"You name it, we got it," Dave said as they reached the bar.

"What are you drinking?" Mike Sabara asked.

"Scotch. Some kind her father liked. He bought it by the truckload."

"I'll have what Captain Pekach is drinking," Sabara said. "Lois?"

"Wine, I think. Have you any red wine?"

"There's a California Cabernet Sauvignon, madam, and a very nice Moroccan burgundy that Miss Martha likes," Nathaniel said.

"I'll have the burgundy, please."

Staff Inspector Peter Wohl and Lieutenant John J. Malone entered the family dining room next.

"Who's he?" Lois asked softly, as they walked toward the bar.

"Jack Malone. New lieutenant," her husband told her.

"He's the one with the wife trouble, right?"

"Jesus Christ, Lois!"

"Where's the lady of the house?" Wohl asked.

"I guess she's checking on the food," Pekach said. "Thank you for coming, Inspector. And welcome, Jack."

"The inspector said it would be all right," Malone said.

"Absolutely."

"You don't know Mike's wife, do you, Jack?" Wohl said. "Lois, this is Jack Malone."

"How do you do?" Lois Sabara said.

Madam Sabara, Wohl thought, *has obviously heard the gossip vis-à-vis Mrs. Malone. Her tone of voice would freeze a penguin.*

"We just ran past Monahan's house," Wohl offered. "Things seem well in hand."

"And Payne?" Sabara asked.

"Officer Payne is dining at the FOP," Wohl said.

"Can he get around well enough for that?" Lois asked. "I thought he was shot in the leg?"

"He will not be the first young police officer to crawl into the FOP," Wohl said. "For that matter, I've seen some pretty old ones crawl in there."

"May I get you gentlemen a cocktail?" Nathaniel asked.

"I'll have Scotch, light on the ice and water, please," Wohl said.

He saw the hesitancy in Malone's eyes, and made the quick decision that when Lois, as she certainly would, recounted her encounter with Lieutenant-Jack-Malone-the-Wife-Beater to her peers, it would be better if she could not crow, "Well, at least he wasn't drinking," from a position of moral superiority.

"Try the Scotch, Jack," he said. "David's been bragging about it."

"Same for me, then," Malone said.

Martha came through a door Wohl hadn't noticed. He approved of what he saw, both sartorially—Martha was wearing a simple black dress with a double string of pearls—and on her face: She was a happy woman.

A wholesome one too, he thought. *Dave's going to have a hard time adjusting to life in the palace, and she's going to have a hard time being a cop's wife, but Dave is a decent human being, and I think he's just what this poor little rich girl really needs.*

"Good evening, Inspector," she said. "I'm so glad you could come."

"Thank you for asking me," Wohl said. "And David said, when I told him I didn't have a lady to bring, to bring somebody. This is somebody, Lieutenant Jack Malone."

"David's told me about you, Lieutenant," Martha said, shaking his hand.

I wonder how much? Wohl thought.

Farnsworth and Helene Stillwell appeared in the room.

"I don't know him well," Martha said, quickly and softly to Wohl, "but my father knew her father. And I thought that since you're working together, having them would be appropriate."

"Absolutely," Wohl said.

What she's doing—good for her—is trying to foster Dave's career. If she's as smart as I think she is, I will be working for Dave in a couple of years.

He next had a somewhat less upbeat thought when he took a good look at Helene Stillwell.

That one has had a couple of little nips to give her courage to face the party.

"Small world, Peter, eh?" Stillwell greeted him.

"It looks that way, doesn't it?"

"You remember my wife, of course?"

"Yes of course. Nice to see you, Mrs. Stillwell."

"Oh, please call me Helene."

Helene Stillwell was wearing a black dress, almost an exact duplicate of Martha's, and a similar string of pearls.

The necessary introductions were made and drinks offered and comments about the foul weather exchanged.

I wonder why Martha Peebles doesn't talk that way, using the teeth-clenched diction Stillwell's wife does? Peter Wohl wondered.

According to Matt Payne, Martha has more money than God, and this house makes it rather obvious that she didn't make it last week. Ergo, she too should talk through her nose and as if she has lockjaw.

But she doesn't. Martha sounds, if not like Lois Sabara, at least like my mother, and Stillwell's wife sounds exactly like the horny married lady from Bala Cynwyd on Matt's answering machine.

"And how, Inspector Wohl, is Officer Payne?" Helene asked.

Jesus H. Christ! Don't let your dirty imagination run away with you!

"It's quarter to eight, Helene. By now I'd say he's on the third pitcher of beer and con-vinced, given the chance, he could solve all the problems of the Police Department."

"I don't quite follow you?"

"He's on the town, more or less."

"I thought he was—that you had him under protection in some mysterious place. And he's on the town?"

"No mysterious place. He's in his apartment. And tonight he's at the FOP—the Fraternal Order of Police building, on Spring Garden Street. Jack Malone, who is in charge of his security, decided that if there was any place more secure than Matt's apart-ment, it would be downstairs in the FOP, where there are generally at least a hundred armed cops."

"Yes, of course," Helene said through clenched teeth and sounding exactly like the horny lady from Bala Cynwyd on Matt's answering machine.

Except, of course, we don't know that she's from Bala Cynwyd. Warren Lomax said she sounded like she was from Bala Cynwyd.

"I'm going to drop in on him tomorrow morning," Wohl said. "I'll tell him you were asking about him."

"Yes, please. He's such a nice young man."

And such a comfort to a bored teeth clencher to boot? And that is a martini you're drinking, Helene, isn't it?

"Peter," Farnsworth Stillwell said, walking up. "I really do have to have a word with you."

"Certainly."

"Martha, I need a few minutes alone with Inspector Wohl. Is there somewhere?"

"David, darling, would you take them into the library?"

"Sure," Pekach said.

"Thank you, David darling," Wohl said softly as he followed Pekach out of the room.

Pekach glared at him, and then smiled and shook his head.

"Do I detect a certain element of jealousy, Inspector?"

"Absolutely, David."

Do I really think that Matt is fucking Stillwell's wife? And presuming for the sake of argument that I do, am I annoyed because that's a pretty fucking dumb thing for him to be doing? Or because he's getting in where Peter Wohl ain't?

"I hope, Farnsworth," Wohl said as he followed Pekach into the library, "that this won't take long. My glass seems to have a hole in it."

"No problem," Pekach said. "Martha's father never liked to get far from the sauce."

He heaved on what looked like a chest. It unfolded upward into a bar.

"There's even a refrigerator and running water in this thing," Pekach said, demonstrating.

"How nice," Stillwell said.

And thank you, Farnsworth Stillwell. I was just about to say, "It must be nice to be rich," and that would have been a dumb thing to say.

"I think Martha's about to serve dinner," Pekach said.

"This won't take long," Stillwell said.

Wohl went to the bar, poured more Scotch into his glass, and added a little water. By then Pekach had left the library and closed the door after himself.

"Now, there's a man who knows what to do with an opportunity," Stillwell said, nod-ding toward the door through which Pekach had left.

"How do you mean?"

"Unless she is smart enough to get an airtight premarital agreement, and floating on the wings of love as she is at the moment, I rather doubt if she will be, your man Pekach is shortly going to be co-owner of half the anthracite coal in Northeast Pennsylvania."

I will be on my good behavior. I will not get into it with this cynical wiseass sonofabitch.

"It couldn't happen to a nicer guy."

"Don't misunderstand me, Peter," Stillwell said. "I like Dave Pekach, and I admire people who take advantage of opportunities that come their way."

Wohl smiled and nodded.

What is this sonofabitch up to?

"Tomorrow morning, Peter, the governor will hold a press conference at which he will appoint a new deputy attorney general for corporate crime. Nice ring to that, isn't there? *'Corporate crime.'* Everybody knows that the men in corporate boardrooms are robbing the poor people blind. I thought it was one of the governor's brighter moves recently, figuring out for himself that there are more poor people voting than people in corporate boardrooms. I told him so."

"I'm missing something here?"

"A brilliant gumshoe like you? I just can't believe that, Peter."

"I'm not much good at games, either, Farnsworth."

"Okay. The facts and nothing but the facts, right, Sergeant Friday? I am going to be the deputy attorney general for corporate crime."

"Well, in that case, congratulations," Peter said, and put out his hand.

"And you are going to be the new chief investigator for the deputy attorney general for corporate crime," Stillwell went on.

"I am?"

"Starting at a salary that's ten, maybe twelve thousand more than you're making now."

He means this! He's absolutely goddamn serious! And he's looking at me as if he expects me to get down on one knee and kiss his ring.

"Farnsworth, why would you want me to work for you?"

"Very simple answer. I don't know the first goddamn thing about corporate crime. And you do. There doesn't seem to be much question that you are the best white-collar crime investigator in Philadelphia. Your record proves that. If you can do that in Philadelphia, you certainly can do it elsewhere in Pennsylvania. I want the best, and you're it."

There is a certain element of truth in that, he understands, with overwhelming immodesty.

"When did all this come up?"

"Yesterday and today. What absolutely perfect timing, wouldn't you say?"

"Perfect timing for what?"

"This Islamic Liberation Army thing is just about to blow up in our faces."

"Is it? I'm a little dense. The doers are in jail. We have a witness. And you're going to prosecute."

"I would hate to think you were being sarcastic, Peter."

"Like I said, sometimes I'm dense. You tell me. Why is it going to blow up in our faces?"

"Armando C. Giacomo, for one thing. More important, whatever shadowy faces in the background have come up with the money to engage Mr. Giacomo's professional services."

"I don't think you're saying that anytime a sleazeball, or a group of sleazeballs, comes up with the money to hire Giacomo, the DA's office should roll over and apologize for having them arrested in the first place."

He saw in Stillwell's eyes that he was becoming annoyed, at what he perceived to be his naiveté.

Fuck you, Farnsworth!

"I heard—I have some contacts in the FBI, the Justice Department—that the Coalition for Equitable Law Enforcement has filed a petition demanding an investigation of Officer Payne, alleging that he violated the civil rights of Charles David Stevens."

"The what?"

"The Coalition for Equitable Law Enforcement. It's one of those lunatic bleeding heart groups. One of the more articulate ones, unfortunately."

"That shooting was not only justifiable use of force, it was self-defense."

"The allegation will be investigated. It will get in the papers. Arthur Nelson—in both the *Ledger* and over WGHA-TV—will be overjoyed with the opportunity to paint Officer Payne as a trigger-happy killer murdering the innocent. He will gleefully point out that Mr. Stevens's unfortunate demise was the second notch on Payne's gun."

"The bottom line will be—if it gets as far as a Grand Jury—"

"It will," Stillwell interrupted.

"—that the shooting was justified."

"I am surprised that I have to remind you, of all people, Peter, that all it will take is *one* juror—during the ILA trial I mean—to come to the conclusion that since the police were so willing to murder in cold blood one of the alleged robbers, they are entirely capable of coming up with manufactured evidence and a perjuring witness, that they have not, in the immortal words of Perry Mason, proved their case beyond a reasonable doubt."

Wohl took a long pull on his drink, but didn't reply.

"I would rate the chances of a conviction in the ILA case as no better than fifty percent," Stillworth said. "And that is if we can get Monahan into court. I don't like those odds, Peter. I don't want to be thought of as the assistant district attorney who was unable to get a conviction of the niggers who robbed Goldblatt's and killed the watchman or whatever he was."

"You want to be governor, right?"

"Is there something wrong with that? Wouldn't you like to be police commissioner?" Wohl met his eyes. "The police commissioner is an appointive post. I don't think it's impossible, some years down the pike, that the mayor of Philadelphia would want to appoint to that position someone who both had earned a reputation state-wide as a highly successful investigator of corporate crime, and who also had been a respected police officer in Philadelphia for many years."

The odds are that no matter what you say now, you will later regret it.

"Such a hypothetical person might even have a high recommendation from a hypothetical governor, right?"

Stillwell laughed.

"Farnsworth, frankly, you've taken me by surprise."

"I've noticed."

"I'll need some time to think this over."

"There isn't much time, Peter. I've scheduled a press conference for ten tomorrow morning, at which I will announce my acceptance of the governor's appointment. I'd like to be able to say, at that time, who my chief investigator will be."

"Let me sleep on this," Wohl said. "I'll get back to you first thing in the morning."

"Deal," Stillwell said, offering his hand. "I admire, within reason of course, people who look before they leap. Now let us go back in there and share the joy of Romeo and Juliet."

Officer Charles McFadden, who, on his fifth cup of black coffee, was watching an Edward G. Robinson/Jimmy Cagney gangster movie on the *Late, Late Show,* was startled when the telephone rang. It was, according to the clock on the mantelpiece, a few minutes before three A.M.

He got quickly out of the chair and went to the telephone.

"Hello?"

"Who is this?"

"Who's this?"

"This is Inspector Wohl. Who's that, McFadden?"

"Yes, sir."

"Everything under control, McFadden?"

"Yes, sir."

"Is Officer Payne there?"

"Yes, sir."

"Put him on, please."

"He's asleep, Inspector."

"Then I suppose it will be necessary to wake him up, won't it?"

"Yes, sir. Sir, is anything wrong?"

"No. Not at all. The world, Officer McFadden, is getting, day by day, in every way, better and better. You might keep that in mind."

"Yes, sir. Hold on, Inspector. I'll go wake Payne up."

Officer McFadden had some difficulty in waking Officer Payne. Officer Payne had consumed pitchers of FOP beer like a sponge earlier on. He now smelled like a brewery.

"Jesus Christ, Matt, wake up! Wohl's on the phone!"

Officer Payne managed to get into a semireclining position in his bed.

"What the hell is going on?" he demanded. He looked up at the time projected on the ceiling by the clock Amy had given him. "It's three o'clock in the morning, for Christ's sake!" he protested.

"Wohl's on the phone."

"What the hell does he want?"

"I don't know. He sounds crocked."

"Jesus!"

Officer Payne, with some difficulty, finally managed to make it from a semireclining to a fully sitting-up position. Officer McFadden then removed the handset of the newly installed telephone and handed it to him.

"Yes, sir?" Matt said.

"Sorry to trouble you at this late hour, Officer Payne," Inspector Wohl said, his syllables sufficiently slurred to remind Officer Payne that Officer McFadden had said, "He sounds crocked."

"No problem, sir."

"But I have to have an answer to a certain question that has come up."

"Yes, sir."

"Allegations have reached me, Officer Payne, that you have had, on one or more occasions, carnal knowledge of a female to whom you are not joined in lawful marriage."

What the hell is this all about?

"Sir?"

"And that, on the other hand, the lady in question is married. Not to you, of course."

Christ, he knows about Helene! And he's crocked! And pissed, otherwise he would not be calling at three o'clock in the morning.

"Sir?"

"I am about to ask you a question. I want you to carefully consider your answer before giving it."

"Yes, sir."

"Officer Payne, have you been conducting an illicit affair with Mrs. Helene Stillwell?"

Matt did not reply, because he was absolutely sure that whatever answer he gave was going to get him up to his ears in the deep shit.

"You do know the lady? Helene? The beloved wife of our beloved assistant district attorney?"

"Yes, sir."

"Well, yes or no, Officer Payne? Have you been fucking Farnsworth Stillwell's wife or not?"

"Yes, sir," Matt confessed.

"Good boy!" Inspector Wohl said, and hung up.

———

At 5:51 A.M., it was visually pleasant on the 5600 block of Sylvester Street, east of Roosevelt Boulevard not far from Oxford Circle. It had snowed, on and off, during the night, and the streets and sidewalks were blanketed in white. Here and there, light came from windows in the row houses, as people began their day. Those windows, and the streetlights, seemed to glow as there came the first hint of daylight.

Physically, it was not quite so pleasant. The reason it had stopped snowing was that the temperature had dropped; it was now twenty-six degrees Fahrenheit, six degrees below freezing. There was a steady northerly wind, powerful enough to move the recently fallen powder snow around.

Officer Richard Kallanan, of the three-man Special Operations team charged with protecting the residence and person of Mr. Albert J. Monahan, had found the wind and the blowing snow particularly uncomfortable during his turn on foot patrol around the Monahan residence. His ears and nose were perhaps unusually sensitive to cold. He had tried walking his route both ways, passing through the alley from Bridge Street to Sanger Street in a northeast direction, and then down Sylvester in a southwestern path, and the reverse. He could detect no difference in perceived cold.

It was a cold sonofabitch in the alley, no matter which way he walked, and he was, therefore, understandably pleased when he turned onto Sylvester Street one more time and saw that there were now two substantially identical dark blue Plymouth RPCs at the curb, one house up from Monahan's house.

Their relief had arrived.

A couple of minutes early, instead of a couple of minutes late. Thank God!

Kallanan picked up his pace a little, slapping his gloved hands together as he moved. As he passed the replacement RPC, he waved and glanced in the window. The side windows were covered with ice, and he could not make out any of the faces inside.

Not that it would have mattered. Kallanan was a relative newcomer to Special Operations, transferred in from the 11th District, where he had spent six of his seven years on the job, and he had not yet had time to make that many new friends.

He could see enough, however, to notice that two of the guys in the relief car were wearing winter hats, Renfrew of the Royal Canadian Mounted Police hats.

They're going to need them.

When Kallanan reached his RPC, he knocked on the window, and Officer Richard O. Totts, who was sitting in the front passenger seat, turned and reached into the back and opened the door for him. Kallanan glanced at the relief car, and gave its occupants a cheerful farewell wave. The driver, a black guy whose window was clear, waved back. Kallanan got in the backseat and pulled the door closed.

"Jesus, it's cold out there," he said.

"I think there's a little coffee left," Officer Duane Jones, who was behind the wheel, said. Totts handed a thermos bottle into the backseat. Kallanan unscrewed the top, which was also the cup, and as Duane Jones got the car moving, he emptied the thermos into it. There was not much coffee left in the thermos.

"Hungry, Kallanan?" Jones asked.

"What I would like is a cup of hot coffee. With a stiff shot in it. There's nothing in here."

"I know a place," Totts offered.

"I'm going to turn in the car first," Jones said. "I hear Pekach is a real sonofabitch if you get caught drinking."

"Hey, we've been relieved," Kallanan said.

"We're still in the goddamn car," Jones said. "You can wait."

At 6:06 A.M., Special Operations Radio Patrol Car W-22 (Radio Call, William Twenty-Two) carrying Officers Rudolph McPhail, Paul Hennis, and John Wilhite turned right off Castor Avenue onto Bridge Street, and then right again on Sylvester Street.

"I don't see the car," Officer Wilhite, who was driving, said. "You don't suppose they took off without waiting for us?"

"Shit, we're only a couple of minutes late," Officer Hennis said.

"Hey, Monahan's house is all lit up," Officer McPhail said, from the backseat.

The radio went off:

"BEEP BEEP BEEP. 5600 block Sylvester Street. Report of shooting and hospital case. Civilian by phone."

"BEEP BEEP BEEP. 5600 block Sylvester Street. Report of shooting and hospital case. Civilian by phone."

"Holy shit!" Officer Hennis said.

Officer Wilhite picked up the microphone.

"William Twenty-Two, in on that. On the scene. There is no other car in sight at this location."

The three of them literally leaped out of the car and ran as fast as they could toward the residence of Albert J. Monahan.

"Wohl," Staff Inspector Peter Wohl, his mouth as dry as the Sahara Desert, said into the phone at his bedside.

"Inspector, this is Lieutenant Farr. We have a report of a shooting and hospital case at Monahan's."

"What?"

"We have a report of a shooting and hospital case at Monahan's house."

"Did they get Monahan?"

"I think so."

"On my way. Notify Captains Sabara and Pekach, Lieutenant Malone, and Sergeant Washington. Have them meet me there."

"Yes, sir."

"And check with the people sitting on Payne. Send a Highway car there, in any event."

"Yes, sir."

Wohl hung up without saying anything else, kicked the blankets off himself, and got out of bed.

25.

"Inspector," the Emergency Room physician at Nazareth Hospital said, "I don't know why this man died—I suspect he suffered a coronary occlusion, a heart attack—but I am sure that he wasn't shot. Or for that matter, suffered any other kind of a traumatic wound."

Wohl looked at her in disbelief. She was what he thought of as a pale redhead, as opposed to the more robust, Hungarian variety. She was slight and delicate, with pale blue eyes. Probably, he guessed, the near side of forty.

"Doctor, we have an eyewitness who said she *saw* him *being* shot. His *wife*. She said she saw the gun, heard a noise, and then saw her husband fall down."

He received a look of utter contempt.

The doctor pulled down the green sheet that covered the now naked remains of Albert J. Monahan, leaving only the legs below the knees covered.

"There is no wound," she said. "Gunshots, as you probably know, make at least entrance wounds. So do knives. Will you take my word that I have carefully examined the body? Or would you like me to turn him over?"

"What about the head?"

"I checked the head."

"Doctor, what about a very small caliber wound? A .22. That's less than a quarter of an inch in diameter?"

"Closer to a fifth of an inch, actually," the doctor said dryly. "Let me tell you what happened: The cops in the van brought this man in here. They said he had been shot. A superficial examination showed no wound. But—there was time; he was dead on arrival—and though I had no obligation to do so, I checked for a wound. I was thinking .22. We get a lot of them in here. There is no puncture wound of any kind. Sorry."

"And you think he had a heart attack?"

"Your guess is as good as mine. The autopsy will come up with the answer, I'm sure." She picked up the green sheet. "Seen enough?"

"Yes, thank you."

She pulled the sheet up over Albert J. Monahan.

More than enough. I'm going to remember this one a long time. This one I'm responsible for. The phrase is "dereliction of duty."

Jesus H. Christ, what's going on around here?

A Highway Patrolman pushed open the swinging door.

"You said to tell you when Washington got here, Inspector."

"Thank you, Doctor," Wohl said.

She responded with a just perceptible nod of her head.

When he stepped into the corridor he saw Jason Washington walking down it toward him, and Tony Harris turning off into a side corridor.

"What's he doing here?" Wohl snapped.

"He's going to talk to the widow," Washington said evenly. "He knows the hospital priest. The chapel is down that way. Or do you mean, 'what's *he* doing here'? The answer to which is that until I hear differently from you, he works for me. I am under the assumption that means I say where and when."

"I'm sorry," Wohl said after a moment. "I'm on edge. I picked last night to tie one on."

"You look like hell," Washington said.

"I have just been informed that there are no puncture wounds in the body—"

"There have to be," Washington interrupted him.

"—the doctor says she thinks he probably had a heart attack."

"Wilhite told me that Mrs. Monahan told him she saw him being shot. By a cop."

"He's one of those who came on duty?"

Washington nodded.

"Where is he, where are they, all of them, the three going off duty, now?"

"At Bustleton and Bowler."

"I want them separated," Wohl said.

"Sergeant Carter was on the scene. I told him to keep the two groups—the three going off and the three coming on—apart. Or do you mean separated from each other?"

"I would be happier with separated from each other, but I suppose it's too late for that now."

"You think they really had something to do with this?"

"I honest to God don't know what to think. But something, goddammit, went wrong."

"Well, let's go get you a fried egg sandwich."

"What?"

"You need something in your stomach. Besides black coffee. The only food, in my experience, that hospital cafeterias can't screw up is a fried egg sandwich."

"I'll eat later."

"I told Tony to come to the cafeteria after he's talked to Mrs. Monahan. Before I go charging off anywhere, I want to hear what Tony says."

Wohl looked at him.

"Peter, come on. What you have to do is calm down."

"Okay," Wohl said after a moment. "You're probably right."

"A little Sen-Sen might be in order too," Washington said. "And I hope you have an electric razor in your car."

"That bad, huh?"

"What was the occasion?"

"Stillwell got me alone at Dave Pekach's—*Martha Peebles's*—house. There was a little party. They're going to get married. Anyway, he told me that he's getting appointed a state assistant DA. He offered me a job as his chief investigator."

"You've lost me somewhere," Washington said as they entered the cafeteria. "Go find a table. I'll get it."

Wohl sat down at a table, then spotted a soft drink machine. He went to it and deposited coins and got a can of 7-Up, which he drank down quickly. The cold produced a sharp pain in his sinus.

He remembered, as he pressed his fingers against his forehead, the telephone call he had made to Matt Payne sometime during the evening.

"Oh, *shit!*" he said aloud.

He deposited more coins and carried a second can of 7-Up back to the table.

Washington appeared carrying a tray with two mugs of coffee and four fried egg sandwiches wrapped in waxed paper on it.

Wohl took one. When the waxed paper was open his mouth salivated.

Jesus Christ, of all the times to tie one on!

"What, if anything, I think I have to ask, has been done about notifying anybody else?" Washington asked. "Specifically, the commissioner?"

"Mike Sabara called Lowenstein and Coughlin. I told him to ask Lowenstein to notify the commissioner, and I told him to tell both of them that I am trying to find out what the hell happened."

"Then you're not in as bad shape as you look," Washington said.

"Oh, yes, I am," Wohl said.

"You'll feel better with something in your stomach and some coffee," Washington said.

Wohl had eaten two fried egg sandwiches, emptied the second can of 7-Up, and had sipped half his mug of coffee before Tony Harris came into the cafeteria.

"Good morning, Inspector," he said.

That's pretty formal. That's because of the ass-chewing I gave him yesterday about the evils of alcohol. What Detective Harris is now thinking is, What a fucking hypocrite is Inspector Wohl.

"Get anything out of Mrs. Monahan, Tony?" he asked.

"She said he wasn't sleeping well. At about six o'clock, he got out of bed to take a piss. This apparently woke her up. On the way back to bed, he heard something outside on the street. He pushed the curtains aside, looked out, and told her 'the cops have just changed again,' or words to that effect. Then he got back in bed. Then the doorbell rang. He went down to open it. She told him to stay in bed, she would see what they wanted. He went anyway. She got out of bed and put a robe on, because she knew that whenever the cops knocked on the door, Monahan would offer them coffee, and she wanted to make it. So she got to the head of the stairs in time to see him peek through the peephole in the door. Then he took the chain off the door, and opened it. A cop started to come inside. He took a gun from his coat pocket and shot him. Then he closed the door and went away. She went down the stairs, saw that he, Monahan, was unconscious, and called the cops."

"The number we gave her or Police Emergency?" Washington asked.

"Police Emergency. She said our number was next to the bed, and she used the phone in the kitchen."

"She get a good look at the cop?"

"White guy."

"Would she recognize him if she saw him again?"

"She doesn't know; she doesn't think so. I think she means that. I mean, I don't think she would be afraid to point her finger at the doer."

"Did she see the two cars outside?" Wohl asked.

"No. *He* looked out the window. *He* said 'the cops have changed again.' I think you have to figure he saw the two cars. Otherwise how would he know they were going off and coming on?"

"You couldn't get more precise times out of her?" Washington asked.

"No. 'Around six.' "

"She said she saw the gun?"

"Right."

"And saw him shoot it?"

"Right. And then he fell."

"There are no puncture wounds in the body," Wohl said.

"There would have to be."

"The doctor says she looked. The doctor says she thinks he died of a heart attack."

"What the hell?"

"Get on the radio, Tony," Washington ordered. "Tell the lab people to *really* look for a bullet—how many shots did she say she heard?"

"One. Said it sounded like a .22."

"Yeah," Washington said. "Tell the lab people to look very carefully for a bullet hole. In the carpets, in the furniture."

"You think the medical examiner will find the wound, Jason?" Wohl asked.

"I have no idea what he'll find. But if Mrs. Monahan said she heard a shot—"

"Where are you going to be?" Harris asked.

"The inspector and I are going to talk to the cops who were on the job."

"There's bullshit in there somewhere," Tony said as he got up from the table. "The cops going off the job say they were relieved. The cops coming on the job say there was nobody there when they got there."

"Tony," Washington said. "Check with the district and see what their RPCs who rolled by there just before six saw. And the same from Highway. I'll be at Bustleton and Bowler for the next hour or so."

Harris nodded his understanding and walked out of the cafeteria.

"What was that you were saying before about Stillwell?" Washington asked.

"He's being appointed a deputy attorney general for corporate crime," Wohl replied. "He told me last night. He wants me to become his chief investigator."

"Are you going to take it?"

"Last night, it was all I could do to keep myself from telling him to go fuck himself. Now, after this, I may need the job."

"That's why you tied one on?"

"He said he doesn't think we can get a conviction. And that was before we lost Monahan. But he did say that the feds are going after Payne."

"I don't understand that."

"You ever hear of the Coalition of Equitable Law Enforcement? Something like that, anyway?"

"Yeah. I know who they are."

"They have requested that the Justice Department investigate the shooting of Charles David Stevens, alleging that it violated his civil rights."

"And the feds are going along with it?"

"According to Stillwell, they are," Wohl said. "But to answer your question, Jason, I don't know why I got drunk. But at the time, it seemed like a marvelous idea."

"I don't think Matt's got anything to worry about. That was an absolutely justified shooting; Stevens had shot at him—*hit* him—before Matt shot."

"Tell that to the Coalition for Equitable Law Enforcement."

"I don't know what, if anything, this means, but I just remembered hearing that they—the Coalition—were just about out of business, going broke, when Arthur Nelson rescued them with a substantial donation."

"That figures, knowing Nelson's interest in equitable law enforcement," Wohl said bitterly. "Jesus, what a field day that sonofabitch is going to have with this!"

"I hadn't even thought about that," Washington said, shook his head, and then asked, "You know what's going to happen now?"

"Those sleazeballs are going to walk."

"You're going to the Athletic Club, where you will take a steam bath, followed by a shave and haircut."

"Am I?"

"You're going to have to face Czernich and the mayor, and soon. Don't give Czernich the opportunity to point out to Carlucci that you were hungover. I'll try to get to the bottom of which cops were where and when. And by then, maybe the medical examiner can tell us what happened to Monahan."

"He got shot, is what happened to Monahan," Wohl said. "Because I fucked up his protection."

"Wait until we sort it out before you start kicking yourself. Right now, go sweat the whiskey out of you."

"A good long shower will do as well as a steam bath," Wohl said. "Besides, I've got to go home anyway to dress properly before I meet the firing squad."

"Then don't answer your phone. Or the radios in your car."

Wohl nodded, and then pushed himself up from the table.

In the ten minutes Peter Wohl had been in his car en route from his apartment to Special Operations, there had been three calls for W-William One.

That meant, he believed, that the police radio operator had been instructed, most likely by the Hon. Taddeus Czernich, commissioner of police, but possibly by the Hon. Jerry Carlucci, mayor of the City of Philadelphia, to keep trying to locate Staff Inspector Peter Wohl until you find him.

He had not responded to the calls for W-William One because he was absolutely sure that the message for him would be to immediately report to the commissioner. It was bad enough that Monahan had been killed while he was charged with his protection; he didn't want to face Czernich and/or the mayor and have to tell him that although Mrs. Monahan said she saw a cop shoot him, there were no wounds in the body, or that the two groups of cops who were supposed to be sitting on Monahan told conflicting stories and he wasn't sure who was telling the truth.

There had also been two calls on the Supervisor Band that he had listened to with half a mind. They were not intended for him. Someone was trying to reach I-Isaac Seventeen. The only reason he paid any attention to the calls at all was that, in the happy, happy days of yore when he had not been W-William One, commanding officer of the Special Operations Division, he had been I-Isaac Seventeen, just one more simple staff inspector.

I wonder who I-Isaac Seventeen is now, and I wonder why W-William Seven wants to talk to him.

Jesus H. Christ! As far as turning my brain back on is concerned, that shower didn't do me a goddamn bit of good.

He grabbed the microphone.

"W-William Seven, I-Isaac Seventeen."

"Isaac Seventeen, can you meet me at the medical examiner's?"

Even with the frequency-clipped tones of the radio, Jason Washington's deep melodic voice was unmistakable.

"Isaac Seventeen, on the way."

Wohl tossed the microphone onto the seat beside him, braked sharply, and then made a wide sweeping U-turn, tires squealing in protest, and headed for the medical examiner's office.

Jason wouldn't want me there unless he has learned something.

The ME probably found the bullet puncture that damned redhead couldn't find. It's not much, but it's something!

Jason Washington was sitting in his car outside the medical examiner's office when Wohl pulled into the parking lot. There was a space next to him. Wohl pulled into it, and then got in Washington's car.

"I suspect when you walk in there," Washington said, "there will be a message for you to call the commissioner immediately. So let's take a minute here."

"They've been calling me on the radio every three minutes," Wohl said. "That Isaac Seventeen business was clever, Jason, thank you."

"It will prove to be clever if Czernich, or somebody else who remembers you used to be Isaac Seventeen and will run to Czernich, wasn't listening to the radio."

"I thought of that too. I owe you another one, Jason."

"I talked to the cops who were sitting on Mr. Monahan," Washington said, cutting him off. "I think they're all telling the truth."

"How can that be?"

"A guy named Kallanan was taking his turn walking around the house just before six. I happen to know him. When I did my civic duty in the Black Police Officers' Association, I worked with him. I was treasurer when he was secretary. Good man."

"Okay. I'll take your word."

"He said it was a couple of minutes before six when he came out of the alley and started down Sylvester Street. He said that the relief RPC was already there. He said he couldn't see into the relief RPC clearly—the side windows were mostly frozen over—but he remembers that two of the guys inside were wearing—what do you call those hats with earflaps?"

"I know what you mean."

"Okay. Two guys were wearing winter hats, for lack of a better word. And that the driver was black. He could see that well."

"He didn't recognize anybody?"

"No. It was still pretty dark. The windshield was fogged over. He saw what I just told you."

"Okay."

"The other two guys in the car getting relieved didn't say anything except that there was a car. When Kallanan got in the car, they drove off. They're either all much better liars than I think is credible, or they're telling the truth."

"And the relief car?"

"The guy driving was John Wilhite. He said they were a little late—"

"Why? Did he say?"

"They stopped at a McDonald's to get their coffee thermoses filled. They had to wait until they made coffee. He said it was five, six minutes after six when they got to the scene. And there was no car there."

Wohl shrugged.

"The other two guys in the relief car were a guy named McPhail and a guy named Hennis. They're white. So is Wilhite."

"And Kallanan said the guy driving the relief car was black?"

"Right."

"And he said it was a couple of minutes *before* six when the relief car got there? And

Wilhite says he was five, six minutes *late* getting there? Which means we have ten minutes that needs explaining."

"Scenario, Peter: The doers show up at five minutes to six, pretending to be the relief RPC. The guys on the job, who are expecting relief, see an RPC and think they're relieved and drive off. When they are around the corner, somebody gets out of the RPC, rings Monahan's doorbell, shoots him, gets back in the car, and they drive off. A couple of minutes after that, the real relief RPC shows up."

"W-William Seven," the radio went off.

Washington looked at Wohl, who gestured for him to reply.

"William Seven," Washington said to his microphone.

"William Seven, have you a location on William One?"

Washington again looked at Wohl for instruction. Wohl nodded yes.

"I'm at the medical examiner's. William One is en route to this location."

"William Seven, advise William One to contact C-Charlie One by telephone as soon as possible."

"Will do," Washington said. "I expect him here in about ten minutes."

"W-William One. W-William One," the radio said. Washington reached to the controls and turned it off.

"Was it an RPC?" Wohl asked. "Or did Kallanan just presume it was an RPC because it was a four-door Ford or whatever?"

"He says there was no question in his mind that it was an RPC," Washington said. "A new one. One of ours. I think, consciously or subconsciously, he would have picked up on it if it wasn't a bona fide RPC."

"Jesus, you know what we're saying, Jason?" Wohl said.

"I'm not saying anything yet," Washington said.

"Mrs. Monahan said she saw a *cop* shoot her husband," Wohl said.

"Yeah, but the doctor said she could find no puncture wounds. Let's find out about that first, before we start saying anything."

He opened his door.

"What's going on here?"

"The ME called me. He's an old pal. He said I wasn't going to believe what he had to show me."

"Did you ask him if he found an entrance wound?"

"Just before he told me I wasn't going to believe what he had to show me," Washington said as he got out of the car.

Chief Inspectors Dennis V. Coughlin and Matt Lowenstein were in the office of Police Commissioner Taddeus Czernich when Staff Inspector Peter Wohl came into it. The mayor was not. Wohl wondered where he was.

The odds are that in the next five or ten minutes, either Lowenstein or Coughlin will be ordered to temporarily assume command of Special Operations, pending the naming of a permanent new commanding officer.

"Good morning, sir," Wohl said.

"You're a hard man to locate, Wohl," Czernich said.

"I'm sorry about that, sir."

"Sorry won't cut it, Wohl," Czernich said. "You know that someone with your responsibilities can't simply vanish from the face of the earth for three hours."

"Yes, sir."

"You're not going to try to tell me you weren't aware I had sent out a call for you?"

"I am now, sir."

The door opened and Mayor Carlucci walked in, drying his hands on a paper towel. Everybody stood up.

The mayor finished wiping his hands, looking around for a wastebasket, and, finding none, carefully laid the towel in Czernich's OUT basket and turned to Wohl.

"My mother used to tell me if you looked hard enough, you could always find something nice about anybody," he said. "I can find a few nice things about you, Peter. For one thing, you're here. That took some balls; I wouldn't have been surprised if you had just mailed in your resignation. And you look remarkably crisp and well turned out for someone who, I am reliably informed, arrived at the scene of the Monahan shooting looking and smelling as if he had spent the night on a saloon floor."

Wohl forced himself to meet the mayor's eyes. Their eyes locked for a moment, and then the mayor looked away.

"No denial?" he asked softly.

"I drank too much last night, sir."

"The third nice thing I have to say about you is that you seemed to be able to instill a high, hell, incredibly high, level of loyalty in people who work for you. It took a lot of balls from Jack Malone, especially considering the trouble he's in already, to march into my office and tell me that if anyone was to blame for this colossal fuckup, it was him, not you."

"He did what?" Czernich asked indignantly.

"You heard what I said," the mayor said. "And if you're thinking about doing anything to him for coming to see me, forget it."

"The responsibility is mine, Mr. Mayor," Wohl said, "not Lieutenant Malone's."

"Yeah, that's what I told him," Carlucci said. "Okay, Peter, you're here. Tell me what the fuck happened."

"All I can do is tell you what I know so far, sir."

Carlucci sat down on the edge of Czernich's desk and made a "come on" gesture with both hands.

"A few minutes before six this morning, an unmarked car pulled up behind the unmarked car on protection duty outside Mr. Malone's home. In the belief their relief had arrived, the officers on duty drove away—"

"If you had used Highway Patrol as I told you to," Commissioner Czernich said, "none of this would have happened!"

"We believe that as soon as the RPC going off duty turned the corner, an individual in police uniform—"

"Answer the commissioner's question, Peter," the mayor said.

"I wasn't aware that it was a question, sir."

"Don't add insolence to everything else, Peter," the mayor said.

"I didn't use Highway because I thought using Special Operations officers was a more efficient utilization of manpower. And because I didn't want a Highway car parked there all night, every night."

"But you do now admit that was faulty judgment?" Czernich said.

"No, sir. I do not. I would do the same thing again. And I don't think it would have made a bit of difference if a Highway car had been given the job. The same thing would have happened."

"Now, that's bullsh—"

"He answered your question, Tad," the mayor interrupted. "Now let me ask one: What, if it was still your responsibility, would you do to the cops who took off before they were properly relieved?"

The question took Wohl by surprise. He tried to shift mental gears to consider it.

"They took off without checking to see that the cops who were relieving them were really cops. That got Monahan killed, and makes the entire Department look ridiculous," the mayor said.

"I don't think I'd do anything to them, sir. I hope you don't. If I had been in that car and saw another car with uniformed cops in it show up when I expected a car with uniformed cops in it to show up, I would have presumed I had been relieved."

"And you would have been wrong."

"Malone's plan was pretty thorough. I reviewed it. There was nothing in it about having the cops on the job check the IDs of the cops relieving them. That's my fault. Not Malone's and certainly not theirs."

The mayor shrugged, but said nothing. He made another "come on" gesture with his hands.

"We believe," Wohl continued, "that as soon as the RPC, the one going off the job, turned the corner, an individual wearing a police uniform rang Mr. Monahan's doorbell, and when Mr. Monahan answered the doorbell, he shot him, if that's the correct word, with a stun gun."

"What?" Chief Lowenstein asked incredulously. "What did you say, 'stun gun'?"

"What the hell is a stun gun?" the mayor asked.

"What it is, Jerry," Chief Coughlin said, "is a thing that throws little darts at you. There's wires, and when it hits you, you get shocked. It's supposed to be nonlethal."

"You know what this thing is?" Carlucci asked him incredulously.

"They had a booth at the IACP (International Association of Chiefs of Police) Convention," Chief Coughlin said. "They demonstrated them. They're supposed to be used places where you don't want to fire a gun."

"And Monahan was shot with one of these things?" the mayor asked.

"That's what the medical examiner believes, sir," Wohl said. "Mr. Monahan died of a heart attack. The ME thinks it was caused by getting hit with a stun gun. There are two small bruises on his chest."

"How come the ME knows about these things?" the mayor asked.

"They've been trying to sell them to us," Coughlin said.

"We buy any of these things, Tad?" the mayor asked.

"I would have to check, Mr. Mayor."

"There are three at the range at the Academy," Wohl said. "On loan from the dealer, or the manufacturer, I'm not sure which."

"Let me get this straight: You're telling me Monahan was shot by a cop with a Mickey Mouse Buck Rogers stun gun we borrowed from somebody?"

"No, sir. I checked with the Academy. The ones out there are inoperative; they're waiting for the manufacturer, or the dealer, to come fix them."

"So where did the one who shot Monahan come from?" the mayor asked, and then, before Wohl could frame a reply, thought of something else: "I thought Coughlin just said they're nonlethal?"

"They're supposed to be, Jerry," Coughlin repeated. "That's what they said at the convention. They're supposed to knock you on your ass for a couple of minutes, but they're not supposed to kill you."

"Monahan's dead," the mayor said.

"They're not classified as firearms, Mr. Mayor," Wohl said. "So they're available on the open market. I called Colosimo's. They said they didn't have any, never had, but they had heard that a place in Camden had them, and some store in Bucks County. I've got people checking that out."

"How do we know Monahan was shot by a cop?" the mayor asked.

"We don't. Mrs. Monahan said that she saw a police officer take a gun from his coat—"

"These things look like guns?"

"I don't know, sir. I've never seen one."

"In dim light, or if you don't know all that much about guns," Coughlin said, "it would look, maybe, to Mrs. Monahan, like a gun."

"Do they make any noise? Where do they get the electricity to shock you?"

"They go 'splat,' " Coughlin said. "Or like that. Not like a .38."

"Like a .22, Chief?" Wohl asked.

"Something. Sure. It could be mistaken for a .22."

"Mrs. Monahan said it sounded like a .22," Wohl said.

"Why would they use something like this?"

"So there wouldn't be the sound of a gun going off," Lowenstein said.

"If it makes as much noise as a .22, then why not use a .22?" the mayor asked. He did not wait for a reply, but asked another question: "What is it, Peter? The guy who shot Monahan with this thing, the people in the car, were they cops or not?"

"They had an RPC, Mr. Mayor. An unmarked RPC."

"How do we know that? And if so, where did they get it?"

"We *don't* know. But Washington said, and I think he's right, that if it wasn't an RPC, I mean if it was just a similar Ford, the cop who walked past it would have picked up on that, either consciously or subconsciously: The tires would have been wrong, it wouldn't have had an antenna, or the right antenna—"

"So if it was a bona fide car, that makes it look as if a cop, cops, were the doers, doesn't it?" Carlucci interrupted.

"That sounds entirely credible," Wohl said. "As to where it came from, it probably came out of the parking lot at Bustleton and Bowler."

The mayor turned to Lowenstein and pointed a finger at him.

"I want those bastards, Matt!"

"Yes, sir," Lowenstein said softly, coldly, "so do I."

Carlucci turned back to Wohl. "What I'm thinking now is that it would be best, until he can give some real thought to your replacement, that we have Mike Sabara fill in for you. Is there something wrong with that?"

"No, sir. Sabara is a good man."

"Is there some way you can put off going to Harrisburg for a day or two? I'd like you to be available to Lowenstein."

"I'm not going to Harrisburg," Wohl said.

Carlucci looked at him in surprise, and then the look seemed to turn to anger.

"That's strange, Peter," he said. "Not half an hour ago, your pal Farnsworth Stillwell was on the phone. He wanted to be sure there would be no hard feelings about you going with him. He said you really didn't want to go, and that to get you he had to offer you a hell of a lot of money."

"I saw him last night. He offered me a job as his chief investigator. I told him I'd have to think it over, and I'd get back to him before he had his press conference this morning."

"He told me you had accepted. Period."

"I never thought of accepting. The reason I didn't call him this morning to tell him was that I was busy."

"Look at me, Peter," Carlucci said. Wohl met his eyes. "Now tell me again, when did you decide?"

"When he made the offer," Wohl said evenly. "I was afraid I would say something I would regret if I said anything last night."

Carlucci looked at him intently for a full thirty seconds before he spoke again.

"Okay. That obviously changes things," he said, finally, and then looked around the table. "Since Inspector Wohl is not resigning from the Department, there is no need to name a replacement for him at Special Operations at this time—"

"Mr. Mayor!" Czernich said.

"—temporary or otherwise," Carlucci went on coldly. Then he looked at Wohl. "There will be, Peter, unless you get this mess straightened out. *Capisce?*"

"Yes, sir."

"Keep me informed," the mayor said, and got up and walked out of the room.

26.

Officer Foster H. Lewis, Jr., sat, as quietly and as inconspicuously as possible, on a folding steel chair in the small office that housed the Special Investigations Section of the Special Operations Division. He was very much afraid that he would, at any moment, be ordered out of the room on some minor errand or other, and he very much wanted to hear what was being said in the room.

The entire staff of the Special Investigations Section, that is to say Sergeant Jason Washington, Detective Anthony Harris, and himself, was in the room.

The night before, Officer Lewis had spent just about an hour making up an organizational chart for the Special Investigations Section using a drafting set he had last used in high school. There were three boxes on the chart, one on top of the other. The uppermost enclosed Sergeant Washington's name. The one in the middle read, Det. Harris, and the one on the bottom, PO Lewis. Black lines indicated the chain of authority.

It was sort of, but not entirely, a joke. Every other bureaucratic subdivision of the Special Operations Division had an organizational chart. It had been Tiny's intention, when Sergeant Washington saw the new organizational chart thumbtacked to the corkboard and, as he almost certainly would, asked, *"What the hell is that?"* to reply, *"We may be small, but we're bureaucratically up to standards."*

Tiny Lewis had come to believe there was a small but credible hope that he could manage to stay assigned to the Special Investigations Section rather than find himself back in uniform and riding around in one of the Special Operations RPCs, which was the most likely scenario.

For one thing, the Officer Magnella murder job was no closer to a solution than it had ever been, and since it was the murder of a cop, it would continue to be worked. Tony Harris would continue to need his services as an errand runner. For another, now that they were officially caught up in the bureaucracy, there would be paperwork, that which was now being done by Inspector Wohl's administrative sergeant. He could take that over. Certainly the Black Buddha wouldn't want to do it, nor Tony Harris. If he could make himself useful, his temporary assignment just might become permanent.

And my God, what a way to see how detectives worked! Even Pop says Tony is nearly as good as Washington, and everybody knows Washington is as good as they come.

It hadn't gone exactly as planned. The Black Buddha had come into the office to find Tiny waiting for him, nodded at him idly, and then looked at the corkboard.

"What the hell is that?"

"That's our organizational chart."

"Jesus Christ!" Washington had offered contemptuously before asking, "Is there any coffee?"

"Yes, sir."

That was, of course, because of what had happened to Monahan. Washington, almost visibly, was thinking of nothing but that. The only other thing he had said before Harris came into the office was, as he pointed to the phone, "Wohl, Sabara, Pekach, and nobody else. Lowenstein and Coughlin too."

"Yes, sir."

Running telephone interference had provided the excuse to stay in the office and watch them brainstorm the job. It had been absolutely fascinating to Tiny, as much for the way the two of them worked together as for the various scenarios they came up with.

They seemed to have a telepathic, or at least a shorthand, means of communication.

They exchanged ideas with very few words, as if both knew the way the other one's brain worked.

And Tiny got to listen.

"From the beginning," Washington had begun. "The firebomb."

"Somebody knew the Highway car was sent there."

"And why."

"Off the air?"

"No."

"Payne's car bothers me."

"Could have been anybody."

"Anybody who knew (1) Porsche (2) where he lived."

"Oh."

"Back to somebody with access."

"They could have been watching Monahan's house."

"Different people driving by."

"Too many drive-bys."

"Back to somebody with access."

"Somebody pretty sure of his own smarts."

"The stun gun?"

"Why didn't they just pop him?"

"Hold that one a minute."

"No noise?"

"They could have hit him with an ax."

"They didn't want to kill him?"

"Hold that one too."

"They didn't give a shit when they blew the watchman away."

"Maintenance man. Not watchman."

"Did they think the firebomb would not be lethal?"

"Are they?"

"Hold that one too."

"Why don't burglars go armed?"

"Because breaking and entering isn't murder one."

"Christ, they already committed murder."

"Define 'they.' "

"The ones who hit Goldblatt & Sons Credit Furniture & Appliances, Inc."

"What if we had caught the guy with the firebomb."

"Huh?"

"What would it be? Not more than assault. Maybe even creating a public nuisance."

"Hold *that* one."

"Defining 'they' again. Are those clowns in the bathrobes smart enough to stage what happened this morning?"

"Not getting their hands on an unmarked car."

"Back to someone with access."

"That means someone here."

"Someone here would be too smart to rob Goldblatt's: no money."

"Back to the burglar. What happened at Goldblatt's was potentially murder caused in connection with another felony. What the hell?"

"Where did the money come from for Giacomo?"

"What the hell are they after?"

"I thought about that. More robberies, banks, maybe, with witnesses scared off by what happened at Goldblatt's."

"Back to the goddamn Liberation Army."

"Back to defining 'they.' Are the Goldblatt doers smart enough for the press releases?"

"The organized telephone calls to Payne?"

"There are now two kinds of 'they.' The ones who are calling the shots—"

"Including setting up the clowns to rob Goldblatt's."

"I can't see anybody here doing that."

"We have somebody here. That's a given."

" 'They' is now three. The sleazeballs at Goldblatt's; somebody here; and somebody calling the shots for the first two. Somebody with enough money to hire Giacomo."

"That would be the ILA."

"The ILA is bullshit. There is no ILA."

"Hold that too."

"They knew the firebomb wasn't good for murder; they knew the stun gun—"

"They *thought* the stun gun—"

"—would be nonlethal. Somebody here would think that."

"And cover his ass."

"They would have convinced Monahan that police protection or not they could get to him whenever they wanted to."

"But if they hadn't killed him, he would have had a face."

"A face wouldn't do him much good if it wasn't a cop's face."

"Bingo!"

"It's an opening. Not 'Bingo.' "

"We're talking about a white face here, by the way. She said it was a white guy she saw shoot him."

"Interesting."

"It could be a light-skinned Cuban or something."

"Not Cuban. The white doesn't fit, but not Cuban. Very few Muslims, make-believe or otherwise, among the Cubans. Or for that matter, Latinos."

Both Washington and Harris fell silent for what seemed like a very long time, but was probably no more than sixty seconds.

Finally Washington raised his head and looked at Officer Foster H. Lewis.

"What are you thinking?" Harris asked.

"I am thinking I have a task for Officer Lewis."

"Yes, sir?"

"I want you to check with the corporal. Get his sheets on unmarked cars for yesterday. Check the incoming mileage against the outgoing today."

Tiny Lewis realized he had absolutely no idea what Washington wanted. As he was trying to frame a reply that might just possibly make him look like less of an ignorant asshole than he felt himself to be, Washington correctly read the expression on his face.

"What I'm looking for, Foster," he said patiently, "is a discrepancy between the mileage recorded when the driver of the unmarked car turned it in yesterday, and the mileage recorded when the car was taken out today."

"Unscrew the speedometer cable. Takes ten seconds," Harris said.

"Do you understand now, Foster?"

"Yes, sir."

"Tiny, then contact everybody who took an unmarked RPC out of here this morning," Harris said. "Ask them if there was any indication that it hadn't sat out there in the snow and ice all night."

"Unless somebody here is driving the car he took to Goldblatt's."

"Sergeant," Tiny said hesitantly.

"Come on, Foster, pay attention!"

"I went out to warm up my car when I got here. Did either of you drive it last night?"

"I gather somebody had?" Jason Washington asked softly.

"Bingo!" Harris said.

Washington reached for the telephone.

"Lieutenant Lomax, please," he said when his party answered. "Sergeant Washington is calling."

Tiny Lewis understood enough of the one side of the conversation he heard to know that Lieutenant Lomax had told Sergeant Washington that it would be best to leave the car where it was; that if that was going to be impossible, the next best was to have it towed to the nearest police garage; and that in no event should the car be driven or entered again.

Sergeant Washington returned the phone to its cradle.

"Officer Lewis," he said, "you will now go stand by the hood of the car until a police wrecker comes to haul it off. If you somehow could convey the impression that it has a mysterious malady, fine. But in no event let anyone touch it, much less get inside."

"Yes, sir."

Assistant Special Agent in Charge (Criminal Affairs) Frank F. Young came into the morning Senior Staff Conference ten minutes late.

"Sorry to be late, Chief," he said as he took a chair at the table that butted against Special Agent in Charge Walter F. Davis's desk and made a vague but unmistakable gesture of dismissal to Special Agent F. Charles Vorhiss, who had been filling in for him.

Davis waited until Vorhiss had left the room before replying, "It's all right, Frank, we know what difficulty you have getting up before noon."

Not quite sure whether Davis was cracking witty or had some other agenda, Young said, "I was just having the most fascinating conversation with Agent Matthews, who *was* out carousing until the wee hours."

"With the cops, you mean?"

"In the FOP," Young said.

"We were, just coincidentally, talking about the police," Davis said, and slid a copy of the Philadelphia *Ledger* across the desk to him. "Have you seen this?"

"No," Young said, and since he suspected he was expected to, he read the front-page story.

ASSASSINS GET PAST
POLICE TO MURDER
WITNESS AGAINST ILA
By Charles E. Whaley
Ledger Staff Writer

Albert J. Monahan, 56, was shot to death before his wife's eyes early this morning at his home in the 5600 block of Sylvester Street according to a highly placed police official who declined to be identified.

Monahan was shot with a small-caliber weapon, according to the same police official, when he opened his door to an assassin who had somehow gotten past three officers of the "elite" Special Operations Division that was charged with his round-the-clock protection.

Staff Inspector Peter F. Wohl, commanding officer of the Special Operations Division, which was formed, reportedly at the orders of Mayor Jerry Carlucci, late last year to combat the growing crime in Philadelphia, was "not available to the press" for comment.

Monahan, who was employed by Goldblatt & Sons Credit Furniture & Appliances, Inc., was scheduled to appear before the Grand Jury next Monday. Assistant District Attorney Farnsworth Stillwell was to seek an indictment for murder against six men for a shooting death during a robbery at the South Street furniture store. Monahan reportedly had positively identified seven men presently being held in the Detention Center as being involved.

"Prosecution now seems unlikely," the police official said, "with the death of Mr. Monahan, and Mr. Stillwell off the case." He was apparently referring to the appointment, announced today, of Stillwell to the staff of the state attorney general in Harrisburg. (See "Governor Names Stillwell As Corporate Crime Prosecutor," Page B-1).

Police have thrown up a barrier of silence around the incident. Police Captain Michael J. Sabara, deputy commander of Special Operations, the only senior police official willing to speak officially to the press at all, would say only that "the incident is under investigation and no information can be released at this time."

Sabara also refused to discuss rumors circulating throughout the Police Department that the Justice Department is investigating Officer M. M. Payne, Inspector Wohl's administrative assistant. During the arrest of the eight men charged in the Goldblatt robbery, Payne shot to death one of the alleged bandits, Charles David Stevens. It has been said the Justice Department is investigating allegations that Payne, who has something of a reputation for being too quick to use his pistol, exceeded Police Department criteria governing the use of force. If the allegations are true, Payne could be charged with violating Stevens's civil rights, a federal offense.

"Jesus!" Young said. "I wonder how that happened?"

"How about gross incompetence?" Glenn Williamson, A-SAC (Administration), asked rhetorically.

"I would think it's a case of having underestimated the opposition," SAC Davis said. "What do we have on the ILA? Did you check with Washington?"

"There's three of them," A-SAC (Counterintelligence) Isaac J. Towne said. "One in New York, one in Chicago, and one in Berkeley, California. There is no known connection between the three, and no known connection between any of them and anyone in Philadelphia."

"Have we got anybody in with them?"

"In all three. That's where we got what I came up with."

"Any of them ever into anything like this?"

"They're mostly into protest marches," Towne said. "Talk and protest marches."

"I'd like to help Wohl if I could," SAC Davis said.

"There was something I heard—" Towne said, stopped, and then went on. "I heard that Wohl was going with Farnsworth Stillwell. As his chief investigator."

"Really?" Davis asked.

"He might as well," Young said. "I'll bet Carlucci throws him to the wolves."

"You think that 'unnamed police official' was Carlucci?"

"I think it was somebody close to Czernich. Maybe even Czernich himself."

"Not Czernich," Davis said. "Czernich wouldn't do that, unless Carlucci told him to. But somebody close to Czernich—"

"If Carlucci isn't behind it, and finds out who the big mouth is, he's in more trouble than Wohl."

"I don't think anyone's in more trouble than Wohl," Davis said. "How good was your source about Wohl going with Stillwell?"

"I just heard it. I can't even remember where. Maybe on one of those radio talk shows driving to work."

"See what you can find out for sure, Isaac, will you, please?" Davis said.

"Yes, sir," Towne said.

"I'll tell you what I can see," Davis said. "Armed robberies of banks, with witnesses afraid to testify because of this case, because of what happened to Mr. Monahan."

"You really think so, Chief?" Young asked.

"I think it's a credible possibility," Davis said. "I think this could be a dry run for something like that."

"Well, there goes our bank robbery solution rate," A-SAC Williamson said.

"I wasn't trying to be funny, Glenn," Davis said.

"Chief, neither was I," Williamson said. "I'm very much afraid you're absolutely right."

"I hope not," Davis said.

It was evident to the others that Davis did not violently object to being told he was absolutely right.

"This isn't exactly on the same subject—" Young said.

"But?" Davis prodded.

"I told you the reason I was late was because I was talking with Jack Matthews. He heard something last night that might, just might, affect one of our ongoing investigations."

"Which one?"

"Bob Holland."

"Oh, Jesus, that's all we need! We're getting pretty close to the end of that, aren't we?"

"At the cost of I don't like to think how much money and man-hours," A-SAC Williamson said, "I have been assured that we are beginning to see light at the end of the tunnel."

"Well, spit it out, Frank, what did young Matthews hear?"

"Nothing specific. But what he did hear made him think he should bring me in on it. He went drinking with young Payne, his bodyguard, and another young cop—"

"What the hell is *that* all about?" Williamson interrupted. "He went out drinking with the cops? I've been telling my people to maintain a polite, cordial, but distant—"

"I sent him," Davis said, annoyance in his voice. "Okay, Glenn? Go on, Frank."

"Well, toward the end of the evening, when Matthews mentioned that he was working on interstate auto theft, he said the ears of both Payne and one of the cops—Mc-Something—perked up, and they started asking all sorts of questions about how the Bureau runs a car theft investigation. From the nature of their questions, Jack thought that they could be talking about Bob Holland's operation."

"What kind of questions?" A-SAC Towne asked.

"Why don't we go to the source?" SAC Davis said. He picked up his telephone. "Carolyn, would you please ask Special Agent Matthews to come in here?"

"Who's that?" Officer Robert Hartzog said into the microphone of the new intercom on the wall of Matt Payne's kitchen.

"Inspector Wohl."

"Be right there, Inspector," Hartzog said. He then went down the stairs two at a time.

Wohl appeared a moment later at the head of the stairs, carrying Hartzog's shotgun.

"I told him to take a couple of laps around Rittenhouse Square," Wohl said, resting the shotgun against the closet door. "And how are *you* this morning, Casanova?"

"I heard about what happened," Matt said. "I'm sorry."

"For me or Monahan?"

"Both."

"I'm sorry for Malone and Monahan, and for me. I'm even sorry for you. Everybody's sorry for someone else."

"Why are you sorry for me?" Matt asked.

"I would desperately like to have a cold beer," Wohl said, as if he hadn't heard the question. "For purely medicinal purposes."

"Help yourself," Matt said, gesturing toward the kitchen. "Bring me one too, please."

"You want a glass?" Wohl called the kitchen.

"Absolutely. A good beer, like a decent wine, needs to breathe."

"Oh, *God!*"

"It's true," Matt said.

Wohl came into the living room with two bottles of Tuborg, glasses sitting upside down on their necks.

"And there is a way to get the beer from the bottle to the glass," Matt said, demonstrating. "One pours the glass approximately half full by decanting against the side of the glass, and then, at the precise moment, allowing the incoming liquid to fall into the middle, thus providing the proper head."

He looked at Wohl, smiling. Wohl did not return the smile.

"You're going to be investigated by the FBI, for the Justice Department, for violating the civil rights of Charles David Stevens."

"I know. The FBI told me last night."

"They were here already?" Wohl asked, surprised.

"They sent a young FBI agent, Jack Matthews, to tell me. On the QT."

"How nice of the FBI," Wohl said. "I wonder why they are being so friendly?"

"I've been wondering the same thing myself."

"I wouldn't worry about this, Matt."

"You know the joke?"

"What joke?"

"The doctor about to perform major surgery looks down at the patient and says, *'I wouldn't worry about this,'* and the patient looks up and says, *'If I wasn't lying here, I wouldn't be worried either.'* "

"Well, I mean it. It's a defense tactic, a sleazy one, but that's all it is."

"I was worried about it," Matt said. "But I just got off the telephone with Colonel Mawson. He said he's going to sue the—what is it?—Coalition for Something?"

"Equitable Law Enforcement."

"He's going to sue them for ninety-nine million dollars, the minute the FBI actually shows up here. I think he's delighted it happened."

Wohl smiled.

"I had a few too many drinks last night."

"The Tuborg will fix that," Matt said.

"I shouldn't have made that early morning call."

"Why don't we both forget it? I just hope, among other things, that the knowledge won't make it awkward for you with Stillwell. How the hell did you find out, anyhow?"

"Why should it be awkward for me?"

"In Harrisburg, I mean."

"I'm not going to Harrisburg."

"That's not what it said on the radio. The radio said you had been appointed chief investigator to Stillworth, who was just appointed to some bullshit position with the attorney general."

"The radio is wrong. Never believe what you hear on the radio. For that matter, never believe what you read in the newspaper, especially the *Ledger.*"

"Really?"

"Dave Pekach proposed to Martha Peebles. Surprising no one at all, she accepted. She had a few of his friends, Mike Sabara and his wife, Jack Malone, and me, plus Mr. and Mrs. Farnsworth Stillwell in for a little intimate supper."

"And that's where you found out?" Matt asked. "Christ, how?"

"Your *paramour*—is that the word?"

"For the sake of discussion only, it will do."

"Your *paramour,* as I said, was there. She sounded very much like a lady who left erotic messages on your answering machine. Being the clever fellow I am, I put two and two together. And being the horse's ass I seem to be when I'm drinking, I—I called you."

"Christ, does anybody else know?"

"I don't think so. But that wasn't the smartest thing you ever did, Matt."

"You ever hear that a stiff prick has no conscience?"

"How deep are you in with her?"

"It happened just once," Matt said. "She was at a party downstairs. She saw my gun and got turned on by it. She was a little drunk."

"Are you going to pursue it?" Wohl asked, and then, before Matt could reply, asked, "What do you mean she got turned on by your gun?"

"It was a little frightening. She wanted to know if it was the gun I used on the serial rapist. It aroused her."

"Well, *are* you going to pursue it?"

"What do you do to get out of something like this?"

"You thank God the lady's leaving town. In the meantime, don't answer your telephone."

"Anything like this ever happen to you?"

"You mean a gun fetishist?"

"I mean a married woman."

"Yeah. Once. It was very painful."

Matt picked up his glass and leaned back in the leather armchair, looking thoughtfully into his beer.

I wonder why I told him that? Wohl thought. *I damned sure never told anybody else.*

"I don't want to sound like I didn't know what I was doing, but I didn't actually seduce her," Matt said.

"No man has ever seduced a mature woman," Wohl said. "And probably very few virgins have ever been seduced. The way it works is that *they* decide who *they* want to have take them to bed, and then *they* arrange to be seduced."

Matt looked up at him.

"You really believe that?"

I don't know if I do or not. It sounds plausible. But what I was really trying to do was cheer him up. More than that, to point him onto Ye Olde Straight and Narrow.

Why the hell am I doing that? What the hell am I doing here, anyway? I could have told him about the FBI investigation on the phone.

The answer, obviously, is that I am very fond of this kid. He is, I suppose, the little brother that I never had. So what's wrong with that?

"It sounds plausible," Wohl said with a grin.

"So I'm not on your shitlist?"

"You're not on mine, but *I'm* apparently on everybody else's."

"They're not blaming you for what happened?"

"It's a question of who had the responsibility. That's spelled WOHL."

"You couldn't be expected to sit outside his house yourself," Payne argued. "If it's anybody's fault, it's Jack Malone's."

"Malone works for me," Wohl said. "Whatever he does, or doesn't do, is my responsibility."

"Loyalty down and loyalty up, huh?"

"Is something wrong with that?"

Matt shrugged and looked uncomfortable.

"Come on, Matt, out with it."

Payne met his eyes.

"Did you tell Malone to lay off trying to catch Bob Holland?"

"Not specifically," Wohl replied. "I'm sure he got the message, though." And then he understood the meaning of Payne's question. "What do you know that I don't, Matt?"

"I promised him if I decided to tell you, I would tell him first."

"This isn't the Boy Scouts. You can't have it both ways."

"Charley caught him surveilling Holland's body shop, the one up by Temple."

"What do you mean, caught him?"

"McFadden—off duty, he had just dropped Margaret off at work at Temple—"

"Margaret being his girlfriend?"

"Right. So he saw this old car with somebody in it parked near Holland's body shop. And he checked it out. It was Malone. He, Malone, told Charley not to tell anybody about it."

"Which proves what?"

"The night you had me measuring the school building, Malone showed up there. Charley was with me. He offered to buy us a cheese-steak, and I brought him here. Both of them. And he admitted that what he was trying to do was catch Holland."

"And you decided not to tell me, right?"

Matt nodded.

"I don't know what I would have done if I hadn't gone to play Dick Tracy and gotten myself shot, but that night, I told Malone I was going to sleep on it, that I would probably decide I had to tell you, but if I did, I would tell him first."

"You must have had a reason," Wohl said, more than a little annoyed. "You work for me, getting back to that loyalty business."

"He convinced the both us that Holland is a thief," Matt said.

"You and McFadden, of course, being experts in the area of car theft."

"Open the goddamn door!" the intercom speaker erupted. "Michael J. O'Hara is gracing these crummy premises with his presence."

"Oh, shit!" Wohl said, even though he had to smile. "The last guy in Philadelphia I want to see is Mickey."

"You want to hide in the bedroom while I get rid of him?"

"No," Wohl said, after a moment's hesitation. "I've always thought, said, Mickey can be trusted. Let's put it to the test."

He walked quickly to the stairwell, and down it, to let O'Hara in.

27.

"I must be getting old," Michael J. O'Hara said to Inspector Peter Wohl as Wohl handed him a bottle of Tuborg. "I should have guessed you would be here."

"I'm not here, Mickey. You didn't see me."

O'Hara looked at him intently for a moment, and then shrugged and nodded his agreement.

"Okay. Neither of us are here. But if we were here, and I asked you, on or off the record, 'How do you think you're going to like Harrisburg?' what would be your off-the-record, just-between-us-boys reply?"

"*On* the record, I'm not going to Harrisburg."

"That's not what it said—what *he* said, *he* being Farnsworth Stillwell—on the radio."

"As I was just saying to Casanova here, you should never believe everything you hear on the radio, or read in the newspapers, especially the *Ledger.*"

"Give me a for example."

"I just gave you one. I never told Stillwell that I would take that job."

"If I were to write that—'*Staff Inspector Peter Wohl today emphatically denied that he ever intended to resign from the Police Department to become chief investigator for Farnsworth Stillwell, newly appointed deputy attorney general for corporate crime*'—it would make Stillwell look pretty silly."

"How about leaving out the phrase '*to resign from the Police Department*'?"

"How about the making him look silly part?"

"I don't think that would reduce me to tears," Wohl said.

"Is it that bad, Peter? You're really thinking of resigning?"

"We were talking about not always believing what you read in the newspapers. You want another for example?"

"Yeah."

"The records of the medical examiner, so far as I understand it, are public records. If you were to go down there, and pay the small fee—I think it's two dollars—they would give you a copy of Mr. Albert J. Monahan's death certificate. I think you might find that very interesting."

"Why?"

"Why don't you go spend the two dollars?"

"If I didn't know better, I'd think you were trying to get rid of me," O'Hara said.

"Perish the thought. But trust me, Mickey, I think you'd find the death certificate interesting."

"He's dead, right?" O'Hara asked.

"He's dead."

"So what would I find interesting? What did they do, shoot him with a cannon? He wasn't shot? Some jungle bunny threw a spear at him? What?"

"For two dollars, you could find out," Wohl said.

"I can find out cheaper than that," O'Hara said.

He leaned over and picked up the telephone on the table beside Matt's chair. He draped the handset over his shoulder, and then dialed a number.

"Dr. Phane, please. Mickey O'Hara . . ."

"Oh, bullshit. Tell him he owes me one."

He covered the mouthpiece with his hand. "Interesting," he observed, "the bastard doesn't want to talk to me. . . .

"Charley, how the hell are you? . . .

"Well, just put her on hold, all I have is a couple of questions. . . .

"Tell me about Albert J. Monahan. . . .

"Yeah, I know he's dead. What did they shoot him with? . . .

"What are you telling me, Charley? . . .

"And that's what's going on the death certificate? . . .

"Charley, if I print this and it turns out it's not true, I would be very unhappy. It is for that reason I have been recording this call. Just so you can't deny having told me what you just told me."

O'Hara shrugged, hung the handset on his shoulder again, and dialed another number.

"Would you believe that the Most Exalted Poo-Bah of the Knights of Columbus just told me to go fuck myself?" he asked, in hurt innocence, and then his party answered.

"O'Hara," he said. "Are you ready to copy? . . .

"Slug: ILA Witness Dead of Natural Causes, Says Medical Examiner. By Michael J. O'Hara. In an exclusive interview with this reporter, Philadelphia County Medical Examiner Dr. Charles F. Phane refuted reports in another newspaper—break. I'd like to say the Philadelphia *Ledger,* but you'd better run it past legal before you do."

"—in another newspaper that Mr. Albert J. Monahan was shot to death, allegedly by persons connected with the so-called Islamic Liberation Army. Dr. Phane said that a thorough autopsy of Mr. Monahan's body has convinced him, and other medical personnel of his staff, that Mr. Monahan had died of a cardiac arrest, commonly called a heart attack.

"Dr. Phane, who personally conducted the autopsy, also said that tests had been run that ruled out the possibility of poisons.

"Quote Mr. Monahan's heart just stopped beating, Unquote Dr. Phane said. Quote. He had a medical history of heart trouble and it finally took his life. Unquote.

"Got that? . . .

"Yeah, I'm sure. If I wasn't sure, I wouldn't have called it in."

Mickey put the handset back in the cradle, and then set the telephone back on the table.

"Okay, Peter. So you tell me why Mrs. Monahan told me she saw her husband getting shot."

"This has to be off the record, Mickey."

"Off the record."

"I think she did see someone—"

"A cop? She said, *'a white cop.'* "

"—someone, probably a Caucasian, in a police uniform, shoot her husband. But what he was using was a stun gun, not a real one."

"One of those things that shocks people?" Mickey asked. "No shit?"

"There were bruise marks, plus slight indications of electric burns, on his chest."

"Phane didn't say anything about that."

"Phane is a very careful man, Mickey."

"You don't *have* the stun gun, do you?" O'Hara challenged. "This is a *theory?"*

"It's a pretty good theory," Wohl said.

"You tell me why it's a good theory."

"We don't think they were trying to kill Monahan, just scare him."

"I have no idea what you're talking about," O'Hara said.

"I'll tell you what we think this whole thing is about, and where we are, but if you print it, you can really screw things up. Not only for me, but for a lot of other people."

"You prick!" O'Hara said. "You know that after you told me that, I couldn't use it."

"Fuck it," Matt Payne said. "The risk is too great, don't tell him."

Mickey turned to look at him in what looked like hurt surprise. "For the rest of your life, I will misspell your name," he said.

He turned at Wohl. "Does *he* know what's going on?"

"No. He's just worried about me."

"Okay, Peter," O'Hara said after a moment. "Boy Scout's Honor." He held up three fingers as Boy Scouts do when giving their word of honor. "I won't use any of this until you tell me I can."

It took Wohl ten minutes, during which Mickey O'Hara asked a very few questions, all of which struck Matt as being penetrating.

"Okay," Mickey said, finally. "So what are you doing here drinking beer with Wyatt Earp? Why aren't you out catching—better still, shooting by accident, or at least running over—this rogue cop of yours?"

"Two reasons," Wohl said. "For one thing, I think I would probably get caught if I did. More importantly, Jason Washington asked me to make myself scarce until five o'clock. That's what I'm doing."

"Can I stick around?"

"I wish you wouldn't."

"Well, and all this time, I thought we were buddies," O'Hara said. "How would you feel about me interviewing Arthur X? Getting his *Islamic* slant on this?"

"Will he talk to you?"

"Yeah, I think so. He likes being in the newspapers." He saw the look on Wohl's face. "Relax, I won't give anything away."

"If I thought you would, I wouldn't have told you what I did."

"I just had a better idea," O'Hara said. "Fuck Arthur X. I know what he's going to say. I'm going to see Sam Goldblatt and maybe Katz too."

"Who?" Matt asked.

"Sam Goldblatt, of Goldblatt's furniture," O'Hara replied. "Ol' Mr. I-have-to-think-about-my-wife-and-children. The one who covered his ass about these scumbags by having his eyesight conveniently fail. Phil Katz is Goldblatt's nephew."

"Oh," Matt said, and then asked, "Why?"

" 'Mr. Goldblatt, would you tell me how you feel about the people who killed both poor Mr. Cohn and now poor Mr. Monahan escaping punishment because you have bad eyesight? My one point three million readers would like to know. In case they wanted to buy a washing machine, or something, and wanted to make sure they were buying it from somebody who was always thinking about his wife and children.' "

Wohl chuckled. "I really think you would do that."

"You'd better believe it."

"I'll tell you what I did do," Wohl said. "When Goldblatt and Katz walked out of their houses this morning, they found a Highway RPC waiting for them. Highway's going to sit on both of them for the next couple of days, at least."

"To protect them? Or to remind them they need protection?"

"Both."

"Mr. Goldblatt, considering what happened to poor Mr. Monahan, do you think the police are going to be able to protect you from these people you weren't able to see well enough to identify?"

"If you added, 'and your family,' " Wohl said, "that might not be a bad question to ask."

"Consider it asked," O'Hara said.

He stood up, shrugged into his fur-collared overcoat, finished off his bottle of beer, and went down the stairs.

At five minutes past four, just after Officer Charles McFadden had relieved Officer Frank Hartzog on the protection detail of Officer Matthew M. Payne, the doorbell rang.

"Who's there?" McFadden asked, through the intercom.

"Sergeant D'Angelo."

"You know a Sergeant D'Angelo, Inspector?" McFadden asked Wohl.

"Yeah. Let him in."

"Be right down," McFadden said, and went down the stairs.

The face that first appeared at the head of the stairwell a moment later was that of the Hon. Jerry Carlucci, mayor of the City of Brotherly Love. He was followed by a burly, curly-haired man in his late twenties.

"I didn't know anybody lived up here," the mayor thought aloud, and nodded at the occupant, Officer Payne, as he looked around.

"What the hell is this all about, Peter?" he asked.

"Chief Lowenstein said he would be here at four," Wohl said. "He must have been delayed."

"That's not what I asked," the mayor said, but he did not pursue the question. He looked at Matt.

"How's your leg, son?"

"Pretty good, sir. Thank you."

"I don't suppose there's any coffee?"

"I can make some in just a minute," Matt said, and started to get out of his leather armchair.

"Al, make coffee," the mayor ordered.

Sergeant D'Angelo went into the kitchen.

"Coffee's in the cabinet right over the machine," Matt called.

"Got it," D'Angelo called back.

The telephone rang.

"Hello?" Matt answered it.

"Chief Lowenstein. Is Carlucci there?"

"Mr. Mayor," Matt said. "Chief Lowenstein for you, sir."

Carlucci snatched the phone from Payne's hand.

"Lowenstein, what the hell's going on? . . .

"How did that happen? . . .

"I'll be damned," he said, and hung up.

He looked at Wohl.

"That was Lowenstein. He's at the district attorney's. That's why he's late."

"Yes, sir."

"Mr. Samuel Goldblatt just identified from photographs all of the doers of the Goldblatt job, and is prepared to go before the Grand Jury on Monday. And, *and,* get this: Tom Callis just called Giacomo, as a professional courtesy, and informed him he will personally prosecute."

"That's good news, sir," Wohl said.

"Did you know about this, Peter?"

"I'd heard that another attempt to get Mr. Goldblatt to testify would be made, sir."

"Stop the bullshit, Peter, what do you know about this sudden change of heart?"

"Chief Lowenstein told me that he was going to have a talk with Mr. Goldblatt, sir. And I believe that Mickey O'Hara saw him, Goldblatt, today too."

"O'Hara? What about O'Hara?"

"He was here earlier, sir."

"He was here? How is it, Peter, that every sonofabitch and his brother but the police commissioner and me knew where you were?"

"I wasn't aware you were looking for me, sir."

"Czernich was looking for you, and he couldn't find you. Or so he told me."

"Chiefs Coughlin and Lowenstein knew I was here, sir. And so did Captain Sabara."

"I don't like it a goddamn bit the way the three of you treat Czernich like the enemy," Carlucci said. "It has to stop. You understand me?"

"Yes, sir."

"Now, what about O'Hara?"

"Mr. O'Hara led me to believe he was going to ask Mr. Goldblatt and the nephew, Katz, about how they felt about these people going to walk with Monahan dead."

"You got him to do that?"

"It was Mickey's idea, sir."

"Bullshit," the mayor said.

The telephone rang again, and Matt answered it.

"Is that you, Matty?" Chief Inspector Dennis V. Coughlin asked.

"Yes."

"Is the mayor there? Lowenstein?"

"Chief Lowenstein is on his way here from the district attorney's office."

"Who is that?" the mayor asked suspiciously.

"Chief Coughlin, sir."

"Give me the phone," he ordered sharply. Matt handed it over.

"What the hell is this all about, Denny?"

Matt couldn't hear what Coughlin replied.

"If the both of you aren't here in ten minutes, we will adjourn this meeting to the commissioner's office. *Capisce?*" Carlucci said, and hung up.

He turned to Wohl.

"I don't suppose you're going to tell me what the hell is going on around here?"

"I'd prefer to wait until Chief Lowenstein is here, sir."

"In numbers, there is strength, huh?" Carlucci said unpleasantly. "Where the hell is that coffee, Al?"

"It's almost through, sir," Sergeant D'Angelo said.

"Let me ask you something else, Peter," Carlucci said. "Are you conducting an investigation of Bob Holland?"

"No, sir."

"Strange. The FBI thinks you are. Davis called Czernich and asked him. Czernich told him he would ask you about it. You better have a goddamn good answer when he does. Auto theft is none of your business."

"That sonofabitch!" Charley McFadden said.

The mayor looked at him. McFadden, realizing that his mouth had run away with him, looked stricken.

"What sonofabitch is that, son?" Carlucci asked softly, menacingly. "The police commissioner or Mr. Davis of the FBI?"

"There was an FBI agent here last night, Mr. Mayor," Matt said. "We took—"

"What was he doing here? Friend of yours, what?"

"I met him yesterday," Matt said. "He came to confirm rumors that I'm going to be investigated by the Justice Department."

"For what?"

"For shooting Stevens."

"Did you know about this, Peter?"

"Yes, sir."

"How come I don't?"

"I sent a memorandum to Commissioner Czernich, sir."

Carlucci turned back to Matt Payne.

"What about the FBI agent who was here last night?"

"We went to the FOP," Matt said. "During the conversation, when he said that he was working interstate auto theft, I asked him some questions about how that works."

"Me too. I did too," Charley McFadden said.

"What Officer McFadden is suggesting is that Matthews, the FBI guy, reported our interest to his superiors," Matt explained.

" 'Our interest'?" Carlucci snapped. "Just what is 'our interest'?"

"We think Mr. Holland is involved in at least the sale of stolen automobiles," Matt said.

" 'We'? Who's 'we'?"

"Officer McFadden and myself," Matt said.

"On one hand, coming from two rookies with an exaggerated opinion of themselves, that's probably bullshit," the mayor said. "But on the other hand, the FBI wouldn't be trying to tell us to butt out unless they were onto something. Peter, you sure you don't know anything about this?"

The door buzzer went off, sparing Wohl having to reply.

"Who's there?"

"Lowenstein."

"Be right there."

"Peter," the mayor said. "I think it would be very embarrassing to the Police Department if the FBI came up with a case against Bob Holland that we didn't know anything about. You take my meaning?"

"No, sir."

"I mean I want you to find out what these two hotshots of yours think they know."

"And give it to Major Crime?"

"No. Give it to me," Carlucci said, "either these two are imagining things, or Major Crime isn't doing their job."

He then turned his attention to the stairwell, in which a moment later Chief Inspector Matt Lowenstein's head and shoulders appeared.

"Matt," the mayor greeted him. "There better be a goddamn good reason for all this goddamn mystery."

Thirty minutes later, the mayor said, in quiet fury, "What you're telling me is that both the guy who killed Monahan with the stun gun, *and* two guys with him, *and* the miserable sonofabitch out of Bustleton and Bowler are going to get away with it? Everything?"

"We can't go to court with this, Jerry," Lowenstein said. "You can see that."

"On the bright side," Chief Inspector Dennis V. Coughlin said, "the Grand Jury will return a true bill aga'ıst the doers of the Goldblatt job. And Tom Callis is convinced that he can get convictions."

"On the *dim* side, there is *nothing* lower than a cop who would do something like this, and the sonofabitch is going to get away with it!"

He glowered, in turn, at Chief Inspectors Lowenstein and Coughlin and Staff Inspector Wohl, all of whom, in turn, shrugged.

"Jesus *Christ!*" the mayor said in frustration.

"Or," Peter Wohl said. "We could just leave him where he is and watch him."

The mayor considered that a moment before replying. "No. Go ahead with this. I'll clear it with Czernich."

"Yes, sir," Wohl said.

"Maybe that's not smart, but I can't stand the thought of this bastard walking around in a Highway uniform," the mayor said. "Highway means something to me."

"It means something to me too," Peter Wohl heard himself say.

Jesus, he realized with genuine surprise, *I really meant that.*

Sergeant Jason Washington sat slouched behind the wheel of his car until he saw Sergeant Wilson Carter pull into the parking lot. Then he sat up and watched as Carter parked his car. He got out of his car and walked toward the side entrance of the building, timing himself so that he arrived there a few seconds before Carter.

"I was hoping to run into you," he said to Carter.

"Well, hey, Brother. How they hanging? What's on your mind?"

"Let's have a beer," Washington said.

"One," Carter said, after a just perceptible hesitation. "I have plans."

"Sure. I understand. But there's a couple of questions I'd like to ask you."

"What kind of questions?"

"More like advice questions, about what I should do about something."

"Well, then, hell, yes."

"I thought Hellman's? They have booths in the back."

"Give me thirty minutes to check out and I'll meet you there."

"Thanks, Carter, I appreciate it," Washington said, touched Carter's arm, and walked back to his car.

When Sergeant Carter walked into the back room of Hellman's Restaurant, he found Sergeant Jason Washington already there, sitting alone in a booth, his massive hand wrapped around a glass of whiskey.

"You must have a problem," Carter said as he slipped into the bench across from Washington. "Beer, little problem, whiskey, big problem."

"Big problem," Washington agreed.

Carter glanced around the room, looking for a waitress. He couldn't see one, but he saw a familiar face in another booth.

"Richard Kallanan's over there," he said, waving.

Kallanan took his hand from his glass of whiskey long enough to wave back.

A waitress appeared from the barroom. Carter waved to catch her attention.

"Cutty Sark, on the rocks," Carter ordered. "You ready, Jason?"

"Might as well."

"I thought Kallanan was one of those straight home to the wife and kiddies types," Carter said. "I don't think I've ever seen him in here before."

"I don't think he comes in here often," Washington said. "Tonight's sort of special."

"What?"

"You want to know what Kallanan's thinking right now, Carter?"

"What the hell are you talking about?"

"He's thinking, 'Christ, why didn't I recognize Carter in that car?' "

"What car would that be, Washington?"

"The car normally driven by Foster Lewis's boy, the kid we call 'Tiny,' " Washington said. "The one you drove to Monahan's house."

"That sounds like an accusation, Washington."

"Statement of fact. We picked your prints off the plastic behind the front seat. You know where I mean? Where it's flat on top? You must have touched it when you got in. Or maybe when you reached for the seat belt. We got a match on your pinky, ring, and index fingers."

"I don't know what the fuck you're up to, but you could probably find my prints on half the unmarked cars in the parking lot."

"We also got your prints, heel of the hand and four fingers, on the hood of Matt Payne's pretty little Porsche."

"I must have rested my hand on it when I looked down at the tire."

"More likely when you stabbed the tires," Washington said.

"You don't really believe that?"

"Yes, I do."

"You're out of your fucking mind, Washington!"

"Kallanan is a very interesting man," Washington said. "Did you know that he's a lay reader in the Episcopal Church?"

"So what?"

"So he told me that he has to be very careful about not bearing false witness."

"Meaning what?"

"Meaning he's worried about the power of suggestion. In other words, he's afraid that when I asked him if it could have been you driving that car, and he said, *'Oh, yes. That's who it was,'* he's afraid that the reason he now recognizes you *is because* I asked him if it could have been you."

"What the hell is going on here? Are you that fucking desperate? You come up with a couple of matched prints— How many other prints matched?"

"Four sets," Washington said. "And there were prints from two people in that car that don't match any of anybody in Special Operations. We're now running them against every cop in the Department. That'll take a long time, there's six thousand odd cops. I frankly will be surprised if we get a match, but you never know."

"I think I've had enough of this bullshit conversation," Carter said, and stood up and took a wad of money from his pocket.

"How do you think you're going to like it in the 6th District?"

"What's that supposed to mean?"

"You're being transferred, tomorrow, to the 6th District. Where you will work for Lieutenant Foster H. Lewis, Sr."

"I don't know what the fuck you think you're doing, or who the hell you think you are, Washington, but I will not take a transfer to the 6th Division or anywhere else."

"You could resign, of course. That would make a lot of people happy. But if you stay on the job, you're going to the 6th, tomorrow."

"Because you have this nutty idea that I trashed Payne's car? Or that I was involved in what happened to Monahan?"

"There is no question in my mind that you trashed Payne's car, drove the car to Monahan's house the morning he was shot, shot Monahan with a stun gun, and told your friends when I was going to pick Monahan up at Goldblatt's so they could throw a gasoline bomb at me."

"You know how far you would get with this in court? They'd laugh you out of City Hall."

"Did I say anything about taking you to court? All I said was that you were going to the 6th District."

"You try to get me transferred, transferred anywhere, and I'll have the Black Police Officers' Association all over your ass!"

"You know how a complaint gets acted on by the Black Police Officers' Association?" Washington asked, and then went on without waiting for a reply. "It goes to the Executive Committee. The Executive Committee is composed of former officers. Like me, for example. And Richard Kallanan. I really don't think, Brother, that you're going to get a hell of a lot of sympathy from the Black Police Officers' Association."

"Fuck you, Washington!" Sergeant Carter said, tossed a five-dollar bill on the table, and walked away.

As he approached the booth occupied by Officer Richard Kallanan, their eyes met and Kallanan stood up.

Carter stopped at the booth.

"You're still the white man's slave, motherfucker!" he said.

Officer Kallanan thereupon struck Sergeant Carter in the face with his fist, causing him to fall to the floor.

Sergeant Washington rushed from his booth to restrain Officer Kallanan, but this proved unnecessary.

Officer Kallanan was already bending over Sergeant Carter, to assist him to his feet.

"I'm sorry I hit you, Carter," Richard Kallanan said. "I should have remembered what it says in the Bible, 'Judge not, lest ye be judged.' "

Sergeant Carter shook free of Kallanan's hand and walked out of the back room of Hellman's Bar & Grill.

The Philadelphia County Grand Jury returned indictments charging the seven men arrested by the police with murder in the first degree.

Between the Grand Jury indictments and the trial, Hector Carlos Estivez came to an agreement with District Attorney Thomas J. Callis under which Mr. Estivez agreed to testify against those persons charged in the robbery of Goldblatt & Sons Credit Furniture & Appliances, Inc.; the murder that occurred during the robbery; and others, in exchange for immunity from prosecution.

In sworn statements made to the district attorney, Mr. Estivez stated that it was his belief that Charles David Stevens, aka Abu Ben Mohammed, had planned the Goldblatt robbery with the advice and assistance of Omar Ben Kalif, whom he described as a black male, approximately twenty-seven years of age, with a shaven head and a full beard. Mr. Estivez stated that, in his presence, Omar Ben Kalif was identified as a member of the Philadelphia Islamic Temple.

Estivez stated that Charles David Stevens, aka Abu Ben Mohammed, had stated that should anything "go wrong" with the Goldblatt robbery, Omar Ben Kalif, and/or the Philadelphia Islamic Temple, would provide legal counsel, bail money, and other assistance.

The Philadelphia Islamic Temple, through its counsel, categorically denied any involvement of any kind whatever in the robbery/murder that took place at Goldblatt & Sons Credit Furniture & Appliances, Inc. The Temple further categorically denied that there was now, or ever had been, anyone associated with the Temple by the name of Omar Ben Kalif.

In separate trials, and as a result of plea bargaining, the remaining accused were found guilty of murder in the first degree, manslaughter in the first degree, assault, and armed robbery. Sentences ranged from life imprisonment to five years' incarceration.

The Philadelphia County Grand Jury determined that the death by gunfire of Charles David Stevens at the hands of Officer M. M. Payne was an act of self-defense.

Following an investigation by the Justice Department, it was determined there had been no violation of the civil rights of Charles David Stevens by Officer Matthew M. Payne.

A suit for defamation of character and slander brought by Officer M. M. Payne against the Coalition for Equitable Law Enforcement was settled out of court for an undisclosed sum.

Sergeant Wilson Carter resigned from the Philadelphia Police Department four weeks after being transferred to the 6th District. He shortly thereafter had his name changed to Wilson X. He is now serving as personal bodyguard to Arthur X, and as head of the Fruit of Islam.

PROMINENT
AUTO DEALER
CHARGED IN HOT
CAR RING
By Michael J. O'Hara
Bulletin Staff Writer

Robert L. Holland, prominent Delaware Valley auto dealer, was arrested this morning, following a joint FBI–Philadelphia Police investigation, and charged with 106 counts of trafficking in stolen automobiles, falsification of registration documents, and other auto-theft related charges.

"It is one more example of the fine cooperation we have learned to expect from our brother officers in the Philadelphia Police," said Walter F. Davis, Special Agent in Charge of the Philadelphia FBI office.

He had special praise for Philadelphia Police Lieutenant John J. Malone, of the Special Operations Division, who headed the police investigation.

"Malone's professionalism and dedication in a very tough investigation was inspiring," Davis said.

Philadelphia Police Commissioner Taddeus Czernich, who was with Special Agent in Charge Davis when Holland, in handcuffs, was brought to the Central Lockup in the Police Administration building, said the arrest of Holland proved once again how effective a joint effort of federal and local law enforcement can be.

(Photos and additional story on Page B-1.)

THE
ASSASSIN

1.

Marion Claude Wheatley, who was thirty-three years of age, stood just under six feet tall, weighed 165 pounds, and was just starting to lose his hair, had no idea why God wanted to kill the Vice President of the United States, any more than he did why God had selected him to carry out His will in this regard, together with the promise that if he did so, he would be made an angel, and would live forever in the presence of the Lord, experiencing the peace that passeth all understanding.

He had, of course, thought a good deal about it. After all, he had a good education (BA, Swarthmore, cum laude; MBA, Pennsylvania) and as a market analyst (petrochemicals) for First Pennsylvania Bank & Trust, his brain had been trained to first determine the facts and then to draw reasonable inferences from them.

The first fact was that God was all-powerful, which Marion accepted without question. But that raised the question why didn't God, figuratively speaking, of course, just snap his fingers and cause the Vice President to disappear? Or blow up, which is how the Lord had told him He wished the Vice President to die?

Since He had the power to disintegrate the Vice President without any mortal assistance, but had chosen instead to make Marion the instrument of His will, the only conclusion that could be reasonably drawn was that the Lord had his reasons, which naturally he had not elected to share with a simple mortal.

Perhaps, Marion reasoned, later, after he had proven himself worthy by unquestioningly carrying out the Lord's will, the Lord might graciously tell him why He had chosen the course of action He had.

And if that happened, Marion reasoned, it would seem to follow that God might even tell him how the Vice President of the United States had offended the Lord Most High.

There were a thousand ways the Vice President might have caused offense. He was of course a politician, and one did not need divine insight to understand how much evil they caused each and every day.

Marion suspected that whatever the Vice President's offense, it was a case of either one really terrible thing, in the eyes of God, or a series of relatively minor offenses against the Lord's will, the cumulative effect of which equaled one really terrible sin.

When the Lord had spoken with Marion, the subject of repentance and forgiveness vis-à-vis the Vice President had never even come up. Marion, of course, would not have had the presumption to raise the question himself, but certainly, if God wanted the Vice President to repent, to straighten up and fly right, so to speak, it would seem logical to expect that He would have said something along those lines. It was thus reasonable to assume that whatever the Vice President had done to offend the Lord was unforgivable.

But this was not, Marion had decided while having lunch at the Reading Terminal Market, the same thing as saying that the Vice President could not, or should not, make an effort to get himself right with the Lord. If the Lord was merciful, as Marion devoutly believed Him to be, He just might change His mind if the Vice President, figuratively or literally, went to Him on his knees and begged forgiveness.

It was even possible, if unlikely, Marion had concluded, that the Vice President was unaware of how, or to what degree, he had offended the Lord. But if that was the case, it would certainly be a Christian act of compassion, of Christian love, for Marion to let the Vice President know that he was in trouble with the Lord.

The question then became how to do so in such a way that he would not draw attention to himself. Obviously, he could not call the Vice President on the telephone. There would be several layers of people in place to protect the Vice President from every Tom, Dick, and Harry who wanted to talk to him.

The only way to do it, Marion concluded, was to write him a letter. And that was not quite as simple as it sounded. He would have to be careful to make sure the Secret Service, who protected the Vice President, did not find out who he was. Since the Secret Service would have no way of knowing that he was not some kind of nut, rather than working at the specific direction of the Lord, if they found out he had mailed the Vice President a letter telling him that he was about to be blown up, they would come and arrest him.

Going to prison, or a lunatic asylum, was a price Marion was willing to pay for doing the Lord's work, but only *after* he had done it. If he was in prison, obviously, he could not blow the Vice President up.

And from what Marion had seen on television, and read in books, the Secret Service was very skilled in what they did. They would obviously make a great effort to locate him, once the Vice President showed them the letter. He was going to have to strive for anonymity.

On the way back to the office from the Reading Terminal, he went to the Post Office Annex and bought two stamped envelopes. Then he went into one of the discount stores on Market Street and bought a thin pad of typing paper.

He often worked late, so no one was suspicious when he stayed in his office after everyone else had gone home. When he was absolutely sure that there was no one in the office but him, he went to the typing pool and sat down at the first typist's desk. He opened the top drawer and found two spare disposable ribbons.

He took the plastic cover off the typewriter, then opened it, and removed the ribbon on the machine, carefully placing it on the desktop. Then he put in a new ribbon. He addressed the envelope:

The Hon. Vice President of the United States
Senate Office Building
Washington, D.C.

And then he took the envelope out and tore a sheet of paper from the typing paper pad and rolled that into the typewriter. He sat there drumming his fingers on the desk for a moment as he made up his mind how to say what he wanted to say. Then he started to type. He was a good typist, and when he was finished, there wasn't even one strikeover, and Marion was pleased.

Dear Mr. Vice President:

You have offended the Lord, and He has decided, using me as His instrument, to disintegrate you using high explosives.

It is never too late to ask God's forgiveness, and I respectfully suggest that you make your peace with God as soon as possible.

Yours in Our Lord,

A Christian.

Marion carefully folded the letter in thirds, slipped it into the envelope, and then licked the flap and sealed it. He put it into his breast pocket.

Then he removed the ribbon from the typewriter, put the old one back in, and closed the typewriter and covered it with its plastic cover.

He tore off the section of ribbon that had the impressions of the typewriter keys on it and put it into the second stamped envelope he had purchased against the contingency that he would make an error. He carried the envelope, the pad of typing paper, and the ribbon he had used and then removed from the typewriter back into his office. He turned on his shredder and fed first the envelope with the used ribbon inside into it, and then, half a dozen sheets at a time, the typing paper. Next came the cardboard backing and cover sheet of the typing paper pad. The only thing left was the almost intact unused plastic typewriter ribbon. It was too thick to get into the mouth of the shredder, and moreover, he suspected that even if it had fit into it, it probably would have jammed the mechanism.

He took the sterling silver Waterman's ballpoint pen that had been the firm's gift to him at Christmas from his pocket, and held it through the little plastic inside of the typewriter ribbon. Then he fed the loose end of the ribbon into the shredder. The mechanism drew the ribbon between the cutters. It took a long time for all of the ribbon to be drawn into the shredder, but it was somehow fascinating to watch the process, and he was a little disappointed when it was all gone.

He held the plastic center in his hand and left his office for the men's room. He went into a stall and flushed the plastic center down the toilet. Then he carefully washed his hands and left the office.

He bought a Philadelphia *Ledger* from the newsstand at 16th and Chestnut Streets, and grew warm with the knowledge that he had done the right thing and pleased God. There was a headline that said, VICE PRESIDENT TO VISIT.

The meeting in the commissioner's conference room on the third floor of the Police Administration Building, commonly called the Roundhouse, was convened, and presided over, by Arthur C. Marshall, deputy commissioner (Operations) of the Police Department of the City of Philadelphia.

The police commissioner of the City of Philadelphia is a political appointee who serves at the pleasure of the mayor. There are three deputy commissioners in the Philadelphia Police Department. They are the first deputy commissioner, who is the highest-ranking member of the Department under Civil Service regulations, and the two deputy commissioners, Operations and Administration.

Under the deputy commissioner (Operations) are four Bureaus, each commanded by a chief inspector: the Patrol Bureau, the Special Patrol Bureau, the Detective Bureau, and the Command Inspections Bureau.

Present for the Roundhouse meeting were Chief Inspector Matt Lowenstein, of the Detective Bureau, and Chief Inspector Dennis V. Coughlin, of the Command Inspections Bureau, both of whom were subordinate to Deputy Commissioner Marshall. Also present were Chief Inspector Mario C. Delachessi, of the Internal Investigations Bureau; Chief Inspector Paul T. Easterbrook, of the Special Investigations Bureau; Staff Inspector Peter Wohl, commanding officer of the Special Operations Division; and Captain John M. "Jack" Duffy, special assistant to the commissioner for inter-agency liaison.

Internal Investigations, Special Investigations, and Special Operations in theory took their orders from the first deputy commissioner directly. In practice, however, First Deputy Commissioner Marshall and Chiefs Lowenstein and Coughlin exercised more than a little influence in their operations. There was no question in anyone's mind that Lowenstein and Coughlin were the most influential of all the eleven chief inspectors in the Department, and that both were considered ripe candidates for the next opening as a deputy commissioner.

Part of this was because they were first-class police executives and part was because they had long-running close relations with the Honorable Jerry Carlucci, mayor of the City of Philadelphia.

Prior to running for mayor, in his first bid for elective office, Jerry Carlucci had been the police commissioner. And prior to that, the story went, he had held every rank in the Police Department except policewoman. As a result of this, Mayor Carlucci felt that he knew as much, probably more, about the Police Department than anyone else, and consequently was not at all bashful about offering helpful suggestions concerning police operations.

"Okay," Commissioner Marshall said, "let's get this started."

He was a tall, very thin, sharp-featured man with bright, intelligent eyes.

There was a moment's silence broken only by the scratching of a wooden match on the underside of the long, oblong conference table by Chief Lowenstein. The commissioner watched as Lowenstein applied the flame carefully to a long, thin, black cigar.

"Is that all right with you, Matt?" the commissioner asked, gently sarcastic. "Is your rope on fire? We can begin?"

"A woman is only a woman, but a good cigar is a smoke. Remember that, Art," Lowenstein said, unabashed. He and Commissioner Marshall went back a long way too. Lowenstein had been one of Captain Marshall's lieutenants when Marshall had commanded the 19th District.

There were chuckles. Marshall shook his head, and began:

"We have a problem with the Bureau of Narcotics and Dangerous Drugs. . . ."

"So what else is new?" Chief Lowenstein said. He was a large, nearly handsome man, with a full head of curly silver hair, wearing a gray pin-striped suit.

"Let me talk, for Christ's sake, Matt," Marshall said.

"Sorry."

"They've come to Duffy. Officially. They say they have information that drugs, specifically heroin, are getting past the Airport Unit."

"Did they give us the information?" Lowenstein asked.

Marshall shook his head, no.

"You said, 'getting past the Airport Unit,' " Chief Lowenstein said. "Was that an accusation?"

"Jack?" Marshall said.

"They stayed a hairbreadth away from making that an accusation, Chief," Captain Duffy, a florid-faced, nervous-appearing forty-five-year-old, said.

"Paul?" Marshall asked Chief Inspector Easterbrook, under whose Special Investigations Bureau were the Narcotics Unit, the Narcotics Strike Force, and Vice.

Easterbrook was just the near side of being fat. His collar looked too tight.

"Is heroin coming through the airport?" he asked rhetorically. "Sure it is. I haven't heard a word, though, that anybody in the Airport Unit is dirty."

Everyone looked at Chief Inspector Delachessi, a plump, short, natty forty-year-old, among whose Internal Investigations Bureau responsibilities were Internal Affairs, the Organized Crime Intelligence Unit, and the Staff Investigation Unit. Eighteen months before, he had been Staff Inspector Peter Wohl's boss.

"Neither have I," Delachessi said. "Not a whisper. And what is it now—two months ago?—when that Airport Unit corporal got himself killed coming home from the shore, the corporal who was his temporary replacement was one of my guys. He didn't come up with a thing. Having said that, is somebody out there dirty? Could be. I'll have another look."

"Hold off on that, Mario," Commissioner Marshall said.

"What, exactly, is the problem with Narcotics and Dangerous Drugs?" Chief Lowenstein asked. "You said there was a problem."

"They want to send somebody out there, undercover," Marshall said.

"*In* the Airport Unit?" Lowenstein asked incredulously. "As a *cop*?"

Marshall nodded.

"They've made it an official request," Captain Duffy said. "By letter."

"Tell them to go fuck themselves, by official letter," Lowenstein said.

"It's not that easy, Matt," Marshall said. "The commissioner says we'll have to come up with a good reason to turn them down."

"Why doesn't that surprise me?" Lowenstein replied. "There's no way some nice young agent of the Bureau of Narcotics and Dangerous Drugs can pass himself off to anyone in the Airport Unit as a cop. And if there's dirty cops out there, we should catch them, not the feds. Do you think you could explain that to the commissioner?"

"Art and I had an idea, talking this over," Chief Coughlin said.

Ah ha! thought Staff Inspector Peter Wohl, a lithe, well-built, just under six feet tall thirty-five-year-old. *The mystery is about to be explained. This is not a conference. Whatever is going to be done has already been decided upon by Marshall and Coughlin. The rest of us are here to be told what the problem is, and what we are expected to do. I wonder what the hell I'm here for? None of this is any of my business.*

"I'll bet you did," Lowenstein said.

Shame on you, Commissioner Marshall, Wohl thought. *You broke the rules. You are not supposed to present Chief Lowenstein with a fait accompli. You are supposed to involve him in the decision-making process. Otherwise, he is very liable to piss on your sparkling idea.*

"Matt, of course, is right," Chief Coughlin went on. "There is no way a fed could go out to the Airport Unit and pass himself off as a cop. And, no offense, Mario, I personally would be very surprised if the people out there weren't very suspicious of the corporal you sent out there when their corporal got killed."

"He feels very strongly that no one suspected he worked for me," Chief Delachessi said.

"What did you expect him to say?" Lowenstein said, somewhat unpleasantly. " 'Boy, Chief, sending me out there was really dumb. They made me right away'?"

"So what we need out there is a real cop . . ." Coughlin said.

"Are you inferring, Denny, there's something wrong with the guy I sent out there?" Chief Delachessi interrupted.

"Come on, Mario, you know I didn't mean anything like that," Coughlin said placatingly.

"That's what it sounded like!"

"Then I apologize," Coughlin said, sounding genuinely contrite.

"What Chief Coughlin meant to say, I think," Commissioner Marshall said, "was that if we're to uncover anything dirty going on out there—and I'm *not* saying anything is—we need somebody out there who will (a) not make people suspicious and (b) who will be there for the long haul, not just a temporary assignment, like Mario's corporal."

The rest of you guys might as well surrender, Peter Wohl thought. *If Marshall and Coughlin have come up with this brilliant idea, whatever it is, there's only one guy who can shoot it down, and he's got a sign on his desk reading Mayor Jerry Carlucci.*

"Where are you going to get this guy?" Lowenstein asked.

"We think we have him," Coughlin said. "We wanted to get your input."

Yeah, you did. As long as the input is "Jesus, what a great idea, why didn't I think of that?"

"We need an officer out there," Commissioner Marshall said, "whose assignment will not make anybody suspicious, and an officer who is experienced in working undercover."

"You remember the two undercover officers, from Narcotics, who bagged the guy who shot Dutch Moffitt?" Chief Coughlin asked.

"Mutt and Jeff," Lowenstein said.

Now I know why I was invited, Peter Wohl thought.

The officers in question were Police Officers Charles McFadden and Jesus Martinez, who had been assigned to Narcotics right out of the Police Academy. McFadden was a very large Irish lad from South Philadelphia, in whom, Wohl was sure, Chief Coughlin saw a clone of himself. Martinez was very small, barely over departmental minimum height and weight requirements, of Puerto Rican ancestry. They were called "Mutt and Jeff" because of their size.

Staff Inspector Peter Wohl knew a good deal about both officers. They had been assigned to Special Operations after they had run to earth an Irish junkie from Northeast Philadelphia who had shot Captain Dutch Moffitt, then the Highway Patrol commander, to death, and thus blown their cover. Assigned, he now reminded himself, through the influence of Chief Inspector Dennis V. Coughlin.

"They now work for Peter," Coughlin said.

"Doing what, Peter?" Captain Delachessi asked.

"They're Highway Patrolmen," Wohl replied.

"They won't be for long," Coughlin said.

"Sir?" Wohl asked, surprised.

"We got the results of the detective exam today," Commissioner Marshall said. "Both of them passed in the top twenty."

"So, incidentally, Peter, did Matt Payne," Chief Coughlin added. "He was third."

Officer Matthew M. Payne was Peter Wohl's administrative assistant, another gift from Chief Dennis V. Coughlin.

"I thought he might squeeze past," Wohl replied. Matt Payne had graduated from the University of Pennsylvania cum laude. Wohl didn't think he would have trouble with the detective's examination.

"Well, hold off on congratulating him," Coughlin said. "Any of them. The results of the examination are confidential until Civil Service people make the announcement. No word of who passed is to leave this room, if I have to say that."

"Let's try this scenario on for size," Commissioner Marshall said. "And see if it binds in the crotch. Martinez's name does not appear on the examination list as having passed. He is disappointed, maybe even a little bitter. And he asks for a transfer. They've been riding his ass in Highway, Denny tells me, because of his size. He doesn't seem to fit in. But he's still the guy who got the guy who killed Dutch Moffitt, and he deserves a little better than getting sent to some district to work school crossings or in a sector car. So Denny sends him out to the Airport Unit."

Both Commissioner Marshall and Chief Inspector Coughlin looked very pleased with themselves.

If there's going to be an objection to this, it will have to come from Lowenstein. He's the only one who would be willing to stand up against these two.

Chief Lowenstein leaned forward and tapped a three-quarter-inch ash into an ashtray.

"That'd work," he said. "Martinez is a mean little fucker. Not too dumb, either."

From you, Chief Lowenstein, that is indeed praise of the highest order.

"Do you think he would be willing, Chief?" Wohl asked.

"Yeah, I think so," Coughlin said. "I already had a little talk with him. No specifics. Just would he take an interesting undercover assignment?"

You sonofabitch, Denny Coughlin! You did that, went directly to one of my men, with something like this, without saying a word to me?

"What we would like from you gentlemen," Commissioner Marshall said, "is to play devil's advocate."

"Will the commissioner hold still for this?" Lowenstein said.

"No problem," Commissioner Marshall said.

The translation of that is that there was a third party, by the name of Carlucci, involved in this brainstorm. The commissioner either knows that, or will shortly be told, and will then devoutly believe the idea was divinely inspired.

"What we thought," Coughlin went on, "is that Peter can serve as the connection. We don't want anyone to connect Martinez with Internal Affairs, or Organized Crime, or Narcotics. If Martinez comes up with something for them, or vice versa, they'll pass it through Peter. You see any problems with that, Peter?"

"No, sir."

"Anyone else got anything?" Commissioner Marshall asked.

There was nothing.

"Then all that remains to be done," Coughlin said, "is to get with Martinez and drop the other shoe. What I suggest, Peter, is that you have Martinez meet us here."

"Yes, sir. When?"

"Now's as good a time as any, wouldn't you say?"

Officer Matthew M. Payne, a pleasant-looking young man of twenty-two, who looked far more like a University of Pennsylvania student, which eighteen months before he had been, than what comes to mind when the words "cop" or "police officer" are used, was waiting near the elevators, with the other "drivers" of those attending the first deputy commissioner's meeting. They were all in civilian clothing.

Technically, Officer Payne was not a "driver," for drivers are a privilege accorded only to chief inspectors or better, and his boss was only a staff inspector. His official title was administrative assistant.

There is a military analogy. There is a military rank structure within the Police Department. On the very rare occasions when Peter Wohl wore a uniform, it carried on its epaulets gold oak leaves, essentially identical to those worn by majors in the armed forces. Inspectors wore silver oak leaves, like those of lieutenant colonels, and chief inspectors, an eagle, like those worn by colonels.

Drivers functioned very much like aides-de-camp to general officers in the armed forces. They relieved the man they worked for of annoying details, served as chauffeurs, and performed other services. And, like their counterparts in the armed forces, they were chosen as much for their potential use to the Department down the line as they were for their ability to perform their current duties. It was presumed that they were learning how the Department worked at the upper echelons by observing their bosses in action.

Most of the other drivers waiting for the meeting to end were sergeants. One, Chief Lowenstein's driver, was a police officer. Matt Payne was both the youngest of the drivers and, as a police officer, held the lowest rank in the Department.

There was a hissing sound, and one of the drivers gestured to the corridor toward what was in effect the executive suite of the Police Administration Building. The meeting was over, the bosses were coming out.

Chief Delachessi came first, gestured to his driver, and got on the elevator. Next came Chief Coughlin, who walked up to his driver, a young Irish sergeant named Tom Mahon.

"Meet me outside Shank & Evelyn's in an hour and a half," he ordered. "I'll catch a ride with Inspector Wohl."

Shank & Evelyn's was a restaurant in the Italian section of South Philadelphia.

"Yes, sir," Sergeant Mahon said.

Then Chief Coughlin walked to Officer Payne and shook his hand.

"Nice suit, Matty," he said.

"Thank you."

For all of his life, Officer Payne had called Chief Coughlin "Uncle Denny," and still did when they were alone.

Staff Inspector Wohl walked up to them.

"Officer Martinez is on his way to meet me in the parking lot," he said to Officer Payne. "You meet him, give him the keys to my car, and tell him that Chief Coughlin and I will be down in a couple of minutes. You catch a ride in the Highway car back to the Schoolhouse. I'll be there in a couple of hours. I'll be, if someone really has to get to me, at Shank & Evelyn's."

"Yes, sir," Officer Payne said.

Chief Coughlin and Inspector Wohl went back down the corridor toward the office of the police commissioner and his deputies. Sergeant Mahon and Officer Payne got on the elevator and rode to the lobby.

"What the hell is that all about?" Mahon asked.

"I think Coughlin and Wohl are being nice guys," Matt Payne said. "The results of the detective exam are back. Martinez didn't pass it."

"Oh, shit. He wanted it bad?"

"Real bad."

"You saw the list?"

"I respectfully decline to answer on the grounds that it may tend to incriminate me," Matt Payne said.

Mahon chuckled.

"How'd you do?"

"Third."

"Hey, congratulations!"

"If you quote me, I'll deny it. But thank you."

Matt Payne had to wait only a minute or two on the concrete ramp outside the rear door of the Roundhouse before a Highway Patrol RPC pulled up to the curb.

He went the rest of the way down the ramp to meet it. The driver, a lean, athletic-looking man in his early thirties, whom he knew by sight, but not by name, rolled down the window as Highway patrolman Jesus Martinez got out of the passenger side.

"How goes it, Hay-zus?" Payne called.

Martinez nodded, but did not reply. Or smile.

"We had a call to meet the inspector, Payne," the driver said. While the reverse was not true, just about everybody in Highway and Special Operations knew the inspector's "administrative assistant" by name and sight.

Payne squatted beside the car. "He'll be down in a minute," he said. "I'm to give Hay-zus the keys to his car; you're supposed to give me a ride to the Schoolhouse."

The driver nodded.

I wish to hell I was better about names.

Payne stood up, fished the car keys from his pocket, and tossed them to Martinez.

"Back row, Hay-zus," he said, and pointed. "I'd bring it over here. If anyone asks, tell them you're waiting for Chief Coughlin."

Martinez nodded, but didn't say anything.

I am not one of Officer Martinez's favorite people. And now that he busted the detective exam, and Charley and I passed it, that's going to get worse. Well, fuck it, there's nothing I can do about it.

He walked around the front of the car and got in the front seat. Martinez walked away, toward the rear of the parking lot. The driver put the car in gear and drove away.

"You have to get right out to the Schoolhouse?" Matt asked.

"No."

"You had lunch?"

"No. You want to stop someplace?"

"Good idea. Johnny's Hots okay with you?"

"Fine."

"You have an idea where McFadden's riding?"

"Thirteen, I think," the driver said.

Matt checked the controls of the radio to make sure the frequency was set to that of the Highway Patrol, then picked up the microphone.

"Highway Thirteen, Highway Nine."

"Thirteen," a voice immediately replied. Matt recognized it as Charley McFadden's.

"Thirteen, can you meet us at Johnny's Hots?"

"On the way," McFadden's voice said. "Highway Thirteen. Let me have lunch at Delaware and Penn Street."

"Okay, Thirteen," the J-band radio operator said. J-band, the city-wide band, is the fre-

quency Highway units usually listen to. It gives them the opportunity to go in on any interesting call anywhere in the city.

"Highway Nine. Hold us out to lunch at the same location."

Matt dropped the microphone onto the seat.

"I guess you and McFadden are buying, huh?" the driver asked.

"Why should we do that?"

"You both passed the exam, didn't you?"

"You heard that, did you?"

"I also heard that Martinez didn't."

"I think that's what the business at the Roundhouse is all about. The inspector and
Chief Coughlin are going to break it to him easy."

"I tried the corporal's exam three years ago and didn't make it," the driver said. "Then
I figured, fuck it, I'd rather be doing this than working in an office anyhow."

Was that simply a conversational interchange, or have I just been zinged?

"I'm surprised Hay-zus didn't make it," Matt said.

"Yeah, I was too. But I guess some people can pass exams, and some people can't."

"You're right. You think McFadden knows we passed?"

"He told me this morning at roll call."

"So that means Martinez knows too, I guess?"

"Yeah, I'm sure he knows."

Was that why Hay-zus cut me cold, or was that on general principles?

2.

Detective Matthew M. Payne, of East Detectives, pulled his unmarked car to the curb just
beyond the intersection of 12th and Butler Streets in the Tioga section of Philadelphia.

There was a three-year-old Ford station wagon parked at the curb. Payne reached over
and picked up a clipboard from the passenger seat, and examined the Hot Sheet. It was a
sheet of eight-and-a-half-by-eleven-inch paper, printed on both sides, which listed the tag
numbers of stolen vehicles in alphanumeric order.

There were three categories of stolen vehicles. If a double asterisk followed the
number, this was a warning to police officers that if persons were seen in the stolen
vehicle they were to be regarded as armed and dangerous. A single asterisk meant that if
and when the car was recovered, it was to be guarded until technicians could examine it
for fingerprints. No asterisks meant that it was an ordinary run-of-the-mill hot car that
nobody but its owner really gave a damn about.

The license number recorded on the Hot Sheet corresponded with the license plate on
the Ford station, which had been reported stolen twenty-eight hours previously. There
were no asterisks following the listing. Two hours previously, Radio Patrol Car 2517, of
the 25th Police District, on routine patrol had noticed the Ford station wagon, and upon
inquiry had determined that it had been reported as a stolen car.

The reason, obviously, that this Ford station wagon had attracted the attention of the
guys in the blue-and-white was not hard for someone of Detective Payne's vast experience—he had been a detective for three whole weeks—to deduce. The wheels and tires
had been removed from the vehicle, and the hood was open, suggesting that other items of
value on the resale market had been removed from the engine compartment.

The officer who had found the stolen car had then filled out Philadelphia Police Department Form 75-48, on which was listed the location, the time the car had been found, the
tag number and the VIN (Vehicle Identification Number), and the condition (if it had been
burned, stripped, or was reasonably intact).

If he had recovered the vehicle intact, that is to say drivable, he would have disabled it by removing the coil wire or letting the air out of one or more tires. It is very embarrassing to the police for them to triumphantly inform a citizen that his stolen car has been recovered at, say, 12th and Butler, and then to have the car stolen again before the citizen can get to 12th and Butler.

The officer who had found the car had turned in Form 75-48 to one of the trainees in the Operations Room of the 25th District, at Front and Westmoreland Streets, because the corporal in charge was otherwise occupied. The term "trainee" is somewhat misleading. It suggests someone who is learning a job and, by inference, someone young. One of the trainees in the Operations Room of the 25th District had in fact been on the job longer than Detective Payne was old, and had been working as a trainee for eleven years.

The trainee did not feel it necessary to ask the corporal for guidance as to what should be done with the Form 75-48. The corporal, in fact, would have been surprised, even shocked, if he had.

If the car had been stolen inside the city limits of Philadelphia, the trainee would have simply notified the owner, and, in the name of the district, canceled the listing on the Hot Sheet. But this Ford had been stolen from a citizen of Jenkintown, Pennsylvania, just north of Philadelphia. It thus became an OJ, for Other Jurisdiction.

First, he assigned a DC (for District Control) Number to it. In this case it was 74-25-004765. Seventy-four was the year, twenty-five stood for the 25th District, and 004765 meant that it was the four thousandth seven hundredth sixty-fifth incident of this nature occurring since the first of the year.

Then the trainee carried the paperwork upstairs in the building, where EDD (East Detective Division) maintained their offices, and turned it over to the EDD desk man, who then assigned the case an EDD Control Number, much like the DC Number.

The EDD desk man then placed the report before Sergeant Aloysius J. Sutton, who then assigned the investigation of the recovered stolen vehicle to Detective Matthew M. Payne, the newest member of his squad.

Theoretically, the investigation should have been assigned to the detective "next up on the Wheel." "The Wheel" was a figure of speech; actually, it was a sheet of lined paper on a pad, on which the names of all the detectives of the squad available for duty were written. As jobs came into East Detectives, they were assigned in turn, according to the list. The idea was that the workload would thus be equally shared.

In practice, however, especially when there was a brand-new detective on the squad, the Wheel was ignored. Sergeant Sutton was not about to assign, say, an armed robbery job to a detective who had completed Promotional Training at the Police Academy the week, or three weeks, before. Neither, with an armed robbery job to deal with, was Sergeant Sutton about to assign a recovered stolen vehicle investigation to a detective who had been on the job for ten or twelve years, especially if there was a rookie available to do it.

Since he had reported for duty at East Detectives, Detective Payne had investigated eight recovered stolen vehicles. During that time, nine had been reported to East Detectives for appropriate action.

Actually, Detective Payne knew more about auto theft than all but one of the detectives who had passed the most recent examination and gone to Promotional Training with him. In his previous assignment, he had had occasion to discuss at some length auto theft with Lieutenant Jack Malone, who had at one time headed the Auto Theft Squad in the Major Crimes Division of the Philadelphia Police Department.

Lieutenant Malone had recently received some attention in the press for an investigation he had conducted that had resulted in the Grand Jury indictment of Robert L. Holland, a prominent Delaware Valley automobile dealer, on 106 counts of trafficking in stolen automobiles, falsification of registration documents, and other auto-theft-related charges.

Detective Payne had learned a great deal from Lieutenant Malone about big-time auto theft. He knew how chop-shops operated; how Vehicle Identification Number tags could be forged; how authentic-looking bills of sale and title could be obtained; and he even had a rather detailed knowledge of how stolen vehicles could be illegally exported through the Port of Philadelphia for sale in Latin and South American countries.

None of this knowledge, unfortunately, was of any value whatever in the investigation Detective Payne was now charged with conducting.

Detective Payne had also learned from Lieutenant Malone that the great majority of vehicular thefts could be divided into two categories: those cars stolen by joyriders, kids who found the keys in a car and went riding in it for a couple of hours; and those stolen by sort of amateur, apprentice choppers. These thieves had neither the knowledge of the trade nor the premises or equipment to actually break a car down into component pieces for resale. They did, however, know people who would purchase wheels and tires, generators, air-conditioning compressors, batteries, carburetors, radios, and other readily detachable parts, no questions asked.

Very few thieves in either category were ever brought before the bench of the Common Pleas Court. Only a few joyriders were ever caught, usually when they ran into something, such as a bridge abutment or a station wagon full of nuns, and these thieves were almost always juveniles, who were treated as wayward children, and instead of going to jail entered a program intended to turn them into productive, law-abiding adults.

Very few strippers were ever caught, either, because they were skilled enough to strip a car of everything worth a couple of dollars in less than half an hour. They waited for the local RPC to drive past, in other words, and then stripped the car they had boosted secure in the knowledge that the RPC wouldn't be back in under an hour.

But under the law, it was felony theft and had to be investigated with the same degree of thoroughness as, say, a liquor store burglary.

In practice, Detective Payne had learned, such investigations were assigned to detectives such as himself, in the belief that not only did it save experienced detectives for more important jobs, but also might, in time, teach rookies to be able to really find their asses with both hands.

Carrying the clipboard with him, Detective Payne got out of his car and walked to the station wagon. He was not surprised when he put his head into the window to see that the radio was gone from the dash, and that the keys were still in the ignition.

Moreover, these thieves had been inconsiderate. If they had been considerate, they would have dumped this car by a deserted lot, or in Fairmount Park or someplace not surrounded by occupied dwellings. Now he would have to go knock on doors and ask people if they had seen anyone taking the tires and wheels off the Ford station wagon down the street, and if so, what did they look like.

An hour later, he finished conducting the neighborhood survey. Surprising him not at all, none of the six people he interviewed had seen anything at all.

He got back in the unmarked car and drove back to East Detectives. Not without difficulty, he found a place to park the car in the tiny parking lot, went inside, found an empty desk and a typewriter not in use, and began to complete the paperwork. Once completed, he knew, it would be carefully filed and would never be seen by human eyes again.

At five minutes to four, when his eight-to-four tour would be over, Detective Payne became aware that someone was standing behind him. He turned from the typewriter and looked over his shoulder. Sergeant Aloysius J. Sutton, a ruddy-faced, red-haired, stocky man in his late thirties, his boss, was smiling at him.

"I wish I could type that fast," Sergeant Sutton said admiringly.

"You should see me on a typewriter built after 1929," Payne replied.

Sutton chuckled. "You got time for a beer when we quit?"

"Sure."

The invitation surprised him. Having a beer with his newest rookie detective did not seem to be Sutton's style. But it was obviously a command performance. Rookie detectives did not refuse an invitation from their sergeant.

"Tom & Frieda's, you know it?"

Matt Payne nodded. It was a bar at Lee and Westmoreland, fifty yards from East Detectives.

"See you there."

Sergeant Sutton walked away, back to his desk just outside Captain Eames's office, and started cleaning up the stuff on the desk.

What the hell is this all about? Jesus Christ, have I fucked up somehow? Broken some unwritten rule? It has to be something like that. I am about to get a word-to-the-wise. But what about?

At five past four, Matt Payne left the squad room of East Detectives and walked down the street to Tom & Frieda's. Sergeant Sutton was not in the bar and grill when he got there, and for a moment, Matt was afraid that he had been there, grown tired of waiting, and left. Left more than a little annoyed with Detective Payne.

But then Sutton, who had apparently been in the gentlemen's rest facility, touched his arm.

"I'm sorry I'm late, Sergeant."

"In here, you can call me Al. We're . . . more or less . . . off duty."

"Okay. Thank you."

"Ortlieb's from the tap all right?"

"Fine."

"What you have to do is find a bar where they sell a lot of beer, so what they give you is fresh. Most draft beer tastes like horse piss because it's been sitting around forever."

He is making conversation. He did not bring me here because he likes me, or to deliver a lecture on the merits of fresh beer on draft. I wish to hell he would get to it.

"You got anything going that won't hold for three days?" Sergeant Al Sutton asked as he signaled the bartender.

Matt thought that over briefly. "No."

"Good. As of tomorrow, you're on three days' special assignment at the Roundhouse. Report to Sergeant McElroy in Chief Lowenstein's office."

Matt looked at Sutton for amplification. None came.

"Can you tell me what this is all about?" Matt asked.

Sutton looked at him carefully. "I thought maybe you could tell me," he said, finally.

Matt shook his head from side to side.

"I'll tell you what I know," Sutton said. "Harry McElroy . . . you know who he is?"

"I know him."

"Harry called down for Captain Eames, and I took the call because he wasn't there. He said the chief wants you down there starting tomorrow morning, for three days, maybe four, and the fewer people know about it, the better."

Matt shrugged again. That had told him nothing.

"So I asked him, what was it all about, and Harry said if anybody asked, they needed somebody to help out with paperwork, that you were good at that."

Matt grunted.

"So if anybody asks, that's the story," Sutton said.

"I know what it is," Matt said. "Based on my brilliant record as the recovered car expert of East Detectives, they're going to transfer me to Homicide."

Sutton looked at him, and after a moment laughed.

"It's a dirty job, kid," he said, "but somebody has to do it."

"Well, it can't be worse, whatever it is, than recovered cars," Matt said.

"I got to get home. We have to go to a wake. Jerry Sullivan, retired as a lieutenant out of the 9th District a year ago. Just dropped dead."

"I didn't know him."

"They had just sold their house; they were going to move to Wildwood," Sutton said.

He pushed himself off the bar stool, picked up his change, nodded at Matt, and walked out of the bar.

Detective Matthew M. Payne lived in a very small apartment on the top floor of a brownstone mansion on Rittenhouse Square, in what is known in Philadelphia as Center City. The three main floors of the mansion had three years before been converted to office space, all of which had been leased to the Delaware Valley Cancer Society.

It had never entered the owner's mind when he had authorized the expense of converting the attic, not suitable for use as offices, into an apartment that it would house a policeman. He thought that he could earn a small rent by renting the tiny rooms to an elderly couple, or a widow or widower, someone of limited means who worked downtown, perhaps in the Franklin Institute or the Free Public Library, and who would be willing to put up with the inconvenience of access and the slanting walls and limited space because it was convenient and, possibly more important, because the building was protected around the clock by the rent-a-cops of the Holmes Security Service. Downtown Philadelphia was not a very safe place at night for people getting on in years.

Neither, at the time of the attic's conversion, had it ever entered the owner's mind that his son, then a senior at the University of Pennsylvania, would become a policeman. Brewster Cortland Payne II had then believed, with reason, that Matt, after a three-year tour of duty as a Marine officer, would go to law school and join the law firm of Mawson, Payne, Stockton, McAdoo & Lester, of which he was a founding partner.

Matt's precommissioning physical, however, had found something wrong with his eyes. Nothing serious, but sufficient to deny him his commission. Brewster Payne had been privately relieved. He understood what a blow it was to a twenty-one-year-old's ego to be informed that you don't measure up to Marine Corps standards, but Matt was an unusually bright kid, and time would heal that wound. In the meantime, a word in the right ear would see Matt accepted in whatever law school he wanted to attend.

Despite a life at Pennsylvania that seemed to Brewster C. Payne to have been devoted primarily to drinking beer and lifting skirts, Matt had graduated cum laude.

And then Captain Richard C. "Dutch" Moffitt, commanding officer of the Highway Patrol of the Pennsylvania Police Department, had been shot to death while trying to stop an armed robbery.

It was the second death in the line of duty for the Moffitt family. Twenty-two years before, his brother, Sergeant John Xavier Moffitt, had been shot to death answering a silent alarm call. Six months after his death, Sergeant Moffitt's widow had given birth to their son.

Four months after that, having spent the last trimester of her pregnancy learning to type, and the four months since her son had been born learning shorthand, Sergeant Moffitt's widow had found employment as a typist trainee with the law firm of Lowerie, Tant, Foster, Pedigill & Payne.

There was a police pension, of course, and there had been some insurance, but Patricia Moffitt had known that it would not be enough to give her son all that she wanted to give him.

On a Sunday afternoon two months after entering the employ of Lowerie, Tant, Foster, Pedigill & Payne, while pushing her son in a stroller near the Franklin Institute, Patricia Moffitt ran into Brewster Cortland Payne II, whom she recognized as the heir apparent to Lowerie, Tant, Foster, Pedigill & Payne. She had been informed that Young Mr. Payne was not only the son of the presiding partner of the firm, but the grandson of one of the founding partners.

Despite this distinguished lineage, Brewster Cortland Payne II was obviously in waters beyond his depth outside the Franklin Institute. He was pushing a stroller, carrying a two-year-old boy, and leading a four-and-half-year-old girl on what looked like a dog harness and leash.

As Mrs. Moffitt and Mr. Payne exchanged brief greetings (she had twice typed letters for him) the girl announced somewhat self-righteously that "Foster has poo-pooed his pants and Daddy didn't bring a diaper."

Mrs. Moffitt took pity on Mr. Payne and took the boy into a rest room in the Franklin Institute and diapered him. When she returned, Mr. Payne told her, he was "rather much in the same situation as yourself, Mrs. Moffitt."

Specifically, he told her that Mrs. Brewster Cortland Payne II had died in a traffic accident eight months before, returning from their country place in the Poconos.

Three months after that, Mrs. Moffitt and Mr. Payne had shocked and/or enraged the Payne family, the Moffitt family, and assorted friends and relatives on both sides by driving themselves and their children to Bethesda, Maryland, on Friday after work and getting married.

Six months after their marriage, Brewster had adopted Patricia's son, in the process changing Matthew Mark Moffitt's name to Payne.

When, the day after Captain Dutch Moffitt had been laid to rest in the cemetery of St. Monica's Roman Catholic Church, Matt Payne had joined the Philadelphia Police Department, Brewster Payne did not have to hear the professional psychiatric opinion of his daughter, Amelia Payne, M.D., that Matt had done so to prove that he was a man, to overcome the psychological castration of his rejection by the Marines. He had figured that out himself.

And so had Chief Inspector Dennis V. Coughlin of the Philadelphia Police Department. Denny Coughlin had been Sergeant John X. Moffitt's best friend, and over the years had become quite close to Brewster Payne, as they dealt with the problem of Mother Moffitt, Matt's grandmother, a bellicose German-Irish woman who sincerely believed that Brewster Cortland Payne II would burn in hell for seducing her son's widow into abandoning Holy Mother Church for Protestantism, and raising her grandson as a heathen.

Over more whiskey than was probably good for them in the bar at the Union League, Denny Coughlin and Brewster Payne had agreed that Matt's idea that he wanted to be a cop was understandable, but once he found out how things were, he would come to his senses. A couple of weeks, no more than a month, in the Police Academy would open his eyes to what he had let himself in for, and he would resign.

Matt did not resign. On his graduation, Denny Coughlin used his influence to have him assigned to clerical duties in the newly formed Special Operations Division. He had knocked on Patricia Moffitt's door to tell her that her husband had been killed in the line of duty. He had no intention of knocking on Patricia M. Payne's door to tell her her son had been killed.

He had explained the situation to the commanding officer of the Special Operations Division, Staff Inspector Peter Wohl. Coughlin believed, with some reason, that Peter Wohl was the smartest cop in the Department. Peter Wohl had been a homicide detective, the youngest sergeant ever in Highway Patrol, and had been the youngest ever staff inspector working in Internal Affairs when the mayor had set up Special Operations and put him in charge. Wohl's father was Chief Inspector Augustus Wohl, retired, for whom both Denny Coughlin and Jerry Carlucci had worked early on in their careers.

Peter Wohl understood the situation even better than Denny Coughlin thought. He understood that Matt Payne was the son Denny Coughlin had never had. And his father had told him that Denny Coughlin had been waiting a suitable period of time before proposing marriage to John X. Moffitt's widow when she surprised everybody by marrying the Main Line lawyer.

Inspector Wohl decided it would pose no major problem to keep Officer Matthew M.

Payne gainfully, and safely, employed shuffling paper until the kid came to his senses, resigned, and went to law school, where he belonged.

That hadn't worked out as planned, either. Ninety-five percent of police officers complete their careers without ever once having drawn and fired their service revolver in anger. In the nineteen months Officer Payne had been assigned to Special Operations, he had shot to death two armed felons.

Both incidents, certainly, were unusual happenstances. In the first, Wohl had loaned Young Payne to veteran Homicide detective Jason Washington as a gofer. Washington was working the Northwest Philadelphia serial rapist job, where a looney tune who had started out assaulting women in their apartments had graduated to carrying them off in his van and then cutting various portions of their bodies off. Washington needed someone to make telephone calls for him, run errands, do whatever was necessary to free his time and mind to run the rapist/murderer down.

Officer Payne had been involved in nothing more adventurous, or life-threatening, than reporting to Inspector Wohl that Detective Washington had secured plaster casts of the doer's van's tires, and that he had just delivered said casts to the Forensic Laboratory when he happened upon the van. The very first time that Officer Payne had ever identified himself to a member of the public as a police officer, the citizen he attempted to speak with had tried to run him over with his van.

Payne emptied his revolver at the van, and one bullet had entered the cranial cavity of his assailant, causing his instant death. In the back of the van, under a canvas tarpaulin, was his next intended victim, naked, gagged, and tied up with lamp cord.

The second incident occurred during the early morning roundup of a group of armed robbers who elected to call themselves the Islamic Liberation Army. Officer Payne's intended role in this operation was to accompany Mr. Mickey O'Hara, a police reporter for the Philadelphia *Bulletin*. His orders were to deter Mr. O'Hara, by sitting on him if necessary, from entering the premises until the person to be arrested was safely in the custody of Homicide detectives and officers of the Special Operations Division.

The person whom it was intended to arrest quietly somehow learned what was going on, suddenly appeared in the alley where Officer Payne was waiting with Mr. O'Hara for the arrest to be completed, and started shooting. One of his .45 ACP caliber bullets ricocheted off a brick wall before striking Officer Payne in the leg, and another caused brick splinters to open Officer Payne's forehead and make it bleed profusely. Despite his wounds, Payne got his pistol in action and got off five shots at this assailant, two of which hit him and caused fatal wounds.

The circumstances didn't matter. What mattered was that Payne had blown the serial murderer/rapist's brains all over the windshield of his van, thus saving a naked woman from being raped and dismembered, and that he had been photographed by Mr. O'Hara as he stood, blood streaming down his face, over the scumbag who had opened fire on him with his .45 and lost the shoot-out.

Denny Coughlin had been spared having to tell Patricia Moffitt Payne that her son had just been shot in the line of duty only because Brewster Payne had answered the phone.

There had been another long conversation over a good many drinks in the Union League between Denny Coughlin and Brewster C. Payne about the results of the most recent examination for promotion to detective. There had been no way that Officer Payne, who had the requisite time on the job, could be kept from taking the examination. And neither Chief Coughlin nor Mr. Payne doubted he would pass.

It was obvious to both of them that Matt was not going to resign from the Department. And within a matter of a month or so, perhaps within a couple of weeks, he would be promoted to detective. He had never issued a traffic ticket, been called upon to settle a domestic dispute, manned the barricades against an assault by brick-throwing citizens exercising their constitutional right to peaceably demonstrate against whatever governmental outrage it was currently chic to oppose, worked a sector car, or done any of the things that normally a rookie cop would do in his first couple of years on the job.

"The East Detective captain is a friend of mine, Brewster," Denny Coughlin said, finally. "I think Personnel will send Matt there. He'll have a chance to work with some good people, really learn the trade. He needs the experience, and they'll keep an eye out for him."

Brewster Payne knew Denny Coughlin well enough to understand that if he said he thought Personnel would send Matt somewhere, it was already arranged, and with the understanding that Chief Inspector Dennis V. Coughlin would be keeping an eye on the people keeping an eye on Matt.

"Thank you, Denny," Brewster Cortland Payne II had said.

When Matt drove the Bug into the parking garage beneath the Delaware Valley Cancer Building (and the buildings to the right and left of it) he found that someone was in his reserved parking spot. Ordinarily, this would have caused him to use foul language, but he recognized the Cadillac Fleetwood. He knew it was registered to Brewster C. Payne, Providence Road, Wallingford.

When he had moved into the apartment, his father had told him that he had reserved two parking spaces in the underground garage for the resident of the attic apartment, primarily as a token of his affection, of course, and only incidentally because it would also provide a parking space for his mother, or other family members, when they had business around Rittenhouse Square.

Until three weeks before it had never posed a problem, because Matt had kept only one car in the garage. Not the battered twelve-year-old Volkswagen Beetle he was now driving, but a glistening, year-old, silver Porsche 911. It had been his graduation present from his father. From the time he had been given the Porsche, the Bug—which had also been a present from his father, six years before, when he had gotten his driver's license—had sat, rotted actually, in the garage in Wallingford. He had for some reason been reluctant to sell it.

Three weeks before, as he sat taking his promotion physical, he had realized that not selling it had been one of the few wise decisions he had made in his lifetime.

One of the dumber things he had ever done, when assigned to Special Operations out of the Police Academy, was to drive to work in the Porsche. It had immediately identified him as the rich kid from the Main Line who was playing at being a cop. He would not make that same mistake when reporting to East Detectives as a rookie detective.

The battery had been dead, understandably, when he rode out to Wallingford with his father to claim the car, but once he'd put the charger on it, it had jumped to life. He'd changed the oil, replaced two tires, and the Bug was ready to provide sensible, appropriate transportation for him back and forth to work.

The Porsche was sitting in the parking spot closest to the elevator, beside the Cadillac, which meant that he had no place to park the Bug, since his mother had chosen to exercise her right to the "extra" parking space. He was sure it was his mother, because his father commuted to Philadelphia by train.

There were several empty parking spaces, and after a moment's indecision, he pulled the Bug into the one reserved for the executive director. With a little bit of luck, Matt reasoned, that gentleman would have exercised his right to quit for the day whenever he wanted to, and would no longer require his space.

He walked up the stairs to the first floor, however, found the rent-a-cop, and handed hm the keys to the Bug.

"I had to park my Bug in the executive director's slot; my mother's in mine."

"Your *father*," the rent-a-cop said. He was a retired police officer. "He said if I saw you, to tell you he wants to see you. He'll be in the Rittenhouse Club until six. I stuck a note under your door."

"Thank you," Matt said.

"I'll take care of the car, don't worry about it. I think he's gone for the day."

"Thank you," Matt said, and got on the elevator and rode up to the third floor, wondering what was going on. He had a premonition, not that the sky was falling in, but that something was about to happen that he was not going to like.

He unlocked the door to the stairway, opened it, and picked up the envelope on the floor.

4:20 P.M.

Matt:

If this comes to hand after six, when I will have left the Rittenhouse, please call me at home no matter what the hour. This is rather important.

Dad.

He jammed the note in his pocket and went up the stairs. The red light on his answering machine was blinking. There were two messages. The first was from someone who wished to sell him burglar bars at a special, one-time reduced rate, and the second was a familiar voice:

"I tried to call you at work, but you had already left. Your dad and I are going to have a drink in the Rittenhouse Club. You need to be there. If you don't get this until after six, call him or me when you finally do."

The caller had not identified himself. Chief Inspector Dennis V. Coughlin did not like to waste words, and he correctly assumed that his voice would be recognized.

And, Matt thought, *there had been something in his voice suggesting there was something wrong in a new detective having gone off shift at the called-for time.*

What the hell is going on?

Matt picked up the telephone and dialed a number from memory.

"Yeah?" Detective Charley McFadden was not about to win an award for telephone courtesy.

"This is Sears Roebuck. We're running a sale on previously owned wedding gowns."

Detective McFadden was not amused. "Hi, Matt, what's up?"

"I don't know, but I'm not going to be able to meet you at six. You going to be home later?"

"How much later?"

"Maybe six-thirty, quarter to seven?"

"Call me at McGee's. I'll probably still be there."

"Sorry, Charley."

"Yeah, well, what the hell. We'll see what happens. Maybe I'll get lucky without you."

Matt hung up, looked at his watch, and then quickly left his apartment.

Matt walked up the stairs of the Rittenhouse Club, pushed open the heavy door, and went into the foyer. He looked up at the board behind the porter's counter, on which the names of all the members were listed, together with a sliding indicator that told whether or not they were in the club.

"Your father's in the lounge, Mr. Payne," the porter said to him.

"Thank you," Matt said.

Brewster Cortland Payne II, a tall, angular, distinguished-looking man who was actually far wittier than his appearance suggested, saw him the moment he entered the lounge and raised his hand. Chief Inspector Dennis V. Coughlin, a heavyset, ruddy-faced man in a well-fitting pin-striped suit, turned to look, and then smiled. They were sitting in rather small leather-upholstered armchairs between which sat a small table. There were squat whiskey glasses, small glass water pitchers, a silver bowl full of mixed nuts, and a battered, but well-shined, brass ashtray with a box of wooden matches in a holder on it on the table.

"Good," Brewster Payne said, smiling and rising from his chair to touch Matt softly and affectionately on the arm. "We caught you."

"Dad. Uncle Denny."

"Matty, I tried to call you at East Detectives," Coughlin said, sitting back down. "You had already gone."

"I left at five *after* four, Uncle Denny. The City got their full measure of my flesh for their day's pay."

An elderly waiter in a white jacket appeared.

"Denny's drinking Irish and the power of suggestion got to me," Brewster Payne said. "But have what you'd like."

"Irish is fine with me."

"All around, please, Philip," Brewster Payne said.

I have just had a premonition: I am not going to like whatever is going to happen. Whatever this is all about, it is not "let's call Good Ol' Matt and buy him a drink at the Rittenhouse Club."

3.

"Are we celebrating something, or is this boys' night out?" Matt asked.

Coughlin chuckled.

"Well, more or less, we're celebrating something," Brewster Payne said. "Penny's coming home."

"Is she really?" Matt said, and the moment the words were out of his mouth, he realized that not only had he been making noise, rather than responding, but that his disinterest had not only been apparent to his father, but had annoyed him, perhaps hurt him, as well.

Penny was Miss Penelope Alice Detweiler of Chestnut Hill. Matt now recalled hearing from someone, probably his sister Amy, that she had been moved from The Institute of Living, a psychiatric hospital in Connecticut, to another funny farm out west somewhere. Arizona, Nevada, someplace like that.

Matt had known Penny Detweiler all his life. Penny's father and his had been schoolmates at Episcopal Academy and Princeton, and one of the major—almost certainly the most lucrative—clients of Mawson, Payne, Stockton, McAdoo & Lester, his father's law firm, was Nesfoods International, Philadelphia's largest employer, H. Richard Detweiler, president and chief executive officer.

After a somewhat pained silence, Brewster Payne said, "I was under the impression that you were fond of Penny."

"I am," Matt said quickly.

I'm not at all sure that's true. I am not, now that I think about it, at all fond of Penny. She's just been around forever, like the walls. I've never even thought of her as a girl, really.

He corrected himself: *There was that incident when we were four or five when I talked her into showing me hers and her mother caught us at it, and had hysterically shrieked at me that I was a filthy little boy, an opinion of me I strongly suspect she still holds.*

But fond? No. The cold truth is that I now regard Precious Penny (to use her father's somewhat nauseating appellation) very much as I would regard a run-over dog. I am dismayed and repelled by what she did.

"You certainly managed to conceal your joy at the news they feel she can leave The Lindens."

The Lindens, Matt recalled, *is the name of the new funny farm. And it's in* Nevada, *not Arizona. She's been there what? Five months? Six?*

There was another of what Matt thought of as "Dad's Significant Silences." He dreaded them. His father did not correct or chastise him. He just looked at the worm before him until the worm, squirming, figured out himself the error, or the bad manners, he had just manifested to God and Brewster Cortland Payne II.

Finally, Brewster Payne went on: "According to Amy, and according to the people at The Lindens, the problem of her physical addiction to narcotics is pretty much under control."

Matt kept his mouth shut, but in looking away from his father, to keep him from seeing Matt's reaction to that on his face, Matt found himself looking at Dennis V. Coughlin, who just perceptibly shook his head. The meaning was clear: *You and I don't believe that, we know that no more than one junkie in fifty ever gets the problem under control, but this is not the time or place to say so.*

"I'm really glad to hear that," Matt said.

"Which is not to say that her problems are over," Brewster Payne went on. "There is specifically the problem of the notoriety that went with this whole unfortunate business."

The newspapers in Philadelphia, in the correct belief that their readers would be interested, indeed, fascinated, had reported in great detail that the good-looking blonde who had been wounded when her boyfriend—a gentleman named Anthony J. "Tony the Zee" DeZego, whom it was alleged had connections to organized crime—had been assassinated in a downtown parking garage was none other than Miss Penelope Detweiler, only child of the Chestnut Hill/Nesfoods International Detweilers.

"That's yesterday's news," Matt said. "That was seven months ago."

"Dick Detweiler doesn't think so," Brewster Payne said. "That's where this whole thing started."

"Excuse me?"

"Dick Detweiler didn't want Penny to get off the airliner and find herself facing a mob of reporters shoving cameras in her face."

"Why doesn't he send the company airplane after her?" Matt wondered aloud. "Have it land at Northeast Philadelphia?"

"That was the original idea, but Amy said that she considered it important that Penny not think that her return home was nothing more than a continuation of her hospitalization."

"I'm lost, Dad."

"I don't completely understand Amy's reasoning either, frankly, but I think the general idea is that Penny should feel, when she leaves The Lindens, that she is closing the door on her hospitalization and returning to a normal life. Hence, no company plane. Equally important, no nurse, not even Amy, to accompany her, which would carry with it the suggestion that she's still under care."

"Amy just wants to turn her loose in Nevada?" Matt asked incredulously. "How far is the funny farm from Las Vegas?"

Brewster Payne's face tightened.

"I don't at all like your choice of words, Matt. That was not only uncalled for, it was despicable!" he said icily.

"Christ, Matty!" Dennis V. Coughlin said, seemingly torn between disgust and anger.

"I'm sorry," Matt said, genuinely contrite. "That just . . . came out. But just turning her loose, alone, *that's* insane."

"It would, everyone agrees, be *ill-advised,*" Brewster Payne said. "That's where you come in, Matt."

"I beg your pardon?"

"Amy's reasoning here, and in this I am in complete agreement, is that you are the ideal person to go out there and bring her home . . ."

"No. Absolutely not!"

". . . for these reasons," Brewster Payne went on, ignoring him. "For one thing, Penny thinks of you as her brother. . . ."

"She thinks of me as the guy who pinned the tail on her," Matt said. "If it weren't for me, no one would have known she's a junkie."

"I don't like that term, either, Matt, but that's Amy's point. If you appear out there, in a nonjudgmental role, as her friend, welcoming her back to her life . . ."

"I can't believe you're going along with this," Matt said. "For one thing, Penny does not think of me as her brother. I'm just a guy she's known for a long time who betrayed her, turned her in. If I had been locked up out there for six months in that funny farm, I would really hate me."

"The reason Amy, and the people at The Lindens, feel that Penny is ready to resume her life is because, in her counseling, they have caused her to see things as they really are. To see you, specifically, as someone who was trying to help, not hurt her."

I just don't believe this bullshit, and I especially don't believe my dad going along with it.

"Dad, this is so much bullshit."

"Amy said that would probably be your reaction," Brewster Payne said. "I can see she was right."

"Anyway, it's a moot point. I couldn't go out there if I wanted to," Matt said. "Uncle Denny, tell him that I just can't call up my sergeant and tell him that I won't be in for a couple of days. . . ."

"I'm disappointed in you, Matty," Chief Coughlin said. "I thought by now you would have put two and two together."

I'm a little disappointed in me myself, now that the mystery of my temporary assignment, report to Sergeant McElroy, has been cleared up.

"What did Detweiler do, call you?"

"He called the mayor," Coughlin said. "And the mayor called Chief Lowenstein and me."

"I don't think it entered Dick Detweiler's mind, it certainly never entered mine, that you would have any reservations at all about helping Penny in any way you could," Brewster Payne said. Matt looked across the table at him. "But if you feel this strongly about it, I'll call Amy and . . ."

Matt held up both hands. "I surrender."

"I'm not sure that's the attitude we're all looking for."

Matt met his father's eyes.

"I'll do whatever I can to help Penny," he said.

There was another Significant Silence, and then Brewster C. Payne reached in his breast pocket and took out an envelope.

"These are the tickets. You're on American Airlines Flight 485 tomorrow morning at eight-fifteen. A car will meet you at the airport in Las Vegas. You will spend the night there . . ."

"At The Lindens?"

"Presumably. And return the next morning."

Shortly afterward, after having concluded their business with Detective Payne, Chief Coughlin and Brewster C. Payne went their respective ways.

Matt spent the balance of the evening in McGee's Saloon, in the company of Detective Charley McFadden of Northwest Detectives.

Perhaps naturally, their conversation dealt with their professional duties. Detective McFadden, who had been seven places below Matt on the detective examination listing, told Matt what he was doing in Northwest Detectives.

Charley had been an undercover Narc right out of the Police Academy, before he'd gone to Special Operations where he and Matt had become friends. On his very first assignment as a rookie detective, he found that his lieutenant was a supervisor (then a sergeant) he'd worked under in Narcotics, and who treated him like a detective, not a rookie detective. His interesting case of the day had been the investigation of a shooting of a numbers runner by a client who felt that he had cheated.

Matt had not felt that Detective McFadden would be thrilled to hear of his specialization in investigating recovered stolen automobiles, and spared him a recounting. Neither had he been fascinated with Detective McFadden's report on the plans for his upcoming wedding, and the ritual litany of his intended's many virtues.

The result of this was that Matt had a lot to drink, and woke up with a hangover and just enough time to dress, throw some clothes in a bag, and catch a cab to the airport, but not to have any breakfast.

At the very last minute, specifically at 7:40 A.M., as he handed his small suitcase to the attendant at the American Airlines counter, Detective Payne realized that he had, as either a Pavlovian reflex, or because he was more than a little hungover, picked up his Chief's Special revolver and its holster from the mantelpiece and clipped it to his waistband before leaving the apartment.

Carrying a pistol aboard an airliner was in conflict with federal law, which prohibited any passenger, cop or not, to go armed except on official business, with written permission.

"Hold it, please," Officer Payne said to the counter attendant. She looked at him with annoyance, and then with wide-eyed interest as he took out his pistol, opened the cylinder, and ejected the cartridges.

"Sir, what are you doing?"

"Putting this in my suitcase," he said, and then added, when he saw the look on her face, "I'm a police officer."

That, to judge from the look on her face, was either an unsatisfactory reply, or one she was not willing to accept. He found his badge and ID and showed her that. She gave him a wan smile and quickly walked away. A moment later someone higher in the American Airlines hierarchy appeared.

"Sir, I understand you've placed a weapon in your luggage," he said.

"I'm a police officer," Matt said, and produced his ID again.

"We have to inspect the weapon to make sure it is unloaded," the American Airlines man said.

"I just unloaded it," Matt said, and offered the handful of cartridges as proof.

"We do not permit passengers to possess ammunition in the passenger cabins of our aircraft," the American Airlines man said.

Matt opened the suitcase again, handed the Chief's Special to the man, who accepted it as if it were obviously soaked in leper suppuration, and finally handed it back. Matt returned it to the suitcase and dumped the cartridges in an interior pocket.

By then, the American Airlines man had a form for Matt to sign, swearing that the firearm he had in his luggage was unloaded. When he had signed it, the man from American Airlines affixed a red tag to the suitcase handle reading UNLOADED FIREARM.

If I were a thief, Detective Payne thought, *and looking for something to steal, I think I'd make my best shot at a suitcase advertising that it contained a gun. You can get a lot more from a fence for a gun than you can get for three sets of worn underwear.*

"Thank you, sir," the man from American Airlines said. "Have a pleasant flight."

A stewardess squatted in the aisle beside him.

"May I get you something before we take off, sir?"

"How about a Bloody Mary?"

"Certainly, sir," she said, but managed to make it clear that anyone who needed a Bloody Mary at eight o'clock in the morning was at least an alcoholic, and most probably was going to cause trouble on the flight for the *nice* passengers in first class.

The Bloody Mary he had on the ground before they took off had made him feel a little better, and the Bloody Mary he had once they were in the air made him feel even better. It also helped him doze off. He became aware of this when a painful pressure in his ears woke him and alerted him to the fact that the airliner was making its descent to Las Vegas. The stewardess, obviously, had decided that someone who drank a Bloody Mary and a half at eight A.M., and then passed out, had no interest in breakfast.

Primarily to make sure that he still had it, he took an envelope containing the tickets from his pocket. There was something, a smaller, banknote-sized envelope, in the *NES-FOODS INTERNATIONAL Office of the President* envelope he had not noticed before.

He tore it open. There were five crisp one-hundred-dollar bills, obviously expense money, and a note:

Dear Matt:

I am not much good at saying "Thank You," but I want you to know that Grace and I will always have you in our hearts and in our prayers for your selfless, loving support of Penny in her troubles. Our family is truly blessed to have a friend like you.

                                                                              Dick

---

"Oh, shit," Matt moaned.

"Please put your chair in the upright position and fasten your seat belt," the stewardess said.

There was a man wearing a chauffeur's cap holding a sign for MR. PAYNE when Matt stepped out of the airway into the terminal.

"I'm Matt Payne."

"If you'll give me your baggage checks, Mr. Payne, I'll take care of the luggage. The car is parked just outside Baggage Claim. A cream Cadillac."

"If you don't mind," Matt said, "I'll just tag along with you."

"Whatever you say, sir."

Matt looked around the terminal with interest. It was his first visit to Las Vegas. He saw that it was true that there were slot machines all over. There was also a clock on the wall. It said it was 10:15, and it was probably working, for he could see the second hand jerk, although his wristwatch told him it was 1:15.

It took him a moment to understand. He had been in the air four and a half or five hours. It was 1:15 in Philadelphia, which meant that he had missed lunch as well as breakfast. But they had changed time zones.

His bag was the very last bag to show up on the carousel, and the red UNLOADED FIREARM tag on it attracted the attention of a muscular young man with closely cropped hair, who was wearing blue jeans and a baggy sweater worn outside the jeans. He looked at the chauffeur, and then at Matt, when he saw he was with the chauffeur, with great interest, and then followed them out of the baggage room and watched them get into the cream-colored Cadillac limousine.

Clever fellow that I am, Matt thought, *I will offer odds of three to one that the guy in the crew cut is a plainclothesman on the airport detail. He is professionally curious why a nice, clean-cut young man such as myself is arriving in Las Vegas with an UNLOADED FIREARM in his luggage.*

The chauffeur installed Matt, whose stomach was now giving audible notice that it hadn't been fed in some time, in the back seat and then drove away from the airport.

I'm going to have to get something to eat, and right now.

He pushed himself off the seat, and with some difficulty found the switch that lowered the glass divider.

"How far is this place? I've got to get something to eat."

"The Lindens, sir, or the Flamingo?"

"What about the Flamingo?"

"My instructions are to take you to the Flamingo, sir, and then pick you up there at seven-fifteen tomorrow morning and take you out to The Lindens."

"Oh."

"They have very nice restaurants in the Flamingo, sir. It's about fifteen, twenty minutes. But I can stop . . ."

The Flamingo, Matt recalled, was a world-famous den of iniquity, a gambling hall where Frank Sinatra, Dean Martin, and other people of that ilk entertained the suckers while they were being parted from their money at the roulette and blackjack tables. He also recalled hearing that the world's best-looking hookers plied their trade in the better Las Vegas dens of iniquity.

"No. That's fine. I can wait."

There was a basket of fruit and a bottle of champagne in a cooler in Suite 9012, which consisted of a sitting room overlooking what Matt decided was The Strip of fame and legend, and a bedroom with the largest bed, with a mirrored headboard, Matt had ever seen.

The bellman also showed him a small bar, stocked with miniature bottles of liquor, and a refrigerator that held wine and beer. As soon as he had tipped the bellman, he headed for the refrigerator and opened a bottle of Tuborg, and drank deeply from it.

A moment later he felt a little dizzy.

Christ, I haven't had anything to eat since that cheese-steak in McGee's. No wonder the beer's making me dizzy.

He ripped the cellophane off the basket of fruit and peeled a banana. And noticed that there was an envelope in the basket.

Flamingo Hotel & Casino

Dear Mr. Payne:

Welcome to the Flamingo! It is always a pleasure to have a guest of Mr. Detweiler in the house.

A $10,000 line of credit has been established for you. Should you wish to test Lady Luck at our tables, simply present yourself at the cashier's window and you will be allowed to draw chips up to that amount.

If there is any way I can help to make your stay more enjoyable, please call me.

Good luck!

James Crawford
General Manager

It took Matt only a second or two to conclude that Mr. James Crawford had made a serious error. Dick and Grace Detweiler might feel themselves blessed to have a friend like him, and they might really have him in their prayers, but there was no way they were going to give him ten thousand dollars to gamble with.

Detweiler probably entertains major clients out here, and the general manger made the natural mistake of thinking I'm one of them, someone in a position to buy a trainload of tomato soup or fifty tons of canned chicken.

The possibilities boggle the mind, but what this nice, young, nongambling police officer is going to do is find someplace to eat and then come back up here and crap out in that polo-field-sized bed.

To get to the restaurant from the lobby, it was necessary to walk past what he estimated to be at least a thousand slot machines, followed by a formidable array of craps tables, blackjack tables, and roulette tables.

He felt rather naive. As far as gambling was concerned, he had lost his fair share, and then some, of money playing both blackjack and poker, but he really had no idea how one actually shot craps, and roulette looked like something you saw in an old movie, with men in dinner jackets and women in low-cut dresses betting the ancestral estates in some Eastern European principality on where the ball would fall into the hole.

The restaurant surprised and pleased him. The menu was enormous. He broke his unintended fast with a filet mignon, hash-brown potatoes, two eggs sunny side up, and two glasses of milk. It was first rate, and it was surprisingly cheap.

He started to pay for it, but then decided to hell with it, and signed the bill with his room number.

Why should I spend my money when I'm out here doing an unpleasant errand for Dick Detweiler?

He walked past the blackjack, craps, and roulette tables and was almost past the slot machines when he decided that it would really be foolish to have been out here in Las Vegas, in one of the most famous gambling dens of them all, without having once played a slot machine.

He looked in his wallet and found that he had a single dollar bill and several twenties. There were also, he knew, two fifties, folded as small as possible, hidden in a recess of the wallet, against the possibility that some girl would get fresh and he would have to walk home.

He took one of the twenties and gave it to a young woman in a very short shirt who had a bus driver's change machine strapped around her waist.

She handed him a short, squat stack of what looked like coins, but what, on examination, turned out to be one-dollar slugs.

He found a slot machine and dropped one of the slugs in and pulled the handle. He did this again seventeen times with no result, except that the oranges and lemons and cherries spun around. On the nineteenth pull, however, the machine made a noise he had not heard before, and then began noisily spitting out a stream of slugs into a sort of a shelf on the bottom of the machine.

"Jesus Christ!"

There were more slugs than he could hold in both hands. But the purpose of the waxed paper bucket he had noticed between his machine and the next now became apparent. Successful gamblers such as himself put their winnings in them.

And wise successful gamblers such as myself know when to quit. I will take all these slugs—Jesus, there must be two hundred of them—to the cashier and turn them in for real money.

He didn't make it to the cashier's cage. His route took him past a roulette table, and he stopped to look. After a minute or two he decided that it wasn't quite as exotic or complicated as it looked in the movies about the Man Who Broke the Bank at Monte Carlo.

There were thirty-six numbers, plus 0 and 00, for a total of thirty-eight. The guy with the stick—the *croupier,* he recalled somewhat smugly—paid thirty-six to one if your number came up. Since there were thirty-eight numbers, that gave the house a one-in-nineteen advantage, roughly five percent.

That didn't seem too unfair. And in another minute or two he had figured out that you could make other bets, one through twelve, for example, or thirteen to twenty-four, or odd or even, or red or black, that gave you a greater chance of winning, but paid lower odds.

Since 0 and 00 were neither odd or even, and were green, rather than black or red, the house, Matt decided, got its five percent no matter how the suckers bet.

And he also decided that since he had already made the mental decision to throw twenty dollars away, so that he could say he had gambled in Las Vegas, there was no reason to change simply because the slot machine had paid off.

He would now be able to say, he thought, as he put five of the slot machine slugs on EVEN, that he had lost his shirt at roulette. That sounded better than having lost his shirt at the slot machines.

Six came up.

The croupier looked at him.

"Pennies or nickels?"

What the hell does that mean?

"Nickels," Matt said.

The croupier took his slot machine slugs and laid two chips in their place.

Obviously, a "nickel" means that chip is the equivalent of five slot machine slugs.

Matt let his two-nickel bet ride. Twenty-six came up. The croupier added two chips to the two on the board. Matt decided it was time to quit, since he was ahead. He picked up the four chips, and felt rather wise when the ball fell into a slot marked with a seven.

He waited until the wheel had been spun again, odd again, and then placed another five slot machine slugs on the green felt, this time on One to Twelve.

Nine came up. The croupier took the slot machine slugs and replaced them with three nickel chips.

"Sir, would you like me to change your coins for you?"

Obviously, it was for some reason impolite to play roulette with slot machine slugs.

"Please," Matt said, and pushed the waxed paper bucket to the croupier.

"All nickels?"

"Nickels and dimes," Matt said.

Two small stacks of chips were pushed across the table to him.

Matt yawned, and then again.

Jesus, what's the matter with me? I was just going to get something to eat and then crap out. How long have I been doing this?

His watch said that it was quarter to six.

Time to quit.

He watched the ball circle the wheel and then bounce around the slots before finally dropping in one.

Obviously, it is time to quit. I have been betting on 00 every fourth or fifth bet since I have been here, and that's the first time I ever won.

As the croupier counted out chips to place beside the chip he had laid on 00, Matt said, "Quit when you're ahead, I always say."

"You want to cash in, sir?"

"Please," Matt said, and pushed the stacks of chips, nickels, dimes, and quarters in front of him to the croupier.

He wondered where the cashier kept the real money to cash him out. There was no money, no cash box, in sight.

The croupier put all the chips in neat little stacks, and then said "Cash out." A man in a suit who had been hovering around in the background came up behind the croupier, looked, nodded, wrote something on a clipboard, and then smiled at Matt.

The croupier pushed a stack of chips, including some oblong ones Matt hadn't noticed before, across the felt to him.

"What do I do with these?" he wondered aloud.

"Take them to the cashier, sir," the croupier said.

Matt reclaimed his waxed paper bucket, and as he dumped the chips into it, he recalled that the polite thing to do was tip the croupier. He pushed one of the oblong chips across the table to the croupier.

"Thank you very much, sir," the croupier said. It was the first time, Matt noticed, that he had sounded at all friendly.

He walked to the cashier's cage and pushed the waxed paper bucket through what looked like a bank teller's window to a gray-haired, middle-aged woman.

She put all the chips in neat little stacks and then counted to herself, moving her lips. She looked at him.

"Would you like me to draw a check, sir?"

What the hell would I do with a check? I couldn't cash a check out here.

"I'd rather have the cash, if that would be all right."

The gray-haired woman took a stack of bills from a drawer and started counting them out. Matt was surprised to see that the bills were hundred-dollar bills, and then astonished to see how many of them she was counting out into thousand-dollar stacks. When she was finished there were four one-thousand-dollar stacks, one stack with six hundred-dollar bills in it, and a sixth stack with eighty-five dollars in it, four twenties and a five.

"Four thousand six hundred eighty-five," the gray-haired woman said.

"Thank you very much."

"Thank *you*, sir."

I don't believe this.

Matt divided the money into two wads, put one in each pocket, and walked out of the casino.

The first thing Matt Payne experienced when he woke up was annoyance. He had fallen asleep with his clothes on. And then he remembered the money and sat up abruptly. It was still there on the bed. No longer in the one thick wad into which he had counted it, three or four times, but there.

He counted it again. $4,685.

Jesus H. Christ!

He put the stack of bills in the drawer of the bedside table, then undressed and took a shower. He wrapped himself in a terry-cloth robe, went back into the bedroom, sat on the enormous bed, took the money from the bedside table, and counted it again.

Then he lay on the bed with his hands laced behind his head and thought about it.

The first thing he thought was that he was a natural-born gambler, that his quick mind gave him an edge over people who lost at roulette. He knew when to bet and when not to bet.

That's so much bullshit! You were just incredibly lucky, that's all. Dumb beginner's luck. Period. If you go back down there and try to do that again, you will lose every dime of that, plus the two fifties mad money.

The thing to do is put the money someplace safe and forget about it.

He figured that he might as well round it off, to forty-five hundred, keeping one hundred eighty-five to play with, and then he changed that to rounding it off to four thousand even, which left him six hundred eighty-five to play with, which meant lose.

He took out his toilet kit, and with some effort managed to cram forty hundred-dollar bills into the chrome soap dish.

He looked at his watch. It was quarter after three. That was Philadelphia time. It was only a little after midnight here, but it explained why he was hungry again.

With his luck, the restaurants would be closed at this hour. He would be denied another meal.

That's not true. With my *luck, the restaurant will not only be open, but the headwaiter will show me to my table with a flourish of trumpets.*

The headwaiter made him wait for a table, as the restaurant was even more crowded at midnight, Las Vegas time, then it had been when he'd had lunch, or breakfast, or whatever meal that had been. He had a martini, a shrimp cocktail, and another filet mignon, and then went back to the casino.

He went to the same roulette table and gave the croupier one hundred eighty-five dollars, specifying nickels, and promptly lost it all.

He moved away from the table and decided he would see if he could figure out how one bet at a craps table, as he had figured out how one bet at roulette.

There was a man at the head of the table rolling dice. He looked like a gambler, Matt decided. He had gold rings on both hands, and a long-collared shirt unbuttoned nearly to his navel, so as to display his hairy chest and a large gold medallion. And he had, one on each side of him, a pair of what Matt decided must be Las Vegas hookers of fame and legend.

Matt moved to what he hoped was an unobtrusive distance from the gambler and tried to figure out what was going on. Ten minutes later, the only thing he was fairly sure of was that the gambler was a fellow Philadelphian. The accent was unmistakable.

"Sir, if you are not going to wager, would you mind stepping aside and making room for someone who would like to play?"

"Sorry," Matt said, and pulled his wad of hundred-dollar bills from his pocket and laid one somewhere, anywhere, on the felt of the craps table. The gambler threw the dice. The hooker on his left said "ooooh" and the one on his right kissed him and gave him a little hug.

The croupier picked up Matt's one-hundred-dollar bill . . .

I lost. Why did I bet a hundred?

. . . and held a handful of chips over it.

"Quarters all right, sir?"

I won. I'll be goddamned. What did I bet on?

"Quarters are fine, thank you."

He picked up the stack of quarters, there were twelve of them, and walked away from the table.

If you have no idea what you're betting on, you have no business betting.

"Stick around," the gambler said. "I'm on a roll."

The temptation was nearly irresistible. The hooker on the left was smiling at him with invitation in her eyes. He had never been with a hooker.

Was this the time and place?

Get thee behind me, Satan! Back to the roulette table.

The Lindens was a forty-five-minute drive from the Flamingo. Matt was sorry that he had let himself be ushered into the back seat of the limousine. He certainly could have seen more of Las Vegas and the desert up front than he could see from the back seat, through the deeply tinted windows.

But he had been more than a little groggy when he left the Flamingo. He had lost the seven hundred dollars he had walked away from the craps table with, gone to bed, woken up, and—absolute insanity—decided he could take a chance with another five hundred, and then had compounded that insanity by taking a thousand dollars, not five hundred, from the soap dish and going back to the casino with it.

When he'd finally left the table, at quarter past six, Las Vegas time, he had worked the thousand up to thirty-seven hundred. Since that obviously wouldn't fit into the soap dish,

W . E . B . G R I F F I N

and he didn't want to have that much money in his pockets, or put it in the suitcase, he told the man in the cashier's cage to give him a check for his winnings.

By the time they had made out the check, and he'd taken another quick shower, they had called from the desk and told him his limousine was waiting for him.

There was nothing he could see for miles around The Lindens, which turned out to be a rambling, vaguely Spanish-looking collection of connected buildings built on a barren mountainside. There was a private road, a mile and a half long, from a secondary highway.

There was no fence around the place. Probably, he decided, because you would have to be out of your mind to try to walk away from The Lindens. There was nothing but desert.

In front of the main building, in an improbably lush patch of grass, were six trees. Lindens, he decided, as in Unter den Linden.

A hefty, middle-aged man in a blazer with retired cop written all over him saw him get out of the limousine and unlocked a double door as Matt walked up to it.

"Mr. Payne?"

"Right."

"Dr. Newberry is expecting you, sir. Will you follow me, please?"

He locked the door again before he headed inside the building.

Dr. Newberry was a woman in a white coat who looked very much like the cashier in the Flamingo.

"You look very much like your sister," Dr. Newberry greeted him cordially. Matt did not think he should inform her that that must be a genetic anomaly, because he and Amy shared no genes. He nodded politely.

"It was very good of you to come out to be with Penelope on her trip home."

"Not at all."

"We believe, as I'm sure Dr. Payne has told you, that we've done all we can for Penelope here. We've talked her through her problems, and of course, we believe that her physical addiction is under control."

"Yes, ma'am."

"We've tried to convince her that the best thing she can do is put what happened behind her, that she's not the only young woman who has had difficulty like this in her life, and that she will not be the only one to overcome it."

"Yes, ma'am."

"What I'm trying to get across is that I hope you can behave in a natural manner toward Penelope. While neither you nor she can deny that she has had problems, or has spent time with us, the less you dwell upon it, the better. Do you understand?"

"Yes, ma'am. I think so."

Dr. Newberry got up and smiled.

"Well, let's go get her. She's been waiting for you."

She led him through a series of wide corridors furnished with simple, heavy furniture and finally to a wide door. She pushed it open.

Penny was sitting on a chair. Her shoulder-length blond hair was parted in the middle. She was wearing a skirt and two sweaters. A single strand of pearls hung around her neck. There was a suitcase beside the chair.

It was a fairly large room with a wall of narrow, ceiling-high windows providing a view of the desert and mountains. Matt saw the windows were not wide enough for anyone to climb out.

"Your friend is here, dear," Dr. Newberry said.

Penny got to her feet.

"Hello, Matt," she said, and walked to him.

Christ, she expects me to kiss her.

He put his hands on her arms and kissed her cheek. He could smell her perfume. Or maybe it was soap. A female smell, anyway.

"How goes it, Penny?"

"I'm sorry you had to come out here," she said.

"Ah, hell, don't be silly."

"Shall I have someone come for your bag?"

"I can handle the bag," Matt said.

"Well, then, Penelope, you're all ready to go. I'll say good-bye to you now, dear."

"Thank you, Dr. Newberry, for everything."

"It's been my pleasure," Dr. Newberry said, smiled at Matt, and walked out of the room. Penny looked at Matt.

"God, I hate that woman!" she said.

He could think of no reply to make.

"Have you got any money?" she asked.

"Why?"

"Some people have been nice to me. I'd like to give them something."

What did they do, smuggle you junk?

"I don't think you're supposed to tip nurses and people like that."

"For God's sake, Matt, let me have some money. You know you'll get it back."

"When you get home, you can write them a check," Matt said.

"What are you thinking, that I'm going to take the money and run?"

As a matter of fact, perhaps subconsciously, that is just what I was thinking.

"I don't know what to think, Penny. But I'm not going to give you any money."

"Fuck you, Matt!"

He wondered if she had used language like that before she had met Tony the Zee DeZego, or whether she had learned it from him.

She picked up her bag and marched out of her room. He followed her. The rent-a-cop in the blue blazer, who, Matt thought, probably had a title like director of Internal Security Services, was at the front door. He unlocked it.

"Good-bye, Miss Detweiler," he said. "Good luck."

Penny didn't reply.

Matt got in the back seat of the limousine with her.

"Well, so how was the food?"

"Fuck you, Matt," Penny said again.

4.

It is accepted almost as an article of faith by police officers assigned to McCarran International Air Field, Las Vegas—which does not mean that it is true—that the decision to have a large number of plainclothes officers, as opposed to uniformed officers, patrolling the passenger terminal was based on the experience of a very senior Las Vegas police officer in the French Quarter of New Orleans, Louisiana.

The legend has it that the senior officer (three names are bandied about) was relaxing at a Bourbon Street bar after a hard day's work at the National Convention of the International Association of Chiefs of Police when an unshaven sleazeball in greasy jeans and leather vest approached him and very politely said, "Excuse me, sir, I believe this is yours."

He thereupon handed the senior police officer his wallet. (In some versions of the story, the sleazeball handed him his wallet, his ID folder, his wristwatch, and his diamond-studded Masonic ring.) It came out that the sleazeball was a plainclothes cop who had been watching the dip (pickpocket) ply his trade. (In some versions of the story, the dip was a stunning blond transvestite with whom the senior police officer had just been dancing.)

In any event, the senior police officer returned to Las Vegas with the notion, which he had the authority to turn into policy, that the way to protect the tourists moving through

McCarran was the way the cops in New Orleans protected the tourists moving down Bourbon Street, with plainclothes people.

They could, the senior police said, protect the public without giving the public the idea that Las Vegas was so crime-ridden a place that you needed police officers stationed every fifty yards along the way from the airway to the limo and taxi stands to keep the local critters from separating them from their worldly goods before the casino operators got a shot at them.

And so it came to pass that Officer Frank J. Oakes, an ex-paratrooper who had been on the job for almost six years, was standing on the sidewalk outside the American Airlines terminal in plainclothes when the white Cadillac limo pulled up. Oakes was wearing sports clothes and carrying a plastic bag bearing the logotype of the Marina Motel & Casino. The bag held his walkie-talkie.

The white Cadillac limo attracted his attention. Even before he took a look at the license plate to make sure, he was sure that it was a *real* limo, as he thought of it, as opposed to one of the livery limos, or one operated by one of the casinos to make the high rollers feel good. For one thing, it wasn't beat up. For another, it did not have a TV antenna on the trunk. Most important, it wasn't a stretch limo, large enough to transport all of a rock-and-roll band and their lady friends. It looked to him like a real, rich people's private limo, an analysis that seemed to be confirmed when the chauffeur got out wearing a neat suit and white shirt and chauffeur's cap and quickly walked around the front to open the curbside door.

The first person to get out was a female Caucasian, early twenties, five feet three, 115 pounds. She wore her shoulder-length blond hair parted in the middle, a light blue linen skirt, a pullover sweater, and a jacket-type sweater unbuttoned. There was a single strand of pearls around her neck. She did not have a spectacular breastworks, but Officer Oakes found her hips and tail attractive.

A male Caucasian, early twenties, maybe 165, right at six feet, followed her out of the limo. He was wearing a tweed coat, a tieless white shirt, gray flannel slacks, and loafers. Oakes thought that the two of them sort of fit the limo, that something about them smelled of money and position.

The chauffeur took a couple of bags from the limo trunk and handed them to the American Airlines guy. Then he went to the young guy, who handed him the tickets. Then the young guy looked at Officer Oakes, first casually, then gave him a closer look. Then he smiled and winked.

It was ten to one that he wasn't a fag, so the only thing that was left was that he had made Oakes as a cop. Oakes didn't like to be made, and he wondered how this guy had made him.

The chauffeur got the tickets back from the American Airlines guy, handed them to the young guy, and then tipped his hat. The blonde went to the chauffeur and smiled at him and shook his hand. No tip, which confirmed Oakes's belief that it was a private limo.

The chauffeur got behind the wheel and drove off. The blond and well-dressed young guy walked into the terminal. The more he thought about it, Oakes was sure that he was right. The guy had made him as a cop on the job.

Another limo, this one a sort of pink-colored livery limo that looked like it was maybe five thousand miles away from the salvage yard, pulled into the space left by the real limo.

A real gonzo got out of it, a white male Caucasian in his late twenties or early thirties, maybe five-ten and 170, swarthy skin with facial scars, probably acne. He was wearing a maroon shirt with long collar points, unbuttoned halfway down to expose his hairy chest and a gold chain with some kind of medal. He had on a pair of yellow pants and white patent-leather loafers with a chain across the instep. He had a gold wristwatch around the wrist of the other.

He got out and looked around as if he had just bought the place, made a big deal of checking the time, so everybody would see the gold watch, and then waited for the limo driver to get his bags from the trunk. Cheap luggage. He waited until the guy had carried his bags to the American Airlines counter, then pulled out a thick wad of bills, hundreds outside, and then counted out four twenties.

"Here you go, my man," the gonzo said.

A limo, no matter at what hotel you were staying, was no more than fifty bucks, so the last of the big spenders was laying a large tip on the driver. The gonzo had apparently done well at the tables.

The Las Vegas Chamber of Commerce, Oakes knew, would be happy. There was no better advertisement than some gonzo like this going home and telling the other gonzos what a killing he'd made in Vegas.

Officer Oakes's attention was diverted from the gonzo by the sound of a strident female voice, offering her anything but flattering opinion of the gentleman with her. Drunk probably, Oakes decided.

He stepped into a doorway, unzipped his Marina Hotel & Casino plastic bag, and took out the radio and called for a uniformed officer to deal with the disturbance at American Airlines Arrival.

By the time the uniforms, two of them, got there, the female Caucasian, five-three, maybe 135, 140, brown hair, had warmed to the subject of what a despicable, untrustworthy sonofabitch the gentleman with her was, and Officer Oakes put the blonde with the nice ass, the gonzo, and the good-looking young guy he was sure had made him as cop from his mind.

Matt caught up with Penny as she marched through the airport and took her arm.

"Is that really necessary?"

"I've got to make a phone call," he said.

He guided her to a row of pay telephones, took a dime from his pocket, dropped it in the slot, gave the operator a number, told her it was collect, that his name was Matthew Payne, and that he would speak with anyone.

"Who are you calling?" Penny asked, almost civilly.

"My father."

"Why?"

"Because I was told to call when I was sure the plane was leaving on schedule," Matt Payne replied, and then turned his attention to the telephone.

"Hello, Mrs. Craig. Would you please tell that slave driver you work for that American Airlines Flight 6766 is leaving on schedule?"

There was brief pause and then he went on:

"Everything's fine. Aside from the fact that I lost my car and next year's salary at the craps tables."

There was a reply, and he chuckled and hung up.

"Why did you call your father?" Penny asked.

"Because I thought he would be better able to deal with a collect call than yours," Matt Payne replied, then took her arm again. "There's what I have been looking for."

He led her to a cocktail lounge and set her down at a tiny table in a relatively uncrowded part of the room.

A waitress almost immediately came to the table.

"Have you got any Tuborg?" Matt Payne asked.

The waitress nodded.

"Penny?" he asked.

"I think a 7-Up, please."

"Sprite okay?"

"Yes, thank you," Penny said. Then, turning to Matt: "You were kidding, right, about losing a lot of money gambling?"

"As a matter of fact, I made so much money, I don't believe it."

"Really?"

He took the Flamingo's check for $3,700 from his pocket and showed it to her.

"My God!"

"And that's not all of it," he said.

"What were you playing?"

"Roulette."

"Roulette? What do you know about playing roulette?"

"Absolutely nothing, that's why I won," Matt said.

She smiled. The anger seemed to be gone. He had a policeman's cynical thought. *Is she charming me?*

"When did you get here?" Penny asked.

"A little after ten yesterday morning."

"Then why didn't you come get me yesterday?"

"Because I was told to get you this morning," he said. "Mine is not to reason why, et cetera, et cetera."

"So instead you went gambling."

"Right. I quit half an hour before the limousine came back for me." When he saw the look on her face, he went on solemnly, "Las Vegas never sleeps, you know. They don't even have clocks."

"I really wouldn't know. I didn't get to go to town."

He did not respond.

"You really gambled all night?" she asked.

"I took a couple of naps and a shower, but yes, I guess I did."

"Well, I'm glad you had fun."

"Thank you."

"You were the last person I expected to see," Penny said.

"You could have been knocked over with a fender, right?"

She smiled dutifully.

"What are you doing out here, Matt? I mean, why you?"

The waitress appeared with their drinks. Matt handed her a credit card and waited for her to leave before replying.

"My father called me up and asked me to have a drink at the Rittenhouse. When I got there, Chief Coughlin was with him . . ."

"That's the man you call 'Uncle Denny'?"

"Right. My father told me it had been decided by your father and Amy that I was the obvious choice to come out here and bring you home. I told him that while the thought of being able to be of some small service to you naturally thrilled me, I would have to regretfully decline, as I had to work. Then Denny Coughlin told me your father had talked to the mayor, and that was no problem. So here I am."

"You're still a . . ." Penny asked, stopped just in time from saying "cop," and finished, ". . . policeman?"

"No, Precious Penny," Matt said. "I am no longer a simple police officer. You have the great privilege of sitting here with one of Philadelphia's newest detectives. M. M. Payne, East Detective Division, at your service, ma'am. Just the facts, please."

She smiled dutifully again.

He smiled back and took a healthy swallow of his beer.

Matt Payne felt nowhere near as bright and clever as he was trying to appear. As a matter of fact, he could recall few times in his twenty-two years when he had been more uncomfortable.

"Then congratulations, Matt," Penny said.

"Thank you, ma'am," he said.

"But that doesn't answer why you? Out here, I mean?"

"I think the idea, I think *Amy's* idea, is that I am the best person to be with you as you begin your passage back into the real world. Amy, I hope you know, is calling the shots."

"She's been coming out here," Penny said.

"Yeah, I know," Payne said. "For whatever the hell it's worth, Penny, even if she is my sister, the word on the street is that she's a pretty good shrink."

That was the truth: Amelia Payne, M.D., *was* a highly regarded psychiatrist.

" 'The word on the street'?" Penny asked, gently mocking him.

"The consensus is," he corrected himself.

"I don't understand . . ." Penny said.

"Neither do I," he said, "but to coin a phrase, 'mine not to reason why, mine but to ride into the valley of the hustlers'. . ."

"Well, thanks anyway for coming out here, even if you didn't want to."

"Better me than Madame D, right?"

Matt Payne had been calling Grace (Mrs. H. Richard) Detweiler "Madame D" since he had been about twelve, primarily because he knew it greatly annoyed her.

Penny laughed.

"Oh, God, I don't think I could have handled my mother out here."

"You better prepare yourself, she'll be at the airport."

"And then what?"

"Jesus Christ, Penny, I don't know. Knowing her as I do, I suspect she'll be a pain in the ass."

"I've always liked your tact and charm, Matt," Penny said, and then, "God, that beer looks good."

"You want one?"

"I'm a *substance abuser,*" Penny said. "Don't tell me you haven't heard."

"You're a . . . you *were* a junkie, not a drunk."

"Alcohol is a drug," Penny said, as if reciting something she had memorized.

"So is aspirin," Matt said, and pushed his beer glass to her.

She met his eyes, and looked into them, and it was only with a good deal of effort that he could keep himself from looking away.

Then she picked up his glass and took a swallow.

"If you're going to start throwing things, or taking your clothes off, or whatever, try to give me a little notice, will you?" Matt said.

"Go to hell, Matt," Penny said, then almost immediately, first touching his hand, added, "I don't mean that. My God, I was so glad to see you this morning!"

"You were always a tough little girl, Penny," Matt said after a moment. "I think you're going to be all right."

Did I mean that, or did I just say it to be kind?

"I wish I was sure you meant that," Penny said.

He shrugged, and then looked around for the waitress and, when he had caught her eye, signaled for another beer.

"On the way to the airplane, we're going to have to get you some Sen-Sen or something. I don't want Amy or your mother to smell booze on your breath."

"Did they tell you to make sure I didn't get . . . anything I wasn't supposed to have?"

"They knew I wouldn't give you, or let you get, anything to suck up your nose."

"Detective Payne, right?"

He nodded.

"And what did they say about talking to me about . . . about what happened?"

"About what, what happened?"

"You know what I mean," she said, somewhat snappishly. "About *who* I mean. Anthony."

The waitress delivered the beer.

"Get me the bill, please," Matt said.

Penny waited until the waitress was out of earshot.

"I loved him, Matt."

"Jesus Christ!" he said disgustedly.

"I'd hoped you would understand. I guess I should have known better."

"DeZego, Anthony J., 'Tony the Zee,' " Matt recited bitterly, "truck driver, soldier in the Savarese family. I'm not even sure that he had made his bones. And incidentally, loving husband and beloved father of three."

"You're a sonofabitch!"

"For Christ's sake, Penny. He's dead. Let it go at that! Be glad, for Christ's sake!"

She glowered at him. He picked up his beer glass and as he drank from it met her eyes. After a moment she averted hers.

"I don't know what that means," she said softly, after a moment, "what you said about bones."

"In order to be a real mobster, you have to kill somebody," Matt said evenly. "They call it 'making your bones.' "

"In other words, you really think he was a gangster?"

"Mobster. There's a difference. He was a low-level mobster. We can't even find out why they hit him."

"And the people who did it? They're just going to get away with it?"

He looked at her for a long moment before deciding to answer her.

"The bodies of two people with reputations as hit men, almost certainly the people who hit your boyfriend, have turned up, one in Detroit and one in Chicago. The mob doesn't like it when innocent civilians, especially rich ones with powerful fathers like you, get hurt when they're hitting people."

"They're dead?" she asked.

He nodded.

"Good!"

Something between contempt and pity flashed in Matt's eyes. He stood up and looked around impatiently for the waitress. When she came to the table, he quickly signed the bill and reclaimed his credit card.

"I haven't finished my beer," Penny said coldly.

"You can have another on the airplane," he said, as coldly. "Let's go."

"Yes, sir, Mr. Detective, sir," Penny said. The waitress gave the both of them a confused look.

"You're in luck, Mr. Lanza," the not-too-bad-looking ticket clerk at the American counter said. "This is the last first-class seat on 6766."

"When you're on a roll, you're on a roll," Vito Joseph Lanza said with a smile. He pulled the wad of bills with the hundreds on the outside from the side pocket of his yellow slacks, flicked it open, and waited for her to tell him how much it was going to cost him to upgrade the return portion of his thirty-days-in-advance, tourist-class, round-trip ticket to first class. Then he counted out what she told him.

She made change, handed him the upgraded ticket and a boarding pass, and said, "Gate 28. They're probably just about to board. Thank you, Mr. Lanza."

"Yeah. Right. Sure," Vito said, stuffed the wad back in his trousers, and looked around for directions to Gate 28.

They were not yet boarding Flight 6766, non-stop service to Philadelphia, when he reached Gate 28. He leaned against the wall and lit a Pall Mall with the gold Dunhill lighter he'd bought in the casino gift shop just before going to bed about three that morning.

I probably could have picked up another couple of grand, if I'd have stuck around, he thought, *but the cards had started to run against me, and the one thing a good gambler has to know is when to quit. I certainly wouldn't have lost it all back, but I would probably have lost some, and quitting the way I did, I sort of have the Dunhill to show for quitting when that was the smart thing to do.*

He had taken only a couple of puffs when the ticket lady got on the loudspeaker and announced that they were preboarding. Women with small children, people who needed assistance in boarding, and of course passengers holding first-class tickets, who could board at their leisure.

Vito had to wait until a couple of old people on canes and what looked like a real Indian-Indian lady with three kids got on, but he was the first passenger in the first-class cabin. He checked his boarding pass, and then found his seat, on the aisle, on the left, right against the bulkhead that separated the first-class compartment from the tourist-class section.

As soon as he'd dug the seat belt out from where someone had stuffed it between the seats, a stewardess appeared, squatted in the aisle, and asked if she could get him something to drink before they took off.

They don't do that in the back of the airplane, he thought.

"Scotch, rocks," Vito said.

She smiled and went forward and returned almost immediately with his drink. Two things surprised him, first that it came in a plastic cup—*Jesus, for what they charge you to sit up here, you'd think they'd at least give you a real glass*—and that she didn't hold her hand out for any money. First he thought that they maybe ran a tab, but then he remembered that drinks in first class were on the house.

He examined his surroundings.

Class, he decided. *The seats are wide and comfortable, and real leather. This is the way to travel.*

He reached up and touched the back of the seat in front of him. That was real leather too.

He watched the other passengers get on. A lot of them looked, he noticed, at the only passenger in first class. He wondered for a moment if the ticket counter had been handing him a line about being lucky to get the only remaining seat in first class, but then some other first-class passengers got on and he decided that maybe she had been telling him the truth.

A good-looking blonde came into the cabin. *Nice ass,* Vito thought. For some reason she looked familiar. *Not a movie or TV star,* he decided. *She isn't good-looking enough for that. But I'm almost sure I seen her someplace.*

A Main Line type came on behind her, wearing a tweed jacket and a dress shirt with no tie. He had the boarding pass stubs in his hand. He glanced at them and stopped the blonde at the second row of seats from the front on the right, asked her did she want the aisle or the window. As she was getting in to sit in the window seat, the young guy looked around the cabin and smiled and nodded at Vito.

I remember him. He was at the craps table in the Flamingo when I was really hot. She wasn't there. I would have remembered her. Neither of them is wearing a wedding ring. She doesn't look like the kind of girl who would go off to Vegas with some guy she isn't married to for a couple of days. Maybe they're brother and sister.

He watched as the stewardess took their order, and then came back with a couple of cans of beer.

Jesus, if it's free booze up here, why drink beer?

Vito Lanza woke up when his ears hurt because they were coming down to land. His mouth was dry. He remembered—*what the hell, it was free*—that he'd had a lot to drink before they served dinner, and wine with the dinner, and he remembered that they had started to show the movie, and decided that he had fallen asleep during the movie.

Ten minutes later, the airplane landed. Vito was a little disappointed, for they had not flown over Philadelphia. The wind was blowing the wrong way or something, and all he could see out the window was Delaware and the oil refineries around Chester.

When they finally taxied up to the terminal building, Vito looked out the window and saw something that caught his attention. There was an Airport Unit Jeep and a limousine and what looked like an unmarked detective's car sitting down there, with the baggage carts and the other airport equipment.

What the hell is that all about?

"Ladies and gentlemen," the stewardess said over the public address system, "the captain has not yet turned off the FASTEN SEAT BELTS sign. Please remain in your seats until he does."

When the stewardess finally got the door open, a stocky, red-faced man wearing the uniform of a lieutenant of the Philadelphia Police Department stepped into the cabin and looked around. Vito knew who he was, Lieutenant Paul Ardell of the Airport Unit.

Ardell looked around the first-class cabin, did a double take when he saw Vito, and then looked down at the Main Line type in the second row. He said something to him— Vito couldn't hear what—and the Main Line type got up, backed up a little in the aisle to let the blonde with the nice ass out, and then they both followed Ardell out the door.

A moment later Vito saw the two of them walking toward the limousine. The door opened and a gray-haired guy got out and put his arms around the blonde and hugged her. Then she got into the limousine and the gray-haired guy shook the Main Line type's hand and then gave him a little hug.

The Main Line type then walked out of Vito's sight, under the airplane. Vito guessed, correctly, that he was going to intercept their luggage before it got from the airplane to the baggage conveyor, but he didn't get to see this. The FASTEN SEAT BELTS sign went off, and the stewardess gave her little speech about how happy American Airlines was that they had chosen American, and hoped they would do so again in the future, and people started getting off.

Joe Marchessi, and the new guy, the little Spic, was working the baggage claim room when Vito got there. Until somebody who transferred into the Airport Unit got to know his way around, they paired him with somebody with experience.

The Airport Unit was different. In other areas you could move a cop from one district to another, and just about put him right to work. But things were different at the Airport; it was a whole new ballgame. You had to learn what to look for, and what you looked for at the Airport was not what you looked for in an ordinary district.

Airport Unit cops were something special. For one thing, they were sworn in as officers both in Philadelphia and Tinnicum Township, which is in Delaware County. Some parts of the runways and their approaches are in Tinnicum Township, and they need the authority to operate there too.

The mob, over the years, had found the Tinnicum Marshes a good place to dump bodies. But aside from that, there was not much violent crime at the Airport.

Most of what you had to deal with was people stealing luggage, and they were most often professional thieves, not some kid who saw something he decided he could get away with stealing and stole it. Or keeping thieves, professional and amateur, from helping themselves to the air freight in "Cargo City."

Then there was smuggling, but that was handled by the feds, the Immigration and Naturalization Service, and the Customs Service, and sometimes the Bureau of Narcotics and Dangerous Drugs, and they usually made the arrest, and all the Airport Unit had to do was arrange for the prisoners to be transported.

All things considered, working the job in the Airport Unit was a pretty good job. Most of the time you got to stay inside the terminal, instead of either freezing your balls or getting a heat stroke outside.

Vito didn't think much of Marchessi: He had been on the job ten, twelve years, never even thought about taking the examination for corporal or detective and bettering himself, just wanted to put in his eight hours a day doing as little as possible, inside where it was warm, until he was old enough to retire and get a job as a rent-a-cop or something.

And Officer Marchessi did not, in Vito's opinion, treat him with the respect to which he was entitled as a corporal.

Vito walked up to them. "Whaddaya say, Marchessi?"

"How's it going, Lanza?"

It should have been "Corporal," but Vito let it ride.

"You're Martinez, right?"

"That's right, Corporal."

"Well, what do you think of Airport?"

"So far, I like it."

"It'll get worse, you can bet on that," Lanza said.

At least he calls me "Corporal." He's got the right attitude. I wonder what makes a little fuck like him want to be a cop?

"You were in Las Vegas, somebody said?" Marchessi asked. "Win any money?"

Vito pulled the wad of bills from his pocket and let Marchessi have a look.

"Can't complain. Can't complain a goddamn bit," Vito said. He saw the little Spic's eyes widen when he saw his roll.

Vito stuffed the money back in his pocket.

"What was going on just now on the ramp?" he asked.

From the looks on their faces, it was apparent to Corporal Vito Lanza that neither Officer Joseph Marchessi nor Officer Whatsisname Martinez had a fucking clue what he was talking about.

"Lieutenant Ardell come on the plane, American from Vegas, Gate 23, and took a good-looking blonde and some Main Line asshole off it," Lanza explained. "There was a limousine, one of our cars, and a detective car on the ramp."

"Oh," Marchessi said. "Yeah. That must have been the—Whatsername?—*Detweiler* girl. You remember, three, four months ago, when the mob hit Tony the Zee DeZego in the parking garage downtown?"

Vito remembered. DeZego had been taken down with a shotgun in a mob hit. The word on the street was that the doers were a couple of pros, from Chicago or someplace.

"So?"

"She got wounded or something when that happened. She's been in a hospital out west. They didn't want the press getting at her."

"Who's they?"

"Chief Lowenstein himself was down here a couple of hours ago," Marchessi said.

Vito knew who Chief Lowenstein was. Of all the chief inspectors, it was six one way and half a dozen the other if Lowenstein or Chief Inspector Dennis V. Coughlin had the most clout. It was unusual that Lowenstein would personally concern himself with seeing that some young woman was not bothered with the press.

"How come the special treatment?"

Marchessi said, more than a little sarcastically, "I guess if your father runs and maybe owns a big piece of Nesfoods, you get a little special treatment."

The bell rang, signaling that the luggage conveyor was about to start moving. Vito nodded at Marchessi and Martinez and walked to the conveyor and waited until his luggage appeared. He grabbed it, then went back into the terminal and walked through it to the Airport Unit office. He walked past without going in, and went to the parking area reserved for police officers either working the Airport Unit or visiting it, where he had left his car.

His car, a five-year-old Buick coupe, gave him a hard time starting. He had about given up on it when it finally gasped into life.

"Piece of shit!" he said aloud, and then had a pleasant thought: When he was finished work tomorrow, he would get rid of the sonofabitch. What he would like to have was a four-door Cadillac. He could probably make a good deal on one a year, eighteen months old. That would mean only twelve, fifteen thousand miles. A Caddy is just starting to get broken in with a lousy fifteen thousand miles on the clock, and you save a bunch of money.

Just because you did all right at the tables, Vito Lanza thought, *is no reason to throw money away on a new car. Most people can't tell the fucking difference between a new one and one a year, eighteen months old, anyway.*

Corporal Vito Lanza lived with his widowed mother, Magdelana, a tiny, intense, silver-haired woman of sixty-six, in the house in which he had grown up. She managed to remind him at least once a day that the row house in the 400 block of Ritner Street in South Philadelphia was in her name, and that he was living there, rent free, only out of the goodness of her heart.

When he finally found a place to park the goddamned Buick and walked up to the house, Magdelana Lanza was sitting on a folding aluminum and plastic webbing lawn chair on the sidewalk, in the company of Mrs. D'Angelo (two houses down toward South Broad Street) and Mrs. Marino (the house next door, toward the Delaware River). She had an aluminum colander in her lap, into which she was breaking green beans from a paper bag on the sidewalk beside her.

Vito nodded at Mrs. D'Angelo and Mrs. Marino and kissed his mother and said, "Hi, Ma" and handed her a two-pound box of Italian chocolates he had bought for her in the gift shop at the Flamingo in Vegas.

She nodded her head, but that was all the thanks he got.

"The toilet's running again," Mrs. Lanza said. "And there's rust in the hot water. You either got to fix it, or give me the money to call the plumber."

"I'll look at it," Vito said, and went into the house.

To the right was the living room, a long, dark room full of heavy furniture. A lithograph of Jesus Christ with his arms held out in front of him hung on the wall. Immediately in front of him was the narrow stairway to the second floor, and the equally narrow passageway that led to the kitchen in the rear of the house. Off the kitchen was the small dark dining room furnished with a table, six chairs, and a china cabinet.

He went up the stairs and a few steps down the corridor to his room. It was furnished with a single bed, a dresser, a small desk, and a floor lamp. There were pictures on the wall, showing Vito when he made his first communion at Our Lady of Mount Carmel Church, his graduation class at Mount Carmel Parochial School, Vito in his graduation gown and tasseled hat at Bishop John Newmann High School, and Vito in police uniform and his father the day he graduated from the Philadelphia Police Academy. There was also an eighteen-inch-long plaster representation of Jesus Christ on his crucifix.

Vito tossed his bags on the bed and went down the corridor to the bathroom. He voided his bladder, flushed the toilet, and waited to see if the toilet was indeed running.

It was, and he took the top off the water box and looked at the mechanism.

He didn't know what the fuck was wrong with it. He jiggled the works, and it stopped running. Then he ran the hot water in the sink, letting it fill the bowl. When he had, he couldn't even see the fucking drain in the bottom.

Sonofabitch!

The simplest thing to do would be to give his mother the money and tell her to call the plumber. But if he did that, there was certain to be some crack about his father, May He Rest In Peace, never having once in all the years they were married called a plumber.

After work tomorrow, Vito decided, *I'll go by Sears and get one of those goddamned repair kits. And see what they want to replace the fucking hot water heater.*

5.

"Mayor Carlucci's residence," Violetta Forchetti said, clearly but with a distinct accent when she picked up the telephone.

Violetta was thirty-five but looked older. She was slight of build, and somewhat sharp-faced. She had come to the United States from Naples seventeen years before to marry Salvatore Forchetti, who was twenty-five and had himself immigrated four years previously.

There had just been time for them to get married, and for Violetta to become with child when, crossing 9th and Mifflin Streets in South Philadelphia, they were both struck by a hit-and-run driver. Salvatore died instantly, and Violetta, who lost the child, had spent four months in St. Agnes's Hospital.

The then commander of the 6th District of the Philadelphia Police Department, Captain Jerry Carlucci, had taken the incident personally. He was himself of Neapolitan heritage, had known Sal, who had found work as a butcher, and been a guest at their wedding.

He had suggested to his wife that it might be a nice thing for her to go to St. Agnes's Hospital, see what the poor woman needed, and tell her she had his word that he would find the hit-and-run driver and see that he got what was coming to him.

Angeline Carlucci, who looked something like Violetta Forchetti, returned from the hospital and told him things were even worse than they looked. Violetta's parents were dead. The relatives who had arranged for her to come to America and marry Salvatore didn't want her back in Naples. She was penniless, a widow in a strange country.

When Violetta got out of the hospital, she moved in temporarily with Captain and Mrs. Carlucci, Jerry's idea being that when he caught the sonofabitch who had run them down, he would get enough money out of the bastard's insurance company to take care of Violetta, to make her look like a desirable wife to some other hardworking young man.

They never found the sonofabitch who had been driving the car. So when Jerry and Angeline, right after he'd made inspector, moved out of their house on South Rosewood Street in South Philly to the new house (actually it was thirty years old) on Crefield Street, Violetta went with them. She was good with the kids, the kids loved her, and Angeline needed a little help around the house.

A number of young, hardworking, respectable men were introduced to Violetta, but she just wasn't interested in any of them. She had found her place in life, working for the Carluccis, almost a member of the family.

When, as police commissioner, Jerry bought the big house in Chestnut Hill, and did it over, they turned three rooms in the attic into an apartment for Violetta, and she just about took over running the place, the things that Angeline no longer had the time to do herself.

It was said, and it was probably true, that Violetta would kill for the Carlucci family. It was true that Violetta did a better job of working the mayor's phone than any secretary he'd ever had in the Roundhouse or City Hall. When she handed him the phone, he knew that it was somebody he should talk to, not some nut or ding-a-ling.

"Matt Lowenstein, Violetta," the caller said. "How are you?"

"Just a minute, Chief," Violetta said. Chief Inspector Lowenstein was one of the very few people who got to talk to the mayor whenever he called, even in the middle of the night, when she had to put her robe on and go downstairs and wake him up.

The Honorable Jerry Carlucci, who was fifty-one years old and had an almost massive body and dark brown hair and eyes, was wearing an apron with CHIEF COOK painted on it when Violetta went into the kitchen of the Chestnut Hill mansion. He was in the act of examining with great interest one of two chicken halves he had been marinating for the past two hours, and which, when he had concluded they had been soaked enough, he planned to broil on a charcoal stove for himself and Angeline.

"Excellence, it is Chief Lowenstein," Violetta said.

Violetta had firm Italianate ideas about the social structure of the world. Jerry had never been able to get her to call him "Mister." It had at first been "Captain," which was obviously more prestigious than "Mister," then "Inspector," as he had worked his way up the hierarchy from staff inspector through inspector to chief inspector, and then "Excellence" from the time he'd been made a deputy commissioner.

He joked with Angeline that Violetta had run out of titles with "Excellence." There were only two more prestigious: "Your Majesty" and "Your Holiness," plus maybe "Your Grace," none of which, obviously, fit.

"Grazie," he said and went to the wall-mounted telephone by the door.

"How's my favorite Hebrew?" the mayor said.

He and Matt Lowenstein went way back. And he was fully aware that behind his back, Matt Lowenstein referred to him as "The Dago."

"The package from Las Vegas, Mr. Mayor, arrived safely at the airport, and two minutes ago passed through the gates in Chestnut Hill."

"No press?"

"Ardell—Paul Ardell, the Airport lieutenant?—"

"I know who he is."

"He said he didn't see any press. We probably attracted more attention taking her off the plane that way than if we'd just let Payne walk her through the terminal."

"Yeah, maybe. But this way, Matt, we did Detweiler a favor. And if Payne had walked her into the airport and there had been a dozen assholes from the TV and the newspapers . . ."

"You're right, of course."

"I'm always right, you should remember that."

"Yes, sir, Mr. Mayor."

"You free for lunch tomorrow?"

That's cant, Matt Lowenstein thought, having recently discovered that cant without the apostrophe meant that what was said was deceitful or hypocritical. *What Jerry Carlucci was really saying was, "If you had something you wanted to do for lunch tomorrow, forget it."*

"Yeah, sure."

"Probably the Union League at twelve-thirty. If there's a change, I'll have my driver call yours."

"Okay. Anything special?"

"Czernich called an hour or so ago," the mayor said. "The Secret Service told him what I already knew. The Vice President's going to honor Philadelphia with his presence."

Taddeus Czernich was police commissioner of the City of Philadelphia.

"It was in the papers."

"Maybe Czernich's driver was too busy to read the papers to him," the mayor said.

Jerry Carlucci was not saying unkind things behind Commissioner Czernich's back. He regularly got that sort of abuse in person. Matt Lowenstein had long ago decided that Carlucci not only really did not like Czernich, but held him in a great deal of contempt.

But Lowenstein had also long ago figured out that Czernich would probably be around as commissioner as long as Carlucci was the mayor. His loyalty to Carlucci was unquestioned, almost certainly because he very much liked being the police commissioner, and was very much aware that he served at Carlucci's pleasure.

"Half past twelve at the Union League," Lowenstein said. "I'll look forward to it."

Carlucci laughed.

"Don't bullshit a bullshitter, Matt," he said, and then added, "I just had an idea about Payne too."

"Excuse me?"

"I'm still thinking about it. I'll tell you tomorrow. You call—Whatsisname?—At the airport?"

"Paul Ardell?"

"Yeah, right. And tell him I said thanks for a job well done."

"Yes, sir."

"Good night, Matt. Thank you."

"Good night, Mr. Mayor."

Marion Claude Wheatley made pork chops, green beans, applesauce, and mashed potatoes for his supper. He liked to cook, was good at it, and when he made his own supper not only was it almost certainly going to be better than what he could get at one of the neighborhood restaurants, but it spared him both having to eat alone in public and from anything unpleasant that might happen on the way home from the restaurant.

Marion lived in the house in which he had grown up, in the 5000 block of Beaumont Street, just a few blocks off Baltimore Avenue and not far from the 49th Street Station. There was no point in pretending that the neighborhood was not deteriorating, but that didn't mean his house was deteriorating. He took a justifiable pride in knowing that he was just as conscientious about taking care of the house as his father had been.

If something needed painting, it got painted. If one of the faucets started dripping, he went to the workshop in the basement and got the proper tools and parts and fixed it.

About the only difference in the house between now and when Mom and Dad had been alive was the burglar bars and the burglar alarm system. Marion had had to have a contractor install the burglar bars, which were actually rather attractive, he thought, wrought iron. The burglar alarm system he had installed himself.

Marion had been taught about electrical circuits in the Army. He could almost certainly have avoided service by staying in college, but that would have been dishonorable. His father had served in World War II as a major with the 28th Division. He would have been shamed if his son had avoided service when his country called upon him.

He had taken Basic Training at Fort Dix, and then gone to Fort Riley for Officer Candidate School, and been commissioned into the Ordnance Corps. He had been trained as an ammunition supply officer, and then they had asked him if he would be interested in volunteering to become an Explosive Ordnance Disposal officer before he went to Vietnam. Marion hadn't even known what that meant when they asked him. They told him that EOD officers commanded small detachments of specialists who were charged with disposing of enemy and our own ordnance, which he understood to mean artillery and mortar shells, primarily, which had been fired but which for some reason hadn't exploded when they landed.

Sometimes shells and rockets could be disarmed, which meant that their detonating mechanisms were rendered inoperative, but sometimes that wasn't possible, and the explosive ordnance had to be "blown in place."

That meant that Explosive Ordnance Disposal people had to be trained in explosives, even though, as an officer, he wouldn't be expected to do the work himself, but instead would supervise the enlisted specialists.

That training had included quite a bit about electrical circuits, about which Marion had previously known absolutely nothing.

But what he had learned in the Army was more than enough for him to easily install the burglar alarm. Actually, it was plural. Alarms. There was one system that detected intrusion of the house on the first floor. If the alarm system was active, and any window, or outside door, on the first floor was opened, that set off one warning buzzer and a light on the control panel Marion had set up in what had been Mom and Dad's bedroom, but was now his.

The second system did the same thing for windows on the second floor and the two dormer windows in the attic. The third system protected the powder magazine only. The powder magazine was in the basement. It had originally been a larder where Mom had stored tomatoes mostly, but beans too, and chow-chow and things like that. Marion liked cooking, but he wasn't about to start canning things the way Mom had. It wasn't worth it.

The first time he had put something in the powder magazine, it was still a larder. That was when he had come from Vietnam on emergency leave when Mom had gotten so sick. At the time, he had wondered why it was so important that he knew he had to bring twenty-seven pounds of Czechoslovakian *plastique* and two dozen detonators home with him. Now, of course, he knew. It was all part of God's plan.

If God hadn't wanted him to bring the *plastique* home, then when the MPs at Tan Son

Nhut had randomly inspected outbound transient luggage, they would have selected his to inspect, and taken it away from him.

Marion hadn't then yet learned that when something odd or out of the ordinary happens, that he didn't have to worry about it, because it was invariably God's plan, and sooner or later, he would come to understand what the Lord had had in mind.

When he'd come home, Mom was already in University Hospital, but there was a colored lady taking care of the house, and he didn't want her hurting herself in any way, so he had put the *plastique* and the detonators in the larder and put a padlock on the door.

God had put off taking Mom into Heaven until they had had a chance to say good-bye, but not much more than that. He had been home seventy-two hours when the Lord called her home. And then he'd had those embarrassing weeping sessions whenever he thought of Mom or Dad or all the kids (he thought of them as kids, although they weren't much younger than he was) who'd fouled up, or been unlucky and been disintegrated, and they hadn't sent him back to Vietnam, but instead to Fort Eustis, Virginia, as an instructor in demolitions to young officers in the Engineer Basic Officer School.

They used mostly Composition C-4 at Eustis, which wasn't as good as the Czechoslovakian *plastique* the Viet Cong used, and sometimes just ordinary dynamite, and when he was setting up the demonstrations, he often slipped a little Composition C-4, or a stick of dynamite, or a length of primer cord, in his field jacket pocket and then brought it to Philadelphia and put it in the larder when he came home on weekends.

God, of course, had been making him do that, even though at the time he hadn't understood it.

One of the first things he did when he was released from active duty was to turn the larder into a proper powder magazine. This meant not only reinforcing the door with steel bars and installing some really good locks, but also installing a small exhaust fan for ventilation that turned on automatically for five minutes every hour, and, after a good deal of experimentation and consulting a humidity gauge, one 100-watt and one 40-watt bulb that burned all the time and kept the humidity down below twenty percent.

After Marion had his supper, he put the leftover green beans in the refrigerator, and the leftover mashed potatoes and the pork chop bones in the garbage, and then washed his dishes.

He then went to watch the CBS Evening News, to see if there would be anything on it about the Vice President coming to Philadelphia. There was not, but it had been in the newspapers, and therefore it was true.

He turned the television off, and then went down the stairs to the cellar. He took the keys to the powder magazine from their hiding place, on top of the second from the left rafter, and unlocked the door.

Everything seemed to be in good shape. The humidity gauge said there was twelve percent humidity and that it was fifty-nine degrees Fahrenheit in the magazines. That was well within the recommended parameters for humidity and temperature. He carefully locked the door again, put the keys back in their hiding place, and went back upstairs and turned the television back on.

Maybe he would be lucky, and there would be a decent program for him to watch. Everything these days seemed to be what they called T&A. For Teats and Ass. He thought that was a funny phrase. He knew the T&A offended God, but he thought that God would not be offended because he thought T&A was funny. He had learned words like that in the Army, and he wouldn't have been in the Army if God hadn't wanted him to be.

Vito Lanza went back to his room and emptied his pockets, tossing everything on the bed. Everything included the wad of bills he had left over after he'd had the Flamingo cashier give him a check for most of the money he'd won. There was almost five hundred dollars, two hundreds, two fifties, and a bunch of twenties and tens, plus some singles.

It sure looked good.

He unpacked his luggage, dividing the clothing into two piles, the underwear and socks and shirts his mother would wash, and the good shirts and trousers and jackets that would have to go to the dry cleaners.

The money looked good. He collected it all together and made a little wad of it, with the hundreds outside, and stuck them in his pocket.

The one goddamned thing I don't want to do is stick around here and have Ma give me that crap about not understanding why I have to go somewhere to relax.

He made a bundle of the clothing that had to go to the dry cleaners, and then picked up one of the jackets on the bed and put that on. He went to the upper right-hand drawer of the dresser and took out his Colt snubnose, and his badge and photo ID. From the drawer underneath, he took out a clip holster and six .38 Special cartridges. He loaded the Colt, put it in the holster, and then clipped the holster to his belt.

"You just got home," his mother said when he went out of the house, "where are you going?"

"To the dry cleaners, and then I got some stuff to do."

He decided to walk. He had found a place to park the goddamned Buick, and if he took it now, sure as Christ made little apples, there would be no parking place for blocks when he came back.

Vito dropped the clothes off at the Martinizer place on South Broad Street and then headed for Terry's Bar & Grill. Then he changed his mind. He wasn't in the mood for Terry's. It was a neighborhood joint, and Vito was still in a Flamingo Hotel & Casino mood.

He stepped off the curb and looked down South Broad in the direction of the navy yard until he could flag a cab. He got in and told the driver to take him to the Warwick Hotel. There was usually some gash in the nightclub in the Warwick, provided you had the money—and he did—to spring for expensive drinks.

The cab dropped him off at the Warwick right outside the bar. The hotel bar is on the right side of the building, off the lobby. The nightclub is a large area on the left side of the building, past the desk and the drugstore. Vito decided he would check out the hotel bar, maybe there would be something interesting in there, and then go to the nightclub.

He found a seat at the bar, ordered a Johnnie Walker on the rocks, and laid one of the fifty-dollar bills on the bar to pay for it.

Francesco Guttermo, who was seated at a small table near the door to the street in the Warwick Bar, leaned forward in his chair, then motioned for Ricco Baltazari to move his head closer, so that others would not hear what he had to say.

"The guy what just come in, at the end of the bar, he's got a gun," Mr. Guttermo, who was known as "Frankie the Gut," said. The appellation had been his since high school, when even then he had been portly with a large stomach.

Mr. Baltazari, who was listed in the records of the City of Philadelphia as the owner of Ristorante Alfredo, one of Center City's best Italian restaurants (northern Italian cuisine, no spaghetti with marinara sauce or crap like that), was expensively and rather tastefully dressed. He nodded his head to signify that he had understood what Frankie the Gut had said, and then relaxed back into his chair, taking the opportunity to let his hand graze across the knee of the young woman beside him.

She was a rather spectacularly bosomed blonde, whose name was Antoinette, but who preferred to be called "Tony." She slapped his hand, but didn't seem to be offended.

After a moment Mr. Baltazari turned his head just far enough to be able to look at the man with the gun, his backside and, in the bar's mirror, his face.

Then he leaned forward again toward Mr. Guttermo, who moved to meet him.

"He's probably a cop," Mr. Baltazari said.

"He paid for the drink with a fifty from a wad," Mr. Guttermo said.

"Maybe he hit his number," Mr. Baltazari said with a smile. "Maybe that's your fifty he's blowing."

It was generally believed by, among others, the Intelligence Unit and the Chief Inspector's Vice Squad of the Philadelphia Police Department that Mr. Guttermo, who had no other visible means of support, was engaged in the operation of a Numbers Book.

"You don't think he's interested in us?" Frankie the Gut asked.

"We're not doing anything wrong," Mr. Baltazari said. "Why should he be interested in us? You're a worrier, Frankie."

"You say so," Frankie the Gut replied.

"All we're doing is having a couple of drinks, right, Tony?" Mr. Baltazari said, touching her knee again.

"You said it, baby," Tony replied.

But Mr. Baltazari, who hadn't gotten where he was by being careless, nevertheless kept an eye on the guy with a gun who was probably a cop, and when the guy finished his drink and picked up his change and walked out of the bar, a slight frown of concern crossed his face.

"Go see where he went, Tony," he said.

"Huh?"

"You heard me. Go see where that guy went."

Tony got up and walked out of the bar into the hotel lobby.

"What are you thinking, Ricco?" Frankie the Gut asked. "That cops don't buy drinks with fifties?"

"Some cops don't," Mr. Baltazari said.

Tony came back and sat down and turned to face Mr. Baltazari.

"He went into The Palms," she said.

Mr. Baltazari was silent for a long moment. It was evident that he was thinking.

"I would like to know more about him," he said, finally.

"You think he was interested in us?" Frankie the Gut said.

"I said I would like to know more about him," Mr. Baltazari said.

"How are you going to do that, baby?" Tony asked.

"You're going to do it for me," Mr. Baltazari said.

"What do you mean?" Tony asked suspiciously.

Mr. Baltazari reached in his pocket and took out a wad of crisp bills. He found a ten, and handed it to Tony.

"I want you to go in there, I think it's five bucks to get in, find him, and be friendly," he said.

"Aaaah, Ricco," Tony protested.

"When you are friendly with people, they tell you things," Mr. Baltazari observed. "Be friendly, Tony. We'll wait for you."

"Do I really have to?"

"Do it, Tony," Mr. Baltazari said.

Tony was gone almost half an hour.

"Let's get out of here," she said. "I told him I had to go to the ladies'."

"What did you find out?" Mr. Baltazari asked.

"Can't we leave? What if he comes looking for me?"

"What did you find out?"

"He's a cop. He's a corporal. He just made a killing in Vegas."

"Did he say where he worked?"

"At the airport."

"Did he say how much of a killing?"

"Enough to buy a Caddy. He said he's going out and buy a Cadillac tomorrow."

Mr. Baltazari thought that over, long enough for Tony to find the courage to repeat her request that they leave before the cop came looking for her.

"No," Mr. Baltazari said. "No. What I want you to do, Tony, is go back in there and give him this."

He took a finely bound leather notebook from the monogrammed pocket of his white-on-white shirt, wrote something on it, tore the page out, and handed it to her.

"What's this?"

"Joe Fierello is your uncle. He's going to give your friend a deal on a Cadillac."

"You're kidding me, right?"

"No, I'm not. You go back in there and be nice to him, and tell him you think your uncle Joe will give him a deal on a Caddy."

"You mean *stay* with him?"

"I gotta go home now anyway, my wife's been on my ass."

"Jesus, Ricco!" Tony protested.

Mr. Baltazari took out his wad of bills again, found a fifty, and handed it to Tony.

"Buy yourself an ice-cream cone or something," he said.

Tony looked indecisive for a moment, then took the bill and folded it and stuffed it into her brassiere.

"I thought we were going to my place," she said.

"I'll make it up to you, baby," Mr. Baltazari said.

Detective Payne had fallen asleep in his armchair watching Fred Astaire and Ginger Rogers gracefully swooping around what was supposed to be the terrace of a New York City penthouse on WCAU-TV's Million Dollar Movie.

He woke up with a dry mouth, a sore neck, a left leg that had apparently been asleep so long it was nearly gangrenous, and a growling hunger in his stomach. He looked at the clock on the fireplace mantel. It was quarter to eight. That meant it was probably the worst time of the day to seek sustenance in his neighborhood. The hole-in-the-wall greasy spoons that catered to the office breakfast and lunch crowd had closed for the day.

That left the real restaurants, including the one in the Rittenhouse Club, which was the closest. That attracted his interest for a moment, as they did a very nice London broil, but then his interest waned as he realized he would have to put on a jacket and tie, then stand in line to be seated, and then eat alone.

The jacket-and-tie and eating-alone considerations also ruled out the other nice restaurants in the vicinity. Without much hope, he checked his cupboard. It was, as he was afraid it would be, nearly bare and, in the case of two eggs, three remaining slices of bread, and a carton of milk, more than likely dangerous. He nearly gagged disposing of the milk, eggs, and green bread down the Disposall.

He had a sudden, literally mouthwatering image of a large glass of cold milk to wash down a western omelette. And there was no question that his mother would be delighted to prepare such an omelette for him.

He went into his bedroom, pulled a baggy sweater over his head, and headed for the door, stopping only long enough to take his pistol, a Smith & Wesson .38 Special caliber "Chief's Special," and the leather folder that held his badge and photo ID from the mantelpiece. The holster had a clip, which allowed him to carry the weapon inside his waistband. If he remembered not to take his sweater off, his mother wouldn't even see the pistol.

He went down the narrow stairway to the third floor of the building, then rode the elevator to the basement, and after a moment's hesitation made the mature decision to drive the Bug to Wallingford. It would have been much nicer to drive the Porsche but the Bug had been sitting for two days, and unless it was driven, the battery would likely be dead in the morning when he had to drive it to work.

As he drove out Baltimore Avenue, which he always thought of as The Chester Pike, he made another mature decision. He drove past an Acme Supermarket, noticed idly that the parking lot was nearly empty, and then did a quick U-turn and went back.

He could make a quick stop, no more than five minutes, pick up a half gallon of milk, a dozen eggs, a loaf of bread, and a package of Taylor Ham, maybe even some orange juice, and be prepared to make his own breakfast in the morning. He would be, as he had learned in the Boy Scouts to be, prepared.

The store was, as he had cleverly deduced from the near-empty parking lot, nearly deserted. There were probably no more than twenty people in the place.

He was halfway down the far-side aisle, bread and Taylor Ham already in the shopping cart, moving toward the eggs-and-milk section, when he ran into Mrs. Glover.

"Hi!" he said cheerfully.

It was obvious from the hesitant smile on her face that Mrs. Glover was having trouble placing him. That was certainly understandable. While Mrs. Glover, who presided over the Special Collections desk at the U of P library, had attracted the rapt attention of just about every heterosexual male student because of her habitual costume of white translucent blouse and skirt, it did not logically follow that she would remember any particular one of her hundreds of admirers.

"Matt Payne. Pre-Constitutional Law," he said. He had occasion to partake of Mrs. Glover's professional services frequently when he was writing a term paper on what had happened, and who had been responsible for it, when the fledgling united colonies had been adapting British common law to American use.

"Oh, yes, of course," she said, and he thought her smile reflected not only relief that he was not putting the make on her, but genuine pleasure at seeing him. "How are you, Matt?"

"Very well, thank you," Matt said. "It's nice to see you, Mrs. Glover."

"Nice to see you too," she said, and pushed her cart past him.

She was wearing a sweater over her blouse, Matt Payne noticed, but the blouse was still translucent and her breastworks were as spectacular as he remembered them.

"This is the police," an electronically amplified voice announced. "Drop your weapons and put your hands on your head!"

"Oh, shit!" Matt Payne said.

There was the sound of firearms. First a couple of loud pops, and then the deep booming of a shotgun. There was a moment's silence, and then the sound of breaking glass.

Matt turned and ran and caught up with Mrs. Glover, and put his hands on her shoulders.

"Get on the floor!" he ordered.

She looked at him with terror in her eyes, and let him push her first to her knees and then flat on her stomach.

As he pushed his sweater aside to get at his pistol, and then fumbled to find his badge, he saw her looking at him with shock in her eyes.

There was the sound of another handgun firing twice.

"Motherfucker!" a male voice shouted angrily, and there was another double booming of a shotgun being fired twice. A moment later there was the sound of a car crash.

"Everybody all right?" a voice of authority demanded loudly.

A moment later the same voice, now electronically amplified, went on: "This is the police. It's all over. There is no danger. Please stay right where you are until a police officer tells you what to do."

Matt got to his feet, and holding his badge in front of him walked toward the front of the store.

As he reached the end of the aisle, he called out, "Three six nine, three six nine," and held the badge out as he carefully stepped into the checkout area.

"Who the hell are you?" a lieutenant holding a shotgun in one hand and a portable loudspeaker in the other demanded. He and three other cops in sight were wearing the peculiar uniform, including bulletproof vests, Stakeout wore on the job.

"Payne, East Detectives, sir."

"What are you doing in here?"

"I came to get milk and eggs," Matt said.

"You see what happened?"

"I didn't see anything," Matt said truthfully.

There were flashing lights, and the sound of dying sirens, and Matt looked through the shattered plate-glass window and saw the first of a line of police vehicles pull up to the door.

The lieutenant made a vague gesture toward the last checkout counter. Matt saw a pair of feet extending into the aisle, and a puddle of blood.

"One there and another outside, in his car," the lieutenant said. "They had their chance to drop their guns and surrender, but they probably thought it would be like the movies. Jesus Christ!"

There was more contempt for the critters he had dropped than compassion, Matt thought.

That's the way it is. Not like the movies, either, where the cops are paralyzed with regret for having had to drop somebody. The bad dreams I have had about my shootings have been about those assholes getting me, not the other way around.

Matt looked through the hole where the plate-glass window had been. Three uniforms were in the act of pulling a man from his car. The car-crashing noise he had heard had apparently come when the doer, trying to flee, had crashed into one of the cars parked in the lot.

Matt had twice gone through the interviews conducted by the Homicide shooting team of officers involved in a fatal shooting. He blurted what popped into his mind.

"You'll spend the next six hours in Homicide."

The lieutenant's eyebrows rose.

"You been through this?" he asked.

"It goes on for goddamned ever," Matt said, and then added, "Christ, I'll be there all night too, and I didn't even see what happened."

The lieutenant met his eyes.

"You want to go, get out of here, now."

Matt had a quick mental image of Mrs. Glover, who looked to be on the edge of hysteria, getting carried down to the Homicide Bureau, in the Roundhouse, in a district wagon and then sitting around until one of the Homicide detectives had time to take her statement.

"I'm with somebody," Matt said. "A woman."

"Get out of here now, then," the lieutenant repeated. "Homicide, or the brass, will be coming in on this any minute."

"I owe you one," Matt said, and trotted back to where he had left Mrs. Glover lying on the floor.

She was still lying on the floor.

"It's all right," he said, and reached down and helped her to her feet. "Did you see anything? Anything at all?"

She shook her head, no.

"I told them you're with me," he said.

There was confusion in her eyes.

"We can go. Otherwise, you'll be taken to the Roundhouse and be there for hours."

"Are you a policeman or something?" she asked incredulously.

"I'm a detective," he said. "You all right? Can you walk?"

"I'm all right," she said. "What do we do about the groceries?"

"Leave them," he said, and took Mrs. Glover's arm and led her out the front of the store.

"Oh, my God!" Mrs. Glover said. "That's my car!"

And then she was clinging to him, whimpering. She had looked at the ground beside her car, where the second robber Stakeout had taken down was on his back in the middle of a spreading pool of blood. He had taken a load, Matt decided, maybe two loads, of double aught buckshot.

Well, that blows any chance we had to get away from here. Shit!

6.

"My car's over there," Matt said, and started to lead Mrs. Glover toward it.

Mrs. Glover seemed to want the reassurance of his arm around her, and stayed close to him. He was very much aware of her body against his.

He put her in the car.

"Listen," he said. "We can't leave now. Let me talk to the lieutenant, and I'll come back."

The lieutenant told him there was nothing he could do now but wait for Homicide and the brass to show up.

That means instead of Mother's western omelette, I will have to find sustenance in a cup of coffee in a paper cup, and if I'm lucky, a stale doughnut.

The first Homicide detective to arrive at the crime scene was Detective Joe D'Amata. Matt knew him. He waited until D'Amata had taken a quick look around inside, and then gone to the body in the parking lot, and then walked up to him.

"Hey, Joe."

"Matthew, my boy," D'Amata said, smiling. "Don't tell me you did this."

"I came in to get a dozen eggs."

"You see what happened?"

"No. But I know who owns this car, the one he ran into."

"Oh?"

"She's a librarian at U of P. Nice lady. She saw the body and she's nearly hysterical."

"I would be too," D'Amata said. "Do you think she saw anything?"

"She saw what I saw, zilch. We were in the back of the store."

"We'll need your statements," D'Amata said. "But I don't see why you couldn't take her to the Roundhouse before the mob gets there. I'll let them know you're coming."

"I owe you one, Joe."

"Yeah. Don't forget."

Matt went back to his Bug and got behind the wheel and turned to Mrs. Glover.

"What happens now?" she asked.

"I know one of the Homicide detectives. He's fixed it so that we can go to the Roundhouse now, before the crowd gets there, and make our statements."

"But I didn't see anything."

"That's your statement. And they'll want to know about your car."

"What am I going to do about my car?"

"They'll want to take pictures of it. Maybe, if we're lucky, we can get them to turn it loose when they're finished. We can ask."

"What would have happened if you weren't here?"

"They'd have taken you, when they got around to it, to the Roundhouse in a car."

"What's this 'Roundhouse' you keep talking about?"

"The Police Administration Building. At 8th and Race. That's where Homicide is." He paused. "You all right, Mrs. Glover?"

"I'll be all right," she said.

He started the Bug and drove downtown to the Roundhouse.

It was quarter to twelve when they left. Captain Quaire, the commanding officer of Homicide, had come in, and he authorized the release of Mrs. Glover's car to her when the Mobile Crime Lab was through with it.

When they got back to the Acme parking lot, they were told that it would be at least an hour before the car could be released.

"I'm sorry," Matt told Mrs. Glover. "But that's the way it is. I'll take you home and then bring you back in an hour."

"You're sweet, Matt. I appreciate all this," Mrs. Glover said, and touched his arm.

He started the car and asked her where she lived. She gave him an address in Upper Darby Township.

"It's not far," Mrs. Glover said. "But I appreciate the offer to take me back there."

"I'll take your husband back," Matt said. "What you should do is make yourself a stiff drink, and then go to bed, and forget this whole thing."

He saw they had crossed into Upper Darby Township. "You're going to have to start giving me directions."

It was a fairly nice ranch house in a subdivision, the sort of house he would have expected people like the Glovers to have. He remembered hearing that Mr. Glover, probably *Doctor* Glover, was some sort of professor. There was a light on in the carport, and there were lights in the living room, behind the curtain that covered the picture window.

"I don't see a car," Matt said. "It looks like Dr. Glover's not home."

"Not here, he's not," Mrs. Glover said, more than a little bitterly.

Oh!

"Could you use one of those stiff drinks you recommended for me?" Mrs. Glover asked. "Or are you on duty?"

"Yes, ma'am."

"Well, you're going to have to watch while I have one, I'm afraid. I'm shaking like a leaf."

"I meant that 'no drinking on duty' business is only in the movies, or on TV cop shows. And anyway I'm not. On duty, I mean."

She got out of the car and went to the door that opened off the carport into the kitchen. He followed her inside. She snapped on fluorescent lights and pulled open a cabinet over the sink.

"I'm not much of a drinker," she said, taking out four bottles. "But this is an occasion, isn't it?" She turned to him. "What do you recommend?"

There was a bottle of gin, a bottle of blended whiskey, a bottle of Southern Comfort, and, surprisingly, an unopened bottle of Martel cognac.

"The cognac, if that would be all right," Matt said.

"I've even got the glasses for it," she said. "They're probably a little dusty."

She went farther into the house and returned with two snifters that were, in fact, dusty. She wiped them with a paper towel and set them on the kitchen counter.

"Do you need a corkscrew?"

"No, I don't think so," he said, and twisted the metal foil off the neck. The bottle was closed with a cork, but the kind that can be pulled loose.

He poured cognac in both glasses, and handed her one.

"You don't mix it with anything?"

"My father says it's a sin to do that," Matt said. "But my mother drinks hers with soda water."

"I've got ginger ale. Would that be all right?"

"That would be a sin," he said.

"I think I'll be a sinner," she said, and went into the refrigerator and took out a bottle of ginger ale, and poured some into her glass. Then she held the glass out to touch his.

"I'm glad you were there, Matt," she said. "This whole experience has been horrible. I would have hated to have had to go through it alone."

He smiled and took a sip from his glass. She took a tentative sip of hers. She smiled. "That's not so bad."

He took another swallow and felt the warmth course through his body.

"Funny," Mrs. Glover said, "you don't look like a detective."

"Probably because I've only been a detective a couple of weeks."

"Or a policeman," she said. "I thought you were one of those who was going in the Marines?"

He was surprised that she had paid enough attention to him to have known that.

"I flunked the physical," he said.

"Oh," she said. "And do you like being a policeman?"

"Most of the time," he said. "Not tonight."

She hugged herself, which caused the material of her blouse to draw taut over her bosom.

"That warms you, doesn't it?" she said.

"Yes, it does."

"My husband's father gave him that when he was promoted."

"Oh."

"I was tempted to throw it out when he left, but I decided that would be a waste, that sooner or later, I'd need it. For an occasion. I didn't have something like this in mind."

"Well, it's over," Matt said. "Put it out of your mind."

"I'm not letting you get on with whatever you were about to do when this happened."

"Don't worry about it."

"Where do you live?"

"In Center City. I was driving past the Acme, saw the parking lot was pretty empty, and thought it would be a good time to get a dozen eggs and a loaf of bread."

"Me too," she said, and upended her brandy snifter and drained it. "I went there to get something for my supper. Have you eaten?"

He shook his head, no.

"The least I can do is feed you," she said. "There should be something in the freezer."

She found two Swanson Frozen Turkey Breast Dinners and put them in the oven.

"It'll take thirty-five minutes," she said. "Is that going to make you terribly late where you were going?"

"I just won't go," he said. "It wasn't important."

She made herself another cognac and ginger ale and extended the bottle to him.

"Well, we'll eat the leathery turkey, and then you can drive me back there."

"Fine."

"I'm now going to do something else I rarely do," Mrs. Glover said. "I'm going to smoke a cigarette."

"I'm sorry, I don't have any."

"I've got some somewhere," she said, and went farther into the house again. She immediately returned. "I'm sorry. Why are we in the kitchen? Come on in the living room."

An hour later, they drove back to the Acme Supermarket. Her car was gone, and so had just about everybody else. There was a uniformed cop by the shattered plate-glass window.

Matt showed him his badge.

"Where's the car, the victim's car the doer ran into?"

The uniformed cop shrugged. "I guess they took it to an impound area. Maybe at the district."

Matt returned to the Bug and told Mrs. Glover that the authority they had to reclaim their car was useless. It was somewhat in limbo, and there was nothing that could be done until the morning.

"What do I do now?" Mrs. Glover asked. "Can you take me home again?"

"Of course."

She wanted an explanation of where in "limbo" her car actually was, so it seemed perfectly natural that he follow her into the house again and have another cognac.

"I was thinking," Mrs. Glover said an hour later, dipping her index finger into her cognac snifter to stir the ginger ale in the cognac, "I mean it's just an idea. But if you stayed here, there's a guest room, you could drive me down to the Roundhouse in the morning."

She is not making a pass at me. She is at least thirty years old, maybe thirty-five, and . . .

"And the truth of the matter seems to be that we've both had more of this cognac than is good for us," she added.

"Well, if it wouldn't inconvenience you."

"Don't be silly," she said. "I'll just get sheets and make up the spare bed."

"I'm sorry I don't have any pajamas to offer you," Mrs. Glover said at the door to the spare bedroom.

"I don't wear them anyway. I'll be all right."

"If you need anything, just ask," she said, and gave him her hand. "And thank you for everything."

"I didn't do anything," he said.

She smiled at him and pulled the door closed.

He looked around the room, and then went and sat on the bed and took his clothing off. He rummaged in the bedside table and came up with a year-old copy of *Scientific American.* He propped the pillows up and flipped through it.

He could hear the sound of a shower running, and had an interesting mental image of Mrs. Glover at her ablutions.

"Shit," he said aloud, turned the light off, and rearranged the pillow.

He had a profound thought: *No good deed goes unpunished.*

The sound of the shower stopped after a couple of minutes. He had an interesting mental image of Mrs. Glover toweling her bosom.

A moment later he heard the bedroom door open.

"Matt, are you asleep?"

"No."

He sensed rather than heard her approach the bed. When she sat on it, he could smell soap and perfume.

Maybe perfumed soap?

She found his face with her hand.

"I've been separated from my husband for eleven months," Mrs. Glover said. "I haven't been near a man in all that time. Not until now."

He reached up and touched her hand. She caught his hand, locked fingers with him, and then moved his hand to the opening of her robe, directed it inside, and then let go.

His fingers found her breast and her nipple, which was erect. She put her hand to the back of his head and pulled his face to her breast.

When he tried to pull her down onto the bed, she resisted, then stood up.

"Not here," Mrs. Glover said throatily. "In my bed."

At quarter to seven the next morning, Detective Matt Payne drove into the garage beneath the Delaware Valley Cancer Society Building, and turned to look at Mrs. Glover, whose Christian name, he had learned two hours before, was Evelyn.

"What is this?" she asked.

"This is where I live. Where I have to change clothes."

"The signs says this is the Cancer Society."

"There's an attic apartment," he said.

"Oh."

"Come on up. It won't take me a minute."

"I'm not so sure that's a good idea."

"You mean, you don't want to see my etchings?"

"What happened last night was obviously insane. Maybe we better leave it at that."

"I liked what happened last night."

"You should be running around with girls your own age, not having an affair with someone my age. And vice versa."

"I don't seem to have much in common with girls my own age," Matt said. "And I don't think that was the first time in the recorded history of mankind that . . ."

"A woman my age took a man your age into her bed?"

"Right."

"Go change your clothes, Matt. I'll wait here."

"You don't want to do that."

"Yes, I do."

"Whatever you say," Matt said, and got out of the Bug and went to the elevator.

When he reached the top step of the narrow stairway leading into his apartment, he saw the red light blinking on his telephone answering machine. He pulled his sweater over his head, tossed it onto the couch, went to the answering machine, and pushed the PLAY MESSAGES switch.

"Matt, I know you're there, pick up the damned telephone."

That was Amelia Payne, M.D. He wondered what the hell she wanted, and then realized she probably wanted a report on Penny Detweiler's trip home.

Then Brewster Cortland Payne II's voice: "Matt. Amy insisted I try to get you to call her. She's positive you're there and just not picking up. She wants to talk to you about Penny. Will you call her, please? Whenever you get home?"

The next voice was Charley McFadden's: "Matt, Charley. Give me a call as soon as you can. I gotta talk to you about something. Oh. How was Las Vegas?"

Something's wrong. I wonder what? Well, it'll have to wait.

"Matt, this is Penny. I just wanted to say 'thank you' for coming out there to get me. I forgot to thank you at the airport. When you have a minute, call me, and I'll buy you an ice-cream cone or lunch or something. Ciao."

Oh, Christ, I don't want to get sucked into that!

"Matt, this is Joe D'Amata. They took your lady friend's car to the Plymouth place in Upper Darby. I called her house, and there was no answer. If we'd left it at the scene, there would be nothing left but the ignition switch."

Jesus, why didn't I think about just calling Joe from her house? Because you were thinking with your dick again, Matthew!

"Payne, this is Al Sutton. If you were thinking of coming to work this morning, don't. They want you in Chief Lowenstein's office at half past one."

Now, what the hell is that about? Something to do with last night?

He pushed the REWIND button and went into his bedroom and laid out fresh clothes on his bed. He picked a light brown suit, since he was possibly going to see Chief Lowenstein and did not want to look like Joe College. Then he took his clothing off.

The doorbell rang.

He searched for and found his bathrobe and went to the intercom.

"Yeah?"

"You were right, I don't want to wait down there," Mrs. Glover said. "May I come up?"

He pushed the door release button and heard it open. She came up the stairs.

"That wasn't exactly true," she said. "Curiosity got the best of me."

"They took your car to the Plymouth place in Upper Darby," Matt said. "There was a message on the machine. Let me grab a shower, and I'll take you out there."

"They don't open until nine-thirty," she said.

"Well, we'll just have to wait."

He smiled uneasily at her, and then walked back in the apartment toward his bedroom.

"Matt . . ."

He turned.

"Was that true, what you said, about you don't have much in common with girls your own age?"

"Yes, it was."

"You're really a nice guy. Be patient. Someone will come along."

"I hope so," he said, and turned again and went and had his shower.

When he came out, he sensed movement in his kitchen. He cracked the door open. Mrs. Glover was leaning against the refrigerator. She had a cheese glass in one hand, and a bottle of his cognac in the other.

"I hope you don't mind."

"Of course not."

"You want one?"

"No. I don't want to smell of booze when I go to work."

"When do you have to be at work? Is taking me back to Upper Darby going to make you late?"

"No. I've got until half past one."

She looked at him, and then away, and then drained the cheese glass.

"What I said before," she said, "was what my father told me when Ken and I broke up. That I was a nice girl, that I should be patient, that someone would come along."

What the hell is she leading up to? Am I the someone?

"I'm sure he's right."

"Now, you and I are obviously not right for reach other . . ."

Damn!

". . . but what I've been thinking, very possibly because I've had more to drink in the last twelve hours than I've had in the last six months, is that, until someone comes along for you, and someone comes along for me . . ."

"The sky wouldn't fall? There will not be a bolt of lightning to punish the sinners?"

She raised her head and met his eyes.

"What do you think?"

"I think I know how we can kill the time until the Plymouth place opens."

"I'll bet you do," she said, and set the cheese glass and the bottle of cognac on the sink and then started to unbutton her blouse.

As Matt Payne was climbing the stairs to his apartment at quarter to seven, across town, in Chestnut Hill, Peter Wohl stepped out of the shower in his apartment and started to towel himself dry.

The chimes activated by his doorbell button went off. They played "Be It Ever So Humble, There's No Place Like Home." One of what Wohl thought of as the "xylophone bars" was out of whack, so the musical rendition was discordant. He had no idea how to fix it, and privately, he hated chimes generally and "Be It Ever So Humble" specifically, but there was nothing he could do about the chimes. They had been a gift from his mother, and installed by his father.

He said a word that he would not have liked to have his mother hear, wrapped the towel around his middle, and left the bathroom. He went through the bedroom, and then through his living room, the most prominent furnishings of which were a white leather couch, a plate-glass coffee table, a massive, Victorian mahogany service bar, and a very large oil painting of a Rubenesque naked lady resting on her side, one arm cocked coyly behind her head.

The ultrachic white leather couch and plate-glass coffee table were the sole remnants of a romantic involvement Peter Wohl had once had with an interior decorator, now a young suburban matron married to a lawyer. The bar and the painting of the naked lady he had acquired at an auction of the furnishings of a Center City's men's club that had gone belly up.

He unlatched the door and pulled it open. A very neat, very wholesome-looking young man in a blue suit stood on the landing.

"Good morning, Inspector," the young man said. His name was Paul T. (for Thomas) O'Mara, and he was a police officer of the Philadelphia Police Department. Specifically, he was Wohl's new administrative assistant.

Telling him, Peter Wohl thought, *that when I say between seven and seven-fifteen, I don't mean quarter to seven, would be like kicking a Labrador puppy who has just retrieved his first tennis ball.*

"Good morning, Paul," Wohl said. "Come on in. There's coffee in the kitchen."

"Thank you, sir."

Officer O'Mara was a recent addition to Peter Wohl's staff. Like Peter Wohl, he was from a police family. His father was a captain, who commanded the 17th District. His brother was a sergeant in Civil Affairs. His grandfather, like Peter Wohl's father and grandfather, had retired from the Philadelphia Police Department.

More important, his father was a friend of both Chief Inspector Dennis V. Coughlin and Chief Inspector (Retired) Augustus Wohl. When Officer O'Mara, who had five years on the job in the Traffic Division, had failed, for the second time, to pass the examination for corporal, both Chief Coughlin and Chief Wohl had had a private word with Inspector Wohl.

They had pointed out to him that just because someone has a little trouble with promotion examinations doesn't mean he's not a good cop, with potential. It just means that he has trouble passing examinations.

Not like you, Peter, the inference had been. *You're not really all that smart, you're just good at taking examinations.*

One or the other or both of them had suggested that what Officer O'Mara needed was a little broader experience than he was getting in the Traffic Division, such as he might get if it could be arranged to have him assigned to Special Operations as your administrative assistant.

"Now that you've lost Young Payne . . ." his father had said.

"Now that Matt's gone to East Detectives . . ." Chief Coughlin had said.

In chorus: "You're going to need someone to replace him. And you know what a good guy, and a good cop, his father is."

And so Officer O'Mara had taken off his uniform, with the distinctive white Traffic Division brimmed cap, and donned a trio of suits Inspector Wohl somewhat unkindly suspected were left over from his high school graduation and/or obtained from the Final Clearance rack at Sears Roebuck and come to work for Special Operations.

Peter Wohl was sitting on his bed, pulling his socks on, when Officer O'Mara walked in with a cup of coffee.

"I couldn't find any cream, Inspector, but I put one spoon of sugar in there. Is that okay?"

Inspector Wohl decided that telling Officer O'Mara that he always took his coffee black would be both unkind and fruitless: He had told him the same thing ten or fifteen times in the office.

"Thank you," he said.

"Stakeout got two critters at the Acme on Baltimore Avenue last night. It was on TV," Officer O'Mara said.

" 'Got two critters'?"

"Blew them away," O'Mara said, admiration in his voice.

"Any police or civilians get hurt?"

"They didn't say anything on TV."

Wohl noticed that Officer O'Mara did not have any coffee.

"Aren't you having any coffee, Paul?"

"I thought you just told me to get you some," O'Mara said.

"Help yourself, Paul. Have you had breakfast?"

"I had a doughnut."

"Well, we're going to the Roundhouse. We can get some breakfast on the way."

"Yes, sir," O'Mara said, and walked out of the bedroom.

Peter Wohl walked to his closet and after a moment's hesitation selected a gray flannel suit. He added to it a light blue button-down-collar shirt and a regimentally striped tie.

Clothes make the man, he thought somewhat cynically. *First impressions are important. Particularly when one is summoned to meet with the commissioner, and one doesn't have a clue what the sonofabitch wants.*

There was no parking space in the parking lot behind the Police Administration Building reserved for the commanding officer, Special Operations, as there were for the chief inspectors of Patrol Bureau (North), Patrol Bureau (South), Command Inspections Bureau, Administration, Internal Affairs, Detective Bureau, and even the Community Relations Bureau.

Neither could Paul O'Mara park Peter Wohl's official nearly new Ford sedan in spots reserved for CHIEF INSPECTORS AND INSPECTORS ONLY, because Wohl was only a staff inspector, one rank below inspector. The senior brass of the Police Department were jealous of the prerogatives of their ranks and titles and would have been offended to see a lowly staff inspector taking privileges that were not rightly his.

Wohl suspected that if a poll were taken, anonymously, of the deputy commissioners, chief inspectors, and inspectors, the consensus would be that his appointment as commanding officer, Special Operations Division, reporting directly to the deputy commissioner, Operations, had been a major mistake, acting to the detriment of overall department efficiency, not to mention what harm it had done to the morale of officers senior to Staff Inspector Wohl, who had naturally felt themselves to be in line for the job.

If, however, he also suspected, asked to identify themselves before replying to the same question, to a man they would say that it was a splendid idea, and that there was no better man in the Department for the job.

They all knew that the Hon. Jerry Carlucci, mayor of the City of Philadelphia, had suggested to Police Commissioner Taddeus Czernich that Wohl be given the job. And they all knew that Mayor Carlucci sincerely—and not without reason—believed himself to know more about what was good for the Police Department than anybody else in Philadelphia.

A "suggestion" from Mayor Carlucci to Commissioner Czernich regarding what he should do in the exercise of his office was the equivalent of an announcement on faith and morals issued by the pope, ex cathedra. It was not open for discussion, much less debate.

Peter Wohl had not wanted the job. He had been the youngest, ever, of the fourteen staff inspectors of the Staff Investigations Unit, and had liked very much what he was doing. The penal system of the Commonwealth of Pennsylvania was now housing more than thirty former judges, city commissioners, and other high-level bureaucrats and political office holders whom Peter Wohl had caught with their hands either in the public treasury or outstretched to accept contributions from the citizenry in exchange for special treatment.

He had even thought about passing up the opportunity to take the examination for inspector. There had been little question in his mind that he could pass the examination and be promoted, but he suspected that if he did, with only a couple of years as a staff inspector behind him, with the promotion would come an assignment to duties he would rather not have, for example, as commanding officer of the Traffic Division, or the Civil Affairs Division, or even the Juvenile Division.

Department politics would, he had believed, keep him from getting an assignment as an inspector he would really like, which would have included commanding one of the nine Police Divisions (under which were all the police districts) or one of the two Detective Field Divisions (under which were the seven Detective Divisions) or the Tactical Division, under which were Highway Patrol, the Airport, Stakeout, Ordnance Disposal, the police boats in the Marine Unit, the dogs of the Canine Unit, and a unit whose function he did not fully understand called Special Operations.

And then Mayor Carlucci had a little chat with Commissioner Czernich. There was a chance for the Philadelphia Police Department to get its hands on some federal money, from the Justice Department. Some Washington bureaucrat had decided that the way to fight crime was to overwhelm the criminal element by sheer numbers. Under the acronym ACT, for Anti-Crime Team, federal money would allow local police departments to dispatch to heavy-crime areas large numbers of policemen.

Philadelphia already was trying the same tactic, more or less, with the Highway Patrol, an elite, specially uniformed, two-men-in-a-car unit who normally practiced fighting crime by going to heavy-crime areas. But they were, of course, paying for it themselves.

There was a way, Mayor Carlucci suggested, to enlist the financial support of the federal government in the never-ending war against crime. The Philadelphia Police Department would form an ACT unit. It would be placed in the already existing Special Operations Division. And Special Operations, the mayor suggested, would be taken out from under the control of the Special Investigations Bureau, made a division, and placed under the direct command of the police commissioner himself.

And the mayor suggested that they needed somebody who was really bright to head up the new division, and what did the commissioner think of Peter Wohl?

The police commissioner knew that as Mayor Carlucci had worked his way up through the ranks of the Police Department, his rabbi had been Chief Inspector Augustus Wohl, retired. And he know that Peter Wohl had just done a hell of a fine job putting Superior Court Judge Moses Findermann into the long-term custody of the state penal system. But most important, he understood that when His Honor the Mayor gave a hint like that, it well behooved him to act on it, and he did.

Paul O'Mara, on his second trip through the parking lot, finally found a place, against the rear fence, to park the Ford. He and Staff Inspector Wohl got out of the car and walked to what had been designed as the rear door, but was now the only functioning door, of the Police Administration Building.

A corporal sitting behind a thick plastic window recognized Inspector Wohl and activated the solenoid that unlocked the door to the main lobby. Officer O'Mara pushed it open and held it for Staff Inspector Wohl, an action that made Wohl feel just a bit uncomfortable. Officer Payne had not hovered over him. He was willing to admit he missed Officer Payne.

They rode the curved elevator to the third (actually the fourth) floor of the Roundhouse and walked down the corridor to where a uniformed police officer sat at a counter guarding access to what amounted to the executive suite. Officer O'Mara announced, somewhat triumphantly, their business: "Inspector Wohl to see the commissioner."

The commissioner, Peter Wohl was not surprised to learn, was tied up but would be with him shortly.

The door to the commissioner's conference room was open, and Wohl saw Captain Henry C. Quaire, the head of the Homicide Division, whom he liked, leaning on the conference table, sipping a cup of coffee.

He walked in, and was immediately sorry he had, for Captain Quaire was not alone in the room. Inspector J. Howard Porter, commanding officer of the Tactical Division, was with him.

Inspector Porter had, when word of the federal money and the upgrading of Special Operations had spread through the Department, naturally considered himself a, perhaps the, prime candidate for the command of Special Operations. He not only had the appropriate rank, but his Tactical Division included Highway Patrol.

He had not been given the Special Operations Division, and Highway Patrol had been taken away from Tactical and given to Special Operations. Peter Wohl did not think he could include Inspector Porter in his legion of admirers.

"Good morning, Inspector," Wohl said politely.

"Wohl."

"Hello, Henry."

"Inspector."

"Do you know Paul O'Mara?"

"I know your dad," Quaire said, offering O'Mara his hand.

Inspector Porter nodded at Officer O'Mara but said nothing, and did not offer to shake hands.

What is that, Wohl thought, *guilt by association? Or is shaking hands with a lowly police officer beneath your dignity?*

He glanced at Quaire, and their eyes met for a moment.

I don't think Quaire likes Porter any more than I do.

"I saw your predecessor last night," Captain Quaire said, as much to Wohl as to O'Mara. "You heard about what happened at the Acme on Baltimore Avenue?"

"I didn't hear Payne shot them," Wohl said without thinking about it.

Quaire laughed. "Not this time, Peter. He was just a spectator."

"I'm glad to hear that."

"That's why we're here," Quaire said. "The commissioner wants to be absolutely sure the shooting was justified."

"Was there a question?"

"Hell no. Both of the doers fired first."

The commissioner's secretary appeared in the conference room door.

"The commissioner will see you now, Inspector," she said, and then realized there were two men answering to that title in the room, and added, ". . . Wohl."

"Thank you," Peter Wohl said.

If I needed one more nail in my coffin, that was it. Porter knows I just walked in here. And I get to enter the throne room first.

7.

"Good morning, Peter," Commissioner Czernich said, smiling broadly. He was a large, stocky, well-tailored man with a full head of silver hair. "Sit down."

"Good morning, sir."

"Would you like some coffee?"

"Please."

"Black, right?"

"Yes, sir."

I don't think I am about to have my head handed to me on a platter. But on the other hand, I don't think he called me in here to express his appreciation for my all-around splendid performance of duty. And nothing has gone wrong in Special Operations, or I would have heard about it.

"How's your dad?"

"Fine, thank you. I had dinner with him on Monday."

"Give him my regards, the next time you see him."

"I'll do that, thank you."

"You see the Overnights, Peter?"

The Overnights were a summary of major crimes, and/or significant events affecting the Police Department that were compiled from reports from the districts, the Detective Divisions, and major Bureaus, and then distributed to senior commanders.

"No, sir. I came here first thing."

Obviously, I've missed something, and I am about to hear what it is, and why it is my fault.

"Stakeout took down two critters at an Acme on the Baltimore Pike," Czernich said. "It's almost a sure thing these were the characters we've been looking for. If it was a good shooting, we're home free."

"I did hear about that, sir. And from what I heard, I think it was a good shooting."

"Every once in a while, Peter, we do do something right, don't we?"

I'll be damned. I didn't do anything wrong.

"Yes, sir, we do."

"The Vice President's coming to town."

"I saw it in the newspaper."

"He's coming by airplane. He's going to do something at Independence Hall. Then he wants to make a triumphal march up Market Street to 30th Street Station, and get on a train."

" 'March,' sir?"

"Figure of speech. What do they call it, 'motorcade'?"

"Yes, sir."

"I talked to the Secret Service guy. He really wants a Highway escort. On wheels, I mean. I think he thinks, or at least the Vice President does, that that makes them look good on the TV."

"Well, there's nothing I know of, sir, that would keep us from giving Dignitary Protection all the wheels they want."

Highway Patrol, as its name suggested, had been formed before World War II, as "The Bandit Chasers." That had evolved into the "Motor Bandit Patrol" and finally into the Highway Patrol. It had originally been equipped with motorcycles ("wheels") only, and its members authorized a special uniform suitable for motorcyclists, breeches, leather boots, leather jackets, and billed caps with an unstiffened crown.

It had evolved over the years into an elite unit that, although it patrolled the Schuylkill Expressway and the interstate highways, spent most of its effort patrolling high-crime areas in two-man RPCs. Other RPCs in the Department were manned by only one police officer, and patrolled only in the district to which they were assigned.

The evolution had begun when command of Highway had been given to Captain Jerry Carlucci, and had continued under his benevolent, and growing, influence as he rose through the ranks to commissioner, and continued now that he was mayor.

Applying for, being selected for, and then serving a tour in Highway was considered an almost essential career step for officers who had ambition for higher rank. Peter Wohl had been a Highway sergeant before his promotion to lieutenant and assignment to the Organized Crime Intelligence Unit.

Highway still had its wheels, and every man in Highway was a graduate of the Motorcycle Training Program (known as "Wheel School"), and continued to wear, although months often passed between times that a Highway Patrolman actually straddled a motorcycle, the special Highway uniform.

Dignitary Protection was ordinarily an inactive function; a sergeant or a lieutenant in the Intelligence Division of the Detective Bureau performed the function and answered that phone number in addition to his other duties.

When a dignitary showed up who needed protection, a more senior officer, sometimes, depending on the dignitary, even a chief inspector, took over and coordinated and commanded whatever police units and personnel were considered necessary.

"What I've been thinking, Peter," Commissioner Czernich said, "is that Dignitary Protection should really be under you. I mean, really, it's a special function, a special operation, am I right? And you have Special Operations."

Carlucci strikes again, Peter Wohl thought. *Czernich might even have come by himself to the conclusion that Dignitary Protection should come under Special Operations, but he would have kept that conclusion to himself. He would not have done anything about it himself, or even suggested it to the mayor, because the mayor might not like the idea, or come to the conclusion that Czernich was getting a little too big for his britches.*

"Yes, I'm sure you're right," Wohl said. "Dignitary Protection is a special function, a special operation."

"And there's something else," Czernich went on. "I don't think it would be a bad idea at all to show the feds where all that ACT money is going."

"Yes, sir."

"What I thought I'd do, Peter . . . Do you know Sergeant Henkels?"

"No, sir. I don't think so."

"He's the man in Chief Lowenstein's office who handles Dignitary Protection. I thought I'd ask Lowenstein to get the paperwork going and transfer him and his paperwork out to the Schoolhouse."

When the Special Operations Division had been formed from the Special Operations Unit, there had been no thought given to providing a place for it to exist. Since there was no other place to go, Peter Wohl had set up his first office in what had been the Highway Patrol captain's office in a building Highway shared with the 7th District at Bustleton Avenue and Bowler Street in Northeast Philadelphia.

There really had not been room in the building for both the District and Highway, and the addition of the ever-growing Special Operations staff made things impossible. His complaints had fallen on deaf ears for a long time, but then, somewhat triumphantly, he had been told that the City was willing to transfer a building at Frankford and Castor Avenues from the Board of Education to the Police Department, and Special Operations could have it for their very own.

There was a slight problem. The reason the Board of Education was being so generous was that the Board of Health had determined that the Frankford Grammar School (built A.D. 1892) posed a health threat to its faculty and student population, and had ordered it abandoned. There were, of course, no funds available in the Police Department budget for repairs or rehabilitation.

But since a building had been provided for Special Operations, Staff Inspector Wohl was soon led to understand, it would be considered impolite for him to complain that he was no better off than he had been. It was also pointed out that the health standards that applied to students and teachers did not apply to policemen.

And then Staff Inspector Wohl's administrative assistant, Officer M. M. Payne, who apparently had nothing more pressing to do at the time, read the fine print in the documents that outlined how the ACT funds could be spent. Up to $250,000 of the federal government's money could be expended for emergency *repairs* to, but not *replacement* of, equipment and facilities. He brought this to Wohl's attention, and Wohl, although he was not of the Roman Catholic persuasion, decided that it was time to adopt a Jesuit attitude to his problem: *The end justifies the means.*

Replacing broken *windowpanes* was obviously proscribed, and could not be done. But emergency *repairs* to windows (which incidentally might involve replacing a couple of panes here and there) were permissible. Similarly, *replacing* shingles on the roof was proscribed, but *repairing* the roof was permissible. *Repairing* the walls, floor, and plumbing system as a necessary emergency measure similarly posed no insurmountable legal or moral problems vis-à-vis the terms of the federal grant.

But the building's heating system posed a major problem. The existing coal-fired furnaces, after seventy-odd years of service, were beyond repair. In what he seriously regarded as the most dishonest act of his life, Peter Wohl chose not to notice that the *repairs* to the "heating system" consisted of "removing malfunctioning components" (the coal furnaces) and "installing replacement components" (gas-fired devices that provided both heat and air-conditioning).

He had also circumvented the City's bureaucracy in the matter of awarding the various contracts. On one hand, his experience as a staff inspector had left him convinced that kickbacks were standard procedure when the City awarded contracts. The price quoted for services to be rendered to the City included the amount of the kickback. On the other hand, he knew that the law required every contract over $10,000 to be awarded on the basis of the lowest bid. He was, in fact, consciously breaking the law.

He had come to understand, further, that it wasn't a question of if he would be caught, but when. He didn't think there would be an attempt to indict him, but there had been a very good chance that he would either be fired, or asked to resign, or, at a minimum, relieved of his new command when the Department of Public Property finally found out what he had done.

That hadn't happened. The mayor had visited the Schoolhouse and liked what he found. And from a source Peter Wohl had in the Department of Public Property, Peter learned that the mayor had shortly thereafter visited the Department of Public Property and made it clear to the commissioner that he didn't want to hear any complaints, to him, or to the newspapers, about how the old Frankford Grammar School building had been *repaired.*

There were several reasons, Wohl had concluded, why the mayor could have chosen to do that. For one thing, it would have been politically embarrassing for him had there been a fuss in the newspapers. He had appointed Wohl to command Special Operations, and look what happened!

Another possibility was that it was repayment of a debt of honor. Peter didn't know all the details, or even many of them, but he had heard enough veiled references to be sure that when Jerry Carlucci had been an up-and-coming lieutenant and captain and inspector, Chief Inspector Augustus Wohl had gone out on the limb a number of times to save Carlucci's ass.

Another obvious possibility was that since Carlucci had saved his ass, he was now deeply in Carlucci's debt.

The last possibility was the nicest to consider, that the mayor understood that while Peter was bending, even breaking, the law he was not doing it for himself, but for the betterment of the Department. Peter didn't like to accept this possibility; it let him off the hook too easily.

The road to hell, or more precisely to the Commonwealth of Pennsylvania's penal system, was paved, his experience had taught him, *if not entirely with good intentions, then with good intentions and the rationalization you aren't doing something really crooked, but rather something that other people do all the time and get away with.*

"Is that all there is, Commissioner, one sergeant?"

"He just holds down the desk until there's a dignitary to protect," Czernich said. "You didn't know?"

"No, sir. I didn't."

"You don't have any objections to this, Peter, do you?"

"No, sir. If you think this makes sense, I'll give it my best shot."

"If you run into problems, Peter, you know my door is always open."

"Yes, sir. I know that, and I appreciate it, Commissioner."

The commissioner stood up and offered his hand.

"Always good to see you, Peter," he said. "Ask my girl to send Inspector Porter and Captain Quaire in, will you?"

"Yes, sir."

There was a Plymouth station wagon in the driveway of Evelyn Glover's ranch house in Upper Darby when Matt turned into it in the Porsche.

"You've got a visitor," he said.

Evelyn tried to make a joke of it. "That's no visitor, that's my husband."

As Matt stopped the car, a man, forty years old, tall, skinny, tweedy, whom Matt vaguely remembered having seen somewhere before, and who had apparently been peering into the kitchen door, came down the driveway.

Evelyn fumbled around until she found the tiny door latch, opened the door, and got out.

Matt felt a strong urge to shove the stick in reverse and get the hell out of here, but that, obviously, was something he could not do. He opened his door and got out.

He heard the tail end of what Evelyn's husband was saying: ". . . so I called the library, and when they said they had no idea where you were, I got worried and came here."

He looked at Matt with unabashed curiosity.

"Mr. Payne," Evelyn said, "this is my husband. He saw my car at Darby Plymouth."

Professor Glover offered his hand to Matt.

"Harry, this is Detective Payne," Evelyn said. "He's been helping me. We just came from Darby Plymouth."

"How do you do?" Professor Glover said, and then blurted what was on his mind: "That's quite a police car."

"It's my car," Matt said. "I'm off duty."

"Oh," Professor Glover said.

"Well, if there's nothing else I can do for you, Mrs. Glover . . ."

"You've already done more for me than I had any right to expect," Evelyn said, and offered him her hand. "I don't know how to thank you."

"Don't mention it," Matt said. "Sorry you had the trouble. Nice to meet you, Professor."

"Yes," Professor Glover said.

Jesus Christ, he knows!

Matt got back in the Porsche, and backed out of the driveway. He glanced at the house and saw Professor Glover following his wife into the house.

Officer Paul O'Mara dropped Staff Inspector Wohl at a door over which was carved in stone, GIRLS' ENTRANCE, at the former Frankford Grammar School, and then drove around to the cracked cement now covering what at one time had been the lawn in front of the building and parked the Ford.

Captain Michael Sabara, a swarthy, acne-scarred, stocky man in his forties, who was wearing a white civilian shirt and yellow V-neck sweater, and Captain David Pekach, a slight, fair-skinned man of thirty-six, who was wearing the special Highway Patrol uniform, were both waiting for Wohl when he walked into his (formerly the principal's) office.

Captain Mike Sabara was Wohl's deputy. He had been the senior lieutenant in Highway, and awaiting promotion to captain when Captain Dutch Moffitt had been killed. He had naturally expected to step into Moffitt's shoes. Dave Pekach, who had been in Narcotics, had just been promoted to captain, and transferred to Special Operations.

Enraging many of the people in Highway, including, Wohl was sure, Mike Sabara, he had named Sabara his deputy and given Highway to Pekach. But that had been almost a year ago, and it had worked out well. It had probably taken Sabara, Wohl thought, no more than a week to realize that the alternative to his being named Wohl's deputy was a transfer elsewhere in the Department, and probably another month to believe what Wohl had told him when he took over Special Operations, that he would be of greater usefulness to the Department as his deputy than he would have been commanding Highway.

Wohl understood the Highway mystique. He still had in his closet his Highway sergeant's leather jacket and soft-crowned billet cap, unable to bring himself to sell, or even give them away, although there was absolutely no way he would ever wear either again. But it had been time for Sabara to take off his Highway breeches, and for Pekach, who had worn a pigtail in his plainclothes Narcotics assignment, to get back in uniform.

"Good morning, Inspector," they said, almost in chorus.

Wohl smiled and motioned for them to follow them into his office.

"I hope you brought your notebooks," he said. "I have just come from the Fountain of All Knowledge."

"I don't like the sound of that," Sabara said.

Pekach closed the office door behind him.

"What did the Polack want, Peter?" he asked.

Wohl did not respond directly.

"Is Jack Malone around?" he asked. "I'd rather go through this just once."

"He went over to the garage," Sabara said, stepping to Wohl's desk as he spoke and picking up a telephone. "Have you got a location on Lieutenant Malone?" He put the phone back in its cradle. "He just drove in the gate."

Wohl sat down at his desk and took the Overnight from his IN box. He read it. He raised his eyes to Pekach.

"We have anybody in on the shooting at the Acme?"

"One car, plus a sergeant who was in the area."

"Did you talk to them? Was it a good shooting?"

"It looks that way. They shot first. The lieutenant—what the hell is his name?—"

Wohl and Sabara shrugged their shoulders.

"—not only identified himself as a police officer, but used an electronic megaphone to do it. One of the doers *then* shot at him and another Stakeout guy. When he was down, the other doer started shooting. It looks to me like it was clearly justified."

"The commissioner seemed a little unsure," Wohl said. "Open the door, Dave, and see if O'Mara's out there. If he is, have him lasso Jack."

"I'll tell you who was also at the Acme, Peter, in case you haven't heard. Matt Payne."

"I heard. I saw Henry Quaire in the Roundhouse."

"This time he was a spectator," Sabara said.

Pekach came back into the office, followed by a uniformed lieutenant, John J. "Jack" Malone, who showed signs of entering middle age. His hairline was starting to recede; there was the suggestion of forming jowls, and he was getting a little thick around the middle.

"Good morning, sir," he said.

"Close the doors, Jack, please," Wohl said. "Gentlemen, I don't believe you've met the new commanding officer of Dignitary Protection?"

Malone misinterpreted what Wohl had intended as a little witticism. The smile vanished from his face. It grew more than sad, bitter.

"When did that happen, sir?" he asked.

Wohl saw that his little joke had laid an egg, and he was furious with himself for trying to be clever. Malone thought he was being told, kindly, that he was being transferred out of Special Operations. And with that came the inference that he had been found wanting.

"About ten minutes ago, Jack," Wohl said, "which is ten minutes after the commissioner told me we now have Dignitary Protection. Have you got something against taking it over?"

"Not here," Malone said, visibly relieved. "I thought I was being sent to the Roundhouse."

Well, that's flattering. He likes it here.

"Do you know a sergeant by the name of Henkels?"

"Yes, sir, I know him."

"There is something in your tone that suggests that you are not especially impressed with the sergeant."

"There used to be a Sergeant Henkels in Central Cell Room," Pekach volunteered. "If it's the same guy, he has a room temperature IQ."

"That's him, Captain. I guess they moved him upstairs," Malone said.

The Central Cell Room was in the Police Administration Building.

"Well, Sergeant Henkels and his Dignitary Protection files are about to be transferred out here. Into your capable command, Lieutenant Malone."

"Oh, God. He's a real dummy, Inspector. God only knows how he got to be a sergeant."

"Well, I'm sure you will find a way to keep the sergeant usefully occupied."

"How about sending him to Wheel School and praying he breaks his neck?" Malone suggested.

"I don't think there will be time to do that before the Vice President comes to town," Wohl said.

"I saw that in the papers," Malone said. "We're going to have that? There's not a hell of a lot of time . . ."

"We'll have to manage somehow."

"Who are they going to move into command?" Malone asked. "Did the commissioner say?"

Wohl shook his head, no. He was more than a little embarrassed that he hadn't considered that.

"One of the chiefs probably," Mike Sabara said. "It's the Vice President."

"They're not going to move anybody in," Peter Wohl said, softly but firmly. "If this is a Special Operations responsibility, we'll be responsible."

"You'd be putting your neck on the line, Peter," Mike Sabara said. "Let them send somebody in, somebody who's familiar with this sort of operation."

"Let them send someone in here with the authority to tell our people what to do?" Wohl replied. "No way, Mike. We'll do it. Discussion closed."

Corporal Vito Lanza had not been the star pupil in Bishop John Newmann High School's Basic, Intermediate, and Advanced Typing courses, but he had tried hard enough not to get kicked out of the class. Being dropped from Typing would have meant assignment as a library monitor (putting books back on shelves), or as a laboratory monitor (washing all that shit out of test tubes and Erlenmeyer flasks), neither of which had great appeal to him.

Almost despite himself, he had become a fairly competent typist, a skill he thought he would never use in real life after graduation, and certainly not as a cop, chasing criminals down the street on his Highway Patrol Harley-Davidson motorcycle.

There was a two-and-a-half-year period after graduation from Bishop Newmann High, until he turned twenty-one and could apply for the cops, during which Vito had had a number of jobs. He worked in three different service stations, worked in a taxi garage, and got a job cleaning Eastern airliners between flights at the airport. He hated all of them, and prayed after he took the Civil Service Examination for the cops that he would not be found wanting.

Officer Lanza had quickly learned that being a cop was not what he thought it would be. Right out of the Academy, he had been assigned to the 18th District at 55th and Pine Streets. He spent eight months riding around the district in a battered Ford van, with another rookie police officer. Hauling prisoners (a great many of whom were drunks, not even guys who'd done a stickup) from where they had been arrested to the holding cells in the District Station was not exactly what he'd had in mind when he had become a law enforcement officer. Neither was hauling sick people from their houses to a hospital.

(Philadelphia Police, unlike the police of other major American cities, respond to every call for help. The citizens of Philadelphia have learned over the years that what one does when Junior falls off the porch and cracks his head open, or Grandma falls on an icy sidewalk, or Mama scalds herself with boiling water on the stove, is to call the cops.)

And Vito learned that while it was certainly possible that he could become a Highway Patrolman and race around the streets on a Harley, or in one of the antennae-festooned special Highway Radio Patrol Cars, fighting crime, that would have to be some time in the future. *After* he had four, five, six *good* years on the job, he could *apply* for Highway. It was police folklore—which is not always accurate—that unless you had done something spectacular, like personally catch a bank robber, or unless you knew somebody in Highway, or had a rabbi, some white shirt who liked you, your chances of getting in Highway were about as good as they were to win the Irish Sweepstakes.

But one night, after he had been pushing the van for eight months, the sergeant at roll call had asked, "Does anybody know how to type good?"

Vito had always thought that typing was something girls did, and was reluctant to publicly confess that he could do that sort of thing, but maybe it would get him out of the fucking van for the night.

"Over here, Sergeant," Officer Lanza had said, raising his hand.

"Okay," the sergeant had said. "See the corporal. Sweitzer, you take his place in the van."

"Shit," Officer Sweitzer said.

The district was behind in its paperwork, the corporal told Officer Lanza, and the captain was on his ass, because the inspector was on his ass.

It had not taken Officer Lanza long to figure out that (a) while he was not a really good typist, compared to anybody in the district he was a world fucking champion and (b) that sitting behind a desk in the district building pushing a typewriter was way ahead of staggering around in the ice and slush loading a fat lady into the back of a van.

That particular typing job had taken three days. Over the next two years, Officer Lanza had spent more and more time behind a typewriter in the office than he had spent in an emergency patrol wagon, in an RPC, or walking a beat.

When he had almost three years on the job, he had taken the examinations for both detective and corporal. He hadn't expected to pass either first time out—he just wanted to see what the fuck the examinations were like—and he didn't. He found that the detective examination was tougher than the corporal examination. Probably, he deduced, because he had been doing so much paperwork, which is what corporals did, that he had come to understand a lot of it.

Two years later, when there was another examination for both detective and corporal, he figured fuck the detective, I think I'd rather be a corporal anyhow, detectives spend a lot of time standing around in the mud and snow.

He passed the corporal's examination, way down on the numerical list, so it was another year almost before he actually got promoted. He did four months working the desk in the Central Cell Room in the Roundhouse, and then they transferred him upstairs to the Traffic Division, where he had met Lieutenant Schnair, who was a pretty good guy for a Jew, and was supposed to have Chief Inspector Matt Lowenstein, the chief inspector of the Detective Division, for a rabbi.

Obviously, pushing a typewriter for the Traffic Division in the Roundhouse was a lot better than standing in the snow and blowing your whistle at tractor trailers at some accident scene for the Traffic Division, and Vito tried hard to please Lieutenant Schnair.

When Schnair got promoted to captain, and they gave him the Airport Unit (which, so far as Vito was concerned, proved Chief Lowenstein *was* his rabbi), he arranged for Corporal Lanza to be transferred to Airport too, after one of the corporals there got himself killed driving home from the shore.

It was a good job. All he had to do was keep on top of the paperwork, and everybody left him alone. The lieutenants and the sergeants and the other corporals knew how good he got along with Captain Schnair. If he came in a little late, or left a little early, no one said anything to him.

It never entered Corporal Vito Lanza's mind to ask permission to leave his desk in the Airport Unit office at 11:15. He simply *told* the lieutenant on duty, Lieutenant Ardell, that he was going to lunch.

He would get back when he got back. He was going to have a real lunch, not a sandwich or a hot dog, which meant getting out of the airport, where they charged crazy fucking prices. Just because he had a bundle of Las Vegas money was no excuse to pay five dollars for something worth two-fifty.

The Buick surprised him by starting right off. Now that he was going to dump the sonofabitch, it had decided to turn reliable. It was like when you went to the dentist, your teeth stopped hurting.

Thinking of dumping the Buick reminded him that he was supposed to meet Antoinette after work and go see her uncle, who had a car lot. He'd told her, of course, that he'd had a little luck in Vegas and was going to look around for a Caddy, and she told him her uncle had a car lot with a lot of Caddys on it.

He hadn't been sure then whether she had been trying to be nice to him, or just steering her uncle some business. After she'd taken him to her apartment, he decided that she really did like him, and maybe this thing with her uncle would turn out all right.

It also made him feel like a fool for slipping that bimbo in Vegas two hundred dollars. He didn't really have to pay for it, and now he couldn't understand why he had. Except, of course, that he was on a high from what had happened at the tables.

Antoinette had told him her uncle's car lot was one of those in the "Auto Mall" at 67th Street and Essington Avenue. Just past the ballpark on South Broad, he decided that it wouldn't hurt to just drive past the uncle's car lot, it wasn't far, to see what he had. If he was some sleazeball with a dozen cars or so, that would mean that Antoinette was trying to push some business his way, and when he saw her after work, he would tell her he had made other arrangements. Tell her nice. The last thing in the world he wanted to do was piss her off. She was really much better in the sack than the bimbo in Vegas he'd given the two hundred dollars to.

Fierello's Fine Cars, on Essington Avenue, was no sleaze operation. Vito thought there must be a hundred, maybe a hundred fifty cars on the lot, which was paved and had lights and everything and even a little office building that was a real building, not just a trailer. And there were at least twenty Caddys, and they all looked like nearly new.

He drove past it twice, and then started back to the airport. He didn't get the real lunch he started out to get—he stopped at Oregon Steaks at Oregon Avenue and Juniper Street and had a sausage and peppers sandwich and a beer—but he was in a good mood and it didn't bother him. Not only was he probably going to drive home tonight in a new Caddy, but on the way, the odds were that he might spend some time in Antoinette's apartment.

He was still on a roll, no question about it.

Marion Claude Wheatley, the Hon. Jerry Carlucci, and Detective M. M. Payne all had lunch at the Union League Club on South Broad Street, but not together.

Mr. Wheatley was the guest of Mr. D. Logan Hammersmith, Jr., who was a vice president and senior trust officer of the First Pennsylvania Bank & Trust Company and who, like Mr. Wheatley, held an MBA from the University of Pennsylvania.

Mr. Hammersmith did not really know what to think of Mr. Wheatley beyond the obvious, which was that he was one hell of an analyst; not only was his knowledge of the petrochemical industry encyclopedic, but he had demonstrated over the years a remarkable ability to predict upturns and downturns. Acting on Mr. Wheatley's recommendations, Mr. Hammersmith had been able to make a lot of money for the trusts under his control, and he was perfectly willing to admit that this success had been a factor, indeed a major factor, in his recent promotion to senior trust officer, which carried with it the titular promotion to vice president.

(While he was willing to concede that it was true that First Philadelphia dispensed titular promotions instead of salary increases, it was, nevertheless, rather nice to have the bronze name plate reading D. LOGAN HAMMERSMITH, JR. VICE PRESIDENT sitting on his desk.)

Logan Hammersmith was not the only one around First Pennsylvania who had noticed that M. C. Wheatley had never married. But there never had been any talk that he was perhaps light on his feet. For one thing, the contents of his personnel file, although they were supposed to be confidential, were well known. One is not prone to jump to the conclusion that someone who has served, with great distinction, was twice wounded and three times decorated, as an Army officer in Vietnam is a fag simply because he has not marched to the marriage altar.

And he didn't have effeminate mannerisms, either. He drank his whiskey straight and sometimes smoked cigars. Hammersmith's final, best guess was that Wheatley was either very shy, and incapable of pursuing women, or, more likely, asexual.

And, of course, for all that anybody really *knew,* Marion Claude Wheatley might be carrying on, discreetly, with a married woman, or for that matter with a belly dancer in Atlantic City. He had a country place, a farm, or what had years before been a farm, acquired by inheritance, in that area of New Jersey known as the Pine Barrens. He spent many of his weekends there, and presumably his summer vacations.

Hammersmith, over the years, had had Marion C. Wheatley out to the house in Bryn Mawr a number of times for dinner. His behavior had been impeccable. He'd brought the right sort of wine as a gift, and he didn't get plastered, or try to grope some shapely knee under the table. But he was not a brilliant, or even mediocre, conversationalist. He was, as Bootsie (Mrs. D. Logan, Jr.) Hammersmith had put it, a crashing bore.

It had been, Hammersmith thought, as he handed the menu back and told the waiter he'd have the Boston scrod, well over a year since Wheatley had been out to the house. He would have to do something about that.

"I think the same for me, please," Marion C. Wheatley said.

"Do you think the building would fall down if we walked back in reeking of gin?" Hammersmith asked.

Employees of First Pennsylvania were expected not to take alcohol at lunch. *Officers* were under no such unwritten proscription.

"I think a martini would be a splendid idea," Marion said with a smile.

Hammersmith held up two fingers to the waiter, and then his eyes fell on a familiar face.

"We are in the presence of the mayor," he said, and discreetly nodded his head in the mayor's direction.

After a moment Marion C. Wheatley looked.

"Is he a member, do you think?"

"I think ex-officio," Hammersmith said. "For the obvious reasons. Speaking of the upper crust, Bootsie and I were invited to the Peebles wedding."

Marion C. Wheatley looked at him curiously.

"Peebles," Hammersmith repeated. "As in Tamaqua Mining."

"Oh," Wheatley said.

That rang a bell, Hammersmith thought. *I thought it would. Tamaqua Mining owned somewhere between ten and twelve percent of the known anthracite reserves of the United States. Anthracite coal was still an important part of petrochemicals, and according to Marion Claude Wheatley it would grow in financial importance. Miss Martha Peebles owned all of the outstanding shares of Tamaqua Mining, and Wheatley would know that.*

After a moment Marion Claude Wheatley asked, "Is that in a trust?"

"No. She manages it herself. With Mawson, Payne, Stockton, McAdoo & Lester's assistance, of course."

"You know her, then?" Wheatley asked.

Hammersmith was pleased they had found something to talk about. Making conversation with Wheatley was often difficult. Or impossible.

"No. I know the brother. Alexander Peebles, Jr."

Wheatley's face showed that he didn't understand.

"When the old man died, he, in the classic phrase, cut the boy off without a dime. There is an unpleasant story that the son, how should I phrase this delicately?"

"He's a fairy," Marion Claude Wheatley said. "Now that you mention it, I've heard that." *I don't think he would have used that word if he was queer himself.*

"Not from me," Hammersmith said. "Anyway, he left everything to the daughter. There was a nasty lawsuit but he was up against Mawson, Payne, Stockton, McAdoo & Lester, and he lost. Then the sister set up a trust fund for him. With us. Specifically with me. We couldn't have Alexander Peebles, Jr., sleeping in the subway."

"And he invited you?"

"I don't know. I guess he's been told to show up and behave at the wedding. Brewster Payne's going to give her away, and I suspect he was responsible for the invitation."

"Who is she marrying?"

"The story gets curiouser and curiouser," Hammersmith said. "A cop."

"A *cop?*"

"Well, a captain. A fellow named Pekach. He's the head of Highway Patrol."

"Where did she meet him?"

"The story as I understand it is that her place in Chestnut Hill kept getting burglarized. She complained to the mayor, or Payne complained to the mayor for her, and the mayor sent the Highway Patrol. . . ."

"Carlucci's Commandos," Wheatley interrupted. "That's what the *Ledger* calls the Highway Patrol."

"Right. So, as the story goes, His Honor the Mayor sent the head commando, this Captain Pekach, to calm the lady down, and it was love at first sight."

"What does this lady look like?"

"Actually, she's rather attractive."

"Then why didn't you arrange for me to meet her?"

"You don't have a motorcycle and a large pistol. The lady probably wouldn't have been interested in you."

"I could have gone out and bought them," Marion Claude Wheatley said. "In a good cause."

He smiled at Hammersmith and Hammersmith smiled back. He was pleased that he had decided to take Wheatley to lunch. There was no longer a gnawing suspicion that Wheatley was queer. It could have been awkward at First Pennsylvania if that had come out. Everyone knew that he relied heavily on Wheatley's advice, and there would have been talk if something embarrassing had developed.

8.

Detective Matthew M. Payne was the guest of Brewster C. Payne for lunch at the Union League. On the way into Philadelphia from Upper Darby, while pumping gas into the Porsche, he had seen a pay telephone and remembered that his father had left a message on the answering machine to which he had not responded. He'd called him and been invited to lunch.

He had hung up the phone thinking that virtue *was* its own reward. He had nobly been the dutiful son, and only in the middle of the conversation realized that his father would have the solution to what he should do with his Las Vegas winnings.

Brewster Payne arrived first and was asked by the headwaiter how many would be in his party.

"Just my son, Charley."

"Then you wouldn't mind sitting at small table?"

"Not at all."

One of the prerogatives of being a member of the Board of Governors was being able to walk into the dining room anytime before twelve-thirty without a reservation and finding a good four-place table with a RESERVED sign on it was available to you.

Brewster Payne had just been served, without having to ask for it, a Famous Grouse with an equal amount of water and just a little ice, when he saw his son stop at the entrance and look around for him.

He thought, as he very often did, *it is incredible that that well-dressed, very nice young man is a policeman with a gun concealed somewhere on his person. A gun, even more incredibly, with which he has killed two people.*

Matt spotted him and smiled and walked across the room. Brewster Payne got to his feet and extended his hand. At the last moment, he moved his hand to his son's shoulders and gave him a brief hug.

"I didn't know how long I would have to wait, so I ordered a drink."

"I am ninety seconds late, just for the record."

A waiter appeared.

"I'll have a Tuborg, please," Matt ordered.

"Your sister is annoyed with you."

"Anything else new?"

"Have you called her?"

"No."

"I think you should have. She wanted to know how things went in Las Vegas."

"Vis-à-vis Precious Penny, more smoothly than I would have thought," Matt said. "She only said 'Fuck you, Matt' twice."

"What was that about?"

"Idle conversation," Matt said. "She left a message on the machine, very sweetly thanking me for going out there and fetching her home. I didn't really have anything to tell Amy; that's why I didn't call her."

"That you had nothing to report would have been useful in itself."

"Okay, I'll call her."

"You don't have to now. She went out to Chestnut Hill this morning and saw her."

"Great," Matt said. "Then that's over. Ask me what else happened in Las Vegas."

"What else happened in Las Vegas?"

Matt reached in his pocket and handed his father the $3,700 check from the Flamingo.

"And I have another three thousand in cash," Matt said as soon as he saw his father's eyebrows raise in surprise.

Brewster Payne looked at him.

"Three thousand more in cash?"

Matt nodded. "What do I do with it?"

"What were you playing?"

"Roulette."

"I didn't know you knew how to play roulette."

"Now you do. I think I have found my niche in life." He saw the look in his father's eyes and added: "Hey, I'm kidding."

"I hope so. How did this happen?"

"I started out to lose twenty dollars and got lucky and lost my mind."

"Lost your mind?"

"If I had been thinking clearly, I would have quit when I was four thousand odd ahead. But I didn't, and went back to the tables and won another twenty-seven hundred."

"Then you were smart enough to quit?"

"Then it was time to go get Penny."

Brewster Payne shook his head and tapped the check with a long, thin finger.

"The first thing you do is put enough of this in escrow to pay your taxes."

"What taxes?"

"Income taxes. Gambling winnings are taxable."

"That's outrageous!"

Brewster Payne smiled at his son's righteous indignation.

" 'The law is an ass,' right?"

"That sums it up nicely," Matt said. And then he had a thought. "How does the IRS know I won? Or how much I won?"

Brewster Payne held the check up.

"You'll notice your social security number is on here. They're required to inform the IRS, and they do."

"What about the three thousand in cash?"

"An unethical lawyer might suggest to you that you could probably conceal that from the IRS and get away with it. I am not an unethical lawyer, and *you* are an officer of the law."

"Jesus H. Christ!"

"Pay the two dollars, Matt. Sleep easy."

"It's not *two* dollars!"

"You're a big boy. Do what you like."

"So what do I do with it?"

"My advice would be to put it in tax-free municipals. You've already got a good deal of money in them. If you'd like, I'll take care of it for you."

Matt's indignation had not run completely down.

"You win, we get our pound of flesh. You *lose,* tough luck, right?"

"Essentially," Brewster Payne said. "And if you would like some additional advice?"

"Sure."

"I would not tell your mother about this. Right now she thinks of you as her saintly son who went out to the desert to help a sick girl. I would rather have her think that than to have a mental picture of you at the Las Vegas craps tables . . ."

"Roulette."

". . . *roulette tables,* surrounded by scantily dressed chorus girls."

"It's true."

"What's true?"

"They have some really good-looking hookers out there."

"But you, being virtuous, had nothing to do with them, and were rewarded by good luck at the roulette tables?"

"Absolutely. I have the strength of ten because in my heart, I'm pure."

"When do you go back to work?"

"Tomorrow, probably. I've got to go to Chief Lowenstein's office at half past one. I suspect that someone is going to tell me that when I go back to work, I say I was doing paperwork in the Roundhouse, not running out to Vegas to fetch Precious Penny."

The waiter appeared and interrupted the conversation to take their order."

"Have you plans for tonight?"

"No, sir."

"I think your mother would like to have you for dinner. She's making a leg of lamb."

"Thank you."

"Amy will be there."

"I have just been sandbagged."

"Yes," Brewster Payne said. "I had that in mind when I mentioned the lamb." He handed Matt the Flamingo check. "Take this, and the cash, to the bank. Cash this, and have them give you a cashier's check for the entire amount of money, payable to First Philadelphia. Give it to me tonight, and I'll take care of it from there."

Matt nodded, and took the check back.

"How much in taxes are they going to get?"

"You don't really want to know. It would ruin your lunch."

"I'll have the vegetable soup and the calves' liver, please," Chief Inspector Matt Lowenstein told the waiter.

"Shrimp cocktail and the luncheon steak, pink in the middle," the Honorable Jerry Carlucci ordered.

When the waiter had gone, the mayor said, "You should have had the shrimp and steak. I'm buying."

"Most of the time when you say you're buying I wind up with the check. Besides, I like the way they do liver in here."

"I had a call from H. Richard Detweiler this morning," the mayor said.

"And?"

"And he said he wanted me to know he was very grateful for our letting the Payne kid go out there and bring his daughter home, and if there was ever anything he could for me I should not hesitate to let him know."

"You should hold off calling that marker in until you're running for governor or the Senate. Or the White House."

"All I want to do is be mayor of Philadelphia."

"Isn't that what you said when they appointed you police commissioner? That all you wanted to be was commissioner?"

"What is this, Beat Up On Jerry Carlucci Day?"

"You want a straight answer to that?"

"No, lie to me."

"I sent word to Payne to meet me in my office at half past one. I'm going to tell him, when he goes back on the job, that what he was doing was paperwork in the Roundhouse, not running out to Las Vegas, for Christ's sake, baby-sitting Detweiler's daughter. He's going to have a hard enough time proving himself over at East as it is . . ."

"I've been in a detective division. Right there in East Detectives, as a matter of fact. You don't have to tell me about detective divisions."

". . . . without us pulling him out of there every time somebody like Detweiler wants a favor from you," Lowenstein finished.

"I'm not as dumb as I look, Matt," the mayor said. "I'm even one or two steps ahead of you."

"Are you?"

"Yes, I am. I thought you and Denny Coughlin did a dumb thing when you sent him to East Detectives in the first place."

"He made detective. What you do with new detectives is send them out to the Academy to learn the new forms, and then to a division, to learn how to *be* a detective. You tell me, why is that dumb?"

"Because he is who he is."

"You tell me, who is he?"

"He's the guy who took down the Northwest Philadelphia serial rapist, and the guy who shot it out with that Islamic Liberation Army jackass and won. That makes him different, without the other things. Like I said, I've been in a detective division. They're really going to stay on his ass to remind him he's a rookie, until he proves himself."

"He's a good kid. He can handle that."

"Sure he can, and what have we got then? I'll tell you what we'll have—one more detective who can probably work a crime scene about as good as any other detective."

"I don't know what the hell you're talking about."

"The Good of the Department is what I'm talking about."

"Then you have lost me somewhere along the way."

"Do you know how many college graduates have applied for the Department in the last year?"

"No."

"Fifty-three."

"So?"

"Do you know how many college graduates applied, in the three years previous to this one?"

"I have no idea."

"Seventeen. Not each year. Total."

"Now I'm really lost."

"Public relations," the mayor said significantly.

"What does that mean?"

"That a lot of young men, fifty-three young men, with college degrees, with the potential to become really good cops, saw Payne's picture in the newspapers and decided they might like being a cop themselves."

"Do you know that? Or just think that?"

"I checked it out," the mayor said.

"So what are you saying, Jerry? That we should put Payne on recruiting duty?"

"I'm saying you and Coughlin should have left him right where he was, in Special Operations."

"A," Lowenstein said, "you always transfer people who get promoted. B, there are no detectives in Special Operations."

"A, that 'transfer people when they get promoted' didn't come off the mountain with Moses, engraved on stone, and B, as of today, there are two detectives assigned to Special Operations."

"Two detectives who should have been sent back to Homicide where they belong," Lowenstein said.

"If you mean Jason Washington, he's a sergeant now. He got promoted, and he didn't get transferred out of Special Operations. I said two *detectives*. One of whom is Tony Harris, who would probably go back to being a drunk if we sent him back to Homicide."

Lowenstein took a deep swallow of his Jack Daniel's and water. He was impressed again with Jerry Carlucci's intimate knowledge of what was going on in the Department.

Detectives Jason Washington and Tony Harris, in Lowenstein's judgment the two best Homicide detectives, had been "temporarily" assigned to the then newly formed Special Operations Division when Mayor Carlucci had taken away the Northwest serial rapist job from Northwest Detectives and given it to Peter Wohl.

Other special jobs had come up, and they had never gone back to Homicide, which had been a continuing source of annoyance to Matt Lowenstein. The only good thing about it was that Tony Harris seemed to have gotten his bottle problem under control working for Wohl. Until just now, Matt Lowenstein had believed that Harris's boozing was known to only a few people, not including the mayor.

"You said 'two detectives,' " Lowenstein said, finally. "The other one's name is Payne, right?"

"You're a clever fellow. Maybe you should be a detective or something," Jerry Carlucci said.

Lowenstein did not reply.

"He can learn as much watching Washington and Harris as he could have learned in

East Detectives, and probably quicker," Carlucci said. "And he'll be available, without a lot of bullshit and resentment, the next time the Department needs to do somebody who can do the Department a lot of good a favor."

"Oh, shit," Matt Lowenstein said.

"You don't like it?" the mayor said. There was just a hint of coldness in his voice.

"What I don't like is that you're right," Lowenstein said. "It wasn't fair to either East Detectives or Payne to send him there. I don't know if he'll stay on the job or not, but if he does, it wouldn't be at East Detectives."

"I thought about that too," Carlucci said. "Whether he would stay. I decided he would. He's been around long enough, done enough, to have it get in his blood."

"You make it sound like syphilis," Lowenstein said.

Mr. Ricco Baltazari had his luncheon, a dozen cherrystone clams, a double thick lamb chop, medium rare with mint sauce, and a sliced tomato with olive oil and vinegar in his place of business, the Ristorante Alfredo, in Center City, Philadelphia, three blocks east of the Union League.

A table in the rear of the establishment had been especially laid for the occasion, for Mr. Gian-Carlo Rosselli had called Mr. Baltazari with the announcement that Mr. S. thought he would like to have a little fish for his lunch and was that going to pose any problems?

Mr. Baltazari had told Mr. Rosselli that it would be no problem at all, and what time was Mr. S. thinking of having his lunch?

"Twelve-thirty, one," Mr. Rosselli had replied and then hung up without saying another word.

Mr. Baltazari had personally inspected the table after it was set, to make sure there wasn't any grease or lipstick or whatever the dishwasher had missed; that there were no chips on the dishes or glasses; and that there were no spots on the tablecloth or napkins the laundry hadn't washed out. Then he went into the kitchen and personally first selected the slice of swordfish that would be served to Mr. S., and then the wines he thought Mr. S. might like. After a moment's thought, he added a third bottle, of sparkling wine, to his original selections and had it put into the refrigerator to cool. Sometimes Mr. S. liked sparkling wine.

As a final preparation, Mr. Baltazari walked two blocks farther east, toward the Delaware River, where he had a shave and a trim and had his shoes shined.

Mr. S., whose full name was Vincenzo Carlos Savarese, was more than just a customer. Despite what it said on Ristorante Alfredo's restaurant and liquor licenses, that Ricco Baltazari was the owner and licensee, it was really owned by Mr. Savarese. Mr. Baltazari operated it for him, it being understood between them that no matter what it said on the books about salary and profits, that Mr. S. was to be paid, in cash, once a month, fifty percent of gross receipts less the cost of food, liquor, rent, salaries, and laundry.

Out of his fifty percent, Mr. Baltazari was expected to pay all other expenses. Anything left over after that was his.

There was no written agreement. They were men of honor, and it was understood between them that if it ever came to Mr. S.'s attention that Mr. Baltazari had been fucking with the books, taking cash out of the register, or in any other way, no matter how, depriving Mr. S. of his full return on his investment, Mr. Baltazari could expect to find himself floating facedown in the Delaware River, or stuffed into the trunk of his Cadillac with twenty-dollar bills inserted into his nostrils and other cranial cavities.

Mr. Savarese, a slightly built, silver-haired, superbly tailored and shod man in his early sixties, arrived at Ristorante Alfredo at five minutes to one. He took great pride in his personal appearance, believing that a businessman, such as himself, should look the part.

He had, ten years before, arranged the immigration from Rome of a journeyman gentlemen's tailor and set him up in business in a downtown office building. At Mr. S.'s recommendation, a number of his business associates had begun to patronize the tailor, and he had found financial security and a good life in the new world. It was understood between the tailor and Mr. Savarese that the tailor would not offer to cut a suit for anyone else from a bolt of cloth from which he had cut a suit for Mr. Savarese.

Shoes were something else. Mr. Savarese was a good enough businessman to understand there was not a sufficient market in Philadelphia to support a custom bootmaker, no matter how skilled, so he had his shoes made in Palermo on a last carved there for him on a visit he had made years before attending the funeral of a great-aunt.

Mr. Savarese did not own an automobile, and rarely drove himself, although he took pains to make sure his driver's license did not lapse. The Lincoln sedan in which he arrived at Ristorante Alfredo was owned by Classic Livery, which supplied limousines to the funeral trade, and which was owned, in much the same sort of arrangement as that which Mr. Saverese had with Mr. Baltazari vis-à-vis Ristorante Alfredo, by Mr. Paulo Cassandro. Mr. Cassandro, as now, habitually assigned his brother, Pietro, to drive the automobile he made available for Mr. Savarese's use.

Mr. Savarese, as now, was habitually accompanied by Mr. Gian-Carlo Rosselli, a tall, heavyset gentleman in his middle thirties.

When the Lincoln pulled to the curb before the marquee of Ristorante Alfredo, Mr. Rosselli, who was riding in the front seat, got out of the car and walked around the front to the sidewalk. He glanced up and down the street, and then nodded at Mr. Cassandro. Mr. Cassandro then got from behind the wheel and opened the rear door for Mr. Savarese.

By the time Mr. Savarese reached the door of the restaurant, Mr. Rosselli had pulled the door open for him. He stepped inside, where Mr. Baltazari was waiting for him. They shook hands. Mr. Baltazari was always very careful when shaking hands with Mr. Savarese, for his hands were very large and strong, and Mr. Savarese's rather delicate. Mr. Savarese played the violin and the violoncello, primarily for his own pleasure, but sometimes for friends, say at a wedding or an anniversary celebration. It was considered a great honor to have him play at such gatherings.

Mr. Baltazari led Mr. Savarese and Mr. Rosselli to the table, where the maître d'hôtel was standing behind the chair in which Mr. Savarese would sit, and a waiter (not the wine steward; that sonofabitch having this day, of all goddamned days, with Mr. S. coming in, called in sick) stood before two wine coolers on legs.

Mr. Savarese sat down, and the headwaiter pushed his chair in for him. He looked up at Mr. Rosselli, who was obviously waiting for direction, and made a little gesture with his hand, signaling that Mr. Rosselli should sit down.

"What are you going to feed me, Ricco?" Mr. Savarese asked with a smile.

"I thought some cherrystones," Mr. Baltazari said. "And there is some very nice swordfish?"

"I leave myself in your hands."

"I have a nice white wine . . ."

"Anything you think . . ."

"And some nice Fiore e Fiore sparkling . . ."

"The sparkling. It always goes so well with the clams, I think."

Mr. Baltazari snapped his fingers and the waiter who was standing in for the goddamned wine steward who'd chosen today to fuck off twisted the wire holding the cork in the sparkling wine off, popped the cork, and poured a little in a champagne glass whose stem was hollow to the bottom and cost a fucking fortune and was only taken out of the cabinet when Mr. S. was in the place.

Mr. Savarese tasted the sparkling wine.

"That's very nice, Ricco," he said.

"Thank you," Mr. Baltazari said, beaming, and then added, to the headwaiter, "Put a case of that in Mr. S.'s car."

"You're very kind," Mr. Savarese said.

The waiter filled Mr. Savarese's glass with the Fiore e Fiore, and then poured some in Mr. Baltazari's and Mr. Rosselli's glasses.

Mr. Baltazari then raised his glass, and Mr. Rosselli followed suit.

"Health and long life," Mr. Baltazari said.

Mr. Savarese smiled.

"What is it the Irish say? 'May the sun'—or is it the wind?—'always be at your back.' I like that."

"I think 'the wind,' Mr. S.," Mr. Rosselli said.

"I think it's the sun," Mr. Savarese said.

"Now that I think about it, I'm sure you're right," Mr. Rosselli said.

"It doesn't matter, either way," Mr. Savarese said graciously.

"The cherrystones and the swordfish for Mr. Savarese, right?" the maître d'hôtel asked. "And for you, sir?"

"What are you eating, Ricco?" Mr. Rosselli asked.

"Lamb chops."

"Same for me," Mr. Rosselli said. "Sometimes swordfish don't agree with me."

"How would you like them cooked, sir?"

"Pink in the middle."

The clams, on a bed of ice, were served. While they were eating them, Mr. Savarese inquired as to the health of Mr. Baltazari's wife and children, and Mr. Baltazari asked Mr. Savarese to pass on his best respects to Mr. Savarese's wife and mother.

The clams were cleared away, and the entrée served.

Mr. Baltazari made a gesture, and a folding screen was put in place, screening the table from the view of anyone in the front part of the restaurant.

"Open another bottle of the Fiore e Fiore," Mr. Baltazari ordered, "and then leave us alone."

Mr. Savarese delicately placed a piece of the swordfish into his mouth, chewed, and nodded.

"This is very nice, Ricco," he said.

"I'm glad you're pleased, Mr. S."

"It has to be fresh," Mr. Saverese said. "Otherwise, when it's been on ice too long, it gets mushy."

"That was swimming in the Gulf of Mexico two days ago, Mr. S."

"Tell me why you told Joe Fierello to make the police officer a good deal," Mr. Savarese said as he placed another piece of swordfish into his mouth. "Tell me about the police officer, is what I want."

"I was going to call you this morning, but then Carlo called and said you was coming, and I figured it could wait until I could tell you in person."

Mr. Savarese nodded, and then gestured with his fork for Mr. Baltazari to continue.

"I try to keep my eyes open," Mr. Baltazari said. "So when I saw this cop flashing a wad in the Warwick . . ."

"How did you know he was a police officer?" Mr. Savarese interrupted.

"I can tell a cop, Mr. S.," Mr. Baltazari said, a bit smugly. "So I checked him out."

"How?"

"I happened to be with a lady," Mr. Baltazari said, just a little uneasily. "I had her do it for me."

"Can this lady be trusted?"

"She's a divorced lady, Mr. S. With a kid. She has a hard time making out on what they pay her at the phone company, so I help her out from time to time."

Mr. Savarese nodded, and Mr. Baltazari went on.

"She struck up a conversation with this guy, like I told her, and come back and told me he's a corporal, working at the airport, and that he just come home from Vegas, where he won a lot of money . . ."

"How much?"

"I don't know exactly, but he was talking about buying a Caddy, so I figure fifteen, twenty big ones, maybe a little more."

Mr. Savarese nodded his understanding again.

"So I figured this was one of those times when you have to do something right away, or forget it," Mr. Baltazari went on. "So I sent the lady back to the cop and told her to tell him she has an uncle who has a car lot who would give him a good deal."

"Is this police officer married?" Mr. Savarese asked.

"I don't *know,* Mr. S. He told Antoinette he's a bachelor."

"It would be better if he was married," Mr. Savarese said.

"I'll find out for sure and let you know, Mr. S. Anyway, I figured if this wasn't such a hot idea, no harm. So I called Joe, and told him. . . ."

"What you should have done, Ricco," Mr. Savarese said, "was call me and let me talk to Joe."

"I wasn't sure if you would have time to talk with me today, Mr. S."

"Joe called me," Mr. Savarese said, "and asked exactly what was going on. I didn't know, and that was very embarrassing. So I told him I would talk to you and get back to him."

"If I stepped out of line, Mr. S., I'm really sorry. But like I said, I figured no harm . . ."

Mr. Savarese interrupted Mr. Baltazari by holding up the hand with the fork in it.

"Gian-Carlo," he said. "Get on the phone to Joe. Tell him there was a slight misunderstanding. Tell him I have absolute faith in Ricco's judgment."

Mr. Rosselli laid down his knife and fork and pushed himself away from the table.

"There's a pay station in the candy store on the corner," Mr. Savarese said.

"Right, Mr. S.," Mr. Rosselli said.

When he had gone, Mr. Savarese laid his hand on that of Mr. Baltazari.

"Ricco," he said. "This may be more important than you know. This police officer works at the airport. You're sure of that?"

"That's what he told Antoinette."

"Do you recall reading, or seeing on the television, two months back, about the police officer who was killed in an auto accident on the way from the shore?"

"I seem to remember something about that, Mr. S."

"He was a friend of ours, Ricco."

"I didn't know that, Mr. S."

"And he worked at the airport. And now that he's gone, we don't have a friend at the airport. That's posing certain problems for us. Serious problems, right now."

"Oh."

"This police officer you found could be very useful to us, Ricco."

"I understand."

"Whatever is done with him has to be done very carefully, you understand. But at the same time, so long as we don't have a friend at the airport, the problems we are having there are not going to go away."

"I understand," Mr. Baltazari said, although he had no idea what Mr. S. had going at the airport.

"I want you to let me know what goes on, when it happens, Ricco. And while I trust your judgment, whenever there is any question at all in your mind about what to do, I want you to call me and we'll decide what to do together. You understand, Ricco?"

"Absolutely, Mr. S."

"Why don't you go get us some coffee, Ricco?"

"Certainly, Mr. S."

Marion Claude Wheatley did not own an automobile, and had not for several years. He suspected, and then had proved by putting all the figures down on paper, that it was much cheaper, considering the price of automobiles and their required maintenance and especially the price of insurance, to rent a car when he needed one.

And the inconveniences—particularly that of getting groceries from the supermarket checkout counter to the house—were overwhelmed by the elimination of annoyances not owning an automobile provided.

Paying his automobile insurance had especially annoyed him. There were, he was quite sure, actuarial reasons for the insurance company's classifications of people they insured. They were, after all, a business, not a charitable organization. Statistically, it could be proved that an unmarried male between twenty-one and thirty-five living in Philadelphia could be expected to cost the insurance company far more in settling claims than a thirty-six-year-old who was married and lived, say, in New Hope or Paoli. But there was an exception to every rule, and they should have acknowledged that.

He had never had a traffic violation in his life, had never been involved in an accident, and did not use his automobile to commute to work. He drove it back and forth to the supermarket and every month to New Jersey to check on the farm. Sometimes, on rare occasions, such as when Hammersmith, or someone like him, felt obliged to have him to dinner, he drove it at night out to Bryn Mawr, or someplace.

But most of the time the car had sat in the garage, letting its battery discharge.

He had tried to make this point to his insurance broker, who had not only been unsympathetic to his reasoning but had practically laughed at him.

He had solved both problems by selling the car and changing insurance brokers. Marion believed that when you know something is right, you do it.

And he had learned that while renting a car wasn't as cheap as the rental companies advertising would have one believe, it was possible, by carefully reading the advertisements and taking advantage of discounts of one kind or another, to rent a car at perfectly reasonable figures.

When he returned to his office from having lunch with Hammersmith at the Union League, he spent the next forty-five minutes calling around and arranging a car for the weekend. The best price was offered, this time, by Hertz. If he picked up the car at the airport, not downtown, after six-thirty on Friday, and returned it not later than eleven-thirty on Saturday, they would charge him for only one twenty-four-hour day, providing he did not add more than two hundred miles to the odometer. They would also provide him a "standard" size car, for the price of a "compact."

It averaged between 178.8 and 192.4 miles, round trip (he didn't really understand why there should be a difference, unless the odometers themselves were inaccurate) from the airport to the farm, so he would be within the 200-mile limitation. And since he was getting a standard-sized car, that meant he could conceal the equipment he was taking to the farm in the trunk.

Marion Claude Wheatley knew enough about explosives to know that the greater distance one can put between detonators and explosives the better. He didn't think the Lord would cause an accident now, but it was better to be safe than sorry. Marion knew that the Lord would probably not be at all forgiving, if through his own carelessness he had an accident, and hurt—or disintegrated—himself while having a test run of the demolition program for the Vice President at the farm.

The only risky part would be getting from the house to the airport in the taxicab to pick up the car. He would have to have the detonators, half a dozen of them, in his suit jacket breast pocket. They were getting pretty old now, and with age came instability. There were half a dozen ways in which they could be inadvertently set off. He would carry the Composition C-4 in his attaché case, as usual. The cabdriver might look askance if he asked to put the attaché case in the trunk, with the suitcases, particularly if it was a small taxi, and there would not be a lot of room.

The risk was that something would set off one of the detonators. If that happened, it was a certainty that the other five detonators would also detonate. The technical phrase was "sympathetic detonation." If one detonator went off, and then, microseconds later, the other five, it was a possibility, even a likelihood, that the Composition C-4 would detonate sympathetically.

It was a risk that would have to be taken. The more he thought about it, the less worried he became. If something happened in the taxicab, the Lord, who knew everything, would understand that he had been doing the best he knew how. And if he permitted Marion to be disintegrated, who would be available to disintegrate the Vice President?

9.

Joe Fierello did not like Paulo Cassandro. The sonofabitch had always been arrogant, long before he'd made his bones and become a made man, and now he was fucking insufferable. Joe didn't really understand why they had made the sonofabitch a made man.

But that didn't matter. What was was, and you don't let a made man know that you think he's really an ignorant asshole.

"Paulo!" Joe called happily when, around half past two, Paulo got out of the back seat of his Jaguar sedan and walked up to the office. "How are you, pal? What can I do for you?"

"A mutual friend wanted to make sure that nothing goes wrong when your niece comes in later."

"Nothing will, Paulo. I talked with Gian-Carlo not more than a hour ago."

"I just talked with Mr. S., and he suggested I come down here and explain exactly what has to be done."

Joe Fierello was more than a little curious about that. When Gian-Carlo Rosselli said something, you knew it was direct from Mr. S. So what was Paulo Cassandro doing here?

"Let me know what I can do," Joe said.

"You know this guy coming is a cop?"

Joe nodded.

"What Mr. S. wants you to do is sell him a really nice car . . ."

"I was going to."

". . . at a special price. Like a thousand, fifteen hundred under Blue Book loan."

The Blue Book was a small, shirt-pocket-size listing of recent automobile transactions, published for the automotive trade. It listed the average retail sale price of an automobile, the average amount of money a bank or finance company had loaned for an installment purchase, and the average price dealers had paid as a trade-in.

"You got it."

"And he wants you to pay him at least a grand more for his trade-in than it's worth."

"Any friend of Mr. S.'s . . ."

"Don't be a wiseass, Joe. This is business."

"Sorry."

"Yeah. You got a Xerox machine, right?"

"Sure."

"We're going to make up a little file on this cop. In it will be copies of this week's Blue Book showing what his trade is worth, and what the car you're going to sell him is worth. And then, on Tuesday, when you run his trade-in through the auction, where you will give it away, we want a Xerox of that too."

"This has all been explained to me, Paulo," Joe said.

"Yeah, well, Mr. S. obviously figured somebody better explain it again, so there would be no mistakes, which is why I'm here, okay?"

"Absolutely."

"And in addition to everything else you're going to do nice for this cop," Paulo went on, "you're going to give him this."

He handed him a printed form. Joe looked at it without understanding. It bore the logotype of the Oaks and Pines Resort Lodge in the Poconos, and it said that the Bearer was entitled to have a room and all meals, plus unlimited free tennis and two rounds of golf.

"What is this?"

"It's what they call a comp," Paulo explained. "This place is owned by a friend of Mr. S.'s. Let's say, for example, they buy a case of soap to wash the dishes. Or two cases, something worth a couple of hundred bucks. Instead of paying them cash, the lodge people give them one of these. *Retail,* it's worth more than the two hundred. *Cost-wise* maybe a hundred. So the guy who came up with the soap gets more than the soap is worth, and the lodge people get the soap for less than the guy wanted. *Capisce?"*

"I seen a comp coupon before, Paulo," Joe said. "What I was asking was, is this cop gonna be a tennis player? Or a golf player?"

"He gets to take the girl to a hotel," Paulo said. "He don't give a fuck about golf."

Joe still looked confused, and Paulo took pity on him.

"There's a story going around, I personally don't know if it's true or not, that in some of these lodge places in the Poconos you can gamble in the back room."

Joe now nodded his understanding.

"You tell this guy you shoot a little craps at this place from time to time, and they sent you the comp coupon, and you can't use it, so he can have it."

"Right."

"Don't fuck this up, Joe. Mr. S. is personally interested in this."

"You tell Mr. S. not to worry."

"He's not worrying. I'm not worrying. You should be the one that's worrying."

Antoinette Marie Wolinski Schermer had moved back in with her parents when Eddie, that sonofabitch, had moved out on her and Brian, which was all she could do, suspecting correctly that getting child support out of Eddie was going to be like pulling teeth.

That hadn't worked out. Her mother, especially, and her father were Catholic and didn't believe in divorce no matter what a sonofabitch you were married to, no matter if he slapped you around whenever he had two beers in him. What they expected her to do was go to work, save her money, and wait around the house for the time when she could straighten things out with Eddie.

No going out, in other words.

She had met Ricco Baltazari in the Reading Terminal Market on Market Street. She had gone there for lunch, and so had he. She decided later, when she found out that he owned Ristorante Alfredo, which was before she found out that he was connected with the Mob, that he had probably got bored with the fancy food in his restaurant and wanted a hot Italian sausage with onions and peppers, which was what she was having when she saw him looking at her.

She had noticed him too, saw that he was a really good-looking guy, that he was dressed real nice, and that when he paid for his sausage and pepper and onions, he had a wad of fifties and hundreds as thick as his thumb.

It probably had something to do, too, with what people said about opposites attracting. She was blonde (she only had to touch it up to keep it light, not dye it, the way most blondes had to) and fair-skinned, and he was sort of dark olive-skinned with really black hair.

The first time she noticed him, she wondered what it would be like doing it with him, never suspecting that she would find out that same night.

The first night, he picked her up outside work in his Cadillac and they went first to a real nice restaurant in Jersey, outside Cherry Hill, where everybody seemed to know him, and the manager or whatever sent a bottle of champagne to the table. Ricco told her right out that he was married, but didn't get along with his old lady, but couldn't divorce her because his mother was old and a Catholic, and you know how Catholics feel about divorce.

After dinner, they went to a motel, not one of the el cheapos that lined Admiral Wilson

Boulevard, but to the Cherry Hill Inn, which was real nice, and had in the bathroom the first whatchamacallit that Antoinette had ever seen. She had to ask Ricco what it was for.

The truth of the matter was that when he was driving her back to her parents' house she thought she had blown it, that she had been too easy to pick up, that she had gone to the motel with him on the First Date, and that once there, she had been a little too enthusiastic. She hadn't been with anybody in months, and the two whiskey sours and then the champagne and then the two Amaretto liqueurs afterward had put her more than a little into the bag.

Antoinette figured, in other words, that Ricco had got what he wanted (probably more than he expected) and that was the last she would ever see of him. She could have played it smarter, she supposed, but the vice versa was also true. She had got what she wanted too, a nice dinner, a nice ride in a Caddy, and then what happened in the motel, which she had needed and wanted from the moment she first saw him trying to look down her blouse.

But then a week later, when she walked out of the building after work, there he was at the curb, looking real nice, and smiling at her, and holding the door of his Caddy open for her.

He told her that he would have called her sooner, but his wife was being a bitch, and he couldn't arrange it. She told him that she understood, she had been married to someone like that herself, a real bastard.

He told her he would like to show her his restaurant, but that she understood why he couldn't do that, with his wife and all, and she told him she understood. The second night, they had gone to the bar in the Warwick Hotel, and then across the street to a bar that had a piano player, and then back across the street to the Warwick, to a nice hotel suite he said a business associate kept all the time so he could use it when he was in town.

When she went home that night, her father and mother were waiting up for her like she was sixteen or seventeen, instead of a woman who was twenty-three and had a kid, and said she looked like a whore and smelled like a drunk and they weren't going to put up with that. And who was the Guinea in the Cadillac, some gangster?

The next time she saw Ricco, three days later, she told him what had happened, and that if they were going to do anything, they would have to do it early, so she wouldn't get hell when she got home.

He asked her why she still lived at home, and she told him about Eddie and Brian, and how Eddie, that sonofabitch, wasn't paying child support. He told her maybe something could be worked out; he would look into it.

The first thing that happened was that Eddie, out of the goddamned blue, sent a Western Union money order for four hundred bucks, which wasn't all he owed, of course, but was four hundred Antoinette didn't expect to get.

And then she heard from her mother that she had heard from Eddie's mother that Eddie had gotten mugged going home from work, that two white guys had done a real job on him, knocked out a couple of teeth, and broken his glasses and a couple of ribs, and taken all his money.

Antoinette wasn't stupid. She knew that the last thing Eddie would have done if he had got mugged and they took all his money would suddenly decide to send child support. And three days after the Western Union money order came, there was one from the Post Office, what he owed for two weeks' child support, plus twenty dollars on account.

The only way Eddie would suddenly decide to start doing what was right was because somebody had convinced him that he better do right, and Antoinette suspected that Ricco was that somebody.

Ricco wouldn't admit it, of course, but what he said was that bastards who won't support their own children deserve whatever happens to them, like losing a couple of teeth.

The second thing that happened was that Ricco said he knew where she could get a nice apartment, a couple of blocks from the Warwick, the only problem being she couldn't have a kid in there. Antoinette told him it didn't matter whether she could have Brian or not, on what the phone company was paying her, she couldn't afford it. He said he would be happy to help out with the whole thing.

Her mother and father threw a fit when she said she was moving out, and her father said he knew it had something to do with that Guinea gangster with the shiny Cadillac, and her mother said she was making the mistake of her life, because Eddie was straightening himself out, like for example paying the child support for one thing. But she moved out anyway, and came to believe that her mother and father were really glad she had, because that way, except when she saw him on weekends, they had Brian all to themselves.

The apartment was nice, and Ricco not only picked up the rent, but was always slipping her a fifty or a hundred and telling her to buy herself something. She knew that she was kidding herself whenever she thought about maybe getting him to marry her. He was going to stay married to his Guinea princess for ever.

The only thing that had ever really bothered her was the first time he told her that he had a friend from Chicago that was coming to town and he wanted her to be very nice to him, and she knew what very nice meant. That made her feel like a hooker, but she had just moved into the apartment, and couldn't just move back home again, so she did it. It wasn't as bad as she thought, the guy was nicer than she thought he would be, and to tell the truth, he was pretty good between the sheets, and when he went back to Chicago, Ricco handed her four fifties and told her to buy herself a cheese-steak or something.

And it didn't happen often, maybe two, three, four times a year. It wasn't as if he was telling her to go stand on a sidewalk someplace and wink at strange men, just be very nice to people who were important to Ricco. That didn't seem to be, considering, all that much for him to ask of her.

This Vito Lanza the cop was something else. This was the first time something like this had happened. But if Ricco wanted her to do it, it was important. And what the hell, the truth was Vito was kind of cute, and not too bad in the bedroom department, either. It wasn't as if he made her want to throw up, like that.

Ricco told her he wanted her to be very nice to Vito the cop until he told her different. He said the cop was in a position to be useful to some business associates of his, and part of that meant getting him to figure that he owed her something.

It was pretty clear to Antoinette that it had something to do with his being a cop at the airport. They wanted him to be looking the other way when something happened, something like that. It wasn't as if they were *after* Vito, anything like that. If they were after him, the same thing that had happened to Eddie would already have happened to him.

Vito was waiting for her outside the apartment in his Buick when she got home from work. He acted like he wanted to go up to the apartment with her, and then go see her uncle Joe, but she told him that her uncle expected them now, before he had to go home, and they could come back to the apartment later.

Take care of business first. Antoinette had learned that from Ricco. Ricco was always saying that.

Marion reached the farm about quarter to nine. There had been no cars on the highway when he turned off onto the dirt country road, and he encountered no cars on the dirt road as he drove to the farm.

There are approximately 1,200,000 acres in that portion of southern New Jersey known as the Pine Barrens. Statistically speaking, the built-up portions of southern New Jersey represent a very small fraction of the total land area. The term "Pine Barrens," Marion had learned, had been applied to the area from the earliest days of colonization. "Barrens" meant the area was barren, except for stunted pine trees.

There were some exceptions, of course. Some people had acquired title to land within the Barrens with the intention of farming it. Some had succeeded, including, for a time, some of Marion's maternal ancestors. It was a mystery to Marion how they had managed to eke a living out of their double section (1,280 acres, more or less, as the deed described it), but there was no question that they had, from the early 1800s for almost a century.

The house, as closely as he had been able to determine, had been built circa 1810, and the farm had been in use until just before World War I. He had no idea why it had not been sold, but it hadn't, and it had come to him via inheritance.

For a long time, he had thought that the reason he had not sold it was because no one wanted it. The house was 6.3 miles from the nearest paved road. There was a well, but the water was foul-tasting, and while Marion did not pretend to understand things like this, he suspected it was somehow contaminated. The taxes were negligible, and he had simply kept the farm.

Now he knew, of course, that it hadn't been his decision at all, but the Lord's. The Lord had had plans for the farm all along.

The fences, except for vestiges here and there, had long ago disappeared, as had the wooden portions of the farmhouse, and the barns and other outlying structures. What was left was a three-room building, partly constructed from field stone and partly from crude brick.

Marion's father had replaced the windows in the building, and installed a tin roof when Marion was a little boy. Marion now understood that his father had had some half-baked idea of making the farmhouse into some sort of vacation cabin, but that idea had sort of petered out. Marion's mother had not liked driving into the Pine Barrens to spend the weekend cooking on a camping stove and using an outside privy. There was absolutely nothing to do at the farm but sit around and talk and look out at stunted pine trees.

She had, he now understood, tried. She had planted various kinds of flowers and bushes, most of which had died, but some of which, roses and some bushes the names of which he had never known, had survived and even flourished. You couldn't see the farm-house, behind the vegetation, until you were within a hundred yards.

There were unpaved roads running along the south and north property lines, main-tained as little as possible by the county, who showed up once a year with road scrapers. There were two roads, more properly described as paths, leading from the unpaved roads. One of them led to the farmhouse, and the other, nothing more than earth beaten into two tracks, simply crossed between the two unpaved county roads.

When Marion reached the house, he parked the car behind the house, and then, using a flashlight to light his way, walked around to the front, unlocked the padlock, removed it from the hasp, and let himself in.

He flashed the light around the room. There were no signs of intruders. Standing the flashlight on its end, he took a Coleman lantern from a shelf, filled the tank from a gallon can of Coleman Fluid, pumped it up and got it going. Then he extinguished the flashlight, and carried the Coleman lantern and the can of Coleman Fluid into the bedroom, where he repeated the fueling and lighting procedure for a second Coleman lantern.

He then returned to the front room, where he refueled a Coleman stove with Coleman liquid. Unless properly handled, the Coleman lanterns and stoves were dangerous. Marion could not understand why people were blind to that. The newspapers were always full of stories of people who were burned when they tried to refuel lanterns and stoves while they were still hot.

He then went out to the rental car and brought the six detonators into the house. He carefully placed them in a drawer of the dresser in the bedroom, lying them on a bed of work shirts and underwear, for a cushion under them, and then carefully placed more work shirts and underwear on top of them. Marion knew that there was no such thing as being too careful with detonators.

Then he returned to the car again, took his suitcase out of it, and carefully locked it. In the interests of safety, it was better to leave the Composition C-4 right where it was, in the car.

He went into the bedroom, and changed out of his suit and dress shirt into what he thought of as his farm clothes, a flannel shirt, denim overalls, and ankle-high work shoes.

Then he made another trip out to the car, unlocked it, took out the groceries he'd bought just outside of Camden, locked the car again, and carried the groceries into the house.

He pumped up the Coleman stove, got it going, and cooked his supper, a hamburger steak with onions, instant mashed potatoes, lima beans, and coffee. For dessert he had ice cream. It was cold, but no longer frozen, but that couldn't be helped. It was just too much of a nuisance to carry ice to the farm.

After he finished eating, he washed the dishes and the pots and pans and put the garbage into one of the grocery bags. He would take it to the garbage dump in the morning.

If, he thought, making a wry little joke with himself, if there was still any place to dump garbage in his garbage dump.

The problem with the farm, Marion often thought, was exactly opposite from the problem he had with the house in Philadelphia. In the city, people were always trying— and often succeeding—in taking away things that belonged to him. At the farm, people were always giving him things he hadn't asked for and didn't want. Such as worn-out automobile tires, refrigerators, mattresses, and bed springs.

He didn't like it, of course. No civilized person could be anything but annoyed with the transformation of one's private property into a public dump. But he understood why it had happened, and why the police couldn't do much about it.

While the land was mostly flat, there were two depressions, each more than two acres in size, both of them touching the road that cut across the property from one country road to the other. The garbage dumpers simply backed their trucks up to the edge of the depressions and unloaded their worn-out mattresses, rusty bed springs, old tires, and broken refrigerators.

Marion had from time to time complained to the authorities about the unauthorized dumping, but to no avail. They told him that if he, or they, caught someone dumping, they would of course deal with the matter. But since there was no one living in the area, police patrols seldom visited it, their presence being required elsewhere.

His only solution, they told him, was to both fence and post the property. Fencing 1,280 acres was of course for financial reasons out of the question. And when he had put up PRIVATE PROPERTY—TRESPASSERS WILL BE PROSECUTED signs where the paths began at the county roads, the only response had been that the garbage dumpers, or someone else, had used them for target practice. It had been a waste of money.

Four months before, on one of his monthly weekends at the farm, he had taken the canvas tarpaulin off the old Fordson tractor his father had bought years before, jump-started it with jumper cables from his rented Chevrolet, and driven it around the farm on what he thought of as his quarterly inspection of the property.

This time there had been something new in the larger of the two garbage dumps. Lockers. They appeared to have been in a fire. There were approximately fifty of them, each about three feet square. They were painted green, and they were constructed in units of three.

Curiosity had overcome his disgust and annoyance, and he'd gotten off the Fordson, leaving it running, and gone down in the depression and opened them. It was only then, when he found keys in most of them, that he recognized them for what they were. They were the lockers one found in railroad stations, where travelers stored their suitcases. You put a quarter in the slot, which allowed you to withdraw the key. When you returned to the locker for your belongings and put the key back in the lock, the door could be opened, but the mechanism now seized the key and would hold it until another quarter was deposited.

Marion had happened to have two quarters in his pocket, and tested two of the lockers. They were operable.

He had then regretted having thrown the fifty cents away, and climbed out of the depression and got back on the Fordson and drove back to the farmhouse. He had made his supper, and then got on his knees and prayed for the souls of those of his men whom the Lord had chosen to take unto Him in 'Nam.

He would have thought that he would have given no further thought to the lockers than he had to the refrigerators and worn-out tires or the other garbage, but they stayed in his mind. Where had they come from? He thought he would have heard if there had been a fire in a railroad station. Why, since some of them had hardly been damaged, had they been discarded?

He had thought of the lockers not only during that weekend on the farm, but often afterward. There had been no answers until he had read in *The Philadelphia Inquirer* that the Vice President was going to arrive in Philadelphia and depart from Philadelphia by train, at the 30th Street Station.

Then, of course, it had all become quite clear. The reason the lockers had been dumped on the farm was because the Lord wanted him to have the lockers to use when he disintegrated the Vice President.

The moment this had popped into his mind, Marion knew that it was true. There was no need to get on his knees and beg the Lord for a sign. The Lord had already given him a sign, back in 'Nam. Marion had personally gone to the locker room of the Hotel de Indochine to investigate the explosion that had taken the lives of twenty-six American civilian technicians. The Vietcong had set off explosives, almost certainly Composition C-4, in half a dozen lockers. He thought that each charge had probably been a half pound of C-4, around which chain had been wrapped. Each charge had functioned like an oversize fragmentation hand grenade. The American civilians had literally been disintegrated.

The lockers in the Hotel de Indochine were not identical to the ones that had been dumped in the depression—they had been eighteen inches by five feet, not three feet square. But that was a detail that didn't seem to matter.

There were rows of lockers like the ones that had been dumped all over 30th Street Station. All he was going to have to do was install a device in one locker in each of the rows. And then be in a position to see the Vice President, so that he could detonate the explosive device that would disintegrate him.

It was possible, even probable, Marion knew, that people who had not offended the Lord would also be disintegrated. But there were two ways to look at that. It couldn't be helped, for one thing, and certainly the Lord would somehow compensate in Heaven those whose premature deaths had been made necessary in order to carry out His will.

Marion had realized that it was becoming more and more clear why the Lord had chosen him as His instrument to carry out His will. There were not that many people around with his level of expertise in making lethal devices from readily available material. And there were not very many people around with access to a testing area. You can't cause an explosion in very many places without causing a good deal of curiosity. The farm, in the middle of the Pine Barrens, was one of the very few places where an explosion would not be heard.

After Marion had put the garbage from the meal into the paper bag from the grocery store, he turned off the Coleman lantern in the kitchen and went into the bedroom.

He made the bed, laid out fresh underwear and socks for the morning, took off his clothes, and then turned off the other Coleman lantern. He dropped to his knees by the side of the bed, and prayed the Lord's grace on himself as he began to carry out His will, and then for the souls of the boys who the Lord had taken into Heaven from Vietnam, and then he got in bed and was almost instantly asleep.

Marion woke at first light. He changed into the linen he had laid out the night before, and then made his breakfast. Bacon, two fried eggs, fried "toast," coffee, and a small can of tomato juice. After he ate he washed the dishes and pots and pans, and added the refuse to the garbage from supper.

He then began to lay out on the table everything he would need to make the devices. There were two large rolls of duct tape, approximately thirty feet of one-inch link chain, the shortwave receivers from Radio Shack, and an assortment of tools, including a large bolt cutter. Then he went out to the car and brought in the Composition C-4.

The basic device would be two quarter-pound blocks of Composition C-4, which looked not unlike sticks of butter, except of course they were gray in color, and had a hole to accommodate the detonator. He didn't have as many detonators as he would have liked to have had, so for the testing, he would use one detonator per device. The devices he would install in the lockers in 30th Street Station would have two detonators per device. Redundancy was the term. The chances of two detonators failing to function were infinitesimal.

First he taped a dozen blocks of Composition C-4 together, two blocks to a unit. Then he wound chain around one of the double blocks, as tightly as he could, twisting the links so that they sort of doubled up on each other. Then, holding the last link carefully in his hand, he unwound the chain. He took the bolt cutter and cut the link he had held in his hand.

Then he measured off five more lengths of chain, using the first length as a template. He then wound the chain around the six double blocks of Composition C-4, and then wound that with the duct tape.

That was all that he felt he should do, in the interests of safety, in the house. The rest he would do on site.

He put the partially constructed devices into a canvas satchel, and carried that outside to where the Fordson sat under its tarpaulin. He removed the tarpaulin, and checked to see that there was sufficient fuel in the tank. Then from a small, two-wheel trailer attached to the rear of the tractor, he took a set of jumper cables.

He then started the rental car, drove it to the tractor, opened the hood, and connected the jumper cables. The tractor started almost immediately, which Marion interpreted as a good omen. He set the throttle at fast idle.

He then put the satchel with the partially constructed devices in the utility trailer, and then, in four trips into the house, took the garbage, the shortwave equipment from Radio Shack, and most of the tools from the table and loaded it into the trailer. Finally he went into the bedroom and took the detonators from the dresser. He wrapped each very carefully in two socks, one outside the other, and then put the padded detonators in a tin Saltines box.

He took two pillows from the bed, and carried them and the Saltines tin box with the detonators to the trailer, where he carefully laid the Saltines box on one pillow, covered it with the second pillow, and then put the bricks on the upper pillow to keep it in place.

Then he disconnected the jumper cables from the tractor, got on it, and drove off between the stunted pines. He drove very carefully, so there would be no great risk of somehow, despite all his precautions, setting off one of the detonators.

When he reached the garbage dump, he decided that the first order of business was making sure the shortwave transmitter and the receivers worked. He had tested them in Philadelphia, but electronic equipment didn't like to be bounced around and it was better to be sure.

He dug out the Saltines box from between the pillows, and carried it carefully two hundred yards into the pines as a safety precaution. Then he returned to the garbage dump and carefully rigged the test setup.

When he pressed the key on the transmitter, the capacitors that he had installed in the receiver where the speaker had been began to accumulate electrical energy and then discharged. The 15-watt 110-volt refrigerator bulb Marion had installed where the detonator would ultimately be glowed brightly for a moment. There would be more than enough juice to fire the detonator.

He disconnected everything, in the interest of safety, walked back into the pines, and took one detonator from the Saltines box. He went back to the garbage dump and carefully slipped the detonator into one of the double blocks of Composition C-4. He taped this, except for the leads, into place with duct tape.

Then he carried this down into the garbage dump, to one of the lockers, and propped the door open with his shoulder as he inserted the device, then hooked the receiver up to the exposed leads.

He then closed the locker door, put a quarter in the slot, removed the key, and climbed up out of the garbage dump. He got back on the tractor and drove what he estimated to be two hundred yards away, and then stopped. Carrying the transmitter with him, he walked fifty feet from the tractor and then turned on the Radio Shack transmitter.

He depressed the key. Nothing happened.

Kaboom!

Marion smiled.

10.

Staff Inspector Peter Wohl, wearing a faded green polo shirt and somewhat frayed khaki trousers, both liberally stained with oil spots and various colors of paint, was in the process of filling a stainless-steel thermos bottle with coffee when his door buzzer went off.

He went quickly to it and pulled it open. A slight, olive-skinned twenty-four-year-old was standing there, dressed in a somewhat flashy suit and obviously fresh from the barber.

"Hello, Hay-zus," Wohl said. "Come on in."

"Good morning, sir," Martinez said.

"You pulled your car in the garage?"

"Yes, sir."

"I just made coffee. Will you have some?"

"Thank you, please."

Wohl gestured for Martinez to have a seat on the couch under the oil painting of the naked Rubenesque lady, took two mugs from a kitchen cabinet, carried them to the coffee table, fetched the thermos, and sat down beside Martinez on the couch.

"So how are things at the airport?" Wohl asked with a smile.

The question had been intended to put Martinez at ease. It had, Wohl saw, almost the opposite reaction. Martinez was almost visibly uncomfortable.

"I'm not pushing you, Hay-zus," Wohl said. "You've only been out there a couple of weeks. I don't think anybody expected you to learn very much in that short a time."

"Yes, sir," Jesus said, then blurted: "I think I figured out how I would get drugs, or for that matter anything else, out of there."

"How?"

"For little packages, anyway. Coke. Heroin. Are they still trying to smuggle diamonds, jewels, into this country?"

I really don't know, Wohl thought. *That's the first time jewelry has come up.*

"All the Bureau of Narcotics and Dangerous Drugs mentioned was drugs," Wohl said. "You think someone is smuggling diamonds, gemstones, through the airport?"

"The way it works, on international flights, is that the plane lands and comes up to the terminal. The baggage handlers come out, they open doors in the bottom of the airplane. On the big airplanes, one guy, maybe two guys, actually get in the baggage compartment. Nobody can see them from the ground. If they knew which suitcase had the stuff, they could open it, take out a small package, packages, conceal it on their person, and then send the luggage onto the conveyor belt over to the customs area."

"Hay-zus," Wohl said. "I want to show you something."

He got up and walked to his desk, unlocked a drawer and took out a vinyl-covered loose-leaf notebook. On it was stamped:

Martinez looked at the cover, then opened the manual and flipped through it, and then looked at Wohl for an explanation.

"They sent that over, they thought it would be helpful."

Martinez nodded.

"I took a look at it," Wohl said. "They refer to what you just described as a common means of smuggling."

"I guess it is," Martinez said. "I didn't exactly feel like Sherlock Holmes."

"Maybe not Sherlock Holmes," Wohl said. "But maybe Dick Tracy. It didn't take you long to figure that out."

That was intended, too, to put Martinez at ease. This time, Wohl saw in Martinez's face, it worked.

"When you leave, take this with you. I don't think I have to tell you not to let anybody see it."

"Yeah," Martinez said. "Thank you."

"Okay. So tell me what you've figured out about how someone, a baggage handler, or anyone else, would get a small package out of the airport."

"Well, there's all sorts of people keeping an eye on the baggage handlers. The airline has their security people. Customs is there, and the drug guys, and, of course, our guys. When the baggage handlers come to work, they change into uniforms, coveralls, or whatever, in their locker room. They change back into their regular clothes when they leave work. They have spot checks, they actually search them. What they're looking for is stuff they might have stolen, tools, stuff like that, but if the airlines security people should find a small package, they would damned sure know what it was."

"Unless they were part of the system," Wohl said thoughtfully.

"Yeah, but they're subject to the same sort of spot checks when *they* leave, and also, I think, when they're working. I thought about that. What they *could* do, once one of the baggage handlers had this stuff, is take it from them, and then move into the terminal and pass it to somebody, a passenger, for example. Once they got it into the terminal, that wouldn't be hard."

"You think that's the way it's being done?"

Martinez did not reply directly.

"Another way it could be done, which would not involve the airlines security people, I mean, them being in on it, would be to put the package in another piece of luggage, one being either unloaded off, or being put on, a domestic flight. They don't search domestic luggage."

"But they do have drug-sniffing dogs working domestic luggage."

"Not every place," Martinez argued. "Like, for example, Allentown-Bethlehem-Easton. Or Harrisburg."

"Yeah," Wohl agreed.

"The risk the baggage handlers would run would be getting caught with this stuff before they could get rid of it. Which means they would have to know when the plane with the drugs was arriving, and when the plane for, say, Allentown was leaving. And then they would have to arrange it so they worked that plane too."

"How do you think it's being done? Or do you think it's being done?"

"It's being done, all right," Martinez said. "And I think we have a dirty cop involved in it."

"How?" Wohl asked.

"Nobody searches the cops. And nobody, except maybe the sergeant, or one of the lieutenants, asks a cop what he's doing. He's got keys to get onto the ramp, and keys to open the doors leading off the ramp onto the conveyors and into the terminal. I went onto the ramp and watched them unload arriving international airplanes, and nobody said beans to me. I could have been handed, say, three-, four-, even five-kilo bags of coke or heroin, and just walked away with it."

"Five kilos is ten, eleven pounds," Wohl said thoughtfully.

"Worth twenty, twenty-five thousand a K," Martinez said.

"How would you have gotten it out of the airport?"

"Passed it to somebody in the terminal. Put it in a locker, and passed the key to some-body. Or just put it in my car."

"Let me throw this at you," Wohl said. "Add this to the equation. I had a long talk with a BNDD agent. I got him to tell me something his boss didn't happen to mention. There have been two incidents of unclaimed luggage. Both about five weeks ago. Each piece had four Ks of heroin. That's why they're so sure it's coming into Philadelphia."

"The luggage is marked in some way, a name tag, probably with a phony name. If the baggage handler gets to take the stuff out of the bag, he also removes the tag. When the mule gets to the carousel, and sees his baggage, and the tag is still on it, he just doesn't pick it up."

He didn't think about that before replying, Wohl thought. *He'd already figured that out as a possibility. He's as smart as a whip.*

"That means giving up four Ks, a hundred thousand dollars' worth of drugs."

"The cost of doing business," Martinez replied.

"I don't suppose you have any idea which cop is dirty?" Wohl asked.

"No," Martinez said.

That was too quick, Wohl thought.

"I'm not asking for an accusation," Wohl said. "Just a suspicion, a gut feeling. And nothing leaves this room."

"Nothing yet," Martinez said.

That was not the truth. The moment Jesus Martinez had laid eyes on Corporal Vito Lanza, he had had the feeling that something was not right about him. But you don't accuse a brother officer, or even admit you have suspicions about him, unless you have more to go on than the fact that he gambles big money in Las Vegas, and dresses and behaves like a Guinea gangster.

Wohl suspected that Martinez was concealing something from him, but realized he could not press him any more than he had.

One of the telephones in his bedroom rang. Wohl could tell by the sound of the ring that it was his personal, rather than his official, telephone.

That makes it fairly certain, he thought as he turned toward the bedroom, *that I am not to be informed that one of my stalwart Highway Patrolmen has just run through a red light into a station wagon full of nuns.*

He had used that for instance as the criterion for telephoning him at his home on week-ends. Any catastrophe of less monumental proportions, he had ordered, should be referred to either Captain Michael Sabara, his deputy, or to Captain David Pekach, commanding officer of the Highway Patrol, for appropriate action.

"Excuse me," Wohl said, and went into his bedroom.

The fact that this is on my personal line, he thought as he sat down on his bed and reached for the telephone, *does not meant that I am not about to hear something I do not wish to hear, such as Mother reminding me that I have not been to Sunday dinner in a month, so how about tomorrow?*

"Hello?"

"From that tone of voice," his caller said, "what I think I should do is just hang up, but I hate it when people do that to me."

"Hello, Matt," Wohl said, smiling. "What's up?"

"I was wondering how welcome I would be if I drove over there."

Not at all welcome, with Martinez here. And from the tone of your voice, Detective Payne, I think the smartest thing I could do is tell you, "Sorry, I was just walking out the door."

"You would be very welcome. As a matter of fact, I was thinking of calling you. I am about to polish the Jaguar and I hate to do that alone. A weak mind and a strong back is just what I need."

"I'll be there in half an hour. Thank you," Detective Payne said, and hung up.

It is possible, Wohl thought, *that Matt is coming over here simply as a friend. The reason he sounds so insecure is that he's not sure of the tribal rites. Can a lowly detective and an exalted staff inspector be friends? The answer is sure, but he doesn't know that. And the truth of the matter is, I was glad to hear his voice and I miss him around the office.*

But clever detective that I am, I don't think that a social visit is all he has in mind. His tone of voice and the "thank you" is not consistent with that.

Is he in trouble? Nothing serious, or I would have heard about it. And if he was in a jam, wouldn't he go first to Denny Coughlin?

There is a distinct possibility, now that I think about it, that Detective Payne has, now that he's been leading the exciting, romantic life of a real-life detective in the famous East Detective Division for two months, decided that law enforcement is not how he really wants to spend the rest of his life. Unless things have changed a hell of a lot, he has spent his time on recovered stolen vehicles, with maybe a few good burglary of autos thrown in for good measure.

If he did decide to quit, he would feel some sort of an obligation to tell me. That would be consistent with his polite asking if he could come over, and then saying "thank you."

So what will I do? Tell him to hang in there, things will get better? Or jump on the wise elders bandwagon with his father and Denny Coughlin, and tell him to go to law school?

The telephone rang again.

"A Highway car ran the light at Broad and Olney, broadsided a station wagon full of nuns, and knocked it into a bus carrying the Philadelphia Rabbinical Council," his caller announced without any opening salutation.

Wohl chuckled. "Good morning, Captain Pekach," he said. "You better be kidding."

"Am I interrupting anything, boss?"

"No. What's up, Dave?"

"It's a beautiful day. Martha's got some shrimp and steaks and we're going to barbecue lunch. Mike and his wife are coming, and I thought maybe you'd be free?"

Is he inviting me because he likes me, or because I am the boss? Why the hell are you so cynical? Dave is a good guy, and you like Martha. And they are friends. He is not sucking up to the boss.

Your cynicism just might have something to do with last night. When are you going to learn, Peter Wohl, that blond hair and splendid boobs do not a nice lady make?

"I've got somebody coming over, Dave."

"Bring her, the more the merrier."

"It's a him. Specifically, Matt Payne."

"I thought maybe he'd be in touch . . ."

What the hell does that mean?

". . . so bring him too. Martha likes him, and we've got plenty."

"I don't know what his plans are, but I'll be there. Thank you, Dave. When?"

"Noon. Anytime around there."

"Can I bring anything?"

"Nothing but an appetite."

Wohl walked back to his living room, where Martinez was reading the BNDD Investigator's Manual.

"That was Matt Payne," Wohl said. "The first call."

"How's he doing?"

"I understand he's become the East Detectives' specialist on recovered stolen cars," Wohl said, and then added: "He's coming over here."

Martinez closed the BNDD notebook and stood up.

"Then I better get going, huh?"

"I don't think it would be a good idea if he saw you here."

Martinez held up the notebook.

"How soon do you want this back?"

"Whenever you're finished with it. Take your time."

Martinez nodded.

"You're doing a good job, Hay-zus," Wohl said. "I think it's just a question of hanging in there with your eyes open."

"Yes, sir."

"Anytime you want to talk, Hay-zus, about anything at all, you have my personal number."

"Yes, sir."

Martinez stood up, looked at Wohl for a moment, long enough for Wohl to suspect that he was about to say something else, but then, as if he had changed his mind, nodded at Wohl.

"Good morning, sir."

Wohl walked to the door with him and touched his shoulder in a gesture of friendliness as Martinez opened it and stepped outside.

Wohl had just about finished carefully washing his Jaguar when Detective Payne drove onto the cobblestone driveway in his silver Porsche. It showed signs of just having gone through a car wash. The way Payne was dressed, Wohl thought, he looked like he was about to pose for an advertisement in *Esquire*—for either Porsche automobiles, twenty-five-year-old Ambassador Scotch, or Hart, Schaffner & Marx clothing.

Payne handed Wohl a paper bag.

"Present," he said.

"What is it?"

"The latest miracle automobile polish. It's supposed to go on and off with no percep-tible effort, and last for a thousand years."

I am not going to ask him what's on his mind. In his own time, he will tell me.

"And you believe this?"

"Also in the tooth fairy. But hope springs eternal. I didn't think you would be willing to try it on the Jag, but I thought we could run a comparison test. I'll do mine with this stuff, and you do the Jag with your old-fashioned junk . . ."

"Which comes all the way from England and costs me five ninety-five a can . . ."

". . . and we'll see which lasts longer. You'll notice mine is also freshly washed."

"In a car wash," Wohl said. "I'm surprised you do that. Those brushes are supposed to be hell on a finish. They grind somebody else's dirt into your paint."

He's looking at me as if I just told him I don't know how to read.

"You don't believe that?" Wohl asked.

"You know the car wash on Germantown Avenue, right off Easton Road?"

Wohl nodded.

"For four ninety-five, they'll wash your car by hand."

"I didn't know that," Wohl confessed.

"They don't do a bad job, either," Matt said, gesturing toward the Porsche.

Wisdom from the mouth of babes, Wohl thought. *One is supposed to never be too old to learn.*

"So I see," Wohl said.

Payne took off his linen jacket, and then rolled up the sleeves of his light blue button-down collar shirt. Then he extended his can of car polish toward Wohl.

"You want to do a fender, or the hood, with this? Then you could really tell."

"The *bonnet,*" Wohl said. "On a Jaguar the hood is the *bonnet.* And thank you, no."

Matt opened the hood of his rear-engined Porsche, which was of course the trunk, and took out a package of cheese cloth.

Why don't I spend the two bucks? Instead of using old T-shirts? Except when I can't find an old T-shirt and have to use a towel that costs more than two bucks?

"So how is life treating you, Matt?" Wohl asked.

"I thought you would never ask," Matt said. "The good news is that I won six thousand bucks, actually sixty-seven hundred, in Las Vegas, and the bad news is that the IRS gets their share."

He is not pulling my leg. Jesus Christ, six thousand dollars! Nearer seven!

"What were you doing in Las Vegas?"

"I was sent out there to bring Penny Detweiler home from the funny farm."

That was a surprising announcement, and Wohl wondered aloud: "How did you get time off?"

"Ostensibly, I was helping with the paperwork in Chief Lowenstein's office. That is the official version."

"Start from the beginning," Wohl said.

Payne examined a layer of polish he had just applied to the front of the Porsche before replying. Then he looked at Wohl.

"My father asked me to meet him for drinks. When I got there, Denny Coughlin was there. They asked me how I would like to go to Nevada and bring Penny home, and I said I would love that, but unfortunately, I couldn't get the time off. Then Uncle Denny said, 'That's been taken care of,' and Dad said, 'Here's your tickets.' "

I wonder what Matt Lowenstein thought about that? Not to mention Matt's sergeant, lieutenant, and captain in EDD.

"They won't hassle you in East Detectives, Matt, if that's what you're worrying about. That couldn't have happened without Chief Lowenstein knowing about it, ordering it. Your response should be the classic 'mine not to reason why, mine but to do what I'm told.' "

"I'm not worried about East Detectives. What I'm wondering about is how you feel about me coming back to Special Operations."

Shit! That's disappointing. I didn't think he'd ask to get transferred back. I thought he was smart enough to know that would be a lousy idea, and I didn't think he would impose on our friendship for a favor. Helping him out of a jam is one thing, doing something for him that would be blatant special treatment is something entirely different. But, on the other hand, the only thing he's known since he's joined the Department is special treatment.

"Matt," Wohl said carefully. "I think your coming back to Special Operations would be, at the very least, ill-advised. And let me clear the air between us. I'm a little disappointed that you can't see that, and even more disappointed that you would ask."

Wohl saw on Matt's face that what he had said had stung. He hated that. But he had said what had to be said.

Matt bent over the front of the Porsche and applied wax to another two square feet. Then he straightened and looked at Wohl again.

"Well, I suspected that I might not be welcomed like the prodigal returning to the fold, but just to clear the air between us, Inspector, I didn't ask to come back. You or anybody else. I was told to report to Chief Lowenstein's office at half past one yesterday, and when I got there, a sergeant told me to clean out my locker in East and report to Special Operations Monday morning."

"God*dammit!*" Wohl exploded.

"I could resign, I suppose. Suicide seems a bit more than the situation calls for," Matt said.

"You can knock off the 'Inspector' crap. I apologize for thinking what I was thinking. I should have known better."

"Yeah, you should have known better," Matt said. It was not the sort of thing a very junior detective should say, and it wasn't expressed in the tone of voice a junior detective should use to a staff inspector who was also his division commander. But Wohl was not offended.

For one thing, I deserve it. For another, in a strange perverted way, that was a remark by one friend to another.

"I wouldn't have said what I said, obviously, if I had known you were coming back," Wohl said. "This is the first I've heard of it."

"It was on the teletype," Matt said, and reached into the Porsche and handed Wohl a sheet of teletype paper. "Charley McFadden took that home from Northwest Detectives."

```
GENERAL: 1365 04/23/74 17:20 FROM COMMISSIONER
RECEIPT NO. 107
PAGE 1 OF 1

THE FOLLOWING TRANSFERS WILL BE EFFECTIVE 1201 AM
MON 04/23/74


NAME        RANK  PAYROLL  FROM        TO
****        ****  *******  ****        **

ROBERT J. FODE   LT   108988   9TH DISTRICT   PLANS & ANALYSIS

MATTHEW M. PAYNE   DET   126786   EAST DETECTIVE SPECIAL OPERATIONS

TADDEUS CZERNICH
POLICE COMMISSIONER
```

"I wonder," Wohl said, and there was sarcasm and anger in his voice, "why no one thought I would be interested in this?"

"Maybe what you need is a good administrative assistant, to keep something like this from happening again," Matt said.

"No," Wohl said. "I've got an administrative assistant. Until I figure out what to do with you, you can work for Jason Washington."

Before the words were out of his mouth, Wohl had modified that quick decision. Matt would possibly wind up working for Jason somewhere down the line, he decided, but where he would go to work immediately was for Jack Malone.

Malone could use some help, certainly, in his new role in Dignitary Protection. And if Matt were working for him, he would not only learn something that would broaden his general education, but also just might keep Malone from doing something stupid. Malone was a good cop, but working with the feds was always risky.

Wohl decided this was not the time to tell Matt he had changed his mind. Instead, he changed the subject.

"We're invited to a party," he said.

"Oh?"

"Steak, you know, barbecue, at Martha Peebles's. Dave Pekach called up right after you did, invited me and, when I said you were coming over, said to bring you too."

"Fine," Matt said. "Maybe *he'll* be glad to have me back."

"It is not nice to mock your superiors. Detective Payne. Make a note of that. Carve it in your forehead with a dull knife, for example."

Payne laughed, and Wohl smiled back at him.

I am glad he's back.

He remembered an insight he'd had about Matt Payne several months before, when Matt was still in Special Operations and had found himself in trouble not of his own making, and Wohl had jumped in with both feet in his defense before asking why. The reason, he had finally concluded, was that he thought of Matt as his younger brother.

"How is the Detweiler girl?" Wohl asked.

"She looks all right," Matt said.

"People do lick their drug problems, Matt."

"And I'll bet if you looked hard enough, you could find a pig who really can whistle."

"Is that a general feeling, or is there something specific?"

Matt looked at him and shrugged helplessly.

"She told me she was in love with Tony the Zee," Matt said.

"Have you considered that may be simple female insanity, not connected with narcotics?"

Matt laughed again.

"No," he said. "But isn't that a cheerful thought?"

Peter Wohl was not prepared to admit that Matt Payne's miracle auto polish was better in every way than his imported British wax, but there was no doubt that it went on and off faster, and with less effort.

For at least the last fifteen minutes, Detective Payne had been leaning on his gleaming Porsche, sucking on a bottle of beer and smiling smugly as he waited for Staff Inspector Wohl to finish waxing his Jaguar.

"Mine will last longer," Wohl said, when he had finally finished.

"We don't know that, do we?" Matt replied. "And you will notice that *I* am not sweating."

"No one loves a smart-ass."

"It is difficult for someone like myself to be humble," Matt said.

"I wonder what a contract on the mayor would cost?"

Matt picked up on that immediately.

"You think he was responsible for sending me back to Special Operations?"

Wohl put the galvanized steel bucket, the car polish, and the rags into the garage, came out again, closed the door, and motioned for Matt to follow him into his apartment before replying.

"Who else? Not only does it smell like one of his friendly suggestions for general improvement of departmental operations, but who else would dare challenge the collective wisdom of Lowenstein and Coughlin—and my dad, by the way—that the best place for you to learn how to be a detective was to send you to East Detectives?"

He turned on the stairs and looked back at Payne.

"I'd say five thousand dollars," Matt said. "I understand the price goes up if the guy to be hit is known to go around armed."

Mayor Carlucci was known to never feel completely dressed unless he had a Smith & Wesson Chief's Special .38 caliber snubnose on his hip.

"Maybe we could take up a collection," Wohl said. "Put a pickle jar in every district."

He pushed open the door to his apartment and went inside.

"I need a shower," he said. "If you haven't already drunk it all, help yourself to a beer, and then call the tour lieutenant and tell him I'll be at Pekach's . . . *Martha Peebles's.*"

"Yes, sir," Matt said.

He sat down on the white leather couch and pulled the telephone to him. There were lipstick-stained cigarette butts in the ashtray.

"You forgot to conceal the evidence," he called. "How did you do with whoever likes Purple Passion lipstick?"

"And clean the ashtrays," Wohl called back. "And not that it's any of your business, but she told me she was not that kind of girl. She was deeply annoyed that I thought she would do that sort of thing on the fifth date."

Matt chuckled and dialed, from memory, the number of the lieutenant on duty at Special Operations.

"Special Operations, Lieutenant Wisser."

Must be somebody new. I don't know that name.

"Lieutenant, Inspector Wohl asked me to call in that until further notice, he'll be at the Peebles's residence in Chestnut Hill. The number's on the list under the glass on his desk."

"Who is this?"

"My name is Payne, sir. Detective Payne."

"I've been trying to reach the inspector. Is he with you?"

Matt could hear the sound of the shower.

"No, sir. But I can get a message to him in a couple of minutes."

"Tell him that Chief Wohl has been trying to get him. That he's to call. He said it was important."

"Yes, sir, I'll tell him."

"Do I know you, Payne?"

"I don't think so, sir."

The phone went dead in Matt's ear.

He replaced the telephone in the cradle, carried the ashtray into the kitchen, emptied it, took another Ortlieb's beer from the refrigerator, and sat on the couch with it and the current copy of *Playboy* until Wohl reappeared.

"Your dad wants you to call," Matt reported. "Lieutenant Wisser said he said it was important."

Wohl sat on the couch beside him and dialed the telephone.

Matt could only guess at what the conversation was, but there was no mistaking that Wohl's attitude changed from concern to annoyance, and then resignation.

"Okay, Dad. Six-thirty, maybe a little later. Okay. Six-thirty, *no later*," he concluded, and hung up, and turned to Matt: "If you can find the hit man, tell him the mayor will probably be at 8231 Rockwell Avenue from about half past six."

"Oh?"

"It may just be for a friendly evening with old friends, and then again, it may not be," Wohl said.

Matt waited for more of an explanation, but none was forthcoming.

11.

There was a light-skinned black man in a white coat standing under the portico of the Peebleses' turn-of-the-century mansion when Wohl drove up.

"Good afternoon, sir. I'll take care of your car. Miss Peebles is at the barbecue pit."

He gestured toward a brick path leading from the house to a grove of trees.

Peter Wohl did not permit anyone else to drive his car. He had spent three years and more money than he liked to remember rebuilding it from the frame up, and had no intention of having it damaged by someone else.

"I'll park it, thank you. Around the back?"

"Beside the carriage house, if you please, sir."

Matt, who had followed him to the estate, now followed him to the carriage house.

There were two cars already parked there. One, a nearly new Ford four-door sedan both Matt and Wohl recognized as the unmarked Department car assigned to Captain Mike Sabara, Wohl's deputy. The other was a four-year-old Chevrolet with a Fraternal Order of Police sticker in the rear windshield.

They each noticed the other looking at it, and then shrugged almost simultaneously, indicating that neither recognized it.

They walked across the cobblestones past the carriage house (now a four-car garage) to the brick wall and toward the barbecue pit. They were almost out of sight of the house when they heard another car arrive.

It was a Buick Roadmaster Estate Wagon, and at the moment Matt decided that it looked vaguely familiar, there was proof. The Buick wagon stopped at the portico of the mansion and Miss Penelope Detweiler got out.

"Shit," Matt said.

"Someone you know, I gather?" Wohl said.

"Precious Penny Detweiler," Matt said.

"Really?" Wohl sounded surprised.

"Before we send the hit man to the mayor's house, do you suppose he'd have time to do a job on Pekach's girlfriend?"

They reached the barbecue pit. It was a circular area perhaps fifty feet across, with brick benches, now covered with flowered cushions, at the perimeter. There were several cast-iron tables and matching chairs, each topped with a large umbrella. Each table had been set with place mats and a full set of silver and glassware.

A bar had been set up, and another black man in a white jacket stood behind that. A third black man, older and wearing a gray jacket, whom Matt recognized as Evans, Martha Peebles's butler, was, assisted by Captain Pekach, adjusting the rack over a large bed of charcoal in the grill itself, a brick structure in the center of the circle.

"God," Wohl said softly, "ain't getting back to simple nature wonderful?"

Martha Peebles came up to them when they stepped inside the circle.

"I'm so glad you could come," she said. "David is fixing the fire."

She gave her cheek to Matt, who kissed it, and then to Wohl, who followed suit.

"I think I should warn you, Martha," Matt said. "That when he's at work, we don't let the captain play with matches."

"Penny Detweiler's coming," Martha said. "She should be here any minute."

"She's here."

"I ran into her and her mother at the butcher's, and I asked them to join us. . . ."

Matt smiled insincerely.

"And Grace said she and Dick were tied up, but Penny . . ."

"Would just love to come, right?" Matt said.

"And I told Grace you would drive her home, afterward. Is that all right?"

The bartender approached them.

"Can I get you gentlemen something?"

"How are you fixed for strychnine?"

"I'm beginning to suspect that wasn't the smartest thing I've ever done," Martha said. "If I did the wrong thing, Matt, I'm sorry. It was just that I knew she is just home . . ."

"I don't think you're capable of doing the wrong thing, Martha," Matt said. "On the other hand, I'm famous for being ill-mannered. Sure, I'll take her home." He turned to the bartender: "I'll have a beer, please. Ortlieb's, if you have it."

"The same for me, please," Wohl said.

Officer Paul T. O'Mara, holding a bottle of Pabst, walked up. He was in civilian clothing, a sports coat, and slacks.

"Hello, Paul," Wohl said.

Matt decided Wohl was surprised and not entirely pleased to see whoever this guy was.

"Inspector, would you please call your father?"

"How old is that request?" Wohl asked.

"He called me at my dad's house about ten," O'Mara said. "He said he couldn't find you at your apartment. I called Captain Sabara . . ."

"And he said I'd probably be here?"

"Yes, sir."

"He got through to me," Wohl said. "But good job, Paul, running me down."

"Yes, sir. Miss Peebles asked me to stay . . ."

"How lucky for you."

"Captain Sabara said it would be all right."

"Paul, this is Matt Payne," Wohl said.

"Yes, sir, I know who he is." He put out his hand. "Nice to meet you, Payne."

"Paul took your job, Matt," Wohl said. "So far he's been doing a much better job than you ever did."

"Thanks a lot," Matt said.

Captain Mike Sabara, whose acne-scarred olive skin gave him a somewhat menacing appearance, walked up to them, trailed by his wife.

"How goes it, boss?" Sabara asked.

"Inspector," Mrs. Sabara said.

"Hello, Helen," Wohl said. "It's good to see you."

"How are you, Matt? How's things at East Detectives?"

"Take a note, O'Mara," Wohl said. "The inspector desires that supervisors read departmental teletypes."

Sabara looked confused and possibly a little worried, but before he could question the remark, Captain Dave Pekach came up.

"I'm glad you could come," he said. "Both of you. How's East Detectives, Matt?"

"O'Mara," Wohl said. "Take two notes. Same subject."

"Excuse me?" Pekach said.

"Gentlemen, permit me to introduce the latest addition to our happy little family. Detective Payne. The reason I know this is Detective Payne showed me the teletype transferring him. Which was nice, because it was apparently never sent to Special Operations, or if it was, nobody ever thought to tell me about it."

"Jesus, Peter, I didn't see it," Mike Sabara said.

"Me, either," Pekach confessed.

"Inspector, I did," O'Mara said. "I guess I should have told you, but I just thought you would know."

"I would have thought so too," Wohl said.

"Dammit," Dave Pekach said, and then stopped as Miss Penelope Detweiler walked up to them.

She took Matt's arm, leaned up and kissed his cheek, and then laid her head against his shoulder.

"Hi," she said. "I'm Penny."

"You know our hostess, of course," Matt said. "These delightful folks are Mrs. Mike Sabara, Captain Sabara, Captain Pekach, Officer O'Mara, and the boss, Inspector Wohl."

"How do you do, Miss Detweiler?" Mike Sabara said.

From the look on your face, Mrs. Sabara, Matt thought, *it is evident that you have just identified the sweet-looking blonde you thought was my girlfriend as the poor little rich girl who took dope, and was involved with the Guinea gangster, and was just freed from the loony bin.*

"Couldn't you just call me 'Penny'?" she asked plaintively.

"Hi, Penny," Wohl said. "Call me Peter."

"I'm Dave," Captain Pekach said.

"I like him, Martha," Penny said. "He's even nicer-looking than you told Mother."

"I like him too," Martha said, and kissed Captain Pekach on the cheek, an act that seemed to embarrass him.

"Please call me Helen," Mrs. Sabara said.

"My name is Tom," Officer O'Mara said.

"Hi, Tom," Penny said, and smiled at him.

Officer O'Mara, Matt thought, *looks as stunned as Madame Sabara. I think he has just fallen in love.*

"I think we're all here now," Martha said. "I thought we'd have some munchies and a drink or two to work up an appetite and then Dave will do the steaks."

"May I help in some way, Martha?" Penny asked.

"It's all been done, dear, thank you just the same."

I wish to hell she would let go of my arm, Matt thought. *As a matter of fact, I devoutly wish she weren't here at all.* And then he considered that for a moment. *You are really a prick, Matthew Payne. She isn't at all interested in you as a male. She is hanging on to you because she's scared to death. She's floating around all alone in strange waters, and you're the only life preserver in sight. You* are, *whether you like it or not, the closest thing she has to a brother, and you have a clear obligation to try to help her.*

"Nonsense," Matt said. "Put her to work. If nothing else, get her a broom and have her sweep the place up."

"Matt, that's terrible!" Martha said.

"No, it's not," Penny said. "I learned a long time ago that saying something rude is Matt's perverse way of showing affection."

She leaned up and kissed his cheek again.

"So go get a broom," Matt said.

"I won't get a broom, but I will pass the . . . what did you say, Martha, 'the munchies'?"

Matt glanced at Peter Wohl and found Wohl's thoughtful eyes already on him.

There was the muted sound of a telephone ringing, and Evans opened a small door in the low brick wall and took out a telephone.

"One moment, please, sir," he said, and covered the mouthpiece with his hand. "Are you available to take a call from a Lieutenant Malone, Inspector?"

"Sure," Wohl said, and got up and took the telephone from Evans.

"God," Pekach said. "I didn't think to ask him! Peter, let me talk to him when you're through."

"Hello, Mike," Wohl said. "What's up?" He paused. "Wait a minute, Captain Pekach wants to talk to you." He covered the microphone with his hand. "He says he needs to talk to me."

Pekach nodded, and took the phone.

"Mike, where are you? I've been trying to get you on the phone." There was a reply. "Okay, well, you come over here. No, you won't be intruding."

He handed the telephone back to Evans and turned to Wohl.

"He was over at your place. He'll be here in ten minutes. He say what was on his mind?"

Wohl shook his head no. "Thank you, David. I really didn't want to leave before the steak."

"I should have invited him, anyway. I don't know why I didn't."

"Probably for the same reason you don't read departmental teletypes," Wohl said. He saw on Pekach's face that he had stung him more than he intended, and quickly added: "You're in love. People in love are unreliable."

"I don't think like that," Martha said in mock indignation.

Lieutenant Malone, in slacks and a cotton jacket, drove up the drive ten minutes later in his personal automobile, a battered Mustang that always made Peter Wohl wonder what

Malone had on the State Certified Inspection Station garage that had certified it as safe for passage on the Commonwealth of Pennsylvania's public roads.

"I didn't mean to intrude," he said, when he came into the barbecue pit.

"You're not," Martha said. "David's been trying to get you on the phone ever since we decided to do this. Will what you have to tell Peter wait until after you've had a drink?"

"Unless one of Dave's cars has run into a station wagon full of nuns it will," Wohl said.

"Yes, thank you. Scotch, please."

Malone spotted Matt and smiled at him.

"Hello, Matt," he said.

"How are you, Lieutenant?"

Malone spotted Penelope Detweiler, looked hard to make sure it was she, and then looked away.

Wohl went to Penny, put his arm around her shoulders, and led her to Malone.

"Penny, I want you to meet the man who put one of your father's golf partners in jail," he said. "This is Lieutenant Jack Malone."

"One of Daddy's golf partners? Really? Who?"

"Bob Holland," Wohl said. "Philadelphia's Friendliest Car Dealer of Integrity."

"Oh, I heard about that!" Penny said. "He was stealing cars, wasn't he?"

"By the hundreds," Wohl said. "And Jack was the guy who caught him."

Malone looked torn between pleasure and embarrassment.

But he had also decided, Matt saw, that being somewhere with Penny Detweiler was no cause for being uncomfortable. If Peter Wohl had a friendly arm around her shoulders, she was all right.

That was a goddamned nice thing for you to do, boss. And if it incidentally makes me feel like a shit, I deserve it.

"Is what's on your mind going to take long, Jack?" Wohl asked.

"No, sir."

"Then why don't we take our drinks and wander off in the woods for a minute and get it over with? Will you excuse us, Penny?"

"Certainly," Penny said. "Nice to have met you, Lieutenant. I can't wait to tell my father."

When Wohl and Malone were out of earshot, Penny touched Matt's arm and when he looked at her, she said, "He's really nice, isn't he? I like your friends, Matt."

Wohl led Malone fifty yards away from the barbecue pit and then stopped.

"Okay, let's have it," he said.

"I had a call from the Secret Service this morning," Malone replied. "A guy named H. Charles Larkin. *Supervisory Special Agent* H. Charles Larkin."

"How did he get to you?"

"I told you that Dignitary Protection sergeant, Henkels, has a room temperature IQ. Larkin called him, and he gave him my number."

"What did this guy want?"

"He said that he was the guy in charge of the Vice President's security; that he was coming up here by train in the morning; and that I'm 'invited' to the Philly office of the Secret Service at nine-thirty to discuss the Vice President's visit."

"Tomorrow's Sunday," Wohl thought aloud, "and I can't believe this guy doesn't know he's supposed to go through Captain Whatsisname Duffy in the Roundhouse."

"*Jack* Duffy," Malone furnished. "Special assistant to the commissioner for inter-agency liaison."

Wohl looked at him and grunted. "What did you tell this guy?"

"That I would get back to him. And then I started looking for you."

"Have you got this guy's number?"

Malone nodded, and Wohl made a "follow me" gesture with his hand and led him back to the barbecue pit.

"Martha," he said. "I have to call Washington. May I use the phone? I'll have it billed to the Department, of course."

"Don't be silly. Just use the phone."

"Thank you," Wohl said, going to the cubicle in the brick wall where Evans had stored the telephone.

"Dave," he called. "I want you and Mike to hear this. And you too, Matt."

Pekach and Sabara walked over to him. Officer O'Mara, Matt thought, looked like he had just been told the Big Boys didn't want to play with him. And then Wohl saw the look on O'Mara's face too:

"And, of course, you too, O'Mara. You're supposed to be able to remind me of what I said."

"Yes, sir."

Wohl pointed to the phone. Malone took a notebook from his pocket, opened it, and found the number he had.

"Person to person, Jack," Wohl ordered.

The call went through very quickly. Malone put his hand over the microphone.

"They're ringing him."

Wohl took the telephone from Malone, and held it slightly way from his ear so the others would be able to hear both sides of the conversation.

"Larkin," a somewhat brusque voice said.

"Mr. Larkin, this is Inspector Peter Wohl of the Special Operations Division of the Philadelphia Police Department."

"What can I do for you, Inspector?"

"That's what I intended to ask you. You called one of my people, Lieutenant Malone, an hour or so ago."

"Oh, yeah. I asked him to come by our Philadelphia office in the morning. Is there a problem with that?"

"I'm afraid there is. I'm not free at that time."

"Is there sort of an inference in that that I should have called you, not this lieutenant?"

"That would have been nice. Dignitary Protection is under Special Operations. I run Special Operations."

"I thought it was run out of the commissioner's office."

"Not anymore."

"Oh, shit," Larkin said. "Okay, Inspector. You tell me. How do I make this right?"

"Are you open to suggestion?"

"Wide open."

"I was going to suggest . . . I understand you're coming by train?"

"Right. Arriving at 30th Street at nine-oh-five."

"I was going to suggest that I have one of my men, Detective Payne, pick you up at 30th Street and bring you by my office. By then, with a little luck, I can have my desk cleared for you."

There was a long pause before Larkin replied.

"That's very kind of you, Inspector," he said, finally.

"Detective Payne will be waiting for you at the information booth in the main waiting room," Wohl said.

"How will I know him? What does he look like?"

Wohl's mouth ran away with him: "Like a Brooks Brothers advertisement. What about you?"

Larkin chuckled. "Like a Brooks Brothers advertisement? Tell him to look for a bald fat man in a rumpled suit. Thanks for the call, Inspector."

There was a click on the line.

Wohl took the handset from his ear, held it in front of him, and looked at it for a moment before replacing it in its cradle.

"Tom," he said to Officer O'Mara as he tossed him a set of keys, "either tonight or first thing in the morning go get a car from the Schoolhouse, drop it at my apartment, and take my Department car. Pick Payne up at no later than eight-fifteen at his apartment. He lives on Rittenhouse Square, he'll tell you where."

"Yes, sir."

"Jack, I want you in uniform tomorrow."

"Yes, sir."

"And I would be grateful if you two," he said, nodding at Pekach and Sabara, "could just happen to drop by the Schoolhouse a little after nine. You in uniform, Dave."

Pekach nodded.

"And between now and nine tomorrow morning, I want the more lurid graffiti removed from the men's room walls. *Supervisory Special Agent* Larkin may experience the call of nature, and we don't want to offend him."

"I'll drop by the Schoolhouse on my way home," Sabara said, "and be outraged at what I find on the toilet's walls."

"We are not about to start a guerrilla war against the Secret Service," Wohl said. "But on the other hand, I want to make sure that Larkin understands that Special Operations is a division of the Philadelphia Police Department, not of the Secret Service."

"I think you made that point, Peter," Sabara said.

Matt saw H. Richard Detweiler and Brewster C. Payne II sitting at a cast-iron table on the flagstone area outside the library of the Detweiler mansion, dressed in what Matt thought of as their drive-to-the-golf-club clothes, when he drove up.

There goes any chance I had of just dropping Penny off. Damn!

"Your dad's here," Penny said.

"I saw them," Matt said, and turned the ignition off and got out of the car and started up the shallow flight of stairs to the front door.

Miss Penelope Detweiler waited in vain for Matt to open her door, finally opened it herself, got out, and walked after him.

Grace Detweiler came into the foyer as they entered. Behind her, in the "small" sitting room, he saw his mother, who saw him and waved cheerfully.

"Well, did you have a good time?" Grace Detweiler asked.

"Oh, yes!" Penny said enthusiastically.

"She especially liked the part where Dave Pekach bit the head off the rooster," Matt said.

"Matt!" Grace Detweiler said indignantly.

Matt saw his mother smiling. They shared a sense of humor. It was one of many reasons that he was extraordinarily fond of her.

"If you will excuse me, ladies, I will now go kiss my frail and aged mother."

"You can go to hell, Matthew Payne," Patricia Payne said, getting up and tilting her cheek to him for a kiss. " 'Frail and aged'!"

She took his arm and led him toward the door to the library.

"You look very nice," she said. "Was that for Penny's benefit?"

"I didn't even know she was going to be there. Madame D. and Martha Peebles sand-bagged me with that."

His mother looked at him for a moment and then said, "Well, thank you for not making that clear to Penny. Obviously, she had a good time, and that was good for her."

"I get a gold star to take home to Mommy, right?"

"Daddy," his mother replied. "He's with Penny's father out there." She made a gesture toward the veranda outside the library, then added, "Matt, it's always nice if you can make someone happy, particularly someone who needs, desperately, a little happiness."

She squeezed his arm, and then turned back toward the "small" sitting room. *The* sitting room of the Detweiler mansion was on the second floor, and Matt could never remember ever seeing anyone in it, except during parties.

H. Richard Detweiler got out of his chair and, beaming, offered Matt his hand.

"Hello, Matt," he said. "Sit down and help us finish the bottle."

That's my gold star. Your usual greeting is a curt nod of the head. Until I became He-Upon-Whose-Strong-Shoulder-Precious-Penny-Leans, I was tolerated only because of Dad.

"Hello, Mr. Detweiler."

"He's only being generous because he took all my money at the club," Brewster Payne said. "I couldn't stay out of the sand traps."

"Or the water," Detweiler said. "Scotch all right, Matt?"

"Fine. Thank you."

Matt reached into his pocket and took out his wallet, and then five one-hundred-dollar bills. When Detweiler handed him the drink, Matt handed him the money.

"What's this?"

"The expense money. I didn't need it."

Detweiler took the money and held it for a moment before tucking it in the pocket of his open-collared plaid shirt.

"I didn't expect any back, and I was just about to say, 'Matt, go buy yourself something,' but you don't try to pay dear friends for an act of love, do you?"

Oh, shit!

Matt turned away in embarrassment, saw a cast-iron love seat, walked to it, and sat down.

"He doesn't need your money, Dick," Brewster C. Payne said. "He made a killing at the tables."

"Really?"

"More than six thousand," Brewster Payne said.

"I didn't know you were a gambler," Detweiler said.

"I'm not. That was my first time. Beginner's luck."

Detweiler, Matt thought, seemed relieved.

"You understand that the money I took from your father today," Detweiler went on, "is not really gambling."

"More beginner's luck?" Matt asked innocently.

His father laughed heartily.

"I meant, not really gambling. Gambling can get you in a lot of trouble in a hurry."

That's why you give your guests at the Flamingo a ten-thousand-dollar line of credit, right? So they'll get in a lot of trouble in a hurry?

"Yes, sir," Matt said. He took a sip of his Scotch. "Nice booze."

"It's a straight malt, whatever that means," Detweiler said. "It suggests there's a crooked malt."

Penny Detweiler, trailed by her mother and Mrs. Payne, came onto the veranda. She had a long-necked bottle of Ortlieb's and a glass in her hands.

"What's that?" Detweiler asked.

"It's what Matt's been drinking all afternoon," Penny said. "When did you start drinking whiskey?"

"As nearly as I can remember, when I was eleven or twelve."

"No, he didn't," Patricia Payne said.

"Yes, he did, dear," Brewster Payne said. "We just managed to keep it from you."

Penny sat beside Matt on the cast-iron love seat.

"What am I supposed to do with this?" she asked.

"You might try drinking it," Matt said.

"Penny . . ." Grace Detweiler said warningly.

"A glass of beer isn't going to hurt her," her father said. "She's with friends and family."

There was a moment's awkward silence, and then Penny put the glass on the flagstone floor and put the neck of the bottle to her mouth. Her mother looked very uncomfortable.

"Did you have a good time at Martha Peebles's, Precious?" Detweiler asked.

"Very nice," she said. "And her captain is just darling!"

"Polish, isn't he?" Detweiler said.

"Don't be a snob, Daddy," Penny said. "He's very nice, and they're very much in love."

"I'm happy for her," Patricia Payne said. "She's at the age where she should have a little romance in her life. And living in that big house all alone . . ."

"I would have bet she'd never get married," Detweiler said. "Her father was one hell of a man. Alexander Peebles is a tough act to follow."

"I thought about that," Penny said. "And I think that it has a lot to do with Captain Pekach being a cop." She stopped and turned to Matt, and her hand dropped onto his leg. "Does that embarrass you, Matt?"

"Not at all. I thought everyone knew that women find cops irresistible."

"Good God!" his father said.

"I mean it," Penny went on. "I was talking with Matt's boss, Inspector Wohl, and he's darling too. . . ."

"Ex-boss," Brewster Payne interrupted.

"Please let me finish, Uncle Brew," Penny said.

"Sorry."

"I was talking to Inspector Wohl, and he moved, his jacket moved, and I could see that he was carrying a gun, and it occurred to me that every man in the barbecue pit, Martha's Captain Pekach, Captain Sabara, Lieutenant Malone, Matt, and even a young Irish boy who works for Inspector Wohl, was carrying a gun."

"They have to, I believe, Penny," Brewster C. Payne said. "Even off duty."

"Not here, I hope," Grace Detweiler said.

"Even here, Madame D.," Matt said.

"As I was saying," Penny went on, annoyance at being interrupted in her voice, "I realized that although they looked like ordinary people, they weren't."

For one thing, Matt thought, *they make a hell of a lot less money than the people you think of as ordinary do.*

He said, "We only bite the heads off roosters on special occasions, Penny. Barbecues. Wakes. Bar Mitzvahs. Things like that. We probably won't do it again for a month."

She turned to him again, and again her hand dropped to his leg.

"Will you stop?" she giggled. "I'm trying to say something flattering."

"Then proceed, by all means."

"I realized that they were all—what was it you said about Mr. Peebles, Daddy?—'One hell of a man.' They're all special men. I can understand why Martha fell in love with Captain Pekach. He's one hell of a man."

I am wholly convinced that your hand on my leg, Precious Penny, is absolutely innocent; you have always been one of those kiss-kiss, touch-touch airheads. Nevertheless, I wish you would take it off. You are about to give me a hard-on.

Matt stood up and went to the table and splashed more Scotch into his glass. He did not return to the cast-iron love seat.

"You may very well be right, dear," Matt's mother said.

"Thank you," Penny said. She looked over at Matt. "You do work for Inspector Wohl, don't you, Matt?"

He nodded.

"Then what did you mean, Uncle Brew, when you said 'ex-boss'?"

"I've been transferred back to Special Operations, Dad," Matt said.

"When did that happen?"

"Yesterday."

"What are you going to do over there, as a detective?"

"Well, for one thing," Penny said proudly, "he's going to protect the Vice President when he comes to Philadelphia."

Jesus, you have ears like a fox, don't you?

"What I'm going to do," Matt said quickly, "is meet the *Secret Service guy* who is going to protect the Vice President at 30th Street Station."

And that gives me my excuse to get out of here.

"I don't understand," Brewster Payne said.

"He and Wohl are playing King of the Mountain," Matt said. "He wanted our guy to go to the Secret Service office. Wohl wanted him to come to his. Wohl won. I pick up this guy at 30th Street Station in the morning, and drive him to see Wohl." He looked at his watch. "Which means I have to leave now if I am to have a nice clean suit to wear to meet this guy."

"Oh, finish your drink," H. Richard Detweiler said. "And are you sure you don't want something to eat?"

"I had a steak an hour ago that must have weighed three pounds," Matt said. "Thank you, no."

He drained his drink and set it on the table.

"I know you're busy, dear," his mother said, "but if you could try to find time in your schedule to come see your frail and aged mother, I would be so grateful."

H. Richard Detweiler stood up and shook Matt's hand in both of his.

"Thank you, Matt. Don't be a stranger."

"Thank you, sir."

"I think I left my scarf in your car," Penny said. "I'll walk you out."

When they got to the Porsche, she said, "I didn't have a scarf. I just wanted to thank you for being so nice to me."

"No thanks necessary," he said, and then his mouth ran away with him. "Whenever I'm with a pretty blonde, I automatically shift into the seduce mode. Nothing personal."

She seemed startled for a moment, but only for a moment.

"Just to clear the air," Penny said. "It worked."

And her hand, ever so lightly, but obviously intentionally, grazed his crotch.

"I'd let you kiss me, but they're watching."

She stepped away from him, and said, loud enough for their parents to hear, "You heard what Daddy said, don't be a stranger."

He got quickly into the Porsche and drove away.

12.

Peter Wohl was only mildly surprised when he turned onto Rockwell Avenue and saw a gleaming black Cadillac limousine parked before the comfortable house in which he had grown up. He didn't have to look at the license plate to identify it as the official vehicle provided by the City of Philadelphia to transport its mayor; the trunk was festooned with shortwave antennae, and the driver, now leaning on the front fender conversing with two other similarly dressed, neat-appearing young men, was obviously a police officer. There were two other cars, almost identical to Wohl's, parked just beyond the Cadillac.

He didn't recognize the drivers, but there was little doubt in his mind that the cars were those assigned to Chief Inspectors Matt Lowenstein and Dennis V. Coughlin,.

I am about to get one of three things, good news, bad news, or a Dutch Uncle speech. I don't know of anything I've done, or anyone else in Special Operations has done, that should have me on the carpet, but that simply means I don't know about it, not that there is nothing. And the reverse is true. I can't think of a thing I've done that would cause the mayor to show up to tell me what a good job I've been doing.

He pulled the Jaguar to the curb behind the limousine and got out.

The two drivers who had been leaning on the Cadillac pushed themselves erect.

"Good evening, Inspector."

"I guess the party can start now," Wohl said, smiling, "I'm here."

"They been in there the better part of an hour, Inspector," one of the drivers said.

That was immediately evident when his mother opened the door to his ring. There was hearty laughter from the living room, and when he walked in there, the faces of all four men were unnaturally, if slightly, flushed.

There were liquor and soft drink bottles and an insulated ice bucket on the coffee table, and the dining-room table was covered with cold cuts and bowls of potato salad.

"Well, here he is," Chief Inspector Augustus Wohl, retired, said. "As always, ten minutes late and a dollar short."

"Mr. Mayor," Wohl said, and then, nodding his head at Lowenstein and Coughlin, in turn, said, "Chief."

"Always the fashion plate, aren't you, Peter?" the mayor said as he shook Wohl's hand. "Even when you were a little boy."

"I've been out hobnobbing with the hoi polloi, Mr. Mayor."

"Which hoi polloi would that be?" the mayor asked, chuckling.

"Captain Pekach's fiancée."

"Oh, yes, Miss Peebles."

"And Miss Penelope Detweiler was there, too," Wohl said.

"Is Pekach doing a little matchmaking?" the mayor said, and then went on without waiting for a reply. "You could do worse, Peter. It's about time you found a nice girl and settled down."

"Miss Peebles is doing the matchmaking, but her target, I think, is Detective Payne. The Detweiler girl is a little young for me."

"He was there too?"

"He was at my place when Dave Pekach called. He said to bring him along. He came to tell me he had been reassigned to Special Operations."

"Oh, yeah. That was one of the things I was going to mention to you. I heard the commissioner was thinking of sending him back over there."

Do you really expect me to believe that was Czernich's idea, and you knew nothing about it?

And "one of the things" you were going to mention to me? What else, Mr. Mayor?

Wohl's father handed him a drink.

"Thank you," Peter said, and took a sip.

"Jerry was just telling me that Neil Jasper's going to retire," Chief Wohl said.

It took a moment for Wohl to identify Neil Jasper as an inspector working somewhere in the Roundhouse bureaucracy.

Christ, is he going to tell me "the commissioner is thinking" of making me Jasper's replacement?

"A lot of people, Peter, including the commissioner," the mayor said, looking directly at him, "think Special Operations is getting too big to be commanded by a staff inspector."

"I'm sorry the Commissioner feels that way," Wohl said.

"Well, I'm afraid he's right," the mayor said.

Oh, shit! I have just been told that I'm going to lose Special Operations. That's what this is all about. Jerry Carlucci is softening the blow by letting me know ahead of time, and is about to throw me a bone: Pick a job, Peter, any job. I owe your father.

"Do I read you correctly, Peter? You don't want to work in the Roundhouse?"

"I would rather not work in the Roundhouse, Mr. Mayor."

"That's what I told Czernich," the mayor said. "That I didn't think you'd like that."

So what does that leave? Back to Staff Investigations? Probably not. If Carlucci is throwing the dog a bone, and tells Czernich not to give me a job in the Roundhouse, there's not really much left for a staff inspector. Maybe as an assistant to Lowenstein in the Detective Bureau, or to Coughlin in Special Patrol. Why else would they be here?

"May I ask who the commissioner's thinking of sending in to take over Special Operations?"

"That's pretty much up to you, Peter," the mayor replied.

What the hell does he mean by that?

"Unless, of course, you'd like to stay there," the mayor said.

"You just said that it had been decided Special Operations should have a full inspector. . . ."

"And so it should," the mayor said. "You were what, when you took the Inspector's exam."

"Seventh," Wohl replied, without thinking.

"And they promoted five people off the list, right? That's what Czernich said."

"I think that's right," Wohl replied.

You know damned well it's right. Why are you being a hypocrite? You watched the promotions off the list like a hawk, until the two-year life of the list ran out and you knew you weren't going to get promoted from it.

"Commissioner Czernich came to me with an idea," the mayor said. "He said that Marty Hornstein was number six, in other words next up, on the last Inspector's List, and said that it would be a pretty good idea if I could ask the Civil Service Board to extend the life of the list, so that Hornstein could be promoted and take Jasper's place."

Wohl was aware that the mayor was pleased with himself, and exchanging glances with Chiefs Wohl, Lowenstein, and Coughlin.

What the hell is that all about?

"Now you have been around long enough, Peter, to know that I don't like to go to the Civil Service Board and ask them for a favor. They do something for you, you got to do something for them. But, on the other hand, I try to oblige Commissioner Czernich whenever I can. So I thought it over, and what I decided was that if I had to go to all the trouble of going to the Board to ask them to extend the life of the Inspector's List so that we could promote one guy off it, why not promote two guys off it?"

Jesus H. Christ!

The last board made it pretty clear to me that they didn't think I was old enough to be a captain, much less a staff inspector trying for inspector. I squeezed by that one only because they believed the list would be long expired before I got anywhere near the top of it, and that I would spend the next five years or so as a staff inspector investigator. If they had known I'd be given command of Special Operations after eighteen months, they would have found some reason to keep me off the list, or at least put me near, or at, the bottom.

"If you can find time in your busy schedule, Peter," the mayor said. "Why don't you drop by the commissioner's office next Tuesday at, say, nine-thirty? Wear a nice suit. They'll probably want to take your picture. Yours and Hornstein's. But keep this under your hat until then."

I have just been promoted. By mayoral edict, screw the established procedure.

A massive arm went around his shoulders, and then Peter felt his father's stubbly cheek against his as he was wrapped in an affectionate embrace.

"You better have another drink, Peter," the mayor said. "You look as shocked as if you'd just been goosed by a nun."

The telephone was ringing when Matt climbed the narrow stairway to his apartment. He walked quickly to it, but at the last moment decided not to pick it up. On the fifth ring, there was a click, and then his voice, giving the *I'm Not Home* message. There was a beep, and then a click. His caller had elected not to leave a message.

The red *You Have Messages* light was blinking. He pushed the PLAY button. There were four buzz and click sounds, which meant that four other people had called, gotten his *I'm Not Home* message, and hung up.

Evelyn, he thought. *It has to be her.*

Why are you so sure it's her? Because the gentle sex, contrary to popular opinion, does not have an exclusive monopoly on intuition, and also because everybody, anybody, else would have left a message.

If you call her back, there is a very good chance that you can wind up between, or on top of, the sheets with her. Why doesn't that fill you with joyous anticipation?

The answer came to him with a sudden, very clear mental image of Professor Harry Glover outside the house in Upper Darby, specifically of the look in his eyes that said, *"I know you have been fooling around with my wife."*

Jesus Christ, could it be him? "Stay away from my wife, you bastard!"

Conclusions: You did the right thing, Matthew, my boy, because God takes care of fools and drunks, and you qualify on both counts, in not picking up the telephone. You neither want to discuss with Professor Glover your relationship with his wife, or diddle the lady.

And why not? Because he knows? Or because Precious Penny has made it quite clear that she would be willing, indeed pleased, to roll around on the sheets with you?

Oh, shit!

He turned on the television, sat down in his armchair, flicked through the channels, got up, and went to the refrigerator for a beer.

The telephone rang again.

He walked to the chair-side table, looked down at the telephone, and picked it up on the third ring.

"Payne."

"This is your friendly neighborhood FBI agent," a familiar voice said. "We have a report of a sexual deviate living at that address. Would you care to comment?"

"The word is 'athlete,' not 'deviate.' Guilty. What are you up to, Jack?"

Jack Matthews, a tall, muscular, fair-skinned man in his late twenties, was a special agent of the FBI. When Matt had been wounded by a member of the so-called Islamic Liberation Army, Jack had shown up to express the FBI's sympathy, and, Matt, was sure, to find out what the Philadelphia Police knew about the Islamic Liberation Army and might not be telling the FBI. In addition, Lari Matsi, a nurse in the hospital who had raised Matt's temperature at least four degrees simply by handing him an aspirin, had suddenly found Matt invisible after a thirty-second look at the pride of the Justice Department.

Despite this, however, Matt liked Jack Matthews. He watched what he said about police activity when they were together, but they shared a sense of humor, and he had become convinced that there was a certain honest affection on Jack's part for him and Charley McFadden, whose fiancée and Lari Matsi were pals.

"I'm sitting at the FOP bar with a morose Irish detective," Jack said. "Who is threatening to sing, 'I'll take you home again, Kathleen.'" McFadden wants you to come over here and sing harmony."

"You sound like you've been there for a while."

"Only since it opened," Jack said. "The girls are working."

"Did you call before, Jack?"

"No. Why?"

"No reason. Yeah, give me twenty minutes."

"Bring some of that Las Vegas money with you," Jack said, and hung up.

Matt went into his bedroom and changed into khakis and a sweatshirt. As he was reclaiming his pistol from the mantelpiece, the telephone rang again. He looked at it for a moment, and then went down the stairs.

———

Jack Matthews and Charley McFadden, a very large, pleasant-faced young man, were sitting at a table near the door of the bar in the basement of the Fraternal Order of Police Building on Spring Garden Street, just off North Broad Street, when Matt walked in.

There was a third man at the table, Jesus Martinez, in a suit Matt thought was predictably flashy, and whom he was surprised to see, although when he thought about it, he wondered why.

Charley McFadden and Jesus Martinez had been partners, working as undercover Narcs. When their anonymity had been destroyed when they ran to earth the junkie who had shot Captain Dutch Moffitt, they had been transferred to Special Operations. Charley and Martinez had been friends and, more important, partners, since before Matt had come on the job.

"How are you, Hay-zus?" Matt said, offering his hand and smiling at Officer Jesus Martinez of the Airport Unit.

"Whaddaya say, Payne?" Jesus replied.

Both our smiles are forced, Matt thought. *He doesn't like me, for no good reason that I can think of, and I am not especially fond of him. We are on our good behavior because Charley likes both of us, and we both like Charley.*

Matthews and McFadden were dressed much like Matt. Charley was wearing a zippered nylon jacket and blue jeans, and Matthews was wearing blue jeans and a sweatshirt with the legend PROPERTY OF THE SING-SING ATHLETIC DEPARTMENT. A loose-fitting upper garment of some sort is required to conceal revolvers.

They both had their feet up on chairs, and were watching the dancers on the floor, at least a half dozen of whom appeared to have their slacks and blouses painted on.

"We have a new rule," Jack said. "People who win a lot of money gambling have to buy the beer."

"Right," McFadden said.

They're both plastered. I think Jack is here because he wants to be, not because the FBI told him to hang around the cops with his eyes and ears open.

"Does that apply to guys who can tell certain females that their boyfriends spent Saturday night ogling the broads in the FOP bar?"

"You have a point, sir," Jack said. "I will buy the beer."

"Sit down," Matt said. "Ortlieb's, right? What are you drinking, Hay-zus?"

Martinez picked up a glass that almost certainly held straight 7-Up.

"I'm okay. Thanks."

Matt crossed the room to the bar and picked up three bottles of Ortlieb's beer and a bottle of 7-Up and returned to the table.

When he passed the 7-Up to Jesus, Martinez snapped, "I told you I was okay."

"I'm the last of the big spenders, all right?" Matt countered, and then his annoyance overwhelmed him. "Drink it. Maybe it'll help you grow."

Martinez was instantly to his feet.

"I'm big enough to whip your ass anytime, hotshot."

"Don't fuck with me, Martinez, I've had a bad day."

"Shut-up, Hay-zus," Charley said. "Shut up and sit down."

"Fuck him!" Martinez snarled. "Fucking hotshot!"

"Hey!" an authoritative voice called from somewhere in the large, dark, low-ceilinged room. "Watch the goddamned language. There's ladies in here, for Christ's sake."

Martinez turned on his heel and went quickly out the door. Matt could hear his shoes on the concrete stairs. They made a sort of metallic ringing sound.

"What was that all about?" Matthews asked.

"You shouldn't have made that crack about him growing, Matt," Charley said.

"All he had to do was say 'thank you' for the goddamn 7-Up. Or say nothing. He didn't have to bite my ass. I don't have to put up with his shit. Or yours, either."

"Oh, boy," Matthews said. "I'm going to get to see a real barroom brawl."

"He never liked you for openers," Charley said, "and then you passed the exam, and he didn't."

"What am I supposed to do, apologize for passing the exam?"

"Just show a little consideration for his feelings is all," Charley said, almost plaintively.

Matt laughed and sat down.

"What's so funny?"

"Let it go, Charley," Matthews said.

"I want to know what he thinks is so funny!"

"Drink your beer, Charley," Matthews said.

"Jesus," Charley said, and sat down.

"I want to say something to you, Charley," Matt said.

"Yeah?" McFadden asked suspiciously. "What would that be?"

"I don't want you telling Mary, if she comes in here and finds you lying on the floor, that I held you down and poured booze down your throat."

McFadden glowered at him for a moment and then said, "Fuck you, Matt."

There was affection in his voice.

"And so what's new with you, Detective Payne?" Matthews asked. "Aside from you going back to Special Operations, I mean?"

"That upset Hay-zus too," Charley interrupted. "When he heard that you're going back out there. Sort of rubbing it in his face. With him flunking the exam."

"Loyalty, thy name is McFadden," Matt said.

"Something wrong with that?"

"Not a thing, pal. I admire it," Matt said, and then turned to Matthews. "How about the FBI? Arrested anybody interesting lately?"

"No, but I'm hot on the trail of a big-time gambler. Was he pulling my leg, or did you really win six thousand bucks out there?"

"Sixty-seven hundred, he tells you, in the interests of accuracy."

"And what if you had lost?"

"I was going to quit when I lost a hundred," Matt said. "But I didn't lose it."

"You went out there to bring the Detweiler girl home?"

"Right."

"How is she?"

"I don't know," Matt said. "She seems perfectly normal. As normal as she ever was."

The question and his response made him uncomfortable. He stood up.

"I need another beer."

He was surprised when Jack Matthews showed up at his elbow while he was waiting for his turn with the bartender.

"My turn to buy," Jack said.

He wants something. How do I know that?

"I thought you would never say that," Matt replied.

Matthews took money from his pocket.

"I understand Special Operations now runs Dignitary Protection," he said.

"I don't know. I haven't reported in yet. Why do you ask?"

"Oh, I've been assigned to liaise between the Bureau and the Secret Service for the Vice President's visit."

"What does that mean?"

"Well, for example, when the Secret Service big shot arrives at 30th Street Station from Washington tomorrow morning, I will be a member of the official welcoming party."

"You get to carry his bags? Boy, you are moving up in the FBI, aren't you?"

Why am I unwilling to tell him, "Whoopee, what a coincidence, me too!"

"Screw you, Matt," Matthews said, chuckling. "Look, if you can find out who's going to run this for the Police Department, it would be helpful to me. Okay?"

"Yeah, sure, Jack. I'll ask around."

At quarter to seven the next morning, half an hour early, Officer Tom O'Mara pulled Staff Inspector Peter Wohl's unmarked car to the curb in front of the Delaware Valley Cancer Society Building.

And then he didn't know what to do. It was an office building, and it was Sunday, and it was closed. Detective Payne had told him he lived on the top floor. That was a little strange to begin with. Who lived in an office building?

He got out of the car and walked to the plate-glass door and looked in. There was a deserted lobby, with a polishing machine next to a receptionist's desk, and nothing else. O'Mara walked to the edge of the sidewalk and looked up. He couldn't see anything. But then when he glanced back at the building, he saw a doorbell, mounted on the bricks next to the door where you could hardly see it.

He went to it and pushed it. He couldn't hear anything ringing. He decided the only thing he could do was just wait. He went to the car and leaned on the fender.

A minute or so later, a Holmes Service rent-a-cop appeared in the lobby and looked out curiously. O'Mara walked to the door as the rent-a-cop unlocked it.

"Can I help you?"

"I'm a police officer," O'Mara said.

"I never would have guessed," the rent-a-cop said, and then when he saw the look on O'Mara's face added, "I retired in 1965 out of the Third District."

"Does a detective named Payne live here?"

The rent-a-cop motioned him into the building and pointed at an elevator.

"Take a ride to the third floor. Payne lives up there. You'll see a doorway with an intercom."

"Thank you."

Matt Payne, obviously fresh from a shower, was buttoning his shirt when O'Mara climbed the flight of stairs from the third floor.

"I decided making coffee would be a waste of effort, sorry," he said.

"Nice apartment," O'Mara said.

"If you're a midget," Payne said. "Give me a minute to get my pants on."

"I'm early."

"You get the worm, then," Payne said as he walked to the rear of the apartment.

O'Mara looked around the apartment. There was an oil painting of a naked lady mounted to the bricks of the fireplace.

It would be nice, Officer O'Mara thought, to have a place like this to bring a girl to. He had thought of getting an apartment, but every time he brought the subject up, his mother had a fit. There would be enough time to get his own apartment later, when he was married. The thing he had to do now was learn to save his money, and renting an apartment when there was a perfectly good room for him to use at home would be like throwing money down the toilet.

He wondered if Payne brought the Detweiler girl here. She seemed to be a nice girl, even after what he'd heard about her being on drugs.

"I like your picture," O'Mara said. "The inspector's got one like it."

"Yeah, I know," Payne said. "Mrs. Washington gave me that one."

"Sergeant Washington's wife?"

"Yeah," Payne said, walking to the fireplace mantel and picking up his Chief's Special snub-nosed revolver and slipping it into a holster that fit inside his waistband.

"Is it hard to get through the qualification?" O'Mara asked.

"What?"

O'Mara pushed his coat aside to reveal his standard-issue Smith & Wesson Military and Police revolver, which had a six-inch barrel and was time and a half as large as the snubnose.

In order to carry anything but the issue revolver, it was necessary to go through a test—"the qualification"—at the range at the Police Academy.

"The Range guys make a big deal of it," Payne said. "It helps if you know one of them."

"I got a cousin works out there," O'Mara said.

"Then talk to him," Payne said as he shrugged into his jacket. "Where are you parked?"

"Out in front."

"I should have told you to come around the back, there's a garage in the basement. Sorry."

"No problem."

"How'd you get in?"

"I rang the doorbell. A rent-a-cop let me in."

"The guy who usually works the building on Sundays is a retired cop," Matt said.

"He told me."

The telephone rang.

O'Mara saw that Payne was reluctant to answer it, that he was really making up his mind whether or not he would, and he wondered what that was all about. Finally, Payne shrugged and picked it up.

"Hello."

"You sound grumpy," Evelyn said. "Did I wake you up?"

"Hi. No. As a matter of fact, I was just about to walk out the door." There was a silence, and then Matt added: "Hey, I mean that. I've got to work. Women work from sun to sun, a policeman's work is never done."

"I was going to ask you to dinner. Is that out of the question?"

"I'll have to call you. I don't know how long this will take."

"How long what will take? Or is it bad form to ask?"

"I've got to pick up a VIP at 30th Street Station and drive him to see my boss."

"Oh."

"I may be through at ten, ten-thirty, and I may not be through until five or six."

"Matt, it would be kinder, if you'd rather break this off, for you to come out and say so."

"There is nothing I would rather do than come out there right now," Matt said. "Don't be silly."

"You mean that, or you're being polite?"

"Of course I mean it."

"Will you call me, please, when you know something?"

"As soon as I find out."

"I bought steaks yesterday," Evelyn said. "I thought you'd like a steak."

Then she hung up.

You bought steaks, and then you went home and started calling me, apparently every half hour. Jesus!

Why the hell didn't you take the out she gave you?

He put the handset in its cradle, and turned away from the table. The phone rang again.

Jesus, now what does she want?

"Hello."

"I just wanted to make sure you were out of bed," Peter Wohl said. "O'Mara should be there any minute."

"He's here now. We were just about to leave."

"No suggestion that either one of you is unreliable," Wohl said. "But things happen, and I didn't want the Secret Service standing around 30th Street feeling unloved."

"You want me to kiss him when he gets off the train?"

"That would be nice," Wohl said, and hung up.

Matt hung up again and looked at O'Mara.

"That was the boss. He wanted to be sure I was out of bed."

There are those who feel that Philadelphia's 30th Street Station is one of the world's most attractive railroad stations. It was built before World War II when the Pennsylvania Railroad was growing richer by the day, and the airplane was regarded as a novelty, not a threat for passenger business. And even after the airplane had killed the long-distance railroad passenger business in other areas, along the New York–Washington corridor, going by train remained quicker and more convenient.

There were a lot of people going in and out of the doors at the west exit of 30th Street Station when Tom O'Mara pulled up in a NO STANDING ZONE.

"If a white hat tries to run you off," Matt said. "Tell him you're waiting for Chief Coughlin."

"Chief Coughlin?" O'Mara asked.

"Everybody's afraid of Chief Coughlin," Matt said as he opened the door and got out.

He had almost reached the doors to the main waiting room when a voice called out, "Detective Payne?"

He turned and saw a Highway Patrol sergeant walking up to him. He was a good-looking young Irishman, and Matt now recalled seeing him with Pekach, but he couldn't come up with a name.

"Jerry O'Dowd," the sergeant said, putting out his hand. "I work for Captain Pekach."

"How are you, Jerry? What's up?"

"I got the captain's car. I was told to see if you showed up, and if not, to stand by the information booth and look for a bald fat man in a rumpled suit, named Supervisory Special Agent H. Charles Larkin, and then drive him to the Schoolhouse. You're here. What do you think I should do?"

"I think maybe you should stick around in case the battery in Wohl's car goes dead or something."

"Sure."

"Why don't you call in and say I'm here."

"Captain Pekach said this guy's a Secret Service big shot?"

"That's all I know about him too."

"I'm across the street, you want me to pull up behind your car?"

"No. This guy's in the Secret Service, not a movie star."

Matt was standing beside the information booth in the center of the main waiting room at 9:05, his eyes fixed on the wide stairway that led down to the tracks below.

At 9:06, a crowd of people began to come up the stairway. After a moment, he had trouble seeing through them, and started to walk to the head of the stairs, but changed his mind. He had been told to be at the information booth.

At 9:08, a voice behind him said, "Excuse me, sir, but is that a Brooks Brothers suit?"

Matt turned and saw a man whose hair was thin, but who could not be called bald, who was heavyset, but could not be called fat, and whose suit appeared comfortable, but was not rumpled. He was surrounded by half a dozen neatly dressed men, one of whom was Special Agent Matthews of the FBI, and all of whom seemed baffled by the behavior of the man they had come to 30th Street Station to meet.

"Actually, it's from Tripler. Have I the privilege of addressing Mr. H. Charles Larkin?"

"Yes, you do," Larkin said, smiling conspiratorially at him.

"Welcome to Philadelphia, Mr. Larkin."

"Thank you very much. It's nice to be here."

Larkin turned to the men with him.

"I am going with this gentleman. I don't know where, but if you can't trust the Philadelphia Police Department, who can you trust?"

"Excuse me, sir?" one of the men standing behind him asked.

"Detective Payne, do you happen to know any of these gentlemen?"

"I have the privilege of Special Agent Matthew's acquaintance, sir. Good morning, Special Agent Matthews."

Jack Matthews looked embarrassed. Or annoyed. Or both. He nodded curtly at Matt but didn't say anything.

"How strange," Larkin said. "I was led to believe that the FBI and the Philadelphia Police Department were not on speaking terms."

"We talk to some of them, sir," Matt said.

"Well, shall we be on our way, Detective Payne?"

"The car is right outside, sir," Matt said, and pointed.

"I'll be in touch," Larkin said, and marched off toward the doors to the street. Matt walked quickly to catch up with him. Behind him, he heard one of the men left behind say, "Jesus *Christ!*"

O'Mara saw them coming and opened the rear door of the car. Larkin smiled at him, and then pulled open the front door and got in the front seat. Matt had no choice but to get in the back.

O'Mara walked quickly around the front of the car and got behind the wheel and drove off.

"Mr. Larkin, this is Officer O'Mara. Tom, this is Supervisory Special Agent Larkin of the Secret Service."

"Good morning," Larkin said, and then turned on the seat to face Matt. "I understand you're pretty close to Denny Coughlin."

The announcement surprised Matt.

"Yes, sir, I am."

"First chance you get, give him a call. I think he'll tell you I'm not the arrogant prick your boss apparently thinks I am. Not that Wohl has a reputation for being a shrinking violet himself."

"May I ask how you know Chief Coughlin, sir?"

"Ten, twelve, Christ, it must be fifteen years ago, there was a guy making funny money on Frankford Avenue. Wedding announcements in the daytime, funny money at night. First-class engraver. We had a hell of a time catching him. Denny was then working Major Crimes. Good arrest. We got indictments for twelve people, and ten convictions. He's a hell of a good cop."

"Yes, sir, he is."

"So am I," Larkin said. "Am I going to have to have Denny Coughlin tell Wohl that, or do you think we can make friends by ourselves?"

"Sir, I think that you and Inspector Wohl will have no trouble becoming friends. Sir, can I ask you how you knew I know Chief Coughlin?"

"Our office here keeps files. One of them is on you. You're a very interesting young man, Payne."

Matt would have loved to have an amplification of that, but he suspected that none would be offered, and none was.

"Does Chief Coughlin know you're in town, sir?"

"No. I thought I would put that off until I met your Inspector Wohl," Larkin said, and then turned to O'Mara: "Are you speeding, son?"

O'Mara dropped his eyes quickly to the speedometer, before replying righteously, "No, sir."

"There's a Highway car following us," Larkin said. "If you're not speeding, what do you think he wants?"

Matt laughed. "He's there in case we get a flat or something," he said.

Larkin looked at him and smiled. "That's what the file said," he said. "Wohl is very careful, very thorough. And very bright."

"You have pretty good files, Mr. Larkin," Matt said.

"Yeah, we do," Larkin said.

13.

It took Vito Lanza several seconds to realize where he was when he woke up, several seconds more to reconstruct what had happened the night before, a few seconds more to realize that he was alone in the revolving circular bed, and a final second or two to grasp that the revolving bed was still revolving.

It didn't *spin* around, or anything like that, you really had to work at deciding it was really moving, but it did move, the proof of which was that he was now looking out the window, and the last he remembered, he had been facing toward the bathroom, waiting for Tony to come out.

The bed was also supposed to vibrate, but the switch for that was either busted, or they didn't know how to work it. They were both pretty blasted when they tried that.

He'd had too much to drink, *way* too much to drink, there was no question about that. He'd had a little trouble getting it up, *that* much to drink, and that hardly ever happened. And much too much to be doing any serious gambling, and he'd done that too.

It had started on the way up. Tony had said she hadn't had anything for breakfast but toast and coffee and was getting just a little hungry, so they stopped at a place just the Poconos side of Easton on US 611 for an early lunch. And he'd fed her a couple of drinks, and had a couple himself thinking it would probably put her in the mood for what he had in mind when they got to the Oaks and Pines Resort Lodge.

He had half expected the coupon Tony's uncle Joe had given them for the Oaks and Pines Resort Lodge to be a gimmick; that when they got there there either wouldn't be a room for them, or there would be "service charges" or some bullshit like that that would add up to mean it wasn't going to be free at all.

But it hadn't been that way. They didn't get a free *room,* they got a free *suite,* on the top floor, a bedroom with the revolving bed and a mirror on the ceiling; a living room, or whatever it was called, complete to a bar and great big color TV, and a bathroom with a bathtub big enough for the both of them at once made out of tiles and shaped like a heart, and with water jets or whatever they were called you could turn on and make the water swirl around you.

And when they got to the room, there was a bottle of champagne in an ice bucket sitting on the bar, so they'd drunk that, and then tried out the bathtub, and that had really put Tony in the mood for what he had in mind.

And that was before they'd found out that the bed revolved.

After, they had gone down to the cocktail lounge, where the Oaks and Pines Resort Lodge had an old broad—not too bad-looking, nice teats, mostly showing—playing the piano, and they'd had a couple of drinks there.

That was when the assistant manager had come up to him and handed him a card.

"Just show this to the man at the door, Mr. Lanza," he said, nodding his head toward the rear of the cocktail lounge where there had been a door with no sign on it or anything, and a guy in a waiter suit standing by it. "He'll take care of you. Good luck."

They didn't go back there until after dinner. Whoever ran the place sent another bottle of champagne to the table, compliments of the house, and the dinner of course went with the coupon. Vito had clams and roast beef. Tony had a shrimp cocktail and a filet mignon with some kind of sauce on it. She gave him a little taste, and the steak was all right, but if he'd had a choice he would rather have had A-1 Sauce.

And then they had a couple of Benedictines and brandies, and danced a little, and he had tried to get her to go back to the room, but she said it was early, and it was going to be a long night, and he didn't push it.

Then he'd asked her if it would be all right if he went into the back room, and Tony said, sure, go ahead, she had to go to the room, and she would come down when she was done.

It wasn't Vegas behind the door. No slots, for one thing. And no roulette. But there was blackjack, two tables for that, and there were three tables where people were playing poker, with the house taking their cut out of each pot, and of course craps. Two tables. Pretty well crowded.

By the time Tony came down from the room, he had made maybe two hundred, maybe a little more, making five- and ten-dollar bets against the shooter. When she showed up, he didn't want to look like an amateur making five-dollar bets, so he started betting twenty-five, sometimes fifty, the same way, against the shooter.

When he decided it was time to quit, he had close to five thousand, over and above the thousand he had started with and was prepared to lose.

"You're going to quit, on a roll?" Tony had asked him, and he told her that was when smart people quit, when they were on a roll, and what he needed right now was a little nap.

So they'd had a little nap, and a couple of drinks, and that was when they fooled around with the switch Tony had found on the carpet when she'd fallen off the bed, and then they'd gotten dressed again and went back downstairs and to the room in the back.

And this time the dice had turned against him. He was sure it was that, not that he was blasted or anything. Sometimes, you just have lousy luck, and with him betting C-notes, and sometimes double C-notes, letting the bet ride, it hadn't taken long to go through the five big ones he'd won, plus the thousand he had brought with him.

That was when the pit boss told him that if he wanted, they would take his marker, that Mr. Fierello had vouched for him, said his markers were good.

So what the hell, he'd figured that as bad as his luck had been, it had to change, it was a question of probability, so he'd asked how much of a marker he could sign, and the guy said as much as he wanted, and he hadn't wanted to look like a piker in front of Tony, so he signed a marker for six big ones, what he was out, and they gave him the money, in hundreds.

When he lost that, he knew it was time to quit, so he quit. If he had really been blasted, he would have signed another marker, because his credit was good, and that would have been stupid. The way to look at it was that he had dropped seven big ones. That was a lot of money, sure, but he'd come home from Vegas with twenty-two big ones. So he was still ahead. He was still on a roll.

He had the Caddy, and about ten thousand in cash, and, of course, Tony. If that wasn't being on a roll, what was?

Vito focused his eyes on the mirror over the bed, and then pulled the sheet modestly over his groin.

Then he got out of bed and walked to the bathroom.

Tony was in the tub, and it was full of bubbles, a bubble bath. It was the first bubble bath Vito had ever seen, except of course in the movies.

"Jees, honey," Tony said, "I didn't wake you, did I? I tried to be quiet."

"Don't worry about it."

"How about this?" Tony said, splashing the bubbles, moving them just enough so that he could see her teats. "I found a bottle of bubble stuff on the dresser. You just pour it in, and turn on them squirter things, and—bubbles!"

"There still room in there for me?"

"Oh, I don't know. Maybe there is, maybe there isn't."

Vito walked to the edge of the tub, dropped his shorts, and got in with Tony.

"You know what I would like to do later?" Tony asked.

"I know what *I'd* like to do later. Or for that matter, right now."

"Behave yourself! What I would like to do is get one of them golf things. . . ."

"What golf things?"

"The buggies, or whatever."

"You mean a golf cart," he said.

"Yeah. Could we get one and just take a ride in it?"

He thought that over.

"Why the hell not?" he said, finally.

"You know what else I would like?"

"What?"

"Champagne."

"Christ, before breakfast?"

"Well, I figured champagne and bubble baths go together. You can eat breakfast any-time. How many times does a person get a chance to do something like this?"

"You want champagne," Vito said, and hoisted himself out of the tub, "you get champagne."

Marion Claude Wheatley had slept soundly and for almost twelve hours. That was, he decided, because no matter what else one could say about the Pine Barrens, it was quiet out here. No blaring horns, or sirens, no screeching tires, and one was not required to listen to other people's radios or televisions.

But on reflection, he thought as he got out of bed and started to fold the bedding to take back to Philadelphia with him, it was probably more than that. He had noticed, ever since he had understood what the Lord wanted him to do, and especially when he was actually involved in something to carry out the Lord's will, that he was peaceful. It probably wasn't the "Peace That Passeth All Understanding," to which the prayer book of the Protestant Episcopal Church referred so frequently, and which the Lord had promised he would experience in Heaven, but it was a peace of mind that he had never before experienced in his life.

It seemed perfectly logical that if one was experiencing such an extraordinary peace, one would be able to sleep like a log.

Before he made his breakfast, he put the bedding into a suitcase, turned the mattress, and then carried the suitcase out and put it in the trunk of the rental car.

He fired up the Coleman stove and made his breakfast. Bacon and eggs, sunny side up, basted with the bacon fat, the way Mother used to make them for him when he was a kid, served on top of a slice of toast. Mother had thought dipping toast into an egg yolk was rather vulgar; placing the egg on a slice of toast, so that when the yolk was cut it ran onto the toast, accomplished the same purpose and was more refined.

He didn't have toast, of course. There was no toaster. And if there had been, there was no electricity to power a toaster. He thought again of the pluses and minuses of getting a gasoline-powered generator and bringing it out here to the farm. There was a new genera-tion of small, truly portable generators. He had spent the better part of an hour taking a close look at the ones Sears Roebuck now had.

The one he liked best advertised that it produced 110-volt alternating current at five amperes, and burned one-half gallon of unleaded gasoline per hour. The recommended load was up to 1,500 watts. That was more than enough to power a toaster. It was enough to power a small television. And it would pose no problem, if he had such a generator, to install some simple wiring and have electric lighting over the sink, next to his chair, and in the bedroom.

That would mean, he had thought at first, that he could do away with the Coleman lanterns, which would be nice. But then he realized that 1.5 KW was not adequate to power more than one electric hotplate, which meant that the procurement of a generator would not mean that he could dispense with the Coleman stove.

And then he realized that he didn't really want to come out here and watch television, so there was no point in getting a generator to provide power for that purpose.

And then, of course, there were the obvious downsides to having a generator. For one thing, it would make noise. He didn't think that he would really be willing to put up with the sound of a lawn-mower engine running at two-thirds power hour after hour. And it would, of course, require fuel. He would have to bring at least five gallons of unleaded gasoline every time he came to the farm. Carrying gasoline in cans was very dangerous.

It would be much better, he concluded again, not to get a generator. Besides, if he went ahead and got one, there was a very good chance that he wouldn't get to use it very much. Once he had disintegrated the Vice President, all sorts of law enforcement people would begin to look for him. He thought there was very little chance that they would not sooner or later find him.

If indeed, in carrying out the Lord's will at Pennsylvania Station, he didn't end his mortal life.

When he finished breakfast, he pumped the pump and filled the sink in the kitchen with foul-tasting water, added liquid Palmolive dish soap, and washed the plates and flatware and pots and pans he had soiled since his arrival. He put everything in its proper place in the cabinets, and then made up the garbage package.

Until he had finally realized how to solve the problem—like most solutions, once reached, he was surprised at how long it had taken him to figure it out—he had ridden the tractor to the depression carrying the paper bags full of garbage in his arm. It was difficult to drive the tractor with one hand, and sometimes, despite trying to be very careful, he had hit a bump and lost the damn bag anyway, but that was all he could see to do. If he put the garbage in the trailer, by the time he got to the depression, the vibration caused the garbage to come out of the paper sack and spread out all over the trailer. Or even bounce out of the trailer.

The solution was simplicity itself. He made up a garbage package, or packages, by placing one paper sack inside another, and when it was full, sealing it with duct tape. He had then been able to place the sealed bag in the trailer, and then drive, with both hands free, the tractor to the depression.

Ordinarily, when Marion took care of the garbage, he simply drove to the edge of the depression and stood on the edge and threw the garbage packages down the slope.

Today, however, he decided that it would be a good idea if he took another look at the lockers. He had examined them yesterday, of course, but that had been right after he'd set off the devices, and there had been a good deal of smoke and even several small smoldering fires. By now, everything would have cooled down, and if any of the fires were still smoldering, he could be sure they were extinguished.

Throughout the Pine Barrens were areas that smoldering fires had left blackened and ugly. And one could not completely dismiss the possibility that a smoldering fire could reach the farmhouse, although that was unlikely.

There was still the smell of smoke in the depression, but he could not find any smoke, and it was probably that the converse of "where there's smoke there's fire" was true. No smoke, so to speak, no fire.

He was pleased when he examined the lockers. The devices had functioned perfectly, and with evidence of greater explosive power than he would have thought. The doors of the lockers in which the devices had been detonated had, except for one that hung on a hinge, been blown off. The chain that had been wrapped around the Composition C-4 had functioned as he had hoped it would. The lockers in which the devices had been placed were shredded, as were the adjacent lockers. He found only a couple of dozen chain links, and he found none where more than two links remained attached.

Marion climbed back up the slope of the depression, drove the tractor back to the farmhouse, replaced the tarpaulin over the tractor, and then went into the house. He took a careful look around to make sure that he hadn't forgotten anything, and then left, carefully locking the padlock on the door.

He got in the rental car and started the engine. He looked at his watch. Things couldn't be better. He would get home in plenty of time to do the laundry, go to the grocery store, and then get the rental car back to the airport in time to qualify for the special weekend rate. And then he could get back home in time to watch Masterpiece Theater on the public television station.

That was the television program he really hated to miss.

Tom O'Mara stopped the car in front of the building that was the headquarters of the Special Operations Division of the Philadelphia Police Department. Over the door there was a legend chiseled in granite: FRANKFORD GRAMMAR SCHOOL A.D. 1892.

Before O'Mara could apply the parking brake and open his door, Supervisory Special Agent H. Charles Larkin said, "This must be the place," and got out of the car.

Matt hurried after him, and managed to beat Larkin to the door and pull it open for him.

"Right this way, Mr. Larkin," he said.

He led him down the corridor to the private door of what had been the principal's office, knocked, and then pushed the door open.

"Mr. Larkin is here, Inspector."

"Fine. Would you ask him to wait just a minute, please, Detective Payne?"

"Yes, sir," Matt said, and turned to Larkin. "The inspector will be with you in just a minute, sir."

"How good of him," Larkin said, expressionless.

Matt knew from checking his watch that Wohl kept Larkin waiting for two minutes, but it seemed like much longer before Wohl pulled his door open.

"Mr. Larkin, I'm Staff Inspector Peter Wohl. Won't you please come in?"

"Thank you."

Wohl gestured for Matt to come in, and then waved Larkin into an armchair.

"Any problems picking you up, sir?"

"None whatever."

"May I offer you a cup of coffee? A soft drink?"

"No, thank you," Larkin said. "But may I use your telephone?"

"Of course," Wohl said, and pushed one of the phones on his desk to Larkin. Larkin consulted a small leather-bound notebook, and then dialed a number.

Matt could hear the phone ringing.

"Olga? Charley Larkin. How are you, sweetheart?"

Matt saw Wohl looking at him strangely.

"Is that guy you live with around? Sober?"

There was a brief pause.

"How the hell are you, Augie?" Larkin asked.

Staff Inspector Peter Wohl's eyes rolled up toward the ceiling; he shook his head from side to side, smiled faintly, and exhaled audibly.

"I'm in Philadelphia, and I need a favor," Supervisory Special Agent Larkin went on. "I need a good word. For some reason, I got off on the wrong foot with one of your guys, and I'd like to set it right."

"I appreciate it, pal. Hold on a minute."

Larkin handed the telephone to Peter Wohl.

"Chief Wohl would like a word with you, Inspector," he said.

Peter Wohl took the telephone.

"Good morning, Dad," he said.

Larkin, beaming smugly, tapped his fingertips together.

"Yes, I'm afraid Mr. Larkin was talking about me. Obviously, there has been what they call a communications problem, Dad. Nothing that can't be fixed."

Chief Wohl spoke for almost a minute, before Peter Wohl replied, "I'll do what I can, Dad. I don't know his schedule."

He handed the phone back to Larkin.

"Chief Wohl would like to talk to you again, Mr. Larkin."

"I don't know what his plans are for lunch, Augie, but I'm free, and I accept. Okay. Bookbinder's at twelve. Look forward to it."

He reached over and replaced the handset in its cradle.

They looked at each other for a moment, and then Wohl chuckled, and then laughed. Larkin joined in.

"I thought my guy here said 'Wall,' " Larkin said. "I don't know anybody named 'Wall.' "

"Well, while you and my dad have a lobster, that I'll pay for, I'll have a boiled crow," Wohl said. "Will that set things right?"

"I'm sorry I used that phrase," Larkin said. "Nothing has gone wrong yet, but I'm glad I saw your father's picture on the wall. I think you and I could have crossed swords, and that would have been unfortunate. Can I ask a question?"

"Certainly."

"Have you got a hard-on for the feds generally, or is there someone in particular who's been giving you trouble? One of our guys, maybe?"

Wohl, almost visibly, carefully chose his words.

"I think the bottom line, Mr. Larkin, is that I was being overprotective of my turf. They just gave me Dignitary Protection, and I wanted to make sure it was understood who was running it. I really feel like a fool."

"Don't. The Secret Service is a nasty bureaucracy too. I understand how that works."

"When you're aware of your ignorance, you tend to gather your wagons in a circle," Wohl said.

"Well, I'm not the Indians," Larkin said. "And now that we both know that, could you bring yourself to call me Charley?"

"My dad might decide I was being disrespectful," Wohl said.

"Peter, if you keep calling me 'Mr. Larkin,' your dad will think we still have a communications problem."

"Matt," Wohl said. "Go get Captains Sabara and Pekach. I want them to meet Charley here."

"Yes, sir. Lieutenant Malone?"

"Him too," Wohl said.

As Matt started down the corridor to Sabara's office, where he suspected they would all be, he heard Larkin say, "Nice-looking kid."

"I think he'll make a pretty good cop."

That's very nice. But it's sort of a left-handed compliment. It suggests I will probably be a pretty good cop sometime in the future. So what does that make me now?

Wohl made the introductions, and they all shook hands.

"There is a new game plan," Wohl said. "There is something I didn't know until a few minutes ago about Mr. Larkin. He and my dad are old pals, and that changes his status from one of them to one of us. And I've already told him that we don't know zilch about what's expected of us. So we're all here to learn. The basic rule is what he asks for, he gets. Mr. Larkin?"

"The first thing you have to understand," Larkin said seriously, "is that the Secret Service never makes a mistake. Our people here in Philadelphia told me that the man in charge of this operation was Inspector Wall. Peter has promised to have his birth certificate altered so that our record will not be tarnished."

He got the chuckles he expected.

"The way this usually works," Larkin went on, "is that our special agent in charge here will come up with the protection plan. I'll get a copy of it, to see if he missed anything, then we present it to you guys and ask for your cooperation. Then, a day or so before the actual visit, either me, or one of my guys, will come to town and check everything again, and check in with your people."

He paused, and looked in turn at everyone in the room—including Matt, which Matt found flattering.

"This time," he went on, "there's what I'm afraid may be a potential problem. Which is why I'm here, and so early."

He picked his briefcase up from the floor, laid it on his lap, opened it, and took out a plastic envelope.

"This is the original," he said, handing it to Wohl. "I had some Xeroxes made."

He passed the Xeroxes around to the others. They showed an envelope addressed to the Vice President of the United States, and the letter that envelope had held.

> Dear Mr. Vice President:
>
> You have offended the Lord, and He has decided, using me as His instrument, to disintegrate you using high explosives.
>
> It is never too late to ask God's forgiveness, and I respectfully suggest that you make your peace with God as soon as possible.
>
> Yours in Our Lord,
>
> A Christian.

"Is this for real?" Mike Sabara asked.

Wohl gave him a disdainful look. Matt was glad that Sabara had spoken before he had a chance to open his mouth. He had been on the verge of asking the same question.

"If you're getting a little long in the tooth," Larkin said, "and you've been in this business awhile, you start to think you can intuit whether a threat is real or not. My gut feeling is that it's real; that this guy is dangerous."

"I don't think I quite follow you," Wohl said.

"The Vice President and, of course, the President get all kinds of threatening letters," Larkin said. "There's a surprisingly large number of lunatics out there who get their kicks just writing letters, people in other words who have no intention of doing what they threaten to do. Then there are the mental incompetents. Then there are those with some kind of gripe, something they blame, in this case, on the Vice President—and want fixed."

Larkin paused long enough for that to sink in.

"Everybody, I suppose, has seen *Casablanca?*" He looked around as they nodded. "There was a great line, Claude Rains said, 'round up the usual suspects,' or something like that. We have a list of suspects, people we think need to be watched, or in some cases taken out of circulation while the man we're protecting is around. This guy is not on our list."

"How could he be on a list?" Matt blurted. "He didn't sign his name."

He glanced at Wohl, and saw Wohl's eyes chill, but then move to Larkin. It was a valid question, and Larkin immediately confirmed this:

"Good question. If they don't have a name, we give them one. For example, No Pension Check. Jew-Hater. Irish-Hater. Sometimes, it gets to be Jew-Hater, Chicago, Number Seventeen. Understand?"

"I think so," Matt said.

"We keep pretty good files. Cross-referenced. As good as we can make them. This guy doesn't appear anywhere."

"What makes you think he's dangerous?" Dave Pekach asked.

"For one thing, he's in Philadelphia, and the Vice President will be in Philadelphia in eight days, a week from Monday. We don't have much time."

"I meant, why do you think he's dangerous, and not just a guy who writes letters to get his kicks?" Pekach persisted.

"Primarily, because he sees himself as an instrument of the Lord. God is on his side; he's doing God's bidding, and that removes all questions of right and wrong from the equation. If God tells you to quote 'disintegrate' somebody, that's not murder."

"Interesting word," Sabara said thoughtfully, " 'disintegrate.' "

Larkin glanced at him. Matt thought he saw approval in his eyes.

"I thought so too," he said.

"So is 'instrument,' " Wohl chimed in. "God using this fellow as his 'instrument.' "

"Yeah," Larkin said. "I sent this off, as a matter of routine, to a psychiatrist for a pro-file. I'll be interested to hear what he has to say. Incidentally, if you have a good shrink, I'd be interested in what he thinks too."

"Her," Wohl said. "Not a departmental shrink. But she was very helpful when we had a serial rapist, ultimately serial murderer, running around the northwest. When we finally ran him down, it was uncanny to compare what she had to say about him based on almost nothing, and what we learned about him once we had stopped him."

"Interesting," Larkin said.

"Payne's sister. Dr. Amelia Payne. She teaches at the University."

"What's even more interesting, Mr. Larkin . . ." Pekach said.

"Charley, please," Larkin interrupted.

". . . is that Matt, Detective Payne, got this guy. With his next victim already tied up in the back of his van," Pekach concluded.

"Fascinating," Larkin said, looking at Matt.

He already knew that, Matt thought. *He's not going to shut Pekach up, but he knew. He really must have some files.*

"Okay, Matt," Wohl ordered. "As a first order of business, run this letter past Dr. Payne, will you, please?"

"Yes, sir."

"Mike, how are we fixed for cars?"

"Not good. Worse than not good."

"Matt's going to be doing a lot of running around," Wohl said. "He's going to need a car."

"Let him use mine," Pekach volunteered. "With or without Sergeant O'Dowd. I can get a ride if I need one."

"With your sergeant," Wohl said. "Matt, take the Xerox—before you go, make half a dozen copies—to Amy. Explain what we need, and why we need it yesterday. On the way, explain this to Sergeant O'Dowd, ask him for suggestions. The minute you can get through to him, call Chief Coughlin and ask him if he can meet us, make sure you tell him Mr. Larkin will be there, at Bookbinder's for lunch. I'll see if I can get Chief Lowenstein to come too."

"It's Sunday. There's no telling where Amy might be."

"Find her," Wohl ordered. "And keep me advised, step by step."

"Yes, sir."

14.

"There are some other things I think we can safely say about this guy," Larkin said after Matt had gone. "For one thing, he's intelligent, and he's well educated. The two don't always go together. You'll notice that he correctly capitalizes all references to the deity. 'His instrument,' for example, has a capital 'H.' "

Sabara grunted.

"And there are no typos on either the letter or the envelope, which were typed on an IBM typewriter. One of those with the ball. So he both knows how to type and has access to an IBM typewriter. Which means probably in an office. Which would mean that he would also have access to a blank sheet of paper, and probably an envelope. He used instead a sheet of typing paper from one of those pads you buy in Woolworth's or McCrory's. There are traces of an animal-based adhesive on the top edge. Actually the bottom, which just means that after he ripped the sheet free, he put it in the typewriter upside down. And he used an envelope from the Post Office. Which probably means that he knows somebody was going to take a good close look at both the letter and the envelope and didn't want us to be able to find him by tracing the paper or envelope."

"Then why write the letter in the first place? Take that risk?" Sabara asked.

"Because he believes that he is a Christian, and is worried about the Vice President's soul," Larkin said. "Which brings us back to someone who thinks he's doing the Lord's work being a very dangerous character, indeed."

"We keep saying 'he,' " Wohl said, but it was a question.

"Two things. Both unscientific," Larkin replied. "Women don't normally do this sort of thing. And there is, in my judgment, a masculine character to the tone of the letter. It doesn't sound as if it's written by a female. But I could be wrong."

"Yeah," Wohl said thoughtfully.

"One more speculation," Larkin said. " 'High explosives.' Technically, there are low-yield explosives and high-yield explosives. Maybe he knows the difference. That could suggest that this guy has some experience with explosives. It could just as easily mean, of course, that he doesn't know the difference, but just heard the term."

"But the whole letter suggests that he isn't thinking of taking a shot at the Vice President," Wohl said.

"Presuming, for the sake of argument, that you're right, that's a mixed blessing. Getting close enough to the Vice President to take a shot at him wouldn't be easy. Using explosives—and I don't think we can dismiss military ordnance, hand grenades, mines, that sort of thing—is something else. And since this guy is doing God's work, I don't think he's worrying about how many other people might have to be 'disintegrated.' "

"I don't suppose there's any chance of having the Vice President put off his visit until we can get our hands on this guy?" Wohl asked.

"No," Larkin said. "Not a chance."

"Has he seen this letter?"

Larkin shook his head, no.

"Well, you tell us, Charley," Wohl said. "How can we help?"

"That's a little delicate . . ."

"You'd rather discuss that in private, is that what you mean?"

Larkin nodded.

"Charley, anything that you want to say to me, you can say in front of these people," Wohl said.

Larkin hesitated, and then said, "You are like your dad, Peter. He once told me he never had anyone working for him he couldn't trust."

"There are some I trust less than others," Wohl said. "These I trust, period."

"Okay," Larkin said. "The word that gets back to me is that there is some bad feeling between the Police Department and the feds, the FBI in particular, but the feds generally."

"I can't imagine why anyone would think that," Wohl said, lightly sarcastic.

Larkin snorted.

"There's a story going around that both you, the Department, I mean, and the FBI were going after a big-time car thief. And the first time that either of you knew the other guys were working the job was when your cars ran into each other when you were picking him up."

"Not true," Wohl said.

Larkin looked at him in surprise.

"The real story is that nobody in the Department, except one hard-nosed Irishman, believed that the car thief could possibly be a car thief. We were wrong, and the FBI was right."

"One of your guys, the hard-nosed Irishman?"

Wohl pointed at Jack Malone.

"And I don't believe him, either," Wohl said. "Walter Davis and I had a long talk to see if we couldn't keep something like that from happening again."

Walter Davis was the SAC, the special agent in charge, of the Philadelphia office of the FBI.

"You get along with Davis all right, Peter?"

"As well as any simple local cop can get along with the FBI," Wohl said.

"Did you almost say 'the feds'?"

"No."

"Out of school," Larkin said. "I hear that part of the problem is a Captain Jack Duffy."

"Out of school, did you hear what Captain Duffy is supposed to have done?"

"What he doesn't do is the problem, is what I hear. Phrased delicately, both Walter Davis and our SAC here . . . Joe Toner, you know him, our supervisory agent in charge?"

Wohl shook his head, no.

". . . tell me that in the best of all possible worlds, Captain Duffy would be a bit more enthusiastically cooperative than he is."

"That's delicately phrased," Wohl said. "But I don't think it's Duffy personally. He takes his guidance from the commissioner."

"Okay. Confession time," Larkin said. "Joe Toner found out somehow that Dignitary Protection had been given to something called Special Operations, which was under an Inspector Wall. So, when I began to suspect that this vice presidential visit was going to present serious problems, I decided I was going to bypass Captain Duffy. I called the Dignitary Protection sergeant . . . you know who I mean, the caretaker sergeant?"

"Henkels," Wohl furnished.

"Sergeant Henkels. And I told him that I wanted to see the supervisor in charge in our office. There, I was going to make sure he found out somehow that Denny Coughlin and I are old pals. The logic being that Henkels and the lieutenant were going to be more impressed with, and more worried about annoying, Chief Coughlin than they would about Duffy. In other words, they would enthusiastically cooperate."

"You think the danger this guy poses is worth really pissing off Duffy and the commissioner?"

"I would rather have both love me, but yes, I do."

"And if getting Henkels and Malone to circumvent normal channels incidentally got them in deep trouble, too bad?"

"My job is to keep the Vice President alive, Peter. If I have to step on some toes . . ."

"You can't simply cut Duffy out of the picture, even if you wanted to," Wohl said.

"Joe Toner's deputy has an appointment with Duffy at eight o'clock Monday morning. We will go through the motions. But what I hoped to get first from Malone, and then from you, was more cooperation than I'm liable to get from Duffy. This is not one of those times when it would be all right for you to say, 'Fuck the feds.' We've got to find this guy before he has a chance to 'disintegrate' the Vice President, and in the process probably a bunch of civilians."

Wohl's face was expressionless, but obviously, Mike Sabara decided, he was giving his response a good deal of thought. Finally, Wohl reached for his coffee cup, picked it up, and then looked directly at Larkin.

"How, specifically, do you think we could help?"

"Some cop in this town has a line on this guy. Either somebody in Intelligence, Sex Crimes, Civil Affairs, something else esoteric, or a detective somewhere, or a beat cop. He's done something suspicious. If we're lucky, done something really out of the ordinary, like buying explosives, maybe. Had some kind of trouble with his neighbors. Done something that would make a good cop suspicious of him, but nothing he would make official."

"If you gave Jack Duffy," Wohl replied, "or, better yet, the commissioner himself what you've just given us, it would be brought up at the very next roll call."

"And laughed at," Larkin said. "But that's what Toner's deputy is going to do tomorrow morning, tell Duffy everything. I told you, we're going to go through the motions. And maybe we'll get lucky. But maybe lucky won't cut it."

"So what do you want from us?" Wohl asked.

"I thought maybe you could tell me what you could do," Larkin said.

The question surprised Wohl; it was evident on his face.

"My dad was not a fan of police vehicles," he said after a moment. "He always said the beat cop, who knew everybody on his beat, could usually stop trouble before it happened. Unfortunately, we don't have many beat cops these days. But that strikes me as the way to go."

"Excuse me?" Larkin said.

"We'll need a good profile, written in simple English, not like a psychiatrist's case record, of this guy. We spread that around the Department, into every district, every unit. 'Does anybody think they know this guy?' And I'll have Dave distribute it, using the Highway Patrol. They're in and out of districts all over the city; they have friends everywhere, in other words. Make it look like a job, not like the brass in the Roundhouse are smoking funny cigarettes."

"Could you do that?" Larkin asked.

"Not without stepping on Duffy's toes, and a lot of other people's," Wohl said. "Do you know Chief Lowenstein?"

"Only that he runs the Detective Division."

"As a fiefdom," Wohl said. "How soon are you going to have the psychological profile you mentioned?"

"Ours, probably tomorrow, the day after. And the FBI's a day or two after that."

"Can that be speeded up?"

"I can have them in your hands, hand carried, within an hour of their delivery to my office in Washington," Larkin said. "Sooner, if you want it read over the phone. But I can't rush our shrink, and certainly not the FBI's."

"Okay. Then we'll have to go with Amy," Wohl said.

"Who?" Larkin asked.

"Dr. Payne. Detective Payne's sister."

"Oh, yeah."

"She'll give us a profile. I'll translate it into English."

The doorman of the large, luxurious apartment building in the 2600 block of the Parkway in which Amelia Alice Payne, M.D., lived paid only casual attention to the blue Ford as it dropped a passenger, a nicely dressed young man, outside his heavy plate-glass doors.

But then, as the young man stepped inside the lobby, the doorman saw, out of the corner of his eye, that the Ford, instead of driving onto the road leading to the parking lot and/or the Parkway had moved into an area close to the door where parking was prohibited to all but the management of the building and those tenants whose generosity to the doorman deserved a little reward.

"Hey!" the doorman called after the nicely dressed young man. "Your friend can't park there."

Matt Payne's childhood and youth had been punctuated frequently by the parental folklore that hay was for horses, and was not a suitable form of address for fellow human beings, the result of which being that he did not like to be addressed as "Hey!"

He turned to the doorman.

"Oh, I think he can," he said.

"Hey, he either moves the car, or I call the cops."

"There's a cop," Matt said helpfully as Jerry O'Dowd, in the full regalia of a sergeant of the Highway Patrol, got out of the car and strode purposefully toward the door.

"What's going on here?" the doorman asked.

"We're finally going to close the floating craps game on the tenth floor," Matt said. "Gambling is illegal, you know."

Sergeant Jerry O'Dowd, who was by nature a very cordial person, at that moment came through the plate-glass door, smiled at the doorman, and said, "Good morning. Nice day, isn't it?"

He then followed Matt to the bank of elevators and into one of them.

The doorman went to the elevator the moment the door closed and watched in some fascination as the indicator needle over the door moved in an arc and finally stopped at ten.

There were four apartments on the tenth floor. The two larger ones were occupied by a dentist and his family, and a lawyer and his family. The two smaller apartments were occupied by single people. One was a male, who, now that the doorman thought of it, did walk a little strangely, but was not the sort of guy who acted like a gambler.

The other was a female, a medical doctor, who he seemed to recall hearing was a teacher at the University of Pennsylvania, even if she didn't look old enough to be a doctor, much less a teacher. The only suspicious thing about her was that ten minutes before the cops showed up a really good-looking blonde had been dropped off by a chauffeur-driven Buick station wagon, asked for the doctor by name, and gone up.

The blonde didn't look like a hooker, but you weren't supposed to be able to tell anymore just by looks. Two young women and two young guys seemed to add up. Mr. Whatsisname in 10D didn't look like he even liked women.

The doorman decided he would just have to wait and see who got off the elevator, later. And then he decided that the young guy was probably pulling his chain. The cop might be a cop, but he was off duty, and the two of them were just going to see their girlfriends.

Just to be sure, he went out and looked at the blue Ford. It looked like a regular car, except that there was at least one extra radio antenna, and when he looked close, he saw a microphone lying on the seat, its cord disappearing into the glove compartment, and when he looked even closer, he could see a speaker mounted under the dashboard.

So it was a cop car. So what it *probably really* was that the sergeant was on duty, and it was Sunday morning, and nothing was going on, so he picked up his buddy and they came to see the girls. And parked wherever the hell they wanted to!

Goddamned cops!

Amy Payne, a slight, just this side of pretty, brown-haired twenty-seven-year-old, peered through the peephole in her door, and then, somewhat reluctantly, opened it just wide enough to look out.

"You are really the last person I expected to see here this morning, Matt," she said.

There was absolutely no suggestion that she intended to open the door.

"I've got to talk to you, Amy," Matt said.

"You've heard of the telephone? People get on the telephone and say, 'Would it be convenient for me to drop by?' "

"This is important," Matt said.

"How did you get past the doorman, come to think of it? Flash your badge at him?"

"Yeah, as a matter of fact. I'm on business, Amy. May we come in?"

She shrugged, and stepped out of the way.

"Amy, Jerry O'Dowd."

"How do you do, Doctor?"

"Why do I suspect you've been talking about me?" Amy said. "I hope you have a sister of your own, Sergeant, so that you will understand that despite the way I talk to him, I really loathe and detest him."

Jerry O'Dowd laughed. "He said you were feisty," O'Dowd said.

Amy realized that she was smiling back at him.

"I'll be with you in a minute," she said. "Go in the living room, Matt, you know where it is. I've got a little surprise for you too."

The surprise was Miss Penelope Detweiler, who was standing by the expanse of glass opening onto the Parkway and the Museum of Art.

"I thought that was your voice!" she said, seemingly torn between surprise and pleasure. "What are you doing here?"

"That's none of your damned business, Matt!" Amy called from her bedroom. "Who do you think you are, asking a question like that?"

"Oh, I just dropped in to see Amy," Penny said, somewhat lamely.

Yeah, like hell. Your relationship is professional. Doctor and patient. The only thing personal about it is that you get to come here to Amy's apartment because you are a friend of the family.

"Penny, this is Sergeant Jerry O'Dowd," Matt said. "Jerry, this is Penny Detweiler, an old buddy of mine and my sister's."

"Hi," Penny said.

"Hello," O'Dowd said. Matt watched his face to see if he made the connection between the pretty blonde and Tony the Zee's junkie girlfriend. There was nothing on his face to suggest that he did.

"We were just having coffee," Penny said. "Real coffee. Amy even grinds the beans just before she makes it. Would you like some?"

"Please," Matt said.

Penny headed for the kitchen, probably, Matt thought, to get cups and saucers. Matt went and looked out the window. O'Dowd followed him.

"Nice view!" he said enthusiastically.

"Yeah, it is."

"Is that who I think it is?"

"Yeah."

"Pretty girl."

And you're a good cop. I was trying to read your face and couldn't.

"Where were you before you went to work for Pekach?" Matt asked.

"Central Detectives, until I made sergeant, and before that in Narcotics. When Pekach was a lieutenant."

"And now Highway? You like riding a motorcycle?"

"You'll notice I'm not riding one. Pekach told me that if Highway was going to be good for his career, it should be good for mine."

"If I have to go to Wheel School and spend time in Highway, I think I'll stay a detective."

"You haven't been a detective long enough, have you, to make that kind of a judgment?"

"No, I haven't."

Amy came into the room, stopping their conversation.

"Okay, Matt," Amy said, "now what's this all about?" She didn't give him time to reply before she noticed that Penny was not in sight. "Where's Penny?"

"She went to get cups and saucers," Matt said. "What did you think?"

Amy ignored the question.

"What is that you're waving around like a field marshal's baton?" she asked.

O'Dowd chuckled. Amy found herself smiling at him again.

"There's nobody nicer anywhere than someone who thinks you're a wit," Matt said.

"Dad said that, not you," Amy said.

Matt peeled one of the Xeroxes from the roll of them he had been carrying in his hand.

"What's this . . ." Amy asked as she took a quick glance, and then she broke off in mid-sentence. Almost absently, she backed away from Matt and Jerry and sat down on the side arm of her couch.

"My God!" she said, finally. "This is a sick man."

"We'd sort of figured that out," Matt said. "What we need from you is a profile."

"Who's 'we,' you and the sergeant?"

"Peter Wohl, for one. The head of the Vice President's Secret Service detail, for another."

"The Secret Service have their own psychiatrists," Amy said. "I met one of them at Menninger one time. Why me?"

"Wohl said to tell you we need a profile yesterday," Matt said. "We won't get one from the Secret Service until tomorrow. If then."

"Secret Service?" Penny said, coming back into the room with cups and saucers. "That sounds interesting!"

"That's right," Amy said, ignoring Penny, "he is coming to town, isn't he? Next week?"

"Right," O'Dowd said.

"I think I have just been more or less politely told that what's going on here is none of my business," Penny said.

Matt looked at her, saw the hurt in her eyes, and surprised himself by handing her one of the Xeroxes.

"Not to be spread around the Merion Cricket Club, okay, Penny?"

"Thank you," Penny said, and Matt understood that it was not simply ritual courtesy for having been handed a piece of paper. He glanced at O'Dowd and saw in his eyes that he did not approve of what he had done.

And you're right, Sergeant. I should not have passed that official document to a junkie three days out of the funny farm. And I thank you for not saying so, and humiliating me in front of my sister.

"You have no idea who this man is?" Amy asked.

"None. That's why we need the profile."

"What are you going to do with it?"

"Circulate it in the Department, 'Do you know someone who fits this description?' "

"Not in public? Not in the newspapers?"

"That didn't come up," Matt said.

"Probably not," O'Dowd said. "That would tend to set off the copycats."

"Yes," Amy said thoughtfully. She looked directly at O'Dowd. "This letter doesn't give me much to go on, you understand?"

"I understand, Doctor," O'Dowd said. "But whatever you could tell us would be helpful."

He sounds like Jason Washington, Matt thought. *Stroking the interviewee.*

Jason Washington, late of Homicide, now a sergeant heading up Special Operations Division's Special Investigation Section, considered himself to be the best detective in the Philadelphia Police Department. So did Peter Wohl and Matt Payne.

And then as Matt watched Jerry O'Dowd skillfully draw from his sister a profile of the looney tune who wanted to blow up the Vice President, he had another series of thoughts, which ranged from humbling to humiliating:

Wohl didn't send Pekach's driver with me so that I could ask him questions. He sent me with Jerry O'Dowd because I could get O'Dowd in to see Amy. My sole role in this was to get him into her presence. She might have, probably would have, told anyone else to call her office and arrange an appointment.

Pekach didn't pick this guy to be his driver for auld lang syne, but rather because Jerry O'Dowd is a very bright guy, an experienced detective, and now a sergeant. Both Pekach, when he volunteered O'Dowd to "drive me," and Wohl, when he accepted the offer, knew damned well O'Dowd would take over this little interview sooner or later, probably sooner, and in any event the instant Rookie Detective Payne started to fuck it up.

Penny handed him a cup of coffee.

"Black, right?"

"Right. Thank you."

"Sergeant?"

"Black is fine with me."

And that's why O'Dowd was at 30th Street Station when I picked Larkin up. Pekach was not about to tell Wohl that he thought he was making a mistake sending me on an important errand, but he felt obliged to protect his boss by sending O'Dowd there in case I fucked that up.

Matt had a clear mental image of him patronizing O'Dowd outside the station: *"How are you, Jerry? What's up?"*

Did your reputation precede you, Detective Payne? Did Captain Pekach say a soft word in Sergeant O'Dowd's ear before he sent him to the station, or did he think that was unnecessary, it would only be a matter of a minute or two before O'Dowd would be able to conclude for himself that Matthew M. Payne was a first-class, supercilious horse's ass?

"Sergeant, excuse me," Matt Payne said. "I think I'd better call Chief Coughlin, and then check in with Inspector Wohl."

Sergeant O'Dowd looked at Detective Payne with something in his eyes that hadn't been there before.

"Yeah, Matt, please. Go ahead. Tell the inspector that what we're getting from Dr. Payne is very valuable."

Pekach answered Wohl's private number.

"Captain Pekach."

"Payne, sir. I was told to check in."

"The inspector took Mr. Larkin down to Intelligence," Pekach said. "How's things going?"

"Chief Coughlin will meet us for lunch. And Sergeant O'Dowd said to say that what we're getting from my sister is valuable."

"The reservations are for twelve noon. The inspector wants O'Dowd there. Tell him it would be nice if he could get into civilian clothing by then."

"Yes, sir. I have the feeling we're about finished here. There should be time."

In the elevator, Matt said, "Sergeant, Captain Pekach said that you're to go to Bookbinder's, and that if there's time, he'd like you to get out of uniform."

"The inspector probably wants to hear two versions of what we got from your sister," O'Dowd thought out loud, and looked at his watch. "There will be time. I live in Ashton Acres, right by the entrance to Northeast Airport."

The elevator door whooshed open, and they walked to the main door, past the doorman, who made no effort to rush to the door and open it for them.

"See you again," O'Dowd said cheerfully to the doorman, who snorted and pretended to find something on his little desk to be absolutely fascinating.

"I wonder what's wrong with him? Tight shoes?" O'Dowd asked as they were walking to the car.

"Beats me," Matt said. His brilliant repartee earlier with the doorman now seemed nowhere near as witty as it had.

When they were on the Parkway, headed east, O'Dowd said, "Give them a call, tell them where we're going."

Matt picked up the microphone, and then started to open the glove compartment to make sure he was on the right frequency.

"We're on the J-band," O'Dowd said, reading his mind. "And this is the boss's car."

"Highway One-A to Radio," Matt said.

"Highway One-A," the Highway radio dispatcher came back.

"Have you got anything for us?"

"Nothing, Highway One-A."

Matt laid the microphone back on the seat.

"Predictably, I suppose," O'Dowd said, "the only really interesting thing your sister said was when you were on the phone. She said she thinks this guy is asexual. I asked her if she thought that was the cause of his problems, and she said no, she thought it was something else, but that he was asexual, and we should keep that in mind. Do you have any idea what she meant by that?"

"Sergeant, I rarely have any idea what my sister is talking about."

"Have I pissed you off somehow, Payne?"

"Of course not."

"What happened to 'Jerry'?"

"It finally dawned on me that I was out of line at 30th Street Station this morning. A rookie detective should not call a sergeant by his first name."

"I'm not at all shy. If you had been out of line, I would have let you know."

"Thank you."

"So what do you think your sister meant when she said we should keep in mind that this guy is asexual?"

"Beats the shit out of me, Jerry."

O'Dowd laughed. "Better," he said. "Better."

15.

Bookbinder's Restaurant provided a private dining room for the luncheon party, and senior members of the landmark restaurant's hierarchy stopped by twice to shake hands and make sure everything was satisfactory.

But, Matt thought, *that's as far as manifestations of respect for the upper echelons of the Police Department are going to go. They might grab the tab if Coughlin or Lowenstein came in here alone. But they are not going to pick up the tab for a party as large as this one. For one thing, it would be too much money, and for another, it would set an unfortunate precedent:* Hey, let's get the guys together and go down to Bookbinder's for a free lobster!

So what does that mean? That we go Dutch treat, which would make the most sense, or is Peter Wohl going to get stuck with the tab?

Fortunately, that is not my problem. So why am I worrying about it?

He concentrated on his steamed clams, boiled lobster, and on making his two beers last through everything.

It would be inappropriate for Matthew M. Payne, the junior police officer present, to get sloshed during lunch with his betters.

Second *junior police officer,* he corrected himself: *I am no longer low man on the Special Operations totem pole. Officer Tom O'Mara is.*

O'Mara, Matt thought, somewhat surprised, *does not seem at all uncomfortable in the presence of all the white shirts, and heavy-hitter white shirts, at that. You'd think he would be; for the ordinary cop, chief inspectors are sort of a mix between the cardinal of the Spanish Inquisition and God himself.*

But, when you think twice, Tom O'Mara is not an ordinary police officer in the sense that Charley McFadden was—and for that matter, detective or not, still is—an ordinary cop. He belongs to the club. His father is a captain. The reputation is hereditary: Until proven otherwise, the son of a good cop is a good cop.

Some of that, now that I think about it, also applies to me. In a sense, I am a hereditary member of the club. Because of Denny Coughlin, and/or because both my biological father and my uncle Dutch got killed on duty.

The correct term is "fraternity," an association of brothers, from the Latin word meaning brother, as in Delta Phi Omicron *at the University of Pennsylvania, where, despite your noble, two years service as Treasurer, you didn't have a fucking clue what the word* "fraternity" *really meant.*

"You look deep in thought, Matty," Chief Coughlin said, breaking abruptly into his mental meandering. "You all right?"

"I don't think I should have had the second dozen steamed clams," Matt replied. "But aside from that, I'm fine."

"You should have three dozen, Payne," Mr. Larkin said. "I'm paying."

"No, you're not!" Staff Inspector Peter Wohl said.

"We'll have none of that!" Chief Inspector Augustus Wohl said.

"Don't be silly, Charley," Chief Inspector Dennis V. Coughlin said.

"I'll tell you what I'll do, just so we all stay friends," Larkin said, "I'll flip anybody else here with a representation allowance. Loser pays."

"What the hell is a 'representation allowance'?" Chief Wohl asked.

"Your tax dollars at work, Augie," Larkin said. "When high-ranking Secret Service people such as myself are forced to go out with the local Keystone Cops, we're supposed to keep them happy by grabbing the tab. They call it a 'representation allowance.' "

"Screw you, Charley," Coughlin said, laughing. " 'Keystone Cops'!"

"Shut up, Denny. Let him pay," Chief Lowenstein said. "But order another round first." There was laughter.

"Except for him," Peter Wohl said, pointing at Matt. "I want him sober when he translates that psychological profile into English."

"Sir, I can go out to the Schoolhouse right now, if you'd like."

"What I was thinking, Matt," Wohl said seriously, "was that the most efficient way to handle it would be for you to take it to your apartment and translate it there. Then O'Mara could run it by my dad's house, where we can have a look at it. Then Tom can take it out to the Schoolhouse, retype it, and duplicate it. By then Captain Pekach will have been able to set up distribution by Highway."

"Yes, sir," Matt said. "You don't want me to come by Chief Wohl's house?"

"I don't see any reason for you to come out there," Wohl said.

Am I being told I don't belong there, or is he giving me time off?

"Yes, sir," Matt said. "Thank you for lunch, Mr. Larkin."

"Thanks for the ride, Matt," Mr. Larkin said.

The only place there was room in Matt's apartment for a desk was in his bedroom, and even there he had to look long and hard for a desk small enough to fit. He'd finally found an unpainted "student's desk" in Sears Roebuck that fit, but wasn't quite sturdy enough for the standard IBM electric typewriter he had inherited from his father's office. Every time the carriage slammed back and forth for a new line, the desk shifted with a painful squeak.

Tom O'Mara made himself comfortable on Matt's bed, first by sitting on it, and then, when he became bored with that, by lying down on it and watching television with the sound turned off, so as not to disturb Matt's mental labor.

It took him the better part of an hour to translate first Amy's really incredibly bad handwriting, and then to reorganize what she had written, and then finally to incorporate what Wohl and Larkin had brought up in their meeting. Finally, he was satisfied that he had come up with what Wohl and Larkin wanted. He typed one more copy, pulled it from the typewriter, and handed it to O'Mara.

This individual is <u>almost certainly</u>:

Mentally unbalanced, believing that he has a special relationship with God. He may believe that God speaks to him directly.

IMPORTANTLY: He would not make a public announcement of this relationship.

Highly intelligent.

Well educated, most likely a college graduate, but almost certainly has some college education.

Well spoken, possessed of a good vocabulary.

An expert typist, with access to a current model IBM typewriter (one with a "type ball").

This individual is <u>probably</u>:

A male Caucasian.

Twenty-five to forty years old.

Asexual (that is, he's unmarried, and has no wife, or homo- or heterosexual partner or sex life).

"A loner" (that is, has very few, or no friends).

Living alone.

Neat and orderly, possibly to an excessive degree, and dresses conservatively.

Of ordinary, or slightly less than ordinary, physical appearance. A chess player, not a football player.

Self-assured, possibly to an excessive degree. (That is, tends to become annoyed, even angry, with anyone who disagrees with him.)

An Episcopalian, Presbyterian, Methodist, (less likely, a Roman Catholic) but not an active member of any church group.

Works in an office.

A nondrinker.

Either a nonsmoker or a chain cigarette smoker.

This individual is <u>possibly</u>:

An engineer, either civil or electronic, or an accountant, or someone who works with figures.

A veteran, possibly discharged for medical (including psychological) reasons. Possibly a former junior officer.

Someone who has come to the attention of the authorities as the result of a complaint <u>he has made</u> when he has felt he has been wronged. (For example, complaining about neighbor's loud party, or loud radio, damage to his lawn, et cetera, by neighborhood children.)

As O'Mara read it, Matt glanced up at the silent TV mounted on a hospital-room shelf over the door. O'Mara had been watching an old cops-and-robbers movie.

I wonder how he can tell the good guys from the bad guys? They all look like 1930s-era gangsters.

"Your sister was able to come up with all this just from that nutty note that screwball wrote?" O'Mara asked, visibly awed.

"My sister is a genius. It runs in the family."

"Shit!" O'Mara said.

After a pause, Matt thought, *while he decided I was not serious.*

"Well, I'd better run this out to the brass," O'Mara said, and finally pushed himself upright and got off the bed.

At the head of the stairs, O'Mara stopped. "How do I get out?"

Matt recalled that O'Mara had parked Wohl's car in front of the building. Despite the NO PARKING signs, no white hat was going to ticket what was obviously the unmarked car of a senior white shirt. He had unlocked the plate-glass door to the lobby with his key, and then locked it again after them. It would now be necessary to repeat the process to let O'Mara out.

"I'll let you out," Matt said, and went down the stairs ahead of him.

Matt went into the kitchen and took a bottle of beer from the refrigerator and went into the living room, slumped in his chair and picked up a copy of *Playboy.* He looked at his answering machine. The red *You Have Messages* light was flashing.

I really don't want to hear my messages. But on the other hand, Wohl may be wondering what the hell took me so long.

He reached over and pushed the PLAY button.

There were six calls, five of them from people—

People, hell, Evelyn is at it again!

—who had not chosen to leave a message, and one from Jack Matthews, who wanted him to call the first chance he got.

And I know what you want, Jack Matthews. The FBI wants to know what the hell the Keystone Cops are doing with the Secret Service big shot from Washington. Fuck you!

As the tape was rewinding, the doorbell, the one from the third floor, at the foot of his stairs, buzzed.

Now what, O'Mara? Did you forget something?

He got out of his chair, and pushed the button that operated the solenoid, and then looked down the stairs to see what O'Mara wanted.

Mrs. Evelyn Glover came through the door and smiled up at him.

Jesus H. Christ!

"Am I disturbing anything?"

"No," Matt lied. "I was just about to call you. Come on up."

There was an awkward moment at the head of the stairs, when Matt considered if he had some sort of obligation to kiss her and decided against it.

"I guess I shouldn't have done this, should I?" Evelyn asked.

"Don't be silly, I'm glad to see you. Would you like a drink?"

"Yes. Yes, I would."

"Cognac?"

"Yes, please."

She followed him into the kitchen, and stood close, but somewhat awkwardly, as he found the bottle and a snifter and poured her a drink.

"Aren't you having one?"

"I've got a beer in the living room."

"I owe you an apology," Evelyn said.

"How come?"

"I didn't really believe you when you said you had to work," she said. "I thought you were . . . trying to get rid of me."

"Why would I want to do that?"

Because even as stupid as you are in matters of the heart, you can see where this one is about to get out of control.

"But then, when I happened to drive by and saw the police car parked in front . . ."

"He just left."

As if you didn't know. What have you been doing, Evelyn, circling the block?

"Forgive me?" Evelyn asked coyly.

"There's nothing to forgive."

She had moved close to him, and now there was no question at all that she expected to be kissed.

There was just a momentary flicker of her tongue when he kissed her. She pulled her face away just far enough to be able to look into his eyes and smiled wickedly. He kissed her again, and this time she responded hungrily, her mouth open on his, her body pressing against his.

When she felt him stiffen, she caught his hand, directed it to her breast, and then moved her hand to his groin.

She moved her mouth to his ear, stuck her tongue in, and whispered huskily, pleased, "Well, he's not mad at me, is he?"

"Obviously not," Matt said.

To hell with it!

He put his hand under her sweater and moved it up to the fastener on her brassiere.

Marion Claude Wheatley turned the rental car back in to the Hertz people at the airport in plenty of time to qualify for the special rate, but there was, according to the mental defective on duty, 212 miles on the odometer, twelve more than was permitted under the rental agreement. The turn-in booth functionary insisted that Marion would have to pay for the extra miles at twenty-five cents a mile. He was stone deaf to Marion's argument that he'd made the trip fifty times before, and it had never exceeded 130 miles.

It wasn't the three dollars, it was the principle of the matter. Obviously, the odometer in the car was in error, and that was Hertz's fault, not his. Finally, a supervisor was summoned from the airport. He was only minimally brighter than the mental defective at the turn-in booth, but after Marion threatened to turn the entire matter over not only to Hertz management, but also to the Better Business Bureau and the police, he finally backed down, and Marion was able to get in a taxi and go home.

When he got to the house, Marion carefully checked everything, paying particular attention to the powder magazine, to make sure there had been no intruders during his absence.

Then he unpacked the suitcases, and took his soiled linen, bedclothes, and his overalls to the basement, and ran them through the washer, using the ALL COLD and LOW WATER settings. He watched the machine as it went through the various cycles, using the time to make up a list of things he would need in the future.

First of all, he would need batteries, and he made a note to be sure to check the expiration date to be sure that he would be buying the freshest batteries possible for both the detonation mechanism and for the radio transmitter.

He would need more chain, as well. He was very pleased to learn how well the chain had functioned. He would need six lengths of chain, five for the five devices, and one as a reserve. Each length had to be between twenty and twenty-two inches in length.

He would need two 50-yard rolls of duct tape, and two 25-yard rolls of a good-quality electrical tape, tape that would have both high electrical and adhesive qualities. He wouldn't need anywhere near even twenty-five yards of electrical tape, but one tended to misplace small rolls of tape, and he would have a spare if that happened. One tended to lose the larger rolls of duct tape less often, but it wouldn't hurt to be careful.

And he would need five pieces of luggage in which to place the devices. As he had driven back from the Pine Barrens, Marion had decided that what had been "AWOL bags" in the Army would be the thing to get. They were of canvas construction, nine or ten inches wide, probably eighteen inches or two feet long, and closed with a zipper.

It would be necessary to get them with brass, or steel, zippers, not plastic or aluminum. By attaching a wire between a steel or brass zipper and the antennae of the devices, it would be possible to increase the sensitivity of the radio receivers' antennae.

He would also need an attaché case in which to carry the shortwave transmitter. He had seen some for sale in one of the trashy stores along Market Street, east of City Hall. They were supposed to be genuine leather, but Marion doubted that, considering the price they were asking. It didn't matter, really, but there was no sense in buying a genuine leather attaché case when one that looked like leather would accomplish the same purpose.

Marion made two more notes, one to remind himself not to buy the AWOL bags all in one place, which might raise questions, and the other to make sure they all were of different colors and, if possible, of slightly different design.

He was finished making up the list a good five minutes before the washing machine completed the last cycle, and he was tempted to just leave the sheets and everything in the machine, and come back later and hang them up to dry, but then decided that the best way to go, doing anything, was to finish one task completely before going on to another.

He waited patiently until the washing machine finally clunked to a final stop, and then removed everything and hung it on a cord stretched across the basement. Things took longer, it seemed like forever, to dry in the basement, but on the other hand, no one had ever stolen anything from the cord in the basement the way things were stolen from the cord in the backyard.

When he came out of the basement, he changed into a suit and tie, and then walked to the 30th Street Station. He wanted to make sure that his memory wouldn't play tricks on him about the general layout of the station, and what was located where. He had been coming to the 30th Street Station since he had been a child, and therefore should know it like the back of his hand. But the operative word there was "should," and it simply made sense to have another careful look, in case changes had been made or there was some other potential problem.

He spent thirty minutes inside the station, including ten minutes he spent at the fast-food counter off the main waiting room, sitting at a dirty little table from which he could look around.

The Vice President would certainly want to march right down the center of the main waiting room, after he rode up the escalator from the train platform.

Unfortunately, there were no rows of lockers on the platform itself, which would have simplified matters a great deal. If there had been lockers, all he would have had to do was wait until the Vice President walked past where he could have concealed one of the devices, and then detonate it.

He consoled himself by thinking that if there had been lockers there, the Secret Service, who were not fools, would almost certainly make sure they didn't contain anything they shouldn't.

Once the Vice President and his entourage reached the main waiting room level of the station, there were three possible routes to where he would enter his official car. There were east, west, and south entrances.

The logical place would be the east exit, but that did not mean he would use it. There were a number of factors that would be considered by those in charge of the Vice President's movements, and there was just no telling, with any degree of certainty, which one would be used.

All three routes would have to be covered. The east and west routes, conveniently, had rows of lockers. If he placed in each of two lockers on both the east and west routes one device, the lethal zone of the devices would be entirely effective. The south route did not have a row of lockers.

Marion thought that it was entirely likely the Lord was sending him a message via the lockers in the Pine Barrens. In other words, why the symbolism of the lockers if they were not in some way connected with the disintegration of the Vice President?

It was unlikely, following that line of thought, that the Vice President would take the south, locker-less route.

But on the other hand, it was also possible that he was wrong. It was also clear that the Lord expected him to be as thorough as humanly possible. That meant, obviously, that he was going to have to cover the south route, even if the Vice President would probably not use it.

There was, of course, a solution. There was always a solution when doing the Lord's work. One simply had to give it some thought. Often some prayerful thought.

There was a large metal refuse container against the wall in the passage between the main waiting room and the doors of the south exit. All he would have to do is put the fifth device in the refuse container. For all he knew—and there was no way to *know* without conducting a test—the metal refuse container would produce every bit as much shrapnel as one of the lockers.

The only problem, which Marion decided could be solved as he left 30th Street Station, was to make sure the metal refuse container would accept one of the AWOL bags through its opening.

Marion bought one of the last copies of the Sunday edition of *The Philadelphia Inquirer* on sale at the newsstand. He sat down on one of the benches in the main waiting room and flipped through it for three or four minutes. Then he left the station by the south route, stopping at the metal refuse container to place the newspaper in it.

He kept the first section. First he opened it and laid it on the opening horizontally, and then tore the paper to mark how wide the opening was. Then he held the paper vertically, and tore it again, this time marking how tall the opening was.

Then he folded the newspaper, tucked it under his arm, and walked out of the station and home.

He had thirty minutes to spare before Masterpiece Theater came on the television.

Magdelana Lanza was waiting for her son Vito on the sidewalk in front of the house on Ritner Street.

"I had to call the plumber," she announced.

"I told you I would go by Sears when I got off work."

"The hot water thing is busted; there was water all over the basement. And the pipes is bad."

"What pipes?"

"What pipes do you think, sonny? The *water* pipes is what pipes."

"What do you mean they're bad?"

"They're all clogged up; they got to go. We have to have new pipes."

That sonofabitch of a plumber! What he did was figure he could sell an old woman anything he told her she needed. I'll fix his ass!

"I'll have a look, Mama."

"Don't use the toilet. There's no water; it won't flush."

"Okay, Mama. I'll have a look."

No water, my ass. What can go wrong with pipes? What I'm going to find when I go in the basement is that this sonofabitch has turned the valve off.

Vito went in the house and went to his room and took off the good clothes he had worn to take Tony to the Poconos and put on a pair of khaki trousers and an old pair of shoes.

I got to take a leak. What did you expect? The minute she tells you the toilet won't flush, you have to piss so bad your back teeth are floating.

He went into the bathroom and looked at the toilet. There was water in the bowl.

Nothing wrong with this toilet. What the hell was she talking about?

He voided his bladder, and pulled the chain. Water emptied from the reservoir into the toilet bowl. It flushed. But there was no rush of clean water. The toilet sort of burped, and when he looked down there was hardly any water in the bowl at all, and none was coming in.

Vito dropped to his knees and looked behind the bowl at the valve on the thin copper pipe that fed water to the reservoir, and then put his hand on it.

There was a momentary feeling of triumph.

The fucking thing's turned off! That sonofabitching plumber! Wait 'til I get my hands on you, pal!

He turned the valve, opening it fully. No water entered the reservoir. He waited a moment, thinking maybe it would take a second or two to come on, like it took a while for the water to come hot when you turned it on.

Nothing! Shit!

Three hours ago, I was in a bathroom with a carpet on the floor and a toilet you couldn't even hear flushing or filling, and now look where I am!

Wait a minute! He wouldn't shut it off here, he'd shut it off in the basement, where nobody would see. I didn't turn that valve on, I turned it off!

He cranked the valve as far it would go in the opposite direction, and then went down the stairs to the first floor two at a time, and then more carefully down the stairs to the basement, because Mama kept brooms and mops and buckets and stuff like that on the cellar stairs.

His foot slipped on the basement floor, and he only barely kept from falling down. When he finally found the chain hanging from the light switch and got the bare bulb turned on, he saw that the floor was slick wet. Here and there there were little puddles. And it smelled rotten too, not as bad as a backed-up toilet, but bad.

He found the place at the rear of the basement where the water pipes came in through the wall from the water meter out back. And again there was a feeling of triumph.

There's the fucking valve, and it's off!

It didn't have a handle, like the valve on the toilet upstairs, just a piece of iron sticking up that you needed a wrench, or a pair of pliers, to turn. He turned and started for the front of the basement, where there was sort of a workbench, and where he knew he could find a wrench.

It was then that he saw the water heater had been disconnected, and moved from the concrete blocks on which it normally rested. Both the water and gas pipes connected to it had been disconnected.

He took a good close look.

Well, shit, if I was the fucking plumber, I would disconnect the water heater. How the hell would an old lady know whether or not it was really busted? A plumber tells an old lady it's busted, she thinks it's busted.

And then he saw something else out of the ordinary. There were two pieces of pipe, one with a connection on one end, and the other end sawed off, and a second piece, with both ends showing signs of having just been cut, lying on the floor near the water heater. . . .

What the fuck did he have to do that for?

He picked one piece of pipe up, and confirmed that the connection on one end indeed matched the connection on top of the water heater. Then he took the sawed end, and held it up against the pipe that carried the hot water upstairs.

It matched, like he thought it would. Then he saw where there was a break in the cold water pipe, where the other piece had been cut from. Just to be sure, he picked up the other piece of pipe and held it up to see if it fit. It did. And then for no good reason at all, he put the piece of pipe to his eye and looked through it.

You can hardly see through the sonofabitch! What the fuck?

He carried it to the bare lightbulb fixture and looked through it again.

And saw that it was almost entirely clogged with some kind of shit. Rust. Whatever.

That's what she meant when she said "the pipes are clogged. They got to go." Jesus Christ! What the fuck is that going to cost?

Magdelana Lanza was waiting at the head of the cellar stairs when Vito came up.

"I told you not to flush the toilet," she said. "That there's no water. So now what am I supposed to do?"

"Use Mrs. Marino's toilet," he said.

"The plumber wants two thousand dollars' deposit."

"What?"

"He says, you don't get him two thousand dollars by nine tomorrow morning, he'll have to go on to another job, and we'll have to wait. He don't know when he could get back."

"Two thousand dollars?"

"He said that'll almost cover materials, labor will be extra, but he won't order the materials until you give him two thousand dollars, and you pay the rest when he's finished."

"Jesus, Mary, and Joseph!"

"Watch your language!"

"And what if I don't have two thousand dollars?"

"Then sell your Cadillac automobile, Mr. Big Shot, you got to have water in the house."

"Who'd you call, Mama, the plumber?"

"Rosselli Brothers, who else?"

"I'll go there in the morning."

"You can get off work? Give me a check, and I'll take it over there."

"I go on four-to-midnight today, Mama. I'll be off in the morning."

"You got two thousand dollars in the bank? After you bought your fancy Cadillac automobile?"

"Don't worry about it, Mama, okay? I told you I would take care of it."

Vito realized that he did not have two thousand dollars in his Philadelphia Savings Fund Society checking account. Maybe a little over a thousand, maybe even twelve hundred, but not two big ones.

Upstairs, under the second drawer in the dresser, of course, there is some real money. Ten big ones.

But shit, I signed a marker for six big ones, which means I got four big ones, not ten. And when I pay the fucking plumber two big ones in the morning, that'll take me down to two.

Jesus Christ, where the fuck did it all go? I got off the airplane from Vegas with all the fucking money in the world, and now I'm damned near broke again.

"You got to take care of it," Magdelana Lanza said. "We got to have a toilet and hot water."

"Mama, I said I'd take care of it. Don't worry about it."

Magdelana Lanza snorted.

"Mama, can you stay with Mrs. Marino tonight? I mean you can't stay here with no water."

"Tonight, I can stay with Mrs. Marino. But I can't stay there forever."

"Okay. One day at a time. I'll see what the plumber says tomorrow, how long it will take him. Now I got to get dressed and go to work. Okay?"

"I'll go ask Mrs. Marino if it would be an imposition."

"You'd do it for her, right? What's the problem?"

"I'll go ask her, would it be an imposition."

She walked out the front door and Vito climbed the stairs to the second floor. He took the second drawer from his dresser, and then took the money he had concealed in the dresser out and sat on his bed and counted it.

It wasn't ten big ones. It was only ninety-four hundred bucks. When there had been twenty-two big ones, six hundred bucks hadn't seemed like much.

Now it means that I don't even have two big ones, just fourteen lousy hundred. Plus, the eleven hundred in PSFS, that's only twenty-five hundred.

Jesus H. Christ!

He changed into his uniform.

The plumber and his helpers will be all over the house. I better take this money with me; it will be safer than here.

16.

Officer Jesus Martinez drove into the parking lot of the Airport Police Station in his five-year-old Oldsmobile 98 about two minutes before Corporal Vito Lanza pulled in at the wheel of his not-quite-a-year-old Cadillac Fleetwood.

Martinez would not have seen Lanza arrive had he not noticed that his power antenna hadn't completely retracted. Jesus took great pride in his car, and things like that bothered him. He unlocked the car and got back in and turned the ignition on and ran the antenna up and down by turning the radio on and off.

It retracted completely the last couple of times, which made him think, to his relief, that there was nothing wrong with the antenna, that it was probably just a little dirty. As soon as he got home, he would get some alcohol and wet a rag with it, and wipe the antenna clean, and then lubricate it with some silicone lubricant.

He was in the process of relocking the Olds's door when Corporal Lanza pulled in beside him.

That's a new Cadillac. Where the fuck does he get the money for a new Cadillac?

"Whaddaya say, Corporal?"

"Hey! How they hanging, Gomez?"

"It's Martinez, Corporal."

"Sorry."

"Nice wheels."

"Yeah, it's all right. Nothing like a Caddy."

"What's something like that worth?"

"What the fuck is the matter with you? It's not polite to ask people what things cost."

"Sorry, Corporal. Just curious."

"A lot," Lanza said. "Save your pennies, Martinez."

"Yeah."

"Or get lucky, which is how I got that fucker."

"Excuse me?"

"Las Vegas. You want a Caddy like that, you go to Las Vegas and get lucky."

"Yeah, I guess."

"So how do you like the Airport?"

"I haven't been out here long enough to really know. So far it's great. I was in Highway."

How the fuck did a little Spic like you get into Highway? You don't look big enough to straddle a motorcycle.

"Yeah, I heard. So why did you leave Highway?"

"They made it plain to me that maybe I would be happier someplace else. Which was all right with me. I wasn't too happy in Highway."

They didn't want you in Highway as little as you are. Those fuckers all think they're John Wayne. And John Wayne you're not, Gom—Martinez.

"Well, walking around an air-conditioned building telling tourists where they can find the pisser sure beats riding a motorcycle in the rain."

"You said it, Corporal."

'The next time they announce a corporal's exam, you ought to have a shot at it."

"Yeah, well, I'm not too good at taking examinations."

"Some people are, and some people aren't. Don't worry about it."

It wasn't until a few minutes after midnight, when he put the key in the Caddy's door, that Vito, with a sinking feeling in his stomach, realized that he had done something really fucking stupid.

He pulled the door open and slid across the seat, and then, cursing, lifted the fold-down armrest out of the way and put his finger on the glove compartment button.

Shit, it's locked. I don't remember locking the sonofabitch.

He found the key and unlocked the glove compartment, and exhaled audibly with relief. The Flamingo Hotel & Casino envelope was still there, right where he'd shoved it when he got in the car.

He took it out and glanced into it. There was enough light from the tiny glove compartment bulb to see the comforting thick wad of fifties and hundreds. He closed the envelope and stuck it in his pocket.

Not that much of it is still mine anymore.

I know goddamned well I didn't lock that compartment. Maybe, this is a Caddy, after all, it locks automatically.

He closed the glove compartment door, slid back across the seat behind the wheel, put the ignition key in, and started the engine.

Starts right fucking off! There really is nothing like a Caddy.

He backed out of the parking slot, noticed that the old Olds the Spic kid drove was still there. Well, at least he knew what he was doing in the Airport Unit. The little fucker was too dumb to pass the detective's exam, and too little to be a real Highway Patrolman, so they eased him out. They tossed him Airport Unit as a bone. He wondered if the little Spic was smart enough to know how lucky he was to be in Airport; they could just as easily have sent him to one of the districts, or somewhere else really shitty.

Vito decided he would be nice to the kid. Make sure he knows what a good deal he had fallen into. He might come in useful sometime.

He drove up South Broad Street and then made an illegal left turn onto Spruce.

What the hell it was after midnight, there was no traffic, and he was in his uniform, nobody was going to give him a ticket, even if some cop saw him.

He did decide to put the Caddy in a parking garage. If he didn't, sure as Christ made little apples, some asshole, jealous of the Caddy, would run a key down the side or across the hood. Or steal the fucking hubcaps.

When he parked the car, he remembered this was the garage where the mob blew away a guy, one of their own, who had pissed somebody off. Tony the Zee DeZego. They got him with a shotgun.

Tony met him at the door of her apartment in a negligee. Nice-looking one. Vito had never seen her in it before.

"You didn't have to wait up for me, baby," Vito said.

"I went to bed," she said, kissing him, but moving her body away when he tried to slip his hand under the negligee, "but Uncle Joe called me, and then I couldn't get back to sleep."

"What did he want?"

"He's worried about those markers you signed at Oaks and Pines Lodge."

"Why should he be worried? I'm good for them. And he set it up too, didn't he?"

"Well, that's what happened. He didn't set it up. They just thought he did. But because he sent you there, they told him they were holding him responsible. So he's worried. Six thousand dollars is a lot of money."

"Hey! I'm good for it. I got it in my pocket. You call him up and ask if he wants me to come over there right now with it, or whether he can wait until the morning."

"I'm sure it will be okay," Tony said.

"Call him!" Vito said. "Tell him the only reason I didn't make those markers good sooner was that I had to work."

"Okay, honey," Tony said. "Whatever you say."

Penelope Detweiler, wearing only the most brief of underpants, her naked bosom bouncing not at all unattractively, was chasing Matthew M. Payne around the upstairs sitting room of the Detweiler mansion in Chestnut Hill when the doorbell, actually a rather unpleasant-sounding buzzer, went off.

Matt Payne sat up in his bed suddenly.

Who the hell is that?

He looked up at the ceiling, where a clever little clock his sister Amy had given him projected the time by a beam of light. It was almost half past one.

Christ, don't tell me Evelyn's come back!

He threw the blankets back angrily and marched naked through the kitchen to the button by the head of the stairs that operated the door lock solenoid and pushed it.

The door opened and Detective Charley McFadden started up the stairs. On his heels was Officer Jesus Martinez, in uniform.

"You took your fucking time answering the doorbell," Detective McFadden said, by way of apology for disturbing Matt's sleep.

"I'll try to do better the next time."

"I thought maybe you had a broad up here," McFadden said as he reached the head of the stairs.

Not anymore. She finally went home, after reluctantly concluding that the only way she was going to be able to make it stand up again was to put it in a splint.

That being the case, where did that erotic dream about Precious Penny come from?

"If there was, you'd still be down there leaning on the doorbell." Matt said. "What do you say, Hay-zus?"

Martinez did not reply.

"You got a beer or something?" McFadden asked. "And why don't you put a bathrobe on or something?"

"Are we going to have a party?"

"No. This is business. We got to talk."

"You know where the beer is," Matt said, and went in the bedroom for his robe.

It smells in here. Essence de Sex.

"You got a Coke or something?" Martinez asked.

"There's ginger ale, Hay-zus," Matt said. "I don't think there's any Coke."

He went to the refrigerator and found a small bottle of ginger ale and handed it to Martinez.

"Thank you."

"Hay-zus thinks he's found a dirty cop at the airport," McFadden said.

Then he probably has. But why tell me?

"Tell Internal Affairs," Matt said.

"I can't go to Internal Affairs. I haven't caught him doing anything, but I got the gut feeling he's dirty," Martinez said.

"I don't understand what you're doing here," Matt said.

"Charley said I should talk to you."

"I don't have the faintest idea what you're talking about," Matt said. "You want to take it from the beginning?"

"Tell him what you told me, Hay-zus," Charley said, lowering himself with a grunt into Matt's upholstered chair.

"There's a corporal out there," Jesus said. "A flashy Guinea named Lanza, Vito Lanza."

Matt did not reply.

"Just bought himself a new Cadillac," Jesus said. "You can't buy a Caddy on a corporal's pay."

"Maybe his number hit," Matt said, slightly sarcastic.

"He said he won the money in Las Vegas," Jesus said.

"That's possible," Matt said.

"Look at him. He won six thousand when he was out there," McFadden said.

"Yeah, I thought about that. But he's not Lanza."

"What does that mean?" Matt asked.

"You're fucking rich. You don't really give a shit whether you win or lose, and you came home with only six thousand."

"*Only* six thousand? I wish to Christ I had won six thousand," Charley said.

"There's more," Jesus said.

"Like what more?"

"He had almost ten thousand in cash, ninety-four hundred, to be exact, in his car tonight."

"How do you know that?"

"I looked."

"What do you mean, you looked?"

"When Charley and I were in Narcotics, we stopped a guy one night and took a car thief's friend from him," Jesus said. "I kept it."

A car thief's friend, sometimes called a "Slim-Jim," was a flat piece of metal, most commonly stainless steel, suitably shaped so that when inserted into an automobile door, sliding it downward in the window channel, it defeated the door lock.

"In other words, you broke into this guy's car, is that what you're saying?"

"Yeah, and he had ninety-four hundred dollars in an envelope in the glove compartment, an ashtray full of cigarette butts with lipstick on them, and this."

Martinez threw something at Matt, who caught it. It was a book of matches. *Oaks and Pines Resort Lodge.*

"What's this?"

"It's a fancy place in the Poconos," Jesus said.

"So?"

"I called a guy I know in Vice and asked him did he ever hear about it, and he told me that there's a room in the back for high rollers; that the word is that the Mob owns it."

"So?"

"This doesn't smell to you, Payne?" Martinez said, seemingly torn between surprise and contempt.

"I take back what I said before. You should not go to Internal Affairs. What you have is a guy that gambles. At this lodge, and in Las Vegas. And right now, he's lucky. The only thing I can see he's done illegally is gamble in the Poconos. That's a misdemeanor, as opposed to a felony. Like being in possession of burglar tools is a felony."

"What did I tell you he'd say, Hay-zus?" Charley McFadden said.

"I got the *feeling,* Charley," Jesus said. "This guy is dirty."

"What's he doing?"

"They're smuggling drugs through the airport, most likely off Eastern Airlines flights from Puerto Rico, and probably from Mexico City flights too."

"You *know* this?"

"Everybody knows it, Matt," Charley said. "The feds, Customs Service, and the Bureau of Drugs and Dangerous Narcotics. . . ."

"Narcotics and Dangerous Drugs," Jesus interrupted to correct him.

"Whatever the fuck they are, they're all over the place."

"They haven't caught this guy, then, have they?" Matt responded.

"*I* want to catch this fucker," Jesus said.

You're not a detective, Martinez. You're a simple police officer who took the detective's exam and flunked it.

You are an arrogant, self-satisfied shit, aren't you, Matthew Payne? Martinez is not only not a rookie, he's spent a lot of time dealing with drug people when he was in Narcotics. He knows what he's talking about.

"What do you want from me, Hay-zus?"

"I told him he ought to go to Wohl," Charley said. "He says he doesn't want to."

"Why not?" Matt asked, meeting Martinez's eyes.

"I don't work for Wohl anymore, for one thing. And even if I did, how the hell could I go to Wohl and tell him the reason I know this fucker runs around with almost ten thousand in his glove compartment is because I looked?"

" 'Broke into his car' are the words you're looking for," Matt said.

"I told Hay-zus Wohl, or at least Pekach, would listen to him. And he could tell them the car was unlocked."

"That's splitting a hair," Matt thought out loud. "That wouldn't wash with either Wohl or Pekach. And I suppose you know that if you'd found ten thousand dollars' worth of cocaine in his glove compartment, it would be inadmissible evidence."

"Hey, I was a Narc when you were Mr. Joe College Payne," Jesus said. "I know what's admissible and what isn't."

"Hay-zus, you don't have a thing on this guy," Matt said.

"He wants to follow him, and *get* something on him," Charley said.

"You mean, he wants *us* to surveil this guy, right?"

"I told you he'd tell us to go fuck ourselves," Martinez said.

"He can't do it himself, this Dago knows him."

"We're wasting our time. Let's get out of here," Martinez said.

"Hay-zus is usually right, when he smells something," McFadden went on.

"Come on, let's get out of here," Martinez repeated.

"What do you expect to find, Martinez, if we start to follow this guy around?" Matt asked.

"Association with known criminals," Martinez said. "That would give me enough to go to Wohl or Internal Affairs."

He keeps bringing up Wohl. Why? He doesn't work for Wohl anymore. But I do. That's what this is all about. He figures I could go to Wohl.

"For the sake of argument, Hay-zus," Matt said. "Let's suppose we follow this guy, and either he spots us before we catch him with some Mob type, or that you're wrong. He'd really be pissed. And we would have some explaining to do."

"In other words, no, right?"

"I didn't say that," Matt said. "I said what if."

"Then I would take my lumps."

"*We* all would take *our* lumps," Matt said.

"This guy is dirty," Martinez said. "We're cops."

Matt exhaled audibly.

"What have you got in mind?"

"You don't look like a cop," Martinez said. "You drive a Porsche. You could get into this place in the Poconos."

"How would we know when he was going to be there? And if we did, what am I supposed to do, tell Wohl I want the day off to take a ride to the Poconos?"

"I don't think he'd be going up there in the daytime," Martinez said. "Except over the weekend. He's got Friday-Saturday off. With a little bit of luck, he'd go up there then."

"And what if he just came across this book of matches someplace? Picked it up in a bar or something? You don't *know* that he's ever even been in this place." Matt picked up the matchbook. "Oaks and Pines Resort Lodge."

"Then I'll think of something else," Martinez said.

"Okay, Hay-zus," Matt said. "Let me know what you want me to do, and when you want me to do it."

"See, Hay-zus," McFadden said. "I told you."

"But don't let your Latin-American temper get out of joint if I can't jump when you call. I may be doing a lot of overtime."

"Overtime, you?" McFadden asked.

That was an honest question, Matt decided, *not a challenge.*

"Special Operations has been given Dignitary Protection. The Vice President's coming to Philly. There's a looney tune out there that wants to blow him up."

"No shit?" McFadden asked.

"Yeah, and the Secret Service thinks this guy is for real."

"What's that got to do with you?"

"Malone is in charge. For the time being, I'm working for Malone."

"We'll just have to see what happens," Martinez said. "If you're working, you're working."

When Joe Fierello drove his Mercedes-Benz onto the lot of Fierello Fine Cars at quarter to nine in the morning, he found Vito Lanza waiting for him.

"Don't tell me," Joe said as he got out of his car, "the transmission fell out."

"Not yet," Vito said. "I wanted to take care of my markers."

"Tony tell you I called?" Joe asked, but before Vito could answer, he went on, "Come on in the office. I'm not worth a shit in the morning until I have my coffee."

Fierello's secretary smiled at them as they walked past.

"Darlene, get us some coffee, will you?" Joe said, and as he walked behind his desk, he waved Vito into a chair in front of his desk. "Take a load off. You take anything in your coffee?"

Vito shook his head, no.

"Black both times, darling," Joe called out.

Darlene delivered the coffee and then left, closing the door behind her.

"Nice," Vito said.

"My wife's sister's girl," Joe said. "A *nice* girl."

"That's what I meant," Vito said.

Joe Fierello smiled at Vito. Vito did not like the smile.

"Like Tony," he said.

"Darlene doesn't go off overnight to the Poconos," Joe said. "You understand?"

"Absolutely."

"Don't misunderstand me, Tony's a nice girl. She's over twenty-one and she can do what she likes."

"I'm sorry there was that confusion about the markers," Joe said.

"They offered me the markers," Vito said. "I didn't ask for them."

"You went up there as my guest; they're holding me responsible for the markers. You're a nice fellow, Vito, but I don't like you six big ones worth. How soon can you make them good?"

"Right now, Joe. That's what I came here for."

He reached in his pocket and took out the envelope from the Flamingo.

"Hey, what are you doing?"

"I'm making good my markers," Vito said, now very confused.

"You don't understand," Joe said. "I'm a businessman. You don't make your markers good with me."

"With who, then?"

"You really don't know, do you?"

"You got me pretty confused, to tell you the truth," Vito confessed.

"Let me make a call," Joe said.

He took a small leather notebook from his jacket pocket, found a number, and dialed it.

"This is Joe Fierello," he said when someone answered. "Could I talk to Mr. Cassandro, please?" He covered the microphone with his hand. "Mr. Cassandro is sort of like the local business agent, you know what I mean?"

Vito nodded.

Business agent, my ass; this Cassandro guy is with the Mob.

"Paulo? Joe Fierello. You know those financial documents you were a little concerned about? Well, don't worry. They're good. Mr. Lanza is right here with me now, and he's anxious to take care of them."

He started nodding, and again covered the microphone with his hand. "He says he's sorry, I don't know what the fuck he means."

He removed his hand from the microphone.

"I'm sure Mr. Lanza would be perfectly willing to come wherever you tell him, Paulo," Fierello said, and there was a reply, and then he went on: "Whatever you say, Paulo. He'll be here."

He hung up the telephone and looked at Vito.

"He's coming right over. He said there was some kind of a mix-up, and he wants to make it right. It'll take him five, ten minutes. You got to be someplace else?"

Vito shook his head. "I really don't understand this," he said.

"Neither do I," Joe Fierello said. "So we'll have our cup of coffee, and in five, ten minutes, we'll both know."

Ten minutes later, a silver Jaguar drove up the driveway into Fierello Fine Cars, and stopped beside Joe Fierello's Mercedes-Benz. Paulo Cassandro, wearing a turtleneck sweater and a tweed sports coat with matching cap, got out of the back seat.

He looked toward the window of Joe Fierello's office.

"I think he wants you to come out there," Joe said.

Somewhat uncomfortable, but not quite sure why he was, Vito nodded at Joe Fierello and walked out of the building and down the stairs.

Joe Fierello opened the drawer of his desk, took out a 35-mm camera in a leather case, went to the window, and started snapping pictures.

"Mr. Lanza, I'm Paulo Cassandro," Paulo said. "I'm sorry about this."

"I don't understand," Vito said.

"We thought you were somebody else," Paulo said. "Lanza is a pretty common name. You, Mario the singer, and a lot of other people, right?"

"I guess so."

"I hate to tell you this," Paulo said, draping a friendly arm around Vito's shoulders, "but one of your cousins, maybe a second cousin, is a deadbeat. He owes everybody and his fucking brother. We thought it was you."

"I can't think of who that would be," Vito said.

"It doesn't matter. With a little bit of luck, you'll never run into him."

"Yeah," Vito said.

"We're sorry we made the mistake. We never should have bothered you or Joe with this. I hope you ain't pissed?"

"No. Of course not. I just want to make my markers good."

"There's no hurry. Take your time. Once we found out you wasn't *Anthony* Lanza, we asked around a little, and *your* credit is as good as gold."

"I always try to pay my debts," Vito said. "I like to think I got a good reputation."

"And now we know that," Paulo said. "So, whenever it's convenient, make the markers good. It don't have to be now. Next month sometime would be fine."

"Let me take care of them now," Vito said. "I already brung the cash."

"You don't have to, but if you got it, and it's convenient, that'd straighten everything out."

Vito handed him the six thousand dollars. Paulo very carefully counted it.

"No offense, me counting it?"

"No. Not at all."

"Watch the fifties, and the hundreds will take care of themselves, right?"

"Right."

Paulo put the money in the pocket of his tweed jacket.

"I want to give you this," he said, and took out a business card. "You want to loan me your back?"

Vito, after a moment, understood that Cassandro wanted to use his back as a desk, and turned around.

"Okay," Paulo said, and Vito turned around again.

Cassandro handed him the card. Vito read it. It said *Paulo Cassandro, President, Classic Livery, Distinguished Motor Cars For All Occasions.*

"You ever get back up to the Lodge, you just give that to the manager," Paulo said. "Turn it over."

Vito turned it over. On it, Cassandro had written, *"Vito Lanza is a friend of mine. And I owe him a big one."*

"You didn't have to do nothing like this," Vito said, embarrassed.

"I don't have to do nothing but pay taxes and die," Paulo said. "Just take that as my apology for making a mistake. Maybe they'll give you a free ice cream or something."

"Well, thank you," Vito said.

"I'm glad we could straighten this out," Paulo said, and wrapped his arm around Vito's shoulder.

Vito felt pretty good until he got to the goddamned plumber's. The sonofabitch was waiting for him, and overnight, he'd gone back on his word. Now he wanted twenty-five hundred before he would fix a fucking thing at the house. That left him with nine hundred. The plumber said it would probably run another thousand, maybe fifteen hundred, for the labor and incidentals.

There isn't a plumber in the fucking world who ever brought a job in for less than the estimate, and even if this sonofabitch did, that would leave me, if he wants fifteen hundred, six hundred short.

I've got eleven, twelve hundred in the PSFS account, and I can always borrow against the Caddy.

Jesus, I hate to put a loan against the Caddy.

Why the fuck didn't I take Cassandro's offer to take my time making the markers good? I really didn't have to pay them off that quick. My credit is good.

The absence of inhabitants in most of the Pine Barrens does not obviate the need for police patrols. The physical principle that nature abhors a vacuum has a tangential application to an unoccupied area. People tend to dump things that they would rather not be connected to in areas where they believe they are unlikely to be found in the near future.

Enterprising youth, for example, who wish to earn a little pocket money by stealing someone's automobile, and removing therefrom parts that have resale value, drive the cars into the Pine Barrens and strip them there.

And, in the winter, more than one passionate back seat dalliance in an auto with a leaking exhaust system has ended in tragedy by carbon monoxide poisoning.

And the Pine Barrens is a good place to shoot someone and dispose of the body. The chances that a shot will be heard are remote, and a shallow grave even desultorily concealed stands a very good chance of never being discovered.

There had been an incident of this nature just about a year before, which Deputy Sheriff Daniel J. Springs was thinking about as he drove, touching sixty, on a routine patrol in his three-year-old Ford, down one of the dirt roads that crosses the Barrens.

Dan Springs, a heavyset, somewhat jowly man who was fifty and had been with the Sheriff's Department more than twenty years, tried to cover all the roads in his area at least once every three days. Nine times out of ten, he saw nothing but the scrubby pines and the dirt road, and his mind tended to wander.

One of Springs's fellow deputies, making a routine patrol not far from here, had come across a nearly new Jaguar sedan abandoned by the side of the road, the keys still in the ignition, battery hot, with half a tank full of gas.

That meant somebody had dumped the car there, and driven away in a second car. They'd put the Pennsylvania plate on the FBI's NCIC (National Crime Information Center) computer and got a hit.

The cops in Philadelphia were looking for the car. It was owned by a rich guy, a white guy, who had been found carved up in his apartment. The cops were looking for the car, and for the white guy's black boyfriend.

Springs had been called in on the job then, to help with working the crime scene, and to keep civilians from getting in the way. Springs never ceased to be amazed how civilians came out of the woodwork, even in the Pine Barrens, when something happened.

Everybody came in on that job. The State Police, and even the FBI. There was a possibility of a kidnapping, which was a federal offense, even if state lines didn't get crossed, and here it was pretty evident, with a Philadelphia car abandoned in New Jersey, that state lines had been crossed.

Plus, of course, the Philadelphia Homicide detectives working the job. Springs remembered one of them, an enormous black guy dressed like a banker. Springs remembered him because he was the only one of the hotshots who did not go along with the thinking that because the car had been found *here,* that if there *was* a body, it had been dumped/buried anywhere *but* here, and the chances of finding it were zilch.

The black Philadelphia Homicide detective had said he was pretty sure (a) that there was a body and (b) they were going to find it right around where they had found the Jaguar.

And they had. Not a hundred yards from the Jaguar they had found a shallow grave with a black guy in it.

Springs had spoken to the big Homicide detective:

"How come you were so sure we'd find a body, and find it here?"

"I'm Detective Jason Washington," the black guy had said, introducing himself, offering a hand that could conceal a baseball. "How do you do, Deputy Springs? We're grateful for your cooperation."

"Why did you know the body would be here?" Springs had pursued as he shook hands. "Call me Dan."

"I didn't know it would be here," Washington had explained. "But I thought it would be."

"Why?"

"Well, I started with the idea that the doers were not very smart. They would never have stolen the Jaguar, an easy-to-spot vehicle, for example, if they were smart. And I'm reasonably sure they were drunk. And people who get drunk doing something wrong invariably sober up, and then get worried about what they've done. That would apply whether they shot this fellow back in Philadelphia, en route here, or here. They would therefore be anxious to get rid of the car, and the body, as quickly as possible. I would not have been surprised if we had found the body in, or beside, the car. And they are both lazy, and by now hungover. I thought it unlikely that they would drag a two-hundred-odd-pound corpse very far."

Just like Sherlock Holmes, Springs had thought. He had *deduced* what probably had happened. Smart guy, as smart as Springs had ever met.

They'd caught the guys, two colored guys, who had shot the one in the Barrens, a couple of days later, in Atlantic City. They had been using the dead white guy's credit cards, which proved Detective Washington's theory that they were not very smart.

They'd copped a plea, and been sentenced to twenty years to life, which meant they would be out in seven, eight years, but Springs now recalled hearing somewhere that they had been indicted for kidnapping, and were to be tried in federal court for that. The white boy's father had political clout, he owned a newspaper, newspapers, and he wanted to make sure that the guys who chopped up his son didn't get out in seven or eight years.

Deputy Springs was thinking of the enormous black Homicide detective who dressed like a banker and talked like a college professor, wondering if he was still around Philadelphia, when suddenly the steering wheel was torn out of his hands, and the Ford skidded out of control off the dirt road and into a scraggly pine tree before he could do anything about it.

He hit the four-inch-thick pine tree squarely. He was thrown forward onto the steering wheel, and felt the air being knocked out of him. The Ford bent the pine tree, and then rode up the trunk for a couple feet, and then the tree trunk snapped, and the car settled on the stump.

"Jesus, Mary, and Joseph!" Deputy Springs exclaimed. For a moment, he could see the branches of the pine tree, and then, accompanied by the smell of the water/antifreeze mixture turning to steam, the windshield clouded over.

There was a screeching from the engine compartment as the blades of the fan dug into the radiator.

Springs switched off the ignition, unfastened his seat belt, and pushed his door open. He got out and walked several feet away from the car and stood there for a moment, taking tentative deep breaths to see if he'd broken a rib or something, and bending his knees to see if they were all right.

Then he walked around the front of the car and examined the bumper.

They're not bumpers, they're goddamned decoration is all they are. Look at the way that "bumper" is bent!

He walked to the right side of the car and saw what had happened.

He'd blown a tire. The wheel was off the ground, and still spinning, and he could see the steel and nylon, or polyethylene or whatever they were, cords just hanging out of the tire.

That sonofabitch really blew. It must have been defective from the factory. Christ, it could have blown when I was chasing some speeder on the highway, and I would have been up shit creek.

He walked back to the driver's side and got behind the wheel and turned the ignition key on. The radio lights went on.

He called in, reporting that he'd had an accident, and approximately where, and that he'd need a wrecker.

They said they'd send someone as quick as they could, and asked if he was hurt. He told them no, he was all right, he had been lucky. He also told them he was going off the air, that he didn't want to have the ignition and the radios on, he might have got a gas line.

They told him to take it easy, they were going to send a State Trooper who was only ten, fifteen miles away, and that the wrecker should be there in thirty, thirty-five minutes.

He turned the ignition off and got out of the car again. He took another look at the shredded tire, and then walked twenty yards away and sat down against another pine tree.

He then offered a little prayer of thanks for not getting hurt or killed, and settled down to wait for the Trooper and the wrecker.

17.

Detective Matthew M. Payne parked his Bug in the Special Operations parking lot at five minutes to eight Monday morning. At precisely eight, he pushed open a door—on the frosted glass door of which had been etched, before he was born, "Principal's Office."

There was a very natty sergeant, face unfamiliar, sitting inside the door, a stocky man who looked as if he was holding the war against middle-aged fat to a draw.

"May I help you, sir?" the sergeant asked politely.

"Sergeant, I'm Detective Payne, I'm reporting in."

"Oh, yes," the sergeant said, and stood up and offered his hand. "I'm Sergeant Rawlins, Dick Rawlins, the administrative sergeant."

"How do you do?"

"I just had a quick look at your records," Rawlins said. "Haven't had the time for more than a quick look. But I did pick up that you were third on the detective's exam, and that speaks well of you."

"Thank you."

"Have a seat, Payne," Rawlins said. "The captain will see you when he's free."

He gestured toward the door, on which could still be faintly seen faded gilt lettering, *Principal. Private.*

"The captain" was obviously Mike Sabara, whose small office opened off Peter Wohl's office. Captain Dave Pekach's office was down the corridor.

"I wonder what he wants?" Matt thought aloud.

Rawlins's smile faded.

"I'm sure the captain will tell you what he wants, Detective," he said.

You have just had your knuckles rapped, Detective Payne, and you will not get a gold star for behavior to take home to Mommy.

I wonder what Sabara wants with me? He was there when Wohl told me I would be working with Jack Malone. And Malone left a message on the machine that he wanted to see me at eight.

Five minutes later, the door opened and Mike Sabara stuck his head out. Then, surprised, he saw Matt.

"Hi, Matt. You waiting to see me?"

"Sir, Sergeant Rawlins told me you wanted to see me."

"Come on in," Sabara said, and then added, to Rawlins, "Sergeant, if you see the inspector before I do, would you have him call Chief Coughlin?"

"Yes, sir."

Sabara closed the door to his office behind him.

"Sergeant Rawlins comes to us highly recommended from Criminal Records," he said dryly. "That 'see the captain' business is so either the inspector or I can eyeball newcomers. It didn't apply to you, obviously, and he should have known that. I'm already getting the feeling that he's every bit as bright as that Sergeant Henkels we got stuck with. Does that tell you enough, or should I draw a diagram?"

"I think I get the point, sir."

"Well, our time is not entirely wasted. This gives me the chance to tell you that the inspector was impressed with Sergeant O'Dowd, so for the time being, he'll be working for Jack Malone too, full-time, on the lunatic. And so will Washington, although, of course, with the Black Buddha, the way we say that is 'will be working *with*.' "

"Yes, sir," Matt said, chuckling.

"I think catching this lunatic with the bomb is the first thing that's really interested Jason since Wohl transferred him here. He and Malone are going, maybe have gone, to Intelligence. I don't know what Malone has planned for you, but I think you'd better go down there and see."

"Yes, sir."

"Matt, that was a good job on the lunatic profile."

"That was my sister, not me," Matt said, "but thank you anyway."

"I'm glad you're back. You—or at least your car—lends the place some class."

"I'm driving my Volkswagen, Captain."

"Get out of here," Sabara said.

Matt went back in the outer office as Staff Inspector Wohl came into it from the corridor.

Sergeant Rawlins stood up.

"Good morning, Inspector," he said. "Sir, Captain Sabara said that you are to call Chief Coughlin at your earliest opportunity. And, sir, this is Detective Payne."

"Is it?" Wohl asked, a wicked gleam in his eye.

"Good morning, sir," Matt said.

"Good morning, Detective Payne," Wohl said, and then turned to Rawlins. "Is Captain Sabara in there?"

"Yes, sir. He just interviewed Detective Payne."

"I'm sorry I missed that," Wohl said, and went into his office.

"Did the captain happen to tell you where you will be working, Detective?" Rawlins asked.

"For Lieutenant Malone," Matt said.

"That would be in Plans and Training," Rawlins replied, after consulting an organizational chart. "I'll make a note of that."

"What can I do for you?" Sergeant Maxwell Henkels demanded, making it more of a challenge than a question, as Detective Matthew M. Payne walked through a door on the second floor of the building, above which hung a sign, *Plans and Training Section.*

Henkels was just this side of fat, a flabby man who could have been anywhere from forty to fifty, florid-faced, with what Matt thought of as booze tracks on his nose.

"I'm looking for Lieutenant Malone, Sergeant."

"What for, and who are you?"

Why, I'm the visiting inspector for the Courtesy in Police Work Program, Sergeant. And you have just won the booby prize.

"My name is Payne, Sergeant. Detective Payne."

"The lieutenant and Sergeant Washington were waiting for you," Henkels said. "When you didn't show up, they went to Intelligence. He wants you to meet him there."

"I just transferred in this morning . . ."

"Yeah, I heard."

". . . and the administrative sergeant said I had to report to Captain Sabara before I came here."

"You should have called me," Sergeant Henkels said. "You're to let me know where you are all the time, understand?"

Oh, shit!

Matt nodded.

"Did Lieutenant Malone say anything about a car for me?"

"No."

"I'd better get going."

Sergeant Henkels snorted.

Matt went down the corridor, the oiled wooden boards of which creaked under his footsteps, to another former classroom, this one now the office space provided for the Special

Investigations Section of the Special Operations Division. He knew he could both use the phone there and receive a friendly welcome.

This time the uniformed sergeant behind the door was smiling genuinely.

"I told you he'd show up here," Sergeant Jerry O'Dowd said to Officer Foster H. Lewis, Jr., who was even larger than Sergeant Jason Washington, and thus had inevitably been dubbed "Tiny."

"I didn't expect to find you here," Matt said. "You guys know each other?"

"His dad was my first sergeant on my first job out of the Academy," O'Dowd said. "I knew him before he ate the magic growth pills."

"Hey, Matt," Tiny Lewis said, "welcome home."

They shook hands.

"Sergeant Rawlins just introduced me to Inspector Wohl," Matt said.

"Introduced you to Wohl?" Tiny asked.

"That was after my 'welcome to Special Operations' speech from Sabara. And *then* I met Sergeant Henkels."

Lewis and O'Dowd chuckled.

"Which is why I decided to hang out up here," O'Dowd said.

"Was . . . is . . . Malone and/or Washington looking for me?" Matt asked.

"Was," Tiny said.

"They went down to Intelligence," Jerry O'Dowd explained. "What they wanted to tell you was that I'm now working for Malone, and we're going to work together."

Well, that's good news. And I really appreciate "work together"; he had every right to say "you'll be working for me."

"Doing what?"

"Right now, we're waiting for the phone to ring," O'Dowd said, pointing to a desk with a brand-new telephone on it. "That's new. That's the number we're asking people to call in case they think they have a line on our lunatic. If it sounds at all . . . what? credible? possible? . . . we're to go talk to the guy who called it in, and then, if it still looks promising, call Washington and/or Sabara and/or Pekach."

"In that case, I guess I've got time for a cup of coffee."

"You'll have to make it," Tiny said, pointing at the coffee machine. "Unless you want to drink that black whatever from the machine."

"I'll make it," Matt said.

"Rough night, Detective Payne?" O'Dowd asked.

"At half past one," Matt said, more to Tiny Lewis than to O'Dowd, "Detective McFadden and Officer Martinez paid a social call."

"What did Mutt and Jeff have on their minds, so-called?" Tiny asked.

I cannot tell either of them what Hay-zus has in mind. Is that deceit or discretion?

"Not much," Matt said. "I think they simply decided that I should not be asleep while they were awake."

"Tough about Hay-zus failing the detective exam," Tiny said.

"Yeah, that surprised me," Matt said.

He went to the coffee machine, picked up the water reservoir and went down the corridor to the door with BOYS lettered on it, and filled it.

Matt Payne, mostly privately, was very much aware of his inadequate capabilities to be a detective. It was a long list of characteristics he didn't have, including experience, but headed by impatience. He had learned, even before Jason Washington had made the point aloud, that a good detective absolutely has to have nearly infinite patience.

The special line telephone did not ring, after either the Highway patrols had come off their seven P.M. to three A.M. tour, or the district patrols had come off their midnight-to-eight tours. Neither did Malone nor Washington call.

His new assignment as one of the inner circle of Special Operations people looking for the lunatic who wanted to disintegrate the Vice President was turning out to be just as thrilling as his assignment as recovered stolen car specialist in East Detectives had been.

His mind began to wander.

His relationship with Evelyn came quickly to mind, with all its potential for disaster, long and near term, and specifically what he was going to do about her tonight, when he got off work, and she would be waiting by her phone for him to call, and if he didn't call, circling Rittenhouse Square until she decided to come up to the apartment and console him in his loneliness and sexual deprivation.

And he thought of Jesus and his dirty corporal at the airport. Going into the guy's car was a monumental act of stupidity. If someone had seen him, the excreta would really have hit the rapidly revolving blades of the electromechanical cooling device.

But maybe that was the way a good cop worked, fighting fire with fire. A dirty cop had to be stopped, even if you bent the law, taking a big chance, in the process.

There would be rewards, of course, if he was right. Maybe that was Jesus' motivation. Failing the detective exam had certainly been humiliating for him.

If this guy is *dirty, is, if nothing else, associating with known criminals, and Hay-zus caught him at it, it would be, to coin a phrase, a feather in his cap. It wouldn't get him a detective's badge, of course, he's going to have to pass the exam to get promoted, but it might get him a better job, maybe in plainclothes someplace, than looking for baggage thieves at the airport.*

Except that Hay-zus wants me *to catch this guy associating with known criminals at the—what the hell is it?—*

He fished through his pockets until he came up with the matchbook from the Oaks and Pines Lodge.

—Oaks and Pines Lodge, Gourmet Cuisine, Championship Golf, Tennis, Heated Pool, Riding, 340 Wooded Acres Only 12.5 miles North of Stroudsburg on Penna. Highway 402. . . .

Plus, of course, if Hay-zus is to be believed—and he's probably right—fun and games for high rollers in the back room.

What am I supposed to do, just walk into this place and ask where the roulette tables are, and does there happen to be a dirty cop on the premises? I am again functioning from a bottomless pit of ignorance, but I suspect that you have to know someone to get into the back room. I doubt, even considering Hay-zus' opinion that I don't look like a cop, that the management is simply going to let a single guy who wanders into the place into the back room.

I may not look like a cop, but I damned well could be an FBI agent, or an IRS agent, or some other kind of fed. Who handles gambling for the feds?

I could not get in there alone. I would have to be with either a bunch of guys, out for a good time—that wouldn't work, if there were a bunch of guys, they would expect at least one of them to be able to furnish a reference . . .

Or a girl. A guy out with a date, who had heard you could play a little roulette in the back room. A guy driving a Porsche and with a nice-looking girl would probably work.

What girl? Evelyn? Evelyn would love to take a ride to the Poconos for dinner, to be followed by several hours of mattress bouncing in a lodge in the oaks and pines.

But (a) Evelyn doesn't look young enough to be my girl and (b) I don't want to take Evelyn anywhere.

Who, then? Precious Penny, maybe? Jesus H. Christ, what a lunatic idea!

But on the other hand, Penny is a bona fide airhead. There's no way she could be suspected of being an undercover FBI agent. With Penny, you see what you get, an overprivileged, expensively dressed inhabitant of Chestnut Hill, the kind of young woman, were I the operator of an illegal gaming house for high rollers, I would be anxious to acquire as a client.

But what if they spotted her as Penelope Detweiler, aka the ex-girlfriend of the late Tony the Zee?

That would either fuck things up completely, or the opposite. They would know she was a wild little rich girl who would be looking for something exciting, like gambling, to do.

You don't know, Matthew, how well acquainted she is among the Mob. On the other hand, you don't know which Mob controls Oaks and Pines Lodge, either. It could be a family out of New York, or Wilkes-Barre.

Very probably, now that I think of it, she probably is not well acquainted with the Mob. Tony the Zee would neither want to share her with his associates, or to run the risk of one of his associates telling Mrs. DeZego about Tony's blond girlfriend. Say what you like about the Mob, they are staunch defenders of the family.

Next question: Do you really want to involve Penny in something like this?

Involve her in what? All you would be doing would be taking her out to dinner in the Poconos. It would certainly be ill-advised to inform her you were checking out a dirty cop, so she wouldn't know what was going on, beyond being taken out to dinner, by the loyal family friend. And all you would be doing would be checking out the Oaks and Pines. Unless everything fell in place, you might not even inquire about gambling. Just take a look around and give them a face to remember—the guy with the Porsche who was in here a couple of days with the blonde—if you should go and ask about making a few small wagers.

And if you were in the Poconos with Penny, the odds are that by, say, midnight, Evelyn would finally become discouraged and stop calling and/or circling Rittenhouse Square.

Why not? What is there to lose?

Martin's Ford and Modern Chevrolet, both of Glassboro, N.J., shared the pleasure of the Sheriff's Department's business. By an amazing coincidence, going back at least fifteen years, when the sheriff announced for competitive bid his need for six suitably equipped for police service automobiles—which he did every year, replacing his eighteen vehicles on a three-year basis—Martin's Ford would submit the lowest bid one year, and Modern Chevrolet the next.

Maintenance of all county light automotive vehicles, including as-needed wrecker service, was similarly awarded, on a competitive bid basis, annually. And by another amazing coincidence, Modern Chevrolet seemed to submit the lowest bid one year, and Martin's Ford the next.

On a purely unofficial basis, both dealerships seemed to feel that it was a manifestation of efficiency in business to "subcontract" repairs to the brand agency. In other words, if, as was the case when Deputy Springs wrecked his Ford patrol car, Modern Chevrolet had that year's county maintenance contract, Modern would "subcontract" the Ford's repairs to Martin's. The next year, if a county-owned Chevrolet needed repair, and Martin's had the contract, Martin's would "subcontract" the repairs to Modern.

And so it came to pass when Modern Chevrolet's wrecker went out in the Pine Barrens to haul Deputy Springs's wrecked Ford off, it never entered the driver's mind to bring the car to Modern Chevrolet; he hauled it directly into the maintenance bay at Martin's Ford and lowered it onto the grease-stained concrete.

Greg Tomer, Martin's Ford's chief mechanic and service adviser, walked up and shook the hand of Tommy Fallon, the Modern Chevrolet's chief mechanic and wrecker driver. On the first Tuesday of each month, at seven-thirty P.M., they were respectively the senior vice commander and adjutant quartermaster of Casey Daniel Post 2139, Veterans of Foreign Wars.

"What the hell did he hit, Tommy?"

"He blew a tire. Going through the Barrens. Went right off the road. Hit a tree square in the middle. It broke. Had a hell of a time getting the sonofabitch off the tree. Fucked up the pan, I'm sure."

"Springs all right?"

"Yeah, I guess he was wearing his seat belt."

Greg Tomer dropped to his knees and peered under the car.

"Just missed the drive shaft," he said. "But, yeah, he fucked up the pan. I don't think it can be straightened."

"Radiator's gone too. And the fan."

"Maybe the insurance adjuster will says it's totaled. I sure don't want to try to fix it." He got off his knees and leaned in the driver's window. "Sixty-seven thousand on the clock. And no telling whether that's the second time around or the third."

"Well, he was lucky he wasn't hurt, is all I can say."

"Yeah."

"I gotta go, Greg."

"We appreciate your business, Mr. Fallon. Come in again soon."

Tommy Fallon touched Greg Tomer's arm, and then got in the cab on the wrecker, got it into low with a clash of gears, and drove out the back door of the maintenance bay.

"Shit," Greg Tomer said aloud, "I should have asked him to dump it out in back."

He had two options. He could fire up the Martin's Ford wrecker, pick the car up, and haul it out in back himself, or he could change the wheel with the blown tire on it, and push it into a corner of the maintenance bay.

He opened the trunk. There was a spare.

"Harry," he called to the closest of Martin's Ford's three mechanics, "get a jack and change the wheel here, and then we'll push it in the corner."

Harry rolled a hydraulic jack over to the Ford, maneuvered it into place, and raised the car in the bay. As he went to get an air-powered wrench, Tomer jerked the spare from the trunk and rested it against the passenger side door.

Harry removed the wheel with quick expertise, and then stuck his head in the wheel well to see what damage the wreck had caused.

"What the hell is that?" he wondered aloud.

A moment later, after a grunt, he came out of the wheel with something in his hand and handed it to Tomer.

"Look at that."

"What am I looking at?" Tomer asked. "Where did this come from?"

In his hand was a piece of steel plate, a rough oblong about ten inches long and five inches wide. One edge of the steel was bent at roughly a ninety-degree angle. There were several perforations of the steel, and in one of them was stuck what looked like a link of one-inch chain.

"I took it out of the wheel well, behind the rubber sheet, or whatever they call it," Harry said. "That's what blew his tire. There was nothing wrong with the tire. Look."

He took the piece of steel back from Tomer and laid it on the floor of the garage.

Tomer looked.

"That would certainly blow a tire all right," he said. "Like somebody swinging an ax. I wonder what the hell it is?"

"And it went into the tire far enough so that it got thrown into the wheel well, behind the rubber," Harry said. "I don't know what the hell it is. A piece of junk metal."

"When you get the spare on, Harry, have somebody help you push it into the corner." He pointed. "I'm going to walk across the street to the courthouse and give this to Springs. Souvenir."

"You think he'll want a souvenir?"

"Who can tell."

When Tomer went into the Patrol Division of the Sheriff's Department, they told him that Deputy Springs had slammed his chest into the steering wheel harder than he thought, that they'd x-rayed him at the hospital, nothing was broke, but the sheriff told him to take a couple of days off.

Tomer left the piece of steel, with the sawlike edge and the piece of chain wedged into it, and then walked back across the street to Martin's Ford and went back to work.

There were no telephone calls at all for Sergeant O'Dowd or Detective Payne all morning, until just before lunch, when Lieutenant Malone telephoned to say that he and Detective Washington were going to see Mr. Larkin at the Secret Service office, and that they should wait for their phone to ring; maybe something would happen when the eight-to-four tour came off duty.

Detective Payne and Officer Lewis took luncheon at Roy Rogers' Western Hamburger emporium. When they returned to the office, Sergeant O'Dowd went for his lunch. As soon as he was out the door, Detective Payne called Miss Penelope Detweiler at her residence and asked if she would like to go up to the Poconos for dinner.

Miss Detweiler accepted immediately, and with such obvious delight that it made Detective Payne a bit uneasy. He next called the residence of Mrs. Evelyn Glover and left a message on her answering machine that he had to work, and that if he got off at a reasonable hour, say before nine, he would call.

When he put the telephone back in its cradle, he felt Tiny Lewis's eyes on him, and looked at him.

"The last of the great swordsmen at work, huh?"

"Would you believe me, Officer Lewis, if I gave you my word as a gentleman that carnal activity with either lady is the one thing I don't want?"

"No," Officer Lewis said. "I would not."

It wasn't until Matt went into the parking lot to claim his car that he remembered he was driving the Bug. He glanced at his watch, even though he was fully aware that it was only a minute or two after five.

There would not be time to drive all the way downtown to the apartment to get the Porsche. He had told Penny he would pick her up at five-fifteen, and please not to make him wait, it was going to be at least a two-hour drive to the Poconos.

He fired up the Bug and drove crosstown to Chestnut Hill. The Bug was not going to be a problem, he could park it, probably, where no one would see it at Oaks and Pines Lodge, and if Penny didn't like it, screw her, let her see up close how the other half lived.

It didn't work out that way.

Surprising him not at all, H. Richard Detweiler answered the door of the Detweiler mansion himself, and informed him first that Penny would be down in a moment.

"Your Porsche is down?" he asked, and then as if that was self-evident went on without giving Matt a chance to reply, "Your dad told me you couldn't bring yourself to sell the Volkswagen."

"An old friend, tried and true," Matt said. "It would have been like selling Amy."

Detweiler smiled a little uncomfortably.

"Tell you what," Mr. Detweiler said. "The Mercedes man was here today. Yesterday. Doing Penny's car. It hadn't been moved, since . . . uh . . . you brought it out here."

The Philadelphia Police Department (specifically then Officer M. M. Payne and then Detective Jason Washington) had returned the victim's automobile, a 1973 Mercedes-Benz 380 SL roadster, to her residence after it had been processed by the forensics experts of the Mobile Crime Lab at the scene of the crime. The scene of the crime had been a Center City parking lot where the victim had been wounded by a shotgun during a homicide in which Mr. Anthony J. DeZego had been fatally shot by unknown person or persons.

Jesus, that's a great idea! I really didn't want to roll up to the Oaks and Pines in the Bug.

"It really should be driven," Mr. Detweiler said. "Why don't you take it? It's a long way to Allentown."

"Allentown"? What the hell does he mean, "Allentown"? And now that I think about

it, it's a lousy idea. I don't want Precious Penny reminded of Tony the Zee lying on the concrete with his stomach blown out his back.

"Is that a good idea?" Matt said. "Bad memories?"

"I thought of that," H. Richard Detweiler said, somewhat impatiently. He touched Matt's shoulder. "Replace bad memories with a good one, right?"

He waited until Matt nodded, then pushed him toward the door.

"Come on in and have a drink, one drink, and I'll have Jensen get the car while we're having it."

Jensen was the Detweilers' chauffeur.

Detweiler led Matt onto the veranda outside the small sitting room where, predictably, Grace Detweiler was also waiting.

"How are you, Matt? You look very nice."

Matt, as he was expected to, kissed her cheek.

Detweiler picked up the telephone.

"Florence," he ordered, "would you please ask Jensen to bring Penny's car around to the front?"

"What's that all about?" Grace Detweiler asked.

"Matt's car is down," Detweiler said. "He's driving his Volkswagen, which is visibly on its last legs. Or tires. I suggested that he take Penny's car."

"Is that a good idea?" Grace challenged.

"He's a policeman now," Detweiler said. "He doesn't get tickets, he gives them."

"That's not what I meant."

"I know what you meant," Detweiler snapped. "Leave it lie, Grace. They're taking the Mercedes."

"Well, excuse me!"

"Scotch all right, Matt?"

"A weak one, please," Matt said.

Penny and the chauffeur came onto the veranda together.

"Whenever you're ready, Mr. Detweiler," Jensen said.

"Communications problem again," Detweiler said. "Mr. Matt and Penny will be taking the car. I'm not going anywhere."

Penny walked to Matt and leaned up and kissed his cheek. She was wearing a crisp-looking cord suit with a frilly blouse under the jacket.

Giving the devil his—the deviless her—due, she's not a bad-looking female.

He had a quick, clear mental image of her in his erotic dream and wondered, almost idly, if she really looked that way, au naturel.

The next line in this little scenario of life in Chestnut HIll will be Detweiler telling me to make sure I get Precious Penny home by twelve, or maybe twelve-thirty.

"I'll put your bag in the car, Miss Penny," Jensen said.

"Thank you, Jensen." Penny smiled sweetly.

"Bag"? What bag? And what was that about Allentown?

"Well, Matt," Penny said. "You said not to keep you waiting. Here I am. Are we going to go or what?"

"One or the other," Matt said. "I don't know what you mean by 'what.' "

"We'll see you later," Penny said, and caught Matt's hand and led him off the veranda.

"Have a good time," Grace Detweiler called after them.

Jensen was waiting by the Mercedes, waiting to close Penny's door. Both doors were open.

Matt got behind the wheel, adjusted the seat, and waited for Penny to get it. The moment she closed the door he could smell her perfume.

A gas expands to the limits of its containment; there ain't a hell of a lot of space in here. Be nice.

"You smell good," Matt said.

"Oh, I'm *so* glad you noticed!" Penny said.

Is that sarcasm?

Matt looked over at her. Penny was bent over, fixing the carpet, or something, on the floorboard. He got a quick, unintentional look down her blouse. A white brassiere. For some reason, he had always found crisp white feminine undergarments to have a certain erotic quality.

He put the car in gear and started down the driveway.

"You want to tell me what the bag, and Allentown, are all about?"

"I'm glad you waited until we were out of there before you asked that."

"Which means?"

"That in case anybody asks, I was asked by a dear friend of mine, who understands my problems, whose mother is a dear friend of my mother's, GiGi Howser, who lives in *Allentown,* to come to a party. And I called you, and asked you to take me, and you agreed."

"We're going to a place called the Oaks and Pines Lodge," Matt said, without thinking.

"Wherever," Penny said. "I'm helpless in your hands."

"What's with Allentown? And what's with the bag?"

"If the party's fun, and lasts until late, and you have more to drink than you should, we may sleep over."

"Jesus Christ!"

"I thought you'd be pleased," Penny said. "You were the one who told me you automatically shift into the seduce mode."

What we are going to do is go to the Oaks and Pines and have dinner, and then we are going to come back here and tell the Detweilers we had a lousy time.

"We're not sleeping over anywhere. I have to be at work at eight o'clock in the morning."

"I don't mind getting up early," Penny said. "I told Mother that might happen. She understands. She'd much rather have you bring me home early in the morning than us get in a wreck because you had too much to drink, the way you usually do."

"And what if she calls your *GiGi* and asks to speak to you?"

"We will have just gone out for pizza or something, and will have to call back. When we get where you're taking me, I'll have to call GiGi and let her know where we are. Don't worry. GiGi is very reliable."

He glanced at her and found that she had shifted on her seat so that she was turned to him. She smiled naughtily at him.

By ten minutes after five, there were very few people left on the tenth floor of the First Pennsylvania Bank & Trust Company, and it would probably be possible to exit the building without being jammed together in an elevator, but Marion Claude Wheatley liked to be sure of things, so he waited until 5:25 before locking his desk and his filing cabinets and walking to the bank of elevators.

Except for a stop at the seventh floor, where it picked up two women—probably secretaries, they seemed a little too bright to be simple clerks—the elevator went directly to the lobby, and it really could not be called crowded with only the three of them on it, and Marion was pleased that he had decided to wait the additional fifteen minutes.

When he left the South Broad Street entrance of the building he turned right, toward City Hall, until he reached Sansom Street, and then walked east on Sansom to South 12th, and then north to Market. That way, he had learned, he could avoid the rush of people headed toward City Hall at this hour of the day.

On Market Street, he turned east, toward the Delaware, and then changed his plans when he saw the Reading Terminal. He had planned to do some of the necessary shopping, take the things home, and then do something about supper. But now it seemed to make more sense to have a little something to eat at one of the concessionaire stands in the

Reading Terminal Market before shopping. That would obviate having to worry about supper when he got home. He would, so to speak, be killing two birds with one stone.

Marion believed that the efficient use of one's time was a key to success.

He sat at a counter and had a very nice hot roast beef sandwich with french fried potatoes and a sliced tomato, finishing up with a cup of decaffeinated coffee.

Then he went back out onto Market Street, crossed it again, and after looking in the window of the Super Drugstore on the corner of 11th Street and seeing exactly what he wanted, he went in and bought an AWOL bag. It was on sale, for $3.95, and it had a metal zipper, which was important.

The reason it was on sale, he decided, was because it had a picture of a fish jumping out of the waves on it, with the legend, *Souvenir of Asbury Park, N.J.* Whoever had first ordered the bags had apparently overestimated the demand for them, and had had to put the excess up for sale, probably at a loss.

Overestimating demand, Marion thought, was a common fault with many small businesses. The petroleum business did not have, simplistically, that problem. They didn't have to produce their raw material, pump oil from the ground, until they were almost certain of a market. And even if that market collapsed, it was rarely that oil had to be put up for immediate sale. It could be stored relatively inexpensively until a demand, inevitably, arose.

He insisted on getting a paper bag for the AWOL bag—he was not the sort of person who wished to be seen walking through Center City, Philadelphia, with a reddish-orange bag labeled *Souvenir of Asbury Park, N.J.*—and then continued walking east on Market Street.

A very short distance away, just where he had remembered seeing them, which pleased him, there was a tacky little store with a window full of "leather" attaché cases, on SPECIAL SALE.

Special Sale, my left foot, Marion thought. It was a special sale only because money would change hands. He went in the store, and spent fifteen minutes choosing an attaché case that (a) looked reasonably like genuine leather, (b) was deep and wide enough to hold the shortwave transmitter, (c) had its handles fastened to the case securely. The last thing he could afford was to have a handle pull loose, so that he would drop the shortwave transmitter onto the marble floors of 30th Street Station.

He did not insist on a paper bag for the attaché case. He thought he would submit that to a little test. He would stop in on the way home, in one of the cocktail lounges along Chestnut Street that catered to people in the financial industry. He would put the "leather" attaché case out where people who customarily carried genuine leather attaché cases could see it, and see if anyone looked at it strangely.

He had solved the problem of supper, had one AWOL bag and the attaché case, and there was time, so why not?

18.

North of Doylestown, on US Route 611, approaching Kintnersville, Matt became aware of a faint siren. When he glanced in the rearview mirror, he saw that it was mounted in a State Police car, and that the gumball machine on the roof was flashing brightly.

"Shit," he said.

Penny turned in her seat and giggled.

There was no place to pull safely to the side of the road where they were, so Matt put a hand over his head in a gesture of surrender, slowed, and drove another mile or so until he found a place to stop.

"Mother will not be at all surprised that we wound up in jail," Penny said cheerfully. "She expects it of you."

Matt got out of the car, making an effort to keep both hands in view, and then went back to the State Police car. A very large State Policeman, about thirty-five, got out, and straightened his Smoky-the-Bear hat.

"Good evening, sir," the State Policeman said, with the perfect courtesy that suggested he was not at all unhappy to be forced to cite a Mercedes driver for being twenty-five or thirty miles over the speed limit.

"Good evening," Matt replied, and took his driver's license from his wallet. "There's my license."

"I'll need the registration too, please, sir."

Matt took out the leather folder holding his badge and photo ID and handed that over.

"That's what I do for a living. How fraternal are you feeling tonight?"

The State Policeman examined the photo on the ID card carefully, then handed it back.

"Being a Philly detective must pay better than they do us. That's quite a set of wheels."

"The wheels belong to the lady."

The State Policeman took a long look at Penny, who, resting her chin on her hands on the back of her seat, was looking back at them, smiling sweetly.

"I don't think I'd have given her a ticket, either," he said. "Very nice."

"Thank you."

"You're welcome," the State Policeman said, and turned back to his car.

Matt got back in the Mercedes.

"We're not going to jail?"

"I told the nice officer that I was rushing you to the hospital to deliver our firstborn," Matt said.

"You would do something like that too, you bastard," Penny said, laughing. "But that's an interesting thought. I wonder what our firstborn would look like?"

The question made Matt uncomfortable.

"I didn't have any lunch," Penny went on. "You're going to have to get me something to eat, or you're going to have to carry me into wherever you're taking me."

"I'm taking you to a restaurant, can't you wait?"

"How far?"

"About an hour from here, I suppose."

"Then no. But I will settle for something simple."

I don't have dinner reservations for this place, Matt suddenly thought. *For that matter, I don't even know if it's open to the public for dinner. I better find a phone and call.*

Ten minutes later, just south of Easton, he saw the flashing neon sign of a restaurant between the highway and Delaware River. Penny saw it at the same time.

"Clams!" she cried. "I want steamed clams! Steamed clams and a beer! *Please,* Matthew!"

"Your wish, mademoiselle, is my command."

Inside the restaurant, they found a cheerful bar at which a half dozen people sat, half of them with platters of steamed clams before them.

Penny hopped onto a bar stool.

"Two dozen clams and an Ortlieb's for me," she ordered, "and two dozen for him. I don't know if he wants a beer or not. He may be on duty."

The bartender took it as a joke.

"Two beers, please," Matt said.

Two frosted mugs and two bottles of beer appeared immediately.

"And while I'm waiting for the clams, I'll have a pickled egg," Penny said.

"Two," Matt said.

"You're being very agreeable. That must mean you want something from me."

"Not a thing, but your company," Matt said.

"Bullshit," Penny said. "I am not quite as stupid as you think I am. You didn't invite me to dinner in the sticks because you love food or drives through the country, and you've made it perfectly clear that you're not lusting after my body, so what is going on?"

Her eyes were on him, over the rim of her beer mug.

"I want to take a look at the Oaks and Pines Lodge," he said.

"In your line of work, you mean, not idle curiosity?"

Matt nodded.

"You going to tell me why?"

He shook his head, no.

"What I thought was that I would attract less attention if I had a girl, a pretty girl, with me."

She considered that for a moment.

"Okay," she said. "I'm using you, too. I would have gone to watch the Budapest Quintet with you—and you know how I hate fiddle music—if it had gotten me out of the house."

"Pretty bad, is it, at home?"

"Mother's counting the aspirin," Penny said.

"I'm sorry."

"I think you really are," Penny said. "So tell me, is there anything I can do to help you do whatever it is you're not going to tell me you're doing?"

The answer came immediately, but Matt waited until he had taken the time to take a long pull at his beer before he replied.

"I don't even know if this place is open to the public for dinner. Some of them aren't. And I don't have reservations."

"You never were too good at planning ahead, were you?"

"I thought I'd call from here and ask about reservations. . . ."

"But?"

"It would be better, it would look better, if I called and asked for a room."

She smiled at him.

"This is the first time that anyone has proposed taking me to a hotel room, said he did not have sex in mind, and meant it. But okay, Matthew."

"Thank you, Penny," Matt said.

"Why is that, Matt? Because I was on drugs? Because of Tony DeZego? Or is it that you simply don't find me appealing?"

"I find you appealing," Matt blurted. "I just think it would be a lousy idea."

Before she had a chance to reply, he got off his bar stool and went to the pay phone he had seen in the entrance.

When he returned, having learned that he was in luck, the Oaks and Pines Lodge, having had a last-minute cancellation, would be able to accommodate Mr. and Mrs. Payne in the Birch Suite, the clams had been served, and Penny was playing airhead with the bartender, who was clearly taken with her.

Charley Larkin, jacket off, tie pulled down, was sitting behind the very nice mahogany desk and SAC Joseph J. Toner was sitting on the couch with Wohl.

Mr. H. Charles Larkin, Wohl thought, *has taken over the office of the supervisory agent in charge of the Secret Service's Philadelphia office.*

Is it a question of priorities or rank? Certainly, keeping the Vice President from being disintegrated has a higher Secret Service priority than catching somebody who prints his own money or other negotiable instruments, and it would follow that the guy in charge of that job would be the one giving the orders. But it might be rank too. Larkin has been in the Secret Service a long time. He probably outranks Toner too. What difference does it make?

One of the telephones on Toner's desk rang. Larkin looked to see which one it was, and then picked it up.

"Larkin," he said, and then a moment later, "Ask them to come in, please."

Lieutenant Jack Malone, in plainclothes, and Sergeant Jason Washington, in a superbly tailored, faintly plaided gray suit, came into the office.

"Charley, you know Jack," Wohl said. "The slight, delicate gentleman in the raggedy clothes is Sergeant Jason Washington. Jason, Charley Larkin. Watch out for him, he and my father and Chief Coughlin are old pals."

Larkin walked around the desk to shake Washington's hand.

"You know the line, 'your reputation precedes you'?" he asked. "I'm glad you're working with us on this, Sergeant. Do you know Joe Toner?"

"Only by reputation, sir," Washington said. He turned to Toner, who, obviously as an afterthought, stood up and put out his hand.

"How are you, Sergeant?"

"Pretty frustrated, right now, as a matter of fact, Mr. Toner," Washington said.

"I'm Joe Toner, Lieutenant," Toner said, and gave his hand to Malone.

"You mean you didn't come here to report we have our mad bomber in a padded cell, and we can all go home?" Wohl asked.

"Boss, we laid an egg," Washington replied. "We've been through everything in every file cabinet in Philadelphia, and we didn't turn up a looney tune who comes within a mile of that profile."

"And we just checked the Schoolhouse. There has been no, zero, zilch, response from anybody to the profiles we passed around the districts."

"Who's holding the phone down?" Wohl asked.

"Lieutenant Wisser," Malone replied. "Until two. Then a Lieutenant Seaham?"

"Sealyham?" Wohl asked.

"I think so. Captain Sabara arranged for it. He'll do midnight to eight, and then O'Dowd will come back on," Malone said. "We stopped by the Schoolhouse, and talked to them. *Sealyham* on the phone. If they get anything that looks interesting, they're going to call either Washington or me."

Wohl nodded his approval.

"You've had a busy day," he said.

"Spinning our wheels," Jason said.

"I don't offer this with much hope," Charley Larkin said, "but this is the profile the FBI came up with. Did you stumble on anyone who comes anywhere near this?"

He handed copies to both Washington and Malone.

"There's coffee," Larkin said. "Excuse me, I should have offered you some."

Both Malone and Washington declined, silently, shaking their heads, but Washington, not taking his eyes from the sheet of paper, lowered himself onto the couch between Wohl and Toner. The couch was now crowded.

"This is just about what Matt's sister came up with," Washington said.

" 'Matt's sister'?" Toner asked.

"Dr. Payne, sir," Washington said. "A psychiatrist at the University of Pennsylvania. She's been helpful before. Her brother is a detective, Matt Payne."

"Oh," Toner said.

"The FBI says that this guy is probably a 'sexual deviate,' " Malone quoted, "Dr. Payne says he's 'asexual.' What's the difference?"

"Not much," Washington replied. " 'Celibacy is the most unusual of all the perversions,' Oscar Wilde."

Larkin and Wohl chuckled. Toner and Malone looked confused.

"And anyway," Washington went on, "Jack and I went through the files in Sex Crimes too. Same result, zero."

"Who's Oscar Wilde?" Malone asked.

"An English gentleman of exquisite grace," Washington said. "Deceased."

"Oh."

"Sergeant Washington," Larkin said. "Would you mind if I called you 'Jason'?"

"No, sir."

"Jason, I'd like to hear your wild hairs," Larkin said. "I think we all would."

"Yeah," Wohl agreed.

"This chap is going to be hard to find," Washington said. "He's the classic face in the crowd. Law-abiding. Respectable. Few, if any, outward signs of his mental problems."

"We know that," Wohl said, a touch of impatience in his voice.

"Possibly a rude question: How wide have we thrown the net?" Washington asked.

"Meaning?" Toner asked.

"Wilmington, New Jersey, even Baltimore. For that matter, Doylestown, Allentown? Is there a record that matches the profile right over the city border in Cheltenham?"

"Our people, Sergeant," Toner said, somewhat coldly, "have taken care of that. Plus seeking cooperation from other federal agencies, making that profile available to them."

"It was a question worth asking, Jason," Wohl said, flashing Toner an icy look.

"Please ask whatever pops into your mind," Larkin said.

"What about the Army? For that matter, the Navy, the Marines? Coal companies, whatever? Have there been any reports of stolen explosives?"

"Not according to Alcohol, Tobacco and Firearms," Larkin said. "Or the State Board of Mines, in Harrisburg."

Washington shrugged.

"I don't even have any more wild hairs," he said.

"In that case, there is obviously only one thing to do," Larkin said, and waited until the others were all looking at him. "Consult with John Barleycorn. It would not be the first time in recorded history that a good idea was born in a saloon."

Supervisory Special Agent Toner, Wohl thought, *looks shocked at the suggestion. But Larkin means that, and Christ, he may be right.*

"I'll drink to that," Wohl said, and pushed himself up off the couch.

"We don't have any luggage," Matt said as he drove up the curving road to the Oaks and Pines Lodge Resort. "That's going to look funny."

"Yes, we do," Penny replied. "And neither the bellhop nor the desk clerk will suspect that there's nothing in there but my clothes, including, incidentally, a rather risqué negligee."

Matt remembered Jensen saying he would put her bag in the car. He looked in the back seat. There was a fairly large suitcase, made out of what looked like a Persian rug.

"You really came prepared, didn't you?" he asked.

"Life is full of little surprises," Penny said. "What's wrong with being prepared?"

A bellman came out to the Mercedes in front of the lodge.

"Good evening, sir," he said. "Checking in?"

"Yes."

"I'll take the luggage, sir, and I'll take care of the car. If you'll just leave the keys?"

Penny took his arm as they walked across the lobby to the desk.

"My name is Payne," Matt said to the man behind the desk. "I have a reservation."

"Yes, sir, I spoke to you on the phone."

Matt handed him his American Express card.

"I have to be in Philadelphia at eight," he said. "Which means I—*we*—will have to leave here in the middle of the night. Is that going to pose any problems?"

"None at all, sir. Let me run your card through the machine. And then just leave, whenever you wish. We'll mail the bill to your home."

He pushed a registration card across the marble to him, and handed him a pen. At the very last moment, Matt remembered to write "M/M," for "Mr. & Mrs.," in front of his name.

"Thank you," the desk man said, and then raised his voice. "Take Mr. and Mrs. Payne to the Birch Suite, please."

They followed the bellman to the elevator, and then to a suite on the third floor. The Birch Suite consisted of a large, comfortably furnished sitting room, a bedroom with a large double bed, and a bath, with both a sunken bathtub and a separate tile shower.

Matt tipped the bellman and he left.

"The furniture's oak," Matt said. "They should call it 'the oak suite.' "

"Don't be critical," Penny called from the bedroom.

"I'm not being critical. It's very nice."

"The food's good too."

"How do you know that?"

"I've been here before, obviously."

With Tony the Zee? Is this where that Guinea gangster brought you? Why not? It's supposed to have a Mob connection.

"With my parents," Penny said. "Not what you were thinking."

"How do you know what I was thinking?"

"I usually know what you're thinking," Penny said. "Come look at this."

If you're referring to the double bed, I've seen it.

He walked to the bedroom door. Penny pointed at a bottle of champagne in a cooler, placed conveniently close to the bed.

"For what they're charging for this, a hundred and a half a night, they can afford to throw in a bottle of champagne," Matt said.

"How ever do you afford all this high living on a policeman's pay, Matthew?"

"Don't start being a bitch, Penny."

"Sorry," she said, sounding as if she meant it. "I'm curious. Have you got some kind of an expense account?"

"Not for this, no," Matt replied. "What were your parents doing here?"

"Daddy likes to gamble here."

Why does that surprise me? It shouldn't. He apparently is no stranger in Las Vegas. But why the hell is he gambling? With all his money, what's the point? He really can't care if he wins or loses.

"You didn't say anything, before, when I told you we were coming here."

"I didn't want to spoil your little surprise. You said we were coming here, you will recall, before you made it clear that whatever you had in mind, it was not rolling around between the sheets with me."

"I want to get a look inside the gambling place."

"That shouldn't be a problem."

"You still hungry?"

"Always," she said.

"Come on, then, we'll go have a drink at the bar and then have dinner."

"And save that for later?" she asked, pointing at the champagne.

"We could have it now, if you would like."

"I'd really rather have a beer," she said. "If you romanced me like this more often, Matt, you'd learn that I'm really a cheap date."

"Economical," he responded without thinking, "not cheap."

"Why, thank you, Matthew."

She walked past him out of the bedroom and to the corridor door.

They sat at the bar where Penny drank two bottles of Heineken's beer, which for some reason surprised him, and he had two drinks of Scotch.

The entertainment was a pianist, a middle-aged woman trying to look younger, who wasn't half bad. Much better, he thought, than the trio who replaced her when they went to a table for dinner.

And Penny was right. The food was first class. Penny said she remembered the chateaubriand for two was really good, and he indulged her, and it was much better than he expected it to be, a perfectly roasted filet, surrounded by what looked like one each of every known variety of vegetable. They had a bottle of California Cabernet Sauvignon with that, and somehow it was suddenly all gone.

"If you'd like, we could have another," Penny said as he mocked shaking the last couple of drops into his glass. "And have cheese afterward, and listen to the music. I don't think the gambling gets going until later."

The cheese was good, something the waiter recommended, something he'd never had before, sort of a combination of Camembert and Roquefort. They ate one serving, spreading it on crackers and then taking a swallow of the wine before chewing, and then had another.

Penny said she would like a liqueur to finish the meal, and he passed, saying he'd already had too much drink, and instead drank a cup of very black, very strong coffee.

When he'd finished that, Penny inclined her head toward the rear of the room.

"It's over there, if you want to give it a try," she said.

Matt looked and saw a closed double door, draped with red curtain and guarded by a large man in a dinner jacket.

As they walked to it, Penny leaned up and whispered in his ear: "You did remember to bring money?"

"Absolutely," he said, although he wasn't really sure.

The man in the dinner jacket blocked their way.

"May I help you?" he asked.

"We want to go in there," Penny said.

"That's a private party, I'm afraid, madam."

"Oh, come on. I've been in there before."

"Are you a club member?"

"I'm not, but if there's a club, my father probably is."

"And your name, madam?"

"My maiden name was Detweiler," Penny said.

That rang a bell, Matt thought, *if widening eyes and raised eyebrows are any criteria.*

"First name?"

"Richard. H. Richard."

"Just a moment, please, madam," the man in the dinner jacket said. He pulled open a cabinet door in the wall Matt hadn't noticed—it was covered with wallpaper—and spoke softly into a telephone. After a moment, he hung up and pushed the door closed.

"Sorry for the delay, Miss Detweiler," he said as he pulled the door open. "Good luck!"

"Mrs. Payne," Penny corrected him, smiling sweetly at Matt.

There were very few people in the room, although croupiers stood waiting for customers behind every table.

Do you call the guys who run the craps game and the blackjack "croupiers" too? Matt wondered. *Or does that term apply only to roulette? If not, what do you call the guy who runs the craps table? The crapier?*

"Roulette all right with you, Penny?"

"It's fine with me," she replied. "But I'm surprised, I thought you would be a craps shooter."

Matt took out his wallet. He had one hundred-dollar bill and four fifties and some smaller bills.

The hundred must be left over from the Flamingo in Las Vegas. I never take hundreds from the bank. You can never get anyone to change one.

He put the hundred-dollar bill on the green baize beside the roulette wheel.

"Nickles," he said.

The croupier slid a small stack of chips to him.

He placed two of them on the board, both on One to Twelve. The croupier spun the wheel, twenty-three came up, and he picked up Matt's chips.

Matt made the same bet again.

"There's a marvelous story," Penny said. "A fellow brought a girl here, or to a place like this, and gave her chips, and she said, 'I don't know what to bet,' so he said, 'Bet your age,' so she put fifty dollars on twenty-three. Twenty-nine came up. The girl said, 'Oh, *shit!'* "

The croupier laughed softly. Matt didn't understand. Penny saw this: "The moral of the story, Matthew darling, is 'Truth pays off.' "

He laughed.

Thirty-three came up, and the croupier picked up Matt's chips again.

"You're not too good at this, are you, darling?"

"Just getting warmed up," Matt said. He put five chips on 00.

Sixteen came up.

"Have you ever considered getting an honest job?" Penny asked.

Not only isn't this much fun, but I've seen about all of this place that there is to see. It's about as wicked as a bingo game in the basement of McFadden's parish church.

Hay-zus is off base on this one. There's nobody in this room who looks like a mobster; my fellow gamblers look like they all belong to the Kiwanis. And/or the Bible Study Group.

I will buy Penny a drink, and try to show her the wisdom of driving back to Philadelphia now, rather than in the morning. We can get back by one, maybe a little sooner.

When the croupier had removed his five chips from 00, Matt pushed what was left of his stack onto 00.

"I don't think this is my night," Matt said to the croupier.

"You never can tell," the croupier said.

00 came up.

"And we have a winner," the croupier said.

"There must be some sort of mistake," Penny said. "Clearly, God doesn't want him to win."

"God must have changed His mind," the croupier said. "Would you like some quarters, sir? That's going to be a lot of nickels."

"I think I'd rather cash out. I'm too shocked to play anymore."

A pit boss appeared, saw what happened, and nodded his approval. The croupier wrote something on a slip of paper, handed it to the pit boss, who signed it and handed it back. The croupier handed Matt the slip of paper. On it was written $2035.

"Thank you," Matt said. "Where's the cashier?"

The croupier inclined his head, and Matt followed his eyes and saw a barred window near the entrance door. At the last moment, he remembered that winning gentlemen gamblers tip the croupier. He took a fifty-dollar bill from his wallet and handed it to the croupier.

"Is this what's known as quitting when you're ahead?" Penny asked.

"You got it."

He took the chit to the cashier, exchanged it for a nice thick wad of hundred-dollar bills, put them in his inside jacket pocket, and then led Penny out of the casino and toward the bar.

"Are we going to the bar?" Penny asked.

"I thought we'd have a drink to celebrate."

"We have a bottle of champagne in the room," Penny said.

We have to go to the room anyway to get her bag. And there will be no one in the room, as there would be at the bar, to eavesdrop on our conversation, and wonder why a healthy-appearing young man was trying to talk a good-looking healthy blonde out of spending the night in a hotel.

"I forgot," Matt said as he nudged her toward the elevator.

While they had been downstairs, the bed had been turned down. There was a piece of chocolate precisely in the center of each of the pillows.

"Open the champagne," Penny said as she went into the bathroom. "See if it's still cold."

It was still cold. Whoever had turned down the bed had also refilled the cooler with ice. As he wrestled with the cork, he could hear the toilet flush and then water running.

The cork popped and he poured champagne into the glasses. He sipped his.

Nice. He looked at the label, California champagne, a brand he'd never heard of.

Methode Champenoise, whatever the hell that means. What did you expect, Moet et Chandon?

He heard, or at least sensed, the bathroom door opening, and turned with Penny's glass extended.

She had—*Jesus, how did she do that so quickly?*—taken off her clothes and changed into a negligee—or peignoir, whatever a pale blue, lacy, nearly transparent garment of seduction was called—and brushed her hair so that it hung straight down to her shoulders.

The light in the bathroom was still on, which served to illuminate the thin material of her negligee from the rear. She was, for all visual purposes, quite naked.

"Jesus, Penny!"

"I figured, what the hell? Matt knows all my secrets. What have I got to lose?"

She came into the bedroom, took the champagne glass from him, and walked to the draped window.

"I guess it didn't work, huh?" she said after a moment.

What the fuck am I supposed to do now?

I can't see through her nightgown anymore. Jesus, that made my heart jump!

He saw her raise and drain her champagne glass, and then she turned.

"Go and wait in the other room," she said, her voice flat and bitter. "I'll get dressed, and we can go."

She walked toward him.

"Go on, Matt. Get out of here."

Tears were running down her cheeks.

He put his hand to her face.

"Don't," she said. "Don't pity me, you sonofabitch!"

"It would be stupid, Penny."

"*Life* is stupid, you jackass. It's a bitch, and then you die."

He chuckled.

She raised her eyes to his.

And then her hand came up and touched his cheek.

"What are you thinking, Matt?"

"You don't want to know what I'm thinking."

I am thinking that I could cheerfully spend the rest of my life like this, with my arm around you, my fingers on your backbone, your face on my chest, your absolutely magnificent breasts pressing on me, the smell of your hair in my nostrils. Feeling the way I do. Jesus, what made it so good? The champagne?

"Yes, I do."

"Great set of boobs on this broad."

"Fuck you!"

"We've already done that."

"And no comment about that? You usually have an opinion about everything."

Matt kissed the top of her head.

She raised her head.

"Is that in lieu of a comment?"

He kissed her. It was exquisitely tender. She shifted her body against his, so that her mouth was in his neck.

"The reason I'm curious," Penny said softly, carefully, "is because I really don't know what it's supposed to be like."

"I don't understand."

"There was Kellogg Winters," Penny said softly. "And then Anthony. And now you."

"Kellogg Winters? He's an ass."

Is she telling me I'm the third?

"Yes, he is. But I was seventeen, and I wanted to, so I let him. In the back seat of a car at Rose Tree Hunt Club. It was his birthday."

"Kellogg *Winters?*" he chuckled.

"And I thought, if this is what everybody's so excited about, that's really much ado about nothing."

Without thinking, horrified as he heard his own words, he asked, "And Tony the Zee? What was that like?"

He felt her body tense, and then relax.

"Different. Better."

"And Matthew Payne?"

"It was not like anything else. Is it always like that for you?"

Oh, shit!

Tell her the truth. If you make a four-star ass of yourself, so what?

"It has never been, before, like it was with you."

For a moment she didn't reply or move. Then she raised her head and looked down into his eyes.

"Really? God, please don't try to be charming, Matt!"

"I'm not being charming, I'm trying to figure it out."

She looked into his eyes for a long moment, and then lowered her head into his neck again.

"I'm going to take an enormous chance and believe you," she said. Her arm slowly tightened around him. He held her as tightly as he could.

A long moment later, Matt asked throatily, "How would you feel about seeing if we can do the same thing again?"

"Really?" She giggled in his ear. "Could you?" Her hand slid down over his chest and stomach. "Oh, how nice!"

She rolled over on her back, and pulled him onto her.

"Look in my eyes!" she ordered. He did. He felt her guiding him into her body.

"Oh, God, Matt!" she called softly.

19.

Penny started to go through the door of the Birch Suite into the corridor, but then stopped and looked around.

"If I had my druthers," she said, "we would just stay here for a while longer. Like forever."

"We've already had that discussion. What we're going to do is take one more look around Las Vegas East, and then we go back to Philadelphia."

"You still haven't told me what we're—what *you're*—looking for."

"I really don't know. I think this is a bum lead, but I want to be sure before I go back and say so."

"That doesn't make much sense," she said as she walked past him and out into the corridor.

Matt went to the desk, settled the bill, and then handed a bellman Penny's bag and five dollars and told him to bring the Mercedes to the door.

"I'll be out in a few minutes," he said. "I'm going to give you a chance to get a little of your money back."

From the uncomfortable smile on the desk clerk's face, Matt understood that making references to the casino was not considered good form.

He glanced at his watch as they approached the casino door. It was quarter to two.

If it was nearly deserted at half past nine, I'll give you five to one that it will be me and the croupier again.

He was wrong. The room was not crowded, but there were gamblers at all but one of the tables.

He reached into his jacket and took out some of the hundred-dollar bills. He looked and counted. There were six.

"Here," he said, handing them to Penny.

She took the money, looked at it, and then at him, then shrugged.

"Is that the going rate?" she asked. "Or is that five hundred, plus a hundred tip?"

"Oh, Jesus Christ!"

"Sorry," she said, again sounding as if she meant it. She touched his arm, just above the elbow, and gently squeezed it. "Our new relationship is going to take some getting used to."

That, madam, qualifies as the understatement of the millennium.

She turned from him and walked directly to the blackjack table. He followed her and got there in time to watch her hand the money to the dealer.

"Quarters," she said,

This is not the first time she's done this.

He looked around the room, and then at the others at the blackjack table.

There are some people in here now who look like gamblers, as opposed to the Bible Study Group who was in here earlier. But where is it written that a gambler has to wear a two-tone coat and a pastel shirt open to his navel, like that clown at the end of the table? Or, for that matter, where is it written that a Mafioso cannot buy his clothes at Brooks Brothers and look like he went to Princeton?

He watched Penny gamble. She grew intense, to the point of pursing her lips. He had watched her apply lipstick in the room, after she had put on her underwear, before she had put her dress back on. It had been a curious mixture of innocence and eroticism. She had seen him watching her in the mirror and pursed her lips in a kiss.

She quickly lost most of her chips, and then as quickly began to increase the size of the two stacks before her, subconsciously making the stacks even as the game progressed.

She's good at this. Better than I am. I always lose my shirt playing blackjack.

She bumped her rear end against him, and when he looked down, she nodded her head toward her chips.

"Not only economical," she said. "But maybe even profitable."

"The evening is young," he said.

He saw that the clown in the pastel shirt at the end of the table was looking at him curiously.

You could be a mobster, my friend. The question is, have you made me as a cop?

"Nature calls, Penny," he said. "I'll be right back."

She nodded absently.

He glanced around the room, found the rest rooms sign, and walked to it. The men's room was empty. He relieved himself, and then looked at himself in the mirror.

You don't look like a cop. Hay-zus was right about that. On the other hand, you have achieved a certain fame, or infamy, for taking down Mr. Warren K. Fletcher, aka the Northwest serial rapist, and also by getting yourself shot, getting your picture in the newspapers and everything. Is that why El Mafioso has made you?

You don't know he's made you. He may just be wondering where a nice, clean-cut young man like you gets the money to play games in here. Or he may be wondering how he can get a good-looking blonde like the one you're playing with.

And why are you so sure that guy is wrong? He probably has a used car lot in Wilkes-Barre or someplace.

Matt turned from the men's room mirror and went back into the casino. He looked around the room again, but didn't see anyone who attracted his interest. The only guy who was at all interesting was the Mafioso Used Car Salesman at Penny's table.

Penny turned and smiled when she sensed he was again standing behind her.

"Whatever you were doing, do it again," she said. "Look!"

She now had four stacks of chips in front of her, each ten, eleven, maybe twelve chips high.

"You want to quit when you're ahead?"

"Can I have fifteen more minutes?"

"Sure."

A waitress appeared, in a regular uniform, not the short skirt and mesh stockings of Las Vegas, and asked if she could get them something to drink.

"Not for me, thank you," Penny said.

"Could I get some black coffee?" Matt asked.

When the waitress delivered the coffee, Matt felt the eyes of the Used Car Salesman Mafioso on him again, and this time met his glance. The man smiled at him.

Now what the hell does that mean? That he's made me? And is laughing at me? Or that he thinks maybe we went to elementary school together, but isn't sure?

Matt, just perceptibly, nodded his head.

His eyes dropped to the chips in front of his new friend. He was playing quarters too, but he wasn't having the luck Penny was. He was down to six chips, and he lost those in the next two hands.

He turned from the table and walked toward the cashier's window. A woman, a peroxide blonde with spectacular breastworks, trailed after him.

How come you didn't notice that before? You always react to bosoms such as those as if they were electromagnets. Matthew, my boy, you are sated, that is why. Or maybe because you have changed your criteria for magnificent breasts. After tonight, you will always define magnificent breasts as rather small, pink-tipped, and astonishingly firm.

"Time's up," Matt said to Penny. "Daddy has to go into the office early tomorrow."

"Okay," Penny said, without argument. She slid two quarter chips across the table to the dealer, and then scooped up the rest. There were so many she could barely hold them.

"He would have cashed those for you."

"I wanted to carry them," Penny said. "To savor my triumph."

The Mafioso Used Car Salesman was leaning over the cashier's marble counter.

He's signing a—what do you call it?—an IOU? He needs more chips. He's been losing.

That bulge under his arm is a gun. In a shoulder holster. He is a Mafioso. Only Mafiosos and cops carry guns.

Christ, he's a cop! That's what's wrong with him!

The Mafioso/Cop slid the IOU, or whatever it was properly called, under the cashier's grill, and she slid a plastic tray full of quarter chips back out to him.

There were eight stacks of chips, each of ten chips, each chip worth twenty-five dollars. Matt did the math quickly in his head.

That tray is worth two thousand dollars! Cops can't afford that kind of gambling money. Bingo!

Vito Lanza turned from the cashier's window. The guy who looked familiar was standing behind him in line.

With the blonde who also looks familiar. And she's been doing a lot better than I have. Well, hell, maybe with her going, my luck will change, Vito thought.

"Don't I know you from somewhere, pal?" Vito asked the young guy.

"I don't think so."

"You look kind of familiar, you know?"

"I was thinking the same thing."

"You come here a lot?"

"Second time."

"Well . . . Vegas! You ever go to Vegas?"

"Yeah, sure."

"And you was there last week, right?" Vito asked triumphantly.

"Right."

"At the Flamingo, right?"

"Right again."

"And you flew back to Philadelphia on American, right? The both of you. In first class?"

"Right," Matt said. "So that's where it was. I knew I'd seen you somewhere."

"Well, how about that!" Vito said.

"How about that," Matt parroted.

"Small world, right?" Vito said. He handed the tray of chips to Tony, and put out his hand. "Vito Lanza. This is Tony."

"Matt Payne, this is Penny."

"Pleased to meet you," Tony said.

"Hi!" Penny said.

"How's your luck, Vito?" Matt asked.

"Aw, you know how it goes. Win a little, lose a little. The night's young."

"That's what I keep telling him," Penny said, and walked between Vito and Tony to the cashier's window and dumped her chips on the cashier's counter.

"Well, see you around," Vito said.

"See you around."

In the Mercedes, Penny leaned over and stuffed bills into Matt's jacket pocket.

"You didn't have to do that," he said.

"Yes, I did. If you're going to buy me off, it's going to take a lot more than a lousy six hundred dollars. Besides, I've got twenty-two hundred more."

"My God, that much?"

"That much," she said. "Tonight, in more ways than one, has been my lucky night."

"I think we had better proceed very, very slowly," Matt said.

"I thought you would say something like that once you'd had your wicked way with me," Penny said. "That was him, wasn't it? Who you were looking for all the time?"

He looked at her in surprise, then nodded.

"You going to tell me about it?"

"No."

"Well, I'm glad I was able to be helpful," she said. She caught his hand, and moved it to her mouth, and kissed it.

The large, illuminated clock mounted on the Strawbridge & Clothier Department Store in Jenkintown showed quarter to five when Matt looked up at it from Penny's Mercedes.

That meant he would be at her place at five, or a few minutes after. He looked over at her, expecting to find her still curled up asleep.

She was not asleep. She was awake and had apparently been reading his mind again.

"I think we could make this little deception of ours more credible if I arrived home at, say, seven," she said. "We having left GiGi's at, say, five. What time to you have to be at work?"

"Eight."

"We could find an all-night diner, I suppose," Penny said. "Or we could go to your apartment. I've never been to your apartment."

"I've got to change clothes," Matt said. "And reclaim my car."

"Or we could go to your apartment," Penny repeated.

Where we are likely to find Evelyn circling the block, looking for her missing lover. That does not rank as one of the good ideas of all time.

"Is that an indecent proposal?"

"More like female curiosity," Penny said. "Would your delicate male ego be crushed if I told you that I have had enough romance for the next day or two?"

He chuckled.

She reached out her hand and rubbed her fingers across his cheek.

"Make that *'physical* romance,' " she said. "You can hold my hand, if you want."

She moved her hand to his on the steering wheel and caught it and moved it to her chest.

That is a tender, as opposed to erotic, gesture.

"You need a shave," she said. "Are you going to take me to your apartment, Matthew?"

"I suppose that's best, even for someone whose delicate male ego has just been crushed flat."

"Women have the right to change their minds," she said cheerfully. "Didn't anyone ever tell you that?"

She suddenly let go of his hand and sat up.

"I know. Look for an all-night grocery store. We'll get eggs and bacon, or maybe Taylor Ham, and coffee and orange juice, and I'll make us breakfast."

"You're hungry again?"

"I can't imagine why."

"It would be easier to find a diner."

"I want to make us breakfast!"

"It's tiny," Penny said. "Where did you ever find this place?"

The red light on the answering machine, surprising Matt not at all, was blinking.

"My father owns it," he said. "The kitchen is that place back there with all the white things."

He motioned her ahead of him, and then ducked and pulled the answering machine's plug out of its socket.

"Does it have a toilet?"

"Off the bedroom," he said, catching up with her and pointing.

He unpacked the groceries, setting them on the kitchen counter. Then he went to the refrigerator and threw away all the food he had purchased with the noble intention of making his own meals, and which was now spoiled.

She came back into the kitchen.

"Would it help your crushed ego to learn that I am very sore?"

"Jesus," he said. "I'm sorry."

She walked quickly to him and kissed him lightly on the lips.

"I'm not," she said. "Cheap at twice the price."

He put his hands on her shoulders, and then slid them down to her waist and pulled her against him. He ran the balls of his fingers along her spine and wondered why he found that so erotic.

After a moment, she pushed him away.

"Tarzan sit," Penny said. "Jane make food."

He went into the living room and put his pistol on the mantelpiece, and then sat down in his armchair. He looked at the dead answering machine.

And then he reached for the telephone, lifted it up, and consulted a typewritten list of telephone numbers.

Officer Jesus Martinez answered, sleepily, on the third ring.

"Martinez."

"This guy you're interested in: dark-skinned, maybe thirty, thirty-five, five-nine or . . ."

"Payne?" Jesus asked incredulously.

"... five-nine or -ten. Maybe one-seventy. Wears his shirts unbuttoned to the navel?"

"What the hell?"

"You said his name is Lanzo, Lanza, something like that?"

"Lanza, Vito Lanza. What about him?"

"At two o'clock this morning, he was signing a two-thousand-dollar IOU in the back room at the Oaks and Pines Lodge," Matt said.

There was a long silence.

"*Marker,*" Martinez said, finally. "Not an IOU, a marker."

"I stand corrected."

"What were you doing up there?"

"Is this your guy, Hay-zus?"

"Yeah. I'm sure. How did *you* know who he was?"

"He was carrying. I made him as a cop. And he made me . . ."

"Shit!"

"Not as a cop. I was in Las Vegas when he was. He recognized me from Vegas and spoke to me."

"You're sure he didn't make you as a cop?"

"As you're so fond of telling me, Hay-zus, I don't look like a cop."

There was another pause.

"Payne, keep this under your hat, will you?"

"Who would I tell? What would I tell? 'Inspector, I just happened to be in an illegal gambling joint, and you know what, I wasn't the only cop in there'?"

"Just keep it under your hat, Payne, okay?"

"Okay. Are you forgetting something, Hay-zus?"

"What?"

"Try, 'Thank you very much, Detective Payne.' "

"Thanks, Payne," Jesus said. "I'll get back to you."

He hung up.

Matt said, "You're welcome, Hay-zus," and put the phone back in its cradle. He pushed himself out of the chair and went into the kitchen.

Penny was at the stove, and there was the peculiar smell of frying Taylor Ham.

"One egg or two? Over light or sunny side up?"

"Two. Up. Have I got time for a shower?"

"A quick one."

When he came back into the kitchen, Penny was in the process of wiping up the last of her egg yolk with a piece of toast.

"Boy, for a fat girl, you sure don't eat much."

"Your eggs are probably cold, which serves you right. What is that I smell?"

"Some kind of after-shave that comes from the Virgin Islands or somewhere. I get a ritual bottle of it from Amy on suitable occasions."

"Nice," she said. "Who's 'Hay-zus'?"

"Martinez. A cop."

"You don't like him much, do you? I could tell from the tone of your voice."

"No, I don't suppose I do like him. He's a good cop, though."

"Are you a good cop?"

"You haven't been reading the newspapers. I'm a goddamned Dick Tracy."

"You almost got killed, didn't you?"

"Yes, I guess I did."

"You know I don't understand you being a cop at all, don't you?"

"There's a good deal about you I don't understand, either."

"Was that a simple statement of fact, or are we back to Tony? And other things?"

"Are we going to fight now? Are things back to normal?"

"I don't know if we're going to fight or not, but I don't think things are ever going to be the same between us." She paused. "Do you?"

"No. How could they be?"

"If you can keep your lust under control, you can kiss me, Matthew."

He leaned across the table and kissed her lightly on the lips.

"I like kissing you better than fighting with you," Penny said. "Let's try that for a while and see what happens."

Peter Wohl, lying in his bed, had just decided that his delicate condition, the session with Larkin, Washington, Malone, and John Barleycorn having lasted until after ten, indicated a couple of soft-boiled eggs on toast, rather than a restaurant breakfast, when his door buzzer sounded.

Who the hell is that, at quarter to seven?

He got out of bed, put on a bathrobe, and walked barefoot to the door.

"Hello, Hay-zus," he said. "How are you? Come on in."

What the hell do you want? That you couldn't have said on the telephone?

"I brought this back," Martinez said, thrusting the loose-leaf notebook with BUREAU OF NARCOTICS AND DANGEROUS DRUGS Investigator's Manual FOR INTERNAL USE ONLY stamped on its cover at Wohl.

At seven o'clock in the goddamned morning?

"Thank you," Wohl said.

"And I wanted to talk to you," Martinez said a little uncomfortably. "I thought it would be better if I came. Instead of calling, I mean."

"Absolutely. Do you know how to make coffee?"

"Yes, sir."

"You make the coffee, then, while I catch a quick shower," Wohl said, and pointed toward his kitchen.

"Yes, sir."

"What's on your mind, Hay-zus?" Wohl asked, walking into the kitchen buttoning the cuff of his shirt.

"Inspector, the last time I was here . . . sir, you asked me if I had a gut feeling about anybody, anybody dirty, I mean, and I told you I didn't."

And now you're going to tell me, right?

"I remember."

"I did, but I didn't want to say anything."

"I understand. What's your gut feeling, Hay-zus?"

"There's a corporal out there, name of Vito Lanza."

"And you think he's dirty? Why?"

"He just came back from Las Vegas with a lot of money. Enough to buy a new Cadillac."

"Your pal Matt Payne was just in Vegas and did about the same thing."

"Payne's different. Payne's got money. He can afford that kind of money to gamble."

"Is that all you've got to go on, Hay-zus?"

"The day before yesterday, this Lanza had a lot of money, in cash, ninety-four hundred dollars, in his glove compartment."

Maybe he is onto something. That's a lot of money. Christ knows, I never had ninety-four hundred dollars in cash. But then I never gambled in Las Vegas, either. And how the hell does he know that?

"How do you know that?"

Martinez's face flushed.

The reason he knows that is that he went into this guy's car. My God!

"Forget I asked that question. That way you won't have to lie to me," Wohl said. "Anything else?"

"There was also a matchbook from a place in the Poconos, called the Oaks and Pines Lodge," Martinez said. "I called a guy I know in Vice and asked him about it, and he said they gamble in the back room of that place."

"Fortunately, that's no concern of ours, our jurisdiction ending as it does at the city line."

Why did you do that? This guy is trying, and sarcasm is not in order.

"At two o'clock this morning, Lanza signed a marker for two thousand dollars at this place."

"How do you know that? What did you do, for Christ's sake, follow him?"

"No, sir. But I got it from a good source."

"You're supposed to be undercover, Martinez. That means you don't talk to people about what you're doing. Who's your source?"

"I don't want to get him in trouble, Inspector."

"Cut the crap, Martinez. Who's your source?"

"Well, I knew I never could get in this place. And even if I did, Lanza would recognize me. I had to find out."

"Once again, Martinez, cut the crap. Let's have it."

"Payne went up there, Inspector."

"You asked Payne to follow this guy?" Wohl asked incredulously.

"I asked him if he would, if I found out Lanza was going up there."

"And you heard he was going up there?"

"No. Payne went up there on his own. Last night. And he called me about five this morning and told me he saw Lanza sign a marker for two thousand dollars."

"How did he know who Lanza was?"

"He was carrying, and Payne made him as a cop, and then Lanza recognized Payne. . . ."

"Lanza made Payne?"

"Not as a cop. He recognized him from Las Vegas, or something like that. But Payne said he was sure Lanza did not make him as a cop."

I don't need this. A bona fide lunatic is trying to disintegrate the Vice President of the United States, and we have no idea who he is or where he is, and I don't need to be distracted by a possibly dirty cop at the airport, or another proof that Matt Payne has a dangerous tendency to charge off doing something stupid.

"What we have here is a lucky gambler. The only law we know he's broken is to gamble in the Poconos. We wouldn't have a police department if every cop who gambles got fired."

"This guy is dirty, Inspector. I know it," Martinez said.

On the other hand we have here a guy who gambles big time in Las Vegas, had almost ten thousand dollars in cash in his glove compartment yesterday, and yet was signing a marker for two thousand in a joint in the Poconos. Which means, unless he used the ten thousand to pay off his mortgage or something, that he lost it, and signed a marker for more. The money bothers me. Cops do not have that kind of money. Honest cops don't.

And Martinez is not Matt Payne. He had two years undercover in Narcotics, and was damned good at it. He's had the time to develop the intuition. And he's not going off half-cocked, either, strictly on intuition. The last time he was here, he wouldn't give me this guy's name.

Wohl got up from the table and went into his bedroom. He took a small notebook from his bedside table, looked up a number, and dialed it.

"Chief Marchessi, this is Peter Wohl. Sorry to disturb you at home, sir. I think our man has come up with something. Have you got time in your schedule this morning to talk to us, sir?"

There was a pause.

"Thank you, Chief. We'll be there."

He hung up and went back in the kitchen.

"At half past eight, Hay-zus, we're going to see Chief Inspector Marchessi at Internal Affairs. You know where it is?"

"Yes, sir. At Third and Race."

"Be there."

"Yes, sir."

When Martinez had gone, Wohl went to the phone on the coffee table in his living room and dialed another number, this one from memory.

There was no answer on Detective Payne's line, and his answering machine did not kick in, although Wohl let it ring a long time.

Finally, he hung up and looked at his watch.

Christ, I won't get any breakfast at all!

At ten minutes past seven, Matt Payne very nearly drove Miss Penelope Detweiler's Mercedes into the wrought-iron gate of the Detweiler estate in Chestnut Hill.

He stopped so suddenly that Penny was thrown against the dashboard.

"When the hell did you start closing the goddamned gate?"

"No, I don't think I'm hurt, but thank you for asking, darling."

"Sorry. Are you all right?"

"I'm going to be sore all over," Penny said innocently. "If it's not one thing, it's another. Whatever am I going to do about you, Matthew darling?"

"What's with the gate?"

"There's some kind of a machine on it. It closes automatically at ten, something like that, and then opens automatically when it gets light in the morning."

"Not this morning."

He got out of the car and went to the telephone box and lifted a telephone receiver. It rang automatically.

"May I help you?" a voice said.

"Princess Penelope seeks entrance to the castle," Matt said.

"Yes, sir," the voice, which Matt now recognized as that of Jensen, the chauffeur, said. He did not seem amused.

The right half of the double gates creaked majestically open.

"I'll tell you something else that gate does," Matt said as he drove through it. "It permits your parents to know when your boyfriends bring you home."

"Don't be silly," she said.

H. Richard Detweiler, in a quilted silk dressing gown, came out of the front door as Matt drove up, holding a cup of coffee.

"He doesn't do that too well, does he?" Penny said.

"Do what?"

"Manage to look like he just happened to be there?"

Matt drove right past Detweiler, waving cheerfully at him, and around to the garage. His Volkswagen was parked to one side.

"You lie to your father," Matt said. "I'm getting out of here."

"You're underestimating him. I'll bet there's no keys in your Bug."

There was not.

It was necessary to walk back to the house, where Penny gave an entirely credible, but wholly false, report of GiGi's party, and why they had decided to stay over and come back first thing in the morning.

Matt was at first amused. Then it occurred to him that if Penny could lie that easily to her father, she could lie as easily to someone else, say M. Payne, Esq., and it no longer seemed amusing.

And then he realized that H. Richard Detweiler didn't believe a word Penny had told him.

He has no idea where we really were, but he knows damned well we were not at GiGi's. So why isn't he mad? Aren't fathers supposed to be furious when young men screw their daughters?

As a general rule of thumb, yes. But not when the young gentleman is an old, dear, and more importantly, responsible friend of the family, and the young lady in question has previously been involved in things that make a night between the sheets seem quite innocent, indeed.

"I really have to go."

"I'll have Jensen bring your car around," Detweiler said.

"Just get me the keys, please, I can get it myself."

"Thank you for a lovely evening, Matt," Penny said. "Ask me again, soon."

When she was sure her father's back was turned, she winked lewdly at him.

At two minutes before eight, Matt Payne pushed open the door to the Special Investigations Section. Two sergeants were waiting for him.

"Payne," Sergeant Maxwell Henkels said, "I told you once before. This is the second time, I'm not going to tell you again. I want to know where you are located all the time."

Somebody, obviously, has been looking for me.

"I wasn't aware that applied when I'm off duty," Matt said.

"Yeah, well, now you do. You understand me, I'm not going to tell you again?"

"I understand, Sergeant."

"Payne," Sergeant Jerry O'Dowd said uncomfortably, a strange smile on his face. "You have thirty-one minutes to meet Inspector Wohl at Chief Marchessi's office in Internal Affairs."

"What?"

"What are you, deaf or what?" Sergeant Maxwell Henkels demanded.

"I'll handle this, Sergeant," O'Dowd said. "And to make things easier for everybody concerned, I'll keep track of Detective Payne's whereabouts. Will that be all right with you?"

"The inspector asked me where he was, and I felt like an asshole when I didn't know."

"Well, that won't happen again. Payne will keep me advised of his location, on and off duty, won't you, Payne?"

"Right."

Henkels left the office.

"You'd better get moving, Payne," O'Dowd said. "With the early morning traffic, you're going to have to push it."

"Do you know what this is all about?"

"No. But right now, you're not one of his favorite people. He made that pretty clear."

Matt tried to figure that out, but came up with nothing.

"I guess nothing happened overnight? About the lunatic?"

"Not a thing."

"Well, Sergeant," Matt said. "You know where I'll be."

Jerry O'Dowd nodded.

20.

At twenty-nine minutes after eight, Matt entered the outer office of Chief Inspector Mario Marchessi, of the Internal Investigations Bureau, which was housed in a building about as old as the Schoolhouse, literally under the Benjamin Franklin Bridge, which connects Philadelphia with Camden, N.J.

Staff Inspector Peter Wohl and Officer Jesus Martinez were already there.

"Good morning, sir," Matt said.

Wohl did not reply. He gestured for Martinez and Payne to follow him out into the corridor.

"I want to make this clear before we go in to see Chief Marchessi," Wohl said. "This is to see what, if anything, can be salvaged as a result of you two going off like you thought you were the heroes in a cops-and-robbers movie on TV. Do you understand what I'm saying?"

"No, sir," Matt said. Martinez shook his head no.

"Jesus!" Wohl said disgustedly. "Martinez, you were sent to the airport to keep your eyes and ears open, and to report what you thought you heard or saw to me . . ."

What does he mean, "Martinez, you were sent to the airport"?

". . . but when I asked you to tell me your gut feelings, you decided, to hell with him, I'll play it close to my chest; I'm Super Cop. I'll catch this dirty cop by myself."

Matt looked at Martinez, who looked crushed.

"And you!" Wohl turned to Matt. "Whatever gave you the idea that you could, without orders, surveil anyone, much less a police corporal of a district you have absolutely no connection with at all, anywhere, much less to somewhere in another county, for Christ's sake, where you knew illegal gambling was going on?"

"Inspector, I didn't . . ."

"Shut up, Matt!"

". . . follow anyone anywhere."

"I told you to shut up," Wohl said. "I meant it."

He went back into Chief Marchessi's outer office.

Matt looked at Jesus Martinez.

"What did he mean when he said you were sent to the airport?"

Martinez raised his eyes to his, but didn't reply.

"Well?" Matt asked impatiently.

Wohl put his head back out into the corridor.

"Okay, let's go," he said.

They followed Wohl into Chief Marchessi's office. He pointed to where he wanted them to stand, facing Marchessi's desk, then closed the door to the outer office, then sat down on a battered couch.

"Okay, Peter, what's going on?" Chief Marchessi asked.

"My primary mistake, Chief, was in assuming that Detectives Martinez and Payne . . ."

Detectives Martinez and Payne?

". . . had a good deal more common sense than is the case."

"I don't follow you, Peter," Marchessi said.

"At two o'clock this morning, Detective Payne, having followed him there, observed an Airport Unit corporal signing a marker for two thousand dollars in a gambling joint in the Poconos."

"What gambling joint?" Marchessi asked.

"What was the name of this place, Payne?" Wohl asked.

"The Oaks and Pines Lodge," Matt replied. "Sir, I didn't follow . . ."

"Speak when you're spoken to," Wohl said.

"Let him talk," Marchessi said. "What were you saying?"

Wohl didn't let him.

"The reason he followed the fellow to the Oaks and Pines," Wohl went on, "was because Detective Martinez asked him to."

Marchessi put up his hand, palm out, to silence Wohl.

"Did you follow this Corporal . . . have we got a name?"

"Lanza, sir. Vito Lanza," Martinez said.

"Did you follow this Corporal Lanza to this place in the Poconos?" Marchessi asked.

"No, sir."

"Inspector Wohl thinks you did."

"The inspector is mistaken, sir. May I explain?"

"I wish somebody would."

"Officer Martinez believes . . ." Matt began.

"Detective Martinez," Marchessi interrupted. "Let's get that, at least, straight."

Jesus! That means Hay-zus was working the Airport undercover, and *as a detective.*

"Detective Martinez became suspicious of Corporal Lanza, sir," Matt started again.

"Whoa!" Marchessi said. "Why were you suspicious of Corporal Lanza, Martinez?"

"His life-style, sir," Martinez said. "He had too much money. And a new Cadillac. And he gambles."

Marchessi looked at Wohl.

"That's all?" he asked.

"He had almost ten thousand dollars in cash in the glove compartment of his Cadillac, Chief," Martinez said.

"How do you know that?"

"I saw it."

"He showed it to you?"

"No, sir."

"Does this Corporal . . . Lanza . . . know you know he had all this cash?"

"We hope not," Wohl said sarcastically. "We think Detective Martinez's breaking and entering of Corporal Lanza's personal automobile went undetected."

Marchessi snapped his head to look at Martinez. He was on the verge of saying something, but, visibly, changed his mind.

"And with all this somewhat less than incriminating evidence in hand," Marchessi said, "you enlisted the aid of Detective Payne to surveil Corporal Lanza, and he followed him to this lodge in the Poconos?"

"Not exactly, sir," Jesus said.

"Tell me, *exactly.*"

"I asked Detective Payne if he would be willing to follow Lanza there if I found out he was going."

"Why?"

"You mean why did I ask Payne?"

Marchessi nodded.

"Because my friend in Vice said it was a high-class place and I figured Payne could get in. I couldn't follow him myself."

"And did you tell Detective Payne what you're doing at the Airport Unit?"

"No, sir. Just that I thought I found a dirty cop."

"And you learned that Lanza was going to this place, and told Payne, and Payne followed him up there. Is that correct?"

"No, sir," Matt said.

"I'm asking Martinez," Marchessi said.

"I didn't tell him Lanza was going there," Martinez said. "He went up there on his own."

Was that a simple statement of fact, Hay-zus, or are you trying to stick it in me?

"Why did you do that, Payne?"

"Hay-zus is a good cop, sir . . ."

"Who the hell is *'Hay-zus'?"* Marchessi interrupted.

"That's the Spanish pronunciation of 'Jesus,' sir."

"Whether *'Hay-zus'* is a good cop seems to be open to discussion," Marchessi said. "Go on."

"I thought if he said he had a dirty cop, he probably had one."

"Just as an aside, Detective Payne, there is a departmental policy that states that police officers having reason to suspect brother officers of dishonesty will—*will,* not *may*—bring this to the attention of Internal Affairs."

"Yes, sir. Martinez asked me if I would be willing to go to this place to see if Lanza was associating with known criminals . . ."

"And if he was, I was going to tell you his name, Inspector," Martinez said to Wohl.

". . . and I agreed," Matt went on. "Then it occurred to me it would make sense if I knew where I was going. To take a look at the place before I followed Lanza there, in other words. So I went up there."

"No one, correct me if I'm wrong, told you to do so. Just your buddy Martinez asked you, right?"

"Yes, sir."

"Is there anyone else involved in this? Another buddy?"

Martinez and Matt looked at each other.

"Okay, who?" Marchessi asked, correctly interpreting the exchanged glances.

"He didn't do anything, sir," Martinez said.

"Who, dammit?"

"I talked about Lanza to Detective McFadden, sir."

"He's the officer you worked with in Narcotics?" Marchessi asked.

"Yes, sir."

If he knows that, Matt thought, *he knows that it was Hay-zus and Charley who brought down the guy who killed Uncle Dutch. That ought to be worth something.*

"Anybody else?"

"No, sir."

"Just the three of you, huh? Your own private detective squad within the Department, huh?"

Marchessi looked between them until it was clear that neither dared reply to that, and then went on.

"You have any trouble getting in this place, Payne?"

"No, sir."

"It's open to the public?"

"I believe it's operated as a club, sir. I was with someone who belonged."

"That could be interpreted to mean that you are associating with known criminals."

"Not in this case, sir," Matt said quickly.

But that's bullshit. Penny is a known narcotics addict, as well as someone known to associate with known criminals. Jesus!

"And this Corporal Lanza was there?"

"Yes, sir."

"Associating with known criminals?"

"I don't know, sir."

"The truth of the matter, Payne," Wohl said, "is that, with the possible exception of somebody like Vincenzo Savarese, you wouldn't recognize a known criminal if you fell over one. Isn't that so?"

"Yes, sir."

"Tell me about the two-thousand-dollar marker," Marchessi said.

"Sir, as I was cashing out, I saw Lanza sign a marker for two thousand dollars' worth of chips. He was in the line ahead of me."

"I thought you said you didn't follow him up there."

"I didn't. He was there."

"You knew him by sight? That would suggest he knows you by sight."

"Yes, sir. But not the way that sounds, sir."

"Clarify it for me."

"I didn't know who he was. But I made him as a cop. He was carrying."

"People, other than policemen, sometimes go about armed."

"I had a gut feeling he was a cop, sir, and then he spoke to me."

"What did he say?"

"I had apparently run into him in Las Vegas, sir. And on the airplane from Las Vegas home. He recognized me. Not as a cop."

"You made him, is that what you're saying, as a cop, but he didn't make you as a cop?"

"I'm sure I could have told if he had, sir."

"I admire your confidence in your own judgment, Payne," Marchessi said. "And then what did you do?"

"I came back to Philadelphia and called off . . . *Detective* Martinez and told him (a) that Lanza had been in the Oaks and Pines and (b) had signed a marker for two thousand dollars."

"And then I went to see you, sir," Martinez said to Wohl.

"Tell me, Martinez," Marchessi said. "Have you any *evidence* to connect Corporal Lanza with the smuggling of narcotics, or, for that matter, of anything else, or any other criminal activity, at the airport?"

"No evidence, sir. But it has to be him."

" 'Has' to be him?" Marchessi replied, softly sarcastic.

He looked at Wohl, who shrugged his shoulders.

"You two wait outside. In the corridor," Marchessi said.

Matt and Martinez turned around and left his office.

"You want some coffee, Peter?" Marchessi asked.

"What I would like is a stiff drink."

"At this hour of the morning?"

"Figure of speech," Wohl said.

"Both of them talked about 'gut feelings,' or implied it," Marchessi said. "My gut feeling is that they've found who we're looking for."

"But have they blown it?" Wohl asked. "Dammit, I asked him to give me a name."

"Give him the benefit of the doubt. He didn't want to point a finger until he was sure."

"And while he was making sure, there was a good chance this guy would smell that he was being watched. And breaking into his car was absolute stupidity."

Marchessi chuckled.

"There was a story going around that one of my staff inspectors, carried away with enthusiasm, tapped the line of a Superior Court judge without getting the necessary warrant."

"Ouch!" Peter said.

"I didn't believe it, of course," Marchessi said. "I don't know what I would have done if somebody had discovered the tap."

"What, to change the subject, Chief, do we do about this?"

"Well, I think we've already been shifted into high gear, whether or not we like it," Marchessi said.

He pushed one of the buttons on his telephone, then picked up the receiver.

"Ollie, can you come in here a minute?" he said, and hung up.

Less than a minute later, Captain Richard Olsen, a large, blond-haired man of forty, wearing a blue blazer and a striped necktie, opened Marchessi's door without knocking.

"Sir?"

"Come in and close the door, Ollie. You remember Peter, of course?"

"What brings you slumming, Inspector?"

Captain Olsen, whose exact title Wohl could not remember, provided administrative services to the fourteen staff inspectors assigned to the Internal Investigations Bureau. The staff inspectors, from whose ranks Wohl had been transferred to command of Special Operations, handled sensitive investigations, most often involving governmental corruption. Wohl liked and respected him.

"How are you, Ollie?"

"Ollie," Marchessi asked, "if I wanted around-the-clock, moving surveillance of an off-duty Airport Unit corporal, starting right now, what kind of problems would that cause?"

Olsen thought that over for a minute.

"What squad is he assigned to?"

"Three squad, four to midnight," Wohl furnished.

"I can handle the next twenty-four hours, forty-eight, with no trouble. After that, I'll need some bodies. What are we looking for?"

"For openers, association with known criminals. Ultimately, to catch him smuggling drugs out of the airport."

"Watching him on the job would be difficult."

"I'm wondering if I can strike a deal with the feds. I know goddamned well they have people undercover out there. If I told them I'll give them a name, if they let us have the arrest . . ."

"And if they won't go along?" Wohl asked.

"That would bring us back to Hay-zus, wouldn't it, Peter?" Marchessi said thoughtfully.

"Yeah," Wohl said.

"You call it, Peter, you know him better than I do."

"We'd be betting that Lanza has accepted the story that Martinez is out there because he failed the detective's examination," Wohl thought aloud. "And I would have to impress on Martinez that all, absolutely all, that he's to do is watch him on the job. . . . Screw the feds. I don't like the idea of having the feds catch one of our cops dirty. Let's go with Martinez."

"I have no idea," Olsen said, "who or what either of you are talking about."

"I think we should bring Martinez back in here," Marchessi said. "I don't think we need Payne. Except to tell him to keep his nose out of this."

"I'll handle Payne," Wohl said. "I don't think you need me, either, do you, Chief?"

"No. And you're on the mad bomber too, aren't you? How're you doing?"

"We don't have a clue who he is," Wohl said, getting off the couch. "Thank you very much, Chief. You've been very understanding."

"I have some experience, Peter, with bright young men who sometimes get carried away. Every once in a while, they even catch the bad guys. You might keep that in mind."

"Just between you, me, and the Swede here, I'm not nearly as angry with those two as I hope they think I am," Wohl said.

"You could have fooled me," Marchessi said. "Send in Martinez, will you, Peter?"

"I guess I'll be seeing you, Peter?" Olsen said, extending his hand.

"More than you'll want to, Ollie," Wohl said.

At 9:24, Mr. Pietro Cassandro pulled up before Ristorante Alfredo's entrance at the wheel of a Lincoln that had been delivered to Classic Livery only the day before. On the way from his home, Mr. Vincenzo Savarese had been concerned that there was something wrong with the car. It smelled of something burning.

Mr. Cassandro had assured Mr. S. that there was no cause for concern, that he had personally checked the car out himself, that it was absolutely okay, and that what Mr. S. was smelling was the preservatives and paint and stuff that comes with a new car, and burns off after a few miles. Like stickers and oil, for example, on the muffler.

Mr. S. had seemed only partially satisfied with Pietro's explanation, and Pietro had decided that maybe he'd made a mistake in picking up Mr. S. in the car before he'd put some miles on it. He would never do so again. The next time Mr. S. was sent a new car, it would have, say, two hundred miles on it, and wouldn't smell of burning anything.

Mr. Gian-Carlo Rosselli got out of the passenger seat and walked quickly to the door. Ristorante Alfredo didn't open until half-past eleven, and Pietro hoped that Ricco Baltazari had enough brains to have somebody waiting to open the door when Rosselli knocked on it. Mr. S. did not like to be kept waiting in a car when he wanted to go someplace, especially when the people knew he was coming.

Mr. Cassandro's concerns were put to rest when the door was opened by Ricco Baltazari himself before Rosselli reached it. Rosselli turned and looked up and down the street, and then nodded to Pietro, who got quickly out from behind the wheel and opened the door for Mr. S.

Mr. S. didn't say "thank you" the way he usually did, or even nod his head, but just walked quickly across the sidewalk and into the restaurant. Pietro was almost sure that was because he had business on his mind, and not because he was pissed that the car smelled, but he wasn't positive.

He wondered, as he got back behind the wheel, if he raced the engine, would that speed up the burn-the-crap-off process, so that the car wouldn't smell when Mr. S. came out.

He decided against doing so. What was likely to happen was that, sitting still, the smoke would just get more in the car than it would if he just let things take their natural way.

But then he decided that he could take a couple of laps around the block and burn it off that way. Mr. S. probably wasn't going to come out in the next couple of minutes, and if Rosselli looked out and saw the car wasn't there, he would think the cop on the beat had made him move the car.

Sometimes, the cops would leave you alone, let you sit at the curb, if there was somebody behind the wheel, but other times, they would be a pain in the ass and tell you to move on.

Pietro put the Lincoln in gear and drove off. At the first red light, he raced the engine. A cop gave him a strange look. Fuck him!

"Good morning, Mr. S.," Ricco Baltazari said as he carefully shook Mr. S.'s hand. "I got some nice fresh coffee, and I sent out for a little pastry."

"Just the coffee, thank you, Ricco," Mr. S. said, and then changed his mind. "What kind of pastry?"

"I sent out to the French place. I got croissants, and eclairs, and . . ."

"Maybe an eclair. Thank you very much," Mr. S. said.

"Would you like to go to the office? Or maybe a table?"

"This will do nicely," Mr. S. said and sat down at a table along the wall.

Gian-Carlo Rosselli looked as if he didn't know what he should do, and Mr. S. saw this.

"Sit down, Gian-Carlo, and have a pastry and some coffee. I want you to hear this."

"I'll get the stuff," Ricco said.

When he came back, Mr. S. asked after his family.

"Everybody's doing just fine, Mr. S."

Mr. Savarese nodded, then leaned forward and added cream and sugar to the cup of coffee Ricco had poured for him.

"There's a little business problem, Ricco," Mr. S. said.

"With the restaurant?" Ricco asked, concern evident in his voice. He glanced nervously at Gian-Carlo.

Mr. S. looked at him for a moment, expressionless, before replying and when he did it was not directly.

"I had a telephone call yesterday from a business associate in Baltimore," he said. "A man who has always been willing to help me when I asked for a favor. Now he wants a favor from me."

"How can I help, Mr. S.?"

"His problem, he tells me, is that the feds, the Customs people, and the Narcotics and Dangerous Drugs people have been making a nuisance of themselves at Friendship. You know Friendship? The airport in Baltimore?"

"I know it, Mr. S."

"He says that he don't think it will last, that what they're doing is fishing, not looking for something specific, but he has decided that it would be best if he didn't try to bring anything through Friendship for the next week or ten days. As a precaution, you understand."

"Certainly."

"And he asked me, would I do him a favor of handling this merchandise through Philadelphia. The point of origin is San Juan, Puerto Rico."

"We don't have anybody at the airport. . . ."

"There are two reasons I told this man I would be happy to help him," Mr. S. said. "The first being that I owe him, and when he asks . . . And the second being that I did not want it to get around, and it would if I told him, that at this moment, I don't have anybody at the airport."

"I understand."

"So what I want to know from you, Ricco, how are things going with your friend who works at the airport?"

"I had a telephone call at eight this morning, Mr. S. Our friend was up there last night and he had bad luck, and he signed four thousand dollars' worth of markers."

"You ever think, Ricco, that somebody's bad luck is almost always somebody else's good luck?"

"That's very true, Mr. S."

"So you have these markers?"

"No, sir. They're going to have a truck coming to Philadelphia today, this afternoon, and they'll bring the markers with them then."

"I think I would like to have them sooner than that. Do you think you could call them up and ask them, as a favor to you, if they could maybe put somebody in a car and get them down here right away?"

"Or we could send a car up there, Mr. S.," Gian-Carlo suggested.

"Let them, as a favor to Ricco, bring the markers here to the restaurant. Then, when they come, Ricco can call me, at the house, and say that he has the papers you were looking for, and you'll come pick them up, and take them, and also those photographs Joe Fierello took at the car lot, over to Paulo, and then Paulo can go have a talk with this cop."

"Right, Mr. S."

"Where would you say this cop would be, Ricco, in, say, three hours?"

"I don't know, Mr. S., to tell you the truth."

"You know where he is now? I thought I asked you to have that girl keep an eye on him."

"He's at her apartment now, Mr. S. But what you asked is where he'll be at about noon. He may be there. He may go by his house, Tony told me he had to have new pipes put in, or he may just stay at Tony's apartment until it's time for him to go to work. I just have no way of telling."

"I understand. All right. The first thing you do is you get on the phone and ask them to please send the markers right away to here. Then, can you do this, you call the girl, and you tell her if she can to keep the cop in her apartment as long as she can, and if she can't, she's to call you the minute he leaves, and tell you where he's going. And I think it would be best if you made the calls from a pay phone someplace."

"I'll have to leave the keys to the restaurant with Gian-Carlo, otherwise you'd be locked in."

"There's nobody else here?"

"The fewer people around the better, I always say."

"And you're right. But I'll tell you what. We'll leave, and then you go find a pay phone and make the call, and when you find out something, you call the house and all you have to say is 'yes' or 'no.' You understand?"

"That would work nicely."

"And besides, if I stayed here, I'd eat all this pastry, it's very good, but it's not good for me, too much of it."

"I understand, Mr. S."

Gian-Carlo got up and walked to the door and pushed the curtain aside and looked for Pietro.

"He's not out there, Mr. S."

"He probably had to drive around the block," Mr. S. said. "He'll be there in a minute."

For the next three minutes, Gian-Carlo, at fifteen-second intervals, pushed the curtain aside and looked to see if Pietro and the Lincoln had returned.

Finally he had.

"He's out there, Mr. S.," Gian-Carlo said.

Mr. Savarese stood up.

"Thank you for the pastry, even if it wasn't good for me," he said, and shook Ricco's hand.

Then he walked out of the restaurant and quickly across the sidewalk and got into the Lincoln. As soon as Gian-Carlo had got in beside him in the front seat, Pietro drove off.

"I'll tell you, Pietro, if anything, it smells worse than before."

"As soon as I get a chance, Mr. S., I'll take it to the garage and swap it."

"Why don't you do that?" Mr. S. replied.

"Anthony, something has come up," Mr. Ricco Baltazari, proprietor of Ristorante Alfredo, said to Mr. Anthony Clark (formerly Cagliari), resident manager of the Oaks and Pines Lodge, over the telephone. Mr. Clark was in his office overlooking the third tee of the Oaks and Pines Championship Golf Course. Mr. Baltazari was in a pay telephone booth in the lower lobby of the First Philadelphia Bank & Trust Building on South Broad Street.

"What's that?"

"The financial documents you're going to send me . . ."

"They're on their way, Ricco, relax. The van just left, not more than a couple minutes ago."

"That's not good enough. It'll take him for fucking ever to get to Philly."

"What do you want me to do, get in my car and bring them my fucking self?" Mr. Clark said, a slight tone of petulance creeping into his voice.

"It's not what I want, Anthony. It's what you know who, our mutual friend, wants," Mr. Baltazari said. "He wants those financial documents right fucking now."

There was a moment's silence.

"The only thing I could do, Ricco," Mr. Clark said, "is put somebody in my car and send him after the van, see if he could catch it, you understand?"

"Do it, Anthony. Our mutual friend is very anxious to get his hands on those financial documents just as soon as he can."

"If I had known he wanted those documents in a hurry, I would have brought them myself, you understand that?"

"If I had known he wanted them, I would have come up and got the fuckers myself," Mr. Baltazari replied. "I just left him. He said I should tell you he wants them, as a special favor, right now."

"I'll do what I can, Ricco. You want I should call our friend and tell him what I'm doing, in case my guy can't catch the van? Or will you do that?"

"He don't give a shit what you're doing. All he wants is the fucking markers. How you do that is your business."

"I tell my guy to take them right to our mutual friend?"

"You tell your guy to bring them to me, at the restaurant. When I got them, I'm to call our friend."

"Ricco, I would be very unhappy if I was to learn that you weren't telling me the whole truth about this."

"Anthony, get your guy on the way, for Christ's sake!"

"Yeah," Mr. Clark said, and hung up.

Mr. Clark took a pad of Oaks and Pines notepaper from his desk, and a pen from his desk set.

On one sheet of paper, he wrote, "Give Tommy the envelope I gave you, A.C." and on the other he wrote Ristorante Alfredo, Ricco Baltazari, and the address and telephone number.

Then Mr. Clark went down to the money room off the casino. There he found Mr. Thomas Dolbare sitting all alone on one of the stools in front of the money counting table, on which now sat a small stack of plastic bank envelopes. Mr. Dolbare, a very large and muscular twenty-eight-year-old, was charged with the security of last night's take until the messenger arrived from Wilkes-Barre to take it for deposit into six different, innocently named bank accounts in Hazelton and Wilkes-Barre.

"Tommy," Mr. Clark said, "what I want you to do is take my car and chase down the van. He just left. He always goes down Route 611. Stop him, give him this, and he'll give you an envelope. You then take the envelope to Mr. Baltazari. I wrote down the address and phone number."

Mr. Clark gave Mr. Dolbare both notes.

"Right."

"As soon as you have it, go to a pay phone and call me. Or if you can't catch the van, call me and tell me that too."

"I'll catch it," Mr. Dolbare said confidently. He was pleased that he was being given greater responsibility than sitting around in a fucking windowless room watching money bags.

"Don't take a gun," Mr. Clark said. "You won't need it in Philadelphia."

"Right," Mr. Dolbare said, and took off his jacket and the .357 Magnum Colt Trooper in its shoulder holster, and then put his jacket back on.

"Don't drive like a fucking idiot and get arrested, or bang up my car," Mr. Clark said.

"Right," Mr. Dolbare said.

The van that Mr. Dolbare intercepted on Highway 611 between Delaware Water Gap and Mount Bethel was a year-old Ford, which had the Oaks and Pines Lodge logotype painted on both its doors and the sides. It made a daily, except Sunday, run to Philadelphia where it picked up seafood and beef and veal from M. Alcatore & Sons Quality Wholesale and Retail Meats in South Philadelphia.

M. Alcatore & Sons was a wholly owned subsidiary of Food Services, Inc., which was a wholly owned subsidiary of South Street Enterprises, Inc., in which, it was believed by various law enforcement agencies, Mr. Vincenzo Savarese held a substantial interest.

It was also believed by various law enforcement agencies that through some very creative accounting the interlocked corporations were both depriving the federal, state, and city governments of all sorts of taxes, and at the same time laundering through them profits from a rather long list of illegal enterprises.

So far, no law enforcement agency, city, state, or federal, had come up with anything any of the respective governmental attorneys believed would be worth taking to court.

Tommy Dolbare gave the van driver Mr. Clark's note, and the van driver gave him a sealed blank envelope.

Tommy got back in Mr. Clark's Cadillac Sedan de Ville, and continued down Highway 611 to Easton, where he had to take a piss, and stopped at a gas station. He decided, on his way back to the car, that Mr. Clark would probably like to hear that he had intercepted the van, so he went into a telephone booth and called Oaks and Pines Lodge.

Then he got back in the Sedan de Ville and continued down US Highway 611 toward Philadelphia. It is one of the oldest highways in the nation, and from Easton south for twenty miles or so parallels the Delaware Canal.

Shortly after Mr. Dolbare passed the turnoff to Durham, a tiny village of historical significance because it was at Durham that Benjamin Franklin established the first stop of his new postal service, and from the canal at Durham that George Washington took the Durham Boats on which he floated across the Delaware to attack the British in Princeton, Mr. Dolbare took his eyes from the road a moment to locate the cigarette lighter.

When he looked out the windshield again, there was a dog on the road. Mr. Dolbare, although he did not have one himself, liked dogs, and did not wish to run over one. He applied the brakes as hard as he could, and simultaneously attempted to steer around the dog.

The Cadillac went out of control and skidded into the post-and-cable fence that separates Highway 611 from the Delaware Canal.

The fence functioned as designed. The Cadillac did not go into the Delaware Canal. The cables held it from doing so. Only the front wheels left the road. Mr. Dolbare was able to back onto the road, but when he did so, one of the cables, which had become entangled with the grille of the car, did not become unentangled, and held. This caused the grille of the Cadillac, and the sheet metal that held the grille and the radiator in place, to pull loose from the Cadillac.

There was a scream of tortured metal as the fan blades struck something where the radiator had been, and then antifreeze erupted from the displaced radiator hose against the engine block.

"Oh, shit!" Mr. Dolbare said.

He got out of the car. He looked in both directions down the highway. He could see nothing but the narrow road in either direction. He did not recall what lay in the direction of Philadelphia, but he estimated that it was not more than a couple of miles back toward Easton where he had seen a gas station and a bar, which would have a telephone.

He slammed the door of Mr. Clark's Cadillac as hard as he could, and started walking back up Highway 611 toward Easton, his heart heavy with the knowledge that he had really fucked up, and that he was now in deep shit.

Mr. Dolbare had just passed a sign announcing that the Riegelsville Kiwanis met every Tuesday at the Riegelsville Inn and had just learned that the Riegelsville American Legion welcomed him to Riegelsville when he saw a familiar vehicle coming down Highway 611.

He stepped into the road and flagged it down.

"What the fuck are you doing walking down the highway?" the driver inquired of him.

"We have to find a phone," Mr. Dolbare said. "You see one back there?"

"What the hell happened?"

"Some asshole forced me off the road; I had an accident."

"You wrecked Clark's car?" the Oaks and Pines van driver replied, adding unnecessarily, "Boy, is your ass in deep shit."

"No shit? Get me to a fucking phone."

Fifteen minutes later, Mr. Anthony Clark telephoned to Mr. Ricco Baltazari, at the Ristorante Alfredo, to inform him that there had been an accident, some asshole had forced his guy off the road in the sticks, but that the van had caught up with him, and those financial documents they had been talking about were at this very minute on their way to him.

Mr. Baltazari told Mr. Clark, unnecessarily, that he would pass the progress report along to their mutual friend, who wasn't going to like it one fucking bit.

"He's going to want to know, Anthony, if you didn't have somebody reliable to do this favor for him, why you didn't do it yourself."

"Accidents happen, Ricco, for Christ's sake!"

"Yeah," Mr. Baltazari said, and hung up.

He looked at his watch. It was quarter to twelve. He thought that although it wasn't his fault, Mr. S. was going to be pissed to hear that the goddamned markers were still somewhere the other side of Doylestown.

Somewhat reluctantly, he dialed Mr. S.'s number.

21.

Chief Marchessi had ordered surveillance of Corporal Vito Lanza "starting right now." Captain Swede Olsen had done his best to comply with his orders, but Internal Affairs does not have a room full of investigators just sitting around with nothing else to do until summoned to duty, so it was twenty minutes after eleven before a nondescript four-year-old Pontiac turned down the 400 block of Ritner Street in South Philadelphia.

"There it is," Officer Howard Hansen said, pointing to Corporal Lanza's residence. "With the plumber's truck in front."

"Where the hell am I going to park?" Sergeant Bill Sanders responded. "Jesus, South Philly is unbelievable."

Officer Hansen and Sergeant Sanders were in civilian clothing. Hansen, who had been handling complaints from the public about police misbehavior, was wearing a suit and tie, and Sanders, who had been investigating a no-harm-done discharge of firearms involving two police officers and a married lady who had promised absolute fidelity to both of them, was wearing a cotton jacket and a plaid, tieless shirt.

"Go around the block, maybe something'll open up," Hansen said.

"I don't see a new Cadillac, either."

"If you had a new Cadillac, would you want to park it around here?"

"We don't even know if he's here," Sanders said as he drove slowly and carefully down Ritner Street, where cars were parked, half on the sidewalk, along both sides.

Suddenly he stopped.

"Go in the bar," he ordered, pointing. "See if you can get a seat where you can see his house. I'll find someplace to park."

Hansen got quickly out of the car and walked in the bar. He saw that if he sat at the end of the bar by the entrance, he could see over the curtain on the plate-glass window, and would have a view of most of the block, including the doorway to Lanza's house.

He ordered a beer and a piece of pickled sausage.

Sergeant Sanders walked in ten minutes later.

"Well, I'll be damned," he said. "Long time no see!"

They shook hands.

"Let me buy you a beer," Hansen said.

"I accept. Schaefers," he said to the bartender, and then to Hansen: "I got to make a call."

The bartender pointed to a phone, and then drew his beer.

Sanders consulted the inside of a matchbook, then dropped a coin in the slot and dialed a number.

On the fourth ring, a somewhat snappy female voice picked up.

"Hello?"

"Is Vito there, Mrs. Lanza?"

"Who's this?"

"Jerry, Mrs. Lanza. Can I talk to Vito?"

"If you can find him, you can talk to him. I don't know where he is. Nobody is here but me and the plumbers."

"I'll try him later, Mrs. Lanza, thank you."

"You see him, you tell him he's got to come home and talk to these plumbers."

"I'll do that, Mrs. Lanza," Sanders said, and hung up.

He walked back to the bar.

"His mother doesn't know where he is. She's all alone with the plumbers."

Hansen nodded, and took a small sip of his beer.

"Is there anything on the TV?" he called to the bartender.

"What do you want?"

"Anything but the soap opera. I have enough trouble with my own love life; I don't have to watch somebody else's trouble."

The bartender started flipping through the channels.

At five minutes to twelve, Marion Claude Wheatley left his office in the First Pennsylvania Bank & Trust Company, rode down in the elevator, and walked north on South Broad Street to the City Hall, and then east on Market Street toward the Delaware River.

He returned to the Super Drugstore on the corner of 11th Street where he had previously purchased the *Souvenir of Asbury Park, N.J.* AWOL bag, and bought two more of them, another *Souvenir of Asbury Park, N.J.* and one with the same fish jumping out of the waves, but marked *Souvenir of Panama City Beach, Fla.* He thought it would be interesting to know just how many different places were stamped on AWOL bags the Super Drugstore had in the back room.

And then he thought that Super Drugstore was really a misnomer. There was a place where one presumably could have a prescription filled, way in the back of the place, and there were rows of patent medicines, but he would have guessed that at least eighty percent of the available space in the Super Drugstore was given over to nonpharmaceutical items.

It was more of a Woolworth's Five and Dime, he thought, than a Super Drugstore. They really should not be allowed to call it a drugstore; it was deceptive, if not downright dishonest.

He had almost reached the entrance when he saw a display of flashlight batteries, under a flamboyant *S A L E !* sign. He knew all that meant, of course, was that the items were available for sale, not on sale at a reduced price. But he headed for the display anyway, and saw that he was wrong.

The Eveready Battery Corporation, as opposed to the Super Drugstore itself, was having a promotional sale. He could tell that, because there were point-of-purchase promotional materials from Eveready, reading "As Advertised On TV!"

The philosophy behind the promotion, rather clever, he thought, was *"Are you sure your batteries are fresh? Be Sure With Eveready!"*

This was tied in, Marion noticed, with a pricing policy that reduced the individual price of batteries in a sliding scale tied to how many total batteries one bought.

This triggered another thought. Certainly, there would be nothing suspicious if he acted as if he were someone taken in by Eveready's advertising and bought all the batteries he was going to need.

And then he had a sudden, entirely pleasing insight. There was more to his having come across this display than mere happenstance. The Lord had arranged for him to pass by this display. He had, of course, planned to *Be Sure* his batteries were fresh. But he had planned to buy four batteries here, and four batteries there, not all twenty-four at once.

The Lord had made it possible for him to buy everything he needed to *Be Sure With Eveready* at one place, and in such a manner that no one would wonder what he was doing with all those batteries.

He paid for the batteries, and then put them in the *Souvenir of Asbury Park, N.J.* AWOL bag, and then folded that and put it in the *Souvenir of Panama City Beach, Fla.* AWOL bag, and then asked the girl at the cashier's counter for a bag to put everything in.

He didn't want to walk back to the office, much less into the office, carrying a bag with *Souvenir of Panama City Beach, Fla.* painted on it.

When he got back to the office, he got out the telephone book, and a map of Phila-delphia, and carefully marked on the map the location of all hardware stores that could reasonably be expected to sell chain, which were located within a reasonable walking dis-tance of the house.

He would, he decided, hurry home after work, leave the lunchtime purchases just inside the door, and see how much chain he could acquire before he really got hungry, and the headaches would come back, and he would have to eat.

At twenty-five minutes past one o'clock, Mrs. Antoinette Marie Wolinski Schermer tele-phoned to Mr. Ricco Baltazari at the Ristorante Alfredo and informed him that Corporal Vito Lanza had just left her apartment.

"Jesus Christ! I told you to keep him there!"

"Don't snap at me, Ricco, I did everything I could. He said he had to go by his house and see the plumbers."

"I didn't mean to snap at you, baby," Mr. Baltazari said, sounding very contrite. "But this was important. This was business. You sure he went to his house?"

"I'm not sure, that's what he said."

"Okay, I'll get back to you."

Mr. Baltazari was thoughtfully drumming his fingers on his desk, trying to phrase how he could most safely report this latest development to Mr. S., when there was a knock at the door.

"What?"

"Mr. Baltazari, it's Tommy Dolbare."

Mr. Baltazari jumped up and went to the door and jerked it open.

"I got this envelope for you," Tommy said.

Mr. Baltazari snatched the extended envelope from Mr. Dolbare's hand and looked into it.

"Where the fuck have you been, asshole?" he inquired.

"I had a wreck. I got forced off the road," Tommy said, hoping that he sounded sincere and credible.

"Get the fuck out of here," Mr. Baltazari said, and closed the door in Mr. Dolbare's face.

Mr. Baltazari then telephoned Mr. S.'s home. Mr. Gian-Carlo Rosselli answered the telephone.

"I got those financial documents Mr. S. was interested in," Mr. Baltazari reported. "They just this minute got here. Our friend's guy got in a wreck on the way down. Or so he said."

"Fuck!" Mr. Rosselli said.

"I just talked to the broad. She says our other friend just left there to go home, to talk to the plumbers."

"She was supposed to keep him there," Mr. Rosselli said.

"She said she couldn't."

"I'll get back to you, Ricco," Mr. Rosselli said, and hung up.

"That was Ricco," Mr. Rosselli said to Mr. Savarese, who was reading *The Wall Street Journal.* He waited until Mr. S. lowered the newspaper. "He's got the markers. That bimbo of his called him and said that the cop left her place; he had to go to his house and talk to the plumbers. What do you want me to do?"

Mr. Savarese, after a moment, asked, "Did he say why it took so long to get the markers?"

"He said something about Anthony Cagliari's guy . . ."

"Clark," Mr. Savarese interrupted. "If Anthony wants to call himself Clark, we should respect that."

". . . Anthony's guy getting in a wreck on the way down from the Poconos."

"This was important. I told Ricco to tell Anthony it was important. Either Ricco didn't do that, or he didn't make it clear to Anthony. Otherwise Anthony would have brought those markers himself."

"You're right."

"Maybe you had better say something to Ricco," Mr. Savarese said. "When things are important, they're important."

"I'll do that, Mr. S. Right now, if you want."

"What I want you to do right now is go get the markers from Ricco. Take the photographs and give them to Paulo. You know where this cop lives?"

"Yes."

"I don't know what this business with the plumbers is," Mr. Savarese said. "If possible, without attracting attention, you and Paulo try to have a talk with the cop. But I don't want a fuss in the neighborhood, you understand?"

"I understand, Mr. S."

"You tell Paulo I said that. You tell him I said it would have been better if you could have talked to the cop in the girl's apartment. But sometimes things happen. Anthony's driver had a wreck; the cop's toilet is stopped up. It's not the end of the world. If you can't talk to him at his house, it might even be *better* if Paulo and you talked to him at this woman's apartment. Use your best judgment, Gian-Carlo. Just make sure that we get what we're after."

"I'll do my best, Mr. S."

Mr. Savarese nodded and raised *The Wall Street Journal* from his lap and resumed reading it.

"Ricco," Mr. Rosselli said to Mr. Baltazari when he answered the telephone. "What I want you to be doing is standing on the sidewalk in ten minutes with those things in your hand, so I don't have to waste my time coming in there and getting them, you understand?"

"Right," Mr. Baltazari said. "I'll be waiting for you."

"There's a new Cadillac parking," Sergeant Bill Sanders said to Officer Howard Hansen. "Is that our guy?"

Hansen consulted a notebook, stuck into which was a photograph of Corporal Vito Lanza.

"Yeah, that's him."

"If I was dirty, and lived in this neighborhood," Sergeant Sanders said, "I think I would take what that Cadillac cost and move out of this neighborhood."

"But then you wouldn't be able to impress the neighbors with your new Caddy," Hansen said. "Why be dirty if you can't impress your neighbors?"

"Did you hear what this guy is supposed to have done? I mean, anything besides he may be taking stuff out of the airport?"

"Olsen said that Peter Wohl was in the chief's office first thing this morning. He had the kid—he just made detective, by the way—that got himself shot by the Islamic Liberation Army, Payne, and some little Puerto Rican with him. I worked with Wohl on the job where he put Judge Findermann away. He does not go off half-cocked."

"The little Puerto Rican was a cop?"

"I think he was the guy, one of the guys, who got the junkie who shot Captain Dutch Moffitt."

Sanders nodded.

"You think to bring the camera from the car?"

Hansen nodded, and patted his breast pocket.

"Just in case we lose this guy when he leaves, I think you'd better take his picture."

Hansen nodded again.

———

"There's not *a* plumber," Mr. Paulo Cassandro said, looking out the back window of his Jaguar as it moved slowly down the 400 block of Ritner Street, "there's a whole fucking army of them."

"These houses is old; the pipes wear out," Mr. Rosselli replied absently.

On the way here, Mr. Cassandro had given some thought to how he was going to handle the situation if the place was full of plumbers, or Lanza's mother, or whatever. He had what, after some reflection, seemed to be a pretty good idea.

Starting with the bill of sale for the Cadillac, all the paperwork involved in dealing with the cop had been Xeroxed. It was the businesslike thing to do, in case something should get lost, or fucked up, or whatever. Including the bill for the comped room at the Oaks and Pines, and the markers, both the ones he'd paid, and the ones he'd just signed.

The thing they had to do now was make the cop nervous. He thought he had figured out just how to do that.

I will just go in the cop's house, and hand him the markers from last night. And tell him I want to talk to him, and why don't you let me buy you a drink when you get off work, say in the bar in the Warwick. He probably won't come, he wants to bang the broad, but he will wonder all fucking day what getting handed the markers is all about, and what I want to talk about. And if he don't show up at the Warwick by say one o'clock, I know where to find the fucker. Rosselli and I will go to the broad's apartment.

"Let me out of the car, Jimmy," Mr. Cassandro said to his driver, "and then drive around the block until I come out."

"You don't want me to come with you?" Mr. Rosselli asked.

"I want you to drive around the block with Jimmy until I come out."

"You will never believe who I just got a picture of getting out of a Jaguar and walking toward Lanza's house," Officer Howard Hansen said softly as he returned to the bar where Sergeant Bill Sanders was watching a quiz program on the television.

"Who?"

"Paulo Cassandro."

"You sure?" Sergeant Sanders asked.

Hansen nodded.

"And, unless I'm mistaken, the guy driving the Jaguar was Jimmy Gnesci, 'Jimmy the Knees,' and—what the hell is his name?—*Gian-Carlo* Rosselli was in the back seat with Cassandro."

"You get his picture, *their pictures* too?"

Hansen nodded.

"This is getting interesting," Sanders said.

"I told you, I've been on the job with Wohl. He don't go off half-cocked."

The fucking plumbers had just told Vita Lanza that it would be at least three days until there was cold water to flush the toilets, and probably a day more until there was hot water and he could take a bath and shave, when he heard somebody call, "Yo, Vito! You in here?" upstairs at the front door.

He went up the stairs and there was Paulo Cassandro standing there, just inside the open door. He was smiling.

"What the hell have you got going here, Vito? You really need all these plumbers?"

"Well, hello. How are you?"

Paulo Cassandro was the last person Vito expected to see inside his house, and for a moment there was concern that Paulo was there about the markers he had signed at the Oaks and Pines.

He shook Cassandro's hand.

"You wouldn't believe what they're charging me," Vito said.

"I would believe. There's only two kinds of plumbers, good expensive plumbers and bad expensive plumbers. I've been through this."

"So what can I do for you, Mr. Cassandro?"

"You can call me 'Paulo' for one thing," Cassandro said. "I just happened to be in the neighborhood, I was down by Veterans' Stadium, and I had these, and I thought, what the hell, I'll see if Vito's home and give them to him."

He handed Vito the markers, four thousand dollars' worth of markers, that he had signed early that morning at Oaks and Pines.

"To tell you the truth, Paulo, until I can get to the bank, I can't cover these."

I don't have anywhere near enough money in the bank to cover those markers. My fucking luck has been really bad!

"Did I ask for money? I know you're good for them. Take care of them at your convenience. But I had them, and I figured, what the hell, why carry them around and maybe lose them. You know what I mean?"

"Absolutely."

"And we know where you live, right?"

"Yeah."

"So I'll see you around, Vito," Paulo said, and started to leave, and then, as if it was a thought that had suddenly occurred to him, turned back to Vito. "What time do you get off?"

"Eleven," Vito said.

What the hell does he want to know that for?

"That's what I thought," Paulo said. "Hey, Vito. We're all going to be at the bar at the Warwick a little after midnight. Why don't you come by, and we'll have a shooter or two?"

"Jees, that's nice, but when I get off work, I'm kind of beat. And I went up to the Poconos last night. I think I'm just going to tuck it in tonight. Let me have a raincheck."

"Absolutely. I understand. But if you change your mind, the Warwick Bar. On the house. We like to take care of our good customers."

Paulo pinched Vito in a friendly manner on the arm, smiled warmly at him, and walked out of his house.

He stood on the curb for almost five minutes until his Jaguar came around the block and pulled to the curb.

The relationship between the Federal Bureau of Alcohol, Tobacco and Firearms and local law enforcement agencies has rarely been a glowing example of intergovernmental cooperation.

This is not a new development, but goes back to the earliest days of the Republic when Secretary of the Treasury Alexander Hamilton convinced the Congress to pass a tax on distilled spirits. Some of the very first federal revenue officers were tarred and feathered when they tried to collect the tax, more than once as local sheriffs and constables stood by looking in the opposite direction.

In July 1794, five hundred armed men attacked the home of General John Neville, the regional tax collector for Pennsylvania, and burned it to the ground. Since local law enforcement officers seemed more than reluctant to arrest the arsonists, President George Washington was forced to mobilize the militia in Virginia, Maryland, New Jersey, and Pennsylvania to put the Whiskey Rebellion down.

During Prohibition, the New Jersey Pine Barrens served both as a convenient place to conceal illegally imported intoxicants from the federal government, prior to shipment to Philadelphia and New York, and as a place to manufacture distilled spirits far from prying eyes. And again, local law enforcement officers did not enforce the liquor laws with what the federal government considered appropriate enthusiasm. Part of this was probably because most cops and deputy sheriffs both liked a little nip themselves and thought Prohibition was insane, and part was because, it has been alleged, the makers of illegally distilled intoxicants were prone to make generous gifts, either in cash or in kind, to the law enforcement community as a token of their respect and admiration.

Even with the repeal of Prohibition the problem did not go away. High-quality, locally distilled corn whiskey, or grain neutral spirits, it was learned, could be liberally mixed with fully taxed bourbon, blended whiskey, gin, and vodka and most people in Atlantic City bars and saloons could not tell the difference. Except the bartenders and tavern keepers, who could get a gallon or more of untaxed spirits for the price of a quart of the same with a federal tax stamp affixed to the neck of the bottle.

And the illegal distillers still had enough of a profit to be able to comfortably maintain their now traditional generosity toward the local law enforcement community.

While the local law enforcement community did not actively assist the moonshine makers in their illegal enterprise, neither did they drop their other law enforcement obligations to rush to the assistance of what had become the Bureau of Alcohol, Tobacco and Firearms in their relentless pursuit of illegal stills.

It boiled down to a definition of crime. If they learned that someone was smuggling firearms to Latin America, the locals would be as cooperative as could be desired. And since the illegal movement of cigarettes from North Carolina, where they were made and hardly taxed at all, to Atlantic City, where they were heavily taxed by both the state and city, cut into New Jersey's tax revenues, the locals were again as cooperative as could be expected in helping to stamp out this sort of crime.

And if they happened to walk into a still in the Pine Barrens, the operator, if he could be found, would of course be hauled before the bar of justice. It was simply that other aspects of law enforcement normally precluded a vigorous prosecution of illegal distilling.

Additionally, there was—there is—a certain resentment in the local law enforcement community toward neatly dressed young men who had joined ATF right out of college, at a starting salary that almost invariably greatly exceeded that of, for example, a deputy sheriff who had been on the job ten years.

Whatever else may be said about them, ATF agents are not stupid. They know that they need the support of the local law enforcement community more than it needs theirs. They are taught to be grateful for that support, and made aware that it would be very foolish indeed to make impolitic allegations, much less investigations.

When Special Agent C. V. Glynes, of the Atlantic City office of the Bureau of Alcohol, Tobacco and Firearms, making a routine call, just to keep in touch, walked into the Sheriff's Department in the basement of the county courthouse, he knew very well that if he was going to leave with any information he had not previously had, it would be volunteered by either the sheriff himself, or one of his deputies, and not the result of any investigative genius he might demonstrate.

He waved a friendly greeting at the sheriff, behind his glass-walled office, and then bought a Coca-Cola from the machine against the wall.

He studied the bulletin board, which was more devoted to lawn mowers, mixed collie and Labrador puppies, washing machines and other household products for sale, than to criminal matters until the sheriff, having decided he had made the fed wait long enough, waved him into his office.

"Good morning, Sheriff," Special Agent Glynes said.

"How are you, Glynes? I like your suit."

"There was a going-out-of-business sale, Machman's, on the Boardwalk? Fifty percent off. I got two of them for a hundred and twenty bucks each."

The sheriff leaned forward and felt the material.

"That's the real stuff. None of that plastic shit."

"Yeah. And I got some shirts too, one hundred percent cotton Arrow. Fifty percent off."

"Anything special on your mind?"

Glynes shook his head, no.

"Just passing through. I thought I'd stop in and ask about Dan Springs. How is he?"

"He must have really hit his steering wheel. If he hadn't been wearing his seat belt, he'd probably have killed himself. He's got three cracked ribs. He said it doesn't hurt except when he breathes."

Glynes chuckled. "What happened?"

"He was out in the Barrens," the sheriff said, "and he run over something. Blew his right front tire, run off the road, and slammed into a tree."

"Jesus!"

The sheriff raised his voice and called, "Jerry!"

A uniformed deputy put his head in the office.

"Jerry, you know Mr. Glynes?"

The deputy shook his head, no.

"Revenoooooer," the sheriff said. "Don't let him catch you with any homemade beer."

"How do you do, Mr. Glynes? Jerry Resmann."

"Chuck," Special Agent Glynes said, smiling and shaking Resmann's hand firmly. "Pleased to meet you."

"Jerry, is that piece of scrap metal still on Springs's desk?" the sheriff asked.

Deputy Resmann went to the door and looked into the outer office.

"Yeah, it's there."

"Why don't you go get it, and give our visiting Revenooooer a look?"

"Right."

Resmann went into the outer office and returned and handed the twisted piece of metal to Glynes.

"Can you believe that thing?" the sheriff asked. "They found it in the wheel well, up behind that plastic sheeting, when they hauled Dan's car in. No wonder he blew his tire."

Jesus Christ! What the hell is this? That's one-eighth, maybe three-sixteenth-inch steel. And it's been in an explosion. One hell of an explosion, otherwise that link of chain wouldn't be stuck in it.

"You have any idea what this is, Sheriff?"

"It's what blew Dan's tire," the sheriff said. "A piece of junk metal. Probably fell off a truck when some asshole was dumping garbage out in the Barrens, and then Dan drove over it."

"You know, it looks as if it's been in an explosion," Glynes said.

"Why do you say that?" Resmann asked.

"Look at this link of chain stuck in it. The only way that could happen is if it struck it with great velocity."

The sheriff took the piece of metal from Glynes.

"There's burned areas too," the sheriff said. "I read one time that in a hurricane, the wind gets blowing so hard, so fast, that it'll stick pieces of straw three inches deep into a telephone pole."

Glynes took the piece of steel back and lifted it to his nose, and then, carefully, touched the edge of the burned area with his fingertip, and then looked at his fingertip. There was a black smudge. When he touched his finger to it, it smeared.

"The explosion happened recently," he said, handing the steel to the sheriff. "You can smell it, and the burned area is still moist."

The sheriff sniffed. "I'll be damned. I wonder what it is?"

"I'd like to know. I'd like to run it by our laboratory. You think I could have this for a while?"

"Would we get it back?"

"Sure."

"I know Dan would want that for a souvenir."

"I can have it back here before he comes back to work."

"What do you think it is?"

"You tell me. Have there been any industrial explosions, anything like that around here?"

The sheriff considered that for a moment, and then shook his head, no.

"Take it along with you, Chuck, if you want. But I really want it back."

"I understand."

Special Agent Glynes was halfway to Atlantic City when he pulled to the side of the road.

I don't need the goddamned laboratory to tell me that piece of metal has been involved in the detonation of high explosives. What I want to know is where it came from.

It could be nothing. But on the other hand, if somebody is blowing things up around here with high explosives, I damned sure want to know who and why.

He made a U-turn, stopped at the first bar he encountered, bought a get-well bottle of Seagram's 7-Crown for Deputy Springs, and asked for the telephone book.

He found a listing for *Springs, Daniel J.,* which was both unusual and pleased him. Most law enforcement officers, including Special Agent Glynes, did not like to have their telephone numbers in the book. It was an invitation to every wife/mother/girlfriend and male relative/acquaintance of those whom one had met, *professionally,* so to speak, to call up, usually at two A.M., the sonofabitch who put Poor Harry in jail.

He carefully wrote down Springs's number and address, but he did not telephone to inquire whether it would be convenient for him to call. It was likely that either Dan Springs or his wife would, politely, tell him that it would be inconvenient, and he was now determined to see him. If he showed up at the front door with a smile and a bottle of whiskey, it was unlikely that he would be turned away.

Glynes had been on the job nearly fifteen years. When he saw advertisements in the newspapers of colleges offering credit for practical experience, he often thought of applying. He had enough practical experience to be awarded a Ph.D., summa cum laude, in Practical Psychology.

He found Springs's house without difficulty. There was no car in the carport, which was disappointing. He thought about that a moment, then decided the thing to do was leave the whiskey bottle, with a calling card, *"Dan, Hope you're feeling better. Chuck."* That just might put Springs in a charitable frame of mind when he came back in the morning.

But he heard the sound of the television when he walked up to the door, and pushed the doorbell. Chimes sounded inside, and a few moments later a plump, comfortable-looking gray-haired woman wearing an apron opened the door.

"Mrs. Springs, I'm Chuck Glynes. I work sometimes with Dan, and I just heard what happened."

"Oh," she seemed uncomfortable.

Why is she uncomfortable? Ah ha. Dear Old Dan isn't as incapacitated as he would have the sheriff believe.

"I'm not with the Sheriff's Department, Mrs. Springs. I work for the federal government in Atlantic City. I brought something in case Dan needed something stronger than an aspirin."

"Dan went to the store for a minute," Mrs. Springs said. "My arthritis's been acting up, and I didn't think I should be driving."

"Well, maybe I can offer some of this to you."

"Come in," she said, making up her mind. "He shouldn't be long."

Deputy Springs walked into his kitchen twenty minutes later.

He's not carrying any packages. And his nose is glowing. If I were a suspicious man, I might suspect he was down at the VFW, treating his pain with a couple of shooters, not at the Acme Supermarket.

"How are you, Mr. Glynes?"

"The question, Dan, is how are you? And when did you start calling me 'Mr. Glynes'? My name is Chuck."

"Cracked some ribs," Dan said. "But it only hurts when I breathe."

Glynes laughed appreciatively.

"Doris get you something to drink, Chuck?"

"Yes, she did, thank you very much," Glynes said.

"I think I might have one myself," Springs said.

"Well, then, let's open this," Glynes said, and pushed the paper sack with the Seagram's 7-Crown across the table toward him.

"I don't know what happened," Dan Springs said, ten minutes later, as he freshened up Chuck Glynes's drink. "I'm riding down the road one second, and the next second I'm off the road, straddling a tree."

"I know what happened," Glynes said.

"You do?" Springs asked, surprised.

"Let me go out to the car a minute and I'll get it," Glynes said.

Springs walked out to the car with him. Glynes handed him the explosive-torn chunk of metal.

"You ran over that," Glynes said. "It opened your tire like an ax."

"Jesus, I wonder where that came from?"

"Well, they found it in your wheel well, up behind that rubber sheet. But I'd like to know, professionally, where it came from."

"Excuse me?"

"That piece of steel has been in an explosion, Dan. Look at that link of chain stuck in it."

"I'll be damned!"

"I'd really like to see where you had the wreck."

"Out in the Pine Barrens."

"Could you find the spot again?"

"Sure," Springs said. "But not tonight. By the time we got there, it would be dark."

"Would you feel up to going out there tomorrow?"

"I'm on sick leave."

"Well, hell, the sheriff wouldn't have to know."

"Yeah," Springs said, after a moment's thought. "I could take you out there tomorrow, I guess."

"I'd appreciate it, Dan. We like to know who's blowing what up."

"Yeah, and so would I."

Mrs. Springs insisted that Chuck stay for supper. He said he would stay only if she let him buy them dinner.

At dinner, when he said he would have to head back to Atlantic City, Mrs. Springs said there was no reason at all for him to drive all that way just to have to come back in the morning, they had a spare bedroom just going to waste. He said he wouldn't want to put her out, and she said he shouldn't be silly.

22.

"I have just had one of my profound thoughts," Officer Howard Hansen said to Sergeant Bill Sanders as they watched Corporal Vito Lanza drive his Cadillac into the area reserved for police officers on duty at the airport.

"And you're going to tell me, right?"

"I'm not saying Lanza is a nuclear physicist, but he's not really a cretin, either. . . ."

"What's a cretin?"

"A high-level moron."

"Really?"

"Take my word for it, a cretin is a high-level moron. You want to hear this or not?"

"I wouldn't miss it for the world."

"So for the sake of argument, let's say Lanza is smart enough to know that people, especially other cops, are going to ask questions about that Cadillac of his. 'Where did he get the money?' "

"So?"

"He doesn't seem to give a damn, does he?"

"Howard, what are you talking about?"

"If I were dirty and had bought a Cadillac with dirty money, I wouldn't drive it to work."

"Maybe you're smarter than Lanza."

"And maybe he inherited the money and isn't dirty, and if somebody asks him, he can say 'I got it from my mother's estate,' or something."

"And what about those Guinea gangsters we saw at his house? What were they doing, selling Girl Scout cookies?"

"If I was dirty, I think I'd be smart enough to tell the Mob to stay away from my house. And the Mob, I think, is smart enough to figure that out themselves."

Sergeant Sanders grunted, but did not reply.

After a moment, Hansen said, "Well, what do you think?"

"I think I'm going to call Swede Olsen and tell him that after Lanza bought Girl Scout cookies from Paulo Cassandro, Jimmy the Knees, and Gian-Carlo Rosselli, he went to work, and does he want us to keep sitting on him or what."

He opened the door of the Pontiac and went looking for a telephone.

Officer Paul O'Mara stuck his head in Peter Wohl's office.

"Inspector," he said, "there's a Captain Olsen on 312. You want to talk to him?"

"Paul, for your general fund of useful knowledge," Wohl replied as he reached for his telephone, "unless the commissioner is in my office, or the building's on fire, I always want to talk to Captain Olsen."

He punched the button for 312.

"How are you, Swede? What's up?"

"Inspector, I put Bill Sanders and Howard Hansen on Lanza. You know them?"

"Hansen, I do. Good cop. Smart. What about them?"

"Sanders is a sergeant. Good man. He just called from the airport. Lanza just went to work. They picked him up at his house. Before he went to work, Paulo Cassandro paid him a visit at his house."

"Vincenzo Savarese's Paulo Cassandro?" Wohl asked, and then, before Olsen could reply, went on, "We're sure about that?"

"Sanders said he went in, was inside maybe five minutes, and while he was, Gian-Carlo Rosselli and Jimmy the Knees Gnesci rode around the block in Rosselli's Jaguar."

"I suppose it's too much to hope, Swede, that we have photographs?"

"We have undeveloped film," Olsen said. "But Hansen's pretty good with a camera."

"I know. How soon can we have prints?"

"As soon as I can get it to the lab in the Roundhouse. Our lab is temporarily out of business, which is really why I called. I'm out of people, Inspector, I was hoping maybe you could help me out."

"When are you *not* going to be out of people?"

"I had the feeling this was special, and that we should have good people on it. I'll be out of *good* people until about eight o'clock tonight . . ."

"This is special," Wohl interrupted without meaning to.

". . . when I have two good people coming in. What I need between now and then is some way to get Hansen's film to the Roundhouse lab. And if possible to relieve them."

"They don't like overtime?"

"I like to change people. I don't want Lanza to remember seeing them on Ritner Street."

"Yes, of course," Wohl said, feeling more than a little stupid. "Swede, let me get right back to you. Where are you? Give me the number."

He wrote the number down, put the telephone in its cradle, and then sat there for a moment, thinking.

I need one, better two, good men from now until eight. Who's available? Jason Washington won't do. Every cop in the Department knows him. Tony Harris? Jerry O'Dowd?

He pushed himself out of his chair and walked quickly out of his office, stopping at O'Mara's desk.

"Call the duty lieutenant and find out what kind of an unmarked car we have that doesn't look like an unmarked car," he ordered, and then walked out without further explanation.

He walked quickly down the corridor to the door of the Special Investigations Section and pushed it open. Detective Tony Harris was there, and so were Sergeant Jerry O'Dowd, Officer Tiny Lewis, and Detective Matthew M. Payne. Only Lewis was in uniform.

"Tony," Wohl began without preliminaries, "do you know a cop named Vito Lanza, now a corporal at the airport?"

"Yeah, I know him. He's sort of an asshole."

"Damn! Jerry?"

"No," O'Dowd said, after a moment to think it over. "I don't think so."

"What's going on around here?" Wohl asked.

"We're waiting for the phone to ring," Matt Payne said.

"I'm beginning to suspect the mad bomber is not going to call," Tony Harris said.

"Spare me the sarcasm, please," Wohl snapped.

"Sorry," Harris said, sounding more or less contrite.

"I need somebody to surveil Lanza from right now until about eight," Wohl said. "O'Dowd, I think you're elected."

"Yes, sir."

"You know a Sergeant Sanders? Officer Hansen?"

"Both."

"Okay. They're sitting on Lanza, who went on duty at three at the airport. I presume they're parked someplace where they can watch Lanza's car."

"Yes, sir."

"I've got O'Mara looking for an unmarked car for you."

"I've got my car here, Inspector, if that would help."

"No. You might have to follow this guy, and you'd need a radio."

"Let him take mine," Harris said.

You have tried, Detective Harris, and succeeded in making amends, for letting your loose mouth express your dissatisfaction for being here, instead of in Homicide.

"Good idea. Thank you, Tony," Wohl said. "How are you with a camera, O'Dowd?"

"I can work one."

"Take Larsen's camera from him," Wohl ordered. "Payne, you follow him down there. On the way, unless there's some around here, get some film. I'm sure it's 35mm. Sergeant O'Dowd will have the rolls of film Hansen has shot. Take them to the Roundhouse, have them developed and printed. Four copies, five by seven. Right then. If they give you any trouble, call me. Take a look at the pictures. See if you recognize anybody from your trip to the Poconos. If you do, call me. In fact, call me in any case. Then take three copies of the prints to Captain Olsen, in Internal Affairs. Bring the fourth set out here, and leave them on my desk."

"Yes, sir."

"Could I help, sir?" Officer Lewis asked.

"Looking for a little overtime, Tiny? Or are you bored waiting for the phone to ring?"

The moment the words were out of his mouth, Wohl regretted them, and wondered why he had snapped at Lewis.

"More the bored than the overtime, sir," Tiny Lewis said. There was a hurt tone in his voice.

"When do you knock off here?"

"Five, sir."

"When your replacement comes, change into civilian clothing, and then go see if you can make yourself useful to Sergeant O'Dowd. You don't know Corporal Lanza, do you?"

"No, sir."

"Tony, you sit on the phone. I'll have the duty lieutenant send somebody to help you. Or maybe O'Mara?"

"O'Mara would be fine," Harris said.

Wohl had another thought.

"Let me throw some names at you two," he said, nodding at O'Dowd and Lewis. "Do you know Paulo Cassandro, Gian-Carlo Rosselli, or Jimmy the Knees Gnesci?"

Tiny Lewis shook his head, no, and looked embarrassed.

"Cassandro, sure," O'Dowd said. "The other two, no."

"Five sets of prints, Matt," Wohl ordered. "The first three to Captain Olsen, then take a set to the airport and give them to Sergeant O'Dowd, and then bring the last set here. Got it?"

"Yes, sir."

"We have," Wohl explained, "photographs of these three going into Corporal Lanza's house. If he leaves the airport before you're relieved, follow him. See if he sees these guys again."

"And if he does?"

"Try to get a picture of them together. But not if there is any chance he'll see you. Pictures would be nice, but we already have some. Understand?"

"Yes, sir."

"Get going, this is important. You think you can find Sergeant Sanders?"

"It would be helpful to know where he is."

"Near where Lanza would park his car. If you can't find him, call me."

"Yes, sir."

For some reason, the words to "Sweet Lorraine" had been running through Marion Claude Wheatley's mind all afternoon, to the point of interfering with his concentration.

Something like that rarely happened. He often thought that if there was one personal characteristic responsible for his success, it was his ability to concentrate on the intellectual task before him.

This was true, he had reflected, not only at First Pennsylvania Bank & Trust, but had also been true earlier on, at the University of Pennsylvania, and even in Officer Candidate School in the Army. When he put his mind to something, he was able to shut everything else out, from the noises and incredibly terrible music in his barracks, to the normal distractions, visual and audible, one encountered in an office environment.

He had been working on a projection of how increasing production costs in the anthracite fields, coupled with decreased demand (which would negatively affect prices to an unknown degree), would, in turn, affect return on capital investment (and thus stock prices) in a range of time frames. (One year, two years, five years, and ten years.)

It was the sort of thing he was not only very good at, but really enjoyed doing, because of the variable factors involved. Normally, working on something like this, nothing short of an earthquake or a nuclear attack could distract him.

But "Sweet Lorraine" kept coming into his mind. For that matter, into his voice. He several times caught himself humming the melody.

He had no particular feelings regarding the melody. He neither actively disliked it, nor regarded it as a classic popular musical work.

That left, of course, the possibility that the Lord was sending him a message. He considered that possibility several times, and could make no sense of it.

He thought he had it once; it might be the name of someone close to the Vice President, but that wasn't it. He called the Free Public Library and a research librarian told him the Vice President's wife's name was Sally. And she couldn't help him when he asked if she happened to know if there was someone on the Vice President's staff named Lorraine, maybe his secretary.

She had the secretary's name, Patricia, and she said, as far as she could tell, everyone else on the Vice President's staff was a male.

That left only one possibility, presuming that it was not simply an aberration, that the Lord was alerting him to something that would happen later, something that, when he saw it, would answer the mystery.

Once he had come to that analysis, he had been able to return to *A Projection of Anthracite Production Economic Considerations* without having his concentration disrupted. He made good progress, and was very nearly finished when the sounds of people getting ready to go home broke into his concentration again.

Marion was so close to being finished with the *One-Year Time Frame* that he considered staying and finishing it, but finally decided against that. He knew himself well enough to know that if he finished the *One-Year* he would be tempted to just keep going.

The priority, of course, was to get the things on the list not yet acquired. The list was just about complete. All he needed now was the chain and two more AWOL bags. He would get the chain today, and the remaining two AWOL bags tomorrow. It would not be wise to return to the Super Drugstore at all, and certainly not so soon.

First the chain and then the AWOL bags. Perhaps, when he went shopping for the chain, he would see another store that had AWOL bags on sale. Perhaps even bags that met the metal zipper and other criteria, but which at least would not have *Souvenir of Someplace* painted on them, and with a little bit of luck would be of a different design.

Marion waited, of course, until the office herd had thundered out and ridden the cattle cars down to the lobby before putting the *A Projection of Anthracite Production Economic Considerations* material back into its folders and then into his desk file.

When he came out onto Broad Street, he had an interesting thought. Instead of looking for a hardware store in the streets down toward the river, he would get on a bus and ride up North Broad Street.

He vaguely remembered seeing a decent-looking hardware store in a row of shops on the west side of North Broad Street, five or six blocks north of the North Philadelphia Station of the Pennsylvania Railroad.

He started to walk up South Broad Street toward City Hall. As he approached it, he decided he would let the Lord decide, by His timing of the traffic lights that controlled the counterclockwise movement of vehicular traffic around City Hall, whether He wanted him to go to North Broad Street by walking through the City Hall passageways, or if He preferred that Marion turn right at Market Street and walk the long way around, on the sidewalk past John Wanamakers, et cetera.

The Lord apparently wanted him to get to North Broad Street quickly, for just as he approached Market Street, the vehicular light turned to red, the pedestrian light turned to green, and without breaking stride he was able to cross the street and enter the archway of City Hall.

The same thing happened as he emerged from the north archway. The vehicular light turned to red and the pedestrian to green just as he reached the street, and he was again able to keep walking without stopping at all.

And then as he reached the bus stop at the next corner, a bus was just swallowing the last of the line of people who had been waiting for it. Marion climbed aboard without having to break pace.

He thought for a moment that the Lord had wanted him to board this particular bus, but then decided that wasn't true. There was only one empty seat, and that was on the right side of the bus. If the Lord had wanted him to get on this bus, He would have saved him a seat on the left side, from which he could look for the hardware store he remembered seeing somewhere past the North Philadelphia Station.

Perhaps, Marion thought, *by the time we get to the North Philadelphia Station, someone now sitting on the left side will have gotten off the bus and I can move over.*

Sometime later, Marion wasn't sure how much later, because he had been thinking that he had forgotten to factor into *A Projection of Anthracite Production Economic Considerations* the cost of new federal government mine safety regulations, he became aware that the bus was not moving.

He looked out the window. They were stopped at Ridge Avenue. The bus was now filled with mutterings. His fellow passengers were growing angry that the bus wasn't moving. Marion raised himself in his seat and tried to look out the windshield. There was a long line of cars in front of the bus, but he could see nothing that explained why they weren't moving.

Marion glanced out the side window again, and saw that they were stopped in front of the hotel that belonged to that rather amusing, viewed in one light, and rather pathetic, viewed in another, religious sect founded by a Philadelphia black man who called himself Father Divine.

Father Divine had convinced an amazing number of colored people, and even some white people, that he had been anointed by the Lord to bring them out of their misery, spiritual and temporal, primarily by turning over all of their assets to him.

His wife, Marion recalled, had been a white woman, and she had lived rather well as the mate of Father Divine. They were supposed to own property and businesses all over Philadelphia. And New York too. And Washington, D.C.

He wondered if Mrs. Father Divine was still living well, now that Father Divine had been called to Heaven.

I wonder what Father Divine said to Saint Peter?

There really had been a lot of money. The hotel, before they bought it, with cash, closed the bar, and renamed it, after Mrs. Divine, of course, the Divine Lorraine *Hotel, had been a rather decent hotel.*

The Divine Lorraine *Hotel!*

The bus began to move.

Marion broke out in a sweat.

When the bus stopped in front of the old Reading Railroad Terminal at Lehigh Avenue, not far at all from the Pennsylvania Railroad's North Philadelphia Station, the four people sitting in the two seats to the left of Marion all got up at once and exited the bus.

Marion quickly moved across the aisle. The sweating had stopped, but it left him feeling clammy and uncomfortable.

There is no question that the Lord wants me to do something in connection with the Divine Lorraine Hotel. But what?

Three blocks past the North Philadelphia Station, Marion saw the hardware store he thought he remembered. And it was even larger, and thus more likely to carry what he needed to complete the list, than he had remembered.

He got off the bus at the next stop, crossed North Broad Street, and walked back toward the hardware store.

He passed a Super Discount Store, the windows of which were emblazoned with huge signs reading SALE!

And in one of the windows, under a SALE! sign with an arrow pointing downward there was a stack of AWOL bags. These were not only of better quality than the three he had bought on Market Street, but of different design. Their straps went completely around the bag. They had metal zippers, and they did not have *Souvenir of Asbury Park, N.J.,* and a fish leaping out of the surf gaudily painted on their sides.

Marion went into the Super Discount Store and bought two of the AWOL bags, one in a rather nice shade of dark blue, the other in sort of a rusty brown. He put the blue one inside the brown one, and thought that he would have plenty of space left over for the chain.

The clerk in the hardware store told Marion that they stocked a wide variety of chains, and if Marion would tell him what he wanted the chain for, six lengths each twenty-two inches long, they could make sure he was getting the right thing.

Marion was fairly certain that the man was more garrulous than suspicious, but he could not, of course, tell him what he really wanted the chain for. He had considered this sort of question coming up, of course, and was ready for him. He told the clerk that he had to lock six steel casement windows, and that he would also need six padlocks.

The clerk told him that not only did the store stock a wide array of padlocks, but that he thought it would be possible to furnish six locks all of which would operate with the same key.

Marion told him that would be unnecessary but nice.

The clerk was similarly garrulous when Marion informed him that he would need both duct and electrical tape. Marion was astonished at the wide selection available, and made his choice by selecting the most expensive tapes he was shown. That would, he believed, make the clerk happy.

Marion was not annoyed with the clerk. Quite to the contrary. In this day and age it was a pleasant surprise to find a clerk who seemed genuinely interested in pleasing the customer.

He paid for the tape and the chain, and put it all in the AWOL bag, shook the clerk's hand, thanked him for his courtesy, and went back out onto Broad Street.

That completed acquisition of the items on the list.

But now there was a new problem. The Divine Lorraine Hotel.

Was that simply coincidence? Thinking of "Sweet Lorraine" to the point of distraction all day? Or is the Lord telling me something?

Marion stood on the curb for a minute or two, considering that problem.

A taxicab, thinking he was seeking a ride, pulled to the curb.

Marion was on the verge of waving it away, when he suddenly had a thought, almost as if the Lord had put it there.

There were half a dozen ways to get from where I stand to the house. Only one of them leads back past the Divine Lorraine Hotel. If the Lord has nothing in mind vis-à-vis the Divine Lorraine Hotel, the chances are five, or more, out of six that the taxi driver will elect not to pass in front of the Divine Lorraine Hotel. On the other hand, if the taxi driver elects to drive past the Divine Lorraine Hotel, the odds that the Lord wishes me to do something involving the hotel would certainly be on the order of six to one.

Marion got in the taxicab and gave him his address.

The driver headed right down North Broad Street. When they reached Ridge Avenue, the traffic light was red. Marion looked out the window at the Divine Lorraine Hotel.

When the traffic light turned green, and the taxi driver put his foot to the accelerator, the car stalled.

Marion broke out in another sweat.

He looked at the Divine Lorraine Hotel again. A very large colored lady with some kind of white napkin or something wrapped around her head and neck smiled at him.

Marion smiled back.

A taxi pulled up in front of the hotel, and a man got out and carried suitcases toward the door.

It is a hotel still, I forgot that. A hotel that caters, apparently, to those who believe in Father Divine, whom they believe is either God, or close to Him. It would follow, therefore, that a Christian of that persuasion would stay at the Divine Lorraine Hotel.

Any Christian! That's what it is, of course. How could I have been so stupid? The Lord wants me to go there. But why? It is not mine to question the Lord, but it would help me carry out His will if I knew what He wanted of me.

The answer came: *I have probably made an error somewhere, and the Secret Service is looking for me. Or will be looking for me at the house after I carry out the Lord's will and disintegrate the Vice President.*

No one would think of looking for Marion Claude Wheatley in the Divine Lorraine Hotel.

Thank you, Lord! Forgive me for taking so long to understand what it was You wanted of me.

The taxi driver got the motor running again.

Marion leaned back against the cushions. He felt euphoric.

I am in the Lord's hands. I walk through the valley of the shadow of death, I shall fear no evil, for Thou art with me.

Matt's Volkswagen started with difficulty, and he made the immediate decision to swap cars at his apartment as his first order of business. The one thing he did not need was to have the Bug die on him when he was running errands for Peter Wohl.

The Bug performed flawlessly on the way from the Schoolhouse to the basement garage of his apartment and he wondered if swapping cars was now such a good idea. Silver Porsche 911s attracted attention; battered Bugs did not.

He walked out of the basement garage, waving at the rent-a-cop on duty, went to the convenience store around the corner and bought five rolls of 36-exposure ASA 200 Kodak black-and-white film, and went back to the garage.

The Porsche was conspicuous, but on the other hand, people didn't think of cops when they saw one. And the Bug might just have been teasing me when it ran so well on the way down here.

He drove out to the airport, and found Sergeant Jerry O'Dowd with less trouble than he thought he would have. O'Dowd gave him a roll of film, then told him to wait a second, and removed the film from the camera and gave him that too.

"I haven't taken any pictures," O'Dowd said. "But I forgot to ask Hansen if he had."

"I'll be back as soon as I can."

O'Dowd handed him several bills.

"How about stopping at a Colonel Sanders and getting my supper? You better get something for Lewis too."

"Sergeant, you don't make enough money to feed Tiny," Matt said.

He drove to the Roundhouse and for once found a parking spot without trouble. And there was no trouble getting the film souped and printed right away, either.

"Inspector Wohl called," the civilian in charge behind the counter said. "It'll take me forty-five minutes, if you have something else to do."

There was no fried chicken place anywhere near the Roundhouse that Matt could think of. And Jerry O'Dowd had specified fried chicken. But on the other hand, Jerry was a gentleman of taste, and as such would certainly prefer Chinese to fried chicken, no matter how many spices and flavors it was coated with.

He walked to Chinatown, bought a Family Dinner For Four, and went back to the photo laboratory.

The prints were already coming off the large, polished stainless-steel dryer. Matt looked at all of them. He recognized no one but Corporal Vito Lanza, and decided that he would not have recognized Lanza in uniform if he didn't know who he was looking at. Corporal Lanza did not look like the guy on the airplane home from Vegas or in the back rooms of the Oaks and Pines Lodge.

He called Peter Wohl from the photo lab, first at the Schoolhouse and then at his apartment.

Wohl only grunted when he told him he recognized no one but Lanza, but then said, "Remind Sergeant O'Dowd of what I said about making sure Lanza, or anyone else, doesn't see him taking pictures."

"Yes, sir."

"I'll wait here for you, Matt," Wohl said, and hung up.

Matt delivered three sets of photographs to Captain Olsen in Internal Affairs, and then drove back to the airport. Tiny Lewis had joined O'Dowd while he had been gone, and had had the foresight to bring supper—barbecued ribs—for the both of them with him.

Tiny was not at all reluctant to add a little Chinese to his supper menu, however, and accepted half of the food Matt had brought with him.

It will not be wasted, Matt decided, as he headed for Peter Wohl's apartment in Chestnut Hill. *Wohl likes Chinese. What I should have done was get some of Tiny's ribs.*

Peter Wohl, a crisp white shirt and shaving cream behind his ears indicating he was dressed to go out, was not only not at all interested in the Chinese, but didn't even invite Matt in, much less in for a beer. He just took the envelope of photographs from Matt, muttered "thank you," and started to close the door.

"Is there anything else you need me for, sir?"

Wohl looked at him.

"I think you have made quite enough of a contribution to the Department in the last twenty-four hours for one detective, Payne. Why don't you go home? And stay there?"

He closed the door.

Matt, as well as he knew Wohl, was not sure whether Wohl was pulling his chain, or whether Wohl was still sore about his having gone to the Oaks and Pines Lodge.

Matt got back in the Porsche and drove back to Center City. He was almost at Rittenhouse Square before he thought of Evelyn.

She probably ran the answering machine out of tape, he thought as he drove into the underground garage. *What the* hell *am I going to do about her?*

The red light on the answering machine was blinking, and when he played the tape, there had been thirteen callers who had elected not to leave their names, plus two calls from, of all people, Amelia Payne, M.D., who sounded, he thought, as if she had just sat on a nail, and demanded that he call her the moment he got in.

"Screw you, Sister Mine," Matt said aloud. "I am not in the mood for you."

He carefully arranged the Chinese goldfish buckets on his coffee table, got a cold beer from the refrigerator, and sat down to his supper.

The Chinese was cold.

He carried everything to the kitchen and warmed it in the microwave, carried it back to the coffee table, and sat down again.

The doorbell sounded.

Evelyn, Jesus Christ! Well, if she's at the door, she knows I'm here. I might as well face the music.

He went to the head of the stairs and pushed the button that activated the solenoid.

His visitor came through the door.

She looked up at him and called: "You miserable sonofabitch, how could you?"

It was not Evelyn, it was Amelia Payne, M.D.

"That would depend on which of my many mortal sins you have in mind. Come on in, Amy. Soup's on, and it's always a joy to see you."

"I have been angry with you before," Amy said as she reached the top stair. "And disgusted, but this really is despicable."

He was concerned.

Amy is really angry, and that means she thinks I have done something really despicable. But I haven't.

"Are you going to tell me what you're talking about?"

The telephone rang. Without thinking, he picked it up.

"Hello?"

"Hello, Matt," Evelyn said.

"I can't talk to you right now. Let me call you back."

"But you won't, will you?" Evelyn said, her voice loaded with hurt, and then she hung up.

"Jesus!" Matt said. He looked at Amy. "How about an egg roll?"

"What I'm talking about, Matt," Amy said, back in control of her temper, "is you going to bed with Penny."

Jesus Christ! How did she hear about that? The answer to that, obviously, is that Penny told her. Patients tell their psychiatrists everything.

"What in the world were you thinking?" Amy demanded.

She has shifted into her Counselor of Mankind tone of voice.

"I don't know," he said, his mouth running away with him. "What do you think about when you hop in bed with some guy?"

Amy slapped him. His vision blurred, his ears rang, and his eyes watered.

He looked at her for a moment as his eyes came back into focus.

"I should not have done that," Amy announced. But it was as if she was talking to herself.

"You're goddamned right you shouldn't have," he replied angrily. "You slap a cop, you're likely to get slapped right back."

"Is that what it was, Matt?" Amy asked. "Just Detective Payne hopping into bed with the nearest available female?"

"It happened, Amy," Matt said.

"Like hell 'it happened.' You didn't take her to dinner in the Poconos to look at the trees. Matt, she's a sick girl. And you know she is."

"You can believe this or not, but taking . . . but taking Penny to bed was the last thing I had in mind when we went up there."

"Why did you go up there, then?"

He met her eyes.

"I was working. I needed a girl to look legitimate."

She is not going to believe that, and that's all I'm going to tell her.

"Oddly enough, I believe you," Amy said, after a moment. "That doesn't make things any better, but I have the odd notion you're telling the truth."

"I am."

"She's in love with you," Amy said. "Or thinks she is, which is the same thing. The one thing she doesn't need right now is that kind of stress."

"She was behaving perfectly normal up there. I did not seduce the village idiot girl. Amy, she *wanted* to."

"And your monumental ego got in the way, right? It never occurred to you that she wanted the approval of the Rock of Gibraltar, complete to badge and gun, wanted it so desperately that she was willing to pay for it by going to bed with you?"

He did not reply.

"So what are you going to do about it?" Amy asked.

"How does suicide strike you? I could jump out the window."

"God *damn* you! Don't be flip!"

"What am I going to do about what?"

"You haven't been listening to me. How are you going to deal with this notion of hers that she's in love with you?"

"I don't know," Matt said.

"Obviously, you're not in love with her."

Now that you bring it up, I really don't know how I feel about that.

He had a sudden, painfully clear mental image of Penny naked in his arms. Of how good that felt.

"May I speak?" Matt asked.

"I'm waiting."

"I'm not going to hurt Penny. Period. I don't really think that . . . what happened . . . hurt her."

"And what are you going to do when she realizes that you don't love her?"

"I never told her I did."

"When she learns about the rest of your harem?" Amy asked, and pointed to the telephone. "Like the one who just called?"

Matt shrugged.

"I can only repeat that I will not hurt her," Matt said.

"You've already set the stage to do exactly that. She sees you as a life preserver, someone she can lean on. I don't know how she's going to react when she finds out, inevitably, that's not true. Certainly, you're not willing to assume emotional responsibility for her. And even if you were, I don't think you could handle it."

He didn't reply.

"Penny cannot be just one more notch on your gun, Matt."

"I never thought of her that way," Matt interrupted.

Amy ignored his response.

"You can't, when she becomes an inconvenience, tell Penny, the way you told that woman on the telephone just now, 'I can't talk to you right now. I'll call you right back.' She cannot take that kind of rejection, for that matter, any rejection right now. It would put her right back in The Lindens."

"Okay, you made your point."

"You're going to have to disabuse her of the notion that she's in love with you very gently."

"I told you, you made your point."

Amy glowered at him, but after a moment her face softened.

"Okay, Matt. I *have* made my point. And you're not really a sonofabitch. You're incredibly stupid and insensitive, of course, and you do most of your thinking with your penis. A typical male, I would say."

He looked at her and smiled.

"How about an egg roll?"

"You bastard!" Amy said, but she sat beside him on the couch and helped herself to an egg roll.

When she left, half an hour later, and he steeled himself to call Evelyn back, there was no answer.

He knew that if he stayed in the apartment he would get drunk, so he called Charley McFadden, and Charley's mother said he was out with his girlfriend.

He walked up Rittenhouse Square to the Rittenhouse Club, and stood at the bar and ordered a Scotch. There were some people there whom he knew vaguely, and who smiled at him. He moved down the bar and tried to join their conversation.

Before he finished his first drink, he realized that he was wholly disinterested in what they were talking about.

I look like them. I act like them. I am a product of the same socioeconomic background. But I am no longer like them. I'm a cop.

So where does that leave me with Penny?

He motioned to the bartender, so that he could sign the chit, and then he went back to his apartment.

23.

Matt woke instantly at the first ring of the telephone, and was instantly wide awake, and aware that he was in his armchair in the living room. He glanced at the clock on the mantelpiece. It was quarter past eleven.

The telephone rang a second time. On the third ring, the answering machine would kick in.

Evelyn, of course. Who else? And Jesus, I don't want to talk to her!

He picked up the telephone a half second after the answering machine began to play his message.

He spoke over it. "I'm here. Hang on until the machine does its thing."

"Did I wake you up?" Sergeant Jerry O'Dowd asked.

"Yeah, but it's all right. What's up?"

"I thought if you didn't have anything better to do, you might want to put in some unpaid overtime."

No, as a matter of fact, I would not *want to put in some overtime, paid or otherwise. But he wouldn't ask if it wasn't important.*

"Sure. What's up?"

"Not to be repeated, okay?"

"Sure."

"I was not impressed with the two guys Olsen sent to relieve us at the airport. I know one of them, and he couldn't be trusted to follow an elephant down Broad Street."

"You want me to go out there? Lanza knows me."

"I thought about that. And decided it was worth the risk. But I wouldn't drive the Porsche."

Wohl doesn't know about this. If he did, he would tell me to stay at least five miles away from the airport.

As if he had read Matt's mind, O'Dowd said, "If there is any static, from Wohl especially, I'll take the heat. With a little bit of luck, no one will ever know about this but you and me. I'll be proven wrong about the guy I know."

"You'll have to explain that."

"If I'm wrong, and I hope I will be, the guys on Lanza will be able to follow him. If they can follow him, wherever he's going, fine, we'll hang it up. But if they lose him, which wouldn't be surprising, at midnight in that area, I want to be on him. Then I'll get on the radio and tell the other guys where he is."

"You want me to go with you?"

"No. I want both of us to follow him. That would have three people following him. I don't think all three of us would lose him. But if they did, and I did, and you didn't . . ."

"Okay. Where do I meet you?"

"There's an all-night diner on South Broad right across from the stadium. You know it?"

"Uh-huh."

"Twenty minutes?"

"I'll be there."

"Thanks, Matt. I've got one of those feelings about tonight."

"Twenty minutes," Matt repeated. "You still have Tony Harris's car?"

"Yeah," O'Dowd said, and hung up.

———

At ten minutes after eleven, Corporal Vito Lanza came out of the Airport Unit, went to the parking lot, unlocked his Cadillac, and entered the sparse stream of traffic leaving the airport in the direction of Philadelphia.

So did a four-year-old Pontiac, with two men in it; a new Ford sedan with one man in it; and a twelve-year-old Volkswagen driven by Detective M. M. Payne, who brought up the tail of the line.

Corporal Lanza took Penrose Avenue, sometimes known as Bridge Avenue, which carried him across the Schuylkill River to the stoplight at the intersection of Pattison Avenue. Until this point, he had been driving in the left lane, and so had the Pontiac and the Ford. At the last moment, Corporal Lanza jerked the Cadillac into the right lane, and as the light turned red, he turned right onto Pattison Avenue.

The line of traffic closed up, and left the Pontiac and the Ford with no choice but to wait for the light to turn green again, with the hope that Corporal Lanza intended to get on South Broad Street, and that they could intercept him by following Penrose as it turns into Moyamensing Avenue, which angles to the right, and intersects South Broad Street at Oregon Avenue just north of Marconi Plaza.

Detective Payne, in the twelve-year-old Volkswagen, had not been able to get in line behind the Pontiac and the Ford in the left lane, and consequently was already in the right lane when Corporal Lanza abruptly moved into it.

He saw that the Pontiac and the Ford were trapped in the left lane, and thought, as the drivers of the Pontiac and the Ford did, that they could probably catch up with Lanza at South Broad and Oregon. But in the meantime, there was only one possible course of action for him to take, and he took it.

He drove the Bug onto the sidewalk, down the sidewalk to Pattison Avenue, and then down Pattison past the U.S. Naval Hospital and Franklin Delano Roosevelt Park to South Broad Street.

As he approached South Broad, as he saw Lanza's Cadillac turn left onto South Broad Street, the traffic light turned orange and then red. Matt ran it, which caused the horns of several automobiles to sound angrily. But he did not lose Lanza, even though Lanza was driving like hell.

Policemen tend to do that, Matt thought wryly, remembering his encounter with the State Trooper on the way to the Oaks and Pines Lodge, *secure in the knowledge they are unlikely to get a ticket from a brother officer.*

The traffic lights at first Oregon Avenue and then Snyder Avenue were green, permitting the Lanza Cadillac and the Payne Volkswagen to sail through without stopping. They were stopped at Passyunk Avenue and South Broad Street, however, which gave Detective Payne the opportunity to search in vain in his rearview mirror for either a Ford or a Pontiac.

Corporal Lanza turned left at the intersection of South Broad and Spruce Streets, and then wove his way around to the Penn-Services Parking garage, which he entered.

Detective Payne was familiar with the Penn-Services Parking garage, which was around the corner from the Bellvue-Stratford Hotel and not far from his apartment and the Union League Club. It was in the Penn-Services Parking garage that Mr. Anthony "Tony the Zee" DeZego had met his untimely end at the hand of assassin or assassins unknown. Where Matt found Miss Penelope Detweiler lying in a pool of her own blood.

Matt drove around the block until he saw Corporal Lanza come out of the building. Lanza did not look at the Volkswagen as it passed him.

Matt parked the Volkswagen illegally in an alley and ran down the alley and saw Lanza crossing a street. He followed him as discreetly as he could, very much afraid that Lanza would sense his presence and turn around.

But he didn't. He walked purposefully down a street and entered an apartment building. Matt looked around for a pay telephone but couldn't see one.

He backtracked to the next block and found a tavern. He went inside, went to the phone booth, and searched his pockets futilely for coins. The bartender was visibly reluctant to make change for someone who didn't even buy a lousy beer, but finally came through.

Matt called Police Radio and asked the dispatcher to pass to William Five (Harris's radio call sign) his location.

Sergeant Jerry O'Dowd, in Tony Harris's Ford, pulled up in front of the tavern less than ten minutes later. Before he was completely out of the car, the Pontiac pulled up behind him, and two men Matt had never seen before got out of it.

"Lanza's in an apartment around the corner," Matt said to O'Dowd.

"Good man," O'Dowd said.

"Until you called me on the radio, O'Dowd, I didn't know you were in on this," one of the two men from the Pontiac said. He pointed at Matt. "Or him. He works for you?"

"Excuse me," O'Dowd said politely. "Sergeant Framm, Detective Pillare, this is Detective Payne."

Both men shook Matt's hand.

"It's a good thing we were, wouldn't you say, Framm?" O'Dowd asked. "You lost Lanza before you got to the Naval Hospital."

There was no doubt in Matt's mind that Sergeant Framm was the man O'Dowd would not trust to follow an elephant down Broad Street.

"I got caught in traffic . . ." Framm began.

"Nobody, Olsen or Wohl, has to know about this," O'Dowd interrupted. "Payne did not lose Lanza. Everything is fine."

"Yeah, well . . . Hell, all's well that ends well, right?"

"Show us the apartment, Matt," O'Dowd said, "and then you can get some sleep."

When Matt got back to the apartment, the red light on the answering machine was flashing.

"I knew you wouldn't call me back," Evelyn's recorded voice said. "What have I done wrong, Matt?"

Mssrs. Paulo Cassandro, Joseph Fierello, Francesco Guttermo, Ricco Baltazari, and Gian-Carlo Rosselli were sitting at a table at the end of the bar off the lobby of the Hotel Warwick.

Mr. Rosselli took an appreciative sip of his Ambassador 24 Scotch, set the glass delicately down on the marble tabletop, and consulted his Rolex Oyster wristwatch.

"It's almost one," he announced, and then inquired, "How long does it take to drive from the airport?"

"At this time of night," Frankie the Gut replied, "twenty minutes, thirty tops."

"You're saying you don't think he's coming here?" Mr. Cassandro asked.

"Do you see him?" Mr. Rosselli asked. He turned to Mr. Fierello. "Why don't you call your 'niece' and see if he's there?"

"I don't have the number."

"I got it," Mr. Baltazari said, and took a gold Parker ballpoint pen from his pocket, wrote a number inside a Hotel Warwick matchbook, and handed it to Mr. Fierello.

"That's right," Mr. Rosselli said, "I forgot. You know Joe's niece, don't you, Ricco?"

Mr. Fierello and Mr. Cassandro laughed, but it was evident that Mr. Baltazari did not consider the remark amusing.

Mr. Fierello got up from the table and went to one of the pay telephones in the lobby. He was back at the table in less than two minutes.

"He's there."

Mr. Rosselli nodded. He sat thoughtfully for a moment and then nodded again. He stood up.

"Just in case, Ricco, I think you'd better give me the key to the apartment."

"You don't want me to go?"

"Paulo and I can handle it," Mr. Rosselli said. "And I wouldn't want that your jealousy should get in the way."

Mr. Cassandro and Mr. Guttermo laughed.

"Shit!" Mr. Baltazari said.

He removed a key from a ring and handed it to Mr. Rosselli.

"Take care of the bill, will you, Frankie?" Mr. Rosselli asked.

"My pleasure," Mr. Guttermo said.

Mr. Rosselli and Mr. Cassandro left the bar by the door leading directly to the street. They turned south.

"What do you want to do about the car, Carlo?" Mr. Cassandro asked.

"Leave it in the garage," Mr. Rosselli said, his tone suggesting the answer should have been evident. "Jesus, Paulo, you leave a car like a Jaguar on the street, you come back, it'll either be gone or there'll be nothing left but the windshield."

"Yeah," Mr. Cassandro agreed, his tone suggesting that he regretted raising the question.

They walked to the apartment building in which Mrs. Antoinette Marie Wolinksi Schermer maintained her residence. There was a four-year-old Pontiac parked halfway down the block on the other side of the street, but neither gentleman paid it more than cursory attention.

The interior lobby door was locked. Mr. Cassandro took a small, silver pocketknife, which was engraved with his initials, from his pocket, opened it, and slipped the blade into the lock. He then pushed open the door and held it for Mr. Rosselli to pass inside.

They took the elevator to the fifth floor, and walked down the corridor.

"Here it is," Mr. Cassandro said, stopping before the door to Apartment 5-F.

"Ring the bell," Mr. Rosselli ordered.

Sixty seconds later, Mrs. Antoinette Marie Wolinksi Schermer, wearing a bathrobe, opened the door.

"Hi, ya, Tony," Mr. Rosselli said. "Sorry to disturb you. But we have to talk to Vito. Is he here?"

Mrs. Schermer looked distinctly uncomfortable. She stepped back from the door, and waited for them to come into the apartment, then closed the door after them.

"Yo, Vito! It's Gian-Carlo Rosselli. You there?"

"He's in the bedroom," Tony Schermer said. "Give him a minute."

"Take your time, Vito," Mr. Rosselli called cheerfully. "Put your pants on."

Mr. Cassandro chuckled.

"Can I offer you something?" Tony asked.

"You got a little Scotch and water, I wouldn't say no. Paulo?"

"Yeah, me too."

Tony went into the kitchen.

Corporal Lanza came out of the bedroom, which opened onto the living room, barefoot, wearing a T-shirt and his uniform trousers.

"Hey," he greeted his callers somewhat uncomfortably. "What's up?"

"Well, when you didn't show up at the Warwick, we figured, what the hell, we'll go see him. I hope we didn't interrupt anything?"

"Nah. The reason I didn't come over there—I wanted to—was I didn't have any decent clothes to change into at the airport, and I can't be seen drinking in uniform. They'd have my ass."

"I understand," Mr. Rosselli said. "Anyway, a cop would make the customers nervous."

"Yeah."

Tony came into the room carrying two glasses.

"Can I fix you one, honey?" Tony asked.

"Why not?" Vito replied.

There were several minutes of somewhat awkward silence while Tony went into the kitchen and made Vito a drink.

"Honey, there's no reason for you to lose your beauty sleep," Mr. Rosselli said. "We're just going to sit around and have a couple of shooters. Why don't you go to bed? When we need another, Vito'll make it. Right, Vito?"

"Right," Vito said.

"Okay, then," Tony said. "If you're sure you don't mind, Vito."

"Go to bed," Vito said.

When she had closed the door behind her, Mr. Rosselli said, "I like her. She's a nice girl, Vito."

"Yeah, Tony's all right," Vito agreed.

"Vito, I'm going to tell you something, and I hope you'll believe me," Mr. Rosselli said.

"Why shouldn't I believe you?"

"You should. When I asked you to come by the Warwick for a couple of shooters, a couple of laughs, that was all I had in mind. You believe me?"

"Absolutely. And I wanted to come, and if I had the clothes, I would have. Next time."

"Right. Next time," Mr. Rosselli said. "But between the time I seen you and the plumbers . . . what's all that going to cost you, by the way?"

"A fucking bundle is what it's going to cost me. Those bastards know they've got you by the short hair."

"Yeah, I figured. Well, what the hell are you going to do? You can bitch all you want, but in the end, you end up paying, right?"

"Right."

"Like I was saying, Vito, between the time I was at your house and tonight, something has come up. We got a little problem that maybe you can help us with."

"What kind of a problem?"

"You ever hear of the guy that broke the bank at Monte Carlo?" He waited until Vito nodded, and then went on: "We had a guy between nine o'clock and nine-fifteen tonight, that goddamned near broke the bank at Oaks and Pines."

"No shit?"

"Sonofabitch was drunk, which probably had a lot to do with it, a sober guy wouldn't have bet the way he did."

"Like how?"

"He was playing roulette. He bet a hundred, split between Zero and Double Zero. He hit. That gave him eighteen hundred. He let that ride. He hit again . . ."

"Jesus!"

"That gave him, what? Thirty thousand, thirty-two thousand, something like that."

Vito thought: *Jesus Christ, that's the kind of luck I need!*

He said, "I'll be goddamned!"

"Yeah," Mr. Rosselli agreed. "At that point, right, a good gambler, a good *sober* gambler, would know it was time to quit, right?"

"You said it!"

"This guy let it ride," Mr. Rosselli said, awe in his voice.

"Don't tell me he hit again?"

"Okay, I won't tell you. With the kind of luck you've been having, it would be painful for you."

"He hit?" Vito asked incredulously.

"You understand how this works, Vito? Let me tell you how it works: A small place, like Oaks and Pines, it's not the Flamingo in Las Vegas, we have to have table limits."

"Sure," Vito said understandingly.

"On roulette, it's a thousand, unless the pit boss okays it, and then it's twenty-five hundred. Except . . ."

"Except what?"

"You can let your bet ride if you win," Mr. Rosselli explained. "You're a gambler, you understand odds. The chances of anybody hitting the same number twice in a row are enormous. And hitting it three times in a row? Forget it."

"Right," Vito said.

"The house understands the odds. And it would be bad business to tell the players when they're on a roll, that they can't bet no more, you understand?"

"I understand. Sure."

"By now, the pit boss is watching the action. They do that. That's what they're paid for, to make judgments, and to keep the games honest . . . you would be surprised, even being a cop, how many crooks try to hustle someplace like Oaks and Pines . . ."

"I wouldn't be surprised," Vito said solemnly.

"So the pit boss is watching when this guy hits three times in a row. And he knows he's not a crook. He's a rich guy, coal mines or something, from up around Hazleton. But when this guy says 'let it ride' . . . and he's got thirty-two thousand, thirty-three, something like that, the pit boss knows he can't make that kind of a decision, so he suspends play and calls Mr. Clark. You know Mr. Clark?"

Vito shook his head, no.

"Mr. Clark is the general manager of Oaks and Pines. Very fine guy. So the pit boss calls Mr. Clark, and Mr. Clark sees what's going on, and he makes his call. First of all, he knows that the odds against this guy making it four times in a row are like . . . like what? Like Paulo here getting elected pope. And this guy is a good customer, who'll be pissed if they tell him he can't make the bet. So he says, 'Okay.' Guess what?

"You won't believe it. Double Zero. It pays sixteen times the thirty-two, thirty-three big ones this guy has riding."

"Jesus!" Vito said, exhaling audibly.

"Can you believe this?" Mr. Cassandro asked rhetorically.

"So that's eighteen times thirty-three, which comes to what?"

"Five hundred big ones," Vito offered, making a rough mental calculation.

"Closer to six," Mr. Rosselli said.

One of these days, Vito thought, *I'm going to get on a roll like that.*

"So, as I understand it, this is what happened next," Mr. Rosselli went on. "Mr. Clark has just decided he cannot let this guy let six hundred big ones ride. Maybe the fucking wheel is broken. Maybe this is one of those things that happens. But Oaks and Pines can't cover a bet like that, and even if it means pissing this guy off, Mr. Clark is going to give him the money he's won . . . you understand, Vito, we have to do that. We run an absolutely honest casino operation. Mr. Clark has just decided to tell this guy he's sorry, that's all the casino can handle . . ."

"I understand."

"When the guy starts pulling all the chips toward him, Mr. Clark figures the problem has solved itself, so he don't say nothing. The biggest problem he figures he has is how to tell this guy that he don't have six hundred big ones in cash in the house, and he's going to have to wait until tomorrow . . . you understand how that works, don't you?"

"I'm not sure what you mean," Vito confessed.

"I'm surprised, you being a cop," Mr. Rosselli said. "But let me tell you. If there is a raid, by the local cops, the state cops, or the feds, and the feds are the ones that cause the trouble, they're always after gamblers when they should be out looking for terrorists . . . If there's a raid, they confiscate the equipment and whatever money they find. So naturally, you don't keep any more money around than you think you're going to need."

"Yeah," Vito said thoughtfully.

"I don't mind telling you how this works, because you're a good guy and we trust you. What we do up there is keep maybe fifty big ones in the cashier's cage. If somebody has a run of luck, and there's a big dent in the fifty, which sometimes happens, then we have more money someplace a couple of miles away. We send somebody for it. You understand?"

"Yeah, sure."

"In the other place, there's a lot of money. Two hundred big ones, at least. But not enough to pay off this character who's won six hundred big ones. You understand?"

"So what do you do?" Vito asked, genuinely curious.

"You know what the interest is on one hundred big ones a day?"

"What?"

"I asked if you ever thought how much the interest on a hundred thousand dollars is by the day?"

"No," Vito said, now sounding a little confused.

"A lot of money," Mr. Rosselli said seriously. "And on a million, it's ten times that a lot of money."

"Right."

"So keeping two hundred thousand around in a safe, without getting no interest, is one thing, it's the cost of doing business. But a million dollars is something else. You can't afford to keep a million dollars sitting around in a safe someplace not earning no interest, just because maybe someday you're going to need it. Right?"

"Right," Vito replied.

"My glass's got a hole in it or something," Mr. Rosselli said. "You suppose I could have another one of these, Vito?"

"Absolutely. Excuse me, I should have seen it was empty."

"Get Paulo one too, if you don't mind. He looks dry."

Vito took the glasses and went into the kitchen and made fresh drinks.

He wondered for a moment what Gian-Carlo Rosselli wanted from him, wondered if despite what he had said at the house about not having to worry about making the markers good, he was here to tell him that had changed and he wanted the money, but that was quickly supplanted by the excitement of thinking about this guy at Oaks and Pines who had hit four times in a row.

Jesus Christ, winning six hundred big ones in four, five minutes! If I had that kind of luck, I could get my own place somewhere, maybe in Bucks County. And have enough left over to invest, so there would be a check every month, and I wouldn't have to raise a finger.

He carried the drinks back into Tony's living room. Gian-carlo Rosselli had moved to the couch, and now had his feet up on the cocktail table. Vito, after a moment's hesitation, sat down beside him.

"I was telling you about this guy who hit his number four times in a row," Mr. Rosselli said.

"Yeah. I sure could use a little of that kind of luck."

"Yeah, you could," Mr. Rosselli said significantly. "Luck's been running against you, hasn't it? How much are you down? You mind my asking?"

"No. I don't mind. I'm down about twelve big ones."

"What the hell, it happens, but twelve thousand is a lot of money, isn't it? And what are your markers?"

"I think it's four thousand," Vito said, hoping that it looked as if it was unimportant to him, and that he had to think a moment before he could come up with the figure.

"Yeah, right. Four thousand," Mr. Rosselli said. "Pity it's not a hell of a lot more. We could call them, and pay off the million two we owe the guy at the Oaks and Pines."

"Million two?" Vito asked. "I thought you said he won six hundred big ones."

Mr. Rosselli looked as if he were surprised for a moment, and then said, "No. It's a million two."

"You said the general manager cut him off," Vito said.

"Mr. Clark. What I said, I guess I stopped before I was finished, was that Mr. Clark *was* going to cut him off, but when he started collecting his chips, he figured he didn't have to. And then the guy changed his mind . . ."

"He bet six hundred big ones?"

"No. Just the bet. Just the thirty-two thousand whatever it was. He took the nearly six hundred thousand off the table, and then said, 'One more time, just to see what happens' and bet the thirty-two thousand."

"Don't tell me he won?"

"He won. Which meant another nearly six hundred thousand we owed him. Altogether, it comes to a million two."

"And then the manager shut him off?"

"Then the guy said he was going to quit when he was ahead."

"And walked out with a million two?"

"No. He's a good customer. He knows how it works, and he sure didn't want to take a check. You pass a check for that kind of money through a bank, and the IRS is all over you."

"Yeah," Vito said. "So what did Mr. Clark do?"

"He took the croupier out in the woods and shot him in the ear," Mr. Rosselli said, smiling broadly.

Mr. Cassandro laughed appreciatively.

"Kidding, of course," Mr. Rosselli went on. "No, what Mr. Clark did was make a couple of phone calls to get the money."

"I thought you said there was only a couple of hundred big ones in the other place," Vito asked.

"There was," Mr. Rosselli replied, and then asked, "Vito, what do you know about off-shore banks?"

"Not a hell of a lot," Vito confessed.

"The thing they got going for them is their banking laws," Mr. Rosselli explained. "They don't have to tell the fucking IRS anything. How about that?"

"I heard something about that," Vito said. "Fuck the IRS."

"You said it. So what happens is that if you have to have, say, a couple of million dollars where you can get your hands on it right away, instead of a safe, where it don't earn no interest, you put it in an offshore bank, where it does. Understand?"

"Yeah," Vito said appreciatively.

"So Mr. Clark makes the telephone calls, and says he needs a million two right away to pay a winner, and it's set up. It's really no big deal, it happens all the time, not a million two, but five, six hundred big ones. Once a month, sometimes once a week. It goes the other way too, of course. Some high roller drops a bundle, and we put money *in* the offshore banks."

"Yeah, sure," Vito replied.

"But this time, we run into a little trouble," Mr. Rosselli said.

"No million two in the bank?" Vito asked with a smile.

"That's not the problem. The problem is moving the money. A million two is twelve thousand hundred-dollar bills. That's a *lot* of green paper. You can't get that much money in an envelope, and drop it in a mailbox."

Vito tried to form a mental image of twelve thousand one-hundred-dollar bills. He couldn't remember whether there were fifty or one hundred bills in one of those packages of money with the paper band around them. But either way, it was a hell of a lot of paper stacks of one-hundred-dollar bills.

"So what we have is people who carry the money for us," Mr. Rosselli said. "I guess, you're a cop, you know all about this?"

"No," Vito said honestly. "I figured it had to be something like that, but this is the first time I really heard how it works."

"It's a problem, finding the right people for the job," Mr. Rosselli said. "First of all, you don't hand a million dollars to just anybody. And then, with IRS and Customs watching—they're not stupid, they know how this is done—you can't use the same guy all the time, you understand?"

"I can see how that would work," Vito said.

"Anyway, the way it usually works, we take the money out of the bank, offshore, and give it to one of our guys, and he goes to Puerto Rico, and gets on the plane to Philly, and somebody meets him and takes the bag."

"Yeah," Vito said.

"The problem we have is that we think that IRS is watching the only guy we have available," Mr. Rosselli said.

"Oh," Vito said.

"So the way those IRS bastards work it is they make an anonymous telephone call, anonymous my ass, to either Customs or the Bureau of Narcotics and Dangerous Drugs, and tell them somebody, they give a description of our guy, is smuggling drugs. So when he's picking up his bag at the carousel, they search his bag. The Narcotics guys don't have to have the same, what do you call it, probable cause, that other cops do. You know what I mean."

"Probable cause," Vito said. "You need it to get a search warrant."

"Well, they don't need that. They can just search your bags, 'looking for drugs.' They don't find no drugs, of course, but they do find all that money."

"And then what happens? You lose the money?"

"No. Nothing like that. It's just a big pain in the ass, is all. They take it, of course. And then you have to go to court and swear you won it gambling in Barbados or someplace. And you have to pay a fine for not declaring you have more than ten thousand in cash on you, and then you have to pay income tax on the money. Gambling income is income, as I guess you know."

"Yeah, right. The bastards."

"But there's no big deal, like if they caught somebody smuggling drugs or something illegal. The worst that can happen is that they keep the money as long as they can, and you have to pay the fine."

Mr. Rosselli took a sip of his drink.

"Vito, you got anything against making a quick ten big ones?" Mr. Rosselli asked.

Vito looked at him, but did not reply.

"The four you owe us on the markers, and six in cash. It'd pay for your plumbing problem."

"I don't understand," Vito said softly, after a moment.

"Now, we don't know for a fact that this is going to happen," Mr. Rosselli said. "But let's just say that the IRS does know our guy who will have the million two in his suitcase. And let's just say they do make their anonymous fucking telephone call to Customs or the Narcotics cops, giving them his description and flight number. Now, we don't *know* that's going to happen, but we're businessmen, and we have to plan for things like that."

"Yeah," Vito said softly.

"So what would happen? They would wait for him at the baggage carousel and search his bags, right?"

"Right. I've seen them do that. Sometimes they call it a random search."

"Right."

"So they search his bags and find the money, and we have to go through the bullshit of paying the fine and the income tax on a million two. And also have to get another million two out of the bank to pay the guy in the Poconos. Right?"

"Yeah, I understand."

"So, I figured we could help each other. We don't want to take the chance of having to go through the bullshit that *might* happen. Including paying the IRS tax on a million two of gambling earnings. And you need money for your fucking plumbing, and to make good the four big ones you owe us."

"What do you want me to do?"

"Just make sure when our guy's airplane lands at Philadelphia, one of his bags don't make it to the carousel. There will be nothing in his other bag but underwear, *if*, and I keep saying, *if* they search it."

Mr. Rosselli paused.

"Look, Vito, we know you're a cop and an honest cop. We wouldn't ask you to do nothing *really* against the law, something that would get you in trouble with the Department. But you got a problem, we got a problem, and I thought maybe we could help each other out. If you think this is something you wouldn't want to do, just say so, and that'll be it. No hard feelings."

Vito Lanza looked first at Mr. Rosselli and then at his hands, and then back at Mr. Rosselli.

"How would I know which bag?" he asked, finally.

"Jesus, Carlo," Mr. Cassandro said to Mr. Rosselli as they left the apartment building. "I got to hand it to you. You played him like a fucking violin!"

"That did go pretty well, didn't it?" Mr. Rosselli replied. "And he wants in. That's a lot better than having to show him the photographs and the Xeroxes and all that shit."

"Yeah," Mr. Cassandro agreed.

"It's always better," Mr. Rosselli observed philosophically, "to talk people into doing something. If it's their idea, they don't change their minds."

Neither Mr. Rosselli nor Mr. Cassandro noticed that the four-year-old Pontiac was still parked halfway down the block on the other side of the street.

24.

Special Agent C. V. Glynes woke at seven A.M., which, considering how far they had lowered the level in the bottle of Seagram's 7-Crown before they went to bed, was surprising.

He went down the corridor to the bathroom and made as much noise as possible voiding his bladder, flushing twice, and dropping the toilet seat back into the horizontal position as loudly as he could manage.

He heard the creak of bed springs and other sounds of activity in the Springs's bedroom, and went back to his room to finish dressing and to wait for the Springs's announcement that breakfast was ready.

Logic told him that he was not likely to find anything at all, much less anything of interest to the Bureau of Alcohol, Tobacco and Firearms when he got Deputy Dan Springs out into the Pine Barrens. And that meant that this whole business would have been a waste of time, and moreover would cause some minor difficulty with H. Howard Samm, Jr., the special agent in charge of the Atlantic City office of the Bureau of Alcohol, Tobacco and Firearms.

"Sam Junior," as he was known by his not-too-admiring staff, liked to have what he called "his team" present each morning for an eight-thirty conference, aka "the pep talk," and Glynes knew he wasn't going to make that.

On the other hand, finding a chunk of three-eighth-inch steel with a link of chain embedded in it by the force of high explosives was not an everyday occurrence, and Glynes had a hunch he was onto something. Sometimes his hunches worked, and sometimes they didn't—more often than not they didn't—but they had over the years worked often enough so that he knew that he shouldn't ignore them.

Sam Junior's pontifical pronouncements vis-à-vis scientific crime detection to the contrary, Glynes believed what really did the bad guys in was almost always sweat, experience, luck, and following hunches, in just about that order.

In other words, Glynes felt, he just might find something of professional interest to ATF out in the Pine Barrens. He was either right or wrong, but in either case, the sooner he got out in the Pine Barrens the better.

Overnight, Marion Claude Wheatley had given a good deal of thought to the Lord having directed him to the Divine Lorraine Hotel.

There had to be a reason, of course. The Lord was not whimsical. One possibility was that the Lord knew that once the Vice President had been disintegrated the Secret Service and the FBI would learn that Marion had been responsible, and come looking for him. If he was not in his office, or at the house, but rather in the Divine Lorraine Hotel, obviously they would not be able to find him.

If that scenario were true, the Lord would certainly furnish him additional information and assistance once the disintegration had been accomplished.

But after more reflection, Marion came to believe that the Lord was concerned that the Secret Service was already, somehow—they were not stupid, quite the contrary—aware of Marion's existence and intentions. And that they would somehow keep him from carrying out the disintegration.

Before or after the disintegration, the last place, obviously, except perhaps the cells in the Police Administration Building, that the authorities would think to look for Marion Claude Wheatley would be in the Divine Lorraine Hotel.

At eight A.M. Marion got out the telephone book, and laid it on his desk. He took a paper clip from the desk drawer, and straightened one end. He held the clip in his left hand, then closed his eyes and opened the telephone book with his right hand. He stabbed it with the paper clip and then opened his eyes. The paper clip indicated EDMONDS, RICHARD 8201 HENRY AVENUE, 438-1299.

Marion thought about that for a moment, and then, being careful not to disturb the position of the paper clip, took a notebook and a ballpoint from the desk and began to write:

> Richard H. Edmonds
> Henry R. Edmonds
> Edmund R. Henry
> Henry E. Richards

Then he looked elsewhere in the telephone book until he found the number, and then telephoned to the Divine Lorraine Hotel.

"Divine Lorraine Hotel. Praise Jesus!"

That, Marion decided, *is a colored lady.*

He had a mental image of a large colored lady wearing one of those white whatever-they-were-called on her head.

"I'm calling with regard to finding accommodations for the next few days."

"Excuse me, sir, but do you know about the Divine Lorraine Hotel?"

"Yes, of course, I do," Marion said.

What an odd question, Marion thought. And then he understood: *As I heard in her voice that she's colored, she heard in mine that I am white.*

"This is a Christian hotel, you understand," the woman pursued. "No drinking, no smoking, nothing that violates the Ten Commandments and the teachings of Father Divine."

"I understand," Marion said, and then added, "I am about the Lord's work."

"Well, we can put you up. No credit cards."

"I'm prepared to pay cash."

"When was you thinking of coming?"

"This morning, if that would be convenient."

"We can put you up," the woman said. "What did you say your name was?"

"Henry E. Richards," Marion said.

"We'll be expecting you, Brother Richard. Praise Jesus!"

"That's 'Richards,' " Marion said. "With an 'S.' Praise the Lord."

At half past eight, Captain Michael Sabara picked up the private line in his office in the Schoolhouse.

"Captain Sabara."

"Peter Wohl, Mike."

"Good morning, sir."

"Something's come up, Mike. When I get off, Call Swede Olsen in Internal Affairs. I just got off from talking to him. He'll bring you up-to-date on what's going on. I don't think anything's going to happen this morning, but if it does, just use your own good judgment."

"Yes, sir. I guess you're not coming in?"

"No."

"Is there anyplace I can reach you?"

Wohl hesitated.

"For your ears only, Mike," he said, finally. "I'm in the Roundhouse. I made inspector. My dad and my mother are here. We're waiting for the mayor."

"Jesus, Peter, that's good news. Congratulations!"

"Thank you, Mike. I'll call in when I'm through. But if anyone asks, I'm at the dentist's."

"Yes, sir, *Inspector!*"

"Thanks," Wohl said, and hung up.

At five minutes to nine, Special Agent Glynes placed a collect call, he would speak with anyone, to the Atlantic City office of the Bureau of Alcohol, Tobacco and Firearms from a pay telephone in a Shell gasoline station in Hammonton, N.J.

"Odd that you should call, Glynes," Special Agent Tommy Thomas, an old pal, said, "Mr. Samm has been wondering where you are. He at first presumed that you had fallen ill, and had simply forgotten to telephone, but when *he* telephoned your residence, there was no answer, so he knew that couldn't be it."

"Is he there, Tommy?"

"Yes, indeed."

"Put him on."

Special Agent Thomas turned his back to Special Agent in Charge Samm and whispered into the phone: "Careful, Chuck. He's got a hair up his ass."

Then he spun his chair around again to face Special Agent in Charge Samm, who was standing by the coffee machine across the room, and raised his voice.

"It's Glynes, sir."

"Good," Mr. Samm said, coming quickly across the room and snatching the telephone from Thomas. "Glynes?"

"Yes, sir."

"How is it that you were neither at the eight-thirty meeting or called in?"

"Sir, I was in the Pine Barrens. There was no phone."

"What are you doing in the Pine Barrens?"

"I've got something out here I think is very interesting."

"And what is that?"

"I've got six, maybe more, pay lockers, you know, the kind they have in airports and railroad stations, that, in what I would say the last week, maybe the last couple of days, have been blown up with high explosives."

There was a very long pause, so long that Glynes suspected the line had gone out.

"Sir?" he asked.

"Chuck, I have been trying to phrase this adequately," Mr. Samm said. "I confess that I have suspected you never even read the teletype. And that teletype isn't even twenty-four hours old, and you're onto something."

What the hell, Special Agent C. V. Glynes wondered, *is that little asshole talking about?*

"You're confident, Chuck, that it is high explosives?"

"Yes, sir. Nothing but high-intensity explosive could do this kind of damage."

"Good man, Chuck," Mr. Samm said. "Thomas, pick up on 303. Get this all down accurately."

Tommy Thomas's voice came on the line. "Ready, sir."

"Thomas," Mr. Samm said, "with reference to that Request for All Information teletype of yesterday, Glynes has come up with something."

"Yes, sir," Thomas said, his tone of voice suggesting to Glynes that Thomas hadn't read the teletype either.

"Okay, Chuck," Mr. Samm sent on. "Give Thomas your location. I'm going to get on another phone and get in touch with the Secret Service and the FBI."

"Yes, sir."

"And, Glynes, make sure you keep the scene clean. Keep the locals out."

"Yes, sir."

"I'll be there as soon as I can."

"Yes, sir."

"Good work, Glynes. Good work."

At two minutes past nine o'clock, Marion Claude Wheatley telephoned Mr. D. Logan Hammersmith, Jr., vice president and senior trust officer of the First Pennsylvania Bank & Trust Company and told him he had come down with some sort of virus and would not be able to come into work today, and probably not for the next few days.

Mr. Hammersmith expressed concern, told Marion he should err on the side of caution and see his physician, viruses were tricky, and that if there was anything at all that he could do, he should not hesitate to give him a call.

"Thank you," Marion said. "I'm sure I'll be all right in a day or two."

"No sense taking a chance, Marion. Go see your doctor," Mr. Hammersmith said, added "Good-bye," and hung up.

Marion called for a taxi, and while he was waiting for it to come, he took all his luggage from where he had stacked it by the front door and carried it out of the house and down the stairs and stacked it on the second step up from the sidewalk.

When the taxi came, he helped the driver load everything into the trunk and, when it would hold no more, into the back seat. Finally, he returned to the steps and picked up the two attaché cases, one of which held the detonators and the other the shortwave transmitter (batteries disconnected, of course, there was no such thing as being too careful around detonators) and took them with him into the rear seat.

"The airport," he ordered. "Eastern Airlines. No hurry. I have plenty of time."

At the airport, he secured the services of a skycap, and told him he needed to put his luggage in a locker. The skycap rolled his cart to a row of lockers. Marion needed two to store what he was going to temporarily leave at the airport. He kept out the attaché case with the detonators, and two suitcases, one of which held what he thought would be enough clothing for a week, and the other half of the devices.

He paid off the skycap, tipping him two dollars, and then carried the two suitcases and the attaché case to a coffee shop where he had a cup of black coffee and two jelly-filled doughnuts. While he ate, he flipped through a copy of the *Washington Post* that a previous customer had left on the banquette cushion.

He then got up and carried his luggage down to the taxi station, waited in line for a cab, and when it was finally his turn, he told the driver to take him to the Divine Lorraine Hotel.

The driver turned and looked at him in disbelief.

"The Divine Lorraine Hotel?"

Marion smiled.

"I'm going to North Broad and Ridge," he explained. "Some drivers don't know where that is. *Everybody* knows where the Divine Lorraine Hotel is."

"You had me going there for a minute," the driver said. "You didn't look like one of Father Divine's people."

I'll have to remember that, Marion thought. *Someone such as myself, who does not fit in with the Divine Lorraine Hotel, would naturally attract curiosity and attention by taking a taxi there.*

But no harm done, and a lesson learned.

When they reached Ridge Avenue, Marion told the driver to turn right. A block down Ridge, he told the driver to let him out at the corner.

He walked down Ridge Avenue until the taxi was out of sight, then crossed the street and walked back to North Broad Street and into the Divine Lorraine Hotel.

There was a colored lady wearing sort of a robe and a white cloth, or whatever, behind the desk.

"My name is Richards, Henry E. Richards," Marion said. "I have a reservation."

"Yes, sir, we've been expecting you," the colored lady said. She was not, to judge from her voice, the same one he had spoken with on the telephone.

She gave him a registration card to sign, and he filled it out, and she said she could either give him a single room with a single bed, or a single room with a double bed, or a small suite with a double bed in the bedroom and a sitting room.

"Does the small suite have a desk?" Marion asked.

"Yes, and so does the single with a double bed," the woman said.

"Then the single with the double bed, please," Marion said. "I need a desk."

She told him how much, and he asked if there was a weekly rate, and she told him there was, so he paid for a week in advance, and asked for a receipt.

He counted the money in his wallet while she was making out the receipt. He had only one hundred and four dollars.

I probably will not need more, Marion decided, *but it is always good to be prepared. When I go out later, I will find a branch of Girard Trust Bank and cash a check.*

Another colored lady in a robe and a white whatchamacallit around her head appeared and tried to take his suitcases.

He was made uncomfortable by the notion of a woman carrying his bags.

"I'll take those," Marion said.

"You take one, and I'll take the other," she said with a smile.

She led him to the elevator, which she operated herself, and took him to a very nice room on the sixth floor that overlooked North Broad Street.

He gave her a dollar.

"For the Lord's work, you understand," she said.

"Of course."

"I hope you enjoy your stay with us."

"Thank you."

"Praise Jesus!"

"Praise the Lord!"

The room, Marion found on inspection, was immaculate. Everything seemed a bit old, and well worn, but the state of cleanliness left nothing to be desired.

Cleanliness, Marion thought, *is next to godliness.*

He went to the suitcases, hung up the clothing they contained, and then picked up the Bible that was neatly centered on the desk. He sat down in an upholstered chair.

He closed his eyes, and then opened the Bible, and then put his finger on a page.

If the Lord wants to send me a message, what better way? And then, in an hour or so, I'll go back out to the airport and get the rest of my things. This time I will have the driver drop me two blocks farther up North Broad Street.

He opened his eyes to see what passage of Holy Scripture the Lord might have selected for him.

He saw that he was in the second chapter of Haggai, the seventeenth verse.

Marion was not very familiar with Haggai.

"17. I smote you with blasting and with mildew and with hail in all the labours of your hands; yet ye turned not to me, saith the Lord."

Marion read it again and again and again, trying to understand what it meant.

At quarter to ten the private number on the desk of Staff Inspector Peter Wohl rang. Officer Paul O'Mara answered it in the prescribed manner.

"Inspector Wohl's office, Officer O'Mara speaking, sir."

"This is H. Charles Larkin, Secret Service. May I speak with the inspector, please?"

"I'm sorry, sir. The inspector is not available."

"This is important. Where can I reach him?"

"Just a moment, sir."

O'Mara went quickly to Captain Sabara's office.

"Captain, that Secret Service guy is on the inspector's private line. He says it's important."

"Does he have a name?"

"Mr. Larkin, sir."

Sabara went into Wohl's office and picked up the telephone.

"Good morning, Mr. Larkin. Mike Sabara. Can I help you?"

"I really wanted to talk to Peter, Mike."

"He won't be here until after lunch, and I don't really know how to reach him."

"That's not a polite way of saying he doesn't want to talk to me, is it?"

"No," Sabara said. "I . . . Not for dissemination, he's been promoted to Inspector. He's in the Commissioner's office."

"Well, good for him," Larkin said, then added, "Something has come up. *May* have come up. An ATF guy from Atlantic City has found evidence of a recent series of high-explosive detonations under odd circumstances."

"Really?"

"I just this minute got the call. It may or not be our guy. But on the other hand, it's all anybody's turned up. I'm going to the scene . . . it's in the Pine Barrens in Jersey . . . and I'd sort of hoped Peter would either go with me, or send somebody else."

"I can't leave," Sabara said.

"What about Malone?"

"He's at the Roundhouse, and I don't expect him back for at least an hour."

"What about Payne? He at least knows what we're up against."

"When and where do you want him?"

"Here. Ten minutes ago."

"He'll be twenty minutes late. He's on his way."

"Thank you, Mike. I appreciate the cooperation," Larkin said, and hung up.

En route from the Schoolhouse to the Federal Courts Building in Captain Mike Sabara's unmarked car, Detective Payne realized that he had no idea where in the Federal Courts Building he was to meet Supervisory Special Agent H. Charles Larkin. For that matter, he didn't know where in the building the Secret Service maintained its offices, and he suspected that he would not be allowed to drive a car into the building's basement garage without the proper stickers on its windshield.

Fuck it, he decided. *I'll park right in front of the place, and worry about fixing the ticket later.*

His concerns were not justified. When he pulled to the curb, Larkin was standing there waiting for him. He pulled open the passenger side door and got in.

"Good morning, Detective Payne," he said cheerfully. "And how are you this bright and sunny morning?"

Matt opened his mouth to reply, but before a word came out, Larkin went on: "Has this thing got a whistle?"

He means "siren," Detective Payne mentally translated.

He looked down at the row of switches mounted below the dash. He saw Larkin's finger flip one up and the siren began to howl.

"A Jersey State Trooper is waiting for us on the Jersey side of the Ben Franklin Bridge," Larkin said.

Matt looked into his rearview mirror and pulled into the stream of traffic.

No one got out of his way, despite the wailing siren, and, Matt presumed, flashing lights concealed behind the grille.

Larkin read his mind:

"If you think this is bad, try doing it in New York City. They get out of the way of a whistle only when it's mounted on a thirty-ton fire truck."

There was a New Jersey State Trooper car waiting in a toll booth lane on the Jersey side of the bridge, the lights on its bubble gum machine flashing. As Matt pulled up behind it, a State Trooper, his brimmed cap so low on his nose that Matt wondered how he could see, came up.

"Secret Service?"

"Larkin," Larkin said, holding out a leather identification folder. "I appreciate the cooperation."

"We're on our way," the Trooper said and trotted to his car.

There were more vehicles than Matt could count around what looked like a depression off a dirt road in the Pine Barrens, so many that a deputy sheriff had been detailed to direct traffic. He waved them to a stop.

"I'm Larkin, Secret Service," Larkin said, leaning across Matt to speak to him.

"Yes, sir, we've been waiting for you," the sheriff said. "Pull it over there. Everybody's in the garbage dump."

Matt parked the car and then followed Larkin to the depression, which he saw was in fact a garbage dump.

A tall, slender man with rimless glasses detached himself from a group of men, half in one kind or another of police uniform, a few in civilian clothes, and several in overalls with FEDERAL AGENT printed in large letters across their backs.

"Mr. Larkin?" the man asked, and when Larkin nodded, he went on, "I'm Howard Samm, I have the Atlantic City office of ATF."

"I'm very glad to meet you," Larkin said. "I can't tell you how much I appreciate your help with this."

"I like to think we have a pretty good team," Sam said. "And Agent Glynes was really on the ball with this, wasn't he? We didn't get that Request for All Information teletype until yesterday."

"He certainly was," Larkin said. "Mr. Samm, this is Detective Payne of the Philadelphia Police Department. He's working with us."

Samm shook Matt's hand.

Well, that's very nice of you, Mr. Larkin, but it's bullshit. Unless driving you around and running errands is "working with you."

"Well, what have we got?" Larkin asked.

"Somebody has been blowing things—specifically metal lockers, the kind you find in airports, bus stations—up with high explosives. My senior technician—the large fellow, in the coveralls?—says he's almost sure it's Composition C-4."

"When will we know for sure?"

"We just finished making sure the rest of the lockers weren't booby-trapped. The next step is taking a locker to the lab."

He pointed. Matt looked. Two of the men in coveralls were dragging a cable from a wrecker with MODERN CHEVROLET painted on its doors down to the remnants of a row of rental lockers. A Dodge van with no identifying marks on it waited for it, its rear doors open.

"We have any idea who's been doing this?" Larkin asked.

"That's going to be a problem, I'm afraid," Samms said.

"Not even a wild hair?" Larkin asked. "Who owns this property? Has anybody talked to him?"

"We don't know who owns the property. One of the deputies found a cabin a quarter of a mile over there. But there's no signs of life in it."

"A deserted cabin?"

"Well, of course, we haven't been able to go inside. So I really don't know."

"You haven't gone inside?"

"We don't have a search warrant."

"We'll go inside," Larkin said. "I'll take the responsibility."

Samm, visibly, did not like that.

"Christ," Larkin said. "Don't you think we have reasonable cause, even if there wasn't a threat to the Vice President?"

"You're right, of course," Samm said. He raised his voice. "Meador!"

The large man in the coveralls with FEDERAL AGENT on the back looked at him. Samm waved him over.

"This is Mr. Larkin of the Secret Service," he said. "He wants to have a look inside that house. Will you check it for booby traps, please?"

"No search warrant?" Meador asked.

"Just open the place for me, please," Larkin said. "I'll worry about a search warrant."

"Okay," Meador said.

Meador, with Larkin, Samm, and Matt following him, went to the van and took a toolbox from it, and led the way to the house. They stood to one side as he carefully probed a window for trip wires, and then smashed a pane with a screwdriver.

When he had the window open, he crawled through it. He was inside a minute or two, and then crawled back out.

"The door's clean," he said. "What do I do with the padlock?"

"You got any bolt cutters in that box?" Larkin asked.

Meador was putting bolt cutter in place on the padlock when two men in business suits walked up. Matt was surprised to see Jack Matthews, who was also surprised to see him. The other man, somewhat older, was a redhead, pale-faced, and on the edge between muscular and plump.

"Mr. Larkin," he said, "I'm Frank Young, Criminal A-SAC [Assistant Special Agent in Charge] for the FBI in Philadelphia."

"I think we've met, Frank, haven't we?" Larkin said.

"Yes, sir, now that I see you, I think we have met. Maybe Quantico?"

"How about Denver?" Larkin asked.

"Right. I was in the Denver field office. This is Special Agent Jack Matthews."

"We've met," Larkin said. "And I think you know Matthews too, don't you, Matt?"

"Yes, indeed," Matt said. "How nice to see you, Special Agent Matthews."

"Why do I think he's needling him?" Larkin said. "Payne is a Philadelphia detective. Do you know each other?"

"I know who he is," Young said, and shook Matt's hand. "What are we doing here?"

"Well, Frank, if you're the Criminal A-SAC, this will be right down your alley," Larkin said. "Detective Payne and I were walking through the woods and came across this building. Into which, I believe, person or persons unknown have recently broken in. We were just about to have a look."

Meador of ATF looked at Larkin and smiled.

"I wouldn't be at all surprised," he said as he lowered his bolt cutters, "if the burglar used a bolt cutter to cut through that padlock."

"That's very astute of you," Larkin said.

"What are we looking for?" Young asked.

"Signs of occupancy. If we get lucky, a name. So we can ask if he's noticed anything strange, like loud explosions, around here."

"There are tractor tracks that look fresh," Jack Matthews said, pointing.

"Take a look at the dipstick in the tractor engine," Young ordered. "I'll take a look inside."

"Yes, sir."

"Don't open any doors or cabinets until Meador here checks them," Larkin said. "And it would probably be a good idea to watch for trip wires."

"You think this is your bomber?" Young asked.

"I don't know that it's not," Larkin said.

Matthews came into the cabin after a minute or two to report that the tractor battery was charged, and from the condition of the dipstick, he thought the engine had been run in the last week or ten days.

Matt wondered how he could tell that, but was damned if he would reveal his ignorance by asking.

Jack Matthews moved quickly and efficiently around the cabin, and seemed to know exactly what he was looking for. Matt felt ignorant.

There were no trip wires or booby traps, but there was evidence of recent occupancy.

"There is something about this place that bothers me," Larkin said thoughtfully. "It's too damned neat and clean for a cabin in the boondocks."

"Yeah," Young agreed thoughtfully.

"I think we have to find out who owns this, who comes here."

"County courthouse?" Young said.

"Unless one of the deputies knows offhand," Larkin said.

"Are you going back to Philadelphia?" Young asked.

"I don't see what else I can do here," Larkin said.

"Why don't I send Jack to the county courthouse with my car?" Young asked. "And catch a ride back with you?"

"Great," Larkin said. He turned to Meador of ATF. "Meador, look into your crystal ball and tell me what he used for detonators."

"The explosive looks like C-4," Meador said. "Somebody with access to C-4 would probably have access to military detonators. I'll know for sure when I'm finished in the laboratory."

"Depressing thought," Larkin said.

"Sir?"

"Somebody with access to C-4 and military detonators who blew up those lockers the way he did knows how to use that stuff, wouldn't you say?"

"Yeah," Meador said.

"Well, at least it gives us a lead or two," Larkin said. "Which is a lead or two more than we had when I woke up this morning."

He put his hand out to H. Howard Samm.

"Your team really did a fine job, Samm. I think my boss would like to write a letter of commendation."

"Why," Samm said. "That would be very nice, but unnecessary."

"Nonsense. A commendation is in order," Larkin said, and then touched Matt's shoulder. "Let's go home, Matthew."

A moment after they turned off the dirt road onto the highway, Larkin said, "You noticed, Frank, how Mr. Samm was so anxious to make sure that his guy who found that place got the credit?"

"I noticed. His name wasn't mentioned."

"His names is Glynes," Larkin said. "C. V. Glynes."

"And he gets the commendation?"

"They both do. And Meador too. But on his, Samm gets his name misspelled," Larkin said.

Young laughed, and Larkin joined in.

"I don't know why we're laughing," Young said. "Now we *know* we have a lunatic on our hands who knows what he's doing with high explosives, and presumably has more in his kitchen closet."

25.

Inspector Peter F. Wohl, of the Philadelphia Police Department, who had, ten minutes before, been Staff Inspector Wohl, came out of Commissioner Czernich's office in the company of Chief Inspector (retired) and Mrs. Augustus Wohl.

They are happy about this, Peter Wohl thought, *but they are in the minority. Czernich, despite the warm smile and the hearty handshake, didn't like it at all. And a lot of other people aren't going to like it either, when they hear about it.*

Part of this, he felt, was because before he had become a staff inspector, he had been the youngest captain in the Department. And there was the matter of the anomaly in the rank structure of the Philadelphia Police Department: Captains are immediately subordinate to staff inspectors, who are immediately subordinate to Inspectors. The insignia of the ranks parallels that of the Army and Marine Corps. Captains wear two gold bars, "railroad tracks"; staff inspectors wear gold oak leaves, corresponding to military majors; and inspectors wear, like military lieutenant colonels, silver oak leaves.

There were only sixteen staff inspectors in the Department, all of them (with the sole exception of Wohl, Peter F.) assigned to the Staff Inspection Office of the Internal Affairs Division. There they handled "sensitive" investigations, which translated to mean they were a group of really first-rate investigators who went after criminals who were also high governmental officials, elected, appointed, or civil service.

Being a staff inspector is considered both prestigious and a good, interesting job. Many staff inspectors consider it the apex of their police careers.

Consequently, the promotion path from captain to inspector for most officers usually skips staff inspector. A lieutenant is promoted to captain, and spends the next five or six or even ten years commanding a District, or in a special unit, and/or working somewhere in administration until finally he ranks high enough on an inspector's examination—given every two years—to be promoted off it.

Peter Wohl, who everyone was willing to admit was one of the better staff inspectors, had been transferred out of Internal Affairs to command of the newly formed Special Operations Division. Officially, this was a decision of Police Commissioner Taddeus Czernich. Anyone who had been on the job more than six months suspected, correctly, that Wohl's transfer had been made at the "suggestion" of Mayor Jerry Carlucci, whose suggestions carried about as much weight with Czernich as a Papal pronouncement, ex cathedra.

Anyone who had been on the job six months also was aware that Wohl had friends in high places. Chief Inspector Augustus Wohl, retired, it was generally conceded, had been

Mayor Carlucci's rabbi as the mayor had climbed through the ranks of the Department. And Peter Wohl was close to Chief Inspectors Lowenstein and Coughlin. It was far easier, and much more satisfying for personal egos, to conclude that Wohl's rapid rise in rank was due to his closeness to the mayor than to give the mayor the benefit of the doubt, and to believe Carlucci had given Wohl Special Operations, and had the expired Inspector's List reopened, because he really believed Wohl was the best man in the Department for the job, and that he deserved the promotion.

When the Wohls came out of the Commissioner's office door into one of the curving corridors of the Roundhouse, and started walking toward the elevators, Captain Richard Olsen of Internal Affairs walked up to them.

"Looking for me, Swede?" Wohl asked.

"Yes, sir."

"I guess you know my dad? What about my mother?"

"Chief," Olsen said. "Good to see you again. How do you do, Mrs. Wohl?"

"I'm doing very well, thank you, after what just happened in there," Olga Wohl said.

"And just what happened in there?"

"Say hello to the newest inspector," Chief Wohl said.

"No kidding?" Olsen said. "Jesus, Peter, congratulations. Well deserved."

He took Wohl's hand and shook it with enthusiasm.

Swede seems genuinely pleased. But my fans are still outnumbered by maybe ten to one.

"Thanks, Swede. It will not be necessary for you to kiss my ring."

"Peter!" Olga Wohl said. "Really!"

"What's up, Swede? You *were* looking for me?"

"First of all, don't jump on Mike Sabara for telling me where I could find you. I practically had to get down on my knees and beg."

"That's not good enough," Wohl said. "As my first official act as an inspector, I'll have him shot at sunrise. Did your guys come up with something last night?"

"Yeah. Could you give me a minute?"

"Peter, I understand," Chief Wohl said. "We'll get out of your way."

He hugged his son briefly, but affectionately, and then, after she'd kissed her son, propelled Olga Wohl toward the elevator.

"You want to go get a cup of coffee or something?" Olsen asked.

"I didn't have any breakfast," Wohl said. "So I need some, which I think, under the circumstances, I'll even pay for."

"I know just the place," Olsen said. "If that was an invitation."

Olsen led him, on foot, to The Mall, a bar and restaurant on 9th Street. It was popular not only with the Internal Affairs people, but also with Homicide detectives. Wohl had spent a lot of time and money in The Mall as both a staff inspector and when he'd been in Homicide. It was just what he wanted now, for it offered a nice menu and comfortable chairs at a table where their conversation would not be overheard.

He ordered Taylor ham and eggs, hash browns and coffee.

"Same for me, please," Olsen said, and waited for the waitress to leave.

"I sent for Sergeant Framm and Detective Pillare first thing this morning . . ." Olsen began.

"They're the two you had on Lanza?" Wohl interrupted.

Olsen nodded.

". . . Framm opened the conversation by saying, 'It couldn't be helped, Captain, he dodged through traffic.' "

"Oh, shit, they lost him?"

"They did," Olsen said. "And your Sergeant O'Dowd did . . ."

"O'Dowd was there too?"

Olsen nodded again. "And he lost him too, but your man Payne stayed with him."

"Detective Payne was there too?"

Goddammit, Lanza knows Matt, and he shouldn't have been anywhere near him. I am going to have to sit on him, and hard.

"And he followed him to an apartment house in Center City, and then arranged for a somewhat chagrined Sergeant Framm, Detective Pillare, and Sergeant O'Dowd to join him."

If O'Dowd was there, and what the hell was he doing there, he knew Payne was there, and should not have been there. Unless, of course, O'Dowd told Matt to be there. Jesus Christ!

"You lose people. It happens to everybody. It's certainly happened to me," Wohl said.

"Shortly after Lanza got to the apartment building, Mr. Gian-carlo Rosselli *and* Mr. Paulo Cassandro entered the premises, stayed approximately twenty minutes, and then left, obviously pleased with themselves, and went to the bar at the Hotel Warwick where they stayed until closing."

"Who did Lanza see in the apartment building?"

"A lady," Olsen said, and handed Wohl a photograph. "Brilliant detective work by myself this morning identified her as Antoinette Mari Wolinski Schermer, believed by Organized Crime to be the girlfriend of Mr. Ricco Baltazari, proprietor of Ristorante Alfredo."

"What's she doing with Lanza? He spend the night there?"

"Yeah, and it's not the first time."

The waitress delivered the coffee.

"I'm going to need another one of these," Wohl said to her.

She nodded and left. Wohl took a sip, then another, then looked at Olsen.

"It would seem he has nice friends, our Corporal Lanza," Wohl said.

"Yeah, doesn't he?" Olsen replied. "So I took this to Chief Marchessi . . ."

"Right," Wohl said.

"Peter, I didn't mention to him that Framm and Pillare lost Lanza. He's . . . Framm is, this is not the first time he's lost somebody . . . and he's already on the chief's shit list."

If Olsen is covering for Framm, he has his reasons, and it's not because Framm's a nice guy.

"He wasn't lost, that's all that counts," Wohl said.

"Thank you," Olsen said. "The chief asked what you thought of all this, and I told him you were unavailable . . . At this point in time, Mike Sabara was still stonewalling me."

"Good for him," Wohl said.

"So the chief said that what we should do is bring the airline security people in on this. You remember Dickie Lowell?"

"Sure."

Before my time, Wohl thought. *But I remember him. H. Dickenson Lowell had been one of the first, if not the first, black staff inspectors. And then he made inspector. Well, dammit, I am* not *the first staff inspector to have the gall to try to get myself promoted.*

"Well, they had him running the Headquarters Division in the Detective Bureau and he didn't like it, all the paperwork, so he took retirement. He's chief of security for Eastern at the airport. More important, he and Marchessi are old pals."

"He was a good cop, as I recall," Wohl said.

"Marchessi called him, and explained the situation. Lowell is going to have his people keep an eye on Lanza, and he told Marchessi he has some friends, other airlines security, that he can go to. He will not go to the feds, which is important to Marchessi . . ."

"And me," Wohl interjected.

". . . but he will call Marchessi or me if Lanza does something suspicious. And we'll keep sitting on Lanza when he's not on the job."

"Good," Wohl said. "Very good."

"And then the chief told me to find you and bring you in on this and see if it's all right with you, or if you had anything, a suggestion, or what."

Wohl didn't reply for a moment, then he said, "There's only two loose ends that I can think of. This woman, Schermer, you said?"

Olsen nodded.

"I'd like to know if she was the woman Payne saw with Lanza in the Poconos. And then there's Martinez. I don't want him to go off half-cocked and screw anything up."

"The chief said maybe I should mention Martinez to you."

The waitress appeared with their ham and eggs.

Wohl looked at his plate, and then stood up.

"I think I know how to kill two birds with one stone," he said, and walked to a pay telephone.

Five minutes later he was back.

"That didn't work," he said.

"What didn't work?"

"I called the Schoolhouse. I was going to tell Payne to find Martinez, and bring him here. Payne could have told us whether that was the woman Lanza had with him in the Poconos, and we both could have impressed on both of them that neither of them are to get anywhere near Lanza until we finish this."

"What happened?"

"Payne is in New Jersey with the Secret Service, they may have a lead on the guy who wants to blow up the Vice President, and when I called Martinez, his mother told me he's got the flu, and called in sick."

"You've got Payne working on the screwball?" Olsen asked, surprised.

"Mike sent him," Wohl said. "When I have him shot in the morning, I'll have them pick up the body and shoot him again."

He looked at Olsen.

"And my eggs are probably cold. I think this is going to be one of those days."

At five minutes past one, Marion Claude Wheatley left his room in the Divine Lorraine Hotel, rode the elevator to the lobby, left his key at the desk, and walked out onto North Broad Street.

He turned north, walked three blocks, and then crossed the street. There he waited for a bus, rode it downtown into Center City, got off, and walked to Suburban Station. He went downstairs, picked up a Pennsylvania Railroad Timetable from a rack, and went back out to the street.

He flagged a cab and had himself driven to the airport, giving American Airlines as his destination. Inside the airport, he went to a fast-food restaurant and had a hot dog with sauerkraut and mustard and a medium root beer.

When he was finished, he went to the locker where he had left his things earlier, picked them up, and went to the taxi stand.

He gave the driver an address on Ridge Avenue, and when he got there, carried his luggage into a small office building until he was sure the cab had driven away.

Then he went back to the Divine Lorraine Hotel, sorted everything out on the bed, repacked everything, and put it in the closet. The closet had a key, which he thought was fortuitous, and he removed it and put it in his pocket.

Then he sat down at the desk and looked at the Bible again, and reread the passage the Lord had directed him to. He could by now practically recite Haggai 2:17 by heart, but he was no closer to understanding what "17. I smote you with blasting and with mildew and with hail in all the labours of your hands; yet ye turned not to me, saith the Lord" meant than he had been when the Lord had first directed his attention to it.

Marion decided the only thing to do was pray.

He knelt by the bed, and with the Bible before him, he prayed for understanding.

———

When Inspector Wohl walked into his office, a few minutes after two, it was immediately apparent to Captain Mike Sabara that he had a hair up his ass about something, and Sabara wondered if he had done the wrong thing in sending Matt Payne off with the man from the Secret Service.

"Do you have any word from Payne, Mike?" Wohl asked.

"No, sir."

"When he gets back, let me know," Wohl said, and went into his office and closed the door.

Twenty minutes later, Officer O'Mara put his head in Wohl's door and said that Mr. Larkin was here, and could the inspector see him?

"Ask him to come in," Wohl said, "and if Payne is out there, don't let him get away."

"Yes, sir," Officer O'Mara replied crisply, and then promptly misinterpreted his instructions. Detective Payne, at Officer O'Mara's bidding, followed Supervisory Special Agent Larkin into Inspector Wohl's office.

"Well, Peter," Larkin asked as they shook hands, "how did the promotion ceremony go?"

Does everybody in Philadelphia know I've been promoted? And what the hell is Matt doing in here?

"I did all right until the Commissioner kissed me."

He stopped.

I'll show Payne the photograph and then throw him out.

"Yes, sir?"

"Excuse me, Charley. This won't take a minute," Wohl said, and handed Matt the photograph. "You ever see this woman before?"

Matt looked at it.

"That's the girl Lanza had in the Poconos."

"Okay. Call Captain Olsen in Internal Affairs and tell him that," Wohl ordered.

"Right now?"

"Right now," Wohl said sharply.

"Peter," Larkin said. "Excuse me, but is that as important as our lunatic?"

No, of course it isn't. I am just having one of my goddamned bad days. What the hell is the matter with me?

"No, of course not," Wohl said. "Sorry. Payne, that will wait."

"Yes, sir."

"I'm reasonably sure, Peter, that we know where our man has been," Larkin said. "But we don't have an idea who he is, or where."

"What happened in New Jersey?"

"A deputy sheriff came across a piece of steel that showed evidence of having been involved in a high-explosive detonation," Larkin said. "Actually, he ran over it. Anyway, an ATF guy out of Atlantic City ran it down, and they called us. What we found, in a garbage dump in the middle of the Pine Barrens, were half a dozen railroad station, airline terminal, bus station rental lockers that had been, recently, blown up. The ATF expert said he was almost sure it was Composition C-4, and that it was set up with GI detonators. This guy knows his way around explosives."

"That's not good news, is it?"

"It may not be all bad. It may give us a line on him. We're already back-checking with the military. And if he knows what he's doing, that would lessen the chance of his explosives going off accidentally."

"But you don't know who he is?"

"That's the bad news. Where we stand is that the FBI is searching records in the county courthouse over there to find out who owns the property. There's a house, more of a cabin, on the property. Someone has been there in the past week or ten days, which coincides with when the ATF explosives guy says the explosions took place. And, for a cabin, the place was out-of-the-ordinary neat and clean. Which ties in with the psychological profile. Both of them. Ours and Dr. Payne's. I have a gut feeling he could be our guy."

"But no name?"

"Not yet. And I could be wrong. Maybe the people who own the property have nothing to do with what happened there. But that's all we have to go on, unless we get a name from the Defense Department, some explosives guy with mental problems."

"How can we help?" Wohl asked.

"*If* we come up with a name, we're going to have to move fast. It would help if we had a search warrant that had the important parts left blank."

"Denny Coughlin," Wohl said. "I'll call him. He's good at that. He knows every judge in the city."

"You're not?"

"There's a Superior Court judge named Findermann in the slam," Wohl said. "Since I put him there, I have not been too popular with the bench."

"The only people worse than doctors and Congressmen when it comes to protecting their own are judges," Larkin said, and then went on: "If we get a name and an address, *and* a search warrant, we'll need some explosives people, maybe even a booby-trap expert."

"I thought of that," Wohl said. "We call it 'Ordnance Disposal.' It's in the Special Patrol Bureau. When I called over there, they told me, 'You tell us where, and we'll be there in ten minutes.' "

"Good. I appreciate your cooperation, Peter."

"You keep saying that."

"I keep saying it because I mean it. We couldn't handle this by ourselves."

"I have the simple solution to this problem," Wohl said. "Tell the Vice President to stay the hell home."

"No way," Larkin chuckled. "What I think I should do now is go back to the office and see if I can lean on the Defense Department to come up with some names. Can Matt take me?"

"Sure. On your way back, go see Hay-zus Martinez. Tell him . . ." He stopped, and then went on. "Hell, when all else fails, tell the truth. Tell Hay-zus that other people are watching Lanza. If he goes back to work, he is to stay away from Lanza. If he sees him doing something, he is to telephone either Captain Olsen or me. He's not to do anything about it."

"If he goes back to work?" Matt asked.

"His mother said he has the flu. Make sure he understands the message, Matt."

"Yes, sir."

"If he goes off half-cocked, he's liable to blow the whole thing," Wohl went on.

"I'll tell him, sir."

"And then come back here, of course, so Captain Sabara can have his car back."

"Yes, sir."

The red light was blinking on the answering machine when Matt came into his apartment at twenty minutes after five.

I don't want to listen to any goddamned messages. I'm just going to have to bite the goddamned bullet.

He reached down and pushed the ERASE button before he could change his mind. Nothing happened.

You have to play the goddamned messages before you can erase them! Damn!

He pushed the PLAY button and walked into the kitchen and took a beer from the refrigerator. He could hear that there had again been a number of callers who had elected not to leave their names.

Nature called, and he went to the bathroom off his bedroom. He had just begun to void his bladder when there was a familiar voice, somewhat metallically distorted.

Penny! Jesus, I can't understand a word she's saying! I wonder what the hell she wanted?

By the time he had zipped up his fly and returned to the answering machine, all the recorded messages, including the hangups, had played.

Do I want to push REWIND *so that I can hear what Precious Penny wants? No, I do not want to hear what Precious Penny wants.*

He pushed the ERASE button, and this time it worked.

Banishing forever into the infinite mystery of rearranged microscopic metallic particles whatever Penny wanted to tell me. Why did I do that?

He went into the kitchen, picked up the beer bottle, returned to the telephone, and dialed Evelyn's number.

It was a brief, but enormously painful conversation, punctuated by long, painful silences.

He told Evelyn the truth. He could not see her tonight because he was on orders to keep himself available. That was the truth, the whole truth, and nothing but the truth. Peter Wohl had even told him to take an unmarked car home with him in case he would need a car with radios and a siren.

Evelyn, her voice made it quite plain, did not believe a word he was saying. Nor did Evelyn believe him when he said he really didn't know about tomorrow, but that he thought the same thing would be true then. That was also the unvarnished truth. Until they found the lunatic who wanted to disintegrate the Vice President, everyone would be either working or keeping themselves available around the clock for a summons.

But he couldn't tell Evelyn that, of course. Not just on general principles, but because Wohl had made it an order. They didn't want the lunatic knowing they were looking for him, which he would if it got into the newspapers or on television.

He told her he would call her when he was free, and Evelyn didn't believe that, either. In this latter incidence, he had not told her the truth, the whole truth, and nothing but the truth. Even as he spoke, he had wondered if maybe Evelyn would take a hint, that her feminine pride would be offended, and if he didn't call, she would give up.

He strongly suspected that Evelyn was crying when she hung up.

"Shit!" he said aloud after he slammed the handset into its cradle.

Then he went into the kitchen and put a cork in the beer bottle and put it back into the refrigerator. He took down a bottle of Scotch and after carefully pouring a dollop into a shot glass, he tossed it down. And then had another.

All it did was make him feel hungry.

And I don't want to be shit-faced if Wohl summons me to single-handedly place into custody our lunatic. Or more likely, orders me to play taxi driver to Mr. Larkin again.

What I will do is grab a shower, change clothes, call in and say I'm going to supper, and then go either to the Rittenhouse Club or the Ribs Place and have my supper, not washing anything down with wine or anything else.

He was vaguely aware, as he showered, of a noise that could very possibly be the sound of his doorbell, but he wasn't sure, and he wasn't concerned. It could not be Evelyn. There was no way she could have made it into Center City from Upper Darby that quickly. And if Wohl or anybody else at Special Operations wanted him, they would have phoned. It could be Charley McFadden, or Jack Matthews, but in that happenstance, fuck 'em, let 'em wait.

When he turned the shower off, there was no longer a question whether the doorbell was being run. Whoever was pushing it was playing "Shave and a Haircut, Two Bits" on it.

Still dripping, Matt wrapped a towel around his waist and headed for the solenoid button. The doorbell musician played another verse of "Shave and a Haircut" before he got to the button.

"Keep your goddamned pants on!" he called as he looked down the stairwell.

The door opened. Penny came in.

"Tired of me so soon, are you?"

"Jesus! Penny, this is a very bad time."

She stopped halfway up the stairs. She saw that he was dressed in a towel.

"Am I interrupting anything?" she asked, and Matt did not like either her tone of voice or the kicked puppy look in her eyes.

"Come on in," he said. "There's always room for one more in an orgy."

"Is someone with you, Matt?" Penny asked, quite seriously.

"Hell, no. Come on in. You caught me in the shower."

Her face changed. The smile came back on her face and into her voice.

"I knew you were here, the guard told me," she said.

Jesus, she looks good!

"Make yourself at home," Matt said. "Let me get some clothes on."

She was by then at the head of the stairs.

"You called," she said. "And said that if I came into Center City, we could go to the movies."

"Did I?"

"And Daddy, over Mommy's objections, said he thought it would be all right, if I came home right after the movie, if I drove myself."

He looked at her. Their eyes met.

"Are you sore, Matt?" Penny asked softly.

"No, of course not," he said.

And then somehow, his arms went around her, and her face was on his chest, and he could feel her breath and smell her hair.

"I was sort of hoping you'd do that," she said, and then pushed him away. "For God's sake!" she said furiously. "Don't you dry yourself when you get out of your shower? I'm soaked!"

"Sorry," he said.

"Big date tonight?" Penny asked.

"I'm on call," he said.

"Which means?"

"Just what it sounds like. I have to make myself available. They'll probably call me before long."

"Oh."

"I was just about to go out and get something to eat. Ribs, I thought. Sound interesting?"

"How hungry are you?"

"What?"

"You said they were probably going to call you before long."

"I don't know what the hell you're talking about."

"Think about it, Matthew," Penny said, and then, a naughty look in her eyes, she put her hand to the towel around his waist and snatched it away.

"Jesus!" he said.

"You ever hear of first things first?" she said.

A very large man of about thirty-five who had been sitting with what the General Services Administration called a Chair, Metal, Executive, w/arms FSN 453 232234900 tilted as far back as it would go, and with his feet on what the GSA called a Desk, Metal, Office, w/six drawers, FSN 453 232291330, moved with surprising speed and grace when one of the three telephones on the desk rang, snatching the handset from the cradle before the second ring.

"Six Seven Three Nineteen Nineteen," he said.

"Mr. Larkin, please," the caller said.

"May I ask who's calling?" the large man said, then covered the microphone with his large hand. "For you, sir," he called.

Across the room, H. Charles Larkin, who had been lying, in fact half dozing, on what the GSA called a Couch, Office, Upholstered, w/three cushions, FSN 453 232291009, pushed himself to an erect position. He looked at the clock on the wall. It was 6:52.

"My name is Young, I'm the Criminal A-SAC, FBI, for Philadelphia."

"Young, FBI," the large man said, and took his hand off the microphone. "One moment, please, Mr. Young."

Larkin walked to the desk, grunting, his hand on the small of his back.

I'm getting old, he thought. *Too old for that goddamned couch.*

He took the phone from the large man.

"Hello, Frank."

"Charley, we have a name," Young said. "Matthews just called. That property is owned by Richard W. and Marianne Wheatley, husband and wife."

"Spell it, please," Larkin said, snatching a ballpoint pen extended in the hand of the large man.

"What about an address?" Larkin asked when he had written the name down.

"No. Just the address of the property."

"Damn!"

"And we've checked the Philadelphia area, plus Camden and Wilmington phone books. No Richard W. Wheatley."

"Maybe the Philadelphia cops can help," Larkin said. "Let me get back to you, Frank. Where are you?"

"I'm in the office about to go home. Let me give you that number. I've told our night guy what's going on."

Larkin wrote down Young's home phone number, and repeated, "Let me get back to you, Frank. And thank you."

He hung up, and turned to the large man.

"Get on the phone to Washington. Have them send somebody over to the Pentagon. Tell them that Richard W. and Marianne might be parents' names. Tell them to get me anything with Wheatley."

"You don't think the FBI will be on that?"

"I think they will, but I don't know they will," Larkin said sharply. "Just do it."

He took out his notebook, found Peter Wohl's home telephone number, and dialed it.

Detective Matthew M. Payne thought that one of the great erotic sights in the world had to be a blonde wearing a man's white shirt, and nothing else, especially when, whenever she leaned forward to help herself to the contents of one of the goldfish boxes from the Chinese Take-out, it fell away from her body and he could see an absolutely perfect breastworks.

"Here," Penny said, putting an egg roll in his mouth. "This is the last one. You can have one bite."

"Your generosity overwhelms me," Matt said.

"I try to please."

"Are you going to tell my sister that you came here and seduced me?"

"Meaning what?"

"You told her what happened in the Poconos."

"She's my shrink," Penny said. "She said I seemed very happy, and wanted to know why, so I told her. I didn't think she'd tell you!"

"She is convinced that I'm taking advantage of you."

"I can't imagine where she got that idea."

"She was pretty goddamned mad," Matt said.

"I'm pretty goddamned mad that she told you I told her."

"She's afraid that . . . that this won't be good for you."

"That's my problem, not hers. How did we get on this subject?"

"Penny, the last thing I want to do is hurt you."

"Relax. I'm making no demands on you. But that does raise the question I've had in the back of my mind."

"Which is?"

"Have you got someone?"

"No," he said.

"I didn't think so," Penny said. "Otherwise you would have taken her to the Poconos." She looked at him, and she was close enough to kiss, and he did so, tenderly.

The phone rang.

"Damn!" Penny said.

Please God, don't let that be Evelyn!

"Payne," Matt said to the telephone.

"We have a name," Peter Wohl said, without any preliminaries. "Just a name. Do you know where Tiny Lewis lives?"

"Yes, sir."

"Go pick him up, he'll be waiting, and then come to Chief Lowenstein's office in the Roundhouse."

"Yes, sir."

Wohl hung up.

Matt put the telephone down.

"I've been called."

"So I gathered."

He swung his legs out of the bed and went searching for underwear in his chest of drawers.

Penny watched him get dressed.

"You want to take me to the movies again, sometime?"

"Why not?" he asked.

"Would it be all right with you if I hung around here until the movie would be over?"

"Of course. There's an *Inquirer* in the living room. Go look up what we saw, so we can keep our stories straight."

She got out of bed with what he considered to be a very attractive display of thighs and buttocks and went into the living room.

When he had tied his tie and slipped into a jacket he went after her.

"They're showing *Casablanca* for the thousandth time. How about us having seen that?"

" 'Round up the usual suspects,' " he quoted. "Sure. Why not?"

He went to the mantelpiece and picked up his revolver and slipped it into a holster.

"I suppose that's what cops' wives go through every day, isn't it?"

"What?"

"Watching their man pick up his gun and go out, God only knows where."

"You are not a cop's wife, and you are very unlikely to become a cop's wife."

"You said it," she said.

He went and bent and kissed her, intending that it be almost casual, but she returned it with a strange fervor that was somehow frightening.

"I'll call you," he said.

"Enjoy the movie," Penny said.

He went down the stairs.

Penny looked at the mantel clock and did the mental calculations. She had an hour and a half to kill, before she went home after an early supper and the movies.

She gave in to feminine curiosity and went around the apartment opening closets and cabinets, and when she had finished, she sat down in Matt's chair and read the *Inquirer*.

The doorbell sounded.

"Damn!" she said aloud. "What do I do about that?"

She went to the solenoid button and pushed it and looked down the stairwell.

A woman came in, and looked up at her in surprise.

"Who are you?" Evelyn asked.

"To judge by the look on your face, I'm the other woman," Penny said. "Come on up, and we'll talk about the lying sonofabitch."

26.

The commissioner's conference room in the Police Administration Building was jammed with people. Every seat at the long table was filled, chairs had been dragged in from other offices, and people were standing up and leaning against the wall. There were far too many people to fit in Lowenstein's office, which was why they were in the commissioner's conference room.

"You run this, Peter," Chief Inspector Matt Lowenstein declared from his chair at the head of the commissioner's conference table. "Denny Coughlin and I are here only to see how we can help you, Charley, and Frank."

Chief Inspector Dennis V. Coughlin, Supervisory Special Agent H. Charles Larkin of the Secret Service, and Assistant Special Agent in Charge (Criminal Affairs) Frank F. Young of the FBI were seated around him.

And if I fuck up, right, you're off the hook? "Wohl was running the show."

Peter Wohl immediately regretted the thought: *While that might apply to some, most, maybe, of the other chief inspectors, it was not fair to apply it to either Lowenstein or Coughlin.*

Worse, almost certainly Lowenstein had taken the seat at the head of the table to establish his own authority, and then delegating it to me. Lowenstein is one of the good guys. And I know that.

"Yes, sir. Thank you," Wohl said. He looked around the table. With the exception of Captain Jack Duffy, the special assistant to the commissioner for inter-agency liaison, only Captain Dave Pekach and Lieutenant Harry Wisser of Highway Patrol were in uniform.

"Indulge me for a minute, please," Wohl began. "I really don't know who knows what, so let me recap it. An ATF agent from Atlantic City, in response to a 'furnish any information' teletype from the Secret Service, came up with evidence of high-explosive destruction of a bunch of rental lockers. We're still waiting for the lab report, but the ATF explosives expert says he's pretty sure the explosive used was Composition C-4, and the detonators were also military. He also said that whoever rigged the charges knows what he's doing.

"Mr. Larkin went down there. There is a house, a cabin, on the property. Mr. Larkin feels that the unusual neatness, cleanliness, of the cabin fits in with the psychological profile the psychiatrists have given us of this guy.

"The FBI has come up with the names of the people who own the property. Richard W. and Marianne Wheatley. No address. I don't know how many Wheatleys there are in Philadelphia . . ."

"Ninety-six, Inspector," Detective Payne interrupted. Wohl looked at him coldly. He saw that he had a telephone book open on the table before him.

"None of them," Matt went on, "either Richard W. or Marianne. Not even an R. W."

"I was about to say a hell of a lot of them," Wohl said, adding with not quite gentle sarcasm, "Thank you, Payne. If I may continue?"

"Sorry," Matt said.

"And of course we don't know if these people live in Philadelphia, or Camden, or Atlantic City."

"Peter," Frank Young said. "Our office in Atlantic City has already asked the local authorities for their help."

"I'll handle Camden," Denny Coughlin announced. "I'm owed a couple of favors over there."

"What about Wilmington, Chester, the suburbs?" Wohl asked him.

"I'll handle that," Coughlin said.

"Then that leaves us, if we are to believe Detective Payne, ninety-six people to check out in Philadelphia. It may be a wild-goose chase, but we can't take the chance that it's not."

"How do you want to handle it, Peter?"

"Ring doorbells," Wohl said. "I'd rather have detectives ringing them."

"Done," Lowenstein said.

"What I think they should do, Chief," Wohl said, "is ring the doorbell, ask whoever answers it if their name is Wheatley, and then ask if they own property in the Pine Barrens. If they say they do, they'll either ask why the cops want to know, and the detective will reply—or volunteer, if they don't ask—that the Jersey cops, better yet, the sheriff has called. There has been a fire in the house. The people have to be notified, and since Richard W. and Marianne Wheatley are not in the book, they are checking out all Wheatleys."

"What if it's the guy?" Captain Duffy asked.

"I don't really think," Wohl said, aware that he was furious at the stupidity of the question, and trying to restrain his temper, "that the guy is going to say, 'Right, I'm Wheatley, I own the garbage dump, and I've been using it to practice blowing up the Vice President' do you, Jack?"

"If I may, Peter?" Larkin asked.

"Certainly."

"We have to presume this fellow is mentally unstable. And we know he's at least competent, and possibly expert, around explosives. *If* we find him, we have to be very careful how we take him."

"Yes, sir," Captain Duffy said. "I can see that."

"Let me lay this out as I see it," Wohl said. "The reason I want detectives to ring the bell, Chief Lowenstein, is that most people who answer the doorbell are going to say 'No, I don't own a farm in Jersey' and any detective should be able to detect any hesitation. For the sake of argument, they find this guy. There will have to be a reaction to a detective showing up at his door. The detective does his best to calm his down. There was a fire, he's simply delivering a message. The detective goes away. Then we figure how to take him."

"We'd like to be in on that, Peter," Frank F. Young of the FBI said.

"How do you want to handle it, Peter?" Chief Lowenstein said.

"Depends on where and what the detective who's suspicious has to say, of course," Wohl replied. "But I think Stakeout, backed up by Highway."

"We've got warrants," Chief Coughlin said. "We just take the door, is that what you're saying?"

"It'd take us up to an hour to set it up," Wohl said. "Ordnance Disposal would be involved. And the district, of course another field Detective Division. By then, I hope, he would relax. And taking the doors would be, I think, the way to do it."

Coughlin grunted his agreement.

"And in the meantime, sit on him?" Lowenstein said.

"Different detectives," Wohl said, "in case he leaves."

"And what if nobody's home?" Mike Sabara asked.

"Then we sit on that address," Wohl said. "An unmarked Special Operations car, until we run out of them, and then, if nothing else, a district RPC." He looked at Lowenstein and Coughlin, and then around the table. "I'm open to suggestion."

"I suggest," Lowenstein said, breaking the silence, "that Detective Payne slide that phone book down the table to me, and somebody get me a pen, and we'll find out where these ninety-six Wheatleys all live."

The telephone book, still open, was passed down the table to Chief Lowenstein. Sergeant Tom Mahon, Chief Coughlin's driver, leaned over him and handed Chief Lowenstein two ballpoint pens.

As if they had rehearsed what they were doing, Chief Lowenstein read aloud a listing from the telephone directory, the whole thing, name, address, and telephone number, then said, "North Central" or "West" or another name of one of the seven Detective Divisions.

Most of the time, Coughlin would either grunt his acceptance of the location, or repeat it in agreement, but every once in a while they would have a short discussion as to the precise district boundaries. Finally, they would be in agreement, and Lowenstein would very carefully print the name of the Detective Division having jurisdiction over that address in the margin.

Everyone in the room watched in silence as they went through the ninety-six names.

They could have taken that to Radio, Peter Wohl thought. *Any radio dispatcher could have done the same thing.*

But then he changed his mind. *These two old cops know every street and alley in Philadelphia better than any radio dispatcher. They're doing this because it's the quickest way to get it done, and done correctly. But I don't really think they are unaware that everybody at this table has been impressed with their encyclopedic knowledge.*

When he had written the last entry, Lowenstein pushed the telephone book to Coughlin, who examined it carefully.

"Take this, Matty," Coughlin said, finally, holding up the telephone book. "Type it up, broken down into districts. Tom, you go with him. As soon as he's finished a page, Xerox it. Twenty-five copies, and bring it in here."

"Yes, sir," Sergeant Mahon said.

The two left the commissioner's conference room.

"Peter, are you open to suggestion?" Lowenstein asked.

"Yes, sir. Certainly."

"There's three of us, you, Coughlin, and me. I think that list, when he's finished sorting it out, we can break down into thirds. I'll take one, you take one, and Denny can take the third. We'll have the detective teams, I think we should send two to each doorbell, report to whichever of us it is. That make sense to you?"

"Yes, sir. It does."

"Sort of supervisory teams, right?" Frank F. Young of the FBI said. "Do you think it would be a good idea if I went with one of them, with you, Chief Lowenstein, and I'll get two other special agents to go with Chief Coughlin and Inspector Wohl."

"Better yet," Lowenstein said, "why don't you and Charley go with Peter? He's the man in overall charge."

"Whatever you say, of course," Young said, visibly disappointed.

Wohl thought he saw Coughlin, not entirely successfully, try to hide a smile.

When the neatly typed and Xeroxed lists were passed around, it was evident that the Wheatleys were scattered all over Philadelphia. Lowenstein, after first tactfully making it a suggestion to Wohl, assigned himself to supervise the operation in the Central and North Central detective districts. He also "suggested" that Chief Coughlin supervise the operation in the South and West Detective Divisions, which left Wohl to supervise the detectives who would be working in the East, Northeast, and Northwest Detective Divisions.

At that point, although the CONFERENCE IN PROGRESS—DO NOT ENTER sign was on display outside the conference room, the door suddenly opened and the Honorable Jerry Carlucci, mayor of Philadelphia, marched into the room.

"What's all this going to cost in overtime?" he asked, by way of greeting. "I suppose it's too much to expect that anybody would think of telling me, or for that matter the commissioner, what the hell is going on?"

"I was going to call you, Jerry . . ." Lowenstein began.

"Mr. Mayor to you, Chief, thank you very much."

". . . right about now. Peter just decided how this is going to work."

"So you tell me, Peter."

Wohl described the operation to the mayor.

He listened carefully, asked a few specific questions, grunted approval several times, and then when Wohl was finished, he stood leaning against the wall thinking it all over.

"What do the warrants say?" he asked finally.

"As little as legally possible," Lowenstein said. "Denny got them."

"They're city warrants?" Carlucci asked.

"Right," Coughlin said.

"Not federal?" the mayor asked, looking right at Frank F. Young of the FBI.

"Reasonable belief that party or parties unknown by name have in their possession certain explosives and explosive devices in violation of Section whateveritis of the state penal code," Coughlin said.

"That, of course," Young said, "unlawful possession of explosive devices is a violation of federal law."

"Have you got any warrants, Charley?" the mayor asked H. Charles Larkin.

"Mr. Mayor, we haven't tied, this is presuming we can find the guy with the explosives, we haven't tied him to the threatening letter sent to the Vice President. So far as we're concerned, getting this lunatic off the streets, separated from his explosives, solves our problem."

"So, if you want to look at it this way, Charley, you're here just as an observer?"

"That's right, Mr. Mayor."

"Would that describe the FBI's role in this, Mr. Young?" the mayor asked.

"Pretty well," Young said uncomfortably. "The FBI, of course, stands ready to provide whatever assistance we can offer."

"We appreciate that," the mayor said. "And I'm sure Inspector Wohl will call on you if he thinks he needs something."

He looked at Young to make sure that he had made his point. Then he turned to Peter Wohl.

"Before you take any doors, let me know," the mayor said. "I think I would like to be in on it."

"Yes, sir."

With that, the mayor walked out of the conference room.

I wonder, Peter Wohl thought, *if the mayor just happened to hear about this meeting via somebody on the night shift here, or whether Lowenstein or Coughlin called him up, and told him what was going on, sure that he would be anxious to keep the arrest, if there was one, from being taken over by the FBI or the Secret Service. Now that I think about it, Charley Larkin didn't seem very surprised when the mayor honored us with his presence.*

The food in the dining room of the Lorraine Hotel was simple, but quite tasty, and, Marion thought, very reasonably priced. There was no coffee or tea. Apparently, Marion reasoned, Father Divine had interpreted Holy Scriptures to mean that coffee was somehow sinful. He wondered how Father Divine had felt about what had been reported by Saint Timothy vis-à-vis Jesus Christ's attitude toward fermented grapes. There was no wine list, either, in the Divine Lorraine Dining Room.

It was not going to be a problem, Marion thought. He habitually took a little walk after dinner to settle his stomach. He would take one now, and was certain to come across someplace where he could get a cup of coffee.

On his way through the lobby to North Broad Street, he saw that the bulletin board in the lobby announced, *"Sacred Harp Singing, Main Ball Room, 7:30. All Welcome!"*

He wondered what in the world that meant.

When he returned from his walk, which included two cups of coffee and a very nice piece of lemon meringue pie at a Bigger Burger, the lobby was full of pleasant voices, singing, a cappella, "We Will Gather at the River."

He followed the sound of the voices, passing and noticing for the first time an oil portrait of a white middle-aged woman, wearing the whateveritwas these people wore on their heads. He wondered if that was Mrs. Father Divine, and then if she was called "Mother Divine."

He found the source of voices. It was in the main ballroom. A neatly dressed black man put out his hand, said, "Welcome, brother. Make yourself at home. Praise the Lord."

"Praise the Lord," Marion replied, and went into the ballroom and took a mimeographed program, which included the words to the hymns and spirituals on the program, from a folding chair.

He was a little uncomfortable at first but the music was lovely, and the sincerity and enthusiasm of the singers rather touching, and after a few minutes, he was quite caught up in the whole thing.

He had always liked "Rock of Ages," and other what he thought of as traditional hymns, and he had never before had the opportunity to not only hear Negro spirituals, but to join in with the singers.

Afterward, when he went to his room, he wondered if perhaps somehow the last two hours, which certainly could be interpreted as worship, would now give him an insight into Haggai 2:17.

He read it again, standing up at the desk where he had left the Bible open to it: "17. I smote you with blasting and with mildew and with hail in all the labours of your hands; yet ye turned not to me, saith the Lord."

He thought perhaps he had an insight. Viewed from one perspective, it was possible, even likely, that it was what the Lord might be saying to the Vice President, rather than directed to him.

That made a certain sense vis-à-vis "blasting," but while one might be smitten with "blasting" and "hail," being smitten with mildew made no sense. Mildew was what grew in the grouting around the tiles of a bathroom.

He undressed and took a shower, and then took the Bible to bed with him. But even after praying for insight, Haggai 2:17 made no sense to him at all.

Marion Claude Wheatley dropped off to sleep, propped up against the headboard, with the Holy Bible open on his lap.

Mr. Vincenzo Savarese, Mr. Paulo Cassandro, Mr. Gian-Carlo Rosselli, and Mr. Ricco Baltazari were seated at a table in the rear of Ristorante Alfredo. A screen had been erected around the table, to keep the customers from staring. No place had been set for Mr. Baltazari, the proprietor, who thought it might be considered disrespectful to break bread with Mr. Savarese uninvited.

"I like your Chicken Breast Alfredo," Mr. Savarese said to Mr. Baltazari, "how is it made?"

"It's really very simple, Mr. S.," Mr. Baltazari said. "Some oregano, some thyme, some chervil, a little sweet paprika for color, you grind them up, then add maybe a half cup olive oil; you marinate maybe an hour, then you broil, and then, at the last minute, a slice of cheese on top, and that's it."

"Not only is it nice, I see by the price on the menu that it probably makes a nice profit."

"Absolutely, chicken is always good that way. I'm pleased that you're pleased."

"Ricco, I have to make a decision," Mr. Savarese said. "I want your advice."

"I'm honored that you would ask me, Mr. S.," Mr. Baltazari said.

"You understand that I am under an obligation to some friends in Baltimore," Mr. Savarese said. "An obligation that I would like to meet."

"I understand," Mr. Baltazari said.

"They telephoned me just before I came here," Mr. Savarese said. "They are very anxious to make the shipment we talked about. Their man is waiting word that it's all right to come to Philadelphia."

Mr. Baltazari nodded his understanding.

"Gian-Carlo and Paulo tell me that they think everything is arranged with our new friend at the airport," Mr. Savarese said. "And on one hand, I trust their judgment. But on the other hand, I am a cautious man. I am always concerned when things seem to be going too easily. You understand?"

"Yes, Mr. Savarese, I understand."

"There are two things that concern me here," Mr. Savarese said. "One may be as important as the other. We think we have this policeman's cooperation. *Think.* It would be very embarrassing for me if he changed his mind at the last minute. And costly. If the shipment was lost, I would, as a man of honor, have to make good the loss. You understand?"

"I understand, Mr. S."

"The second thing that concerns me is the possibility that if he is not what Paulo tells me he believes he is, that, in other words, if he went either to the Narcotics Division or to the Federal Narcotics people . . . You understand?"

"Mr. S.," Mr. Rosselli said very carefully, "that word never even came up. Narcotics."

"Mr. S.," Mr. Cassandro added, "he thinks the shipment is money."

"So you have told me," Mr. Savarese said. "My question is, would he be tempted by that much money? We certainly could not complain to the authorities that we had lost a large sum of money, could we?"

"He's not that smart, Mr. S.," Mr. Rosselli said.

"Yes. He is not smart. That worries me. He is a fool, a fool without money. Fools without money do foolish, desperate things."

"I see what you mean, Mr. S.," Mr. Rosselli said.

"We could test him," Mr. Savarese said. "That is one option. I could tell my associates in Baltimore that in the interests of safety, we should have nothing of interest to the authorities in the bag, just to be sure."

"That's an idea," Mr. Baltazari said.

"But that would make me look as if I don't have things under control here, wouldn't it?"

"I can see what you mean," Mr. Baltazari said seriously.

"Or, we can take the chance. I will tell Gian-Carlo to telephone Baltimore and tell them everything is in order. So my question to you, Ricco, is what should I do?"

Mr. Baltazari thought it over for a very long moment before he replied.

"Mr. S.," he said carefully. "You asked me, and I will tell you what I honestly think. I think we have to trust Gian-Carlo's and Paulo's judgment. If they say the cop is going to be all right, so far as I'm concerned, that's it."

Mr. Baltazari felt a flush of excitement.

I handled that perfect, he thought. *If I had said,* "I go for the test," *that would have meant that I thought Gian-Carlo and Paulo were wrong, that they were going to get Mr. S. in trouble. That would have really pissed them off. This way, they set it up, it fucks up somehow, it's their fault, and I'm out of it.*

Mr. Savarese nodded, then put another piece of Chicken Breast Alfredo into his mouth and chewed it slowly.

"I thank you for your honest opinion," he said, finally. "So this is what we're going to do. I'm going to have Gian-Carlo call the people in Baltimore and tell them to go ahead."

"There's not going to be a problem with the cop, Mr. S.," Mr. Rosselli said. "He needs to get out from under them markers, and he needs the cash so bad, he's pissing his pants."

"Give Ricco the information," Mr. Savarese said.

Mr. Rosselli handed Mr. Baltazari a sheet of notepaper. On it was written, "Eastern 4302. 9:45."

"That's from San Juan," Mr. Savarese explained. "Tomorrow night, it arrives. The shipment will be in a blue American Tourister plastic suitcase. On both sides of the suitcase will be two strips of adhesive tape with shine on it."

Mr. Baltazari then asked the question foremost in his mind. He held up the piece of paper with "Eastern 4302" on it. "Mr. S., what am I supposed to do with this?"

"I value your judgment, Ricco," Mr. Savarese said. "I want you to give that to the cop. Tell him about the tape with the shine on the blue American Tourister suitcase. Look at his eyes. Make up your mind, is he reliable or not? If it smells like bad fish, then we do the test. It'll be a little embarrassing for me to have to call Baltimore, but there'll be plenty of time if you see the cop when he gets off duty, and better a little embarrassment than taking a loss like that, or worse. You agree?"

"Right, Mr. S.," Mr. Baltazari said.

His stomach suddenly hurt.

"You go see him after midnight, at that woman's apartment, and then you call Gian-Carlo. If you make the judgment that everything will be all right, then that's it. If he sees something wrong, Gian-Carlo, then you call me at the house, understand?"

"Right, Mr. S.," Mr. Rosselli said.

"I feel better," Mr. Savarese said. "Now that we've talked this over. I think I might even have a little cognac. You got a nice cognac, Ricco?"

"Absolutely, Mr. S.," Mr. Baltazari said, and got up from the table.

In the kitchen, he put a teaspoon of baking soda in half a glass of water, dissolved it, and drank it down.

Then he went and got a fresh bottle of Rémy Martin VSOP, which he knew Mr. Savarese preferred, and carried it back to the table.

At about the same time that his reliability was being discussed in Ristorante Alfredo, Corporal Vito Lanza told Officer Jerzy Masnik, his trainee, that he was going to take a break, get some coffee and a doughnut, get the hell out of the office for a few minutes, he was getting a headache.

He made his way to the Eastern Airlines area of the airport, and used his passkey to open a door marked CLOSED TO THE PUBLIC—DO NOT ENTER.

It opened on a flight of stairs, which took him down to the level of the ramp. He walked to the office from which the Eastern baggage handling operation was directed, and asked the man in charge if it would be all right if he borrowed one of the baggage train tractors for a couple of minutes.

"Help yourself," the Eastern supervisor told him.

Vito drove slowly among the airplanes parked at the lines of airways, watching as baggage handlers loaded luggage into, and off-loaded it from, the bellies of the airplanes. Twice, he stopped the tractor and got off, for a closer examination. Once he actually went inside the fuselage of a Lockheed 10-11.

No one questioned his presence. Cops are expected to be in strange places.

The way to get a particular piece of luggage off a particular airplane, Vito decided, was to stand by the conveyor belt and watch for it as it was off-loaded from the airplane, seeing on which of the carts of the baggage train it had been placed.

Once he knew that, he would drive his tractor to the door where luggage was taken from the baggage carts and loaded on the conveyor belt that would transport it, beneath the terminal, to the baggage carousel.

Taking it from the airplane or the baggage carts at the airplane would look suspicious. But with the baggage handlers busy throwing bags on the conveyor belt under the terminal, no one would notice if he removed a bag from the other side of the cart.

And if they did notice him, and someone actually asked him what he was doing, he would say that it was his mother's, or his sister's, and he was just saving her a trip to the baggage carousel.

Nobody questioned what a cop did. And he was only going to do this once. If he did it all the time, somebody might say something about it.

Vito told himself that there were laws and laws. Everybody broke some kind of law, except maybe the pope. And screwing the IRS was something everybody did. And that's all he was going to be doing, was keeping the IRS from making a pain in the ass of itself. It wasn't like he was smuggling drugs or jewels. He wouldn't be able to do that.

What he was doing, Vito convinced himself, was helping a friend, repaying a favor.

It wasn't anything worse than some chief inspector fixing a speeding ticket for his next-door neighbor.

The reason Gian-Carlo Rosselli, or really the people who own the Oaks and Pines, are willing to come up with ten big ones, the four I owe them on the markers, and six besides, is like them buying insurance. It's the cost of them doing business. It's not like they're bribing me or anything. They want all that money to arrive safely so they can pay that coal-mine guy—that lucky sonofabitch, he probably doesn't even need it—what he won.

It was just lucky. They knew me, and I needed the money. That fucking plumber is going to want his money, and with my luck lately, I just don't have it. So this way, everybody is happy. The plumbers, the people who own Oaks and Pines, and especially that fucker with the coal mines who hit his number four times in a row.

And my run of bad luck can't keep on for fucking ever!

Vito drove around the aircraft parking area a few minutes more, trying to figure the best way to get the suitcase, once he had taken it from the baggage cart, out to his car. That turned out to be simplicity itself.

There was a gate leading from the work area under the terminal to the outside. There was a rent-a-cop working it. No rent-a-cop was going to stop a real cop and ask him what he was doing.

I'll just drive one of these goddamned tractors out the gate, go to the parking lot, put the suitcase in the trunk of the Caddy, and drive back in and give them their tractor back.

He decided to try it. It worked like a jewel. He went out of the gate, drove to the parking lot, went in the trunk of the Caddy, got back on the tractor, and drove back through the gate. The rent-a-cop didn't look at him twice.

Why should he? I'm a police corporal. If I'm riding around on an Eastern Airlines tractor, so what? What business was that of a rent-a-cop?

Vito drove the tractor back to the Eastern office and told the guy he'd returned it.

"Anytime," the Eastern guy said. "Support your local sheriff, right?"

Starting at fifteen minutes to midnight, within minutes of each other, automobiles carrying Chief Inspectors Matt Lowenstein and Denny Coughlin, Supervisory Special Agent H. Charles Larkin of the Secret Service, and A-SAC (Criminal) Frank F. Young of the FBI arrived at the headquarters of the Special Operations Division.

The building, and especially the corridor outside Peter Wohl's—what had been the principal's—office, and the office itself were crowded with senior police officers. All the participants in the earlier meeting in the commissioner's office, except Mayor Carlucci, were present. In addition, the commanding officers of Central, North Central, and Northwest Detective Divisions; the commanding officers of Ordnance Disposal and Stakeout; and Captain Jack Duffy, the special assistant to the commissioner for inter-agency liaison, had either been summoned or had naturally migrated to the Schoolhouse as the center of the operation.

Three inspectors, who had been neither summoned nor invited, were also in Peter Wohl's office when Chief Lowenstein marched in. They were the commanding officers of the South and North Detective Divisions and the Tactical Division. Their subordinates had made known to them the orders they had received from Chiefs Lowenstein and Coughlin, and they wanted to know what was going on.

Lowenstein ordered everyone out of Wohl's office but Coughlin, Wohl, and the three inspectors and the federal agents.

"Peter and I decided to hold this here, rather than in the Roundhouse," Lowenstein began, "for a couple of reasons. First of all, it's on my way home . . ."

He paused for the expected chuckle.

"Peter and I decided"? Wohl thought. *Inspector Peter Wohl is not only outranked by you, but, until very recently, by everybody else in this room. Despite his reputation within the Department as a real hard-ass, Lowenstein sometimes can be very gracious and kind.*

". . . and for another, all these white shirts showing up at the Roundhouse at midnight might give the gentlemen of the press the idea that something's going on. Charley Larkin thinks, and I agree, that the less the press is involved until we catch this guy, the better."

"The less the press is involved, the better, period," Inspector Wally Jenks said.

There were chuckles and grunts of approval.

"There's a real nasty copycat aspect to something like this," Charley Larkin said. "A lunatic who has been sitting around harmlessly studying his navel sees another lunatic is getting a lot of attention in the papers and on TV, and promptly decides the thing for him to do to get some attention is also blow something up. If I had my druthers, not a word of this would appear in the papers."

"Sometimes, Charley," Frank F. Young of the FBI said, "it's a good idea to let the tax-payers know where their money is going."

"Let me bring everybody up-to-date on where we stand," Lowenstein said, cutting off what could have been an argument about dealing with the press.

He went on: "We had ninety-six Wheatleys on the list. Eighty-nine of them have been contacted, and are off the list, which means we are down to seven. These are Wheatleys who were not at home when we rang doorbells. Or didn't answer the doorbell.

"We have detectives in unmarked cars sitting on the seven, backed up by Highway RPCs. If anyone leaves those seven houses, we will talk to them.

"Of the seven, two look more promising than the others. One is listed under the name of Wheatley, Stephen J., in the 5600 block of Frazier Avenue, and the other is Wheatley, M. C., in the 120 block of Farragut. Both these houses are in middle-class neighborhoods, which fits in both with somebody owning property in the sticks in Jersey and with the psychological profile we have of this guy. He's well educated, and it would figure he's making a decent living.

"Inspector Wohl believes, and Chief Coughlin and I agree, that taking either of these doors tonight would probably be counterproductive."

"Can I ask why?" Inspector Jenks asked.

"Worst-case scenario, Inspector," Wohl said. "He's in there. He's got explosives. He sets them off, and takes half the neighborhood with him."

"Next-worse-case scenario, Wally," Chief Coughlin said. "He's not in there. He's the editor of the *Catholic Messenger*. On his way to complain to the cardinal archbishop that while he and wife were having a retreat at Sacred Heart Monastery, the cops took his front and back doors and scared hell out of his cat, he stops by the Philadelphia *Ledger* to tell Arthur Nelson what Carlucci's Commandos have done to him."

That produced more outright laughter than chuckles.

"And Jerry Carlucci, Wally," Lowenstein added, "said he wants to be there if we take anybody's door."

"I agree with Inspector Wohl too," H. Charles Larkin said. "I don't think, if our man is in one of these houses, that he's liable to do anything tonight. Unless, of course, we panic him. Then all bets are off."

"So what Peter has come up with is this," Lowenstein went on. "At half past seven tomorrow morning, it gets light at six-fifty, we are going to send detectives to the houses adjacent to the houses in question and see what the neighbors know about Wheatley, Stephen J., and Wheatley, M. C. If it looks at all that there's a chance he's our guy, we evacuate the houses in the area, and then we take the door. Stakeout will take the door, backed up by Highway and Ordnance Disposal."

"And what if he's not our man?" Inspector Jenks asked.

"Then we take a look at the other five houses where nobody was home. There will be people still on them, of course."

And if we shoot blanks there too, Wohl thought, *we're back to square one.*

"So what happens now?" Inspector Jenks asked.

"I don't know about you, Wally," Coughlin said, "but I'm going to go home and go to bed."

"You each, you and Chief Lowenstein, are going to take one of these houses?" Jenks asked.

"That's up to Inspector Wohl," Lowenstein said. "Peter?"

"I'm going to be between the two houses," Wohl said. "Which door we take first, if we take any at all, will depend on what the detectives come up with when they talk to the neighbors. We'll do them one at a time."

"And the mayor's going to be there?"

"Yes, sir. That's what he said."

"And we'll be with Peter and the mayor," Lowenstein said. "Denny's going to pick him up at his house in Chestnut Hill at seven."

Lowenstein put a match to a large black cigar, then turned to Wohl.

"Is that about it, Peter?"

"Yes, sir. All that remains to be done is to pass the word."

"Then I'm going home," Lowenstein said, and walked out of the room.

The meeting was over.

27.

As Mr. Ricco Baltazari walked down the corridor to the door of Mrs. Antoinette Marie Wolinski Schermer's apartment, at quarter to one in the morning, he was aware that several things were bothering him.

There was the obvious, of course, that he was between the rock (Mr. Savarese) and the hard place (Mssrs. Gian-Carlo Rosselli and Paulo Cassandro) about this goddamned cop. If the cop either didn't look like he could handle what was required of him or, worse, that he was maybe setting them up, he would have to tell Mr. S. that he thought so, or risk winding up pushing up grass in the Tinnicum Swamps out by the airport, if something went wrong.

But if he did that, it was the same thing as saying that Gian-Carlo and Paulo were a couple of assholes who were going to get Mr. S. in trouble. They would be insulted, and they both had long memories.

And that wasn't all. There was the business between the goddamned cop and Tony. He was having trouble remembering that all she was, was a dumb Polack who he liked to screw and nothing more. That had been possible as long as he hadn't actually seen what was going on.

But now he was going to be in her apartment, actually *their* apartment, where they'd had some really great times in the sack, and where she was now fucking the goddamned cop.

Well, shit, there's nothing I can do about it.

He pushed her doorbell and in a moment Tony answered it, wearing a fancy nightgown he'd bought her, and which he now clearly remembered taking off her.

"Whaddaya say, Tony?"

"Hello, Ricco."

"Your boyfriend here? I'd like a word with him."

"Come on in, Ricco," Tony said, and then raised her voice. "Vito, honey, it's Mr. Baltazari. He wants to talk to you."

"It's who?"

"I'm a friend of Mr. Rosselli, Vito," Ricco said.

The goddamned cop came into the living room in his underwear.

My *living room, I'm paying the freight. And* my *girl, I'm paying the freight there too. And here's this sonofabitch* in his underwear.

"Vito," Ricco said, putting out his hand, "Mr. Rosselli got tied up. He had to go to the Poconos, as a matter of fact, and he asked me to drop by and pass a little information to you."

"What did you say your name was?"

"Baltazari, Ricco Baltazari. I run the Ristorante Alfredo."

"Oh," the goddamned cop said. He did not offer to shake hands. "You know Tony?"

"We seen each other around, right, Tony?"

"You could put it that way, I guess," Tony said.

"So what's the message?"

"Tony, could you give us a minute alone? Get yourself a beer or something?"

"Whatever you say, Mr. Baltazari," Tony said and went into the bedroom. She turned as she closed the door and gave him a look.

"That shipment you and Mr. Rosselli was talking about?" Ricco began.

"What about it?"

"It's coming tomorrow night. I mean tonight, it's already today, ain't it? On Eastern Flight 4302 from San Juan. At nine forty-five."

Vito Lanza nodded.

"It's going to be in a blue American Tourister suitcase, one of the plastic ones, and there will be two red reflective strips on each side of the suitcase," Ricco went on.

Vito nodded again.

"That going to pose any problems for you, Vito?"

"What kind of problems?"

"You're not going to write that down, or anything?"

"I can remember Eastern 4302 at nine forty-five."

"From San Juan."

"Eastern 4302 is always from San Juan," Vito said. "Every day but Sunday."

He's a wiseass. He's an asshole who gambles with money he doesn't have, a fucking cop too dumb to know he's being set up, or that the only reason he's fucking Tony is because I told her to fuck him, and he's a wiseass.

"I'm going to ask you again, Vito. Is that going to pose any problems?"

"What kind of problems?"

"Money does funny things to people. Nothing personal, you understand. But you understand why I have to ask."

"I understand."

"I'm sure you're not that kind of a guy. Mr. Rosselli speaks very well of you, but there are some people, when they get around that kind of money, they do foolish things. Foolish things that could get them killed."

"I'm not that kind of guy," Vito said evenly.

"I'm sure you're not," Ricco said.

"But I do have a couple of questions."

"What kind of questions?"

"Two questions. What do I do with the suitcase once I get it out of the airport?"

Jesus Christ, I don't know. Didn't they tell him, for Christ's sake?

"Didn't Mr. Rosselli tell you what to do with it?"

"If he had told me, I wouldn't be asking," Vito said calmly.

"Then I guess we'll have to ask him, won't we?" Ricco replied. "What was the other question?"

"When and where do I get my money?"

You're a greedy sonofabitch too, aren't you? Well, I guess if I was into Oaks and Pines for four grand worth of markers, four grand that I didn't have, I'd be a little greedy myself.

"You don't worry about that, Vito. You carry out your end of the deal, Mr. Rosselli will carry out his."

"Yeah."

Ricco walked to the telephone and dialed Gian-Carlo Rosselli's number.

"Yeah?"

"Ricco. I'm with our friend."

"How's things going?"

"He wants to know what he should do with the basket of fruit."

"Shit, I didn't think about that," Rosselli said. There was a long pause. "Ask him if he could take it home, and we'll arrange to pick it up there."

Ricco covered the microphone with his hand.

"Mr. Rosselli says you should take it home, and he'll arrange to have it picked up. You got any problem with that?"

"No," Vito said, after thinking it over for a moment. "That'd be all right."

"He says that's fine," Ricco said.

"Okay. And everything else is fine too, right?"

"Everything else is fine too."

Mr. Rosselli hung up on Mr. Baltazari.

"Okay," Ricco said. "Everything's fine. I'll get out of your hair."

Vito Lanza nodded.

Ricco turned and walked to the door and opened it. Then he turned.

"I got to make the point," he said. "You know what happens to people who do foolish things, right?"

"Yeah, I know," Vito said. "And I already told you I'm not foolish."

"Good," Ricco said and went through the door.

When, a few minutes before one A.M., Matt Payne drove into the underground garage at his apartment at the wheel of the unmarked Special Operations Division car he had been given for the business tomorrow morning, he was surprised to find that the space where he normally parked the Bug was empty.

As if I need another reminder that my ass is dragging, I have no idea where the Bug is. It's almost certainly at the Schoolhouse—where else would it be?—but I'll be damned if I remember leaving it there.

He parked the Ford, and rode the elevator to the third floor, and then walked up the stairs to his apartment.

The red light on the answering machine, which he had come to hate with an amazing passion toward an inanimate object, was blinking.

I don't want to hear what messages are waiting for me. They will be, for one thing, probably not messages at all, but the buzz, hummm, click indication that my callers had not elected to leave a message, in other words, that Evelyn was back dialing my number. Or it might actually be a message from Evelyn, which would be even worse.

On the other hand, it might be a bulletin from the Schoolhouse; Wohl might have thought of some other way in which I can be useful before I meet O'Dowd at half past six, which is 5.5 hours from now.

He was still debating whether to push the PLAY button when the phone rang.

It has to be either Wohl or O'Dowd. And if it's not, if it's Evelyn, I'll just hang up.

"Payne."

"Christ, where the hell have you been?" Charley McFadden's voice demanded.

"What the hell do you want?"

"Have you been at the sauce?"

"No, as a matter of fact, I haven't. But it seems like a splendid idea. You running a survey, or what?"

"Matt, you better get your ass out here, right now," Charley said.

"Out where, and why?"

"I'm on the job. Northwest Detectives. Just get your ass out here, right now," McFadden said, and hung up.

What the hell is that all about?

But Charley's not pulling my chain. I can tell from his voice when he's doing that. Whatever this is, it is not a manifestation of Irish and/or police humor.

He had, in what he thought of as a Pavlovian reflex, laid his revolver on the mantelpiece. He reclaimed it and went down the stairs and took the elevator to the basement.

The Porsche was where he remembered parking it, and he took the keys to it from his pocket and was about to put them in the door when he reconsidered.

Whatever Charley McFadden wants, it's personal, and I don't want to be about personal business when I run into one of Wohl's station wagons full of nuns. But on the other hand, it was made goddamned clear to me that Wohl wants to know where I am, second by second, and there's no radio in the Porsche. The minute I drive the Porsche out of here, Wohl will call, and when he gets the answering machine, will get on the radio. And I won't answer.

He got in the unmarked car and drove out of the garage. There wasn't much traffic, and he was lucky with the lights. The only one he caught was at North Broad Street and Ridge Avenue, which gave him a chance to look at the Divine Lorraine Hotel, and wonder what the hell went on in there.

Wouldn't the bishop of the Episcopal Diocese of Philadelphia have a heart attack if there was suddenly a booming voice from heaven saying, "You're wrong, Bishop; my boy Father Divine has it right"?

He remembered he hadn't reported in. He switched to the J frequency and told Police Radio that William Fourteen was en route to Northwest Detectives.

He then wondered, as he continued up North Broad Street, whether what Charley was so upset about was the missing Bug.

I know goddamned well I left it at the apartment. Stolen? Out of the basement, past the rent-a-cop, who knows who it belongs to? And who the hell would steal the Bug when the Porsche was sitting right next to it? Who would steal the Bug if nothing was sitting right next to it?

That impeccable logical analysis of the situation collapsed immediately upon Detective Payne's entering the parking lot of Northwest Detectives, which shares quarters with the 35th District at Broad and Champlost Streets.

There was the Bug.

Jesus, what the hell is this all about?

He went in the building and took the stairs to the second floor two at a time.

"I'm Detective Payne of Special Operations," Matt said, smiling at the desk man just inside the squad room. "Charley . . ."

"I know who you are," the desk man said with something less than overwhelming charm. He raised his voice: "McFadden!"

Charley appeared around the corner of a wall inside.

"What's with my car?" Matt asked.

McFadden, who looked very uncomfortable, didn't reply. He came to Matt, and motioned for him to follow him down the stairs.

They went into the district holding cells.

"You got him?" Matt asked. "Brilliant work, Detective McFadden!"

"You better take a look at this," Charley said, pointing at one of the cells.

A very faint bulb illuminated the cell interior just enough for Matt to be able to make out a figure lying on the sheet steel bunk. As his eyes adjusted to the gloom, Matt saw that the figure was in a skirt, and thus a female, and there was just enough time for the thought, *Christ, a* woman *stole my Bug?* when he recognized the woman.

"Jesus Christ!" he said.

Charley McFadden tugged on his sleeve and pulled him out of the detention cell area.

"Okay, what happened?" Matt asked, hoping that he was managing to sound matter-of-fact and professional.

"I was out, serving a warrant, and when I brought the critter in here, two Narcotics undercover guys, I know both of them, brought her in."

"On what charges?"

McFadden did not reply directly.

"They were watching a house on Bouvier, near Susquehanna," he said, avoiding Matt's eyes. "Thinking maybe they'd get lucky and be able to grab the delivery boy."

"What delivery boy? What are you talking about?"

"You know where I mean? Bouvier, near Susquehanna?"

Matt searched his memory and came up with nothing specific, just a vague picture of Susquehanna Avenue as it moved through the slums of North Philadelphia near Temple University.

"No," Mat confessed. "Not exactly."

"You don't go in there alone, you understand?" Charley said.

Matt understood. He was not talking about it being the sort of place it was unwise for Miss Penelope Detweiler of Chestnut Hill to visit alone, he was talking about a place where an armed police officer did not go alone, for fear of his life.

He nodded.

"So they see this white girl in a Volkswagen come down Bouvier, and that attracts their attention. So she circles the block, they think looking for the house they're sitting on. And weaving. They think she's either drunk or stoned. These are not nice guys, Matt, do-gooders. But the thought of what was liable to happen to a white girl, stoned or drunk, going in that house was too much."

"Oh, God!"

"So one of them got out of the car and ran down the block, and the next time she came around, he flagged her down. She almost ran over him. But he stopped her, and saw she was drunk. . . ."

"Drunk?" Matt asked.

Please, God! Drunk, *not drugged.*

"Drunk," Charley said. "So he put cuffs on her and got in her car. She told them she's your girlfriend. So they tried to call you, and when they couldn't find you, brought her here. They know we're pals."

"They know who she is?"

"No. Just that she's your girl. She didn't have an ID. For that matter, not even a purse. Just a couple of hundred-dollar bills in her underwear."

"What's she charged with?"

"Right now, nothing. I called in some favors."

"Jesus, Charley!"

"Yeah, well, you'd do the same for me," McFadden said.

Absolutely. The very next time that your girlfriend, Miss Mary-Margaret McCarthy, R.N., who is probably the only virgin over thirteen that I know, gets herself hauled in by an undercover Narcotics officer, I'll pull in whatever favors I can to get her off.

Christ, I feel like crying.

"I don't suppose you have any handcuffs, do you?"

Jesus Christ, handcuffs? What for?

Matt shook his head, no.

McFadden reached behind him, where he wore his handcuffs draped over his belt. He handed them to Matt.

"You got a key?"

Matt nodded.

The cuffs are so it will appear to the uniforms in the lobby that I'm taking her out of here under arrest.

"She's . . . uh. She was pretty drunk, Matt. And mad about being in here."

"You're saying, I'm going to need the cuffs?"

McFadden nodded.

"She's passed out. But if she wakes up in the car, I think you'd be better off if she was cuffed."

"God!"

"Dailey!" McFadden called.

The turnkey, a tired-looking uniform who looked to be about fifty, came up to them.

"Pete Dailey, Matt Payne," McFadden made the introductions. The two men shook hands, but neither said a word.

"Open it up, please, Pete," McFadden said.

The turnkey unlocked the cell, slid the barred door open, and then walked away.

Penny Detweiler did not stir.

Charley went into the cell. Matt followed him. Charley looked at Matt, then put out his hand for the handcuffs. When Matt gave them to him, he pulled Penny's wrists behind her, and put the cuffs on her wrists.

The smell in the cell was foul. Matt wondered if he was going to further embarrass himself by being sick. And then he realized that the smell was coming from Penny.

She had lost control of her bowels, and probably her bladder as well.

The proper word for that, Detective Payne thought, *is "incontinent."*

And then he was swept by nausea, and barely made it to the lidless toilet in the corner of the cell in time.

After a moment, as he became aware that he was soaked in a clammy sweat, he heard Charley ask, "You okay, buddy?"

"Yeah," Matt said, and forced himself to his feet.

He went to the bunk, and the two men pulled Penny erect. She was limp, and surprisingly heavy.

Jesus, she stinks!

They half carried, half dragged her from the detention cell area to the desk.

Officer Peter Dailey appeared with a newspaper.

"What are you driving?" he asked.

"A blue unmarked Ford," Matt said.

Officer Dailey preceded them out of the building and to the car, where he opened the rear door and spread the newspaper over the seat.

"I'll take her shoulders," Charley McFadden said. "You take her feet."

McFadden backed into the rear seat, dragging Penny after him, and then exited the car by the other door.

He came around the back as Matt was closing the opposite door.

"You going to be able to handle her?" Charley asked.

"Yeah," Matt said.

What the hell am I going to do with her? I can't take her home in this condition. And I can't take her to the apartment. What would I do with her when I have to go to work?

"I can get off to go with you."

"Charley, what you can do is call my sister. She's not in the book. The number is 928-5923. Call her and tell her I'm on my way."

"Nine Two Eight, Five Nine Two Three," Charley repeated, setting the number in his memory. "Do I tell her why?"

"Tell her I need some help," Matt said. "Tell her to come down into the lobby and wait for me."

"I can go with you, buddy."

"I can handle it," Matt said. "Thank you, Charley."

"Forget it," McFadden said, and touched Matt's arm gently. "I'm sorry, Matt."

Matt walked around the front of the Ford and got behind the wheel.

He had not gone more than four blocks south on North Broad Street before there was the sound of retching and the smell of vomitus was added to the smell of feces and urine.

He rolled down his window so that he would not be sick again.

Amelia Payne, M.D., fully dressed, came out of the plate-glass doors leading to the lobby of 2601 Parkway as Matt pulled up.

He got out of the car.

"Where is she, in the back?"

Did Charley tell her what happened? Or did she figure that out herself?

"Yes. She's in pretty bad shape."

"What did she take, do you know? She may have overdosed. You should have taken her to University Hospital."

"I think she's just drunk," Matt said. "I don't know. Can you tell?"

"Just drunk? How fortunate for you," Amy said.

She pulled open the rear door and climbed in. Matt saw the bright light of a flashlight, and when he looked, saw that Amy had pushed Penny's eyes open and was shining the light into her eyes. Then she slapped her, twice, three times.

"What have you taken?" Matt heard Amy ask, several times, but could not hear a reply, if there was one.

Amy backed out of the car.

"Let's get her upstairs," she said. "Can you manage? Should I get the doorman?"

"Just make sure the doors are open," Matt said.

He reached in the car and pulled Penny out, bent and threw her over his shoulder in the fireman's carry, and carried her into the lobby and into the elevator.

Amy followed him in and pushed the button. The door closed and the elevator began to rise. Amy turned to face him.

"You sonofabitch, I told you this was liable to happen!" she said bitterly.

"I don't know what happened. She came to the apartment, we had Chinese, and then I went to work."

"I'll tell you what happened. One of your harem showed up at your apartment. Penny called me about nine-thirty."

He didn't reply.

"God *damn* you, Matt," Amy said as the elevator door opened at her floor. She walked off the elevator and down the corridor and by the time Matt got there had the door open.

"Take her in the bathroom," Amy ordered, and led the way.

She turned on the bathtub faucets, then turned to Matt.

"We're going to have to get those things off her wrists and undress her," Amy said. "How we're going to do that in here, I don't know. Can you lower her to the floor?"

"I can try," Matt said.

He dropped to his knees, and then Amy turned from the tub and helped him lower Penny to the tiles of the bathroom floor. He unlocked the handcuffs.

"Help me undress her," Amy said, and then when she saw the look on his face: "Don't look shocked, dammit, you've seen her naked before. And it's your fault she's like this."

Amy, somewhere in the process, disappeared for a moment and returned with a roll of paper towels, with which she cleaned up most of the mess around Penny's groin. Then Matt lowered Penny into the tub, and Amy finished the cleaning process.

Penny made noises, not quite groans, but much like them, but was not fully conscious. Once, she slipped down in the tub and Amy ordered Matt to slide her back up.

Finally, rather coldly, Matt thought, Amy turned on the shower, and as the water drained, she used it to rinse Penny off, as a hose might be used to clear a sidewalk.

"Get her out of there," she said, finally. "Be careful. She's slippery."

Matt got Penny out of the tub and held her up by locking his hands under her arms and breasts. Amy made a halfhearted effort to dry her with a towel, then bent and picked up her feet, and they carried her into Amy's spare bedroom and put her between the sheets.

"For what the hell it's worth," Matt said. "I'm sorry."

"So am I," Amy said. "And for what the hell it's worth, it just occurred to me that if you were not a cop, this would probably be more of a disaster than it is."

"What happens now?"

"You get out of here. I call the Detweilers, who probably need a padded cell themselves by now, and tell them Penny is here with me. What happens in the morning, God knows."

"From what I understand, the Narcs got her before she could buy any drugs," Matt said.

"You sound as if you actually care," Amy said.

"Fuck you, Amy! God damn you! Of course I care."

"Get out of here, Matt," Amy said.

When he got back to the underground garage at his apartment, Matt took the newspaper from the back seat. They had protected the upholstery from Penny's incontinence, but when she had vomited, that had gone onto the floor carpet, where there were no newspapers.

He went up to his apartment and returned with Lysol and everything else in the under-the-sink cabinet he thought might be helpful in cleaning the carpet and getting rid of the smell.

It still smelled like vomitus, so he went back to the apartment and got the bottle of Lime after-shave Amy had given him for Christmas and sprinkled all that was left over the interior of the car.

It was three when he climbed the stairs for the last time.

The fucking smell has followed me up here!

He then realized that his suit was soiled, probably ruined.

Can you get that shit, accurate word, shit, out of suiting material?

He took his clothing off, down to his skin, put on a bathrobe, and then carried the suit, the shirt, the necktie, and the underwear down to the basement and jammed it into one of the commercial garbage cans.

Then he went back to his apartment and showered and shaved and waited for it to grow light by watching television. He fell asleep in his armchair at four-thirty. At five-thirty, the alarm went off.

At ten minutes to six, as Peter Wohl was measuring coffee grounds into the basket of his machine, his out-of-tune "Be It Ever So Humble" door chimes sounded.

He went quickly through the door, wondering who the hell it could be. Usually, a telephone call preceded an early morning call.

Unless, of course, it's my father, who, I suspect, really hopes to catch me with some lovely in here.

It was Captain Richard Olsen, of Internal Affairs.

"Good morning, Swede," Wohl said. "What gets you out of bed at this hour?"

"I need to talk to you, and I didn't want it to be over the phone."

Olsen wouldn't do this unless he thought it was necessary.

"Come on in. I'm just making coffee."

"It's been a long time since I've been here. I remember the couch. What was her name?"

"What was whose name?"

"That interior decorator. You really had the hots for her."

"I forget," Wohl said.

"The hell you do," Olsen chuckled.

"You had breakfast?"

"No. But that doesn't mean you have to feed me."

"There's bacon and eggs. That all right?"

"Fine. Can I help?"

"You can make bacon and eggs while I get dressed," Wohl said. "And I'll finish the coffee."

"Lanza is dirty," Olsen said. "Or it goddamned well looks that way."

"I hope it won't require action between seven and nine this morning," Wohl said.

"No."

"Good, then I can get dressed," Wohl said, and went into his bedroom.

When he came out, he said, "What I really am curious about is why you couldn't have told me that on the phone?"

"We have a wiretap of questionable legality," Olsen said.

"How questionable?"

"Absolutely illegal," Olsen said.

"Oh, shit," Wohl said. "And it was found? Are you in trouble, Swede?"

"The tap is gone, and we were not caught."

"Who's we? You knew about this?"

"No, of course not. Can I start at the beginning?"

"The bacon's burning," Wohl said.

Olsen quickly took the pan off the burner and quickly forked bacon strips out of it.

"Well done, not destroyed," he said.

"Thank God for small blessings," Wohl said. *"I'll* make the eggs. Can you handle the toaster?"

"I don't know. I used to think I could fry bacon without a problem."

"Give it a try. Tell me about the tap."

"You remember I told you about Sergeant Framm and Detective Pillare losing Lanza at the airport, and your man Payne saving their ass?"

"Yeah."

"Yeah, well, Framm was humiliated by that. So he thought he'd make up for it by being Super Cop. He tapped the Schermer woman's line."

"How did you find out?"

"You really want to know?"

"Yeah, I think I better know."

"He told me," Olsen said.

"Oh, Jesus! Now I'm sorry I asked."

"He means well, Peter. I think he just watches too many cop shows on the TV. *They* don't have to get a warrant for a tap."

"We do. I hope you told him that."

"What do you think?"

"Not that we could use it, but what did he hear?"

"They tailed Lanza from the airport when he went off tour at midnight. He went to the Schermer woman's apartment. At quarter to one, he was visited by Mr. Ricco Baltazari. . . ."

"The Ristorante Alfredo Ricco Baltazari?"

"One and the same. He stayed about ten minutes. While he was there, a male, almost certainly Baltazari, called somebody, no name, but Organized Crime told me the number is the unlisted number of Mr. Gian-Carlo Rosselli."

"You didn't tell Organized Crime why you wanted to know, I hope?"

"No. Just asked if they had a name to go with the number."

Olsen took a notebook from his pocket, and opened it.

"Ricco told the no-name guy he was with quote, our friend, end quote, and that the friend, quote, wants to know what he should do with the basket of fruit, unquote."

"Swede, did you listen to the tape?"

"What tape?"

"Is that how you're going to play it?"

Olsen shrugged helplessly.

"Was there a reply?" Wohl asked.

"No name replied, quote, Ask him if he could take it home, and we'll arrange to pick it up there, unquote. Then Ricco replied, quote, He says that's fine, unquote."

Wohl grunted.

"That's all?"

"Two more lines: Unnamed, quote, Okay. And everything else is fine too, right? unquote, to which Ricco replies, quote, Everything else is fine too, unquote."

"Being the clever detective that I am, I don't think the basket of fruit is oranges and grapefruit and things of that nature," Wohl said. "Drugs?"

"What else?" Olsen said. "Rosselli is a heavy hitter."

"Lanza is going to somehow get his hands on this 'fruit basket' at the airport, get it away from the airport, and take it home. Where Rosselli will arrange to have it picked up, right?"

"That's how I see it, Peter."

"God, I'd like to bag Rosselli and Baltazari picking it up," Wohl said.

"Maybe we can," Olsen said.

"Don't hold your breath," Wohl said. "They'll send some punk. They don't take risks."

"Maybe we'll get lucky," Olsen said.

"I have the feeling this will happen tonight," Olsen said.

"Then get Sergeant Whatsisname off the job."

"Framm. He's gone. I have a suggestion, or maybe I'm asking for a favor . . ."

"Either way, what?"

"Sergeant O'Dowd. Can I have him?"

"Sure," Wohl replied after a just perceptible hesitation. "Can I make a suggestion?"

"Of course."

"Have somebody, preferably two men, on both Lanza's house and the girlfriend's apartment, from right now until whatever happens with the fruit basket happens."

"That may take two or three days, longer."

"So what? I don't want this to go wrong. Maybe we *can* catch Rosselli or Baltazari too."

"I don't suppose there's anybody else you could let me have?"

"Not until we catch this fruitcake who wants to disintegrate the Vice President."

"How's that going?"

"At eight o'clock, we may or may not take a couple of doors behind which he may or may not be hiding. Not well, in other words."

"I'll handle the Lanza thing myself if it comes down to that. If I haven't forgotten how to surveil somebody."

"I'll send Tony Harris down to you. I'll have him call you. You tell him when and where. I really would like to put one of these Mafiosos in the slam with our dirty cop."

"Thank you," Olsen said.

"I didn't hear anything you said about an illegal tap, Swede. The bacon was burning or something."

"Thank you, Peter."

28.

At 7:25 A.M., as they sat in a nearly new Ford sedan in the 1100 block of Farragut Street, a very large, expensively tailored police officer turned to a somewhat smaller, but equally expensively tailored police officer and smiled.

"You are really quite dapper this morning, Matthew, my boy," Sergeant Jason Washington said approvingly. "I like that suit. Tripler?"

"Brooks Brothers. Just following orders, Sergeant: You told me to dress like a lawyer."

"And so you have. But despite looking like one of the more successful legal counsel to the Mafioso, somehow I suspect that all is not perfect in your world. Is there anything I can do?"

"Things are not, as a matter of fact, getting better and better, every day, in every way," Matt said.

"My question, Matthew, my boy, was, 'Is there anything I can do?' "

"I wish there were," Matt said.

"Try me," Washington said. "What is the precise nature of your problem? An *affaire de coeur,* perhaps?"

"A couple of undercover guys from Narcotics arrested Penny Detweiler last night, as she was cruising in the vicinity of Susquehanna and Bouvier."

The joking tone was gone from Washington's voice when he replied, replaced with genuine concern.

"Damn! I'm sorry to hear that. I'd hoped that—what was that place they sent her? In Nevada?—would help her."

"The Lindens. Apparently the fix didn't take."

"What have they charged her with?"

"Nothing. They picked her up for drunk driving before she was able to make her connection. She gave them my name. They couldn't find me, but they knew that Charley McFadden and I are close, so they took her to Northwest Detectives, and he got them to turn her loose to me."

"Aside from trying to make a buy, there is no other reason I can think of that she would be in that area," Washington said.

"No, there's not. She was trying to make a buy. And according to McFadden, if the undercover guys hadn't taken her in, she'd probably have had her throat cut."

"If she was lucky," Washington said. "I'm sorry, Matt. That slipped out. But McFadden is right. Where is she now?"

"I took her to my sister. My sister the shrink."

"*I* admire your sister," Washington said. "That was the thing to do."

"William Seven," the radio went off. "William One."

Matt grabbed the microphone.

"Seven," he said.

"It's that time," Wohl's voice metallically announced.

Matt looked at Washington, who nodded.

"On our way," Matt said into the microphone.

They got out of the Ford. Washington opened the trunk and took out a briefcase, and then a second, and handed one to Matt.

They walked up Farragut Street, hoping they looked like two successful real estate salesmen beginning their day early, crossed the intersection, and walked halfway down the block.

There they climbed the stairs of a house, crossed the porch, and rang the doorbell.

They could hear footsteps inside, but it was a long minute before the door was finally opened to them by a woman maybe thirty-five, obviously caught three quarters of the way through getting dressed for work.

"Yes, what is it?" she asked, somewhat shy of graciously, looking with curiosity between them.

Washington held out his identification.

"Madam, I'm Sergeant Washington of the Police Department and this is Detective Payne. We would very much like a moment of your time. May we please come in?"

The woman turned and raised her voice.

"Bernie, it's the cops!"

"The cops?" an incredulous voice replied.

A moment later Bernie, a very thin, stylishly dressed, or half-dressed, man, appeared.

"Sir, I'm Sergeant Washington of the Police Department and this is Detective Payne. We would very much like a moment of your time. May we please come in?"

"Yeah, sure. Come on in. Is something the matter?"

"Thank you very much," Jason Washington said. "You're Mr. and Mrs. Crowne, is that right?"

"I'm Bernie Crowne," Bernie said.

The woman colored slightly.

You are not, I deduce brilliantly, Matt thought, Mrs. *Crowne.*

"Say, my wife's not behind this, is she? My ex-wife?" Bernie Crowne asked.

"No, sir. This inquiry has to do with your neighbor, Mr. Wheatley."

"Marion?" Bernie asked. "What about him?"

"We've been trying to get in touch with Mr. Wheatley for several days now, Mr. Crowne, and we can't seem to catch him at home."

"What did he do? Rob a bank?"

"Oh, no. Nothing like that. Actually, we're not even sure we have the right Mr. Wheatley. There has been a fire in New Jersey, at a summer place, in what they call the Pine Barrens. The New Jersey State Police are trying to locate the owner. And they don't have a first name."

"Bullshit," Mr. Crowne said. "They don't send sergeants and detectives out to do that. My brother is a lieutenant in the 9th District, Sergeant. So you tell me what this is all about, or I'll call him, and he'll find out."

"Call him," Washington said flatly. "If he has any questions about what I'm doing here, tell him to call Chief Inspector Lowenstein."

Bernie looked at Washington for a moment.

"Okay. So go on. Marion's got a house in Jersey that burned down?"

"Do you have any idea where we could find Mr. Wheatley?"

"He works somewhere downtown. In a bank, I think."

"And Mrs. Wheatley?"

"There is no Mrs. Wheatley," the woman said.

Bernie held his hand at the level of his neck and made a waving motion with it, and then let his wrist fall limp.

"You don't *know* that, Bernie," the woman said.

"If it walks like a duck, quacks like a duck, right, Sergeant?"

"Most of the time," Washington agreed.

"Say," the woman said suddenly, triumphantly, pointing at Matt. "I thought you looked familiar. I know who you are! You're the detective who shot the Liberation Army, *Islamic* Liberation Army guy in the alley, aren't you?"

"Actually," Matt said, "the ILA guy shot me."

"Yeah," Bernie said. "But *then* you shot *him,* and killed the bastard. My brother, the lieutenant, thinks you're all right. You know Lieutenant Harry Crowne?"

"I'm afraid not," Matt said.

"Harry and I are old pals," Jason Washington said. "But can we talk about Mr. Wheatley now?"

"Well, I'll tell you this," the woman said. "The one thing Marion isn't is some Islamic nut. He's Mr. Goody Two Shoes. I don't know if he's what Bernie thinks he is, but he's not some revolutionary. He wouldn't hurt a fly."

"Well, I'm glad to hear that," Washington said. "Is there anything else you can tell us about him?"

"I hardly ever see him to talk to," Bernie said. "He mostly keeps to himself."

"You wouldn't happen to know," Jason asked, "if he was in the Army?"

"Yeah, that I know. He was. We were both in 'Nam at the same time. He told me, it could be bullshit, excuse the language, Doris, he told me he was a lieutenant in EOD. That means Explosive Ordnance Disposal."

"Yes, I know," Washington said. "Give me the radio, Matt."

Matt opened his briefcase and handed Washington the radio.

"William One, William Seven."

"One."

"Mr. Wheatley is a bachelor who has told his neighbor he served as a lieutenant in EOD in Vietnam," Washington said.

"Bingo!" Wohl said. "Stay where you are, Jason."

Marion Claude Wheatley was wakened at half past seven by the sound of screeching brakes and tearing metal. He got out of bed, went to the window, and looked down at the intersection of Ridge Avenue and North Broad Street.

Even though he looked carefully up and down both streets as far as he could, he could see no sign of an auto accident.

He turned from the window, took off his pajamas and carefully hung them on a hanger in the closet, then took a shower and shaved and got dressed.

He went down to the restaurant and had two poached eggs on toast, pineapple juice, and a glass of milk for breakfast. He ate slowly, for he had at least half an hour to kill; he hadn't planned to get up until eight, and had carefully set his travel alarm clock to do that. The wreck, or whatever it was, had upset his schedule.

But there really wasn't much that one can do to stretch out two poached eggs on toast, so when he checked his watch when he went back to his room, he saw that he was still running twenty minutes ahead of schedule.

And, of course, into the schedule, he had built in extra time to take care of unforeseen contingencies. With that it mind, he was probably forty-five minutes ahead of what the real time schedule would turn out to be.

He decided he would do everything that had to be done but actually leave the room, and then wait until the real time schedule had time to catch up with the projected schedule.

That didn't burn up much time, either. AWOL bag #1 (one of those with *Souvenir of Asbury Park, N.J.* on it) was already prepared, and it took just a moment to open it and make sure that the explosive device and the receiver were in place, and that the soiled linen in which it was wrapped was not likely to come free.

He sighed. All he could do now was keep looking at his watch until it was time to go.

And then he saw the Bible on the bed. He picked it up and carried it to the desk, and sat down.

"Dear God," he prayed aloud. "I pray that you will give me insight as I prepare to go about your business."

He read, "17. I smote you with blasting and with mildew and with hail in all the labours of your hands; yet ye turned not to me, saith the Lord," and then he read it aloud.

Haggai 2:17 made no more sense to him now than it ever had.

He wondered if he had made some kind of mistake, if the Lord really intended for him to read Haggai 2:17, but decided that couldn't be. If the Lord didn't want him to read it, the Lord would not have attracted his attention to it.

It was obviously his failing, not the Lord's.

Supervisory Special Agent H. Charles Larkin of the Secret Service walked across the intersection of Kingsessing Avenue and Farragut and looked down the 1200 block.

He was honestly impressed with the efficiency with which Peter Wohl's men were evacuating the residents of the houses surrounding the residence of M. C. Wheatley. There was no panic, no excitement.

Obviously, Larkin decided, *because the people being evacuated were being handled by cops who were both smiling and confident, and seemed to know exactly what they were doing. If the man in the blue suit, the figure of authority, looks as if he is about to become hysterical, that's contagious.*

And since Wohl was really a nice guy, Charley Larkin decided it wouldn't hurt a thing to offer his genuine approval out loud, in the hearing of the Honorable Jerry Carlucci, mayor of the City of Brotherly Love, who had shown up five minutes after he had heard that Wohl intended to take M. C. Wheatley's door.

Larkin turned around, crossed Farragut Street again, and returned to where Carlucci and Wohl were standing by Wohl's car, just out of sight of the residence of M. C. Wheatley.

"I think they're about done," Larkin said. "I'm impressed with the way they're doing that, Peter," he said.

The mayor looked first at Larkin and then at Wohl.

"So am I," Wohl said. "Jack Malone set it up. He put them through a couple of dry runs in the dark at the Schoolhouse."

I suppose that proves, Larkin thought, *that while you can't cheat an honest man, you can't get him to take somebody else's credit, either.*

"Peter does a hell of a job with Special Operations, Charley," His Honor said. "I think we can now all say that it was an idea that worked. It. And Peter going in to command it."

" 'The Mayor said,' " Wohl replied, " 'just before the 1200 block of Farragut Street disappeared in a mushroom cloud.' "

"You think he's got it wired, Peter?" Mayor Carlucci asked.

"I believe he's crazy," Wohl said. "Crazy people scare me."

"William One, William Eleven," the radio in Wohl's car went on. William Eleven was Lieutenant Jack Malone.

Officer Paul O'Mara, sitting behind the wheel, handed Wohl the microphone.

"William One," Wohl said.

"All done here."

"Seven?" Wohl said.

"Seven," Jason Washington's voice came back.

"Have you seen any signs of life in there?"

"Nothing. I don't think anybody's in there."

"Your call, Jason. How do you want to take the door?"

"You did say, 'my call'?"

"Right."

"I'll get back to you," Washington said.

"Jason?"

There was no answer.

"Jason?"

"Jason. William Seven, William One."

There was no reply.

"That will teach you, Peter," Mayor Carlucci said. "Never tell Jason 'your call.' "

"William Eleven, William One."

"Eleven."

"Can you see Seven?"

"Payne just jumped onto the porch roof."

"Say again?"

"Payne came out onto the roof over the porch of the house next door, jumped over to the next one, and just smashed the window and went inside."

A bell began to clang.

"What did he say about Payne?" the Mayor asked.

"I hope I didn't hear that right," Wohl said.

He tossed the microphone to Officer O'Mara and quickly got in the front seat beside him, gesturing for him to get moving.

They were halfway down Farragut Street toward the residence of M. C. Wheatley when the radio went off:

"William One, Seven."

Wohl grabbed the microphone and barked, "One," as O'Mara pulled up, with a screech of brakes, in front of the house.

"Boss," Washington's voice came over the radio, "you want to send somebody in here to turn off the burglar alarm?"

There were more screeching brakes. A van skidded to a stop, and discharged half a dozen police officers, two of them buried beneath the layers of miracle plastic that, it was hoped, absorbed the effects of explosions, and all of them wearing yellow jackets with POLICE in large letters on their backs.

As the two Ordnance Disposal experts ran awkwardly up the stairs, the mayoral Cadillac limousine pulled in beside Peter Wohl's car, and Sergeant Jason Washington walked casually out onto the porch.

"Jason, what the hell happened?" Wohl called.

"When Payne let me in, the burglar alarm went off," Washington said innocently.

"That's not what I mean, and you know it," Wohl shouted. "God *damn* the both of you!"

"Where's that mushroom cloud you were talking about, Peter?" the mayor asked, at Wohl's elbow.

"God *damn* them!" Wohl said.

"I don't think he really means that, Charley, do you?" the mayor asked.

"Mr. Mayor," Wohl said. "I think you'd better stay right here."

"Hey, Peter," the mayor said as he started quickly up the stairs of the residence of Mr. M. C. Wheatley. "The way that works is that *I'm* the mayor. I tell *you* what to do."

At 8:25, as the schedule called for, Marion Claude Wheatley picked up AWOL bag #1, left his room in the Divine Lorraine Hotel, caught a bus at Ridge Avenue and North Broad Street, and rode it to the North Philadelphia Station of the Pennsylvania Railroad.

There he purchased a coach ticket to Wilmington, Delaware, went up the stairs to the track, and waited for the train, a local that, according to the schedule, would arrive at North Philadelphia at 9:03, depart North Philadelphia at 9:05, and arrive at 30th Street Station at 9:12. Marion didn't care when it would depart 30th Street Station for Chester, and then Wilmington. He wasn't going to Chester or Wilmington.

At 9:12, right on schedule, the train arrived at 30th Street Station. The conductor hadn't even asked for his ticket.

Marion rode the escalator to the main waiting room, walked across it, deposited two quarters in one of the lockers in the passageway to the south exit, deposited AWOL bag #1 in Locker 7870, and put the key into his watch pocket.

Then he went back to the main waiting room, bought a newspaper, and went to the snack bar, where he had two cups of black coffee and two pieces of coffee cake.

There was no coffee cake in the dining room of the Divine Lorraine Hotel, Marion reasoned, because there was no coffee in the dining room of the Divine Lorraine Hotel. He wondered if that was it, or whether Father Divine had found something in Holy Scripture that he thought proscribed pastry as well as alcohol, tobacco, and coffee.

When he had finished his coffee, Marion left the coffee shop and left 30th Street Station by the west exit. He walked to Market Street, and since it was such a nice morning, and since the really important aspect of trip #1, placing AWOL bag #1 in a locker, had been accomplished, he decided he would walk down Market Street, rather than take a bus, as the schedule called for.

The exercise, he thought, would do him good.

"Well, goddammit, then get it from Kansas City!" Supervisory Special Agent H. Charles Larkin said, nearly shouted, furiously. "I want a description, and preferably a photograph, of this sonofabitch here in an hour!"

He slammed the telephone into its cradle.

"I think Charley's mad about something," Chief Inspector Matt Lowenstein said drolly. "Doesn't he seem mad about something to you, Denny?"

"What was that all about, Charley?" Chief Inspector Coughlin asked, chuckling.

"The Army has the records of our guy—his name is Marion Claude, by the way, his first names—in the Depository in Kansas City," Larkin said. "So instead of calling Kansas City to get us a goddamn description and a picture, he calls me!"

"We have a man in Kansas City who does nothing but maintain liaison with the Army Records Depository," Mr. Frank F. Young of the FBI said. "Shall I give him a call, Charley?"

"So do we, Frank," Larkin said. "Don't take this the wrong way, but if we get your guy involved, that's liable to fuck things up even more than they are now."

"I think we can say," Young said, "that we're making progress."

"Yeah," Wohl said. "We now *know* that he has a lot of explosives, and from the way those burglar alarms were wired, even if he hadn't been in EOD, that he knows how to set them off. We don't know what he looks like, or where he is."

One of the telephones on the commissioner's conference table rang.

"Commissioner's conference room, Sergeant Washington," Jason said, grabbing it on the second ring. "Okay, let me have it!" He scribbled quickly on a pad of lined yellow paper, said "Thank you," and hung up.

The others at the table looked at him.

"Marion Claude Wheatley is employed as a petrochemicals market analyst at First Pennsylvania Bank & Trust, main office, on South Broad," Washington said. "A guy from Central Detectives just found out."

"Do they have a photograph of him?" Larkin asked.

"They're being difficult," Washington said. He looked at Peter Wohl. "You want me to go over there, Inspector?"

"You bet I do," Wohl said.

"Can I take Payne with me?"

"If you think you can keep him from playing Tarzan," Wohl said. "And jumping from roof to roof."

"Sergeant, would you mind if I went with you?" H. Charles Larkin asked. "If they're being difficult, I'll show them difficult."

"No, sir," Washington said. "Come along."

Washington doesn't want him, Wohl thought, *but there's nothing I can do to stop him.*

"Would four be a crowd?" Frank F. Young asked.

"No, sir," Washington said.

The four quickly left the room.

"What about that guy Young?" Denny Coughlin asked, when the door was closed.

"He either is very anxious to render whatever assistance the FBI can on this job," Lowenstein said, "or he wants to play detective."

"Now that we're alone," Wohl said. "It looks like Lanza, the corporal at the airport, *is* dirty."

"Oh, shit," Coughlin said. "What have you got, Peter?"

"He's been having middle-of-the-night meetings with various Mafioso scumbags. Gian-Carlo Rosselli, Paula Cassandro, and others. They have been talking about a fruit basket coming in."

"How do you know that, Peter? About the fruit basket?" Lowenstein asked.

"Please don't ask me that question, Chief," Wohl said.

Lowenstein and Coughlin exchanged glances.

"He's under surveillance?" Lowenstein asked.

"By Internal Affairs when he's off the job. And Dickinson Lowell, who's chief of security for Eastern at the airport, has people watching him when he's on the job. Chief Marchessi set that up. He and Lowell are old pals."

"Dickie Lowell is, was, a good cop," Coughlin said. "You have any idea when this 'fruit basket' is coming in?"

"Nine forty-five tonight," Wohl replied. "Eastern Flight 4302 from San Juan."

"You picked that information up, right, from ordinary, routine, legal surveillance of Corporal Lanza, right?" Chief Lowenstein asked.

Wohl hesitated a moment, and then did not reply directly.

"The surveillance of Corporal Lanza leads us to believe that he is spending a lot of time with a lady by the name of Antoinette Marie Wolinski Schermer," he said. "Spends his nights with her. We find this interesting because Organized Crime says Mrs. Schermer is ordinarily the squeeze of Ricco Baltazari, the well-known restaurateur."

"When you take Lanza, can you take any of the scumbags with him?" Coughlin asked.

"More important, are you sure you can take Lanza?" Lowenstein asked.

"We'll just have to see, Chief," Wohl said.

"You have good people doing the surveillance?" Lowenstein asked.

"Internal Affairs is providing most of it," Wohl replied. "And I loaned them Sergeant O'Dowd, but my priority, of course, is finding this Wheatley screwball before he hurts somebody."

"For all of us," Denny said.

"I want this dirty corporal, Peter," Lowenstein said. "Rather than blow it, I would just as soon let this 'fruit basket' tonight slip through. If there's one, there'll be others."

"I'll keep that in mind, Chief."

"We have a minute, with Larkin and Young gone, to talk about what we do now that we know who this Wheatley nut is, but not where he is," Coughlin said.

"Which means you've been thinking about it," Lowenstein said. "Go on, Denny."

"Worst-case scenario," Coughlin said. "Despite one hell of an effort by everybody concerned to find this guy, and the only way I know to do that is by running down any and every lead we come across, ringing every other doorbell in the city, we don't find him. The odds are that Washington *will* turn up something at the bank, or from his neighbors. But let's say that doesn't happen."

"Worst-case scenario, right?" Lowenstein said sarcastically.

Coughlin's face darkened, but he decided to let the sarcasm pass.

"When Peter said we have to catch Wheatley before he hurts somebody," he went on, "he wasn't talking about just the Vice President. This guy has the means, and I think is just crazy enough, to hurt a lot of people. You heard what Charley said his expert said, that he's probably going to set off his bomb, *bombs,* by radio?"

Both Wohl and Lowenstein nodded.

"That means he could be walking up Market Street with his bomb under his arm and *his* radio in Camden, and somebody turns on a shortwave radio, maybe in an RPC, and off the bomb goes."

"I don't know what we can do about that," Lowenstein said.

"Or he could be walking up Market Street with his bomb under one arm, and his radio under the other, and he spots somebody who looks like the Secret Service, or the FBI, and he pushes the button."

"I don't know where you're going, Denny," Lowenstein confessed.

"Well, I said, 'Market Street' but I don't think he's going to try to set his bomb off on Market Street. He may be a nut, but he's smart. And I don't think he plans to commit suicide when he—what did he say, *'disintegrates'?*—the Vice President. That means he has to put the bomb someplace where he can see it, and the Vice President, from someplace he'll be safe when it goes off."

"Okay," Lowenstein said after a moment.

"There aren't very many places he can do that on Market Street," Coughlin went on. "The only place you could hide a bomb would be, for example, an empty store or a trash can or a mailbox."

"The Post Office will send somebody to open all mailboxes an hour before the Vice President arrives," Wohl replied. "Then they'll chain them shut. Larkin set that up with the postal inspectors. And I, actually Jack Malone, arranged with the City to have every trash basket, et cetera, in which a bomb could be hidden, removed by nine A.M., two hours before the Vice President gets here. And we'll check the stores, empty and otherwise."

"I don't think he's thinking about Market Street anyway," Coughlin said. "He'd have only a second or two to set the bomb off. That's not much margin for error." He paused. "But I damned sure could be wrong. So we're going to have to have Market Street covered from the river to 30th Street Station."

"Which leaves Independence Square and 30th Street Station," Wohl said. "I don't think Independence Square. He knows that we're going to have people all over there, and that he will have a hard time getting close to the Vice President, close enough to hurt him with a bomb."

"That presumes Denny's right about him not wanting to commit suicide," Lowenstein said. "Maybe he likes the idea of being a martyr."

"I think we can let the Secret Service handle somebody rushing up to the Vice President," Coughlin said. "They're very good at that. I keep getting back to 30th Street Station."

"Okay. But tell me why?"

"Well, we can't close it off, for one thing. Trains are going to arrive and depart. They will be carrying people, and many, if not most, of those people will be carrying some kind of luggage, either a briefcase, if they're commuters, or suitcases. Are we going to stop everybody and search their luggage?"

"I don't suppose there's any chance, now that we know this guy is for real, that the Vice President can be talked out of this goddamned motorcade?" Lowenstein asked.

"None," Coughlin said. "I was there when Larkin called Washington."

Lowenstein shrugged and struck a wooden match and relit his cigar.

"We're listening, Denny," he said.

"And there's a lot of places in 30th Street Station to hide a bomb, half a dozen bombs," Coughlin went on. "Places our guy can see from half a dozen places he'd be hard to spot. You follow?"

"Not only do I follow, but I have been wondering if you think Larkin doesn't know all this."

"Larkin knows. We've talked."

"Ah *ha!* And I'll bet that you're about to tell us what you and the Secret Service have come up with, aren't you?"

"What *I* came up with, Matt," Coughlin said. "And what Larkin is willing to go along with."

"Inspector Wohl," Lowenstein said, "why do you think I think the genial Irishman here has just been sold the toll concession on the Benjamin Franklin Bridge?"

"Goddammit, do you always have to be such a cynical sonofabitch? You can be a real pain in the ass, Matt!" the genial Irishman flared. "There *are* some good feds, and Charley Larkin happens to be one of them. If you're too dumb to see that, I'm sorry."

"If I have in any way offended you, Chief Coughlin, please accept my most profound apologies," Lowenstein said innocently. "Please proceed."

"Goddammit, you won't quit, will you?"

They glared at each other for a moment.

Finally, Lowenstein said, "Okay. Sorry, Denny. Let's hear it."

"We are going to have police officers every twenty feet all along the motorcade route, and every ten feet, every five feet, in 30th Street Station and at Independence Hall."

Lowenstein looked at him with incredulity on his face, and then in his voice: "That's it? That's the brilliant plan you and the Secret Service came up with?"

"You have a better idea?"

"How many men is it going to take if we saturate that large an area for what, four hours?" Lowenstein asked.

"We figure six hours," Coughlin said.

"Has Charley Larkin offered to come up with the money to pay for all that overtime?" Lowenstein asked. "Or are we going to move cops in from all over the city, and pray that nothing happens elsewhere?"

"We are going to bring in every uniform in Special Operations," Coughlin began, and then stopped. "This is the idea, Peter. Subject, of course, to your approval."

I know, Wohl thought, *and he knows I know, that me arguing against this would be like me telling the pope he's wrong about the Virgin Mary.*

"Go on, please, Chief," Wohl said.

"That's the whole idea of Special Operations, the federal grants we got for it," Coughlin said. "To have police force available anywhere in the city. . . ."

"There's not that many people in Special Operations to put one every ten feet up and down Market Street," Lowenstein said. "The feds pay the bills, and then they tell us what to do, right?" Lowenstein said. "I was against those goddamn grants from the beginning."

On the other hand, Wohl thought, *we have the grants all the time, and they don't ask for our help all the time.*

"There will be men available from the districts, and I thought the Detective Bureau would make detectives available."

Lowenstein grunted.

"Plus undercover officers, primarily from Narcotics, but from anyplace else we can find them," Coughlin went on.

He looked at Lowenstein for his reply. Lowenstein grunted, and then looked at Wohl.

"Peter?"

"I don't have a better idea," Wohl said.

"Neither do I," Lowenstein said. "Okay. Next question. Do you think the commissioner will go along with this?"

"The commissioner, I think, is going to hide under his desk until this is all over," Coughlin said. "If we catch this guy, or at least keep him from disintegrating the Vice President, he will hold a press conference to modestly announce how pleased he is his plan worked. If the Vice President is disintegrated, it's Peter's fault. He was never in favor of Special Operations in the first place."

"Was that a crack at me, Denny?"

"If the shoe fits, Cinderella."

"Gentlemen," Mr. H. Logan Hammersmith of First Pennsylvania Bank & Trust said, "while I don't mean to appear to be difficult, I'm simply unable to permit you access to our personnel records. The question of confidentiality . . ."

"Mr. Hammersmith," Jason Washington began softly. "I understand your position. But . . ."

"Fuck it, Jason," Mr. H. Charles Larkin interrupted. "I've had enough of this bastard's bullshit."

Mr. Hammersmith was obviously not used to being addressed in that tone of voice, or with such vulgarity and obscenity, which is precisely why Mr. Larkin had chosen that tone of voice and vocabulary.

"I want Marion Claude Wheatley's personnel records, all of them, on your desk in three minutes, or I'm going to take you out of here in handcuffs," Mr. Larkin continued.

"You can't do that!" Mr. Hammersmith said, without very much conviction. "I haven't done anything."

"You're interfering with a federal investigation," Mr. Frank F. Young said.

"Now, we can get a search warrant for this," Larkin said. "It'll take us about an hour. But to preclude the possibility that Mr. Hammerhead here . . ."

"Hammer*smith,*" Hammersmith interjected.

". . . who, in my professional judgment, is acting very strangely, does not, in the meantime, conceal, destroy, or otherwise hinder our access to these records, I believe we should take him into custody."

"I agree," Frank F. Young said.

"May I borrow your handcuffs, please, Jason?" Larkin asked politely.

"Yes, sir."

"Would you please stand up, Mr. Hammerhead, and place your hands behind your back?"

"Now just a moment, please," Mr. Hammersmith said. He reached up and picked up his telephone.

"Mrs. Berkowitz, will you please go to Personnel and get Mr. Wheatley's entire personnel file? And bring it to me, right away."

"We very much appreciate your cooperation, Mr. Hammersmith," Mr. Larkin said.

The personnel records of Marion Claude Wheatley included a photograph. But either the photographic paper was faulty, or the processing had been, for the photograph stapled to his records was entirely black.

Neither were his records of any help at all in suggesting where he might be found. He listed his parents as next of kin, and Mr. Hammersmith told them he was sure they had passed on.

Mr. Young arranged for FBI agents to go out to the University of Pennsylvania, to examine Wheatley's records there. They found a photograph, but it was stapled to Mr. Wheatley's application for admission, and showed him at age seventeen.

When Mr. Wheatley's records in Kansas City were finally exhumed and examined, the only photograph of Mr. Wheatley they contained, a Secret Service agent reported to Mr. Larkin, had been taken during his Army basic training. It was not a good photograph, and for all practical purposes, Army barbers had turned him bald.

"Wire it anyway," Mr. Larkin replied. "We're desperate."

29.

Supervisory Special Agent H. Charles Larkin, Chief Inspector (retired) Augustus Wohl, and Chief Inspector Dennis V. Coughlin were seated around Coughlin's dining-room table when Inspector Peter Wohl came into the apartment a few minutes before ten P.M.

On the table were two telephones, a bottle of Scotch, a bottle of bourbon, and clear evidence that the ordinance of the Commonwealth of Pennsylvania that prohibited gaming, such as poker, was being violated.

"Who's winning?"

"Your father, of course," Charley Larkin replied.

"Deal you in, Peter?" Chief Wohl asked.

"Why not?" Wohl said.

"You want a drink, Peter?" Coughlin asked.

"I better not," Wohl said. "I want to go back to the Schoolhouse before I go home. I hate to have whiskey on my breath."

His father ignored him. He made him a drink of Scotch and handed it to him.

"You look like you need this," he said.

"I corrupt easily," Peter said, taking it, and added, "In case anybody's been wondering, we have come up with zilch, zero."

"That include the airport too?" Coughlin asked.

"Yeah. I gave them this number, Chief, in case something does happen."

"What's going on at the airport?" Larkin asked.

Peter Wohl looked at Coughlin.

"I'm afraid we have a dirty cop out there," Coughlin said.

"I'm sorry," Larkin said.

"We're playing seven-card stud," Chief Wohl said. "Put your money on the table, Peter."

Peter had just taken two twenty-dollar bills and four singles from his wallet when one of the telephones rang.

Coughlin grabbed it on the second ring.

"Coughlin," he said. "Yes, just a moment, he's here." He started to hand the telephone to Peter and then changed his mind. "Is this Dickie Lowell? I thought I recognized your voice. This is Denny Coughlin, Dickie. How the hell are you?"

Then he handed the phone to Peter.

"Peter Wohl," he said, and then listened.

"Have you spoken with Captain Olsen?" he asked. There was a brief pause, and then: "Thank you very much. I owe you one."

He hung up.

"Dickie Lowell?" Chief Wohl asked as he dealt cards. "Retired out of Headquarters Division in the Detective Bureau?"

"He got a job running security for Eastern Airlines," Coughlin said. "He's got his people watching our dirty cop. Peter set it up."

"Chief Marchessi set it up," Peter said. "Lowell's people just saw our dirty cop take a suitcase off Eastern Flight 4302. Specifically, remove a suitcase from a baggage trailer after it had been removed from Eastern 4302."

"So what are you going to do, Peter?" Coughlin asked.

Wohl hesitated, and then shrugged.

"Resist the temptation to get on my horse and charge out to the airport," he said. "Where I probably would fuck things up. I sent Sergeant Jerry O'Dowd . . . you know him?"

His father and Chief Coughlin shook their heads, no.

"He works for Dave Pekach. Good man. He's going to follow our dirty cop when he comes off duty. We already have people watching his house and his girlfriend's apartment."

"Sometimes the smartest thing to do is keep your nose out of the tent," Coughlin said. "I think they call that delegation of authority."

"And I think what we have there is the pot calling the kettle black," Chief Wohl said. "Denny was an inspector before he stopped turning off fire hydrants in the summer."

"Go to hell, Augie!"

"What's in the suitcase?" Larkin said. "Drugs?"

"What else?" Coughlin said.

"I didn't know you handled drugs, Peter," Larkin said.

"Normally, I don't," Peter replied. "Drugs or dirty cops. Thank God. This was Commissioner Marshall's answer to the feds wanting to send their people out there masquerading as cops. He gave the job to me."

"Because you get along so well with we feds, right?" Larkin asked, chuckling.

"There's an exception to every rule, Charley," Coughlin said. "Just be grateful it's you."

"Are we going to play cards or what?" Chief Wohl asked.

Peter Wohl was surprised to find Detective Matthew M. Payne in the Special Investigations office at Special Operations when he walked in at quarter past midnight. He said nothing, however.

Maybe Jack Malone called him in.

"How are we doing?" he asked.

"Well," Lieutenant Malone said tiredly, "Mr. Wheatley is not registered in any of

Philadelphia's many hotels, motels, or flop houses," Malone said. "Nor did anybody in the aforementioned remember seeing anyone who looked like either of the two artists' representations of Mr. Wheatley."

The Philadelphia Police Department had an artist whose ability to make a sketch of an individual from a description was uncanny. The Secret Service had an artist who Mr. H. Charles Larkin announced was the best he had ever seen. In the interest of getting a picture of Mr. Wheatley out on the street as quickly as possible, the Department artist had made a sketch of Wheatley based on his neighbor's, Mr. Crowne's, description of him, while the Secret Service artist had drawn a sketch of Mr. Wheatley based on Mr. Wheatley's boss, Mr. H. Logan Hammersmith's, description of him.

There was only a very vague similarity between the two sketches. Rather than try to come up with a third sketch that would be a compromise, Wohl had ordered that both sketches be distributed.

"Too bad," Wohl said.

"The sonofabitch apparently doesn't have any friends," Malone said. "The neighbor, two houses down, lived there fifteen years, couldn't even remember seeing him."

"He's got to be somewhere, Jack," Wohl said.

"I sent Tony Harris to Vice," Malone said. "They went to all the fag bars with the pictures."

"We don't know he's homosexual."

"I thought maybe he's a closet queen, who has an apartment somewhere," Malone said.

"Good thought, Jack, I didn't think about that."

"They struck out too," Malone said.

"And how's your batting record, Detective Payne?"

It was intended as a joke. Payne looked very uncomfortable.

"I just thought maybe I could make myself useful, so I came in," Payne said.

That's bullshit.

The telephone rang. Malone grabbed it and handed it to Wohl.

"Jerry O'Dowd, Inspector," his caller said. "I'm calling from the tavern down the corner from our friend's house. He drove straight here, with the suitcase, and took it into the house."

"Good man," Wohl said.

"Oooops, there he comes."

"With the suitcase?"

"No. He doesn't have it. He's changed out of his uniform."

"You're going to stay there, right?"

"Right. He's walking back to his car. But Captain Olsen can see him. No problem."

"Olsen is on him?" Wohl asked, surprised.

"Yes, sir. Olsen won't lose him."

"If anything happens, call this number, they'll know where to get me."

"Yes, sir."

"I'm going to send somebody to back you up," Wohl said. "In case somebody interesting comes to pick up the suitcase."

"Yes, sir."

"Good job, Jerry," Wohl said, and hung up.

If Olsen can work this job himself, why can't I? I'd love to catch Ricco Baltazari or one of his pals walking down Ritner Street with that suitcase in his hand.

Dangerous thought. No!

"Jack, can we get our hands on Tony Harris?"

"Yes, sir."

"Get on the horn to him and tell him to go back up O'Dowd."

"Yes, sir."

"And then turn this over to the duty lieutenant and go home and get some sleep."

"Yes, sir."

"That applies to you too, Detective Payne. With all the jumping from roof to roof, and through windows, you've done today, I'm sure you're worn out. Go home and go to bed. I want you here at eight A.M., bright-eyed and bushy-tailed."

That, to judge by the kicked puppy look in your eyes, was another failed attempt to be jocular.

"Yes, sir."

Or is there something else wrong with him? Something is wrong.

"Jack, you want to go somewhere for a nightcap?" Wohl asked. "The reason I am being so generous is that I just took forty bucks from my father and Chief Coughlin, who don't play poker nearly as well as they think they do."

"I accept, Inspector. Thank you."

"The invitation includes you, Detective Payne, if you promise not to jump through a window or otherwise embarrass Lieutenant Malone and me."

"Thank you, I'll try to behave."

The look of gratitude in your eyes now, Matt, is almost pathetic. What the hell is wrong with you?

Jack Malone had two drinks, the second reluctantly, and then said he had to get to bed before he went to sleep at the bar.

"I'm going to call the Schoolhouse, and see what happened to Lanza," Wohl said. "And then I'm going home. Order one more, please, Matt."

Two minutes later, Wohl got back on the bar stool beside Payne.

"Lanza went to the Schermer woman's apartment. The lights went out, and Olsen figures he's in for the night," he reported.

"And you're hoping that somebody will show up at his house for the suitcase?" Payne asked.

Wohl nodded. "We may get lucky."

"Why didn't he take it with him? Isn't that woman involved?"

"I don't know how much she's involved, and I don't know why he left the suitcase at his house. These people are very careful."

Payne nodded.

"And now that Malone has gone home, and I don't have to be officially outraged—as opposed to personally admiring—at your roof-jumping escapade, are you going to tell me what's bothering you?"

"Jesus, does it show?"

"Yeah, it shows."

Matt looked at him for a moment, and then at his drink for a longer moment, before finally saying, "Penny Detweiler is in the psycho ward at University Hospital."

"I'm sorry to hear that," Wohl said.

But not surprised. A junkie is a junkie is a junkie.

"I put her there," Matt said.

"What do you mean, you put her there?"

"You really don't want to hear this."

You're right. I really don't want to hear this.

"I'm not trying to pry, Matt. But, hell, sometimes if you talk things over, when you're finished, they don't seem to be as bad."

It was quarter to two when Inspector Wohl, not without misgivings, installed Detective Payne behind the wheel of the unmarked Ford and sent him home with the admonition to try not to run any stoplights or into a station wagon full of nuns.

I believed what I told him, that if it hadn't been the other woman showing up at his apartment, it would have been something else. That being turned loose from a drug addiction program does not *mean the addiction is cured, just that, so far as they can tell, it's on hold.*

But clearly, if the horny little bastard wasn't fucking every woman in town, it would not have happened. Taking the Detweiler girl to bed was idiotic. He has earned every ounce of the weight of shameful regret he's carrying.

But his wallowing in guilt isn't going to do anybody any good.

Sometimes, Peter Wohl, you are so smart, so Solomon-like, I want to throw up.

He started home to Chestnut Hill, then suddenly changed his mind, got on first Roosevelt Boulevard and then the Schuylkill Expressway and headed for Ritner Street.

I don't want to go to bed. I don't want to delegate authority. I want to put that dirty cop and the Mafioso he's running around with away. And right now there's nobody who can tell me to butt out.

Wohl drove slowly down Ritner Street, saw where Sergeant O'Dowd was parked, and made a left at the next corner and parked the car.

O'Dowd had been alone when he had driven past, but as he walked up to the car now, he first saw another head, and then recognized it as that of Detective Tony Harris, sitting beside O'Dowd.

Wohl opened the rear door and got in.

"I thought that was you driving by," O'Dowd said. "Something come up?"

"I got curious, is all," Wohl said. "I just happened to be in the neighborhood."

"There's somebody in the house," Tony Harris said. "I was out in back. You know how these houses are laid out, Inspector? With the bathroom at the back of the house?"

"Yeah, sure."

"First a dull light, which means a light on in one of the bedrooms, shining into the hall. Then a bright light. Somebody's in the bathroom. I figure it's his mother, taking a piss. Then the bright light goes out, and then the dim light, and I figure she's back in bed."

"Okay. So what?"

"So nothing. So that's what's been going on here."

"There's more, Tony. What are you thinking?"

"I don't think Paulo Cassandro or Ricco Baltazari or any other Mafioso is going to come waltzing down Ritner Street tonight to pick up that suitcase. Those bastards aren't stupid. There's been half a dozen cars come by here, any one of who could have been taking a look, and if they were, they saw us."

"Oh, ye of little faith!" Wohl said.

Why did you say that? Jesus, that was dumb! Three drinks and your mouth gallops away with you!

"You're the boss. You say sit on the house, we'll sit on the house."

"Tell me what you think is going to happen, Tony," Wohl said.

"I'll tell you what I *don't* think is going to happen," Harris said.

"Okay. Tell me what's not going to happen."

"I don't think we're going to catch anybody but this dirty cop. The Mob is going to come up with some pretty clever way to get their hands on that suitcase without us catching them at it."

"Okay. So what would you do if you were me?"

"Let's say we catch Lanza actually handing the suitcase to, say, Ricco Baltazari. We arrest them. They have the best lawyers around. They say we set them up. They ask all kinds of questions of how come we were watching Lanza in the first place. The guy has a spotless record, et cetera. And Lanza is not, I'll bet my ass on it, going to pass the suitcase to anybody. If they send somebody for it, or they tell Lanza to carry it someplace and give it to somebody, we arrest him, it will be some jerk we can't tie to Baltazari or anybody else. And Lanza pleads the Fifth and won't help either. He takes the fall. He pleads guilty to stealing a suitcase. He doesn't know anything about drugs, he just stole a suitcase. First offense, what'll he get?"

"What I asked, Tony, is what you would do if you were in charge?"

"You really want to know, or are we just sitting here killing time bullshitting?"

"I really want to know."

"I go up to the door, I say 'Sorry to bother you this time of night, Mrs. Lanza, but Vito brought my suitcase here, and I'm here to collect it.' She gives me the suitcase, while you and O'Dowd watch, and O'Dowd takes pictures, and then we bust her for possession of cocaine, or whatever shit is in the suitcase. And then we go get Vito out of his girlfriend's bed and tell him he better go down to Central lockup and see what he can do for his mother, who's charged with possession with the intent to distribute. And the Mob is out however much shit they was trying to ship in."

There was a long silence.

"Not you, Tony," Wohl said, finally. "Martinez. In uniform."

"Martinez, the little Spic? What's he got to do with this?"

"*Detective* Martinez, Detective Harris, has been working undercover at the airport, trying to catch whoever has been smuggling drugs."

"No shit?"

"If Mrs. Lanza asked him questions about the airport, he would know the answers," Wohl said.

"Yeah," Harris said thoughtfully.

"That saloon is closed," Wohl said, after looking out the rear window. "Where can I find a telephone around here?"

"There's a pay station on Broad Street. If somebody hasn't ripped it off the wall."

"Hello?"

"You awake, Matt?"

"Yes, sir. What's up?"

"You know Martinez's home phone and where he lives?"

"Yes, sir."

"Call him up. Tell him to put his uniform on, then pick him up, and meet me at Moyamensing and South Broad."

"Right now?"

"Right now."

The door to the apartment of Mrs. Antoinette Marie Wolinski Schermer opened just a crack. It was evident that she had the chain in place.

"What is it?" Mrs. Schermer asked, her tone mingled annoyance and concern.

"It's the police, Mrs. Schermer," Captain Swede Olsen said. "We're here to talk to Corporal Lanza."

When there was no immediate response, Captain Olsen added, "We know he's here, Tony. Open the door."

The door closed. It remained closed for about a minute, but it seemed much longer than that. And then it opened.

Vito, wearing a sleeveless undershirt and trousers, his hair mussed, stood inside the door.

"Corporal Lanza," Olsen said, "I'm Captain Olsen of Internal Affairs. These are Detectives Martinez and Payne. I think you can guess why we're here."

Vito looked at Martinez and Payne. His surprise registered in his eyes, but then they grew cold and wary.

"What's going on?"

"We want you to get dressed and come with us, Corporal," Olsen said conversationally.

"What for?"

"You know what for, Lanza," Olsen said.

"You got a warrant?"

"No. We don't have a warrant. We don't need a warrant."

"What's the charge?"

"That's going to depend in large part on you, Lanza. For the moment, you can consider yourself under arrest for theft of luggage from Eastern Airlines."

Lanza's face whitened.

"I don't know what you're talking about," Lanza said.

"Detective Martinez," Olsen said, "will you go with Corporal Lanza while he puts his clothes on? Take his pistol."

"Yes, sir."

"This is some kind of mistake," Vito Lanza said.

"Get your clothes on, Lanza," Olsen said.

"You're a detective?" Lanza asked Martinez.

"Yeah, I'm a detective."

"Get your clothes on," Captain Olsen repeated. "It's over, Lanza."

Lanza turned and went into the apartment. Martinez followed him.

"Mrs. Schermer," Captain Olsen said. "Detectives are going to want to talk to you later today. They will call you either here, or at work, and set up a time."

"I don't know what this is all about," Tony said.

"You can talk about that with the detectives," Captain Olsen said.

The three stood at the door for the two or three minutes it took Vito to put his shoes and socks and a shirt on.

Finally he came back to the door, followed by Jesus Martinez, who carried Vito's off-duty snub-nosed revolver and its holster in his hand.

"Give the pistol to Detective Payne," Captain Olsen ordered. "And put handcuffs on Corporal Lanza."

They walked down the corridor to the elevator, where Vito saw that the door was being held open by a Highway Patrolman. There was another Highway Patrolman in the lobby, and when they got to the street, there were two Highway RPCs, the lights on their bubble gum machines flashing. There were two unmarked cars on the street, their behind-the-grilles blue lights flashing, and three or four people in plainclothes Vito had been a cop long enough to know were fellow police officers.

Vito Lanza, for a moment, thought he was going to throw up, then he felt hands on his arms, and a Highway Patrolman put his hand on the top of Vito's head, and pushed down, so that Vito wouldn't bang his head on the door as he got into the back seat of one of the Highway RPCs.

"Watch your fucking head, scumbag," the Highway officer said.

Ricco Baltazari's voice, when he answered the telephone, was sleepy and annoyed.

"Yeah?" he snarled.

"Ricco?" Tony asked.

He recognized the voice. His tone changed to concern and anger.

"What are you doing, calling here?"

"Who is it?" Mrs. Baltazari asked, rolling over on her back.

"Ricco, the cops were just here. They arrested Vito."

"What?"

"A guy who said he was a captain, and two detectives, and they told him to get dressed, and they took his gun away and put handcuffs on him, and when I looked out the window, there was cop cars all over the street."

"Jesus, Mary, and Joseph!"

"What *is* it, honey?" Mrs. Baltazari asked. "Who is that?"

"Go back to sleep, for Christ's sake," Ricco said. "Okay. I'll take care of it. You just keep your mouth shut, Tony, you understand?"

"Ricco, I'm scared!"

"Just keep your goddamned mouth shut!" Ricco said, and hung up.

He got out of bed, and found a cigarette, but no matches.

He walked to the bedroom door.

"Where are you *going?*" Mrs. Baltazari demanded.

"Just, goddammit, go back to sleep."

Mr. Baltazari then went downstairs and into the kitchen and found a match for his cigarette, and lit it, and then banged his fist on the sink and said, "Shit!"

He then picked up the handset of the wall telephone and started to dial a number, but then hung up angrily.

If the cops have the cop, they maybe have this line tapped. I can't call from here. I'm going to have to go to a pay phone.

But shit, if the cops have the cop, they're as likely to have Gian-Carlo's phone tapped as they are to have this one tapped.

I'm going to have to go to Gian-Carlo's house and wake him up and tell him the cops have the cop. And that means they have the shipment for the people in Baltimore!

Jesus Christ! He's not going to like this worth a fuck! And Mr. Savarese!

It's not my fucking fault! I don't know what happened, but it's not my fucking fault!

But they're not going to believe that!

Oh, Jesus Christ!

Salvatore J. Riccuito, Esq., a slightly built, olive-skinned thirty-two-year-old, was a recent addition to the district attorney's staff. Prior to his admission to the bar, he had spent eleven years as a police officer, mostly in the 6th District, passing up opportunities to take examinations for promotion in order to find time to graduate from LaSalle College and then the Temple University School of Law, both at night.

Understandably, because he knew how cops thought and behaved, if he was available, he was assigned cases involving the prosecution of police officers. When this case had come up, via a 3:15 A.M. telephone call from Thomas J. "Tommy" Callis, the district attorney himself, Sal had pleaded unavailability. Callis had been unsympathetic.

"We'll rearrange your schedule. Get down to Narcotics and see Inspector Peter Wohl."

Sal knew there was no point in arguing. Wohl had been the investigator in the case that resulted in Judge Findermann taking a long-term lease in the Pennsylvania Penal System. Callis had prosecuted himself. The publicity would probably help him get reelected.

In a way, Sal thought as he drove to the Narcotics Unit, it was flattering. Wohl almost certainly had not asked for "an assistant DA." He had either asked for "a good assistant DA" or possibly even for him by name.

"Let me tell you how things are, Vito," Sal, who had grown up six blocks from Vito, but didn't know him personally, said.

Vito was sitting handcuffed to a steel captain's chair in one of the interview rooms in the headquarters of the Narcotics unit. He was slightly mussed, as it had been necessary to physically restrain him on his arrival at Narcotics, when he had seen his mother similarly handcuffed to a steel captain's chair.

"Tell me how things are," Vito said with a bluster that was almost pathetically transparent.

"You're dead. That's how things are. They saw you steal the suitcase. They saw you sneak it out to the parking lot. They have *photographs."*

"The sonsofbitches, fucking cocksuckers, had no right to do that to my mother!"

"Let's talk about your mother," Sal said. "She gave the suitcase to Detective Martinez. They have photographs. They have witnesses, a detective, a sergeant, *a staff inspector.* The chain of evidence, with your mother, is intact. The suitcase contained about twenty pounds of cocaine. Nine Ks. They just got the lab report. It's good stuff. If they decide to prosecute, she's going down. Simple possession is all it takes for a conviction."

"She didn't know anything about it," Lanza said. "They tricked her. Can they do that?"

"The little Mexican said, quote, Can I have the suitcase Vito brought? end quote, and she gave it to him. No illegal search and seizure, if that's what you're asking."

"Sonsofbitches!"

"They will not prosecute your mother if you cooperate."

"Fuck 'em!"

"You want your mother to ride downtown to Central Detection? You got the money to make her bail? You got ten thousand dollars to pay a bondsman? And that's what the bail will be for that much cocaine. Or do you want her to spend the next six months waiting for her trial in the House of Detention?"

"Why the fuck should I trust them after what they did to my mother?"

"You're not trusting them. You're trusting me. *I'm* the assistant DA. You cooperate, and I'll have your mother out of here in ten minutes. I'll even see she gets home safe."

"Okay, okay," Vito said. He tried to put his right hand to his eyes to stem the tears that were starting, but it was held fast by handcuffs. He put his left hand to his eyes.

Sal handed Vito a handkerchief.

"Take a minute," Sal said. "Then we'll get a steno in here."

At 8:45 A.M. Marion Claude Wheatley finished his breakfast of poached eggs on toast and milk, left a fifty-cent tip under his plate in the dining room of the Divine Lorraine Hotel, and rode the elevator up to his room.

He unlocked the closet, and took AWOL bag #4 of the three remaining AWOL bags— another one with *Souvenir of Asbury Park, N.J.* airbrushed on its sides—from the closet and locked the closet door again.

He was pleased that he had had the foresight to prepare all of the AWOL bags at once. Now all he had to do was take them from the closet as he began the delivery process.

He looked around the room, and, although he really didn't think it would do any good, walked to the Bible on the desk and read Haggai 2:17 again, seeking insight.

"I smote you with blasting and with mildew and with hail in all the labours of your hands; yet ye turned not to me, saith the Lord," made no more sense now than it ever had.

Marion picked up AWOL bag #4 and left his room, carefully locking the door after him, and went down in the elevator to the lobby.

He left his key with the colored lady behind the desk. He had learned that her name was Sister Fortitude, and he used it now.

"It looks, praise the Lord, as if we're going to have another fine day, doesn't it, Sister Fortitude?"

"Yes, it does," Sister Fortitude said.

She doesn't seem very friendly, Marion thought. *I wonder if that is because I'm not colored? Or am I just imagining it?*

Marion walked out onto North Broad Street and crossed it, and walked up half a block to the little fast-food place he'd found where he could get a cup of coffee and a Danish pastry to begin the day, and went in.

Sister Fortitude walked from behind the desk and went and stood by the door beside the revolving door and watched as Marion took a seat at the counter and ordered his coffee.

I knew there was something about that man, she thought.

She watched until Marion had finished a second cup of coffee and left the restaurant and walked, north, out of sight.

Then she went to the elevator and went up to Marion's room and unlocked the door and went inside. She knew what the room should contain, in terms of hotel property, and a quick look showed nothing missing.

But Sister Fortitude, who had read several magazine articles about how professional hotel thieves operated, knew that did not mean that he hadn't stolen whatever he was stealing from another room.

There was nothing in the closet that the white man could steal but wire hangers, but Sister Fortitude decided to check it anyway. When she found that it was locked, her suspicions grew. She went into the adjacent room, took the key from that closet door, and carried it back to Marion's room. It didn't work.

Sister Fortitude had to get, and try, four different closet keys from four different rooms before one operated the lock in the white man's room.

Two minutes later, Sister Fortitude ran out onto North Broad Street, looking for a policeman.

You never could find one when you needed one, she thought.

And then she saw one, in the coffee shop where the white man had gone to get the coffee he couldn't get in the Divine Lorraine Hotel Restaurant.

She walked quickly across Broad Street.

"I want you to come with me," Sister Fortitude said to the policeman. "I got something to show you."

At ten minutes past nine A.M., Sergeant Jerry O'Dowd and Detective Matt Payne were driving up North Broad Street in O'Dowd's unmarked car. They had finally been released at Internal Affairs, and although Matt thought he was about to fall asleep on his feet, he knew he had to go back to Northwest Detectives and get his Bug before all sorts of questions he didn't want to answer would be asked.

There was considerable police activity at the intersection of Broad and Ridge; Broad Street was blocked off, and a white cap was directing traffic in a detour.

When they finally got to the white cap, Jerry rolled the window down in idle curiosity to ask him what was going on.

And then he saw, at the same moment Matt Payne saw, the large blue and white Ordnance Disposal van, with the Explosive Containment trailer hitched to the rear of it.

Without exchanging a word, they both got out of the car and ran toward the Divine Lorraine Hotel.

"You can't just leave your car here!" the white cap called after them.

There was a uniformed lieutenant standing with a large black woman at the desk.

"What's going on here?" O'Dowd asked as he pinned his badge to his jacket.

"And who the hell are you, Sergeant?"

"Watch your mouth, we don't tolerate that sort of talk in here," Sister Fortitude said.

"I'm Sergeant O'Dowd, sir, of Special Operations. We're working on the bomb threat."

Matt took the artists' drawings of Marion Claude Wheatley from his pocket and gave them to Sister Fortitude.

"Ma'am, do you recognize these?"

Sister Fortitude studied both pictures carefully, and then held one out.

"This one, I do. I never saw the other one."

"This is the man who . . . what, rented a room?" Matt asked.

"Said he was about the Lord's work. Satan's work is more like it."

"Where is the bomb?" O'Dowd asked.

"Six-eighteen," Sister Fortitude said.

The elevators were not running. The hotel's electric service had been shut off to make sure no stray electric current would trigger the bomb's detonators.

Matt and O'Dowd were panting when they reached the sixth floor. O'Dowd pulled open the fire door on the landing, and they entered the dark corridor, now lit only by police portable floodlights and what natural light there was.

Halfway down the corridor Matt saw two Bomb Squad men in their distinctive, almost black coveralls. He remembered hearing at the Academy that they were made of special material that did not generate static electricity.

O'Dowd shook hands with one of the Bomb Squad men.

"Hey, Bill. What have we got?"

"Enough C-4, wrapped with chain, to do a lot of damage."

"Bill Raybold, Matt Payne," O'Dowd said.

"Yeah, I know who you are," Raybold said, shaking Matt's hand.

He knows me by reputation. Is that reputation that of the brave and heroic police officer who won the shoot-out in the alley, or that of the poor sonofabitch who's got a junkie for a girlfriend?

"The lady at the desk downstairs says the guy who rented 618 is the guy we're looking for," Matt said. "I showed her the police artist's drawing."

"This guy knows what he's doing with explosives," Raybold replied. "The explosive is Composition C-4. It's military, and as safe as it gets. Your man may be crazy, but he's not stupid. He's got them all ready to go except for the detonators. It would take him no more than ten seconds to hook them up."

"Detonators?" O'Dowd asked.

"Not close to here. Jimmy Samuels was in here with his dog, and the only time the dog got happy was when he sniffed the closet. After we get the hotel cleared, we'll take a really good look."

"Bill," O'Dowd said. "If our guy sees the dog and pony show outside, he'll disappear again."

Raybold considered that for a moment.

"Yeah," he said, after a moment. "I don't see why we couldn't leave this stuff here for a while. It's safe. But that don't mean the district captain would go along. And it's his call."

"Sergeant, I don't know who you think you are," the district captain said. "But nobody tells me to throw the book away. We got a crime scene here, and we're going to work it."

"Captain," Detective Payne said, "sir, I've got Chief Coughlin on the line. He'd like to talk to you."

At fifteen minutes to eleven A.M., Marion Claude Wheatley got off the bus and walked across Ridge Avenue and into the lobby of the Divine Lorraine Hotel.

He smiled at Sister Fortitude but she didn't smile back, just nodded.

I wonder if I have done, or said, something that has offended her?

Marion got on the elevator and rode to his floor. He had bought a newspaper in 30th Street Station, and he planned to read it as he tried to move his bowels. He was suffering from constipation, and had decided it was a combination of his usual bowel movement schedule being disrupted and the food in the Divine Lorraine Hotel Restaurant. He had decided he would take the next several meals elsewhere to see if that would clear his elimination tract.

There was a man sitting in the upholstered chair in the room. He smiled.

"Hello, Marion," he said. "We've been waiting for you."

"Who are you? What do you want?"

"The Lord sent us, Marion. I'm Brother Jerome, and that is Brother Matthew," the man said.

Marion turned and saw another man, a younger one, almost a boy, nicely dressed, standing behind him, just inside the door.

"The Lord sent you?"

"Yes, He did," Brother Jerome said.

"Why?"

"You misunderstood the Lord's message, Marion," Brother Jerome said. "You have the Lord's method out of sequence."

"I don't understand," Marion said.

O'Dowd picked up the Bible from the desk and read aloud: " 'I smote you with blasting and with mildew and with hail in all the labours of your hands; yet ye turned not to me.' "

"Haggai 2:17," Marion said.

"Precisely," Brother Jerome said, adding kindly, "First mildew, Marion. Then hail, and only *finally* blasting."

"Oh," Marion said. *"Oh!* Now I understand."

"Marion, could I see your newspaper, please?" the younger man asked.

"Certainly," Marion said and gave it to him. Then he turned back to Brother Jerome. "I knew the Lord wanted to tell me something," he said.

Brother Matthew patted the newspaper as if he expected to find something in it. Brother Jerome gave him a dirty look. Brother Matthew shook his head, no, and shrugged.

"Well, the Lord understands, Marion," Brother Jerome said. "You were trying, and the Lord knows that."

"Marion, where's the transmitter?" Brother Matthew asked.

Brother Jerome closed his eyes.

"It's in the 30th Street Station," Marion said. "Why do you want to know?"

"The Lord wants us to take over from here, Marion," Brother Jerome said. "He knows how hard you've been working. Where's the transmitter in 30th Street Station?"

"In a locker," Marion said, and reached in his watch pocket and took out several keys. "I really can't tell you which of these keys . . ."

"It's all right, Marion," Brother Jerome said, taking the keys from him. "We'll find it."

At 7:45 P.M., Detective Matthew M. Payne got off the elevator in the Psychiatric Wing of the University of Pennsylvania Hospital.

One of the nurses at the Nursing Station, a formidable red-haired harridan, told him that Miss Detweiler was in 9023, but he couldn't see her because his name wasn't on the list, and anyway, her doctor was in there.

"Dr. Payne is expecting me," Matt said. "Ninety twenty-three, you said?"

Penny was sitting in a chrome, vinyl-upholstered chair by the window. She was wearing a hospital gown and, he could not help but notice, absolutely nothing else. Amelia Payne, M.D., was sitting on the bed.

"What are you doing here?" Dr. Payne snapped.

"I heard this is where the action is," Matt said.

"I don't think this is a good idea," Amy said. "I think you had better leave."

"Please, Amy!" Penny said.

"Take a walk, Amy," Matt said.

Dr. Payne considered that for a long moment, and then pushed herself off the bed and walked to the door, where she turned.

"Five minutes," she said, and left.

Matt walked over to Penny and handed her a grease-stained paper bag.

"Ribs," he said. "They're cold by now, but I'll bet they'll be better than what they serve in here."

"I don't suppose I could have eaten roses, but candy would have been nice," Penny said. "Matt, are you disgusted with me?"

"I was," he blurted. "Until just now. When I saw you."

"My parents blame you for the whole thing, you know," she said.

"I figured that would happen."

"Amy says it was my fault."

"Amy's right," Matt said. "If you had thrown something at me, even taken a shot at me, that would have been my fault. But what you did to yourself . . ."

Penny suddenly pushed herself out of the chair. She threw the bag of ribs at the garbage can and missed. She turned to the window. Matt could see her backbone and the crack of her buttocks. He looked away, then headed for the door.

"Amy's right. I shouldn't have come here."

Penny turned.

"Matt!"

He looked at her.

"Matt, don't leave me!"

After a long moment, he said, his voice on the edge of breaking, "Penny, I don't know what to do with you!"

"Give me a chance," she said. "Give *us* a chance!"

Then she walked, almost ran to him, stopped and looked up at him.

"Please, Matt," she said, and then his arms went around her.

I love her.

A junkie is a junkie is a junkie.

Oh, shit!

District Attorney Thomas J. Callis, after a psychiatric examination of Marion Claude Wheatley, petitioned the court for Mr. Wheatley's involuntary commitment to a psychiatric institution for the criminally insane. The petition was granted.

District Attorney Callis, after studying the available evidence, decided that it was insufficient to bring Mr. Paulo Cassandro, Mr. Ricco Baltazari, Mr. Gian-Carlo Rosselli, or any of the others mentioned in Mr. Vito Lanza's sworn statements to trial.

Mr. Vito Lanza, on a plea of guilty to charges of possession of controlled substances with the intention to distribute, was sentenced to two years imprisonment. At Mr. Callis's recommendation, no charges were brought against Mrs. Magdelana Lanza.

Inspector Peter Wohl retained command of the Special Operations Division of the Philadelphia Police Department.

Detective Matthew M. Payne was led to believe by Supervisory Special Agent H. Charles Larkin of the Secret Service that his application for appointment to the Secret Service would be favorably received. Detective Payne declined to make such an application.

Mr. Ricco Baltazari was found shot to death in a drainage ditch in the Tinnicum Swamps near Philadelphia International Airport. No arrests have been made to date in the case.

THE
MURDERERS

1.

Officer Jerry Kellog, who was on the Five Squad of the Narcotics Unit of the Philadelphia Police Department, had heard somewhere that if something went wrong, and you found yourself looking down the barrel of a gun, the best thing to do was smile. Smiling was supposed to make the guy holding the gun on you less nervous, less likely to use the gun just because he was scared.

He had never had the chance to put the theory to the test before—the last goddamned place in the world he expected to find some scumbag holding a gun on him was in his own kitchen—but he raised his hands to shoulder level, palms out, and smiled.

"No problem," Jerry said. "Whatever you want, you got it."

"You got a ankle holster, motherfucker?" the man with the gun demanded.

Jerry's brain went on automatic, and filed away. *White male, 25–30, 165 pounds, five feet eight, medium build, light brown hair, no significant scars or distinguishing marks, blue .38 Special, five-inch barrel, Smith & Wesson, dark blue turtleneck, dark blue zipper jacket, blue jeans, high-topped work shoes.*

"No. I mean, I got one. But I don't wear it. It rubs my ankle."

That was true.

Christ, that's my gun! I hung it on the hall rack when I came in. This scumbag grabbed it. And that's why he wants to know if I have another one!

"Pull your pants up," the scumbag said.

"Right. You got it," Jerry said, and reached down and pulled up his left trousers leg, and then the right.

Jerry remembered to smile, and said, "Look, we got what could be a bad situation here. So far, it's not as bad as it could—"

"Shut your fucking mouth!"

"Right."

"Who else is here?"

"Nobody," Jerry answered, and when he thought he saw suspicion or disbelief in the scumbag's eyes, quickly added, "No shit. My wife moved out on me. I live here alone."

"I seen the dishes in the sink," the scumbag said, accepting the three or four days' accumulation of unwashed dishes as proof.

"Ran off with another cop, would you believe it?"

The scumbag looked at him, shrugged, and then said, "Turn around."

He's going to hit me in the back of the head. Jesus Christ, that's dangerous. It's not like in the fucking movies. You hit somebody in the head, you're liable to fracture his skull, kill him.

Jerry turned around, his hands still held at shoulder level.

Maybe I should have tried to kick the gun out of his hands. But if I had done that, he'd have tried to kill me.

Jerry felt his shoulders tense in anticipation of the blow.

The scumbag raised the Smith & Wesson to arm's length and fired it into the back of Jerry's head, and then, when Jerry had slumped to the floor, fired it again, leaning slightly over to make sure the second bullet would also enter the brain.

Then he lowered the Smith & Wesson and let it slip from his fingers onto the linoleum of Jerry Kellog's kitchen floor.

———

"Where the hell," Sergeant Patrick J. Dolan of the Narcotics Unit demanded in a loud voice, paused long enough to make sure he had the attention of the seven men in the crowded squad room of Five Squad, and then finished the question, "is Kellog?"

There was no reply beyond a couple of shrugs.

"I told that sonofabitch I wanted to see him at quarter after eight," Sergeant Dolan announced. "I'll have his ass!"

He glowered indignantly around the squad room, turned around, and left the room.

Sergeant Patrick J. Dolan was not regarded by the officers of the Five Squad of the Narcotics Unit—or, for that matter, by anyone else in the entire Narcotics Unit, with the possible exception of Lieutenant Michael J. "Mick" Mikkles—as an all-around splendid fellow and fine police officer with whom it was a pleasure to serve. The reverse was true. If a poll of the officers in Narcotics were to be conducted, asking each officer to come up with one word to describe Sergeant Dolan, the most common choice would be "prick," with "sonofabitch" running a close second.

This is not to say that he was not a good police officer. He had been on the job more than twenty years, a sergeant for ten, and in Narcotics for seven. He was a skilled investigator, reasonably intelligent, and a hard worker. He seldom made mistakes or errors of judgment. Dolan's problem, Officer Tom Coogan had once proclaimed, to general agreement, in the Allgood Bar, across the street from Five Squad's office at Twenty-second and Hunting Park Avenue, where Narcotics officers frequently went after they had finished for the day, was that Dolan devoutly believed that not only did he never make mistakes or errors of judgment but that he was incapable of doing so.

Tom Coogan had been on the job eight years, five of them in plain clothes in Narcotics. For reasons neither he nor his peers understood, he had been unable to make a high enough grade on either of the two detective's examinations he had taken to make a promotion list. Sometimes this bothered him, as he was convinced that he was at least as smart and just as good an investigator as, say, half the detectives he knew. On the other hand, he consoled himself, he would much rather be doing what he was doing than, for example, investigating burglaries in Northeast Detectives, and with the overtime he had in Narcotics he was making as much money as a sergeant or a lieutenant in one of the districts, so what the hell difference did it make?

Coogan had absolutely no idea why Dolan had summoned Jerry Kellog to an early-morning meeting, or why Kellog hadn't shown up when he was supposed to, but a number of possibilities occurred to him, the most likely of which being that Kellog had simply forgotten about it. Another, slightly less likely possibility was that Kellog had overslept. Since his wife had moved out on him, he had been at the sauce more heavily and more often than was good for him.

It wasn't just that his wife had moved out on him—broken marriages are not uncommon in the police community—but that she had moved in with another cop. A police officer whose wife leaves the nuptial couch because she has decided that the life of a cop's wife is not for her can expect the understanding commiseration of his peers. Kellog's wife, however, had moved out of a plainclothes narc's bed into the bed of a Homicide detective. That was different. There was an unspoken suggestion that maybe she had reasons—ranging from bad behavior on Kellog's part to the possibility that the Homicide detective was giving her something in the sack that Kellog hadn't been able to deliver.

The one thing Jerry Kellog didn't need right now was trouble from Sergeant Patrick J. Dolan, which could range from a single ass-chewing to telling the Lieutenant he wasn't where he was supposed to be when he was supposed to be, to something official, bringing him up on charges.

Tom Coogan wasn't a special pal of Jerry Kellog, but they worked together, and Kellog had covered Coogan's ass more than once, so he owed him. He picked up his telephone, pulled out the little shelf with the celluloid-covered list of phone numbers on it, found Kellog's, and dialed it.

The line was busy.

Two minutes later, Coogan tried it again. Still busy.

Who the hell is he talking to? His wife, maybe? Some other broad? His mother? Something connected with the job?

Fuck it! The important thing is to get him over here and get Dolan off his back.

He tried it one more time, and when he got the busy signal broke the connection with his finger and dialed the operator.

"This is Police Officer Thomas Coogan, badge number 3621. I have been trying to reach 555-2330. This is an emergency. Will you break in, please?"

"There's no one on the line, sir," the operator reported thirty seconds later. "The phone is probably off the hook."

"Thank you," Coogan said.

The fact that the phone is off the hook doesn't mean he's not there. He could have come home shitfaced, knocked it off falling into bed, or on purpose so that he wouldn't be disturbed. He's probably lying there in bed, sleeping it off.

That posed the problem of what to do next. He realized he didn't want to drive all the way over to Kellog's house to wake him up, for a number of reasons, including the big one, that Sergeant Dolan was liable to ask him where the fuck he was going.

He thought a moment, then reached for his telephone.

"Twenty-fifth District, Officer Greene."

"Tom Coogan, Narcotics. Who's the supervisor?"

"Corporal Young."

"Let me talk to him, will you?"

He knew Corporal Eddie Young.

"Tom Coogan, Eddie. How are you?"

"Can't complain, Tom. What's up?"

"Need a favor."

"Try me. All I can say is 'no.' "

"One of our guys, Jerry Kellog, you know him?"

"No, I don't think so."

"He lives at 300 West Luray Street. He's supposed to be here. Our Sergeant is shitting a brick. Could you send somebody over to his house and see if he's there and wake him up and tell him to get his ass over here? I've been trying to call him. His phone is off the hook. I think he's probably sleeping one off."

"Give me the address again and it's done, and you owe me one."

A nearly new Buick turned off Seventh Street and into the parking lot at the rear of the Police Administration Building of the City of Philadelphia. The driver, Mr. Michael J. O'Hara, a wiry, curly-haired man in his late thirties, made a quick sweep through the parking lot, found no parking spot he considered convenient enough, pulled to the curb directly in front of the rear entrance to the building, and got out.

A young police officer who had been on the job just over a year, and assigned to duty at the PAB three days before, intercepted Mr. O'Hara as he headed toward the door.

"Excuse me, sir," he said. "You can't leave your car there."

Mr. O'Hara smiled at what he considered the young officer's rather charming naivete.

"It's OK, son," he said. "I'm Commissioner Czernich's bookie."

"Excuse me?" the young officer said, not quite believing what he heard.

"The Commissioner," Mr. O'Hara went on, now enjoying himself, "put two bucks on a long shot. It paid a hundred ninety-eight eighty. When I come here to pay him off, he says I can park anywhere I want."

The young officer's uneasiness was made worse by the appearance of Chief Inspector Heinrich "Heine" Matdorf, Chief of Training for the Philadelphia Police Department, whom the young officer remembered very clearly from his days at the Police Academy. It was the first time the young officer had ever seen him smile.

"What did you tell him?" Chief Matdorf asked.

"I told him I was Czernich's bookie."

"Jesus Christ, Mickey!" Matdorf laughed, patting him on the back as he did so.

As the young police officer had begun to suspect, the driver of the Buick was not a bookmaker. Mr. Michael J. "Mickey" O'Hara was in fact a Pulitzer Prize–winning reporter employed by the *Philadelphia Bulletin.* There was little question in the minds of his peers—and absolutely none in his own mind—that he was the best police reporter between Boston and Washington, and possibly in an even larger geographical area.

Mickey O'Hara extended his hand to Matdorf's driver, a sergeant.

"How are you, Mr. O'Hara?" the Sergeant asked, a respectful tone in his voice.

"Heine," O'Hara asked, "have you got enough pull around here to tell this fine young officer I can park here?"

"The minute he goes inside," Chief Matdorf instructed the young officer, "let the air out of his tires."

"Thanks a lot, Heine."

"What's going on, Mickey?"

"I hoped maybe you could tell me," O'Hara said.

"So far as I know, not much. There was nothing on the radio."

"I know," O'Hara said.

"Going in, Mickey?" Matdorf asked.

"I got to pay off the Commissioner," O'Hara said. "And I thought I might take a look at the Overnights."

The Overnights were reports from the various districts and other bureaucratic divisions of the Philadelphia Police Department of out-of-the-ordinary police activity overnight furnished to senior police officials for their general information.

They were internal Police Department correspondence not made available to the public or the press. Mr. Michael J. O'Hara, as a civilian, and especially as a journalist, was not entitled to be privy to them.

But Mickey O'Hara enjoyed a special relationship with the Police Department. He was not in their pocket, devoting his journalistic skills to puff pieces, but on the other hand, neither did he spend all of his time looking for stories that made the Department or its officers look bad. Most important, he could be trusted. If he was told something off the record, it stayed off the record.

"Come on in, then," Chief Matdorf said. "I'll even buy you a cup of coffee."

He touched O'Hara's arm and they started toward the rear door of the building. There is a front entrance, overlooking Metropolitan Hospital, but it is normally locked. The rear door opens onto a small foyer. Just inside is a uniformed police officer sitting behind a heavy plate-glass window controlling access to the building's lobby with a solenoid switch.

To the right is a corridor leading past the Bail Clerk's Office and the Arraignment Room to the Holding Room. The Municipal Judge's Court is a small, somewhat narrow room separated from the corridor by heavy glass. There are seats for spectators in the corridor. Farther to the right is the entrance to the Holding Room, in effect a holding prison, to which prisoners brought from the various police districts and initially locked up in cells in the basement are brought to be booked and to face a Municipal Court Judge, who sets bail. Those prisoners for whom bail is denied, or who can't make it, are moved, males to the Detention Center, females to the House of Correction.

When the corporal on duty behind the plate-glass window saw Chief Matdorf, he activated the solenoid, the lock buzzed, and Matdorf pushed the door open and waved O'Hara through it ahead of him into the lobby of the PAB, where the general civilian populace is not allowed.

They walked toward the elevators, past the wall display of photographs of police officers who have been killed in the line of duty. As they approached the elevator, the door opened and discharged a half-dozen people, among them Chief Inspector Dennis V. Coughlin and Inspector Peter Wohl.

"Hey, whaddaya say, Mickey?" Chief Coughlin greeted him with a smile, and offered his hand.

"Hello, Mick," Wohl said, as he offered his hand first to O'Hara and then to Chief Matdorf.

Mickey O'Hara had not earned the admiration of his peers, or the Pulitzer Prize, by being wholly immune to the significance of body language.

Despite that warm greeting, neither of these two is at all happy to see me. That means that something is going on that they would rather not tell me about just now. And what are the two of them doing together this early in the morning?

"What's up, Mickey?" Chief Coughlin asked.

"I hoped maybe you would tell me."

Chief Coughlin shrugged, indicating nothing.

Bullshit, Denny.

"I thought I'd take a look at the Overnights," O'Hara said.

"They're on my desk, Mick. Tell Veronica I said you could have a look," Coughlin said.

Veronica Casey was Coughlin's secretary.

"Thanks, Denny," O'Hara said. "Good to see you. And you too, Peter."

They shook hands again. Chief Coughlin and Inspector Wohl walked out the rear entrance. Mickey got on the elevator with Chief Matdorf and his driver.

"Jesus, I forgot something in the car," O'Hara said, and got off the elevator.

He went through the rear door in time to see Coughlin and Wohl walking with what he judged to be unusual speed toward their cars. He stayed just inside the door until they were both in their cars and moving, then went out and quickly got behind the wheel of his Buick and followed them out of the parking lot.

Those two are going somewhere interesting together, somewhere they hope I won't show up.

He turned on all three of the shortwave receivers mounted under the dashboard. The receivers in Mickey O'Hara's car were the best the *Bulletin*'s money could buy. They were each capable of being switched to receive any of the ten different frequencies utilized by the Police Department.

One of these was the universal band (called the J-Band) to which every police vehicle had access. Each of Philadelphia's seven police divisions had its own radio frequency. An eighth frequency (the H-Band) was assigned for the exclusive use of investigative units (detectives' cars, and those assigned to Narcotics, Intelligence, Organized Crime, et cetera). And since Mayor Jerry Carlucci had gotten all that lovely ACT Grant money from Congress, there was a new special band (the W-Band) for the exclusive use of Special Operations (including the Highway Patrol).

Ordinary police cars were limited to the use of two bands, the Universal J Band, and either one of the division frequencies, or the H (Detective) Band.

Mickey switched one of his radios to the J (Universal) Band, the second to the H (Detective) Band, and the third to the W (Special Operations) Band, a little smugly deciding that if anything interesting was happening, or if Wohl and Coughlin wanted to talk to each other, the odds were that it would come over one of the three.

It quickly became clear that wherever the two of them were going, they were going together and in a hurry. Wohl stayed on Coughlin's bumper as they drove through Center City and then out the Parkway and along the Schuylkill.

Nothing of interest came over the radio, however, as they left Center City behind them, and an interesting thought destroyed some of Mickey's good feeling that he had outwitted Denny Coughlin and Peter Wohl.

It is entirely possible that those two bastards have decided to pull my chain. They saw me watch them leave the Roundhouse, and before I got into my car one or the other of them got on his radio and said, "If Mickey follows us, let's take him on a tour of Greater Philadelphia." They're probably headed nowhere special at all, and after I follow them to hell and gone, they will pull into a diner someplace for a cup of coffee, and wait for me with a broad smile.

He had just about decided this was a very good possibility when there was activity on the radio.

"William One."

"William One," Peter Wohl's voice responded.

"William Two requests a location."

Mickey knew that William Two was the call sign of Captain Mike Sabara, Wohl's second-in-command.

"Inform William Two I'm on my way to Chestnut Hill and I'll phone him from there."

Damn, they got me! The two of them are headed for Dave Pekach's girlfriend's house. She's having an engagement party the day after tomorrow. It has to be that. Why else would the two of them be going to Chestnut Hill at this time of the morning?

Mickey turned off the Schuylkill Expressway onto the Roosevelt Boulevard extension.

I'll go get some breakfast at the Franklin Diner and then I'll go home.

He reached down and moved the switch on the third of his radio receivers from the Special Operations frequency so that it would receive police communications of the East Division. He did this without thinking, in what was really a Pavlovian reflex, whenever he drove out of one police division into another.

And there was something going on in the Twenty-fifth District.

"Twenty-five Seventeen," a voice said.

"Twenty-five Seventeen," a male police-radio operator responded immediately.

"Give me a supervisor at this location. This is a Five Two Nine Two, an off-duty Three Six Nine."

Mickey knew police-radio shorthand as well as any police officer. A Five Two Nine Two, an off-duty Three Six Nine, meant the officer was reporting the discovery of a body, that of an off-duty cop.

A "dead body," even of a cop, was not necessarily front-page news, but Mickey's ears perked up.

"Twenty-five A," the police radio operator called.

"Twenty-five A," the Twenty-fifth District sergeant on patrol responded. "What's that location?"

"300 West Luray Street."

"I got it," Twenty-five A announced. "En route."

And then Mickey's memory turned on.

Mickey glanced in his rearview mirror, hit the brakes, made a tire-squealing U-turn, and headed for 300 West Luray Street.

One of the unofficial perquisites of being the Commanding Officer of Highway Patrol was that of being picked up at your home and driven to work, normally a privilege accorded only to Chief Inspectors. A Highway car just seemed to be coincidentally in the neighborhood of the Commanding Officer every day at the time the Commanding Officer would be leaving for work. Captain David Pekach, however, normally chose to forgo this courtesy. He said that it would be inappropriate, especially since Inspector Peter Wohl, his superior, usually drove himself.

While this was of course true, Captain Pekach had another reason for waiving the privilege of being picked up at home and driven to work, and then being driven home again when the day's work was over. This was because it had been a rare night indeed, since he had met Miss Martha Peebles, that he had laid his weary head to rest on his own pillow in his small apartment.

He believed that any police supervisor—and he was Commanding Officer of Highway, which made him a special sort of supervisor—should set an example in both his professional and personal life for his subordinates. The officers of Highway would not understand that his relationship with Martha was love of the most pure sort, and a relationship which he intended to dignify before God and man in holy matrimony in the very near future.

He was painfully sensitive to the thoughts of his peers—the most cruel "joke" he had heard was that "the way to get rich was to have a dong like a mule and find yourself a thirty-five-year-old rich-as-hell virgin"—and if they, his friends, his fellow captains, were unable to understand what he and Martha shared, certainly he could not expect more from rank-and-file officers.

Obviously, if he was picked up and dropped off every day at Martha's house, there would be talk. So he drove himself. And it was nobody's business but his own that he had arranged with the telephone company to have the number assigned to his apartment transferred to Martha's house, so that if anyone called his apartment, he would get the call in Chestnut Hill.

In just five weeks, he thought as he got into his assigned Highway Patrol car and backed it out of the five-car garage behind Martha's house, the problem would be solved, and the deception no longer necessary. They would be married.

They would already be married if they were both Catholic or, for that matter, both Episcopal. Both Martha and his mother had climbed up on a high horse about what was the one true faith. His mother said she would witness her son getting married in a heathen ceremony over her dead body, and Martha had said that she was sorry, she had promised her late father she would be married where he had married, and his father before him, in St. Mark's Church in Center City Philadelphia.

Her father would, she said, tears in her eyes, which really hurt Dave Pekach, turn over in his grave if she broke her word to him, and worse, were married according to the rules of the Church of Rome, which would have required her to promise any children of their union to be raised in the Roman Catholic faith.

Extensive appeals through the channels of the Archdiocese of Philadelphia, lasting months, had resulted in a compromise. After extensive negotiations, with the prospective groom being represented by Father Kaminski, his family's parish priest, and the prospective bride by Brewster Cortland Payne II, Esq., the compromise had been reached in a ninety-second, first-person conversation between the Cardinal of the Archdiocese of Philadelphia and his good friend the Bishop of the Episcopal Diocese of Philadelphia, with enough time left over to schedule eighteen holes at Merion Golf Course and a steak supper the following Wednesday.

It had been mutually agreed that the wedding would be an ecumenical service jointly conducted by the Episcopal Bishop and a Roman Catholic Monsignor, and the prospective bride would be required only to promise that she would raise any fruit of their union as "Christians."

Mother Pekach had been, not without difficulty, won over to the compromise by Father Kaminski, who reminded her what St. Paul had said about it being better to marry than to burn, and argued that if the Cardinal himself was going to send Monsignor O'Hallohan, the Chancellor of the Archdiocese, himself, to St. Mark's Church for the wedding, it really couldn't be called a heathen ceremony in a heathen church.

There would be a formal announcement of their engagement the day after tomorrow, at a party, with the wedding to follow a month later.

Captain Pekach drove out the gates of the Peebles estate at 606 Glengarry Lane in

Chestnut Hill, and tried to decide the best way to get from there to Frankford and Castor avenues at this time of the morning. He decided he would have a shot at going down North Broad, and then cutting over to Frankford. There was no *good* way to get from here to there.

He reached under the dashboard without really thinking about it and turned on both of the radios with which his car, and those of half a dozen other Special Operations/Highway Patrol cars, were equipped.

As he approached North Broad and Roosevelt Boulevard, the part of his brain which was subconsciously listening to the normal early-morning radio traffic was suddenly wide awake.

"Give me a supervisor at this location. This is a Five Two Nine Two, an off-duty Three Six Nine."

"Twenty-five A," the police radio operator called.

"Twenty-five A," the Twenty-fifth District sergeant on patrol responded. "What's that location?"

"300 West Luray Street."

300 West Luray Street? My God, that's Jerry Kellog's address. Jerry Kellog? Dead? Jesus, Mary and Joseph!

"I got it," Twenty-five A announced. "En route."

Without really being aware of what he was doing, Captain Pekach reached down and turned on the lights and siren and pushed the accelerator to the floor.

It took him less than three minutes to reach 300 West Luray Street, but that was enough time for him to have second thoughts about his rushing to the scene.

For one thing, it's none of my business.

But on the other hand, anything that happens anywhere in the City of Philadelphia is Highway's business, and I'm the Highway Commander.

That's bullshit and you know it.

But Jerry Kellog is one of my guys.

Not anymore he's not. You're no longer a Narcotics Lieutenant, but the Highway Captain.

Yeah, but somebody has to notify Helene, and who better than me?

Jesus, I heard there was bad trouble between them. You don't think . . .

There was a Twenty-fifth District RPC at the curb, and as Pekach got out of his car, a Twenty-fifth District sergeant's car pulled up beside him.

"Good morning, sir," the Sergeant said, saluting him. He was obviously surprised to see Pekach. "Sergeant Manning, Twenty-fifth District."

"I heard this on the radio," Pekach said. "Jerry Kellog used to work for me in Narcotics. What's going on?"

"I seen him around," Sergeant Manning said. "I didn't know he was working Narcotics."

The front door of the house opened and a District uniform came out and walked up to them. And he too saluted and looked at Pekach curiously.

"He's in the kitchen, Sergeant," he said.

"Anything?"

"No. When I got here—"

"What brought you here?" Pekach interrupted.

"He wasn't answering his phone, sir. Somebody from Narcotics asked us to check on him." Pekach nodded. "When I got here, the back door was open, and I looked in and saw him."

"You check the premises?" the Sergeant asked.

"Yeah. Nobody was inside."

"You should have asked for backup," the Sergeant said, in mild reprimand.

"I'm going to have a look," Pekach announced.

Pekach went through the open front door. He found the body, lying on its face, between the kitchen and the "dining area," which was the rear portion of the living room.

Kellog was on his stomach, sprawled out. His head was in a large pool of blood, now dried nearly black. Pekach recognized him from his chin and mustache. The rest of his head was pretty well shattered.

Somebody shot him, maybe more than once, in the back of his head. Probably *more than once.*

What the hell happened here? Was Narcotics involved? Christ, it has to be.

"Well," Sergeant Manning said, coming up behind Pekach, "he didn't do that to himself. I'm going to call it in to Homicide."

"I've got to get to a phone myself," Pekach said, thinking out loud.

"Sir?"

No, I don't. You're not going to call Bob Talley and volunteer to go with him to tell Helene that Jerry's dead.

"I'm going to get out of everybody's way. If Homicide wants a statement from me, they know where to find me."

"Yes, sir," Sergeant Manning said.

Dave Pekach turned and walked out of the house and got back in his car.

2.

When the call came into the Homicide Unit of the Philadelphia Police Department from Police Radio that Officer Jerome H. Kellog had been found shot to death in his home in the Twenty-fifth District, Detective Joseph P. D'Amata was holding down the desk.

D'Amata took down the information quickly, hung up, and then called, "We've got a job."

When there was no response, D'Amata looked around the room, which is on the second floor of the Roundhouse, its windows opening to the south and overlooking the parking lot behind the building. It was just about empty.

"Where the hell is everybody?" D'Amata, a slightly built, natty, olive-skinned thirty-eight-year-old, wondered aloud.

D'Amata walked across the room and stuck his head in the open door of Lieutenant Louis Natali's office. Natali, who was also olive-skinned, dapper, and in his mid-thirties, looked something like D'Amata. He was with Sergeant Zachary Hobbs, a stocky, ruddy-faced forty-four-year-old. Both looked up from whatever they were doing on Natali's desk.

"We've got a job. In the Twenty-fifth. A cop. A plainclothes narc by the name of Kellog."

"What happened to him?"

"Shot in the back of his head in his kitchen."

"And?" Natali asked, a hint of impatience in his voice.

"Joe said his name was Kellog, Lieutenant," Hobbs said delicately.

"Kellog?" Natali asked. And then his memory made the connection. "Jesus Christ! Is there more?"

D'Amata shook his head.

There was a just-perceptible hesitation.

"Where's Milham?"

Hobbs shrugged.

"Lieutenant, there's nobody out there but me," D'Amata said.

"Is Captain Quaire in his office?"

"Yes, sir," D'Amata said.

"Hobbs, see if you can find out where Milham is," Natali ordered. "You get out to the scene, Joe. Right now. We'll get you some help."

"Yes, sir."

Natali walked to Captain Henry C. Quaire's office, where he found him at his desk, visibly deep in concentration.

"Boss," Natali said. It took a moment to get Quaire's attention, but he finally looked up.

"Sorry. What's up, Lou?"

"Radio just called in a homicide. In the Twenty-fifth. The victim is a police officer. Jerome H. Kellog. The name mean anything to you?"

"He worked plainclothes in Narcotics?"

Natali nodded. "He was found with at least one bullet wound to the head in his house."

"You don't think . . . ?"

"I don't know, Boss."

"We better do this one by the book, Lou."

"Yes, sir. D'Amata was holding down the desk. He's on his way." He gestured across the room to where D'Amata was taking his service revolver from a cabinet in a small file room. "And so am I."

"Give me a call when you get there," Quaire ordered.

"Yes, sir."

There were two Twenty-fifth District RPCs, a District van, a Twenty-fifth District sergeant's, and a battered unmarked car D'Amata correctly guessed belonged to East Detectives in front of Kellog's house when D'Amata turned onto West Luray Street.

A Twenty-fifth District uniform waved him into a parking spot at the curb.

Joe got out of his car and walked to the front door, where a detective D'Amata knew, Arnold Zigler from East Detectives, was talking to the District uniform guarding the door. Joe knew the uniform's face but couldn't recall his name. Zigler smiled in recognition.

"Well, I see that East Detectives is already here, walking all over my evidence," D'Amata said.

"Screw you, Joe," Zigler said.

"What happened?"

"What I hear is that when he didn't show up at work, somebody in Narcotics called the Twenty-fifth, and they sent an RPC—Officer Hastings here—over to see if he overslept or something. The back door was open, so Hastings went in. He found him on the floor, and called it in."

"Hastings, you found the *back* door was open?"

"Right."

Kellog's row house was about in the middle of the block. D'Amata decided he could look at the back door from the inside, rather than walk to the end of the block and come in that way.

D'Amata smiled at Officer Hastings, touched his arm, and went into the house.

"Hey, Joe," Sergeant Manning said. "How are you?"

Again D'Amata recognized the face of the Sergeant but could not recall his name.

"Underpaid and overworked," D'Amata said with a smile. "How are you, pal?"

"Underpaid, my ass!" the Sergeant snorted.

D'Amata squatted by Kellog's body long enough to determine that there were two entrance wounds in the back of his skull, then carefully stepped over it and the pool of blood around the head, and went into the kitchen.

The kitchen door was open. There were signs of forced entry.

Which might mean that someone had forced the door. Or might mean that someone who had a key to the house—an estranged wife, for example—wanted the police to think that someone had broken in.

Without consciously doing so, he put *We Know For Sure Fact #1* into his mental case file: Officer Jerome H. Kellog was intentionally killed, by someone who fired two shots into his skull at close range.

He looked around the kitchen. The telephone, mounted on the wall, caught his eye. There were extra wires coming from the wall plate. He walked over for a closer look.

The wires led to a cabinet above the sink.

D'Amata took a pencil from his pocket and used it to pull on the cabinet latch. Inside the cabinet was a cassette tape recorder. He stood on his toes to get a better look. The door of the machine was open. There was no cassette inside. There was another machine beside the tape recorder, and a small carton that had once held an Economy-Pak of a half-dozen Radio Shack ninety-minute cassette tapes. It was empty.

He couldn't be sure, of course, and he didn't want to touch it to get a better look until the Mobile Crime Lab guys went over it for prints, but he had a pretty good idea that the second machine was one of those clever gadgets you saw in Radio Shack and places like that would turn the recorder on whenever the telephone was picked up.

There were no tapes in the cabinet, nor, when he carefully opened the drawers of the lower cabinets, in any of them, either. He noticed that, instead of being plugged into a wall outlet, the tape recorder had been wired to it.

Probably to make sure nobody knocked the plug out of the wall.

But where the hell are the tapes?

What the hell was on the tapes?

"Joe?" a male voice called. "You in here?"

"In the kitchen," D'Amata replied.

"Jesus, who did this?" the voice asked. There were hints of repugnance in the voice, which D'Amata now recognized as that of a civilian police photographer from the Mobile Crime Lab.

"Somebody who didn't like him," D'Amata said.

"What is that supposed to be, humor?"

"There's a tape recorder in the kitchen cabinet. I want some shots of that, and the cabinets," D'Amata said. "And make sure they dust it for prints."

"Any other instructions, Detective?" the photographer, a very tall, very thin man, asked sarcastically.

"What have I done, hurt your delicate feelings again?"

"I do this for a living. Sometimes you forget that."

"And you wanted to be a concert pianist, right?"

"Oh, fuck you, Joe," the photographer said with a smile. "Get out of my way."

"Narcotics, Sergeant Dolan," Dolan, a stocky, ruddy-faced man in his late forties, answered the telephone.

"This is Captain Samuels, of the Twenty-fifth District. Is Captain Talley around? He doesn't answer his phone."

"I think he's probably in the can," Sergeant Dolan said. "Just a second, here he comes."

Samuels heard Dolan call, "Captain, Captain Samuels for you on Three Six," and then Captain Robert F. Talley, the Commanding Officer of the Narcotics Bureau, came on the line.

"Hello, Fred. What can I do for you?"

"I've got some bad news, and a problem, Bob," Samuels said. "They just found Officer Jerome Kellog's body in his house. He was shot in the head."

"Jesus Christ!" Talley said. "Self-inflicted?"

Talley, like most good supervisors, knew a good deal about the personal lives of his men, often more than he would have preferred to know. He knew in the case of Officer Jerome Kellog that he was having trouble, serious trouble, with his wife. And his experience had taught him the unpleasant truth that policemen with problems they could not deal with often ate their revolvers.

"No. Somebody shot him. Twice, from what I hear."

"Do we know who?"

"No," Samuels said. "Bob, you know the routine. He lived in my district."

Talley knew the routine. In the case of an officer killed on the job, the body was taken to a hospital. The Commanding Officer of the District where the dead officer lived drove to his home, informed his wife, or next of kin, that he had been injured, and drove her to the hospital.

By the time they got there, the Commissioner, if he was in the City, or the senior of the Deputy Commissioners, and the Chief Inspector of his branch of the Police Department— and more often than not, the Mayor—would be there. And so would be, if it was at all possible to arrange it, the dead officer's parish priest, or minister, or rabbi, and if not one of these, then the Departmental Chaplain of the appropriate faith. They would break the news to the widow or next of kin.

"And you can't find his wife?" Talley asked.

"No. Bob, there's some unpleasant gossip—"

"All of it probably true," Talley interrupted.

"You've heard it?"

"Yeah. Fred, where are you? In your office?"

"Yeah. Bob, I know that you and Henry Quaire are pretty close—"

Captain Henry Quaire was Commanding Officer of the Homicide Unit.

"I'll call him, Fred, and get back to you," Talley said. He broke the connection with his finger, and started to dial a number. Then, sensing Sergeant Dolan's eyes on him, quickly decided that telling him something of what he knew made more sense than keeping it to himself, and letting Dolan guess. Dolan had a big mouth and a wild imagination.

"They just found Jerry Kellog shot to death in his house," he said.

"Jesus, Mary, and Joseph!" Dolan said. "They know who did it?"

"All I know is what I told you," Talley said. "I'm going to call Captain Quaire and see what I can find out."

"You heard the talk?" Dolan asked.

"Talk is cheap, Dolan," Talley said shortly. He walked across the room to his office, closed the door, and dialed a number from memory.

"Homicide, Sergeant Hobbs."

"Captain Talley, Sergeant. Let me talk to Captain Quaire. His private line is always busy."

"Sir, the Captain's tied up at the moment. Maybe I could help you?"

"I know what he's tied up with, Hobbs. Tell him I need to talk to him."

"Captain, Chief Lowenstein's in there with him."

"Tell him I'd like to talk to him," Talley repeated.

"Yes, sir. Hang on a minute, please."

Sergeant Hobbs walked through the outer office to the office of the Commanding Officer and knocked at it.

The three men inside—Captain Henry Quaire, a stocky, balding man in his late forties; Chief Inspector of Detectives Matt Lowenstein, a stocky, barrel-chested man of fifty-five; and Lieutenant Louis Natali—all looked at him with annoyance.

"It's Captain Talley," Sergeant Hobbs called, loud enough to be heard through the door.

"I thought we might be hearing from him," Chief Lowenstein said, then raised his voice loud enough to be heard by Hobbs. "On what, Hobbs?"

"One Seven Seven, Chief," Hobbs replied.

Lowenstein turned one of the telephones on Quaire's desk around so that he could read the extension numbers and pushed the button marked 177.

"Chief Lowenstein, Talley. I guess you heard about Officer Kellog?"

"Yes, sir. Captain Samuels of the Twenty-fifth called. He's—"

"Having trouble finding the Widow Kellog?"

"Yes, sir."

"Detective Milham, who's working a job, has been asked to come in to see Captain Quaire and myself to see if he might be able to shed light on that question. If he can, I will call Captain Samuels. And for your general fund of information, Detective Milham was not up for the Kellog job. Does that answer all the questions you might have?"

Sergeant Harry McElroy, a wiry, sandy-haired thirty-eight-year-old, had been "temporarily" assigned as driver to Chief Matt Lowenstein three years before. He had then been a detective, assigned to East Detectives, and didn't want the job. Like most detectives, he viewed the Chief of Detectives with a little fear. Lowenstein had a well-earned reputation for a quick temper, going strictly by the book, and an inability to suffer fools.

The term "driver" wasn't an accurate description of what a driver did. In military parlance, a driver was somewhere between an aide-de-camp and a chief of staff. His function was to relieve his chief of details, sparing him for more important things.

During Harry's thirty-day temporary assignment, Lowenstein had done nothing to make Harry think he had made a favorable impression on him. He had been genuinely surprised when Lowenstein asked him how he felt about "sticking around, and not going back to East."

Since that possibility had never entered Harry's mind, he could not—although he himself had a well-earned reputation for being able to think on his feet—think of any excuse he could offer Lowenstein to turn down the offer.

Over the next eleven months, as he waited for his name to appear on the promotion list to sergeant—he had placed sixteenth on the exam, and was fairly sure the promotion would come through—he told himself that all he had to do was keep his nose clean and all would be well. He had come to believe that Lowenstein wasn't really as much of a sonofabitch as most people thought, and when his promotion came through, he would be reassigned.

He would, so to speak, while greatly feeling the threat of evil, have safely passed through the Valley of Death. And he knew that he had learned a hell of a lot from his close association with Lowenstein that he could have learned nowhere else.

McElroy learned that his name had come up on a promotion list from Chief Lowenstein himself, the morning of the day the list would become public.

"There's a vacancy for sergeant in Major Crimes," Lowenstein had added. "And they want you. But what I've been thinking is that you could learn more staying right where you are. Your decision."

That, too, had been totally unexpected, and by then he had come to know Lowenstein well enough to know that when he asked for a decision, Lowenstein wanted it right then, that moment.

"Thank you, Chief," Harry had said. "I'd like that."

McElroy now had his own reputation, not only as Lowenstein's shadow, but for knowing how Chief Lowenstein thought, and what he was likely to do in any given situation.

His telephone often rang with conversations that began, "Harry, how do you think the Chief would feel about . . ."

He did, he came to understand, really have an insight into how Lowenstein thought, and what Lowenstein wanted.

Usually, Harry went wherever Lowenstein went. This morning, however, he sensed without a hint of any kind from Lowenstein that he would not be welcome in Captain Henry Quaire's office when the Chief went in there to discuss the murder of Officer Jerome H. Kellog with Quaire and Lieutenant Natali.

He got himself a cup of coffee and stationed himself near the entrance to the Homicide Unit, where he could both keep an eye on Quaire's office and intercept anybody who thought they had to see the Chief.

Chief Lowenstein came suddenly out of Quaire's office and marched out of Homicide. As he passed Harry, he said, "I've got to go see the Dago."

"Yes, sir."

The Dago was the Mayor of the City of Philadelphia, the Honorable Jerry Carlucci.

They rode down to the lobby in the elevator, and out the door to where Harry had parked the Chief's official Oldsmobile, by the CHIEF INSPECTOR DETECTIVE BUREAU sign at the door.

The police band radios came to life with the starting of the engine, and there was traffic on the command band:

"Mary One, William Five, at the Zoo parking lot," one metallic voice announced.

"A couple of minutes," a second metallic voice replied.

"Mary One" was the call sign of the limousine used by the Mayor of Philadelphia, "William" the identification code assigned to Special Operations.

"Who's William Five?" Sergeant McElroy asked thoughtfully.

"Probably Tony Harris," Lowenstein said. "Washington is William Four. But what I'd really like to know is why Special Operations is meeting the Mayor, or vice versa, in the Zoo parking lot. I wonder what wouldn't wait until the Mayor got to his office."

"Yeah," McElroy grunted thoughtfully.

"Well, at least we know where to wait for the Mayor. City Hall, Harry."

"Yes, sir."

"Did Weisbach call in this morning?"

"No, sir."

"When we get to City Hall, you find a phone, get a location on Weisbach, call him, and tell him to stay wherever he is until I get back to him."

"Yes, sir."

When the mayoral Cadillac limousine rolled onto the sidewalk on the northeast corner of Philadelphia City Hall, which sits in the middle of the junction of Broad and Market streets in what is known as Center City, Chief Lowenstein was leaning against the right front fender of his Oldsmobile waiting for him.

He knew that Police Commissioner Taddeus Czernich habitually began his day by waiting in Mayor Carlucci's office for his daily orders, and he wanted to see Mayor Carlucci alone.

Lowenstein walked quickly to the side of the long black Cadillac, reaching it just as Lieutenant Jack Fellows pulled the door open. He saw that his presence surprised Fellows, and a moment later, as he came out of the car, Mayor Carlucci as well.

"Morning, Matt," Carlucci said. He was a tall, large-boned, heavyset man, wearing a well-tailored, dark blue suit, a stiffly starched, bright-white shirt, a dark, finely figured necktie, and highly polished black wing-tip shoes.

He did not seem at all pleased to see Lowenstein.

"I need a minute of your time, Mr. Mayor."

"Here, you mean," Carlucci said, on the edge of unpleasantness, gesturing around at the traffic circling City Hall.

A citizen recognized His Honor and blew his horn. Carlucci smiled warmly and waved.

"Yes, sir," Lowenstein said.

Carlucci hesitated a moment, then got back in the limousine and waved at Lowenstein to join him. Fellows, after hesitating a moment, got back in the front seat. The Mayor activated the switch that raised the divider glass.

"OK, Matt," Carlucci said.

"A police officer has been shot," Lowenstein began.

"Dead?" the Mayor interrupted. There was concern and indignation in the one word.

"Yes, sir. Shot in the back of his head."

"Line of duty?"

"His name is Kellog, Mr. Mayor. He was an undercover officer assigned to the Narcotics Unit. He was found in his home about an hour ago."

"By who?"

"When he didn't show up for work, they sent a Twenty-fifth District car to check on him."

"He wasn't married?"

"Separated."

"Has she been notified?"

"They are trying to locate her."

"Get to the goddamned point, Matt."

"The story is that she's moved in with another detective."

"Oh, Jesus! Do you know who?"

"Detective Wallace J. Milham, of Homicide."

"Isn't he the sonofabitch whose wife left him because she caught him screwing around with her sister?"

Mayor Carlucci's intimate knowledge of the personal lives of police officers was legendary, but this display of instant recall surprised Lowenstein.

"Yes, sir."

"Is what you're trying to tell me that this guy, or the wife, is involved?"

"We don't know, sir. That is, of course, possible."

"You realize the goddamned spot this puts me in?" the Mayor asked rhetorically. "I show up, or Czernich shows up, to console the widow, and there is a story in the goddamned newspapers, and the day after that it comes out—and wouldn't the *Ledger* have a ball with that?—that she's really a tramp, shacked up with a Homicide detective, and they're the doers?"

"Yes, sir. That's why I thought I'd better get to you right away with this."

"And if I don't show up, or Czernich doesn't, then what?" the Mayor went on. He turned to Lowenstein. "So what are you doing, Matt?"

"Detective Milham is on the street somewhere. They're looking for him. A good man, Joe D'Amata, is the assigned detective. Lou Natali's already on his way to the scene, and probably Henry Quaire, too."

"You ever hear the story of the fox protecting the chicken coop?" Carlucci asked nastily. "If you haven't, you can bet that the *Ledger* has."

"Henry Quaire is a straight arrow," Lowenstein said.

"I didn't say he wasn't. I'm talking about appearances. I'm talking about what the *Ledger*'s going to write."

"I don't think Wally Milham has had anything to do with this. I think we're going to find it's Narcotics-related."

"A man who would slip the salami to his wife's sister is capable of anything," the Mayor said. "I have to think that maybe he did. Or the wife did, and if he's shacked up with her . . ."

"So what do you want me to do, give it to Peter Wohl?"

"Wohl's got enough on his back right now," the Mayor said.

You mean running an investigation of corruption that I'm not even supposed to know about, even though I'm the guy charged with precisely that responsibility?

"What's the name of that mousy-looking staff inspector? Weis-something?"

"Mike Weisbach?"

"Him. He's good, and he's a straight arrow."

You used to think I was a straight arrow, Jerry. What the hell happened to change your mind?

"What are you going to do? Have him take over the investigation?"

"The Commissioner's going to tell him to *observe* the investigation, to tell you every day what's going on, and then you tell me every day what's going on."

The Mayor pushed himself off the cushions and started to crawl out of the car, over Lowenstein. He stopped, halfway out, and looked at Lowenstein, whose face was no more than six inches from his.

"I hope, for everybody's sake, Matt, that your Homicide detective who can't keep his pecker in his pocket isn't involved in this."

Lowenstein nodded.

The Mayor got out of the limousine and walked briskly toward the entrance to City Hall. Lieutenant Fellows got quickly out of the front seat and ran after him.

Lowenstein waited until the two of them disappeared from sight, then got out of the limousine, walked to his Oldsmobile, and got in the front seat beside Harry McElroy.

"You get a location on Weisbach?"

"He's in his car, at the Federal Courthouse, waiting to hear from you."

Lowenstein picked a microphone up from the seat.

"Isaac Fourteen, Isaac One."

"Fourteen."

"Meet me at Broad and Hunting Park," Lowenstein said.

"En route."

Staff Inspector Michael Weisbach's unmarked year-old Plymouth was parked on Hunting Park, pointing east toward Roosevelt Boulevard, when Chief Inspector Lowenstein's Oldsmobile pulled up behind it.

"We'll follow you to the scene," Lowenstein said to Harry McElroy as he opened the door. "You know where it is?"

"I'll find out," McElroy said.

Lowenstein walked to Weisbach's car and got in beside him.

"Good morning, Chief," Weisbach said.

He was a slight man of thirty-eight, who had started losing his never-very-luxuriant light brown hair in his late twenties. He wore glasses in mock tortoise frames, and had a slightly rumpled appearance. His wife, Natalie, with whom he had two children, Sharon (now eleven) and Milton (six), said that thirty minutes after putting on a fresh shirt, he looked as if he had been wearing it for three days.

"Mike," Lowenstein replied, offering his hand. "Follow Harry."

"Where are we going?"

"A police officer named Kellog was found an hour or so ago shot in the back of his head."

"I heard it on the radio," Weisbach said as he pulled into the line of traffic.

"You are going to—*observe* the investigation. You are going to report to me once a day, more often if necessary, if anything interesting develops." He looked at Weisbach and continued. "And I will report to the Mayor."

"What's this all about?"

"It seems that Officer Kellog's wife—he's been working plainclothes in Narcotics, by the way—moved out of his bed into Detective Milham's."

"Wally Milham's a suspect?" Weisbach asked disbelievingly.

"He's out on the street somewhere. Quaire is looking for him. I want you to sit in on the interview."

"Then he is a suspect?"

"He's going to be interviewed. The Mayor doesn't want to be embarrassed by this. He wants to be one step ahead of the *Ledger*. If a staff inspector is involved, he thinks it won't be as easy for the *Ledger* to accuse Homicide, the Department—him—of a cover-up."

"Why me?" Weisbach asked.

"What the Mayor said was, 'He's good and he's a straight arrow,' " Lowenstein replied, and then he met Weisbach's eyes and smiled. "He knows that about you, but he doesn't know your name. He referred to you as 'that mousy-looking staff inspector, Weis-something.' "

Weisbach chuckled.

"He knows your name, Mike," Lowenstein said. "What we both have to keep in mind is that the real name of the game is getting Jerry Carlucci reelected."

"Yeah," Weisbach said, a tone that could have been either resignation or disgust in his voice.

Staff Inspector Michael Weisbach, who was one of the sixteen staff inspectors in the Philadelphia Police Department, had never really wanted to be a cop until he had almost five years on the job.

His father operated a small, mostly wholesale, findings store, Weisbach's Buttons and Zipper World, on South Ninth Street in Center City Philadelphia, and the family lived in a row house on Higbee Street, near Oxford Circle. By the time he had finished high school, Mike had decided, with his parents' approval, that he wanted to be a lawyer.

He had obtained, on a partial scholarship, in just over three years, a bachelor of arts degree from Temple University, by going to school year round and supporting himself primarily by working the graveyard shift managing a White Tower hamburger emporium on the northwest corner of Broad and Olney. The job paid just a little more than his father's business could afford to pay, and there was time in the early-morning hours, when business was practically nonexistent, to study.

Sometime during this period, Natalie had changed from being the Little Abramowitz Girl Down the Block into the woman with whom Michael knew he wanted to share his life. And starting right then—when he saw her in her bathing suit, he thought of the Song of Solomon—not after he finished law school and took the bar exams and managed to build a practice that would support them.

The thing for them to do, he and Natalie decided, was for him to get a job. Maybe a day job with the City, or the Gas Company, that would pay more than he was making at White Tower, not require a hell of a lot of work from him, and permit him to go to law school at night. With what she could earn working in her new job as a clerical assistant at the Bursar's Office of the University of Pennsylvania, there would be enough money for an apartment. That was important, because they didn't want to live with his family or hers.

He filed employment applications with just about every branch of city government, and because there didn't seem to be a reason not to, took both the Police and Fire Department entrance examinations.

When the postcard came in the mail saying that he had been selected for appointment to the Police Academy, they really hadn't known what to do. He had never seriously considered becoming a cop, and his mother said he was out of his mind, as big as he was, what was going to happen if he became a cop was that some six foot four Schwartzer was going to cut his throat with a razor; or some guy on drugs would shoot him; or some gangster from the Mafia in South Philly would stand him in a bucket full of concrete until it hardened and then drop him into the Delaware River.

Michael graduated from the Philadelphia Police Academy and was assigned to the Seventh District, in the Far Northeast region of Philadelphia. For the first year, he was assigned as the Recorder in a two-man van, transporting prisoners from the District to Central Lockup in the Roundhouse, and carrying people and bodies to various hospitals.

The second year he spent operating an RPC, turning off fire hydrants in the summer and working school crossings. He took the examination for promotion to detective primarily because it was announced two weeks after he had become eligible to take it. At the time, he would have been much happier to take the corporal's exam, because corporals, as a rule of thumb, handled administration inside districts. But there had been no announcement of a corporal's exam, so he took the detective's examination.

If he passed it, he reasoned, there would be the two years of increased pay while he finished law school.

Detective Michael Weisbach was assigned first to the Central Detective District, which covers Center City. There, almost to his surprise, he not only proved adept at his unchosen profession, but was actually happy to go to work, which had not been the case when he'd been working the van or walking his beat in the Seventh District.

His performance of duty attracted the attention of Lieutenant Harry Abraham, whose rabbi, it was said, was then Inspector Matt Lowenstein of Internal Affairs. When Abraham was promoted to captain and assigned to the Major Crimes Unit, he arranged for Weisbach to be transferred with him.

Detective Weisbach was promoted to sergeant three weeks before he passed the bar examination. With it came a transfer to the office of just-promoted Chief Inspector Matt Lowenstein, who had become Chief of the Detective Division.

It just made sense, he told Natalie, to stick around the Department for a little longer. If he was going to go into private practice, they would need a nest egg to furnish an office, pay the rent, and to keep afloat until his practice reached the point where it would support them.

By then, although he was really afraid to tell even Natalie, much less his mother, he was honest enough to admit to himself that the idea of practicing law, handling people's messy divorces, trying to keep some scumbag from going to prison, that sort of thing, did not have the appeal for him that being a cop did.

When he passed the lieutenant's examination, Chief Lowenstein actually took him out and bought him lunch and told him that if he kept up the good work, there was no telling how high he could rise in the Department. Natalie said that Chief Lowenstein was probably just being polite. But when the promotion list came out, and he was assigned to the Intelligence Unit, instead of in uniform in one of the districts, he told Natalie he knew Lowenstein had arranged it, and that he had meant what he said.

There had been a shake-up in the Department, massive retirements in connection with a scandal, and he had made captain much sooner than he had expected to. With that promotion came an assignment in uniform, to the Nineteenth District, as commanding officer. The truth was that he rather liked the reflection he saw in the mirror of Captain Mike Weisbach in a crisp white shirt, and captain's bars glistening on his shoulders, but Natalie said she liked him better in plain clothes.

More vacancies were created two years later in the upper echelons of the Department, as sort of an aftershock to the scandal and the retirements the original upheaval had caused. Three staff inspectors, two of whom told Mike they had never planned to leave the Internal Affairs Division, were encouraged to take the inspector's examination. That of course meant there were now three vacancies for staff inspectors, and Mike had already decided to take the exam even before Chief Lowenstein called him up and said that it would be a good idea for him to do so.

And like the men he had replaced, Mike Weisbach thought he had found his final home in the Department. He had some vague notion that, a couple of years before his retirement rolled around, if there was an inspector's exam, he would take it. There would be a larger retirement check if he went out as an inspector, but he preferred to do what he was doing now to doing what the Department might have him do—he didn't want to wind up in some office in the Roundhouse, for example—if he became an inspector now.

Staff inspectors, who were sometimes called—not pejoratively—"supercops," or "superdetectives," had, Weisbach believed, the most interesting, most satisfying jobs in the Department. They handled complicated investigations, often involving prominent government officials. It was the sort of work Mike Weisbach liked to do, and which he knew he was good at.

He still went to work in the morning looking forward to what the day would bring. It was only rarely that he was handed a job he would rather not do.

This "observation" of a Homicide investigation fell into that category. It was the worst kind of job. The moment he showed up on the scene, whichever Homicide detective had the job—for that matter, the whole Homicide Unit—would immediately and correctly deduce that they were not being trusted to do their job the way it should be done.

And he would feel their justified resentment, not Lowenstein or Mayor Carlucci.

As he followed Harry McElroy, crossing over Old York Road and onto Hunting Park Avenue, then onto Ninth Street, he tried to be philosophical about it. There was no sense moaning over something he couldn't control.

The street in front of Officer Kellog's home was now crowded with police vehicles of all descriptions, and Mike was not surprised to see Mickey O'Hara's antenna-festooned Buick among them.

"I don't have to tell you what to do," Chief Lowenstein said as he got out of the car. "Call me after the Milham interview."

"Yes, sir," Mike said, and walked toward the District cop standing at the door of the row house.

The cop looked uncomfortable. He recognized the unmarked Plymouth as a police vehicle, and was wise enough in the ways of the Department to know that a nearly new unmarked car was almost certain to have been assigned to a senior white-shirt, but this rumpled little man was a stranger to him.

"I'm Staff Inspector Weisbach. I know your orders are to keep everybody out, but Chief Lowenstein wants me to go in."

"Yes, sir."

Captain Henry Quaire and Lieutenant Lou Natali were in the kitchen, trying to stand out of the way of the crew of laboratory technicians.

They don't have any more business here than I do. You don't get to be a Homicide detective unless you know just about everything there is to know about working a crime scene. Homicide detectives don't need to be supervised.

"Good morning, Henry, Lou."

"Hello, Mike," Quaire replied. His face registered his surprise, and a moment later his annoyance, at seeing Weisbach.

"Inspector," Natali said.

Weisbach looked at the body and the pool of blood and quickly turned away. He was beyond the point of becoming nauseous at the sight of a violated body, but it was very unpleasant for him. His brief glance would stay a painfully clear memory for a long time.

"Shot twice, it looks, at close range," Quaire offered.

"I don't suppose you know who did it?" a voice behind Mike asked.

Mike turned to face Mr. Michael J. O'Hara of the *Bulletin*.

"Not yet, Mickey," Quaire said. "The uniform was told to keep people out of here."

"I have friends in high places, Henry," O'Hara said. "Not only do I know Staff Inspector Weisbach here well enough to ask him what the hell he's doing here, but I know the legendary Chief Lowenstein himself. Lowenstein told the uniform to let me in, Henry. He wouldn't have, otherwise."

"He's out there?" Quaire asked.

O'Hara nodded.

"Talking to Captain Talley."

"I want to talk to Talley too," Quaire said, and walked toward the front door.

"So what are you doing here, Mike?" O'Hara asked.

" 'Observing,' " Weisbach said. He saw the displeased reaction on Lieutenant Lou Natali's face.

"Is that between you and me, or for public consumption?" O'Hara asked.

"Spell my name right, please."

" 'Observing'? Or 'supervising'?"

"Observing."

"Exactly what does that mean?"

"Why don't you ask Chief Lowenstein? I'm not sure, myself."

"OK. I get the picture. But—this is for both of you, off the record, if you want—do you have any idea who shot Kellog?"

"No," Natali said quickly.

"I just got here, Mike."

"Is there anything to the story that the Widow Kellog is—how do I phrase this delicately?—*personally involved* with Wally Milham?"

"I don't know how to answer that delicately," Natali said.

"Mike?"

"I heard that gossip for the first time about fifteen minutes ago," Weisbach said. "I don't know if it's true or not."

His eye fell on something in the open cabinet behind Natali's head.

"What's that?" he asked, and pushed by Natali for a closer look.

"It's a tape recorder. With a gadget that turns it on whenever the phone is used," Weisbach said. "Has that been dusted for prints, Lou?"

"Yes, sir."

Weisbach pulled the recorder out of the cabinet and saw that there was no cassette inside.

"Anything on the tape?" he asked.

"There was no tape in it when D'Amata found it," Natali said. "And no tape anywhere around it. There was an empty box for tapes, but no tapes."

"That's strange," Weisbach thought out loud. "The thing is turned on." He held it up to show the red On light. "Did the lab guys turn it on?"

"D'Amata said you can't turn it off, it's wired to the light socket."

"Strange," Weisbach said.

"Yeah," Mickey O'Hara agreed. "Very strange."

A uniformed officer came into the kitchen.

"Lieutenant, the Captain said that Detective Milham is on his way to the Roundhouse."

"Thank you," Natali said.

"I want to sit in on the interview," Weisbach said.

"You're going to question Milham?" Mickey O'Hara asked.

"Yes, sir," Natali said, not quite succeeding in concealing his displeasure.

"Routinely, Mick," Weisbach said. "If there's anything, I'll call you. All right?"

O'Hara thought that over for a second.

"You have an honest face, Mike, and I am a trusting soul. OK. And in the meantime, I will write that at this point the police have no idea who shot Kellog."

"We don't," Weisbach said.

3.

Detective Wallace J. Milham, a dapper thirty-five-year-old, who was five feet eleven inches tall, weighed 160 pounds, and adorned his upper lip with a carefully manicured pencil-line mustache, reached over the waist-high wooden barrier to the Homicide Unit's office and tripped the lock of the door with his fingers.

He turned to the left and walked toward the office of Captain Henry C. Quaire, the Homicide commander. When he had come out of the First Philadelphia Building, Police Radio had been calling him. When he answered the call, the message had been to see Captain Quaire as soon as possible.

Quaire wasn't in his office. But Lieutenant Louis Natali was, and when he saw Milham, waved at him to come in.

Milham regarded Natali, one of five lieutenants assigned to Homicide, as the one closest to Captain Quaire, and in effect, if not officially, his deputy. He liked him.

"I got the word the Captain wanted to see me," Milham said as he pushed open the door.

"Where were you, Wally? We've been looking for you for an hour."

"At the insurance bureau in the First Philadelphia Building," Milham replied, then when he sensed Natali wanted more information, went on: "On the Grover job."

A week before, Mrs. Katherine Grover had hysterically reported to Police Radio that there had been a terrible accident at her home in Mt. Airy. When a radio patrol car of the Fourteenth District had responded, Officer John Sarabello had found Mr. Arthur Grover, her husband, dead against the wall of their garage. Mrs. Grover told Officer Sarabello that her foot had slipped off the brake onto the accelerator, causing their Plymouth station wagon to jump forward.

Neither Officer Sarabello, his sergeant, or the Northwest Detective Division detective who further investigated the incident were completely satisfied with Mrs. Grover's explanation of what had transpired, and the job was referred to the Homicide Unit. Detective Milham got the job, as he was next up on the wheel.

"I know she did it," Detective Milham went on. "And she knows I know she did it. But she is one tough little cookie."

"The insurance turn up anything?"

"Nothing here in the last eighteen months. They're going to check Hartford for me."

While it might be argued that the interest of the insurance industry in a homicide involving someone whose life they have insured may be more financial than moral—if it turned out, for example, that Mrs. Grover had feloniously taken the life of her husband, they would be relieved of paying her off as the beneficiary of his life insurance policy— the industry for whatever reasons cooperates wholeheartedly with police conducting a homicide investigation.

"You weren't listening to the radio?"

Milham shook his head.

"You know a cop named Kellog?"

Milham nodded.

"They found him, this morning, in the kitchen of his house," Natali said. "Somebody shot him, twice, in the back of his head."

"Jesus Christ!"

"He'd probably been dead about six hours."

"Who did it?"

"They had trouble finding his wife. She apparently didn't live with him. So the neighbors say. They just found her a half an hour ago."

"She works for the City," Milham said. "The neighbors should have known that."

"I think that's where they finally got it, from the neighbors," Natali said. "Where were you last night, Wally, from, say, midnight to six in the morning?"

"So that's what this is all about."

"Where were you, Wally?"

"He was an asshole, Lieutenant. I think he was also dirty. But I didn't shoot the son-ofabitch."

"So tell me where you were last night from midnight on."

"Jesus Christ, Lieutenant! I was home."

"Were you alone?"

"No."

"Was she with you?"

Milham looked at Natali for a moment before replying.

"Yeah, she was."

"She wouldn't make a very credible alibi, Wally."

"I told you I didn't do it."

"I didn't think *you* did," Natali said.

"She was with me, I told you that."

"You wouldn't make a very credible witness either, Wally, under the circumstances."

"So we're both suspects? Is that what you're telling me?"

"Of course you are," Natali said. "Think about it, Wally."

"So what are you telling me?"

"You're going to have to give a formal statement. Joe D'Amata was up on the wheel for the job. I'll do the interview. You know Mike Weisbach?"

"Sure."

"He'll sit in on it. Chief Lowenstein has assigned him to 'observe' the investigation. He's upstairs with the Captain and Chief Coughlin. They ought to be here in a minute."

"OK."

"Unless you want to claim the Fifth."

"If I do?"

"You know how it works, Wally."

"I'm not claiming the Fifth. I didn't do it."

"I don't think you did, either."

"What's with Weisbach?"

"I guess they want to make sure we do our job. I don't like that any more than you like being interviewed. You want a little advice?"

"Sure."

"Go through the motions. Don't lose your temper in there. And then go back to work and forget about it."

Milham met Natali's eyes.

"I start midnights tonight," he said absently.

"I don't think that anybody thinks you had anything to do with it. We're just doing this strictly by the book."

"A staff inspector 'observing' is by the book?"

STATEMENT OF: Detective Wallace J. Milham Badge 626

DATE AND TIME: 1105 AM May 19, 1975

PLACE: Homicide Unit, Police Admin. Bldg. Room A.

CONCERNING: Death by Shooting of Police Officer Jerome H. Kellog

IN PRESENCE OF:
Det. Joseph P. D'Amata, Badge 769
Staff Inspector Michael Weisbach

INTERROGATED BY: Lieutenant Louis Natali Badge 233

RECORDED BY: Mrs. Jo-Ellen Garcia-Romez, Clerk/Typist

I AM Lieutenant Natali and this is Inspector Weisbach, Detective D'Amata and Mrs. Garcia-Romez, who will be recording everything we say on the typewriter.

We are questioning you concerning your involvement in the fatal shooting of Police Officer Jerome H. Kellog.

We have a duty to explain to you and to warn you that you have the following legal rights:

A. You have the right to remain silent and do not have to say anything at all.

B. Anything you say can and will be used against you in Court.

75-331D (Rev.7/70)   Page 1

C. You have a right to talk to a lawyer of your own choice before we ask you any questions, and also to have a lawyer here with you while we ask questions.

D. If you cannot afford to hire a lawyer, and you want one, we will see that you have a lawyer provided to you, free of charge, before we ask you any questions.

E. If you are willing to give us a statement, you have a right to stop anytime you wish.

1. Q. Do you understand that you have a right to keep quiet and do not have to say anything at all?
   A. Yes, of course.

2. Q. Do you understand that anything you say can and will be used against you?
   A. Yes.

3. Q. Do you want to remain silent?
   A. No.

4. Q. Do you understand you have a right to talk to a lawyer before we ask you any questions?
   A. Yes, I do.

5. Q. Do you understand that if you cannot afford to hire a lawyer, and you want one, we will not ask you any questions until a lawyer is appointed for you free of charge?
   A. Yes, I do.

6. Q. Do you want to talk to a lawyer at this time, or to have a lawyer with you while we ask you questions?
   A. I don't want a lawyer, thank you.

7. Q. Are you willing to answer questions of your own free will, without force or fear, and without any threats and promises having been made to you?
   A. Yes, I am.

8. Q. State your name, city of residence, and employment?
   A. Wallace J. Milham, Philadelphia. I am a detective.

9. Q. State your badge number and duty assignment?
   A. Badge Number 626. Homicide Unit.

10. Q. Did you know Police Officer Jerome H. Kellog?
    A. Yes.

11. Q. Was he a friend of yours?
    A. No.

12. Q. What was the nature of your relationship to him?
    A. He was married to a friend of mine.

75-331D (Rev.7/70)   Page 2

13. Q. Who is that?
    A. Mrs. Helene Kellog.

14. Q. What is the nature of your relationship to Mrs. Helene Kellog?
    A. We're very good friends. She is estranged from her husband.

(Captain Henry C. Quaire entered the room and became an additional witness to the interrogation at this point.)

15. Q. (Captain Quaire) Wally, you have any problem with me sitting in on this?
    A. No, Sir. I'd rather have you in here than looking through the mirror.

16. Q. Would it be fair to categorize your relationship with Mrs. Kellog as romantic in nature?
    A. Yes.

17. Q. You seemed to hesitate. Why was that?
    A. I was deciding whether or not to answer it.

18. Q. Was Officer Kellog aware of your relationship with his wife?
    A. I suppose so. I never had a fight with him about it or anything. But I think, sure, he knew. She moved out on him.

19. Q. How long have you had this relationship with Mrs. Kellog?
    A. About a year. A little less.

20. Q. You are aware that Officer Kellog was found shot to death in his home this morning?
    A. I am.

21. Q. How did you first learn of his death?
    A. Lieutenant Natali informed me of it a few minutes ago.

22. Q. That is Lieutenant Louis Natali of the Homicide Unit?
    A. Yes.

23. Q. Did you shoot Officer Kellog?
    A. No.

24. Q. Do you have any knowledge whatsoever of the shooting of Officer Kellog?
    A. No. None whatsoever.

25. Q. How would you categorize the relationship of Officer Kellog and his wife?
    A. They were estranged.

26. Q. Do you know where Mrs. Kellog went to live when she left the home of her husband?
    A. With me.

27. Q. Do you have a department-issued firearm, and if so, what kind?
    A. Yes, a .38 Special Caliber Colt snub nose.

28. Q. Where is this firearm now?
   A. In the gun locker.

29. Q. Would you be willing to turn this firearm over to me now for ballistics and other testing in connection with this investigation?
   A. Captain, I go on at midnight. when would I get it back?

(Captain Quaire) I've got a Cobra in my desk. You can use that.

30. Q. Do you own, or have access to, any other firearms?
   A. Yes, I have several guns at my house.

31. Q. You have stated that Mrs. Kellog resides in your home. That being the case, would Mrs. Kellog have access to the firearms you have stated you have in your home?
   A. Yes.

32. Q. Precisely what firearms do you have in your home?
   A. I've got a .45. An Army Model 1911A1 automatic. And an S & W Chief's Special. And a Savage .32 automatic. And there's a .22, a rifle. A Winchester Model 12 shotgun, 12 gauge. And a Remington Model 70 .30–06 deer rifle.

33. Q. And Mrs. Kellog has had access to these firearms?
   A. Yes.

34. Q. Do you believe Mrs. Kellog had anything whatsoever to do with the shooting of her husband?
   A. I do not.

35. Q. Would you be willing to turn over any or all of the firearms in your home to me for ballistic and other testing in connection with this investigation?
   A. Yes.

36. Q. Would you be willing to do so immediately after this interview is completed? Go there with myself or another detective and turn them over?
   A. Yes.

37. Q. Where were you between the hours of six pm last evening and ten o'clock this morning?
   A. I don't remember where I was at six, but from seven to about eight-thirty, I was interviewing people in connection with the Grover job.

38. Q. You were on duty, conducting an official investigation?
   A. Right.

39. Q. And then what happened? When you went off duty at half past eight?
   A. I went home, had some dinner, watched TV, and went to bed.

40. Q. Were you alone?

A. No. Helene, Mrs. Kellog, was with me. She was home when I got there.

41. Q. Mrs. Kellog was with you all the time?

A. Yes. From the time I got home, a little before nine, until we went to work this morning.

42. Q. You were not out of each other's company from say nine pm until say 8 am this morning?

A. Correct.

43. Q. Did you see anyone else during that period, 9 pm last night until 8 am today?

A. No.

44. Q. Is there anything at all that you could tell me that might shed light on the shooting death of Officer Kellog?

A. No.

45. Q. You have no opinion at all?

A. He was working Narcotics. If you find who did this, I'd bet it'll have something to do with that.

46. Q. Can you expand on that?

A. I don't know anything, if that's what you mean. But I've heard the same talk you have.

47. Q. Captain Quaire?

A. (Captain Quaire) I can't think of anything. Anybody else?
(There was no reply.)

48. Q. Thank you, Detective Milham.

A. Captain, I'm going to probably need some vacation time off.

A. (Captain Quaire) Sure, Wally. Just check in.

A. (Det. Milham) I don't like sitting in here like this.

A. (Capt. Quaire) None of us like it, Wally.

75-331D (Rev.7/70)   Page 5

"Thanks, Henry," Staff Inspector Mike Weisbach said, taking a cup of coffee from Captain Henry Quaire in Quaire's office.

Quaire made a "It's nothing, you're welcome" shrug, and then met Weisbach's eyes. "Is there anything else we can do for you, Inspector?"

"Tell me how you call this, Henry," Weisbach said. "Out of school."

"I don't think Wally Milham's involved."

"And the Widow Kellog?"

Quaire shrugged. "I don't know her."

"Would it be all right with you if I went with D'Amata when he interviews her?"

"What if I said no, Mike?" Quaire asked, smiling.

"Then I would go anyway, and you could go back to calling me 'Inspector,' " Weisbach said, smiling back. "Can I presume that you have finally figured out that I don't want to be here any more than you want me to?"

"Sometimes I'm a little slow. It made me mad. My guys would throw the Pope in Central Lockup if they thought he was a doer, and Lowenstein knows it, and he still sends you in here to look over our shoulder."

"That came from the Mayor."

"The Mayor knows that my people are straight arrows."

"I think he's trying to make sure the *Ledger* has no grounds to use the word 'cover-up.' "

"That means he thinks it's possible that we would."

"I don't think so, Henry. I think he's just covering his behind."

Quaire shrugged.

"I know you didn't ask for the job," he said.

Weisbach guessed the Widow Kellog was twenty-eight, twenty-nine, something like that, which would make her three years younger than the late Officer Kellog. She was a slender, not-unattractive woman with very pale skin—her lipstick was a red slash across her face, and her rouge did little to simulate the healthy blush of nature.

She was wearing a black suit with a white blouse, silk stockings, high heels, a hat with a veil, and sunglasses. No gloves, which gave Weisbach the opportunity to notice that she was wearing both a wedding and an engagement ring. They had obviously gotten here, to her apartment, just in time. She was on her way out.

"Mrs. Kellog," Joe D'Amata said, showing her his badge, "I'm Detective D'Amata and this is Inspector Weisbach."

She looked at both of them but didn't reply.

"We're very sorry about what happened to your husband," D'Amata said. "And we hate to intrude at a time like this, but I'm sure you understand that the sooner we find out who did this to Jerry, the better."

"Did you know him?" she asked.

"Not well," D'Amata said. "Let me ask the hard question. Do you have any idea who might have done this to him?"

"No."

"Not even a suspicion?"

"It had something to do with drugs, I'm pretty sure of that."

"When was the last time you saw your husband?"

"A couple of weeks ago."

"You didn't see him at all yesterday?"

"No."

"Just for the record, would you mind telling me where you were last night? Say, from six o'clock last night."

"I was with a friend."

"All that time? I mean, all night?"

She nodded.

"Would you be willing to give me that friend's name?"

"I was with Wally Milham. I think you probably already knew that."

"I hope you understand we have to ask these questions. What, exactly, is your relationship with Detective Milham?"

"Jerry and I were having trouble, serious trouble. Can we leave it at that?"

"Mrs. Kellog," Weisbach said. "When we were in your house, where we found Officer Kellog, we noticed a tape recorder."

D'Amata doesn't like me putting my two cents in. But the last thing we want to do is make her angry. And she would have been angry if he had kept pressing her. And for what purpose? Milham told us they're sleeping together.

"What about it?" Mrs. Kellog asked.

"I just wondered about it. It turned on whenever the phone was picked up, right?"

"He recorded every phone call," she said. "It was his, not mine."

"You mean, he used it in his work?"

"Yes. You know that he did."

"Do you happen to know where he kept the tapes?"

"There was a box of them in the cabinet. They're gone?"

"We're trying to make sure we have all of them," Weisbach said.

"All the ones I know about, he kept right there with the recorder."

"Did your husband ever talk to you about what he did?" Weisbach asked. "I mean, can you think of anything he ever said that might help us find whoever did this to him?"

"He never brought the job home," she said. "He didn't want to tell me about what he was doing, and I didn't want to know."

"My wife's the same way," Weisbach said.

"And you don't work Narcotics," she said. "Listen, how long is this going to last? I've got to go to the funeral home and pick out a casket."

"I think we're about finished," Weisbach said. "Can we offer you a lift? Is there anything else we can do for you?"

"I've got a car, thank you."

"Thank you for your time, Mrs. Kellog," Weisbach said. "And again, we're very sorry that this happened."

"We had our problems," she said. "But he didn't deserve to have this happen to him."

Detective Anthony C. "Tony" Harris, after thinking about it, decided that discretion dictated that he park the car in the parking garage at South Broad and Locust streets and walk to the Bellvue-Stratford Hotel, even though that meant he would have to get a receipt from the garage to get his money back, and that he would almost certainly lose the damned receipt, or forget to turn it in, and have to pay for parking the car himself.

Things were getting pretty close to the end, and he didn't want to blow the whole damned thing because one of the Vice scumbags—they were, after all, cops—spotted the unmarked Ford on the street, or in the alley behind the Bellvue-Stratford, where he had planned to leave it, and started wondering what it was doing around the hotel at that hour of the night.

Tony Harris was not a very impressive man physically. He was a slight and wiry man of thirty-six, already starting to bald, his face already starting to crease and line. His shirt collar and the cuffs of his sports jacket were frayed, his tie showed evidence of frequent trips to the dry cleaners, his trousers needed to be pressed, and his shoes needed both a shine and new heels.

He enjoyed, however, the reputation among his peers of being one of the best detectives in the Philadelphia Police Department, where for nine of his fifteen years on the job he had been assigned to the Homicide Unit. It had taken him five years on the job to make it to Homicide—an unusually short time—and he would have been perfectly satisfied to spend the rest of his time there. Eighteen months ago, over his angry objections, he had been transferred to the Special Operations Division.

He had mixed emotions about what he was doing now. Bad guys are supposed to be bad guys, not fellow cops, not guys you knew for a fact were—or at least had been—good cops.

On one hand, now that he had been forced to think about it, he was and always had been a straight arrow. And just about all of his friends were straight arrows. He personally had never taken a dime. Even when he was fresh out of the Academy, walking a beat in the Twenty-third District, he had been made uncomfortable when merchants had given him hams and turkeys and whiskey at Christmas.

Taking a ham or a turkey or a bottle of booze at Christmas wasn't really being on the take, but even then, when he was walking a beat, he had drawn the line at taking cash, refusing with a smile the offer of a folded twenty-dollar bill or an envelope with money in it.

There was something wrong, he thought, in a cop taking money for doing his job.

What these sleazeballs were doing was taking money, big-time money, for *not* doing their jobs. Worse, for doing crap behind their badges they knew goddamned well was dirty.

That was one side—they were dirty, and they deserved whatever was going to happen to them.

The other side was, they were cops, brother officers, and doing what he was doing made him uncomfortable.

When Tony had been on the sauce, brother officers had turned him loose a half-dozen times when they would have locked up a civilian for drunken driving, or belting some guy in a bar and making a general asshole of himself.

It wasn't, in other words, like he was Mr. Pure himself.

Washington, Sergeant Jason Washington, his longtime partner in Homicide, and now his supervisor, was Mr. Pure. And so was Inspector Wohl, who was running this job. About the only thing they had ever taken because they were wearing a badge was the professional courtesy they got from a brother officer who stopped them for speeding.

And the kids he was supervising now were pure too. Payne would never take money because he didn't have to, he was rich, and Lewis was pure because he'd got that from his father. Lieutenant Foster H. Lewis, Jr., was so pure and such a straight arrow that they made jokes about it; said that he would turn himself in if he got a goober stuck in his throat and had to spit on the sidewalk.

Tony knew that what he was doing was right, and that it had to be done. He just wished somebody else was doing it.

He entered the Bellvue-Stratford Hotel by the side entrance on Walnut Street, into the cocktail lounge. He stood just inside the door long enough to check for a familiar face at the bar, and then, after walking through it, checked the lobby before walking quickly across to the bank of elevators. He told the operator to take him to twelve.

He tried the key he had to 1204, but it was latched—as it should have been—from inside, and he had to wait until Officer Foster H. Lewis, Jr., who was an enormous black kid, six three, two hundred twenty, two hundred thirty even, came to it and peered through the cracked door and then closed it to take the latch off and let him in.

When he opened the door, Lewis was walking quickly across the room to the window, a set of earphones on his head still connected by a long coiled cord to one of the two reel-to-reel tape recorders set up on the chest of drawers.

"What's going on, Tiny?" Harris asked, and then before Lewis could reply, "Where's Payne?"

Tiny replied by pointing, out the window and up.

Harris crossed the room, noticing as he did a room-service cart with a silver pot of coffee and what looked like the leftovers from a room-service steak dinner.

Payne, of course. It wouldn't occur to him to take a quick trip to McDonald's or some other fast-food joint and bring a couple of hamburgers and some paper cups full of coffee to the room. He's in a hotel room, call room service and order up a couple of steaks, medium rare. Fuck what it costs.

Detective Tony Harris looked out the window and saw Detective Matthew M. Payne.

"Jesus H. Christ!" he exclaimed. "What the fuck does he think he's doing?"

"The lady opened the window," Officer Lewis replied, "which dislodged the suction cup."

"Did she see the wire?" Harris wondered out loud, and was immediately sorry he had.

Dumb question. If she had seen the wire, Payne would not be standing on a twelve-inch ledge thirteen floors up, trying to put the suction cup back on the window.

"I don't think so," Tiny said.

"Did we get anything?"

"If we had a movie camera instead of just a microphone, we would have a really blue movie," Tiny Lewis said.

"Is he crazy or what, to try that?"

"I told him he was. He said he could do it."

"How did he get out there?"

"There have been no lights in Twelve Sixteen all night. Two doors down from Twelve Eighteen. He said he thought he could get in."

"You mean pick the lock?" Harris asked, and again without giving Officer Lewis a chance to reply, went on. "What if someone had seen him in the corridor?"

"For one thing, from what was coming over the wire before the lady knocked the mike off, we didn't think the Lieutenant was quite ready to go home to his wife and kiddies, and for another, Matt's wearing a hotel-maintenance uniform, and says he doesn't think the Lieutenant knows him anyway."

"Yeah, but what if he had?"

"He's got it!" Lewis said.

He took the earphones from his head and held them out to Tony Harris.

Harris took them and put them on.

The sounds of sexual activity made Harris uncomfortable.

"I've been wondering if the fact that I find some of that rather exciting makes me a pervert," Tiny said.

"We're trying to catch him with one of the mobsters, not with his cock in some hooker's mouth."

"Unfortunately, at the moment, all we have is him and the lady. Maybe Martinez and Whatsisname will get lucky when they relieve us," Tiny said, and then added: "He's back inside. I agree with you, that was crazy."

"Your pal is crazy," Harris said.

"I think he prefers to think of it as devotion to duty," Tiny said. "You know, 'Neither heat, nor rain, nor thirteen stories off the ground will deter this courier . . .' "

"Oh, shit," Harris said, chuckling. "I'd never try something like that."

"Neither would I. But I don't want to be Police Commissioner before I'm forty."

Harris looked at him and smiled.

"You think that's what he wants? Really?"

"I don't know. Sometimes I think he's just playing cop . . ."

Harris snorted.

"Other times, I think he takes the job as seriously as my old man. You know, the thin blue line, protecting the citizens from the savages. We know he's not doing it for the money."

There was a knock at the door.

"What did he do? Run back?" Harris asked.

"Hay-zus, more likely," Tiny said, and went to the door.

It was in fact Detective Jesus Martinez, a small—barely above departmental minimums for height and weight—olive-skinned man with a penchant for gold jewelry and sharply tailored suits from Krass Brothers.

"What's up?" he said by way of greeting.

"X-rated audiotapes," Tiny said.

"And your buddy's been playing Supercop."

There was no love lost between Detectives Payne and Martinez, and Tony Harris knew it.

"Where is he?"

"The last we saw him, he was on a ledge outside the love-nest," Tony said.

"Doing what?"

"Putting the mike back. The hooker opened the window and knocked the suction cup off."

Martinez went to the window and looked out.

"No shit? Is it working now?"

"Yeah. The Lieutenant's having a really good time," Tiny said, offering Martinez the headset.

Martinez took the headset and held one of the phones to his ear. He listened for nearly a minute, then handed it back.

"Payne really went out on that ledge to put it back?"

" 'Neither heat nor rain . . .' " Tiny began to recite, stopping when there was another knock at the door.

Martinez opened it.

Detective Matthew M. Payne stood there. He was a tall, lithe twenty-five-year-old with dark, thick hair and intelligent eyes, wearing the gray cotton shirt and trousers work uniform of the hotel-maintenance staff.

"What do you say, Hay-zus?" Payne said. "Strangely enough, I'm delighted to see you."

Martinez didn't respond.

"Is it working?" Payne asked Tiny Lewis. Lewis nodded.

"Tony, now that Detective Martinez is here," Payne said, "and the goddamned microphone is back where it's supposed to be, can I take off?"

Harris did not respond directly. He looked at Tiny Lewis.

"Anything on what you have so far?"

"You mean in addition to the grunts, wheezes, and other sighs of passion? No. No names were mentioned, and the subject of money never came up."

"Washington will want to hear them anyway," Harris said, and turned to Payne. "You take the tapes to Washington, and you can take off. Let Martinez know where you are."

"OK, it's a deal."

"Going out on that ledge was dumb," Harris said.

"The Lieutenant's inamorata knocked the microphone off," Payne replied. "No ledge, no tape."

"The Lieutenant's what?" Tiny asked.

"I believe the word is defined as 'doxy, paramour, lover,' " Payne said.

"In other words, 'hooker'?"

"A hooker, by definition, does it for money," Payne said. "We can't even bust this one for that. No money has changed hands. The last I heard, accepting free samples of available merchandise is not against the law. When you think about it, for all we know, it was true love at first sight between the Lieutenant and the inamorata."

Harris laughed.

"Get out of here, Payne," Harris said. "You want to take off, Tiny, I'll stick around until the other guy—what the hell is his name?—gets here."

"Pederson," Martinez furnished. "Pederson with a *d.*"

"I'll wait. I find this all fascinating."

"You're a dirty young man, Tiny," Payne said. "I'm off."

4.

At just about the same time—9:35 P.M.—Detective Matthew M. Payne left the Bellvue-Stratford Hotel by the rear service entrance and walked quickly, almost trotted, up Walnut Street toward his apartment on Rittenhouse Square, Mr. John Francis "Frankie" Foley walked, almost swaggered, into the Reading Terminal Market four blocks away at Twelfth and Market streets.

Mr. Foley was also twenty-five years of age, but at six feet one inch tall and 189 pounds, was perceptibly larger than Detective Payne. Mr. Foley was wearing a two-toned jacket (reddish plaid body, dark blue sleeves and collar) and a blue sports shirt with the collar open and neatly arranged over the collar of his jacket.

Mr. Foley walked purposefully through the Market, appreciatively sniffing the smells from the various food counters, until he reached the counter of Max's Cheese Steaks. Waiting for him there, sitting on a high, backless stool, facing a draft beer, a plate of french-fried potatoes, and one of Max's almost-famous cheese steak sandwiches, was Mr. Gerald North "Gerry" Atchison, who was forty-two, five feet eight inches tall, and weighed 187 pounds.

Mr. Atchison, who thought of himself as a businessman and restaurateur—he owned and operated the Inferno Lounge in the 1900 block of Market Street—and believed that appearances were important, was wearing a dark blue double-breasted suit, a crisp white shirt, a finely figured silk necktie, and well-polished black wing-tip shoes.

Both gentlemen were armed, Mr. Atchison with a Colt Cobra .38 Special caliber revolver, carried in a belt holster, and Mr. Foley with a .45 ACP caliber Colt Model 1911A1 semiautomatic pistol that he carried in the waistband of his trousers at the small of his back. Mr. Atchison was legally armed, having obtained from the Sheriff of Delaware County, Pennsylvania, where he maintained his home, a license to carry a concealed weapon for the purpose of personal protection.

Mr. Atchison had told the Chief of Police that he often left his place of business late at night carrying large sums of cash and was concerned with the possibility of being robbed. The Chief of Police knew that the 1900 block of Market Street was an unsavory neighborhood and that Mr. Atchison was not only a law-abiding citizen, but a captain in the Pennsylvania Air National Guard, in which he was himself an officer, and granted the license to carry.

It is extremely difficult in Philadelphia for any private citizen to get a license to carry a concealed weapon, but Philadelphia honors concealed-weapons permits issued by other police jurisdictions. Mr. Atchison, therefore, was in violation of no law for having his pistol.

Mr. Foley, on the other hand, did not have a license to carry a concealed weapon. He had applied for one, with the notion that all the cops could say was "no," in which case he would be no worse off than he already was. And for a while, it looked as if he might actually get the detective to give him one. The detective he had talked to when he went to fill out the application forms had a USMC *Semper Fi!* decalcomania affixed to his desk and Frankie had told him he'd been in the Crotch himself, and they talked about Parris Island and Quantico and 29 Palms, and the detective said he wasn't promising anything because permits were goddamned hard to get approved—but maybe something could be worked out. He told Frankie to bring in his DD-214, showing his weapons qualifications, so a copy of that could be attached to the application; that might help.

Frankie explained that while he would be happy to bring in his Form DD-214, which showed that he had qualified as Expert with the .45, there was a small problem. A fag had come on to him in a slop chute at 29 Palms, and he had kicked the shit out of him, and what his Form DD-214 said about the character of his release from service was "Bad Conduct," which was not as bad as "Dishonorable," but wasn't like "Honorable" either.

Frankie could tell from the way the detective's attitude had changed when he told him he'd gotten a "Bad Conduct" discharge from the Crotch that bringing in his DD-214 would be a waste of fucking time, so he never went back.

He was, therefore, by the act of carrying a concealed firearm, in violation of Section 6106 of the Crimes Code of Pennsylvania, and Sections 907 (Possession of Instrument of Crime), and 908 (Possession of Offensive Weapon) of the Uniform Firearms Act, each of which is a misdemeanor of the first degree punishable by imprisonment of not more than five years and/ or a fine of not more than $10,000.

Mr. Foley was not concerned with the possible ramifications of being arrested for carrying a concealed weapon. Primarily, he accepted the folklore of the streets of Philadelphia that on your first bust you got a walk, unless your first bust was for something like raping a nun. The prisons were crowded, and judges commonly gave first offenders a talking-to and a second chance, rather than put them behind bars. Frankie had never been arrested for anything more serious than several traffic violations, once for shoplifting, and once for drunk and disorderly.

And even if that were not the case, he trusted Mr. Atchison, who did carry a gun, about as far as he could throw the sonofabitch—*what kind of a shitheel would hire somebody to kill his own wife?*—and he was not going to be around him anywhere at night without something to protect himself.

More important, the purpose of their meeting was to finalize the details of the verbal contract they had made between themselves, the very planning of which, not to mention the execution, was a far more serious violation of the Crimes Code of Pennsylvania than carrying a gun without a permit.

In exchange for five thousand dollars, half to be paid now at Max's, and the other half when the job was done, Mr. Foley had agreed to "eliminate" Mrs. Alicia Atchison, Mr. Atchison's twenty-five-year-old wife, who Mr. Atchison said had been unfaithful to him, and Mr. Anthony J. Marcuzzi, fifty-two, Mr. Atchison's business partner, who, Mr. Atchison said, had been stealing from him.

Frankie wasn't sure whether Marcuzzi had really been stealing from the Inferno—it was more likely that Atchison just wanted him out of the way. Maybe *he* was stealing from Marcuzzi, and was afraid Marcuzzi was catching on—but he was sure that his wife's fucking around on him wasn't the reason Atchison wanted her taken care of. Atchison had another broad Frankie knew about, another young one, and probably he figured that since he was having Marcuzzi taken care of, he might as well get rid of them both at once. Or maybe he thought it would look more convincing if she got knocked off when Marcuzzi got it. Or maybe there was insurance on her or something.

But whatever his reasons, it wasn't because he was really pissed off that she had let somebody get into her pants. Two weeks after Frankie had met Gerry Atchison, *before* Atchison had talked to him about taking care of his wife and Marcuzzi, he had just about come right out and said that if Frankie wanted to fuck Alicia, that was all right with him.

Frankie had been tempted—Alicia wasn't at all bad-looking, nice boobs and legs—but had decided against it, as it wasn't professional. He didn't want to get involved with somebody he was going to take out.

On his part, Mr. Foley had not been entirely truthful with Mr. Atchison, either. He was not, as he had led Mr. Atchison, and others, to believe, an experienced hit man who accepted contracts from the mob in Philadelphia (and elsewhere, like New York and Las Vegas) that for one reason or another they would rather not handle themselves.

This job, in fact, would be his first.

It was, as he thought of it, putting his foot on the ladder to a successful criminal career. He'd given it a lot of thought when they'd thrown him out of the Crotch. There was a lot of money to be made as a professional criminal. The trouble was, you had to start out doing stupid things like breaking in someplace, or stealing a truck. If you got caught, you spent a long time in jail. And even if you didn't get caught, unless you had the right connections, you didn't get shit—a dime on the dollar, if you were lucky—for what you stole.

You had to get on the inside, and to do that, you needed a reputation. The most prestigious member of the professional criminal community, Frankie had concluded, was the guy who everybody knew took people out. Nobody fucked with a hit man. So clearly the thing to do was become a hit man, and the way to do that was obviously to hit somebody.

The problem there was to find somebody who wanted somebody hit and was willing to give you the job. Frankie was proud of the way he had handled that. He knew a guy, Sonny Boyle, from the neighborhood, since they were kids. Sonny was now running numbers; only on the edges of doing something important, but he knew the important people.

Frankie picked up their friendship again, hanging out in bars with him, and not telling Sonny what he was doing to pay the rent, which was working in the John Wanamaker's warehouse, loading furniture on trucks. He let it out to Sonny that he had been kicked out of the Crotch for killing a guy—actually it had been because they caught him stealing from wall lockers—and when Sonny asked what he was doing told him he was in business, and nothing else.

And then the next time he had seen in the newspapers that the mob had popped some-body—the cops found a body out by the airport with .22 holes in his temples—he went to Sonny Boyle and told him he needed a big favor, and when Sonny asked him what, he told Sonny that if the cops or anybody else asked, they had been together from ten at night until at least three o'clock in the morning, and that they hadn't gone anywhere near the airport during that time.

And when Sonny had asked what he'd been doing, he told Sonny he didn't want to know, and that if he would give him an alibi, he would owe him a big one.

That got the word spreading—Sonny had diarrhea of the mouth, and always had, which is what Frankie had counted on—and then he did exactly the same thing the next time the mob shot somebody, and there was one of them "police report they believe the murder had a connection to organized crime" crime stories by Mickey O'Hara in the *Bulletin;* he went to Sonny and told him he needed an alibi.

Three weeks after that happened, Sonny took him to the Inferno Lounge and said there was somebody there, the guy who owned it, Gerry Atchison, that he wanted him to meet.

He'd known right off, from the way Atchison charmed him and bought him drinks, shit, even as much as told him he could have a shot at fucking his wife, that Sonny had been telling Atchison about his pal the hit man and that Atchison had swallowed it whole.

There were to be other compensations for taking the contract in addition to the agreed-upon five thousand dollars. Frankie would become sort of a mixture of headwaiter and bouncer at the Inferno Lounge. The money wasn't great, not much more than he was get-ting from Wanamaker's, but he told Atchison that he was looking for a job like that, not for the money, but so he could tell the cops, when they asked, that he had an honest job.

That would be nice too. He could quit the fucking Wanamaker's warehouse job and be available, where people could find him. Frankie Foley was sure that when the word spread around, as he knew it would, that he'd done a contract on Atchison's wife and Marcuzzi, his professional services would be in demand.

Mr. Foley slid onto the backless high stool next to Mr. Atchison. Atchison seemed slightly startled to see him.

"You got something that belongs to me, Gerry?" Frankie Foley asked Gerry Atchison, whereupon Mr. Atchison handed Mr. Foley a sealed, white, business-size envelope, which Mr. Foley then put into the lower left of the four pockets on his two-tone jacket.

"We got everything straight, right?" Mr. Atchison inquired, somewhat nervously.

Mr. Foley nodded.

Mr. Atchison did not regard the nod as entirely satisfactory. He looked around to see that the counterman was wholly occupied trying to look down the dress of a peroxide blonde, and then leaned close to Frankie.

"You will come in for a drink just before eleven," he said softly. "I'll show you where you can find the ordnance. Then you will leave. Then, just after midnight, you will walk down Market, and look in the little window in the door, like you're wondering why the Inferno's closed. If all you see is me, then you'll know I sent Marcuzzi downstairs to count the cash, and her down to watch him, and that I left the back door open."

"We been over this twenty times," Mr. Foley said, getting off the stool. "What you should be worried about is whether you can count to twenty-five hundred. Twice."

"Jesus, Frankie!" Mr. Atchison indignantly protested the insinuation that he might try to shortchange someone in a business transaction.

"And you lay off the booze from right now. Not so much as another beer, understand?" Mr. Foley said, and walked away from Max's Cheese Steaks.

Mr. Paulo Cassandro, who was thirty-six years of age, six feet one inches tall, and weighed 185 pounds, and was President of Classic Livery, Inc., had dined at the Ris-torante Alfredo, one of the better restaurants in Center City Philadelphia, with Mr. Vincenzo Savarese, a well-known Philadelphia businessman, who was sixty-four, five feet eight inches tall and weighed 152 pounds.

Mr. Savarese had a number of business interests, including participation in both Ristorante Alfredo and Classic Livery, Inc. His name, however, did not appear anywhere in the corporate documents of either, or for that matter in perhaps ninety percent of his other participations. Rather, almost all of Mr. Savarese's business participations were understandings between men of honor.

Over a very nice veal Marsala, Mr. Cassandro told Mr. Savarese that he had a small problem, one that he thought he should bring to Mr. Savarese for his counsel. Mr. Cassandro said that he had just learned from a business associate, Mrs. Harriet Osadchy, that an agreement that had been made between Mrs. Osadchy and a certain police officer and his associates was no longer considered by the police officer to be adequate.

"As I recall that agreement," Mr. Savarese said, thoughtfully, "it was more than generous."

"Yes, it was," Mr. Cassandro said, and went on: "He said that his expenses have risen, and he needs more money."

Mr. Savarese shook his head, took a sip of Asti Fumante from a very nice crystal glass, and waited for Mr. Cassandro to continue.

"Mrs. Osadchy feels, and I agree with her, that not only is a deal a deal, but if we increase the amount agreed upon, it will only feed the bastard's appetite."

Mr. Cassandro was immediately sorry. Mr. Savarese was a refined gentleman of the old school and was offended by profanity and vulgarity.

"Excuse me," Mr. Cassandro said.

Mr. Savarese waved his hand in acceptance of the apology for the breach of good manners.

"It would be, so to speak, the nose of the camel under the flap of the tent?" Mr. Savarese asked with a chuckle.

Mr. Cassandro smiled at Mr. Savarese to register his appreciation of Mr. Savarese's wit.

"How would you like me to handle this, Mr. S?"

"If at all possible," Mr. Savarese replied, "I don't want to terminate the arrangement. I think of it as an annuity. If it is not disturbed, it will continue to be reasonably profitable for all concerned. I will leave how to deal with this problem to your judgment."

"I'll have a word with him," Mr. Cassandro said. "And reason with him."

"Soon," Mr. Savarese said.

"Tonight, if possible. If not tonight, then tomorrow."

"Good," Mr. Savarese said.

Mr. Cassandro was fully conversant not only with the terms of the arrangement but with its history.

Mrs. Harriet Osadchy, a statuesque thirty-four-year-old blonde of Estonian heritage, had come to Philadelphia from Hazleton, in the Pennsylvania coal region, four years before, in the correct belief that the practice of her profession would be more lucrative in Philadelphia. Both a decrease in the demand for anthracite coal and increasing mechanization of what mines were still in operation had substantially reduced the workforce and consequently the disposable income available in the region.

She had first practiced her profession as a freelance entrepreneur, until, inevitably, her nightly presence in the lounges of the better Center City hotels had come to the attention of the plainclothes vice officers assigned to the Inspector of Central Police Division.

Following her third conviction, which resulted in a thirty-day sentence at the House of Correction for violation of Sections 5902 (Prostitution) and 5503 (Disorderly Conduct) of the Crimes Code of Pennsylvania, she realized that she would either have to go out of business or change her method of doing business. By then, she had come to know both many of her fellow freelance practitioners of the world's oldest profession, and several gentlemen who she correctly believed had a certain influence in certain areas in Philadelphia.

With a high degree of tact, she managed to get to meet Mr. Cassandro, and to outline her plan for the future. If it would not interfere in any way with any similar arrangement in which any of Mr. Cassandro's friends and his associates had an interest, she believed the establishment of a very high-class escort service would fill a genuine need in Philadelphia.

Since she was unaware of how things were done in Philadelphia, and was a woman alone, she would require both advice, in such things as finding suitable legal and medical services, and protection from unsavory characters who might wish to prey upon her. She said she believed that ten percent of gross receipts would be a fair price to pay for such advice and protection.

Mr. Cassandro had told Mrs. Osadchy that he would consider the question, make certain inquiries, and get back to her.

He then sought an audience with Mr. Savarese and reported the proposal to him. After thinking it over for several days Mr. Savarese told Mr. Cassandro that he believed Mrs. Osadchy's proposal had some merit, and that he should encourage her to cautiously proceed with it.

It was agreed between them as men of honor that Mr. Savarese would receive twenty-five percent of the ten percent of gross proceeds Mrs. Osadchy would pay to Mr. Cassandro, in payment for his counsel.

The business prospered from the start. Mrs. Osadchy chose both her workforce and her clientele with great care. She also understood the absolute necessity of maintaining good relations with the administrative personnel of the hotels—not limited to security personnel—where her workforce practiced their profession.

For example, if she anticipated a large volume of business from, say, a convention of attorneys, or vascular surgeons, or a like group of affluent professionals, she would engage a room (or even, for a large convention, a small suite) in the hotel for the duration of the convention. No business was conducted *in* the room. But between professional engagements, her workforce would use it as a base of operations. This both increased efficiency and eliminated what would otherwise have been a parade of unaccompanied attractive young women marching back and forth through the hotel lobby.

And Mrs. Osadchy was of course wise enough to be scrupulously honest when it came to making the weekly payments of ten percent of gross income to Mr. Cassandro.

For his part, Mr. Cassandro introduced Mrs. Osadchy to several attorneys and physicians who could be relied upon to meet the needs of Mrs. Osadchy and her workforce with both efficacy and confidentiality. And, more important, he let the word get out that Mrs. Osadchy was a very good friend of his, and thus entitled to a certain degree of respect. An insult to her would be considered an insult to him.

It was a smooth-running operation, and everybody had been happy with it.

And now this fucking cop was getting greedy, which could fuck everything up, and was moreover a personal embarrassment to Mr. Cassandro, who had not liked having to go to Mr. Savarese with the problem.

I should have known, when he started wanting to help himself to the hookers, Mr. Cassandro thought angrily, *that this sonofabitch was going to cause me trouble.*

He's a real sleazeball, and now it's starting to show. And cause me trouble.

What I have to remember, because I keep forgetting it, is that Lieutenant Seymour Meyer is a cop, a cop on the take, and not a businessman, and consequently can be expected to act like an asshole.

When Mr. Cassandro left Mr. Savarese in the Ristorante Alfredo, instead of getting into the car that was waiting for him outside, he walked to the Benjamin Franklin Hotel on Chestnut Street and entered a pay telephone booth in the lobby.

He telephoned to Mrs. Harriet Osadchy and told her that he was working on their problem, that he had been given permission to deal with it.

"I'm really glad to hear that," Mrs. Osadchy replied. "He's really getting obnoxious."

"Financially speaking, you mean?" Mr. Cassandro asked, laughing. "Or generally speaking?"

"He called up about an hour ago, and asked what the room number was at the Bellvue. So I told him. And then he said the reason he wanted to know was because it was a slow night, and he was a little bored, so why didn't I send Marianne over there, so they could have a little party."

"He's a real shit, Harriet," Mr. Cassandro sympathized.

"It's not just the money that he don't pay the girls and I have to. He's a sicko with the girls. I had a hard time making Marianne go."

"He's a real shit," Mr. Cassandro repeated, and then he had a pleasant thought. "Harriet, why don't you call over there?"

"What?"

"Tell her to keep him there. I want to talk to him. That's as good a place as any."

"I'll call her," Harriet said dubiously. "But I don't want her involved in anything, Paulo."

"Trust me, Harriet," Mr. Cassandro said, and hung up.

Detective Matt Payne turned off the Parkway into the curved drive of a luxury apartment building and stopped with a squeal of tires right in front of the door. The uniformed doorman standing inside looked at him in annoyance.

The car was a silver Porsche 911. It had been Matt's graduation present, three years before, when he had finished his undergraduate studies, cum laude, at the University of Pennsylvania.

Miss Penelope Detweiler, who was his fiancée in everything but formal announcement and ring-on-her-finger, frequently accused him, with some justification, of showering far more attention on it than he did on her.

He was still wearing the gray cotton uniform of the Bellvue-Stratford Hotel Maintenance Staff. By the time he had gone from the hotel to his apartment on Rittenhouse Square, which is five blocks west of the Bellvue-Stratford Hotel, to get the car, he had concluded (a) the smart thing for him to have done was to have prevailed yet again on Tiny Lewis's good nature and asked him to take the damned tapes to Washington, and (b) that since he had failed to do so he was going to be so late that changing his clothing was out of the question. He had gone directly to the basement garage and taken his car.

"I'll just be a minute," he said to the doorman, who, accustomed to Payne's frequent, brief, nocturnal visits, simply grunted and picked up his telephone to inform Ten Oh Six that a visitor was on his way up.

Mrs. Martha Washington, a very tall, lithe, sharply featured woman, who looked, Matt often thought, like one of the women portrayed on the Egyptian bas-reliefs in the museum, opened the door to him. She was wearing a loose, ankle-length silver lamé gown.

"He's not here, Matt," she said, giving him her cheek to kiss. "I just opened a nice bottle of California red, if you'd like to come in and wait. He was supposed to be here by now."

"I'm already late for dinner, thank you," he said. "Would you give him this, please?"

He handed her a large, sealed manila envelope.

"Dinner, dressed like that?" she said, indicating his maintenance department uniform. "It looks like you've been fixing stopped-up sinks. What in the world have you been up to?"

She saw the uncomfortable look on his face, and quickly added: "Sorry, forget I asked."

"I'll take a rain check on the California red," Matt said. "I don't know where we're going for dinner, but I'll be home early if he wants me."

"I'll tell him."

Ten minutes later, Matt pulled the Porsche to a stop at the black painted aluminum pole, hinged at one end, which barred access to a narrow cobblestone street in Society Hill, not far from Independence Hall and the Liberty Bell. A neatly lettered sign reading "Stockton

Place—Private Property—No Thoroughfare" hung on short lengths of chain from the pole. A Wachenhut Private Security officer came out of a Colonial-style redbrick guard shack and walked to the Porsche.

"May I help you, sir?"

"Matthew Payne, to see Mr. Nesbitt."

"One moment, sir, I'll check," the Wachenhut Security officer said, and went back into his shack.

It was said that, before renovation, the area known as Society Hill, not far from the Delaware River, had been going downhill since Benjamin Franklin—whose grave was nearby in the Christ Church Cemetery at Fifth and Arch streets—had walked its narrow streets. Before renovation had begun, it was an unpleasant slum.

Now it was an upscale neighborhood, with again some of the highest real estate values in Philadelphia. The Revolutionary-era buildings had been completely renovated—often the renovations consisted of discarding just about everything but the building's facades—and turned into luxury apartments and town houses.

One of the developers, while doing title research, had been pleasantly surprised to learn that a narrow alley between two blocks of buildings had never been deeded to the City. That provided the legal right for them to bar the public from it, something they correctly suspected would have an appeal to the sort of people they hoped to interest in their property.

They promptly dubbed the alley "Stockton Place," closed one end of it, and put a Colonial-style guard shack at the other.

Having been informed that Mr. Chadwick Thomas Nesbitt IV, who with his wife occupied Number Nine B Stockton Place—an apartment stretching across what had been the second floor of three Revolutionary-era buildings—did in fact expect a Mr. Payne to call, the Wachenhut Security officer pressed a switch on his control console which caused the barrier pole to rise.

Matt drove nearly to the end of Stockton Place, carefully eased the right wheels of the Porsche onto the sidewalk, walked quickly into the lobby of Number Nine, and then quickly up a wide carpeted stairway to the second floor.

The door to Nine B opened as he reached the landing. Standing in it, looking more than a little annoyed, was Miss Penelope Detweiler, who was twenty-four, blond, and just this side of beautiful. She was wearing a simple black dress, adorned with a string of pearls and a golden pin, a representation of a parrot.

"Where the *hell* have you been?" Miss Detweiler asked, and then, seeing how Detective Payne was attired, went on: "Matt, for Christ's sake, we're going to dinner!"

"Hi!" Detective Payne said.

"Don't 'Hi' me, you bastard! We had reservations for nine-thirty, you're not even here at nine-thirty, and when you finally show up, you're dressed like that!"

He tried to kiss her cheek; she evaded him, then turned and walked ahead of him into the living room of the apartment. Wide glass windows offered a view of the Benjamin Franklin Bridge, the Delaware River, and an enormous sign atop a huge brick warehouse on the far—New Jersey—side of the river showing a representation of a can of chicken soup and the words NESFOODS INTERNATIONAL.

"I would hazard to guess, old buddy, that you are on the lady's shitlist," said Mr. Chadwick Thomas Nesbitt IV, who was sprawled on a green leather couch. Sitting somewhat awkwardly beside him was his wife, the former Daphne Elizabeth Browne, who was visibly in the terminal stages of pregnancy.

A thick plate-glass coffee table in front of the couch held a bottle of champagne in a glass cooler.

"What are we celebrating?" Matt asked.

"Look at how he's dressed!" Penny Detweiler snapped.

"Never fear, Chadwick is here, the problem will be solved," Chad Nesbitt said, waving his champagne glass as he rose from the couch. "Will you have a little of this, Matthew?"

"What are we celebrating?" Matt asked again.

"I am no longer peddling soup store by store," Nesbitt said. "I will tell you all about it as you change out of your costume."

Chadwick Thomas Nesbitt IV and Matthew Mark Payne had been best friends since they had met, at age seven, at Episcopal Academy. They had been classmates and fraternity brothers at the University of Pennsylvania, and Matt had been Chad's best man when he married.

Nesbitt grabbed the champagne bottle from its cooler by its neck, snatched up a glass, handed it to Matt, then led him down a corridor to his bedroom. There he gestured toward a walk-in closet and arranged himself against the headboard of his king-sized bed.

"What the hell are you dressed up for?" he asked. "Or as?"

"I was on the job."

"Unstopping toilets?"

"That's not original. I was asked the same question just fifteen minutes ago," Matt said as he selected a shirt and tie from Chad Nesbitt's closet.

"In other words, it's secret police business, right? Not to be shared with the public?"

"Right."

"I wouldn't count on dipping your wick tonight, Matthew. Penny's really pissed."

"I told her I didn't know when I could get here," Matt said.

"Your tardy appearance is a symptom of what she's pissed about, not the root cause."

"So what else is new?"

"How long are you going to go on playing cop?"

"I am not playing cop, goddamn it! And you. This is what I do. I'm good at it. I like it. Don't you start, too."

"I'm afraid I have contributed to the lady's discontent," Nesbitt said. "The champagne is because you are looking at the newest Assistant Vice President of Nesfoods International."

"Really?"

"Yeah. I hate to admit it, but the old man was right. The whole goddamned business does ride on the shoulders of the guys who are out there every day fighting for shelf space. And the only way to really understand that is to go out on the streets and do it yourself."

The business to which Mr. Nesbitt referred was Philadelphia's largest single employer, Nesfoods International. Four generations before, George Detweiler had gone into partnership with Chadwick Thomas Nesbitt to found what was then called The Nesbitt Potted Meats & Preserved Vegetables Company. It was now Nesfoods International, listed just above the middle of the Fortune 500 companies and still tightly held. C.T. Nesbitt III was Chairman of the Executive Committee and H. Richard Detweiler, Penny's father, was President and Chief Executive Officer.

"Newest Assistant Vice President of what?" Matt asked.

"Merchandising."

"Congratulations," Matt said.

"A little more enthusiasm would not be out of order," Chad said. "Vice President, even *Assistant* Vice President, has a certain ring to it."

Matt threw a pair of Nesbitt's trousers and a tweed sports coat on the bed, then started to take his gray uniform trousers off. He had trouble with the right leg, which he finally solved by sitting on the bed, pulling the trousers leg up, and unstrapping an ankle holster.

"Doesn't that thing bother your leg?" Chad asked.

"Only when I'm taking my pants off. I meant it, Chad. Congratulations."

"Penny was already here when I got home," Chad said. "When I made the grand announcement, her response was, 'And Matt is still childishly playing policeman,' or words to that effect."

"If I had gone into the Marine Corps with you, I would just be finishing my first year in law school," Matt replied. "I wonder what she would call that."

"Sensible," Chad said. "Your first foot on the first rung of your ladder to legal and/or corporate success. Anyway, if she is bitchy tonight, you know who to blame."

"I don't want to be a lawyer, and I don't—especially don't—want to work for Nesfoods International."

"*'Especially don't'?* What are you going to do when you marry Penny? It's a family business, for Christ's sake."

"Your family. Her family. Not mine."

"That's bullshit and you know it," Chad said. "She's an only child. I don't know how much stock she owns now, but . . ."

"Let it go, Chad!"

". . . eventually, she'll inherit . . ."

"Goddamn it, quit!"

"Your old man sits on the board," Chad went on. "Mawson, Payne, Stockton, McAdoo and Lester's biggest client is Nesfoods."

"Just for the record, it is not," Matt said. "Now, are you going to quit, or do you want to celebrate your vice presidency all by yourself?"

Nesbitt sensed the threat wasn't idle.

"One final comment," he said. "And then I'll shut up. Please?"

After a moment, as he closed the zipper of Chad's gray flannel slacks, Matt nodded.

"I liked the Marine Corps. I was, I thought, a damned good officer. I really wanted to stay. But I couldn't, Matt. For the same reasons you can't ignore who you are, and who Penny is. I think they call that maturity."

"You're now finished, I hope?"

"Yeah."

"Good. Now we'll go out and celebrate your vice-presidency. I can handle you alone, or Penny, but not the both of you together."

"OK."

"Where are we going?"

"There's a new Italian place down by the river. Northern Italian. I think that means without tomato sauce."

Matt pulled up his trousers leg and strapped his ankle holster in place.

"You really have to carry that with you all the time?" Chad asked.

"I'm a cop," Matt said. "Write that on the palm of your hand."

Mr. John Francis "Frankie" Foley checked his watch as he circled City Hall and headed west on Kennedy Boulevard. It was ten forty-five. He had told Mr. Gerald North "Gerry" Atchison "between quarter of eleven and eleven," so he was right on time.

Mr. Foley considered that a good omen. It was his experience that if things went right from the start, whatever you were doing would usually go right. If little things went wrong, like for example you busted a shoelace or spilled spaghetti sauce on your shirt, or the car wouldn't start, whatever, so that you were a little late, you could almost count on the big things being fucked up, too.

And he felt good about what he was going to do, too, calm, *professional.* He'd spent a good long time thinking the whole thing through, trying to figure out what, or who, could fuck up. His old man used to say, "No chain is stronger than its weakest link," and say what you want to say about that nasty sonofabitch, he was right about that.

And the weak link in this chain, Mr. Foley knew, was Mr. Gerry Atchison. For one thing, Frankie was pretty well convinced that he could trust Atchison about half as far as he could throw the slimy sonofabitch. I mean, what kind of a shitheel would offer somebody you just met a chance to fuck his wife, even if you were planning to get rid of her for business purposes?

The first thing that Frankie thought of was that maybe what Atchison was planning on doing was letting him do the wife and the business partner, and then he would shoot Frankie. That would be the smart thing for him to do. He would have his wife and partner out of the way, and if the shooter was dead, too, with the fucking gun in his hand, Atchison could tell the cops that when he heard the shots in the basement office he went to investigate and shot the dirty sonofabitch who had shot his wife and his best friend and business partner. And with Frankie dead, not only couldn't he—not that he would, of course—tell the cops what had really happened, but Atchison wouldn't have to come up with the twenty-five hundred Frankie was due when he did the wife and the business partner.

Frankie didn't think Atchison would have the balls to do that, but the sonofabitch was certainly smart enough to figure out that he *could* do something like that. So he'd covered those angles, too. For one thing, the first thing he was going to do when he saw Atchison now was make sure that sonofabitch had the other twenty-five hundred ready, and the way he had asked for it, in used bills, nothing bigger than a twenty.

If he didn't have the dough ready, then he would know the fucker was trying to screw him. He really hoped that wouldn't happen, he wanted this whole thing to happen, and if Atchison didn't have the dough ready, he didn't know what he'd do about it, except maybe smack the sonofabitch alongside his head with the .45.

But Atchison could have the dough ready, Frankie reasoned, and still be planning to do him after he had done the wife and the partner. He had figured out the way to deal with the whole thing: first, make sure that he had the dough, and second, when he came back to do the contract, either make sure that Atchison didn't have a gun, or, which is what most likely would happen, make sure that he always had the drop on Atchison.

All he had to be was calm and professional.

Frankie steered his five-year-old Buick convertible into the left lane, turned left off Kennedy Boulevard onto South Nineteenth Street, crossed Market Street, and then made another left turn into the parking lot at South Nineteenth and Ludlow Street. During the day, you had to pay to park there, but not at this time of night. There were only half a dozen cars in the place. He got out of the car, walked back to Market Street, and turned right.

He caught a glimpse of himself reflected in a storefront window. He was pleased with what he saw. There was nothing about the way he was dressed (in a brown sports coat with an open-collared maroon sports shirt and light brown slacks) that made him look any different from anyone else walking up Market Street to have a couple of drinks and maybe try to get laid. No one would remember him because he was dressed flashy or anything like that.

He pushed open the door to the Inferno Lounge and walked in. There were a couple of people at the bar, and in the back of the place he saw Atchison glad-handing a tableful of people.

"Scotch, rocks," Frankie said to the bartender as he slid onto a bar stool.

The bartender served the drink, and when Frankie didn't decorate the mahogany with a bill, said, "Would you mind settling the bill now, sir? I go off at eleven."

"You mean you're closing at eleven?"

"The guy who works eleven 'til closing isn't coming in tonight. The boss, that's him in the back, will fill in for him," the bartender said.

"Hell, you had me worried. The night's just beginning," Frankie said, and took a twenty—his last—from his wallet and laid it on the bar.

So far, so good. Atchison said tonight was the late-night bartender's night off.

Frankie pushed a buck from his stack of change toward the bartender and then picked up his drink. There was a mirror behind the bar, but he couldn't see Atchison in it, and he didn't want to turn around and make it evident that he was looking for him.

Frankie wondered where whatsername, the wife—*Alicia*—was, and the partner.

I wonder if I should have fucked her. She's not bad-looking.

Goddamn it, you know better than that. That would have really been dumb.

"What do you say, Frankie?" Gerry Atchison said, laying a hand on his shoulder. Frankie was a little startled; he hadn't heard or sensed him coming up.

"Gerry, how are you?"

"I got something for you."

"I hoped you would. How's the wife, Gerry?"

Atchison gave him a funny look before replying, "Just fine, thanks. She'll be here in a little while. She went somewhere with Tony."

Tony is the partner, Anthony J. Marcuzzi. What did he do, send her off to fuck the partner?

"Tommy," Gerry Atchison called to the bartender. "Stick around a couple of minutes, will you? I got a little business with Mr. Foley here."

There was nothing Tommy could do but fake a smile and say sure.

Atchison started walking to the rear of the Inferno. Frankie followed him. They went down a narrow flight of stairs to the basement and then down a corridor to the office.

Atchison closed and bolted the office door behind them, then went to a battered wooden desk, and unlocked the right-side lower drawer. He took from it a small corrugated paper box and laid it on the desk.

He unwrapped dark red mechanic's wiping towels, exposing three guns. One was a Colt .38 Special caliber revolver with a five-inch barrel. The second was what Frankie thought of as a cowboy gun. In this case it was a Spanish copy of a Colt Peacemaker, six-shot, single-action .44 Russian caliber revolver. The third was a Savage Model 1911 .32 ACP caliber semiautomatic.

"There they are," he announced.

"Where's the money?" Frankie asked.

"In the desk. Same drawer."

"Let's see it."

"You don't trust me?" Atchison asked with a smile, to make like it was a joke.

"Let's see the money, Gerry," Frankie said.

He picked up the Colt and opened the cylinder and dumped the cartridges in his hand. Then he closed the cylinder and dry-snapped the revolver. The cylinder revolved the way it was supposed to.

The noise of the dry snapping upset Gerry Atchison.

"What are you doing?"

"Making sure these things work."

"You didn't have to do that. I checked them out."

Yeah, but you don't know diddly-shit about guns. You just think you do.

The Colt was to be the primary weapon. He would do both the wife and the partner with the Colt. The cowboy gun was the backup, in case something went wrong. Better safe than sorry, like they say. The Savage was to wound Atchison in the leg. Frankie would have rather shot him with the .38 Special Colt, but Atchison insisted on the smaller .32 ACP Savage.

Atchison held out an envelope to Frankie.

"You get this on delivery, you understand?"

Frankie took the envelope and thumbed through the thick stack of bills.

"You leave it in the desk," Frankie ordered, handing the envelope back to Atchison. "If it's there when I come back, I do it."

Frankie next checked the functioning of the .44 Russian cowboy six-shooter, and finally the .32 Savage automatic.

He put them back in the corrugated paper box and folded the mechanic's rags back over them.

"I sort of wish you'd take those with you," Atchison said. "What if somebody comes down here and maybe finds them?"

"You see that don't happen. I'm not going to wander around Center City with three guns."

Atchison looked like he was going to say something, but changed his mind.

"I'll show you the door," he said.

Frankie followed him out of the office and farther down the corridor to the rear of the building. There a shallow flight of stairs rose toward a steel double door.

With Frankie watching carefully, Atchison removed a chain-and-padlock from the steel doors, then opened the left double door far enough to insert the padlock so that there would be room for Frankie's fingers when he opened the door from the outside.

"Be careful when you do that. You let the door slip, you'll never get it open."

"I'm always careful, Gerry," Frankie said.

Atchison took the corrugated paper box with the pistols from Frankie and put it on the top stair, just below the steel door.

He turned and sighed audibly. Then he smiled and put out his hand to Frankie.

"Jesus!" Frankie said with contempt. "Make sure that envelope is where it's supposed to be," he said, then turned and walked purposefully down the narrow corridor toward the stairs.

5.

Detective Wallace H. Milham reported for duty in the Homicide Unit in the Roundhouse at midnight as his duty schedule called for. The alternative, he knew, was sitting around his apartment alone with a bottle of bourbon. Or sitting around in a bar somewhere, alone, which he thought would be an even dumber thing to do than getting plastered all by himself in his apartment.

It had been a really lousy day.

Wally told himself that he should have expected something lousy to happen—not something as lousy as this, but something—the other shoe to drop, so to speak, because things lately had been going so damned well. For eighteen months, things had really been lousy.

In what he was perfectly willing to admit was about the dumbest thing Wally had ever done in his life, he had gotten involved with his wife Adelaide's sister, Monica. Monica lived in Jersey, in Ocean City. Her husband was a short fat guy who sold insurance. Adelaide's and Monica's mother and dad owned a cottage close to the beach in Wildwood.

Everybody in the family—Adelaide's family; Wally was an only child—got to use the cottage. Adelaide had one other sister besides Monica, and two brothers. The Old Man—Adelaide's father—wouldn't take any money when anybody used it, which sort of bothered Wally, who liked to pay his own way and not be indebted to anybody. So when the place needed a paint job, he volunteered to do that. He told the Old Man that the way his schedule worked, there were often two or three days he had off in the middle of the week, when Adelaide was working in the library, and he would rather do something useful with that time than sit around the house watching the TV.

Which was true. When he offered to paint the cottage in Wildwood, that was all he had in mind, pay his way. Monica didn't come into his thinking at all.

But Charles, Monica's husband, got in the act. He said that if Wally was going to drive all the way over from Philly to do the labor, the least he could do was provide the materials. So he did. And Monica drove the paint down in their station wagon because Charles of course was at work.

And he didn't think about that either. The first two days he spent painting the cottage, he used up most of the paint that Charles had Monica drive down to give him, so he told Adelaide to call Monica to ask Charles if he wanted to provide more paint, or have Wally get it, in which case he would have to know where he'd gotten the first three gallons, so they could mix up some more that would match.

Adelaide told him that Charles said that the paint would be there waiting for him the next time he went to Wildwood. It wasn't, so he started painting with what was left, and just before noon Monica showed up with the paint, and said that Charles had told her to take him out to lunch, and not to take no for an answer, it was the least they could do for him.

So they went out for lunch, and he was surprised when Monica tossed down three martinis, one after the other. He had never seen her take more than one drink at a time. And she started talking—women with a couple of drinks in them tend to do that—and she started out by saying that she was a little jealous of Adelaide because Adelaide was married to a man who had an exciting career, catching murderers, and Charles was a bore.

In more ways than one, she said, if Wally took her meaning.

And he told her that being a Homicide detective wasn't as exciting as people who didn't know thought it was, that most of it was pretty ordinary stuff, just asking questions until somebody came up with the answer.

She said, yeah, but he got to meet interesting, exciting people, and she asked him if he ever met any exciting women, and he told her no, but she said he was just saying that, and she'd bet that if he told her the truth, he got to meet a lot of exciting women.

That's when he realized what was going on, and if he had had half the sense he was born with, he would have stopped it right there, but he'd had three martinis too.

In her car on the way back to the Old Man's cottage, she kept letting her hand fall on his leg, and ten minutes after they got back to the cottage, they were having at it in the Old Man's and Grandma's bed.

Afterward, Monica told him she didn't know what had come over her, it must have been the martinis, and they could never let anything like that happen again. But the way she stuck her tongue down his throat when she kissed him good-bye, he knew that was what she was saying, not what she meant.

So far as he was concerned, that was it, the one time. It would be a long time before he ever let himself be alone with her again.

Two weeks after that, at eleven o'clock in the morning, he had just gotten out of bed and made himself a cup of coffee when the doorbell at the house rang and there was Monica.

She was in Philly to do some shopping, she said, and she thought she would take a chance and see if maybe Adelaide hadn't gone to work at the library and they could go together.

He told her no, Adelaide had gone to work, and wouldn't be home until five, five-thirty.

And she asked what about the kids, and he told her they were both at school and wouldn't be home until quarter to four.

And then she said that she just couldn't get him out of her mind, and since he hadn't called her or anything, she had come to see him.

Three weeks after that, Adelaide walked in on them and caught them in her bed, right in the middle of doing it.

The way Adelaide saw it, it was all his fault, and maybe, he thought, in a way it was. He had known what was going on.

Adelaide said she hoped that he would at least have the decency to get a civilized divorce, so that nobody in her family knew that it was Monica he was taking advantage of, and ruin her life too. She said that she would hate to tell the children what an unmitigated immoral sonofabitch their father was, and hoped he wouldn't make her.

There was a clause in the divorce that said he had to pay a certain amount to her, in addition to child support, so that she could learn a trade or a profession. She decided she would go back to college and get a degree in library science, and get a better job than the one she had, which was "clerical assistant," which meant that he would be giving her money for two years, maybe three. Or more. She was going only part time.

And then she met Greg. Greg was a great big good-looking guy who sold trucks for a living, and who made a hell of a lot more money doing that than Wally had ever made, even in Homicide.

Adelaide started to spend nights in Greg's apartment whenever Wally had the kids over the weekend or she could get the Old Man and Grandma to take them. Wally knew that, because he sometimes drove by Greg's apartment at midnight and saw her car, and then drove past again at three in the morning, and again at seven, and it was still there.

But she wasn't going to marry Greg, because the minute she married him, that was the end of her training for a new career at his expense. She as much as told him that, and let him know if he made any trouble for her about how she conducted her private affairs, she would have to tell the kids what a sonofabitch he was, seducing her own sister, caring only for himself and not for his family.

And then Adelaide had really surprised him two and a half months before by calling him up—she sounded like she was half in the bag on the phone—and telling him she had just come back from Elkton, Maryland, where she and Greg had tied the knot.

Which meant that he could stop paying for her career education and move out of the one-room apartment, which was all he could afford on what was left of his pay, into something at least decent.

And then he went to Lieutenant Sackerman's funeral, and met Helene. Jack Sackerman was an old-time Homicide detective, a good one. When Wally had first gone to Homicide, he had taken him under his wing and showed him how to operate. Wally thought that if it hadn't been for Jack Sackerman, he probably never would have gotten to stay in Homicide.

When Jack had started thinking about retirement, he knew he had to leave Homicide. Homicide detectives make good money, damned good money, because of all the overtime, but when they retire, they get the same retirement pay as any other detective, and that's not much. So Jack had taken the examination for sergeant, and passed that, and they assigned him to Narcotics. Then he took the lieutenant's examination, and passed that, and they kept him in Narcotics. He was getting ready for the captain's examination when they discovered the cancer. And that, of course, was that.

Everybody from Narcotics was at Jack's viewing, of course, and that's when he met Helene and her husband. Captain Talley, the Narcotics Commander, introduced them. Her husband, Officer Kellog, had on a suit and a tie, but he still looked like a bum. Anybody who worked Plainclothes Narcotics had to dress like he was part of the drug business, so it was understandable—when Lieutenant Pekach, who was now a Captain in Special Operations, was running Undercover Narcotics, he actually had a pigtail—but he still looked like a bum.

He met Helene first at the viewing, and then the next day at the reception at Sackerman's house after the funeral, and a third time at Emmett's Place bar, where a bunch of the mourners went after they left Sackerman's house. Jack had had a lot of friends.

Her husband wasn't with her at Emmett's Place, but they seemed to wind up together and started talking. Wally was attracted to her, but didn't come on to her. Only a stupid bird dirties his own nest, and she was married to a cop.

After that, they kept bumping into each other. She worked for the City in the Municipal Services Building in Center City, and he was always around the City Hall courtrooms or the DA's Office, in the same area, so that was understandable. Wally ran into Helene one time on his way to the Reading Terminal Market for lunch and asked her if she wanted a cheese steak or something, and she said yes and went with him.

After that, they started meeting once or twice a week for lunch, or sometimes dinner, and she let him understand that things weren't perfect with her husband, but she never told him—and he didn't ask—what specifically was wrong between them. He told her about Adelaide, what had happened. And absolutely nothing happened between them, he didn't so much as try to hold her hand, until the night she called him, three days after he'd moved into the new apartment, and sounded as if she was crying.

Wally asked her what the matter was, and she said she was calling from the Roosevelt Motor Inn, on Roosevelt Boulevard, that what had happened was that she had finally left the sonofabitch—he remembered that she had used that word, because it was the first time she had ever said anything nasty about him—and needed to talk to somebody.

He said sure, and did she want him to come out there and pick her up and they could go somewhere for a drink, and she said it wouldn't look right, in case somebody saw them, for him to pick her up at the motel. And as far as that went, wouldn't look right if somebody saw them having a drink someplace the very night she moved out on her husband.

So Wally had asked her, did she maybe want to come to his apartment, and Helene said she didn't know, what did he think, and she didn't want to impose or anything.

So he told her to get in a taxi and come down. And she did. And before she got there, he went to a Chinese restaurant and got some takeout to go with the bottle of wine he knew he had somewhere at home. He didn't want to offer her a drink of whiskey, to keep her from getting the wrong idea. All he wanted to be was a friend, offering her something to eat and wine, and a sympathetic ear.

She didn't even take the wine when he offered it to her, but she wolfed down the Chinese, and he was glad he thought of that, and while he watched her eat, he decided that if she wanted to talk about her husband, fine, and if she didn't, fine, too.

When she finished, she smiled at him and asked him if he thought she would be terrible if she asked for a drink. She really needed a drink.

So he made her one and handed it to her, and she started to take a sip and then started crying and he put his arm around her, and one thing led to another, and that was the way they started.

Whatever was wrong between her and her husband wasn't that she was frigid, or anything like that.

And she told him, afterward, that the truth of the matter was that she had been thinking about him and her like that from the very first time she saw him, at Lieutenant Sackerman's viewing; that he was really an attractive man.

So at five o'clock in the morning, he took her back to the Roosevelt Motor Inn on Roosevelt Boulevard, and met her in City Hall at noon, after she'd talked to a lawyer, and they went to his apartment so they could talk without worrying about people at the next table in a restaurant listening in. They didn't do much talking about what the lawyer said, except that it was going to be harder getting a divorce than she thought it would be.

She took a tiny apartment so that her family wouldn't ask questions, but from the first they lived together, and they got along just fine, and without coming right out and talking about it, they understood that as soon as she got him to agree to the divorce, they would get married. With what they made between them, they could live pretty well. They talked about getting a larger apartment, maybe even a house, so there would be room for his kids when he had them on weekends or whenever.

They never talked much about what bad had happened between her and Kellog, but he got the feeling it had something to do with Kellog being dirty on the job. She knew something, and Wally knew if he pressed her he could get it out of her.

But then what? For one thing, she might not know what she was talking about, and for another, dirty cops are Internal Affairs' business, not his. If he learned something he felt he had to tell somebody about, it would come out that he and Helene were living together, and it would look as if he was trying to frame the sonofabitch.

And then the sonofabitch gets himself shot. And guess who they think had something to with it?

Kellog was in Narcotics. If they ever found out who the doer, or doers, were, it was ten-to-one it would have something to do with Narcotics. But they might not ever find the doers, and until they did, Helene was going to be a suspect, and so was he.

The interview in Homicide was the most humiliating thing that Wally could remember ever having to go through. Except maybe being driven to his apartment by Ken Summers to pick up his guns, and having Ken look around "professionally" to see what he could see that might connect him with the Kellog shooting.

And when he finally got to see Helene, he could see that she had been crying, and she told him that D'Amata and Staff Inspector Weisbach had been to see her, and that she thought it would be better for everybody concerned if they didn't see each other until things settled down, at least until after the funeral, and that she was going to the apartment right then to pick up her things and take them to her apartment. And that she thought it would be better if he didn't try to see her, or even telephone, until she thought it would be all right, and when she thought it would be she would telephone him.

She didn't even kiss him before she walked away.

Wally did the only thing he could think of doing. He worked on the Grover job. And nothing. Not from interviewing neighbors or friends, or what he learned from New Haven. She did not have an insurance policy on her husband, except for the ones she told him about. And neither did anyone else.

But she did him. Wally was sure about that. Somehow, he was going to get her.

He went to the apartment about six and had a beer and made himself a hamburger, and it was pretty goddamned lonely. Then he tried to sleep, setting the alarm for eleven. With nothing else to do, he might as well go to work.

He woke up at nine-thirty, alone in their bed, and couldn't get back to sleep, and got up and drank a beer, and then he thought about going to a bar and having a couple of drinks, and fuck going to work. Captain Quaire had told him to take off what time he needed.

But he knew that would be dumb, so he just had the one beer, and took a shower and a shave and left the apartment at half past eleven for the Roundhouse.

A new Plymouth sedan slowed to a near stop in front of the Delaware Valley Cancer Society Building on Rittenhouse Square, and then slowly and carefully put the right-side wheels on the curb, finally stopping equidistant between two signs announcing that this was a No Parking At Any Time Tow Away Zone.

The door opened and a very large, black, impeccably dressed gentleman got out. He was Sergeant Jason Washington of the Special Operations Division of the Philadelphia Police Department, known—behind his back, of course—to his peers as "the Black Buddha."

He believed himself to be the best investigator in the Philadelphia Police Department. This opinion was shared by a number of others, including the Honorable Jerome H. "Jerry" Carlucci, Mayor of the City of Brotherly Love, by Inspector Peter Wohl, Commanding Officer of the Special Operations Division, for whom Washington worked, and by Detective Matthew M. Payne, who worked for Sergeant Washington.

Sergeant Washington was wearing a light gray pin-striped suit. His Countess Mara necktie was fixed precisely in place at the collar of a custom-made crisply starched white Egyptian cotton shirt, and gold cuff links bearing his initials gleamed at the shirt's cuffs.

For most of their married life, Jason Washington and his wife had lived frugally, although their combined income had been above average. He had spent most of his career in Homicide, where overtime routinely meant a paycheck at least as large as an inspector's, and Martha had a very decent salary as an artist for a Center City advertising agency.

They had put money away faithfully for the education of their only child, a daughter, and they had invested what they could carefully, and, it turned out, wisely.

In the last three or four years, they had become affluent. Their daughter had married (much too young, they agreed) an electrical engineer, at whom (they also agreed) RCA in Cherry Hill seemed to throw money. Her marriage had, of course, relieved them of the expense of her college education, and at about the same time, what had begun as Martha's dabbling in the art market had suddenly blossomed into the amazingly profitable Washington Galleries on Chestnut Street.

They could afford to live well, and did.

Sergeant Washington walked to the plate-glass door of the Cancer Society Building and waited until it was opened to him by the rent-a-cop on duty.

"Is Supercop at home?" Sergeant Washington greeted him. The rent-a-cop was a retired police officer whom Washington had known for years.

"Came in about ten minutes ago. What's he done now?"

"Since he works for me, I'm embarrassed to tell you," Washington said, and then had a sudden thought: "Did he come home alone?"

"For once," the rent-a-cop said.

"Good. I would not like to redden the ears of his girlfriend with what I have to say to him," Washington said, smiling, as he got into the elevator.

He rode to the third floor, then pushed a doorbell beside a closed door.

"Yes?" A voice came over an intercom.

"Would you please let me in, Matthew?"

"Hey, Jason, sure."

The door's solenoid buzzed and Washington opened the door. He climbed a steep, narrow flight of stairs. Matt Payne waited for him, smiling.

"Don't smile," Washington said. "I just had a call from Tony Harris vis-à-vis your human-fly stunt, you goddamned fool! What the hell is the matter with you?"

"The Lieutenant's lady friend opened the window and knocked the mike suction cup loose. We weren't getting anything at all."

"These people are not plotting the overthrow of Christian society as we know it, you damned fool! We have some dirty cops, that's all. Not one of them, not this whole investigation, is worth risking your life over."

"Yes, sir."

"Good God, Matt! What were you thinking?"

Matt didn't reply.

"I would hate to think that you were trying to prove your all-around manhood," Washington said.

It was a reference to one of the reasons offered for a nice young man from the Main Line electing to follow a police career instead of a legal one. He had failed, at the last minute before entering upon active duty, the Marine Corps' Pre-Commissioning Physical Exam. He had then, the theory went, joined the Police Department as a means to prove his masculinity.

"I was thinking I could put the mike back without getting hurt," Matt said coldly. "And I did."

Washington saw in his eyes that he had gotten through to him. He fixed him with an icy glance for another thirty seconds, which seemed much longer.

Then he smiled, just a little.

"It would seem to me, considering the sacrifice it has meant for me to come here at this late hour to offer you my wise counsel, that the least you could do would be to offer me a small libation. Perhaps some of the Famous Grouse scotch?"

"Sure, sorry," Matt said, smiling. He went into his kitchen. As he opened first one, and then another over-the-sink cabinet, he called, "What are you doing out this late?"

"Our beloved Mayor has been gracious enough to find time to offer me *his* wise counsel."

"Really?"

"Specifically, he is of the opinion that we should go to Officers Crater and Palmerston and offer them immunity from prosecution in exchange for their testimony against Captain Cazerra and Lieutenant Meyer."

"Jason," Matt said, "I can't find a bottle of any kind of scotch. Not even Irish."

"I am not surprised," Washington said. "It's been one of those days. Get your coat. We will pub crawl for a brief period."

"There's some rum and gin. And vermouth. I could make you a martini."

"Get your coat, Matthew," Washington said. "I accept your kind offer of a drink at the Rittenhouse Club bar."

"Oh, thank you, kind sir," Matt said, mockingly, and started shrugging into Chad Nesbitt's tweed jacket. "I think the Mayor's idea stinks."

"Why?"

"Because any lawyer six weeks out of law school could tear them up on the stand, and we know Cazerra and Meyer's lawyers will be good."

"Armando C. Giacomo, Esquire," Washington agreed, citing the name of Philadelphia's most competent criminal lawyer. "Or someone of his ilk. Perhaps even the legendary Colonel J. Dunlop Mawson, Esquire."

Matt laughed. "No way. My father would go ballistic. I'm ready."

"I made that point to His Honor," Washington said as he pushed himself out of one of Matt's small armchairs.

"And?"

"And as usual got nowhere. Or almost nowhere. We have two weeks to get something on Cazerra and Meyer that will stand up in court. He wants those two in jail."

"Or what?"

"We work Crater and Palmerston over, figuratively speaking of course, with a rubber hose."

"What does Wohl say?" Matt asked as he waved Washington ahead of him down the stairs.

"I haven't told him yet. I figured I would ruin tomorrow for him by doing that first thing in the morning."

The Rittenhouse Club was closed when they got there.

"What do we do now?" Matt asked.

"Why don't we take a stroll down Market Street?" Washington replied. "It will both give us a chance to see how the other half lives, and trigger memories of those happy days when Officer Washington was walking his first beat."

"You walked a beat on Market Street?" Matt asked. It was difficult for him to imagine Washington in a police officer's uniform, patrolling Market Street.

Officer Friendly Black Buddha, he thought, *impeccably tailored and shined, smiling somewhat menacingly as he slapped his palm with his nightstick.*

"Indeed I did. Under the able leadership of Lieutenant Dennis V. Coughlin. And on *our* watch," Washington announced sonorously, "the thieves and mountebanks plied their trade in someone else's district."

"Police Emergency," David Meach said into his headset.

"This is the Inferno Lounge," his caller announced. "1908 Market. There's been a shooting, and somebody may be dead."

"Your name, sir, please?"

"Shit!" the caller responded and hung up.

David Meach had been on the job six years, long enough to be able to unconsciously make judgments regarding the validity of a call, based on not only what was said, but how it was said. Whether, for example, the caller sounded mature (as opposed to an excited kid wanting to give the cops a little exercise) and whether or not there was excitement or tension or a certain numbness in his voice. This call sounded legitimate; he didn't think he'd be sending police cars racing through downtown Philadelphia for no purpose.

He checked to see what was available.

RPC Nine Ten seemed closest to the scene. Meach pressed a key to send two short attention beeps across the airways, then activated his microphone:

"All cars stand by. 1908 Market Street, the Inferno Lounge, report of a shooting and a hospital case. Nine Ten, you have the assignment."

The response was immediate.

"Nine Ten, got it," Officer Edward Schirmer called into the microphone of Radio Patrol Car Number Ten of the Ninth District, as Officer Lewis Roberts, who was driving the car down Walnut Street, reached down to the dashboard and activated the siren and flashing lights.

"Nine Seven in on that," another voice reported, that of Officer Frederick E. Rogers, in RPC Nine Seven.

"Highway Thirteen, in on the 1908 Market," responded Officer David Fowler.

"Nine Oh One, got it," responded Officer Adolphus Hart, who was riding in one of the two vans assigned to the Ninth District.

Nine Oh One had five minutes before left the Police Administration Building at Eighth and Race streets, after having transferred two prisoners from the holding cells at the Ninth District to Central Lockup.

Officer Thomas Daniels, who was driving Nine Oh One, had for no good reason at all elected to drive up Market Street and was by happenstance able to be the first police vehicle responding to the "Shooting and Hospital Case" call to reach the scene.

There was nothing at all unusual about the location when they pulled to the curb. The Inferno Lounge's neon-flames sign was not illuminated, and the establishment seemed to be closed for the night.

He stopped just long enough to permit Officer Hart to jump out of the van and walk quickly to the door of the Inferno, and to see if Hart could open the door. He couldn't. Then he turned left on Ludlow Street, so that he could block the rear entrance.

Two civilians, a very large black man and a tall young white man, both very well dressed, were walking down Nineteenth Street, toward Market. They could have, Officer Daniels reasoned, just come out of the alley behind the Inferno.

Officer Daniels, sounding his horn, drove the van into the alley, blocking it, and jumped out of the van.

"Hold it right there, please!" he called out.

His order proved to be unnecessary. The two civilians had stopped, turned, and were looking at him with curiosity.

While a Pedestrian Stop was of course necessary, Officer Daniels made the snap judgment that it was unlikely that these two had anything to do with whatever—if anything—had happened at the Inferno. They hadn't run, for one thing, and they didn't look uncomfortable.

Officer Daniels had an unkind thought: This area was an unusual place to take a stroll after midnight, unless, of course, the two were cruising for women. Or men. Maybe they had just found each other.

"Excuse me, sir," Daniels said. "May I please see some identification?"

The younger man laughed. Daniels glowered at him.

"We're police officers," the black man said. "What have you got?"

The younger one exhibited a detective's badge.

"What's going on here, Officer?" the black man asked.

Officer Daniels hesitated just perceptibly before replying: "Shooting and hospital case inside the Inferno."

"Was the front door open?" the black man asked.

"No."

"I'll go block the front," the black man said. "The rear door to this place is halfway down the alley. There's usually a garbage can full of beer bottles, and so on." He turned to the young white man. "You go with him, Matt."

The young man sort of stooped, and when he stood erect again, there was a snub-nose revolver in his hand.

Officer Daniels looked dubiously at the black man.

"I told you to go with him," the black man said to Officer Daniels, a tone of command in his voice. Then he started to trot toward Market Street.

Officer Daniels ran after the young white man and caught up with him.

"Who is that guy?" he asked.

"That is Sergeant Jason Washington. He just told me he used to walk this beat."

"He doesn't have any authority here."

"You tell him that," Matt said, chuckling as he continued down the alley.

The sound of dying sirens and the squeal of tires announced the arrival of other police vehicles.

The alley between the buildings was pitch dark, and twice Matt stumbled over something he hadn't seen. There was more light when he reached the end of the alley, coming down what had been in Colonial times a cobblestone street but was now not much more than a garbage-littered alley.

He found the Inferno Lounge's garbage cans. As Jason had said they would be, they were filled to overflowing with kitchen scraps and beer bottles.

He went to a metal door and tried it. It opened.

If there was somebody in here, they're probably gone. The door would ordinarily be locked.

He stepped to one side, hiding, so to speak, behind the bricks of the building, and then pulled the door fully open.

"Police officers!" he called.

There was no response.

He looked very carefully around the bricks. There was no one in sight, but he could see a corridor dimly illuminated by the lights burning in the kitchen, and beyond that, in the public areas of the bar, or restaurant, or whatever the hell this place was.

"Stay here," he ordered Officer Daniels, and then entered the building and started down the corridor. Halfway down it, he saw a flight of stairs leading to the basement, and saw lights down there. It was possible that someone was down in the basement; he was pleased with himself for having told the wagon uniform to stay at the back door.

He went carefully through the kitchen, and then into the public area of the restaurant. There was banging on the closed front door of the place, and someone—not Jason, but to judge by the depth of his voice, not the young guy in the wagon, either—was calling, not quite shouting, "Police, open up."

The door was closed with a keyed dead bolt. There were keys in it. It was hard to unlock. Matt had shoved his pistol in his hip pocket and used both hands to get it open.

There was a uniformed sergeant standing there, and two Highway Patrolmen. Behind them Matt could see Jason Washington looking for all the world like a curious civilian.

"What have you got, Payne?" one of the Highway Patrolmen said. Matt recalled having met him somewhere. He couldn't recall his name.

"Nothing yet. I figured I'd better let you guys in."

"How'd you get in?"

"Back door was unlocked. The wagon guy's covering it."

"Who are you?" the uniformed sergeant asked.

"He's Detective Payne of Special Operations," Jason answered for him. "And I am Sergeant Washington. Nothing, Matt?"

"Nothing on the floor. There's a basement, I didn't get down there."

"I think we should have a look," Washington said, and moving with a quick grace, suddenly appeared in front of the two Highway Patrolmen and the uniformed sergeant. "Lead on, Matthew!"

Matt turned and walked quickly back through the bar, the restaurant, and the kitchen to the corridor, then started down the stairs. Washington stopped him with a massive hand on his shoulder.

"Announce your arrival," he said softly. "You don't know what you're going to find down there, and if the proprietor, for example, is down there, you want to be sure he knows the man coming down the stairs is a police officer."

"Police!" Matt called.

"Down here!" a male voice called.

The stairs led to a narrow corridor, and the corridor to a small office.

The first thing Matt saw was a somewhat stocky man in his forties sitting behind a battered desk, in the act of taking a pull from the neck of a bottle of Seagram's VO. There was a Colt Cobra revolver lying on the desk.

The next thing Matt saw, as he entered the office, was a young female, white, sitting in a chair. Her head was hanging limply back. Her eyes were open and her head, neck, and chest were covered with blood. She was obviously dead. On the floor, lying on his side in a thick pool of blood, was the body of a heavy man. His arm was stretched out, nearly touching the desk.

Matt looked at the man behind the desk.

"What happened here?"

"I was held up," the man said.

"By who?"

Matt looked at the office door and saw that Jason Washington and one of the Highway Patrolmen had stopped inside the office.

"Two white guys."

"Are you all right?"

"I was shot in the leg," the man said.

Matt crossed to him and saw that he had his right leg extended, and that the trouser leg between the knee and the groin was soaked in blood.

"Can you describe the men?" Matt asked.

"There was two of them," the man said. "One was a short, stocky sonofabitch, and the other was about as big as I am."

"How were they dressed?"

"The little fucker was in a suit; the other one was wearing a zipper jacket."

"Mustaches, beards, anything like that?"

The man shook his head.

Jason Washington turned to the Highway Patrolman standing beside him.

"Get out a flash on that," he said softly. "And tell Police Radio that Sergeant Washington and Detective Payne of Special Operations are at the scene of what appears to be an armed robbery and double homicide."

6.

"That was interesting," Sergeant Edward McCarthy of the Homicide Unit said to Detective Wallace J. Milham as he walked up to a desk where Milham was trying to catch up with his paperwork. Milham looked at McCarthy with mingled curiosity and annoyance at having been disturbed.

"Radio just told me we have a *double* homicide at the Inferno Lounge," McCarthy said. "No names on the victims yet, but the report came from Police by radio. A Ninth District van, relaying a message from none other than Sergeant Jason Washington of Special Operations, who is apparently on the scene."

"I wonder what that's all about." Milham chuckled. "That neighborhood, and especially that joint, is not the Black Buddha's style. Who's got the job?"

"You're the assigned detective, Detective Milham," McCarthy said.

"Give me thirty seconds," Milham said. "Let me finish this page."

"Take your time. The victims aren't going anywhere," McCarthy said, and added, "I'm going to see if I can find the Captain."

Captain Henry C. Quaire, Commanding Officer of the Homicide Unit, was located attending a social function—the annual dinner of the vestry of St. John's Lutheran Church—in the Bellvue-Stratford Hotel with his wife when Sergeant McCarthy reached him.

"Where are you, Mac?"

"In the Roundhouse."

"Pick me up outside. I'll be waiting for you."

"Yes, sir."

Preoccupied with his concern about what his wife would say when he told her she would have to drive herself home—a dire prediction of tight lips and a back turned coldly toward him in their bed when he finally got home, a prediction that was to come true—Captain Quaire neglected to inquire of Sergeant McCarthy whether or not he had gotten in touch with Chief Inspector Matthew Lowenstein. The Chief liked to be notified of all interesting jobs, no matter what the hour, and a double willful killing would qualify by itself. With Washington somehow involved, he would be even more interested.

He would, he decided, try to get on a phone while waiting for McCarthy to pick him up. That idea went out the window when he stepped off the elevator and saw Mac's car waiting for him outside on South Broad Street.

"I don't suppose you got in touch with the Chief?" he asked as he got in the car.

McCarthy turned on the flashing lights and the siren and made a U-turn on Broad Street.

"I didn't have to," McCarthy replied. "I got a call from Radio, saying the Chief was going in on this, and would somebody call his wife and tell her he was delayed."

"Who are the victims? Do we know yet?"

"I'm praying that it was a family dispute," McCarthy said.

Quaire chuckled. Sergeant McCarthy was not referring to a disagreement between husband and wife, but to one between members of Philadelphia's often violent Mafia.

"Who's assigned?" Quaire asked.

"Wally Milham. You didn't say anything . . ."

"Sure. He was up, he got the job. I don't think he had anything to do with Kellog."

"I wonder who did that."

"Nothing's turned up?"

"Not a thing."

By the time Detective Milham pulled up in front of the Inferno Lounge, there were nine police vehicles, including three unmarked cars, parked on Market Street. Without consciously doing so, he picked out the anomaly. The three unmarked cars were battered and worn. Therefore, none of them belonged to Sergeant Jason Washington, whose brand-new unmarked car had been the subject of much conversation in the Homicide Unit.

Wally wondered if McCarthy had been pulling his chain about Washington being in on this; or if someone had been pulling McCarthy's chain.

There was a uniformed cop standing at the door who recognized Milham and let him in. Inside the Inferno, Milham saw three detectives whom he knew: David Rocco of the Central Detective Division; John Hanson of the Major Theft Unit; and Wilfred "Wee Willy" Malone, a six-foot-four-inch giant of a man assigned to the Intelligence Unit. That explained the three unmarked cars.

Rocco and Hanson gave him a wave. Wee Willy looked at him strangely. Wally wondered if he had heard about Kellog; that he had been interviewed and that they were checking his guns at Ballistics.

"We're glad you're here," Rocco said. *"Sergeant* Washington is with the victims, protecting the scene until the arrival of the hotshots—one of which presumably is you, Wally—of Homicide."

"If you less important people would learn not to walk all over our evidence, that wouldn't be necessary," Wally replied, and then, not seeing Washington: "Where's the Black Buddha?"

"Oh, shit," Hanson said, and laughed and then pointed. "There's a stairway off the corridor in back. There's an office downstairs."

Wally found the stairs and went down them. Washington heard him coming, and turned with an impatient look on his face until he recognized him.

"Good morning, Detective Milham," Washington said.

"Hello, Jason. What have we got?"

"Have you the acquaintance of Detective Payne?"

"Only by reputation," Milham said, and offered the young detective his hand.

"Detective Payne and myself, by pure coincidence," Washington went on, "were taking the air on Nineteenth Street when the first police vehicle to respond to the call— Officers Adolphus Hart and Thomas Daniels, in Wagon Nine Oh One, they are upstairs— arrived. In the absence of anyone more senior, I took charge of the scene, and being aware that the front door of the premises was steel and locked, ordered Detective Payne to attempt to enter the building from the rear, and sent Officer Daniels with him. Detective Payne was able to gain entrance. He left Officer Daniels to guard the rear door, proceeded through the building, and opened the front door, which was locked from the inside, and admitted me. With Detective Payne leading the way, we searched the building, and came upon the scene of the crime.

"We found Mr. Gerald Atchison, one of the proprietors of this establishment, sitting behind the desk. Mr. Atchison told us he was in the bar upstairs when he heard the sound, a popping noise, of what he now presumes was gunfire. When he went to investigate, he encountered in the corridor upstairs two white males, armed—a flash has gone out with their descriptions—who fired upon him, striking him in the leg. He drew his own pistol . . ."

Jason paused.

"Matthew, give Detective Milham the pistol, please."

Matt turned to a filing cabinet. Carefully placing his fingers on the checkered wooden handles, he picked up a Colt Cobra revolver and extended it to Milham. Wally took a plastic bag from his jacket pocket and held it open until Matt dropped the revolver into it.

". . . which Mr. Atchison is licensed by the Sheriff of Delaware County to carry," Washington went on, "and a gun battle during which Mr. Atchison suffered the wound to his leg ensued. Mr. Atchison fell to the floor. He lay there he doesn't know how long."

"It's starting to hurt," Atchison said.

"A police wagon is outside, Mr. Atchison," Washington said. "In just a moment, you will be transported to a hospital. Have I reported the essence of your discussion with Detective Payne accurately?"

"A short fucker and big one did this," Atchison replied.

"After he knows not how long he laid on the floor, Mr. Atchison reports that he recovered sufficiently to become aware that his assailants were no longer present. He then descended the stairs to the office, where he found the bodies of his wife and his business partner. He thereupon sat down at his desk, called Police Emergency to report what had happened, and then took a drink of whiskey against the pain of his wound. Am I still correct, Mr. Atchison?"

"I knew they were dead," Mr. Atchison said.

"Yes, of course, you could see that," Washington said, and then continued: "I then instructed a Highway officer to report to Police Radio that I had come upon evidence of a double homicide. I then secured the scene of the crime, pending the arrival of someone from the Homicide Unit. No one but Detective Payne and myself have entered the scene. And unless there is some other question you would like to ask of either of us, Detective

Payne and myself will now be on our way. Barring stringent objections, we will prepare statements regarding our involvement in this incident, and have them at Homicide Unit before noon tomorrow. Do you have any questions, Wally?"

"No, Jason," Milham said, smiling. "That covers everything neatly."

The day Wally had reported for duty as a Homicide detective, during his "welcome aboard" interview with then Lieutenant Quaire, Quaire had pulled a Homicide Investigation binder from the file and handed it to him.

"Don't let him know I showed you this, Milham, his ego is bad enough as it is, but this is what you should try for."

"What is it, sir?"

"It's a real Homicide report, Detective Jason Washington's, of a homicide in the course of an armed robbery, but it's also a textbook example of what a completed Homicide binder should be. Everything is in it, in the right sequence, there's no ambivalence, there's no duplication, there's no procedural errors, no spelling or grammatical mistakes, and if there are any type-overs, I can't find one."

"That being the case, Wally, I leave this matter in your capable hands. Shall we be on our way, Matt?"

"I got to get medical attention," Mr. Atchison said. "My goddamned leg is starting to hurt."

"We regret the delay, Mr. Atchison," Washington said. "But I am sure that you are even more interested than we are in apprehending the people who murdered your wife and business associate, and it was necessary for me to put what information I have regarding this tragic incident in the hands of the police officer who will be in charge of the investigation."

"Yeah. I want those bastards caught. And fried."

"Good night, sir," Washington said. "Thank you for your patience."

He turned, and met Wally Milham's eyes. Then he wrinkled his nose, as if smelling something rotten.

"Good night, Detective Milham," he said, and took Matt's arm and propelled him out of the room.

There were well over a dozen police vehicles of all kinds, among them Chief Inspector Matthew Lowenstein's Oldsmobile sedan, parked on the street and on the sidewalk in front of the Inferno Lounge, when Captain Quaire and Sergeant McCarthy arrived.

Captain Thomas Curran of the Central Detective Division was standing on the sidewalk with Staff Inspector Michael Weisbach and Captain Alexander Smith of the Ninth District, but neither Chief Lowenstein nor his driver was anywhere in sight.

"The Chief is inside," Curran explained. "Enter at your own risk. He told us to wait out here, and Weisbach was with him when he drove up. He is not in a good mood."

"Washington's in there?" Quaire asked.

"Which may explain his mood." Curran nodded. "Washington, and that kid, Payne, who shot the rapist. And Milham. Milham just got here."

"You better wait, too, Mac," Quaire said, and walked to the entrance of the Inferno Lounge, where a uniform pulled the door open for him.

Quaire found Chief Lowenstein not where he expected to find him, wherever the bodies were, but in the restaurant area of the Inferno, sitting at a table with Sergeant Jason Washington and Detective Matthew M. Payne.

"Good evening, sir," Quaire said.

"Sergeant Washington's sole function in this has been to keep Highway from walking all over the evidence," Lowenstein said. "The bodies are downstairs. Milham's down there."

"Who are the victims?" Quaire asked.

"One white female, Alicia Atchison," Washington answered. "The wife of the proprietor, one Gerry Atchison. And Mr. Atchison's business partner, one Anthony J. Marcuzzi."

Mr. Atchison contends that two white males shot them in the course of a robbery, during which he was himself shot, as he bravely attempted to defend his wife, his property, and his friend and business associate."

He pinched his nose with his thumb and his index finger, which might have been a simple, innocent gesture, or might have been an indication that he believed Mr. Atchison's version of what had transpired smelled like rotten fish.

"I'll go have a look," Quaire said.

"Take Detective Payne with you," Lowenstein said. "He might be useful—he was first on the scene—and he might learn something."

Matt Payne, looking a little surprised, stood up.

Chief Lowenstein waited until Quaire and Payne were out of earshot, then turned to Washington.

"Jason, we've been friends for a long time."

" 'Uh-oh,' the Apache warrior said, aware that he was about to be schmoozed by the Big Chief,' " Washington said.

Lowenstein smiled, and then the smile vanished.

"I know what you're doing, Jason."

"Excuse me?"

"And for what it's worth, if I had to pick somebody to do it, it would be you. Or Peter Wohl. Or the both of you, which is the way I hear it is."

"Chief, we have been friends a long time, and what you're doing is putting me on a hell of a spot."

"Yeah, and I know it. But goddamn it . . ."

Washington looked at him, met his eyes, but said nothing.

"I'm going to ask you some questions. If you feel you can answer them, answer them. If you feel you can't, don't."

Washington didn't reply, but after a moment, nodded his head.

"How bad is it?"

Washington, after ten seconds, which seemed like much longer, said, "Bad."

"How high does it go?"

"There's a captain involved."

"Suspicion, or something that can be proved?"

Washington thought that question over before replying.

"There will be indictments."

Lowenstein met his eyes and exhaled audibly.

"Anybody I know?"

"Chief, you know a lot of people."

"If I ran some names by you, would you nod your head?"

"No."

"Mike Weisbach heard some talk about Vito Cazerra."

Washington didn't reply.

"He's working on it. Weisbach's a damned good investigator."

Washington remained silent, his face fixed.

"The name of Seymour Meyer also came up."

"Chief, we're not having this conversation," Washington said. "If we were, I'd have to report it."

Lowenstein met Washington's eyes.

"How much time do I have?"

Washington shrugged, then said, "Very little."

"Are you going to tell the Mayor I cornered you and we had this little chat?"

"What little chat?"

"OK, Jason," Lowenstein said. "Thanks."

Washington made a deprecating gesture.

Lowenstein stood up and looked down at Washington.

"Does Denny Coughlin know what's going on?" he asked.

It was a moment before Washington, just perceptibly, shook his head no.

Lowenstein considered that, nodded his head, and turned and walked out of the Inferno Lounge.

Wally Milham was not surprised to see Captain Henry Quaire come into the basement office of the Inferno Lounge. Quaire routinely showed up at the scene of an interesting murder, and this double murder qualified. Wally was surprised and annoyed, however, to see Detective Payne with him.

"What have we got, Wally?" Quaire asked.

Wally told him, ending his synopsis with the announcement that he was about to have Mr. Atchison transported to Hahnemann Hospital for treatment of his leg wound.

"You're ready for the technicians?" Quaire asked. "They're here."

"Yes, sir."

"I'll go get them," Quaire said. "We want to do this by the book. Chief Lowenstein's here, too. Keep me posted on this one, Wally."

"Yes, sir."

Since Detective Payne had arrived with Captain Quaire, Detective Milham reasonably presumed that he would leave with him. He didn't.

What the hell is he hanging around for?

"I've been thinking that maybe I better talk to my lawyer," Mr. Atchison said. "With something like this happening, I'm not thinking too clear."

"Certainly," Wally said. "I understand."

"How long do you think it will take at the hospital?" Mr. Atchison asked.

"No telling," Wally replied. "An hour, anyway. There'd be time for him to meet you there, if that's what you're thinking."

"And I'm going to need a ride home," Mr. Atchison said. "I can't drive with my leg like this."

"Have you got his number? Would you like me to call him for you?" Wally asked solicitously.

"I'll call him," Atchison said, and, grunting, sat up and moved toward the desk.

"It would be better if you didn't use that phone, sir," Matt said, and when Atchison looked at him, continued: "We'd like our technicians to see if there are any fingerprints on it. That would be helpful, when we find the men who did this to you, to prove that they were here in this room."

What's this "we" shit? This is my job, pal, not yours. Butt the hell out.

"Yeah, sure."

"There will be a telephone in the hospital, I'm sure," Matt went on. "Or, if you would like us to, we can get word to him to meet you at Hahnemann Hospital."

More of this "we" shit! Just who the hell do you think you are, Payne?

"That's very nice of you," Atchison said. "His name is Sidney Margolis. I got his number here in the card file."

He started to reach for it, and Matt stopped him.

"It would be better, Mr. Atchison, if you didn't touch that, either, until the technicians have done their thing. Is he in the phone book? Or is his number unlisted?"

"I remember it," Atchison said, triumphantly calling it forth from his memory.

"If you give that to me again," Matt said, "I'd be happy to call him for you."

"Would you, please? Tell him what happened here, and ask him to meet me at Hahnemann."

Matt took a small notebook from his pocket and wrote the number down.

"Can I see you a minute, Payne?" Wally said, and took Matt's arm and led him out of the office. "Be right with you, Mr. Atchison."

He led Matt a dozen steps down the corridor, then stopped.

"I don't know who the hell you think you are, Payne," he snapped. "But shut your fucking mouth. This is my job. When I want some help, I'll ask for it."

"Sorry," Matt said. "I was just trying to help."

"Do me a favor. Don't."

"OK. Sorry."

Wally's anger had not subsided.

"I'll tell you what I do want you to do," he said. "First, give me that lawyer's phone number, and then get your ass down to the Roundhouse and wait for me there. I want your statement. I may have to put up with that 'I'll get my statement to you in the morning' shit from Washington, but I don't have to put up with it from you."

Matt, his face red, tore the page with the phone number from his notebook and handed it to Wally. Wally took it and went back down the corridor.

Matt watched him a moment, then went up the stairs, as two uniformed officers, one carrying a stretcher, came down them.

Chief Lowenstein was gone. Jason Washington, alone at the table where they had been sitting, stood up when he saw Matt.

"Well, did you learn anything?"

"A," Matt replied, "Detective Milham has all the charm of a constipated alligator, and B, he wants my statement tonight, not tomorrow."

Washington's right eyebrow rose in surprise.

"Shall I have a word with him?"

"No. No, thanks. Now that I think of it, I'd just as soon get it over with now. I've got a busy day tomorrow."

"All right. Walk me back to your place, and I'll drop you off at the Roundhouse on my way home. Or you can get your car."

"I'll take the ride, thanks. And catch a cab home later."

Jason Washington was surprised and just a little alarmed when he quietly let himself into his apartment to see that there were lights on in the living room.

Not only is the love of my life angry, but angry to the point where she has decided that marital justice demands that she wait up for me to express her displeasure personally, immediately, and in some detail.

As he walked down the corridor, he heard Martha say, somewhat formally, "I think that's him."

Someone's with her. Someone she doesn't know well. Who? And who else would it be at this hour of the morning?

He walked into the living room. Martha, in a dressing gown, was sitting on the couch. There was a coffee service on the coffee table. And a somewhat distraught-looking woman sitting in one of the armchairs, holding a coffee cup in her hands.

"Martha, I'm sorry to be so late. I was tied up."

"That happens, doesn't it?" Martha replied, the tone of her voice making it clear she thought he had been tied up by a slow-moving bartender.

"Good evening," Jason said to the distraught-looking woman.

"More accurately, 'good morning,' " Martha said. "Jason, this is Mrs. Kellog."

"How do you do?" Jason said.

Kellog? As in Officer Kellog?

"I'm sorry to have come here like this," Mrs. Kellog said. "But I just had to."

"How may I help you, Mrs. Kellog?"

"Jerry Kellog was my husband," she said.

That's precisely what I feared. And what are you doing here, in my home?

"May I offer my condolences on your loss, Mrs. Kellog?"

"I didn't have anything to do with him being killed," she said. "And neither did Wally."

Washington nodded sympathetically.

"Martha, I'm sure you're tired," he said.

"No. Not at all," Martha said, smiling sweetly, letting Jason know that even if this was business he wasn't going to dismiss her so lightly in her own home.

"Wally told me, not only Wally, but Lieutenant Sackerman, too, especially him, that you're not only the best Homicide detective . . ."

"That was very gracious of Jack Sackerman," Washington said, "we were friends for a long time."

". . . but the only cop you *know* is honest."

"That's very kind, but I cannot accept the blanket indictment of the rest of the Police Department," Washington said. "I like to think we're something like Ivory Soap: ninety-nine and forty-four one hundredths pure."

Helene Kellog ignored him.

"That's why I came to you," she said. "I didn't know where else to go." She looked at him, took a deep breath, and went on: "Jerry was dirty. I know that. And—what happened to him—had something to do with that. They're all dirty, the whole Five Squad is dirty."

"Mrs. Kellog, when you were interviewed by detectives investigating the death of your husband, did you tell any of them what you just told me?"

She snorted.

"Of course not. They all acted like they think that I had something to do with it. Or that Wally did. I wouldn't be a bit surprised if they were in on it."

"In on what?"

"Covering up. Maybe trying to pin it on Wally or me. Wally *and* me."

"Does Detective Milham know that you've come to see me?"

"Of course not!"

"Why do you think anyone would want to 'pin' what happened to your husband on you? Or Detective Milham?"

"I just told you! To cover up. To protect themselves. They're all dirty. The whole damned Five Squad is dirty! That's probably why Jerry was killed. He never really wanted to get involved with that. They made him! And maybe he was going to tell somebody or do something."

"By dirty, you mean you believe your husband was taking money from someone?"

"Yes, of course."

"Did he tell you he was?"

"No. He wouldn't talk about it at all."

"Then how do you know?"

"He was getting the money from someplace."

"What money?"

"All of the money. All of a sudden we've got lots of money. You're a cop. You know how much a cop, even with overtime, makes."

"And Jerry had large sums of money?"

"We—*he*—bought a condo at the shore, and there's a boat. And he paid cash. He didn't get that kind of money from the Police Department."

"Did you ask him where the money came from?"

"He wouldn't tell me. That's when we started to have trouble, when he wouldn't tell me."

"Have you told anything about this to Detective Milham?"

"No."

"May I ask why not?"

"Because if I did, he would have done something about it. He's an honest cop."

"Then wouldn't he logically be the person to tell?"

"I didn't want Jerry to go to jail," she said. "And besides, what would it look like, coming from me? Me living with Wally. I'd look like a bitch of a wife trying to make trouble."

"Did you come to me for advice, Mrs. Kellog?" Washington asked.

"For help. For advice."

"If what you told me is true . . ."

"Of course it's true!" she interrupted.

". . . then the information you have should be placed in the hands of the people who can do something about it. I'm sure you know that we have an Internal Affairs Division . . ."

"If I thought I could trust Internal Affairs, I wouldn't be here," she said. "They're all in on it."

"Mrs. Kellog, I can understand why you're upset, but believe me, you can trust Internal Affairs."

At this moment, unfortunately, I'm not absolutely sure that's true. And neither am I sure that what I so glibly said before, that the Department is ninety-nine and forty-four one hundredths percent pure, is true, either.

She snorted.

"If I gave you the name of a staff inspector in Internal Affairs whom I can personally vouch for . . ."

Helene Kellog stood up.

"I guess I should have known better than to come here," she said, on the edge of tears. "I'm sorry to have wasted your time." She turned to Martha Washington. "Thank you."

"Mrs. Kellog, there's really nothing I can do to help you. I have nothing to do with either Homicide or Narcotics or Internal Affairs."

"Like I said, I'm sorry I wasted your time," she said. "That's the way out, right?"

"I'll see you to the door," Washington said, and went with her.

At the door, she turned to him.

"Do me one favor, all right? Don't tell Wally that I came to see you."

"If you wish, Mrs. Kellog."

She turned her back on him and walked down the corridor to the elevator.

Martha was waiting for him in the living room.

"I'm sorry about that, honey," he said.

"I think she was telling the truth."

"She believed what she was saying," Jason said after a moment. "That is not always the same thing as the whole truth."

"I felt sorry for her."

"So did I."

"But you're not going to do anything about what she said?"

"I'll do something about it," he said.

"What?"

"I haven't decided that yet. I don't happen to think that Wally Milham had anything to do with her husband's murder; he's not the type. I saw him tonight, by the way. That's where I was."

"Excuse me?"

"I went to see Matt. We tried to go to the Rittenhouse Club for a drink, but it was closed, so we took a walk, and walked up on a double homicide. On Market Street. And we got involved in that. Wally Milham had the job."

"You mean, you were involved in a shooting?"

"No. We got there after the fact."

"What was so important that you had to see Matt at midnight?" Martha asked. "And be warned that 'police business' will not be an acceptable reply."

He met her eyes, smiled, and shook his head.

"We're conducting a surveillance. Earlier tonight, the microphone we had in place on a hotel window was dislodged. I learned from Tony Harris that Matt climbed out on a ledge thirteen floors up to replace the damned thing."

"My God! At the Bellvue? When he was here, he was wearing a Bellvue maintenance uniform."

Jason ignored the question.

"I wanted to bawl him out for that. And alone."

"So you went to the bar at the Rittenhouse Club?"

"That was after I bawled him out."

"After you bawled him out, you felt sorry for him?"

"I felt sorry for myself. I wanted a drink, and he didn't have anything."

"I'm going to give you the benefit of the doubt," Martha said, "and accept that story."

"Thank you."

"Do you want something to eat? Coffee? Another drink?"

"If I told you what I really want, you'd accuse me of . . ."

"Oddly enough, I was thinking along those lines myself," Martha said. "Why don't you get one of those champagne splits from the fridge, while I turn off the lights."

When Detective Wallace J. Milham walked into the Homicide Division, he saw Detective Matthew M. Payne sitting at an unoccupied desk reading the *Daily News*. When Payne saw him, he closed the newspaper and stood up.

Wally beckoned to him with his finger and led him into one of the interview rooms, remembering as he passed through the door that he had the previous morning given a statement of his own in the same goddamn room.

Milham sat down in the interviewee's chair, a steel version of a captain's chair, firmly bolted to the floor, with a pair of handcuffs locked to it through a hole in the seat.

He motioned for Payne to close the door.

Payne handed him two sheets of typewriter paper.

"I didn't know how you wanted to handle this," Payne said. "But I went ahead and typed out this."

Milham read Matt's synopsis of what had happened at the Inferno Lounge. It wasn't up to Washington's standards, but he was impressed with the clarity, organization, and completeness. And with the typing. There were no strike-overs.

Why the hell am I surprised? He works for Washington.

"What do you do for Washington?" he wondered aloud.

Payne looked uncomfortable.

"Whatever he tells me to do," he said. "That wasn't intended to be a flip answer."

He doesn't want to talk about what he does for Washington. That shouldn't surprise me either. I don't know what they've got Jason doing, but whatever it is, somebody thinks it's more valuable to the Department than his working Homicide. And this guy works for him.

"Payne, I'm sorry I jumped on your ass at the Inferno. I had a really bad day yesterday, but I shouldn't have taken it out on you."

"No. I was out of line. You were right."

There was a knock at the door. Wally pushed himself out of the steel captain's chair and went to it and opened it.

A portly detective Matt recognized stood there.

"Mr. Atchison and his attorney, Mr. Sidney Margolis, are here," he said formally, and then he recognized Matt. "Whaddayasay, Payne?"

Summers shrugged, a gesture Milham interpreted to mean *Fuck you, too,* and went out of the interview room.

"You know Summers?"

"The sonofabitch and another one named Kramer had me in here when I shot Stevens. The way they acted, I thought they were his big brothers."

"When you did what? 'Shot Stevens'?"

"Charles D. Stevens, a.k.a. Abu Ben Mohammed. He was one of the, quote, Arabs, unquote, on the Goldblatt Furniture job."

"I remember that," Wally said. "He tried to shoot his way out of an alley in North Philly when they went to pick him up?"

"Right."

"And shot a cop, who then put three rounds in him? That was you?"

Matt nodded. "I took a ricochet off a wall."

"I didn't make the connection with you," Wally said. And then, surprising himself, he added, "You hear about the plainclothes Narcotics guy getting shot?"

"Washington said something about it."

"Summers had me in here earlier today. 'What did you know about the death of Officer Jerome H. Kellog?' "

"I heard."

"Kellog's wife—they were separated—and I are pretty close. They had me in here. Sitting in that chair is a real bitch."

"Yeah," Matt agreed.

"And you took out the North Philly Serial Rapist, too, didn't you?" Wally said, remembering.

Matt nodded.

Jesus, Wally thought, *as long as I've been on the job, I've never once had to use my gun. And this kid has twice saved the City the price of a trial.*

"If I give you Boy Scout's Honor to keep my runaway mouth shut, could I hang around here?" Matt asked.

"Why would you want to do that?"

"Washington said you're a damned good investigator. I'd like to see you work."

Washington said that about me? I'll be damned!

"Sure. Be my guest."

"Where has, quote, the victim, unquote, been up to now?"

"Probably in the Hahnemann Hospital parking lot being told what not to say by his lawyer. Or deciding if it would be smarter to take the Fifth."

"Wouldn't he be? I had the feeling Jason Washington didn't believe what he had to say."

"Oh, this guy did it," Milham responded matter-of-factly. "Or had it done. There's not much question about that. *Proving* it is not going to be easy. He's smart, and tough, and he's got a good lawyer. But I think I'll nail the sonofabitch."

"Is that intuition on your part? Or Jason's? Or did I miss something?"

"I don't know about Washington. He sees things, senses things, that the rest of us miss. But what I saw was first of all a guy who didn't seem all that upset to be sitting around across a desk from his wife, who had just had her brains blown out. And there's his business partner on the floor, with bullet holes in him, too. I didn't hear one word about 'poor whatsisname.' Did you?"

"Marcuzzi, Anthony J." Matt furnished, shaking his head, no.

" 'Poor Tony, he was more than a business partner. We were very close friends. I loved him,' " Milham said mockingly.

Matt chuckled.

"On the way to Hahnemann Hospital," Milham went on, "I guess he thought about that: 'Jesus, I should remember that I'm supposed to be sorry as hell about this!' He started crying in the wagon. He wasn't all that bad, either. I almost felt sorry for him."

"Do you think he knows that you suspect him?"

"I don't know," Milham replied thoughtfully. "Probably about now, yeah, I think he's realized we haven't swallowed his bullshit. There's always something you forget when you set up something like this. I don't know what the hell he forgot, not yet, but he knows. I'd say right about now, he's getting worried."

"What I wondered about . . ." Matt said. "When I got hit, it hurt like hell. He didn't seem to be hurting much."

"I was not surprised when the bullet they took out of him at Hahnemann," Wally said, and dug in his pocket and came out with a plastic bag, handed it to Matt, then continued, "turned out to be a .32. Or that he had been shot only once. Whoever shot the wife and the partner made damned sure they were dead."

Matt examined the bullet and handed the plastic envelope back.

"And I won't be surprised, judging by the damage they caused, when we get the bullets in the bodies from the Medical Examiner, if they are *not* .32s. At least .38s, maybe even .45s, which do more damage. If I were a suspicious person, which is what the City pays me to be, I would wonder about that. How come the survivor has one small wound in the leg, and . . ."

"Yeah," Matt said thoughtfully.

"I think it's about time we ask them to come in," Wally said. "You want to stick around, stick around."

Milham got out of the captain's chair and went to the door and opened it.

"Would you please come in, Mr. Atchison?" he asked politely.

A moment later, Atchison, his arm around the shoulder of a short, portly, balding man, appeared in the interview-room door.

"Feeling a little better, Mr. Atchison?" Wally asked.

"How the fuck do you think I feel?" Atchison said.

Margolis looked coldly, but without much curiosity, at Matt.

"Howareya?" he said.

Matt noticed that despite the hour—it was reasonable to presume that when Milham called him, he had been in bed—Margolis was freshly shaven and his hair carefully arranged in a manner he apparently thought best concealed his deeply receded hairline. His trousers were mussed, however, and did not match his jacket, and his white shirt was not fresh. He was not wearing a tie.

Margolis led Atchison to the captain's chair and eased him down into it.

Matt saw that Atchison was wearing a fresh shirt and other—if not fresh—trousers. There were no bloodstains on the ones he was wearing.

"I object to having my client have to sit in that goddamned chair like you think he's guilty of something. He just suffered a gunshot wound, for Christ's sake!" Margolis said.

"We really don't have anything more comfortable, Mr. Atchison," Wally said. "But I'll ask Detective Payne to get another chair in here so you can rest your leg on it. Would that be satisfactory?"

"It wouldn't hurt. Let's get this over, for God's sake," Atchison said. "My leg is starting to throb."

"We'll get through this as quickly as we can," Matt heard Wally say as he went in search of another chair. "We appreciate your coming in here, Mr. Atchison."

Matt found a straight-back chair and carried it into the interview room. He arranged it in front of the captain's chair, and with a groan, Atchison lifted his leg up and rested it on it.

Matt glanced at Atchison. Atchison was examining him carefully, and Matt remembered what Wally had just said about "I think he's realized we haven't swallowed his bullshit."

When Matt looked at Milham, Milham, with a nod of his head, told him to stand against the wall, behind Atchison in the captain's chair.

A slight, gray-haired woman, carrying a stenographer's notebook in one hand and a metal folding chair in the other, came into the room.

"This is Mrs. Carnelli," Milham said. "A police stenographer. She'll record this interview. Unless, of course, Mr. Atchison, you have an objection to that?"

Atchison looked at Margolis.

"Let's get on with it," Margolis said.

"Thank you," Milham said. He waited to see that Mrs. Carnelli was ready for him, and then spoke, slightly raising his voice. "This is an interview conducted in the Homicide Unit May 20, at 2:30 A.M. of Mr. Gerald N. Atchison, by Detective Wallace J. Milham, badge 626, concerning the willfully caused deaths of Mrs. Alicia Atchison and Mr. Anthony Marcuzzi. Present are Mr. Sidney Margolis, Mr. Atchison's attorney, and Detective Payne . . . first name and badge number, Payne?"

"Matthew M. Payne, badge number 701," Matt furnished.

"Mr. Atchison, I am Detective Milham of the Homicide Unit," Milham began. "We are questioning you concerning the willful deaths of Mrs. Alicia Atchison and Mr. Anthony Marcuzzi."

7.

Mrs. Martha Washington was not surprised, when she woke up, that her husband was not in bed beside her. They had been married for more than a quarter century and she was as accustomed to finding herself alone in bed—even after a romantic interlude—as she was to the witticisms regarding her married name. She didn't like either worth a damn, but since there was nothing she could do about it, there was no sense in feeling sorry for herself.

She was surprised, when she looked at her bedside clock, to see how early it was: twenty minutes past seven. She rarely woke that early. And then she had the explanation: the sound of a typewriter clattering in the living room. *Her* typewriter, an IBM Electric, brought home from the Washington Galleries, Inc., when IBM wouldn't give her a decent trade-in when she'd bought new Selectrics.

"Damn him!" she said.

She pushed herself out of bed and, with a languorous, unintentionally somewhat erotic movement, pulled her nightgown over her head and tossed it onto the bed. Naked, showing a trim, firm figure that gave her, at forty-seven, nothing whatever to be unhappy about, she walked into the marble-walled bathroom and turned on the faucets in the glass-walled shower.

When she came out of the shower, she toweled her short hair vigorously in front of the partially steamed-over mirror. She had large dark eyes, a sharp, somewhat hooked nose, and smooth, light brown skin. After Matt had made the crack that she looked like the women in the Egyptian bas-reliefs in the collection of the Philadelphia Art Museum, she had begun to consider that there might actually be something to it, if the blood of an Egyptian queen—or at least an Egyptian courtesan; some of the women in those bas-reliefs looked as though they knew the way to a man's heart wasn't really through his stomach—might really flow in her veins.

She wrapped herself in a silk robe and went through the bedroom into the living room. Her red IBM Electric and a tiny tape recorder were on the plate-glass coffee table before the couch. Her husband, a thin earplug cord dangling from his ear, was sitting—somewhat uncomfortably, she thought—on the edge of the leather couch before it, his face showing deep concentration.

She went to the ceiling-to-floor windows overlooking the Art Museum, the Schuylkill River, and the Parkway and threw a switch. With a muted hum, electric motors opened the curtains.

"How many times have I asked you not to put things on the coffee table? Heavy things?"

"How many times have I told you that I called and asked how much weight this will safely support?" her husband replied, completely unabashed.

He was nearly dressed to go to work. All he would have to do to be prepared to face the world would be to put on his shoulder holster (on the coffee table beside the IBM Selectric) and his jacket (on the couch).

"Am I allowed to ask what you're doing?"

"Ask? Yes. Am I going to tell you? No."

"You can make your own coffee."

"I already have, and if you are a good girl, you may have a cup."

"You wouldn't like me if I was a good girl."

"That would depend on what you were good at," he said. "And there are some things, my dear, at which you are very good indeed."

The typewriter continued to clatter during the exchange. She was fascinated with his ability to do two things, several things, at once. He was, she realized, listening to whatever was on the tapes, selecting what he wanted to type out, and talking to her, all at the same time.

"I really hate to see you put the typewriter there," Martha said.

"Then don't look," he said, and leaving one hand to tap steadily at the keyboard, removed the earplug, took the telephone receiver from its cradle, and dialed a number from memory with the other. "Stay in bed."

She went into the kitchen and poured coffee.

"Good morning, Inspector," she heard him say. "I hope I didn't wake you."

The Inspector, Martha felt, was probably Peter Wohl. Whatever Wohl replied, it caused her husband to chuckle, which came out a deep rumble.

"I have something I think you ought to see and hear, and as soon as possible," she heard her husband say. "What would be most convenient for you?"

I wonder what that's all about? What wouldn't wait until he saw Wohl in his office?

"This won't take long, Peter," Washington said.

And then Martha intuited what this was all about. She walked to the kitchen door and looked at him.

"I'll be outside waiting for you," Jason said. Then he dropped the telephone in its cradle.

He looked up at her.

"Did you tape-record that pathetic woman last night?"

Jason didn't reply.

"You did," Martha said, shock and disgust in her voice. "Jason, she came to you in confidence."

"She came to me looking for help. That's what I'm trying to do."

"That's not only illegal—and you're an officer of the law—it's disgusting! She wouldn't have told you what she did if she knew you were recording it!"

He looked at her a long moment.

"I wanted to make sure I really understood what she said," he said. "Watch!"

He pushed the Erase button on the machine.

"No tape, Martha," he said. "I just wanted to make sure I had it all."

He stood up and started to put on his shoulder holster.

She turned angrily and went back to the stove.

He appeared in the kitchen door, now fully dressed. She recognized his jacket as a new one, a woolen tweed from Uruguay, of all places.

"You ever hear about the ancient custom of killing the messenger who bears the bad news?" Jason replied. "Be kind to me, Martha."

"Don't try to be clever. Whatever it is, Peter Wohl won't blame you."

"I'm talking about the Mayor."

She met his eyes for a moment, turned away from him, and then back again, this time offering a mug of coffee.

"Do you have time for this?" she asked. "Or is the drawing and quartering scheduled in the next five minutes?"

"It's not a hearty meal, but the condemned man is grateful nonetheless."

He took the coffee, took a sip, and then set it down.

"What's all this about?" Martha asked. "What that woman said last night? Dirty cops in Narcotics?"

"We're working on dirty cops elsewhere in the Department."

"I thought Internal Affairs was supposed to police the Police Department."

"They are."

She considered that a moment.

"Oh, which explains why you and Peter are involved."

He nodded.

"And now this. I think Mrs. Kellog was telling the truth. It will not make the Mayor's day." Martha shook her head.

"Am I going to be honored with your company later today?" Martha asked. "At any time later today? Or maybe sometime this week?"

"I know what you should do. You should go back to bed and try this again. This time, get up with a smile, and with nothing in your heart but compassion for your overworked and underappreciated husband."

"We haven't had any time together for weeks. And even when you're here, you're not. You're working."

"I know. This will be over soon, Martha. And we'll go to the shore for a couple of days."

"I've heard that before," she said, but she went to him and kissed his cheek. "Get that stuff off my table. Put the damned typewriter back where you found it."

"Yes, Ma'am," Jason said. He put the typewriter back where he had found it, in a small closet in the kitchen, and then, carrying the tape recorder, left the apartment, pausing only long enough to pat his wife on her rump.

"Good morning, Jason," Wohl said as Washington got into the front seat of Wohl's car.

"I'm sorry about this, but I really thought I should get this to you as soon as I could."

"What's up?"

"About midnight last night, Matt and I walked up on a double homicide on Market Street."

"Really? What in the world were you two doing walking on Market Street at midnight?"

"For a quick answer, the bar at the Rittenhouse Club was closed."

"Tell me about the homicide."

"Two victims. What looks like large-caliber-bullet wounds to the cranium. One victim was the wife of one of the owners of the Inferno Lounge . . ."

"I know where it is."

"And the other the partner. It was called in by the other partner, who suffered a small-caliber-bullet wound in what he says was an encounter with the doers, two vaguely described white males."

He didn't call me here to tell me this. Why? Because he thinks that it wasn't an armed robbery, that the husband was the doer? And the Homicide detective is accepting the husband's story?

"We got there right after a Ninth District wagon responded to the call. Chief Lowenstein also came to the scene, and then got me alone. He knows what's going on."

I knew that he wouldn't have bothered me if it wasn't important!

"His finding out was inevitable. How much did you have to tell him?"

"Not much. He knows the names. Most of them. I told him I couldn't talk about it. The only time he really leaned on me was to ask how much time he had."

"What did you tell him?"

"Quote, not much, unquote."

"That's true, isn't it?"

"Yes, sir. Peter, I told him that we didn't have the conversation, that if we had it, I would have to report it."

"Is that what you're doing?"

"That's up to you, Peter. I'll play it any way you want me to."

"I like Matt Lowenstein. There has been absolutely nothing to suggest he's done anything wrong. What purpose would it serve to go to Carlucci with this?"

"You heard what the Mayor said, Peter. If anyone came to you or me asking—asking *anything*—about the investigation, he wanted to know about it."

"The call is yours, Jason. Was Chief Lowenstein—what word am I looking for?— *pissed* that you wouldn't tell him anything?"

"No. He seemed to understand he was putting me on a spot."

"My gut reaction, repeating the call is yours, is that you didn't talk to Chief Lowenstein about anything but the double homicide."

"OK. That's it. We didn't have this conversation, either."

"What conversation?" Wohl asked, with exaggerated innocence.

"I'm not through, I'm afraid," Washington said.

"What else?" Wohl asked tiredly as he pulled the door shut again.

"Chief Lowenstein got rid of Matt, so that he could talk to me, by sending him to the crime scene—the victims were in a downstairs office—with Henry Quaire when Quaire came to the scene. I don't know what happened between Matt and Milham, but Milham pulled the rule book on him and insisted on getting Matt's statement that night—God, that's something else I have to do this morning, get my statement to Homicide—so Matt went to the Roundhouse, and I went home, and when I got there the Widow Kellog was there."

"The widow of the undercover Narcotics guy?"

Washington nodded.

"Who was found with two bullets in his head in his house. Detective Milham's close friend's estranged husband."

"She was at your place?" Wohl asked, surprised.

"Right. And she is convinced that her husband's death is connected with drugs . . ."

"You don't think Milham had anything to do with it, do you?"

"No. I don't think so. But the Widow Kellog thinks it was done by somebody in Narcotics, because they—they being the Five Squad—are all dirty."

"The Narcotics Five Squad, according to Dave Pekach, are knights in shining armor, waging the good war against controlled substances. A lot of esprit de corps, which I gather means they think they're better than other cops, including the other four Narcotics squads. In other words, a bunch of hotshots who do big buys, make raids, take doors, that sort of thing. They're supposed to be pretty effective. It's hard to believe that any of them would be dirty, much less kill one of their own."

"That's what the lady is saying."

"You believe her?"

"She said there's all kinds of money floating around. She said she, she and her husband, bought a house at the shore and paid cash for it."

"That could be checked out, it would seem to me, without much trouble. Did she tell Homicide about this? Or anybody else?"

"No. She thinks everybody's dirty."

"What did you tell her?"

"I told her I knew a staff inspector I knew was honest, and she should go to him; that I would set it up."

"And she doesn't want to go to him?"

"No," Washington said. "Absolutely out of the question."

"You believe her?"

"I think she's telling the truth. My question is, what do we do with this?"

"If you take it to Internal Affairs . . ." Wohl said.

"Yeah."

"Let me read this," Wohl said, opening the envelope.

Wohl grunted twice while reading the three sheets of paper the envelope contained, then stuffed them back into the envelope.

"This has to go to the Mayor," he said. "As soon as you can get it to him. And then I think you had better have a long talk with Captain Pekach about the Narcotics Five Squad."

Washington nodded.

"Can I tell him I'm doing so at your orders?"

"Everything you do is at my orders. Dave Pekach knows that. Are you getting paranoid, Jason?"

"Simply because one is paranoid doesn't mean that people aren't really saying terrible things about one behind one's back," Washington said sonorously.

Wohl laughed.

"No cop likes the guy who asks the wrong questions about other cops. Me included. I especially hate being the guy who asks the questions," Washington said.

"I know," Wohl said sympathetically. "Please don't tell me there's more, Jason."

"That's enough for one morning, wouldn't you say?"

At five minutes to eight, Sergeant Jason Washington drove into the parking lot of what had been built in 1892 at Frankford and Castor avenues as the Frankford Grammar School, and was now the headquarters of the Special Operations Division of the Philadelphia Police Department.

He pulled into a parking spot near the front entrance of the building marked with a sign reading INSPECTORS. He regarded this as his personal parking space. While he was sure that there were a number of sergeants and lieutenants annoyed that he parked his car where it should not be, and who almost certainly had complained, officially or unofficially about it, nothing had been said to him.

There was a certain military-chain-of-command-like structure in the Special Operations Division. Only one's immediate superior was privileged to point out to one the errors of one's ways. In Jason Washington's case, his immediate superior was the head man, Inspector Peter Wohl, the Commanding Officer of Special Operations. Peter Wohl knew where he parked his car and had said nothing to him. That was, Jason had decided, permission to park by inference.

Sergeant Jason Washington and Inspector Peter Wohl had a unique relationship, which went back to the time Detective Wohl had been assigned to Homicide and been placed under the mentorship of Detective Washington. At that time, Jason Washington—who was not burdened, as his wife often said, with crippling modesty—had decided that Wohl possessed not only an intelligence almost equal to his, but also an innate skill to find the anomalies in a given situation—which was really what investigation was all about, finding what didn't fit—that came astonishingly close to his own extraordinary abilities in that regard.

Washington had predicted that not only would Detective Wohl remain in Homicide (many detectives assigned to Homicide did not quite cut the mustard and were reassigned to other duties) but he would have a long and distinguished career there.

Homicide detectives were the elite members of the Detective Bureau. For many people, Jason Washington among them, service as a Homicide detective represented the most challenging and satisfying career in the Police Department, and the thought of going elsewhere was absurd.

Detective Wohl had not remained in Homicide. He had taken the sergeant's examination, and then, with astonishing rapidity, became the youngest sergeant ever to serve in the Highway Patrol; a lieutenant; the youngest captain ever; and then the youngest staff inspector ever.

And then Special Operations had come along.

It had been formed several years before, it was generally, and essentially correctly, believed as a response to criticism of the Police Department—and by implication, of the Mayor—by the Philadelphia *Ledger,* one of the city's four major newspapers.

Mr. Arthur J. Nelson, Chairman of the Board and Chief Executive Officer of the Daye-Nelson Corporation, which owned the *Ledger* and twelve other newspapers, had never been an admirer of the Hon. Jerry Carlucci, and both the *Ledger* and the Daye-Nelson Corporation's Philadelphia television and radio stations (WGHA-TV, Channel Seven; WGHA-FM 100.2 MHz; and WGHA-AM, 770 KC) had opposed him in the mayoral election.

The dislike by Mr. Nelson of Mayor Carlucci had been considerably exacerbated when Mr. Nelson's only son, Jerome Stanley Nelson, had been found murdered—literally butchered—in his luxurious apartment in a renovated Revolutionary War–era building on Society Hill.

Considering the political ramifications of the case, no one had been at all surprised when the job had been given to Detective Jason Washington, who had quickly determined the prime suspect in the case to be Mr. Jerome Nelson's live-in companion, a twenty-five-year-old black homosexual who called himself "Pierre St. Maury."

When this information had been released to the press by Homicide Unit Lieutenant Edward M. DelRaye—who shortly afterward was transferred out of Homicide, for what his superiors regarded as monumentally bad judgment—it had been published in the *Inquirer,* the *Bulletin,* and the *Daily News,* Philadelphia's other major newspapers, and elsewhere.

Mrs. Arthur J. Nelson suffered a nervous breakdown, which Mr. Nelson attributed as much to the shame and humiliation caused her by the publication of their son's lifestyle as by his death. And if the police had only had the common decency to keep the sordid facts to themselves, rather than feed them to the competition in vindictive retribution for his support of the Mayor's opponent in the mayoral election, of course this would not have happened.

Almost immediately, the *Ledger'*s reporters had begun to examine every aspect of the operation of the Philadelphia Police Department with a very critical eye, and on its editorial page there began a series of editorials—many of them, it was suspected, written by Mr. Nelson himself—that called the public's attention to the Department's many failings.

The Highway Patrol, a special unit within the Department, were often referred to as "Carlucci's Commandos," for example, and in one memorable editorial, making reference to the leather puttees worn by Highway Patrolmen since its inception, when the unit was equipped with motorcycles, they became "Philadelphia's Jackbooted Gestapo."

A splendid opportunity for journalistic criticism of the Police Department presented itself to Mr. Nelson and his employees at this time with the appearance of a sexual psychopath whose practice it was to abduct single young women, transport them to remote areas in his van, and there perform various imaginatively obscene sexual acts on their bodies. The Department experienced some difficulty in apprehending this gentleman, who had been quickly dubbed "the Northwest Philadelphia Serial Rapist."

The *Ledger,* sparing no expense in their efforts to keep the public informed, turned up a rather well-known psychiatrist who said that there was no question in his mind that inevitably the Northwest Philadelphia Serial Rapist would go beyond humiliation of his victims, moving into murder and perhaps even dismemberment.

A lengthy interview with this distinguished practitioner of the healing arts was published in the *Ledger*'s Sunday supplement magazine, under a large banner headline asking, "Why Are Our Police Doing Nothing?"

The Monday after the Sunday supplement article appeared, Police Commissioner Taddeus Czernich summoned to the Commissioner's Conference Room in the Police Administration Building the three deputy commissioners and six of the dozen chief inspectors. There he announced a reorganization of certain units within the Police Department. There would be a new unit, called Special Operations Division. It would report directly to the Deputy Commissioner for Operations. It would deal, as the name suggested, with special situations. Its first task would be to apprehend the Northwest Philadelphia Serial Rapist. Special Operations would be commanded by Staff Inspector Peter Wohl, who would be transferred from the Staff Investigation Bureau of the Internal Affairs Division.

That was the first anomaly. Staff inspectors, who ranked between captains and inspectors in the departmental hierarchy, were regarded as sort of super-detectives whose superior investigative skills qualified them to investigate the most complex, most delicate situations that came up, but they did not serve in positions of command.

Staff Inspector Peter Wohl had recently received some very flattering press attention—except, of course, in the *Ledger*—following his investigation of (and the subsequent conviction of) Superior Court Judge Moses Findermann for various offenses against both the law and judicial ethics.

And Highway Patrol, Commissioner Czernich announced, would be transferred from the bureaucratic command of the Traffic Division and placed under Special Operations. As would other elements and individuals from within the Department as needed to accomplish the mission of the Special Operations Division.

Among those to be immediately transferred, Commissioner Czernich announced, would be newly promoted Captain David Pekach of the Narcotics Bureau. He would replace Captain Michael J. Sabara, the present Highway Patrol Commander, who would become Staff Inspector Wohl's deputy.

In response to the question "What the hell is that all about?" posed by Chief Inspector Matt Lowenstein of the Detective Division, Commissioner Czernich replied:

"Because the Mayor says he thinks Mike Sabara looks like a concentration camp guard and Pekach looks like a Polish altar boy. He's thinking public image, OK?"

There were chuckles. Captain Sabara, a gentle, kindly man who taught Sunday school, did indeed have a menacing appearance. Captain Pekach, who until his recent promotion had spent a good deal of time working the streets in filthy clothing, a scraggly beard, and pigtail, would, indeed, shaved, bathed, and shorn, resemble the Polish altar boy he had once been.

Chief Lowenstein had laughed.

"Don't laugh too quick, Matt," Commissioner Czernich said. "Peter Wohl can have any of your people he thinks he needs for as long as he thinks he needs them. And I know he thinks Jason Washington is the one guy who can catch the rapist."

Lowenstein's smile had vanished.

The assignment of any detective outside the Detective Bureau was another anomaly, just as extraordinary as the assignment of a staff inspector as a commanding officer. Lowenstein looked as if he was going to complain over the loss to Special Operations of Detective Jason Washington, whom he—and just about everyone else—considered to be the best Homicide detective, but he said nothing. There was no use in complaining to Commissioner Czernich. This whole business was not Czernich's brainstorm, but the Mayor's, and Lowenstein had known the Mayor long enough to know that complaining to him would be pissing in the wind.

The next day, Detective Washington and his partner, Detective Tony Harris, over their bluntly expressed objections, had been "temporarily" transferred to Special Operations for the express purpose of stopping the Northwest Serial Rapist.

They had never been returned to Homicide.

Peter Wohl had treated both of them well. There was as much overtime, without question, as they had in Homicide. They were now actually, if not officially, on a five-day-a-week day shift, from whenever they wanted to come in the morning to whenever they decided to take off in the afternoon.

They were each provided with a new unmarked car for their sole use. New unmarked cars usually went to inspectors and up, and were passed down to lesser ranks. Wohl had implied—and Washington knew at the time he had done so that he believed—that the investigations they would be assigned to perform would be important, interesting, and challenging.

That hadn't come to pass. It could be argued, of course, that bringing down police officers who were taking money from the Mafia in exchange for not enforcing the law was important. And certainly, if challenging meant difficult, this was a challenging investigation. But there was something about investigating brother police officers—vastly compounded when it revealed the hands of at least a captain and a lieutenant were indeed covered with filth—that Washington found distasteful.

The hackneyed phrase "It's a dirty job, but someone has to do it!" no longer brought a smile to Washington's face.

Washington got out of his car and entered the building. He first stopped at the office of the Commanding Officer, which looked very much as it had when it had been the Principal's Office of the Frankford Grammar School.

Officer Paul Thomas O'Mara, Inspector Wohl's administrative assistant, attired in a shiny, light blue suit Washington suspected had been acquired from the Bargain Basement at J.C. Penney's, told him that Captain Mike Sabara, Wohl's deputy, had not yet come in.

"Give me a call when he does come in, will you, Tommy?" Washington asked, left the Principal's Office, and climbed stone stairs worn deeply by seventy-odd years of children's shoes to the second floor, where he entered what had been a classroom, over the door of which hung a sign: INVESTIGATION SECTION.

There he found Detective Matthew M. Payne on duty. Payne was attired in a sports coat Jason knew that Detective Payne had acquired at a Preferred Customer 30% Off Sale at Brooks Brothers, a button-down-collar light blue shirt, the necktie of the Goodwill Rowing Club, and well-shined loafers.

He looked like an advertisement for Brooks Brothers, Jason thought. It was a compliment.

"Good morning, Detective Payne," Jason said. "You need a shave."

"I woke late," Payne said, touching his chin. "And took a chance you wouldn't get here until I could shave."

"What happened? Did Milham keep you at Homicide?"

"I was there. But he didn't keep me. He let me sit in on interviewing Atchison."

Washington's face showed that he found that interesting, but he didn't reply.

"We can't have you disgracing yourself and our unit with a slovenly appearance when you meet the Mayor," Washington said.

"Am I going to meet the Mayor?" Payne asked.

"I think so," Jason replied, already dialing a number.

There was a brief conversation with someone named Jack, whom Detective Payne correctly guessed to be Lieutenant J. K. Fellows, the Mayor's bodyguard and confidante, and then Washington hung up.

"Get in your car," he ordered, handing Matt Payne the large envelope. "Head for the Schuylkill Expressway. When you get there, call M-Mary One and get a location. Then either wait for them or catch up with them, and give Lieutenant Fellows this."

"What is it?"

"When I got home last night, Officer Kellog's widow was waiting for me. There is no question in her mind that her husband's death has something to do with Narcotics. She also made a blanket indictment of Five Squad Narcotics. She says they're all dirty. That's a transcript, almost a verbatim one, of what she said."

"You believe her?"

Washington shrugged. "I believe she believes what she told me. Wohl said to get it to the Mayor as soon as we can."

Washington dialed the unlisted private number of the Commanding Officer, Highway Patrol from memory. It was answered on the second ring.

"Captain Pekach."

"Sergeant Washington, sir."

"Honest to God, Jason, I was just thinking about you."

"I was hoping you could spare a few minutes for me, sir."

"That sounds somehow official."

"Yes, sir. Inspector Wohl asked me to talk to you."

"You're in the building?"

"Yes, sir."

"Come on, then. You've got me worried."

When Washington walked into Captain Pekach's office, Pekach was in the special uniform worn only by the Highway Patrol, breeches and boots and a Sam Browne belt going back to the days when the Highway Patrol's primary function had been to patrol major thoroughfares on motorcycles.

Washington thought about that as he walked to Pekach's desk to somewhat formally shake Pekach's offered hand: *They used to be called "the bandit chasers"; now they call them "Carlucci's Commandos." Worse, "The Gestapo."*

"Thank you for seeing me, sir."

"Curiosity overwhelms me, *Sergeant,*" Pekach said. "Coffee, Jason?"

"Thank you," Washington said.

Pekach walked around his desk to a small table holding a coffee machine, poured two mugs, handed one to Washington, and then, waving Washington into one of the two upholstered armchairs, sat down in the other and stretched his booted legs out in front of him.

"OK, what's on your mind?"

"Officer Kellog. The Narcotics Five Squad," Washington said. "The boss suggested I talk to you about both."

"What's our interest in that?"

"This is all out of school," Washington said.

Pekach held up the hand holding his mug in a gesture that meant, *understood.*

"The Widow Kellog came to my apartment last night," Washington said. "She is convinced that her husband's death is Narcotics-related."

"She came to your apartment?" Pekach asked, visibly surprised, and without waiting for a reply, went on: "I think that's a good possibility. Actually, when I said I was thinking about you just before you called, I was going to ask you if Homicide had come up with something along that line. I figured you would know if they had come up with something."

"She is also convinced that Officer Kellog was, and the entire Narcotics Five Squad is, dirty," Washington went on.

This produced, as Washington feared it would, an indignant reaction. Pekach's face tightened, and his eyes turned cold.

"Bullshit," he said. "Jerry Kellog worked for me before he went on the Five Squad. A good, smart, hardworking, *honest* cop. Which is how he got onto the Five Squad. I recommended him."

"How much do you know about the Five Squad?"

"Enough. Before I got promoted, I was the senior lieutenant in Narcotics ... no I wasn't, Lieutenant Mikkles was. But I filled in for Captain Talley enough to know all about the Five Squad. Same thing—good, smart, hardworking, *honest* cops."

Washington didn't reply.

"Christ, Jason, the Narcotics Five Squad is—" He looked for a comparison, and found one: "—the Highway Patrol of Narcotics. The best, most experienced, hardworking people. A lot of pride, esprit de corps. They're the ones who make the raids, take the doors, stick their necks out. Where did Wohl get the idea they're dirty?"

"From me, I'm afraid," Washington said.

Pekach looked at him in first surprise and then anger.

"I'm not saying they're dirty," Washington said. "I don't know—"

"Take my word for it, Jason," Pekach interrupted.

"What I told the Boss was that I believed Mrs. Kellog believed what she was saying."

"She's got an accusation to make, tell her to take it to Internal Affairs."

"She's not willing to do that. She doesn't trust Internal Affairs."

"I suppose both you and Wohl have considered that she might be trying to take the heat off her boyfriend?" Pekach challenged. "What's his name? Milham?"

"That, of course, is a possibility."

"What I think you should do—and if you don't want to tell Wohl, by God, I will—is turn this over to Internal Affairs and mind our own business."

Washington didn't reply.

Pekach's temper was now aroused.

"You know what Internal Affairs would find? Presuming that they didn't see these wild accusations for what they are—a desperate woman trying to turn the heat off her boyfriend—and conducted an investigation, they'd find a record of good busts, busts that stood up in court, put people away, took God only knows how much drugs off the street."

"We can't go to Internal Affairs with this right now," Washington said.

"Why not?" Pekach demanded, looking at him sharply. "Oh, is that what you've all been up to, that nobody's talking about? Investigating Internal Affairs? Is that why you can't take this to them?"

"You're putting me on a spot, Captain," Washington said. "I can't answer that."

"No, of course you can't," Pekach said sarcastically. "But let me tell you this, Jason: If anybody just happened to be investigating Internal Affairs, say, for example, the Mayor's personal detective bureau, I'd say they have a much better chance of finding dirty cops there than anyone investigating the Narcotics Five Squad would find there."

Washington was aware that his own temper was beginning to flare. He waited a moment.

"Captain, I do what the Boss tells me. He told me to have a long talk with you about the Narcotics Five Squad. That's what I'm doing."

"Oh, Christ, Jason, I know that. It just burns me up, is all, that the questions would be asked. I know those guys. I didn't, I really didn't, mean to jump on you."

Washington didn't reply.

"And I'll tell you something else, just between us," Pekach said. "I guess my nose is already a little out of joint. I'm supposed to be the Number Three man in Special Operations, and I don't like not knowing what you and your people are up to. I know that's not your doing, but . . ."

"Just between you and me, Captain Sabara doesn't know either," Washington said. "And also, just between you and me, I know that the decision to keep you and Sabara in the dark wasn't made by Inspector Wohl, and he doesn't like it any more than you do."

"I figured it was probably something like that," Pekach said. "But thank you for telling me."

Washington shrugged.

"What else can I do for you, Jason?"

"I'm a little afraid to ask."

"Don't be."

"I don't know the first think about how the Narcotics Five Squad operates. You do. Would you give some thought to how they could be dirty, and tell me?"

"Jesus Christ!" Pekach said bitterly, and then: "OK, Jason, I will."

"I'd appreciate it," Washington said, and stood up.

"Jason, I hope you understand why I'm sore. And that I'm not sore at you."

"I hope you understand, Captain, that I don't like asking the questions."

"Yeah, I do," Pekach said. "We're still friends, right? Despite my nasty Polish temper?"

"I really hope you still think of me as a friend," Washington said.

When Matt Payne went out the rear door into the parking lot, he saw that it was shift-change time. The lot was jammed with antenna-festooned Highway Patrol cars, somewhat less spectacularly marked Anti-Crime Team (ACT) cars, and a row of unmarked cars. Almost all of the cars were new.

There was more than a little resentment throughout the Department about Special Operations' fleet of new cars. In the districts, radio patrol car odometers were commonly on their second hundred thousand miles, seat cushions sagged, windows were cracked, heaters worked intermittently, and breakdowns of one kind or another were the rule, not the exception.

The general belief held by most District police officers was that Inspector Wohl was the fair-haired boy of the Department, and thus was able to get new cars at the expense of others who did not enjoy his status. Others felt that Special Operations had acquired so many new vehicles because it was the pet of Mayor Carlucci, and was given a more or less blank check on the Department's assets.

The truth, to which Matt Payne was privy—he had been then Staff Inspector Wohl's administrative assistant before becoming a detective—had nothing to do with Inspector Wohl or the fact that Special Operations had been dreamed up by the Mayor, but rather with the Congress of the United States.

Doing something about crime-in-the-streets had, about the time the Mayor had come up with his idea for Special Operations, been a popular subject in Congress. It was a legitimate—that is to say, one the voters were getting noisily concerned about—problem, and Congress had reacted in its usual way by throwing the taxpayers' money at it.

Cash grants were made available to local police departments to experiment with a new concept of law enforcement. This was called the Anti-Crime Team concept, which carried with it the acronym ACT. It meant the flooding of high-crime areas with well-trained policemen, equipped with the very latest equipment and technology, and teamed with special assigned prosecutors within the District Attorney's Office who would push the arrested quickly through the criminal justice system.

The grants were based on need. Philadelphia qualified on a need basis on two accounts. Crime was indeed a major problem in Philadelphia, and Philadelphia needed help. Equally important, the Hon. Jerry Carlucci was a political force whose influence extended far beyond the Mayor's office. Two Senators and a dozen or more Congressmen seeking continued employment needed Jerry Carlucci's influence.

Some of the very first, and most generous, grants were given to the City of Philadelphia. There was a small caveat. Grant money was to be used solely for new, innovative, experimental police operations, not for routine police expenditures. So far as Mayor Carlucci was concerned, the Special Operations Division was new, innovative and experimental. The federal grants could thus legally be, and were, expended on the pay of police officers transferred to Special Operations for duty as Anti-Crime Team police, and for their new and innovative equipment, which of course included new, specially equipped police cars. Since it was, of course, necessary to incorporate the new and innovative ACT personnel and equipment into the old and non-innovative Police Department, federal grant funds could be used for this purpose.

Until investigators from the General Accounting Office had put a stop to it, providing the Highway Patrol, in its new, innovative, and experimental role as a subordinate unit of the new, innovative, and experimental Special Operations Division, with new cars had been, in Mayor Carlucci's opinion, a justifiable expenditure of federal grant funds.

More senior police officers, lieutenants and above, usually, the "white shirts," who understood that money was money, and that if extra money from outside bought Special Operations and Highway cars, then the money which would ordinarily have to eventually be spent for that purpose could be spent elsewhere in the Department, were not as resentful. But this rationale was not very satisfying to a cop in a district whose battered radio patrol car wouldn't start at three o'clock in the morning.

Detective Payne went to a row of eight new, unmarked Ford sedans, which so far as the federal government was concerned were involved in new, innovative, and experimental activities under the ACT concept, and got in one of them. It was one of four such cars assigned to the Investigation Section. Sergeant Jason Washington had one, and Detective Tony Harris the second, on an around-the-clock basis. The two other cars were shared by the others of the Investigation Section.

He drove out of the parking lot and headed up Castor Avenue toward Hunting Park Avenue. He turned off Hunting Park Avenue onto Ninth Street and off Ninth Street onto the ramp for the Roosevelt extension of the Schuylkill Expressway, and then turned south toward the Schuylkill River.

At the first traffic light, he took one of the two microphones mounted just about out of sight under the dash.

"Mary One, William Fourteen."

"You have something for me, Fourteen?" Lieutenant Jack Fellows's voice came back immediately.

"Right."

"Where are you now?"

"Just left Special Operations."

There was a moment's hesitation as Lieutenant Fellows searched his memory for time-and-distance.

"Meet us at the Zoo parking lot," he said.

"On the way," Matt said, and dropped the microphone onto the seat.

Then he reached down and threw a switch which caused both the brake lights and the blue and white lights concealed behind the grille of the Ford to flash, and stepped hard on the accelerator.

The Mayor is a busy man. He doesn't have the time to waste sitting at the Zoo parking lot waiting for a lowly detective. This situation clearly complies with the provisions of paragraph whatever the hell it is of Police Administrative Regulations restricting the use of warning lights and sirens to those clearly necessary situations.

There were a number of small pleasures involved with being a policeman, and one of them, Matt Payne had learned, was being able to turn on warning lights and the siren when you had to get somewhere in a hurry.

He had thought of this during dinner the previous evening, during a somewhat acrimonious discussion of his—their—future with Miss Penelope Detweiler.

It was her position (and that of Mr. and Mrs. Chadwick Thomas Nesbitt IV, who allied themselves with Miss Detweiler in the Noble Cause of Talking Common Sense to Matt) that it was childish and selfish of him, with his education, potential, and background, to remain a policeman, working for peanuts, when he should be thinking of *their* future.

He had known that it would not have been wise to have offered the argument "Yeah, but if I'm not a cop, I won't be able to race down Roosevelt Boulevard with the lights on." She would have correctly decided that he was simply being childish again.

There were other satisfactions in being a policeman, but for some reason, he seemed to become instantly inarticulate whenever he tried to explain them to her. In his own mind, he knew that he had been a policeman long enough so that it was in his blood, and he would never be happy at a routine job.

He reached the Schuylkill River, crossed it, and turned east toward Center City. Then he reached down and turned off the flashing lights. The traffic wasn't that heavy, and if Mary One, the mayoral limousine, beat him to the Zoo parking lot, he wasn't entirely sure if the Mayor would agree with his decision that turning on the lights was justified.

From what he'd heard of the Mayor's career as a policemen, he'd been a really by-the-book cop.

When he got to the Zoo parking lot, he stopped and picked up his microphone.

"Mary One, William Fourteen, at the Zoo."

"A couple of minutes," Lieutenant Fellows's voice came back.

Matt picked the envelope off the floor, and got out of the car and waited for the Mayor.

Two minutes later the limousine pulled up beside him. Matt walked to the front-seat passenger door as the window whooshed down and Lieutenant Fellows came into view.

"Good morning, sir," Matt said, and handed him the envelope.

"Thank you, Payne," Fellows said, and the window started back up. Then the rear window rolled down and he heard the Mayor of the City of Philadelphia order:

"Hold it a minute, Charley," and then the rear door opened and the Mayor got out.

"Long time no see," the Mayor said, offering his hand. "How are you, Matt?"

"Just fine, Mr. Mayor. Thank you."

"Good to see you, Matt," the Mayor said. "And say hello to your mother and dad for me."

"Yes, sir. I will. Thank you."

The Mayor patted his shoulder and got back in the limousine, and in a moment it rolled out of the parking lot.

8.

Matt got back in the unmarked Ford and drove out of the Zoo parking lot, wondering where the hell he was going to find a drugstore and buy the razor he had been ordered to buy.

It had been nice of the Mayor, he thought, to get out of his car to say hello. It was easy to accuse the Mayor of being perfectly willing to wrap his arm around an orangutan and inquire as to the well-being of his parents if that would get him one more vote, but the truth, Matt realized, was that after he had wrapped his arm around *your* shoulder, it made you feel good, and you were not at all inclined to question his motives.

While it was said, and mostly believed, that the Mayor knew the name of every cop in the Department, this was not true. There were eight thousand policemen in the Department, and the Mayor did not know the name or even the face of each of them. But he did know the faces and sometimes the names of every cop who was someone, or who had ever done something, out of the ordinary.

Matt qualified on several counts. One of them was that the Mayor knew his parents, but the most significant way Matt Payne had come to the Mayor's attention was as a cop.

Shortly after the formation of Special Operations, as Detective Washington was getting close enough to the Northwest Serial Rapist to have a cast of his tire tracks and a good description of his van, Mr. Warren K. Fletcher, thirty-one, of Germantown, had attempted to run down Matt with his van when he approached it.

That gave Matt (although he was so terrified at the time that this legal consideration had not entered his mind) the justification to use equal—deadly—force in the apprehension of a suspect. He had drawn his service revolver and fired five times at the van. One of the bullets found and exploded Mr. Fletcher's brain all over the windshield of his van.

It didn't matter that finding what looked like it could possibly be the van could be described only as blind luck, or that when Matt had fired his revolver he had been so terrified that hitting Mr. Fletcher had been pure coincidence. What mattered was that Mr.

Fletcher, at the time of his death, had Mrs. Naomi Schneider, thirty-four, of Germantown, in the back of his van, stripped naked, trussed neatly with telephone wire, and covered with a tarpaulin, and shortly before their trip was interrupted had been regaling her with a description of what he had planned for them as soon as they got somewhere private.

What also mattered a good deal was that Matt Payne was assigned to Special Operations. Even the imaginatively agile minds on the editorial floor of the *Ledger* building had trouble finding Police Department incompetence in the end of Mr. Fletcher's career. The *Ledger* just about ignored the story. The other papers gave it a good deal of play, most of them running a front-page picture of the Mayor at the shooting scene with his arm wrapped cordially around the shoulder of Special Operations Division plainclothes officer Matthew M. Payne.

Several months after that, following a robbery, brutal assault, and senseless murder at Goldblatt's Furniture Store in South Philadelphia, the Special Operations Division was asked by the Detective Bureau to assist them in the simultaneous arrest of eight individuals identified as participants in the robbery-murder.

The eight, who identified themselves as members of something called the Islamic Liberation Army, were at various locations in Philadelphia. Seven of them, in what the press—save again the *Ledger*—generally agreed was a well-planned, perfectly carried out maneuver, were placed in custody without incident. The eighth suspect, in trying to escape, drew a .45 Colt pistol and attempted to shoot his way through officers in an alley. In the process, he wounded a police officer, who drew and fired his service revolver in self-defense, inflicting upon Abu Ben Mohammed (also known as Charles D. Stevens) several wounds which proved to be fatal.

And again there were photographs of Officer Matthew M. Payne on the front pages of the *Daily News,* the *Inquirer,* and the *Bulletin* (but not in the *Ledger*), this time showing him with his face bandaged in a hospital bed and Mayor Carlucci's approving arm around his shoulders.

It was said at the time by senior white shirts that, considering the favorable publicity he had engendered for the Special Operations Division, and thus the Mayor, the young police officer had found a home in Special Operations. The only way he was going to get out of Special Operations was when he either retired or was carried to his grave. Or resigned, when he tired of playing cop.

Matt had heard the stories at the time, but had not been particularly concerned. He planned to take, as soon as he was eligible, the examination leading to promotion to detective. He was reasonably confident that he would pass it, and be promoted. And since the only places that detectives could be assigned within the Police Department were in one of the subordinate units of the Detective Division, that's where they would have to assign him. In the meantime, he liked working for Staff Inspector Wohl as his administrative assistant.

And that came to pass. Police Officer Matthew M. Payne took the Examination for Promotion to Detective, passed it, and with a high enough score (he placed third) so as to earn promotion very soon after the results were published.

He was duly transferred to the East Detective Division, which is on the second floor of the building housing the Twenty-fourth and Twenty-fifth Districts as Front and Westmoreland streets, and there began his career as a detective under the tutelage of Sergeant Aloysius J. Sutton.

His initial war of detection against crime wherever found had consisted almost entirely of investigating recovered stolen vehicles. This, in turn, consisted of going to where the stolen vehicle had been located, and then filling out a half-dozen forms in quadruplicate. None of these forms, he had quickly come to understand, would—once they had passed Sergeant Sutton's examination of them for bureaucratic perfection—ever be seen by human eyes again.

Almost all stolen and then recovered vehicles had been taken either by kids who wished to take a joyride and had no vehicle of their own in which to do so or by kids who wished to remove the tires, wheels, radios from said vehicles with the notion of selling them for a little pocket money. Or a combination of the foregoing.

Stolen and never-recovered vehicles were almost always stolen by professional thieves who either stripped the car to its frame or got it on the boat to Asunción, Paraguay, before the owner realized it was gone.

Theft of an automobile is a felony, however, and investigation of felonies, including the return of recovered stolen property, is a police responsibility. Detective Payne learned in EDD that this responsibility, when the recovered property was an automobile, is normally placed in the hands of the member of the detective squad whose time is least valuable.

There was a sort of sense to this, and he told himself that investigating recovered vehicles was both sort of on-the-job training for more important investigations, and a rite of passage. Every new detective went through it.

And he was prepared to do whatever was asked of him.

But then his assignment to EDD came to an abrupt end. He was reassigned to Special Operations. In theory it was a simple personnel matter, the reassignment of a detective from a unit where his services weren't really required to a unit which had need of his services. Matt quickly learned that he had been reassigned to Special Operations because the Mayor had suggested to Commissioner Czernich that this might be a wise thing to do.

There he found that the table of organization now provided for an investigation section. The supervisor of the investigation section was newly promoted Sergeant Jason Washington. Under him were personnel spaces for five detectives, three of whom had been assigned: Tony Harris, Jesus Martinez, and Matthew M. Payne.

Tony Harris was an experienced homicide detective recruited (Harris and Washington both used the term "shanghaied") from Homicide when they were trying to catch up with Warren K. Fletcher, and kept over their objections because Peter Wohl felt his extraordinary investigative skills would almost certainly be needed in the future.

Jesus Martinez was another young police officer, although far more experienced than Matt. He had begun his police career working undercover in the Narcotics Unit, under then Lieutenant David Pekach. He and another young plainclothes officer named Charles McFadden had—"displaying professional skill and extraordinary initiative far beyond that expected of officers of their rank and experience" according to their departmental citations—located and run to earth "with complete disregard of their personal safety" one Gerald Vincent Gallagher, who had shot to death Captain Richard C. "Dutch" Moffitt during an armed robbery.

The resultant publicity had destroyed their ability to function as undercover Narcotics officers, and for that reason, and as a reward for their effective closing of the case of Captain Moffitt's murder (Mr. Gallagher had been cut into several pieces when run over by a subway train as Officers McFadden and Martinez chased him down the subway tracks), they had been transferred to Highway Patrol.

Highway Patrol was considered a very desirable assignment, and officers were normally not considered for Highway Patrol duty until they had from five to seven years of exemplary service. Inasmuch as Captain Moffitt had been Commanding Officer of Highway at the time of his murder, it was generally agreed that the assignment of Officers McFadden and Martinez to Highway was entirely appropriate, their semi-rookie status notwithstanding.

Officer Martinez had ranked seventh on the Examination for Promotion to Detective when he and several hundred other ambitious police officers had taken it, and had been on the same promotion list which elevated Officer Payne to detective. Officer McFadden had not done nearly as well on the examination, and had been pleasantly surprised to find his the last name on the promotion list when it came out.

Detective Payne and Detective McFadden were friends, as were, of course, Detectives

Martinez and McFadden. Detective Payne and Detective Martinez were not friends. Privately, Detective Payne thought of Detective Martinez as a mean little man with a chip on his shoulder, and Detective Martinez thought of Detective Payne as a rich kid with a lot of pull from the Main Line who was playing cop.

Usually—but by no means all the time—Detectives Payne and Martinez kept their dislike for one another under control.

The fourth Detective Personnel space was filled "temporarily" by Police Officer Foster H. Lewis, Jr., twenty-three, who had been on the job even less time than Detective Payne. Officer Lewis, who stood well over six feet tall and weighed approximately 230 pounds and was thus inevitably known as "Tiny," knew more about the workings of the Police Department than either Detective Payne or Detective Martinez. Not only was his father a policeman, but Tiny had, from the time he was eighteen, worked nights and weekends as a police radio operator in the Police Administration Building. He had been in his first year at Temple University Medical School when he decided that what he really wanted to be was a cop, and not a doctor. This decision had pained and greatly annoyed his father, Lieutenant Foster H. Lewis, Sr.

Lieutenant Lewis was also displeased, for several reasons, with Officer Lewis's assignment to the investigations section of the Special Operations Division. He suspected, for one thing, that because of the growing attention being paid to racial discrimination, his son was the token nigger in Special Operations. Jason Washington might have—indeed, almost certainly had—been selected for his professional ability and not because of the color of his skin, but Lieutenant Lewis could think of no reason but his African heritage that had seen his son assigned to Special Operations practically right out of the Police Academy.

And in plain clothes, with an assigned unmarked car, and what looked like unlimited overtime, which caused his take-home pay (Tiny had somewhat smugly announced) to almost equal that of his father.

Lieutenant Lewis believed that officers should rise within the Department, both with regard to rank and desirable assignment, only after having touched all the bases. Rookies went to work in a district, most often starting out in a van, and gained experience on the street dealing with routine police matters, before being given greater responsibilities. He himself had done so.

The fifth personnel space for a detective with the investigations sections of the Special Operations Division was unfilled.

Detective Payne found a drugstore, purchased a Remington battery-powered electric razor and bottles of Old Spice pre-shave and after-shave lotion, and went back to his car.

This was, he thought, the fifth electric razor he had bought in so many months. While certainly his fellow law-enforcement officers were not thieves, it was apparently true that when they found an unaccompanied electric razor in the men's room at the schoolhouse and it was still there two hours later, they chose to believe that the Beard Fairy had intended it as a present for them.

The black Cadillac limousine provided by the taxpayers of Philadelphia to transport their mayor, the Honorable Jerry Carlucci, about in the execution of his official duties came north on South Broad Street, circled City Hall, which sits in the middle of the intersection of Broad and Market streets in the center of America's fourth-largest city, and turned onto the Parkway, which leads past the Philadelphia Museum of Art to, and then along, the Schuylkill River.

The Mayor was wearing a dark blue suit, a stiffly starched, bright-white shirt, a dark, finely figured necktie, highly polished black shoes, and a Smith & Wesson "Chief's Special" .38 Special caliber revolver in a cutaway leather holster attached to his alligator belt.

He shared the backseat of the limousine with his wife, Angeline, who was wearing a simple black dress with a single strand of pearls and a pillbox hat which she had chosen with great care, knowing that what she chose had to be appropriate for both the events on tonight's social calendar.

The evening had begun with the limousine taking them from their home in Chestnut Hill, in the northwest corner of Philadelphia, to the Carto Funeral Home at 2212 South Broad Street in South Philadelphia.

City Councilman the Hon. Anthony J. Cannatello, a longtime friend and political ally of Mayor Carlucci, had been called to his heavenly home after a long and painful battle with prostate cancer, and an appearance at both the viewing and at the funeral tomorrow was considered a necessary expenditure of the Mayor's valuable and limited time. He had planned to be at Carto's for no more than thirty minutes, but it had been well over an hour before he could break free from those who would have felt slighted if there had not been a chance to at least shake his hand.

Councilman Cannatello's many mourners, the Mayor was fully aware, all voted, and all had relatives who voted, and the way things looked—especially considering what was going to be a front-page story in the Monday editions of Philadelphia's four newspapers— the *Bulletin,* the *Ledger,* the *Inquirer,* and the *Daily News*—he was going to need every last one of their votes.

They were now headed back to Chestnut Hill for an entirely different kind of social gathering, this one a festive occasion at which, the Mayor had been informed, the engagement of Miss Martha Peebles to Mr. David R. Pekach would be announced.

It was going from one end of Philadelphia to the other in both geographical and social terms. The invitations, engraved by Bailey, Banks & Biddle, the city's most prominent jewelers and social printers, requesting "The Pleasure of the Company of The Honorable The Mayor of Philadelphia and Mrs. Jerome H. Carlucci at dinner at 606 Glengarry Lane at half past eight o'clock" had been issued in the name of Mr. and Mrs. Brewster Cortland Payne II.

Mr. Payne, a founding partner of Mawson, Payne, Stockton, McAdoo & Lester, arguably Philadelphia's most prestigious law firm, had been a lifelong friend of Miss Peebles's father, the late Alexander F. Peebles. He had been Alex Peebles's personal attorney, and Mawson, Payne, Stockton, McAdoo & Lester served as corporate counsel to Tamaqua Mining, Inc. In Mr. Peebles's obituary in the *Wall Street Journal,* it was said Mr. Peebles's wholly-owned Tamaqua Mining, Inc., not only owned approximately 11.5 percent of the known anthracite coal reserves in the United States, but had other substantial holdings in petrochemical assets and real estate.

A year after Mr. Peebles's death, it was reported by the *Wall Street Journal* that a suit filed by Mr. Peebles's only son, Stephen, challenging his father's last will and testament, in which he had left his entire estate to his daughter, had been discharged with prejudice by the Third United States Court of Appeals, sitting *en banc.*

As was the case in the Mayor's visit to the viewing of the late City Councilman Cannatello at Carto's, the Mayor had both a personal and a political purpose in attending Martha Peebles's dinner. There would certainly be a larger than ordinary gathering of Philadelphia's social and financial elite there, who not only voted, and had friends and relatives who voted, but who were also in a position to contribute to the Mayor's reelection campaign.

Considering what was going to be in Monday's newspapers, it was important that he appear to Martha Peebles's friends to be aware of the situation, and prepared—more important, competent—to deal with it.

Personally, while he did not have the privilege of a close personal friendship with Miss Peebles, he was acquainted with the groom-to-be, Dave Pekach, and privately accorded him about the highest compliment in his repertoire: Dave Pekach was a hell of a good cop.

The Mayor had a thought.

I think Mickey O'Hara's going to be at the Peebles place, but I don't know. *And*

Mickey's just about as good as I am, getting his hands on things he's not supposed to have. I want him to get this straight from me, not from somebody else, and then have him call me and ask about it. And the time to get it to him is now.

He pushed the switch that lowered the sliding glass partition between the passenger's and chauffeur's sections of the limousine, and slid forward off the seat to get close to the opening.

There was a passenger-to-chauffeur telephone in the limousine, but after trying it once to see if it worked, the Mayor had never used it again. He believed that when you can face somebody when you're talking to them, that's the best way.

The very large black man on the passenger side in the chauffeur's compartment, who carried a photo-identification card and badge in a leather folder stating he was Lieutenant J. K. Fellows of the Philadelphia Police Department, had turned when he heard the dividing glass whoosh downward.

"Mayor?"

"Get on the radio and see if you can get a location on Mickey O'Hara," the Mayor ordered.

Lieutenant Fellows nodded, and reached for one of the two microphones mounted just under the dashboard.

As the Mayor slid back against the cushions, his jacket caught on the butt of his revolver. With an easy gesture, as automatic as checking to see that his tie was in place, he knocked the offending garment out of the way.

Jerry Carlucci rarely went anywhere without his pistol.

There were several theories why he did so. One held that he carried it for self-protection; there was always some nut running loose who wanted to get in the history books by shooting some public servant. The Department had just sent off to Byberry State Hospital a looney-tune who thought God had ordered him to blow up the Vice President of the United States. A perfectly ordinary-looking guy who was a Swarthmore graduate and a financial analyst for a bank, for God's sake, who had a couple of hundred pounds of high explosive in his basement and thought God talked to him!

The Mayor did not like to think how much it had cost the Department in just overtime to put that fruitcake in the bag.

A second theory held that he carried it primarily for public relations purposes. This theory was generally advanced by the Mayor's critics, of whom he had a substantial number. "He's never without at least one cop-bodyguard with-a-gun, so what does he need a gun for? Except to get his picture in the papers, 'protecting us,' waving his gun around as if he thinks he's Wyatt Earp or somebody."

The only person who knew the real reason the Mayor elected to go about armed was his wife.

"Do you need that thing?" Angeline Carlucci had asked several years before, in their bedroom, as she watched him deal with the problem, Where does one wear one's revolver when wearing a cummerbund?

"Honey," the Mayor had replied, "I carried a gun for twenty-six years. I feel kind of funny, sort of half-naked, when I don't have it with me."

Mayor Carlucci had begun his career of public service as a police officer, and had held every rank in the Philadelphia Police Department except policewoman before seeking elective office.

Mrs. Carlucci accepted his explanation. So far as she knew, her husband had never lied to her. If she thought that there were perhaps other reasons—she knew it did not hurt him with the voters when his picture, with pistol visible, at some crime site, was published in the papers—she kept her opinion to herself.

"Mary One," Lieutenant Fellows said into the microphone of the Command Band radio.

The response from Police Radio was immediate.

"Mary One," a pleasant, female-sounding voice replied.

"We need a location on Mickey O'Hara," Lieutenant Fellows said.

"Stand by," Police Radio said, and Lieutenant Fellows hung the microphone up as the dividing glass whooshed back into place.

Police Radio, in the person of thirty-seven-year-old Janet Grosse, a civilian with thirteen years on the job, was very familiar with Mr. O'Hara, as well as with what the Mayor's bodyguard—she had recognized Lieutenant Fellows's voice—wanted. He wanted a location on Mickey O'Hara, that and nothing more. He expected her to be smart enough not to go on the air and inquire of every radio-equipped police vehicle in Philadelphia if they had seen Mickey, and if so, where.

Janet had the capability of doing just that, and if it got down to that, she would have to, the result of which would be that the police frequencies would be full with at least a dozen reports of the last time anyone had seen Mickey's antenna-festooned Buick. While he didn't know every cop in Philadelphia, every cop knew him.

And Mickey would be monitoring his police band radios and would learn that they were looking for him. Fellows had said the mayor wanted a location on him, not that he wanted Mickey to know he wanted to know where he was.

Janet thought a moment and then threw a switch on her console which caused her voice to be transmitted over the Highway Band. Only those vehicles assigned to Highway Patrol, plus a very few of the vehicles of the most senior white-shirts, were equipped with Highway Band radios.

"William One," she said.

William One was the call sign of Inspector Peter Wohl. Janet knew that his official vehicle—an unmarked new Ford, which he customarily drove himself—was equipped with an H-Band radio.

There was no answer, which did not surprise Janet, as she had a good hunch where he was, and what he was doing, and consequently that he would not be listening to his radio. Neither was she surprised when a voice came over the H-Band:

"Radio, this is Highway One. William One is out of service. I can get a message to him."

Highway One was the call sign of the vehicle assigned to the Commanding Officer of the Highway Patrol, which was a subordinate unit of the Special Operations Division.

I thought that would happen. William One, Highway One, and just about every senior white-shirt not on duty is in Chestnut Hill tonight. Wohl is having Highway One take his calls.

"Highway One, are you in Chestnut Hill?"

"Right."

"Is Mickey O'Hara there, too?"

"Right."

Bingo! I am a clever girl. Look for a gathering of white-shirts where the free booze is flowing, and there will be Mickey O'Hara.

"That will be all, Highway One. Thank you," Janet said. She switched to the Command Band.

"Mary One."

"Mary One."

"The gentleman is in Chestnut Hill at a party," Janet reported. "Do you need an address?"

"That was quick," Fellows said, laughter in his voice. "No, thanks, I'm sure we can find him with that. Thank you."

"Have a good time," Janet said, and sat back and waited for another call.

"Mayor, Mickey's already at the party."

Mayor Carlucci nodded.

"When we get there, find him. Give me a couple of minutes to circulate, and then ask Mickey if he has a moment for me," the Mayor said, "and bring him over."

"Yes, sir."

There were uniforms—white hats from the Traffic Division, not policemen from the Fourteenth District, which included Chestnut Hill—directing traffic on Glengarry Lane in
Chestnut Hill. The mayoral limousine was quickly waved to the head of the line of cars
waiting to pass through the ornate gates of the five-acre estate. As the Cadillac rolled past,
each uniform saluted and got a wave from the Mayor in return.

The long, curving drive to the turn-of-the-century Peebles mansion was lined with
parked cars, and there a cluster of chauffeurs gathered around a dozen limousines—
including three Rolls Royces, Jerry Carlucci noticed—parked near the mansion itself.

*If is wasn't for what's going to be on the front page of every newspaper in town
tomorrow,* the Mayor thought, *tonight would be a real opportunity. Now all I can hope for
is to minimize the damage, keep these people from wondering whether they're betting on
the wrong horse.*

There was a man in a dinner jacket collecting invitations just outside the door. He
didn't ask for the Mayor's, confirming the Mayor's suspicion that he looked familiar, and
was probably a retired police officer, now working as a rent-a-cop for Wachenhut Security, or something like that.

The reception line consisted of Mr. and Mrs. Brewster Cortland Payne II, Miss Martha
Peebles, and Mr.—Captain—David Pekach.

"Mrs. Carlucci, Mr. Mayor," Payne said. "How nice to see you."

Payne and Pekach were wearing dinner jackets.

Probably most everybody here will be wearing a monkey suit but me, the Mayor
thought. *But it couldn't be helped. I couldn't have shown up at Tony Connatello's viewing
wearing a monkey suit and looking like I was headed right from the funeral home to a
fancy party.*

"We're happy to be here, Mr. Payne."

"You know my wife, don't you? And Miss Peebles?"

"How are you, Angeline?" Mrs. Patricia Payne said. "I like your dress."

Patricia Payne and Martha Peebles were dressed similarly, in black, off-the-shoulder
cocktail dresses. The Peebles woman had a double string of large pearls reaching to the
valley of her breasts, and Mrs. Payne a single strand of pearls.

Nice chest, the Mayor thought, vis-à-vis Miss Peebles. *Nice-looking woman. She'd be
a real catch for Dave Pekach even without all that money.*

And then, slightly piqued: *Yeah, of course I know your wife. I've known her longer
than you have. I carried her first husband's casket out of St. Dominic's when we buried
him. And as long as we've known each other, isn't it about time you started calling me
"Jerry"?*

"How is it, Patricia," Angeline Carlucci spoke truthfully, "that you still look like
a girl?"

The Mayor had a sudden clear mental image of the white, grief-stricken face of the young
widow of Sergeant John X. Moffitt, blown away by a scumbag when answering a silent
alarm at a gas station, as they lowered his casket into the ground in St. Dominic's cemetery.

*A long time ago. Twenty-five years ago. I was Captain of Highway when Jack Moffitt
got killed.*

*Angie's right. She does look good. Real good. She's a Main Line lady now, a long way
from being a cop's widow living with her family off Roosevelt Boulevard.*

"I'm so glad you could come," Martha Peebles said to Angeline Carlucci.

"Oh, Jerry wouldn't have missed it for the world," Angeline said.

"No, I wouldn't," the Mayor agreed. "Thank you for having us, Miss Peebles."

"Oh, Martha, please," she said as she took his hand.

Then the Mayor put his hand out to Captain Pekach.

"Don't you look spiffy, Dave," he said.

"Mr. Mayor."

"There's a rumor going around that some unfortunate girl who doesn't know what she's getting into has agreed to marry you. Anything to it?"

Martha Peebles giggled. Dave Pekach looked at her and smiled uneasily at the Mayor but didn't reply.

A waiter in a white jacket stood at the end of the reception line holding a tray of champagne glasses. Angeline took one. The waiter, seeing the indecision on the Mayor's face, said, "There is a bar in the sitting room to your left, Mr. Mayor."

"A little champagne will do just fine," the Mayor said, and took a glass. "But thank you."

9.

It took the Mayor five minutes to work his way through the entrance foyer to the bar in the sitting room, and another five to find somebody he could leave Angie with and then to reach his destination.

In descending order of importance, he wished to have a word with Chief Inspector Dennis V. Coughlin, Chief Inspector Matthew Lowenstein, and Inspector Peter Wohl. It would have been his intention to first find Denny or Matt and then send Fellows to fetch the others, but luck was with him. The three were standing together in a corner of the sitting room—*not surprising, birds of a feather, et cetera*—and there was a bonus. With them were Chief Inspector (Retired) August Wohl, Detective Matthew M. Payne, and Mr. Michael J. O'Hara of the *Bulletin*.

Chiefs Coughlin, Lowenstein, and Wohl were in business suits. Inspector Wohl and Detective Payne were in monkey suits. Mr. O'Hara was wearing a plaid sports coat of the type worn by the gentlemen who offer suggestions on the wagers one should make at a racetrack.

Not surprising, the Mayor thought. *Dave Pekach works for Peter Wohl, and Peter would have probably rented a monkey suit for this if he didn't have one, and he probably has his own, because he's a bachelor, and doesn't have a family to support and can afford a monkey suit. And Detective Payne not only is also a bachelor with no family to support, but doesn't have to worry about living on a detective's pay anyway. His father—what was the way they put it? His* adoptive father, *he adopted him when he married Patty Moffitt—is Brewster Cortland Payne II.*

The Mayor handed Inspector Wohl his champagne glass.

"Get rid of this for me, will you, Mac?" he asked, as if he thought anybody in a monkey suit had to be a waiter. "Get me a weak scotch, and get my friends another round of whatever they're drinking."

"Good evening, Mr. Mayor," Peter Wohl said, as the others laughed.

"My God, my mistake!" the Mayor said in mock horror. "What we have here is a cop in a monkey suit. I would never have recognized him."

"Two, Jerry," Chief Wohl said. "Three counting Dave Pekach. The Department's getting some class."

As Mayor Carlucci had risen through the ranks of the Police Department he had had Chief Inspector Wohl as his mentor and protector. The phrase used was that "Wohl was Carlucci's rabbi." It was said, quietly of course, but quite accurately, that Chief Wohl had not only helped Carlucci's career prosper, but had on at least two occasions kept it from being terminated.

And Inspector, and then Chief Inspector, and then Deputy Commissioner, and ultimately Commissioner Carlucci had been rabbi to Chiefs Coughlin and Lowenstein as they had worked their way up in the hierarchy. Detective Payne, it was universally recognized, had two rabbis, Chief Coughlin and Inspector Wohl.

Payne's relationship with Wohl was the traditional one. Wohl saw in him a good cop, one who, with guidance and experience, could become a good senior police official. His relationship with Chief Dennis V. Coughlin was something different. Coughlin had been John Francis Xavier Moffitt's best friend since they had been at the Police Academy. He had been the best man at his wedding, and he had gone to tell Patricia Moffitt, pregnant with Matt, that her husband had been killed. Just about everyone—including Jerry Carlucci—had thought it certain that after a suitable period, the Widow Moffitt would marry her late husband's best friend. You didn't have to be Sherlock Holmes to tell from the way he looked at her, and talked about her, how he felt about her.

Patty Moffitt had instead met Brewster Cortland Payne II, an archetypical Main Line WASP, in whose father's law firm she had found work as a typist. He had been widowed four months previously when his wife had died in a traffic accident returning from their summer cottage in the Poconos.

Their marriage had enraged both families. Having lost a mate was not considered sufficient cause to marry hastily, and across a vast chasm of social and religious differences. It was generally agreed that the marriage would not, could not, last, and that was the reason many offered for Denny Coughlin never having married: he was still waiting for Patty Moffitt.

The marriage endured. Payne adopted Matthew Mark Moffitt and gave him his name and his love. Denny Coughlin never married. He and Brewster Payne became friends, and he was Uncle Denny to all the Payne children.

The Mayor shook everybody's hand. A waiter appeared. The Mayor gave him his champagne glass and asked for a weak scotch. Inspector Wohl and Detective Payne both took champagne from the waiter's tray.

"How ya doing, Mayor?" Mickey O'Hara asked.

"Take a look at this," the Mayor said as he took a newspaper clipping from his pocket and handed it to O'Hara, "and make a guess."

O'Hara read the story, then handed it back to the Mayor, who handed it to Chief Wohl. "You all better read it," the Mayor said.

MORE UNSOLVED MURDERS; NO ARRESTS AND 'NO COMMENT'

By Charles E. Whaley
PHILADELPHIA LEDGER STAFF WRITER

Capt. Henry C. Quaire, commanding officer of the Homicide Unit of the Philadelphia Police Department, refused to comment on rumors circulating through the police department that a homicide detective is under investigation for the brutal murder of Police Officer Jerome H. Kellog. Chief Inspector Matthew Lowenstein, who heads the Detective Bureau of the Police Department, was "out of town on official business" when this reporter attempted to contact him.

Kellog, 33, who was assigned to the Narcotics Unit, was found Friday morning in his home at 300 West Luray Street in the Feltonville section, dead of multiple gunshot wounds to the head. His death has been classified as "a willful death," which is police parlance for murder.

Rumors began almost immediately to circulate that an unnamed Homicide United detective, who is allegedly involved with Officer Kellog's estranged wife, is a prime suspect in the killing.

Although a large number of his fellow police officers called to pay their last respects to Officer Kellog at the John F. Fluehr & Sons Funeral Home this afternoon, including more than a dozen middle-ranking police supervisors, none of the police department's most senior officers were present.

Their absence fueled another rumor, that Officer Kellog was not to be accorded the elaborate funeral rites, sometimes called an "Inspector's Funeral," normally given to a police officer killed in the line of duty.

Capt. Robert F. Talley, Commanding Office of the Narcotics Unit, who made a brief appearance at the funeral home visitation, accompanying Officer Kellog's widow, refused comment.

Captain Quaire, when asked if the denial to Officer Kellog of an "Inspector's Funeral" suggested that his death was not in the line of duty, said that as far as he knew, no decision had been made in the matter. He stated that Police Commissioner Taddeus Czernich was the official who authorized, or denied, an official police funeral, and that all questions on the subject should be referred to him.

Commissioner Czernich's office, when contacted, said the Commissioner was out of the office, and they had no idea when he would be available to answer questions from the press.

Kellog will be buried tomorrow in Lawnview Cemetery, in Rockledge, following funeral services at the Memorial Presbyterian Church of Fox Chase.

Quaire also said that the Homicide Unit was "actively involved" in the investigation of the murders of Mrs. Alicia Atchison and Anthony J. Marcuzzi in a downtown restaurant shortly after midnight last night, but the police as yet have been unable to identify, much less arrest, the two men who were identified by Gerald N. Atchison, Mrs. Atchison's husband, and the proprietor of the restaurant, as the murderers.

"Why are you surprised?" O'Hara asked. "You know the *Ledger*'s after you."

"I don't care if they go after me," the Mayor said, "but putting in the paper that his widow has been messing around, that's pretty goddamned low. Did you hear those rumors?"

O'Hara nodded.

"Did you write about them?" the Mayor asked. "Or feel your readers had the right to know that the widow was carrying on with some cop?"

O'Hara shook his head.

"There you go, Mick," the Mayor said with satisfaction. "In that one goddamn story, that sonofabitch writes that the widow is a tramp . . ."

"That's a little strong, Jerry," Chief Wohl protested.

"What do you call a married woman who sleeps with another man?" the Mayor asked sarcastically. "And while we're on that subject, Lowenstein, how is it that neither you nor Quaire told Detective Milham to keep his pecker in his pocket?"

Chief Lowenstein's face colored.

"Jerry, I don't consider that sort of thing any of my business," he said.

"Maybe you should," the Mayor snapped. "I don't know if I'd want a detective around me whose wife divorced him for carrying on with her sister, and the next thing you know is playing hide-the-salami with a brother officer's wife. It says something about his character, wouldn't you say?"

Lowenstein's face was now red.

Chief Wohl touched Lowenstein's arm to stop any response. The worst possible course of action when dealing with an angry Jerry Carlucci was to argue with him.

"Take it easy, Jerry," Chief Wohl said.

Matt Payne glanced at Chief Coughlin. Coughlin made a movement with his head that could have been a signal for him to leave the group. He was considering this possibility when his attention was diverted by the Mayor's angry voice:

"Who the hell are you to tell me to take it easy?"

"Well, for one thing, I'm bigger than you are," Chief Wohl said with a smile, "and for another, smarter. And better-looking."

Carlucci glowered at him.

"Matty," Chief Coughlin said. "Your girlfriend's looking daggers at you. Maybe you better go pay some attention to her."

Matt looked around but could not find Penny Detweiler. He wasn't surprised. Coughlin was telling him a lowly detective should not be here, where he would be privy to what looked like a major confrontation between senior white-shirts and the Mayor of Philadelphia.

"Excuse me," he said.

"You've been doing some good work, Payne," the Mayor said. "It hasn't gone unnoticed." Carlucci waited until Matt was out of earshot.

"You know what that young man did? Not for publication, Mickey?"

"No," O'Hara replied with a chuckle. "What did that young man do, not for publication?"

"Peter here's been running a surveillance operation," Carlucci began.

"Surveilling who?" O'Hara interrupted.

"I'll get to that in a minute. Anyway, they had a microphone mounted to a window, and it got knocked off. The window was on the thirteenth floor, I forgot to say. So what does Payne do? He goes to the room next door to the one where the mike fell off, goes out on a ledge, and puts it back in place. How's that for balls, Mickey?"

"I hadn't heard about that," Chief Coughlin said, looking at Peter Wohl.

"Either had I," Peter said.

"He knew what had to be done, and he did it," the Mayor said approvingly. "That's the mark of a good cop."

"Or a damned fool," O'Hara said. "It was that important?"

"What the hell could be that important? He could have killed himself," Coughlin said.

"The way it turned out, it was that important," Carlucci said. "If he hadn't put the mike back, we wouldn't have got what we got after he put it back. Tony Harris told me that when he gave me the tapes this morning."

"Which is what?" Coughlin asked.

"Enough, Tony Callis tells me, to just about guarantee a true bill from the grand jury and an indictment."

The Hon. Thomas J. "Tony" Callis was the District Attorney for Philadelphia County.

"Of who?" O'Hara asked.

"Not yet, Mickey, but you will be the first to know, trust me. The warrants are being drawn up. Peter, I think you should let Payne go with you when you and Weisbach serve them; he's entitled."

When I and Weisbach serve them? Wohl thought. *What the hell is that all about?*

"Serve them on who?" O'Hara asked.

"I told you, Mickey, you'll be the first to know, but not right now. For right now, you can have this." The Mayor reached in his pocket and handed O'Hara a folded sheet of paper. "I understand the first of these will be given out first thing in the morning. You don't know where you got that," he said.

O'Hara unfolded the sheet of paper. It was a press release.

POLICE DEPARTMENT

———

CITY OF PHILADELPHIA

———

FOR IMMEDIATE RELEASE:

   Police Commissioner Taddeus Czernich today announced a major reorganization of the self-policing functions of the Police Department, to take effect with the retirement of Chief Inspector Harry Allgood, presently the Commanding Officer of the Internal Affairs Division. Chief Allgood's retirement will become effective tomorrow.

   "The public's faith in the absolute integrity of its police department is our most important weapon in the war against crime," Commissioner Czernich declared.

> "A new unit, the Ethical Affairs Unit (EAU), has been formed. It will be commanded by Staff Inspector Michael Weisbach, who will report directly to me on matters concerning any violation of the high ethical standards of behavior demanded of our police officers by the public, myself and Mayor Carlucci," Commissioner Czernich went on.
>
> "I have directed Inspector Peter Wohl, Commanding Officer of the Special Operations Division, to make available to Staff Inspector Weisbach whatever he requires to accomplish his new mission from the assets of Special Operations, which includes the Highway Patrol, the Anti-Crime Teams, and the Special Operations Investigation Section.
>
> "Internal Affairs will continue to deal with complaints from the public regarding inappropriate actions on the part of police officers," Commissioner Czernich concluded.

"What is that, Jerry?" Chief Wohl asked.

"Show it to him, Mickey," the Mayor replied. O'Hara handed it to him.

"I can use this now, or am I supposed to sit on it until everybody else gets it?" O'Hara asked.

"You can use what? I didn't give you anything," Carlucci said.

"OK," O'Hara replied. "I would like to be there, Peter, when you and Weisbach serve your warrants."

"I'm sure Peter can arrange that, Mickey," the Mayor said. "Can't you, Peter?"

"Yes, sir," Wohl said as he took the press release from his father and started to read it.

"I wouldn't be at all surprised if you could find Staff Inspector Weisbach at Peter's office in the morning," the Mayor said.

"I got to go find a phone," O'Hara said.

"Matt," Carlucci said to Chief Lowenstein, "are you having problems with Commissioner Czernich's reorganization plan?"

" 'Commissioner Czernich's reorganization plan'?" Lowenstein quoted mockingly. "Hell no, Jerry. I know where the Commissioner gets his ideas, and I wouldn't dream of questioning his little inspirations."

Chief Wohl chuckled.

"But I would like to know what the hell's going on," Lowenstein added.

"Well, apparently the Commissioner thought that since Allgood decided to retire, Internal Affairs needed some reorganization."

"Why?" Lowenstein pursued.

"To put a point on it, Matt, because it wasn't doing the job it's supposed to do."

"You got something specific?"

"Yeah, I got something specific," Carlucci said unpleasantly. "That surveillance Peter has been running, that tape I got this morning, because Payne climbed out on a ledge and put the microphone back? It recorded a conversation between Lieutenant Seymour Meyer of Central Police Division's Vice Squad—your friend, Matt—and Paulo Cassandro. You know who Paulo Cassandro is, right?"

"Take it easy, Jerry," Chief Wohl said.

"I know who Paulo Cassandro is," Lowenstein said softly.

"What they were talking about, Matt, was that Meyer and his good buddy, Captain Vito Cazerra—you know Cazerra, don't you, Matt? He commands the Sixth District?"

Lowenstein didn't reply.

"I asked you if you know Captain Cazerra," the Mayor said nastily.

"Yeah. I know him," Lowenstein said.

"As I was saying, we now have a tape of Meyer telling Cassandro that he and Cazerra don't think they're getting a big enough payoff from the mob for letting a Polack whore from Hazleton named Harriet Osadchy run a call-girl operation in our better hotels. You know Harriet Osadchy, Matt?"

"No, I don't know her," Lowenstein said.

"We also have what must be a couple of *miles* of tape of your friend Meyer in the sack with a half-dozen of Harriet Osadchy's whores."

"Jesus!" Lowenstein said.

"Now, I know and you know and Commissioner Czernich knows how hard it is to catch somebody actually taking money. But the Commissioner was very disappointed to learn that Internal Affairs didn't take a close look at Meyer even after they got an anonymous call about the sonofabitch screwing Osadchy's whores in every hotel in Center City."

"They get all kinds of anonymous—"

"Goddamn it, Matt," Carlucci flared, "don't you start to make excuses."

"—calls," Lowenstein went on, undaunted. "A lot of them from disgruntled people just trying to make trouble."

"Yeah, well, this disgruntled person—Peter thinks he's a retired cop working as hotel security—was so disgruntled that after he called Internal Affairs twice and nothing happened, he wrote me a letter."

"And you put your own private detective bureau to work on it," Lowenstein said bitterly.

"My own detective bureau?" Carlucci replied icily. "I don't know what you're talking about, Lowenstein. But if you have a problem with Commissioner Czernich asking Special Operations to look into something I gave him that neither your detective bureau nor Internal Affairs seem to even have heard about, why don't you ask for an appointment with the Commissioner and discuss it with him?"

There was a tense moment when it looked as if Chief Lowenstein, who had locked eyes with the Mayor, was going to reply.

"Jerry, what's the relationship between EAU and Special Operations—I guess I mean between Peter and Weisbach—going to be under this reorganization?" Chief Wohl asked.

Did he ask that to change the subject to something safer? Peter Wohl wondered. *Or does he see it as a threat to my career?*

The question clearly distracted Mayor Carlucci. He glanced at Chief Wohl in confusion.

"Just a minute, Augie," Carlucci said, turning back to lock eyes with Lowenstein again.

"Lowenstein and I were talking about the Commissioner," he went on. "The Commissioner and I were discussing the Overnights this morning. When he can find the time, he brings them by my office, to keep me abreast of things."

It was common knowledge that at whatever time in the morning the Mayor of Philadelphia arrived at his office, he could expect to find the Police Commissioner of Philadelphia waiting for him in his outer office. The Police Commissioner's own day began when the Mayor was through with him.

"And the Commissioner had an idea. You saw the Overnights this morning, Chief Lowenstein?"

Lowenstein nodded.

"Excuse me? I didn't hear you, Chief."

"Yes, sir, I saw the Overnights," Lowenstein said.

"The double murder in the Inferno Lounge on Market Street? Did that catch your eye?"

"I was at the scene."

"Oh, yeah, that's right. Then you know that Detective Payne was the first police officer on the scene?"

"I saw that."

"Well, the Commissioner saw it too, and he asked me, what did I think of asking Peter, when he could spare him, of course, to send Payne over to Homicide to help Detective

Milham on the investigation. Milham has the job, right? Your detective who can't keep his pecker in his pocket?"

"Detective Milham has the job," Lowenstein said, flat-voiced.

"Yeah, right. Well, the Commissioner said that maybe if Peter sent Payne over there, Payne might learn something about how a Homicide investigation is conducted. And he's a bright kid, he might learn some other things, too. About other investigations Homicide is running, for example. Things that would be of interest to Peter and Weisbach in carrying out their new responsibilities."

"You realize the hell of a spot you'd be putting the kid in, Jerry, sending him into Homicide that way? There'd be a lot of resentment," Chief Wohl said.

"Augie, I'm sure the Commissioner has considered that," the Mayor replied. "So anyway, I told the Commissioner that he's the Police Commissioner, he can run the Department any way he pleases, do what he wants. If the Commissioner does decide to ask Inspector Wohl to send Detective Payne over there, are you going to have any problem with that, Chief Lowenstein?"

Lowenstein now had his temper and voice under control.

"I have no problem, Mr. Mayor, with any decision of Commissioner Czernich," he said.

"Good," the Mayor said. "What do they call that? 'Cheerful, willing obedience'?" He turned to Chief Wohl. "You were asking, Augie, what Peter's relationship with the Ethical Affairs Unit is going to be?"

"That press release wasn't very clear about that."

"I thought it was perfectly clear. Peter and Weisbach have worked together before, and I can't imagine they'll have any problems."

Oh, shit! Peter thought. *What that means is that I'll be in the worst possible position. I'll have the responsibility, but no authority.*

"I thought I taught you years ago, Jerry," Chief Wohl said, as if he had been reading his son's mind, "that the worst thing you can do to a supervisor is give him responsibility without the necessary authority."

The Mayor's face suggested he didn't like to be reminded that anyone had ever taught him anything.

"Maybe you're right, Augie," Carlucci said. "Maybe that wasn't clear. I thought it was. Ethical Affairs Unit is under Special Operations. Weisbach reports directly to me, but he works for Peter. You understand that, Peter?"

"Yes, sir."

Carlucci looked around the room.

"Ah, there's Angie," he said. "I better go join her. She doesn't like it when I stay away too long."

He walked away from them.

"Jesus Christ!" Chief Lowenstein said when he was out of earshot.

"My sentiments exactly, Chief," Peter Wohl said.

"That crap about sending Payne to Homicide was a last-minute inspiration of his," Lowenstein said.

"That was to remind you who runs the Department," Chief Wohl said. "He thought maybe you'd forgotten."

"I know who runs the Department," Lowenstein said.

"You shouldn't have argued with him," Chief Wohl said. "First about Seymour Meyer, and then about Wally Milham. He knows that Meyer is dirty, and thinks Milham is. And he's never wrong, especially when he's hot under the collar. You know that, Matt."

"Christ," Lowenstein said.

"That's what the whole business of sending Payne to Homicide is all about," Chief Wohl went on. "He couldn't think of anything, right then, that would piss you off more, and remind you who runs the Department."

"I'm sorry, sir," the stocky man in a dinner jacket said with a smile, as he saw two young formally dressed couples coming down the second-floor corridor of the Peebles mansion, "this part of the house has been closed off for the evening."

"It's all right," Matt Payne replied, "I'm a police officer, checking on the firearms collection."

The reply was clearly not expected by the stocky man.

"I'll have to see some identification, please," he said.

"Certainly," Matt said, showing his badge. "You're Wachenhut?"

Daffy (Mrs. Chadwich T.) Nesbitt IV giggled.

"Pinkerton," the stocky man said, stepping out of the way.

"Thank you," Matt said, putting his badge holder away and reclaiming the hand of Miss Penelope Detweiler. He led her and the Nesbitts almost to the end of the long corridor, and then opened a door to the right.

"You could fight a war with the guns in here," Matt said as he switched on the lights and signaled for Penny to walk in.

"Jesus," Chad said. "Look at them!"

"That was disgusting," Penny said.

"What was disgusting, love of my life?" Matt asked. There was a strain in his voice.

"We're not supposed to be in here," Penny said.

"Look," he said. "Chad wanted to see the guns. If we had gone to Martha—if we had been able to find Martha in that mob downstairs—and asked her if we could look at the guns, she would have said, 'sure,' and we would have come up here, and the Pinkerton guy wouldn't have let us in without written authorization, whereupon I would have showed him my badge. OK?"

"You think that damned badge makes you something special," Penny said.

"Penny, sometimes you're a pain in the ass," Matt said.

"Hey!" Daffy said. "Stop it, you two!"

"The cabinets are locked," Chad said in disappointment.

"They lock up the crown jewels of England, too," Matt said. "Something about them being valuable."

"Are these things valuable?" Penny asked.

"Some of the antiques are really worth money," Matt said. "Museum stuff."

"But what did he do with all of them?" Penny asked.

"Looked at them," Matt said. "Just . . . took pleasure in having them."

"What the hell is this?" Chad asked, looking down into a glass-topped, felt-lined display case. "It looks like a sniper rifle, without a scope."

Matt went and looked.

"That one I know," he said. "The Great White Hunter showed me that one himself. It's a .30 caliber—note that I did not say .30-06—Springfield, Model of 1900. When Roosevelt, the first Roosevelt, came back from Cuba and got himself elected President—"

"What in the world are you talking about?" Penny demanded.

"Turn your mouth off automatic, all right? I'm talking to Chad."

"Screw you!"

"Before I was so rudely interrupted, Chad: When Roosevelt made the Ordnance Corps pay Mauser for a license to manufacture bolt actions based on the Spanish 7mm they used in Cuba, the Springfield Arsenal made a trial run. Twenty rifles, I think he said. One of them they gave to Roosevelt, who was then President. That's it. Christ only knows how much it's worth. Martha's father told me it took him three years to talk Roosevelt's daughter into selling it to him once he found out she had it."

"Are we finished here?" Penny asked.

"Penny!" Daffy said.

"We are not finished here, love of my life," Matt said, not at all pleasantly. "You may be, but I have just begun to give Chad the tour."

"I want to go back downstairs. I'm bored up here."

"And I'm bored down there."

"You didn't seem to be bored when you were sucking up to the Mayor."

"Have a nice time downstairs, Penelope," Matt said. "Don't let the doorknob hit you in the ass on your way out."

Penny extended her right hand, with the center finger in an extended upward position, the others folded, and walked out of the arms room.

"You're right, Matthew my boy," Chadwich Thomas Nesbitt IV said. "On occasion, and this is obviously one of them, our beloved Penny can be a flaming pain in the ass."

"I suspect it may be that time of the month," Matt said.

Chad laughed.

"The both of you are disgusting!" Daffy said. "I'm going with Penny."

"Mind what Matt said about the doorknob, darling," Chad said.

"You bastard!" Mrs. Nesbitt said, and marched out.

"I am tempted," Matt said, "to repeat the old saw that there would be a bounty on them, if they didn't have—"

"Don't!" Chad interrupted, laughing. "I'm too tired to have to fight to defend the honor of the mother-to-be of my children."

Ten minutes later, as Matt, having successfully gotten through the lock on one of the pistol cabinets, was showing Chad a mint-collection, low-serial-numbered Colt Model 1911 self-loader, Inspector Peter Wohl came into the gun room, trailed by Mrs. C. T. Nesbitt IV and Miss Penelope Detweiler.

"My God, she called the cops!" Matt said, the wit of which remark getting through only to Mr. Nesbitt.

"I asked Penny if she knew where you were," Wohl said. "Got a minute, Matt?"

"Yes, sir. Sure. You know Chad, don't you?"

"Hello, Nesbitt. How are you?"

"Inspector."

"Could you give us a minute?"

"Certainly," Chad said. "I'll be outside."

Wohl waited until they had gone and had closed the door behind them.

"You ever see one of these?" Matt asked, holding the Model 1911 out to Wohl.

"I just heard about you climbing out on the ledge at the Bellvue, you damned fool," Wohl said.

After a just-perceptible hesitation, Matt asked, "Who told you? Harris?"

"Actually, it was the Mayor. Harris told the Mayor and the Mayor told me."

"The Mayor?"

"The Mayor thinks it makes you a cop with great big balls," Wohl said. "I wanted to make sure you understand that in my book it makes you a goddamned fool."

Matt didn't reply for a moment.

"Inspector—"

"Just when I start to think that maybe you've started to grow up, you do something like that. Jesus H. Christ, Matt!"

"Are you willing to listen to me telling you that ledge was eighteen inches wide?"

"Be in my office at quarter to seven in the morning," Wohl said.

"Yes, sir."

"You and Staff Inspector Mike Weisbach are going to serve a warrant of arrest on Lieutenant Seymour Meyer."

"We are? All of a sudden? What happened? Who's Weisbach?"

"This is in the nature of a reward," Wohl said. "I have been ordered by the Mayor to let you in on the arrest. He thinks your goddamned fool stunt on the ledge entitles you, because at two A.M., Paulo Cassandro and Meyer had an angry discussion, during which they mentioned names and specific sums and Meyer's oral sexual proclivities, all of which were recorded by the microphone you put back in place."

"No crap? We got 'em?"

"If it was up to me, tomorrow morning you'd be back on recovered stolen automobiles."

"Ah, come on, Inspector!"

"If you had fallen off that ledge, Supercop, or if you had been seen up there, all the time and money and effort we spent trying to get Meyer would have gone down the toilet. The conversation we got, or one just as incriminating, would have been repeated in a day or two. Don't you start patting yourself on the back. You acted like a goddamned fool, not like a detective with enough sense to find his ass with both hands."

He locked eyes with Matt until Matt gave in and shrugged his shoulders in chagrin.

"Quarter to seven, Detective Payne," Wohl said. "Have a nice night."

He walked out of the gun room.

Matt replaced the Colt Model 1911 in its cabinet, and was trying to put the cabinet lock back in place when Chad, Penny, and Daffy came back in the room.

"You are forgiven, Penelope," Matt said. "Out of the goodness of my heart. It will not be necessary for you to grovel in tears at my feet."

"What was that business about a ledge at the Bellvue?" Penny asked.

"Does he often call you a goddamned fool?" Chad inquired.

"No comment," Matt said, chuckling, trying desperately but not quite succeeding in making a joke of it.

"What was that all about?"

"He wants to see me at quarter to seven in his office, that's all."

"That's not what it sounded like, buddy." Chad chuckled.

"Tomorrow we're going to play golf!" Penny said. "Tomorrow's your day off. With Tom and Ginny."

"Tomorrow, like the man said, I will be in Wohl's office at quarter to seven. We'll just have to make our excuses to Tom and Ginny. Are they here?"

"We are going to be at Merion at nine," Penny said flatly.

"Chad, how do you feel about an early round?" Matt asked.

"Matt, I mean it!" Penny said.

"Or what, Penny? This is out of my control. I'm sorry, but I'm a cop."

"*You're sorry?* Your precious Inspector Wohl is not the only one who thinks you're a goddamned fool!" Penny said.

"Would you like the goddamned fool to take you home, Penny? I've had about all of you I can stand for one night."

"I'll get home by myself, thank you very much," Penny said.

"Oh, come on, you two," Daffy said.

"Come on, hell!" Penny said, and walked out of the gun room.

"You better go after her, Matt," Daffy said.

"Why? To get more of the same crap she's been giving me all night?"

"She's really angry with you, Matt."

"Frankly, my dear," Matt said, in decent mimicry of Clark Gable in *Gone With the Wind,* "I don't give a damn."

10.

Chief Inspector Dennis V. Coughlin looked at Chief Inspector August Wohl (Retired) and then at Inspector Peter Wohl, shrugged, and said, "OK. I'll call him."

He leaned forward on Peter Wohl's white leather couch for the telephone. He stopped. "I don't have his home phone," he said.

"I've got it," Peter Wohl said. "In my bedroom."

He pushed himself out of one of the two matching white leather armchairs and walked into his bedroom.

"I don't like this, Augie," Denny Coughlin said.

"It took place on his watch," Chief Wohl said. "He was getting the big bucks to make sure things like this don't happen."

"Big bucks!" Coughlin snorted. "I wonder what's going to happen to him?"

"By one o'clock tomorrow afternoon, he will be transferred to Night Commmand. Unless the Mayor has one of his Italian tantrums again, in which case I don't know."

Peter Wohl came back in his living room with a sheet of paper and handed it to Coughlin.

"How did I wind up having to do this?" Coughlin asked.

"Peter's not senior enough, and the Mayor likes you," Chief Wohl said.

"Jesus," Coughlin said. He ran his fingers down the list of private, official, home telephone numbers of the upper hierarchy of the Philadelphia Police Department, found what he was looking for, and dialed the number of Inspector Gregory F. Sawyer, Jr.

Inspector Sawyer was the Commanding Officer of the Central Police Division, which geographically encompasses Center City Philadelphia south of the City Hall. It supervises the Sixth and Ninth police districts, each of which is commanded by a captain. The Sixth District covers the area between Poplar Street on the north and South Street on the south from Broad Street east to the Delaware River, and the Ninth covers the area west of Broad Street between South and Poplar to the Schuylkill River. Its command is generally regarded as a stepping-stone to higher rank; both Chief Wohl and Chief Coughlin had in the past commanded the Central District.

"Barbara, this is Denny Coughlin," Chief Coughlin said into the telephone. "I hate to bother you at home, but I have to speak to Greg."

Chief Wohl leaned forward from his white leather armchair, picked up a bottle of Bushmills Irish whiskey, and generously replenished the glass in front of Denny Coughlin.

"Greg? Denny. Sorry to bother you at home with this, but I didn't want to take the chance of missing you in the morning. We need you, the Commanding Officer of the Sixth, Sy Meyer, a plainclothesman of his named Palmerston, and a Sixth District uniform named Crater at Peter Wohl's office at eight tomorrow morning."

"What's going on, Denny?" Inspector Sawyer inquired, loudly enough so that Chief Wohl and his son could hear.

"There was an incident," Coughlin began, visibly uncomfortable with having to lie, "involving somebody who had Jerry Carlucci's unlisted number. He wants a report from me by noon tomorrow. I figured Wohl's office was the best place to get everybody together as quietly as possible."

"An incident? What kind of an incident?"

"I don't know. I didn't hear about it myself until I saw the Mayor tonight. I guess we'll all find out tomorrow." He paused. "Greg, I probably don't have to tell you this, but don't start your own investigation tonight, OK?"

"Jesus Christ! I haven't heard a goddamned thing."

"Don't feel bad, either did I. Eight o'clock, Greg."

"I'll be there," Inspector Sawyer said.

"Good night, Greg."

"Good night, Denny."

Coughlin put the telephone back in its cradle and picked up his drink.

"Why the hell is my conscience bothering me?" he asked.

"It shouldn't," Chief Wohl said. "Not your conscience."

———

Officer Charles F. Crater, who lived with his wife Joanne and their two children (Angela, three, and Charles, Jr., eighteen months) in a row house at the 6200 block of Crafton Street in the Mayfair section of Philadelphia, was asleep at 7:15 A.M. when Corporal George T. Peterson of the Sixth District telephoned his home and asked to speak to him.

Mrs. Crater told Corporal Peterson that her husband had worked the four-to-twelve tour and it had been after two when he got home.

"I know, but something has come up, and I have to talk to him," Corporal Peterson replied. "It's important, Mrs. Crater."

Two minutes later, sleepy-eyed, dressed in a cotton bathrobe under which it could be seen that he had been sleeping in his underwear, Officer Crater picked up the telephone.

"What's up?" he asked.

"Charley, do you know where Special Operations Headquarters is?"

"Frankford and Castor?"

"Right. Be there at eight o'clock. See the Sergeant."

"Jesus," Crater said, looking at his watch. "It's quarter after seven. What's going on?"

"Wait a minute," Corporal Peterson said. "Charley, the Sergeant says to send a car for you. Be waiting when it gets there."

"What's going on?"

"Hold it a minute, Charley," Corporal Peterson said.

Sergeant Mario Delacroce came on the line.

"Crater, you didn't get this from me," he said. "All I know is that we got a call from Central Division saying to have you at Special Operations at eight this morning. What I *hear* is that Special Operations has got some operation coming off on your beat, and they want to talk to you."

"What kind of an operation?"

"Charley, Central Division don't confide in me, they just tell me what they want done. There'll be a car at your house in fifteen minutes. Be waiting for it. You want a little advice, put on a clean uniform and have a fresh shave."

"Right," Charley Crater said.

He put the telephone back in its cradle.

"What was that all about?" Joanne Crater asked, concern in her voice.

"Ah, those goddamned Special Operations hotshots are running some kind of operation on my beat, and they want to talk to me," Charley said.

"Talk to you about what?"

"Who knows?" Charley said. "They think their shit don't stink."

"I really wish you'd clean up your language, Charley."

"Sorry," he said. "Honey, I got to catch a quick shave and get dressed. Have I got a fresh uniform?"

"Yeah, there's one I picked up yesterday."

As he went up the stairs to his bedroom, Officer Crater had a very unpleasant thought: *Maybe it has something to do with . . . Nah, if it was something like that, I'd have been told, before I went off last night, to report to Internal Affairs.*

But what the hell does Special Operations want to ask me about?

Nine months before, a building contractor from McKeesport, Pennsylvania, had telephoned the Eastern Pennsylvania Executive Escort Service, saying the service had been recommended to him by a client of the service. After first ascertaining that the building contractor did indeed know the client, and that he understood the price structure, Mrs. Osadchy dispatched to Room 517 of the Benjamin Franklin Hotel one of her associates, who happened to be an employee of the Philadelphia Savings Fund Society, whose husband had deserted her and their two children, and who worked on an irregular basis for the Eastern Pennsylvania Executive Escort Service to augment her income.

When she reached the building contractor's room, it was evident to her that he was very drunk, and when his behavior was unacceptably crude, she attempted to leave. The building contractor thereupon punched her in the face. She screamed, attracting the attention of the occupants of the adjacent room, who called hotel security.

The on-duty hotel security officer, a former police officer, was contacted as he stood on the sidewalk, chatting with Officer Charles F. Crater, of the Sixth District, who was walking his beat.

Officer Crater, ignoring the hotel security officer's argument that he could deal with the situation alone, accompanied him to the building contractor's room, where they found the building contractor somewhat aghast at the damage he had done to the face of the lady from the Eastern Pennsylvania Executive Escort Service, and the lady herself in the bathroom, trying to stanch the flow of blood from her mouth and nose, so that she could leave the premises without attracting horrified attention to herself.

The lady did not look like what Officer Crater believed hookers should look like. She was weeping. She told Officer Crater that her name was Marianne Connelly, and that her husband had deserted her and their two children, and that she had to do this to put food in their mouths. He believed her. She told him that if anyone at the Philadelphia Savings Fund Society heard about this, she would be fired, and then she didn't know what she would do. He believed her.

The building contractor said that he didn't know what had come over him, that he was a family man with children, and if this ever got back to McKeesport, he would lose his family and probably his business.

The hotel security officer suggested to Officer Crater that no real good would come from arresting the building contractor, since there were no witnesses to the assault, and the lady from the Eastern Pennsylvania Executive Escort Service wouldn't humiliate herself, and set herself up to surely get fired, by going to court to testify against him.

What harm would there be, the hotel security officer argued, if they settled this bad situation right here and now? The building contractor would give the lady from the Eastern Pennsylvania Executive Escort Service money, enough not only to pay for her medical bills and the damage to her clothing, but to compensate her for what the sonofabitch had done to her.

The sonofabitch produced a wallet stuffed with large-denomination bills to demonstrate his willingness to go along with this solution to the problem.

"Give it all to her," Officer Crater order.

"I got to keep out a few bucks, for Christ's sake!"

"Give it all to her, you sonofabitch!" Officer Crater ordered angrily, and watched as the building contractor gave the lady from the Eastern Pennsylvania Executive Escort Service all the money in his wallet. Then he turned to the hotel security officer. "You'll see that she gets out of here and home all right, right?"

"Absolutely."

Officer Crater then turned and left the room.

The lady from the Eastern Pennsylvania Executive Escort Service went home and telephoned Mrs. Osadchy to report what had happened.

"How much did he give you, Marianne?"

"Six hundred bucks."

"You keep it, and I promise you, this will never happen again."

Mrs. Osadchy also reported the incident to Mr. Cassandro, who considered the situation a moment and then said, "I think, since the cop was so nice, that we ought to show our appreciation. Give the broad a couple of hundred and tell her to give it to the cop."

"I already told Marianne she could keep the dough she got from the john."

"Then you give her the money for the cop, Harriet. Consider it an investment. Trust me. Do it."

Two days later, while Officer Crater was walking his beat, the lady from the Philadelphia Savings Fund Society who moonlighted at the Eastern Pennsylvania Executive Escort Service approached him.

"I want to thank you for the other night," she said. "I really appreciate it."

"Aaaaaah," Officer Crater said, somewhat embarrassed.

"No, I really mean it," she said. "I really appreciate what you did for me."

"Forget it," Officer Crater said.

The lady handed him what looked like a greeting card.

"What's this?" Officer Crater asked.

"It's a thank-you card. I got it at Hallmark."

"You didn't have to do that," Officer Crater said. "All I was trying to do was make the best of a bad situation."

"You're sweet," the lady said. "What did you say your name was?"

"Crater."

"I mean your first name."

"Charley," Officer Crater replied.

"Mine's Marianne," she said. "Thanks again, Charley." She kissed Officer Crater on the cheek and walked away.

Officer Crater stuffed the Hallmark thank-you card in his pocket and resumed walking his beat. When he got home, he took another look at it. Inside the card were four crisp fifty-dollar bills.

"Jesus Christ!" Officer Crater said. He went to the bathroom and tore the thank-you card in little pieces and flushed the pieces down the toilet. His wife, he knew, would never understand. The two hundred he folded up and put in the little pocket in his wallet which, before he got married, he had used to hold a condom.

The next time he saw her, he told himself, he would give the money back to her. There was no point in making a big deal of the money; telling his sergeant about it would mean having to tell him what he had done in the first place.

A week after that, before he saw the lady again, he had a couple of drinks too many after work in Dave's Bar, at Third Street and Fairmount Avenue, with Officer William C. Palmerston, whom he had worked with in the Sixth District before Palmerston had been transferred to Vice.

He told him, out of school, about the thank-you card with the two hundred bucks in it, and that he intended to return it to the hooker the next time he saw her.

"Don't be a goddamned fool," Palmerston said. "Keep it."

"You're kidding, right?"

"It's not like she bribed you, is it? All you did was what you thought was the right thing to do in that situation, right? I mean, you didn't catch her doing something wrong, right? You didn't say, 'For two hundred bucks, I'll let you go,' did you?"

"No, of course not."

"You did her a favor, she appreciated it. Keep the money."

"You'd keep it?"

Officer Palmerston, in reply, extended his hand, palm upward, to Officer Crater.

"Try me."

"All right, goddamn you, Bill, I will," Officer Crater said, and took two of the fifties from the condom pocket in his wallet and laid them in Officer Palmerston's palm. Officer Palmerston stuffed the bills in his shirt pocket, then called for another round.

"I'll pay," Officer Palmerston said, and laid one of the fifties on the bar.

The next time, several days later, Officer Crater saw the lady from the Eastern Pennsylvania Executive Escort Service he could not, of course, give her the two hundred back, since he'd given half of it to Officer Palmerston.

She came up to him right after he started walking his beat, where he was standing on the corner of Ninth and Chestnut Streets.

"Hi, Charley," she said. "How are you?"

"Hi," he replied, thinking again that Marianne didn't really look like a hooker.

"You ever get a break?" she asked. "For a cup of coffee or something?"

"Sure."

"I was about to have a cup of coffee. I'll buy," the lady said.

He seemed hesitant, and she saw this.

"Charley, all I'm offering is a cup of coffee," she said. "Come on."

Why not? Officer Crater reasoned. *I mean, what the hell is wrong with drinking a cup of coffee with her?*

They had coffee and a couple of doughnuts in a luncheonette. He never could remember afterward what they had talked about until Marianne suddenly looked at her watch and said she had to go. And offered her hand for him to shake, and he took it, and there was something in her hand.

"The lady I work for says thank you, too," Marianne said, and was gone before he could say anything else, or even look at what she had left in his hand.

When he finally looked, it was a neatly folded, crisp one-hundred-dollar bill.

"Jesus Christ!" he said aloud, before quickly putting the bill in his trousers pocket.

When he got off work that night, he went to Dave's Bar before going home, in the hope that he would run into Bill Palmerston.

Palmerston was already in Dave's Bar when he got there, and when he bought Palmerston a drink, he paid for it with the hundred-dollar bill.

Palmerston looked at the bill and then at Crater.

"Where'd you get that?"

"The same place I got the fifties," Crater said.

"Lucky you."

Palmerston watched as the bartender made change, and when he had gone, looked at Crater and asked, "Don't tell me your conscience is bothering you again?"

"A little," Officer Crater confessed.

Officer Palmerston reached toward the stack of bills on the bar and carefully pulled two twenties and a ten from it.

"Feel better?" he asked.

"Jesus, Bill, I don't like this."

"Don't be a damned fool," Palmerston said. "It's not like you're doing something wrong." Then Palmerston had a second thought. "Anybody see her give this to you?"

Crater shook his head.

"Then don't worry about it," Palmerston said. "Nobody's getting hurt. But I'll tell you what I'm going to do. I'm going to ask around."

"Ask around about what?"

"I wonder why this lady is being so nice to you. It sure isn't because of the size of your cock. If I come up with something, I'll let you know."

Two weeks later, as Officer Crater was walking his beat, an unmarked car pulled to the curb beside him.

"Get in the back, Charley," Officer Palmerston, who was in the front passenger seat beside the driver, said.

Charley got in the backseat.

"This is Lieutenant Meyer," Palmerston said.

"How are you, Crater?"

"How do you do, sir?"

"I work for the Lieutenant, Charley," Palmerston said.

"Oh, yeah?"

"Bill tells me you're an all-right guy, Crater. Not too smart, but the kind of a guy you can trust."

Palmerston laughed.

"He also told me about your lady friend, the one you helped out, the one who's been showing her gratitude to you."

For a fleeting moment, Charley was very afraid that Bill Palmerston had turned him in for taking the hundred dollars from Marianne every week. But that passed. The Lieutenant wouldn't be talking the way he was if he was going to arrest him or anything like that.

"That's what I meant about you not being too smart, Charley," Lieutenant Meyer said.

"Sir?"

"You really don't know much about your lady friend's business, do you?"

"No, sir."

"Well, let me tell you what I found out after Bill came to me. What Bill and I found out. Your friend works for a woman named Harriet Osadchy. Her sheet shows three busts for prostitution here, and she has a sheet in Hazleton—you know where Hazleton is, Charley?"

"Out west someplace, in the coal regions."

"Right. Anyway, this Osadchy woman has a sheet as long as you are tall in Hazleton, mostly prostitution, some controlled-substance busts, all nol-prossed, even a couple of drunk and disorderlies. But she's smart. You got to give her that, right, Bill?"

"Yes, sir," Officer Palmerston said.

"We didn't even have a line on this Eastern Pennsylvania Executive Escort Service until you brought it to Bill's attention."

"The what?"

"The Eastern Pennsylvania Executive Escort Service. That's what she calls her operation."

"Oh."

"But like I was saying, now we have a line on her. She's got maybe twenty, twenty-five, maybe more hookers working for her. It's a high-class operation. The minimum price is a hundred dollars. That's for one hour."

"Damn!"

"Bill had a talk with your friend Marianne. She said the split is sixty-forty. For her forty percent, Harriet makes the appointments for the girls, and takes care of what has to be taken care of."

"Excuse me?"

"Her girls know that when they knock on some hotel door, they're not going to find some weirdo inside, or a cop, and that they'll get their money. They even take one of those credit card machines with them, in case—and you'd be surprised how often this happens—the john can put the girl on his expense account as secretarial services, or a rental car, or something like that."

"I didn't know they could use credit cards," Officer Crater confessed.

"There's a lot you don't know," Lieutenant Meyer said. "You got any idea how much money is involved here?"

"Not really. You said a hundred an hour."

"Right. Sometimes they stay more than an hour. Sometimes the john wants something more than a straight fuck. That costs more, of course. But the low side would be that a girl would work three johns a night. Let's say Harriet has twenty girls working. That's three times a hundred bucks times twenty girls."

"Six thousand dollars," Officer Crater said wonderingly.

"Right. Times seven nights a week. That's forty-two thousand gross. Harriet's share of that would come to almost seventeen thousand a week. It's a money machine. Now out of that, she has to pay her expenses. Three, four telephones. The rent on a little apartment she has on Cherry Street where the phones are. She has a couple of lawyers on retainer, and a couple of doctors who make sure the girls are clean, and she takes care of the people in the hotels who could make trouble for her. And then I'm sure she has some arrangement with the mob. Usually that's ten percent."

"With the mob? What for?"

"To be left alone. Years ago, the mob ran whorehouses. The Chinese still have a couple running. We keep shutting them down and they keep opening them up, but the mob found out that whorehouses are really more trouble than they're worth, so they went out of that business. Why the hell not, if they can take, like I said, ten percent of Harriet's forty-two thousand a week for doing nothing more than putting the word out on the street that Harriet is a friend of theirs? A freelance hooker can almost expect to get robbed, but even a really dumb sleazeball thug knows better than to mess with anyone who is a friend of the mob."

Officer Crater grunted.

"OK. So let's talk about where we fit in here," Meyer said. "The first thing you have to understand is that prostitution has been around a long time—they don't call it 'the oldest profession' for nothing—and there's absolutely no way to stop it. All we can do is control it. What the citizens don't want is hookers approaching people on the street, or in a bar. The citizens don't want disease. They don't want to see young girls—or, for that matter, young boys—involved. For the obvious reasons. And I think we do a pretty job of giving the citizens what they want.

"What the citizens also want, and I don't think most people understand this, or if they do, don't want to admit it, is somebody like Harriet Osadchy. The johns pay their money, they get what they want, they don't get a disease, they don't get robbed, nobody gets hurt, and nobody finds out that they're not getting what they should be getting at home."

"Yeah," Officer Crater said. "I see what you mean."

"And the Harriet Osadchys of this world don't give the police any trouble, either. They do their thing, and they do it clean, and we have the time to do what we're hired to do, protect the people. We close down the whorehouses, we keep the hookers from working the streets and the bars, we keep the people from getting a disease or robbed, or blackmailed, all those things."

"I see what you mean."

"So now we get back to you, and your friend Marianne. You did the right thing by her and the guy who beat her up. I mean, what good would it have done if you had run him in? Your friend Marianne would not have testified against him anyway, and he made it right by her by giving her a lot of money, right?"

"I think she would have really lost her job if the PSFS heard about that," Officer Crater said.

"Sure she would have," Lieutenant Meyer agreed. "And her john would have gotten in trouble with his wife, a lot of people would have been hurt, and you solved the problem all around. I would have done exactly the same thing myself."

"I thought it was the right thing to do," Officer Crater said.

"OK. So what happened next? Marianne told Harriet what happened, and Harriet knew that it would have been a real pain in the ass, really hurt her business, if you had gone strictly by the book and hauled either one of them in. So she was grateful, right, and she told Marianne to slip you a couple of hundred bucks right off, and a hundred a week regular after that. A little two-hundred-dollar present to say thank you for not running Marianne in, and a regular little hundred-dollar-a-week present just to remind you that being a good guy, doing what's right, sometimes gets you a little extra money. Nothing wrong with that, right?"

"Not the way you put it," Officer Crater said. "It bothered—"

"Wrong, you stupid shit!" Lieutenant Meyer snarled.

"Excuse me?"

"I explained to you, Crater, that Harriet Osadchy is personally pocketing *at least* seventeen thousand, seventeen thousand tax-free, by the way, each and every week, and you really pull her fucking chestnuts out of the fire, really save her ass, really save her big bucks, and she throws a lousy two hundred bucks at you? And figures she's buying you for a hundred a week? That's fucking *insulting,* Crater, can't you see that?"

Officer Crater did not reply.

"She's paying, as her cost of doing business, and happy to do it, some lawyer maybe a *thousand* a week, and some doctor another *thousand,* and slipping the mob probably *ten percent* of however the fuck much she takes in, and she slips you a lousy, what, a *total* of maybe *five hundred,* and you're not insulted?"

"I guess I never really thought about it," Officer Crater confessed.

"Right. You're goddamned right you didn't think about it," Meyer said.

"I don't know what you want me to say, Lieutenant," Crater said.

"You don't say anything, that's what I want you to say. We'll all be better off if you never open your mouth again. I will tell you what's going to happen, Crater. Your friend Marianne, the next time you see her, is going to give you another envelope. This one will have a thousand dollars in it. You will take two hundred for your trouble and give the rest to Bill. And every week the same goddamned thing. Am I getting through to you?"

"What do I have to do?"

"I already told you. Keep your mouth shut. That's all. And remember, if you're as stupid as I'm beginning to think you are, that if you start thinking about maybe going to Internal Affairs or something, it'd be your word against mine and Bill's. Not only would we deny this conversation ever took place, but Internal Affairs would have your ass for not coming to them the first time your friend Marianne gave you money."

Lieutenant Meyer took his arm off the back of the seat and faced forward and turned the ignition.

"Tell whatsisname he'd better get out of the car now, Bill," he said. "Unless he wants to go with us."

Staff Inspector Mike Weisbach turned off Frankford Avenue onto Castor and then drove into the parking lot of the Special Operations Division. He saw a parking slot against the wall of the turn-of-the-century school building marked RESERVED FOR INSPECTORS and steered his unmarked Plymouth into it.

I usually go on the job looking forward to what the day will bring, he thought as he got out of the car, *but today is different; today, I suspect, I am not going to like at all what the day will bring, and I don't mean because I'm not used to getting up before seven o'clock to go to work.*

He entered the building through the nearest door, above which "BOYS" had been carved in the granite, and found himself in what had been, and was now, a locker room. The difference was that the boys were now all uniformed officers, mostly Highway Patrolmen, and the room was liberally decorated with photographs of young women torn from *Playboy, Hustler,* and other literary magazines.

"How do I find Inspector Wohl's office?" Mike addressed a burly Highway Patrolman sitting on a wooden bench in his undershirt, scrubbing at a spot on his uniform shirt.

"I don't think you're supposed to be in here, sir," the Highway Patrolman said, using the word as he would use it to a civilian he had just stopped for driving twenty-five miles over the speed limit the wrong way down a one-way street. "Visitors is supposed to use the front door."

The Highway Patrolman examined him carefully.

"I know you?"

"I don't believe I've had the pleasure. My name is Mike Weisbach."

The Highway Patrolman stood up.

"Sorry, Inspector," he said. "I didn't recognize you. There's stairs over there. First floor. Used to be the principal's office."

"Thank you," Mike said, and then smiled and said, "Your face is familiar, too. What did you say your name was?"

"Lomax, sir. Charley Lomax."

"Yeah, sure," Mike said, and put out his hand. "Good to see you, Charley. It's been a while."

"Yes, sir. It has," Lomax said.

When he reached the outer office of the Commanding Officer of the Special Operations Division, Weisbach identified himself as Staff Inspector Weisbach to the young officer in plain clothes behind the desk.

"I know he's expecting you, Inspector. I'll see if he's free," the young officer said, and got up and walked to a door marked INSPECTOR WOHL, knocked, and went inside.

Mike's memory, which had drawn a blank vis-à-vis Officer Lomax, now kicked in about Wohl's administrative assistant.

His name is O'Mara, Paul Thomas. His father is Captain Aloysius O'Mara, who commands the Seventeenth District. His brother is Sergeant John F. O'Mara of Civil Affairs. His grandfather had retired from the Philadelphia Police Department. His transfer to Special Operations had been arranged because Special Operations was considered a desirable assignment for a young officer with the proper nepotistic connections.

That's not why I'm here. Lowenstein didn't arrange this transfer for me to enhance my career. I'm here to help Jerry Carlucci get reelected.

Peter Wohl, without a jacket, his sleeves rolled up and his tie pulled down, appeared at the door.

"Come on in, Mike," he said. "Can I have Paul get you a cup of coffee?"

"Please," Mike said.

"Three, Paul, please," Wohl ordered, and held the door open for Weisbach.

"Morning, Mike," Mickey O'Hara called as Weisbach entered the office.

He was sitting on a couch. On the coffee table in front of him was a tape recorder and a heavy manila paper envelope.

"What's good about it, Mick?" Weisbach asked.

"Peter's been telling me that the forces of virtue are about to triumph over the forces of evil," O'Hara replied. "I get an exclusive showing a dirty district captain and a dirty lieutenant on their way to the Central Cellroom. I like that, professionally and personally. So far as I'm concerned, that's not a bad way to start my day."

"Mick," Wohl asked, "how would you feel about going with Mike Sabara when he picks up Paulo Cassandro?"

"Instead of staying here, you mean?" O'Hara replied, and then went on without giving Wohl a chance to reply. "For one thing, Peter, the arrest of second- or third-level gangsters is not what gets on the front page. The arrest of a police captain, a district commander, is. And please don't tell him I said so, but Mike Sabara is not what you could call photogenic."

"It's your call, Mickey."

"I know what you're trying to do, Peter," Mickey said. "Keep a picture of a dirty captain getting arrested out of the papers. But it won't work. That's news, Peter."

"And you're here with Carlucci's blessing, right?"

"Yeah, I am, Peter. Sorry."

"OK. Let's talk about what's going to happen. Chief Coughlin will be here any minute. Inspector Sawyer and the others no later than eight. Sawyer comes in here. Coughlin plays the tape of Meyer and Cassandro for him—"

Wohl pointed to the tape machine.

"Coughlin's going to play the tape for him?" Mickey interrupted, sounding surprised.

"That was my father's idea. He and Coughlin choreographed this for me last night. The tape is damned incriminating. That should, I was told, keep Sawyer from loyally defending his men. And, Mickey, Carlucci's blessing or not, you are not going to be here when that happens."

"OK. Do I get to hear the tape?"

"Can you live with taking my word that it's incriminating?"

"Can I listen to it out of school?"

"OK. Why not?"

"Before?"

"After."

O'Hara shrugged his acceptance.

"Then we go to the Investigation Section, upstairs, where Cazerra, Meyer, and the two officers will be waiting. Inspector Sawyer will arrest Captain Cazerra. I will arrest Lieutenant Meyer. Their badges, IDs, and guns will be taken from them. Staff Inspector Weisbach, assisted by Detectives Payne and Martinez, will arrest the two officers, and take their guns and badges."

"Am I going to get to be there?" O'Hara asked.

"When Inspector Sawyer comes in here, you leave," Wohl said. "Wait outside. When we come out, we will be on our way upstairs. You can come with us."

"Thank you."

"The Fraternal Order of Police will be notified immediately after the arrests," Wohl went on. "It will probably take thirty minutes for them to get an attorney, attorneys, here. When that is over, I will take Captain Cazerra to the Police Administration Building in my car, which will be driven by Sergeant Washington. He will not be placed in a cell. Chief Coughlin has arranged for him to be immediately booked, photographed, fingerprinted, and arraigned. He will almost certainly be released on his own recognizance."

"Nice, smooth operation," O'Hara said.

"The same thing will happen with the others. Weisbach will take Lieutenant Meyer to the Roundhouse in his car, with Officer Lewis driving. Detectives Payne and Martinez will take the two officers in a Special Operations car."

"It would be nice if I could get a shot of Cazerra and Meyer in handcuffs," O'Hara said.

Wohl ignored him.

"It would be a good public relations shot, either one of them in cuffs," O'Hara pursued.

Wohl looked at him and shook his head.

"Mick," he said. "I am aware that there are certain public relations aspects to this, otherwise the Prince of the Fourth Estate would not be sitting in my office with egg spots on his tie and his fly open."

Mickey O'Hara glanced in alarm toward his crotch. His zipper was fastened.

"Screw you, Peter." He laughed. "Question: Don't you think the Mayor would be happier if Captain Cazerra were arrested by the new Chief of the Ethical Affairs Unit?"

"Why would that make the Mayor happier?"

"Maybe assisted by Detective Payne?" Mickey went on, not directly answering the question. "Handsome Matthew is always good copy. That picture, I'm almost sure, would make page one. Isn't that what Carlucci wants? More to the point, why he fixed it for me to be here?"

"I suggested last night that Mike make all the arrests."

"Thanks a lot, Peter," Mike Weisbach said sarcastically.

"Coughlin shot me down," Wohl went on. "There's apparently a sacred protocol here, and Coughlin wants it followed."

"Just trying to be helpful," Mickey said. "For purely selfish reasons. I want to get invited back the next time. I guess the Mayor will have to be happy with a picture of the Black Buddha standing behind Cazerra going into the Roundhouse. That should produce a favorable reaction from the voting segment of the black population, right?"

"Even if it does humiliate every policeman in Philadelphia," Wohl said bitterly. "Mike, you've heard it. See anything wrong with it?"

Weisbach shook his head.

"OK," Wohl said. "Then that's the way we'll do it."

"OK," Weisbach parroted.

"Afterward, Mike, you and I are going to have a long talk about the Ethical Affairs Unit."

"Right," Weisbach said.

Wohl's door opened and Chief Inspector Coughlin walked in.

"Morning," he said.

"Good morning, Chief," Wohl and Weisbach said, almost in unison.

"How are you, Mickey?" Coughlin said cordially, offering his hand.

"No problems," O'Hara said.

"Peter fill you in on what's going to happen?"

"Yep."

"Mick, just now, as I was driving over here, I wondered if you might not want to go with Captain Sabara when he arrests Cassandro."

"Nice try, Denny," O'Hara said. "But like I told Peter, a picture of a third-rate gangster in cuffs isn't news. A District captain getting arrested is."

Officer O'Mara put his head in the door.

"Inspector Sawyer is here, sir."

Wohl looked at Coughlin, who nodded.

"Ask him to come in," Peter said.

Inspector Gregory Sawyer, a somewhat portly, gray-haired man in his early fifties, came in the room.

He was visibly surprised at seeing Mickey O'Hara.

"I'll see you guys later," Mickey said. "How are you, Greg?"

He walked out of the room.

"Greg," Coughlin said. "I wasn't exactly truthful with you last night."

"Excuse me, Chief?"

"That thing ready?" Coughlin asked, pointing at the tape recorder.

"Yes, sir," Wohl said.

"Sit down, Greg," Coughlin said.

"Yes, sir."

"At the orders of the Commissioner, Inspector Wohl has been conducting an investigation of certain allegations involving Captain Cazerra, Lieutenant Meyer, and others in your division. A court order was obtained authorizing electronic surveillance of a room in the Bellvue-Stratford Hotel. What you are about to hear is one of the recordings made," Coughlin said formally. "Turn it on, please," he said, and then walked to Wohl's window and looked out at the lawn in front of the building.

11.

At 7:40 A.M. Miss Penelope Detweiler was sitting up in her canopied four-poster bed in her three-room apartment on the second floor of the Detweiler mansion when Mrs. Violet Rogers, who had been employed as a domestic servant by the Detweilers since Miss Detweiler was in diapers, entered carrying a tray with coffee, toast, and orange juice.

Miss Detweiler was wearing a thin, pale blue, sleeveless nightgown. Her eyes were open, and there was a look of surprise on her face.

There was a length of rubber medical tubing tied around Miss Detweiler's left arm between the elbow and the shoulder. A plastic, throwaway hypodermic injection syringe hung from Miss Detweiler's lower left arm.

"Oh, Penny!" Mrs. Rogers moaned. "Oh, Penny!"

She put the tray on the dully gleaming cherrywood hope chest at the foot of the bed, then stood erect, her arms folded disapprovingly against her rather massive breast, her full, very black face showing mingled compassion, sorrow, and anger.

And then she met Miss Detweiler's eyes.

"Oh, sweet Jesus!" Mrs. Rogers said, moaned, and walked quickly to the bed.

She waved a large, plump hand before Miss Detweiler's eyes. There was no reaction.

She put her hand to Miss Detweiler's forehead, then withdrew it as if the contact had burned.

She put her hands on Miss Detweiler's shoulders and shook her.

"Penny! Penny, honey!"

There was no response.

When Mrs. Rogers removed her hands from Miss Detweiler's shoulders and let her rest again on the pillows against the headboard, Miss Detweiler started to slowly slide to the right.

Mrs. Rogers tried to stop the movement but could not. She watched in horror as Miss Detweiler came to rest on her side. Her head tilted back, and she seemed to be staring at the canopy of her bed.

Mrs. Rogers turned from the bed and walked to the door. In the corridor, the walk became a trot, and then she was running to the end of the corridor, past an oil portrait of Miss Detweiler in her pink debutante gown, past the wide stairway leading down to the entrance foyer of the mansion, into the corridor of the other wing of the mansion, to the door of the apartment of Miss Detweiler's parents.

She opened and went through the door leading to the apartment sitting room without knocking, and through it to the closed double doors of the bedroom. She knocked at the left of the double doors, then went through it without waiting for a response.

H. Richard Detweiler, a tall, thin man in his late forties, was sleeping in the oversize bed, on his side, his back to his wife Grace, who was curled up in the bed, one lower leg outside the sheets and blankets, facing away from her husband.

Mr. Detweiler, who slept lightly, opened his eyes as Mrs. Rogers approached the bed.

"Mr. D," Violet said. "You better come."

"What is it, Violet?" Mr. Detweiler asked in mingled concern and annoyance.

"It's Miss Penny."

H. Richard Detweiler sat up abruptly. He was wearing only pajama bottoms.

"Jesus, now what?"

"You'd better come," Mrs. Rogers repeated.

He swung his feet out of the bed and reached for the dressing gown he had discarded on the floor before turning out the lights. As he put it on, his feet found a pair of slippers.

Mrs. Detweiler, a finely featured, rather thin woman of forty-six, who looked younger, woke, raised her head, and looked around and then sat up. Her breasts were exposed; she had been sleeping wearing only her underpants.

"What is it, Violet?" she asked as she pulled the sheet over her breasts.

"Miss Penny."

"What about Miss Penny?"

H. Richard Detweiler was headed for the door, followed by Violet.

"Dick?" Mrs. Detweiler asked, and then, angrily, "Dick!"

He did not reply.

Grace Detweiler got out of bed and retrieved a thick terry-cloth bathrobe from the floor. It was too large for her, it was her husband's, but she often wore it between the shower and the bed. She put it on, and fumbling with the belt, followed her husband and Violet out of her bedroom.

H. Richard Detweiler entered his daughter's bedroom.

He saw her lying on her side and muttered something unintelligible, then walked toward the canopied bed.

"Penny?"

"I think she's gone, Mr. D," Violet said softly.

He flashed her an almost violently angry glare, then bent over the bed and, grunting, pushed his daughter erect. Her head now lolled to one side.

Detweiler sat on the bed and exhaled audibly.

"Call Jensen," he ordered. "Tell him we have a medical emergency, and to bring the Cadillac to the front door."

Violet went to the bedside and punched the button that would ring the telephone in the chauffeur's apartment over the five-car garage.

H. Richard Detweiler stood up, then squatted and grunted as he picked his daughter up in his arms.

"Call Chestnut Hill Hospital, tell them we're on the way, and then call Dr. Dotson and tell him to meet us there," Detweiler said as he started to carry his daughter across the room.

Mrs. Arne—Beatrice—Jensen answered the telephone on the second ring and told Mrs. Rogers her husband had just left in the Cadillac to take it to Merion Cadillac-Olds for service.

"Mr. D," Mrs. Rogers said, "Jensen took the limousine in for service."

"Go get the Rolls, please, Violet," Detweiler said, as calmly as he could manage.

"Oh, my God!" Mrs. Grace Detweiler wailed as she came into the room and saw her husband with their daughter in his arms. "What's happened?"

"Goddamn it, Grace, don't go to pieces on me," Detweiler said. He turned to Violet.

"Not the Rolls, the station wagon," he said, remembering.

There wasn't enough room in the goddamned Rolls Royce Corniche for two people and a large-sized cat, but Grace had to have a goddamned convertible.

"What's the matter with her?" Grace Detweiler asked.

"God only knows what she took this time," Detweiler said, as much to himself as in reply to his wife.

"Beatrice," Violet said, "get the keys to the station wagon. I'll meet you by the door."

"Oh, my God!" Grace Detweiler said, putting her balled fist to her mouth. "She's unconscious!"

"Baxley has the station wagon," Mrs. Jensen reported. "He's gone shopping."

Baxley was the Detweiler butler. He prided himself that not one bite of food entered the house that he had not personally selected. H. Richard Detweiler suspected that Baxley had a cozy arrangement with the grocer's and the butcher's and so on, but he didn't press the issue. The food was a good deal better than he had expected it would be when Grace had hired the Englishman.

"Baxley's gone with the station wagon," Violet reported.

Goddamn it all to hell! Both of them gone at the same time! And no car, of five, large enough to hold him with Penny in his arms. And nobody to drive the car if there was one.

"Call the police," H. Richard Detweiler ordered. "Tell them we have a medical emergency, and to send an ambulance immediately."

He left the bedroom carrying his daughter in his arms, and went down the corridor, past the oil portrait of his daughter in her pink debutante gown and then down the wide staircase to the entrance foyer.

"Police Radio," Mrs. Leander—Harriet—Polk, a somewhat more than pleasingly plump black lady, said into the microphone of her headset.

"We need an ambulance," Violet said.

Harriet Polk had worked in the Radio Room in the Police Administration Building for nineteen years. Her long experience had told her from the tone of the caller's voice that this was a genuine call, not some lunatic with a sick sense of humor.

"Ma'am, what's the nature of the problem?"

"She's unconscious, not breathing."

"Where are you, Ma'am?"

"928 West Chestnut Hill Avenue," Violet said. "It's the Detweiler estate."

Harriet threw a switch on her console which connected her with the Fire Department dispatcher. Fire Department Rescue Squads are equipped with oxygen and resuscitation equipment, and manned by firemen with special Emergency Medical Treatment training.

"Unconscious female at 928 West Chestnut Hill Avenue," she said.

Then she spoke to her caller.

"A rescue squad is on the way, Ma'am," she said.

"Thank you," Violet said politely.

Nineteen years on the job had also embedded in Harriet Polk's memory a map of the City of Philadelphia, overlaid by Police District boundaries. She knew, without thinking about it, that 928 West Chestnut Hill Avenue was in the Fourteenth Police District. Her board showed her that Radio Patrol Car Twenty-three of the Fourteenth District was in service.

Harriet moved another switch.

"Fourteen Twenty-three," she said. "928 West Chestnut Hill Avenue. A hospital case. Rescue en route."

Police Officer John D. Wells, who also had nineteen years on the job, was sitting in his three-year-old Chevrolet, whose odometer was halfway through its second hundred thousand miles, outside a delicatessen on Germantown Avenue.

He had just failed to have the moral courage to refuse stuffing his face before going off shift and home. He had a wax-paper-wrapped Taylor-ham-and-egg sandwich in his hand, and a large bite from same in his mouth.

He picked up his microphone and, with some difficulty, answered his call: "Fourteen Twenty-three, OK."

He took off the emergency brake and dropped the gearshift into drive.

He had spent most of his police career in North Philadelphia, and had been transferred to "The Hill" only six months before. He thought of it as being "retired before retiring." There was far less activity in affluent Chestnut Hill than in North Philly.

He didn't, in other words, know his district well, but he knew it well enough to instantly recall that West Chestnut Hill Avenue was lined with large houses, mansions, on large plots of ground, very few of which had numbers to identify them.

Where the hell is 928 West Chestnut Hill Avenue?

Officer Wells did not turn on either his flashing lights or siren. There was not much traffic in this area at this time of the morning, and he didn't think it was necessary. But he pressed heavily on the accelerator pedal.

H. Richard Detweiler, now staggering under the hundred-and-nine-pound weight of his daughter, reached the massive oak door of the foyer. He stopped and looked angrily over his shoulder and found his wife.

"Grace, open the goddamned door!"

She did so, and he walked through it, onto the slate-paved area before the door.

Penny was really getting heavy. He looked around, and walked to a wrought-iron couch and sat down in it.

Violet appeared.

"Mr. D," she said, "the police, the ambulance, is coming," she said.

"Thank you," he said.

He looked down at his daughter's face. Penny was looking at him, but she wasn't seeing him.

Oh, my God!

"Violet, please call Mr. Payne and tell him what's happened, and that I'm probably going to need him."

Violet nodded and went back in the house.

Brewster Cortland Payne II, Esq., a tall, well-built—he had played tackle at Princeton in that memorable year when Princeton had lost sixteen of seventeen games played—man in his early fifties, was having breakfast with his wife, Patricia, on the patio outside the breakfast room of his rambling house on a four-acre plot on Providence Road in Wallingford when Mrs. Elizabeth Newman, the Payne housekeeper, appeared carrying a telephone on a long cord.

"It's the Detweilers' Violet," she said.

Mrs. Payne, an attractive forty-four-year-old blonde, who was wearing a pleated skirt and a sweater, put her coffee cup down as she watched her husband take the telephone.

"For you?" she asked, not really expecting a reply.

"Good morning, Violet," Brewster C. Payne said. "How are you?"

"Mr. Detweiler asked me to call," Violet said. "He said he will probably need you."

"What seems to be the problem?"

Payne, who was a founding partner of Mawson, Payne, Stockton, McAdoo & Lester, arguably Philadelphia's most prestigious law firm, was both Mr. H. Richard Detweiler's personal attorney and his most intimate friend. They had been classmates at both Episcopal Academy and Princeton.

Violet told him what the problem was, ending her recitation of what had transpired by almost sobbing, "I think Penny is gone, Mr. Payne. He's sitting outside holding her in his lap, waiting for the ambulance, but I think she's gone."

"Violet, when the ambulance gets there, find out where they're taking Penny. Call here and tell Elizabeth. I'm leaving right away. When I get into Philadelphia, I'll call here and Elizabeth can tell me where to go. Tell Mr. Detweiler I'm on my way."

He broke the connection with his finger, lifted it and waited for a dial tone, and then started dialing again.

"Well, what is it?" Patricia Payne asked.

"Violet went into Penny's room and found her sitting up in bed with a needle hanging out of her arm," Payne replied, evenly. "They're waiting for an ambulance. Violet thinks it's too late."

"Oh, my God!"

A metallic female voice came on the telephone: "Dr. Payne is not available at this time. If you will leave your name and number, she will return your call as soon as possible. Please wait for the tone. Thank you."

He waited for the tone and then said, "Amy, if you're there, please pick up."

"Dad?"

"Penny was found by the maid ten minutes ago with a needle in her arm. Violet thinks she's gone."

"Damn!"

"I think you had better go out there and deal with Grace," Brewster Payne said.

"Goddamn!" Dr. Amelia Payne said.

"Tell her I'm coming," Patricia said.

"Your mother said she's coming to Chestnut Hill," Payne said.

"All right," Amy said, and the connection went dead.

Payne waited for another dial tone and dialed again.

"More than likely by mistake," Matt's voice said metallically, "you have dialed my number. If you're trying to sell me something, you will self-destruct in ten seconds. Otherwise, you may leave a message when the machine goes bleep."

Bleep.

"Matt, pick up."

There was no human voice.

He's probably at work, Payne decided, and replaced the handset in its cradle.

"Elizabeth, please call Mrs. Craig—you'd better try her at home first—and tell her that something has come up and I don't know when I'll be able to come to the office. And ask her to ask Colonel Mawson to let her know where he'll be this morning."

Mrs. Newman nodded.

"Poor Matt," Mrs. Newman said.

"Good God!" Brewster Payne said, and then stood up. His old-fashioned, well-worn briefcase was sitting on the low fieldstone wall surrounding the patio. He picked it up and then jumped over the wall and headed toward the garage. His wife started to follow him, then stopped and called after him: "I've got to get my purse. And I'll try to get Matt at work."

She waited until she saw his head nod, then turned and went into the house.

Officer John D. Wells, in RPC Fourteen Twenty-three, slowed down when he reached the 900 block of West Chestnut Hill Avenue, a little angry that his memory had been correct.

There are no goddamned numbers. Just tall fences that look like rows of spears and fancy gates, all closed. You can't even see the houses from the street.

Then, as he moved past one set of gates, it began to open, slowly and majestically. He slammed on the brakes and backed up, and drove through the gates, up a curving drive lined with hundred-year-old oak trees.

If this isn't the place, I can ask.

It was the place.

There was a man on a patio outside an enormous house sitting on an iron couch holding a girl in her nightgown in his arms.

Wells got quickly out of the car.

"Thank God!" the man said, and then, quickly, angrily: "Where the hell is the ambulance? We called for an ambulance!"

"A rescue squad's on the way, sir," Wells said.

He looked down at the girl. Her eyes were open. Wells had seen enough open lifeless eyes to know this girl was dead. But he leaned over and touched the carotid artery at the rear of her ear, feeling for a pulse, to make sure.

"Can you tell me what happened, sir?" he asked.

"We found her this way, Violet found her this way."

There came the faint wailing of a siren.

"There was a needle in her arm," a large black woman said softly, earning a look of pained betrayal from the man holding the body.

Wells looked. There was no needle, but there was a purple puncture wound in the girl's arm.

"Where did you find her?" Wells asked the black woman.

"Sitting up in her bed," Violet said.

The sound of the ambulance siren had grown much louder. Then it shut off. A moment later the ambulance appeared in the driveway.

Two firemen got quickly out, pulled a stretcher from the back of the van, and, carrying an oxygen bottle and an equipment bag, ran up to the patio.

The taller of them, a very thin man, did exactly what Officer Wells had done, took a quick look at Miss Penelope Detweiler's lifeless eyes and concluded she was dead, and then checked her carotid artery to make sure.

He met Wells's eyes and, just perceptibly, shook his head.

"Sir," he said, very kindly, to H. Richard Detweiler, "I think we'd better get her onto the stretcher."

"There was, the lady said, a needle in her arm," Wells said.

H. Richard Detweiler now gave Officer Wells a very dirty look.

The very thin fireman nodded. The announcement did not surprise him. The Fire Department Rescue Squads of the City of Philadelphia see a good many deaths caused by narcotics overdose.

Officer Wells went to his car and picked up the microphone.

"Fourteen Twenty-three," he said.

"Fourteen Twenty-three," Harriet Polk's voice came back immediately.

"Give me a supervisor at this location. This is a Five Two Nine Two."

Five Two Nine Two was a code that went back to the time before shortwave radio and telephones, when police communications were by telegraph key in police boxes on street corners. It meant "dead body."

"Fourteen B," Harriet called.

Fourteen B was the call sign of one of two sergeants assigned to patrol the Fourteenth Police District.

"Fourteen B," Sergeant John Aloysius Monahan said into his microphone. "I have it. En route."

Officer Wells picked up a clipboard from the floor of the passenger side of his car and then went back onto the patio. The firemen were just finishing lowering Miss Detweiler onto the stretcher.

The tall thin fireman picked up a worn and spotted gray blanket, held it up so that it unfolded of its own weight, and then very gently laid it over the body of Miss Detweiler.

"What are you doing that for?" H. Richard Detweiler demanded angrily.

"Sir," the thin fireman said, "I'm sorry. She's gone."

"She's not!"

"I'm really sorry, sir."

"Oh, Jesus H. fucking Christ!" H. Richard Detweiler wailed.

Mrs. H. Richard Detweiler, who had been standing just inside the door, now began to scream.

Violet went to her and, tears running down her face, wrapped her arms around her.

"What happens now?" H. Richard Detweiler asked.

"I'm afraid I've got to ask you some questions," Officer Wells said. "You're Mr. Detweiler? The girl's father?"

"I mean what happens to . . . my daughter? I suppose I'll have to call the funeral home—"

"Mr. Detweiler," Wells said, "what happens now is that someone from the Medical Examiner's Office will come here and officially pronounce her dead and remove her body to the morgue. Under the circumstances, the detectives will have to conduct an investigation. There will have to be an examination of the remains."

"An autopsy, you mean? Like hell there will be."

"Mr. Detweiler, that's the way it is," Wells said. "It's the law."

"We'll see about that!" Detweiler said. "That's my daughter!"

"Yes, sir. And, sir, a sergeant is on the way here. And there will be a detective. There are some questions we have to ask. And we'll have to see where you found her."

"The hell you will!" Detweiler fumed. "Have you got a search warrant?"

"No, sir," Wells said. There was no requirement for a search warrant. But he did not want to argue with this grief-stricken man. The Sergeant was on the way. Let the Sergeant deal with it.

He searched his memory. John Aloysius Monahan was on the job. Nice guy. Good cop. The sort of a man who could reason with somebody like this girl's father.

Sergeant John Aloysius Monahan got out of his car and started to walk up the wide flight of stairs to the patio. Officer Wells walked down to him. Monahan saw a tall man in a dressing robe sitting on a wrought-iron couch, staring at a blanket-covered body on a stretcher.

"Looks like an overdose," Wells said softly. "The maid found her, the daughter, in her bed with a needle in her arm."

"In her bed? How did she get down here?"

"The father carried her," Wells said. "He was sitting on that couch holding her in his arms when I got here. He's pretty upset. I told him about the M.E., the autopsy, and he said 'no way.' "

"You know who this guy is?" Monahan asked.

Wells shook his head, then gestured toward the mansion. "Somebody important."

"He runs Nesfoods," Monahan said.

"Jesus!"

Monahan walked up the shallow stairs to the patio.

"Mr. Detweiler," he said.

It took a long moment before Detweiler raised his eyes to him.

"I'm Sergeant Monahan from the Fourteenth District, Mr. Detweiler," he said. "I'm very sorry about this."

Detweiler shrugged.

"I'm here to help in any way I can, Mr. Detweiler."

"It's a little late for that now, isn't it?"

"It looks that way, Mr. Detweiler," Monahan agreed. "I'm really sorry." He paused. "Mr. Detweiler, I have to see the room where she was found. Maybe we'll find something there that will help us. Could you bring yourself to take me there?"

"Why not?" H. Richard Detweiler replied. "I'm not doing anybody any good here, am I?"

"That's very good of you, Mr. Detweiler," Sergeant Monahan said. "I appreciate it very much."

He waited until Detweiler had stood up and started into the house, then motioned for Wells to follow them.

"What's your daughter's name, Mr. Detweiler?" Monahan asked gently. "We have to have that for the report."

"Penelope," Mr. Detweiler said. "Penelope Alice."

Behind them, as they crossed the foyer to the stairs, Officer Wells began to write the information down on Police Department Form 75-48.

They walked up the stairs and turned left.

"And who besides yourself and Mrs. Detweiler," Sergeant Monahan asked, "was in the house, sir?"

"Well, Violet, of course," Detweiler replied. "I don't know if the cook is here yet."

"Wells," Sergeant Monahan interrupted.

"I got it, Sergeant," Officer Wells said.

"Excuse me, Mr. Detweiler," Sergeant Monahan said.

Officer Wells let them get a little ahead of them, then, one at a time, he picked two of the half-dozen Louis XIV chairs that were neatly arranged against the walls of the corridor. He placed one over the plastic hypodermic syringe that both he and Sergeant Monahan had spotted, and the second over a length of rubber surgical tubing, to protect them.

Then he walked quickly after Sergeant Monahan and Mr. Detweiler.

Sergeant John Aloysius Monahan was impressed with the size of Miss Penelope Alice Detweiler's apartment. It was as large as the entire upstairs of his row house off Roosevelt Boulevard. The bathroom was as large as his bedroom. He was a little surprised to find that the faucets were stainless steel. He would not have been surprised if they had been gold.

And he was not at all surprised to find, on one of Miss Detweiler's bedside tables, an empty glassine packet, a spoon, a candle, and a small cotton ball.

He touched nothing.

"Is there a telephone I can use, Mr. Detweiler?" he asked.

Detweiler pointed to the telephone on the other bedside table.

"The detectives like it better if we don't touch anything," Monahan said. "Until they've had a look."

"There's one downstairs," Detweiler said. "Sergeant, may I now call my funeral director? I want to get . . . her off the patio. For her mother's sake."

"I think you'd better ask the Medical Examiner about that, Mr. Detweiler," Monahan said. "Can I ask you to show me the telephone?"

"All right," Detweiler said. "I was thinking of Penny's mother."

"Yes, of course," Monahan said. "This is a terrible thing, Mr. Detweiler."

He waited until Detweiler started out of the room, then followed him back downstairs. Officer Wells followed both of them. Detweiler led him to a living room and pointed at a telephone on a table beside a red leather chair.

"Officer Wells here," Monahan said, "has some forms that have to be filled out. I hate to ask you, but could you give him a minute or two?"

"Let's get it over with," Detweiler said.

"Officer Wells, why don't you go with Mr. Detweiler?" Monahan said, waited until they had left the living room, closed the door after them, went to the telephone, and dialed a number from memory.

"Northwest Detectives, Detective McFadden."

Detective Charles McFadden, a very large, pleasant-faced young man, was sitting at a desk at the entrance to the offices of the Northwest Detective Division, on the second floor of the Thirty-fifth Police District building at North Broad and Champlost streets.

"This is Sergeant Monahan, Fourteenth District. Is Captain O'Connor around?"

"He's around here someplace," Detective McFadden said, then raised his voice: "Captain, Sergeant Monahan on Three Four for you."

"What can I do for you, Jack?" Captain Thomas O'Connor said.

"Sir, I'm out on a Five Two Nine Two in Chestnut Hill. The Detweiler estate. It's the Detweiler girl."

"What happened to her?"

"Looks like a drug overdose."

"I'll call Chief Lowenstein," Captain O'Connor said, thinking aloud.

Lowenstein would want to know about this as soon as possible. For one thing, the Detweiler family was among the most influential in the city. The Mayor would want to know about this, and Lowenstein could get the word to him.

Captain O'Connor thought of another political ramification to the case: the Detweiler girl's boyfriend was Detective Matthew Payne. Detective Payne had for a rabbi Chief Inspector Dennis V. Coughlin. It was a toss-up between Coughlin and Lowenstein for the unofficial title of most important chief inspector. O'Connor understood that he would have to tell Coughlin what had happened to the Detweiler girl. And then he realized there was a third police officer who had a personal interest and would have to be told.

"You're just calling it in?" O'Connor asked.

"I thought I'd better report it directly to you."

"Yeah. Right. Good thinking. Consider it reported. I'll get somebody out there right away. A couple of guys just had their court appearances canceled. I don't know who's up on the wheel, but I'll see the right people go out on this job. And I'll go myself."

"The body's still on a Fire Department stretcher," Monahan said. "The father carried it downstairs to wait for the ambulance. I haven't called the M.E. yet."

"You go ahead and call the M.E.," O'Connor said. "Do this strictly by the book. Give me a number where I can get you."

Monahan read it off the telephone cradle and O'Connor recited it back to him.

"Right," Monahan said.

"Thanks for the call, Jack," O'Connor said, and hung up.

He looked down at Detective McFadden.

"Who's next up on the wheel?"

"I am. I'm holding down the desk for Taylor."

"When are Hemmings and Shapiro due in?"

Detective McFadden looked at his watch.

"Any minute. They called in twenty minutes ago."

"Have Taylor take this job when he gets here. I don't think you should."

McFadden's face asked why.

"That was a Five Two Nine Two, Charley. It looks like your friend Payne's girlfriend put a needle in herself one time too many."

"Holy Mother of God!"

"At her house. That's all I have. But I don't think you should take the job."

"Captain, I'm going to need some personal time off."

"Yeah, sure. As soon as Hemmings comes in. Take what you need."

"Thank you."

"I've seen pictures of her," Captain O'Connor said. "What a fucking waste!"

"Chief Coughlin's office, Sergeant Holloran."

"Captain O'Connor, Northwest Detectives. Is the Chief available?"

"He's here, but the door is closed. Inspector Wohl is with him, Captain."

"I think this is important."

"Hold on, Captain."

"Coughlin."

"Chief, this is Tom O'Connor."

"I hope this is important, Tom."

"Sergeant Monahan of the Fourteenth just called in a Five Two Nine Two from the Detweiler estate. The girl. The daughter. Drug overdose."

"Jesus, Mary, and Joseph," Chief Coughlin responded with even more emotion than O'Connor expected. Then, as if he had not quite covered the mouthpiece with his hand, O'Connor heard him say, "Penny Detweiler overdosed. At her house. She's dead."

"I'll be a sonofabitch!" O'Connor heard Inspector Peter Wohl say.

"Chief, I've been trying to get Chief Lowenstein. You don't happen to know where he is, do you?"

"Haven't a clue, Tom. It's ten past eight. He should be in his office by now."

"I'll try him there again," O'Connor said.

"Thanks for the call, Tom."

"Yes, sir."

At 7:55 A.M., Police Commissioner Taddeus Czernich, a tall, heavyset, fifty-seven-year-old with a thick head of silver hair, had been waiting in the inner reception room of the office of the Mayor in the City Hall Building when one of the telephones on the receptionist's desk had rung.

"Mayor Carlucci's office," the receptionist, a thirty-odd-year-old, somewhat plump woman of obvious Italian extraction, had said into the telephone, and then hung up without saying anything else. Czernich thought he knew what the call was. Confirmation came when the receptionist got up and walked to the door of the Mayor's private secretary and announced, "He's entering the building."

The Mayor's secretary, another thirty-odd-year-old woman, also of obvious Italian extraction, who wore her obviously chemically assisted blond hair in an upswing, had arranged for the sergeant in charge of the squad of police assigned to City Hall to telephone the moment the mayoral limousine rolled into the inner courtyard of the City Hall Building.

Czernich stood up and checked the position of the finely printed necktie at his neck. He was wearing a banker's gray double-breasted suit and highly polished black wing-tip shoes. He was an impressive-looking man.

Three minutes later, the door to the inner reception room was pushed open by Lieutenant Jack Fellows. The Mayor marched purposefully into the room.

"Good morning, Mr. Mayor," the Police Commissioner and the receptionist said in chorus.

"Morning," the Mayor said to the receptionist and then turned to the Police Commissioner, whom he did not seem especially overjoyed to see. "Is it important?"

"Yes, Mr. Mayor, I think so," Czernich replied.

"Well, then, come on in. Let's get it over with," the Mayor said, and marched into the inner office, the door to which was now held open by Lieutenant Fellows.

"Good morning," the Mayor said to his personal secretary as he marched past her desk toward the door of his office. By moving very quickly, Lieutenant Fellows reached it just in time to open it for him.

Commissioner Czernich followed the Mayor into his office and took up a position three feet in front of the Mayor's huge, ornately carved antique desk. The Mayor's secretary appeared carrying a steaming mug of coffee bearing the logotype of the Sons of Italy.

The Mayor sat down in his dark green high-backed leather chair, leaned forward to glance at the documents waiting for his attention on the green pad on his desk, lifted several of them to see what was underneath, and then raised his eyes to Czernich.

"What's so important?"

Commissioner Czernich laid a single sheet of paper on the Mayor's desk, carefully placing it so that the Mayor could read it without turning it around.

"Sergeant McElroy brought that to my house while I was having my breakfast," Commissioner Czernich said, a touch of indignation in his voice.

The Mayor took the document and read it.

CITY OF PHILADELPHIA

MEMORANDUM

To: POLICE COMMISSIONER

From: COMMANDING OFFICER, DETECTIVE BUREAU

Subject: COMPENSATORY TIME/RETIREMENT

   1. The undersigned has this date placed himself on leave (compensatory time) for a period of fourteen days.
   2. The undersigned has this date applied for retirement effective immediately.
   3. Inasmuch as the undersigned does not anticipate returning to duty before entering retirement status, the undersigned's identification card and police shield are turned in herewith.

                                        M. L. Lowenstein
                                     Matthew L. Lowenstein
                                         Chief Inspector

       82-S-1AE (Rev. 3/59) RESPONSE TO THIS MEMORANDUM MAY
                    BE MADE HEREON IN LONGHAND

"Damn!" the Mayor said.

Czernich took a step forward and laid a chief inspector's badge and a leather photo identification folder on the Mayor's desk.

"You did not see fit to let me know Chief Lowenstein was involved in your investigation," Czernich said.

"Damn!" the Mayor repeated, this time with utter contempt in his voice, and then raised it. "Jack!"

Lieutenant Fellows pushed the door to the Mayor's office open.

"Yes, Mr. Mayor?"

"Get Chief Lowenstein on the phone," the Mayor ordered. "He's probably at home."

"Yes, sir," Fellows said, and started to withdraw.

"Use this phone," the Mayor said.

Fellows walked to the Mayor's desk and picked up the handset of one of the three telephones on it.

"This makes the situation worse, I take it?" Commissioner Czernich asked.

"Tad, just close your mouth, all right?"

"Mrs. Lowenstein," Fellows said into the telephone. "This is Lieutenant Jack Fellows. I'm calling for the Mayor. He'd like to speak to Chief Lowenstein."

There was a reply, and then Fellows covered the microphone with his hand.

"She says he's not available," he reported.

"Tell her thank you," the Mayor ordered.

"Thank you, Ma'am," Lieutenant Fellows said, and replaced the handset in its cradle and looked to the Mayor for further orders.

"Take a look at this, Jack," the Mayor ordered, and pushed the memorandum toward Fellows.

"My God!" Fellows said.

"I had no idea this mess we're in went that high," Commissioner Czernich said.

"I thought I told you to close your mouth," the Mayor said, then looked at Fellows. "Jack, call down to the courtyard and see if there's an unmarked car down there. If there is, I want it. You drive. If there isn't, call Special Operations and have them meet us with one at Broad and Roosevelt Boulevard."

"Yes, sir," Fellows reported, and picked up the telephone again.

The Mayor watched, his face expressionless, as Fellows called the sergeant in charge of the City Hall detail.

"Inspector Taylor's car is down there, Mr. Mayor," Fellows reported.

"Go get it. I'll be down in a minute," the Mayor ordered.

"Yes, sir."

The Mayor watched Fellows hurry out of his office and then turned to Commissioner Czernich.

"How many people know about that memo?"

"Just yourself and me, Mr. Mayor. And now Jack Fellows."

"Keep—" the Mayor began.

"And Harry McElroy," Czernich interrupted him. "It wasn't even sealed. The envelope, I mean."

"Keep it that way, Tad. You understand me?"

"Yes, of course, Mr. Mayor."

The Mayor stood up and walked out of his office.

"Sarah," the Mayor of the City of Philadelphia said gently to the gray-haired, soft-faced woman standing behind the barely opened door of a row house on Tyson Street, off Roosevelt Boulevard, "I know he's in there."

She just looked at him.

She looks close to tears, the Mayor thought. *Hell, she has been crying. Goddamnitalltohell!*

"What do you want me to do, Sarah?" the Mayor asked very gently. "Take the door?"

The door closed in his face. There was the sound of a door chain rattling, and then the door opened. Sarah Lowenstein stood behind it.

"In the kitchen," she said softly.

"Thank you," the Mayor said, and walked into the house and down the corridor beside the stairs and pushed open the swinging door to the kitchen.

Chief Matthew L. Lowenstein, in a sleeveless undershirt, was sitting at the kitchen table, hunched over a cup of coffee. He looked up when he heard the door open, and then, when he saw the Mayor, quickly averted his gaze.

The Mayor laid Lowenstein's badge and photo ID on the table.

"What is this shit, Matt?"

"I'm trying to remember," Lowenstein said. "I think if you just walked in, that's simple trespassing. If you took the door, that's forcible entry."

"Sarah let me in."

"I told her not to. What's on your mind, Mr. Mayor?"

"I want to know what the hell this is all about."

Lowenstein raised his eyes to look at the Mayor.

"OK," he said. "What it's all about is that you don't need a chief of detectives you don't trust."

"Who said I don't trust you? For God's sake, we go back a long way together, twenty-five years, at least. Of course I trust you."

"That's why you're running your own detective squad, right? And you didn't tell me about it because you trust me? Bullshit, Jerry, you don't trust me. My character or my professional competence."

"That's bullshit!"

"And I don't have to take your bullshit, either. I'm not Taddeus Czernich. I've got my time on the job. I don't need it, in other words."

"What are you pissed off about? What happened at that goddamned party? Matt, for Christ's sake, I was upset."

"You were a pretty good cop, Jerry. Not as good as you think you were, but good. But that doesn't mean that nobody else in the Department is as smart as you, or as honest. I'm as good a cop, probably better—*I* never nearly got thrown out of the Department or indicted—than you ever were. So let me put it another way. I'm sick of your bullshit, I don't have to put up with it, and I don't intend to. I'm out."

"Come on, Matt!"

"I'm out," Lowenstein repeated flatly. "Find somebody else to push around. Make Peter Wohl Chief of Detectives. You really already have."

"So that's it. You're pissed because I gave Wohl Ethical Affairs?"

"That whole Ethical Affairs idea stinks. Internal Affairs, a part of the Detective Bureau, is supposed to find dirty cops. And by and large, they do a pretty good job of it."

"Not this time, they didn't," the Mayor said.

"I was working on it. I was getting close."

"There are political considerations," the Mayor said.

"Yeah, political considerations," Lowenstein said bitterly.

"Yeah, political considerations," Carlucci said. "And don't raise your nose at them. You better hope I get reelected, or you're liable to have a mayor and a police commissioner you'd *really* have trouble with."

"We don't have a police commissioner now. We have a parrot."

"That's true," the Mayor said. "But he takes a good picture, and he doesn't give you any trouble. Admit it."

"An original thought and a cold drink of water would kill the Polack," Lowenstein said.

"But he doesn't give you any trouble, does he, Matt?" the Mayor persisted.

"You give me the goddamned trouble. *Gave* me. Past tense. I'm out."

"You can't quit now."

"Watch me."

"The Department's in trouble. Deep trouble. It needs you. I need you."

"You mean you're in trouble about getting yourself reelected."

"If I don't get reelected, then the Department will be in even worse trouble."

"Has it ever occurred to you that maybe the Department wouldn't be in trouble if you let the people who are supposed to run it actually run it?"

"You know I love the Department, Matt," the Mayor said. "Everything I try to do is for the good of the Department."

"Like I said, make Peter Wohl chief of detectives. He's already investigating everything but recovered stolen vehicles. Jesus, you even sent the Payne kid in to spy on Homicide."

"I sent the Payne kid over there to piss you off. I was already upset about these god-damned scumbags Cazerra and Meyer, and then you give me an argument about your detective who got caught screwing his wife's sister, and whose current girlfriend is probably involved in shooting her husband."

"That's bullshit and you know it."

"I wish I did know it."

Lowenstein looked at the Mayor and then shook his head.

"That's what Augie Wohl said. And Sarah said it, too. That you did that just to piss me off."

"And it worked, didn't it?" the Mayor said, pleased. "Better than I hoped."

"You sonofabitch, Jerry," Lowenstein said.

"Augie and Sarah are only partly right. Pissing you off wasn't the only thing I had in mind."

"What else?"

"I gave Ethical Affairs to Peter Wohl for political considerations, and even if you don't like the phrase, I have to worry about it. Peter's Mr. Clean in the public eye, the guy who put Judge Moses Findermann away. I needed something for the newspapers besides 'Internal Affairs is conducting an investigation of these allegations.' Christ, can't you see that? The papers, especially the *Ledger,* are always crying 'Police cover-up!' If I said that Internal Affairs was now investigating something they should have found out themselves, what would that look like?"

Chief Lowenstein granted the point, somewhat unwillingly, with a shrug.

"What's that got to do with Payne, sending him in to spy on Homicide?"

"Same principle. His picture has been all over the papers. Payne is the kind of cop the public wants. It's like TV and the movies. A good-looking young cop kills the bad guys and doesn't steal money."

There was a faint suggestion of a smile on Lowenstein's lips.

"So I figured if I send Payne to spend some time at Homicide (a) he can't really do any harm over there and (b) if it turns out your man who can't keep his dick in his pocket and/or the widow—and get pissed if you want, Matt, but that wouldn't surprise me a bit if that's the way it turns out—had something to do with Kellog getting himself shot, then what the papers have is another example of one of Mr. Clean's hotshots cleaning up the Police Department."

"I talked to Wally Milham, Jerry. I've seen enough killers and been around enough cops to know a killer and/or a lying cop when I see one. He didn't do it."

"Maybe he didn't, but if she had something to do with it, and he's been fucking her, which is now common knowledge, it's the same thing. You talk to her?"

"No," Lowenstein said.

"Maybe you should," the Mayor said.

"You're not listening to me. I'm going out. I'm going to move to some goddamned place at the shore and walk up and down the beach."

"We haven't even got around to talking about that."

"There's nothing to talk about."

"You haven't even heard my offer."

"I don't want to hear your goddamned offer."

"How do you know until you hear it?"

"Jesus Christ, can't you take no for an answer?"

"No. Not with you. Not when the Department needs you."

The kitchen door swung open.

"I thought maybe you'd need some more coffee," Sarah Lowenstein said a little nervously.

"You still got that stuff you bought to get rid of the rats?" Chief Lowenstein said. "Put two heaping tablespoons, three, in Jerry's cup."

"You two have been friends so long," Sarah said. "It's not right that you should fight."

"Tell him, Sarah," the Mayor said. "I am the spirit of reasonableness and conciliation."

"Four tablespoons, honey," Chief Lowenstein said.

12.

Brewster Cortland Payne II had stopped in a service station on City Line Avenue and called his home. Mrs. Newman had told him there had been no call from Violet, the Detweiler maid, telling him to which hospital Penny had been taken.

If she hadn't been taken to a hospital, he reasoned, there was a chance that the situation wasn't as bad as initially reported; that Penny might have been unconscious—that sometimes happened when drugs were involved—rather than, as Violet had reported, "gone," and had regained consciousness.

If that had happened, Dick Detweiler would have been reluctant to have her taken to a hospital; she could be cared for at home by Dr. Dotson, the family physician, or Amy Payne, M.D., and the incident could be kept quiet.

He got back behind the wheel of the Buick station wagon and drove to West Chestnut Hill Avenue.

He realized the moment he drove through the open gates of the estate that the hope that things weren't as bad as reported had been wishful thinking. There was an ambulance and two police cars parked in front of the house, and a third car, unmarked, but from its black-walled tires and battered appearance almost certainly a police car, pulled in behind him as he was getting out of the station wagon.

The driver got out. Payne saw that he was a police captain.

"Excuse me, sir," the Captain called to him as Payne started up the stairs to the patio.

Payne stopped and turned.

"I'm Captain O'Connor. Northwest Detectives. May I ask who you are, sir?"

"My name is Payne. I am Mr. Detweiler's attorney."

"We've got a pretty unpleasant situation here, Mr. Payne," O'Connor said, offering Payne his hand.

"Just how bad is it?"

"About as bad as it can get, I'm afraid," O'Connor said, and tilted his head toward the patio.

Payne looked and for the first time saw the blanket-covered body on the stretcher.

"Oh, God!"

"Mr. Payne, Chief Inspector Coughlin is on his way here. Do you happen to know . . . ?"

"I know the Chief," Payne said softly.

"I don't have any of the details myself," O'Connor said. "But I'd like to suggest that you . . ."

"I'm going to see my client, Captain," Payne said, softly but firmly. "Unless there is some reason . . . ?"

"I'd guess he's in the house, sir," O'Connor said.

"Thank you," Payne said, and turned and walked onto the patio. The door was closed but unlocked. Payne walked through it and started to cross the foyer. Then he stopped and picked up a telephone mounted in a small alcove beside the door.

He dialed a number from memory.

"Nesfoods International. Good morning."

"Let me have the Chief of Security, please," he said.

"Mr. Schraeder's office."

"My name is Brewster C. Payne. I'm calling for Mr. Richard Detweiler. Mr. Schraeder, please."

"Good morning, Mr. Payne. How can I help you?"

"Mr. Schraeder, just as soon as you can, will you please send some security officers to Mr. Detweiler's home? Six, or eight. I think their services will be required, day and night, for the next four or five days, so I suggest you plan for that."

"I'll have someone there in half an hour, Mr. Payne," Schraeder said. "Would you care to tell me the nature of the problem? Or should I come out there myself?"

"I think it would be helpful if you came here, Mr. Schraeder," Payne said.

"I'm on my way, sir," Schraeder said.

Payne put the telephone back in its cradle and turned from the alcove in the wall.

Captain O'Connor was standing there.

"Dr. Amelia Payne is on her way here," Payne said. "As is my wife. They will wish to be with the Detweilers."

"I understand, sir. No problem."

"Thank you, Captain," Payne said.

"Mr. Detweiler is in there," O'Connor said, pointing toward the downstairs sitting room. "I believe Mrs. Detweiler is upstairs."

"Thank you," Payne said, and walked to the downstairs sitting room and pushed the door open.

H. Richard Detweiler was sitting in a red leather chair—his chair—with his hands folded in his lap, looking at the floor. He raised his eyes.

"Brew," he said, and smiled.

"Dick."

"Everything was going just fine, Brew. The night before last, Penny and Matt had dinner with Chad and Daffy to celebrate Chad's promotion. And last night, they were at Martha Peebles's. And one day, three, four days ago, Matt came out and the two of them made cheese dogs for us. You know, you slit the hot dog and put cheese inside and then wrap it in bacon. They made them for us on the charcoal thing. And then they went to the movies. She seemed so happy, Brew. And now this."

"I'm very sorry, Dick."

"Oh, goddamn it all to hell, Brew," H. Richard Detweiler said. He started to sob. "When I went in there, her eyes were open, but I knew."

He started to weep.

Brewster Cortland Payne went to him and put his arms around him.

"Steady, lad," he said, somewhat brokenly as tears ran down his own cheeks. "Steady."

The Buick station wagon in which Amelia Payne, M.D., drove through the gates of the Detweiler estate was identical in model, color, and even the Rose Tree Hunt and Merion Cricket Club parking decalcomanias on the rear window to the one her father had driven through the gates five minutes before, except that it was two years older, had a large number of dings and dents on the body, a badly damaged right front fender, and was sorely in need of a passage through a car wash.

The car had, in fact, been Dr. Payne's father's car. He had made it available to his daughter at a very good price because, he said, the trade-in allowance on his new car had been grossly inadequate. That was not the whole truth. While Brewster Payne had been quietly incensed at the trade-in price offered for a two-year-old car with less that 15,000 miles on the odometer and in showroom condition, the real reason was that the skillful chauffeuring of an automobile was not among his daughter's many skills and accomplishments.

"She needs something substantial, like the Buick, something that will survive a crash," he confided to his wife. "If I could, I'd get her a tank or an armored car. When Amy gets behind the wheel, she reminds me of that comic-strip character with the black cloud of inevitable disaster floating over his head."

It was not that she was reckless, or had a heavy foot on the accelerator, but rather that she simply didn't seem to care. Her father had decided that this was because Amy had— always had had—things on her mind far more important than the possibility of a dented fender, hers or someone else's.

In the third grade when Amy had been sent to see a psychiatrist for her behavior in class (when she wasn't causing all sorts of trouble, she was in the habit of taking a nap) the psychiatrist quickly determined the cause. She was, according to the three different tests to which he subjected her, a genius. She was bored with the third grade.

At ten, she was admitted to a high school for the intellectually gifted operated by the University of Pennsylvania, and matriculated at the University of Pennsylvania at the age of thirteen, because of her extraordinary mathematical ability.

"Theoretical mathematics, of course," her father joked to intimate friends. "Double Doctor Payne is absolutely unable to balance a checkbook."

That was a reference to her two doctoral degrees, the first a Ph.D. earned at twenty with a dissertation on probability, the second an M.D. earned at twenty-three after she had gone through what her father thought of as a dangerous dalliance with a handsome Jesuit priest nearly twice her age. She emerged from this (so far as he knew platonic) relationship with a need to serve God by serving mankind. Her original intention was to become a surgeon, specializing in trauma injuries, but during her internship at the University of Pennsylvania Hospital, she decided to become a psychiatrist. She trained at the Menninger Clinic, then returned to Philadelphia, where she had a private practice and taught at the University of Pennsylvania School of Medicine.

She was now twenty-nine and had never married, although a steady stream of young men had passed through her life. Her father privately thought she scared them off with her brainpower. He could think of no other reason she was still single. She was attractive, he thought, and charming, and had a sense of humor much like his own.

Amelia Payne, Ph.D., M.D., stopped the Buick in front of the Detweiler mansion, effectively denying the use of the drive to anyone else who wished to use it, and got out. She was wearing a pleated tweed skirt and a sweater, and looked like a typical Main Line Young Matron.

The EMT firemen standing near the blanket-covered body were therefore surprised when she knelt beside the stretcher and started to remove the blanket.

"Hey, lady!"

"I'm Dr. Payne," Amy said, and examined the body very quickly. Then she pulled the blanket back in place and stood up.

"Let's get this into the house," she said. "Out of sight."

"We're waiting for the M.E."

"And while we're waiting, we're going to move the body into the house," Dr. Payne said. "That wasn't a suggestion."

The EMT firemen picked up the stretcher and followed her into the house.

She crossed the foyer and opened the door to the sitting room and saw her father and H. Richard Detweiler talking softly.

"Are you all right, Uncle Dick?" she asked.

"Ginger-peachy, honey," Detweiler replied.

"Grace is upstairs, Amy," her father said.

"I'll look in on her," Amy said, and pulled the door closed. She turned to the firemen. "Over there," she said. "In the dining room."

She crossed the foyer, opened the door to the dining room, and waited inside until the firemen had carried the stretcher inside. Then she issued other orders:

"One of you stay here, the other wait outside for the M.E. When he gets here, send for me. I'll be upstairs with Mrs. Detweiler, the mother."

"Yes, Ma'am," the larger of the two EMTs—whose body weight was approximately twice that of Amy's—said docilely.

Amy went quickly up the stairs to the second floor.

A black Ford Falcon with the seal of the City of Philadelphia and those words in small white letters on its doors passed through the gates of the Detweiler estate and drove to the door of the mansion.

Bernard C. Potter, a middle-aged, balding black man, tieless, wearing a sports coat and carrying a 35mm camera and a small black bag, got out and walked toward the door. Bernie Potter was an investigator for the Office of the Medical Examiner, City of Philadelphia.

This job, Potter thought, judging from the number of police cars—and especially the Fire Department rescue vehicle that normally would have been long gone from the scene—parked in front of the house, *is going to be a little unusual.*

And then Captain O'Connor, who Bernie Potter knew was Commanding Officer of Northwest Detectives, came out the door. This was another indication that something special was going on. Captains of Detectives did not normally go out on routine Five Two Nine Two jobs.

"What do you say, Bernie?"

"What have we got?" Bernie asked as they shook hands.

"Looks like a simple OD, Bernie. Caucasian female, early twenties, whose father happens to own Nesfoods."

"Nice house," Bernie said. "I didn't think these people were on public assistance. Where's the body?"

"In the dining room."

"What are you guys still doing here?" Bernie asked the Fire Department EMT on the patio. It was simple curiosity, not a reprimand.

The EMT looked uncomfortable.

"Like I told you," Captain O'Connor answered for him, "the father owns Nesfoods International." And then he looked down the drive at a new Ford coming up. "And here comes, I think, Chief Coughlin."

"Equal justice under the law, right?" Bernie asked.

"There's a doctor, a lady doctor, in there," the EMT said, "said she wanted to be called when you came."

"What does she want?" Bernie asked.

The EMT shrugged.

Chief Coughlin got out of his car and walked up.

"Good morning, Chief," Tom O'Connor said.

Coughlin shook his hand and then Bernie Potter's.

"Long time no see, Bernie," he said. "You pronounce yet?"

"Haven't seen the body."

"The quicker we can get this over, the better. You call for a wagon, Tom?"

"I didn't. I don't like to get in the way of my people."

"Check and see. If he hasn't called for one, get one here."

"Yes, sir."

"Where's the body?"

"In the dining room," the EMT said.

"I heard it was on the patio here."

"The lady doctor made us move it," the EMT said.

"Let's go have a look at it," Coughlin said. "I know where the dining room is. Tom, you make sure about the wagon."

"Yes, sir."

Coughlin led the way to the dining room.

"How did it get on the stretcher?" Bernie asked.

"What I hear is that the father carried it downstairs," the EMT said. "When we got here, he was sitting outside on one of them metal chairs, couches, holding it in his arms. We took it from him."

A look of pain, or compassion, flashed briefly over Chief Coughlin's face.

"Where did they find it?" Bernie asked.

Dr. Amelia Payne entered the dining room.

"In her bedroom," she answered the question. "In an erect position, with a syringe in her left arm."

"Dr. Payne, this is Mr. Potter, an investigator of the Medical Examiner's Office."

"How do you do?" Amy said. "Death was apparently instantaneous, or nearly so," she went on. "There is a frothy liquid in the nostrils, often encountered in cases of heroin poisoning. The decedent was a known narcotic-substance abuser. In my opinion—"

"Doctor," Bernie interrupted her uncomfortably, "I don't mean to sound hard-nosed, but you don't have any status here. This is the M.E.'s business."

"I am a licensed physician, Mr. Potter," Amy said. "The decedent was my patient, and she died in her home in not-unexpected circumstances. Under those circumstances, I am authorized to pronounce, and to conduct, if in my judgment it is necessary, any post-mortem examination."

"Amy, honey," Chief Coughlin said gently.

"Yes?" She turned to him.

"I know where you're coming from, Amy. But let me tell you how it is. You may be right. You probably are. But while you're fighting the M.E. taking Penny's body, think what's going to happen: It's going to take time, maybe a couple of days, before even your father can get an injunction. Until he gets a judge to issue an order to release it to you, the M.E.'ll hold the body. Let's get it over with, as quickly and painlessly as possible. I already talked to the M.E. He's going to do the autopsy himself, as soon as the body gets there. It can be in the hands of the funeral home in two, three hours."

She didn't respond.

"Grace Detweiler's going to need you," Coughlin went on. "And Matt. That's what's important."

Amy looked at Bernie.

"There's no need for a postmortem," she said. "Everybody in this room knows how this girl killed herself."

"It's the law, Doctor," Bernie said sympathetically.

Amy turned to Dennis Coughlin.

"What about Matt? Does he know?"

"Peter Wohl's waiting for him on North Broad Street. He'll tell him. Unless . . ."

"No," Amy said. "I think Peter's the best one. They have a sibling relationship. And Peter obviously has more experience than my father. You think Matt will come here?"

"I would suppose so."

She turned to Bernie Potter.

"OK, Mr. Potter," she said. "She is pronounced at nine twenty-five A.M." She turned back to Chief Coughlin. "Thank you, Uncle Denny."

She walked out of the dining room.

Chief Coughlin turned to the EMT.

"The wagon's on the way. Wait in here until it gets here."

The EMT nodded.

"I'm going to have to see the bedroom, Chief," Bernie Potter said.

"I'll show you where it is," Chief Coughlin said. "You through here?"

"I haven't seen the body," Potter said.

He squatted beside the stretcher and pulled the blanket off. He looked closely at the eyes and then closed them. He examined the nostrils.

"Yeah," he said, as if to himself. Then, "Give me a hand rolling her over."

The EMT helped him turn the body on its stomach. Bernie Potter tugged and pulled at Penelope Alice Detweiler's nightdress until it was up around her neck.

There was evidence of livor. The lower back and buttocks and the back of her legs were a dark purple color. Gravity drains blood in a corpse to the body's lowest point.

"OK," he said. "No signs of trauma on the back. Now let's turn her the other way."

There was more evidence of livor when the body was again on its back. The abdominal area and groin were a deep purple color.

"No trauma here, either," Bernie Potter said. He picked up the left arm.

"It looks like a needle could have been in here," he said. "It's discolored."

"The maid said there was a syringe in her arm," Captain O'Connor said. "And the district sergeant saw one, and some rubber tubing, on the floor in the corridor upstairs. He put chairs over them."

Bernie Potter nodded. Then he put Penelope's arm back beside her body, tugged at the nightgown so that it covered the body again, replaced the blanket, and stood up.

"OK," he said. "Now let's go see the bedroom. And the needle."

Chief Coughlin led the procession upstairs.

"There it is," Tom O'Connor said when they came to the chairs in the middle of the upstairs corridor. He carefully picked up the chairs Officer Wells had placed over the plastic hypodermic syringe and the surgical rubber tubing and put them against the wall.

Bernie Potter went into his bag and took two plastic bags from it. Then, using a forceps, he picked up the syringe and the tubing from the carpet and carefully placed them into the plastic bags.

Coughlin then led him to Penelope's bedroom. Potter first took several photographs of the bed and the bedside tables, then took another, larger plastic bag from his bag and, using the forceps, moved the spoon, the candle, the cotton ball, and the glassine bag containing a white crystalline substance from Penelope's bedside table into it.

"OK," he said. "I've got everything I need. Let me use a telephone and I'm on my way."

"I'll show you, Bernie," Chief Coughlin said. "There's one by the door downstairs."

As they went down the stairs, the door to the dining room opened and two uniformed police officers came through it, carrying Penelope's body on a stretcher. It was covered with a blanket, but her arm hung down from the side.

"The arm!" Chief Coughlin said.

One of the Fire Department EMTs, who was holding the door open, went quickly and put the arm onto the stretcher.

The policemen carried the stretcher outside and down the stairs from the patio and slid it through the already open doors of a Police Department wagon.

Chief Coughlin pointed to the telephone, then walked out onto the patio.

"Just don't give it to anybody," he called. "It's for Dr. Greene. He expects it."

"Yes, sir," one of the police officers said.

Coughlin went back into the foyer.

Bernie Potter was just hanging up the telephone.

"Thanks, Bernie," Coughlin said, and put out his hand.

"Christ, what a way to begin a day," Bernie said.

"Yeah," Coughlin said.

It would have been reasonable for anyone seeing Inspector Peter Wohl leaning on the trunk of his car, its right wheels off the pavement on the sidewalk, his arms folded on his chest, a look of annoyance on his face, to assume that he was an up-and-coming stock-broker, or lawyer, about to be late for an early-morning appointment because his new car had broken down and the Keystone Automobile Club was taking their own damned sweet time coming to his rescue.

The look of displeasure on his face was in fact not even because he was going to have to tell Matt Payne, of whom he was extraordinarily fond—his mother had once said that Matt was like the little brother she had never been able to give him, and she was, he had realized, right—that the love of his life was dead, but rather because it had just occurred to him that he was really a cold-blooded sonofabitch.

He would, he had realized, be as sympathetic as he could possibly be when Matt showed up, expressing his own personal sense of loss. But the truth of the matter was, he had just been honest enough with himself to admit that he felt Matt was going to be a hell of a lot better off with Penelope Detweiler dead.

It had been his experience, and as a cop, there had been a lot of experience, that a junkie is a junkie is a junkie. And in the case of Penelope Detweiler, if after the best medical and psychiatric treatment that money could, quite literally, buy, she was still sticking needles in herself, for whatever reason, that seemed to be absolutely true.

There would have been no decent future for them. If she hadn't OD'd this morning, she would have OD'd next week, or next month, or next year, or two years from now. There would have been other incidents, sordid beyond the comprehension of people who didn't know the horrors of narcotics addiction firsthand, and each of them would have killed Matt a little.

It was better for Matt that this had happened now, rather than after they had married, after they had children.

The fact that he felt sorry for Penelope Detweiler did not alter the fact that he was glad she had died before she could cause Matt more pain.

But by definition, Peter Wohl thought, *anyone who is glad a twenty-three-year-old woman is dead is a cold-blooded sonofabitch.*

He looked up as a car nearly identical to his flashed its headlights at him and then bounced up on the curb. Detective Jesus Martinez was driving. Detective Matt Payne, smiling, opened the passenger door and got out.

Martinez, annoyance on his face, hurried to follow him.

Why do those two hate each other?

The answer, obviously, is that opposites do not attract.

What do I say to Matt?

When all else fails, try the unvarnished truth.

"Don't tell me, you're broken down again?" Matt Payne said.

Gremlins—or the effects of John Barleycorn over the weekend affecting Monday-morning Ford assembly lines—had been at work on Inspector Wohl's automobiles. His generators failed, the radiators leaked their coolant, the transmissions ground themselves into pieces, usually leaving him stranded in the middle of the night in the middle of nowhere. Most of his subordinates were highly amused. He was now on his third brand-new car in six months.

"Let's get in the car," Wohl said. "Jesus, give us a minute, please?"

Matt looked curious but obeyed the order wordlessly. He closed the door after him and looked at Wohl.

Wohl met Matt's eyes.

"Matt, Penny OD'd," he said.

Matt's face tightened. His eyebrows rose in question, as if seeking a denial of what he had just heard.

Wohl shrugged, and threw his hands up in a gesture of helplessness.

"Matt . . ."

"Oh, shit!" Matt said.

"The maid found her in her bed with a needle in her arm. Death was apparently instantaneous."

"Oh, shit!"

"Tom O'Connor—he commands Northwest Detectives—called Denny Coughlin when they called it in. I happened to be in Denny's office when he got the call. He went out to the house to see how he could help. By now the M.E. has the body."

"Instantaneous?"

Wohl nodded. "So I'm told."

"Oh, shit, Peter!"

"I'm sorry, Matt," Wohl said, and put his arm around Matt's shoulder. "I'm really sorry."

"We had a goddamned fight last night."

"This is not your fault, Matt. Don't start thinking that."

"Same goddamned subject. Our future. Me being a cop."

"If it hadn't been that, it would have been something else. They find an excuse."

"Addicts, you mean?"

Wohl nodded.

"Has Amy been notified?" Matt asked. "This is going to wipe out Mrs. Detweiler."

His reaction is not what I expected. But what did I expect?

"I don't know," Wohl said, and then had a thought. He reached under the dash for a microphone.

"Isaac Three, William One."

"Isaac Three." It was the voice of Sergeant Francis Holloran, Chief Inspector Coughlin's driver.

"Tom, check with the Chief and see if Dr. Payne has been notified."

"She's here, Inspector."

"Thank you," Wohl said, and replaced the microphone. He looked over at Matt.

"I guess I'd better go out there," Matt said.

"Take the car and as much time as you need," Wohl said. "I'll take Martinez with me. Or why don't you give me the keys to your car, and I'll have Martinez or somebody bring it out there and swap."

"I'll go to the schoolhouse and get my car," Matt said. "I'm a coward, Peter. I don't want to go out there at all. With a little bit of luck, maybe I can get myself run over by a bus on my way."

"Matt, this isn't your fault."

Matt shrugged.

"I think I will take the car out there," he said. "Get it over with. I'll have it back at the schoolhouse in an hour or so."

"Take what time you need," Wohl said. "Is there anything else I can do, Matt?"

"No. But thank you."

"See me when you come to the schoolhouse."

Matt nodded.

"I'm really sorry, Matt."

"Yeah. Thank you."

They got out of the car and walked to Martinez.

"Are the keys in that?" Matt asked.

"Yeah, why?"

Without replying, Matt walked to the car, got behind the wheel, and started the engine. Martinez looked at Wohl.

Matt bounced off the curb and, tires chirping, entered the stream of traffic.

"I should have sent you with him," Wohl thought aloud.

"Sir?"

"Penelope Detweiler overdosed about an hour ago."

"Madre de Dios!" Martinez said, and crossed himself.

"Yeah," Wohl said bitterly, then walked back to his car.

Martinez walked to the car but didn't get in.

"Get in, for Christ's sake," Wohl snapped, and was immediately sorry. "Sorry, Jesus. I didn't mean to snap at you."

Martinez shrugged, signaling that he understood.

"That poor sonofabitch," he said.

"Yeah," Wohl agreed.

"Sorry to have kept you waiting," Inspector Peter Wohl said to Staff Inspector Michael Weisbach as he walked into his office. "Something came up."

"The Detweiler girl?" Weisbach asked, and when Wohl nodded, added: "Sabara told me. Awful. For her—what was she, twenty-three, her whole life ahead of her—and for Payne. He was really up when you put out the call for him."

"Up? What for, for having put the cuffs on a crooked cop? He liked that?"

"No. I think he felt sorry for Captain Cazerra. I think he felt *vindicated.* He told me that you, and Washington and Denny Coughlin, had really eaten his ass out for going out on that ledge."

"I wasn't going to let it drop, either—it was damned stupid—until this ... this god-damned overdose came along."

"I imagine he's pretty broken up?"

"I don't know. No outward emotion, which may mean he really has one of those well-bred stiff upper lips we hear about, or that he's in shock."

"Where is he?"

"Out at the estate. He's coming here. I'm going to see that he's not alone."

"There was a kid in here. McFadden, from Northwest Detectives, looking for him."

"Good. I was going to put the arm out for him. They're pals. You think he knows what happened?"

"I'm sure he does. When O'Mara told him Payne wasn't here, he said something about him probably being in Chestnut Hill, and that he would go there."

Wohl picked up his telephone and was eventually connected with O'Connor.

"Captain O'Connor. Inspector Wohl calling," he said, and then: "Peter Wohl, Tom. Need a favor."

Weisbach faintly heard O'Connor say, "Name it."

"If you could see your way clear to give your Detective McFadden a little time off, I'd appreciate it. He and my Detective Payne are friends, and for the next couple of days, Payne, I'm sure you know why, is going to need all the friends he has."

Weisbach heard O'Connor say, "I already told him to take whatever time he needed, Inspector."

"I owe you one, Tom."

"I owe you a lot more than one, Inspector. Glad to help. Christ, what a terrible waste!"

"Isn't it?" Wohl said, added, "Thanks, Tom," and hung up.

He had a second thought, and pushed a button on the telephone that connected him with Officer O'Mara, his administrative assistant.

"Yes, sir?"

"Two things, Paul. Inspector Weisbach and I need some coffee, and while that's brewing, I want you to call Special Agent Jack Matthews at the FBI. Tell him I asked you to tell him what happened in Chestnut Hill this morning, and politely suggest that Detective Payne would probably be grateful for some company. That latter applies to you, too. Why don't you stop by Payne's apartment on your way home?"

Weisbach heard O'Mara say, "Yes, sir."

Wohl looked at Weisbach as he hung up.

"Busy morning. I feel like it's two in the afternoon, and it's only ten to eleven."

"Busier even than I think you know. Did you hear about Lowenstein turning in his papers?"

"Jesus, no! Are you sure?"

The door opened and Paul O'Mara walked in with a tray holding two somewhat battered mugs of coffee, a can of condensed milk, and a saucer holding a dozen paper packets of sugar bearing advertisements suggesting they were souvenirs from McDonald's and Roy Rogers and other fast-food emporiums.

"That was quick," Wohl said. "Thank you, Paul." He waited until O'Mara had left, and then said, "Tell me about Lowenstein."

"The first thing this morning, Harry McElroy delivered Lowenstein's badge and a memorandum announcing his intention to retire to the Commissioner. I got that from McElroy, so that much I know for sure."

"God knows I'm sorry to hear that. But I'm not surprised that he's going out—"

Weisbach held up his hand, interrupting him.

"Just before I came out here," he said, "Lowenstein put out the arm for me. I met him at the Philadelphia Athletic Club on Broad Street. And not only did he not mention going out, but he didn't act like it, either."

"Interesting," Wohl said. "What did he want?"

"I got sort of a pep talk. He told me this Ethical Affairs Unit was a good thing for me, could help my career, and that all I had to do to get anything I wanted from the Detective Division was to ask."

"Lowenstein and the Mayor got into it at David Pekach's engagement party. Got into it bad. Did you hear about that?"

"The Mayor had just seen that Charley Whaley story in the *Ledger*. The 'more unsolved murders, no arrests, no comment' story. You see that?"

"Yeah."

"For some reason, it displeased our mayor," Wohl said, dryly. "The Mayor then announced he wouldn't be surprised if Wally Milham was involved in the Kellog murder, primarily because he thinks that Milham's morals are questionable. You've heard that gossip, I suppose?"

"Milham and Kellog's wife? Yeah, sure."

"The Mayor asked Lowenstein why he hadn't spoken to him about his love life. Lowenstein told the Mayor he didn't think it was any of his business. Then, warming to the subject, defended Milham. And then, really getting sore, Lowenstein made impolitic remarks about, quote, the Mayor's own private detective squad, unquote."

"Ouch!"

"Whereupon the Mayor told him if he didn't like the way things were being run, he should talk it over with the Commissioner. And then—he was really in a lousy mood—to make the point to the Chief who was running the Department, he told him 'the Commissioner' was going to send Matt Payne, who knows zilch about Homicide, over to Homicide to (a) help with the double murder at that gin mill on Market Street—"

"The Inferno?"

"Right. And (b) to see what he could learn about other Homicide investigations, meaning, of course, how Homicide is handling the Kellog job."

"My God!"

"I thought Lowenstein was going to have a heart attack. Or punch out the Mayor. It was that bad. I'm not surprised, now that I hear it, that he turned in his papers."

"I got it from Harry McElroy that he did. But then he didn't act like it when he sent for me."

"OK. How's this for a scenario? Czernich ran to the Mayor with Lowenstein's retirement memorandum. The Mayor hadn't wanted to go that far with Chief Lowenstein.

Christ, they've been friends for years. He didn't want him to quit. So they struck a deal. Lowenstein would stay on the job if certain conditions were met. They apparently were. And since they almost certainly involve you and me, we'll probably hear about them sometime next month."

Weisbach considered what Wohl had said, then nodded his head, accepting the scenario.

"So what do I do this month? Peter, you can't be happy with me—the Ethical Affairs Unit—being suddenly dumped on you."

"I don't have any problems with it," Wohl said. "First of all, it, and/or you, haven't been dumped on me. All I have to do is support you, and I have no problem with that. I think the EAU is a good idea, that you are just the guy to run it, and I think your work is already cut out for you."

"You really think it's a good idea?" Weisbach asked, surprised. Wohl nodded. "And what do you mean my work is already cut out for me?"

"The Widow Kellog showed up at Jason Washington's apartment the night her husband was killed with the announcement that everybody in Five Squad in Narcotics—you know about Five Squad?"

"Not much. I've heard they're very effective." He chuckled, and added: "Sort of an unshaven Highway Patrol, in dirty clothes, beards, and T-shirts—concealing unauthorized weapons—reading 'Legalize Marijuana,' who cast fear into the drug culture by making middle-of-the-night raids."

"Everybody in Five Squad, according to the Widow Kellog, is dirty, and she implied that they did her husband."

"My God!"

"Washington believes her, at least about the whole Five Squad being dirty. Before all this crap happened, I was going to bring you in on it."

"That was nice of you."

"Practically speaking, our priorities are the Mayor's priorities. I don't think he wants to be surprised again by dirty Narcotics people the way he was with Cazerra and company. Internal Affairs dropped the ball on that one, and I don't think we can give them the benefit of the doubt on this one. Yeah, it looks to me that you've got your work cut out for you."

"What kind of help can I have?"

"Anything you want. Washington and Harris, after getting their hands dirty on the Cazerra job, would love to work on a nice clean Homicide, especially of a police officer. And if there is a tie to Narcotics . . . Jesus!"

"What?"

"I forgot about the Mayor ordering Payne into Homicide," Wohl said. He reached for his telephone, pushed a button, and a moment later ordered, "Paul, would you get Chief Lowenstein for me, please?"

He put the telephone down.

"Drink your coffee, Mike," he said. "The first thing you're going to have to do is face the fact that your innocent, happy days as a staff inspector are over. You have just moved into the world of police politics, and you're probably not going to like it at all."

"That thought had already run through my mind," Weisbach said. He picked up his mug and, shaking his head, put it to his mouth.

The telephone rang. Wohl picked it up.

"Good morning, Chief," he said. "I wanted to check with you about sending Detective Payne to Homicide. Is that still on?"

He took the headset from his ear so that Weisbach could hear the Chief's reply.

"Denny Coughlin just told me what happened to the Detweiler girl," Lowenstein said. "I presume you're giving Matt some time off?"

"Yes, sir."

"Well, when he comes back, send him over whenever you can spare him. I've spoken to Captain Quaire. They're waiting for him."

"Yes, sir."

"And please tell him I'm sorry about what happened. That's really a goddamn shame."

"I'll tell him that, sir. Thank you."

"Nice talking to you, Peter," Chief Lowenstein said, and hung up.

"He didn't sound like someone about to retire, did he?" Weisbach said.

"No, he didn't."

One of the telephones on Wohl's desk rang.

"This is what happens when I forget to tell Paul to hold my calls," he said as he reached for it. "Inspector Wohl."

"Ah, Peter," Weisbach overheard. "How is the Beau Brummell of Philadelphia law enforcement this morning?"

"Why is it, Armando, that whenever I hear your voice, I think of King Henry the Sixth?"

"Peter, you are, as you well know, quoting that infamous Shakespearean 'kill all the lawyers' line out of context."

"Well, he had the right idea, anyhow. What can I do for you, Armando?"

"Actually, I was led to believe that Inspector Weisbach could be reached at your office."

"I'd love to know who told you that," Wohl said, and then handed the telephone to Weisbach. "Armando C. Giacomo, Esquire, for you, Inspector."

Giacomo, a slight, lithe, dapper man who wore what was left of his hair plastered to the sides of his tanned skull, was one of the best criminal lawyers in Philadelphia.

Wohl got up from his desk and walked to his window and looked out. He could therefore hear only Weisbach's side of the brief conversation.

"I'll call you back in five minutes," Weisbach concluded, and hung up.

Wohl walked back to his desk.

"Don't tell me," he said. "Giacomo has been asked to represent Mr. Paulo Cassandro."

"I'll bet that he has," Weisbach said. "But he didn't say so. What he said was that it would give him great pleasure if I would have lunch with him today at the Rittenhouse Club, during which he would like to discuss something which would be to our mutual benefit."

"I'd go, if I were you," Wohl said. "They set a very nice table at the Rittenhouse Club."

"Why don't you come with me?"

"I'm not in the mood for lunch, really, even at the Rittenhouse Club."

"He's looking for something, which means he's desperate. I'd like to have you there."

"Yeah," Wohl said, thoughtfully. "If he's looking for a deal, he would have gone to the District Attorney. It might be interesting."

He pushed the button for Paul O'Mara.

"Paul, call Armando C. Giacomo. Tell him that Inspector Weisbach accepts his kind invitation to lunch at the Rittenhouse Club at one, and that he's bringing me with him."

13.

Peter Wohl pushed open the heavy door of the Rittenhouse Club and motioned for Mike Weisbach to go in ahead of him. They climbed a wide, shallow flight of carpeted marble stairs to the lobby, where they were intercepted by the club porter, a dignified black man in his sixties.

"May I help you, gentlemen?"

"Mr. Weisbach and myself as the guests of Mr. Giacomo," Peter said.

"It's nice to see you, Mr. Wohl," the porter said, and glanced at what Peter thought of as the Who's Here Board behind his polished mahogany stand. "I believe Mr. Giacomo is in the club. Would you please have a seat?"

He gestured toward a row of chairs against the wall, then walked into the club.

The Who's Here Board behind the porter's stand listed, alphabetically, the names of the three-hundred-odd members of the Rittenhouse Club. Beside each name was an inch-long piece of brass, which could be slid back and forth in a track. When the marker was next to the member's name, this indicated he was on the premises; when away from it that he was not.

Peter saw Weisbach looking at the board with interest. The list of names represented the power structure, social and business, of Philadelphia. Philadelphia's upper crust belonged to either the Rittenhouse Club or the Union League, or both.

Peter saw that Carlucci, J., an ex officio member, was not in the club. Giacomo, A., was. So was Mawson, J., of Mawson, Payne, Stockton, McAdoo & Lester, who competed with Giacomo, A., for being the best (which translated to mean most expensive) criminal lawyer in the city. Payne, B., Mawson, J.'s, law partner, was not.

And neither, Wohl noticed with interest, was Payne, M.

I didn't know Matt was a member. That's new.

Possibly, he thought, *Detweiler, H., had suggested to Payne, B., that they have a word with the Membership Committee. Since their offspring were about to be married, it was time that Payne, M., should be put up for membership. Young Nesbitt, C. IV, had become a member shortly before his marriage to the daughter of Browne, S.*

Wohl had heard that the Rittenhouse Club initiation fee was something like the old saw about how much a yacht cost: If you had to ask what it cost, you couldn't afford it.

The porter returned.

"Mr. Giacomo is in the bar, Mr. Wohl. You know the way?"

"Yes, thank you," Peter said, and led Weisbach into the club bar, a quiet, deeply carpeted, wood-paneled room, furnished with twenty or so small tables, at each of which were rather small leather-upholstered armchairs. The tables were spaced so that a soft conversation could not be heard at the tables adjacent to it.

Armando C. Giacomo rose, smiling, from one of the chairs when he saw Wohl and Weisbach, and waved them over.

Wohl thought Giacomo was an interesting man. His family had been in Philadelphia from the time of the Revolution. He was a graduate of the University of Pennsylvania and the Yale School of Law. He had flown Corsairs as a Naval Aviator in the Korean War. He could have had a law practice much like Brewster Cortland Payne's, with clientele drawn from banks and insurance companies and familial connections.

He had elected, instead, to become a criminal lawyer, and was known (somewhat unfairly, Wohl thought) as the Mob's Lawyer, which suggested that he himself was involved in criminal activity. So far as Wohl knew, Giacomo's personal ethics were impeccable. He represented those criminals who could afford his services when they were hauled before the bar of justice, and more often than not defended them successfully.

Wohl had come to believe that Giacomo held the mob in just about as much contempt as he did, and that he represented them both because they had the financial resources to pay him, and also because he really believed that an accused was entitled to good legal representation, not so much for himself personally, but as a reinforcement of the Constitution.

Giacomo was also held in high regard by most police officers, primarily because he represented, *pro bono publico,* police officers charged with police brutality and other infractions of the law. He would not, in other words, represent Captain Vito Cazerra, because Cazerra could not afford him. But he would represent an ordinary police officer charged with the use of excessive force or otherwise violating the civil rights of a citizen, and do so without charge.

"Peter," Giacomo said. "I'm delighted that you could join us."

"I didn't want Mike to walk out of here barefoot, Armando, but thank you for your hospitality."

"I only talk other people out of their shoes, Peter, not my friends."

"And the check is in the mail, right?" Weisbach said, laughing as they shook hands.

A waiter appeared.

"I'm drinking a very nice California cabernet sauvignon," Giacomo said. "But don't let that influence you."

"A little wine would be very nice," Wohl said.

"Me, too, thank you," Weisbach said.

"The word has reached these hallowed precincts of the tragic event in Chestnut Hill this morning," Giacomo said. "What a pity."

"Yes, it was," Wohl agreed.

"If I don't have the opportunity before you see him, Peter, would you extend my sympathies to young Payne?"

"Yes, of course."

"He must be devastated."

"He is," Wohl said.

"And her mother and father . . ." Giacomo said, shaking his head sadly.

A waiter in a gray cotton jacket served the wine.

"I think we'll need another bottle of that over lunch, please," Giacomo said. He waited for the waiter to leave, and then said, "I hope you like that. What shall we drink to?"

Wohl shrugged.

"How about good friends?" Giacomo suggested.

"All right," Peter said, raising his glass. "Good friends."

"Better yet, Mike's new job."

"Better yet, Mike's new job," Wohl parroted. He sipped the wine. "Very nice."

"I'd send you a case, if I didn't know you would think I was trying to bribe you," Giacomo said.

"All gifts between friends are not bribes," Wohl said. "Send me a case, and I'll give Mike half. You can't bribe him, either."

"I'll send the both of you a case," Giacomo said, and then added: "Would you prefer to hear what I'd like to say now, or over lunch?"

"Now, please, Armando," Wohl said. "I would really hate to have my lunch in these hallowed precincts ruined."

"I suspected you'd feel that way. They do a very nice mixed grill here, did you know that?"

"Yes, I do. And also a very nice rack of lamb."

"I represent a gentleman named Paulo Cassandro."

"Why am I not surprised?" Weisbach asked.

"Because you are both astute and perceptive, Michael. May I go on?"

"By all means."

"Mr. Cassandro was arrested this morning. I have assured Mr. Cassandro that once I bring the circumstances surrounding his arrest . . . Constitutionally illegal wiretaps head a long list of irregularities . . ."

"Come on, Armando," Weisbach said, laughing.

". . . to the attention of the proper judicial authorities," Giacomo went on, undaunted, "it is highly unlikely that he will ever be brought to trial. And I have further assured him that, in the highly unlikely event he is brought to trial, I have little doubt in my mind that no fair-minded jury would ever convict him."

"He's going away, Armando," Wohl said. "You know that and I know that."

"You tend to underestimate me, Peter. I don't hold it against you; most people do."

"I never underestimate you, Counselor. But that clanging noise you hear in the background is the sound of a jail door slamming," Peter said. "The choir you hear is singing, 'Bye, Bye, Paulo.' "

"If I may continue?"

"Certainly."

"However, this unfortunate business, this travesty of justice, comes at a very awkward time for Mr. Cassandro. It will force him to devote a certain amount of time to it, time he feels he must devote to his business interests."

"Freely translated, Peter," Weisbach said, "what Armando is telling us is that Paulo doesn't want to go to jail."

"I wondered what he was trying to say," Wohl said.

"What he wants to do is get this unfortunate business behind him as soon as possible."

"Tell him probably ten to fifteen years, depending on the judge. If he gets Hanging Harriet, probably fifteen to twenty," Weisbach said.

The Hon. Harriet M. McCandless, a black jurist who passionately believed that civilized society was based on a civil service whose honesty was above question, was famous for her severe sentences.

"You're not listening to me, Michael," Giacomo said. "I am quite confident that, upon hearing how the police department has so outrageously violated the rights of Mr. Cassandro, Judge McCandless, or any other judge, will throw this case out of court."

"God, you're wonderful," Peter said.

"As I was saying, with an eye to putting this unfortunate business behind him as soon as possible, my client would be . . ."

"Armando," Weisbach said, "even if I wanted to, we couldn't deal on this. You want to deal, try the District Attorney. But I'll bet you he'll tell you Cassandro has nothing to deal with. We have him cold and he's going to jail."

"I will, of course, discuss this matter with Mr. Callis. But frankly, it will be a good deal easier for me, when I do speak with him, if I could tell him that I had spoken to you and Peter, and that you share my belief that what I propose would serve the ends of justice."

"Armando," Wohl said, laughing, "not only do I like you, but you are about to not only send me a case of wine, but also buy me a very expensive lunch. What that entitles you to is this: If you will tell me what you want, and how Paulo Cassandro wishes to pay for it, I will give you my honest opinion of how hard Mr. Callis is going to laugh at you before he throws you out of his office."

"Mr. Cassandro, as a public-spirited citizen, is willing to testify against Captain Cazerra. Lieutenant Meyer, and the two police officers. All he asks in exchange is immunity from prosecution."

"Loudly," Weisbach said. "Mr. Callis is going to laugh very loudly when you go to him with that."

"He may even become hysterical," Wohl said.

"*And* against the lady," Giacomo went on. "The madam, what the hell is her name?"

I will be damned, Wohl thought. *He's flustered. Have we really gotten through to Armando C. Giacomo, shattered his famous rocklike confidence?*

"Her name is Osadchy, Armando," Wohl said. "If you have trouble remembering her last name, why don't you associate it with Hanging Harriet? Same Christian name."

"Very funny, Peter."

"By now, Armando, with the egg they have on their face about Mrs. Osadchy," Weisbach said, "I'll bet Vice is paying her a lot of attention. They'll find something, I'm sure, that they can take to the DA."

"Let's talk about that," Giacomo said. "The egg on the face."

"OK," Peter said. "The egg on whose face?"

"The Police Department's."

"Because we had a couple of dirty cops? There might be some egg on our face because of that, but I think we wiped off most of it this morning," Weisbach said.

"Not in a public relations sense, maybe. Let me put that another way. The egg you wiped off this morning is going to reappear when you try Captain Cazerra. The trial will last at least two weeks, and there will be a story in every newspaper in Philadelphia every day of the trial. People will forget that he was arrested by good cops; what they'll remember is that the Department had a dirty captain. And when his trial is over, we will have the trial of Lieutenant Meyer."

"I reluctantly grant the point," Peter said.

"On the other hand, for the sake of friendly argument, if Captain Cazerra were to plead guilty and throw himself upon the mercy of the court because he became aware that Mr. Cassandro's public-spirited testimony was going to see him convicted . . ."

Or if the mob struck a deal with him, Peter thought. *"Take the fall and we'll take care of your family." Which is not such an unlikely idea. I wonder why it's so important that they keep Paulo out of jail. Has he moved up in the mob hierarchy? I'll pass this on to Intelligence and Organized Crime, anyway.*

". . . there would only be, on one day only," Giacomo went on, "a short story, buried in the back pages, that a dishonest policeman had admitted his guilt and had been sentenced. There are people who are wise in public relations, and I would include our beloved mayor among them, who would think that alternative would be preferable to a long and sordid public trial."

I'm agreeing with him again, which means that I am getting in over my head. I am now going to swim for shore before I drown.

"Before we go in for lunch, Armando, and apropos of nothing whatever, I would suggest that if Mr. Cassandro wants any kind of consideration at all from anybody you know, he's going to have to come up with more than a possible solution to a public relations problem."

"I understand, Peter," Armando said smoothly. "Such as what?"

"You've heard about the murder of Officer Jerry Kellog?" Wohl asked.

Giacomo nodded. "Tragic. Shot down in cold blood in his own house, according to the *Ledger.*"

"The *Ledger* also implied that a Homicide detective was involved," Wohl said. "My bet is that it's related to Narcotics. I would be grateful for any information that would lead the Department down that path."

"And then there's the double murder at the Inferno Lounge," Weisbach said. "Some people think that looks like a contract hit. I think the Department might be grateful for information that would help them there."

From the look on his face, Peter Wohl thought, *he thinks there is a mob connection.*

Confirmation came immediately.

"Those people, and you two know this as well as I do, have a code of honor . . ."

"Call it a code, if you like, but the word 'honor' is inappropriate," Peter said.

"Whatever you want to call it, turning in one of their own violates it," Giacomo said.

"They also don't fool around with each other's wives, either, do they?" Weisbach said. "And I wouldn't be at all surprised if they give a percentage of their earnings from prostitution and drugs to worthy causes and the church. Despite what you may have heard, they're really not bad people, are they, Armando?"

Giacomo looked very uncomfortable.

"A top-level decision would have to be made," Peter interrupted. "Who goes to jail? Who is more valuable? Paulo Cassandro or a hit man? Who goes directly to jail without passing 'go'?"

What the hell am I doing? Bargaining with the mob? Making a deal to have the mob do something the Police Department should be doing itself? Cassandro bribed some dirty cops. We caught them. They should all go to jail, not just the cops. Paulo Cassandro should not walk because it will increase Jerry Carlucci's chances of getting reelected.

Wohl stood up.

"Is something wrong?" Giacomo asked.

"I'm not sure I want to eat lunch," he said. "And I know I have enough of this conversation."

Weisbach stood up. Giacomo looked up at them, and then stood up himself.

"I thank you for your indulgence," he said. "I would be deeply pained if this conversation affected our friendship."

Oddly enough, I believe him. Which probably proves I was right about getting in over my head.

"Please, let's not let this ruin a lunch with friends. Come and break bread with me, please," Giacomo said.

Wohl didn't reply for a moment.

"I was about to say, only if I can pay. But I can't pay in here, can I?"

"No. And it is an expulsable offense for a member to let a guest reimburse him. If that's important to you, Peter, would you like to go somewhere else?"

Wohl met his eyes for a moment.

"No," he said finally. "I think we understand each other, Armando. We can eat here."

South Rittenhouse Square—on the south side of Rittenhouse Square in Center City Philadelphia—is no wider than it was when it was laid out at the time of the American Revolution. There are a half-dozen NO PARKING AT ANY TIME—TOW AWAY ZONE signs, warning citizens that if they park there at any time, it is virtually certain that to reclaim their car, it will be necessary for them to somehow make their way halfway across Philadelphia to the Parking Authority impoundment lot at Delaware Avenue and Spring Garden Street and there both pay a hefty fine for illegal parking and generously compensate the City of Brotherly Love for the services of the Parking Authority tow truck that hauled their car away.

Despite this, when Amelia Payne, M.D., drove past the building housing the Delaware Valley Cancer Society, there were seven automobiles parked in front of it, all of them with their right-side wheels on the sidewalk. There was a new Oldsmobile sedan, a battered Volkswagen, a ten-year-old, gleaming Jaguar XK120, a new Mercedes convertible, a new Buick sedan, and two new sedans, a Ford and a Chevrolet.

There's not even room enough for me, Dr. Payne thought somewhat indignantly. Like most of her fellow practitioners of the healing arts, she was in the habit of interpreting rather loosely the privilege granted to physicians of ignoring NO PARKING AT ANY TIME signs when making emergency calls.

And she had intended to do so now, by placing her official PHYSICIAN MAKING CALL card on the dashboard of the Buick station wagon, because the basement garage of the Cancer Society Building, to which she had access, had a very narrow entrance passage that she had difficulty negotiating.

She continued past the Delaware Valley Cancer Society Building, noticing with annoyance the beat cop on the corner, his arms folded on his chest, calmly surveying his domain and oblivious to the multiple violations of parking laws.

Professional courtesy, she thought. *Damn the cops!*

She had recognized four of the cars—the Oldsmobile, the Volkswagen, the Jaguar, and the Mercedes—as belonging respectively to Chief Inspector Dennis V. Coughlin, Detective Charles McFadden, Inspector Peter Wohl, and Captain David Pekach, and had drawn, as the cop obviously had, the natural and correct conclusion that the rest of the cars were also the official or personal automobiles of other policemen (or in the case of Pekach, belonged to his fiancée, Miss Martha Peebles, which was just about the same thing) who regarded parking regulations as applying only to civilians.

She drove to South Nineteenth Street, where she turned right, and then made the next right, and ultimately reached the entrance of the underground garage, which, surprising her not at all, she failed to maneuver through unscathed. This time she scraped the right fender against a wall.

This served to further lower her morale. In addition to the early-morning horror at the Detweilers', she had just come from University Hospital, where a patient of hers, an attractive young woman whom she had originally diagnosed as suffering from routine postpartum depression, was manifesting symptoms of more serious mental illness that Amy simply could not fathom, nor could anyone else she had consulted.

She was not surprised, either, to find both of the reserved parking places she intended to use already occupied. One of them held a silver Porsche 911, and the other a Buick wagon identical to hers, save it was two years younger and unscratched and undented.

The Buick belonged to her father, who could be expected to offer some clever witticism about the dents in her Buick, and the Porsche to her brother. The Delaware Valley Cancer Society Building was owned by her father, and her brother occupied a tiny apartment in what had been the garret before the 1850s building had been gutted and converted into offices behind the original facade.

She parked the Buick—neatly straddling a marking line between spaces—and got out of the car. The elevator did not respond to her summons, and only after a while did she remember that it was late—she consulted her watch and saw that it was well after midnight—and remembered that at this hour, the elevator was locked. It would be necessary to call Matt's apartment by telephone, whereupon he could push a button activating the elevator.

And he took his damned sweet time answering the telephone, and when he did, it wasn't him, but a clipped, metallic voice she did not at first recognize.

"Yes?"

"This is Dr. Payne. Would you please push the elevator button?"

There was the sound of male laughter in the background.

"Just a moment, darlin'," the voice said. "I'll ask Matty how to work it."

She now recognized the voice to be that of chief Inspector Dennis V. Coughlin. Normally, she did not mind his addressing her as "darlin'," but now it annoyed her.

The line went dead, and she stood there for a full minute, waiting for the sound of a buzzer, or whatever, which would bring the elevator to life. It gave her time to consider that what was going on upstairs was really an Irish wake, the males of the clan gathering to console one of their number who had suffered a loss.

She reached for the telephone again, then changed her mind and pushed the elevator button again. This time she was rewarded with the sound of the elevator moving.

It took her to the third floor. A closed door led to the narrow flight of stairs to Matt's apartment. She pushed the button, and in a moment, a solenoid buzzed and she was able to push the door open.

She was greeted again with the sound of male laughter, which for some reason annoyed her, although another part of her mind said that it was probably therapeutic.

She walked up the stairs.

The tiny apartment was jammed. In the living room, she saw Martha Peebles sitting on a small couch with Mary-Margaret McCarthy—Detective Charley McFadden's girlfriend—and a tall young man she recognized as Matt's friend Jack Matthews, an FBI agent. The small table in front of the couch was covered with jackets. It was hot in the apartment, and most of the men had taken off their jackets and pulled down their ties and rolled up their sleeves.

Which also served to reveal that most of them were armed. There were shoulder holsters and waist holsters, most of them carrying snub-nosed .38-caliber revolvers.

The tribal insignia, Amy thought, *like that little purse or whatever Scots wear hanging down over their kilts.*

Matt's two small armchairs held Captain David Pekach and Lieutenant Jack Malone, having what seemed to be a serious conversation; they didn't look at her.

Martha Peebles smiled and stood up when she saw her, and stepped over Mary-Margaret McCarthy and the FBI agent to come to her. Mary-Margaret and the FBI agent smiled at her.

"How's Grace?" Martha Peebles asked softly as she put her cheek next to Amy's.

"I stopped off earlier and gave her something to help her sleep," Amy said.

"How terrible for her!"

Amy nodded.

A large arm gently draped itself around Amy's shoulders. She looked up into the face of Chief Inspector Dennis V. Coughlin.

"I checked with the Medical Examiner," he said softly. "He released the body at noon. Kirk and Nice picked it up at half past twelve."

"I know, Uncle Denny," she said. "Thank you."

She looked around for Matt. He was in the kitchen, leaning against the refrigerator, holding a can of beer. He didn't seem drunk, which could or could not be a good thing. There was no sign that he was armed, but Amy knew better. Matt carried his .38 snub-nose in an ankle holster.

"It was the right way to go, darlin'," Coughlin said. "Thank you for trusting me."

"I always trust you, Uncle Denny," she said sincerely, and with a smile.

He squeezed her shoulder.

"Uncle Denny, I think it might be a good idea to get all these people out of here."

"I was thinking the same thing, darlin'."

"Getting him to take it might be a problem, but I'll try to give him something to help him sleep."

"I'll see to it," Coughlin said, and raised his voice. "David? See you a minute?"

Amy walked into the kitchen. Sitting at the small table, which was covered with whiskey bottles, empty cans, and the remnants of a take-out Chinese buffet were Inspector Peter Wohl, his father, Chief Inspector August Wohl (Retired), Captain Mike Sabara, Detective Charley McFadden, and her father.

"I agree with McFadden," Amy heard Chief Wohl say. "If he'd been hit in the head with a two-by-four, or something, I'd say he walked in on a burglar, but two bullets in the back of the head? That makes it a hit."

Detective McFadden beamed to have the Chief agree with him.

Amy walked up to her brother, and resisted the temptation to kiss him. He looked desolate.

"How're you doing, Sherlock?"

He nodded and raised his beer can.

"OK. You want a beer?"

"Yes," she said after a moment's hesitation. "I think I would. Thank you."

"The beer's been gone for an hour," Peter Wohl said. "We can call and get some. Or would you like something stronger?"

"Hello, Peter," Amy said. "How are you?"

"Long time no see," he said evenly.

"There's scotch, bourbon, and gin, honey," Brewster C. Payne said. "And Irish."

"Yes, of course, Irish," Amy said. "An Irish, please. A short one, over the rocks. And then I think we should call off the wake."

Her father nodded and stood up to make the drink.

"Have you been out to Chestnut Hill?" he asked.

"Not since I saw you there. I gave Grace something to help her sleep, and I called a while ago and Violet said she'd gone to bed. I was tied up at the hospital."

"I left when Dick went to sleep," her father said.

In other words, passed out, Amy thought. *He was three-quarters drunk when I left there.*

"I'll go out there first thing in the morning," Amy said, and then turned to her brother. "I asked you how you're doing?"

He shrugged.

"What a goddamned waste," he said.

"I want a minute with you alone when everybody's gone," she said.

"None of your goddamned pills, Amy."

"I'm trying to help," she said.

"Yeah, I know."

"Your beer must be warm."

"Is that a prescription? Booze in lieu of happy pills?"

"It might help you sleep."

He met her eyes for a moment.

"Dad, could you make two of those, please?" he called.

Their father turned to look over his shoulder at her. She nodded, just perceptibly, and he reached for another glass.

"Charley," Mary-Margaret McCarthy called, "we're going."

There was a tone of command in her voice. She was a nurse, an R.N. who had gone back to school to get a degree, and was, she had once confided in Amy, thinking about going for an M.D.

McFadden immediately stood up.

Matt needs somebody like that, Amy thought. *A strong-willed young woman as smart as he is. He didn't need Penny.*

God, what a terrible thing to even think!

"We're going too," Martha Peebles announced. She already had her David—whom she usually called, to his intense embarrassment, "Precious"—in tow.

One by one, the men filed into the kitchen and shook Matt's hand.

"Circumstances aside, it was good to see you, Amy," Peter Wohl said, and offered her his hand.

"Thank you," she said.

He was almost at the top of the stairs when she went quickly after him.

"Peter, wait a moment," she called, and he stopped. "I'd like to talk to you," Amy said.

"Sure. When? Will it wait until morning?"

"I won't be with Matt more than a minute," she said

"OK," he said with what she interpreted as reluctance, and then went down the stairs.

Her father touched her shoulder.

"You're the doctor. Is there anything I should be doing for Matt?"

"Just what you are doing," she said.

"Should I go out to Chestnut Hill in the morning, or is it better . . ."

"He's your friend, Dad," Amy said. "You'll have to decide."

"Yes, of course."

Finally, after a final hug from Denny Coughlin, Amy was alone with Matt.

He met her eyes, waiting for whatever she had to say.

"This was not your fault, Matt. She had a chemical addiction—"

"She was a junkie."

"—which she was unable to manage."

"And I wasn't a hell of a lot of help, was I?"

"What happened is not your fault, Matt."

"So everyone keeps telling me."

"The best thing you can do—an emotional trauma like this is exhausting—is to get a good night's sleep."

"And things will seem better in the morning, right?"

"I've got something to give you . . ."

"No, thank you."

". . . a mild sedative."

"In case you haven't noticed, I'm not climbing the walls, or hysterical, or . . ."

"It's inside, Matt, it's a pain. It will have to come out. The better shape you're in when it does, the better. That's why you need to sleep."

"You are your father's daughter, aren't you? You never know when to take no for an answer."

"OK. But people, even tough guys like you, have been known to change their minds. I'll leave the pills."

"Take two and call me in the morning?" Matt asked, now smiling.

"If you take two, you won't be able to use a telephone in the morning. One, Matt, with water, preferably not on an empty stomach."

"My stomach is full of Chinese."

"I'll be at home until half past seven or so," Amy said. "If you want to talk."

"Amy, believe it or not, I'm touched by your concern," Matt said. "But all I need is to finish this"—he held up his whiskey glass—"and get in bed."

And then he surprised her by putting his arms around her.

"Who holds your hand when you need it, Doc?" he asked softly. "Don't you ever get it up to here with other people's problems?"

"Yeah," she said, surprised at her emotional reaction. "Just between thee, me, and the lamp pole, I do. But not with your problems, Matt. You're my little brother."

"Chronologically speaking only, of course."

She hugged him, and then broke away.

"Go to bed," she said. "I'll see you tomorrow."

She went down the narrow flight of stairs and turned at the bottom and looked up.

"Try to stay on the black stuff between parked cars, Amy," Matt called down to her with a wave.

"Wiseass," she called back, and closed the door to the stairs. She had just enough time to be surprised to find the landing empty when she heard the whine of the elevator.

That has to be Peter, she thought. *If he said he would wait for me, he will.*

And then she just had time to recognize the depth of her original disappointment when the elevator door opened. It was not Peter, it was Jason Washington.

Where the hell is Peter? Did he decide, "Screw her, I'm going home"?

"Good evening, Doctor," Washington said in his sonorous voice. "Or, more accurately, good morning."

"Mr. Washington."

"Do I correctly surmise from the look of disapproval on your face that now is not a good time to call on Matt?"

"No. As a matter of fact," Amy said with a nervous laugh—Jason Washington was a formidable male—"I think you'd be good for him. He said he was going to bed, but I don't believe him."

"I couldn't get here earlier," he said. "Inspector Wohl—he's with the security officer in the lobby—thought perhaps you . . ."

Peter did wait. Why are you so damned pleased?

"I think you're very kind to come at this hour, and that Matt will be delighted to see you."

"Thank you," Washington said, and waved her onto the elevator.

Peter did not smile when he saw her.

"Thank you for waiting," she said. "I really wanted to talk to you."

"So you said."

"Could we go somewhere for coffee? Or a drink?"

They locked eyes for a moment.

"Most of the places I'd take you to around here are closed."

"Would you have time to stop by my apartment?"

"Somehow I don't think that's an invitation to breakfast."

"Of course it wasn't," she snapped. "I want to talk about Matt. Nothing else."

"We tried the other, right, and it didn't work?"

"It didn't seem to, did it?"

"I'll meet you in your lobby," Peter said. "I hate to follow people."

"Thank you," she said, and got back on the elevator. By the time she turned around, he was already out the door.

"How are you holding up, Matthew?" Jason Washington asked as he reached the top of the steep flight of stairs.

"Most often by leaning against the wall," Matt replied

"He said, masking his pain with humor. I am your friend, Matthew. Answer the question."

"You know the old joke: 'How is your wife?' and the reply, 'Compared to what?' I don't know how I'm supposed to feel."

"Try a one-word reply."

"Empty," Matt said after a moment.

Washington grunted.

"I would suggest that is a normal reaction," he said. "I would have been here earlier, Matthew, but I was about the King's business, protecting our fair city from assorted mountebanks, scoundrels, and scalawags."

Matt chuckled. "Thanks for coming."

"I'm very sorry about Penny, Matt," Washington said.

"Thank you."

"It was originally my intention, and that of my fair lady, to come to add our voices to the chorus of those telling you that you are in no way responsible for what happened."

"Thank you."

"I mean that. I am not just saying it."

"I know," Matt said.

"My lesser half—who is a bitch on wheels when awakened from her slumber in the wee hours—is going to be mightily piqued when I finally show up at home and tell her I have been here alone."

Matt chuckled.

"Considering that sacrifice I have made—you have seen the lady in a state of pique and should be sympathetic—do you think you could find it in your heart to offer me one of whatever it is you're drinking?"

"Sorry," Matt said. "This is Irish. Is that all right?"

"Gaelic chauvinist's scotch will do nicely. Thank you," Washington said.

"You've been on the job?" Matt asked as he walked toward the kitchen.

"Indeed."

"I thought you'd be taking some time off, going to the Shore or something."

"There have been several interesting developments," Washington said. "What opinion did you form of Staff Inspector Weisbach?"

"I liked him. He's smart as hell."

"That's good, because he's our new boss."

"Really?"

"Would you be interested in his opinion of you?"

"Yeah."

"He said you need to be held on a tight leash."

"Is that what he said?"

"That's what he said."

"You said 'our new boss.' Are we going to be involved in this Ethical Affairs business?"

"I think we are the Ethical Affairs Unit."

"That sounds like Internal Affairs by another name."

Matt walked back into his living room and handed Washington the drink.

"Not precisely. Wohl and Weisbach have elected to lend a broad interpretation to their mandate."

"Wohl was here."

"I saw him in the lobby."

"He didn't say anything to me about . . . anything."

"Under the circumstances . . ."

"He did mention half a dozen times that what I have to do is put . . . what happened to Penny . . . behind me, and get on with my life."

"And so you should. Anyway, Armando C. Giacomo had Wohl and Weisbach as his guests for lunch at the Rittenhouse Club."

"He's representing Cassandro?"

"Uh-huh. And Mr. Cassandro really does not wish to go to jail. Mr. Giacomo proposed a deal: Cassandro testifies against Cazerra, Meyer, and company, in exchange for immunity from prosecution."

"They're not going to deal, are they? They don't need his testimony. We have the bastard cold."

"What Peter and Weisbach find interesting is why the deal was proposed. Giacomo can, if he can't get him off completely, delay his trial for forever and a day, and then keep him from actually going to jail, with one appeal or another, for another couple of years. So, what, in other words, is going on?"

"What is?"

"Weisbach and Wohl, taking a shot in the dark, told Giacomo that the only thing we're interested in, vis-à-vis Cassandro, that might accrue to his advantage would be help with the murder of Officer Kellog and what happened at the Inferno Lounge. According to Weisbach, Giacomo acted as if something might be worked out."

"The mob would give us one, or both, doers in exchange for Cassandro?"

Washington nodded. "Which, since that would constitute a gross violation of the Sicilian Code of Honor, again raises the question, Why is Cassandro not going to trial so important? And that is what Weisbach and I have been trying to find out."

"And?"

"Nothing so far."

"Anything turn up on the Inferno Lounge job?"

"No. But I suspect there may be a connection there. Rather obviously, it was a hit, not a robbery. If it was a contract hit, it was expensive. If they give us that doer, that means Cassandro not going to jail is really important, and we're back to why."

Matt grunted.

"Anyway, you'll be close to that one. You're still going to Homicide. Whenever you feel up to coming back on the job."

"If I had my druthers, I'd come back tomorrow morning. I really dread tomorrow."

"At something of a tangent," Washington said, "I have something to say which may sound cruel. But I think I should say it. My first reaction when I heard what happened was relief."

Matt didn't reply at first.

"I've also felt that," he said finally. "It makes me feel like a real sonofabitch."

"I've seen a good many murders, Matt. And more than my fair share of narcotics addicts. I hold the private opinion that a pusher commits a far more heinous crime than— for example—whoever shot Officer Kellog. Or Mrs. Alicia Atchison and Mr. Anthony J.

Marcuzzi at the Inferno. For them, it was over instantaneously. It was brutal, but not as brutal as taking the life of a young woman, in painful stages, over a long period of time."

Matt did not reply.

"The point of this little philosophical observation, Matt, is that Penny was murdered the first time she put a needle in her arm. When you . . . became romantically involved . . . with one another, she was already dead. The man who killed her was the man who gave her her first hard drugs."

"I loved her."

"Yes, I know."

"We had a fight the last time I saw her. About me being a cop."

"If you had agreed to become the Nesfoods International Vice President in Charge of Keeping the Boss's Daughter Happy as of tomorrow morning, Matt," Washington said seriously, "she would have found some other excuse to seek narcotic euphoria. The addiction was out of her control. It had nothing to do with you. You've got to believe that, for the simple reason that it's true."

"I'll never know now, will I?"

Washington met his eyes, then set his drink down.

"Let's go bar-crawling."

"What?" Matt asked, surprised at the suggestion.

"How long have you been up here in the garret?"

Matt thought about that before replying.

"I got here about one-thirty."

"Twelve hours in a smoke-filled room. That's enough. Get your coat."

"Where are we going?"

"The Mall Tavern. At Tenth and Cherry. When I was an honest Homicide detective, I used to go there for a post-duty libation. Let's go listen to the gossip. Maybe we'll hear something interesting."

14.

He doesn't look like a cop, Amy thought when she saw Peter talking to the night manager in the lobby of her apartment building. *Mr. Ramerez has put the well-cut suit and the Jaguar together and decided Dr. Payne is carrying on with a lawyer or a stockbroker.*

"Good evening, Doctor," Peter said.

"Thank you for coming at this hour," Amy replied. "Shall we go up?" She smiled at Mr. Ramerez. "Good evening, Mr. Ramerez."

It is obviously important to me that Mr. Ramerez understand that I am not carrying on with him, cop or stockbroker.

They rode in silence and somewhat awkwardly to Amy's apartment. She unlocked the door, and entered. He followed her.

"Coffee? Or a drink?" she asked.

"Neither, thank you. You said you wanted to talk about Matt."

"I think it important that he not be left alone."

"Tiny Lewis—he's a police officer . . ."

"I know who he is," Amy interrupted.

Peter nodded and went on: ". . . will be at Matt's apartment at seven-fifteen in the morning. If you think he should not be alone tonight, I can go back."

"I think he'll be all right tonight," she said. "Can you keep him busy? Especially for the next few days?"

Wohl nodded.

"He blames himself for Penny," Amy said.

"Yes, I know."

"I don't know if you appreciate it, but he is actually rather sensitive."

"I know."

"You know what he did tonight?" she asked, and went on without waiting for a reply. "He put his arms around me and asked who holds my hand when I need it."

"There has been at least one applicant for that job that I know about. As I recall, you didn't seem interested."

"Damn you, Peter, you're not making this easy."

"I don't know if you appreciate it, but I am actually rather sensitive," Wohl mockingly paraphrased what she had said about Matt.

"You bastard!" she said, but laughed. "Honest to God, Peter, I didn't want to hurt you."

He shrugged.

"I lied," Amy said.

"Not returning calls, not being in, having 'previous plans' when I finally got you on the phone is not exactly lying."

"I mean tonight," Amy said. "Certainly to you, and probably to myself. I knew that you, the Ancient and Honorable Order of Cops, were going to gather protectively around Matt and do more for him than I could."

Wohl looked at her, waiting for her to go on.

"I wanted somebody, to hold my hand. Penny Detweiler was my patient. I failed her."

He looked at her a moment.

"Somebody? Anybody? Or me?"

"I knew you would be there," Amy said.

Peter held his arms open. She took several hesitant steps toward him, and ultimately wound up with her face on his chest.

"Amy, you did everything that could be done for that girl," Peter said, putting his hand on the back of her head, gently caressing it. "Some people are beyond help. Or don't want it."

"Oh, God, Peter! I feel so lousy about it!"

He felt her back stiffen under his hand, and then tremble with repressed sobs.

"Tell you what I'm going to do, Doc," he said gently. "On one condition, I will accept your kind invitation to breakfast."

She pushed away from him and looked up at his face.

"I made no such invitation."

"That I cook breakfast. The culinary arts not being among your many other accomplishments."

"You think that would help?"

"I don't think it would hurt."

"I don't even know if there's anything in the fridge."

"So I'll open a can of spaghetti."

Amy tried to smile, failed, and put her head against his chest. She felt his arms tighten around her.

"Would you rather tear off my clothes here, or should we wait until we get into the bedroom?"

It was half past seven when the ringing of his door buzzer woke Matt Payne.

He fumbled on his bedside table for his wristwatch, saw the time, muttered a sacrilege, and got out of bed.

The buzzer went off again, for about five seconds.

"I'm coming, for Christ's sake," Matt said, although there was no possibility at all that anyone could hear him.

There was ten seconds of silence as he looked around for his discarded underpants—it being his custom to sleep in his birthday suit—and then another five seconds of buzzer.

He was halfway through the kitchen when the buzzer sounded again.

He found the button that activated the door's solenoid, pushed it, and then continued through the kitchen and the living room to the head of the stairs. When he looked down, the bulk of Officer Foster H. Lewis, Jr., attired in a nicely cut dark-blue suit, nearly filled the narrow stairway.

"Tiny, what the hell do you want?" Matt asked, far less than graciously.

"What I want to do is be home in my bed," Tiny Lewis replied. "What I have been told to do is not let you out of my sight."

"By who?"

"Wohl," Tiny said as he reached the head of the stairs. "God, are you always that hard to wake up? I've been sitting on that damned buzzer for ten minutes. I was about to take the door."

"I didn't get to bed until three," Matt said.

Tiny looked uncomfortable.

"Matt, I don't think booze is the solution."

"I was with Washington at the Mall Tavern."

"Doing what?"

"Ostensibly, it was so that he and I could listen to Homicide gossip. About the time he went home, I decided it was to introduce me socially to the Homicide guys; he was playing rabbi for me."

"My father said they're really going to be pissed that the Mayor sent you over there."

"I think their reaction, thanks to Washington, has been reduced from homicidal rage, pun intended, to bitter resentment by Washington's act of charity. Actually, they seemed to understand it wasn't my doing."

"I would have been here yesterday," Tiny said. "Personally, not because Wohl would have sent me. But Washington said there would be enough people here then, and I should come today." Tiny paused. "I'm sorry about what happened, Matt."

"Thank you."

"Anyway, you're stuck with me," Tiny said. "And apropos of nothing whatever, I haven't had my breakfast."

"See what's in the refrigerator while I have a shower," Matt said.

Matt came back into the kitchen ten minutes later to the smell of frying bacon and percolating coffee, and the sight of Tiny Lewis neatly arranging tableware on the kitchen table. He had taken off his suit jacket and put on an apron. It was a full-sized apron, but on Tiny's massive bulk it appeared much smaller. He looked ridiculous, and Matt smiled.

"I'll bet you can iron very well, too," he said.

"Fuck you, you don't get no breakfast," Tiny replied amiably.

"When you're through with that, you can vacuum the living room."

"Fuck you again," Tiny said. "Tell me about the double homicide at the Inferno."

Over breakfast, Matt told him.

"This Atchison guy is very good," he concluded. "Smart and tough. And his lawyer is good, too. Just when Milham was starting to get him, the lawyer—"

"Who's his lawyer?"

"A guy named Sidney Margolis."

Tiny snorted. "I know who he is. A real sleazeball. My father told me he's been reported to the bar association so often he's got his own filing cabinet."

"He's smart. He saw Milham was getting to Atchison, and said, 'Interview over. My client is in great pain.' "

"Was he?"

"After Margolis told him he was, he was. And that was it."

"I wish I could have seen the interview," Tiny said.

"Milham is very good."

"You heard about his lady friend's husband?"

"Yeah."

"Do you think he had anything to do with it?"

"No," Matt said immediately.

"Either does my father," Tiny said. "He said it's two-to-one it's something to do with Narcotics. Heading the long list of things I was absolutely forbidden to do when I came on the job was accept an assignment to Narcotics. He said those guys roll around on the pigsty floor so much, and there's so much money floating around that he's not surprised how many of them are dirty, but how many are straight."

"Charley and the Little Spic were undercover narcs, and so was Captain Pekach. They're straight."

"The exceptions that prove the rule," Tiny said. "So what do we do today?"

"I don't know what you're going to do, but I'm going out to Chestnut Hill in half an hour. Jesus, I hate to face that! The funeral is this afternoon."

"You mean, *we're* going to Chestnut Hill. I have heard my master's voice, and it said I'm not to let you out of my sight."

"Family and intimate friends only," Matt said. "I think it will be my family, the Detweilers, and the Nesbitts. And that's it."

"So what do I tell Wohl, since the riffraff aren't welcome?"

"I'll call him."

"Matt, I don't mind feeling unwelcome. With a suntan like mine, you get pretty used to it. If I can help some way . . ."

"You'd make a lousy situation worse, Tiny, but thanks," Matt said. He got up from the table and started toward the telephone, then stopped. He touched Tiny's shoulder, and Tiny looked up at him. "I appreciate that, pal," Matt said.

"Somehow saying I'm sorry about what happened doesn't seem to be enough."

Matt picked up the telephone and dialed Wohl's home number. When there was no answer, he called the headquarters of the Special Operations Division to see if, as he often did, Wohl had come to work early. When Wohl's private line was not answered by the fifth ring, the call was automatically transferred to the line of the tour lieutenant.

"Special Operations, Lieutenant Suffern."

"Matt Payne, sir. Have you got a location on the Inspector?"

"Yeah. I got a number. Just a minute, Matt," Lieutenant Suffern said, and then his voice changed: "Matt, I was sorry to hear . . ."

"Thank you."

"If there's anything I can do?"

"I can't think of a thing, but thank you. I appreciate the thought."

"Here it is," Suffern said. "One-thirty A.M. this morning until further notice." He then read Matt the telephone number at which Inspector Wohl could be reached.

A look of mingled amusement and annoyance flickered across Matt's face. The number he had been given was familiar to him. It was the one number in Greater Philadelphia where calling Inspector Wohl at this time would be a very bad idea indeed. It was that of the apartment of his sister, Amelia Payne, M.D., Ph.D.

"Thank you, sir."

"When you feel up to it, Matt, we'll go hoist a couple."

"Thank you," Matt said. "I'd like to."

Matt hung up and turned to Tiny, a smile crossing his face at his own wit.

"Wohl can't be reached right now," he said. "He's at the doctor's."

"So what do we do?"

"When all else fails, tell the truth," Matt said. "You go to the schoolhouse and when Wohl shows up you tell him I said 'Thank you, but no thank you. I don't want any company.' "

"I don't know, Matt," Tiny said dubiously. "Wohl wasn't making a suggestion. He told me to sit on you."

"Oh, shit," Matt said, and dialed Amy's number.

"Dr. Payne is not available at this time," her answering machine reported. "If you will leave your name and number, she will return your call as soon as possible. Please wait for the tone. Thank you."

"Amy, I know you're there. I need to talk to Inspector Wohl."

A moment later, Wohl himself came on the line.

"What is it, Matt?"

"Tiny Lewis is here. Having him go with me to the Detweilers' is not such a good idea. The funeral is family and intimate friends only."

"So your sister has been telling me," Wohl said. "He's there? Put him on the line."

Matt held the phone up, and Tiny rose massively from the table and took it.

"Yes, sir?" he said.

Tiny's was the only side of the conversation Matt could hear, and he was curious when Tiny chuckled, a deep rumble, and said, "I would, too. That'd be something to see."

When he hung up, Matt asked, "What would be 'something to see'?"

"The Mayor's face when somebody tells him he can't get in. Wohl said he knows the Mayor's going to the funeral."

"This one he may not get to go to," Matt said. "My father said nobody's been invited, period."

"Wohl also said I was to drive you out there, if you wanted, and then to keep myself available. I was going to do that anyway."

"You can take me over to the Parkway as soon as I get dressed. I'm going to drive my sister out there, in her car."

"Yeah, sure. But listen to what I said. You need me, you know where to find me."

Inspector Peter Wohl was examining the hole gouged in his cheek by Amy Payne's dull razor—and from which an astonishing flow of blood was now escaping—when Amy appeared in the bathroom door.

She was in her underwear. It was white, and what there was of it was mostly lace. He found the sight very appealing, and wondered if that was her everyday underwear, or whether she had worn it for him.

That pleasant notion was immediately shattered by her tone of voice and the look on her face.

"It's for you," she said. "Again. Does everyone in Philadelphia know you're here?"

"Sorry," he said, and quickly tore off a square of toilet paper, pressed it to the wound, and went into her bedroom. He sat on the bed and grabbed the telephone.

"Inspector Wohl."

"I'm sorry to trouble you, sir," Jason Washington's deep, mellifluous voice said.

Washington's the soul of discretion. When he got this number from the tour lieutenant—and with that memory of his, he probably knows whose number it is—unless it was important, he would have waited until I went to work.

"No trouble. I'm just sitting here quietly bleeding to death. Good morning, Jason. What's up?"

"I just had an interesting call. An informant who has been reliable with what he's given me—which hasn't been much—in the past. He said the Inferno murders were a mob contract."

"Interesting. Did he give you a name?"

"Frankie Foley."

"Never heard of him."

Amy sat on the bed beside him and put her hand on his cheek. It was a gesture of affection, but only by implication. She had a cotton swab dipped in some kind of antiseptic. She pulled the toilet paper bandage off and professionally swabbed his gouge.

"Either have I. And neither has Organized Crime or Intelligence."

"Even more interesting."

"What do you want me to do with it?"

It was a moment before Wohl replied.

"Give it to Homicide. And then see if you can make a connection to Cassandro."

"Yes, sir."

Wohl had an unpleasant thought. There was a strong possibility that he would have to remind Washington that a new chain of command was in effect. Washington was used to reporting directly to him. He might not like having to go through Weisbach.

"What did Weisbach say when you told him?"

"He said he thought we better give it to Homicide, but to ask you first."

Thank God! Personnel conflict avoided.

"Write this down, Jason. The true sign of another man's intelligence is the degree to which he agrees with you."

Washington laughed.

"I'll be in touch," he said, and hung up.

"Who was that?" Amy asked.

"Jason Washington."

"I thought so. How did he know you were here? What did you do, put an ad in the *Bulletin?* Who else knows where you spent the night?"

"There is a very short list of people who have to know where I am all the time. The tour lieutenant knows where to find me. Since only Matt and Jason called, to answer your question two people have reason to suspect I spent the night here."

"God!"

"There is a solution to the problem," Peter said. "I could make an honest woman of you."

"Surely you jest," she said after a moment's pause.

"I don't know if I am or not," Peter said. "You better not consider that a firm offer."

She stood up. "Now I'm sorry I fixed your face," she said, and walked toward the bathroom.

"Nice ass," he called after her.

She gave him the finger without turning and went into the bathroom, closing the door.

Jesus, where did that "make an honest woman of you" crack come from?

He stood up and started looking for his clothing.

Lieutenant Foster H. Lewis, Sr., of the Ninth District, a very tall, well-muscled man, was sitting in a wicker armchair on the enclosed porch of his home reading the *Philadelphia Bulletin* when Officer Foster H. Lewis, Jr., of Special Operations, pushed the door open and walked in.

Tiny, who knew his father was working the midnight-out tour, was surprised to see him. It was his father's custom, when he came off the midnight-out tour, to take a shower and go to bed and get his eight hours' sleep. And here he was, in an obviously fresh white shirt, immaculately shaven, looking as if he was about to go on duty.

"I thought you were working the midnight-out," Tiny said.

"Good morning, son. How are you? I am fine, thank you for asking," Lieutenant Lewis said dryly.

"Sorry."

"I was supposed to fill in for Lieutenant Prater, who was ill," Lieutenant Lewis said. "When I got to the office, he had experienced a miraculous recovery. And *I* thought *you* were working days."

"I'm working," Tiny said, and gestured toward the car parked in the drive.

"How can you be working and here?"

"My orders, Lieutenant, sir, are to stay close to the radio, in case I'm needed."

"You needn't be sarcastic, Foster, it was a reasonable question."

"Inspector Wohl told me to give Matt Payne some company," Tiny said. "I wasn't needed."

"What a tragedy!" Lieutenant Lewis said.

"I thought I'd come see Mom," Tiny said.

"Since I would not be here, you mean?"

"Pop, every time I see you, you jump all over me."

"I wasn't aware of that."

"Just now," Tiny said. "The implication that I'm screwing off being here."

"I didn't say that."

"That's what you meant."

"You are driving a departmental vehicle, presumably on duty, visiting your family."

"I'm doing what I'm ordered to do. Pop, I'm a pretty good cop! Inspector Wohl expects me to be available if he needs me. I don't think he expected me to just sit in the car and wait for the radio to go off."

"You believe that, don't you?"

"Believe what?"

"That you're a pretty good cop."

"I'm not as good a cop as you are, but yeah, I'm a pretty good cop."

"I'm sure you will take offense when I say this, but you don't know what being a police officer really means."

"You mean, I never worked in a district?"

"Exactly."

"Come on, Pop. If Inspector Wohl thought I would learn anything riding around in a car, walking a beat, that's what he'd have me doing."

"That sort of thing is beneath you, right?"

"I think we better stop this before either one of us says something we'll be sorry for," Tiny said.

Lieutenant Lewis looked at his son for a moment before replying.

"I'm not saying that what you're doing is not important, or that you don't do it well."

"It is important—we're going to put a dirty captain and a dirty lieutenant away—and I helped. Wohl and Washington wouldn't have let me get close to that job if they didn't think I could handle it."

"All I'm saying, Foster," Lieutenant Lewis said, "is that I am concerned that you have no experience as a police officer on the street. You don't even have any friends who are common, ordinary policemen, do you?"

"I guess not," Tiny said.

"Would you indulge me if I asked you to do something?"

"Within reason."

It came out sarcastically, more disrespectfully than Tiny intended, and there was frost for a moment in his father's eyes. But then apparently he decided to let it pass.

"Did I understand you to say that, so long as you keep yourself available, you're free to move about the city?"

"That's right."

"Go inside, say hello to your mother, tell her you're coming to dinner tonight, and that we're going for a ride. Police business."

"A ride? What police business?"

"We're going to the Thirty-ninth District. I have a friend there, a common ordinary policeman, who I want you to meet. You might even learn something from him."

Police Officer Woodrow Wilson Bailey, Sr., badge number 2554 of the Thirty-ninth District, who had twenty-four years on the job, twenty-two of it in the Thirty-ninth District, wanted only one thing from the Philadelphia Police Department. He wanted to make it to retirement, tell them where to mail his retirement checks, and go back home to Hartsville, South Carolina.

Having done that, it was his devout hope that he would never have to put on a uniform, look at a gun, or see Philadelphia, Pennsylvania, ever again so long as the Good Lord saw fit to let him live.

He thought of it as going back to Hartsville, although in fact he could never remember living there. He had been brought to Philadelphia from Hartsville at the age of three by his father, who had decided that as bad as things might be up north, with the depression and all, they couldn't be any worse than being a sharecropper with a wife and child to feed on a hardscrabble farm in South Carolina.

The first memory of a home that Officer Bailey had was of an attic room in a row house on Sydenham in North Philadelphia. There was a table in it, and two beds, one for Mamma Dear and Daddy, and one for him, and then when Charles David came along, for him and Charles David. There was an electric hot plate, and a galvanized bucket for water. The bathroom was one floor down, and shared with the three families who occupied the five rooms on the second floor.

The room was provided to them by the charity of the Third Abyssinian Baptist Church, to which Officer Bailey and his family still belonged.

He had vague memories of Daddy leaving the apartment in the morning to seek work as a laborer, and much more clear memories of Daddy leaving the room (and later the two-room apartment on the second floor of another row house) carrying his shoe-shine box to walk downtown to station himself at the Market Street Station of the Pennsylvania Railroad to shine the shoes of the rich white folks who rode the train in from places with funny-sounding names like Bala Cynwyd and Glen Riddle.

And he had memories of Hartsville from those times, too. Of going to see Granny Bailey and Granny Smythe back in Hartsville. Mamma Dear and Daddy had believed with the other members of the Third Abyssinian Baptist Church that if it was in the Bible, that was all there was to it, you did what it said, and you spent eternity with the Good Lord, or you didn't, and you spent eternity in the fiery fires of Hell. It said in the Good Book that you were supposed to Honor Thy Mother and Thy Father, and that meant you went to see your mother and your father at least at Christmas, and more often if you could afford it, and affording it meant saving up to buy the bus tickets, and for a few little presents to take with you, even if that meant you didn't get to drink Coca-Cola or go to the movies.

Bailey had liked Hartsville even then, even if he now recognized that Granny Smythe's "farm" was nothing more than a weathered shack without inside plumbing that sat on three acres she had been given in the will of old Mr. Smythe—probably because it wasn't worth the powder to blow it away—whose father had bought Granny Smythe's father at a slave auction in Beaufort.

There were chickens on Granny Smythe's farm, and a couple of dogs, and almost always a couple of pigs, and the whole place had seemed a much nicer place to live than in a row house in North Philadelphia.

He had asked several times why they had to live in Philadelphia, and Daddy had told him that he didn't expect him to understand, but that Philadelphia was a place where you could better yourself, get a good education, and make something of yourself.

Bailey remembered being dropped off with Charles David at the Third Abyssinian Baptist Church by Mamma Dear, wearing a crisp white maid's uniform, so he and Charles David could be cared for, and she could work and make some money and realize her and Daddy's dream of buying a house that would be theirs, instead of paying rent.

He remembered the beating Daddy had given him with a leather belt when he was in the fifth grade at the Dunbar Elementary School and the teacher had come by the house they were then renting and reported that he had not only been cutting school, but giving her talk-back in class, and running around with the wrong crowd.

Charles David, who was now a welder at the Navy Shipyard, still told that story, said that he got through high school because he had been there when Daddy had taken a strap to Woodrow for cutting school and sassing the teacher at Dunbar, and he was smart enough to learn by vicarious experience.

Woodrow had graduated from Dunbar Elementary School and gone on to graduate from William Penn High School. By then, Daddy had gone from shining shoes inside the Market Street Station to shining them in a barbershop on South Ninth Street, and finally to shining them in the gents' room of the Rittenhouse Club on Rittenhouse Square. He was on salary then, paid to be in the gents' room from just before lunch until maybe nine o'clock at night, shining anybody who climbed up on the chair's shoes for free. It was part of what you got being a member of the Rittenhouse Club, getting your shoes shined for free.

The members weren't supposed to pay the shoe-shine boy, but, Daddy had told him, maybe about one in four would hand him a quarter or fifty cents anyway, and at Christmas, about three or four of the members whose shoes he had shined all year would wish him "Merry Christmas" and slip him some folding money. Usually it was ten or twenty dollars, but sometimes more. The first one-hundred-dollar bill Woodrow had ever seen in his life one of the Rittenhouse gentlemen had given to his father at Christmas.

That hundred dollars, and just about everything else Daddy and Mamma Dear could scrape together (what was left, in other words, after they'd given the Good Lord's Tithe to the Third Abyssinian Baptist Church, and after they'd put money away to go home to Hartsville at Christmas and maybe to go home for a funeral or a wedding or something like that), had gone into coming up with the money for the down payment on the house, and then paying the house off.

The house was another reason Woodrow really hated Philadelphia. Daddy and Mamma Dear had worked their hearts out, done without, to pay for the thing, and they had just about paid it off when the neighborhood had started to go to hell.

Woodrow did not like to curse, but *hell* was the only word that fit, and he knew the Good Lord would not think he was being blasphemous.

Trash moved in. Black trash and white trash. Drinkers and adulterers and blasphemers, people who took no pride in the neighborhood or themselves.

It had been bad when Woodrow had finished William Penn High School and was looking for work, it was worse when, at twenty-two, he'd applied for a job on the cops, and it had grown worse ever since. He spent his first two years in the Twenty-second District, learning how to be a cop, and then they had transferred him—they'd asked him first how he would feel about it, to give the devil his due—to the Thirty-ninth District which was then about thirty percent black (they said "Negro" in those days, but it meant the same thing as "nigger" and everybody knew it) and getting blacker.

"You live there, Woodrow," Lieutenant Grogarty, a red-faced Irishman, had asked him. "How would you feel about working there, with your people?"

At the time, truth to tell, Woodrow had thought it would be a pretty good idea. He had still thought then—he was only two years out of the Academy and didn't know better— that a police officer could be a force for good, that a good Christian man could help people.

He thought that one of the problems was that most cops were white men, and colored folks naturally resented that. He thought that maybe it would be different if a colored police officer were handling things.

He'd been wrong about that. His being colored hadn't made a bit of difference. The people he had to deal with didn't care if he was black or yellow or green. He was The Man. He was the badge. He was the guy who was going to put them in jail. They hated him. Worse, he hadn't been able to help anyone that he could tell. Unless arresting some punk *after* he'd hit some old lady in the back of her head, and stolen her groceries and rent money and spent it on loose women, whiskey, or worse could be considered helping.

He had been bitter when he'd finally faced the truth about this, even considered quitting the cops, finding some other job. He didn't know what other kind of job he could get—all he'd ever done after high school before he came on the cops was work unskilled labor jobs—but he thought there had to be something.

He had had a long talk about it with the Pastor Emeritus of the Third Abyssinian Baptist Church, Rev. Dr. Joshua Steele—that fine old gentleman and servant of the Good Lord was still alive then, eat up with cancer but not willing to quit—and Dr. Steele had told him that all the Bible said was that if you prayed, the Good Lord would point out a Christian man's path to him. Nothing was said about that path being easy.

"You ask the Good Lord, Woodrow, if He has other plans for you, and if so, what. If He wants you to do something else, Woodrow, He'll let you know. You'll *know,* boy. In your heart, you'll know."

Woodrow, after prayerful consideration, had decided that if the Good Lord wanted him to do something else, he would have let him know. And since he didn't get a sign or anything, it was logical to conclude that the Lord was perfectly happy having him do what he was doing.

Which wasn't so strange, he came to decide. While he wasn't able to change things much, or help a lot of people, every once in a while he was able to do something for somebody.

And maybe locking up punks who were beating up and robbing old people was really helping. If they were in jail, they at least weren't robbing and beating up on people.

Three months later, Woodrow met Joellen, who had come up from Georgia right after she finished high school. He never told her—she might have laughed at him—but he took meeting her as a sign from the Good Lord that he had done the right thing. Joellen was like a present from the Good Lord. And so was Woodrow Wilson Bailey, Jr., when he come along twenty months later.

The Lord giveth and the Lord taketh away. Woodrow didn't know if he could have handled Mamma Dear and Daddy being taken into heaven within four months of each other if it hadn't been for Joellen, and with her already starting to show what the Good Lord was giving them: Woodrow Wilson, Junior.

That meant two more trips back home to Hartsville. Mamma Dear had told Daddy in the hospital that she had been paying all along for a burial policy, sixty-five cents a week for twenty years and more, that he didn't know about, and that she wanted him to spend the money to send her back to Hartsville and bury her beside her Mamma, Granny Smythe. She didn't want to be buried in Philadelphia, Pennsylvania, beside strangers.

Four months after they buried Mamma Dear, Woodrow buried Daddy beside her. That was really when Woodrow decided he was going to come home to Hartsville, and when he told Joellen what he had decided, she said that was fine with her, she didn't like living up north anyhow.

There was no work he could get in Hartsville that paid anything like what he was making on the cops, and they didn't even know what a pension for colored people was in Hartsville, so that meant he had to stay on the cops, put in his time, and then retire to Hartsville.

That had been a long time ago, and at the time he'd thought he could sell the house that Mamma Dear and Daddy had sacrificed so much for, and maybe buy a little farm in Hartsville. Let somebody else work it on shares, not work it himself.

That hadn't turned out. With the trash moving into the neighborhood, you couldn't sell the place at hardly any price today. But he and Joellen had been able to save some money, and with his police pension, it was going to be all right when they went home to Hartsville.

Several times in the last couple of years, he had been offered different jobs in the Thirty-ninth District. Once the Captain had asked him if he wanted to help the Corporal, be what they called a "trainee" (which sounded like some kid, but wasn't) with the administration, but he told him no thank you, I'd just as soon just work my beat than be inside all day. Another time, another *two* times, they'd asked him did he want to do something called "Community Relations."

"We want people to start thinking about the police as being their friends, Woodrow," a lieutenant had told him, a *colored* lieutenant. "And with your position in the community, your being a deacon at Third Abyssinian Baptist church, for example, we think you're just the man to help us."

He told the Lieutenant, "Thank you, sir, for thinking about me, but I'm not interested in anything like that, I don't think I'd be any good at it."

What Woodrow thought he was good at was what he did, what he wanted to do until he got his time in and could go home to Hartsville, South Carolina. He worked his beat. He protected old people from getting hit in the head and having their grocery money stolen by some punk. He looked for new faces standing around on corners and talked to them, and told them he didn't like funny cigarettes or worse sold on his beat and that he had a good memory for faces.

The punks on the street corner could call him Old Oreo, or Uncle Tom, or whatever they liked, and it didn't bother him much, because he knew he was straight with the Good Lord and that was all that mattered. The Bible said all there was to say about bearing false witness against your neighbor. And also because he knew what else the punks who called him names told the new punks: "Don't cross that mean old nigger, he'll catch you alone when there's nobody around and slap you up aside of the head with his club or his gun and knock you into the middle of next week."

He liked to walk his beat. You could see much more of what was going on just ambling down the street than you could from inside an RPC. A lot of police officers hated to get out of their cars, but Woodrow was just the opposite. He liked to walk, say hello to people, be seen, see things he wouldn't have been able to see driving a car.

Officer Bailey was not surprised to get the call telling him to meet the Sergeant, but when he got there, he was surprised to see Lieutenant Foster H. Lewis, Sr., standing by the car, talking to the Sergeant.

He and Lewis went back together a long time. He was a good man, in Bailey's opinion. God-fearing, honest, hardworking. But Bailey was a little worried when he saw him. Lewis was assigned to the Ninth District.

What's he doing here?

Maybe he's been sent to talk me into taking one of those special jobs in Community Relations the Lieutenant had talked to me about and I turned down.

When the Sergeant saw Bailey coming, he shook Lieutenant Lewis's hand, got back in his car, and drove off. Lieutenant Lewis stood in the middle of the street and waited for Bailey to drive up.

"How are you, Woodrow?" Lieutenant Lewis said, offering his hand.

"Pretty good, Lieutenant. How's yourself?"

"We were riding around—" Lieutenant Lewis said, interrupting himself to point at the new car parked at the curb. Woodrow saw that it was an unmarked car, the kind inspectors and the like got, and that a black man was behind the wheel.

"—and we had some time, and I thought maybe we could have a cup of coffee or something."

"I can always find time to take a cup of coffee with you," Woodrow said. "Right over there's as good a place as any. At least it's clean."

"The Sergeant said it would be all right if you put yourself out of service for half an hour."

"I'll park this," Woodrow said.

When he came back from parking the car, he recognized the man driving the car.

"This your boy, isn't it, Foster? He wasn't nearly so big the last time I saw him."

"How do you do, sir?" Tiny said politely.

"Well, I'll be. I recognized him from his picture in the paper. When they arrested those dirty cops."

They went in the small neighborhood restaurant. An obese woman brought coffee to the table for all of them.

"Miss Kathy, this is Lieutenant Foster, and his boy," Woodrow said. "We go back a long way."

"Way back," Lieutenant Lewis agreed. "When I graduated from the Academy Officer Bailey sort of took me under his wing."

"Is that so?" the woman said, and walked away.

"When Foster here finished the Academy, they sent him right to Special Operations, put him in plain clothes, and gave him a car," Lieutenant Lewis said. "Things have changed, eh, Woodrow?"

"You like what you're doing, boy?"

"Yes, sir."

"I was thinking the other day that if I had to do it all over again, I wouldn't," Bailey said.

Lieutenant Lewis laughed.

"You don't mean that, Woodrow," he said.

"Yes, I do mean it. Don't take this the wrong way, boy, but I'm glad I'm not starting out. I don't think I could take another twenty-some years walking this beat."

"I was telling Foster that walking a beat is what the police are all about," Lieutenant Lewis said.

"Well, then, the country's in trouble," Bailey said. "Because we're losing, Foster, and you know it. Things get a little worse every day, and there doesn't seem to be anything that anybody can do about it."

"What I was trying to get across to Foster was that there's no substitute for the experience an officer like yourself gets," Lieutenant Lewis said.

"Well, maybe you're right, but the only thing my experience does is make me tired. Time was, I used to think I could clean up a place. Now I know better. All I'm doing is slowing down how fast it's getting worse. And I only get to slow it down a little on good days."

Lieutenant Lewis laughed politely.

"I was thinking, Woodrow," he said, "that since Foster hasn't had any experience on the streets, that maybe you'd be good enough to let him ride around with you once in a while. You know, show him the tricks of the trade."

"Good Lord," Officer Bailey laughed, "why would he want to do that?"

Lieutenant Lewis glanced at his son. He saw that it was only with a great effort that Officer Foster H. Lewis, Jr., was able to keep his face straight, not let it show what he was thinking.

"My father is right, Mr. Bailey," Tiny said. "I could probably learn a lot from you."

That response surprised and then delighted Lieutenant Lewis, but the delight was short-lived:

"The only thing you could learn by riding around with me," Officer Bailey said, "is that Satan's having his way, and if you have half the brains you were born with, you already know that."

Officer Lewis looked at his watch.

"Is there a phone around here, Mr. Bailey? I've got to check in."

"There's a pay phone outside," Bailey said. "But most likely somebody ripped the handset off for the fun of it. You go see Miss Kathy, and tell her I said to let you use hers."

"Thank you," Tiny said.

When he was out of earshot, Officer Bailey nodded approvingly.

"Nice boy, Foster," he said. "You should be proud of him."

"I am," Lieutenant Lewis said.

Men in light blue uniforms, suggesting State Police uniforms, with shoulder patches reading "Nesfoods International Security," stood at the gates of the Detweiler estate. They were armed, Matt noticed, with chrome-plated Smith & Wesson .357 caliber revolvers, and their Sam Browne belts held rows of shining cartridges.

"Anyone trying to shoot their way in here's going to have his hands full," Matt said softly as he slowed and lowered the window of Amy's station wagon.

"You really have a strange sense of humor," Amy said, and leaned over him to speak to the security man.

"I'm Dr. Payne," Amy said, "and this is my brother."

One of the two men consulted a clipboard.

"Yes, Ma'am, you're on the list," the security man said, and the left of the tall wrought-iron gates began to open inward.

Matt raised the window.

"And you're back on Peter's list, too, I see," Matt said.

"Matt, I understand that you're under a terrible strain," Amy said tolerantly, either the understanding psychiatrist or the sympathetic older sister, or both, "but please try to control your mouth. Things are going to be difficult enough in here."

"I wonder how long it's going to be before Mother Detweiler decides that if I had only been reasonable, reasonable defined as resigning from the Police Department and taking my rightful position in society, Penny wouldn't have stuck that needle in her arm, and that this whole thing is my fault."

"That's to be expected," Amy said. "The important thing is that you don't accept that line of reasoning."

"In other words, she's already started down that road?"

"What did you expect?" Amy said. "She, and Uncle Dick, have to find someone to blame."

"Give me a straight answer, Doc. I don't feel I'm responsible. What does that make me?"

"Is that your emotional reaction, as opposed to a logical conclusion you've come to?"

"How about both?"

"Straight answer: You're probably still in emotional shock. Have you wept?"

"I haven't had time to," Matt said. "I didn't get to bed until about three."

"More people showed up at your apartment?" Amy said, annoyance in her voice.

"No, I went to the bar where the Homicide detectives hang out with Jason Washington. He was trying to make me palatable to them."

"What does that mean?"

"When I go back on the job, I'm going to spend some time in Homicide."

"What's all that about?"

"It's a long story. What I will ostensibly be doing is working on the Inferno job."

"What's the 'Inferno job'?"

"Washington and I walked up on a double homicide on Market Street, in a gin mill called the Inferno Lounge."

"The bar owner? They killed his wife? I heard something on the radio."

"The wife and business partner had their brains blown out. The husband suffered a .32 flesh wound to the leg."

"Is there something significant in that?" Amy asked.

"Let us say the version of the incident related by the not-so-bereaved husband is not regarded as being wholly true," Matt said.

"But why are you going to Homicide?" Amy asked.

She didn't get an answer.

"Jesus Christ, what's this?" Matt exclaimed. "It looks like a used-car lot."

Amy looked out the windshield. The wide cobblestone drive in front of the Detweiler mansion and the last fifty yards of the road leading to it were crowded with cars, a substantial percentage of them Cadillacs and Lincolns. There were five or six limousines, including two Rolls-Royces.

"Dad said family and intimate friends," Amy said. "It's apparently gotten out of hand."

"Intimate friends, or the morbidly curious?" Matt asked. "With a *soupçon* of social climbers thrown in for good measure?"

"Matt, have those acidulous thoughts if they make you feel better, but for the sake of Uncle Dick and Aunt Grace—and Mother and Dad—please have the decency to keep them to yourself."

"Sorry," he said, sounding contrite.

"What were they supposed to say when someone called, or simply showed up? 'Sorry, you're not welcome'?"

"Oh, shit, there's Chad," Matt said. "And the very pregnant Daffy and friend."

"Why are you surprised, and why 'oh, shit'?"

"I would just as soon not see them just now."

Mr. Chadwick Thomas Nesbitt IV glanced down the drive as the station wagon drove up, recognized the occupants, and touched the arm of his wife. Mrs. Nesbitt in turn touched the arm of Miss Amanda Chase Spencer, a strikingly beautiful blonde who was wearing a black silk suit with a hat and veil nearly identical to Mrs. Nesbitt's. All three stopped and waited on the lower of the shallow steps leading to the flagstone patio before the mansion's front door.

"How are you holding up, buddy?" Chad asked, grasping Matt's arm.

"Oh, Matt," Daffy said. "Poor Matt!"

She embraced him, which caused her swollen belly to push against him.

"Hello, Matt," Amanda said. "I'm so very sorry."

"Thank you," Matt said, reaching around Daffy to take the gloved hand she extended.

"I still can't believe it," Daffy said as she finally released Matt.

"I'm Amelia Payne," Amy said to Amanda.

"How do you do?"

"I thought this was supposed to be family and immediate friends only," Matt said, gesturing at all the cars.

"Matt, I can't believe you said that!" Daffy said, horrified.

Matt looked at her without comprehension.

"Amanda's been staying with us, for Martha Peebles's engagement party," Chad said coldly.

"Oh, Christ, I wasn't talking about you, Amanda," Matt said, finally realizing how what he had said had been interpreted.

"I know you weren't," Amanda said.

"I didn't see you out there," Matt said.

"I didn't want you to," Amanda said simply.

"Penny and Amanda were very close," Daffy said.

"No, we weren't," Amanda corrected her. "We knew each other at Bennington. That's all."

Good for you, Matt thought. *Cut the bullshit.*

Chad Nesbitt gave her a strange look.

"Shall we go in?" he said, taking his wife's arm.

Baxley, the Detweiler butler, opened the door to them. He was a man in his fifties, and wearing a morning coat with a horizontally striped vest.

"Mr. Detweiler's been expecting you, Doctor," he said.

The translation of which is that Mother D is about to lose control. Or has already lost it, Matt thought.

"I'll go up," Amy said. "Thank you, Baxley."

"Coffee has been laid in the library," Baxley said. "Miss Penny is in the siting room."

"Thank you, Baxley," Chad Nesbitt said. He put his hand on Matt's arm.

"Take care of him, Chad," Amy said. "I'll go see Aunt Grace."

"I will," Chad said. "Coffee first, Matt?"

"Yeah."

As they walked across the foyer, Matt glanced through the open door of the sitting room. He could see the foot of a glistening mahogany casket, surrounded by flowers.

Shit, I didn't even think about flowers.

Mother certainly sent some in my name, knowing that I wouldn't do it myself.

Heads turned as the four of them went into the library. There were perhaps twenty-five people in the room, most of whom Matt knew by sight. A long table had been set with silver coffee services and trays of pastry. A man in a gray jacket and two maids stood behind the table. A small table behind them held bottles of whiskey and cognac.

Chad propelled Matt to the table.

"I need a little liquid courage myself to face up to going in there," Chad said, indicating to the manservant to produce a bottle of cognac. "Straight up, Matt? Or do you want something to cut it with?"

I don't want any at all, strangely enough. I don't need any liquid courage to go in there and look at Penny's body. For one thing, it's not Penny. Just a body. And I'm used to bodies. Just the other day, I saw two of them, both with their brains blown all over the room. If that didn't bother me, this certainly won't. I am not anywhere close to the near-state of emotional collapse that everyone seems to think I'm in.

"It's a little early for me, Chad," Matt said. "Maybe later."

"Suit yourself," Chad said, taking the cognac bottle from the man behind the table, pouring half an inch of it into a snifter, and tossing it down.

"I wish I could have one of those," Daffy said.

"Baby, you can't," Chad said sympathetically.

"If it's a girl, I want to name her Penelope," Daffy said.

Matt saw this idea didn't please the prospective father, but that he was wise enough not to argue with his wife here.

"You're not having anything?" Amanda asked, at Matt's elbow.

"Probably later," he said.

"Let's get it over with," Chad said.

"That's a terrible thing . . ." Daffy protested.

"Unless you want to go in alone first, Matt?" Chad asked solicitously.

Anything to get away from these three. Go in there alone, stay what seems to be an appropriate period for profound introspection and grief, and then get the hell out.

"Thank you," Matt said softly.

"Thank you," the hypocrite said, with what he judged to be what his audience expected in grief-stricken tone and facial demeanor.

He smiled wanly at Chad, Daffy, and Amanda and walked away from them, out of the library, across the foyer and into the sitting room. There was a line of people, maybe half a dozen, waiting for their last look at the mortal remains of Miss Penelope Detweiler. He took his place with them, and slowly made his way to the casket, looking for, and finally finding, behind the casket, a floral display bearing a card reading "Matthew Mark Payne" and then noticing the strange mingled smells of expensive perfume on the woman in front of him and from the flowers, and comparing it with what he had smelled in the office of the Inferno Lounge, the last time he'd looked at mortal remains. There it had been the sick sweet smell of the pools of blood under the bodies, mingled with the foul odors of feces and urine released in death.

And then it was his turn to look down at Penny in her coffin.

She looks as if she's asleep, he thought, *which is the effect the cosmetic technologist at the undertaker's was struggling to achieve.*

And then, like a wall falling on him, and without warning, his chest contracted painfully, a wailing moan saying "Oh, shit!" in a voice he recognized as his own came out of it, and his chest began to heave with sobs.

He next became aware that someone was pulling him away from the casket, where his right hand was caressing the cool, unmoving flesh of Penny's cheeks, and then that the someone was Chad, gently saying, "Come on, ol' buddy. Just come along with us," and then that Daffy's swollen belly was pressing against him as they led him out of the sitting room past those next in line, and that, when he looked at her, tears were running down her cheeks, cutting courses through her pancake makeup.

"Inspector Wohl," Peter answered his telephone.

"The funeral's over," Amy said.

"I was hoping you'd call. How did it go?"

"Matt has a way with words. When we got here, he said it was 'intimate friends, and the morbidly curious, with a *soupçon* of social climbers thrown in for good measure.' "

"How did he handle it?"

"He broke down when he saw her in the casket. Really broke down. Chad Nesbitt and his very pregnant wife had to practically carry him out of the room."

There was a moment's silence before Wohl said:

"You said last night you expected something like that to happen."

"That was a clinical opinion; professionally, I'm relieved. It's the first step, acceptance, in managing grief. Personally, he's my little brother. It was awful. I felt so damned sorry for him."

"How's he now? Where is he now?"

"Oh, now he's got his stiff upper lip back in place. He and Chad are into the booze. There's quite a post-interment party going on out here."

"You want me to send someone out there and get him? I sent Tiny Lewis to sit on him, but . . ."

"I know," Amy said. "What I was hoping to hear was you volunteering to come out here and get the both of us."

"It was bad for you?"

"As we were coming back here from the cemetery—I thought Grace Detweiler might need me, so I rode with them—I caught her looking at me as if she had just realized that if I had done my job, Penny would still be here."

"That could be an overactive imagination."

"I don't think so. I got the same look here in the house when I was getting a tranquilizer out of my purse for her. She's decided—seeing how Matt collapsed completely probably had a lot to do with it—that he's still an irresponsible boy, who can't be blamed. She needs somebody to blame. I make a fine candidate to be the real villain, because I really didn't help Penny at all."

There was a moment's silence, and then Wohl said, "I'm on my way, Amy," and the line went dead in her ear.

"It's a good thing I know you're a doctor," Inspector Peter Wohl said to Dr. Amelia Payne as they came off the elevator into the lobby of the Delaware Valley Cancer Society Building on Rittenhouse Square.

"Meaning what?"

"The folklore among us laypersons is don't mix booze and pills."

"That's a good general rule of thumb," Amy said. "What I gave Matt is what we doctor persons prescribe as a sedative when the patient person has been soaking up cognac like a sponge. It is my professional opinion that that patient person will be out like a light for the next twelve to eighteen hours without side effects. Any other questions, layperson?"

Wohl smiled at her.

"How about dinner tonight?"

"Absolutely not."

"I guess that makes breakfast tomorrow out of the question."

"I didn't say that," Amy said. "I said no dinner. I have to make my rounds, and then there's a very sick young woman I want to spend some time with. But I didn't say any-thing about breakfast, or, for that matter, a midnight supper with candles and wine, being out of any question."

"My place or yours, doctor person?"

She didn't reply directly.

"We left my car at the Detweilers'."

"Give me the keys. I'll have someone run me out there, and I'll drop it by—where? The hospital? Your place?"

"Wouldn't it be easier if you took it to your place? When I leave the hospital, I'll catch a cab out there. It'll probably be after eleven."

"Done," he said, putting his hand out for the keys.

"You're headed for the hospital now?" he asked. She nodded. "You want a ride?"

"Where are you going?"

"Wherever you need to go is right on my way."

"I'll catch a cab," she said.

"You're sure?"

She nodded.

Their eyes met, and held. Somewhat hesitantly, Wohl moved his face closer to hers.

"Don't push me, Peter," Amy said, and then moved her face closer to his and kissed him on the lips.

Then she quickly walked away from him, out the door and onto Rittenhouse Square. He started to follow her, then changed his mind.

He went to the receptionist's desk and asked to use her telephone.

"Of course," she said with a smile that suggested she did not find him unattractive.

He smiled at her and dialed a number from memory.

"Inspector Wohl," he said as he watched Amy get into a cab. "Anything for me?"

"Chief Lowenstein's been trying to reach you all afternoon, sir," the tour lieutenant reported.

"Anything else?"

"No, sir."

"I'll call Chief Lowenstein and get back to you."

"Yes, sir."

Wohl broke the connection with his finger and dialed Chief Lowenstein's private number.

"Lowenstein."

"Peter Wohl, Chief."

"Where are you, Peter?"

"Center City. Rittenhouse Square."

"With Matt Payne?"

"I just left him."

"How is he?"

"His sister gave him a pill she said will knock him out until tomorrow."

"I really feel sorry for him," Lowenstein said, and then immediately added: "I need to talk to you, Peter."

"I'm available for you anytime, Chief."

"Why don't you let me buy you a drink at the bar in the Warwick?"

"Yes, sir."

"Ten minutes, Peter," Lowenstein said. "Thank you."

15.

Chief Inspector of Detectives Matthew Lowenstein was sitting, with an eight-inch black cigar in his mouth, on a stool at the street end of the bar in the Warwick Hotel when Inspector Peter Wohl got there.

"Sorry to keep you waiting, Chief."

"What will you have, Peter?" Lowenstein asked, ignoring the apology.

"I would like a triple scotch, but what I'd better have is a beer," Wohl said.

"Bad day for you?" Lowenstein asked, chuckling, and got the bartender's attention. "Give this nice young man one of these. A single."

"Thank you," Peter said.

"I turned in my papers this morning," he said. "You hear about that?"

Wohl nodded.

"Carlucci came out to the house and made me a deal to stay."

Wohl's face was as devoid of expression as he could make it.

"The deal," Lowenstein said, "is that I have his word that you will bring me in on anything interesting his personal detective squad, now called Ethical Affairs Unit, comes up with, and I get to define the term 'interesting.' You have any problem with that, Peter?"

"I had a problem with keeping you out of the Cazerra investigation. That wasn't my idea, Chief."

"So Carlucci told me. I asked you, do you have any problems with the new arrangement?"

"None at all."

"Tell me what interesting things you have heard today, Peter."

"How about yesterday, Chief?"

"Start with yesterday."

"I had lunch with Armando C. Giacomo, Esquire, at the Rittenhouse Club. Weisbach and I did. Mr. Paulo Cassandro really doesn't want to go to jail. As a public-spirited citizen, he is willing to testify against Cazerra in exchange for immunity from prosecution."

Lowenstein snorted.

"Giacomo is pissing in the wind. He knows he has nothing to deal with. And if he did, he would have gone to the District Attorney with it. Why you?"

"I thought that was interesting. Weisbach told him that, offhand, the only thing he could think of that we were interested in was the Inferno doer, or doers. And/or the Kellog doer."

"And how did the dapper little dago react to that?"

"He didn't say no."

"You think either one was a mob hit, Peter?"

"I didn't until Giacomo didn't say no."

"Interesting."

"I thought so. And then Jason Washington called me this morning. One of his informants said that the Inferno was a mob hit, and gave him a name. Frank—Frankie—Foley."

There was a just-perceptible pause as Lowenstein searched his memory.

"Never heard of him."

"Neither has Washington. Or Harris. Or me. Or intelligence or Organized Crime."

"Who's the informant?"

"Washington said that what this guy has given him in the past—which wasn't much—was reliable. I think he would have said something if there was a mob connection."

"Huh!" Lowenstein snorted.

"Going back even further than yesterday, the day Kellog was shot, that night, his widow showed up at Washington's apartment. Did you hear about that?"

"Tell me about it," Lowenstein said.

Which means either that you did hear about it or didn't hear about it, but if you did, you want to hear my version of it anyway.

"She told Washington (a) her husband was dirty, (b) the entire Narcotics Five Squad is dirty, and (c) that they did her husband."

"What did Washington think about it?"

"He said he believes she thinks she's telling the truth."

"So what are you going to do with this? All of this?"

"I told Washington to give the Frankie Foley name to Homicide. By now, they probably have it."

"And the Five Squad allegations?"

"Before Ethical Affairs popped up, I was going to have a quiet word with a staff inspector I know pretty well, and ask him to please keep me out of it."

Lowenstein chuckled. "A staff inspector named Weisbach?"

"Yeah."

"And now?"

"This is the first time I've really thought hard about it. It seems to me the lines of authority are fuzzy. Dirty cops on the Narcotics Five Squad would seem to be Ethical Affairs' business. Somebody on the Narcotics Five Squad doing Officer Kellog would seem to belong to Homicide."

"Are you asking me?"

"Yes."

"What's Washington's role going to be in Ethical Affairs?"

"I have been ordered to give Weisbach whatever support he needs. So far as I'm concerned, that means he gets the Special Operations Investigation Section, which means he gets Washington."

"Why don't you leave it that way? Let Washington run that down independently of Homicide? If he's investigating corruption, and comes across something that looks like the Kellog homicide, he can pass it along."

"That's fine with me."

"And I will have a word with Henry Quaire and suggest that he have Wally Milham run down this—what was the name?—Frankie Foley lead. Assisted by Detective Payne."

"Can I ask why?"

"I think there may be something to it. Gut feeling."

"Really? Why?"

"I just told you: gut feeling. Write this down, Peter: When you don't have a clue, go with your gut feeling."

"Thank you, Chief," Wohl said, smiling.

"And I would like Milham to come up with something, to prove to Carlucci that a detective can have a very active sex life and still be a good detective."

"I've known that all along," Wohl said.

"I'll bet you have." Lowenstein laughed. "I think that when we finally get the true story of Mr. Atchison's recent tragedy, it will turn out that money was involved. Insurance on the wife, maybe. Business problems with the partner. If that's so, that means he would not have the dough to hire a professional hit man. And the mob only does that sort of thing for adequate compensation. And I don't think they'd be interested in doing a contract hit for somebody like Atchison in the first place."

Wohl nodded his head in agreement.

"And following that lead will be instructional for Payne," Lowenstein went on. "He will learn that most homicides are solved wearing out shoe leather, not by brilliant reasoning. Or, in this case, by an anonymous tip that takes a hell of a lot of legwork to come up with what's necessary to make it stand up in court."

"Who do you think did Officer Kellog?"

"If I had to bet, I'd bet on Washington's gut feeling. He thinks the widow's telling the truth. I hope to hell the Narcotics Five Squad is not involved, but I wouldn't be at all surprised if there was a Narcotics connection."

"Either would I," Wohl said, somewhat sadly.

He looked at his drink. It was empty. He idly moved the glass so that ice cubes spun inside.

"Another, Peter?" Lowenstein asked.

"I shouldn't, but I will," Wohl said, and held up the glass to attract the bartender.

When he was to think about it afterward, with more than a little chagrin, Matt Payne realized that if he hadn't been three quarters of the way into the bag, he never would have gone to Homicide at all that night.

At the time, he hadn't been thinking too clearly. The only thing he had been sure about was that he hadn't wanted one of Amy's pills. Pretending to swallow it while she watched was easier than arguing with her about it.

What he would do, he originally thought, was have a couple of drinks, enough to make him sleepy, and then fall in bed.

But by the third Famous Grouse, he thought that maybe it would be a good idea to go to the Fraternal Order of Police bar. By the fifth drink, it seemed to be a splendid idea. So he went down and got in the Porsche.

By the time he got to Broad and Market, going to the FOP bar seemed less a splendid idea. Everybody in the place would have heard about Penny; everybody he knew would be offering sympathy, and he didn't want that.

He drove around City Hall, and headed down South Broad Street, headed for Charley McFadden's house. Charley was working days, he would get him out of bed, and they would have a couple of drinks someplace.

Five blocks down South Broad, he realized that would also be a bad idea, an imposition. Charley would, out of pity, get out of bed and be a good guy. Not fair to Charley.

Dropping in on Peter Wohl was similarly a bad idea. For one thing, Peter lived way the hell out in Chestnut Hill. More importantly, he might have—probably did have—company, spelled A-m-y, and not only would he be an unwelcome guest, but they would correctly surmise that he had not swallowed Amy's pill.

And then he thought of Wally Milham. Milham was working midnight to eight. And Milham's personal life was nearly as fucked up as his own. The Mayor had gotten up on a moral high horse at Martha Peebles's party because Milham had gotten involved with his wife's sister, and, worse, was using this as a basis to suspect that Milham was somehow involved in the Kellog shooting.

Milham, Matt reasoned, would not only be up and awake, but might welcome some company.

Matt made an illegal U-turn on South Broad Street and headed for the Roundhouse.

Matt had been to Homicide often enough to know how to get past the wooden barrier. There was a little button on the inside of the barrier, which activated the solenoid that opened the gate.

There were half a dozen detectives in the room, one of whom looked up, registering surprise when he saw Matt. And then he gestured with his finger across the room to where Wally Milham sat at a desk before a typewriter.

Matt walked over to him. It was a moment before Milham became aware that he was standing there.

"Well, I expected you, but not so soon," Wally Milham said.

"Excuse me?"

Milham pushed a memorandum across his desk. Matt picked it up.

CITY OF PHILADELPHIA

MEMORANDUM

To: SERGEANT ZACHARY HOBBS

FROM: COMMANDING OFFICER, HOMICIDE UNIT

SUBJECT: INFORMANT'S TIP

1. We have an informant's tip on the Inferno job concerning an individual named Frank, or Frankie, Foley. The informant, whose information in the past has been reliable, identifies this subject as a "mob-connected hit man."

2. Neither Records, Intelligence or Organized Crime has anything on him.

3. Assign Detective Milham to investigate this lead, instructing him to continue his investigation, making daily reports to you, until such time as further information is developed, or until he is convinced there is nothing to it.

Detective Payne, of Special Operations, will be working in the Homicide Unit for an indefinite period. When he reports for duty, assign him to assist Detective Milham.

Henry C. Quaire
Henry C. Quaire
Captain

cc: Chief Inspector Lowenstein
82-S-1AE (Rev. 3/59) RESPONSE TO THIS MEMORANDUM MAY
BE MADE HEREON IN LONGHAND

"I didn't expect you for a couple of days," Milham said. "I heard about . . . I thought the funeral was today."

"It was," Matt said.

Milham looked at Matt intently for a moment, then suddenly stood up. He took his coat from the back of the chair he had been sitting on and shrugged into it.

"Come on, Payne," he said.

"Where are we doing?"

"Out," Milham said, and gestured toward the door.

"You drive over here?" Milham asked when they came out of the back door of the Roundhouse.

"Yeah."

"Where'd you park?" Milham asked.

Matt pointed at the Porsche.

"Nice wheels," Milham said. "Leave it, we'll pick it up later."

"Whatever you say," Matt replied.

They got in Milham's unmarked three-year-old Ford, left the parking lot, went south on Eighth Street, crossed Market and turned right on Walnut Street to South Broad, and then left.

"How much have you had to drink?" Milham asked.

"I had a couple."

"More than a couple, to judge from the smell," Milham said. "That wasn't really smart, Payne."

"I couldn't sleep."

"I mean coming into Homicide shitfaced," Milham said. "Lucky for you, Hobbs and Natali went out on a job—a stabbing, two Schwartzers fighting over a tootsie in the East Falls project—and Logan, who was on the desk, either didn't smell you or didn't want to. It could have gone the other way. If it had, Lowenstein would have heard first thing in the morning that you showed up drunk. I get the feeling he would love to tell that to the Mayor."

"Oh, shit!" Matt said.

"I think you were lucky, so forget it. But don't do it again."

"Sorry," Matt said.

"We're going to a bar called Meagan's," Milham said, changing the subject somewhat, "where you are going to have either coffee or a Coke."

Milham handed Matt a clipboard, then turned on the large, specially installed light mounted on the headliner. Matt saw that the clipboard held a pad of lined paper and a Xerox of a page from the telephone book. On closer examination, there were two Xerox pages. There was also a pencil-written list of what looked like bars.

"There are ninety-seven Foleys in the phone book," Milham said. "We may have to check every one of them out. Just because there's no Frank or Francis listed doesn't mean there's nobody at that address named Frank or Francis. In the morning, I'll check driver's licenses in Harrisburg, and see if they have a Frank or Francis matching one of these addresses. Right now, I'm working on a hunch."

"What kind of a hunch?"

"A hunch hunch. There are eleven Foleys in the phone book in a six-block area in South Philly. There are twelve bars in that six-block area. A couple of them will probably still be open. One—Meagan's—I know stays open late. We will ask, 'Is this the place where Ol' Frankie Foley drinks?' "

"What about this tip? Where did it come from? Is it any good?"

"We are probably on a wild-goose chase, but you never know until you know. As to where it came from, I don't know. Not from someone inside Homicide. Who knows? Lowenstein thinks it's worth checking out, that's all that matters."

Meagan's Bar, on Jackson Street, turned out to be an ordinary neighborhood bar. There were half a dozen customers, two of them middle-aged women, sitting at the bar, each with a beer in front of them. There was a jukebox, but no one had fed it coins. A television, with a flickering picture, was showing a man and a peroxide blonde in an apron demonstrating a kitchen device guaranteed to make life in the kitchen a genuine joy.

The bartender, a heavyset man in his fifties, hoisted himself with visible reluctance from his stool by the cash register and walked to them, putting both hands on the bar and wordlessly asking for their order.

"Ortleib's," Milham ordered.

"I think I better have coffee," Matt said.

"No coffee," the bartender said.

"One more, and then I'll drive you home," Milham said.

"What the hell," Matt said. "Why not?"

When the bartender served the beer, Milham laid a five-dollar bill on the bar.

"Where are we?" he asked the bartender.

"What do you mean, where are you? This place is called Meagan's."

"I mean where, where. What is this, Jackson Street?"

"Jackson and Mole streets."

"Doesn't Frank Foley live around here?"

"Frank who?"

"Frankie Foley. My cousin. I thought he lived right around here, on South Mole Street."

"Short fat guy? Works for Strawbridge's?"

"No. Ordinary-sized. Maybe a little bigger. And I thought he worked for Wanamaker's."

"Right. Yeah. He comes in here every once in a while."

"He been in tonight?"

"Haven't seen him in a while."

"Yeah, well, what the hell. Listen, if he does come in, tell him his cousin Marty, from Conshohocken, said hi, will you?"

"Yeah, if I see him, I'll do that."

"I'd be obliged."

"You're a long way from Conshohocken."

"Went to a wake. Jack O'Neill. May he rest in peace."

"Didn't know him."

"He retired from Budd Company."

"Didn't know him," the bartender said, made change, and went back to his stool.

Milham looked at Matt and raised his beer glass.

"Good ol' Jack," he said.

"May he rest in peace," Matt said.

"I think he made me," Milham said when they were back in his car. "He was being cute with that 'short fat guy?' line. And I got lucky when I said Wanamaker's. I'll bet when we finally find Mr. Foley, he will work in Wanamaker's, and now we know he lives around here. It may not be our Frankie, but you never can tell. Sometimes you get lucky."

"If he made you," Matt said, "and was cute, he's going to tell this guy somebody, a cop, was looking for him."

"Good. If it is our Frankie, it will make him nervous. Unless he's got a cousin from Conshohocken. Give me the clipboard."

Milham switched on the light, consulted the Xerox pages of the telephone book, and drew a circle around the name "Foley, Mary" of 2320 South Eighteenth Street.

"Maybe he lives with his mother," Milham said, handing the clipboard back to Matt. He switched off the overhead light and started the engine.

They drove to South Eighteenth Street, and drove slowly by 2320. It was a typical row house, in the center of the block. There were no lights on.

They visited three more bars. Two of them had coffee. None of their bartenders had ever heard of Frank, or Frankie, Foley.

"I don't know what to do with you," Milham said. "On one hand, you still smell like a brewery. On the other, so do I. You want to take a chance on going back to the Round-house with me, to see what everybody else has come up with?"

"Whatever you think is best," Matt said, chagrined.

"What the hell, we have to get your car anyway," Milham said. "Just try not to breathe on anybody."

"Sergeant, this is Detective Payne," Milham said. "Payne, this is Sergeant Zachary Hobbs."

Hobbs offered his hand, and looked at Matt closely.

"We didn't expect you for a couple of days," he said.

"You weren't here," Milham replied for him, "when he came in. Your memo was in my box, so I took him with me."

"You find this Foley guy?"

"I think we know where he lives, and that he works for Wanamaker's."

"The bartender at the Inferno says there was a guy named Foley in there that night," Hobbs said. "That's in your box, too."

Milham nodded.

"Payne, Captain Quaire knows about your, uh, personal problem. You don't have to come to work, is what I'm saying, until you feel up to it," Hobbs said.

"I think I'd rather work than not," Matt said. "But thank you."

"You need anything, you let me know. Did Wally show you the memo?"

"Yes, he did."

"OK. You work with Wally."

Matt nodded.

"I think you'd better see Lieutenant Natali," Hobbs said. "Let him know you're here." He gestured across the room. Matt saw Lieutenant Natali in a small office.

Jesus, I hope he's got a cold or something, and can't smell the booze.

He had met Lieutenant Natali once before. The circumstances flooded his mind.

He had been escorting Miss Amanda Spender to a prewedding dinner honoring Miss Daphne Soames Brown and Mr. Chadwick Thomas Nesbitt IV, at the Union League Club.

No wonder Amanda said I hadn't seen her at Martha Peebles's party; she hadn't wanted me to. I'm trouble, dangerous. If I were her, I wouldn't have wanted to see me either.

When he had pulled the Porsche onto the top floor of the Penn Center Parking Garage, there had been a body lying in a pool of blood, that of a second-rate gangster named Tony the Zee Dezito, who had been taken out with a shotgun blast in what was almost certainly a contract hit by party or parties unknown for reasons unknown.

Nearby was Miss Penelope Detweiler, a lifelong acquaintance, also lying in a pool of blood. Matt's original conclusion that Penny, like him and Amanda en route to Daffy and Chad's party, was an innocent bystander was soon corrected by the facts. She had been in the parking garage to meet Tony the Zee, with whom she was having an affair.

And almost certainly, I know now, to get something from him to stick in her arm, or sniff up her nose. It was that goddamn Dezito who gave Penny her habit.

Narcotics had had a tail on Tony the Zee, and when Matt had gone to Homicide to give them a statement, a Narcotics sergeant, an asshole named Dolan, and another Narcotics asshole had been waiting for him there. They had taken him into the interview room, sat him down in the steel captain's chair with the handcuffs, and as much as accused him of being involved with either Tony the Zee or Narcotics, or both. And then taken him to Narcotics, if not under arrest, then the next thing to it, to continue the interrogation and to search the Porsche.

Lieutenant Natali had been the tour lieutenant in Homicide that night, hadn't liked what he had seen, and had called Peter Wohl. Wohl had come to Narcotics like the Cavalry to the rescue and gotten him out.

Natali had bent, if not regulations, then departmental protocol, and thus stuck his neck out, by calling Peter Wohl. He was therefore, by definition, a proven good guy.

Matt walked to the office and stood in the door until Natali looked up and waved him inside. He stood up and put out his hand.

"I didn't expect to see you so soon, Payne," he said. "I, uh, heard what happened. I'm sorry."

"Thank you," Matt said.

It was evident on Natali's face that he, too, was recalling the circumstances of their first meeting.

"I thought I would rather work than sit around."

That's not true. I'm here because I got shitfaced and didn't want to go to bed. I'm a goddamned hypocrite and a liar.

"Yeah," Natali said. "I understand." He paused and then went on. "Payne, some of the people here are going to resent you being here."

"I thought they would."

"But they know—Captain Quaire passed the word—that you had nothing to do with it. So I don't think it will be a problem. If there is one, you come to me with it."

"Thank you."

"You'll be working with Wally Milham. There's a memo . . ."

"I saw it."

"OK. I don't think you'll have any trouble with Milham. And he's a good Homicide detective. You can learn a lot from him. Homicide works differently. I don't know how much experience you had at East Detectives . . ."

"Not much," Matt said. "Most of it on recovered stolen vehicles."

Natali smiled understandingly.

"I did a few of those myself, when I made detective," he said. "We don't get as many jobs here," Natali went on. "And when one comes in, everybody goes to work on it. There's an assigned detective, of course. Milham, in the case of the Inferno Lounge job. But everybody works on it."

"I understand. Or I think I do."

"You'll catch on in a hurry," Natali said. "If you have any problems, come see me."

"Thank you, sir."

When he went to Wally Milham's desk, Milham was working his way through a thick stack of paper forms. He read one of the forms, and then placed it facedown beside the unread stack.

"You better take a look at these," Milham said, tapping the facedown stack without raising his eyes from the document he was reading.

Matt pulled up a chair and slid the facedown stack to him.

Matt turned over the stack. They were all carbon copies of 75-49s, the standard Police Department Detective Division Investigation Report.

He started to read the first one:

INVESTIGATION REPORT		PHILADELPHIA POLICE DEPARTMENT	
Yr | C.C.# | DIST | COMPL.#		| INITIAL(49) | |DIST/UNIT |	
REPORT DATE	SUPPLEMENTAL	|	PREPARING
CLASSIFICATION	| CODE | CONTINUATION		Homicide/9th Dist.
PREVIOUS CLASSIFICATION	CODE | DATE AND TIME		| PLACE OF OCCURRENCE
COMPLAINANT | AGE | RACE | ADDRESS	| PHONE		| TYPE OF PREMISES
Alicia Atchison	| 25 | W | 320 Wilson Avenue, Media, PA		
DATE AND TIME REPORTED	| REPORTED BY		| ADDRESS
FOUNDED ❐ YES ❐ NO ARREST ❐ CLEARED ❐ EXCEPTIONALLY CLEARED			
STOLEN | ❐ CURRENCY, BONDS, ETC. ❐ FURS ❐ AUTOS | RECOVERED VALUE			
PROPERTY | ❐ JEWELRY, PRECIOUS METAL ❐ CLOTHING ❐ MISC |			
INSURED ❐ YES ❐ NO			
DETAILS			

AUTOPSY: Alicia Atchison

1. Pronouncement: Saturday, May 20, 1975 at 5:39 a.m., at 1908 Market Street, the scene, by Dr. Howard D. Mitchell, Medical Examiners office.

2. Transporting of Body: From the scene to the Medical Examiners Office in Morgue Wagon #61538, manned by Lewis Martin.

3. Post: Saturday, May 20, 1975 at 9:30 a.m., Medical Examiners Office by Dr. Howard D. Mitchell.

4. Findings: Gunshot wounds (4) of head. Craniocerebral Injuries. Manner of Death: Homicide.

INVESTIGATOR (Type and Sign Name)	SERGEANT	LIEUTENANT
Alonzo Kramer	*Zachary Hobbs*	
Alonzo Kramer #967	Zachary Hobbs #396	

75-49 (Rev 3/63)   DETECTIVE DIVISION

The telephone on the desk rang. Without taking his eyes from the 75-49s before him, Milham reached for it.

"Homicide, Milham," he said.

Matt looked up in natural curiosity.

"Hello, honey," Milham said, his voice changing.

The Widow Kellog, Matt decided, *and that makes it none of my business.*

He turned his attention to the second 75-49:

INVESTIGATION REPORT   PHILADELPHIA POLICE DEPARTMENT

Yr	C.C.#	DIST	COMPL.#		INITIAL(49)		DIST/UNIT	
REPORT DATE		SUPPLEMENTAL					PREPARING	
CLASSIFICATION			CODE	CONTINUATION			Homicide/9th Dist.	

PREVIOUS CLASSIFICATION   CODE|DATE AND TIME |PLACE OF OCCURRENCE

COMPLAINANT	AGE	RACE	ADDRESS	PHONE	TYPE OF PREMISES
Anthony J. Marcuzzi	52	W	6105 Palter Avenue		

DATE AND TIME REPORTED | REPORTED BY | ADDRESS

FOUNDED   ❒ YES ❒ NO   ARREST ❒ CLEARED   ❒ EXCEPTIONALLY CLEARED

STOLEN | ❒ CURRENCY, BONDS, ETC. ❒ FURS   ❒ AUTOS | RECOVERED VALUE
PROPERTY | ❒ JEWELRY, PRECIOUS METAL ❒ CLOTHING ❒ MISC |
INSURED   ❒ YES ❒ NO

DETAILS

AUTOPSY: Anthony J. Marcuzzi.

1. Pronouncement: Saturday, May 20, 1975 at 5:39 a.m., at 1908 Market Street, the scene, by Dr. Howard D. Mitchell, Medical Examiners Office.

2. Transporting of Body: From the scene to the Medical Examiners Office in Morgue Wagon #61538, manned by Lewis Martin.

3. Post: Saturday, May 20, 1975 at 9:30 a.m., Medical Examiners Office by Dr. Howard D. Mitchell.

4. Findings: Gunshot wounds (3) of head. Craniocerebral Injuries. Manner of Death: Homicide.

INVESTIGATOR (Type and Sign Name)	SERGEANT	LIEUTENANT
Alonzo Kramer Alonzo Kramer #967	*Zachary Hobbs* Zachary Hobbs #396	
75-49 (Rev 3/63)	DETECTIVE DIVISION	

"Jesus Christ!" Milham said, softly but with such intensity that Matt's noble intention to mind his own business was overwhelmed by curiosity.

"Baby," Milham said. "You stay there. Stay inside. I'll be right there!"

I wonder what the hell that's all about.

Milham hung the telephone up and looked at Matt.

"Something's come up," he said. "I gotta go."

Matt nodded.

"Tell you what, Payne," Milham said, obviously having thought over what he was about to say. "Take that stack with you and go home. You all right to drive?"

"I'm all right."

"I'll call you about ten tomorrow morning. You read that, see if you come up with something."

"Right."

"OK. You'll find some manila envelopes over there," Milham said, pointing. "I really got to go."

"Anything I can do?"

"Yeah, if anybody asks where I went, all you know is I told you to go home."

"OK."

"Ten tomorrow, I'll call you at ten tomorrow," Milham said, and went to retrieve his pistol from a filing cabinet.

16.

Matt left the Police Administration Building and found his car. The interior lights were on. Because, he saw, the door was ajar.

Christ, was I so plastered when I came here that I not only didn't lock the car, but didn't even close the damned door? No wonder Milham was worried if I was all right to drive.

Or did somebody use a Car Thief's Friend and open the door? Did I leave anything inside worth stealing?

He pulled the door fully open and stuck his head inside.

There was no sign of damage; the glove compartment showed no sign that anyone had tried to force it open.

I deduce that no attempt at Vehicular Burglary has occurred. I am forced to conclude that I was shitfaced when I drove in here. Shit!

There was a white tissue on the floor under the steering wheel.

Penny's Kleenex. With her lipstick on it.

He picked it up and looked at it.

What the hell do I do with it? Throw it away? I don't want to do that. Keep it, as a Sacred Relic? I don't want to do that, either.

He patted his pocket and found a book of matches.

He unfolded the Kleenex, struck a match, and set the Kleenex on fire. He held it in his fingers until that became painful, and then let what was left float to the ground. He watched until it was consumed and the embers died.

Then he got in the Porsche and drove out of the Roundhouse parking lot.

His stomach hurt, and he decided that was because he still hadn't had anything to eat. He drove over to the 1400 block of Race Street where he remembered a restaurant was open all night. He ordered two hamburgers, changed his mind to three hamburgers, a cup of coffee, a large french fries, and two containers of milk, all to go.

Then he got back in the Porsche and drove home.

The red light was blinking on his answering machine. He was tempted to ignore it, but finally pushed the Play Messages button.

Predictably, there was a call from his mother, asking if he was all right. And one from his father, same question. And there were seven No Message blurps; someone had called, and elected not to leave a message.

He opened the paper bag from the St. George Restaurant and started to unwrap a hamburger.

The telephone rang.

He debated answering it, but finally ran and grabbed it just before the fifth ring, which would turn on the answering machine.

"Hello?"

There was no reply, but someone was on the line.

"If you're going to talk dirty to me, please start now," Matt said.

There was a click and the line went dead.

"Fuck you, pal," Matt said, hung the telephone up, and went back to the hamburger.

The telephone rang again.

"Goddamn it!"

He snatched the phone from the wall and remembered at the last moment that the caller, this time, might be his mother, and one did not scream obscenities at one's mother.

"Hello?"

And again there was no reply.

"Oh, goddamn it!"

"Were you asleep?" It was a female voice.

Jesus Christ! Amanda?

"Amanda?"

"I was worried about you," Amanda said.

"I'm all right."

"I knew this was going to be a bad idea. I told myself you would be all right."

"I'm glad you called," he said. "What was going to be a bad idea? Jesus, it's quarter after three. Was that you on the machine? You called and didn't leave a message?"

There was no reply, which told him it had indeed been Amanda who had called and elected not to leave a message.

"How long have you been trying to reach me?"

"I got here about eleven," she said, very softly.

"Where's here? Home?"

"No."

"Where are you?"

"In the Warwick Hotel."

"The Warwick? I thought you were staying with Chad?"

"I was. They put me on the train at seven."

"I don't understand."

"What happened is that I kicked myself most of the way to Newark for being afraid what Chad and Daffy would think if I told him I was worried about you and wanted to see you. So I got off in Newark and came back. At the time, it seemed like a reasonable idea."

"Jesus, that was nice of you," he said.

"I haven't had anything to eat," she said. "Damn you. Where were you?"

"On the job. Working."

"I should have guessed that," she said. "I thought maybe you were out getting sloshed."

"I started to," he said. "And then I decided I'd better go to work."

There was a long pause, and then she said:

"This is your town. Is there someplace I can get something to eat this time of the morning?"

"How about a lukewarm hamburger and some limp french fries?"

There was another long pause.

"You mean at your place?"

"I stopped off at a restaurant on my way home," he said.

"I'm so hungry I'm tempted to accept," Amanda said. "But knowing you, you'd get the wrong idea."

"Oh, hell, I wouldn't—Jesus, Amanda!"

"All I want to be is your friend, Matt. OK? I thought you could use one."

"Absolutely. I understand. Nothing else ever entered my mind."

"OK. As long as you understand that."

"I do. Perfectly. Look, you want me to bring the hamburger there?"

"No," she said, after a just-perceptible pause. "I know where you live. Give me ten, fifteen minutes. I have to get dressed again. The last call was going to be the last call."

"I'll come get you."

"I'll be there in ten minutes," Amanda said, and hung up.

"I will be damned," Matt thought aloud. "That was really very nice of her."

He went back to the table, took knives and forks and salt and pepper and plates from cabinets, and laid them on the table. Then he got a pot from under the sink and poured the coffee into it.

At least I can offer her hot coffee!

Then he went into the living room and sat down in his chair. *While I wait, I'll take a look at this stuff:*

INVESTIGATION REPORT   PHILADELPHIA POLICE DEPARTMENT

Yr | C.C.# | DIST | COMPL.# | INITIAL(49) | | DIST/UNIT |
REPORT DATE   SUPPLEMENTAL | PREPARING
CLASSIFICATION | CODE | CONTINUATION   Homicide/9th Dist.

PREVIOUS CLASSIFICATION   CODE | DATE AND TIME | PLACE OF OCCURRENCE

COMPLAINANT | AGE | RACE | ADDRESS | PHONE | TYPE OF PREMISES
Alicia Atchison | 25 | W | 320 Wilson Avenue, Media, PA

DATE AND TIME REPORTED | REPORTED BY | ADDRESS

FOUNDED   ❐ YES ❐ NO   ARREST ❐ CLEARED   ❐ EXCEPTIONALLY CLEARED

STOLEN | ❐ CURRENCY, BONDS, ETC. ❐ FURS   ❐ AUTOS | RECOVERED VALUE
PROPERTY | ❐ JEWELRY, PRECIOUS METAL ❐ CLOTHING ❐ MISC |
INSURED   ❐ YES ❐ NO

DETAILS

A. ORIGIN:

   On Saturday, May 20, 1975 at 4:20 a.m., Sergeant Jason Washington, Special Operations Division, notified Sergeant Edward McCarthy #380 via Police
Radio, that two persons—Alicia Atchison, 25 years, White, 320 Wilson Ave,
Media, Penna., and Anthony J. Marcuzzi, 52 years, White, 6105 Palter Ave.
had been shot and killed and that Gerald N. Atchison had been shot in the leg.
That this shooting occurred inside The Inferno Lounge Bar & Restaurant,
1908 Market Street.

B. ASSIGNMENT:

1. Homicide: At 4:30 a.m., Detective Wallace H. Milham #626 was assigned
by Sergeant Zachary Hobbs #396 and he immediately proceeded to the scene.

2. Division: Detective Edgar Hayes #680 assigned by Sergeant Thomas Spiers
#336 of Central Detective Division.

3. Crime Lab: Technicians William Walters and Doyle Cohan were assigned by
Sergeant Zachary Hobbs of the Homicide Unit.

4. Other Units:

   Major Theft: Detectives Salvatore Domenico #734 and Ellis Davison #927
were assigned on May 20, 1975 at 9:00 A.M.

INVESTIGATOR (Type and Sign Name) | SERGEANT | LIEUTENANT

Alonzo Kramer | *Zachary Hobbs* |
Alonzo Kramer #967 | Zachary Hobbs #396

75-49 (Rev 3/63)   DETECTIVE DIVISION

INVESTIGATION REPORT   PHILADELPHIA POLICE DEPARTMENT

Yr | C.C.# | DIST | COMPL.# | INITIAL(49) | |DIST/UNIT |
REPORT DATE   SUPPLEMENTAL | PREPARING
CLASSIFICATION |CODE |CONTINUATION   Homicide/9th Dist.

PREVIOUS CLASSIFICATION   CODE|DATE AND TIME |PLACE OF OCCURRENCE

COMPLAINANT |AGE|RACE|ADDRESS |PHONE |TYPE OF PREMISES
Alicia Atchison | 25 | W | 320 Wilson Avenue, Media, PA

DATE AND TIME REPORTED |REPORTED BY |ADDRESS

FOUNDED ❒ YES ❒ NO   ARREST ❒ CLEARED   ❒ EXCEPTIONALLY CLEARED

STOLEN |❒ CURRENCY, BONDS, ETC. ❒ FURS   ❒.AUTOS |RECOVERED VALUE
PROPERTY |❒ JEWELRY, PRECIOUS METAL ❒ CLOTHING ❒ MISC |
INSURED   ❒ YES ❒ NO

DETAILS

C. SCENE:

   Intelligence Unit: Detectives Arthur Mason #908 and Robert McGrory #746
were assigned on May 20, 1975 at 10:00 a.m.

   1. Arrival: Sergeant Zachary Hobbs #396 and Detective Wallace H. Milham
#626 arrived at the scene at 5:05 a.m., Saturday, May 20, 1975.

   2 Present: Chief Inspector Matthew Lowenstein Detective Bureau.
                Staff Inspector Michael Weisbach
                Captain Henry C. Quaire #42, Homicide Unit.
                "   "   Thomas Curran #31, Central DD.
                "   "   Alexander Smith #17, 9th District.
                Lieutenant Louis Natali #233, Homicide Unit.
                Sergeant Zachary Hobbs #396, Homicide Unit.
                "   "   James Thom #498, Central DD.
                "   "   Jason Washington #342, Special Operations
                "   "   Edward McCarthy #380, Homicide Unit.
                "   "   Gerald Kennedy #576, 9th District.
                Detective James Whatley #607, Central DD.
                "   "   Adolphus Fowler #792, Central DD.
                "   "   Wallace H. Milham #626, Homicide Unit.
                "   "   David Rocco #615, Central DD.
                "   "   John Hanson #931, Major Theft.
                "   "   Wilfred Malone #772, Intelligence Unit.
                "   "   Edgar Hayes #680, Central DD.

INVESTIGATOR (Type and Sign Name) | SERGEANT | LIEUTENANT

Alonzo Kramer | *Zachary Hobbs* |

Alonzo Kramer #967 | Zachary Hobbs #396

75-49 (Rev 3/63)   DETECTIVE DIVISION

INVESTIGATION REPORT		PHILADELPHIA POLICE DEPARTMENT	

Yr | C.C.# | DIST | COMPL.# | INITIAL(49) | DIST/UNIT |
REPORT DATE   SUPPLEMENTAL | PREPARING
CLASSIFICATION | CODE | CONTINUATION   Homicide/9th Dist.

PREVIOUS CLASSIFICATION   CODE | DATE AND TIME | PLACE OF OCCURRENCE

COMPLAINANT | AGE | RACE | ADDRESS | PHONE | TYPE OF PREMISES
Alicia Atchison | 25 | W | 320 Wilson Avenue, Media, PA

DATE AND TIME REPORTED | REPORTED BY | ADDRESS

FOUNDED   ☐ YES ☐ NO   ARREST ☐ CLEARED   ☐ EXCEPTIONALLY CLEARED

STOLEN | ☐ CURRENCY, BONDS, ETC. ☐ FURS   ☐ AUTOS | RECOVERED VALUE
PROPERTY | ☐ JEWELRY, PRECIOUS METAL ☐ CLOTHING   ☐ MISC |
INSURED   ☐ YES ☐ NO

DETAILS

C. **SCENE:** (Continued)

        Detective James Wood #816, Homicide Unit.
        " "   Matthew Payne #701, Special Operations.
        Policeman Charles Shagren #3243, 9th District.
        " "   Frederick Marchese #4188, 9th District.
        " "   Thomas Daniels #4553, 9th District.
        " "   David Fowler #3665, 9th District.
        " "   Edward Schirmer #2559, 9th District
        " "   Lewis Roberts #3775, 9th District.
        " "   Frederick E. Rogers #4998, 9th District.
        " "   Robert Peters #3784, 9th District.
        Policeman Joseph Hart #2539, 9th District.
        " "   John McDonough #4178, 9th District.
        " "   Paul Kummerling #4228, 9th District.
        Technician Corsey Coy, Crime Lab.
        " "   Wilfred Doyle, Crime Lab.
        " "   David Dennison, Crime Lab.
        " "   Harry Withjack, Crime Lab.
        Dr. Howard D. Mitchell, Medical Examiners Office.
        Photographer Jose Acquila, Medical Examiners Office.

    3. Outside Description:
    1908 Market Street is a one story brick building housing Inferno Lounge &
Restaurant. It is located on the south side of Market Street and is between
multi-story buildings. On the west side of 1908 is a former office building which

INVESTIGATOR (Type and Sign Name) | SERGEANT | LIEUTENANT

Alonzo Kramer | *Zachary Hobbs* |
Alonzo Kramer #967 | Zachary Hobbs #396

75-49 (Rev 3/63)   DETECTIVE DIVISION

INVESTIGATION REPORT				PHILADELPHIA POLICE DEPARTMENT	

Yr | C.C.# | DIST | COMPL.# | INITIAL(49) | DIST/UNIT |
REPORT DATE   SUPPLEMENTAL | PREPARING
CLASSIFICATION | CODE | CONTINUATION   Homicide/9th Dist.

PREVIOUS CLASSIFICATION   CODE | DATE AND TIME | PLACE OF OCCURRENCE

COMPLAINANT | AGE | RACE | ADDRESS | PHONE | TYPE OF PREMISES
Alicia Atchison | 25 | W | 320 Wilson Avenue, Media, PA

DATE AND TIME REPORTED | REPORTED BY | ADDRESS

FOUNDED   ❏ YES ❏ NO   ARREST ❏ CLEARED   ❏ EXCEPTIONALLY CLEARED

STOLEN | ❏ CURRENCY, BONDS, ETC. ❏ FURS   ❏ AUTOS | RECOVERED VALUE
PROPERTY | ❏ JEWELRY, PRECIOUS METAL ❏ CLOTHING   ❏ MISC |
INSURED   ❏ YES ❏ NO

DETAILS

C. SCENE: (Continued)

is now unoccupied. On the east side is a four story commercial building occupied by various businesses. Inferno Lounge & Restaurant runs from Market Street to Ludlow Street. Ranstead Street is located to the south of Market. Entrance to 1908 can be gained from either Market or an alley off Ludlow Street. Market is a one way eastbound street. Parking is restricted to certain hours and when permitted, is on the north side.

Ludlow Street can be entered from 18th or 19th Streets. A parking lot runs from Market to Ludlow Street west of the unoccupied office building.

The rear entrance of The Inferno is on an alley off Ludlow Street. On the west end of the building is a concrete stairway having 6 steps to the door which leads into the hallway. There are two large windows in the wall about 7 feet from the ground which are protected by a heavy wire screen with a metal frame. These windows are in the kitchen. Above the 2nd step of this concrete stairway there is a boarded up window. At the bottom of the stairs there were 2 metal trash cans and a carton of trash containing broken whiskey bottles. Flush with the pavement there was a solid metal door which opened in the middle for entrance into the basement. Underneath this metal door is a well about 4 feet deep. Above this metal door is a heavy metal wire door. These protect the inner wooden door which leads into the basement. The weather was clear and warm.

INVESTIGATOR (Type and Sign Name) | SERGEANT | LIEUTENANT

Alonzo Kramer
Alonzo Kramer #967 | *Zachary Hobbs*
                    | Zachary Hobbs #396 |

75-49 (Rev 3/63)   DETECTIVE DIVISION

INVESTIGATION REPORT			PHILADELPHIA POLICE DEPARTMENT		
Yr	C.C.#	DIST	COMPL.#	INITIAL(49)	DIST/UNIT
REPORT DATE		SUPPLEMENTAL			PREPARING
CLASSIFICATION		CODE	CONTINUATION		Homicide/9th Dist.

PREVIOUS CLASSIFICATION	CODE	DATE AND TIME		PLACE OF OCCURRENCE

COMPLAINANT	AGE	RACE	ADDRESS	PHONE	TYPE OF PREMISES
Alicia Atchison	25	W	320 Wilson Avenue, Media, PA		

DATE AND TIME REPORTED	REPORTED BY	ADDRESS

FOUNDED ☐ YES ☐ NO   ARREST ☐ CLEARED   ☐ EXCEPTIONALLY CLEARED

STOLEN   ☐ CURRENCY, BONDS, ETC. ☐ FURS   ☐ AUTOS   RECOVERED VALUE
PROPERTY ☐ JEWELRY, PRECIOUS METAL ☐ CLOTHING   ☐ MISC
INSURED   ☐ YES ☐ NO

DETAILS

C. SCENE: (Continued)

4. Inside Description:

Entrance to 1908 Market Street is made through a large glass door which opens out north to west and once inside, about 3 feet south, is a large lattice work which makes you turn to the right-east. This is the bar area and the bar is set off to the right. The bar is approximately 22 feet long north to south and 7 feet wide east to west. The building at this point is 14 feet wide east to west and 28 feet in length north to south.

The bar has bar chairs around it and against the west wall, starting from the lattice work, is a cigarette machine, a juke box and two booths with tables that seat two, each.

North of the bar area is a dining room at which point the building is only 12 feet wide east to west and 47 feet in length north to south. Along the west wall of this dining room are six booths with tables, which seat 4 people each. North of the last booth is a piano.

Along the east wall is a seating area made by a bench placed on angles so that four tables can be placed in front of the bench, to make each table a separate party. Each table has two chairs.

INVESTIGATOR (Type and Sign Name)	SERGEANT	LIEUTENANT
Alonzo Kramer	*Zachary Hobbs*	
Alonzo Kramer #967	Zachary Hobbs #396	

75-49 (Rev 3/63)	DETECTIVE DIVISION

INVESTIGATION REPORT   PHILADELPHIA POLICE DEPARTMENT

| Yr | C.C.# | DIST | COMPL.# | | INITIAL(49) | | DIST/UNIT | |
REPORT DATE   SUPPLEMENTAL | PREPARING
CLASSIFICATION | CODE | CONTINUATION   Homicide/9th Dist.

PREVIOUS CLASSIFICATION   CODE| DATE AND TIME | PLACE OF OCCURRENCE

COMPLAINANT | AGE | RACE | ADDRESS | PHONE | TYPE OF PREMISES
Alicia Atchison | 25 | W | 320 Wilson Avenue, Media, PA

DATE AND TIME REPORTED | REPORTED BY | ADDRESS

FOUNDED   ☐ YES ☐ NO   ARREST ☐ CLEARED   ☐ EXCEPTIONALLY CLEARED

STOLEN | ☐ CURRENCY, BONDS, ETC. ☐ FURS   ☐ AUTOS | RECOVERED VALUE
PROPERTY | ☐ JEWELRY, PRECIOUS METAL ☐ CLOTHING ☐ MISC |
INSURED   ☐ YES ☐ NO

DETAILS

C. SCENE: (Continued)

   4. Inside Description: (Continued)
   West of this bench is a service table, then a large potted artificial flower
arrangement, then a stairway having six steps that lead to another dining
room. This stairway is 4 feet wide. There is an iron railing that runs along the
western edge of the stairway. At the top of the stairway the iron railing is
extended until it reaches the western wall. There is a lattice work in front of
the iron railing and extends up to the ceiling. This takes the place of a wall
and it has an opening at the top of the stairway which permits entrance into
the rear dining room.

   In the rear dining room, starting from the stairway, along the east wall
going south to north, is a radiator, a clothes rack and a large air conditioner
which is built into the wall. Next there are two tables each seating four. North
of the tables is a partition that is built out of the east wall about 4 feet, then
turns at a 90° angle going north for about another 4 feet. This is the entrance
to the rest rooms. The building at this point extends about 4 feet further to
the east. In this extension the ladies room is to the south and the mens room
is to the north.

   North of the lattice work that separates the rear dining room from the lower
dining room were two open hutches which contained glasses, dishes, linens,
etc. In the corner there was a table that had a coffee warmer. Against the
west wall going south to north were five tables with chairs, each table seating
four. Then one table that seats two. The first table north of the lattice work

INVESTIGATOR (Type and Sign Name) | SERGEANT | LIEUTENANT

Alonzo Kramer | *Zachary Hobbs* |
Alonzo Kramer #967 | Zachary Hobbs #396

75-49 (Rev 3/63)   DETECTIVE DIVISION

INVESTIGATION REPORT	PHILADELPHIA POLICE DEPARTMENT

Yr   C.C.#   DIST   COMPL.#   INITIAL(49)   DIST/UNIT
REPORT DATE   SUPPLEMENTAL   PREPARING
CLASSIFICATION   CODE   CONTINUATION   Homicide/9th Dist.

PREVIOUS CLASSIFICATION   CODE   DATE AND TIME   PLACE OF OCCURRENCE

COMPLAINANT   AGE   RACE   ADDRESS   PHONE   TYPE OF PREMISES
Alicia Atchison   25   W   320 Wilson Avenue, Media, PA

DATE AND TIME REPORTED   REPORTED BY   ADDRESS

FOUNDED   ☐ YES ☐ NO   ARREST ☐ CLEARED   ☐ EXCEPTIONALLY CLEARED

STOLEN   ☐ CURRENCY, BONDS, ETC. ☐ FURS   ☐ .AUTOS   RECOVERED VALUE
PROPERTY   ☐ JEWELRY, PRECIOUS METAL ☐ CLOTHING   ☐ MISC
INSURED   ☐ YES ☐ NO

DETAILS

C. <u>SCENE:</u> (Continued)

contained two plastic containers which held dirty dishes, glasses, etc. All the other tables were covered with white tablecloths and on the floor was what appeared to be a new green rug. About 6 feet north of the last table there was an entrance to a hallway about 3 feet wide. This hallway leads to the rear exit of the building. The overall length of this hallway is approximately 40 feet long and about 4 feet wide. There was an entrance into the kitchen through a doorway that is about 25 feet from the rear door.

The rear entrance is guarded by two doors. The inner door, which is wooden, opens inwardly from right to left. It has a sliding bolt at the top and bottom, but they were not bolted. The outer door is made of a heavy wire with a metal frame. This door opens outwardly right to left and had two padlocks which were in an open position. These were inserted in the hasp, top and bottom of the door frame.

Going south into the kitchen from the rear service area of the rear dining room is a large double entrance. Going south about 15 feet is a wall to the west that has four shelves on it. At the end of this wall and west about 3 feet is an entrance to the hall for the rear exit. The wall continues west to Ludlow Street. The basement steps are located between the hall wall and the kitchen wall that has the shelves on it.

INVESTIGATOR (Type and Sign Name)   SERGEANT   LIEUTENANT

Alonzo Kramer   *Zachary Hobbs*

Alonzo Kramer #967   Zachary Hobbs #396

75-49 (Rev 3/63)   DETECTIVE DIVISION

INVESTIGATION REPORT	PHILADELPHIA POLICE DEPARTMENT

Yr	C.C.#	DIST	COMPL.#		INITIAL(49)		DIST/UNIT	

REPORT DATE   SUPPLEMENTAL | PREPARING
CLASSIFICATION | CODE | CONTINUATION   Homicide/9th Dist.

PREVIOUS CLASSIFICATION   CODE | DATE AND TIME | PLACE OF OCCURRENCE

COMPLAINANT		AGE	RACE	ADDRESS		PHONE		TYPE OF PREMISES
Alicia Atchison		25	W	320 Wilson Avenue, Media, PA				

DATE AND TIME REPORTED | REPORTED BY | ADDRESS

FOUNDED   ❒ YES ❒ NO   ARREST ❒ CLEARED   ❒ EXCEPTIONALLY CLEARED

STOLEN | ❒ CURRENCY, BONDS, ETC. ❒ FURS   ❒ AUTOS | RECOVERED VALUE
PROPERTY | ❒ JEWELRY, PRECIOUS METAL ❒ CLOTHING   ❒ MISC |
INSURED   ❒ YES ❒ NO

DETAILS

C. <u>SCENE:</u> (Continued)

   4. <u>Inside Description:</u> (Continued)

On the east section of the kitchen is a washing section separated by a small wall and then starts the food and preparation area. The stoves are located against the north wall at the rear of the building.

There is a flight of 14 steps from the kitchen to the basement running north to south and a door at the kitchen that opens into the cellar from left to right.

In the north wall of the basement near the east corner is a wooden door that leads to a well under the pavement on the alley off Ludlow Street. This door and well are used for putting the trash out onto the alley. This well is about 4 feet deep, 4 feet wide and 4 feet long. The well is covered over with 2 metal doors that are flush with the sidewalk.

These metal doors open up from the well from the center. They are locked by a metal sliding bolt that is located under the west metal door. This metal sliding bolt was found to be in an open position.

Also covering the rear cellar door is a heavy metal wire door that protects the top portion of the wooden inner door. This metal door is kept locked by a hasp and padlock which were found to be in a locked position.

INVESTIGATOR (Type and Sign Name)	SERGEANT	LIEUTENANT

Alonzo Kramer | *Zachary Hobbs* |
Alonzo Kramer #967 | Zachary Hobbs #396

75-49 (Rev 3/63)   DETECTIVE DIVISION

INVESTIGATION REPORT	PHILADELPHIA POLICE DEPARTMENT

Yr | C.C.# | DIST | COMPL.# | INITIAL(49) | |DIST/UNIT |
REPORT DATE   SUPPLEMENTAL | PREPARING
CLASSIFICATION |CODE |CONTINUATION   Homicide/9th Dist.

PREVIOUS CLASSIFICATION   CODE|DATE AND TIME |PLACE OF OCCURRENCE

COMPLAINANT |AGE|RACE|ADDRESS |PHONE |TYPE OF PREMISES
Alicia Atchison | 25 | W | 320 Wilson Avenue, Media, PA

DATE AND TIME REPORTED |REPORTED BY |ADDRESS

FOUNDED   ☐ YES ☐ NO   ARREST ☐ CLEARED   ☐ EXCEPTIONALLY CLEARED

STOLEN |☐ CURRENCY, BONDS, ETC. ☐ FURS   ☐.AUTOS |RECOVERED VALUE
PROPERTY |☐ JEWELRY, PRECIOUS METAL ☐ CLOTHING   ☐ MISC |
INSURED   ☐ YES ☐ NO

DETAILS

C. <u>SCENE:</u> (Continued)
    4. <u>Inside Description:</u> (Continued)

    The wooden door opens into the basement from left to right. This door is locked with a latch lock. It was observed that this lock was slightly sprung and can not be securely locked.

    It was observed that a 2 x 4 piece of wood, approximately 3 feet long was against the north wall west of the wooden door. This 2 x 4 is used to place under the doorknob of the wooden door to help secure the door from being opened from the outside.

    From the north wall going south are a number of boxes and debris. The last step of the stairway that leads into the cellar is 25 feet 5 inches south of the north wall. From the north basement wall to the north wall of the office is 33 feet 8 inches.

    Along the outside north wall of the office are racks for storage. South of the steps, along the west wall, is a refrigerator, then an open storage area, an ice machine and then a storeroom that is used by the employees for changing their clothing.

    The office in the basement is built alongside the east wall and has exposed studding on the outside and is enclosed from the inside with sheetrock. The north wall of the office is 7 feet 1 inch wide east to west and the south wall is 9 feet 6 inches wide east to west. The office is 18 feet 8 inches in length north to south and the west wall is offset so that it is wider at the south end.

INVESTIGATOR (Type and Sign Name) | SERGEANT | LIEUTENANT

Alonzo Kramer | *Zachary Hobbs* |
Alonzo Kramer #967 | Zachary Hobbs #396

75-49 (Rev 3/63)   DETECTIVE DIVISION

INVESTIGATION REPORT				PHILADELPHIA POLICE DEPARTMENT	

Yr | C.C.# | DIST | COMPL.# | INITIAL(49) | DIST/UNIT |
REPORT DATE   SUPPLEMENTAL | PREPARING
CLASSIFICATION | CODE | CONTINUATION   Homicide/9th Dist.

PREVIOUS CLASSIFICATION   CODE | DATE AND TIME | PLACE OF OCCURRENCE

COMPLAINANT | AGE | RACE | ADDRESS | PHONE | TYPE OF PREMISES
Alicia Atchison | 25 | W | 320 Wilson Avenue, Media, PA

DATE AND TIME REPORTED | REPORTED BY | ADDRESS

FOUNDED   ❐ YES ❐ NO   ARREST ❐ CLEARED   ❐ EXCEPTIONALLY CLEARED

STOLEN | ❐ CURRENCY, BONDS, ETC. ❐ FURS   ❐ AUTOS | RECOVERED VALUE
PROPERTY | ❐ JEWELRY, PRECIOUS METAL ❐ CLOTHING   ❐ MISC |
INSURED   ❐ YES ❐ NO

DETAILS

C. <u>SCENE:</u> (Continued)

4. <u>Inside Description:</u> (Continued)

Entrance can be gained to the office by a doorway that is 5 feet 5 inches south of the north wall. The door opens in to the office from right to left. Inside the office along the west wall going south, were two boxes behind the open door. Past the south of the entranceway where the west is extended out were liquor shelves divided into two sections, with bottles of assorted liquors and wines on them. Next is a four drawer file, a box, then a chair with a cardboard carton on it, in the southwest corner. Under the first rack of shelves at the entryway is an open safe.

Along the north wall was a coat rack and in the northeast corner was a round board on a milk carton, which is used as a table. Along the east wall, going south, was a sofa and a chair and then a desk. On the wall behind the chair was a large area with what appeared to be blood. On the east wall in the southeast corner was a pay phone. The south wall had an air space knocked out at the top acting as a window. Between the south wall and the desk was a desk chair.

The safe was found open with the door opening from the left to the right. Inside the safe were several rolls of coins, assorted papers and an empty box for a Colt Cobra revolver. In front of the safe on the floor, was a metal container which contained money and papers. At the base of this metal container were marks that appeared to be blood. Alongside this metal container was a

INVESTIGATOR (Type and Sign Name)	SERGEANT	LIEUTENANT

Alonzo Kramer | *Zachary Hobbs* |
Alonzo Kramer #967 | Zachary Hobbs #396

75-49 (Rev 3/63)   DETECTIVE DIVISION

INVESTIGATION REPORT   PHILADELPHIA POLICE DEPARTMENT

Yr | C.C.# | DIST | COMPL.# | INITIAL(49) | |DIST/UNIT |
REPORT DATE   SUPPLEMENTAL | PREPARING
CLASSIFICATION | CODE | CONTINUATION   Homicide/9th Dist.

PREVIOUS CLASSIFICATION   CODE | DATE AND TIME | PLACE OF OCCURRENCE

COMPLAINANT | AGE | RACE | ADDRESS | PHONE | TYPE OF PREMISES
Alicia Atchison | 25 | W | 320 Wilson Avenue, Media, PA

DATE AND TIME REPORTED | REPORTED BY | ADDRESS

FOUNDED   ❐ YES ❐ NO   ARREST ❐ CLEARED   ❐ EXCEPTIONALLY CLEARED

STOLEN | ❐ CURRENCY, BONDS, ETC. ❐ FURS   ❐ .AUTOS | RECOVERED VALUE
PROPERTY | ❐ JEWELRY, PRECIOUS METAL ❐ CLOTHING   ❐ MISC |
INSURED   ❐ YES ❐ NO

DETAILS

C. SCENE: (Continued)

empty paper box and then a lid that is turned up. In front of the metal container and paper box, about 1½ feet east, was an area of splatter blood.

5. Body:

   Alicia Atchison - Found victim to be stretched out in the chair on the east wall
between the desk and sofa. She was stretched out with her body and legs facing
west and her head in an easterly direction tilted back facing up. Her face was
completely covered with blood, both of her arms hanging down. She was wearing a white sweater that was open, a dark blue dress, stockings with no shoe on
her right foot. A white shoe was on her left foot and under the left foot was a
white shoe, which was apparently from this victim. Her clothing, arms, legs and
shoes all had blood on them. Directly under her, on the floor, was an extremely
large pool of blood.

   Anthony J. Marcuzzi - Found victim lying on the floor on his left side, his
legs in a northwest direction and his head in a southeast direction facing
west. His back was leaning up against the sofa and his head was directly
under the body of Alicia Atchison. He was lying in an extremely large pool of
blood. There was blood on the right side of his face around the temple area
and right ear, blood from his nose and mouth which ran down the left side of
his face.

INVESTIGATOR (Type and Sign Name) | SERGEANT | LIEUTENANT

Alonzo Kramer | *Zachary Hobbs* |
Alonzo Kramer #967 | Zachary Hobbs #396

75-49 (Rev 3/63)   DETECTIVE DIVISION

INVESTIGATION REPORT	PHILADELPHIA POLICE DEPARTMENT

Yr | C.C.# | DIST | COMPL.# | INITIAL(49) | DIST/UNIT |
REPORT DATE   SUPPLEMENTAL | PREPARING
CLASSIFICATION | CODE | CONTINUATION   Homicide/9th Dist.

PREVIOUS CLASSIFICATION   CODE | DATE AND TIME | PLACE OF OCCURRENCE

COMPLAINANT | AGE | RACE | ADDRESS | PHONE | TYPE OF PREMISES
Alicia Atchison | 25 | W | 320 Wilson Avenue, Media, PA

DATE AND TIME REPORTED | REPORTED BY | ADDRESS

FOUNDED   ❐ YES ❐ NO   ARREST ❐ CLEARED   ❐ EXCEPTIONALLY CLEARED

STOLEN | ❐ CURRENCY, BONDS, ETC. ❐ FURS   ❐ AUTOS | RECOVERED VALUE
PROPERTY | ❐ JEWELRY, PRECIOUS METAL ❐ CLOTHING   ❐ MISC |
INSURED   ❐ YES ❐ NO

DETAILS

C. SCENE: (Continued)

His left arm was extended out from under his body in a northwest direction and his right arm was folded across his chest. He was wearing a brown suit, white shirt, brown tie and shoes and socks.

6. Crime Lab:

(a) Direction: On Saturday, May 20, 1975, Technicians Corsey Coy and Wilfred Doyle were directed at the crime scene by Sergeant Zachary Hobbs, to take a total of 47 photographs, also to make a sketch of the scene, search same for latent fingerprints and preserve evidence found at scene and submit same.

(b) Latent Prints: Technician Corsey Coy lifted over-laps and partial prints from the safe and a Seagrams V-O bottle that was on the desk, both being inside the office.

Latent Prints were developed from the stem of a glass that was on top of the desk inside the office and from a plain glass that was found on the bar. These prints were checked by Corsey Coy and David Dennison with positive results, both latent prints being of Anthony J. Marcuzzi.

(c) Direction: On Saturday, May 20, 1975, Technicians Harry Withjack and David Dennison were directed to the scene to assist in making a sketch and search of the scene.

INVESTIGATOR (Type and Sign Name)	SERGEANT	LIEUTENANT

Alonzo Kramer | *Zachary Hobbs* |
Alonzo Kramer #967 | Zachary Hobbs #396

75-49 (Rev 3/63)   DETECTIVE DIVISION

When Detective Wally Milham pushed open the door of the Red Robin Diner at Frankford and Levick it was nearly empty, and for at least fifteen seconds, which seemed like much longer, he couldn't find Helene Kellog. But then he saw her, in a booth halfway down the counter, staring into a coffee cup on the table.

She had a kerchief around her head, and was wearing a cotton raincoat.

He walked quickly to the booth and slid onto the seat facing her.

"Hi," he said.

She looked up at him and smiled wanly, but didn't speak, and when he touched her hand, she pulled it away.

"Tell me exactly what happened," he said.

"My mother came into my room. I hadn't heard the phone ring, it's downstairs in the hall. And she told me I had a call—"

"When was this?"

"Just before I called you."

"You were in bed?"

"Of course I was in bed. It was . . . God, I don't know. Late. Of course I was in bed. Everybody was in bed. My mother had to get out of bed to answer the phone . . ."

"Take it easy, honey," Milham said gently.

"I'm frightened, Wally."

"Tell me exactly what happened."

"He said, he said, 'Keep your . . .' Wally, he said, 'Keep your fucking mouth closed, bitch, or you'll get the same thing your fucking husband did.' "

"Sonofabitch," Milham said. "Did you recognize the voice?"

Helene shook her head.

"Honey, do you know something about—what your husband was doing, something dirty, that you haven't told me?"

"No. But, Wally, they must know I went to see Sergeant Washington."

"You did what?"

"Oh, God, I didn't tell you, did I?"

"Didn't tell me what?"

"That I went to see Sergeant Washington."

"No, you didn't," Milham said. "What exactly did you tell Washington?"

"I told him that the Narcotics Five Squad is all dirty, that Jerry was dirty, and that they probably are the ones who killed him."

"Jesus!"

"I didn't tell you because I didn't want to involve you," Helene said.

"Honey, I'm involved," Wally said, and added, "You're probably right. Somebody knows you talked to Washington. What did you do, call him up?"

"I went to see him."

"Well, somebody from Five Squad was at Special Operations, and recognized you, or somebody at Special Operations told somebody at Five Squad . . ."

"I went to his house," Helene said. "I didn't go to Special Operations. Which means that if Five Squad knows, he told them."

Milham considered that for two seconds.

"No. Not Washington. He's a straight arrow. He didn't tell anybody, except maybe somebody at Internal Affairs."

"What's the difference? They know."

"What are they afraid you'll tell somebody?"

Helene shrugged helplessly. "I don't know. I don't know what they're doing dirty, just that they are."

"Your husband never told you where the money came from?"

Helene shook her head.

"Wally, I don't want them to do anything to my mother and father."

"They won't. The dumbest thing they could do is try to do something to you. Or them. The whole Police Department would come down on them."

"Huh!" she snorted. "They don't want to go to jail; there's no telling what they'll do."

"They're just trying to scare you, is all. Christ, I wish you had told me about this. I could have got to Washington and nobody would ever have known."

"I told you, I didn't want to involve you."

"And I told you, I'm involved in whatever you do," Milham said. He reached out for her hand again, and this time she did not move it away.

When he looked at her face, tears were running down her cheeks.

"Honey, don't do that. I can't stand to see you cry."

"Wally, what am I going to do?"

"The question is what are we going to do. You understand?"

"OK. We," Helene said, and tried to smile.

"OK. So you're not going back to your mother's. That's one thing."

"What is she going to say? What do I say to her?"

"What did you say when you left the house?"

"I told her I had to go somewhere, and that I would call. She didn't like it at all."

"OK. So you call her again, and tell her you have to go away for a couple of days, and that you'll call her."

"She won't like it."

"Honey, for Christ's sake! They called you there because they knew you were there."

She nodded a grudging acceptance of that.

"So where do I go?"

"My place," he suggested without much conviction in his voice.

"I can't do that, and you know it," Helene said.

"OK. We'll talk about that later. Tonight we'll go to a motel."

"Not *we,* Wally. I'm not up to anything like that."

"OK. We get you in a motel. You go to bed. Get your rest. I'll think of something."

"Something what?"

"I don't know. Something," Milham said. "One thing at a time."

She looked at him and squeezed his hand.

"Helene," Wally said. "Everything's going to be all right. You're not alone." She squeezed his hand. "I love you," Wally said.

She squeezed his hand again.

He stood up.

"Come on, let's get out of here."

"You think maybe they followed me here?"

"Of course not," he said.

But when they went to his car, he looked up and down the street to make sure there was nothing suspicious, and as they drove to the Sheraton Hotel, on Roosevelt Boulevard and Grant Avenue, he made three or four turns to be absolutely sure no one was following them.

He didn't like the idea of leaving her alone, but he understood why she didn't want him to stay with her, and he knew that he couldn't press her about that; she would think that all he wanted to do was get in bed with her.

He got the key from the desk clerk, who sort of smirked at him, making it clear he thought that what they were up to was a little quickie.

He stood outside the motel door.

"Get the room number off the phone, and I'll call you in the morning," Wally said.

"OK," she said, "wait here."

She came back with the number written inside a matchbook, and handed it to him.

"I'll call you in the morning," he said.

"Yes."

She looked at him, and leaned forward and kissed him on the cheek.

"Thank you, Wally," she said.

"Aaaah. I'll call you in the morning. Just lock the door and get some sleep."

"Right."

"Good night, Helene. I'll call you in the morning."

"Right."

He had taken a dozen steps toward his car when she called his name.

"Wally?"

"Yeah?"

He walked back to her.

"Wally, I love you, too," Helene said.

"I know," he said. "But thank you for saying it."

"I don't want you to go," Helene said.

She took his hand and pulled him into the motel room.

Matt's door buzzer sounded.

He pushed the button that opened the door and went to the top of the stairs to wait for Amanda.

The doorway was filled with a rent-a-cop, a huge one Matt did not know.

"Sorry to bother you, Mr. Payne, but there's a young lady here says you expect her."

"Of course," Matt said, and ran down the stairs.

"Thanks a lot," Matt said to the rent-a-cop.

"Hello," Amanda said softly, and walked quickly past him and up the stairs. She was wearing a suit with a white blouse. He could smell soap.

He closed the door in the face of the rent-a-cop and went after Amanda, carefully averting his eyes so that she wouldn't have any reason at all to suspect he was looking up her skirt as she went up the stairs.

She waited for him at the top of the stairs.

"You know what he thought, don't you?" Amanda asked.

"No. What did he think?"

"He thought I was a call girl."

"Don't be silly."

"I'm not being silly. He as much as accused me in the elevator. And why not? Who else would be going to a bachelor apartment at this hour?"

"A friend," Matt said.

"God. I'm sorry I ever got started on this!"

"I'm not."

"I meant it, Matt, when I said I'm here as a friend."

"Absolutely. I know that."

She met his eyes, and then quickly averted hers.

"Do you know how to warm up a hamburger?" Matt asked. "I put the coffee in a pot, and we can heat that. But the hamburgers are cold."

"You put the meat patty in a frying pan," Amanda said. "You have a frying pan?" He nodded. "And—you said french fries?" Matt nodded again. "You put french fries in the oven."

"I've got one of those, too," Matt said.

"Good," she said. "Show me."

"I'm glad you came," Matt said. "Thank you."

"Just as long as you understand why I came," she said. "OK?"

"Absolutely. I told you that."

She went in the kitchen. He turned the oven on and handed her a frying pan.

When she bent over to put the french fries in the oven, he looked down her blouse and told himself he was really a sonofabitch.

When she stood up, he could tell by the look in her eyes that she knew he had looked down her blouse.

He backed two steps away from her and smiled uneasily.

"If anybody finds out I came here," Amanda said, "they wouldn't understand."

"Nobody will ever find out," Matt said. He held up three fingers in the Boy Scout salute. "Scout's Honor."

"Oh, God," Amanda groaned.

"Bad joke," he said. "Sorry."

"And they would, of course, be right," Amanda said. "Oh, hell! 'In for a penny'—*oh, God!*—'in for a pound.' "

"Excuse me?"

"You know what my reaction was when I heard Penny was dead?"

"What?"

"Thank God. She was going to suck Matt dry and ruin his life." She looked intently at his face, then moaned. "Oh, God. I shouldn't have told you!"

"Isn't that why you came here, to tell me that? Amanda, that's really—decent—of you. And it really took balls."

"Balls?" she parroted, gently mocking.

"It took courage," he corrected himself. "But you're not the only one who felt that way. Penny . . . Penny apparently did not enjoy the universal approval of my friends. Half a dozen people told me exactly, or paraphrased, what you just did."

"That's not why I came," Amanda said. "I wanted to be with you."

"You're a good friend," Matt said.

She met his eyes, then looked away, and then met them again.

"Maybe that, too," Amanda said softly.

"Jesus, Amanda."

"Does that come as such a surprise? Am I making as much of a fool of myself as I think I am?"

He reached out and touched her cheek with his fingers.

She moved her head away and looked to the side.

"For God's sake, don't feel sorry for me," she said.

"What I'm doing is wondering what would happen if I tried to put my arms around you."

She turned her face to look at him. She looked into his eyes for a long moment.

"Why don't you try it and find out?" Amanda asked.

17.

Matt Payne rolled over in bed, grabbed the telephone on the bedside table, and snarled, "Hello."

"Good morning," Amanda Spencer said, a chuckle in her voice. "Somehow I thought you'd be in a better mood than you sound like."

Still half asleep, Matt turned and looked in confusion at where he expected Amanda to be, lying beside him. He was obviously alone in his bed.

"Where are you?"

"Thirtieth Street Station," she said.

"Why?"

"You have to come here to get on a train."

"Jesus H. Christ!"

"I have a job, Matt."

"Call in and tell them you were run over by a truck."

"It was something like that, wasn't it? How do you feel this morning?"

"Right now, desolate."

She chuckled again.

"Don't call me, Matt. I'll call you."

"Did I do something wrong?"

"This is what I think they call the cold, cruel light of day," Amanda said. "I need some time to think."

"Second thoughts, you mean? Morning-after regrets?"

"I said I need some time to think. But no regrets."

"Me either," he said.

He was now fully awake. He picked his watch up from the bedside table. It was ten past eight.

"You could have said something," he said, somewhat petulantly.

"I'm saying it now," Amanda said. "I have a job. I have to go to work, and I need some time to think."

"Damn!"

"If it makes you feel any better, I didn't really want to leave. But it was the sensible thing to do."

"Screw sensible."

"Have you got any morning-after regrets?"

"I'm still in shock, but no regrets."

"We both got a little carried away last night."

"Anything wrong with that?"

"That's what I want to think about," Amanda said. "I'll call you, Matt. Don't call me."

The phone went dead in his ear.

"Damn!"

"Push the damned button, Matt," Inspector Peter Wohl said into the microphone beside Detective Payne's doorbell. "The Wachenhut guy told me he knows you're up there."

A moment later the solenoid buzzed, and Wohl pushed the door open and started up the narrow flight of stairs.

"I didn't know who it was," Matt said from the head of the stairs. He was wearing khaki trousers, a gray, battered University of Pennsylvania sweatshirt, and was obviously fresh from the shower.

He looks more than a little sleepy, Peter thought. *Probably still feeling the pill Amy gave him.*

"How are you doing?"

"I was just about to go out and get some breakfast."

"Not necessary," Wohl said, handing him a large kraft paper bag. "Never let it be said that I do not take care of my underlings."

Matt sniffed it.

"Smells great. What is it?"

"Western omelet, bagels, orange juice, and coffee."

"Thank you, Peter," Matt said.

"I expected to find you still in bed," Wohl said.

"Huh?"

"Amy said that the pill she gave you . . ." Wohl stopped. He had followed Matt into the kitchen and seen the stack of Forms 75-49. "What's this?"

"75-49s on the Inferno job," Matt said. "Milham told me to read them."

"When did you see Milham?"

"Last night. Early this morning. I went over there—"

"You didn't take Amy's pill?" Wohl asked, but it was a statement rather than a question.

"No, I didn't," Matt confessed. "I had a couple of drinks here, decided going to the FOP was a good idea, started out for there, changed my mind, and went to Homicide."

"Why?" Wohl asked, a tone of exasperation in his voice.

"At the time it seemed like a good idea," Matt said.

Wohl reached into his jacket pocket and came out with an interoffice memorandum. He handed it to Matt.

"One of the reasons I came here was to show you this. I guess you've seen it."

Matt glanced at it.

"Yeah. Milham had a copy."

"Lowenstein sent me one," Wohl said, taking the memorandum back and then crumpling it in his fist. He looked around, remembered the garbage can was under the sink, and went to it and dropped the memorandum in it.

"For some reason, I'm not sore at you," Wohl said. "I think I should be."

"I didn't want that damned pill," Matt said.

"That, I understand. But you shouldn't have gone to Homicide until I sent you."

"Sorry," Matt said.

"Oh, hell, I'd have probably done the same thing myself," Wohl said. "Unwrap the omelets."

"Lieutenant Natali was very nice to me," Matt said.

"Natali's a nice fellow," Wohl said. "Where's your cups? I hate coffee in a paper cup."

"In the cabinet."

"Are you really all right? Amy thinks you're still in what she calls a condition called 'grief shock.' "

"Amy's a nice girl," Matt said, gently mocking. "But what I'm in is a condition called 'Oh, what a sonofabitch you are, Matt Payne.' "

"I told you, what Penny did to herself wasn't your fault."

"Somebody came to see me last night," Matt said. "To comfort me in my condition of grief shock."

"Somebody, I gather from the tone of your voice, female. And?"

"She comforted me," Matt said.

Wohl looked at him to make sure he had correctly interpreted what he had said.

"Who?"

"I don't think I want to tell you."

"Nice kind of girl, or the other?"

"Very nice kind of girl."

"Good for you," Wohl said. "But I don't think I'd tell Amy."

"I've been trying to wallow in guilt, but I don't seem to be able to."

"What's in it for the girl?"

"I just think she was being nice. Maybe a little more."

"The one from New York? Amanda, something like that?"

"Jesus Christ!"

"I saw her looking at you at Martha Peebles's."

"I didn't see her at Martha Peebles's."

"I repeat, good for you, Matt. Don't wallow in guilt."

The door buzzer sounded.

Matt looked surprised.

"Detective McFadden, I'll bet," Wohl said. "Here to comfort you in your condition of grief shock, with firm orders to keep you off the sauce."

"You really do take care of me, don't you?" Matt asked.

"Somebody has to, or the first thing you know, you're crawling around on a ledge like an orangutan."

"Thank you, Peter," Matt said, pushing the button to open the door, and walked to the head of the stairs.

It was, instead of Detective McFadden, Detective Milham.

"You're up, I hope?" Milham asked. "I know I said ten . . ."

"Having breakfast. Come on up."

"I've got somebody with me. Is that all right?"

"Sure."

Milham took a step backward and a woman Matt had never seen before, but who he intuited was the Widow Kellog, appeared in the doorway and started up the stairs.

"I know we're intruding," she said as she reached Matt.

"Not at all."

"I'm Helene Kellog," she said.

"Matt Payne," Matt said. "How do you do? Come on in."

He led her to the kitchen.

"Mrs. Kellog, this is Inspector Wohl."

"Oh, God," Helene said.

"How do you do, Mrs. Kellog?" Wohl said politely, standing up.

Milham appeared.

It's a toss-up, Matt thought, *which of them looks unhappier at finding Wohl up here.*

"Hello, Wally," Wohl said. "How are you?"

"Wally, we should leave," Helene said.

"Not on my account, I hope," Wohl said.

"Inspector—" Milham began, and then stopped. Wohl looked at him curiously. "Inspector, Mrs. Kellog got a death threat last night."

"Damn you, Wally," Helene said.

"Did you really?" Wohl asked. "Please sit down, Mrs. Kellog. Let me get you a cup of coffee."

"I don't mean to be rude, but . . ."

"Helene, honey, we just can't pretend it didn't happen."

"Please, sit down," Wohl repeated.

She reluctantly did so.

"Mrs. Kellog, you're with friends," Wohl said.

The door buzzer sounded again. Helene glanced toward the stairway with fright in her eyes.

"That has to be McFadden," Wohl said. "You want to let him in, Matt?"

It was McFadden, laden with a kraft paper bag.

"I stopped by McDonald's and got some Egg McMuffins," he said, handing Matt the bag as he reached the top of the stairs. "I thought maybe you hadn't eaten."

"I really want to go," Helene said, getting up from the table.

"Who's that?" McFadden asked.

"Charley, this is Mrs. Helene Kellog," Wohl said. "Mrs. Kellog, this is Detective McFadden."

"Please, Wally," Helene said.

"I'm going to have to be firm about this," Wohl said. "If you've had a death threat, I want to know about it. If you won't tell me about it, Mrs. Kellog, Wally will have to."

"I knew we shouldn't have come here," Helene said, but, with resignation, she sat back down.

"At least we have enough food," Wohl said. "Have you had any breakfast, Mrs. Kellog?"

"No," she said softly.

"Have an Egg McMuffin and a cup of coffee," Wohl said. "Wally will tell me what's happened, and then you can fill in any blanks."

Milham looked as if he was torn between regret that he had to tell Wohl and relief.

"Helene called me at the Roundhouse last night," he said. "She told me there had been a telephone call."

"Where was she?"

"At my mother's," Helene said. "I mean, I got the call at my mother's. I called Wally from the Red Robin Diner."

"And what exactly did your caller say?"

"He told me that unless I kept my mouth shut, I'd get the same thing that happened to Jerry," Helene said.

"In just about those exact words?"

"He used dirty words," she said.

"You didn't happen to recognize the voice?" Wohl asked.

She shook her head.

"I can understand why you're upset," Wohl said.

"Upset? I'm scared to death. Not only for me. I'm afraid for my mother and father."

"Well, I was about to say, you're safe now. We're friends, Mrs. Kellog. You think this call came from somebody on the Narcotics Five Squad?"

"Of course it did," Helene snapped. "Who else? What I'd like to know . . ."

Wohl waited a moment for her to continue, and when she did not, he asked, gently: "What would you like to know?"

"Nothing, forget it."

"She'd like to know how that damned Five Squad heard she'd talked to Washington," Wally Milham said. "And so would I."

"And so would I," Wohl said. "We'll find out. And until we do, until we get to the bottom of this, you won't be alone, Mrs. Kellog. You're living with your mother for the time being?"

"I was. Not now. I don't want them involved in this."

"So where will you be staying?"

"Helene stayed in a motel last night," Milham said.

"That can get kind of expensive," Wohl thought aloud. "Isn't there some place you can stay?"

Helene and Wally looked at each other helplessly.

"She could stay here," Matt heard himself say. The others looked at him in what was more confusion than surprise. "My mother's been on my back for me to stay with her for a couple of days."

"I couldn't do that," Helene said.

"I know it's not much," Matt said. "But if anybody was looking for you, they wouldn't look for you here. And there's a rent-a-cop downstairs twenty-four hours a day. And it's just going to sit here, empty."

"Jesus, Payne," Milham said. "That's very nice of you, but . . ."

"Why not?" Matt said. "I mean, really, why not?"

"I told you you were among friends, Mrs. Kellog," Wohl said. "I think it's a good idea."

"I just don't know," she said, and started to sniffle.

"I think you should, honey," Milham said.

"OK. It's settled," Matt said.

"Thank you very much," Helene said, formally. "Just for a few days."

"Wally, you take her to get her things, and then come back here," Wohl ordered.

"Right," Milham said, and then, quickly, as if he was afraid she would change her mind, "Come on, honey. Let's go."

"If I'm not here when you get back, I'll leave a key with the rent-a-cop," Matt said.

Helene looked at him.

"Wally was right," she said. "He said you were a very nice guy."

When they had gone down the stairs, and heard the door close after them, Wohl said, "That was nice of you, Matt."

"Christ, they can't afford living in a motel," Matt said.

"And won't your mother be pleasantly surprised to have you at home?" Wohl asked drolly. He stood up and went to the telephone and dialed a number.

"Inspector Wohl for the Chief," he said a moment later, and then: "Chief, I promised to let you know if anything interesting happened. The Widow Kellog got a death threat—specifically, 'Keep your mouth shut, or you'll get the same thing as your husband,' or words to that effect embroidered with obscenity—last night."

The outraged, familiar voice of Chief Inspector Lowenstein could be heard all over the kitchen: "I'll be goddamned! Where is she?"

"With Detective Milham. He took her to fetch some clothing. Matt Payne offered her his apartment to stay in."

"That really burns me up," Lowenstein said, unnecessarily adding, "what happened to her. That was nice of Payne. What are you going to do about it?"

"I'm going, first of all, to have someone sit on her. Discreetly."

"Your people?"

"My people, and since we're going to have to do this around the clock, I'd like to borrow one of yours for as long as this lasts."

"Who?"

"McFadden. He was here, at Payne's apartment, when this came up."

"Northwest Detectives? That McFadden? The one who took down Dutch Moffitt's murderer?"

"That McFadden."

"OK. He's yours. I'll call Northwest Detectives."

"Thank you. And then I'm going to give this to Weisbach and Washington. What I would like to know is who told Narcotics Five Squad that she'd talked to Washington."

"You don't know for sure that they know that," Lowenstein said.

"No. But it strikes me as highly probable."

Lowenstein grunted, and then said: "Peter, if you need anything else, let me know. Keep me posted. And thank you for the call."

"Yes, sir. Thank you."

He hung up the telephone, then leaned against the wall.

"It's time, I think," he said thoughtfully, "that we practice a little psychology. That woman is frightened. I think she knows more about what's going on dirty with that Five Squad than she's told anybody, including Milham, and right now, he's the only cop she really trusts. She trusts Matt a little, because Milham likes him, and because he offered the apartment. And she thinks that Washington is straight, otherwise she would never have gone to him. So we'll try to build a little trust by association."

He turned back to the telephone and dialed a number.

"Jason, is Weisbach there?" he asked, and when the reply was that he wasn't, added: "Put out the arm for him, please, and ask him to meet me at Payne's apartment right away. I want you here, too, Jason. Right away."

They could not hear what Washington replied.

"The Widow Kellog got a death threat telephone call this morning, telling her to keep her mouth shut or get the same thing that happened to her husband. Matt offered his apartment as a place for her to stay. Milham just took her to pick up some clothes. When they come back here, I want her to feel she's surrounded by cops she can trust."

And again, Washington made a reply they couldn't hear.

"Oh, sure, we're going to sit on her. I'm taking that threat very seriously. Be prepared, when you get here, to assign, in her hearing, everybody but Tiny a duty schedule to sit on her. I borrowed McFadden from Lowenstein. If you can find Martinez and Tiny, I'd like them here, too. Once she sees that she's surrounded by cops, I want to leave her alone with you and Weisbach. Maybe you can get her to talk now."

Washington made another inaudible reply, to which Wohl responded, "Yeah."

Then: "Jason, switch me to Captain Pekach, will you?"

"David? Are you in uniform?"

Now Matt and Charley McFadden could hear Pekach's reply: "Yes, I am."

"OK. Good. I want you, in a Highway car, to be parked on the sidewalk in front of Matt

Payne's apartment in twenty minutes. You come up. And I think it would be a good idea to have another Highway car parked with you. Tell them to get out of the car and be standing conspicuously on the sidewalk. I'll explain it all to you when you get here."

He hung up and turned to face Matt and McFadden again.

"In her presence, I will order the Commanding Officer of Highway to have a Highway car pass her parents' home not less than once each half hour," he said, "and to check on any car, or person, who looks halfway suspicious."

"You're really taking that threat seriously, aren't you?" Matt asked.

"Somebody shot her husband," Wohl said. "If they're willing to do that once . . ."

"If somebody is watching her parents' house, they'll probably make the Highway drive-bys."

"Good, let's make them nervous," Wohl said. He paused, almost visibly having another thought. "If I was wondering what Mrs. Kellog told Washington, I think I'd also be worrying what she told Milham. So I think you'd better stick with him, Matt, instead of sitting on her."

"OK."

"I think it would also make her feel better to know he's not walking around alone. Question: Should Milham be here when she talks to Washington or not?"

"She seems to listen to him," McFadden said.

"Yeah," Matt said.

"OK. So you pack your bag, Matt, and be ready to get out when I tell you. Take McFadden with you. Go to Homicide and let him read the 75-49s on Kellog. I'll call Quaire and fix it with him. If anything has come up that looks like it has a connection with this, call me."

"Right."

When Matt returned to the kitchen after getting dressed, and carrying a small suitcase into which he had put his toilet kit and a spare pair of shoes, Charley McFadden was at the kitchen table, reading the 75-49s on the Inferno job. Wohl was in the living room, studiously writing in his notebook.

"Interesting," Charley said. "I've never seen Homicide 75-49s before."

"That's because God doesn't love you," Matt said piously.

McFadden looked at him curiously.

"How are you doing?" he asked.

"Fine," Matt said, cheerfully and immediately, and then, chagrined, remembered he was supposed to be grief-stricken.

"Yeah?" Charley asked suspiciously. "Are you on something? Wohl . . ." He quickly corrected himself, remembering that *Inspector* Wohl was ten feet away: ". . . Inspector Wohl said your sister gave you a pill."

Matt didn't want to get into the subject of the pill, and he didn't want to lie to McFadden. He avoided a direct reply.

"I'm OK, Charley," he said, and leaned over McFadden's shoulder hoping he could find something in the 75-49s that would allow him to change the subject.

He found something, on the page Charley was just about to turn facedown.

"Bingo!"

McFadden looked up at him.

"What the hell does that mean?"

"Look here," Matt said, and pointed toward the bottom of the page. "We had a tip that the doer was somebody named Frankie. Milham and I, starting from zilch, were out looking for him early this morning. We think we found him, on 2320 South Eighteenth Street. And here's a Frankie who was in the Inferno, and there's a description."

"I know that neighborhood," McFadden said, and then was interrupted when the door buzzer sounded.

"This is Captain Pekach," a metallic voice announced.

"Push the button, Charley," Matt said. "I'll stack this stuff together."
He read again the page Charley had been reading:

INVESTIGATION REPORT		PHILADELPHIA POLICE DEPARTMENT

INVESTIGATION REPORT   PHILADELPHIA POLICE DEPARTMENT

Yr | C.C.# | DIST | COMPL.# | INITIAL(49) | | DIST/UNIT |
REPORT DATE   SUPPLEMENTAL | PREPARING
CLASSIFICATION | CODE | CONTINUATION   Homicide/9th Dist.

PREVIOUS CLASSIFICATION   CODE|DATE AND TIME |PLACE OF OCCURRENCE

COMPLAINANT | AGE | RACE | ADDRESS | PHONE | TYPE OF PREMISES
Alicia Atchison | 25 | W | 320 Wilson Avenue, Media, PA

DATE AND TIME REPORTED | REPORTED BY | ADDRESS

FOUNDED   ☐ YES ☐ NO   ARREST ☐ CLEARED   ☐ EXCEPTIONALLY CLEARED

STOLEN | ☐ CURRENCY, BONDS, ETC. ☐ FURS   ☐.AUTOS | RECOVERED VALUE
PROPERTY | ☐ JEWELRY, PRECIOUS METAL ☐ CLOTHING   ☐ MISC |
INSURED   ☐ YES ☐ NO

DETAILS

   D. INTERVIEWS: (Continued)

   Informative Witnesses: (Continued)

   12. Pontalle, Henriette, 37-W, 220 N. 15th Street, interviewed by Detective
Rocco Andretti #743, on May 20, 1975 at 10:05 a.m., inside Homicide Unit
Hdqts.

   Stated - That she is a waitress at the Inferno Lounge & Restaurant, and
that she worked on May 19, 1975 from 12:00 a.m. until 10:00 p.m. She said
business was slow all day. She saw nothing out of the ordinary during her
work. The last time she saw Mrs. Atchison was about 9:00 p.m. when she had
dinner with her husband and Marcuzzi. She left the Inferno with Marcuzzi on
some sort of business. Atchison was in the Inferno when she went off duty.
Stated that as far as she knew, there was no trouble between Atchison and
his wife, or between Atchison and Marcuzzi.

   13. Melrose, Thomas, 20-W, 2733 N. Portman Street, interviewed by Detective Rocco Andretti #743, on May 20, 1975 at 10:45 a.m., inside Homicide
Unit Hdqts.

   Stated - That he is a bartender at the Inferno Lounge & Restaurant, and
that he was working on the night of May 19, 1975. He went to work at 3:00
p.m. and quit work shortly after eleven. He said business was slow. He saw
nothing out of the ordinary during the night. Around eleven p.m., Atchison
asked him to stay a couple of minutes more, as he had business to transact
with a customer named "Frankie" in the office. "Frankie" is a white male approx.

INVESTIGATOR (Type and Sign Name) | SERGEANT | LIEUTENANT

Alonzo Kramer | *Zachary Hobbs* |
Alonzo Kramer #967 | Zachary Hobbs #396

75-49 (Rev 3/63)   DETECTIVE DIVISION

INVESTIGATION REPORT			PHILADELPHIA POLICE DEPARTMENT	

Yr | C.C.# | DIST | COMPL.# | INITIAL(49) | DIST/UNIT |
REPORT DATE   SUPPLEMENTAL   PREPARING
CLASSIFICATION | CODE | CONTINUATION   Homicide/9th Dist.

PREVIOUS CLASSIFICATION   CODE | DATE AND TIME | PLACE OF OCCURRENCE

COMPLAINANT | AGE | RACE | ADDRESS | PHONE | TYPE OF PREMISES
Alicia Atchison | 25 | W | 320 Wilson Avenue, Media, PA

DATE AND TIME REPORTED | REPORTED BY | ADDRESS

FOUNDED   ☐ YES ☐ NO   ARREST ☐ CLEARED   ☐ EXCEPTIONALLY CLEARED

STOLEN | ☐ CURRENCY, BONDS, ETC. ☐ FURS   ☐ .AUTOS | RECOVERED VALUE
PROPERTY | ☐ JEWELRY, PRECIOUS METAL ☐ CLOTHING   ☐ MISC |
INSURED   ☐ YES ☐ NO

DETAILS

D. INTERVIEWS: (Continued)

   Informative Witnesses: (Continued)

25 years old, and sometimes comes into the Inferno. Stated he does not know what was the nature of the business, but that Atchison sometimes made loans. Atchison and "Frankie" returned to the bar from the office a few minutes at 11 p.m. "Frankie" left the Inferno. Atchison took over the bar. Neither Mrs. Atchison or Marcuzzi were in the bar when he left. Stated that as far as he knew, there was no trouble between Atchison and his wife, or between Atchison and Marcuzzi.

INVESTIGATOR (Type and Sign Name) | SERGEANT | LIEUTENANT

Alonzo Kramer | *Zachary Hobbs* |
Alonzo Kramer #967 | Zachary Hobbs #396

75-49 (Rev 3/63)   DETECTIVE DIVISION

"Well, what do we do now? Go back to your place?" Detective McFadden inquired of Detective Payne as they came out of the Detective Bureau in the Roundhouse and waited for the elevator.

There had been nothing in the 75-49s on the Kellog job that Matt thought Wohl would be interested in, and nothing much new on the Inferno job that Matt found in Milham's box.

"I don't think so," Matt said. "I think he'll get on the radio when whatever is going to happen at the apartment has happened."

"So where shall we go in that spanking-new unmarked car? You all have cars like that?"

"God loves us."

"Knock that shit off, will you, Matt? It's blasphemous."

"Sorry," Matt said, meaning it. He had trouble remembering that Charley was almost, if not quite, as devoutly Roman Catholic as Mother Moffitt, his grandmother, and took sincere offense at what he had not thought of as anything approaching blasphemy.

"What are you going to do about that name you picked up on the 75-49?"

"Frankie, you mean?"

"Yeah."

"Wait for Milham, I guess."

"That's my neighborhood, Matt. And I think I know a guy who could probably give us a good line on him. Or are you afraid of spooking him?"

Matt remembered what Milham had said when they had come out of the bar after Milham had told the bartender he was Frankie's cousin from Conshohocken, that he hoped the bartender would tell Frankie a cop had been looking for him, that it would make Frankie nervous.

"No, I get the feeling that Milham would like it if Frankie got a little nervous."

"OK. Let's do that."

"Who are we going to see?"

"Sonny Boyle, we went to St. Monica's at Sixteenth and Porter."

Timothy Francis "Sonny" Boyle, who was twenty-seven years of age, weighed 195 pounds, and stood six feet one inch tall, had not known for the past year or so what to think about Charles Thomas McFadden.

Sonny had decided early on that the world was populated by two kinds of people: those that had to work hard for a living because they weren't too smart, and a small group of the other kind, who didn't have to work hard because they used their heads.

He had been in maybe the second year at Bishop Neuman High School when he had decided he was a member of the small group of the other kind, the kind who lived well by their wits, figuring out the system, and putting it to work for them.

He had known Charley since the second grade at St. Monica's, and liked him, really liked him. But that hadn't stopped him from concluding that Charley was just one more none-too-bright Irish Catholic guy from South Philly who would spend his life doing what other people told him to do, and doing it for peanuts.

He had not been surprised when Charley had gone on the cops. For people like Charley, it was either going into the service, or going on the cops, or becoming a fireman, or maybe in Charley's case, since his father worked in the sewers, getting on with U.G.I., the gas company.

Charley, Sonny had decided when he had heard that Charley had gone on the cops, would spend his life riding around in a prowl car, or standing in the middle of the street up to his ass in snow and carbon monoxide, directing traffic. With a little bit of luck, and the proper connections, he might make sergeant by the time he retired. And in the meantime, he would do what other people told him to do, and for peanuts.

Charley, Sonny had decided, wasn't smart enough to figure out how to make a little extra money as a cop, and if he tried to be smart, he wouldn't be smart enough and would get caught at it.

He had really been surprised to hear that Charley had become a detective. It took him a lot of thought to realize that what it probably was was dumb luck. An asshole named Gerry Gallagher had got himself hooked on drugs, desperately needed money, and had tried to stick up the Waikiki Diner on Roosevelt Boulevard in Northeast Philly.

Tough luck for the both of them, the Commanding Officer of the Highway Patrol, a big mean sonofabitch named Captain "Dutch" Moffitt, had been having his dinner in the Waikiki. He tried to be a hero, and Gallagher was dumb enough to shoot him for trying. Killed him. With a little fucking .22-caliber pistol.

Now the one thing you don't want to do, ever, is shoot a cop, any cop. And Moffitt was a captain, and the Commanding Officer of Highway Patrol. There were eight-thousand-plus cops in Philadelphia, and every last fucking one of them had a hard-on for Gallagher.

If you were white and between sixteen and forty and looked anything like the description the cops put out on the radio, you could count on being stopped by a cop and asked could you prove you weren't at the Waikiki Diner when the Highway Captain got himself shot.

Every cop in Philly was looking for Gallagher. Charley McFadden and his partner, a little Spic named Gonzales or Martinez or one of them Spic names like that, had caught him. They chased him down the subway tracks, near the Frankford-Pratt Station in Northeast Philly where the train is elevated. The dumb sonofabitch slipped and got himself cut in little pieces by a train that had come along at the wrong time.

Now the cops certainly knew, Sonny had reasoned at the time, that McFadden wasn't Sherlock Holmes, and if he had found Gallagher it had to be dumb luck. That didn't matter. Charley was a fucking hero. He was the cop who got the guy who shot Captain Dutch Moffitt. Got his picture in the newspapers with Mayor Carlucci and everything.

The next thing Sonny heard was that Charley was now a Highway Patrolman. Highway Patrolmen, everybody knew, were the sharp cops. They *could* find their asses with only one hand. What the hell, Sonny had reasoned, it was a payback. Even if Charley wasn't too smart, he had done what he did, and Highway would make an exception for the guy who had caught the guy who shot the Highway commander.

The next thing Sonny heard about Charley after that was that he was now a detective. That was surprising. Sonny knew that you had to take a test to be a detective, and unless Charley had changed a whole hell of a lot since Bishop Neuman High School, taking tests was not his strong point.

Then Sonny figured that out, too. Charley hadn't been able to cut it as a Highway Patrolman. You couldn't be a dummy and be a Highway Patrolman, and Highway had probably found out about Charley in two or three days.

So what to do with him? Make him a detective. It sounded good, and despite what you saw on the TV and in the movies, all detectives weren't out solving murders and catching big-money drug dealers. A lot of them did things that didn't take too much brains, like looking for stolen cars, and checking pawnshops with a list of what had been heisted lately, things like that.

And then Sonny had heard that there were some Police Department big shots, chief inspectors and the like, who got to have a chauffeur for their cars and to answer their phones, and that sometimes these gofers were detectives.

That's what Charley McFadden was probably doing, Sonny Boyle reasoned. It fit. The Police Department figured they owed him for catching Gallagher, and there was nothing wrong with being a detective, and he could be useful doing something, like driving some big shot around, that other cops would rather not do themselves.

All of this ran through Timothy Francis Boyle's mind when he saw Charles Thomas McFadden walk into Lou's Crab House at Eleventh and Moyamensing.

What surprised him now was how Charley was dressed. He looked nice. Not as classy as the young guy with him—the other guy was not a cop; you don't buy threads like he's wearing on what they pay cops—but nice. Nice jacket, nice white shirt, nice slacks, even a nice necktie.

And he was also surprised when McFadden headed for the booth where Sonny was waiting for his runners to bring the cash and numbers to him.

Did he just spot me? Or was he looking for me?

"Well, aren't we in luck?" Charley McFadden said as he slid into the booth beside Sonny. "Tomothy Francis Boyle himself, in the flesh!"

"How are you, Charley?" Sonny asked, and smilingly offered his hand. "Nice threads."

"Thanks," Charley said. "Sonny, say hello to my friend Matt Payne."

"Pleased to meet you," Sonny said. He gave the other guy his hand, and was surprised that he wasn't able to give it a real squeeze the way he wanted to. This Payne guy was stronger than he looked like.

"How do you do, Mr. Boyle?" Matt said.

Main Line, Sonny decided. *If he talks like that—like he keeps his teeth together when he talks—and dresses like that, he's from some place like Merion or Bala Cynwyd. I wonder what the fuck he's doing with McFadden.*

"Long time no see," Sonny said. "What brings you down this way?"

Charley put two fingers in his mouth, causing a shrill whistle which attracted the waitress's attention. "Two coffees, darling," he called out. "Put them on Sonny's bill."

"On my bill, my ass," Sonny said.

"For old times' sake, Sonny, right? Besides, I've told Matt you're a successful businessman."

"You did?"

"I told him you are one of the neighborhood's most successful numbers runners and part-time bookies."

"Jesus Christ, Charley, that's not funny."

"Don't be bashful," McFadden said. "He's always been a little bashful, Matt."

"Has he really?" Matt said.

"Yeah. What do you expect, with a name like Francis? That's a girl's name."

"When it's a girl, they spell it with an *e,*" Sonny said. "Damn it, you know that." He looked at Matt Payne. "Charley and me go back a long ways. He's always pulling my leg."

Who the fuck is this guy? What the hell is this all about?

One of Sonny's runners—Pat O'Hallihan, a bright, redheaded eighteen-year-old who worked hard, was honest, and for whom Sonny saw a bright future—came into Lou's Crab House, carrying a small canvas zipper bag with his morning's receipts. He stopped when he saw that Sonny was not alone in the booth. Sonny made what he hoped was a discreet gesture telling him to cool it.

It was not discreet enough.

"Turn around, Matthew," McFadden said. "The kid in the red hair? Three to five he's one of Sonny's runners."

Matt turned and looked.

"Is he really?" he asked.

"Charley, you are not funny," Sonny said.

"Who's trying to be funny?" McFadden said. "I was just filling Detective Payne in on the local scumbags."

"Detective" Payne? Is he telling me this Main Line asshole in the three-hundred-fifty-dollar jacket and the fifty-dollar tie is a cop?

"You're a cop?" Sonny's mouth ran away with him.

"Show him your badge, Matthew," McFadden said. "Sonny—I suppose in his line of work, it's natural—don't trust anybody."

The Main Line asshole reached into the inside breast pocket of his three-hundred-fifty-dollar Harris tweed jacket with leather patches on the elbows and came out with a small folder. He opened it and extended it to Sonny, which afforded Sonny the opportunity to see a Philadelphia Police Department detective's badge and accompanying photo identification.

"You don't look like a cop," Sonny said.

"Don't I really?" Matt asked.

"Detective Payne is with Special Operations," Charley said. "You familiar with Special Operations, Sonny?"

"Sure."

What the fuck is Special Operations? Oh, yeah. That new hotshot outfit. They're over Highway Patrol.

"You know what Detective Payne said when I told him what line of work you're in, Sonny?"

"I don't know what you're talking about."

"Detective Payne said, 'Bookmaking and numbers running is a violation of the law. I think we should find your friend and throw his ass in jail.' Isn't that what you said, Matt?"

"Hmmmm," Matt said thoughtfully. "Yes, that is essentially what I said."

"You're kidding, right?"

"No," Matt said. "I was not speaking in jest."

"I'm getting out of here," Sonny said. "And just for the hell of it, wiseass, you can't search me without a reason, and even if you did, you wouldn't find a thing on me."

"You're not going anywhere, Sonny," McFadden said, and his voice was no longer pleasant. "Until I tell you you can."

"I'll bet, Charles," Matt said, "that if I was to show that young man with the red hair my badge, and ask if he would be kind enough to open his bag for me . . ." He interrupted himself, jumped to his feet, and walked quickly to the redhead.

"I want you to put that bag on that table," he said, showing him his badge. "In sight. And I want you to sit in that booth with your hands flat on the table until I tell you to move. You understand me?"

The redhead followed Matt's pointing, to the last booth in the line.

"Am I busted?" the redhead asked, very nervously.

"If you mean 'arrested,' not yet. And perhaps that can be avoided. It depends on Mr. Boyle."

He waited until the redhead had done what he had ordered him to do, then walked back to the booth and sat down.

"Excuse me, Detective McFadden," he said politely. "Please continue."

"So you bust him, so what?" Sonny said.

"I hope that won't be necessary," Matt said. "But in that unhappy happenstance, you would lose the morning's receipts. That would provide sufficient justification, I would think, Mr. Boyle, for Special Operations to assign whatever police personnel proved to be necessary to save the innocent citizens of this area from gambling czars such as yourself. And I think there is a good possibility that after we have his mother and his parish priest talk to that young man in Central Lockup, he might be willing, to save his soul from eternal damnation, ninety days in prison, and the first entry on his criminal record, to tell us who had given him his present employment, and precisely where and with whom he plied his trade."

"Speaking of which," Charley McFadden said. "The minute the word gets out that the cops have your receipts, you're going to have a lot of winners, Sonny. They're not too smart, but they're smart enough to know if they claim they won, you're either going to have to have a receipt proving they didn't, or pay off. That could be very expensive, Sonny."

"Interesting thought, Detective McFadden," Matt said.

"Thank you, Detective Payne."

Sonny, now visibly nervous, looked between Matt and Charley.

"OK, McFadden," Sonny said. "What do you want?"

"Now that we have you in the right frame of mind, Mr. Boyle," Matt said, "Detective McFadden wishes to probe your presumably extensive knowledge of Philadelphia's criminal community."

"Huh?"

"Tell us about Frankie Foley, Sonny," Charley said.

Oh, shit! I didn't even think about him. What the fuck has Foley done now? Christ, did he hit the Narcotics cop?

"Never heard of him," Sonny said.

"Think hard," Charley said.

Sonny shrugged helplessly.

"Never heard of him, Charley," Sonny said. "I swear to God!"

"You were apparently wrong, Charles," Matt said. "Mr. Boyle will not be cooperative. Mr. Boyle, you are under arrest for violating the laws of the City of Philadelphia and the Commonwealth of Pennsylvania vis-à-vis gambling and participating in an organized gambling enterprise. You have the right to an attorney . . ."

"Jesus Christ, Charley!" Sonny said. "Now wait a minute."

"Remember who he is now, Sonny?" Charley asked.

". . . and if you cannot afford an attorney," Matt went on, "one will be appointed for you." He paused. "I don't seem to have my handcuffs, Charles. Might I borrow yours?"

"Charley, can we talk? Private?" Sonny asked.

"I have other things on my agenda, Mr. Boyle. I don't have time to waste on you," Matt said.

"Matt, Sonny and I go back a long way," Charley said. "Be a good guy. Give me a minute alone with him."

Matt gave this some thought. He looked impatiently at his wristwatch.

"Very well," Matt said. "I will have a word with his accomplice."

He got up and walked to the booth where Pat O'Hallihan sat with his hands obediently on the table.

"I don't like your friend, Charley," Sonny said.

"I don't think he likes you, either. Too bad for you. He's a mean sonofabitch sometimes. You don't know who he is?"

Sonny shook his head.

"He's the guy who popped the Northwest Serial Rapist in the head. Blew his brains out."

"No shit, that's him?"

"That's him."

"Charley, you're going to get me killed," Sonny said. "I'm not shitting you."

"How am I going to get you killed?"

"Frankie Foley's a hit man for the mob. If he finds out I've been talking to you, I'm a dead man."

"An *Irish* hit man for the mob? Come on, Sonny."

"I'm telling you. He does hits they don't want to do themselves."

Sonny looked over at Pat O'Hallihan. Matt Payne had the zipper bag open and was searching through its contents.

"How do you know?" Charley asked.

"I know. I know. Trust me."

" 'How do you know?' I asked."

"He . . . uh, Jesus, Charley, you're going to get me killed."

"Think about it, Sonny," Charley said. "When the word gets out that two cops were in here asking you about Frankie Foley, and then hauled you off, Frankie's going to think you told on him anyway."

Sonny Boyle felt sick to his stomach.

"He's come to me a couple times and told me he needed alibis. Usually right after *somebody* hit one of the Guineas."

"Lately?"

"I ain't seen him, I swear to God, in a month."

"Where does he usually hang out?"

"Meagan's Bar."

"He's in the deep shit now, Sonny."

"You think he hit the narc?"

"You tell me, Sonny."

"I ain't heard nothing, Charley, I swear to God."

"Payne wants to lock you up, Sonny. You're going to have to do better than that."

"Christ, I don't know any more than I told you. And that's enough to get me killed. Those Dagos don't fuck around."

"You're going to have to do better than that," Charley repeated.

"I can ask around," Sonny said. "I hear things sometimes."

"I'll bet you do," Charley said.

"I swear to God, if I hear anything, I'll call you."

"I believe you, Sonny," Charley said. "But I don't know about Payne. He wants this guy. He'll do anything to get him."

"You lock me up, all you get is what I already told you," Sonny argued. "Let me ask around, Charley. It makes sense."

Charley considered that for a moment.

"I'll try, Sonny," he said. "I don't know . . ."

"Talk to him, Charley. I'll make it worth your while."

Charley shrugged and walked over to the booth where Matt was now counting thick, rubber-band-bound stacks of one-dollar bills.

Matt got up and walked with Charley to a corner of the room. Charley began to talk to him. Sonny did not think Payne looked at all happy with what Charley was saying.

But finally, after flashing Sonny Boyle a look of utter contempt, he shrugged and walked out of the restaurant. Charley went back to Boyle's booth.

"That took some doing," he said. "My ass is now on the line. Don't fuck with me about this, Sonny. If that mean sonofabitch comes down on me, I'll really come down on you. You understand?"

"Charley, I understand. The first thing I hear—"

"And you better hear something, and soon," Charley interrupted. He laid a calling card on the table, took out a pen, and wrote another number on it. "My home phone is on there. The one I wrote is Special Operations. Call me there, not at Northwest Detectives."

"You're in Special Operations now?"

"I expect to hear from you soon, Sonny," Charley said, and walked out of the restaurant.

Sonny looked out the window and watched him get into a new Ford unmarked car and drive away.

He walked over to where Pat O'Hallihan sat.

"Jesus Christ, what was that all about?" Pat asked.

"Don't worry about it," Sonny said. "Charley McFadden and I are old pals. We were in the same class at Bishop Neuman High School."

"What about the one with me?"

"You were in pretty fancy company. That was Payne. You remember when a detective shot that sicko in the Northwest who was carving up women?"

"That was him?"

"That was him."

"What was this all about?"

"Nothing. Don't worry about it. Everything's under control. Now, order me a cup of coffee. I got to make a telephone call."

"Right."

Sonny Boyle went to the pay phone by the door to the men's room and called Frankie Foley's house. Frankie's mother said he was at work, and gave him the number of the warehouse at Wanamaker's where Frankie worked.

It took some time to get Frankie on the phone—his boss obviously didn't like him getting personal calls at work—but finally he came on the line and Sonny told him that two Special Operations detectives were asking questions about him, that one of the detectives was a real hotshot, the cop that shot the Northwest Serial Rapist in the head, and that they seemed to think Frankie had something to do with the Narcotics cop who got himself hit.

He assured Frankie that of course he hadn't told them a fucking thing.

18.

The radio went off as Matt Payne and Charley McFadden headed north on South Broad Street.

"William Fourteen."

"That's me," Matt said.

Charley looked around, found the microphone on its hook under the dash, and picked it up.

"Fourteen," he said.

"What's your location?"

"South Broad, near City Hall."

"Meet the Inspector at the schoolhouse."

"En route," Charley said, and replaced the microphone. "Well, at least we know where to go," he said.

"I hope we did the right thing," Matt said. "I'll bet your ol' buddy was on the phone before we turned the corner, telling Foley we were asking about him."

"Hey," Charley said, his tone making it clear he thought it was a naive observation. "What's the difference? Bad guys think there's a cop behind every tree."

Fifteen minutes later, he gave Matt a smug glance when the same question and answer was paraphrased by Inspector Wohl and Sergeant Washington.

"Is this going to cause a problem?" Wohl asked. "Foley will know now we're interested in him."

"Malefactors," Washington intoned solemnly, "in my experience, see the menacing forces of exposure and punishment lurking behind every bush. Often this causes them to do foolish things."

Wohl chuckled.

"I do see a jurisdictional problem," Washington went on. "On one hand, we are interested in Mr. Foley's possible involvement with the Inferno job, which would put him in Wally Milham's basket. On the other, Mr. Boyle suggested Mr. Foley has something to do with Officer Kellog's murder, which would fall into Joe D'Amata's zone of interest. Or possibly mine, if I am to follow allegations of corruption in the Narcotics Five Squad."

Wohl smiled again.

"Going along with your 'menacing forces of exposure and punishment' theory, Jason, it seems to me that you are the most menacing of all."

"I will interpret that as a compliment," Washington said.

"You and Matt were in on the Inferno job from the beginning. So why don't you two go see Mr. Atchison first? Right now, McFadden can go see Joe D'Amata and tell him what Mr. Boyle has had to say, and that I suggest it might be helpful if you were there when he speaks with Mr. Foley."

Washington nodded.

"And then McFadden can go to see Milham at Matt's apartment—"

"Where I devoutly hope he is having at least a modicum of success in trying to convince the Widow Kellog that she should *not* regard me as menacing," Washington interrupted. "And tell me what she knows about Five Squad."

"—and tell him what McFadden's friend has told us about Mr. Foley," Wohl continued. "That will also place Charley at Matt's apartment, where he can work out the sitting-on-Mrs. Kellog schedule with Martinez and Tiny Lewis."

"A masterful display of organizational genius," Washington said.

"And meanwhile, I'll bring Inspector Weisbach in on all this. Any questions?"

McFadden held up his hand.

"How do I get from here to Matt's place, Inspector?"

"Take the car Matt's driving."

"If I went with him, and met Jason . . . where are we going to see Atchison?"

"In the beast's lair," Washington said. "At his home."

"I could pick up my car at the apartment, if I went with Charley."

"Meet me at the Media police station," Washington said. "Where I will be stroking the locals."

"I'll call out there if you like, Jason," Wohl offered.

"Thank you, no. Lieutenant Swann and I are old friends," Washington said. He got to his feet. "I am reluctant to say this, aware as I am of your already monumental egos, but you two done good."

McFadden actually blushed.

"I ally myself with the comments of Sergeant Washington," Wohl said. "Especially the part about your already monumental egos."

Detective Matthew Payne had been inside the Media Police Headquarters before, the circumstances of which came to mind as he pulled the Porsche into a visitors' parking slot outside the redbrick, vaguely Colonial-appearing building in the Philadelphia suburb.

It had been during his last year at Episcopal Academy. He had been in the company of Mr. Chadwick Thomas Nesbitt IV and two females, all of them bound for the Rose Tree Hunt Club. One of the females had been Daffy Browne, he remembered, but he could not recall either the name or the face of the one he'd been with in the backseat of Mr. Chadwick Thomas Nesbitt III's Rolls-Royce Silver Shadow.

He remembered only that he had finally managed to disengage the fastening of her brassiere only moments before a howling siren and flashing lights had announced the presence of the Media Police Department.

Chad was charged with going sixty-eight miles per hour in a forty-mile-per-hour zone; with operating a motor vehicle under the influence of alcohol; with operating a motor vehicle without a valid driver's license in his possession; and operating a motor vehicle without the necessary registration documents therefore.

Chad didn't have a driver's license in his possession because it had been confiscated by his father to make the point that failing two of four Major Curriculum subjects in Mid-Year Examinations was not socially acceptable behavior. He didn't have the registration for the Rolls because he was absolutely forbidden to get behind the wheel of the Rolls under any circumstances, not only while undergoing durance vile. He was driving the Rolls because his parents were spending the weekend in the Bahamas, and he thought they would never know.

Everyone in the Rolls had been charged with unlawful possession of alcoholic beverages by minors. The Rolls was parked on the side of the Baltimore Pike, and all four miscreants (the females sniffling in shame and humiliation) were hauled off to Media Police Headquarters and placed in a holding cell.

It had been necessary to telephone Brewster Cortland Payne II at five minutes to two in the morning. Mr. Payne had arrived at the police station a half hour later, arranged the appropriate bail for the females, and taken them home, leaving a greatly surprised Matt and Chad looking out from behind the holding cell bars.

Brewster Cortland Payne II had a day or two later informed Matt that he had decided spending the night in jail would have a more efficacious effect on Matt (and Chad) than anything he could think of to say at the time.

Matt got out of the Porsche and walked into Police Headquarters.

"Help you?" the sergeant behind the desk asked.

"I'm Detective Payne," Matt said. "I'm supposed to meet Sergeant Washington in Lieutenant Swann's office?"

"Down the corridor, third door on the right."

Washington and Lieutenant Swann, a tall, thin man in his forties, were drinking coffee.

"How are you, Payne?" Lieutenant Swann said after Washington made the introduction. "I know your dad, I think. Providence Road, in Wallingford?"

"Yes, sir," Matt said.

"Known him for years," Lieutenant Swann said.

Is he laughing at me behind that straight face?

"Lieutenant Swann's been telling me that Mr. Atchison is a model citizen," Washington said. "An officer in the National Guard, among other things."

"When we heard about what happened, we thought it was the way it was reported in the papers," Swann said. "This is very interesting."

"Strange things happen," Washington said. "It may have been just the way it was reported in the papers."

"But you don't think so, do you, Jason?"

"I am not wholly convinced of his absolute innocence," Washington said.

"You want me to go over there with you, Jason?"

"I'd rather keep this low-key, if you'll go along," Jason said. "Just drop in to ask him about Mr. Foley."

"Whatever you want, Jason. I owe you a couple."

"The reverse is true, Johnny," Washington said. "I add this to a long list of courtesies to be repaid."

Lieutenant Swann stood up and put out his hand.

"Anytime, Jason. Nice to see you—again—Payne."

Goddamn it, he does remember.

"It was much nicer to come in the front door all by myself," Matt said.

"Well, what the hell," Lieutenant Swann said, laughing. "We all stub our toes once in a while. You seem to be on the straight and narrow now."

"I don't know what that was all about," Washington said, "but appearances, Johnny, can be deceiving."

320 Wilson Avenue, Media, Pennsylvania, was a two-story brick Colonial house sitting in a well-kept lawn on a tree-lined street. A cast-iron jockey on the lawn held a sign reading "320 Wilson, Atchison." There was a black mourning wreath hanging on the door. Decalcomania on the small windows of the white door announced that the occupants had contributed to the Red Cross, United Way, Boy Scouts, and the Girl Scout Cookie Program. When Washington pushed the doorbell, they could hear chimes playing, "Be It Ever So Humble, There's No Place Like Home."

A young black maid in a gray dress answered the door.

"Mr. Atchison, please," Jason said. "My name is Washington."

"Mr. Atchison's not at home," the maid said. The obvious lie made her obviously nervous.

"Please tell Mr. Atchison that Sergeant Washington of the Philadelphia Police Department would be grateful for a few minutes of his time."

She closed the door in their faces. What seemed like a long time later, it reopened. Gerald North Atchison, wearing a crisp white shirt, no tie, slacks, and leaning on a cane, stood there.

"Good afternoon, Mr. Atchison," Washington said cordially. "Do you remember me?"

"Yeah, sure."

"How's the leg?" Washington asked.

For answer, Atchison raised the cane and waved it.

"You remember Detective Payne?"

"Yeah, sure. How are you, Payne?"

"Mr. Atchison."

"We really hate to disturb you at home, Mr. Atchison," Washington said. "But we have a few questions."

"I was hoping you were here to tell me you got the bastards who did . . ."

"We're getting closer, Mr. Atchison. It's getting to be a process of elimination. We think you can probably help us, if you can spare us a minute or two."

"Christ, I don't know. My lawyer told me I wasn't to answer any more questions if he wasn't there."

"Sidney Margolis is protecting your interests, as he should. But we're trying to keep this as informal as possible. To keep you from having to go to Mr. Margolis's office, or ours."

"Yeah, I know. But . . ."

"Let me suggest this, Mr. Atchison, to save us both time and inconvenience. I give you my word that if you find any of my questions are in any way inconvenient, if you have any doubt whatever that you shouldn't answer them without Mr. Margolis's advice, you simply say 'Pass,' and I will drop that question and any similar to it."

"Well, Sergeant, you put me on a spot. You know I want to cooperate, but Margolis said . . ."

"The decision, of course, is yours. And I will understand no matter what you decide."

Atchison hesitated a moment and then swung the door open.

"What the hell," he said. "I want to be as helpful as I can. I want whoever did what they did to my wife and Tony Marcuzzi caught and fried."

"Thank you very much," Washington said. "There's just a few things that we'd like to ask your opinion about."

"Whatever I can do to help," Atchison said. "Can I have the girl get you some coffee? Or something stronger?"

"I don't know about Matt here, but the detective in me tells me it's very likely that a restaurateur would have some drinkable coffee in his house."

"I have some special from Brazil," Atchison said. "*Bean* coffee. Dark roast. I grind it just before I brew it."

"I accept your kind invitation," Washington said.

"And so do I," Matt said.

"Let me show it to you," Atchison said.

They followed him into the kitchen and watched his coffee-brewing ritual.

Washington, Matt thought, looked genuinely interested.

Finally they returned to the living room.

"Sit down," Atchison said. "Let me know how I can help."

Washington sipped his coffee.

"*Very* nice!"

"I'm glad you like it," Atchison said.

"Mr. Atchison," Washington began. "As a general rule of thumb, in cases like this, we've found that usually robbers will observe a place of business carefully before they act. And we're working on the premise that whoever did this were professional criminals."

"They certainly seemed to know what they were doing," Atchison agreed.

"So it would therefore follow that they did, in fact, more than likely, decide to rob your place of business some time, days, weeks, before they actually committed the crime. That they (a) decided that your establishment was worth their time and the risk involved to rob; and (b) planned their robbery carefully."

"I can see what you mean," Atchison said.

"Would you say that it was common knowledge that you sometimes had large amounts of cash on the premises?"

"I think most bars and restaurants do," Atchison said. "They have to. A good customer wants to cash a check for a couple of hundred, even a thousand, you look foolish if you can't accommodate him."

"I thought it would be something like that," Washington said. "That's helpful."

"And I never keep the cash in the register, either, I always keep it downstairs in the safe. You know that neighborhood, Sergeant, I don't have to tell you. Sometimes, when there's a busy night, I even take large amounts of cash out of the register and take it down and put it in the safe."

"In other words, you would say you take the precautions a prudent businessman would take under the circumstances."

"I think you could say that, yes."

"We've found, over the years—and I certainly hope you won't take offense over the question—that in some cases, employees have a connection with robberies of this nature."

"I guess that would happen."

"Would you mind giving me your opinion of Thomas Melrose?" Washington asked. "He was, I believe, the bartender on duty that night?"

"Tommy went off duty before those men came in," Atchison replied, and then hesitated a moment before continuing: "I just can't believe Tommy Melrose would be involved in anything like this."

"But he was aware that you frequently kept large amounts of cash in your office."

"Yes, I guess he was," Atchison said reluctantly.

"How long has Mr. Melrose been working for you?" Washington asked.

"About nine months," Atchison replied, after thinking about it.

"He came well recommended?"

"Oh, absolutely. You have to be very careful about hiring bartenders. An open cash drawer is quite a temptation."

"Do you think you still have his references? I presume you checked them."

"Oh, I checked them, all right. And I suppose they're in a filing cabinet someplace."

"When you feel a little better, Mr. Atchison, do you think we could have a look at them?"

"Certainly."

"Mr. Melrose said that business was slow the night of this incident."

"Yes, it was."

"He said there was, just before he went off duty, only one customer in the place; and that when that last customer left, you took over for him tending bar."

"That's right. I did. You have to stay open in a bar like mine. Even if there's no customers. There might be customers coming in after you closed, and the next time they wanted a late-evening drink, they'd remember you were closed and go someplace else."

"I understand."

"The one customer who left just before you took over from Mr. Melrose: Do you remember him? I mean, was there anything about him? You don't happen to remember his name?"

Atchison appeared to be searching his memory. He shook his head and said, "Sorry."

Washington stood up. "Well, I hate to leave good company, and especially such fine coffee, but that's all I have. Thank you for your time, Mr. Atchison."

"Have another before you go," Atchison said. "One for the road."

"Thank you, no," Washington said. "I think Mr. Melrose said the customer was named Frankie. Does that ring a bell, Mr. Atchison?"

Atchison shook his head again. "No. Sorry."

"Probably not important," Washington said. "I would have been surprised if you had remembered him, Mr. Atchison. Thank you again for your time."

He put his hand out.

"Anything I can do to help, Sergeant," Atchison said.

"Cool customer," Jason Washington said with neither condemnation nor admiration in his voice, making it a simple professional judgment.

"You gave him two chances to remember Frankie Foley," Matt said.

"It will be interesting to see if Mr. Foley remembers Mr. Atchison," Washington said, and then changed the subject: "Did your father really leave you in durance vile overnight?"

"Swann told you, did he?"

"Your father's wisdom made quite an impression on Lieutenant Swann," Washington said. "And you haven't been behind bars since, have you?"

"No," Matt said, and then thought aloud: "Unless you want to count the time those Narcotics assholes hauled me off the night Tony the Zee got himself hit."

"I'm not sure you have considered the possibility that the Narcotics officers were simply doing their job."

"Taking great pleasure in what they were doing."

"Well, the tables have turned, haven't they? They thought they had a dirty cop. And now you're going to see if it can be proved that they are dirty."

"Am I going to work on that?"

"You and everybody else. Compared to coming up with something on the Narcotics Five Squad that will result in indictments, bringing Atchison before a grand jury will be fairly easy."

"How come?"

"We have a crime scene on the Inferno job, and other evidence. We have two good suspects. I think we can get a motive without a great deal of effort. A good deal of shoe leather may be required, but it isn't a question of *if* we will get Atchison, but *when*. So far as the Narcotics Five Squad is concerned, we don't know what they have done, only that they have done it, and we don't know what 'it' is, except the Widow Kellog's definition of 'it' as dirty."

"You can't get any specifics out of her?"

"Not a one," Washington replied. "But I believe she believes she is telling the truth that the whole squad is dirty. And to support that, they do own, without a mortgage, a condominium at the shore, and a boat. Their combined, honestly acquired, income is not enough to pay for those sorts of luxuries. And then we have the threatening telephone call."

"How do you think Five Squad heard she had talked to you?"

"There's no way that they could have. I think the simple explanation for that is that someone on Five Squad knew that Homicide would be talking to her, and they didn't want her volunteering any information."

"And you think that's why Kellog was killed?"

"It looks to me as if there are two possibilities, one of which no one seems to have considered very much. That he was killed in connection with his honest labor as a Narcotics officer. He knew something—where are the tapes from his tape recorder?—and had to be silenced. And of course it is entirely possible that he was killed by someone on the Five Squad for the same reason. His wife had left him. He might have wanted her back bad enough . . ."

"Milham and Mrs. Kellog seem pretty tight; I don't think she was going to go back to her husband."

"I noticed that," Washington said. "But neither of us have any way of knowing what Kellog was thinking, perhaps irrationally. Losing your wife to another man is traumatic. If she left him because of what he was doing, or, more to the point, because of what it was doing to him, and thus to their relationship, it's entirely possible that he thought by *stopping* what he was doing he might be able to get her back. Whatever was on those tapes that we can't find might have been his insurance."

"Excuse me?" Matt interrupted. He was having trouble following Washington's reasoning; the introduction of the missing tapes left him wholly confused.

"I'm quitting, I'm through," Washington said. "I'm not going to squeal, but just to keep anyone from getting any clever ideas, I have tapes of whatever that will wind up in the hands of Internal Affairs if anything happens to me."

"This is starting to sound like a cops show on television," Matt said. "A very convoluted plot."

"Yes," Washington said thoughtfully. "It does. And that bothers me." He was silent for a moment, then changed the subject. "For a number of reasons, including not wanting Wally Milham to think I'm pushing him out of the way, I am not going with you when you chat with Mr. Foley."

"OK," Matt said. "You going to tell me the other reasons?"

"I'll take you back to the Media police station," Washington said, ignoring the question. "We will get Wally Milham on the telephone and decide where you are to meet. Then you can get in your car and meet him. Relay to him in appropriate detail the essence and the ambience of our conversation with Mr. Atchison."

"OK."

Officer Paul Thomas O'Mara, Inspector Wohl's administrative assistant, knocked on Wohl's office door, and then, without waiting for a reply, pushed it open.

"Mr. Giacomo for Inspector Weisbach on Four," he announced.

Staff Inspector Michael Weisbach was sitting slumped on Wohl's couch, his legs stretched out in front of him, balancing a cup of coffee on his chest.

Wohl, behind his desk, picked up one of the telephones and punched a button.

"Peter Wohl, Armando," he said. "How are you? How odd that you should call. Mike and I were just talking about you. Here he is."

Weisbach smiled as he walked behind Wohl's desk and took the telephone. They had not been talking about Giacomo. They had been discussing the time-consuming difficulty they would have in investigating the personal finances of the Narcotics Five Squad, and the inevitability that their interest would soon become known.

"Hello, Armando," Weisbach said. "What can I do for you?"

He moved the receiver off his ear so that Wohl could hear the conversation.

"I wanted you to know I haven't forgotten our conversation at luncheon, Mike, and that I have already begun to accumulate some information—nothing yet that I'd feel comfortable about passing on to you—but I am beginning to hear some interesting things. I need some time, you'll understand, to make certain that what I pass on to you is reliable."

"My heart is always warmed, Armando, when citizens such as yourself go out of their way to assist the police."

Wohl chuckled.

"I consider it my civic duty," Giacomo said.

"Armando, perhaps I could save you some time, keep you from chasing a cat, so to speak, that's already nearly in the bag. In our own plodding way, we have come up with a name. What I'm getting at, Armando, is that it would bother me if you came up with a name we already have, and you would still figure we owed you."

"What's the name?"

"Frankie Foley," Weisbach said.

"He wasn't, between us, one of the names I heard. Frankie Foley?"

"Frankie Foley."

"How interesting."

"Nice to talk to you, Armando," Weisbach said. "I appreciate the call."

He hung up.

"Why did you give him Foley's name?" Wohl asked. "A question, not a criticism."

"By now, Foley probably knows we're looking at him. If he told Giacomo, or the Mob found out some other way, Italian blood being stronger than Irish water, they may have decided to give him to us to keep Cassandro out of jail."

"Michael, you are devious. I say that as a compliment."

"So maybe, with Foley taken off the table, Giacomo may come up with another name."

Frankie Foley waited impatiently, time card in hand, for his turn to punch out. He really hated Wanamaker's, having to spend all day busting open crates, breaking his hump shoving furniture around, and for fucking peanuts.

It would, he consoled himself, soon be over. He could tell Stan Wisznecki, his crew chief, to shove his job up his ass. He would go to work in the Inferno, get himself some decent threads with the money Atchison owed him, and wait for the next business opportunity to come along. And he wasn't going to do the next hit for a lousy five thousand dollars. He'd ask for ten, maybe even more, depending on who he had to hit.

Frankie had been a little disappointed with the attention, or lack of it, paid to the Inferno hit by the newspapers and TV. There had been almost nothing on the TV, and only a couple of stories in the newspapers.

He had, the day after he'd made the Inferno hit, clipped out Michael J. O'Hara's story about it from the *Bulletin* with the idea of keeping it, a souvenir, like of his first professional job.

But after he'd cut it out he realized that might not be too smart. If the cops got his name somehow, and got a search warrant or something, and found it, it would be awkward explaining what he was doing with it.

Not incriminating. What the fuck could they prove just because he'd cut a story out of the newspaper? He could tell them he'd cut it out because he drank in the Inferno. Shit, if they pressed him, he could say he cut it out because he had fucked Alicia Atchison.

But it was smarter not to have it, so he had first crumpled up the clipping and tossed it in the toilet, and then, when he thought that the front page now had a hole in it where the story had been, tore off the whole front page and sliced it up with scissors and flushed the whole damn thing down the toilet. He really hated to throw the story away, but knew that it was the smart thing to do.

And anyway, the word would get out who'd done the hit among the people who mattered. That was what mattered.

He knew he'd done the right thing, not keeping the clipping, when Tim McCarthy, who ran Meagan's Bar for his father-in-law, called him up and told him that a couple of cops had been in the bar, asking about him, and giving Tom some bullshit that one of them was a cousin from Conshohocken.

What that meant, Frankie decided professionally, was that his name had come up somehow. That was to be expected. He drank at the Inferno, and he had been in there the night he'd made the hit. The cops probably had a list of two hundred people who drank in the Inferno. They probably got his name from the bartender. Which was the point. He was only one more name they would check out. And the bartender, if he had given the cops his name, would also have told them that he had left the Inferno long before the hit.

The cops didn't have a fucking thing to connect him with the hit, except Atchison, of course, and Atchison couldn't say a fucking word. It would make him an accessible, or whatever the fuck they called it.

He hadn't been too upset, either, when Sonny Boyle had called him to tell him two detectives had been to see him about him. He had been sort of flattered to learn who they were. One of them was the cop that had caught up with the guy who shot the Highway Patrol captain, and the other detective was the guy who had shot the pervert in Northwest Philly who was cutting the teats off women. What that was, Frankie decided professionally, was that the ordinary cops and detectives was having trouble finding him. He didn't have no record, for one thing, and the phone was in his mother's name. So when the ordinary cops couldn't find him, the hotshots had started looking for him.

Well, fuck the hotshots too. They would eventually find him—it would be kind of interesting to see how long finding him took—and they would ask him questions. *Yeah, I was in the Inferno that night. I go in there all the time. I been talking to Mr. Atchison about maybe becoming his headwaiter. Where was I at midnight? I was home in bed. Ask my mother. No, I don't have no idea who might have shot them two. Sorry.*

The dinge ahead of him in line finally figured out how to get his time card punched and Frankie stepped to the time clock, punched out, put the card in the rack, and walked out of the building.

He had gone maybe thirty feet down the street when there was a guy walking on each side of him. The one on his right had a mustache, one of the thin kind you probably have to trim every day. The other one was much younger. He didn't look much like a cop, more like a college kid.

"Frank Foley?" the one with the mustache asked.

"Who wants to know?"

"We're police officers," the guy with the mustache said.

"No shit? What do you want with me?"

"You are Frank Foley?"

"Yeah, I'm Frank Foley. You got a badge or something?"

The guy with the mustache produced a badge.

"I'm Detective Milham," he said. "And this is Detective Payne."

Frankie took a second look at the kid.

"You the guy who shot that pervert in North Philly? The one who was cutting up all them women?"

"That's him," Milham said.

"I'll be goddamned," Frankie said, putting out his hand. "I thought you'd be older. Let me shake your hand. It's a real pleasure to meet you."

The kid looked uncomfortable.

Modesty, Frankie decided.

Frankie was genuinely pleased to meet Detective Payne.

This guy is a real fucking detective, Frankie decided, *somebody who had also shot somebody. Professionally. When you think about it, what it is is that we're both professionals. We just work the other side of the street, is all.*

"Detective Payne," Milham said, "was also involved in the gun battle with the Islamic Liberation Army. Do you remember that?"

Payne looked at Milham with mingled surprise and annoyance.

"The dinges that robbed Goldblatt's?" Frankie asked. "That was you, too?"

"That was him," Milham said.

"Mr. Foley, we're investigating the shooting at the Inferno Lounge," Matt said.

"Wasn't that a bitch?" Frankie replied. "Jesus, you don't think I had anything to do with that, do you?"

"We just have a few questions we'd like to ask," Matt said.

"Such as?"

"Mr. Foley," Wally Milham said, "would you be willing to come to Police Administration with us to make a statement?"

"A statement about what?"

"We've learned that you were in the Inferno Lounge that night."

"Yeah, I was. I stop in there from time to time. I guess I was there maybe an hour before what happened happened."

"Well, maybe you could help us. Would you be willing to come with us?" Wally asked.

"How long would it take?"

"Not long. We'd just like to get on record what you might have seen when you were there. It might help us to find the people who did it."

The smart thing for me to do is look like I'm willing to help. And what the fuck choice do I have?

"Yeah, I guess I could go with you," Frankie said.

"We've got a car right over there, Mr. Foley," Matt said. "And when we're finished, we'll see that you get wherever you want to go."

Frankie got in the backseat of the car and saw for himself that the story that went around that once you got in the backseat of a cop car, you couldn't get out until they let you; that there was no handles in the backseat was bullshit. This was like a regular car; the handles worked.

He got a little nervous when he saw the two detectives having a little talk before they got in themselves. They had their backs to him, and talked softly, and he didn't hear what Detective Milham said to Detective Payne:

"This asshole thinks you're hot shit, Matt. Sometimes that means they'll run off at the mouth. When we get to the Roundhouse, you interview the sonofabitch. Charm the bastard."

"You think he did it?"

"This fucker is crazy. Let's see what he has to say."

STATEMENT OF: John Francis "Frankie" Foley

DATE AND TIME: 5:40 p.m. May 22, 1975

PLACE: Homicide Division, Police Admin. Bldg. Room A.

CONCERNING: Robbery/Homicide at Inferno Lounge

IN PRESENCE OF: Det. Wallace J. Milham, Badge 626

INTERROGATED BY: Det. Matthew M. Payne, Badge 701

RECORDED BY: Mrs. Jo-Ellen Garcia-Romez, Clerk/typist.

I AM Detective Payne. This is Mrs. Garcia-Romez, who will be recording everything we say on the typewriter.

We are questioning you concerning the murder homicide at the Inferno Lounge.

We have a duty to explain to you and to warn you that you have the following legal rights:

A. You have the right to remain silent and do not have to say anything at all.

B. Anything you say can and will be used against you in Court.

75-331D(Rev.7/70)   Page 1

C. You have a right to talk to a lawyer of your own choice before we ask you any questions, and also to have a lawyer here with you while we ask questions.

D. If you cannot afford to hire a lawyer, and you want one, we will see that you have a lawyer provided to you, free of charge, before we ask you any questions.

E. If you are willing to give us a statement, you have a right to stop anytime you wish.

1. Q. Do you understand that you have a right to keep quiet and do not have to say anything at all?
     A. Yeah. I understand.

2. Q. Do you understand that anything you say can and will be used against you?
     A. Did I miss something? Am I arrested or something?

3. Q. Do you want to remain silent?
     A. No.

4. Q. Do you understand you have a right to talk to a lawyer before we ask you any questions?
     A. Yeah, but what you guys said was just that you wanted to talk to me.

5. Q. Do you understand that if you cannot afford to hire a lawyer, and you want one, we will not ask you any questions until a lawyer is appointed for you free of charge?
     A. Yes, I do.

6. Q. Do you want to talk to a lawyer at this time, or to have a lawyer with you while we ask you questions?
     A. I don't have nothing to hide.

7. Q. Are you willing to answer questions of your own free will, without force or fear, and without any threats and promises having been made to you?
     A. Yeah, yeah, get on with it.

(Det. Milham) Frankie, to clear things up in your mind. That's what they call the Miranda questions. Everybody we talk to gets the same questions.

     A: Am I arrested, for Christ's sake, or not?

(Det. Milham) You are not under arrest.

     A: You had me worried there for a minute.

8. Q. For the record, Mr. Foley, state your name, city of residence, and employment.
     A. Frank Foley, Philadelphia. Right now, I work for Wanamaker's.

9. Q. Mr. Foley, were you in the Inferno Lounge the night there was a double murder there?

A. Yeah, I was. Just before midnight.

10. Q. What were you doing there?

A. I stopped in for a drink. I drink there every once in a while.

11. Q. That's all? Just for a drink?

A. I been talking with Atchison, the guy who owns it, about maybe going to work there as the headwaiter.

12. Q. Does the Inferno have a headwaiter?

A. Well, you know what I mean. I'd sort of keep an eye on things. That's a pretty rough neighborhood, you know what I mean.

12. Q. Oh, you mean sort of be the bouncer?

A. They don't like to use that word. But yeah, sort of a bouncer.

14. Q. You have experience doing that sort of thing?

A. Not really. But I was a Marine. I can take care of myself. Handle things. You know.

15. Q. When you were in Inferno, the night of the shooting, did you talk to Mr. Atchison about your going to work for him?

A. I guess we talked about it. When I came in, we went to his office for a drink. I don't remember exactly what we talked about, but maybe we did. We been talking about it all along.

16. Q. You went to his office? You didn't drink at the bar?

A. Mr. Atchison don't like to buy people drinks at the bar. You know. So we went downstairs to his office.

17. Q. Was Mrs. Atchison in the Inferno when you were there?

A. No. He said she and Marcuzzi went somewheres.

18. Q. You knew Mrs. Atchison?

A. Yeah, you could put it that way. Nice-looking broad. Had a roving eye, you know what I mean?

19. Q. You knew her pretty well, then?

A. Not as well as I would have liked to.

20. Q. Tell us exactly what you did when you went to the Inferno?

A. Well, I went in, and had a drink at the bar, and then Atchison came over, and asked me to go to the office, and we had a drink down there. And then I left.

21. Q. How long would you say you were in the Inferno?

A. Thirty minutes, tops. Ten minutes, maybe, in the bar and then fifteen, twenty minutes down in his office.

22. Q. We've heard that Mr. Atchison used to keep a lot of money in the office. That he used to make loans. You ever hear that?

A. Yeah, sure. He did that. That was one of the reasons we was talking about me working for him. People sometimes don't pay when they're supposed to.

23. Q. And you were going to help him collect his bad debts.

A. Not only that. Just be around the place. Keep the peace. You know.

24. Q. When you were in the Inferno, did you notice anything out of the ordinary?

A. No. If you're asking did I see anybody in there who looked like they might be thinking of sticking the place up, hell no. If I'd have seen anything like that, I would have stuck around.

25. Q. You said Mrs. Atchison had a roving eye. Do you think that what happened there had anything to do with that? Was she playing around on the side, do you think?

A. Well, she may have been. Like I said, she seemed to like men. But I don't know nothing for sure.

26. Q. When you left the Inferno, where did you go?

A. Home. It was late.

27. Q. Have you got any idea who might have robbed the Inferno and killed those two people?

A. There's a lot of people in Philadelphia who do that sort of thing for a living. Have I got a name? No.

28. Q. That's about all I have. Unless Detective Milham . . . ?

A. (Det. Milham) No. I think that's everything. Thank you, Mr. Foley.

29. Q. (Mr. Foley) Could I ask a question?

(Det. Payne) Certainly.

(Mr. Foley) When you shot that nutcase who was cutting up the women, what did you use?

(Det. Payne) My .38 snub-nose.

(Mr. Foley) And on the dinge who did the Goldblatt job? Same gun?

(Det. Payne) Yes.

(Mr. Foley) You got more balls than I do. If my life was on the line, I'd carry a .45 at least. You ever see what a .45'll do to you?

(Det. Payne) Yes, I have. But we can carry only weapons that are authorized by the Department.

(Mr. Foley) That's bullshit.

19.

"Frankie's in love with Matt," Wally Milham said. "He wants to buy him a drink and tell him about guns."

"Jesus Christ!" Matt said.

Jason Washington raised his hand somewhat imperiously and made a circling motion with his extended index finger, as a signal to the waitress that he wanted another cup of espresso.

They were in Café Elana, a new (and rather pretentious, Matt thought) Italian coffeehouse in Society Hill.

"That sometimes happens," Washington said, returning his attention to the table. "I think it has more to do with Matt representing authority than his charming personality. You might find it interesting, Matthew, to discuss the phenomenon with your sister."

"In this case, it's because Matt shoots people," Milham said. "Frankie found that fascinating."

"Frankie found a kindred soul, in other words?" Washington asked, nodding. "Let's think about that."

"There's something wrong with that guy," Matt said.

"There's something wrong, as you put it, with most people who commit homicide," Washington said. "Or did you have something special in mind?"

"He seems detached from reality," Matt said. "The only time he seemed at all concerned with having been picked up and taken to a Homicide interview room was when I went through the Miranda business; that made him worry that he had been arrested. But even that didn't seem to bother him very much. As soon as Wally told him he wasn't under arrest . . ."

"Matthew, you realize, I hope, that the moment he was told that he wasn't under arrest, all the ramifications of his being informed of his Miranda rights became moot."

"I thought going through the routine might unnerve him," Matt said. "And I didn't get anywhere close to asking him about his involvement in either the robberies or the murders. I just asked him if he was in the Inferno, what he was doing there, and if he saw anything out of the ordinary."

"No harm done in this case," Washington said, "but you were close to the edge of the precipice."

"Matt asked me before he gave him the Miranda." Wally came to Matt's defense. "It made sense to me. He's right, there is something wrong with this guy. I agreed that it might shake him up, and I told him not to get into the murder itself. Either the Inferno murders, or Kellog's."

"Then, Wallace," Washington pronounced, "the two of you were teetering on the precipice, in grave risk of providing a defense counsel six weeks out of law school with an issue that would cloud the minds of the jurors."

Washington let the criticism sink in for a moment, then went on: "Having said that, it was not a bad idea. Professor Washington just wanted to make the point in his Homicide 101 Tutorial for Detective Payne that there are enormous risks in dancing around Miranda. In my experience, the more heinous the crime alleged, the greater the concern from the bench about the rights of the accused."

"I didn't turn Matt loose, Jason," Milham said, his annoyance at the lecture visible and growing as he spoke. "And he wasn't a loose cannon. I was prepared to shut him off if he was getting into something he shouldn't have. I didn't have to."

"I intended no offense, Wallace," Washington said. "Nevertheless, my observations were in order. It would offend me if, because of some procedural error, Mr. Foley and Mr. Atchison got away with what they did."

"OK," Milham said.

"I have the feeling that neither of you feel Foley was involved with Officer Kellog's murder. Is that—"

"He's tied to the Inferno," Milham said. "Atchison says he doesn't know Frankie, and Frankie tells us he's going to work there as a bouncer."

"Unless, of course, he is in fact a contract killer," Washington said. "While I was waiting for you two to show up, I considered the anomaly of a nice Irish boy being so employed by the mob. Unusual, of course, but not impossible. I read the 75-49s on the Kellog job. There was nothing of great value stolen from the house. The only thing Mrs. Kellog reported as missing were her wedding and engagement rings. She left them there when she left Officer Kellog. Some other minor items are missing: a silver frame, holding their wedding picture; a portable television; and a silver coffee service. The street value of everything would not exceed two or three hundred dollars. And, of course, the tapes from the telephone recording device. Not enough for a burglar to kill over. The manner, the professional manner, so to speak, in which Officer Kellog was shot suggests assassination, rather than anything else. Perhaps the tapes were what his murderer was after."

"Narcotics Five Squad?" Milham said doubtfully. "Jason, I have trouble thinking . . ."

"As do I. Unless what was on those tapes was so incriminating that desperate measures were required. Or . . ."

"Or what?"

"What was on those tapes was incriminating vis-à-vis the mob. The decision was made to eliminate Officer Kellog and get the tapes. And to put distance between the Mob and any Narcotics involvement, or involvement between the Mob and the Narcotics Five Squad, an outside contract killer was employed. Perhaps Matt's admirer. I don't think we should conclude that Mr. Foley was not involved with Officer Kellog's murder."

"If this character is a hit man, and I have trouble with that—he's not that smart—why the hell is he working at Wanamaker's?" Milham said.

"Interesting question," Washington said. "There are all sorts of possible explanations. For example, let us suppose that Mr. Foley has been engaged, by the Mob, as a loan shark among the Wanamaker's warehouse labor force. He secured the repayment of a loan under such violent conditions that it came to the attention of the Mob that here was a young man of reliability and ambition, perhaps suited for more important things."

"Hell, why not?" Milham said.

"Letting my imagination run free," Washington said, "I tried to come up with a credible scenario as to why Mr. Atchison lied to us about Mr. Foley. He is no fool, and he must have known that we would learn from the bartender that Mr. Foley was in there last night. Let us suppose that Mr. Atchison knows, or suspects, that Mr. Foley has a Mob connection. Let us suppose further that Mr. Atchison has been having difficulty of some sort with the Mob. Or Mr. Marcuzzi was in some sort of difficulty with them. Mr. Marcuzzi was hit, with Mrs. Atchison as an innocent bystander, so to speak. Mr. Atchison was spared, with a warning, explicit or implied, to keep his mouth shut. Knowing or suspecting that Mr. Foley has a Mob connection, he was reluctant to point a finger at him. I was taken with his lack of concern for Mr. Marcuzzi. It is possible that he knew what Marcuzzi had been up to and decided that he had gotten his just deserts."

"You mean, you don't think Frankie did the Inferno job?" Matt asked.

"I didn't say that," Washington said. "What I'm saying is that we have yet to come up with a motive for Mr. Atchison being involved in the deaths of his wife and partner. No large amount of recently acquired insurance, et cetera, et cetera."

"And if we confront Atchison with lying about Foley, he confesses to running a loan-shark operation with Foley as the enforcer," Matt said.

"Precisely," Washington said. "And we have little physical evidence, except for the bullets removed from the bodies of Mrs. Atchison and Mr. Marcuzzi. That's useless unless we have the guns and can tie them to Foley or somebody else. Maybe there were two robbers."

"Well, we could send Matt to have a drink with Frankie and talk about guns," Milham said jokingly.

"He might not be too sharp, but he's shrewd," Matt said. "I don't think I'd get anything from him."

"Neither do I, but let's think that through," Washington said.

"Jesus!" Matt said. "Can I let my imagination run free?"

"Certainly."

"Foley likes to talk. Boast. I have the feeling that working in Wanamaker's embarrasses him."

"So?"

"So maybe he would boast to somebody else."

"I don't follow you, Matthew," Washington said. There was a tone of impatience in his voice.

"A guy comes up to him in a bar. Tells him he's heard that Frankie has connections. Maybe tells him he wants to buy a gun."

"That's stretching, Payne," Milham said. "You don't think he's going to sell the guns he used at the Inferno, do you? They're probably at the bottom of the river."

Matt met Washington's eyes.

"Hay-zus," he said. "Wearing all his gold chains."

It was a full thirty seconds before Washington spoke.

"I think Matthew may have something."

"Hay-zus?" Milham asked.

"Detective Jesus Martinez," Washington said. "Let me run this past Lieutenant Natali, maybe Captain Quaire, too. It would help if I could say the assigned detective had no objections."

"Anything that works," Milham said.

"I would suggest to you, Matthew, that while Mr. Foley presented a picture of complete composure in the Roundhouse, he may start to worry when he has had time to think things over. It is also possible that he may communicate with Mr. Atchison, or vice versa, which may make Mr. Atchison less confident than he was when we left him. In any event, there is nothing else that I can see that any of us can do today. I suggest we hang it up for the night."

"I'll see if I can get anything out of Helene," Milham said. "And I'll check with Homicide and see if anything new has come up."

Every evening except Sunday, between 8:00 and 8:15 P.M. an automobile, most often a new Buick, stopped near the middle of the 1200 block of Ritner Street in South Philadelphia. A man carrying a small zipper bag would get out of the passenger seat, walk to the door of the residence occupied by Mr. and Mrs. Timothy Francis "Sonny" Boyle, and ring the bell.

The door would be opened, the man would enter, and the door would be closed. Usually less than a minute later, the door would reopen, and the man, still carrying what appeared to be the same small zipper bag, would appear, descend the stairs, and get back in the car, which would then drive off.

There were, in fact, two bags. The bag the man carried into the house would more often than not be empty. The bag the man carried from the house would contain the records of Mr. Boyle's business transactions of that day, and the cash proceeds therefrom, less Mr. Boyle's commission.

Mr. Boyle was in the numbers business. His clientele would "buy a number," that is select a number between 000 and 999. The standard purchase price was one dollar. If the number selected "came up," that is, corresponded to the second comma-separated trio of numbers of activity on the New York Stock Exchange for that day, the lucky number holder received $500. For example, if 340,676,000 shares were traded on the stock exchange on one particular day, the winning number would be 676, and anyone who had purchased number 676 could exchange his receipt for his purchase for $500.

The operation of Mr. Boyle's business was quite simple. Most of the sales were conducted through small retail businesses, candy stores, grocery stores, newspaper stands, and the like. Individual customers would buy a number and be given a receipt. The storekeeper would turn over his carbon copy of the number selected, and his cash receipts (less a ten percent commission for his trouble), to one of Mr. Boyle's runners. The numbers runner would in turn pass the carbons and the receipts to Mr. Boyle, for which service he was paid five percent of total receipts. Mr. Boyle would prepare a list of numbers purchased from the carbons, and put the carbons and the cash, less ten percent for his commission, into the zipper bag for collection by the gentleman who called at his home each evening.

Sale of numbers was closed off at half past two in the afternoon. The New York Stock Exchange closed at three. By three-fifteen, the day's transactions had been reported on radio and television, and Mr. Boyle was made aware which number had hit, if any. Or, far more commonly, that no number had been hit. Or, far less commonly, that two or three individuals had purchased numbers that had hit. Only once in Mr. Boyle's experience (and he had been a runner before becoming a "numbers man" himself) had five individuals bought a number that had hit. He considered it far more probable that he would be struck by lightning than for it to happen that six individuals would select the same winning number.

But in any event, the laws of probability were not Mr. Boyle's concern. All winning numbers were paid by his employers and did not come out of his pocket. When a number did hit, Mr. Boyle almost always had sufficient funds from that day's receipts to pay it. If winnings exceeded receipts, a rare happenstance, he would make a telephone call and there would be enough cash in the zipper bag brought to his door to make payment, which was religiously made the next business day.

At 7:15 P.M. Mr. Boyle was sitting in his shirtsleeves at his kitchen table concluding the administration of the day's business when he heard the doorbell ring.

He was idly curious, but did not allow it to disturb his concentration. His work was important, and he took pride in both his accuracy, his absolute honesty, both to his clients and to his employers, and his timeliness. He had failed only twice to be ready when the man with the bag appeared at his door. His wife, Helen, moreover, had strict orders that he was not to be disturbed when he was working unless the house was on fire.

The kitchen table was covered with carbons of numbers selected that day, which would be forwarded, and with stacks of money, folded in half, and kept together with rubber bands. The folded stacks of money—the day's receipts—were predominantly dollar bills, but with the odd five-, ten-, and twenty-dollar bills assembled in their own stack. There were also three stacks of tens, crisp new bills, bound by paper strips bearing the logotype of the Philadelphia Savings Fund Society, and marked "$500."

These crisp new ten-dollar bills would be used to pay yesterday's winners, those whose number had come up. This, Mr. Boyle believed, had a certain public relations aspect.

He could have, of course, paid the winners from the day's receipts. There were a lot of people who would say money is money, it doesn't matter where it comes from, so long as it can be spent. But Sonny believed that winners were happier to receive a stack of crisp new bills than they would be had he paid them with battered old currency, no telling where the hell it's been. It made them feel better, and if they felt better, they would not only keep picking numbers, but would flash the wad of new bills around, very likely encouraging their friends and neighbors to put a buck, or a couple of bucks, on the numbers.

The swinging door from the dining room opened.

"Honey," Helen said, to get his attention.

Sonny looked up at her with annoyance. She knew the rules.

"What?" he asked, less than politely.

"Mr. D'Angelo is here," Helen said.

Marco D'Angelo was Mr. Boyle's immediate supervisor. He normally drove the Buick which appeared ritualistically between 8:00 and 8:15 P.M., looking up and down the street as his assistant went into the Boyles' residence.

As Sonny understood the hierarchy, Mr. D'Angelo worked directly for Mr. Pietro Cassandro. Mr. Pietro Cassandro was the younger brother of Mr. Paulo Cassandro, who was, as Sonny understood it, a made man, and who reported directly to Mr. Vincenzo Savarese, who was, so to speak, the Chairman of the Board.

Sonny didn't *know* this. But it was what was said. And he had not considered it polite to ask specific question.

Sonny glanced at his watch. Marco D'Angelo was not due for another forty-five minutes.

"He's here? Now? What time is it?"

Mr. D'Angelo appeared in the kitchen.

"Whaddaya say, Sonny?" he said. "Sorry to barge in here like this."

"Anytime, Marco," Sonny replied. "Can I get you something?"

"Thank you, no," Mr. D'Angelo said. "Sonny, Mr. Cassandro would like a word with you. Would that be all right?"

"I'm doing the day's business," Sonny said, gesturing at the table.

"This won't take long," Mr. D'Angelo said. "Just leave that. So we'll be a little late, so what, it's not the end of the world. Finish up when you come back."

"Whatever you say, Marco," Sonny said. "Let me get my coat."

Mr. Boyle was not uncomfortable. He had seen Mr. Pietro Cassandro on several occasions but did not *know* him. He searched his memory desperately for something, anything, that he had done that might possibly have been misunderstood. He could think of nothing. If there was something, it had been a mistake, an honest mistake.

The problem, obviously, was to convince Pietro Cassandro of that, to assure him that he had consciously done nothing that would in any way endanger the reputation he had built over the years for reliability and honesty.

Sonny did not recognize the man standing by Marco D'Angelo's black Buick four-door. He was a large man, with a massive neck showing in an open-collared sports shirt spread over his sports-jacket collar. He did not smile at Sonny.

"You wanna get in the back, Sonny?" Mr. D'Angelo ordered. "Big as I am, there ain't room for all of me back there."

"No problem at all," Sonny said.

He got in the backseat. Mr. D'Angelo slammed the door on him and got in the passenger seat.

They drove to La Portabella's Restaurant, at 1200 South Front Street, which Sonny had heard was one of Mr. Paulo Cassandro's business interests. The parking lot looked full, but a man in a business suit, looking like a brother to the man driving Marco D'Angelo's Buick, appeared and waved them to a parking space near the kitchen.

They entered the building through the kitchen. Marco D'Angelo led Sonny past the stoves and food-preparation tables, and the man with the thick neck followed them.

Marco D'Angelo knocked at a closed door.

"Marco, Mr. Cassandro."

"Yeah," a voice replied.

D'Angelo pushed the door open and waved Sonny in ahead of him.

It was an office. But a place had been set on the desk, at which sat another large Italian gentleman, a napkin tucked in his collar. He stood up as Sonny entered the room.

The large Italian gentleman was, Sonny realized with a sinking heart, Mr. Paulo Cassandro, Pietro's brother. He had just had his picture in the newspaper when he had been arrested for something. The *Inquirer* had referred to him as a "reputed mobster."

"Sonny Boyle, right?" Mr. Cassandro asked, smiling and offering his hand.

"That's me," Sonny said.

"Pleased to meet you. Marco's been telling me good things about you."

"He has?"

"I appreciate your coming here like this."

"My pleasure."

"Get him a glass," Paulo Cassandro ordered. "You hungry, Sonny? I get you up from your dinner?"

"No. A glass of wine would be fine. Thank you."

"You're sure you don't want something to eat?"

"No, thank you."

"Well, maybe after we talk. I figure I owe you for getting you here like this. After we talk, you'll have something. It's the least I can do."

"Thank you very much."

"Marco tells me you're pretty well connected in your neighborhood. Know a lot of people. That true?"

"Well, I live in the house my mother was born in, Mr. Cassandro."

"The name Frank Foley mean anything to you, Sonny?"

Sonofabitch! I didn't even think of that!

"I know who he is," Sonny said.

"Me asking looks like it made you nervous," Paulo said. "Did it make you nervous?"

"No. No. Why should it?"

"You tell me. You looked nervous."

Sonny shrugged and waved his hands helplessly.

"Tell me about this guy," Paulo said.

"I don't know much about him," Sonny said.

"Tell me what you do know."

"Well, he's from the neighborhood. I see him around."

"I get the feeling you don't want to talk about him."

"Mr. Cassandro, can I say something?"

"That's what I'm waiting for, Sonny."

"I sort of thought you knew all about him, is what I mean."

"I don't know nothing about him; that's why I'm asking. Why would you think I know all about him?"

"I got the idea somehow that you knew each other, that he was a business associate, is what I meant."

"Where would you get an idea like that?"

"That's what people say," Sonny said. "I got that idea from him. I thought I did. I probably misunderstood him. Got the wrong idea."

"Sonny, I never laid eyes on this guy. I wouldn't know him if he walked in that door right this minute," Paulo said.

"Well, I'm sorry I had the wrong idea."

"Why should you be sorry? We all make mistakes. Tell me, what sort of business associate of mine did you think he was?"

"Nothing specific. I just thought he worked for you."

"You don't know where he works?"

"He works at Wanamaker's."

"Doing what?"

"I don't know. In the warehouse, I think."

"Just between you and me, did you really think I would have somebody working for me who works in the Wanamaker's warehouse?"

"No disrespect intended, Mr. Cassandro."

"I know that, Sonny. Like I told you, Marco's been saying good things about you. Look, I know you were mistaken, and I understand. But when you were mistaken, what did you think this guy did for me?"

Sonny did not immediately reply.

"Hey, you're among friends. What's said in this room stays in this room, OK?"

"I feel like a goddamned fool for not knowing it was bullshit when I heard it," Sonny said. "I should have known better."

"Known better than what, Sonny?" Paulo Cassandro said, and now there was an unmistakable tone of impatience in his voice.

"He sort of hinted that he was a hit man for you," Sonny said, very reluctantly.

"You're right, Sonny," Paulo said. "You should have known it was bullshit when you heard it. You know why?"

Inspiration came, miraculously, to Sonny Boyle. He suddenly knew the right answer to give.

"Because you're a legitimate businessman," he said.

"Right. All that bullshit in the movies about a mob, and hit men, all that bullshit is nothing but bullshit. And you should have known that, Sonny. I'm a little disappointed in you."

"I'm embarrassed. I just didn't think this through."

"Right. You didn't think. That can get a fella in trouble, Sonny."

"I know."

"Ah, well, what the hell. You're among friends. Marco says good things about you. Let's just forget the whole thing."

"Thank you."

"You know what I mean about forgetting the whole thing?"

"I'm not exactly sure."

"You know what you did tonight, Sonny?"

"No."

"You wanted to be nice to the wife. You wanted to surprise her. You know a guy who works in the kitchen out there. You come to the back door and told him to make you two dinners to go. He did."

"Right, Mr. Cassandro."

"That it was on the house is nobody's business but yours and mine, right? And you didn't see nobody but your friend, right?"

"Absolutely, Mr. Cassandro."

"Marco," Paulo Cassandro said. "Get them to make up a takeout. Antipasto, some veal, some pasta, some fish, spumoni, the works, a couple bottles of wine. And then take Sonny here home."

"Yes, Mr. Cassandro."

Paulo Cassandro extended his hand.

"I would say that it was nice to see you, Sonny, but we didn't, right? Keep up the good work. It's appreciated."

"Thank you, Mr. Cassandro."

"You see anybody here by that name, Marco?"

"I don't," Marco D'Angelo said.

"Sorry," Sonny said.

"Ah, get out of here. Enjoy your dinner," Paulo Cassandro said.

Impulsively, when he reached the Media Inn, at the intersection of the Baltimore Pike and Providence Road, Matt continued straight on into Media, instead of turning left onto Providence Road toward the home in Wallingford in which he had grown up.

Except for a lantern-style fixture by the front door, there were no lights on in the brick Colonial house at 320 Wilson Avenue; Mr. Gerald North Atchison, restaurateur and almost certain conspirator in a double murder, was apparently out for the evening.

There was time for Matt to consider, as he slowly approached and rolled past the house, that driving by wasn't the smartest thing he had done lately.

What if he had been home? So what? What did I expect to find?

He pressed harder on the Porsche's accelerator and dropped his hand to the gearshift.

To hell with it. I'll go home, and hope I can look—what did Wohl say Amy said? A condition of "grief shock"?—sufficiently grief-shocked to convince my mother that I am not the sonofabitch I have proven myself to be.

Jesus! What if Amanda calls the apartment and Milham's girlfriend answers the phone? Amanda will decide that I am letting some other kind female soul console me in my grief shock! And be justifiably pissed. Worse than pissed, hurt. I'll have to call her.

And that's not so bad. She said not to call her. But this gives me an excuse. Jesus, I'm glad I thought about that!

There was a sudden light in the rear of the house at 320 Wilson, growing in intensity. Matt looked over his shoulder—it was difficult in the small interior of the Porsche—and saw that the left door of the double garage was going up.

He pulled quickly to the curb, stopped, and turned his lights off. A moment later, a Cadillac Coupe de Ville backed out of the driveway onto the street, turned its tail toward Matt, and drove off in the other direction.

With his lights still off, Matt made a U-turn, swore when his front wheel bounced over the curb he could not see, then set off in pursuit.

Why the hell am I doing this?

Because I think I'm Sherlock Holmes? Or because I really don't want to go home and have Mother comfort me in my grief shock?

Or maybe, just maybe, because I'm a cop, and I'm after that bastard?

Not without difficulty—the traffic on the Baltimore Pike through Clifton Heights and Lansdowne toward Philadelphia was heavy, and there were a number of stoplights, two of which left him stopped as the Cadillac went ahead—he kept Atchison in sight.

Atchison drove to the Yock's Diner at Fifty-seventh and Chestnut, just inside the city limits. Matt drove past the parking lot, saw Atchison get out of his car and walk toward the diner, and then circled the block and entered the parking lot.

Atchison knew him, of course, so he couldn't go in the diner. He walked toward the diner, deciding he would try to look in the windows. He passed a car and idly looked inside. There was a radio mounted below the dash, and when he looked closer, he could see the after-market light mounted on the headliner. An unmarked car.

The occupants of which will see me stalking around out here, rush out, blow whistles, shine flashlights, and accuse me of auto burglary.

There was a three-foot-wide area between the parked unmarked car and the diner itself, planted with some sort of hardy perennial bushes which were thick and had thorns. He scratched both legs painfully, and a grandfather of a thorn ripped a three-inch slash in his jacket.

He found a footing and hoisted himself up to look in the window.

There will be a maiden lady at this table, two maiden ladies, who will see the face in the window, scream, and cause whoever's in the unmarked car to rush to protect society.

The table was unoccupied. Matt twisted his head—clinging to the stainless-steel panels of the diner wall made this difficult—and looked right and then left.

Mr. Gerald North Atchison was sitting at a banquette, alone, studying the menu.

Jesus, why not? What did I expect? People have to eat. Going to a diner is what hungry people do.

He dropped off the wall and turned to fight his way back through the jungle.

You are a goddamn fool, Matthew Payne. The price of your Sherlock Holmes foolishness is your ripped jacket. Be grateful that the guys in the unmarked car didn't see you.

But, Jesus, why did he come all the way here? He could have eaten a hell of a lot closer to his house than this—the Media Inn, for example.

He stood motionless for a second, then turned back to the diner and climbed up again.

Mr. Gerald North Atchison, smiling, was giving his order to a waitress whose hair was piled on top of her head.

What are you doing here, you sonofabitch?

He looked around the diner again.

Frankie Foley was sitting at the diner's counter, the remnants of his meal pushed aside, drinking a cup of coffee, holding the cup in both hands.

"You want to climb down from there, sir, and tell us what you're doing?"

Matt quickly looked over his shoulder. Too quickly. His right foot slipped and he fell backward onto one of the larger perennial thornbushes.

"Shit!" Matt said.

"Jesus!" one of the detectives said, his tone indicating that the strange behavior of civilians still amazed him.

"I'm a Three Six Nine," Matt said.

Both detectives, if that's what they were, entered the thornbush jungle far enough to put their hands on Matt's arm and shoulders and push him out of the thornbush.

"I'm Detective Payne, of Special Operations," Matt said. "Let me get out of here, and I'll show you my identification."

The two eyed him warily as he reached into his jacket for his identification.

The larger of the two took the leather folder, examined it and Matt critically, and finally handed it back.

"What the hell are you doing?" he asked.

"Right now, I need some help," Matt said.

"It sure looks like you do," the second of them said.

"There's a man in there named Gerald North Atchison," Matt said. "You hear about the double homicide at the Inferno?"

"I heard about it," the larger one said.

"It was his wife and partner who were killed," Matt said. "And there is another man in there. Frankie Foley, who we think is involved."

"I thought you said you was Special Operations," the larger detective said. "Isn't that Homicide's business?"

"I'm working the job," Matt said. "I followed Atchison here from his house. I think he's here to meet Foley. That would put a lot of things together."

"What kind of help?" the larger one asked.

"I can't go in there. They both know my face."

"What are you looking for?"

"I don't know," Matt said, aware of how stupid that made him sound. "See if they talk together. Anything. I don't think it's a coincidence that they're both here together."

"If they've got enough brains to pour piss out of a boot," the larger one said, "they'd transact their business out here in the parking lot, where nobody would see them."

It was a valid comment, and Matt could think of no reply to make.

"Harry," the smaller one said, "I could drink another cup of coffee."

"I'd appreciate it," Matt said.

"If you need some help, why don't you get on the radio?" the larger one said.

"I'm driving my own car."

"Where are these guys?"

"Atchison, five eight or nine, a hundred ninety pounds, forty-something, in a suit, is in the second banquette from the kitchen door. Foley, twenty-five, six one, maybe two hundred pounds, is in a two-tone sports coat, third or fourth seat from the far end of the counter."

"We'll have a look," the larger one said. "I'm Harry Cronin, Payne, South Detectives. This is Bob Chesley."

Chesley waved a hand in greeting; Cronin offered his hand.

"You tore the shit out of your jacket, I guess you know," he said, then signaled for Chesley to go into the diner ahead of him.

A minute after that, Cronin followed Chesley into the diner. Matt walked away from the diner, stationing himself behind the second line of cars in the parking lot.

Five minutes later, he saw Foley come out of the diner. Matt ducked behind a car and watched Foley through the windows. Foley went to a battered, somewhat gaudily repainted Oldsmobile two-door and got in. The door closed, and a moment later the interior lights went on.

Matt couldn't see what he was doing at first, but then Foley tapped a stack of money on the dashboard. The door opened wider, and he could see an envelope flutter to the ground. The door closed, the engine cranked, the lights came on, and Foley drove out of the parking lot.

"That one," Detective Cronin reported as he approached Matt, "went into the crapper carrying a package. A heavy package. He came out a minute or two later without it. Then the fat guy went in the crapper, and when he came out, he had the package."

Matt ran over and retrieved the envelope. It was blank, but Matt remembered a lecture at the Police Academy—and it had been a question on the detective's exam—where the technique of lifting fingerprints from paper using nihydrous oxide had been discussed. An envelope with Foley's and Atchison's prints on it would be valuable.

"I'd love to know what's in that package," Matt said when he went back to where Cronin waited.

"It was heavy and tied with string," Cronin said. "It could be a gun. Guns. More than one."

"Shit," Matt said.

"Guns don't help?"

"In the last couple of days, I've had several lectures about not giving defense attorneys an edge," Matt said. "I'm afraid we'd get into an unlawful search-and-seizure, and lose the guns as evidence."

"If they are guns," Cronin said. "That's just a maybe."

"Shit," Matt said.

"I could bump into the fat guy, and maybe the package would fall to the ground and rip open . . ."

"And maybe it wouldn't."

"You call it, Payne."

"I think I had better be very careful," Matt said.

"Whatever. Anything else?"

"I'm going to follow him. I don't suppose you could tag along?"

"I don't know. I'd have to check in."

"Fuck it," Matt thought aloud. "I started this myself, I'll do it myself. Anyway, he might catch on if two cars followed him."

"You know that he hasn't caught on to you already?"

"No, I don't."

They waited in silence for another ten minutes.

"If you saw a gun barrel or something sticking out of a ripped package, that would be sufficient cause for you to ask for a permit, right?" asked Matt.

"Absolutely. A wrapped-up gun is a concealed weapon."

"He's got a permit to carry concealed, but you could get the serial numbers."

"I'll go bump the sonofabitch," Cronin said.

Five minutes after that, Gerald North Atchison came out the Yock's Diner. Detective Cronin stepped from between two parked cars and bumped into him, hard enough to make Atchison stagger. But he didn't drop the package, and he held on to it firmly while Cronin profusely apologized for not watching where he was going, and tried to straighten Atchison's clothing.

Detective Cronin, still apologizing, went into the diner. Atchison watched him, then turned and walked quickly to his car. Matt trotted to his Porsche and followed him out of the parking lot.

Atchison drive back toward Media. Just making the light, he turned left on Providence Road. The line of traffic was such that Matt could not run the stoplight. He fumed impatiently until it finally gave him a green left-turn signal, and then took out after Atchison's Cadillac.

It was nowhere in sight. There weren't even any red taillights glowing in the distance.

Matt put his foot to the floor. When he passed the residence of Mr. and Mrs. Brewster Cortland Payne II, he was going seventy-five miles an hour. There were lights on in the kitchen, and he had a mental picture of his mother and father at the kitchen table.

Just beyond the bridge over the railroad tracks near the Wallingford Station, he was able to pick out the peculiar taillight assembly of a Cadillac. He gradually closed the distance between them.

Atchison drove into and through Chester, to the river, then through a run-down area of former shipyards and no-longer-functioning oil refineries, weaving slowly between enormous potholes and junk strewn on the roadway.

Matt turned off his headlights, which kept, he felt, Atchison from noticing that he was being followed but which also denied him a clear view of the road. He struck several potholes hard enough to worry about blowing a tire, and making a trip to enrich the alignment techniques at the Porsche dealership a certainty.

And then he ran over something metallic, which lodged itself somewhere under the Porsche, set up a terrifying howl of torn metal, and gave off a shower of sparks.

He slammed on the brakes, wondering if he had done so because he was afraid Atchison would hear the screeching or see the sparks, or because it hurt to consider what damage was being done to the Porsche.

He jumped out, looking in frustration at Atchison's disappearing Cadillac. And then the brake lights came on and the Cadillac stopped.

Christ, he saw me!

What do I do now?

There was a sudden light as the Cadillac's door opened. Atchison got out, looked around, seemed fascinated with the Porsche, and then slammed the car door shut.

It took Matt's eyes some time to adjust to the now pitch darkness, but when they did he saw Atchison—nothing more than a silhouette—walking away from the car.

He ran after him. When he got close he saw that they were next to the river, and that Atchison was on a pier extending into it.

He saw Atchison make a move like a basketball player. A shadow of something arced up into the sky, fell, and in a moment, Matt could faintly hear a splash.

Atchison now walked quickly back to the Cadillac, fired it up, and started to turn around. As the headlights swept the area, Matt dropped to the ground. His hands touched something wet and sticky. He put his fingers to his nose. It smelled as foul as it felt.

Atchison's Cadillac rolled past him. It stopped at the Porsche. Atchison got half out of the car, looked around, then got all the way out. It looked for a moment as if he was going to try the door, but then he stumbled over something.

Then he got back in the car and drove rapidly away.

Matt got to his feet, rubbed his hands against his jacket to cleanse them of whatever the hell it was on his hands—the jacket was ruined anyway—and walked back to his car.

He saw what Atchison had stumbled over. A curved automobile bumper.

That which caused that unholy screech and the shower of sparks. With a little bit of luck, Atchison will think that's why the Porsche is here, and not that I ran over the god-damn thing when I was tailing him.

The Cadillac's taillights were no longer visible.

What the hell, he's probably going home anyway.

Matt opened the car door with two fingers, got the keys from the ignition, then opened the hood and took out the jack. It took him fifteen minutes to dislodge the bumper from the car's underpinnings.

20.

Inspector Peter Wohl was visibly disturbed when he opened the door to his apartment and found Detective Payne standing there.

"What the hell do you want? Are you drunk, or what?"

"Atchison threw something I'll bet is guns in the river," Matt said.

"What the hell are you talking about?"

"In Chester," Matt said. "I followed him."

"You did what? What the hell gave you the idea you had that authority?"

"He met Frankie, Frankie gave him a package, and Atchison threw it in the river in Chester."

"I'll want to hear all about this, Detective Payne, but not here, and not when you're obviously shitfaced. I'll see you in my office at eight o'clock."

The door slammed in Detective Payne's face. He waited a moment and then started down the stairs. He was halfway down when light told him the door had reopened. He looked over his shoulder.

Amelia Payne, Ph.D., M.D., attired in a terry-cloth bathrobe, stood at the head of the stairs.

"Matt, what happened to you?"

You may be his lady love, but first of all, you are my big sister, who takes care of her little brother.

"Are you drunk?" Amy asked, more in sympathy than moral outrage.

"Not yet."

"Well, come in here," Amy said. "What does 'not yet' mean?"

"I mean that getting drunk right now seems like a splendid idea, one that I will pursue with enthusiasm, once I have a bath."

"What is that stuff on you?" Wohl demanded, in curiosity, not sympathy.

"I don't think I want to find out."

"Come up here," Amy ordered.

She is now in her healer-of-mankind role.

Matt climbed the stairs.

"It's all over you!" Amy announced.

"I've noticed."

She wiped a finger, professionally, across his forehead.

"There's irritation. It's a caustic of some sort. You need a long hot bath."

"If he's coming in here," Inspector Wohl said, resigned to the inevitable, "he's going to take his clothes off first."

Fifteen minutes later, attired in the robe Amy had been wearing when she appeared at the top of the steps, Detective Payne entered Inspector Wohl's living room. Inspector Wohl and Dr. Payne were now fully clothed.

"I am under instructions to apologize for accusing you of being drunk," Wohl said. "You want a beer?"

"I'd love a beer," Matt said.

Wohl walked into his kitchen, returned with a bottle of Ortleib's, and handed it to Matt.

"I am under further instructions to question you kindly, having been reminded that you are undoubtedly in a condition of grief shock," Wohl said. "So why don't we start at the beginning?"

"I don't like your sarcasm, Peter," Amy said. "Look at his face and hands! He's been burned! Have you got any sort of an antiseptic lotion?"

"Listerine?" Wohl asked. "Where did you get that stuff on you, anyway?"

"No, not Listerine, stupid!"

"On a pier, or near a pier, near the old refineries in Chester," Matt said.

"Where you had followed, you said, Mr. Atchison?"

"That will have to wait until I do something about his face and hands," Amy said. "I probably should take him to an emergency room."

"I'm all right," Matt said.

"You must have something around here," Amy said to Peter Wohl.

"Look in the medicine cabinet," Wohl said. "You were telling me you followed Atchison? And I was asking you where the hell you got the idea—"

"Stop it, Peter," Amy ordered. "For God's sake, what's the matter with you?"

She glowered at him, then marched into the bedroom. Thirty seconds later she was back, triumphantly displaying a tube of medicine.

"This will do," she said. "Why didn't you tell me you had it?"

"I don't even know what it is," Wohl said.

Amy daubed the ointment on Matt's face, then rubbed it on his hands.

"Give me that, I've got a nasty scratch on my leg," Matt said.

Wohl looked.

"I'm just dying to learn where you've been besides on a pier in Chester," he said sweetly.

"I got these in the bushes outside the Yock's Diner on Fifty-Seventh and Chestnut. That's where I saw Atchison and Foley."

"You *have* been a busy little junior Sherlock Holmes, haven't you?"

"Peter, for Christ's sake, at least hear me out!"

Wohl glared at him.

"OK. Fair enough. We're back at square one. Start at the beginning."

Ten minutes later, Wohl dialed a number from memory.

"Tony, I hate to call you at this hour, but this is important. Go out to South Detectives. I'll call out there and tell them you're coming. I want you to get a statement from two detectives. One of them is named Cronin, and the other's name is Chesley. The first thing you say to them is to keep their mouths shut about what happened tonight at the Yock's Diner on Fifty-seventh and Chestnut. If they spread the story around the squad room, it'll be public knowledge in the morning. Then I want you to question them, separately, about what went on at the Yock's Diner. Payne was there, he followed Atchison there. Frankie Foley was there. Frankie arrived with a package. Atchison left with the package. Payne thinks Atchison gave Foley an envelope, and he thinks there was money in the envelope. Atchison then went to the riverfront in Chester and threw a package in the river. Payne suspects the package contained guns. What I want from the detectives are the facts, not what they think or surmise, something they can testify to in court without getting blown out of the witness chair by Atchison's lawyer."

Detective Tony Harris asked a question, during which Inspector Wohl glanced at Detective Payne. Detective Payne's face bore, in addition to a glistening layer of medicated ointment, a look of smug vindication. Inspector Wohl, tempering the gesture with a smile, extended his right hand toward Detective Payne, the palm upward, all but the center finger folded inward.

Detective Payne was not cowed.

"When you're right, you're right," he said.

Inspector Wohl returned his attention to the telephone.

"I know a couple of people in the Chester Police Department," he said. "I'm going to call them, and then Payne and I are coming out there. Payne says he can find the pier; he marked the site with an old bumper. I'm going to ask the Chester cops to guard the site until we can get our divers out there at first light. What I'm hoping, Tony, is that Sherlock Holmes, Junior, got lucky again. I think he may have. Call me when you're finished. I don't care what time it is."

He put the phone back in the cradle.

"What we have, hotshot," he said, turning to Matt, "is a lot of ifs. *If* the package does contain firearms. *If* those firearms can be ballistically connected with the weapons used in the Inferno. *If* we can tie the guns to either Atchison or Foley."

"If all else fails, we can shake the two of them up," Matt argued. "What were they doing together in the Yock's Diner? What did the package Foley gave him contain?"

Wohl could think of no counterargument.

"And when we find your pier, I will drop you off at your family's home in Wallingford," he said.

"He can't go to Wallingford at this hour, looking like that," Amy announced. "Mother and Dad have gone through enough in the last couple of days without him showing up looking like that."

"And you can't go to your apartment, either, can you, with Milham's girlfriend there? That leaves here, doesn't it?" Wohl asked.

"I could go to a hotel."

"No he—" Amy began. Wohl held up his hand to interrupt her. To Matt's surprise, she stopped.

"If this thing works out, I may have to forgive you for a large assortment of sins, but I will not forgive you, Matt, for this."

He gestured around the apartment. Amy took his meaning, and blushed.

Detective Payne smiled.

"Chastity, goodness, and mercy shall follow you all the days of your lives," he paraphrased piously.

"Why, you little sonofabitch!" Amelia Payne, Ph.D., M.D., said.

The Philadelphia Marine Police Unit occupies part of a municipal pier on the Delaware River just south of the Benjamin Franklin Bridge.

When Detective Payne arrived at ten minutes to seven, at the wheel of his Porsche, which shuddered alarmingly whenever he exceeded thirty miles per hour, and looking both as if he had fallen asleep on the beach and was suffering from terminal sunburn, and as if his clothing had shrunken (he was wearing a complete ensemble borrowed from

Inspector Peter Wohl, who was two inches shorter and twenty-five pounds lighter than he was, there having been no time for him to get his own clothing), the parking lot was crowded with personal and official vehicles.

There were two Mobile Crime Laboratory vans, and a similar-size van bearing the insignia of the Marine Police Unit; two radio patrol cars; two unmarked cars (one of which he recognized as belonging to Wally Milham); a green Oldsmobile 98 coupe (which he knew to be the personal automobile of Chief Inspector Dennis V. Coughlin); a police car bearing the insignia of the Chester Police Department; and an assortment of personal automobiles.

That Denny Coughlin was driving his own car, rather than being in his official car chauffeured by Sergeant Francis Holloran, made it clear to Matt that he was present in his role of Loving Uncle in Fact, rather than as a senior member of the Philadelphia police hierarchy.

Chief Coughlin and Detective Milham were standing on the pier. Coughlin waved him over.

"What the hell did you do to your face, Matty?" he asked, his gruffness not quite masking his concern.

"It's not as bad as it looks," Matt said.

"Amy said it'll be gone in a couple of days," Coughlin said, his tone making it clear that he had serious doubts about the accuracy of the diagnosis.

"They're ready for us," Milham said, and gestured over the side of the pier. Matt looked down. There was a forty-foot boat down there, festooned with flood- and spot-lights, a collection of radio antennae, a radar antenna, and what looked like a standard RPC bubble gum machine.

The rear deck was crowded with diving equipment and people, including a neatly uniformed sergeant of the Chester Police Department. His dapper appearance contrasted strongly with the appearance of officers of the Marine Police Unit, who had reported for duty prepared to go to work, which meant that their badges were pinned to work clothing.

There was a lieutenant (presumably the Marine Police Unit commander) standing by the wheel, and a sergeant actually at the boat's controls.

Matt followed Milham down a flight of stairs onto a floating pier and then jumped aboard the boat after him.

"Chief," the Inspector called up to Coughlin. "Would you like to ride along with us, sir?"

It was a pro forma question, asked because lieutenants generally recognize the wisdom of being very courteous under any circumstances to chief inspectors. The expected response would normally have been, "No, thank you. But thank you for asking."

Chief Coughlin looked at his watch, looked thoughtful, then said, "What the hell, there's nothing on my desk that won't wait a couple of hours."

He then quickly came down the flight of stairs onto the floating pier and jumped onto the boat.

"Don't let me get in your way, Lieutenant," he called, then went to the Chester police sergeant. "I'm Chief Coughlin," he said, offering his hand. "We appreciate your courtesy, and especially you coming in here like this."

"Anything we can do to help," the Sergeant said. "I thought I might make it easier to find the site."

"We appreciate it," Coughlin said.

The diesel engines roared, and the boat moved away from the pier and headed downstream. To his left, Matt could see the Nesfoods International complex on the Camden shore, and to his right, on Society Hill, he thought he could make out the apartment of Mr. and Mrs. Chadwick T. Nesbitt IV.

I wonder what Vice President Nesbitt is doing at this hour of the morning? Trying to come up with some clever way to sell another ten billion cans of chicken soup?

Matt watched as Denny Coughlin made his way among the other police officers and technicians. Matt was impressed, but not particularly surprised, that Coughlin knew most of their names. Somewhat unkindly, knowing that it would offend Coughlin if he knew what he was thinking, Matt thought he was working the crowd of cops just about as effectively as Jerry Carlucci worked a crowd of voters.

Then the Sergeant from the Chester Police Department embarrassed him.

"You're Detective Payne, right?"

"Right," Matt said, shaking the Sergeant's hand. "Nice to meet you."

"I don't mean to put down what you did. It was good work," the Sergeant said. "But you know what I was just thinking?"

Matt smiled and shook his head.

"I was thinking it must be nice to work for a police department where there's enough money to surveil somebody like this guy Atchison. We just don't have the dough to pay for twenty-four-hour surveillance, even on a murder job. How many officers did you have on the detail?"

"I really don't know," Matt said.

That is far from the truth. I know precisely how many. Zero. And the surveillance of Mr. Atchison will cost the Philadelphia Police Department zero dollars, because it was not only not authorized, but as Peter pointed out with some emphasis, another manifestation of what's wrong with me; that I am an undisciplined hotshot who goes charging off in all directions without thinking.

The cost of whatever it's going to cost to fix the Porsche, and I don't like to think how much that's going to be, plus the cost of a new jacket, shirts, pants, necktie, and loafers, is going to be borne personally by Detective Matt Payne. I don't even dare to put in for overtime.

It didn't take as long to reach the pier along the Chester waterfront as Matt expected it would.

And finding the pier was easy. There was a Chester police car sitting on it, and it could be seen a half-mile away.

Thirty minutes after the Marine Police Unit boat tied up to the pier, a police diver, wearing a diving helmet, bobbed to the surface with a package. It was a white plastic garbage bag, wrapped in duct tape.

"That it, Matty?" Denny Coughlin asked.

"That looks like what I saw Atchison carry out of the Yock's Diner."

"Good job, Matty."

Unless, of course, it contains something like the records of the loan-shark operation Atchison was operating, and not guns.

A police photographer recorded the diver in the water, the package on the deck, and then as a laboratory technician carefully cut the duct tape away. Inside the plastic garbage bag was a paper bag. Inside the paper bag, wrapped in mechanic's wiping cloths, were three guns. A large revolver, which a ballistics technician identified for another technician to write down as a .44-40 single-action six-shot revolver, of Spanish manufacture, a .38 Special Caliber six-shot Colt revolver, and a Savage .32 ACP semiautomatic pistol.

Officer Woodrow Wilson Bailey, Sr., woke to the smell of brewing coffee and fried ham. It pleased him. He didn't complain or feel sorry for himself most days that he didn't get to eat breakfast with Joellen and Woodrow Junior. Policing was a twenty-four-hour-a-day job, and everybody had to take their fair turn working the four-to-midnight tours, and the midnight-to-eight-in-the-morning tours. And truth to tell, he sort of liked the last-out tour; there was something he liked about cruising around the deserted streets, say, at half past three or four, when all the punks had finally decided to go to bed.

But it was nice when he was working the day shift, and could sit down at the kitchen table and have breakfast with Joellen and Woodrow Junior. Having breakfast like that every day was one of the things Woodrow looked forward to, when he got his time in and went home to Hartsville.

He got out of bed and took a quick shower and a careful shave, then put on his terry-cloth bathrobe and went down to the kitchen. He really hated it when he dribbled coffee or egg or redeye gravy or something on a clean uniform shirt and had to change it, so he ate in his bathrobe. All you had to do if you made a pig of yourself on your bathrobe was throw it in the washing machine. Joellen knew he took pride in the way he looked in his uniform, and always had one clean and pressed waiting for him. That was a lot of work, and Woodrow knew it, and made a genuine effort not to get his uniform duty, so that what Joellen did for him would not be wasted.

"I was about to come see if you were going to take breakfast with us," Joellen said when he walked in the kitchen.

"I could smell that cooking," Woodrow said. "It would wake a dead man."

Joellen smiled and kissed him.

"Good morning, son."

"Good morning, sir," Woodrow Junior said. He was wearing a white shirt and a blue sweater and a necktie. He was a junior at Cardinal Dougherty High School, and they had a dress code there. More important, they taught Christian morals, even if they weren't Protestant Christians. It would have been nicer if Third Abyssinian had a church-run school that Woodrow Junior could have gone to, but they didn't.

And he certainly couldn't have sent Woodrow Junior to a public high school. The corridors of the public schools, Woodrow sometimes thought, were not a bit better than the corners of the neighborhood. You could buy anything in there, and it was no place to send your child unless you didn't care what was going to happen to him, what he would see, what punks would give him trouble.

Woodrow thought it was a truly Christian act on the part of the Catholics to let Protestant Baptist boys like Woodrow into their schools. And there were a lot of them. There was a charge, of course, but in Woodrow's case it was reduced because Joellen went over there every day and helped out in the cafeteria for free.

Woodrow sat down at the kitchen table. Woodrow Junior bent his head, and standing behind her husband, Joellen closed her eyes and bent her head.

"Dear Lord, we thank You for Your bounty which we are now about to receive, and for Thy many other blessings. We ask You to watch over us. Through Thy Son, our Lord and Saviour, Jesus Christ."

Joellen and Woodrow Junior said, "Amen," and Joellen put breakfast on the table: sunny-side-up eggs and ham, redeye gravy and grits, and the biscuits Mamma Dear had taught Joellen to make before the Good Lord took her into heaven.

Then Woodrow went upstairs and put on his uniform, and started to get his gun out of the drawer. He glanced down at his shoes and almost swore. There was a scratch across the toe of the left one, and the toe of the right one was smudged. He wondered when that had happened. He closed the drawer in the dresser where he kept his gun, and went back down to the kitchen.

Joellen watched as he put on a pair of rubber gloves and very carefully polished his shoes.

"Woodrow Junior would have done that if you'd have told him," Joellen said.

"I messed them up, I'll make them right," he said.

Then he went back upstairs, got his gun from the drawer, went back downstairs, kissed Joellen good-bye. He got his uniform cap and his nightstick from the hall clothes hanger and left the house.

It was seven blocks to the District Headquarters at Twenty-second and Hunting Park Avenue.

Woodrow walked briskly, looking to see what he could see, thinking that when roll call was over and he went on patrol he'd cruise the alleys. He'd been off for seventy hours, and there was no telling what might have happened in that time.

It was a morning like any other. There was absolutely nothing different about it that would have made him suspect that before the day was over, he would be in the office of the Northwest Police Division Inspector, getting his hand shook, and having his picture made with the Mayor of the City of Philadelphia.

Having decided *First things first,* Matt limped to Imported Motor Cars, Ltd., Inc., from the Marine Police Unit pier. There the Senior Maintenance Advisor, a somewhat epicene young man in a blazer and bow tie and three maintenance technicians in spotless white thigh-length coats which made them look more, Matt thought, like gynecologists waiting for a patient than automobile mechanics, confirmed his worst fears about the Porsche.

"Whatever did you do to it?" the Senior Maintenance Advisor asked, in what Matt thought was mingled horror and joy as he calculated the size of the repair bill.

Well, I was chasing a murder suspect down by the refineries in Chester, and I had to turn the headlights off so that he wouldn't know he was being followed.

"I ran over a bumper," Matt said.

"I'll say you did!"

"You should have left it where you did it," one of the maintenance technicians volunteered, his tone suggesting Matt deserved a prize for Idiot of the Year. "Called a wrecker. No telling how much damage to the suspension you did driving it in."

Imported Motor Cars, Ltd., Inc., evidently felt such enormous sympathy for him, or figured they could make up the cost when they presented him with the bill, that they gave him a loaner. A new 911 Demonstrator. Matt suspected that sometime in the next day or two he would receive a call from Imported Motor Cars, Ltd., Inc., asking him, taking into consideration what the repair bill for repairing the damage he had done to his old car would be, would he be interested in a very special deal on the car he was now driving?

He then went to his apartment. There was no one there. Helene Kellog had apparently gone off with Wally Milham someplace—Wally had said that it would be three o'clock, maybe later, before the lab was finished testing the guns taken from the river—or possibly had calmed down enough to go to work.

There was evidence of her presence in the apartment—a can of hair spray, a mascara brush, and a jar of deodorant on the sink in his bathroom—when he stripped out of Wohl's clothes and went to take a shower.

That reminded him that he had not telephoned Amanda on the pretense that she should not be concerned if she called the apartment and a woman answered.

The hot water of the shower exacerbated whatever the hell he had been rolling around in on the Chester pier had done to his face and hands. When he wiped the condensation off the mirror to shave, he looked like a lobster. A lobster with a three-square-inch albino white spot on the right cheek, which served to make the rest of his face look even redder.

And shaving hurt, even with an electric razor.

He had just about finished dressing when the telephone rang.

That's obviously Inspector Wohl, calling to apologize for having spoken harshly to me, and to express the gratitude and admiration of the entire Police Department for my brilliant detecting.

Or the President of the United States, (b) being quite as likely as (a).

Jesus, maybe it's Amanda!

"Hello."

"You're a hard man to find, Matt," the familiar voice of Mrs. Irene Craig, his father's secretary, said. "Hold on." Faintly, he could hear her add, presumably over the intercom to his father, "Triumph! Perseverance pays!"

"Matt? Good morning."

"Good morning, Dad."

"I've been concerned about you, and not only because we rather expected to see you at home last night and no one seems to know where you are."

"Sorry, I was working."

"Are you working now?"

"No. I just got out of the shower."

"I don't suppose you would have time to come by the office for a few minutes?"

"Yes, sir, I could."

"Fine, I'll see you shortly," his father said, and hung up.

He did that, Matt hypothesized, correctly, *so that I wouldn't have time to come up with an excuse not to go to his office. I wonder what he wants.*

"What in the world happened to your face?" Brewster Cortland Payne II greeted him twenty minutes later.

"I don't suppose you would believe I fell asleep under a sunlamp?"

"I wouldn't," said Irene Craig. "You'll have to do better than that. Would you like some coffee, Matt?"

"Very much, thank you. Black, please."

His father waved him into one of two green leather-upholstered chairs facing his desk.

"Two, Irene, please, and then hold my calls," his father said.

He waited until Mrs. Craig had served the coffee, left, and closed the door behind her.

"What did happen to your face?"

"I fell into something that, according to Amy, was some kind of caustic."

"Amy's had a look at you?"

Matt nodded.

"How did it happen?"

"I was working."

"That's what I told your mother, that you were probably working. First, when you didn't show up for dinner as promised, and again when you didn't show up by bedtime, and a third time when Amanda Spencer called at midnight."

"Amanda called out there?"

"She was concerned for you," Matt's father said. "Apparently, she called the apartment several times. A woman answered one time, and then she called back and there was a man, who either didn't know where you are or wouldn't tell her."

"God!"

"Your mother said it must have been very difficult for Amanda to call us."

"Oh, boy!"

"I wasn't aware that you and Amanda were close," Matt's father said, carefully.

Matt met his eyes.

"That's been a very recent development," Matt said after a moment. "I don't suppose it makes me any less of a sonofabitch, but . . . there was nothing between us before Penny killed herself."

"I didn't think there had been," his father said. "You've never been duplicitous. Your mother, however, told me that she saw Amanda looking at you, quote, 'in a certain way,' unquote, at Martha Peebles's party."

"Jesus, that's the second time I heard that. I hope the Detweilers didn't see it."

"So do I," his father said. He came around from behind his desk and handed Matt a small sheet of notepaper.

"Your mother told Amanda that she would have you call her as soon as we found you," he said. "The first number is her office number, the second her apartment. I think you'd better call her; she's quite upset."

"What does Mother think of me?"

"I think she's happy for you, Matt," Brewster Cortland Payne II said, and walked toward his door. "I am."

He left the office and closed the door behind him.

Matt reached for the telephone.

21.

There are a number of City Ordinances dealing with the disposition of garbage and an equally large number of City Ordinances dealing with the setting of open fires within the City. A good deal of legal thought has gone into their preparation, and the means by which they were to be enforced.

In theory, citizens were encouraged to place that which they wished to discard in suitable covered containers of prescribed sizes and construction. The containers were to be placed according to a published schedule in designated places in such a manner that garbage-collection personnel could easily empty the containers' contents into the rear collection area of garbage trucks.

The ordinances spelled out in some detail what was "ordinary, acceptable" garbage and what was "special types of refuse" and proscribed, for example, the placing of toxic material or explosive material or liquids in ordinary containers.

The setting of open fires within the City was prohibited under most conditions, with a few exceptions provided, such as the burning of leaves at certain times of the year under carefully delineated conditions.

Violation of most provisions was considered a Summary Offense, the least serious of the three classifications of crimes against the Peace and Dignity of the City and County of Philadelphia and the Commonwealth of Pennsylvania. The other, more serious, classifications were Misdemeanors (for example, simple assault and theft of property worth less than $2000) and Felonies (for example, Murder, Rape, and Armed Robbery).

It was spelled out in some detail what malefactors could expect to receive in the way of punishment for littering the streets with garbage, for example, with small fines growing to potentially large fines, and growing periods of imprisonment for second, third, and subsequent offenses.

Similarly, there were pages of small type outlining the myriad punishments which could be assessed against malefactors who were found guilty of setting open fires in violation of various applicable sections of the ordinances, likewise growing in severity depending on the size and type of fire set, the type material set ablaze, under what circumstances, and the number of times the accused had been previously convicted of offending the Peace and Dignity of the City, County, and Commonwealth by so doing.

As a general rule of thumb, the residents of Officer Woodrow Wilson Bailey's beat were not cognizant of the effort that had been made by their government to carefully balance the rights of the individual against the overall peace and dignity of the community insofar as garbage and setting fires were concerned. Or if they were aware of the applicable ordinances in these regards, they decided that their chances of having to face the stern bar of justice for violating them was at best remote.

If they had a garbage can, or a cardboard box, or some other container that could be used as a substitute, and if they remembered what day the garbageman came, they often—but by no means always, or even routinely—put their garbage on the curb for pickup.

It had been Officer Woodrow Wilson Bailey's experience that a substantial, and growing, number of the trash—white, brown, and black—who had moved into the neighborhood had decided the least difficult means of disposing of their trash was to either carry it into (or throw it out the window into) their backyards and alleys when the garbage cans inside their houses filled to overflowing, or the smell became unbearable.

There was little he could do about this. The criminal justice system of Philadelphia was no longer able to cope with many Summary Offenses, and issuing a citation for littering was nothing more than a waste of his time and the taxpayers' money. He would show up in court, the accused would not, and the magistrates were reluctant to issue a bench warrant for someone accused of littering a back street in North Philadelphia. The police had more important things to do with their time.

He privately thought that if the trash wanted to live in their own filth, so be it.

At a certain point in time, however, backyards became filled to overflowing with refuse. Just about as frequently, the piles of garbage became rat-infested. When either or both of these circumstances occurred, the trash's solution to an immediate problem was to set the garbage on fire. This both chased the rats away and reduced the height of the garbage piles.

It was at this point that Officer Woodrow Wilson Bailey drew the line. This was a violation of the law that presented a clear and present danger to innocent persons.

Even trash had rights. It was not fair or just that they get somebody's else's rats. And not all the people on Woodrow's beat were trash. There were a lot of folks who reminded Woodrow of Mamma Dear and Daddy, hardworking, Christian people who had worked all their lives to buy their own home, and when they'd finally finished, about the time they went on retirement, they found that the neighborhood's having gone to hell meant they couldn't sell their house for beans, and were stuck in the neighborhood with the trash.

It was, in Woodrow's mind, a sin that trash should set fires that could burn down the houses next door, taking all the poor old folks had left in the world.

Woodrow did not think of it, as some people concerned with social justice certainly would, as taking the law into his own hands. He thought of it first as something that had to be done, and rationalized that he was providing a genuine service to the people he had sworn to protect.

He dealt with people who set fires in his own way, without getting the overworked criminal justice system involved. And over the last couple of years, the word had gone out on his beat that burning garbage was socially unacceptable conduct, and that doing so brought swift punishment.

Officer Bailey was thus surprised and angry when through the open window of RPC 3913, as he rode slowly down an alley behind Shedwick Street, his nostrils detected the peculiar smell of burning garbage.

He stopped the car, put his head out the window and sniffed, and then backed the car up.

There was smoke rising above the wooden fence separating the backyard of a row house from the alley.

He was less surprised when he searched his memory and came up with the identity of the occupant of the house. White trash, and a junkie. White trash born right here in Philadelphia. His name, Woodrow recalled, was James Howard Leslie. White Male, twenty-six, 150 pounds, five feet nine. He had been in and out of some kind of confinement since he was twelve. Lived with some brown-trash Puerto Rican woman. Not married to her. Three kids; none of them looked like they ever had a decent meal.

Now he had a mental image of him. Junkie type. Long, dirty hair, looked like he hadn't had a bath—and probably hadn't—in two weeks. Had a little scraggly beard on the point of his chin. Called himself "Speed."

Officer Bailey got out of his car, taking his stick with him. There was a gate in the fence, held shut with a chain and a rusty lock. Woodrow put his stick in the chain and twisted. The chain and rusty lock held; the rotten wood of the fence crushed under the pressure and gave way.

Woodrow pulled the gate open and entered the backyard. His anger grew. The fire was coming from a pile of garbage against the fence. The fire would almost certainly set the fence on fire. He saw a rat scurry out from the pile.

Flames flickered on the garbage pile. There was an old tire on the pile. Once a tire caught fire, you could hardly put it out. Tires burned hot and hard and gave off thick smoke.

First things first; get the fire out.

There was a grease can with a Texaco sign on it. Woodrow picked it up. It was empty, but there was the smell of gasoline.

"Trash!" Woodrow muttered in angry contempt.

Speed had used gasoline to start the fire. That was dangerous.

Moving quickly, Woodrow went to a water spigot. He knew where to find it, even behind the trash. All these houses were alike, like they were stamped out with a cookie cutter.

He rinsed out the Texaco grease bucket twice, then filled it up with water.

It took six buckets of water to put the fire out, and Woodrow threw a seventh one on the garbage, to be sure. As he looked for a hint of smoke, he glanced at his shoes. The shoes he had shined with such care just two hours before were now covered with filth.

Then he went to the rear door of the residence and knocked on it. There was no response. Woodrow knocked again, and again there was no response. Woodrow gave the door a couple of good licks with his stick.

"Who the fuck is that?" a voice demanded in indignation.

"Speed, get your trashy ass out here!"

James Howard Leslie appeared behind the dirty glass of his kitchen door, and then opened it.

He did not seem particularly happy to see Officer Bailey, but neither did he seem at all concerned. He was wearing dirty blue jeans, a bad necklace, and nothing else.

"What's happening?" Mr. Leslie inquired.

Officer Bailey lost his temper. He caught Mr. Leslie's wrist and twisted it behind his back. Then he marched Mr. Leslie off his porch and to the smoldering pile of garbage, and manipulated Mr. Leslie's body so that his nose was perhaps six inches from the garbage.

"That's what's happening, Speed," Officer Bailey said.

"Man, you're hurting me! What the fuck!"

"You trying to burn the neighborhood down. Speed? What's the matter with you? You lost the sense you were born with?"

"What the fuck is the big deal? So I burned some garbage! So what the fuck?"

At this point in similar situations, it was normally Officer Bailey's practice to first hurt the trash a little, either with a slap in the face or by jabbing them in the abdomen with his stick to get their attention. To further get their attention, he would then put handcuffs about their wrists and search them for weapons and illegal substances. Very often he encountered the latter, if only a few specks of spilled marijuana in their pockets.

Then he would explain in some detail what crimes they had committed, with special emphasis on the punishments provided by law. If he had found illegal substances on their persons, so much the better.

By then, the malefactor would be contrite. He did not want to go through the inconvenience he knew would be associated with an arrest: detention in the Thirty-ninth District, followed by transportation way the hell downtown to Central Lockup. And then several hours in Central Lockup before being arraigned before a magistrate.

The malefactors knew that the magistrate would probably release them on their own recognizance, and that if they actually got to trial they would walk, but it was a fucking pain in the ass to go through all that bullshit.

Officer Bailey would at some point shortly thereafter inform the trash there was a way to avoid all the inconvenience. They could make their backyard so clean they could eat off it. Get rid of all the garbage, right down to where there once had been grass. Get it all in plastic bags or something, and put it out on the street so the garbageman could take it off.

And keep it that way from now on, or Officer Bailey, who was going to check, would come down on their trashy asses like a ton of bricks, they could believe that.

Far more often than not, the malefactors would agree to this alternate solution of the problem at hand.

Mr. Leslie had, indeed, heard stories about the old black cop who had a hair up his ass about burning garbage, and had heard stories that if he caught you, he'd make you clean up the whole goddamned place or throw your ass in jail.

He was debating—*Jesus Christ, I'm tired*—whether it would be better to let the cop lock him up, or clean up the yard. It would take fucking forever to get all this shit out of here.

Mr. Leslie was not given the opportunity to make a choice.

Officer Bailey just spun him around and, guiding him with one hand on his arm and the other on his shoulder, led him to the cop car. He opened the door and guided Mr. Leslie to a seat in the rear.

Then he returned to the backyard, and the pile of garbage. He took a mechanical pencil from his pocket, squatted beside the garbage, and began to shove things aside. The first item he uncovered was a wedding picture.

He looked at it carefully.

"Lord almighty!" he said wonderingly.

He stirred the garbage a bit more. He was looking for the frame it was logical to assume would be with a photograph of what was supposed to be the happiest moment of a man's life. He could not find one.

He stopped stirring, and, still squatting, was motionless in thought for about thirty seconds.

Then he stood up and walked to Leslie's house. He rapped on the door with his night-stick until the brown-trash Puerto Rican woman appeared.

She stared at him with contempt.

"Teléfono?" Officer Bailey inquired.

The brown-trash woman just looked at him.

He looked over her shoulder, saw a telephone sitting on top of the refrigerator, pointed to it and repeated, *"Teléfono."*

Her expression didn't change, but she shrugged, which Officer Bailey decided could be interpreted to mean that she had given him permission to enter her home.

And now the phone won't work. They won't have paid that bill either.

There was a dial tone.

"Homicide, Detective Kramer."

"Detective, this is Officer Woodrow W. Bailey, of the Thirty-ninth District."

"What can I do for you, Bailey?"

"I'd like to talk to somebody working the job of that police officer, Kellog, who was murdered."

"What have you got, Bailey?"

"You working the job, Detective?"

"The assigned detective's not here. But I'm working it."

"What I got may not be anything, but I thought it was worth telling you."

"What have you got, Bailey?"

"A fellow named James Howard Leslie—he's a junkie, done some time for burglary—was burning garbage in his backyard."

"And?" Detective Kramer asked, somewhat impatiently.

"I put the fire out, and then I got a good look at what he was burning. I don't know . . ."

"What, Bailey?"

"There was a photograph of Officer Kellog and his wife, on their wedding day, in his garbage."

There was a moment's silence, and then Detective Kramer asked, very carefully: "How do you know it was Officer Kellog?"

"There's a sign on the wall behind him. 'Good Luck Officer Kellog From the Seventeenth District.' And I remembered his picture in the newspapers."

"Where's the picture now?"

"I left it there."

"Where's the guy . . . Leslie, you said?"

"In my car. I arrested him for setting an unlawful fire."

"Where are you?"

"Behind his house. In the alley. The 1900 block of Sedgwick Street."

"I'll be there in ten minutes. Don't let him out of your sight, don't let anybody near where you found the picture, and don't touch nothing you don't have to."

Bailey hung up the telephone, then called the Thirty-ninth District and asked for a supervisor to meet him at the scene.

"What have you got, Bailey?" the Corporal inquired.

"A garbage burner," Bailey said, and hung up.

He nodded at Leslie's Puerto Rican woman, then walked back through the yard to his car and got behind the wheel.

"Hey, Officer, what's happening?" Mr. Leslie inquired, sliding forward with some difficulty on the seat to get closer to the fucking cop.

"You under arrest, Speed," Officer Bailey replied. "For setting a fire in your backyard."

"Oh, Jesus Christ, man! For burning some fucking garbage?"

"If I was you, I'd just sit there and close my mouth," Officer Bailey replied.

As a general rule of thumb, unless the visitor to the Mayor's office was someone really important ("really important" being defined as someone of the ilk of a United States Senator, the Governor of the State of Pennsylvania, or the Cardinal Archbishop of the Diocese of Philadelphia) Mrs. Annette Cossino, the Mayor's secretary, would escort the visitor to the door of the Mayor's office, push it open, and say, "The Mayor will see you now."

The visitor would then be able to see the Mayor deep in concentration, dealing with some document of great importance laid out on his massive desk. After a moment or two, the Mayor would glance toward the door, look surprised and apologetic, and rise to his feet.

"Please excuse me," he would say. "Sometimes . . ."

Visitors would rarely fail to be impressed with the fact that the Mayor was tearing himself from Something Important to receive them.

This afternoon, however, on learning that Chief Inspector Matt Lowenstein had asked for an appointment for himself and Inspector Peter Wohl, His Honor had decided to deviate from the normal routine.

While he could not be fairly accused of being paranoid, the threatened resignation of Chief Lowenstein had caused the Mayor to consider that he really had few friends, people he could really trust, and that Matt Lowenstein was just about at the head of that short list.

"When he comes in, Annette," the Mayor ordered, "you let me know he's here, and I'll come out and get him."

Such a gesture would, the Mayor believed, permit Chief Lowenstein to understand the high personal regard in which he was held. And Peter Wohl would certainly report the manner in which Lowenstein had been welcomed to the Mayor's office to his father. The Mayor was perfectly willing to admit—at least to himself—that his rise through every rank to Commissioner of the Philadelphia Police Department—which, of course, had led to his seeking the mayoralty—would not have been possible had not Chief Inspector Augustus Wohl covered his ass in at least half a dozen really bad situations.

And when he thought about that, he realized that Inspector Peter Wohl was no longer a nice young cop, but getting to be a power in his own right. And that he could safely add him to the short list of people he could trust.

He was pleased with his decision to greet Lowenstein and Wohl in a special manner.

And was thus somewhat annoyed when he pulled the door to his office open, warm smile on his face, his hand extended, and found that Chief Lowenstein was at Annette's desk talking on the telephone.

Finally, Chief Lowenstein hung up and turned around.

"Sorry," Lowenstein said.

"What the hell was that?" Carlucci asked, somewhat sharply.

"Henry Quaire," Lowenstein said. "There may be a break in the Kellog murder."

"What?" the Mayor asked.

He's not being charming, Peter Wohl thought. *When Lowenstein told him that, he went right back on the job. He's a cop, and if there is one thing a cop hates worse than a murdered cop it's a murdered cop with no doers in sight.*

"A uniform in the Thirty-ninth working his beat came across a critter, junkie, petty criminal with a record six feet long, including burglaries, burning garbage in his backyard. In the garbage was Officer Kellog's wedding picture. The uniform called Homicide."

"There was mention of a wedding picture in the 49s," Carlucci said. "In a silver frame."

"Right," Lowenstein said.

"Where else would he get a picture of Kellog?" Carlucci asked, thoughtfully rhetoric. "Have you got the frame?"

"Yeah. That's why Quaire called me. We got a search warrant. They found not only a silver frame, but a dozen—thirteen, actually—tape casettes. They were in the fire, but maybe Forensics can do something with them. If Mrs. Kellog can identify the frame, or there's something on the tapes . . ."

"Where's the critter?"

"Right now, he's on his way from the Thirty-ninth to Homicide," Lowenstein said.

"Who's going to interview him?"

Lowenstein shrugged. "Detective D'Amata is the assigned detective."

"Peter, do you have Jason Washington doing anything he can't put off for a couple of hours?" the Mayor asked, innocently.

That is, Wohl noted mentally, *the first time the Mayor has acknowledged my presence.*

"You want to take it away from D'Amata?" Lowenstein asked.

"I'd like an arrest in that case," Carlucci said. "If you think it would be a good idea to have Washington talk to this critter, Matt, I'd go along with that."

"Shit," Lowenstein said. "You find Washington, Peter," he ordered. "I'll call Quaire."

"Yes, sir," Peter said.

"Only if you think it's a good idea, Matt," the Mayor said. "It was only a suggestion."

"Yeah, right," Lowenstein said, and walked back to Mrs. Annette Cossino's desk and reached for one of the telephones.

"D'Amata will understand, Peter," the Mayor said.

"Yes, sir," Peter said. "I'm sure he will."

"Annette," the Mayor called. "Call the Thirty-ninth. Tell the Commanding Officer I want him and this uniform standing by to come here if I need them."

"Yes, Mr. Mayor," Mrs. Cossino said.

"Henry," Lowenstein said into the telephone. "When they bring in the critter from the Thirty-ninth, handcuff him to a chair in an interview room and leave him there until Washington shows up. Wohl's putting the arm out for him now. I think that's the way to handle the interview, and the Mayor agrees."

He hung the phone up and turned to face Carlucci.

"Are you pissed at me, Matt?" Carlucci, sounding genuinely concerned, asked.

"When am I not pissed at you?" Lowenstein said. "It goes with the territory."

"You don't think it was a good idea?"

"That's the trouble. I think it was a very good idea," Lowenstein said.

"Sergeant Washington is en route to the Roundhouse, Mr. Mayor," Wohl repeated.

"Great!" Carlucci said enthusiastically. Then he smiled broadly. "Let's do this all over."

"What?" Lowenstein asked in confusion.

"Well, Chief Lowenstein," Carlucci said, and grabbed Lowenstein's hand and pumped it. "And Inspector Wohl! How good of you both to come see me! It's always a pleasure to see two of the most valuable members of the Police Department here in my office. Come in and have a cup of coffee and tell me how I may be of assistance!"

Lowenstein shook his head in resignation.

"Jesus Christ!"

"What *can* I do for you, Chief?"

"Stop the bullshit, Jerry," Lowenstein said, chuckling.

"OK," Carlucci said agreeably. "What's up?"

"Last night, a couple of South detectives saw one John Francis Foley pass a package to one Gerald North Atchison. Shortly thereafter, Detective Payne of Special Operations saw Mr. Atchison throw said package off a pier in Chester—"

"How did South detectives get involved in this?" Carlucci asked, and Wohl saw that he had slipped back into being a cop.

"Payne was surveilling Atchison. He ran into the South detectives and asked for their assistance."

"OK," Carlucci said thoughtfully. "Go on."

"The package was retrieved early this morning by a police diver. The lab just came up with a positive ballistics match to the murder weapons."

"Fingerprints?"

Lowenstein shook his head. "Weapons were cleaned. I thought I'd show it to you before I sent someone over to Tom Callis's office with it."

"Let me see," Carlucci said, holding out his hand.

Lowenstein handed the Mayor an envelope. Carlucci made a "come in" gesture with his hand, walked ahead of them into his office, sat down at his desk, and opened the envelope.

FORENSICS LABORATORY REPORT	PHILADELPHIA POLICE DEPARTMENT
REPORT DATE CLASSIFICATION	SUPPLEMENTAL
DATE AND TIME REPORTED	PREPARED BY Tech. Harry Withjack

DETAILS:

The Forensics Laboratory conducted the following examinations of evidence submitted, with results as follows:

(1) Projectiles:
(A) Three (3) bullets taken from the head of Anthony J. Marcuzzi (In envelope marked Case #2397.)

(B) Four (4) bullets taken from the head of Alicia Atchison. (In envelope marked Case #2398.)

(C) One (1) bullet taken from the leg of Gerald N. Atchison. (In envelope marked Case #2399.)

(D) Three (3) .38 Special Caliber bullets fired from Colt Revolver Serial #286955 in the Police Laboratory.

(E) Three (3) .44-40 caliber bullets fired from six-shot single-action revolver (No Manufacturer's Name) probably of Spanish Manufacture, Serial #9133 in the Police Laboratory.

(F) Three (3) .32 ACP bullets fired from Savage semiautomatic pistol Serial #44078 in the Police Laboratory.

Bullets described in (A) and (B) above were removed by Dr. Howard D. Mitchell, Medical Examiners Office, during the course of autopsies performed on the decedents, on Saturday, May 20, 1975 and turned over to Detective Wallace J. Milham. Submitted to Ballistics Lab by Detective Milham on property receipt #201308 on May 20, 1975.

Bullet described in (C) above was taken from the leg of Gerald N. Atchison by K. Lewis Hailey, MD, at Hahnemann Hospital on May 20, 1975, and turned over to Detective Wallace J. Milham. Submitted to Ballistics Lab by Detective Milham on property receipt #201322 on May 20, 1975.

Bullets described in (D), (E), and (F) above were fired by the undersigned under test conditions witnessed by Lieutenant Thomas P. McNamara.

| APPROVED: (Type and Sign Name) | SERGEANT | LIEUTENANT |

Thomas P. McNamara

| | Thomas P. McNamara, Officer In Charge

75-91 (Rev 3/70)

FORENSICS LABORATORY REPORT   PHILADELPHIA POLICE
                                                      DEPARTMENT

REPORT DATE   SUPPLEMENTAL |
CLASSIFICATION |

DATE AND TIME REPORTED | PREPARED BY   Tech. Harry Withjack |

DETAILS:

(2) Analysis:

(A) Ballistic Laboratory Report #640742: (From the head of Anthony J. Marcuzzi):

1. One (1) BULLET SPECIMEN, marked 640742X1 on base area for identification purposes, uncoated lead, caliber .44, bearing one knurled cannelure, weight 198.5 grains, fired from a smokeless powder cartridge, considerably mutilated and distorted, with large piece of bone and flesh tissue adhered. General rifling characteristics: Indeterminable.

2. One (1) BULLET SPECIMEN, marked 640742X2 on base area for identification purposes, uncoated lead, caliber .44, bearing one knurled cannelure, weight 205.8 grains, fired from a smokeless powder cartridge, considerably distorted. General rifling characteristics: five lands and five grooves with a right hand direction of twist.

3. One (1) BULLET SPECIMEN, marked 640742X3 on base area for identification purposes, uncoated lead, caliber .44, bearing one knurled cannelure, weight 215.7 grains, fired from a smokeless powder cartridge, considerably distorted. General rifling characteristics: five lands and five grooves with a right hand direction of twist.

(B) Ballistic Laboratory Report #640743: (From the head of Alicia Atchison):

1. One (1) BULLET SPECIMEN and two bullet fragments, bullet specimen marked 640743X1 on flattened surface and fragments marked x1 for identification purposes, uncoated lead, caliber .38 Special, bearing one knurled cannelure, total weight 142.87 grains, fired from a smokeless powder cartridge, considerably flattened and distorted. General rifling characteristics: five lands and five grooves with a right hand direction of twist.

APPROVED: (Type and Sign Name) | SERGEANT | LIEUTENANT

Thomas P. McNamara

| | Thomas P. McNamara, Officer In Charge

75-91 (Rev 3/70)

FORENSICS LABORATORY REPORT

PHILADELPHIA POLICE DEPARTMENT

REPORT DATE   SUPPLEMENTAL |
CLASSIFICATION |

DATE AND TIME REPORTED | PREPARED BY   Tech. Harry Withjack |

DETAILS:

(2) Analysis: (Continued)

2. One (1) BULLET SPECIMEN, marked 640743X2 on base area for identification purposes, uncoated lead, caliber .38 Special, bearing one knurled cannelure, weight 137.37 grains, fired from a smokeless powder cartridge, considerably mutilated and distorted. General rifling characteristics: five lands and five grooves with a right hand direction of twist.

3. One (1) BULLET SPECIMEN, marked 640743X3 on base area for identification purposes, uncoated lead, caliber .38 Special, bearing one knurled cannelure, weight 127.3 grains, fired from a smokeless powder cartridge, considerably mutilated and distorted. General rifling characteristics: five lands and five grooves with a right hand direction of twist.

4. One (1) BULLET SPECIMEN, marked 640743X4 on base area for identification purposes, uncoated lead, caliber .44, bearing one knurled cannelure, weight 205.5 grains, fired from a smokeless powder cartridge, considerably mutilated and distorted, with large piece of bone and flesh tissue adhered. General rifling characteristics: Indeterminable.

(C) Ballistic Laboratory Report #640744: (From the leg of Gerald N. Atchison):

One (1) BULLET SPECIMEN, marked 640744X1 on base area for identification purposes, uncoated lead, caliber .32, bearing one knurled cannelure, weight 80.25 grains, fired from a smokeless powder cartridge, slightly distorted. General rifling characteristics: six lands and six grooves with a left hand direction of twist.

(3) Determinations:

(A) Microscopic comparative examination of .44 caliber bullets removed from the heads of Anthony J. Marcuzzi and Alicia Atchison shows that all bullets

APPROVED: (Type and Sign Name) | SERGEANT | LIEUTENANT

Thomas P. McNamara

| | Thomas P. McNamara, Officer In Charge

75-91 (Rev 3/70)

FORENSICS LABORATORY REPORT

PHILADELPHIA POLICE DEPARTMENT

REPORT DATE SUPPLEMENTAL |
CLASSIFICATION |

DATE AND TIME REPORTED | PREPARED BY Tech. Harry Withjack |

DETAILS:

(3) Determinations: (Continued)

were fired from the same revolver, Microscopic comparative examination of bullets fired from .44-40 Caliber Revolver Special #9133 in the Police Laboratory with bullets removed from Marcuzzi and Atchison's heads shows identical markings, indicating the .44-40 Revolver #9133 fired all tested bullets.
(B) Microscopic comparative examination of .38 Special caliber bullets removed from the head of Alicia Atchison shows that all bullets were fired from the same revolver. Microscopic comparative examination of bullets fired from .38 Special Caliber Colt Revolver Serial #286955 in the Police Laboratory with bullets removed from Atchison's head shows identical markings, indicating the .38 Special Colt Revolver #286955 fired all tested bullets.

(C) Microscopic comparative examination of .32 ACP bullets removed from the leg of Gerald N. Atchison with bullets fired from Savage .32 ACP semiautomatic pistol, Serial #44078 in the Police Laboratory shows identical markings, indicating the .32 ACP caliber Savage pistol #44078 fired all tested bullets.

APPROVED: (Type and Sign Name) | SERGEANT | LIEUTENANT

Thomas P. McNamara

| | Thomas P. McNamara, Officer In Charge

75-91 (Rev 3/70)

Carlucci carefully stuffed the report back into its envelope, then looked at Lowenstein.

"It may be enough," Carlucci said. "It is for an arrest, anyway."

"I thought so," Lowenstein said. "I'll have it sent to Callis within the hour."

"What the hell, Matt," Carlucci said. "I mean, you're right here in the neighborhood, right? Why don't you, both of you, take this to Tom? See if he has any problems with it? Give him my very best regards when you do."

James Howard Leslie had been sitting in the steel captain's chair in the Homicide Unit interview room, handcuffed to its seat, for almost an hour when the door opened and a very large, important-looking black man walked in.

No one had spoken to him during that time, nor had anyone so much as opened the door to look at him. He suspected that he was being watched through the somewhat fuzzy mirror on the wall, but he couldn't be sure.

"James Howard Leslie?" the black man asked.

Leslie didn't reply.

"Good afternoon," Jason Washington said. "If you'd like, I can remove the handcuff."

"I don't give a fuck one way or the other."

Washington unlocked the handcuff and stood back. Leslie rubbed his wrist.

"I don't even know what the fuck's going on," Leslie said.

"You've been in here some time, I understand." Washington said. "Is there anything I can get for you? Would you like a Coca-Cola, a cup of coffee, a sandwich?"

"What I would like is to know what the hell is going on. All I did was try to burn some garbage."

"I understand. That's why I'm here, to explain to you what's going on. And while we're talking, would you like a Coca-Cola, or a cigarette?"

"I could drink a Coke."

Washington opened the door. "Sergeant," he ordered sternly, "would you please get a Coca-Cola for Mr. Leslie?"

Leslie heard someone reply.

"Fuck him! Let the fucking cop killer drink water!"

"I said get him a Coca-Cola."

"Whose side are you on, anyway?" the voice said.

"That wasn't a suggestion, it was an order," Washington said sharply.

Two minutes later, a slight, dapper man with a pencil-thin mustache entered the interview room with a Coca-Cola, thrust it into Leslie's hand with such violence that liquid erupted from the neck of the bottle and spilled on Leslie's shirt and trousers.

The slight, dapper man then left the interview room. Just before the door slammed shut, Leslie heard the man say, "Fuck Special Operations, too."

Washington handed Leslie a crisp white handkerchief to clean his shirt and trousers.

"He and Officer Kellog were friends," Washington said, in explanation.

"What?"

"It doesn't matter," Washington said. He leaned on the wall by the door, waited until Leslie had finished mopping at himself and started to return the handkerchief.

"Keep it," Washington said. "You may need it again."

"Thanks," Leslie said.

"As I understand what's happened here," Washington said conversationally, "Officer Bailey of the Thirty-ninth District extinguished a fire in the your backyard. In doing so, he found a photograph of Officer Kellog on his wedding day."

"I don't know what the fuck you're talking about. Officer who?"

"The finding of the photograph was, in the opinion of the Honorable Francis X. McGrory, Judge of the Superior Court, sufficient cause for him to issue a search warrant for your home."

"I told you, I don't know what the fuck you're talking about."

"A search of your home was then conducted by detectives of the Homicide Bureau. A silver frame was discovered. It has since been positively identified by Mrs. Helene Kellog as her property. Mrs. Kellog previously reported the framed photograph to have been stolen from her home."

"So what?"

"Mrs. Kellog's husband, Police Officer Jerome H. Kellog, was found dead in his home. Shot to death. Inasmuch as his silver-framed wedding photograph was known to be present in his home prior to the robbery, and missing from his home immediately after the robbery, it is presumed that the framed photograph was stolen during the robbery."

"So what?"

"During the search authorized by Judge McGrory, Homicide detectives found other items among those things you were attempting to burn known to be the property of Police Officer Kellog. Specifically, thirteen recording tapes. And some other items."

"I keep telling you, I don't know what the fuck you're talking about."

"Mr. Leslie, you are presently being held for setting an unlawful fire," Washington said. "And, I believe, for maintaining an unsanitary nuisance."

"Then what the fuck am I doing here?"

"Very shortly, I think you can count on a Homicide detective coming in here and arresting you for the murder of Officer Kellog. I came here to see if I could explain your situation to you."

"What the hell does that mean?"

"If you are arrested for the murder of Officer Kellog, you will receive the required Miranda warning. I understand you have been arrested before, and know what that means. You will be advised of your rights, and provided with an attorney."

"Who the hell are you?"

"I'm a police officer, an investigator for the Special Operations Division. We are sometimes asked, in cases like this, to see if we can't get through a situation like this as smoothly as possible. To save everyone concerned time and money."

"I don't know what the hell you're talking about."

"I'll try to explain it to you. In my judgment, from what the Homicide Bureau Commanding Officer has shown and told me, what Homicide has here is a pretty strong case of circumstantial evidence against you. What I mean by that is that no one actually saw you shoot Officer Kellog. There were no witnesses. That means, when your case comes to trial, the District Attorney—I think I should explain that to you, too."

"Explain what?"

"The District Attorney, Mr. Thomas Callis, rarely goes into court himself. *Assistant* district attorneys actually do the prosecuting. The exception to that rule is when a police officer has been killed. Mr. Callis himself prosecutes such cases. He was a police officer himself when he was a young man. So I think you can expect, when your case comes to trial, that you will be prosecuted by him personally. Do you understand that?"

"I guess so."

"Fine. Well, what Mr. Callis will have to do in your trial will be to convince the jury that although no one actually saw you shoot Officer Kellog—"

"I didn't shoot anybody! I don't know what the fuck this is all about!"

"In that case, you—through your attorney, and I suppose you know that if you can't afford to hire an attorney, one will be assigned to you from the Office of the Public Defender. And I must admit that some of those young men and women are really quite competent. They're young and dedicated, fresh from law school, and really try hard."

"I don't have any fucking money," Leslie said.

"Yes, we know," Washington said. "As I was saying, if you say you are innocent, your defense counsel will enter a plea of not guilty on your behalf. Then it will be up to Mr. Callis to convince the jury that, although no one actually saw you shoot Officer Kellog, the circumstances surrounding the incident prove that you and only you could have done it.

"Mr. Callis will try to convince the jury that the only way you could have come into possession of the silver frame the Homicide detectives found in your home, and tapes they found in your home, and the photograph of Officer Kellog Officer Bailey found in the fire you set—"

"I don't know anything about no fucking photograph!"

"You will be given the chance to explain how tapes made by Officer Kellog, tapes of his voice and telephone calls, came into your possession."

"I don't know nothing about no fucking tapes, either!"

"Your public defender will try to prove that," Washington said. "Mr. Callis will be given the opportunity to try to convince the jury that you stole the framed photograph and the tapes and the other things from Officer Kellog's home, and that in the conduct of that robbery, Officer Kellog came home and you shot him."

"I didn't do nothing like that."

"And then it will be your attorney's turn to convince the jury that it wasn't you. If you can find someone, someone the jury would believe, who will go into court and swear that you were with them during the time of the robbery, that might help. Or if you could explain how the photograph of Officer Kellog and the silver frame and tapes and the other things came into your possession, that would help your case."

"People are always throwing shit over the fence," Leslie said.

"That might explain the photograph," Washington said, reasonably, "but not the frame, which was found inside your house."

Leslie looked uncomfortable.

"Your defense counsel could also have as witnesses people who know you, and would testify to your character, to try to make the point that you're not the sort of fellow who would do something like this," Washington said. "But if he did that, under the law Mr. Callis could introduce evidence to the contrary. You've been arrested, I understand, for burglary on several occasions."

"So what? That doesn't mean I did the cop."

"There is an alternative," Washington said.

"What?"

The door opened and another detective, this one a huge white man wearing cowboy boots, stepped inside.

"Excuse me, Mr. Washington, District Attorney Callis is on the telephone for you."

"I was afraid of that," Washington said. "I don't know how long this will take, Mr. Leslie, but I'll try to come back."

He left the interview room.

"Who the fuck uncuffed you?" the large detective asked rhetorically, walked quickly to Leslie, grabbed his right arm, clamped the handcuff on his wrist, muttered, "Fucking Special Operations hotshot!" under his breath, and stormed out of the interview room, slamming the door closed and leaving Mr. Leslie alone again.

Outside the room, he walked directly to Sergeant Washington, who was sitting on a desk holding a mug of coffee in his hands.

"That's my mug, Jason."

"I won't say I'm sorry, because I am not."

The large detective laughed.

"I didn't think you would be. You think this is going to work?"

"I think we have established in his mind that (a) you don't like him; (b) that shooting a policeman is not socially acceptable conduct; and (c) that he can't beat this unless the nice black man comes up with some solution. The test of these assumptions will come when I go back in."

"You want me to go back in there and accidentally bump him around a little?"

"I think that would be counterproductive. As frightening as you are, Arthur, I think his imagination should be allowed to run free."

"Your call. Changing the subject: There's a story going around that your pal Payne climbed out on a thirteenth-floor ledge of the Bellvue-Stratford to fix a wire?"

"All too true, I'm afraid. I have remonstrated with him."

"What's with him, Jason?"

"He's young. Aside from that, he's a damned good cop."

"I meant, if he's got all the dough everybody thinks he has, why is he a cop?"

"He has all the dough everybody thinks he has," Washington said. "Did you ever think, Arthur, that some people are, so to speak, born to be policemen?"

"You, for example?"

"It's possible. You and me. I can't imagine doing anything else."

"Shit, neither can I. What would I do? Sell used cars?"

"Some of it is the challenge, I think. That explains people like you and me. And probably Payne. But what about people like Officer Bailey? I talked to him before I came here. The reason Leslie is in there is because Bailey, after years on the job, still takes personal pride and satisfaction in protecting people from critters like Leslie. He knows he can't personally clean up the Thirty-ninth District, but 'You don't burn your garbage on my beat.' "

Arthur grunted.

"How long are you going to let the critter's imagination run free?"

"I think fifteen minutes should suffice," Washington said. He looked at his watch. "Another five and a half minutes, to be specific."

"That big guy cuffed me again," Leslie said in some indignation, raising his shackled wrist to demonstrate.

Washington made no move to unlock the handcuff.

"I just came in to tell you I have to leave. I have to go to see Mr. Callis. The decision is yours, Mr. Leslie, and now is when you're going to have to make it."

"What decision?"

"Whether you wish to insist on your innocence, or—"

"Or what?"

"Be cooperative."

"Like what?"

"How serious is your narcotics addiction, Mr. Leslie?"

"I ain't no addict, if that's what you're saying."

"I can't possibly help you, Mr. Leslie, if you don't tell me the truth. Your records show that you have undergone a drug-rehabilitation program. Why lie about it?"

"I got it under control."

"Then you were not under the influence of narcotics when you burglarized Officer Kellog's home? Your defense counsel might be able to introduce that at your trial. 'Diminished capacity' is the term used."

"I don't know what that means."

"It means that if you weren't aware of what you were doing, because of 'diminished capacity' because you were on drugs, you really didn't know what you were doing, and should be judged accordingly."

"Which means what?"

"Let me explain this to you as best I can. If you are not cooperative, they're going to take you to court and ask for the death penalty. In my judgment, they have enough circumstantial evidence to get a conviction."

"And if I'm cooperative, what?"

"You probably would not get the death penalty. It's possible that the District Attorney would be agreeable to having evidence of your drug addiction given to the court, and that the court would take it into consideration when considering your sentence."

"Shit."

"I'm not a lawyer, Mr. Leslie. You should discuss this with a lawyer."

"When do I get a lawyer?"

"When Homicide arrests you for murder, and your Miranda rights come into play. That's going to happen. What you have to decide, *before* you are arrested for murder, is whether you want to cooperate or not."

"I could plead, what did you say, 'diminished capacity'?"

"What I said was that you can either tell the truth, and make it easier on yourself and Homicide, or lie, and make it harder on yourself and Homicide."

"You're not going to be around for this?"

"No. But I've talked to Lieutenant Natali, and explained to him the situation here, and I think the two of you would be able to work something out that would be in everybody's best interests."

"Jesus, I don't know," Leslie said.

"I've got to go. I'll ask Lieutenant Natali to come here and talk to you."

"Jesus, I wish you could stick around."

"I could come to talk some more, later, if you'd like."

"Yeah."

Washington put out his hand. Leslie's right arm was handcuffed to the chair, so he had to shake Washington's hand with his left hand.

"Good luck, Mr. Leslie," Washington said.

"Jesus Christ, I don't know what to do."

"Talk it over with Lieutenant Natali," Washington said. He walked to the door and pulled it open, then closed it.

"Just between us, Mr. Leslie, to satisfy my curiosity. Why did you think you had to shoot Officer Kellog?"

"Well, shit," Leslie said. "I had to. He seen my face. He was a cop. I knew he'd find me sooner or later."

"Yes," Washington said. "Of course, I understand."

"I'm going to hold you to what you said about coming to talk to me," Leslie said.

"I will," Washington said. "I said I would, and I will."

He left the interview room.

Lieutenant Natali and Detective D'Amata came out of the adjacent room. They had been watching through a one-way mirror.

Natali quoted, "I had to. He seen my face. He was a cop."

"Christ!" D'Amata said in a mingled disgust and horror.

"What's really sad," Washington said, "is that he doesn't acknowledge, or even understand, the enormity of what he's done. The only thing he thinks he did wrong is to get caught doing it."

"You don't want to stick around, Jason?" D'Amata said. "I'll probably need your help."

Washington looked at Lieutenant Natali.

"Does Joe know who Mrs. Kellog believed was responsible for her husband's death?"

"You mean Narcotics Five Squad?" D'Amata asked.

"I thought he should know," Natali said. "I told him to keep it under his hat."

"That's what I was doing, Joe, when they sent me here. But to coin a phrase, 'Duty calls.' Or how about, 'It's a dirty job but somebody has to do it'? Do I have to tell you I'd much rather stay here?"

Both Natali and D'Amata shook their heads. Natali touched Washington's arm, and then Washington walked out of Homicide.

The Honorable Thomas J. "Tony" Callis, the District Attorney of the County of Philadelphia, had decided he would personally deal with the case of Messrs. Francis Foley and

Gerald North Atchison rather than entrust it to one of the Assistant District Attorneys subordinate to him.

This was less because of his judgment of the professional skill levels involved (although Mr. Callis, like most lawyers, in his heart of hearts, believed he was as competent an attorney as he had ever met) than because of the political implications involved.

He was very much aware that the Hon. Jerry Carlucci, Mayor of the City of Philadelphia, was taking a personal interest in this case, a personal interest heavily flavored with political implications. The *Ledger,* which was after Carlucci's scalp, had been running scathing editorials bringing to the public's attention the Police Department's inability to arrest whoever had blown Atchison's wife and partner away. (Alternating the "Outrageous Massacre of Center City Restaurateur's Wife and Partner" editorials, Tony Callis had noted, with equally scathing editorials bringing to the public's attention that a cop had been brutally murdered in his kitchen, and the cops didn't seem to know anything about that, either.)

Mr. Callis, a large, silver-haired, ruddy-faced, well-tailored man in his early fifties, had a somewhat tenuous political alliance with Mayor Carlucci. It was understood between the parties that either would abandon the other the moment it appeared that the alliance threatened the reelection chances of either.

As a politician possessed of skills approaching the political skills of the Mayor, The District Attorney had considered the possibility that Mayor Carlucci would be happy to drop the ball, the Inferno ball, into his lap. That he would, in other words, be able to get the *Ledger* off his back by making an arrest in the case on information that might not hold up either before a grand jury or in court.

"My Police Department," the Mayor might well say, "with its usual brilliance, nabbed those villains. If they walked out of court free men, that speaks to the competence of Mr. Callis."

Proof—not that any was needed—that this case had heavy political ramifications came when the police officers sent to the District Attorney's office to present their evidence gathered turned out to be Chief Inspector of Detectives Matthew Lowenstein and Inspector Peter Wohl, Commanding Officer of the Special Operations Division. Mr. Callis—who normally disagreed with anything written in the *Ledger,* which had opposed him in the last election—was forced to admit that there was indeed more than a grain of truth in the *Ledger*'s editorial assertion that the Special Operations Division had become Carlucci's private police force.

And with Chief Lowenstein's opening comment, when he was shown into Callis's office:

"Mr. District Attorney, I bring you the best regards of our mayor, whose office Inspector Wohl and I just left."

"How gracious of our beloved mayor! Please be so kind, Chief Inspector, to pass on my warmest regards to His Honor when you next see him, which no doubt will be shortly after we conclude our little chat."

"It will be my pleasure, Mr. District Attorney."

"How the hell are you, Matt?" Callis asked, chuckling. "We don't see enough of each other these days."

"Can't complain, Tom. How's the wife?"

"Compared to what? How are you, Peter?"

"Mr. Callis," Wohl said.

"You're a big boy now, Peter. A full inspector. You don't have to call me 'Mister.' "

Wohl smiled and shrugged, and raised his hands in a gesture of helplessness.

"My saintly father always told me, when you're with a lawyer, be respectful and keep one hand on your wallet," Wohl said.

Callis chuckled. "Give my regards to the saintly old gentleman, Peter. And your mother."

"Thank you, I will."

"OK. Now what have we got?"

"We have the guns used in the Inferno murders. We have—" Lowenstein began.

"Tell me about the guns, Matt," Callis interrupted.

Lowenstein opened his briefcase. He took a sheaf of Xerox copies from it and laid it on Callis's desk.

"The lab reports, Tom," he said. "They're pretty conclusive."

"Would you mind if I asked Harry Hormel to come in here?" Callis asked. "If I can't find the time to prosecute, it'll almost certainly be Harry."

"By all means," Lowenstein said smoothly. "I'd like to get Harry's opinion."

District Attorney Callis punched his intercom button and very politely asked his secretary to see if she could determine if Mr. Hormel was in the building, and if so, if he could spare a few minutes to come to his office.

A faint smile flickered across Peter Wohl's face. He was perfectly sure that Hormel had been ordered, probably far less courteously, to make himself available.

"Harry," Callis had almost certainly said, "don't leave the office until you check with me. Lowenstein and Wohl are coming over with something on the Inferno murders. I'll need you."

Or words to that effect: Mr. Harrison J. Hormel was an assistant district attorney. He had come to the District Attorney's Office right after passing the bar examination twenty-odd years before and had stayed.

Only a small number of bright young lawyers fresh from law schools stayed on. Many of those who did were those who felt the need of a steady paycheck and were not at all sure they could earn a living in private practice. Hormel, in Peter's opinion, was the exception to that rule of thumb. He was a very good lawyer, and a splendid courtroom performer. Juries trusted him. He could have had a far more lucrative legal career as a defense counsel.

Peter had decided, years before, that Hormel had stayed on, rising to be (at least de facto) the best prosecutor in the DA's Office because he took pride and satisfaction in putting evil people where they could do no more harm.

And Peter knew that whether District Attorney Callis or Assistant District Attorney Hormel prosecuted Foley and Atchison would not be based on professional qualifications—Callis was not a fool, and was honest enough to admit that Hormel was the better prosecutor—but on Callis's weighing of the odds on whether the case could be won or lost. If conviction looked certain, he would prosecute, and take the glory. If there was some doubt, Hormel would be assigned. It was to be hoped that his superior skill would triumph. If Foley and/or Atchison walked, the embarrassment would be Hormel's, not Callis's.

Callis took his glasses, which, suspended around his neck on an elastic cord, had been resting on his chest, and adjusted them on his nose. Then he leaned forward on his desk and began to read, carefully, the report Lowenstein had given him.

Assistant District Attorney Hormel entered Callis's office while Callis was reading the report. He quietly greeted Lowenstein and Wohl, then stretched himself out in a leather armchair to the side of Callis's desk.

Wordlessly, Callis handed him the report, page by page, as he finished reading it. When he himself had finished reading it, he looked at Chief Inspector Lowenstein and made a gesture clearly indicating he was not awed by the report.

Lowenstein handed him another sheaf of Xerox copies.

"The 75-49s on the recovery of the murder weapons," he said.

Callis again placed his glasses on his nose and read the 75-49s carefully, again handing the pages as he finished them to Assistant District Attorney Hormel.

As he read page four, he said: "Denny Coughlin was a witness to the recovery? What was he doing there?"

"Chief Coughlin did not see fit to inform me of his reasons," Lowenstein said. "Inspector Wohl suspects that he thought it would be nice to go yachting at that hour of the morning."

"Oh, shit, Matt." Callis laughed.

Callis finished reading the 75-49s, and then everybody waited for Hormel to finish.

"There are some problems with this," Hormel said.

"Such as?"

"What was this Special Operations detective doing surveilling Mr. Atchison?"

"At the direction of the Commissioner, Detective Payne was detailed to Homicide to assist in the investigation," Lowenstein said.

"I'd love to know what that was all about," Callis said, looking at Lowenstein. "Was that before or after you threatened to retire?"

"Gossip does get around, doesn't it?" Lowenstein said. "I didn't *threaten* to retire. I *considered* retiring. I changed my mind. If you're suggesting I in any way was unhappy with the detail of Detective Payne to Homicide, I was not. He is a very bright young man, as those 75-49s indicate."

"He was assigned to surveil Atchison?"

"He was ordered to assist the assigned detective in whatever way the assigned detective felt would be helpful," Lowenstein replied.

"Presumably," Hormel said, "there was coordination with the Media Police Department?"

"That same afternoon, Detective Payne accompanied Sergeant Washington to interview Mr. Atchison at his home. That was coordinated with the Media Police Department."

"Jason's back working Homicide? I hadn't heard that," Callis said.

"Sergeant Washington and Detective Payne were the first police officers on the scene of the Inferno Lounge murders," Lowenstein said. "Inspector Wohl was kind enough to make them both available to me to assist in the conduct of Homicide's investigation of the murders."

Callis snorted.

" 'Detective Payne,' " Hormel said, obviously playing the role of a defense attorney, " 'you look like a very young man. How long have you been a police officer? How long have you been a detective?' "

" 'How long have you been assigned to Homicide?' " Callis picked up on Hormel's role playing. " 'Oh, you're not assigned to Homicide? Then you really had no previous experience in conducting a surveillance of a murder suspect? Is that what you're telling me?' "

"And then we get to re-direct," Wohl said. "Our distinguished Assistant District Attorney—or perhaps the District Attorney himself—approaches the boy detective on the stand and asks, 'Detective Payne, were you in any way involved in the apprehension of the so-called Northwest Serial Rapist? Oh, was that you who was forced to use deadly force to rescue Mrs. Naomi Schneider from the deadly clutches of that fiend?' "

Callis chuckled.

"Very good, Peter."

" 'And were you involved in any way, Detective Payne, in the apprehension of the persons subsequently convicted in the murders at Goldblatt's Furniture Store? Oh, was that you who was in the deadly gun battle with one of the murderers? Mr. Atchison was not, then, the first murderer with whom you have dealt?' "

"That could be turned against you. It could make him look like a cowboy," Callis said.

"The dark and stormy night is what bothers me," Hormel said. "We have to convince the jury that the package Denny Coughlin saw them take from the river was the same package Atchison tossed in there. That's a tenuous connection."

"The two South detectives saw the package being passed from Foley to Atchison," Lowenstein said.

"No, they didn't," Hormel argued. "There's room for reasonable doubt about that. And it was a dark and stormy night. 'How can you testify under oath, Detective Payne, that the package taken from the river by police divers was the package you saw Mr. Atchison carry out of Yock's Diner? How can you testify under oath that, if the night was as dark as you have testified it was, and you were as far from Mr. Atchison as you say you were, that what he threw, if indeed he threw anything, into the river was that package? You couldn't really see him, could you? You're testifying to what you may honestly believe happened, but, honestly, you didn't really see anything, did you?' "

"Ah, come on, Harry!" Lowenstein protested.

"I'm inclined to go with Harry," Callis said. "This is weak."

Lowenstein stood up.

"Always a pleasure to see you, Tom," he said. "And you, too, Harry."

"Where are you going?"

"To carry out my orders," Lowenstein said. "I was instructed to show you what we have. Then I was instructed to arrest the sonofbitches. Come on, Peter."

Wohl stood up and offered his hand to Harry Hormel.

"Now, wait a minute," Callis said. "I didn't say it was no good. I said it was weak."

"It is," Hormel agreed.

"Harry," the District Attorney said. "You've gone into court with less then this, and won. Peter made a good point. All you have to do is convince the jury that these two were pursued by one of the brightest detectives on the force. A certified hero. If you handle that angle right, you can go for the death penalty and get it."

"It's weak," Harry Hormel repeated.

"Let Harry know when you have them, Matt," Callis said. "I'm sure he would like to be there when you confront them with the guns."

22.

For Frankie Foley, there had been a certain satisfying finality about his meeting with Gerry Atchison in the Yock's Diner the previous night. He had received his final payment for the hit, and he'd gotten rid of the guns. The job was done.

He presumed that Atchison would safely dispose of the weapons somewhere, probably throw them in the Delaware, or bury them in the woods when he was out playing weekend warrior with the National Guard. It didn't matter.

Frankie knew that once Atchison had taken the guns, and once he'd gotten out of the diner without anyone seeing them together, everything was going to be fine.

Frankie personally thought that the bullshit Atchison insisted on going through, making him leave the guns in the garbage can in the toilet of the Yock's Diner, and coming out, and then Atchison going in to get them, was some really silly bullshit. Atchison must have been watching spy movies on the TV or something.

It would have made much more sense for them just to have met someplace, even in the parking lot of the Yock's Diner, for Christ's sake, swapped the dough for the guns, and gotten in their cars and driven away.

On the other hand, which was why Frankie had gone along with the swapping-in-the-crapper bullshit, doing it that way had been safer than meeting him in a dark parking lot someplace.

Frankie didn't trust Atchison. He hadn't trusted him in the Inferno when he'd done the job, and had taken steps to make sure that Atchison hadn't hit him after he'd hit the wife and the partner, which would have been smart, which would have made it look like the dead guy on the floor had robbed the place and killed the partner and the wife, and Atchison was the fucking hero who had killed him.

That "dead men tell no tales" wasn't no bullshit. He was the only guy who could pin the job on Atchison, and Atchison knew it. If he was dead, Atchison could relax. The cops would look for-fucking-ever—or at least until something else came along—for the two robbers Atchison had made up and told the cops about.

Frankie had considered that the reverse was also true, that if Atchison was dead, Atchison couldn't get weak knees or something and tell the cops, "Frankie Foley is the guy who murdered my wife." He considered hitting Atchison. It would be no trouble at all. He could have been waiting for him in the parking lot at the Yock's Diner, put a couple of bullets into his head, and driven off and that would have been the end of it.

Except that maybe it wouldn't have really been the end of it. The cops would look like even bigger assholes if Atchison got hit and they couldn't catch who had done him, either. The *Ledger* was already giving the cops a hard time about that. The cops would get all excited all over again, and maybe they'd get lucky.

Frankie didn't think Atchison would have the balls to try to kill him himself, otherwise he would have killed his wife and the partner by himself, right? And Atchison didn't know no other professional hit men, or else he would have hired one of them to do the job, right?

So the smart thing to do—the professional thing—was just stop right where he was. He had been paid to do a job, and he had done it, and got paid for it, and that should be the end of it. Go on to other things, right?

If he did it that way, in a couple of weeks he could go to work in the Inferno, and tell Wanamaker's what they could do with their fucking warehouse. The word would get out that he had done the job for Atchison, and sooner or later other jobs would come along.

What he would have liked to have done was maybe catch an airplane and go to Las Vegas and see if he would have any luck gambling. Frankie had never been to Vegas, but he had heard there was a lot of pussy that hung around the tables, and that if they thought you were a high roller, they even sent pussy to your room. That would really be nice, go out there, win a lot of money at the crap tables, and get some pussy thrown in for good measure. But that would not have been professional. What he had to do, for a little while anyway, was play it cool.

The cops might be watching him, and they might wonder how come he could afford to quit fucking Wanamaker's, not to mention where he got the money to go to Vegas. In a couple of weeks, about the time he would go see Atchison and remind him about the maître d' job, the cops would lose interest in the Inferno job, and in him. There would be other things for the cops to do.

Neither was he, Frankie decided, going to start to spend the five grand he got right away, get a better car or something, or even some clothes. That would attract attention. When he was working at the Inferno, it would be different. If he turned up with some dough, he could explain it saying he'd won it gambling. Everybody knew that maître d's were right in the middle of the action.

Having decided all this, Frankie then concluded that there would be no real harm in going by Meagan's Bar and having a couple of drinks, and maybe letting Tim McCarthy see that he was walking around with a couple, three, hundred-dollar bills snuggled up in his wallet. Not to mention letting Tim see that he was walking around not giving a tiny fuck that detectives were asking questions about him.

And who knows, there just might be some bored wife in there looking for a little action from some real man. Tim. And if not Tim, then ol' diarrhea mouth himself, Sonny Boyle, were talking about him to people, telling people not to let it get around, but that cops was asking about Frankie Foley. Tim and Sonny would be passing that word around, that was for damn sure, you could bet on it.

Women like dangerous men. Frankie had read that someplace. He thought it was probably true.

Frankie got home from Wanamaker's warehouse a couple of minutes after six. He grabbed a quick shower, put on the two-tone jacket and a clean sports shirt, told his mother he'd catch supper some other place, he had business to do, and walked into Meagan's Bar at ten minutes to seven.

He really would have liked to have had a couple of shooters, maybe a jigger glass of Seagram's-7 dropped into a draft Ortlieb's, but he thought better of it and ordered just the beer.

Not that he was afraid of running off at the mouth or something, but rather that there maybe just might be some bored wife in there looking for a little action—you never could tell, he thought maybe he was on a roll—and if that happened, he didn't want to be half shitfaced and ruin the opportunity.

He paid for the Ortlieb's with one of the three hundred-dollar bills he'd put in his wallet, told Tim to have a little something with him, and when Tim made him his change, just left it there on the bar, like he didn't give a shit about it, there was more where that come from.

He was just about finished with the Ortlieb's, and looking for Tim to order another, when somebody yelled at Tim:

"Hey, Tim, we need a couple of drinks down here. And give Frankie another of whatever he's having."

At the end of the bar, where it right-angled to the wall by the door, were two guys. Guineas, they looked like, wearing shirts and ties and suits. That was strange, you didn't see guineas that often in Meagan's. The guineas had their bars and the Irish had theirs.

But these guys had apparently been in here before. They knew Tim's name, and Tim called back, "Johnnie Walker, right?" which meant he knew them well enough to remember what they drank.

"Johnnie Black, if you got it," one of the guineas called back. "And, what the hell, give Frankie one, too."

What the hell is this all about? Frankie wondered. *What the hell, a couple of guineas playing big shot. They're always doing that kind of shit. Something in their blood, maybe.*

Tim served the drinks, first to the guineas, and then carried another Ortlieb's and the bottle of Johnnie Walker and a shot glass to where Frankie sat.

"You want a chaser with that, or what?" Tim asked as he filled the shot glass with scotch.

"The beer's fine," Frankie said.

He raised the shot glass to his lips and took a sip and looked at the guineas and waved his hand.

One of the guineas came down the bar.

"How are you, Frankie?" he said, putting out his hand. "The scotch all right? I didn't think to ask did you like scotch."

"Fine. Thanks. Do I know you?"

"I dunno. Do you? My name is Joey Fatalgio."

"Don't think I've had the pleasure," Frankie said.

They shook hands.

"I know who you are, of course," Joey Fatalgio said, and winked.

What the fuck is with the wink? This guy don't look like no fag.

"I come in here every once in a while," Frankie said.

"And maybe I seen you at the Inferno," Fatalgio said. "Me and my brother—Dominic—that's him down there, we go in there from time to time."

"Yeah, maybe I seen you in the Inferno," Frankie said. "I hang out there sometimes. And I'm thinking of going to work there."

"Hey, Dominic!" Joey Fatalgio called to his brother. "Bring your glass down here and say hello to Frankie Foley."

Dominic hoisted himself off his stool and made his way down the bar.

"Frankie, Dominic," Joey made the introductions, "Dominic, Frankie."

"How the hell are you, Frankie?" Dominic said. "A pleasure to meet you."

"Likewise," Frankie said.

"Frankie was just telling me he's thinking of going to work at the Inferno," Joey said.

"Going to work? The way I heard it, he already did the job at the Inferno," Dominic said, and he winked at Frankie.

Frankie felt a little nervous.

There were guineas on the cops. Are these two cops?

"Shut the fuck up, for Christ's sake, Dominic," Joey Fatalgio said. "What the fuck's wrong with you?" He turned to Frankie. "You should excuse him, Frankie. Sometimes he gets stupid."

"Fuck you, Joey," Dominic said.

"There are places you talk about certain things, asshole," Joey said, "and places you don't, and this is one of the places you don't. Right, Frankie?"

"Right," Frankie agreed.

"No offense, Frankie," Dominic said.

"Ah, don't worry about it," Frankie said.

"He don't mean no harm, but sometimes he's stupid," Joey said.

"Fuck you, Joey, who do you think you are, Einstein or somebody?"

"Where do you guys work?" Frankie said, both to change the subject—Dominic looked like he was getting pissed at the way his brother was talking to him—and to see what they would say. He didn't think they were cops, but you never really could tell.

"We're drivers," Joey said.

"Truck drivers?"

"I'm a people driver," Joey said. "Asshole here is a stiff driver."

"Huh?"

Joey reached in his wallet and produced a business card, and gave it to Frankie. It was for some company called Classic Livery, Inc., with an address in South Philly, and "Joseph T. Fatalgio, Jr." printed on the bottom.

"What's a livery?" Frankie asked.

"It goes back to horses," Joey explained. "Remember in the cowboy movies where Roy Rogers would park his horse in the livery stables?"

"Yeah," Frankie said, remembering. "I do."

"I think it used to mean 'horses for hire' or something like that," Dominic said. "Now it means limousines."

"Limousines?"

"Yeah. Limousines. Mostly for funerals, but if you want a limousine to get married in, we got white ones. We even got a white Rolls-Royce."

"No shit?"

"Costs a fucking fortune, but you'd be surprised how often it gets rented," Dominic went on.

"Most of our business is funeral homes," Joey said. "Only the bride, usually, gets a limousine ride for a wedding. But if you don't get to follow the casket to the cemetery in a limousine for a funeral, people will think you're the family black sheep."

"I guess that's so," Frankie agreed, and then started to hand the Classic Livery business card back to Joey.

Joey held up his hand to stop him.

"Keep it," he said. "You may need a limousine someday."

"Yeah," Dominic said. "And they'll probably give you a professional discount."

Joey laughed in delight.

"I told you shut up, asshole," he said.

"A professional discount for what?" Frankie asked, overwhelmed by curiosity.

"Shit, you know what for. Increasing business," Dominic said.

Joey laughed.

"I don't know what you're talking about," Frankie said.

"Right," Joey said, and laughed, and winked.

"Yeah, right," Dominic said.

"Actually, Frankie, that's sort of the reason we're here."

"What is?" Frankie asked.

"What you don't know we're talking about," Joey said softly, moving so close to Frankie that Frankie could smell his cologne. "Frankie, there's a fellow we know wants to talk to you."

"Talk to me about what?"

Joey winked at Frankie.

"I don't know," Joey said. "But what I do know about this fellow is that he admires a job well done."

"He's done a job or two himself," Dominic said. "If you know what I mean."

"He already told you he don't know what you're talking about, asshole," Joey said.

"Right," Dominic said.

"What this fellow we know wants to talk to you about, Frankie," Joey said, "is a job."

"What kind of a job?"

"Let's say a job where you could make in an hour about ten times what you make in a month pushing furniture around the Wanamaker's warehouse."

"Yeah?"

"Let's say this fellow we know has a sort of professional admiration for the way you did your last job, and we both know I'm not talking about throwing furniture on the back of some truck."

"Who is this guy?"

"He's like you, Frankie, he lies to sort of maintain a low profile, you know what I mean. Have a sort of public job, and then have another job, like a part-time job, every once in a while, a job that not a hell of a lot of other people can do, you know what I mean."

"Why does he want to talk to me?" Frankie asked.

"Sometimes, what I understand, with his full-time job, he can handle a part-time job, too, when one comes along. But sometimes, you know what I mean, more than one part-time job comes along. Actually, in this case, what I understand is that there's three, four part-time jobs come along, and this fellow can't handle all of them himself. I mean, you'd have to keep your mouth shut—you can keep your mouth shut, can't you, Frankie?"

"Like a fucking clam," Frankie said.

"I figured you could, a fellow in the part-time job business like you would have to keep his mouth shut. What I'm saying here, Frankie, is that you would be like a subcontractor. I mean, you come to some financial understanding with this fellow, you do the job, and the whole thing would be between you two. I mean, the people who hired him for the particular part-time job I think this fellow has in mind wouldn't ever find out that this fellow subcontracted it. They might not like that. I mean, they pay this fellow the kind of money they pay, they expect him to do the job himself, not subcontract it. But what they don't know can't hurt them, right?"

"Right," Frankie said.

"So maybe you would be willing to talk to this fellow, Frankie?" Dominic asked. "I mean, he'd appreciate it. And if you can't come to some sort of mutually satisfactory arrangement, then you walk away, right? No hard feelings. You'd lose nothing, and it might be in your mutual interest to get to know this fellow. You never know what will happen next week."

"What the hell," Frankie said. "Why not?"

Frankie had never seen so many Cadillacs in one place in his life as there were lined up in the garage of Classic Livery, Inc.

He thought there must be maybe a hundred of them, most of them black limousines. There were also a dozen Cadillac hearses, and that many or more flower cars. Plus a whole line of regular Cadillacs and Lincolns, and he saw the white Rolls-Royce Dominic had told him they had.

The floor of the garage was all wet. Frankie decided that they washed the limousines every day, and had probably just finished washing the cars that had been used.

He had never really thought about where the limousines at weddings and funerals had come from, but now he could understand that it must be a pretty good business to be in.

I wonder what they charge for a limousine at a funeral. Probably at least a hundred dollars. And they could probably use the same limousine for more than one funeral in a day. Maybe even more than two. Say a funeral at nine o'clock, and another at eleven, and then at say half past one, and one at say four o'clock.

That's four hundred bucks a day per limousine!

Jesus Christ, somebody around here must be getting rich, even if they had to pay whatever the fuck it costs, thirty thousand bucks or whatever for a limousine. Four hundred bucks a day times five days is two fucking grand a fucking week! After fifteen weeks, you got your money for the limousine back, and all you have to do after that is pay the driver and the gas. How long will a limousine last? Two, three years at least . . .

Joey Fatalgio stopped the regular Cadillac he had parked around the corner from Meagan's Bar, and pointed out the window.

"Through that door, Frankie, the one what says 'No Admittance.' You'll understand that this fellow wants to talk to you alone."

"Yeah, sure," Frankie said.

"I'll go park this and get a cup of coffee or something, and when you're finished, I'll take you back to Meagan's. OK?"

"Fine," Frankie said.

He got out of the car and walked to the door and knocked on it.

"Come in!" a voice said.

Frankie opened the door.

A large, olive-skinned man in a really classy suit was inside, leaning up against what looked like the garage manager's desk.

He looked at Frankie, looked good, up and down, for a good fifteen seconds.

"No names, right?" he said. "You're Mr. Smith and I'm Mr. Jones, right?"

"Right, Mr. Jones," Frankie said.

Jones, my ass. This is Paulo Cassandro. I seen his picture in the papers just a couple of days ago. The cops arrested him for running some big-time whore ring, and bribing some fucking cop captain.

"Thank you for coming to see me, Mr. Smith," Cassandro said.

"Don't mention it, Mr. Jones."

"Look, you'll understand, Mr. Smith, that what you hear about something isn't always what really happened," Cassandro said. "I mean, I understand that you would be reluctant to talk about a job. But on the other hand, for one thing, nobody's going to hear a thing that's said in here but you and me, and from what I hear we're in the same line of business, and for another, you'll understand that, with what I've got riding on this, I have to be damned sure I'm not dealing with no amateur."

"I know what you mean, Mr. Jones," Frankie said.

"You want to check me, or the room, for a wire, I'll understand, Mr. Smith. I'll take no offense."

Jesus Christ, I didn't even think about some sonofabitch recording this!

"No need to do that," Frankie said, feeling quite sophisticated about it. "I trust you."

"That's good. I appreciate that trust. In our line of work, trust is important. You know what I mean."

"Yeah."

"So tell me about the job you did on Atchison and Marcuzzi."

And Frankie Foley did, in great detail. From time to time, Mr. Cassandro asked a question to clarify a point, but most of the time during Frankie's recitation he just nodded his head in what Frankie chose to think was professional approval.

"In other words, you think it was a good, clean job, with no problems?"

"Yeah, I'd say that, Mr. Jones."

"You wouldn't take offense if I pointed out a couple of things to you? A couple of mistakes I think you made?"

"Not at all," Frankie said.

"Well, the first mistake you made, you fucking slimeball, was thinking you're a tough guy," Paulo Cassandro said.

He pushed himself off the desk and walked to the door and opened it.

Joey and Dominic Fatalgio came into the office.

"Break the fingers on his left hand," Paulo Cassandro ordered.

"What?" Frankie asked.

Joey wrapped his arms around Frankie, pinning his arms to his sides. Dominic pulled the fingers of Joey's left hand back. Frankie screamed, and then a moment later screamed much louder as the joints and knuckles were either separated from their joints or the finger bones broken or both.

"Oh, please, Mr. Cassandro," Frankie howled. "For Christ's sake!"

"That was another mistake," Paulo said, and punched Frankie in the face while holding a heavy cast-metal stapler in his hand.

"You never seen me in your life, you understand that, asshole?" Mr. Cassandro said.

Frankie now had his left hand under his right arm. When he opened his mouth to reply, he spit out two teeth. His whole arm seemed to be on fire. He wondered if he was going to faint.

"Yes, sir," he said.

"One of the mistakes you made, you pasty-faced Irish cocksucker, was going around saying untrue things, letting people think, *telling* people, that you were working for some Italian mob. For one thing, there is no Mob, and if there was, there wouldn't be no stupid fucking Irish shit-asses in it. The Italians in Philadelphia are law-abiding businessmen like me. You insulted me. Worse, you insulted my mother and my father when you started spreading bullshit like that around. You understand that, you fucking Mick?"

Frankie nodded his head to indicate that he was willing to grant the point Mr. Cassandro had just made.

Mr. Cassandro struck Mr. Foley again with the heavy cast-metal stapler, this time higher on the face, so that the skin above Mr. Foley's eye was cut open, and he could no longer see out of his left eye.

"Say 'Yes, sir,' you fucking Mick scumbag!"

"Yes, sir," Mr. Foley said.

Mr. Cassandro, with surprising grace of movement, then kicked Mr. Foley in the genital area.

Mr. Foley fell to the floor screaming faintly, but in obvious agony.

Mr. Cassandro watched him contemptuously for a full minute.

"Stop whining, you Irish motherfucker," he said conversationally, "and stand up, or I'll really give you something to cry about."

With some difficulty, Mr. Foley regained his feet. He had great difficulty becoming erect, because of the pain in his groin, and because his entire right side now seemed to be shuddering with pain.

"Now I'm going to tell you something, and I want you to listen carefully, because I don't want to have to repeat myself. You don't even know shit about the law, so I'm going to educate you. You know what happens when you plead guilty to murder?"

Mr. Foley looked at Mr. Cassandro in utter confusion.

"Nine times out of ten, it don't mean shit," Mr. Cassandro said, "when you confess and plead guilty, which is what you're going to do."

That penetrated Mr. Foley's wall of pain.

"Confess?" he asked.

"Right. Confess. What happens is your lawyer can usually come up with something that will make the jury feel sorry for you, so they won't vote for the death penalty. Even if he can't do that, the judge usually knocks down the chair to life without parole, and what that means is that you have to do maybe twenty years."

"Why?" Mr. Foley asked, somewhat piteously.

"I told you. You dishonored the Italian people of Philadelphia. And if there was a Mob, you would have dishonored them too. How would it be if it got around that a stupid Mick asshole like you was associated with the Mob? If there was a Mob."

"I didn't say any—" Mr. Foley began, only to be interrupted again by Mr. Cassandro striking him a third time in the face with the heavy cast-metal stapler. This blow caught him in the corner of the mouth, causing some rupture of mucous membrane and skin tissue and a certain amount of bleeding.

"You know what's worse than going to the slammer for twenty years, Frankie?" Mr. Cassandro asked conversationally after Mr. Foley had again regained his feet. "Even worse, if you think about it, than getting the chair?"

Frankie shook his head no and then muttered something from his swollen and distorted mouth that might have been "No, sir."

"Dying a little bit at a time, is what would be worse," Mr. Cassandro said. "You know what I mean by that?"

Again there came a sound from Mr. Foley and a shake of the head that Mr. Cassandro interpreted to mean that Mr. Foley needed an explanation.

"Show him," Mr. Cassandro said.

Mr. Joey Fatalgio went to Mr. Foley, this time grabbing his left hand, which Mr. Foley was holding against his body with his upper right arm, and twisted it behind his back. Then he grabbed Mr. Foley's right wrist, and forced Mr. Foley to place his right hand, so far undamaged, on the desk at which Mr. Cassandro had been standing.

Mr. Cassandro moved away from the desk. Mr. Dominic Fatalgio then appeared at the desk, holding a red fire ax in his hand, high up by the blade itself. He flattened Mr. Foley's hand on the desk, and struck it with the ax, which served to sever Mr. Foley's little finger between the largest and next largest of its joints.

Mr. Foley screamed again, looked at his bleeding hand, and the severed little finger, and fainted.

Mr. Cassandro looked down at him.

"We don't want him dead," he said conversationally. "Wake him up, wrap a rag or something around his hand, and make sure he understands that if I hear anything at all I don't want to hear, I will cut the rest of his fucking fingers off."

Mr. Dominic Fatalgio nodded his understanding of the orders he had received and began to nudge Mr. Foley with the toe of his shoe.

Mr. Cassandro left the office, and then returned.

"Make sure you clean this place up," he said. "I don't want Mrs. Lucca coming in here in the morning and finding that finger. She'd shit a brick."

Both Mr. Dominic and Mr. Joey Fatalgio laughed. Mr. Cassandro then left again, carefully closing the door behind him.

———

There were a number of problems connected with the arrests of Mr. Atchison and Mr. Foley for the murders of Mrs. Atchison and Mr. Marcuzzi.

The first problem came up when Chief Inspector Matthew Lowenstein telephoned the Hon. Jerry Carlucci, Mayor of the City of Philadelphia, on his unlisted private line, in Chestnut Hill to tell him that the Honorable Thomas Callis, District Attorney of Philadelphia County, had been his usual chickenshit self, but had come around when he had told him that he was going to arrest the two of them whether or not Callis thought there was sufficient evidence.

"He already called me, Matt," the Mayor said. "To let me know what a big favor he was doing me."

"That figures," Lowenstein said.

"Would it cause any problems for you," the Mayor began, which Chief Lowenstein correctly translated to mean, *This is what I want done, you figure out how to do it,* "to bring Mickey O'Hara along when you arrest Atchison and the shooter, preferably both?"

Chief Lowenstein hesitated, trying to find the words to tactfully suggest this might not be such an all-around splendid idea as the Mayor obviously thought it to be.

"When I had Officer Bailey in here this afternoon, to personally congratulate him for his good work in catching that scumbag who shot Officer Kellog, I had the idea Mickey was a little pissed."

"Why should Mickey be pissed?"

"All the other press people were here, too," the Mayor said. "Now, I'm not saying he did anything wrong, there was no way he could have known I figure I owe O'Hara," the Mayor said, "but when Captain Quaire put out the word to the press that we had solved the Officer Kellog job, I think Mickey got the idea I wasn't living up to my word. I'd like to convince him that I take care of my friends."

"No problem. I'll put the arm out for Mickey," Lowenstein said. "He'll have that story all to himself."

"I was thinking maybe both arrests," the Mayor said. "You mind if I ask how you plan to handle them?"

And if I said, "Yeah, Jerry, now that you mention it, I do," then what?

"We're going to pick up Foley first thing in the morning," Lowenstein said. "He's not too smart, and I wouldn't be at all surprised if we could get him to confess before we arrest Atchison."

"At his house?"

"As soon as he walks out the door. I don't like taking doors, and we found out when he goes to work. We'll be waiting."

"Who's we?"

"We is Lieutenant Natali and Detective Milham, backed up by a couple of district uniforms in case we need them. I don't think we will."

"And Atchison?"

"I thought—actually Peter Wohl thought, and I agree with him—that it would avoid all sorts of jurisdictional problems if we could get him into Philadelphia, rather than arresting him at his house in Media. So Jason Washington called his lawyer—"

"Who's his lawyer?"

"Sid Margolis."

The Mayor snorted. "That figures."

"And Washington said he has a couple of questions for him, and he thought Margolis might want to be there when he asked him, and could he ask him at Margolis's office. Margolis called back and set it up for twelve o'clock."

"Good thinking. You open to a couple of suggestions?"

"Of course."

"Well, I think Tom Callis would like to get his picture in the newspapers too, and if I could tell him I had set it up for him and O'Hara to be there when you arrest Atchison . . ."

"No problem. You want to call him, or do you want me to?"

"I'll call him," the Mayor said. "And tell him to call you. And I think it would be a nice gesture if you allowed Detective Payne to go to both arrests. It would show the cooperation between Homicide and Special Operations. And what the hell, the kid deserves a little pat on the back. He did work overtime to catch Atchison with the guns."

"He'll be there. I'll call Peter Wohl and set it up."

"And then, so the rest of the press isn't pissed because Mickey got the exclusive on the arrests, I thought I'd have a little photo opportunity in my office, like the one this afternoon when I congratulated Officer Bailey, and personally thank everybody, everybody including you and Peter, of course."

"And including Detective Milham?"

"Of course including Detective Milham. He's a fine police officer and an outstanding detective who did first-class work on this job."

They call that elective memory, Chief Lowenstein thought. *Our beloved mayor has elected not to recall that the last time we discussed Detective Milham, he was my Homicide detective who can't keep his pecker in his pocket.*

"Good idea," Lowenstein said.

"I'll have Czernich set it up," the Mayor said. "Thanks for the call, Matt, and keep me posted."

"Yes, sir," Chief Lowenstein said.

It was necessary for Chief Lowenstein to telephone Mayor Carlucci at his office at ten-thirty the next morning to report that a small glitch had developed in the well-laid plans to effect the arrest of Mr. John Francis Foley.

His whereabouts, the Chief was forced to inform the Mayor, were unknown. When he had not come out of his house to go to work when he was supposed to, Detectives Milham and Payne had gone to his door and rung the bell.

His mother had told him that she was worried about John Francis. He had gone out the night before and not returned. He rarely did that. If he decided to spend the night with a friend, Mrs. Foley reported, he always telephoned his mother to tell her. John Francis was a good boy, his mother said.

"You're telling me you don't know where this scumbag is?" the Mayor asked.

"Well, we know he's not at the Wanamaker's warehouse," Lowenstein, more than a little embarrassed, reported. "We're working on known associates."

"Speaking of known associates, you do have an idea where Mr. Atchison is right now, don't you?"

"The Media police are watching his house. He's there."

"Find Foley, Matt," the Mayor ordered. "Soon."

"Yes, sir."

"Why don't you call the police," the Mayor said, his sarcasm having been ignited. "Maybe he got himself arrested. Or check the hospitals. Maybe he got run over with a truck. Just find him, Matt!"

"Yes, sir."

Chief Lowenstein replaced the pay telephone in Meagan's Bar into its cradle. He looked thoughtful for a moment, and then asked himself a question, aloud.

"Why the hell not?"

He dropped another coin in the slot, dialed a number, and told the lieutenant who answered to call the hospitals and see if they had a patient, maybe an auto accident or something, named John Francis Foley. And while he was at it, check the districts and see if anybody by that name had been arrested.

INVESTIGATION REPORT		PHILADELPHIA POLICE DEPARTMENT	

Yr | C.C.# | DIST | COMPL.# | INITIAL(49) | DIST/UNIT |
REPORT DATE   SUPPLEMENTAL   PREPARING
CLASSIFICATION | CODE | CONTINUATION   Homicide/9th Dist.

PREVIOUS CLASSIFICATION   CODE | DATE AND TIME | PLACE OF OCCURRENCE

COMPLAINANT | AGE | RACE | ADDRESS | PHONE | TYPE OF PREMISES
Alicia Atchison | 25 | W | 320 Wilson Avenue, Media, PA

DATE AND TIME REPORTED | REPORTED BY | ADDRESS

FOUNDED   ❐ YES ❐ NO   ARREST ❐ CLEARED   ❐ EXCEPTIONALLY CLEARED

STOLEN | ❐ CURRENCY, BONDS, ETC. ❐ FURS   ❐ AUTOS | RECOVERED VALUE
PROPERTY | ❐ JEWELRY, PRECIOUS METAL ❐ CLOTHING   ❐ MISC |
INSURED   ❐ YES ❐ NO

DETAILS

E. Arrests

1. Defendant #1 Foley, John Francis, 25 years, white, 2320 South 18th Street. PP#375783, two previous arrests. Occupation: Laborer (Wanamaker's). Born: 2/5/50. On Thursday, May 25, 1975 at 9:55 a.m., taken into custody at Memorial Hospital by Lieutenant Louis Natali #233; Sergeant Zachary Hobbs #396; Detective Wallace J. Milham #626 and Detective Matthew M. Payne #701.

Description

Foley, John Francis, is a white male, 6'1", 189 lbs., light brown hair, light blue eyes, wearing a hospital gown. He had been taken to the Emergency Room of Memorial Hospital by a Sixth District van after having been found in a semi-conscious state at Chestnut and S. 9th Streets. He was treated by Emergency Room personnel supervised by M.C. Chobenzy, MD, for various injuries and admitted to Memorial Hospital for further treatment and observation.

His left hand had been placed in a cast applied under Dr. Chobenzy's supervision. Finger bones and joints were fractured. His right hand had been placed in a cast and bandaged under Dr. Chobenzy's supervision. The little finger had been recently amputated, it is not known how. He also had a swollen right eye, cut upper lip, lacerations on back of his head, a laceration on the left side of his face at the eye line, and various other bruises and contusions of the face and body.

INVESTIGATOR (Type and Sign Name) | SERGEANT | LIEUTENANT

Wallace J. Milham | *Zachary Hobbs* |
Wallace J. Milham #626 | Zachary Hobbs #396

75-49 (Rev 3/63)   DETECTIVE DIVISION

INVESTIGATION REPORT		PHILADELPHIA POLICE DEPARTMENT	

Yr | C.C.# | DIST | COMPL.# | INITIAL(49) | DIST/UNIT |
REPORT DATE   SUPPLEMENTAL | PREPARING
CLASSIFICATION | CODE | CONTINUATION   Homicide/9th Dist.

PREVIOUS CLASSIFICATION   CODE | DATE AND TIME | PLACE OF OCCURRENCE

COMPLAINANT | AGE | RACE | ADDRESS | PHONE | TYPE OF PREMISES
Alicia Atchison | 25 | W | 320 Wilson Avenue, Media, PA

DATE AND TIME REPORTED | REPORTED BY | ADDRESS

FOUNDED   ☐ YES ☐ NO   ARREST ☐ CLEARED   ☐ EXCEPTIONALLY CLEARED

STOLEN | ☐ CURRENCY, BONDS, ETC. ☐ FURS   ☐ .AUTOS | RECOVERED VALUE
PROPERTY | ☐ JEWELRY, PRECIOUS METAL ☐ CLOTHING   ☐ MISC |
INSURED   ☐ YES ☐ NO

DETAILS

E. <u>ARRESTS</u> (Continued)

   <u>Defendant #1</u> John Francis Foley (Continued)

   <u>Description</u> (Continued)

   It was determined by Long Tay Hu, MD, that his physical condition was such that no further hospitalization was required, and he was discharged from the hospital into police custody.

The clothing he had been wearing at the time of his admission to the hospital was returned to him at that time. There was apparent dried blood on his shirt, trousers, and jacket, and evidence of bloody fecal matter on his under pants.

   He appeared to be sober.

Defendant #1 was taken to the Homicide Division, Police Department Headquarters, Franklin Square for interview.

   2. Defendant #2 Atchison, Gerald North, 42-W, 320 Wilson Avenue, Media, PA, no previous record. Occupation: Bar Owner. Born: 12/25/32. On Thursday, May 25, 1975 at 12:01 p.m., taken into custody at the law offices of Sidney Margolis, Esq., PSFS Building, Phila. by Lieutenant Louis Natali #233, Sergeant Zachary Hobbs #396, Detective Wallace J. Milham #626, and Detective Matthew M. Payne #701, as directed by District Attorney Thomas Callis. Defendant was taken to Room 759, City Hall, Sheriff's Cellroom and

INVESTIGATOR (Type and Sign Name) | SERGEANT | LIEUTENANT

Wallace J. Milham | *Zachary Hobbs* |
Wallace J. Milham #626 | Zachary Hobbs #396

75-49 (Rev 3/63)   DETECTIVE DIVISION

INVESTIGATION REPORT			PHILADELPHIA POLICE DEPARTMENT		

Yr | C.C.# | DIST | COMPL.# | INITIAL(49) | DIST/UNIT |
REPORT DATE   SUPPLEMENTAL | PREPARING
CLASSIFICATION | CODE | CONTINUATION   Homicide/9th Dist.

PREVIOUS CLASSIFICATION   CODE | DATE AND TIME | PLACE OF OCCURRENCE

COMPLAINANT | AGE | RACE | ADDRESS | PHONE | TYPE OF PREMISES
Alicia Atchison | 25 | W | 320 Wilson Avenue, Media, PA

DATE AND TIME REPORTED | REPORTED BY | ADDRESS

FOUNDED   ❒ YES ❒ NO   ARREST ❒ CLEARED   ❒ EXCEPTIONALLY CLEARED

STOLEN | ❒ CURRENCY, BONDS, ETC. ❒ FURS   ❒ AUTOS | RECOVERED VALUE
PROPERTY | ❒ JEWELRY, PRECIOUS METAL ❒ CLOTHING   ❒ MISC |
INSURED   ❒ YES ❒ NO

DETAILS

E. ARRESTS (Continued)

   Defendant #2 Gerald North Atchison (Continued)

then transported to the Police Detention Center, Police Department Headquarters, Franklin Square.

Description

   Defendant #2 is a white male, 5'8", 187 lbs., brown hair, brown eyes, wearing a gray suit, white shirt, black tie, black shoes. He was on crutches at the time. He did not appear to be under the influence of alcohol or drugs.

F. INTERVIEWS

   1. Defendant John Francis Foley

Stated—During the winter of 1974 he went into The Inferno to meet a friend and was introduced to Gerald Atchison. Gerald said that he heard that he was a killer and that he wanted to have somebody killed. The deal was supposed to be for Gerald's wife. Then Marcuzzi came into the picture and Gerald decided that he wanted him killed too. Gerald decided that Alicia and Marcuzzi would be done together in The Inferno.

On Monday, May 15, 1975, he saw Gerald and Gerald gave him a Savage .32, a Spanish .44 and a Colt .38. Gerald didn't want to get hit with a big gun.

INVESTIGATOR (Type and Sign Name) | SERGEANT | LIEUTENANT

Wallace J. Milham | *Zachary Hobbs* |
Wallace J. Milham #626 | Zachary Hobbs #396

75-49 (Rev 3/63)   DETECTIVE DIVISION

INVESTIGATION REPORT   PHILADELPHIA POLICE DEPARTMENT

| Yr | C.C.# | DIST | COMPL.# | | INITIAL(49) | DIST/UNIT | |
REPORT DATE   SUPPLEMENTAL | PREPARING
CLASSIFICATION | CODE | CONTINUATION   Homicide/9th Dist.

PREVIOUS CLASSIFICATION   CODE | DATE AND TIME | PLACE OF OCCURRENCE

| COMPLAINANT | AGE | RACE | ADDRESS | PHONE | TYPE OF PREMISES |
Alicia Atchison | 25 | W | 320 Wilson Avenue, Media, PA

DATE AND TIME REPORTED | REPORTED BY | ADDRESS

FOUNDED ☐ YES ☐ NO   ARREST ☐ CLEARED ☐ EXCEPTIONALLY CLEARED

STOLEN | ☐ CURRENCY, BONDS, ETC. ☐ FURS   ☐ AUTOS | RECOVERED VALUE
PROPERTY | ☐ JEWELRY, PRECIOUS METAL ☐ CLOTHING   ☐ MISC |
INSURED   ☐ YES ☐ NO

DETAILS

F. <u>INTERVIEWS</u> (Continued)

   <u>Defendant #1</u> John Francis Foley (Continued)

Gerald wanted to get hit with something light. He told Gerald that the best place would be the restaurant and that they would work out the details together as to how it would be done.

Gerald said that he would send Alicia downstairs telling her to pretend to read a book and to watch Anthony Marcuzzi with the receipts. He would tell Alicia that he thought that Anthony was cheating him. Gerald would get rid of the bartender, so he would have an excuse not to go with Alicia.

Foley was to go down into the cellar and wait for Alicia and Anthony to get into the office together and Gerald would give the signal with the juke box that it was all clear upstairs. He would then be able to go in and do the killing. Then he was supposed to go upstairs, shoot Gerald, and leave the place.

On Friday, May 19, 1975, sometime around 10:00 pm, he met Gerald in the 12th Street Market. He told Gerald that he had to kill them that night, that he was running out of time and that was going to be the night. Gerald said, OK, and gave him $2500. He still had the guns that Gerald gave him on Monday and he went to The Inferno about 11:30 or 11:45 p.m.

When he went in there, he stayed at the bar for a while, and then Gerald took

| INVESTIGATOR (Type and Sign Name) | SERGEANT | LIEUTENANT |

Wallace J. Milham | *Zachary Hobbs* |

Wallace J. Milham #626 | Zachary Hobbs #396

75-49 (Rev 3/63)   DETECTIVE DIVISION

INVESTIGATION REPORT			PHILADELPHIA POLICE DEPARTMENT	

Yr | C.C.# | DIST | COMPL.# | INITIAL(49) | DIST/UNIT |
REPORT DATE   SUPPLEMENTAL | PREPARING
CLASSIFICATION | CODE | CONTINUATION   Homicide/9th Dist.

PREVIOUS CLASSIFICATION   CODE | DATE AND TIME | PLACE OF OCCURRENCE

COMPLAINANT | AGE | RACE | ADDRESS | PHONE | TYPE OF PREMISES
Alicia Atchison | 25 | W | 320 Wilson Avenue, Media, PA

DATE AND TIME REPORTED | REPORTED BY | ADDRESS

FOUNDED   ❐ YES ❐ NO   ARREST ❐ CLEARED   ❐ EXCEPTIONALLY CLEARED

STOLEN | ❐ CURRENCY, BONDS, ETC. ❐ FURS   ❐.AUTOS | RECOVERED VALUE
PROPERTY | ❐ JEWELRY, PRECIOUS METAL ❐ CLOTHING   ❐ MISC |
INSURED   ❐ YES ❐ NO

DETAILS

F. <u>INTERVIEWS</u> (Continued)

     <u>Defendant #1</u> John Francis Foley (Continued)

him to the office and started cleaning the guns. Gerald started helping to clean the guns but he was kind of nervous and was interested in drinking, so he cleaned the guns himself. He then went to the back of the cellar where the floor drops down where the beer cases are stored, behind a dressing room. He took a beer box and sat it up so that he would be able to sit on it and placed the guns where the floor drops. Gerald fixed the trap door to keep it open a couple of inches. Then Foley and Gerald went upstairs and Foley left The Inferno.

He walked around awhile, and then at 12:30 or so, he is not sure of the time, he went to the rear of The Inferno. He opened the trap door which Gerald had fixed and went into the cellar. He went and got the guns, then sat on the beer box and waited.

In about 5 minutes Alicia came down and she went into the office. Then he waited about 5 minutes more before Anthony Marcuzzi came down and went into the office. Then the juke box started to play and that was Gerald's signal that it was clear upstairs and for him to do the killings.

He waited for about 10 seconds to make sure that the juke box was playing right. He had the .44 in his right hand and the .38 in his left hand and he walked into the office.

INVESTIGATOR (Type and Sign Name) | SERGEANT | LIEUTENANT

Wallace J. Milham | *Zachary Hobbs* |
Wallace J. Milham #626 | Zachary Hobbs #396

75-49 (Rev 3/63)   DETECTIVE DIVISION

INVESTIGATION REPORT		PHILADELPHIA POLICE DEPARTMENT	

Yr | C.C.# | DIST | COMPL.# | INITIAL(49) | DIST/UNIT |
REPORT DATE   SUPPLEMENTAL   PREPARING
CLASSIFICATION | CODE | CONTINUATION   Homicide/9th Dist.

PREVIOUS CLASSIFICATION   CODE | DATE AND TIME | PLACE OF OCCURRENCE

COMPLAINANT | AGE | RACE | ADDRESS | PHONE | TYPE OF PREMISES
Alicia Atchison | 25 | W | 320 Wilson Avenue, Media, PA

DATE AND TIME REPORTED | REPORTED BY | ADDRESS

FOUNDED   ☐ YES ☐ NO   ARREST ☐ CLEARED   ☐ EXCEPTIONALLY CLEARED

STOLEN | ☐ CURRENCY, BONDS, ETC. ☐ FURS   ☐.AUTOS | RECOVERED VALUE
PROPERTY | ☐ JEWELRY, PRECIOUS METAL ☐ CLOTHING   ☐ MISC |
INSURED   ☐ YES ☐ NO

DETAILS

F. <u>INTERVIEWS</u> (Continued)

    <u>Defendant #1</u> John Francis Foley (Continued)

He saw Marcuzzi bending over directly in front of the safe and Alicia was sitting in the chair in front of the desk. He shot Anthony in the head first and Anthony fell directly on his left side. A fraction of a second later he shot Alicia in the head twice and then shot Anthony once more. He thought that Anthony died right away, but Alicia put her head down on the desk on her arm and started talking to him and said, "Gerry, Gerry, what happened?" He (Foley) sat down on the sofa and said to her, "Don't worry about it, it will be over very soon."

While he was talking to Alicia he heard footsteps on the floor overhead and then footsteps returning to the front of the building.

He went upstairs to the kitchen and hit the floor and called out for Gerald. Gerald answered him from up front near the juke box. He was expecting Gerald to make an attempt to kill him. He told Gerald to put his hands up and he walked up to Gerald having both guns in his hands and told Gerald to put his gun in his (Foley's) belt.

Gerald walked in front of him to the kitchen where they stopped and he put the guns down and washed his hands with vinegar, then soap and water. He then picked up the guns and he thinks that he put the .44 in his right hand

INVESTIGATOR (Type and Sign Name)	SERGEANT	LIEUTENANT
Wallace J. Milham Wallace J. Milham #626	| *Zachary Hobbs* | Zachary Hobbs #396	|

75-49 (Rev 3/63)   DETECTIVE DIVISION

INVESTIGATION REPORT					PHILADELPHIA POLICE DEPARTMENT	

Yr | C.C.# | DIST | COMPL.# | INITIAL(49) | |DIST/UNIT |
REPORT DATE   SUPPLEMENTAL | PREPARING
CLASSIFICATION | CODE | CONTINUATION   Homicide/9th Dist.

PREVIOUS CLASSIFICATION   CODE¦DATE AND TIME |PLACE OF OCCURRENCE

COMPLAINANT | AGE | RACE | ADDRESS | PHONE | TYPE OF PREMISES
Alicia Atchison | 25 | W | 320 Wilson Avenue, Media, PA

DATE AND TIME REPORTED | REPORTED BY | ADDRESS

FOUNDED   ❐ YES ❐ NO   ARREST ❐ CLEARED   ❐ EXCEPTIONALLY CLEARED

STOLEN | ❐ CURRENCY, BONDS, ETC. ❐ FURS   ❐.AUTOS | RECOVERED VALUE
PROPERTY | ❐ JEWELRY, PRECIOUS METAL ❐ CLOTHING   ❐ MISC |
INSURED   ❐ YES ❐ NO

DETAILS

    F. INTERVIEWS (Continued)

       Defendant #1 John Francis Foley (Continued)

and the .38 in his left hand, and the .32 in his pocket. He unloaded Gerald's
gun and gave it to him, but kept the bullets.

He and Gerald went down to the cellar and went into the office. Gerald told
him to shoot Alicia and Anthony again, so he did. Alicia was sitting up in the
chair and he shot her on the right side of her face and her head went down
again. She was still moaning so he shot her in the back of the head. With this
shot she straightened up in the chair and spun around and her head fell back
against the wall. Gerald and he went upstairs and Gerald looked out the back
door and then went to check the front door, then they both sat down in a
booth near the bar and waited about 10 minutes. Gerald told him that it was a
good job. Gerald went to the back door again, then threw the key to the back
door on the hallway floor.

They both then went into the dining room and Gerald braced himself and he
shot Gerald in the leg with the .32 and Gerald fell to the floor. After he shot
Gerald he walked to the back and when he got to the hallway, he threw the
bullets, for Gerald's gun back to him, but not close, as he didn't want Gerald
to load his gun and shoot him as he was leaving. Foley left through the back
door and went to the parking lot where he got in his car and drove home,

INVESTIGATOR (Type and Sign Name) | SERGEANT | LIEUTENANT

Wallace J. Milham | *Zachary Hobbs* |
Wallace J. Milham #626 | Zachary Hobbs #396

75-49 (Rev 3/63)   DETECTIVE DIVISION

```
INVESTIGATION REPORT              PHILADELPHIA POLICE DEPARTMENT

Yr | C.C.#    | DIST | COMPL.#           | INITIAL(49)  | | DIST/UNIT  |
REPORT DATE           SUPPLEMENTAL         |              PREPARING
CLASSIFICATION              | CODE  | CONTINUATION    Homicide/9th Dist.

PREVIOUS CLASSIFICATION    CODE | DATE AND TIME      | PLACE OF OCCURRENCE


COMPLAINANT    | AGE | RACE | ADDRESS   | PHONE        | TYPE OF PREMISES
Alicia Atchison        | 25  |  W  | 320 Wilson Avenue, Media, PA

DATE AND TIME REPORTED     | REPORTED BY        | ADDRESS

FOUNDED   ☐ YES ☐ NO   ARREST ☐ CLEARED  ☐ EXCEPTIONALLY CLEARED

STOLEN     | ☐ CURRENCY, BONDS, ETC. ☐ FURS   ☐ AUTOS | RECOVERED VALUE
PROPERTY   | ☐ JEWELRY, PRECIOUS METAL ☐ CLOTHING  ☐ MISC   |
INSURED      ☐ YES ☐ NO

DETAILS
```

stayed up and listened to the radio.

The reason he threw the bullets to Gerald's gun back to Gerald as he was leaving was because it was planned that Gerald would throw a few shots around to make it look like a robbery.

He said that he has had a feeling for the past 2 years that he had to kill someone.

2. Defendant #2 On advice of counsel, Gerald North Atchison declined to answer questions.

```
INVESTIGATOR (Type and Sign Name)  | SERGEANT        | LIEUTENANT

Wallace J. Milham                   | Zachary Hobbs                |
Wallace J. Milham #626              | Zachary Hobbs #396

75-49 (Rev 3/63)          DETECTIVE DIVISION
```

Philadelphia District Attorney Thomas J. Callis was in something of a quandary regarding the prosecution of James Howard Leslie, a.k.a. "Speed," for the murder of Police Officer Jerome H. Kellog.

Option one, of course, was that he would personally assume the responsibility for prosecuting the case. He knew that if he did that, in addition to the satisfaction he knew he would feel if he was able to cause the full weight of the law to come crashing down on the miserable little sonofabitch, there would be certain political advantages.

The trial was certain to attract a good deal of attention from the news media, print, radio, and television. The good people of Philadelphia could not avoid being made aware time and time again that their district attorney was in the front lines of the criminal justice system, personally bringing a terrible person, a cop killer, to the bar of justice.

The problem there was that there was a real possibility that he might not be able to get a conviction. The fact that there was no question Leslie had brutally shot Kellog to death was almost beside the point here. What was necessary was to get twelve people to agree that not only had he done it, but that he knew what he was doing when he did.

Leslie had asked for, and had been provided with, an attorney from the public defender's office immediately after being advised of his rights under the Miranda decision.

That fellow practitioner of the law had turned out to be a somewhat motherly-appearing woman, who had spent seven years as a nun before being released from her vows and going to law school.

She had promptly advised Mr. Leslie to answer no questions, and he had not. Tony Callis had often watched the attorney in question (whom he very privately thought of as That Goddamned Nun) in action, and had come to have a genuine professional admiration for both her mind and her skill. He also believed that she had a personal agenda: She truly believed that murder was a sin, and that the taking of life by the state, as in a sentence to the electric chair, was morally no different from what Leslie had done to Kellog.

Her strategy, Callis thought, would be obvious. She would first attempt to plea-bargain the charge against Leslie down to something which would not result in the death penalty.

Callis could not agree to that, either, from rather deep personal feelings that a cop-killing under any circumstances undermined the very foundations of society and had to be prosecuted vigorously to the full extent of the law. And also because he did not want to see headlines in the *Bulletin,* the *Daily News,* and elsewhere telling the voters he had agreed to permitting a cop killer to get off with nothing more than a slap on the wrist.

When the case then came to trial, That Goddamned Nun, oozing Christian, motherly charity from every pore, would with great skill try to convince the jury that he hadn't done it in the first place—and Callis knew his case was mostly circumstantial—and if he had, he was a poor societal victim of poverty, ignorance, and neglect, which had caused him to seek solace in drugs, and he hadn't known what he was doing, and consequently could not be held responsible.

The headlines in the *Bulletin,* the *Daily News,* and elsewhere would read, "DA Fails in Cop Killer Case; Leslie Acquitted."

Option two was to have one of the assistant DAs take the case to court. In that case it was entirely possible that the Assistant DA would get lucky with a jury, who after ten minutes of deliberation would recommend Leslie be drawn and quartered, and the Assistant DA would get *his* picture in the papers and on the TV, and people would wonder why Callis hadn't done the job he was being paid for.

Inasmuch as he had yet to weigh all the factors involved and come to a decision, Tony Callis was more than a little annoyed when his secretary reported that Inspector Peter Wohl, Staff Inspector Mike Weisbach, and Detective Matthew Payne were in his outer office and sought an immediate audience *in re* evidence in the Leslie case.

On general principle, Callis had them cool their heels for five minutes during which he wondered what the hell Wohl wanted—the Leslie case was a Homicide case—before walking to his door and opening it for them.

"Peter," he said. "Good to see you. Sorry to keep you waiting."

"Thank you for seeing us."

"Mike," Callis went on, shaking Weisbach's hand, and then turned to Payne. "Nice to see you, too. Give my best to your dad."

"Thank you, sir, I will."

"Now what can I do for you?"

"This is confidential, Mr. Callis," Wohl said. "We would appreciate it if what we say doesn't get out of your office."

"I understand."

"Mike, show Mr. Callis the pictures," Wohl ordered.

Weisbach handed Callis a thick manila envelope.

"The first ones are the photographs Homicide had taken in Leslie's backyard," Weisbach said. "They show the photo of Officer Kellog and the tape cassettes in the garbage pile."

"I've seen them."

"Next are individual photographs of each cassette, taken this morning in the Forensics Lab."

Callis flipped quickly through the 8-by-10-inch photographs of the individual cassettes. Each bore a legend stating what was portrayed, and when the photographs were taken.

"OK," Callis said. "So tell me?"

"We have in interesting thing here," Weisbach said. "The cassettes are evidence in the Leslie case. They may also, down the line, be evidence in other cases."

What the hell is he talking about?

"I'm afraid I don't understand, Mike."

"This is what is confidential," Wohl said. "The Widow Kellog appeared at Jason Washington's apartment and announced that the entire Narcotics Five Squad is dirty. She went so far as to suggest they were responsible for her husband's murder."

"We know now, don't we, Peter, that's not the case."

"We know that Leslie murdered Officer Kellog. We don't know if anyone in Narcotics Five Squad is dirty."

"Peter, the gossip going around is that Mrs. Kellog . . . how should I put it?"

"Mrs. Kellog was estranged from her husband," Wohl said.

". . . and—how shall I put it—*'involved'* with Detective Milham. I'm sure that you have considered the possibility that she just might have been . . . how shall I put it?"

" 'Diverting attention from Milham'?" Wohl suggested. "She received a death threat. A telephone call telling her to keep her mouth shut, or she'd get the same thing her husband did."

"Oh, really?"

"And she told Washington that her husband bought a house at the shore, and a boat, both for cash. Very few police officers are in a position to do that. Mike has already checked that out. They own a house and a boat."

It was obvious that Callis was not pleased to hear of this new complication.

"Isn't this sort of thing in Internal Affairs' basket? And what's it got to do with the tapes, in any event?"

"I wish it was in Internal Affairs' basket," Wohl said. "But I had a call this morning from the Commissioner, who gave it to Special Operations."

"You really are the Mayor's private detective bureau, aren't you?" Callis observed. When Wohl did not reply but Callis saw his face tighten, Callis added: "No offense, Peter. I know you didn't ask for it."

"We have reason to suspect," Weisbach said, "that these tapes are recordings made by Officer Kellog of telephone calls to his home. If that's the case, they may contain information bearing on our investigation."

"They may *have* contained anything," Callis said. "Past tense. They're burned up."

"The Forensics Lab thinks maybe they can salvage something," Weisbach said.

"What we would like from you, to preserve the evidence in both cases," Wohl said, "is permission to have Forensics work on them. Photographing each step of the process as they're worked on."

"Destroyed is what you mean," Callis said. "If I was going to be in court with the Leslie case, I'd want to show the jury the tapes as they were in the fire, the actual tapes, not what's left after Forensics takes them apart."

Wohl didn't reply, and Callis let his imagination run:

"A good defense attorney could generate a lot of fog with somebody having fooled around with those tapes," he said, and shifted into a credible mimicry of Bernadette Callahan, Attorney-at-Law, formerly Sister John Anthony:

" 'What were you looking for on these tapes? Oh, you don't know? Or you won't tell me? But you can tell me, under oath, can't you, that you found absolutely nothing on these mysterious tapes that you examined with such care that connected Mr. Leslie in any way with what you're accusing him of.'

"And then," Callis went on, "in final arguments, she could make the jury so damned curious about these damned tapes that they would forget everything else they heard."

"They gave him the Nun to defend him?" Weisbach asked, smiling.

"She probably volunteered," Callis replied. "She has great compassion for people who kill other people."

"Tony," Wohl said. "I need those tapes."

That's the first time he called me by my first name. Interesting.

"I know that . . ."

"If I have to, I'll get a court order," Wohl said.

I'll be damned. He means that. Who the hell does he think he is, threatening the District Attorney with a court order?

The answer to that is that he knows who he is. He's wrapped in the authority of the Honorable Jerry Carlucci.

"Come on, Peter, we're friends, we're just talking. All I'm asking you to do is make sure the chain of evidence remains intact."

"Detective Payne," Wohl said. "You are ordered to take the tapes from the case of Officer Kellog from the Evidence Room to the Forensics Laboratory for examination. You wil not let the tapes out of your sight. You will see that each step of the examination process is photographed. You will then return the tapes to the Evidence Room. You will then personally deliver to Mr. Callis (a) the photographs you will have taken and (b) the results, no matter what they are, of the forensics examination."

"Yes, sir," Matt said.

Wohl looked at Callis.

"OK?"

"Fine."

"Thank you, Tony."

"Anytime, Peter. You know that."

23.

The Forensics Laboratory of the Philadelphia Police Department is in the basement of the Roundhouse. It is crowded with a large array of equipment—some high-tech, and some locally manufactured—with which highly skilled technicians, some sworn police officers, some civilian employees, ply their very specialized profession.

When Detective Wally Milham walked in at half past eight, he found Detective Matt Payne, who had been in the room in compliance with his orders not to leave the cassette tapes out of his sight, for nine hours, sprawled on a table placed against the wall. He had made sort of a backrest from several very large plastic bags holding blood-soaked sheets, pillows, and blankets. It was evidence, one of the uniform technicians had told Matt, from a job where a wife had expressed her umbrage at finding her husband in her bed with the lady next door by striking both multiple times with their son's Boy Scout ax.

Amazingly, the technician had reported, neither had been killed.

Matt was pleased to see Milham. He was bored out of his mind. The forensics process had at first been fascinating. One of the technicians, using a Dremel motor tool, had, with all the finesse of a surgeon, carefully sawed through the heat-distorted tape casettes so that the tape inside could be removed.

The technician, Danny Meadows, was nearly as large as Tiny Lewis, and Matt had been genuinely awed by the delicacy he demonstrated.

And, according to his orders, Matt had ensured that photographs were taken of every cassette being opened, and then of the individual parts the technician managed to separate.

He had been fascinated too, at first, as Danny Meadows attempted to wind the removed tape onto reels taken from dissected new Radio Shack tape cassettes.

And his interest had been maintained at a high level when some of the removed tapes would not unwind, because the heat had melted the tape itself, or the rubber wheels of the cassette had melted and dripped onto the tape, and Danny again displayed his incredible delicacy trying to separate it.

But watching that, too, had grown a little dull after a while, and for the past two hours, as Meadows sat silently bent over a tape-splicing machine, gluing together the "good" sections of tape he had been able to salvage from sections of tape damaged beyond any hope of repair, he had been ready to climb the walls.

He had, at seven-thirty, announced that he was hungry, in the private hope that Danny would look at his watch, decide it was time to go home. A corporal working elsewhere in the laboratory, aware of Matt's orders not to let the tapes out of his sight, had obligingly gone out and returned with two fried-egg sandwiches and a soggy paper cup of lukewarm coffee.

At eight-fifteen, Matt had inquired, in idle conversation, if Danny was perhaps romantically attached. On being informed that he had three months before been married, Matt suggested, out of the goodness of his heart, that perhaps Danny might wish to go home to his bride.

"No problem," Danny had replied. "We can use the overtime money. You have any idea what furniture costs these days?"

"I've been looking all over for you," Wally said.

"I've been right here, in case my expert advice might be required," Matt said.

The technician, without taking his eyes from the tape-splicing machine, chuckled.

"I thought you'd like to have these," Wally said, and handed Matt Xeroxes of 75-49s, "as a souvenir of your time in Homicide."

Jesus, that's right, isn't it? My detail to Homicide is over. I am back to doing something useful, like not letting cassette tapes out of my sight. And rolling around in the mud catching dirty cops.

I'm going to miss Homicide, and it's going to be a long time before I can even think of getting assigned there. Unless, of course, Our Beloved Mayor and Chief Lowenstein get into another lovers' quarrel.

INVESTIGATION REPORT				PHILADELPHIA POLICE DEPARTMENT		
Yr | C.C.# | DIST | COMPL.#				| INITIAL(49) |	| DIST/UNIT |	
REPORT DATE		SUPPLEMENTAL		|	PREPARING	
CLASSIFICATION		| CODE	| CONTINUATION		Homicide/9th Dist.	
PREVIOUS CLASSIFICATION	CODE | DATE AND TIME			| PLACE OF OCCURRENCE		
COMPLAINANT	| AGE	| RACE	| ADDRESS	| PHONE	| TYPE OF PREMISES	
Alicia Atchison	| 25	| W	| 320 Wilson Avenue, Media, PA			
DATE AND TIME REPORTED		| REPORTED BY		| ADDRESS		
FOUNDED ☐ YES ☐ NO ARREST ☐ CLEARED ☐ EXCEPTIONALLY CLEARED						
STOLEN | ☐ CURRENCY, BONDS, ETC. ☐ FURS ☐ AUTOS | RECOVERED VALUE						
PROPERTY | ☐ JEWELRY, PRECIOUS METAL ☐ CLOTHING ☐ MISC |						
INSURED ☐ YES ☐ NO						
DETAILS						

G. Slating

Defendant #1 On Thursday, May 25, 1975 at 3:35 p.m., Foley was slated at the Homicide Unit by Lieutenant Louis Natali #233 for Homicide, 2 counts.

Defendant #2 On Thursday, May 25, 1975 at 3:45 p.m., Atchison was slated at the Central Lockup by Lieutenant Louis Natali #233 for Homicide, 2 counts.

On Thursday, May 25, 1975, at 4:00 p.m., before Judge John Walsh, in the presence of District Attorney Thomas J. Callis, after hearing testimony presented by Detective Wallace J. Milham #626 and Sergeant Zachary Hobbs #396, the defendants were held without bail for Grand Jury. Defendant #1 was not represented by counsel. Defendant #2 was represented by Sidney Margolis, Esq.

INVESTIGATOR (Type and Sign Name)	SERGEANT	LIEUTENANT
Wallace J. Milham	*Zachary Hobbs*	
Wallace J. Milham #626	Zachary Hobbs #396	

75-49 (Rev 3/63)   DETECTIVE DIVISION

INVESTIGATION REPORT   PHILADELPHIA POLICE DEPARTMENT

Yr	C.C.#	DIST	COMPL.#		INITIAL(49)	DIST/UNIT	
REPORT DATE		SUPPLEMENTAL			PREPARING		
CLASSIFICATION		CODE	CONTINUATION		Homicide/9th Dist.		

PREVIOUS CLASSIFICATION   CODE | DATE AND TIME | PLACE OF OCCURRENCE

COMPLAINANT	AGE	RACE	ADDRESS	PHONE	TYPE OF PREMISES
Alicia Atchison	25	W	320 Wilson Avenue, Media, PA		

DATE AND TIME REPORTED | REPORTED BY | ADDRESS

FOUNDED   ❏ YES ❏ NO   ARREST ❏ CLEARED   ❏ EXCEPTIONALLY CLEARED

STOLEN	❏ CURRENCY, BONDS, ETC. ❏ FURS ❏ AUTOS	RECOVERED VALUE
PROPERTY	❏ JEWELRY, PRECIOUS METAL ❏ CLOTHING ❏ MISC	
INSURED	❏ YES ❏ NO	

DETAILS

H. Hearing

Beginning Monday, May 29, 1975 through Wednesday, May 31, 1975, there was an inquest held in Court Room 696, City Hall, in the deaths of Alicia Atchison and Anthony J. Marcuzzi before Medical Examiner Dr. Howard D. Mitchell and District Attorney Thomas J. Callis. After testimony given by numerous witnesses, Mr. Callis ordered the defendants John Francis Foley and Gerald North Atchison to be charged with Homicide by Shooting of the decedents and held them without bail for the Grand Jury. Defendant Foley was not represented by legal counsel. Defendant Atchison was represented by Sidney Margolis, Esq.

I. Grand Jury

On Wednesday, May 31, 1975 at 3:00 p.m., Defendants John Francis Foley
and Gerald North Atchison were indicted by the Grand Jury on true bills
#468, #469 and #470.

INVESTIGATOR (Type and Sign Name)	SERGEANT	LIEUTENANT
Wallace J. Milham Wallace J. Milham #626	*Zachary Hobbs* Zachary Hobbs #396	

75-49 (Rev 3/63)	DETECTIVE DIVISION

"Thank you," Matt said after scanning the reports. "What I'll do with these is have
them framed and hang them on my bathroom wall, so that when I take a leak, I can
remember when they let me play with the big boys."

Milham laughed.

"Come on, Matt, if you hadn't taken one more look at Atchison, we wouldn't have the
guns. That'll be remembered, down the line, when they're looking for people in Homicide. I enjoyed working with you."

"Thank you," Matt said. "Me, too."

"And this," Milham said, handing Matt what in a moment he recognized as the spare
set of keys to his apartment. "I really owe you—both of us do—for that."

"Hell, Wally, keep it as long as you need it."

"Well, that's it. We're not going to need it. I just left Helene there. She's packing. We
had dinner tonight, and she asked me, 'What happens now?' and I said, 'I think we should
get married,' and she said, 'Oh, Wally, what would people think?' and I said, 'Who cares?'
The logic of my argument overwhelmed her."

"Well, good for you. Do I get an invitation?"

"Well, you're welcome, of course, but what we're going to do is drive to Elkton, Maryland, tonight. You can get married there right away. And then come back in the morning, a
done deed."

"Jesus. I have to sit on these goddamned tapes!"

"I know. I figured that after we're back a couple of days, we'll have a little party. A
small party, only those people who didn't think I might have done Kellog. Anyway,
you're invited to that, of course."

"I accept," Matt said, and then changed the subject. "Is she going to help us with this?"
He waved his hand at the technician working on the tapes.

"I don't know. Maybe, after a while, after we're married, she'll change her mind, but
right now she won't talk about the Narcotics Five Squad. I'll work on her, but, Jesus, she's
scared—that telephone call really got to her—and she's got a hard head."

"Well, maybe we'll get something out of the tapes, but I doubt it."

"Why do you say that?"

"Because we're—Danny is—putting so much effort into it. The Matt Payne Theory of
Investigation holds that the more effort put into something, the less you get from it. The
really good stuff falls into your lap."

Danny and Wally both laughed.

And then Danny surprised him.

"You're right, Payne. To hell with it. I've had enough. My eyes are watering, and I don't
know what the hell I'm doing anymore. Let's hang it up and start again in the morning."

"That's the best idea I've heard in eight hours."

By the time Matt got to his apartment—checking the tapes back into the Evidence Room took even longer than checking them out had—Wally Milham and Helene Kellog were gone.

Helene left a thank-you note on the refrigerator door, and when he opened it, he saw that they had stacked it with two six-packs of Ortlieb's, eggs, Taylor ham, and English muffins, which he thought was a really nice gesture.

He was sipping on a beer and frying a slice of the Taylor ham when the telephone rang.

Wohl, he thought, *or Weisbach. They called the Forensics Lab to see how things were going, heard I was gone, and are now calling here.*

"Hello."

"Matt? Where have you been? I've been looking all over for you," Mrs. Chadwick Thomas Nesbitt IV began.

At the top of a long list of people I would rather not talk to right now is Dear Old Daffy.

"The orgy lasted a little longer than I thought it would. I just got home."

"Have you been drinking?" It was more an accusation than a question.

"No."

"You're difficult when you've been drinking, and I want you to be nice," Daffy said.

"Why does you wanting me to be nice worry me?"

"I'm worried about you. Chad and I are worried about you."

"I'm all right, Daffy. Really."

"Chad and I are worried about you being all alone in that terrible little apartment of yours."

"That's very kind of you, Daphne, but there's nothing to worry about."

"You have to get out, Matt. What's done is done."

"I understand."

"Chad says that you'll think we're matchmaking or something like that."

"What's on your convoluted mind, Daffy?" Matt asked not at all pleasantly.

Her reply came all in a rush:

"The thing is, Matt, Amanda is coming to town tomorrow on business. Now, I realize you don't really get along with her, and I have never understood why—she's really a very nice girl—but we'll have to take her to dinner, or have her here for dinner, or whatever, of course, and I thought that it would be nice if you came too. That's all that's on my mind. It would be good for you, and playing Cupid is the last thing on my mind."

"Oh, Daffy," Matt said, "I don't think—"

"Please, Matt. Do it for me. Penny would want you to."

"Well, if you put it that way."

"Wonderful! I'll call you tomorrow and tell you when and where."

The phone went dead.

She hung up before I could change my mind.

Grinning from ear to ear, Matt returned to the kitchen. The Taylor ham was burned black, and the kitchen was full of smoke, but it didn't seem to matter.

He burned his hand transferring the smoking pan to the sink, but that didn't seem to matter either.

He was annoyed when the telephone went off again.

That has *to be Wohl, Weisbach, or Washington about to ruin my good feeling.*

"Hello."

"You don't sound like you're in a very good mood, but at least I know where you are," Amanda said.

"God is in His heaven and all is right with the world. I'm a little surprised He chose Daffy as His messenger, but who am I to question the Almighty?"

She giggled.

"She said she was going to call," Amanda said.

"When am I going to see you?"

"That depends."

"On what?"

"On whether or not you have guests in your apartment."

"No guests. Tomorrow night? How are you going to get away from Daffy?"

"So far as tomorrow night is concerned, I'll think of something. Are you tied up tonight?"

"Where are you?"

"Thirtieth Street Station. I decided to take a chance and come down tonight."

"Jesus!"

"Are you tied up tonight?"

"No, but if you're into that sort of thing, I'm willing to try anything once."

"Matt!"

"You bring the rope; I already have the handcuffs."

"That's not what I meant, and you know it."

"I'll wait for you downstairs."

"OK," she said, and the phone went dead.

He walked quickly into the bedroom.

The bed had been changed, and was neatly turned down.

He went into the living room, put the answering machine on On, shut off the telephone bell, and then went quickly down the stairs.

A conference was held vis-à-vis the investigation of allegations of corruption within the Narcotics Unit after the tapes taken from the pile of burned garbage had been analyzed at some length.

Present were Chief Inspector Matt Lowenstein, Inspector Peter Wohl, Staff Inspector Mike Weisbach, and the Honorable Jerry Carlucci. The conference was held in the living room of Chief Inspector Augustus Wohl (Retired).

It was the consensus that while nothing incriminating had been found on the tapes, it was suspicious

(a) that Officer Kellog had carefully recorded his telephone conversations with other officers of Five Squad;

(b) that the conversations had used sort of a code to describe both past activity and planned activity.

It was also agreed, based on Inspector Wohl's assessment of the reaction of Mrs. Kellog at the time, and on a conversation Staff Inspector Weisbach had had with Detective Milham concerning his wife, that

(a) there had indeed been a life-threatening telephone call to the former Mrs. Kellog shortly after her husband's murder;

(b) that it was reasonable to presume that this call had come from someone on the Narcotics Squad.

Staff Inspector Weisbach also reported that, somewhat reluctantly, Captain David Pekach had come to him with conjecture concerning how members of the Narcotics Five Squad could illegally profit from the performance, or nonperformance, of their official duties.

It was Captain Pekach's opinion that—and official statistics regarding arrests in the area supported this position; the number of "good" arrests resulting in court convictions was extraordinary—the Narcotics Five Squad was not taking payments from drug dealers or others to ignore their criminal activities.

That left one possibility. That, if there was dishonest activity going on, it took place during raids and arrests. Inspector Weisbach felt that the number of times raids and arrests were conducted *without* support from other police units, the districts, Highway Patrol, and ACT teams was unusual.

With no one present during a raid or arrest but fellow members of the Narcotics Five Squad, Captain Pekach said, it was possible that the Narcotics Five Squad was illegally diverting, to their own use, part of the cash and other valuables which would be subject to seizure before it was entered on a property receipt.

"Shit," the Mayor of Philadelphia said, confident that he was among friends and that his vulgarity would not become public, and also because he had really stopped being, for the moment, Mayor and was in his cop role. "That's enough to go on. I want those dirty bastards. The only thing worse than a drug dealer is a dirty cop letting the bastards get away with it. Get them, Peter. Lowenstein will give you whatever help you need."

"Yes, sir," Inspector Wohl said.

INVESTIGATION REPORT	PHILADELPHIA POLICE DEPARTMENT

Yr	C.C.#	DIST	COMPL.#		INITIAL(49)	DIST/UNIT

REPORT DATE   SUPPLEMENTAL | PREPARING

CLASSIFICATION | CODE | CONTINUATION   Homicide/9th Dist.

PREVIOUS CLASSIFICATION   CODE | DATE AND TIME | PLACE OF OCCURRENCE

COMPLAINANT | AGE | RACE | ADDRESS | PHONE | TYPE OF PREMISES

Alicia Atchison | 25 | W | 320 Wilson Avenue, Media, PA

DATE AND TIME REPORTED | REPORTED BY | ADDRESS

FOUNDED   ☐ YES ☐ NO   ARREST ☐ CLEARED   ☐ EXCEPTIONALLY CLEARED

STOLEN | ☐ CURRENCY, BONDS, ETC. ☐ FURS   ☐ AUTOS | RECOVERED VALUE

PROPERTY | ☐ JEWELRY, PRECIOUS METAL ☐ CLOTHING   ☐ MISC |

INSURED   ☐ YES ☐ NO

DETAILS

J. COURT DISPOSITION

1. DEFENDANTS: FOLEY, John Francis, 25-W, 2320 South 18th Street
ATCHISON, Gerald North, 52-W, 320 Wilson Ave., Media, PA

2. PLEAS:

     Defendant Foley: Guilty to Murder in General.
     Defendant Atchison: Not Guilty

3. DISPOSITION: Guilty to 1st degree Murder, Bill #468, 5/75, Homicide of Anthony J. MARCUZZI, Bill #469, 5/75, Homicide of Alicia ATCHISON, Bill #470, 5/75, Conspiracy. Defendants found guilty on all counts and sentenced to death in the electric chair on Bills #468 & #469 and 1 to 3 yrs. on Bill #470.

4. JUDGES: Raymond Pace ALEXANDER, Joseph SLOANE, Alexander BARBIERI.

5. TRIAL DATE: On Monday, October 11, 1975, in Court Room #453, the trial started and continued through till Friday, October 15, 1975. On Tuesday, October 19, 1975 in Court #653, the disposition and sentencing was given.

6. DISTRICT ATTORNEYS: Thomas J. CALLIS and Harrison J. HORMEL

7. DEFENSE ATTORNEYS: Sidney MARGOLIS and Manuel A. MAZERATI

8. WITNESSES: Monday, October 11, 1975, argument was presented by the defense attorneys for Defendant #1 to withdraw his guilty plea, which was turned down by the Court. It was then presented to the Supreme Court in the afternoon and again was turned down.

WENTZ, Fred, read Doctor COLE'S report into the record, regarding the findings of the Doctor's examination of John Francis FOLEY.

D.A. Anthony J. CALLIS, read Doctor Baldwin HANES'S report into the record, regarding the findings of the Doctor's examination of John Francis FOLEY.

Doctor Michael KEYES, testified to the ability of himself and all the other Doctors in Psychiatric study and work.

On Tuesday, October 19, 1975, in Court #653, Judge Raymond Pace ALEXANDER read to the defendants the findings of the Judges and sentenced the defendants to death in the electric chair.

CASE CLOSED.

INVESTIGATOR (Type and Sign Name)	SERGEANT	LIEUTENANT
Wallace J. Milham	*Zachary Hobbs*	
Wallace J. Milham #626	Zachary Hobbs #396	
75-49 (Rev 3/63)	DETECTIVE DIVISION	

THE BENNINGTON ALUMNAE NEWS

PHILADELPHIA REGIONAL CHAPTER

BY PATIENCE DAWES MILLER '70

All of her many friends were saddened to learn of the death of Penelope Alice Detweiler '71, who passed at her home after a short illness May 21.

Penny is survived by her parents, Mr. and Mrs. H. Richard Detweiler (Grace Wilson Thorney '47) of Chestnut Hill, and her fiancé, Matthew Mark Payne.

Funeral services were held at St. Mark's Episcopal Church, Philadelphia, with interment following in the Detweiler tomb in the Merion Cemetery.

* * *

But there was good news, too, from Philadelphia. Mr. and Mrs. Chadwick Thomas Nesbitt IV (Daphne Elizabeth Browne '71) are the proud parents of a beautiful baby girl. The child, their first, was christened Penelope Alice at St. Mark's with Amanda Chase Spencer ('71) and Matthew Mark Payne as godparents.